The Cantatas of J. S. Bach

The Cantatas of J. S. Bach

WITH THEIR LIBRETTOS IN
GERMAN–ENGLISH PARALLEL TEXT

ALFRED DÜRR

Revised and translated by RICHARD D. P. JONES

UNIVERSITY PRESS

OXFORD
UNIVERSITY PRESS

Great Clarendon Street, Oxford OX2 6DP

Oxford University Press is a department of the University of Oxford.
It furthers the University's objective of excellence in research, scholarship,
and education by publishing worldwide in

Oxford New York

Auckland Cape Town Dar es Salaam Hong Kong Karachi Kuala Lumpur
Madrid Melbourne Mexico City Nairobi New Delhi Shanghai Taipei Toronto

With offices in

Argentina Austria Brazil Chile Czech Republic France Greece
Guatemala Hungary Italy Japan South Korea Poland Portugal
Singapore Switzerland Thailand Turkey Ukraine Vietnam

Oxford is a registered trade mark of Oxford University Press
in the UK and in certain other countries

Published in the United States
by Oxford University Press Inc., New York

Translated from the German by arrangment with Bärenreiter-Verlag
Kassel-Basel-London-New York-Prag

The publication of this work was supported by a grant from the Goethe-Institut
Inter Nationes

First published 2005

British Library Cataloguing in Publication Data
Data available

Library of Congress Cataloging in Publication Data
Data available

10 9 8 7 6 5 4 3 2 1

Typeset by RefineCatch Limited, Bungay, Suffolk
Printed in Great Britain by
Antony Rowe Ltd., Chippenham, Wilts

ISBN 0–19–816707–5
EAN 978–0–19–816707–5

Preface

In the course of the twentieth century, the music of Johann Sebastian Bach has undergone a revival with which that of other composers cannot be remotely compared. Even the cantatas, whose Cinderella status was still lamented in the preface to the first edition of this book (1971), have since become more familiar to music lovers through various enterprises, such as complete recordings, radio broadcasts, summer courses and so on.

Owing to its specific relevance to its own time, the Bach cantata is, of course, more tied to its period than the 'timeless' instrumental works. Yet the author takes the view that Bach's cantatas lay claim to our attention as a testimony to supreme art, Christian faith and Western cultural history, and therefore demand that we come to terms with them. This involves not only a sensitive response to their cultural context but also conscientious grappling with the question of their relevance for our time. Whoever follows the music of today with sympathy will surely be unable to deny the same sympathy to Bach's endeavour to give topical immediacy to the church music of his time. It is this attitude that the present commentaries try to instil.

This book will, first of all, serve the interested lay reader as a companion during live performances, radio broadcasts, or recordings, acting as a guide to attentive listening and attempting to render comprehensible whatever is hard to understand. These aims extend to the reproduction of the cantata texts, whose poetic worth should in no way be overestimated, though they should be taken seriously as baroque poetry bound to a specific purpose. Other matters, such as symbolism, the musical doctrine of figures, and the liturgical use of the cantatas today, can be touched upon only occasionally due to the great quantity of material involved; for them the reader must be referred to specialized studies.

In order to facilitate the study of the individual cantatas without overburdening the commentaries with constant repetition, certain frequently recurring ideas and concepts are elucidated in a brief introductory historical survey. The commentary on the individual cantatas that follows this is ordered according to their original occasion (largely in keeping with their assignment to volumes in the *Neue Bach-Ausgabe*). First the sacred cantatas are considered in liturgical order, as if through a single church year (starting with Advent), then church cantatas for other purposes or for no fixed occasion, and finally the secular cantatas. As far as possible the commentaries on the individual cantatas are formulated so that each is readable independently.

Ideally, study of the commentaries should be accompanied by the score, or at least a keyboard reduction, of the work concerned. Since this will not always be possible, however, each commentary is preceded by a synopsis of the relevant cantata movements. Here details of duration are drawn from the *Handbuch der Kantaten J. S. Bachs* (fifth edition, Wiesbaden, 1984) by Werner Neumann, with the kind permission of the author. Details of key are indicated by capital letters for a tonic with a major third and lower-case letters for a tonic with a minor third. Thus capitals denote not only major keys but the Lydian, Mixolydian and Ionian modes (for example, in the case of harmonizations of chorales in the church modes), and lower-case letters not only minor keys but the Dorian, Phrygian and Aeolian modes. Where two (occasionally three) time signatures are given, they are listed in the order in which they appear in the music. The volume ends with a bibliography of literature used here or recommended for further study, a glossary for the elucidation of technical terms (those marked with an asterisk in the main text), an index of names (excluding authors and editors listed in the bibliography), and two indexes of the cantatas, one in alphabetical order of title (i.e. first line of text), the other in order of BWV (*Bach-Werke-Verzeichnis*) numbers.

For the reproduction of the cantata texts, the principles employed in the *Neue Bach-Ausgabe* apply here too: the use of modern orthography but with the retention of original verbal or phonetic forms; and the adoption of original question or exclamation marks (more frequent than those of today). Occasional small corrections nonetheless proved to be necessary in order to preserve clarity. Thus, unless grammatically justified, the dative ending -n, customary in dialect, is replaced by -m, and 'Küßen' by 'Kissen' (if that is what is meant), and so on.

In the case of certain types of information, the author felt compelled to restrict the quantity given in order to avoid unduly overburdening the volume. Thus the texts of lost works that cannot be reconstructed are omitted; textual variants of little significance (for example, in the repeats of portions of text in choruses and arias) are suppressed; and scoring details for individual movements are often given in a generalized form (for example, 'brass ww str bc'), with further details following in the commentary as and where necessary. In particular, the instruments that participate in the continuo are not specified in detail, even if they are clear from the sources or to some extent differ from each other in voice-leading.

Alfred Dürr
Bovenden, 1995

Translator's Preface

The English edition includes the cantata librettos in German–English parallel text. The translator's aim has been to adhere as closely to the original German as is compatible with clear, readable modern English. One constraining factor was the line-for-line approach adopted: for ease of comparison, each line of English corresponds as far as possible with the German line next to it. As a result, the English word order is not always the most natural one, but it is hoped that gross distortions have been avoided. Biblical quotations tend to echo the Authorized Version (1611)—the version most familiar in English-speaking countries—though exact translation of the Lutheran Bible (1534) naturally takes precedence in all cases of different readings. Readers should note that the translation does not match the scansion of the original and is not intended for performance.

The introduction and commentaries have been updated to take account of recent research: in general, the English edition is designed to reflect the state of Bach scholarship by the beginning of the Bach Year 2000. With the approval of the author, all such additions and modifications are woven into the text or its footnotes and consequently remain undifferentiated from the original. The style and scope of this editorial intervention has been limited by two factors. First, the aim has been to preserve the distinctive character of Alfred Dürr's own writings. Second, in a book intended primarily for the ordinary music lover, it was regarded as expedient to restrict scholarly discussion and references to an essential minimum in order not to overwhelm the reader. For further study he or she is referred to the bibliography.

The translator would like to express his gratitude to Joshua Rifkin, David Schulenberg and, above all, Michael Marissen for reading the text in manuscript with great care and making many valuable suggestions for improvements, most of which have been adopted. Any deficiencies that remain are the sole responsibility of the translator.

Richard D. P. Jones
Abingdon, Oxon, 2000

Note to the Reader

Among the details that precede the text of each movement, capital letters denote major keys; lower-case letters, minor. Chorale texts are given in bold print, biblical texts in inverted commas. Formally distinct portions of text, such as the middle section of a da Capo aria, are indented. In the commentaries, asterisks refer the reader to the Index of Terms and Glossary.

Contents

List of illustrations

Abbreviations

A	alto
B	bass
bc	basso continuo
BC	*Bach Compendium: Analytisch-bibliographisches Repertorium der Werke Johann Sebastian Bachs*, ed. H.-J. Schulze and C. Wolff (Leipzig and Frankfurt, 1985 ff.)
BG	Collected Edition of the Bach-Gesellschaft (Leipzig, 1851–99).
BJ	*Bach-Jahrbuch* (Leipzig, 1904 ff.)
bsn	bassoon (fagotto, bassono)
BT	*Sämtliche von Johann Sebastian Bach vertonte Texte*, ed. W. Neumann (Leipzig, 1974)
BWV	*Bach-Werke-Verzeichnis*: Wolfgang Schmieder, *Thematisch-systematisches Verzeichnis der musikalischen Werke von Johann Sebastian Bach* (Leipzig, 1950); 2nd edn, rev. and enlarged (Wiesbaden, 1990); *Kleine Ausgabe* (the 'Little BWV'), ed. A. Dürr and Y. Kobayashi (Wiesbaden, 1998). The numbering of the cantatas is not chronological, but accords with that of the Bach-Gesellschaft edition (reflecting the catalogue's origin as an index of that edition), in which order of publication was determined largely by practical issues, such as the whereabouts of original sources.
CF	*cantus firmus*
conc	*concertato*
cor da t	corno da tirarsi
ctt cttino	cornett, cornettino
DDT	*Denkmäler deutscher Tonkunst* (Leipzig, 1892–1931)
Dok I	*Bach-Dokumente*, Vol. I: *Schriftstücke von der Hand Johann Sebastian Bachs*, ed. W. Neumann and H.-J. Schulze (Kassel and Leipzig, 1963)
Dok II	*Bach-Dokumente*, Vol. II: *Fremdschriftliche und gedruckte Dokumente zur Lebensgeschichte Johann Sebastian Bachs 1685–1750*, ed. W. Neumann and H.-J. Schulze (Kassel and Leipzig, 1969)
Dok III	*Bach-Dokumente*, Vol. III: *Dokumente zum Nachwirken Johann Sebastian Bachs 1750–1800*, ed. H.-J. Schulze (Kassel and Leipzig, 1972)
Dürr Chr 2	A. Dürr, *Zur Chronologie der Leipziger Vokalwerke J. S. Bachs*, 2nd rev. edn of study first published in *BJ* 1957 (Kassel, 1976)

Dürr St 2	A. Dürr, *Studien über die frühen Kantaten Johann Sebastian Bachs*, 2nd rev. edn of dissertation first published in 1951 (Wiesbaden, 1977)
fl	flauto traverso
fl picc	flauto piccolo (a sopranino recorder, not a modern piccolo)
hn	horn (corno, corno da caccia)
hpschd	harpsichord
KB	*Kritischer Bericht* (Critical Report) to the *Neue Bach-Ausgabe*
Kobayashi Chr	Y. Kobayashi, 'Zur Chronologie der Spätwerke Johann Sebastian Bachs: Kompositions- und Aufführungstätigkeit von 1736 bis 1750', *BJ* 1988, 7–72
NBA	*Neue Bach-Ausgabe*: J. S. Bach, *Neue Ausgabe sämtlicher Werke* (Kassel and Leipzig, 1954 ff.). Series I: Cantatas; Series II: Masses, Passions & Oratorios. NBA I/1 = *Neue Bach-Ausgabe*, Series I, Volume 1.
NBR	*The New Bach Reader: A Life of Johann Sebastian Bach in Letters and Documents*, a rev. and enlarged edn, ed. C. Wolff, of a documentary biography ed. H. T. David and A. Mendel, first pub. 1945 (New York and London, 1998).
NT	New Testament
ob	oboe
ob da c	oboe da caccia
ob d'am	oboe d'amore
org	organ
OT	Old Testament
picc	piccolo
rec	recorder
rip	ripieno
S	soprano
SATB	soprano, alto, tenor, bass
Scheide I, II, III	W. H. Scheide, 'Johann Sebastian Bachs Sammlung von Kantaten seines Vetters Johann Ludwig Bach', Part I: *BJ* 1959, 52–94; Part II: *BJ* 1961, 5–24; Part III: *BJ* 1962, 5–32
Smend Kö	F. Smend, *Bach in Köthen* (Berlin, 1951). Eng. trans. by J. Page, rev. and ed. S. Daw (St Louis, 1985)
Spitta I, II	P. Spitta, *Johann Sebastian Bach*, 2 vols (Leipzig, 1873, 1880). Eng. trans. by C. Bell and J. A. Fuller-Maitland, 3 vols (London, 1884–5).
str	strings (as a rule, violin I, II, and viola; continuo instruments are subsumed under the abbreviation bc)
T	tenor
timp	timpani, tamburi

tr	trumpet (tromba, clarino)
tr da t	tromba da tirarsi
trb	trombone
vln	violin
vla	viola
vla da g	viola da gamba
vla d'am	viola d'amore
vc	violoncello
vc picc	violoncello piccolo
vne	violone
ww	woodwind

PART I

Introduction to Bach's Cantatas

I

History of the cantata before Bach

The cantata occupies a prominent position among the musical genres of the seventeenth and early eighteenth centuries. Closely related to opera and oratorio, it originated in Italy as a lyrical counterpart to these dramatic and epic sister-genres. It penetrated into neighbouring countries in the course of the seventeenth century; and in the form of the church cantata it attained a unique high point in Protestant Germany. This culmination is inextricably linked with the name of Johann Sebastian Bach.

Artistic peaks generally owe their origins to a happy concurrence of various contributory factors. Hence a variety of causes may be adduced for the cultivation of the Protestant church cantata. Perhaps the most important of these is the theology of Martin Luther. The conviction that God's Word, as laid down in the Bible, is dead and ineffectual unless it is proclaimed, that everything depends on making it current, increasingly resulted in a new orientation for church music. A close link between words and melody is already found in Luther's own hymns, and in liturgical singing—increasingly in the vernacular rather than in Latin—church musicians fruitfully sought to achieve correct declamation. When the monodic style, invented in Italy around 1600, became known in Germany, composers sought a declamation of the sung word that was no longer merely correct but animated and impassioned, an art that in Protestant Germany found its unsurpassed master in Heinrich Schütz.

At the heart of the Protestant service lies the sermon. Here, according to Luther, the proclamation of God's Word becomes a reality. The history of church music from Schütz to Bach is thus an account of the influx into liturgical singing of sermon-like interpretative and exegetical elements. The simplest way of interpreting a text is to repeat parts of it in order to give them special prominence: for example, the words 'Wer Ohren hat zu hören, der höre' ('Whoever has ears to hear, let him hear') in Schütz's setting of the Parable of the Sower (SWV 408). If new words are added, the principle known to the Middle Ages as 'trope' becomes available—the insertion of freely invented words within a prescribed text, a procedure often found in the works of Bach.[1]

[1] For instance in the chorus 'Wo ist der neugeborne König der Jüden' from the *Christmas Oratorio*, Part V (No. 45), with its interpolated alto recitative 'Sucht ihn in meiner Brust . . .'.

A further possibility is the addition of a chorale either during or after the singing of a biblical or ecclesiastical text. This practice also finds a frequent echo in Bach's works. Finally, new texts can be written that shed an interpretative light upon the text transmitted.

Church musicians were naturally most interested in those parts of the divine service best suited to assuming a sermon-like character. Up to the Reformation, the Ordinary of the Mass had for centuries stimulated composers to ever-new settings. But now Bible readings came to the fore: sometimes the Epistle, but more often the Gospel, which had long been prescribed for clerics as the obligatory text of their sermon at the main service. Even in the Lutheran Church these readings were originally chanted by the minister to a prescribed melodic formula known as the lesson tone. But parts of them, particularly the words of Jesus or other aphoristic passages, were now set to music afresh and sung by the choir. Finally, the stage was reached when the choir no longer sang its 'dictum motet' during the reading but afterwards instead. Here we reach the birthplace of a genre that acquired many different names in contemporary terminology, such as 'motet', 'Kirchenstück' ('church piece'), 'Kirchenmusik' (or simply 'Musik'), 'Musikalische Andacht' ('musical devotion'), 'concerto', and so on. In the end, however, it was called 'cantata', and this name alone has survived for posterity as a description of music fulfilling this function.

The development from Bible reading via dictum motet to cantata, considered here against the background of Protestant theology, corresponds with contemporary changes that took place in the spheres of both text and music. The textual backbone of all the music associated with the reading is naturally the biblical Word itself, to which, as we have already seen, freely invented texts were added. Indeed, these accumulated so much in the course of the decades that in the end the text of the reading itself became superfluous, since it had already been read out from the altar beforehand. What form did these freely invented texts take? Two forms were used above all: the strophic poem and the madrigal. The hymn was itself a strophic poem, and many of the texts that supplemented the biblical Word were, in fact, chorale verses. But the aspiration for deeper piety that spread over wide areas of northern Germany in the second half of the seventeenth century, in association with the rise of Pietism, led to a more widespread devotional poetry in strophic form—designated 'ode' in the poetics of the day—a genre particularly well adapted to musical setting. Just as the poets of such odes often prefaced them with a biblical dictum as motto, so composers favoured a cantata type of the basic form 'biblical word—strophic poem', in accordance with the musical structure 'concerto—aria 1-aria 2-aria 3' (etc.). 'Aria' should here be understood not as the Italian operatic type but as a simple song-like form. Examples of this cantata type and its variants were composed in large numbers by Dietrich Buxtehude and his contemporaries. In Bach's time, however, it was already regarded as antiquated.

More forward-looking was the madrigal, which, having emerged from Italy, underwent a late blossoming in Germany. This should be understood as a song for several voices, based on a non-strophic poem of mainly subjective and, at first, mostly amatory content. An important factor in its assessment is the high significance accorded to the text, which enabled Michael Praetorius to maintain that the word 'madrigal' was '*nomen poematis* und nicht *cantionis*' ('the name of a poem and not a song'). Interest in the madrigal declined appreciably in Italy after 1620. In Germany, however, the poetic form was discovered in the mid-seventeenth century (if we disregard Schein's *Waldliederlein* of 1621) by Caspar Ziegler, who in 1653 published an essay entitled *Von den Madrigalen*, in which he stressed how much musicians would want to set such texts. Characteristic of madrigalian verse are the freedoms permitted, no doubt with a view to prospective musical setting. A fixed number of lines is not prescribed, concealed rhyme is permitted, unequal line lengths are practically a requirement, and changes of metre no rarity. At the end of the madrigal a punchline of some kind, or at least something out of the ordinary, is expected. Ziegler, who also printed a few samples of his madrigals, had successors. Ernst Stockmann made this originally secular form at home in sacred verse too. In his *Madrigalische Schriftlust* of 1660, madrigals are prefaced by biblical quotations. And Salomo Franck, whom we shall later encounter as one of Bach's librettists, published not only individual madrigals but a collection entitled *Madrigalische Seelen-Lust über das heilige Leiden unsers Erlösers* (Madrigalian Soul's Delight on the Holy Passion of our Redeemer, 1697).

The true significance of the madrigal for the development of the Protestant church cantata lies not so much in the genre itself as in the suitability of madrigalian verse for the compositional forms of recitative and da capo aria, both of Italian extraction. For the text of a recitative, or even that of an aria, is composed according to the poetic rules of the madrigal (though, of course, with the omission of the final punchline). This is stated clearly in the poetics taught at the time. Ziegler says that he adheres to

> the aforesaid recitative style, such as the Italians use in the poetry of their sung comedies, for a continually unfolding madrigal, or for many madrigals, within which an arietta, or perhaps an aria of several stanzas, sometimes occurs, over which both poet and composer must then take particular care and alternate them at the right time in order to sweeten the one with the other.[2]

[2] '. . . besagten Stylum recitativum, wie ihn die Italianer in der Poesie zu ihren Singe Comedien gebrauchen vor einen stets werenden Madrigal, oder vor etliche viel Madrigalen, doch solcher gestalt, daß ie zuweilen darzwischen eine Arietta, auch wohl eine Aria von etlichen Stanzen lauffe, welches denn so wohl der Poet als der Componist sonderlich in acht nehmen, und eines mit dem andern zu versüssen, zu rechter zeit abwechseln muß.'

The form of alternating recitative and aria Ziegler alludes to here is that of the Italian chamber cantata. And it is this very form that Erdmann Neumeister transferred to the Protestant church cantata in his librettos of 1700.

Neumeister, born in 1671 at Uichteritz near Weißenfels, was educated at Schulpforta, studied theology at Leipzig from 1689, and became a schoolmaster in 1695. After the publication of a dissertation on poets of the seventeenth century, he gave lectures on poetics in Leipzig. Unknown to Neumeister, these were published in 1707 by his pupil Christian Friedrich Hunold under the title *Die Allerneueste Art, zur Reinen und Galanten Poesie zu gelangen* (The Very Latest Fashion of Arriving at a Pure and *Galant* Poetry). In 1697 Neumeister took up his first appointment as a pastor at Bad Bibra; this was followed by further appointments at Eckartsberg, Weißenfels, Sorau, and finally in 1715 at the Jacobikirche, Hamburg, where he remained till his death in 1756.

Neumeister's first cycle of cantata texts for the entire church year, completed in 1700 and published four years later under the title *Geistliche Cantaten statt einer Kirchen-Music* (Spiritual Cantatas in Place of Church Music), was soon followed by others: four more appeared in the years 1708, 1711, 1714 and 1716, and later still another five. From the third cycle onwards biblical words and chorales were added. In the fifth cycle of 1716 Neumeister even returned to the antiquated form of the ode. Neumeister's librettos, far from outstanding works of art, are nonetheless well suited to their purpose, skilfully laid out in form, free of bombastic excess, and yet alive and figurative. As a theologian Neumeister was strictly orthodox: he took up cudgels against Pietism and on behalf of 'sound doctrine' (BWV 61), and this perhaps explains why in his librettos depth of feeling is less evident than a moralizing learnedness which at times becomes insufferable (BWV 24). Yet, taking everything into account, Neumeister is, in his poetry, not an unworthy advocate of his own innovation.

The introduction of the Italian cantata form into the Protestant church initiated a lively debate.[3] Musicians took up the innovation enthusiastically and found themselves supported by the open enlistment of the orthodox clergy. The Pietists, on the other hand, saw in the adoption of opera-like elements of form an inadmissible invasion of worldliness into the divine service, and they waged war on it of the most vehement kind. In the long run, however, they were unable to hinder it, and so the history of the church cantata in the eighteenth century became an account of the Neumeister type of cantata.

Still more multifarious than the textual foundations of the church cantata—biblical prose, strophic chorale and aria, madrigalian verse—are its musical forms, which unite virtually the entire repertoire of the time. Briefly we shall attempt to characterize the most important of them according to their origin.

[3] A graphic description of these disputes over the introduction of the modern cantata is given in Spitta I, 463–80 (Eng. trans., I, 468–86).

For the delivery of the biblical Word by the choir, the most commonly used form from time immemorial was the motet. Characteristic of this form since the sixteenth century was the division of the text into sections according to the sentence structure, each of which acquired its own musical material and form (designated *a, b* and *c* in the example below). In the second half of the sixteenth century, the heyday of a style of vocal polyphony associated with the name of Palestrina, a basic type of motet had grown up that was characterized by a succession of polyphonic formations according to the following scheme:

Soprano	a__________	b__________	c__________				
Alto		a__________	b__________	c__________			
Tenor			a__________	b__________	c________		etc.
Bass				a__________	b__________	c______	

Decisions regarding the number of voices and the order of entries were left to the discretion of the composer. The motet reproduced in part in Music Example 1 essentially follows the above scheme, though with five-part texture and with differing order of entries from section *b* onwards.

At the beginning of the seventeenth century, the motet was increasingly influenced by the madrigal, whose compositional principles for the setting of secular rhyming verse were transferred to the biblical Word. These involve, above all, an intensive penetration into the substance of the text: text declamation is elevated to an expressive plane; and the images and 'affects' of the text—the surging of waves, the rustling of wind, height and depth, joy and lamentation—are all depicted in musical terms. The compositional means available are, among others, a concentration of contrasting note-values within a confined space, changes of tempo, and a systematic, text-engendered employment of diatonic or chromatic, polyphonic or homophonic passages, larger or smaller intervals, syllabic declamation or extended coloraturas. Even breaking the rules of composition is occasionally permitted if it assists the interpretation of the text. The application or 'significance' of these resources is regulated by a carefully elaborated doctrine of musical figures, whose concepts are borrowed from rhetoric.[4] An illustration of a Protestant dictum motet influenced by the madrigal is given in Music Example 2. By the eighteenth century the motet was already antiquated; only commissioned works, chiefly for funerals, were as a rule newly composed. Nevertheless, the compositional principle of the motet lived on in many choruses from cantatas.

Among the Italian achievements of around 1600 is a compositional principle that decisively influenced the music of the following century, namely the

[4] See the articles 'Figures' and 'Rhetoric and music' in S. Sadie, ed., *The New Grove Dictionary of Music and Musicians*, 2nd edn, 29 vols (London, 2001).

concerto—the opposition of diverse sources of sound. This confrontation between one body and another can take three different forms:

1. Several groups concert with one another, a style frequently cultivated from the era of Venetian polychoral music right up to Bach's *St Matthew Passion*. The principle is employed in both vocal and instrumental music, hence the polychoral motet and the concerto for groups of instruments. An illustration of a double-choral motet (reproduced in part) is given in Music Example 3.
2. A full-textured group is placed in opposition to a single part or several parts. This principle, developed above all in the instrumental sphere, led to the well-known form of the instrumental concerto with one or more solo instruments.
3. Two or more individual parts interact over a continuo bass, hence the 'sacred concerto' for a few parts, which underwent a fertile development during the seventeenth century and became one of the immediate forerunners of the cantata. The first publication in this field was the epoch-making *Cento concerti ecclesiastici* by the Italian Ludovico Grossi da Viadana (Venice, 1602). The make-up of these sacred concertos is that of the motet with a reduced number of voices. The earliest evidence for the reception of this style in German Protestant church music is Johann Hermann Schein's *Opella nova* of 1618—see Music Example 4. A direct line leads from the sacred concertos of composers such as Schein and Schütz to the early cantatas of Bach. Development in the intervening period above all took the form of greater flexibility of voice-leading and increased differentiation in the treatment of participating instruments.

Another compositional principle first made its mark in Italy around 1600, namely the monody with continuo accompaniment. At first it exhibits little formal articulation, but in Giulio Caccini's collection *Le nuove musiche* (Florence, 1602), which contains twelve 'madrigals' and ten 'arias' for voice and continuo, an embryonic distinction is already made which in future would lead from declamatory madrigal to recitative and from simple song-like aria to the elaborate, virtuoso aria of opera and cantata. Caccini's collection is thus the starting-point of the Italian chamber cantata, whose forms, via Neumeister, entered into the Protestant church cantata.

The Bach cantata was not only imprinted with Italian influences, however, for the various forms of *cantus firmus* arrangement—above all the hymn setting—are derived from the German tradition. In compositions for a few parts, the rich *bicinium* and *tricinium* culture of the sixteenth century blended with the achievements of the sacred concerto and turned into the chorale concerto in few parts, of which Schein gives fine specimens in his *Opella nova* (see Music Example 4). In the full-textured chorale arrangement, compositional types range from the plain, chordal, 'cantional' setting intended for congregational participation, as first published by Lukas Osiander in 1568, to the large polychoral chorale concerto that we know from the works of Michael Praetorius, Samuel Scheidt and others. It was not unusual for a chorale to be set *per omnes versus* (each verse in its own polyphonic setting), in which case the various available types of arrangement alternate. Bach's chorale cantatas are thus founded upon an old tradition whose eminent exponents include Samuel Scheidt and Johann Pachelbel. It is also worth mentioning that in Leipzig, when Johann Schelle was Thomascantor (1677–1701), the pastor based each sermon upon a chorale throughout the whole of one church year, and the cantor performed a piece of music specially composed for each occasion on the basis of the same chorale.

Finally, in the second half of the seventeenth century it became popular to combine a chorale verse with some other kind of text, a practice chiefly associated with the motet (see Music Example 3). In cantata composition interest in the chorale dwindled around 1700; and it is no coincidence that it was the motet, sunk to the level of worthy utility music, that became the retreat of the chorale, for only with great hesitation did Neumeister and his successors adopt the chorale in their texts. Bach's own interest in the chorale, and his inexhaustible imagination in the invention of new, individual methods of chorale arrangement, is thus decidedly anachronistic.

Related to the chorale is the strophic aria, a song-like and normally very unpretentious musical setting which, in the form of the pre-Neumeister concerto-aria cantata, was either repeated unaltered for each of the verses of an ode or else varied more or less from verse to verse. Particularly popular was the technique of inventing a different melody for each verse (or for some of the verses) over an unchanging continuo part, or having the same melody sung by voices of corresponding pitch level: soprano and tenor or alto and bass. Often an orchestral ritornello concluded each strophe. By the eighteenth century the strophic aria was so antiquated that, even where the text took the form of an ode, Bach chose to set it in a through-composed manner rather than in strophic form.

The secular cantata in Germany followed its Italian model still more closely than the church cantata. In fact, many German composers wrote cantatas to Italian texts, and two Italian cantatas are transmitted under Bach's name. Secular cantatas to German texts, however, do not differ from them in principle. Contemporary theorists distinguish clearly between the true 'cantata', a work of largely lyrical character and amatory text for one or a few solo voice parts, and the 'serenata' for several voices, often lightly dramatic in character and frequently written as an occasional work for a specific festive event. Later, the term 'serenata' died away and was replaced by 'dramma per musica', a name that still more clearly denotes a usually modest plot, often ending in general congratulation of the person honoured in the festivities.

This, then, was the tradition inherited by Johann Sebastian Bach, born in Eisenach on 21 March 1685. He absorbed it as a choirboy, as a budding organist and violinist, in the domestic music-making of his family, in the compositions of his relatives—which he himself collected together in the so-called *Alt-Bachisches Archiv* (Archive of the Elder Bachs)—and finally during his trips to Hamburg and Lübeck. How fully the youthful Bach absorbed and digested the achievements of his predecessors and contemporaries is testified by his own first works in the field of the cantata.

2

Development of the Bach cantata

2.1 Early forms (*c.* 1707–12)

Bach's cantatas have come down to us in substantially reduced numbers. The obituary by Carl Philipp Emanuel Bach and Johann Friedrich Agricola[1] mentions five cycles of cantatas for the whole church year, but today only three cycles survive virtually complete,[2] plus a few scattered remains of others. Almost two cycles—a good two-fifths of Bach's output of sacred cantatas—are lost. Even heavier are the losses in the sphere of the secular cantata, where the number of works known to have been lost exceeds the number that survive. Any assertions we make about Bach's cantatas must therefore take into account the uncertainty that arises from reduced numbers.

The earliest Bach cantatas that we possess stem from his Mühlhausen period (1707–8), or in one case (BWV 150) possibly earlier still.[3] Formally, they belong to the old, pre-Neumeister type of church cantata, lacking recitatives and arias of the Neapolitan operatic type. Even the first Weimar years (1708–*c.* 1712) reveal no fundamental change, though the dating of the few surviving works from that time is very uncertain. The following cantatas of this older sort have survived:[4]

Nach dir, Herr, verlanget mich, BWV 150 (before 1707?)
Aus der Tiefen rufe ich, BWV 131 (1707)
Gottes Zeit ist die allerbeste Zeit, BWV 106 (1707?)
Gott ist mein König, BWV 71 (1708)
Der Herr denket an uns, BWV 196 (*c.* 1708/9?)
Christ lag in Todes Banden, BWV 4 (*c.* 1707–13?)

Biblical words and chorale form the textual basis of these works, exclusively so in BWV 131, 196 and 4, and almost exclusively in BWV 106. In two of the six

[1] Published in L. C. Mizler, *Neu eröffnete musikalische Bibliothek*, 4/1 (Leipzig, 1754), 158–76; reproduced in Dok III, No. 666 (80–93); Eng. trans. in NBR, No. 306 (297–307).

[2] For Bach in Leipzig a complete cycle may be estimated at about 59 cantatas.

[3] Andreas Glöckner ('Zur Echtheit und Datierung der Kantate BWV 150', *BJ* 1988, 195–203) argues that Cantata 150 might pre-date the Mülhausen cantatas and stem from Bach's Arnstadt years (1703–7). Cantata 15, *Denn du wirst meine Seele nicht in der Hölle lassen*, formerly dated in the Arnstadt period, was in reality composed by Johann Ludwig Bach (see Scheide I).

[4] See Dürr St 2, 221.

surviving works, free verse is added in arias and choruses, mixed with three psalm extracts in BWV 150 and with biblical words and chorale in BWV 71. Strophic poetry occurs only in BWV 71, whose closing chorus consists of two verses of text, set differently. Leaving aside the pure chorale cantata BWV 4, these early works are dominated by biblical words, themselves interpreted by the added ingredients of chorale and free verse, so that in textual terms the type might be designated the 'troping dictum cantata'.

Typical of Bach's setting of these texts is its articulation into brief sections ranged one after another, an obvious legacy of the motet. The thematic relationship between these sections is very loose. In several cases, however, we find a symmetrical overall structure that may be regarded as a manifestation of the basic type: chorus–solos–chorus–solos–chorus. Here we might see a critique of the traditional sectional form and a tendency to draw together the individual sections into larger forms, an endeavour that Bach brought to fruition by diverse means in his later works.

Even within the individual sections, however, a tendency towards unified form is already manifest in these early works. This is especially clear in the design of the fugal sections. The first type of Bachian choral fugue, the so-called 'permutation fugue',[5] dispenses with free episodes such as occur everywhere in instrumental fugues, and arranges a number of subjects in series, each occurring in *dux* and *comes* form according to the following basic scheme (A = *dux* form, B = *comes* form; 1, 2, 3, 4 = four subjects):

	A	B	A	B	A	B	A	B	
Soprano	1	2	3	4	1	2	3	4	
Alto		1	2	3	4	1	2	3	etc.
Tenor			1	2	3	4	1	2	
Bass				1	2	3	4	1	

The opening of a Bach permutation fugue is shown in Music Example 5. Within this strict scheme Bach finds possibilities of variation and enhancement in solo–tutti contrasts (at first each part is solo, the tutti entering after all four subjects), in the resting and re-entry of individual parts, and in the addition of instruments, which either double the voices (*colla parte*) or else proceed independently, in which case they too might take a thematic role.

The principle of *Stimmtausch* (exchange of parts) employed here also plays a substantial part in Bach apart from in fugues. It allows a passage to be repeated in a different key without the individual parts becoming impossibly high or low as a result of the transposition. The basic scheme of such *Stimmtausch* passages might perhaps be represented as follows:

[5] See W. Neumann, *J. S. Bachs Chorfuge: ein Beitrag zur Kompositionstechnik Bachs* (Leipzig, 1938; 3rd edn 1953).

	Tonic	Dominant
Soprano	a	b
Alto	b	a
Tenor	c	d
Bass	d	c

It might apply just as much to brief chordal blocks, repeated a few bars later with interchanged parts, as to extended sections of a movement (the first kind is more typical of Bach's early works, the second of his later works). In principle, however, this technical device enables a more extended part of a movement to be uniformly designed and, at the same time, varied.

In Bach's early cantatas, then, a gradual transformation took place from sectional form in small units to a unified large form. The first technical means employed for this purpose were *Stimmtausch* and permutation fugue; in subsequent years Bach acquired additional means.

2.2 Weimar cantatas of the newer type (1713–16)

In Weimar Bach took his first steps towards the 'modern' cantata form created by Erdmann Neumeister, though the precise date of this cannot be established with certainty. At any rate, by 1714, when we can once more follow Bach's cantata composition closely, the transformation had already taken place. What exactly occurred between 1708 and 1713 remains uncertain; probably the composition of organ music occupied the foreground during this period.

It is perhaps not without significance for Bach's development that in the year 1713 he performed what was, as far as we know, his first secular cantata, *Was mir behagt, ist nur die muntre Jagd*, BWV 208 (commonly known in English as the 'Hunt' Cantata), for the birthday of Duke Christian of Saxe-Weißenfels. Perhaps in the same year (certainly no more than two years later) Bach set a text by Neumeister, the Sexagesima cantata *Gleichwie der Regen und Schnee vom Himmel fällt*, BWV 18. It is also possible that two solo cantatas with texts by Georg Christian Lehms, *Mein Herze schwimmt im Blut*, BWV 199, and *Widerstehe doch der Sünde*, BWV 54, originated as early as 1713—that is, before the composition of church cantatas became one of Bach's regular duties.[6] Both works lack any reference to a specific liturgical occasion in their sources, and thus might have been conceived, in the first instance, as music 'in ogni tempo' (for any occasion), like most of Bach's pre-Weimar cantatas, and like one version of

[6] For the dating of BWV 199 see Y. Kobayashi, 'Quellenkundliche Überlegungen zur Chronologie der Weimarer Vokalwerke Bachs', in K. Heller and H.-J. Schulze (eds), *Das Frühwerk Johann Sebastian Bachs: Kolloquium veranstaltet vom Institut für Musikwissenschaft der Universität Rostock 11–13 September 1990* (Cologne, 1995), 290–310; and for that of BWV 54, C. Wolff, *Kritischer Bericht, NBA* I/8.1–2, 89–90.

Ich hatte viel Bekümmernis, BWV 21, which probably also originated in some form before 1714.

From 2 March 1714 onwards Bach's output of cantatas is easier to survey, for on that day Bach, then chamber musician and organist at the Weimar court, was appointed Concertmaster by Duke Wilhelm Ernst of Saxe-Weimar, with the attendant duty of composing and performing his own cantatas monthly in order to relieve the ailing Capellmeister Johann Samuel Drese. From that time until Drese's death on 1 December 1716, Bach as a rule composed a new cantata every four weeks. The following cantatas survive from this period:[7]

1714: BWV 182, 12, 172, 21, 61, 63, 152
1715: BWV 80a (?), 31, 165, 185, 163, 132
1716: BWV 155, 161, 162, 70a, 186a, 147a

It is curious how often we find apparently sudden rearrangements and contradictions in relation to the date of the texts (by Salomo Franck) in the sources of many of these cantatas (BWV 199, 182, 172, 21, 31, 185, 161 and 162). This raises the question whether or not Bach might have supplied cantatas not only to the court of Weimar but to some other ensemble elsewhere.[8] Klaus Hofmann, however, favours the assumption that the cantatas concerned were revived in 1716 at the Weimar court.[9]

The representative poet of the court, and of most of Bach's Weimar cantatas, was Salomo Franck. Born in Weimar in March 1659, Franck studied law, and probably also theology, at Jena. In 1701, after temporary activities in Zwickau, Arnstadt and Jena, he became Consistory Secretary (and soon Chief Consistory Secretary) at Weimar. He was in charge of the ducal library and numismatic collection, and a member of the poetic society known as the 'Fruchtbringenden Gesellschaft' (Profitable Society). As cantata poet for the Weimar court he was active from at least as early as 1694. At first he wrote librettos of the older type—mostly biblical words and strophic verse—but from 1710 onwards, at the latest, he cultivated a transitional type, modelled on Neumeister's form but without freely versified recitatives: several arias succeed each other without connecting links, so that, despite the non-strophic, madrigalian verse of the arias, an affinity with the old concerto-aria cantata remains clearly perceptible. Finally, from 1715 onwards, Franck wrote cantata texts of the Neumeister type (without biblical words or chorus; partly with and partly without closing chorale). Many of Franck's numerous secular congratulatory poems for the ducal House of

[7] Details, together with discussion of questionable dates and gaps in transmission, are given in Dürr St 2, 63 ff. Various modifications to Dürr's chronology have since been proposed by A. Glöckner, 'Zur Chronologie der Weimarer Kantaten J. S. Bachs', *BJ* 1985, 159–64, by K. Hofmann, 'Neue Überlegungen zu Bachs Weimarer Kantaten-Kalender', *BJ* 1993, 9–29, and by Kobayashi, 'Quellenkundliche Überlegungen'.

[8] See A. Dürr, 'Merkwürdiges in den Quellen zu Weimarer Kantaten Bachs', *BJ* 1987, 151–7.

[9] See Hofmann, 'Neue Überlegungen'.

Weimar are similarly fashioned in cantata form. He also wrote occasional cantatas of various kinds, among which is the text of Bach's aforementioned 'Hunt' Cantata BWV 208 for Weißenfels. Franck was buried in Weimar on 14 June 1725.

Salomo Franck was perhaps the most gifted and original poetic talent with whom Bach collaborated. Formally as skilful as Neumeister, he also had at his disposal a rich vein of fantasy and a depth of feeling that Neumeister lacked. He often imbued his poems with rapturous, indeed mystical traits, in which a link with Pietism can be discerned, though he cannot really be classed as a Pietist. Immediately after Bach's appointment as Concertmaster he set three Franck cantata texts of the transitional type—BWV 182, 12 and 172—followed by Cantata 21, which was evidently based in part on an earlier composition. The church year 1714–15, however, for which Franck wrote a new cycle of texts, *Evangelisches Andachts-Opffer* (Evangelical Devotional Offering), instead opened with a Neumeister cantata (BWV 61); apparently Franck's libretto was not available in time for the First Sunday in Advent. For the Sunday after Christmas (BWV 152), and then probably from the Third Sunday in Lent onwards (BWV 80a), Franck texts set by Bach follow in a regular cycle, though several gaps remain. These are perhaps partly due to losses in transmission and partly to the public mourning that took place in Weimar from 11 August to 9 November 1715 for Prince Johann Ernst, a gifted musician (and a pupil of Bach and J. G. Walther) who died at the age of 18 on 1 August 1715. We are particularly badly informed about Bach's cantata performances in the year 1716. Although Franck wrote a new cycle of cantata texts for the church year 1715–16, *Evangelische Seelen-Lust* (Evangelical Souls' Delight), no Bach settings from it have survived. Instead Bach composed several cantatas from Franck's 1714–15 cycle which had not been set in the previous year (BWV 132, 155 and probably also 161 and 162); but we have no definite information about his remaining cantata performances during the church year 1715–16. When Capellmeister Drese died on 1 December 1716, however, Bach, hoping to be appointed his successor, composed for three successive Sundays in Advent Cantatas 70a, 186a and 147a, all based on texts from Franck's collection *Evangelische Sonn- und Fest-Tages Andachten* (Evangelical Sunday and Feast-Day Devotions) for the church year 1716–17. With its stereotyped order of chorus-four arias-closing chorale, the poetry again represents Franck's transitional type; it is possible, therefore, that it stems from earlier years and was selected in haste. After the opening chorus of BWV 147a Bach's Weimar autograph breaks off; evidently he was surprised by the news that it was not he but Drese's son who was to take over the position of Capellmeister. Upon this decision of the Duke's, Bach discontinued the composition of cantatas for the Weimar court.

In Weimar, then, Bach set Franck's poetry almost exclusively, evidently turning to texts by other poets only when no Franck libretto was at hand. In two cases (BWV 18 and 61) he chose texts by Erdmann Neumeister, whose life and work have been outlined above, and in two other cases (BWV 199 and 54) texts by Lehms,[10] whose verse Bach also set on a number of later occasions in Leipzig.

Georg Christian Lehms was born in 1684 at Liegnitz (now Legnica, Poland), attended school at Görlitz, and studied at the University of Leipzig. At the end of 1710 he took up the post of court poet and librarian at Darmstadt, and before 1713 was appointed to the court council. On 15 May 1717, however, pulmonary tuberculosis brought his life to an untimely end. Lehms is best known for his dictionary *Teuschlands galante Poetinnen* (Germany's *galant* Poetesses; Frankfurt, 1715), yet he also wrote novels, opera librettos, numerous occasional poems, and several church-year cycles of cantata texts for services at the Darmstadt court, set to music by the resident Capellmeisters Christoph Graupner and Gottfried Grünewald. Bach adopted several texts from the first of these cycles, which appeared in print in 1711 under the title *Gottgefälliges Kirchen-Opffer* (Church Offering, Pleasing to God). This publication is divided into two parts: a cycle for the morning service, containing only biblical words, arias, and occasional chorales; and another for the evening service, characterized by its predominance of madrigalian verse, including recitatives. This evening cycle is thus a successor to Neumeister's cycles, and was probably conceived mainly for solo voice. From it, Bach set Cantatas 199 and 54 in Weimar and another seven cantatas later in Leipzig (BWV 57, 151, 16, 32, 13, 170, and 35). From the morning cycle, on the other hand, he set only a single text: Cantata 110 (Leipzig, 1725). An eleventh cantata, *Liebster Gott, vergißt du mich*, BWV Anh. I 209, originated at an unknown date, perhaps in Weimar, but is no longer extant. Other church-year cycles by Lehms survive, dating from 1712, 1715, and 1716, but as far as we know Bach set no texts from them.

From a textual standpoint, then, the following cantata types are represented in Bach's Weimar output:

1. Salomo Franck's transitional type (without recitative verse): BWV 182, 12, 172, 70a, 186a, 147a.
2. The type of Neumeister's first and second cycles (recitatives and arias, without biblical words or chorale): BWV 54, 152 and, related to this type, 199.
3. The type of Neumeister's third and fourth cycles (recitatives and arias, with biblical words or chorale, or both): BWV 18, 21, 61, 80a, 31, 165, 185, 163, 132, 155, 161, 162.

From a musical standpoint, the Italian forms of recitative and aria have now been adopted, and with them came the assimilation to opera so vehemently opposed by Neumeister's adversaries. By Bach's time, both recitative and aria had already undergone a century-long development. Soon after the birth of

[10] See E. Noack, 'Georg Christian Lehms, ein Textdichter Johann Sebastian Bachs', *BJ* 1970, 7–18.

monody around 1600, two types of musical recitation had been established in Italian opera and solo cantata, on the basis of the originally quite formless speech-song with continuo accompaniment: the one dramatic in style, characterized by a predominance of text-engendered syllabic declamation, and termed 'stile recitativo'; the other lyrical and with a melodic tendency, rich in melismas, increasingly articulated in form by the use of recurring passages, and designated 'aria'. Both types had a clearly defined role in opera: recitative had the function of advancing the plot, and aria that of expressing in music, and lyrically dwelling upon, an affect released by the plot—anger, hatred, sorrow, love, contemplative calm, and so on—and thus arousing a corresponding affect within the listener. Musically, recitative also serves as a tonal link between adjoining arias, beginning in the key of the aria just finished (or a related one), and modulating during its course so that it ends in the key of the following aria (or a related one), thus helping to smooth out what would otherwise be an awkward key shift between the two arias.

By the time recitative and aria were introduced into the Protestant church cantata, they had already reached a final stage in their development, characterized by far-reaching standardization. Although Bach never lapsed, like many contemporaries, into the rigid application of formal schemes, even in his case certain definite types may be differentiated. These should now be delineated briefly.

The simplest and most common form of recitative is 'secco' (literally, 'dry'), a type of speech-song notated correctly in rhythm but freely declaimed, and harmonically supported by a continuo accompaniment of the simplest kind—a melody instrument playing the bass line plus a keyboard playing chords according to a series of figures in the score that represented the harmony in shorthand. Bach wrote such figured basses (invariably played as short notes in opera, even where notated as long notes) mostly in the form of long held notes, and in his church music it remains unclear whether held or short chords (or perhaps short chords and long bass notes?) were the rule.[11] The opening of a Bach *secco* recitative (including an arioso passage) is shown in Music Example 6.

If instruments other than those of the continuo are added to the accompaniment of a recitative, we speak of an 'accompagnato'—an accompanied recitative. In the simplest form of *accompagnato*, also known as an 'ausinstrumentiertes Secco' ('instrumentally filled-out *secco*'), the voice is accompanied by held wind or string chords. On the other hand, the accompaniment might be livelier; but as the motion of the accompanying parts increases, so the singer's

[11] See G. Darmstadt, 'Kurz oder lang? Zur Rezitativbegleitung im 18. Jahrhundert', *Musik und Kirche*, 50 (1980), and E. Platen, 'Aufgehoben oder ausgehalten? Zur Ausführung der Rezitativ-Continuopartien in J. S. Bachs Kirchenmusik', in R. Brinkmann (ed.), *Bachforschung und Bachinterpretation heute: Wissenschaftler und Praktiker im Dialog, 53. Bachfest der Neuen Bachgesellschaft, Marburg 1978* (Kassel, 1981), 167–77.

scope for rhythmically flexible delivery is diminished. Sometimes Bach shapes the recitative accompaniment in a uniform fashion out of a single motive, constantly repeated in more or less modified forms, a type aptly named the 'motivgeprägtes Accompagnato' ('motivically imprinted *accompagnato*'). This form of recitative, liberally represented in the *St Matthew Passion* ('Du lieber Heiland, du' etc.), is illustrated in Music Example 7.

The *arioso* occupies an intermediate position between recitative and aria. Of all the types considered here it is the least tied to a definite scheme. At times it approaches aria, but it is far more often close to recitative, with which it is frequently united within the same movement as a component part or conclusion. It differs from recitative in its rhythmically fixed delivery—no longer exclusively syllabic, but enriched with melismas—which entails the possibility of repeating significant portions of text. It also differs in its more clearly profiled instrumental accompaniment: regardless of whether it is played by continuo only or by other instruments as well, this is not only, as a rule, livelier than in recitative (or at least *secco* recitative) but also frequently made up of definite motives. In contrast to the motivically imprinted *accompagnato*, however, in which the motive has a purely accompanying function, the *arioso* often contains motivic imitation between the vocal and instrumental parts. It differs from aria in its lack of a definite theme worked out by various parts in several sections articulated by ritornellos. As a rule, it is shorter than aria and lacks the formal element of extended corresponding passages, though here the borders between the two types are sometimes fluid. An *arioso* section of a recitative is shown in Music Example 6.

The aria in Bach's time, under the influence of soloistic instrumental technique, had left behind its origin in song. The masters of the Neapolitan school of opera, whose chief representative was Alessandro Scarlatti (1660–1725), developed it into a brilliant number—elaborate, sophisticated, at times bravura-like—in which the singer could show his or her capabilities in their true light. Its structure was for the most part crudely schematic: tripartite da capo form (ABA, in which the direction 'da capo'—'from the beginning'—at the end of the B section indicates a repeat of the original A section) is almost universal. In Bach, however, numerous formal variants are found, ranging from varied or abridged da capo to two- or four-section forms. Characteristic of aria style in Bach's day is the virtual equality of voice and instrument. Particularly where one or more *obbligato* instruments are involved (that is, instruments with independent, solo parts), this leads to a lively reciprocal exchange between singers and instrumentalists. The vocal passages are surrounded by purely instrumental ritornellos. The opening ritornello in particular, however, possesses more than a merely articulating function, for within it the thematic material is stated which is then developed in the vocal passages. The voice part often enters with the ritornello theme—an indication of the decidedly instrumental treatment of the human voice—or the theme is remodelled for vocal delivery, or else the voice enters with a new theme. Even in the latter case, however, the ritornello themes are heard in the instruments during the vocal passages, as we shall see in connection with *Vokaleinbau* (vocal insertion). A Bach aria whose brevity allows its reproduction in full is shown in Music Example 8.

The first of Bach's Weimar cantatas of the Neumeister type still show several characteristic transitional features. Very extended *arioso* passages are found in the recitatives, for example; and the arias are still relatively brief, particularly in BWV 18 and 21. In 1714 they are largely structured in pure da capo form, but from 1715 onwards they become formally more complex, with free or abridged da capo, or else without da capo altogether. From the very outset Bach in general avoided the schematism into which recitative and aria composition in the eighteenth century constantly lapsed, and variety of form remains characteristic of his entire output.

The formal structure of the choruses is extraordinarily diverse. Except those of Cantata 21 (perhaps of earlier origin), they are no longer based on biblical words but on free verse. Each of the choruses of 1714 displays a different formal or technical principle: fugue or canon* in Cantata 182, ostinato variations (passacaglia) in No. 12, concerto in No. 172, motet in No. 21, and French overture in No. 61. During Advent 1716 a new compositional technique appears, formerly employed in aria composition: the incorporation of the voice parts within a reprise of the whole or part of the opening ritornello. Passages based on this technique—distinguished by the dominance of the (previously played) instrumental music—as a rule alternate with passages in which the voice parts dominate, while the instruments rest or adopt an accompanying function. This is illustrated in Music Example 8, where the thematic material stated beforehand in the ritornello recurs in the vocal section, partly in the soprano (bb. 8, 11, 14, and 18, where the vocal music is predominant) and partly in the oboe (bb. 9, 12–13, 15, 19–23, and to some extent also 10–11 and 16–17). Even movements whose ritornello themes do not recur with the same frequency in the vocal sections are nonetheless largely structured according to the same formal principle, which governs the majority of Bach's arias and a substantial proportion of his *concertante* choruses.

This incorporation of the voice parts within the reprise of the instrumental introduction is, in choral music, designated *Choreinbau* (choral insertion). Since the same technique is found in aria composition, however, it would be more appropriately described by a less specific term such as *Vokaleinbau* (vocal insertion). It is by no means peculiar to Bach, but is seldom found as often and as consistently as in his works. It contributes to the unified motivic-thematic structure of extended portions of a movement, and thus to the demise of the old motet-like articulation in small units. When combined with fugue, a passage of choral insertion can take on the function of an episode between two expositions, or else that of the non-fugal continuation of a composition.

Even in Bach's earliest cantatas the Protestant chorale was variously employed in combination with *arioso* and chorus. In the Neumeister type of cantata, however, the possibility also arises of including it in an aria (not until his Leipzig period did Bach venture to combine it with recitative). Particularly characteristic of Bach's Weimar cantatas is the textless instrumental quotation of a chorale within an aria. The hymn, whose text is known to the congregation, is thus added as a gloss, as it were, on the aria text. This procedure is ultimately derived from the aforementioned trope principle of the Middle Ages. Where the substance of the text permits, Bach seeks exceptional unification by choosing, for the instrumental chorale quotation, the chorale melody sung in the final movement, as in the following cantatas from Franck's 1715 cycle:

BWV 80a/1 (aria) and 6 (chorale): *Ein feste Burg ist unser Gott*
BWV 31/8 (aria) and 9 (chorale): *Wenn mein Stündlein vorhanden ist*
BWV 185/1 (duet) and 6 (chorale): *Ich ruf zu dir, Herr Jesu Christ*
BWV 161/1 (aria) and 6 (chorale): *Herzlich tut mich verlangen*

By the time Bach's Weimar output of cantatas was complete, the forms of the Bach cantata—both those of the individual movement and of the overall work—were, in all essentials, established. What was new in Cöthen and Leipzig was, above all, an expansion of the existing forms and variation of the available possibilities. A fundamental transformation, however, such as took place in Weimar from the old to the new type of cantata, is no longer evident.

2.3 Cöthen (1717–23)

Since he was not obliged to perform church music in Cöthen, the cantatas Bach composed during this period were mainly secular. The performance of a church cantata for the birthday of Prince Leopold on 10 December 1718 (BWV Anh. I 5; now lost) probably remained an isolated case;[12] at any rate, there is no evidence of any other church cantata from the Cöthen years. A few supplementary performing parts indicate revivals of Cantatas 21 and 199 at that time, but they need not necessarily have taken place in Cöthen itself.

Secular cantatas were performed regularly at least twice a year: at New Year and for the birthday of Prince Leopold on 10 December. A few of these cantatas

[12] Smend Kö takes a different view, assuming the annual performance of at least two church cantatas, but see the review of Smend Kö by A. Dürr in *Die Musikforschung*, 6 (1953), 382–3. It remains possible, of course, that Bach composed other church cantatas in Cöthen that are now lost.

survive, in other cases only the text is transmitted, and still others are completely lost: that they once existed can only be inferred from the general custom of cantata performances at the Cöthen court. The favoured librettist of these cantatas is Christian Friedrich Hunold, the poet who, in 1707, had published Neumeister's poetic lectures.

Hunold, who wrote under the pseudonym Menantes, was born on 29 September 1681 at Wandersleben in Thuringia, attended school at Arnstadt and Weißenfels, and studied law at Jena. In 1700 he broke off his studies due to shortage of money and moved to Hamburg, where he worked as a poet and literary critic. Here he also composed the librettos to operas and to a passion oratorio until he was forced to leave the city due to the threat of legal action. By 1708 he was residing in Halle, where he gave lectures on poetics and (from 1714) on jurisprudence, and made a living out of his poetic activity. He died there on 6 August 1721.

The first evidence of Bach's collaboration with Hunold is dated 10 December 1718. In all, Hunold supplied the texts of the following Bach cantatas:

10.12.1718: BWV 66a (secular; only sacred parodies survive, BWV 66 and 42)
10.12.1718: BWV Anh. I 5 (sacred; music lost)
1.1.1719: BWV 134a
1.1.1720: BWV Anh. I 6 (lost)
10.12.1720: BWV Anh. I 7 (lost)

It is not known who supplied the librettos for Bach's Cöthen cantatas after Hunold's death. The Cöthen birthday cantata BWV 173a cannot be traced among Hunold's poems; and the text of its sister-work BWV 184a—perhaps a New Year cantata—is lost. Both works should perhaps be dated, therefore, either before the Hunold cantatas (to 10.12.1717 and 1.1.1718 respectively) or after them (between 10.12.1721 and 1.1.1723). Other works that perhaps date from the Cöthen period are BWV 194a, the secular original (which can be reconstructed only in part) of the organ consecration cantata *Höchsterwünschtes Freudenfest*, BWV 194, and the lost secular cantata that very likely formed the common source of *Vereinigte Zwietracht der wechselnden Saiten*, BWV 207, Brandenburg Concerto No. 1 in F, BWV 1046, and the Sinfonia in F, BWV 1046a.[13]

Bach's Cöthen congratulatory cantatas chiefly belong to the 'serenata' type. At the time this was understood as a species of mini-opera with modest dramatic action, in which scenic representation was possible but not a *sine qua non*. It mostly consisted of nothing but dialogue between allegorical characters, gods or shepherds, who praise the excellence of the prince and unite at the end in general good wishes. Musically, as might be expected, these secular occasional

[13] The conjectural dating in Smend Kö of various other cantatas, or movements therefrom, within Bach's Cöthen period (BWV 32, 120, 145, 190, and 193) can no longer be upheld.

works assume the lightly draped, cheerful character of their poetic texts.[14] Dance-like melodies are often heard, and BWV 194a is an essay in composing a cantata in the form of a dance suite. The dramatic aspect of the serenata often results in duet passages which not only take a distinctive textual form, such as:

<table>
<tr><td>Fama:
Glückseligkeit
Anhalts:</td><td>Ich weiche</td><td>nun; ich will
nicht; du sollst</td><td>der Erden sagen:</td></tr>
<tr><td></td><td>Nur Tugend kann</td><td>Glückseligkeit
des Landes Wohl</td><td>erjagen.</td></tr>
</table>

<table>
<tr><td>Fame:
Anhalt's
Felicity:</td><td>I yield</td><td>now; I would
not; you shall</td><td>say to Earth:</td></tr>
<tr><td></td><td>Only Virtue can strive for</td><td>felicity.
the land's welfare.</td><td></td></tr>
</table>

but also derive from it their peculiar musical design. Moreover, a reciprocal relationship with the instrumental concerto—so abundantly cultivated in Cöthen—is unmistakable: for example, in the division of the choir in BWV 66a and 134a into concertists and ripienists, and in the probable derivation of the Brandenburg Concerto No. 1 from a lost secular cantata (see below under Cantata 207). In the recitatives there is still a tendency to introduce arioso passages, which we have already recognized as typical of the Weimar cantatas.

2.4 Leipzig cycle I (1723–4)

When Bach put himself forward as an applicant for the post of Thomascantor at Leipzig on Quinquagesima Sunday 1723, he had a cantata ready for the occasion, namely BWV 23, which he had evidently brought with him from Cöthen. The true trial piece, however, was BWV 22, written in Leipzig. Presumably Bach performed both cantatas at his trial service, one before the sermon and the other afterwards. The first Leipzig church-year cycle of cantatas then began with Bach's installation as Cantor on the First Sunday after Trinity 1723. In the following years Bach's cantata cycles seem to have begun on this same Sunday, six months before or after the start of the church year at Advent.[15]

[14] A detailed appreciation of Bach's Cöthen cantata style may be found in Smend Kö, 92 ff.

[15] Thus Picander dates the preface of his 1728 cantata cycle, which was intended for musical setting by Bach, 24 June.

Before we turn to the Leipzig works themselves, the scope and requirements of Bach's new post should be considered here briefly. As is well known, the church cantata had its fixed place in the principal Sunday and feast-day service (the 'Office'), after the Gospel had been read but before the singing of the Lutheran Creed, *Wir glauben all an einen Gott*. If the cantata was in two parts, the second part was performed after the sermon or during the Communion. As we have just seen, the performance of two cantatas, instead of one in two parts, was also not unusual. In addition, sacred cantatas were performed at the annual service to mark the council elections, at weddings and funerals, and on special occasions, such as church consecrations.

The Sunday services available to the people of Leipzig were abundant. Matins had already been celebrated before the Office began at 7 a.m.; and this, in turn, was followed by the *Mittagspredigt* (midday sermon) at 11.30. Since sermons of more than an hour were then no rarity, and since Communion was celebrated during the Office, sometimes with enormous participation, the time available for a cantata performance was barely half an hour, and very seldom could this time be exceeded. On various feast-days the cantata sung in the morning at one

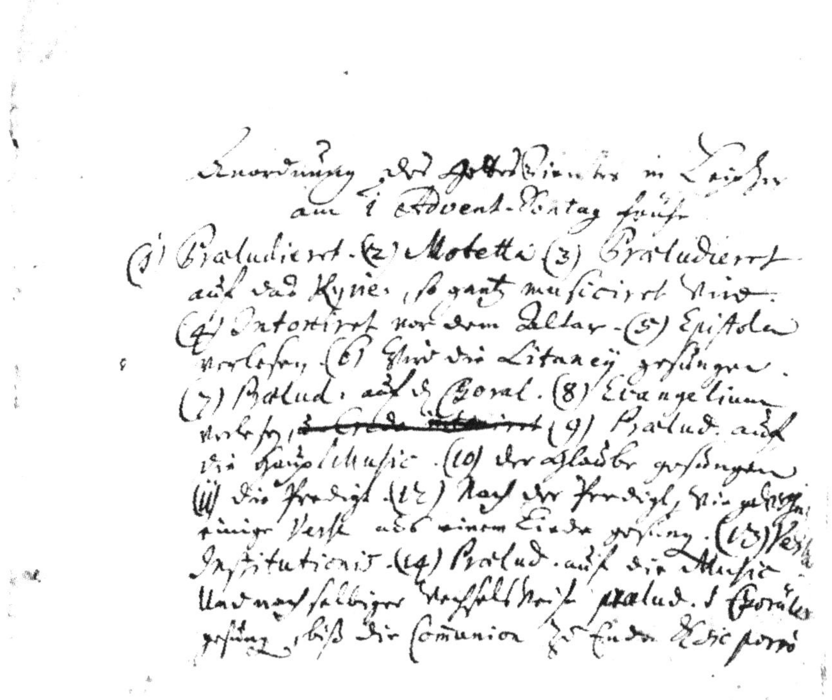
Anordnung des Gottesdienstes in Leipzig
am 1 Advent-Sontag frühe
(1) Praeludiret. (2) Motetta (3) Praeludiret
auf das Kyrie, so gantz musiciret wird.
(4) Intoniret vor dem Altar. (5) Epistola
verlesen. (6) Wird die Litaney gesungen.
(7) Praelud. auf d. Choral. (8) Evangelium
verlesen, ~~Credo intoniret~~ (9) Praelud. auf
die Haupt Music. (10) der Glaube gesungen
(11) die Predigt. (12) Nach der Predigt, wie gewöhnlich
einige Verse aus einem Liede gesungen. (13) Verba
Institutionis. (14) Praelud. auf die Music.
Und nach selbiger wechselsweise praelud. u. Choräle
gesungen, biß die Communion zu Ende et sic porrò

The Leipzig order of service for the First Sunday in Advent, entered in Bach's hand in the score of the cantata *Nun komm, der Heiden Heiland*, BWV 61 (Staatsbibliothek zu Berlin, Preußischer Kulturbesitz, Mus. ms. Bach P 45).

of the two principal churches, the Nicolaikirche or the Thomaskirche, was repeated at the other church during the afternoon service.

The pupils at the Thomasschule were chiefly responsible for the music at the main Leipzig churches. According to school regulations issued in 1723,[16] thirty-two of the fifty-five pupils were expected to participate in church music, and they were to be divided into four cantorates of eight members each. A memorandum in Bach's hand of 18 May 1729[17] shows that he wanted to increase the membership of the first three cantorates to twelve each, a requirement he reiterated (and even tentatively raised to sixteen) in his petition to the Leipzig council of 23 August 1730.[18] The first two cantorates discharged their duties on alternate Sundays in the Thomaskirche and the Nicolaikirche—the latter was the true principal church—while the third cantorate had to sing only motets in the Neue Kirche, and the fourth nothing but unison chorales in the Peterskirche. The first cantorate was musically the most skilled and, as Bach noted in another petition,[19] had to sing mostly cantatas of his own composition, whereas the second cantorate was expected to sing simpler cantatas, on feast-days only. In the performance of Bach's cantatas by the first cantorate, the leading singer, or 'concertist', of each voice type (soprano, alto, tenor or bass) had to sing all the recitatives, arias, choruses and chorales, while the remaining personnel might be variously employed as 'ripienists' (additional singers, doubling in the choruses and chorales only) or as instrumentalists. It is significant that, as a rule, only one copy survives for each voice type in the original performing material.

The rest of the performing body were instrumentalists: four *Stadtpfeifer* (town musicians), three professional string players and one journeyman. Since these did not suffice even for the most modest scoring, however, students or older Thomasschule pupils had to fill the gaps. According to the 1730 petition mentioned above, Bach viewed the following instrumental ensemble as strictly necessary:

violin I, II	2–3 players each	cello	2 players
viola (I, II)	2 players (each)	violone	1 player
oboe I, II, (III)	1 player each	trumpet (I, II, III)	3 players
bassoon	1–2 players	drums	1 player

To this ensemble at least two flautists were to be added on occasion (the organist was present in any case). In all, then, Bach required an ensemble of at least four singers and, depending on the work concerned, from twelve to twenty instrumentalists, plus the organist and the director (Bach himself). Exceptionally—on

[16] See *Die Thomasschule Leipzig zur Zeit Johann Sebastian Bachs: Ordnungen und Gesetze 1634, 1723, 1733*, ed. H.-J. Schulze (Leipzig, 1987), 1723, 73–4.

[17] Dok I, No. 180; Eng. trans. in NBR, No. 144.

[18] Dok I, No. 22; Eng. trans. in NBR, No. 151.

[19] Dok I, No. 34 (especially p. 88); Eng. trans. in NBR, No. 183 (especially p. 176).

special occasions—he may have had larger forces at his disposal, but not for the regular Sunday music; and often enough he had to be content with substantially fewer instrumentalists.

Bach's immediate superior in all church affairs was Superintendent Salomon Deyling (1677–1755), who preached at the principal church, the Nicolaikirche. Here, therefore, the first cantorate of the Thomasschule sang on the first day of each of the three High Feasts, Christmas, Easter and Whit. At all other main services in which concerted music was sung, the first cantorate alternated between the Nicolaikirche and the Thomaskirche. In penitential weeks—the Second, Third and Fourth Sundays in Advent and the Lenten period, from the First Sunday in Lent to Palm Sunday—'high' music was silent for the so-called *tempus clausum*. An exception was the Feast of the Annunciation (25 March), when concerted music was performed even if it took place during Lent. The feast-days celebrated in Leipzig on which cantatas were heard include Epiphany (6 January), the three Marian feasts—the Purification (2 February), the Annunciation (25 March) and the Visitation (2 July)—the Feast of St John the Baptist (24 June), Michaelmas (29 September), and the Reformation Festival (31 October). Moreover, the three High Feasts were each celebrated on three successive feast-days. The overall result is an annual number of about fifty-nine cantata performances, which naturally varied depending on how many of the fixed feast-days fell on a Sunday.

Bach's predecessor Johann Kuhnau also had to take responsibility for church music at the Paulinerkirche, the university church. Since this church had been made accessible to the public in 1710, two different kinds of service were held there: the 'old' service, with cantata performances on the three High Feasts and at the Reformation Festival, and with motet singing at the *Quartalsorationen* (quarterly orations); and the 'new' service, to which every Sunday the non-academic population were also admitted. After Kuhnau's death, but before Bach succeeded him, Johann Gottlieb Görner (1697–1778), organist of the Nicolaikirche, pushed his way into the post of university music director. Only after prolonged wrangling did the newly appointed Thomascantor succeed in securing for himself at least the musical supervision of the 'old' service (which he had, in any case, attended to in good faith from the outset). From 1726 onwards, however, Bach left all the university services to Görner. Before then, from Whit 1723 to Christmas 1725, we have to take into account another Bach cantata performance: in the Paulinerkirche on each of the three High Feasts and at the Reformation Festival.

At the beginning of his career in Leipzig, Bach evidently endeavoured to perform, with the first cantorate of the Thomasschule, exclusively cantatas of his own composition. Even later he seems to have made few exceptions to this rule. Accordingly, during his first few years at Leipzig, he had to compose a new work week after week and have it copied into parts and rehearsed. Only occasionally was he able to fall back on existing compositions from his Weimar period. The cantatas performed by Bach during his first year at Leipzig, grouped together by him to form a church-year cycle (but starting in the middle of the year, as noted above), here designated Cycle I, are as follows:[20]

1723: BWV 75, 76, 21, 24, 185, 167, 147, 186, 136, 105, 46, 179, 199, 69a, 77, 25, 119, 138, 95, 148, 48, 162, 109, 89, 163 (?), 194, 60, 90, 70, 61, 63, 40, 64

1724: BWV 190, 153, 65, 154, 155, 73, 81, 83, 144, 181, 18, 22, 23, 182, Anh. I 199, 4, 66, 134, 67, 104, 12, 166, 86, 37, 44, 172, 59 (?), 173, 184, 194, 165 (?)

It would be helpful to know more about the origin of Bach's texts, but we are completely in the dark about the librettists of his first Leipzig cycle. He appears to have drawn his texts from various sources, for several groups may be differentiated according to textual structure. In the first place, we can account for the cantatas—mostly to texts by Franck, Neumeister and Lehms—that Bach had composed at an earlier period and could revive in Leipzig without major textual alterations: BWV 21, 185, 199, 162, 163 (?), 61, 63, 18, 182, 4 (text by Luther), 12, 172, 59 (?), and 165 (?). BWV 154, whose librettist is unknown, perhaps also belongs to this group. Three additional cantatas, BWV 147, 186, and 70, are also based on Weimar originals, but they were expanded by interpolations and, in places, made more suitable for their new liturgical occasion by means of paraphrase. It has been conjectured, not without reason, that Bach himself might have undertaken these alterations and expansions, but of this there is no firm evidence. Several other cantatas are parodies: here again, an earlier composition—usually a secular cantata—was revived, but it was furnished with a fresh, sacred text (in this musicological usage the term 'parody' does not imply any satirical intent). The works concerned are BWV 66, 134, 173, and 184; BWV 181 should probably be added to the list, and perhaps also BWV 154. In such cases the librettist was confronted with the task of inventing a text which, while suitable for the intended liturgical occasion, nonetheless fitted the existing music as easily as possible. It stands to reason that Bach himself might have been the author of these parody texts, but again we lack evidence.

According to the present state of our knowledge, all the other cantatas of Cycle I are new compositions. With only one exception—BWV 24, which is based on a Neumeister text—the librettists are unknown. As noted above, several groups may be distinguished by the similarity of their textual structure, which invites the conjecture that the texts within a group were written by a single author.[21] However, since the possibilities of variation within cantata forms are not very great, such groupings alone are insufficient to provide a firm

[20] Detailed verification of their chronology may be found in Dürr Chr 2, 56 ff., on which the following remarks are generally based.

[21] With reference to the comments that follow see Scheide II (especially pp. 11 f.) and H. K. Krausse, 'Eine neue Quelle zu drei Kantatentexten J. S. Bachs', *BJ* 1981, 7–22.

classification. Only precise style-critical methods, based on linguistic and theological studies, could aid further clarification, and no such study has yet been made.

A first group is made up of the cantatas for the Eighth to the Fourteenth and Twenty-first to Twenty-second Sundays after Trinity and the Second Sunday after Easter: BWV 136, 105, 46, 179, 69a, 77, 25, 109, 89 and 104. These are characterized by the form: biblical words-recitative-aria-recitative-aria-chorale. A second group includes the cantatas for the Nineteenth Sunday after Trinity, the Second and Third Days of Christmas, the Sunday after New Year, Epiphany, and the First Sunday after Easter: BWV 48, 40, 64, 153, 65 and 67. These adhere to the following basic scheme (more or less varied): biblical words-recitative-chorale-aria-recitative-aria-chorale. In the case of a third group—the cantatas for Septuagesima, the Purification, from Easter Monday to the Sunday after Ascension (except Easter Tuesday and the Third Sunday after Easter), and for the Reformation Festival—we are on firmer ground. These cantatas have in common not only formal elements but clearly tangible characteristics relating to their content. The invariable movement order is: biblical words-aria-chorale-recitative-aria-chorale. A feature worth mentioning among the characteristics relating to content[22] is that the introductory biblical passage is invariably drawn from the Gospel reading for the day, the only exception being the cantata for the Reformation Festival, BWV 79, since no fixed reading had been handed down for this occasion. In each case, the following aria takes up the ideas of the opening biblical passage, often incorporating literal quotations from it. The single recitative is strikingly learned in character and often seems dry to the present-day listener. The aria that follows shows a similar tendency; and, instead of the concluding application to the individual Christian otherwise popular in cantata librettos, it provides a generalized conclusion, valid at all times. No doubt due to their learned character, Rudolf Wustmann has attributed these texts to a theologian, namely Christian Weiß the Elder, to whom he also ascribes various other Bach cantata texts.[23] Weiß (1671–1737) was Pastor of the Thomaskirche, Leipzig, from 1714 until his death. He had formerly been 'ein geschicktes Mitglied des Collegii Anthologici' ('a proficient member of the *Collegium anthologicum*'), a Leipzig learned society that united the three higher faculties. In 1718 he lost his voice, but was able to preach again—with interruptions—from 1723, and then regularly from Easter 1724 onwards. Since the Bach and Weiß families acted as godparents to each other, it is clear that they were well acquainted. However, no conclusive evidence for Wustmann's hypothesis has

[22] In connection with the following remarks see A. Dürr, 'Bachs Kantatentexte: Probleme und Aufgaben der Forschung', *Bach-Studien*, 5 (Leipzig, 1975), 49–61; reprinted in A. Dürr, *Im Mittelpunkt Bach: Ausgewählte Aufsätze und Vorträge* (Kassel: Bärenreiter-Verlag, 1988), 167–77.

[23] Wustmann hypothetically attributes the following cantata texts to Weiß: BWV 37, 44, 67, 75, 76, 81, 86, 104, 154, 166, and 179.

so far been found. The Bach compositions that belong to this group are divided between two cycles:

Cycle I (Septuagesima, Purification, Fourth Sunday after Easter to Sunday after Ascension): BWV 144, Anh. I 199, 166, 86, 37, 44
Cycle II (Easter Monday to Second Sunday after Easter, Reformation Festival): BWV 6, 42, 85, 79

The circumstances might be visualized thus: after an initial setting for Septuagesima, Bach began to set the texts of this librettist regularly on the Fourth Sunday after Easter 1724 (Cycle I); in the following year (Cycle II), after the series of chorale cantatas, he set the texts that were still outstanding. In the case of three additional cantata texts, BWV 69a, 77, and 64, Helmut K. Krausse has established the putative model on which Bach's anonymous librettist evidently relied, namely Johann Knauer's *Gott-geheiligtes Singen und Spielen* (Singing and Playing Sanctified by God; Gotha, 1720), a cycle of cantata texts set by Gottfried Heinrich Stölzel.[24]

For the music of the cantatas of Cycle I, Bach now had at his disposal a richness of form far beyond any standardization. In accordance with his new circumstances, he drew upon the choir to a greater extent than before. The first Leipzig cantatas, in particular, include large-scale choruses, often with solo-tutti contrasts (BWV 75, 76, and 24). It is also noteworthy that, at the very beginning of the Trinity period, Bach often composed cantatas in two parts. Occasionally he seems to have performed two different, originally independent cantatas on the same Sunday, instead of a single work in two parts: BWV 22 and 23 on Quinquagesima Sunday, BWV 24 and 185 on the Fourth Sunday after Trinity, BWV 179 and 199 on the Eleventh Sunday after Trinity, BWV 181 and 18 on Sexagesima Sunday, and BWV Anh. I 199 and 182 at the Feast of the Annunciation. In revivals of older works, Bach now did full justice to his expanded resources—and probably also to the larger available space in the church—by occasional enlargement of the instrumental ensemble: trombones are added in BWV 21, recorders in BWV 18, and additional violins, oboe and violone in BWV 182.

A new development in the first year at Leipzig, as far as we can tell, was a form of solo singing that remained characteristic in later years too, namely a bass solo based on a dictum—a saying of Jesus's, or sometimes words of God from the Old Testament. The preference for the bass voice in such utterances is founded on the liturgical tradition of Passion recitation divided among several singers: Christ's words were invariably sung in bass register, the Evangelist's in tenor register, and those of the other characters in alto register. Ever since, not just in Passion settings but in church music in general, the bass voice was

[24] See above, n. 21.

regarded as the *vox Christi*. Such dicta, sung by soloists, are already encountered in Bach's Weimar cantatas, but there they were composed as recitatives (BWV 18 movement 2, 182/3, 172/2, 61/4; and for alto BWV 12/3). Now, however, Bach's preferred type of setting was a form that lies somewhere between aria and *arioso*. On the whole he leaves such movements untitled; occasionally he uses the non-committal formulation 'Basso Solo', and only seldom do we find the term 'arioso' or 'aria'. The first surviving movement of this kind occurs in the opening movement of the Leipzig audition cantata BWV 22, placed between an introductory tenor recitative and a chorus. After the large choral cantatas of the first weeks—from the Twenty-second Sunday after Trinity onwards—such movements become more frequent, either with orchestral accompaniment (BWV 89/1, 166/1, 86/1) or with continuo only (BWV 153/3, 154/5, 81/4). Related movements with special features of their own are BWV 83/2 and 67/6. Similar pieces occur in the cantatas of the following years.

2.5 Leipzig cycle II (1724–5)

The burden of work during Bach's first year at Leipzig must have been enormous. He received indispensable assistance, not only in rehearsing but in copying out the parts, from the older Thomasschule pupils who stood at his side, above all Johann Andreas Kuhnau, a nephew of Bach's predecessor, who, during the short period from 1723 to the end of 1725, wrote out, or helped to write out, the performing parts of almost half of Bach's complete church cantatas.

The energy and seriousness with which Bach pursued his aim during the first Leipzig years is illustrated by the special task he set himself for Cycle II, an undertaking that largely prevented him from relying on earlier compositions any longer: following an old Leipzig tradition, he based his cantatas on Protestant chorales. Musically, this procedure may be traced back to the old chorale variations *per omnes versus* as practised by, among others, Ludwig Senfl (*c.*1486–1542/3) in his chorale motet *Da Jesus an dem Kreuze stund*, and as still encountered in Cantata 4, *Christ lag in Todes Banden*, by the young Bach.

From a theological standpoint, church musicians of the seventeenth century were induced to set chorales by the *Liederpredigten* (chorale-sermons) which were not unusual at that time.[25] In the age of Lutheran orthodoxy, the so-called pericope constraint generally prevailed: it was the duty of ecclesiastics to take as the text of their Office sermon the Gospel reading for the day. The minister thus had to preach on the same text year after year; and he sought to counter the threat of monotony by employing a different theme—within the framework

[25] With regard to what follows, see A. Niebergall, 'Die Geschichte der christlichen Predigt', *Leiturgia: Handbuch des evangelischen Gottesdienstes*, 2 (Kassel: Bärenreiter, 1955), 181–353.

provided by the reading—for each church-year cycle of sermons. And so the 'emblematic' sermon blossomed, in which exegesis was associated with a symbol that arose from the text. Throughout a whole year, for example, Jesus would be celebrated as the supreme craftsman: he would be described as the model host (Second Sunday after Epiphany—the Wedding at Cana), as well-digger (Second Sunday after Easter), decorator (Ascension), and chimney-sweep (Sixth Sunday after Trinity), and so on. Another method of achieving diversity was the chorale-sermon. In 1690 Johann Benedikt Carpzov, pastor of the Thomaskirche, Leipzig, wrote that during the previous year, alongside the exegesis of the Sunday Gospel, he had

> each time expounded a good, fine old Protestant and Lutheran hymn, and had also instructed that the hymn expounded should be sung publicly in the congregation immediately after the sermon had ended.

In the coming year, he would maintain this practice,

> which the celebrated *Musicus* Mr Johann Schelle, the duly appointed *Director Chori Musici* of our Leipzig churches, will render all the more pleasing and desirable to hear for devout listeners in that he has undertaken, quite willingly, to set each hymn in a charming piece of music, and to let it be heard before the sermon, before the Christian Creed is sung (unless the church *agenda* permits only the chorale, as has to be sung in the Advent and Lent seasons).[26]

It has not so far been established whether Bach's cycle of chorale cantatas should be traced back to a similar collaboration with a preacher, or whether Bach needed any special inducement to follow Schelle's tradition. Bach, of course, not only maintained the tradition but modified it. For since the hymn text was paraphrased in the spirit of the 'modern' cantata, a 'sermon' was made out of it, often incorporating very clear references to the Gospel reading for the day.

The chorale cantatas do not quite extend to the end of Cycle II; they break off with the revival of Cantata 4 at Easter 1725. From the preceding period the following works have come down to us:

1724: BWV 20, 2, 7, 135, 10, 93, 107, 178, 94, 101, 113, 33, 78, 99, 8, 130, 114, 96, 5, 180, 38, 115, 139, 26, 116, 62, 91, 121, 133, 122
1725: BWV 41, 123, 124, 3, 11, 92, 125, 126, 127, 1, 4 (revival)

[26] '. . . jedesmal ein gut, schön, alt, evangelisches und lutherisches Lied . . . erkläret, auch die Verfügung getan, das erklärte Lied in öffentlicher Gemeinde gleich nach geendigter Predigt anzustimmen . . . welches der berühmte Musicus, Herr Johann Schelle, wolverordneter *Director Chori Musici* unserer Leipzigischen Kirchen, andächtigen Zuhörern desto lieblicher und begieriger zu hören machen wird, indem er jedwedes Lied in eine anmutige *music* zu bringen, und solche vor der Predigt, ehe der Christliche glaube gesungen wird (es sey denn, daß vermöge der kirchen-*agenda* nur Choral, wie in der Advent- und Fasten-Zeit gesungen werden müsse), hören zu lassen, ganz willig sich erbothen.' Quoted by A. Schering in DDT 58/9, p. xxxiii.

The cycle concludes with cantatas of the normal type—BWV 249, 6, 42 and 85—followed by the nine cantatas to texts by Mariane von Ziegler: BWV 103, 108, 87, 128, 183, 74, 68, 175 and 176.

We do not know who adapted the hymn texts of the chorale cantatas into the form set by Bach,[27] nor whether one or several writers were involved. The basic form of adaptation remains constant:

First movement: first chorale verse (unchanged)
Second-to-penultimate movements: paraphrase of the second-to-penultimate verses of the chorale to form arias and recitatives, with the occasional preservation of certain lines or verses in their original wording; the text is reduced or expanded, depending on the number of verses.
Last movement: last chorale verse (unchanged)

As an example of the paraphrase of a chorale verse, the second movement of the first chorale cantata, *O Ewigkeit, du Donnerwort*, BWV 20, may be compared with the second verse of the hymn by Johann Rist (1642):

Rist, verse 2	*BWV 20/2 (recitative)*
Kein Unglück ist in aller Welt,	Kein Unglück ist in aller Welt zu finden,
Das endlich mit der Zeit nicht fällt	Das ewig dauernd sei:
Und ganz wird aufgehoben.	Es muß doch endlich mit der Zeit einmal verschwinden.
Die Ewigkeit nur hat kein Ziel,	Ach! aber ach! die Pein der Ewigkeit hat nur kein Ziel;
Sie treibet fort und fort ihr Spiel,	Sie treibet fort und fort ihr Marterspiel;
Läßt nimmer ab zu toben;	
Ja—wie mein Heiland selber spricht—	Ja—wie selbst Jesus spricht—
Aus ihr ist kein Erlösung nicht.	Aus ihr ist kein Erlösung nicht.
There is no misfortune in all the world	No misfortune is to be found in all the world
That does not finally end with time	That lasts for ever:
And is completely eradicated.	It must finally vanish with time.
Only Eternity has no end;	Ah! But alas! the pain of Eternity just has no end;
It drives on and on its play	It drives on and on its play of torment;
And never stops raging;	
Yes—as my Saviour Himself says—	Yes—as Jesus Himself says—
From it there is no redemption.	From it there is no redemption.

[27] According to Schulze, the most likely candidate is Andreas Stübel (1653–1725), conrector of the Thomasschule; see H.-J. Schulze, 'Texte und Textdichter', in C. Wolff (ed.), *Die Welt der Bach-Kantaten*, 3 (Stuttgart, 1999), 116.

Often, however, the paraphrase departs a good deal further from its model; and elsewhere free verse enters as a 'troping' insertion between chorale lines retained in their original wording (in the above example, the last line is preserved in its original form).

The musical structure corresponds with the design of the text. In the first and last movements, the chorale melody is preserved unaltered. The first movement takes the form of a large-scale chorale-chorus, usually with an introductory sinfonia and orchestral episodes between the chorale lines, and with independent instrumental parts in the choral passages. The last movement is a plain four-part chorale setting. The intervening movements depart further from the prescribed chorale; indeed, many recitatives and arias lack even the remotest suggestion of its melody. Sometimes, however, their thematic material is invented in free imitation of the opening of the chorale; now and then, individual chorale lines are heard more or less literally; and occasionally a whole movement is designed as a chorale arrangement. Here the composer acts entirely according to his own judgement, though, as a rough rule of thumb, a passage of hymn text preserved word-for-word tends to bring with it a literal quotation of its associated melody.

At the beginning of the cycle of chorale cantatas we find—uniquely within Bach's output—the rudiments of cyclical composition. In the opening chorus of the first chorale cantata, *O Ewigkeit, du Donnerwort*, BWV 20, a French overture inaugurates the cycle. The opening choruses of the following cantatas are each then designed according to a different compositional principle; and, more remarkably still, in each case the chorale melody lies in a different part, migrating downwards from soprano to bass:

Date	Occasion	BWV	Opening movement	Chorale voice
11.6.1724	1st Sunday after Trinity	20	French overture	Soprano
18.6.1724	2nd Sunday after Trinity	2	Motet-style, c.f.	Alto
24.6.1724	St John's Day	7	'Violin concerto'	Tenor
25.6.1724	3rd Sunday after Trinity	135	Chorale fantasia	Bass

In the cantata for the following Sunday, BWV 10, for the Feast of the Visitation (2 July 1724), the *cantus firmus* again lies in the soprano part, though the melody is no longer that of a hymn but rather the ninth psalm tone.

The composition of chorale cantatas in the form of a church-year cycle concluded at Easter 1725 with the revival of Cantata 4. This probably took place not in the Nicolaikirche but in the university church, the Paulinerkirche, where Bach also had to supply cantatas for services on High Feast days during his first years at Leipzig; for on the same Easter Sunday he performed *Kommt, gehet und eilet*, a rather superficial parody of the Weißenfels pastoral cantata BWV 249a. It is not known why Bach broke off the composition of chorale cantatas. Did he lose his librettist? Or did the preacher alter his theme?[28] However that may be, in the cantatas that followed, Bach at first evidently resorted to a group of librettos, some of which he had already set during the previous year, now composing BWV 6, 42 and 85. But then, having already used the librettos of that group in 1724 for the Fourth Sunday after Easter onwards, he drew upon the poems of Mariane von Ziegler. It is clear that for a short period this poet collaborated closely with Bach; for the very same nine cantata texts that Bach now set—BWV 103, 108, 87, 128, 183, 74, 68, 175 and 176—were published by her in 1728 in the first volume of her poetry, *Versuch in Gebundener Schreib-Art*. In her second volume, of 1729, she completed her cycle by adding the outstanding texts, but as far as we know Bach set no more of them.

This poet, née Christiane Mariane Romanus, was born in Leipzig in June 1695 as daughter of a court councillor who later became a Leipzig burgomaster. As early as 1711 she married Heinrich Levin von Könitz, who, however, died soon afterwards. In 1715 she married again, but her second husband, Captain Georg Friedrich von Ziegler, also died not long afterwards, as did her children from both marriages. In 1722 she surfaces once more in her parents' house in Leipzig; and at this time she began to devote herself zealously to her love of the arts. She wrote poetry and played the clavier, lute and transverse flute. Her house became a centre for local artists, as well as those from elsewhere. When Johann Christoph Gottsched (1700–66) came to Leipzig in 1724, her literary interests grew keener; she published her poems in 1728 and 1729, and a collection of letters followed in 1731. In 1733 she was chosen as poet laureate by the Wittenberg philosophy faculty. In 1741 she married yet again, her third husband being Wolf Balthasar Adolf von Steinwehr, former secretary of the German Society and professor at Frankfurt-on-Oder. She died there on 1 May 1760.

Although the librettos of Mariane von Ziegler are deft and lively, Bach set none of them unaltered, and the changes made are not always altogether felicitous. Evidently he was intent on tightening the substance of the text, and in doing so he shows a striking tendency to lists of words without conjunctions, for example 'Teufel, Tod' ('devil, death') in place of 'Sünd und Tod' ('sin and death'). Another notable feature of the alterations is a preference for words that refer to singing, or even acoustic images. Although it cannot be ruled out that the poet herself made a few changes for publication, many of Bach's readings can be shown to be secondary (because rhyme is destroyed in them), so Bach might be regarded as responsible for most of the alterations. Here are some examples:[29]

[28] It might be significant that Christian Weiß the Elder began to preach again regularly at Easter 1724, so that a cycle of sermons came to an end at Easter 1725.

[29] Note that the rhyme scheme is destroyed in the first example; in the second, note the series of unjoined words—'Frohlocke, sing, scherze', 'Weg Jammer, weg Klagen'—and the inclusion of words with an aural reference: 'sing', 'Jammer', 'Klagen'.

Ziegler (Third Sunday after Easter)	*Bach, BWV 103/4*
Ich traue dem Verheißungswort,	Ich traue dem Verheißungswort,
Daß meine Traurigkeit,	Daß meine Traurigkeit
Und dies vielleicht in kurzer Zeit,	
Nach bäng- und ängstlichen Gebärden	
In Freude soll verkehret werden.	In Freude soll verkehret werden.
I trust the promised word	I trust the promised word
That my sorrow,	That my sorrow
Perhaps in a short time,	
After alarmed and anxious gestures,	
Shall be turned into joy.	Shall be turned into joy.

Ziegler (Whit Monday)	*Bach, BWV 68/2*
Getröstetes Herze,	Mein gläubiges Herze,
Frohlocke und scherze,	Frohlocke, sing, scherze,
Dein Jesus ist da!	Dein Jesus ist da!
Weg Kummer und Plagen,	Weg Jammer, weg Klagen,
Ich will euch nur sagen:	Ich will euch nur sagen:
Mein Jesus ist nah.	Mein Jesus ist nah.
Comforted heart,	My believing heart,
Exult and jest,	Exult, sing, jest,
Your Jesus is here!	Your Jesus is here!
Away with grief and torment;	Away with woe, away with lamentation,
I will say to you only:	I will say to you only:
My Jesus is near.	My Jesus is near.

In his setting of those works from Cycle II that are not designed as chorale cantatas, Bach essentially follows the precedent of Cycle I. As already to some extent in the chorale cantatas themselves, a tendency towards virtuoso treatment of the instruments becomes apparent. Although in Leipzig Bach hardly ever assembled such individual combinations, in terms of sonority, as in his early cantatas (in particular BWV 106, 71, 182, and 152), he seems to have pursued definite aims both in the training of players and in the choice of instruments. For example, the transverse flute, not used in 1723, was introduced only gradually in 1724, but then, from the second half of that year onwards, it received important solo assignments.[30] Moreover, in Cantatas 96 and 103 a 'flauto piccolo'—not a small transverse flute like the modern piccolo, but a recorder of high register—is required.[31] Newly added to the instrumental ensemble of the

[30] As William H. Scheide was the first to observe; see the list of cantatas with extended parts for solo or obbligato flute dating from July to November 1724, given by R. L. Marshall in 'The Compositions for Solo Flute', *The Music of Johann Sebastian Bach* (New York: Schirmer, 1989), 201–25 (see p. 214).

[31] See P. Thalheimer, 'Der Flauto piccolo bei J. S. Bach', *BJ* 1966, 138–46; see also under 'flauto piccolo' in U. Prinz, *Studien zum Instrumentarium J. S. Bachs mit besonderer Berücksichtigung der Kantaten*, diss., University of Tübingen, 1974 (Tübingen, 1979).

cantatas from autumn 1724 onwards, starting with Cantata 180 for the Twentieth Sunday after Trinity, was the violoncello piccolo, an instrument that Bach himself invented. Being held on the arm, it resembled an outsize viola; and it served, in particular, for the rendition of especially lively passages in the bass and tenor registers. The required range varies somewhat, from which we might conclude that Bach experimented with the instrument (or perhaps with several instruments of various design) for some time. Ernst Ludwig Gerber, whose father Heinrich Nicolaus had been a pupil of Bach's in Leipzig at this very period, gave an account of Bach's invention in his biographical dictionary of music published in 1790. Gerber called the instrument viola pomposa, which has led to terminological confusion, for under the names violoncello piccolo and viola pomposa essentially different instruments must be imagined.[32] If we take into account C. P. E. Bach's observation that his father most liked to play the viola in the orchestra, the invention of the violoncello piccolo may be viewed as an expression of his search for lively shaping of the inner parts. The oboe da caccia, another instrument of middle pitch, is also given virtuoso parts in the Ziegler cantatas BWV 183 and 74; and overall a tendency towards richer use of woodwind instruments is apparent in Cantatas 183 (two oboes plus two oboes da caccia) and 175 (three recorders).

Finally, parody procedure again plays a larger part in the cantatas that originated between Easter and Whit 1725. We have already seen how, in Cycle I, Bach fashioned a number of cantatas or movements by making alterations to the texts of existing compositions, a procedure that naturally applies less often to the chorale cantatas. In the period between Good Friday and Whit, great demands were invariably made upon Bach owing to the Passion performance and the large number of successive feast-days. And during that very period in 1725 numerous parodies occur once more. A characteristic of the cantatas to Ziegler texts, however, is that the new text is not modelled on the old one; in other words, it was evidently not written with parody in mind. Consequently, the musical adaptation interferes at a deeper level with the substance of the movement concerned. Moreover, only individual movements could be used as parody models in this fashion, never a complete cantata. A striking example of radical revision of this kind is the aria 'Mein gläubiges Herze' from Cantata 68, a parody of the aria 'Weil die wollenreichen Herden' from the 'Hunt' Cantata, BWV 208.

Bach later removed most of the cantatas for the period from Easter to Whit from the chorale-cantata cycle and incorporated them in Cycle III. Only Cantatas 128 and 68, both of which at least open with a large-scale chorale-chorus, kept their place in Cycle II. Two other cantatas, BWV 112 and 129, were

[32] See Prinz, *Studien zum Instrumentarium J. S. Bachs*, and the relevant literature by H. Husmann, J. Eppelsheim, W. Schrammek, U. Drüner, A. Dürr and M. M. Smith listed in the bibliography.

later added to the cycle in place of the excluded BWV 85 and 176. Nevertheless, it is clear that not all the gaps in the Easter-to-Whit period of the chorale-cantata cycle were filled.

2.6 Leipzig cycle III (1725–7)

In its present state, as transmitted via the estate of C. P. E. Bach, Cycle III is no longer the product of continuous cantata composition in the course of a single year. Either it is a *mixtum compositum* of two cycles (or even three if we take account of the cantatas borrowed from Cycle II), or else suspension of Bach's creativity during the Trinity period of 1725 caused the composition of Cycle III to be spread out over several years so that gaps could be filled. In any event, only a few isolated cantatas are transmitted from the Trinity period concerned: BWV 137 (Twelfth Sunday after Trinity), a late addition to Cycle II, BWV 168 and 164 (Ninth and Thirteenth Sundays after Trinity), and BWV 79 (Reformation Festival). The texts of the cantatas performed between the Third and Sixth Sundays after Trinity were in 1971 rediscovered by Wolf Hobohm in St Petersburg.[33] Since no music by, or belonging to, Bach survives for this period, Andreas Glöckner conjectures that Bach might have been away, leaving the direction of music at the two principal churches to Georg Balthasar Schott, organist of the Neue Kirche.[34] At least three of the five cantatas in question might be by Georg Philipp Telemann, for their texts belong to Erdmann Neumeister's cantata cycle of 1711, which Telemann had set to music throughout. We do not know what cantata Bach performed that year on the First Sunday in Advent; but during the Christmas and Epiphany period of 1725–6 the following works were performed: BWV 110, 57, 151, 28, 16, 32, 13, and 72.

From the Feast of the Purification (2 February 1726) onwards, however, we observe another peculiarity: Bach performed none of his own cantatas, but instead the works of his Meiningen cousin Johann Ludwig Bach (1677–1731). Among them was the Easter cantata *Denn du wirst meine Seele nicht in der Hölle lassen*, formerly regarded as a youthful work by Johann Sebastian (BWV 15).[35] Only isolated works by Bach himself were performed during this period: BWV 43 and perhaps 146; and the gaps in the cycle were later filled by the cantatas of 1725. But from Trinity onwards Bach's own works occur more regularly: BWV 194 (abridged revival), 39, 88, 170, 187, 45, 102, 35, 17, 19, 27, 47, 169, 56, 49, 98, 55, and 52.

[33] See W. Hobohm, 'Neue "Texte zur Leipziger Kirchen-Music" ', *BJ* 1973, 5–32.

[34] See A. Glöckner, 'Bemerkungen zu den Leipziger Kantatenaufführungen vom 3. bis 6. Sonntag nach Trinitatis 1725', *BJ* 1992, 73–6.

[35] See Scheide I.

Early in 1727, Bach performed three more cantatas that may originally have belonged to the same cycle: BWV 58, which, though not a true chorale cantata, was later assigned to Cycle II; BWV 82, which belongs to Cycle III; and BWV 84, whose text belongs to the Picander cycle of 1728, though the work probably originated before then and is transmitted in Cycle III. Cycle III as a whole, as it has come down to us, lacks not only temporal but formal unity. It exhibits no tendency towards cyclical integration according to an overriding principle. All that can be done is to differentiate a number of groups on the basis of shared characteristics. Let us first consider the texts.

In the group of cantatas for the Christmas and Epiphany season of 1725–6, Bach resorted to older texts whose authors are invariably known. Six librettos are drawn from Lehms's 1711 cycle (BWV 110, 57, 151, 16, 32, and 13) and one each from Neumeister's fourth cycle (BWV 28) and Franck's *Evangelisches Andachtsopfer* of 1715 (BWV 72). In the Trinity period of 1726 Bach twice more drew upon Lehms's 1711 cycle (BWV 170 and 35). Apart from these and a few more cantatas by Johann Ludwig Bach, however, the period from Ascension to the Fourteenth Sunday after Trinity is devoted to a group of works whose librettos are drawn from the same cycle as Johann Ludwig Bach's cantatas, a cycle notable for its far-reaching formal uniformity.[36] Of the seven cantatas that belong to this group, one, BWV 43, represents the so-called 'long form' (Scheide) which has the movement order: biblical text (OT)–recitative–aria–biblical text (NT)–strophic poem–chorale. The other six represent the 'short form', in which an aria-recitative pair replaces the strophic poem, giving rise to the following seven-movement order: biblical text (OT)–recitative–aria–biblical text (NT)–aria–recitative–chorale. The overall form may either be conceived as bipartite, since each half is introduced by a biblical text, or else as symmetrical, centred around the New Testament text. The following Bach cantatas exhibit this text structure: BWV 39, 88, 187, 45, 102, and 17.

The form of the dialogue cantata, occasionally used earlier, in which Jesus (bass) and the Soul (soprano) usually form dialogue partners, recurs in Cycle III, twice in texts by Lehms (BWV 57 and 32) and twice in texts by unknown librettists (BWV 49 and 58). In several works from Cycle III—mostly solo cantatas but also one dialogue cantata—it is notable that a line of text from one of the movements recurs in a later movement. It remains an open question whether this textual linking of two movements indicates that one and the same

[36] This observation was first made in Scheide II and confirmed by W. Blankenburg, 'Eine neue Textquelle zu sieben Kantaten J. S. Bachs und achtzehn Kantaten J. L. Bachs', *BJ* 1977, 7–25. The librettist was possibly Duke Ernst Ludwig of Saxe-Meiningen (see K. Küster, 'Meininger Kantatentexte um Johann Ludwig Bach', *BJ* 1987, 159–64); if so, the cycle must have originated around 1704/5.

author was involved, and whether it is right to regard these cantatas as a self-contained group:

BWV	*Recurring line*
169	Gott soll allein mein Herze haben
56	Da leg ich den Kummer auf einmal ins Grab
49	Ich geh und suche mit Verlangen
55	Erbarme dich
82	Ich habe genung
158[37]	Da bleib ich, da hab ich Vergnügen zu wohnen

The musical structure of the cantatas of Cycle III is not essentially different from that of previous years. A particularly notable feature, however, is the borrowing of movements from earlier instrumental works. These movements are mostly used as introductory sinfonias, but also occasionally as choruses or arias with newly composed vocal parts. A closely related characteristic is the frequent use made of obbligato organ, not only in borrowed instrumental pieces, as a replacement for another solo instrument, but even in newly composed vocal movements. These cantatas with obbligato organ were formerly, following Spitta, dated after 1730 and linked with the reconstruction of the organ in the Thomaskirche.[38] It was believed that Bach wanted to give his two eldest sons the opportunity to display their skill as organists. In reality, however, most of these works were performed before 1726, perhaps as a form of trial for the sixteen-year-old Wilhelm Friedemann Bach, though this purpose cannot be verified. Nor can we exclude the possibility that, contrary to the opinion of many scholars,[39] Bach was led to adopt this procedure by purely musical considerations.

A list follows (see top of page 39) of instrumental concerto movements adopted in the cantatas and of instrumental movements with obbligato organ included in cantatas. For the sake of completeness, the list includes a few later compositions that do not belong to Cycle III (these are dated after 1726). Needless to say, the borrowings involved compositional alterations (especially changes of scoring), so that we may speak only of correspondence, not of identity:

[37] The date of origin of this cantata is unknown.

[38] Spitta believed that the Rückpositiv of the Thomaskirche organ had been made playable independently in 1730 (see Spitta II, 112 and 769 f.; Eng. trans., ii, 282 and 675 f.), an hypothesis refuted by B. F. Richter, 'Über J. S. Bachs Kantaten mit obligater Orgel', *BJ* 1908, 49–63.

[39] For instance Richter, 'Über J. S. Bachs Kantaten mit obligater Orgel', p. 51: 'Es ist nicht recht glaubhaft, daß Bach sich von der Neuerung eine besondere Wirkung versprochen habe' ('It is not altogether plausible that Bach hoped for a special effect from the innovation').

Date	BWV	Model	Adaptation
25.12.1725	110/1	BWV 1069/1	with choral insertion and trumpets and drums
12.5.1726 (?)	146/1	original of BWV 1052/1	with obbligato organ
	146/2	original of BWV 1052/2	with obbligato organ and choral insertion
8.9.1726	35/1	original of BWV 1059/1	with obbligato organ
	35/2	original of BWV 1059/2 (?)	with obbligato organ and vocal solo insertion
	35/5	original of BWV 1059/3 (?)	with obbligato organ
20.10.1726	169/1	original of BWV 1053/1	with obbligato organ
	169/5	original of BWV 1053/2	with obbligato organ and vocal solo insertion
3.11.1726	49/1	original of BWV 1053/3	with obbligato organ
24.11.1726	52/1	BWV 1046a/1	
c. 1728	188/1	original of BWV 1052/3	with obbligato organ
c. 1729	156/1	original of BWV 1056/2	with obbligato oboe
6.6.1729	174/1	BWV 1048/1	
c. 1729	120a/4	BWV 1006/1	with obbligato organ and orchestra
27.8.1731	29/4	BWV 1006/1	with obbligato organ and orchestra

A few other cantata movements that might possibly be traced back to lost instrumental pieces are not taken into account here for lack of sufficient evidence. Obbligato organ is used not only in the movements borrowed from instrumental works which are listed above, but also in certain newly composed cantata movements. The following works employ obbligato organ but do not contain borrowings from instrumental works: BWV 170 (28.7.1726), 27 (6.10.1726), and 47 (13.10.1726). In addition, obbligato organ is occasionally used in place of another instrument in revivals of older cantatas: BWV 63 (25.12.1729?), 172 (after 1731) 73 (*c.* 1732–5), and 128 (date unknown).

2.7 Picander and his cycle (1728–9?)

Few traces survive of Cycles IV and V, which, if we are to believe the obituary, Bach wrote in addition to the three we know. The few post-1729 compositions that might conceivably have belonged to Cycle V (BWV 30, 34, 36, and 51) provide insufficient evidence that such a cycle ever existed. As for Cycle IV, the only reasonably distinct trail leads to the cycle of cantata texts published in 1728 by the fluent writer Henrici, who wrote under the pseudonym Picander.[40]

Christian Friedrich Henrici (1700–64) was born in Stolpen, near Dresden, studied at Wittenberg University, and lived from 1720 onwards in Leipzig, first as a private teacher, then as Post Attendant (from 1734, Chief Post Commissioner), and from 1740 as City Receiver of Taxes for Beverages, Wine Inspector, and Exciseman. It can be shown that in 1730 he was a member of a collegium musicum (Bach's?); he therefore not only understood music but himself played an instrument. He began his poetic career in Leipzig as author of satirical, and at times very lascivious, occasional verse and polemical writings, which made him numerous enemies and, in particular, caused a literary feud with Gottsched, who had arrived in Leipzig in 1724. Ostensibly to counter further criticism, he turned to sacred verse, and in 1725 published his *Sammlung Erbaulicher Gedancken, Bey und über die gewöhnlichen Sonn- und Festtags-Evangelien* (Collection of Edifying Thoughts with and on the usual Sunday and Feast-day Gospels), a series of reflections in alexandrines, each followed by a strophic poem to a well-known chorale melody. His collaboration with Bach dates from the same year at the latest (the secular cantata BWV 249a for Weißenfels, 23 February 1725). He wrote a large number of sacred and secular texts for Bach, mostly published in his five-volume collection *Ernst-Schertzhaffte und Satyrische Gedichte* (Earnest, Jocular and Satirical Poems), Leipzig, 1727–51. He was responsible for the texts of the St Matthew and St Mark Passions, and perhaps also for those of the Christmas and Easter Oratorios.

Picander is only a moderately good poet; and where he occasionally shows poetic stature, as for example in the line 'Mond und Licht ist vor Schmerzen untergangen' ('Moon and light are obliterated by pain'), it is tempting to look for external models. What predestined him for collaboration with Bach was an undeniable formal facility and polish plus an apparently profound musical knowledge. This not only afforded him general insight into the demands made of a librettist, but also led him to become a parody poet par excellence. For he tackled with incredible skill this special task of adapting a newly invented text to an existing composition. Even today Bach research is not always unanimous as to which of his texts is original and which parody.

In 1728 Picander published the texts of a cycle of church cantatas under the title *Cantaten auf die Sonn- und Fest-Tage durch das gantze Jahr* (Cantatas on Sundays and Feast-days throughout the whole Year). In the preface he clearly states that these cantatas were to be performed by Bach:

I have undertaken such a project all the more willingly because I flatter myself that perhaps the lack of poetic charm might be compensated by the loveliness of the

[40] On the Picander cycle see the items listed in the bibliography under K. Häfner (1975, 1982, and 1987), W. Blankenburg (1978), and W. H. Scheide (1980 and 1983).

incomparable Capellmeister Mr Bach's music, and that these songs will be sung in the principal churches of devout Leipzig.[41]

This preface is dated 24 June 1728, which corresponds with the dividing line between Bach's cantata cycles: in accordance with the date on which he took up his post, each cycle began on the First Sunday after Trinity.

We have no reason to doubt that Bach set this cycle of texts. Except for a few paltry remains, however, the original scores and parts are lost; and the surviving manuscript copies transmit little more. Bach seems to have set a Picander sacred cantata text as early as 1727: BWV 84, whose text the poet included in his 1728 cycle, whereas Bach, as far as we can tell from the source material, classified the work in Cycle III (to which it belongs according to its date of origin). Assuming that the remaining identifiable works were composed in the course of the usual church-year rotation (which can be established only in the case of BWV 174), we arrive at the following order:

1728: BWV 149, 188, 197a
1729: BWV 171, 156, 159, Anh. I 190 (lost apart from a few bars), 145, 174 (dated '1729')

A few further hints of lost cantatas from this cycle are yielded by a comparison of the chorale texts prescribed by Picander with the collection of Bach four-part chorale settings edited by C. P. E. Bach in 1784–7.[42]

The texts of the cycle follow the enriched Neumeister type and lack special features. From a musical standpoint, the few works that survive form a continuum with Cycle III. In particular, Bach appears to have maintained his tendency to adopt introductory instrumental sinfonias from older instrumental compositions (BWV 188, 156, 174). Cantata 145 is transmitted with an opening chorus whose text ('So du mit deinem Munde bekennest Jesum') is not prescribed by Picander and whose music is drawn from a cantata by Georg Philipp Telemann.

2.8 Other church cantatas

Only isolated church cantatas by Bach survive from the period after the Picander cycle. We cannot say with certainty how great the losses are in these later

[41] 'Ich habe solches Vorhaben desto lieber unternommen, weil ich mir schmeicheln darf, daß vielleicht der Mangel der poetischen Anmuth durch die Lieblichkeit des unvergleichlichen Herrn Capell-Meisters, *Bachs*, dürfte ersetzet, und diese Lieder in den Haupt-Kirchen des andächtigen Leipzigs angestimmet werden.' Quoted from Spitta II, 174 f. (Eng. trans., ii, 345). The only known exemplar was lost in WW II, but the texts themselves (without the preface) are reproduced in Vol. III of Picander's collected verse.

[42] For details see K. Häfner, 'Der Picander-Jahrgang', *BJ* 1975, 70–113.

Leipzig years. It is quite possible, however, that, having an adequate supply of church cantatas at his disposal, Bach's creative will moved in other directions. Thus during these years the four parts of the *Clavierübung* and the Missa (Kyrie and Gloria) in B minor originated; and, in particular, Bach devoted himself, evidently with newly awakened interest, to the student Collegium musicum which he directed from 1729 onwards.[43]

The cantatas that did originate during those years often owe their composition to a special purpose on the part of the composer. One such purpose was that of completing the existing cantata cycles. If, for example, during the original year of a cycle one of the fixed feast-days took place on a Sunday, or if the Epiphany or Trinity season that year included fewer Sundays than usual, several gaps would remain in the cycle; and, when a suitable opportunity arose, cantatas would have to be composed retrospectively if the cycle were to be completed. Such retrospective compositions are chiefly identifiable in the case of Cycle II, the chorale-cantata cycle. They begin soon after the end of the regular cycle and, in some cases, have already been mentioned: BWV 137 (1725), 129 (1726), 112 (1731), 140 (1731), 177 (1732), 14 (1735) and 9 (*c.* 1732–5). Two other retrospective compositions, Cantatas 51 (*c.* 1730) and 30 (*c.* 1738), were probably assigned to Cycle III.

Another special purpose lies behind a group of cantatas that originated as parodies. They owe their existence to the fact that often, as in the case of, for instance, congratulatory, wedding, and funeral music, the function of the work was discharged with a single hearing. If Bach wanted to reuse the music he had composed, sacred parody had much to recommend it, for it allowed the work concerned to be performed again and again within the context of the church year. We have already encountered such parodied works within the first Leipzig cantata cycles. From the later Leipzig years, the following works should be mentioned in particular:

BWV 157: funeral cantata for 6 February 1727; later revived, without textual alteration, for the Feast of the Purification.

BWV 36: cantata for the First Sunday in Advent (1726–31), a parody of the congratulatory cantata BWV 36c of 1725.

BWV 30: cantata for the Feast of St John the Baptist (*c.* 1738), a parody of the homage cantata BWV 30a of 1737.

BWV 191: Latin Christmas music (1745?), a parody of extracts from the Gloria of the Missa in B minor, BWV 232^{I}, of 1733.

BWV 34: cantata for Whit Sunday (*c.* 1746–7), a parody of the wedding cantata BWV 34a of 1726.

[43] See W. Neumann, 'Das "Bachische Collegium musicum" ', *BJ* 1960, 5–27, and H. R. Pankratz, 'J. S. Bach and his Leipzig Collegium musicum', *Musical Quarterly*, 69 (1983), 323–53.

Finally, these later Leipzig years saw the origin of a group of chorale cantatas that differ from those of 1724–5 in that the chorale text is preserved unaltered throughout all verses, and thus all movements. Nearly all the middle movements, however, continue to be set as arias or recitatives as they were in 1724–5, and not as chorale arrangements as they were in the early Cantata 4. The beginnings of this group can be traced back to 1724. It is quite possible that the first of them arose from the unavailability of a paraphrased text, rather than from the intentional creation of a definite type. Later, however, such works occur more frequently and, so it appears, not merely as the solution of a practical dilemma. Several of them have already been mentioned as late compositions written to fill gaps in Cycle II. Four others—BWV 117, 192, 97, and 100—are transmitted outside this cycle and without any stated occasion. It is likely that these four works were originally composed as wedding cantatas, though of course this does not preclude their subsequent use in Sunday services. The late chorale cantatas are listed here for ease of reference:

Date	Occasion	BWV	Text incipit	Cycle
1724	7th Sun. after Trin.	107	Was willst du dich	II
1725	12th Sun. after Trin.	137	Lobe den Herren	II
1726	Trinity Sunday	129	Gelobet sei der Herr	II
1728–31	Wedding?	117	Sei Lob und Ehr	?
1730	Wedding?	192	Nun danket alle Gott	?
1731	2nd Sun. after Easter	112	Der Herr ist mein	II
1732	4th Sun. after Trin.	177	Ich ruf zu dir	II
1734	Wedding?	97	In allen meinen Taten	?
1734–5	Wedding?	100	Was Gott tut	?

From a musical standpoint, it is apparent that the latest of these chorale cantatas, in particular, strongly emphasize the virtuoso element. The arias 'Ich traue seiner Gnaden', BWV 97/4, and 'Was Gott tut, das ist wohlgetan, er wird mich wohl bedenken', BWV 100/3, might be cited as examples.

Apart from the performance of cantatas for the church year, Bach was also obliged to supply church cantatas for special occasions. These include council election cantatas (BWV 119, 193, 120, 29, 69, and several lost works), performed annually at a special service after the new council had been elected. Other occasions of this kind are the jubilee that took place in 1730 to celebrate the bicentenary of the Augsburg Confession (BWV 190a, 120b, and Anh. I 4a), weddings (BWV 34a, 120a, 197, 195, and several lost works, as well as the chorale cantatas mentioned above), funerals (BWV 157 and several lost works), and organ consecrations (BWV 194). However, these cantatas do not differ in principle from those previously described.

2.9 Oratorios (1734–*c.* 1738)

Bach not only constantly endeavoured to diversify his musical forms, he also strove incessantly to break through the stereotype of the conventional cantata text. We know too little about his literary views to say whether this signifies a critique of the ephemeral verse of the time or only the wish to avoid any sterile uniformity. When we consider how ingeniously biblical words and chorale are united to form a 'sermon' in one of Bach's earliest cantatas, the *Actus tragicus*, BWV 106, or in the motet *Jesu, meine Freude*, BWV 227, we begin to understand why in his creative work, even within the 'modern' cantata, he constantly sought orientation around the reference points of scriptural text and hymn. Alongside many individual examples, the chorale cantatas of 1724–5 may be recalled in particular, as well as the later cantatas based on unaltered chorale texts.

In his approach to oratorio, Bach was evidently intent on developing a new domain of church music, more closely linked with the events recorded in the Gospel reading. We do not know whether Bach originally had in mind only the three works of this kind that survive, whether others are lost (one might imagine a 'Whit Oratorio', for example), or whether unknown factors prevented him from undertaking further work in the genre. However this may be, Bach's preoccupation with oratorio may be fairly accurately fixed in time:

Christmas 1734 to Epiphany 1735: the *Christmas Oratorio*, BWV 248
Ascension 1735: the *Ascension Oratorio*, BWV 11
Easter, *c.* 1738: the *Easter Oratorio*, BWV 249, a revision—with relatively slight alterations—of the Easter cantata *Kommt, gehet und eilet* of 1725

Liturgically, these works occupy the same position as cantatas; they differ from them, however, by virtue of their self-contained narrative. It might be disputed whether the works Bach called 'oratorio' are true representatives of their genre. Yet the term 'oratorio' was employed for such diverse works in the eighteenth century that the more epic compositions for Christmas and Ascension, both of which include the characteristic 'testo' or narrator, might just as well be subsumed under the heading as the more dramatically conceived Easter Oratorio.

The librettists of the three oratorios are unknown. For the Easter Oratorio, Picander is an obvious possibility, since he had already supplied the text of its secular model, the pastoral cantata BWV 249a. For the other two oratorios, nothing militates against Picander's authorship, beyond the absence of all three texts in his published collections of verse.

The oratorios for Easter and the Ascension each occupy the dimensions of a single cantata. The Christmas Oratorio, on the other hand, extends over six different services from Christmas to Epiphany. It is nonetheless based on a self-contained narrative, comprising the birth, the announcement to the shepherds, their adoration, the naming of Jesus, the wise men with Herod, and the adoration of the wise men. In order to achieve this narrative unity, Bach on several occasions departs from the divisions of the Gospel readings, as the following comparison shows:

Day	Gospel reading	Christmas Oratorio
Christmas Day	birth; announcement to the shepherds	birth
2nd Day of Christmas	the shepherds at the crib (unless celebrated as St Stephen's Day)	announcement to the shepherds
3rd Day of Christmas	prologue to St John's Gospel (unless celebrated as St John's Day)	the shepherds at the crib
New Year	the naming of Jesus	the naming of Jesus
Sunday after New Year	the flight into Egypt	the wise men with Herod
Epiphany	the wise men from the east	adoration of the wise men

Bach thus eliminates both the prologue to St John's Gospel, which does not belong to the story, and the flight into Egypt, which is anachronistic in this context, and extends the remainder of the Gospel narrative accordingly.

From a musical standpoint, the three oratorios belong to the aforementioned category of works that originated chiefly by parody of older compositions. Yet the Christmas and Ascension Oratorios in particular are adapted with such great care and contain so much newly composed music of their own that their partial origin in parody does not entail a diminution of worth. Among the newly composed movements, mention should be made of the scripture-text recitatives and, in particular, the choruses to biblical words (in the Christmas Oratorio) and the closing chorales (in both works), which are more richly decked out than usual.

By about 1738—over a decade before the composer's death—the development of the Bach church cantata had come to an end. The few works that followed contribute nothing new to the great and many-sided history of the genre. Of course, the church cantata was still zealously cultivated and developed further by other composers in the second half of the century; but by then it had lost its leading place among genres and blossomed in seclusion—that is to say, in the activities of minor masters. After Bach no future great master would ever again say of himself that his aim was to create a 'well regulated church music to the Glory of God' ('eine *regulir*te kirchen *music* zu Gottes Ehren').

2.10 Secular cantatas of the Leipzig period

Although Bach's first years at Leipzig were devoted almost exclusively to the composition of church music, he also found time to compose and perform a number of secular cantatas. These were written for various occasions, among which student events figure prominently. For although Bach's rival Görner had secured for himself the post of university music director, the students were free to ask Bach to compose and perform music for events organized at their own initiative, hence the origin of Cantatas 205, 207, and 36b, as well as the *Trauer-Ode*, BWV 198. Naturally various events in the life of the Thomasschule also offered the opportunity for a cantata performance: for example, the consecration of the renovated school buildings in 1732 (BWV Anh. I 18; music lost), bidding farewell to the Rector in 1734 (BWV Anh. I 210; also lost), greeting his successor in the same year (BWV Anh. I 19; also lost), and perhaps celebrating the birthday of a teacher in 1725 (BWV 36c).

Nobles and prosperous citizens often approached the Thomascantor and *Director musices* with requests for congratulatory cantatas for festive occasions, such as weddings (BWV 216 and 210), birthdays (BWV 249b), or other kinds of homage (BWV 210a, 30a, and 212). Moreover, Bach continued to cultivate his connections with the courts of Weißenfels (BWV 249a) and Cöthen (BWV 36a and the sacred work BWV 244a), often travelling in person from Leipzig.

Bach's composition of secular cantatas received a special boost in 1729 when he took over the directorship of the student Collegium musicum, which had been founded by Telemann. Now, on the one hand, the Dresden sovereign and his family were remembered in cantatas of homage on festive occasions, for example in BWV 213–15, 206, and 207a; and, on the other hand, various cantatas were no doubt heard in the regular concerts of the Collegium in Zimmerman's coffee-house or, during the summer, in the coffee-garden, for example *The Dispute between Phoebus and Pan*, BWV 201, the *Coffee Cantata*, BWV 211, possibly the Italian cantatas BWV 203 and 209, and the cantata *Von der Vergnügsamkeit*, BWV 204, which originated a few years earlier for an unknown occasion.

Bach's librettists include not only many unknown figures and writers employed only once, but also the versatile Picander, who constantly provided Bach with new texts from at least 1725 to 1742. Also noteworthy is his repeated collaboration with Gottsched, though only a single product thereof survives in full with music. Gottsched came to Leipzig in 1724 after taking flight from army impressment in Prussia. At first he received support in Leipzig from the well-known university professor Johann Burkhard Mencke, to whom he showed his gratitude by writing the text of the cantata *Auf, süß entzückende Gewalt*, set to music by Bach (BWV Anh. I 196), for the wedding of his patron's daughter. Unfortunately, Bach's composition is lost, though two arias from it survive in parodied form in the *Ascension Oratorio*, BWV 11. By 1727, when the student

Carl von Kirchbach commissioned Gottsched to write the text of a mourning ode on the death of Christiane Eberhardine, Electress of Saxony, the writer's star was very much in the ascendant. Bach's setting of this work survives, namely the *Trauer-Ode*, BWV 198. Finally, a further collaboration between Bach and Gottsched dates from later years: the students' music of homage on the occasion of a visit to Leipzig by the Elector of Saxony and his family during the Easter Fair of 1738. However, Bach's setting of this bombastic text, *Willkommen, ihr herrschenden Götter der Erden* (BWV Anh. I 13), does not survive.

Formally, the secular cantatas of Bach's Leipzig period may be divided into two groups: the 'dramma per musica' and the true 'cantata' (see above, p. 9). An example of the first group is the Hercules Cantata, BWV 213; by contrast, the lyrical 'cantata' type is illustrated by *Von der Vergnügsamkeit*, BWV 204. A certain intermediate position is occupied by the *Coffee Cantata*, BWV 211, and the *Peasant Cantata*, BWV 212, both of which are designated 'cantata', despite their clear-cut plot. This intermediate type is perhaps the most forward-looking of all, for it deals with a bourgeois subject, in marked contrast with the pompous mythological pseudo-dramas of the *dramma per musica*. At times, it seems as if Bach has here found a strain of human characterization that in some ways genuinely anticipates Mozart: for example, in the languishing arias of Liesgen in the *Coffee Cantata*. Moreover, since the *Peasant Cantata* belongs among Bach's latest cantatas, dating from 1742, it might be asked cautiously whether, in the sphere of the secular cantata, Bach revealed the beginnings of psychological characterization at a time when the development of the sacred cantata lay behind him.

3

Performance practice in Bach's cantatas

Few details of Bach's own performance practice in the cantatas have been handed down to us. Admittedly, we still possess the original performing material of numerous works; but, coming from a time when essential aspects of their realization in sound were not yet fixed in writing but left to improvisation and oral instruction, the original sources provide little more than the plain musical text and contain a minimum of performance indications. It is all the more important to evaluate fully the small amount of information they convey to us.[1]

3.1 Preparation of the performing material

Writing out the parts from Bach's score was invariably done in the greatest haste and shortage of time. This is confirmed by certain dates in the sources: the performing parts for the Whit Monday cantata BWV 174 were not ready till the previous day, Whit Sunday (5 June 1729);[2] and even the score of the *Trauer-Ode*, BWV 198, was not completed till 15 October 1727, two days before the performance. In order that the consequent demands could be met at all, a fixed schedule was almost invariably followed:

1) A copyist, perhaps with the assistance of others, wrote out from the score a single set of parts.
2) Additional copyists prepared from these parts the usual duplicates, namely one extra part for Violin I, one for Violin II, and two for continuo, plus one extra transposed for the organ (which was tuned to *Chorton* or 'choir pitch') in church cantatas.
3) Bach revised the parts and entered the bass figuring in the organ continuo part (or, in secular cantatas, the harpsichord continuo part).

The work involved in stage 3, the last stage and the only one that was not absolutely indispensable, was often carried out in a very cursory manner due to

[1] The following remarks apply to normal circumstances, to which there were occasional (though rare) exceptions.

[2] A graphic picture of the process of preparing the performance material for BWV 174 is given by Arthur Mendel in *Kritischer Bericht*, NBA I/14, 109–15.

lack of time, and not infrequently left undone altogether.[3] As a result, a fearful number of copying errors often remained uncorrected, and very few of them could be put right (perhaps by remembering rehearsals) during performance.

No less informative is what we do *not* find in the original parts of the Bach cantatas. Altogether absent, or almost so, are:

1) Cues of any kind. This means that a singer under Bach would have difficulty recognizing the prevailing key from his copy, let alone the notes that immediately preceded his entry.
2) Markings made by musicians during rehearsals. Corrections not in the copyist's hand were as a rule made by Bach, which stands to reason since Bach had to compare the copy with the score in order to correct it. Far more astonishing is that the same applies to all kinds of performance indications. Thus the rehearsal procedure generally followed today—the conductor gives directions (for example, '*p* in bar 5, please') which are then entered by the player in his copy—did not apply to Bach. On the contrary, since errors certain to be noticed during rehearsal, such as the omission of bars, remain uncorrected, we have to conclude that seldom or never were markings made in the copies during rehearsals.
3) Indications in the vocal copies of solo or choral rendition. It was formerly assumed that, in principle, while recitatives and arias were sung by concertists only (that is, as solos), choruses necessarily involved the participation of additional singers, or ripienists. According to a modern school of thought, however,[4] the choruses also were in the main sung only by the concertist, the principal singer of each voice type. This view rests chiefly on the existence, in most cases, of only one copy for each voice type, coupled with evidence that ripienists did not share concertists' copies. Was the role of ripienists as restricted, then, as the few surviving original ripieno copies (see section 3.3 below) might lead us to believe? It is perhaps conceivable that extended solo and tutti passages alternated in certain choruses as indicated by hand signs, thus without involving differences of notation or textual underlay.[5] But a *detailed* division of choral passages between concertists and ripienists, such as Wilhelm Ehmann recommends for the B minor Mass, for example,[6] is verified only in a few cases, and thus as a rule did not take place. Bach's request, mentioned earlier, that the size of his first three cantorates

[3] Thus the absence of figuring in certain movements or works is not always a well-considered intention of the composer's.

[4] Led by Joshua Rifkin (see bibliography); the arguments are conveniently assembled in A. Parrott, *The Essential Bach Choir* (Woodbridge: Boydell Press, 2000).

[5] However, this theory, which originated with Arnold Schering, has been refuted by Joshua Rifkin: see his 'From Weimar to Leipzig: Concertists and Ripienists in Bach's *Ich hatte viel Bekümmernis* [BWV 21]', *Early Music*, 24 (1996), 583–603 (specifically p. 601, n. 49).

[6] See W. Ehmann, 'Concertisten und Ripienisten in der h-moll-Messe von J. S. Bach', *Musik und Kirche*, 30 (1960), 95–104, 138–47, 227–36, 255–73, and 298–309.

be increased, must therefore be understood as a desire to have reserves available in case of illness, to increase the number of singers available for singing motets and chorales, and to increase the body of instrumentalists, rather than a desire to boost the number of voices singing the concerted choruses of his cantatas.

3.2 Rehearsal

From what has been said so far it is apparent that an intensive rehearsing of Bach's cantatas in preparation for performance may be discounted. The number of errors that remain uncorrected even raises the question whether there was any rehearsal at all. If there was, it must have been under conditions of extreme shortage of time. Perhaps Bach or the choir prefect might have run through the voice parts with the pupils, in so far as time allowed. A rehearsal of this kind could have achieved little more than preventing a disaster. However, we know of no document in which Bach is censured for inadequate preparation of church music.

3.3 Problems of scoring

As indicated above, the number of participants in both the vocal and the instrumental ensemble was, by modern standards, extremely small. Only in nine cases are additional copies preserved for Bach's singers, over and above the concertist's copy: BWV 21, 29, 63, 71, 76, 110, 195, 201, and 245.[7] And even then such ripieno copies, which naturally contain only the choruses, indicate an undifferentiated reinforcement of the principal singers in only a handful of cases (BWV 29, 201, and 245; also the first chorus of BWV 21); elsewhere they serve to effect a 'registration' of the choruses into solo and tutti passages. Compared with our present-day choral and orchestral sound, therefore, Bach's own performances must have sounded decidedly soloistic. And in the instrumental ensemble, due to the small number of violins (at most two or three per part), the wind sound would have been much more dominant than it is today. On the assumption, mentioned earlier, that ripienists played instruments when not singing (which, taking the paucity of surviving ripienists' copies as an indication, must have been almost all of the time), Bach's plea to increase the size of his first three cantorates can be understood principally as a disguised attempt to increase the body of instrumentalists at his disposal.

[7] See Parrott, *The Essential Bach Choir*, p. 61, Table 3a.

The firmly established leader of the performance, and gauge of all uncertainties, was the continuo group.[8] This included organ (or in secular cantatas, harpsichord), violone (a weaker-toned instrument than our double bass, probably tuned an octave lower than the cello), two cellos, and one or two bassoons. Whether Bach invariably had so many players at his disposal is, of course, open to doubt; and it cannot be established with certainty that all instruments would have participated in every movement of a work. Nevertheless, it may be stated categorically that only in rare, exceptional cases is a continuo instrument marked *tacet* in the performing part. Thus, for example, if Bach had used the violone only in choruses, as is often done today, leaving it silent in recitatives and arias, it is quite certain, in view of the shortage of time described, that he would not have had all movements written in all continuo parts with perfect regularity. The same applies to the participation of the bassoon, though many cantatas contain no specific part for this instrument, in which case we have to suppose that the bassoonist, if present, played from the cello part. At least in Bach's Leipzig period, however, those parts expressly written for bassoon that survive (such as, for example, for the *Christmas Oratorio*, Part I) almost invariably contains all the movements of a cantata.

The organ likewise participates in all the movements of a church cantata. However, as the performing parts of several cantatas reveal,[9] Bach seems to have made a temporary exception to this rule around 1732. In these works the organ is *tacet* in certain inner movements scored for only a few parts; but we are unable to say whether or not a player on another instrument, such as harpsichord or lute, played instead. Since Bach later dropped this practice,[10] it had only temporary validity, perhaps on account of special circumstances.

The question to what extent the harpsichord participated in the performance of church cantatas cannot be answered with full certainty. Cases in which harpsichord parts survive are insufficient to establish a rule of general validity. The part concerned is usually one of the two untransposed continuo parts, possibly figured for harpsichord at a later date in order to replace the organ, which might have become unplayable, for some reason, at a revival of the work concerned. In general, then, the harpsichord could have participated regularly only if Bach himself directed the performance from the score at the harpsichord. We do not know whether this was the case, but there is good reason to doubt it. Carl Philipp Emanuel Bach wrote of his father: 'In his youth, and until the approach

[8] On this subject see L. Dreyfus, *Bach's Continuo Group: Players and Practices in his Vocal Works* (Cambridge, Mass., 1987).

[9] To be specific, *tacet* indications are found in the following cantata movements: BWV 129/2–4; 177/2–4; 9/2–4 and 6; 94/2, 4 and 7; 5/2–4 and 6; and 139/2–4 (for Trinity Sunday and the 4th, 6th, 9th, 19th and 23rd Sundays after Trinity respectively), and also in BWV 97/3, 4, and 7, and 100/2, 3, and 5, both for unknown occasions.

[10] As revealed in the organ part provided subsequently for all movements of Cantata 129 and in the lack of similar *tacet* indications in cantatas of later origin.

of old age, he played the violin cleanly and penetratingly, and thus kept the orchestra in better order than he could have done with the harpsichord.'[11]

We have to ask ourselves whether C. P. E. Bach (who was only nine when Bach moved from Cöthen, and therefore must have gained his decisive impressions of his father in Leipzig) would have written this if, every Sunday, he had seen his father direct church music from the harpsichord. Admittedly, it is well established that Bach played the harpsichord during the original performance of the *Trauer-Ode*, BWV 198,[12] and that therefore the evidence is not altogether unanimous. Moreover, Bach might have altered his practice: it is from his late years, specifically, that harpsichord parts survive with greater frequency.

3.4 Performance

From all that has been said it is apparent that a decidedly improvisatory character must have adhered to Bach's performances. Under such a skilled director this might have been quite advantageous, and we may assume that Bach's direction inspired many capable musicians to an artistic perfection that made the deficient preparations seem immaterial. On the other hand, it cannot be denied that a considerable amount of artistic effort must have been focused on the task of achieving a tolerably correct reproduction of the required notes. This view coincides with the picture of Bach sketched by Johann Matthias Gesner, sometime rector of the Thomasschule, in his Quintilian commentary. Gesner describes him

> . . . attending to everything at once and, from a group of thirty or even forty musicians, reminding one of the rhythm and beat by nodding his head, another by stamping his foot, and a third by wagging his finger; giving the right note to one with the top part of his voice, another with the bottom, and a third with the middle; moreover, though he is but one man, with the hardest role of all, while the performers combine to make a great deal of noise, nonetheless noticing immediately if anything sounds wrong, and what is wrong; and holding them all together in due order, stepping in at any point and putting right any unsteadiness, carrying the rhythm in every limb; one man testing every harmony with his sharp ear, one man producing every voice from the confines of his one throat.[13]

Perhaps, therefore, we should imagine Bach's activity as director not merely in rehearsals but to a large extent in the performances themselves.

[11] 'In seiner Jugend bis zum zieml. herannahenden Alter spielte er die Violine rein u. durchdringend u. hielt dadurch das Orchester in einer größeren Ordnung, als er mit dem Flügel hätte ausrichten können.' Dok III, No. 801 (p. 285); Eng. trans. in NBR, No. 394 (especially p. 397).

[12] See Dok II, No. 232 (p. 175); NBR, No. 136 (pp. 136 f.).

[13] See Dok II, No. 432 (p. 333); Eng. trans. from the original Latin kindly supplied by Mr. Peter G. McC. Brown of Trinity College, Oxford.

3.5 Consequences for present-day performance practice

A performance today must be guided by what the composer had in mind, in so far as that can be established, not by the imperfections with which he had to make do in his own time. Thus we should never relinquish the increased opportunities of our time on account of Bach's improvisatory performances. On the other hand, the present-day conductor must ask himself time and again whether, by his actions, he departs from Bach's ideal to the detriment of the work concerned. This applies chiefly to the size of the performing body, but also to the danger of over-differentiating the dynamics of a piece, which would run contrary to the linearity of Bach's compositional structure. In addition, the division of a chorus between concertists and ripienists can only be decided on an *ad hoc* basis (chiefly in passages conceived largely in chordal texture) and should on no account become a habit.

Treatment of the continuo requires special care. Ever since Max Seiffert, disregarding the unambiguous source findings, elevated the aforementioned exceptions of 1732 into a general rule—and went even further by combining the organ with the choral passages only, and the harpsichord with the soloists and instrumental episodes[14]—this practice has never been fully eradicated from our performances, even though Seiffert's thesis was categorically refuted by Arnold Schering as early as 1936.[15] It cannot be emphasized strongly enough, therefore, that the policy of *tacet* organ in movements for few parts and in instrumental passages from choruses, and its replacement by the harpsichord, is a form of *arrangement* that runs contrary to Bach's intentions.

Evidently, the double bass (in Bach, the 'violone') should also take part in all movements in accordance with Bach's Leipzig practice. However, care must be taken to ensure that the instrument used today sounds gentle enough in thin-textured passages. If this cannot be achieved, given the resonance of the modern instrument, in certain circumstances one might prefer the lesser evil and dispense with sixteen-foot bass. Yet this should be regarded as a modern expedient, in no way authorized by Bach's own practice.

It almost goes without saying today that with all other instruments too an anti-baroque, modern tone colour should be avoided as far as possible; for example, recorders should not be thoughtlessly replaced by Böhm flutes. Where re-scorings cannot be avoided, the performer, using all the means at our disposal today, should at least endeavour to find a solution whose justification lies in the work itself and in the sound Bach is thought to have imagined.

14 In his article 'Praktische Bearbeitungen Bachscher Kompositionen', *BJ* 1904, 51–76.

15 See A. Schering, *J. S. Bachs Leipziger Kirchenmusik* (Leipzig, 1936; 2nd edn 1954).

Music Examples for the Introduction

1. Motet in the classic Italian style of vocal polyphony, from the Song of Songs motets (Rome, 1584) by Giovanni Pierluigi da Palestrina (1525/6–94). In principle, the formal structure corresponds with the scheme outlined on p. 7. Each portion of text is set to its own thematic pattern: a) 'Adjuro vos . . .'; b) 'si inveneritis . . .'; c) 'ut nuncietis . . .'.

10
si in - ve -
Je - ru - - sa - lem, si in - ve - ne - ri - tis di -
Je - ru - sa - lem, si in - ve - ne - ri - tis di - le - ctum me -
- - - sa - lem,
ae Je - ru - - - sa - lem, si in - ve - ne - ri - tis di -

14
ne - ri - tis di - le - ctum me - - um, di - le - ctum me - - -
le - ctum me - um, si in - ve - ne - ri - tis di - le - ctum me -
- - - - - - um,
si in - ve - ne - ri - tis di - le - ctum me -
le - ctum me - - - - - - um, ut

18
um, ut nun - ci - e - tis e - i, ut, nun - etc.
um, ut nun - ci - e - tis e - - - - i, etc.
ut nun - ci - e - tis e - - i, ut nun - ci - e - tis e - etc.
um, ut nun - ci - e - tis e - - - - i, etc.
nun - ci - e - tis e - i, ut nun - ci - e - tis e - i, etc.

2. Seventeenth-century Protestant motet for the Twenty-first Sunday after Trinity by Melchior Franck (*c.* 1580–1639), drawn from *Gemmulae Evangeliorum Musicae* (Coburg, 1623). The text is divided into sections set in different ways: part imitatively ('Herr, komm hinab . . .', 'und ging hinab') and part homophonically ('Jesus spricht', 'Geh hin . . .', 'Der Mensch glaubet . . .'). Stylistic means from the doctrine of figures are employed for textual interpretation: downward motion characterizes descent; block chords on 'Jesus' cause the name to stand out emphatically; and triple-time rhythms illustrate the glad tidings.

Note that, for the sake of clarity, Exx. 2–8 are reproduced without their figured bass.

9
mein Kind stir - - bet! Je - sus, Je - sus spricht
Kind stir - - bet! Je - sus, Je - sus spricht
mein Kind stir - - bet! Je - sus, Je - sus spricht
mein Kind stir - - bet! Je - sus, Je - sus spricht

15
zu ihm: Geh hin, dein Sohn le - bet, geh hin, dein Sohn le - bet,
zu ihm: Geh hin, dein Sohn le - bet, geh hin, dein Sohn le - bet,
zu ihm: Geh hin, dein Sohn le - bet, geh hin, dein Sohn le - bet,
zu ihm: Geh hin, dein Sohn le - bet, geh hin, dein Sohn le - bet,

19
dein Sohn le - bet, dein Sohn le - - bet! Der Mensch glau - bet dem
dein Sohn le - bet, dein Sohn le - - bet! Der Mensch glau - bet dem
dein Sohn le - bet, dein Sohn le - - bet! Der Mensch glau - bet dem
dein Sohn le - bet, dein Sohn le - - bet! Der Mensch glau - bet dem

23
Wort, das Je - sus zu ihm sa - get, und ging hin-ab, und ging hin-ab, und ging
Wort, das Je - sus zu ihm sa - get, und ging hin-ab, und ging hin-ab, und
Wort, das Je - sus zu ihm sa - get, und ging hinab, und ging hin- ab, und ging hin-
Wort, das Je - sus zu ihm sa - get, und ging hin-ab, und ging hin-

27
hin - ab, und ging hin - ab, und ging hin - ab, und ging hin - -
ging hin - ab, und ging hin - ab, und ging hin - ab,
ab, und ging hin - ab, und ging hin - ab, und ging hin - ab, und ging hin -
ab, und ging hin - ab, und ging hin - -

29
1. 2.
ab, und ging hinab, und ging hin- ab, und ging hin - ab.. ab.
und ging hin-ab, und ging hin-ab, und ging hin - ab. ab.
ab, und ging hinab, und ging hin- ab, und ging hin- ab, und ging hin - ab. ab.
ab, und ging hin-ab, und ging hin-ab, und ging hin - ab. ab.

3. Seventeenth-century double-choir motet by Johann Michael Bach (1648–94), J. S. Bach's father-in-law. It opens with the two choirs in antiphonal exchange, but from bar 34 there is a transition to a single choir of four parts with chorale *cantus firmus* in the soprano.

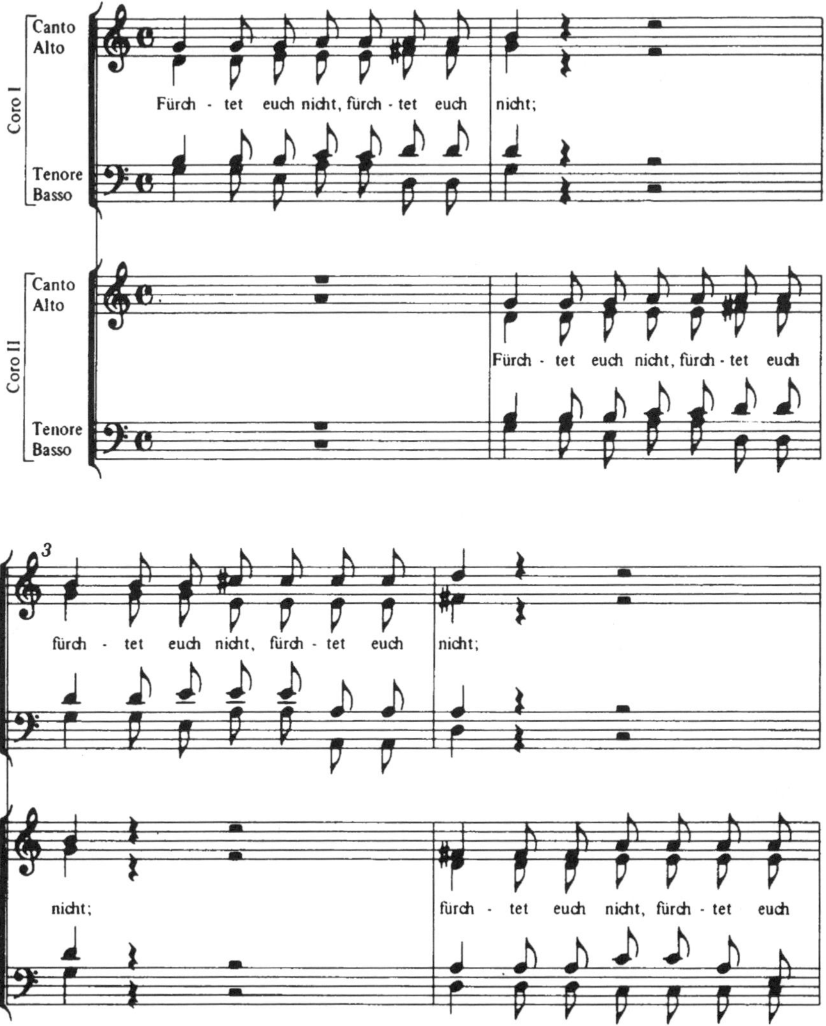

5
sie - he,
etc.
nicht, sie - he, sie - he, ich ver - kün - di - ge euch gro - ße Freu - de.
34
Denn euch, denn euch ist heu - te der Hei - land ge -
Denn euch, denn euch ist heu - te der Hei - land ge -
37
bo - ren, denn euch ist heu - te der Hei - land ge - bo - ren,
bo - ren, denn euch ist heu - te der Hei - land ge - bo - ren,

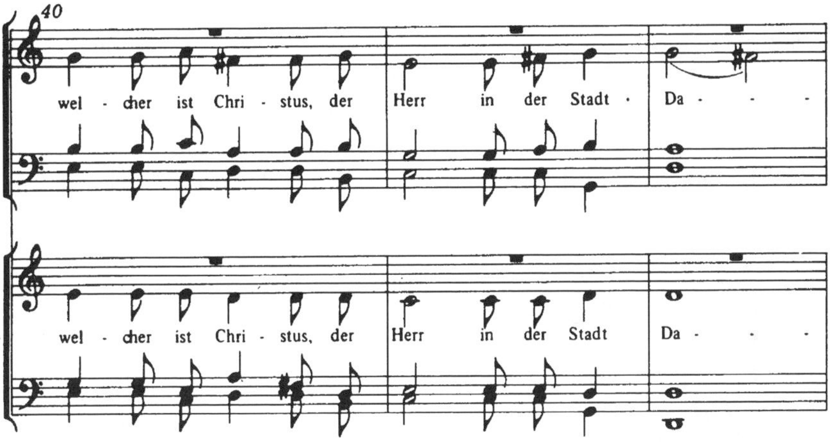

40
wel - cher ist Chri - stus, der Herr in der Stadt · Da - - - -
wel - cher ist Chri - stus, der Herr in der Stadt Da - - - -

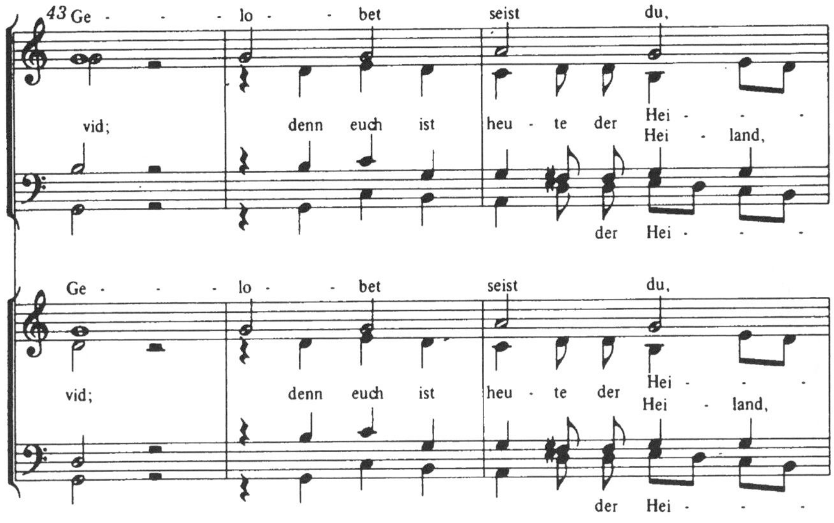

43 Ge - - - lo - - bet seist du,
vid; denn euch ist heu - te der Hei - - -
Hei - land,
der Hei - - -
Ge - - - lo - - bet seist du,
vid; denn euch ist heu - te der Hei - - -
Hei - land,
der Hei - - -

Chor I + II
46 Je - - - - su Christ,
- - - - - land ge - bo - ren,
denn euch ist heu - te der Hei - land ge - bo -
etc.
- - - - - land ge - bo - ren,
etc.

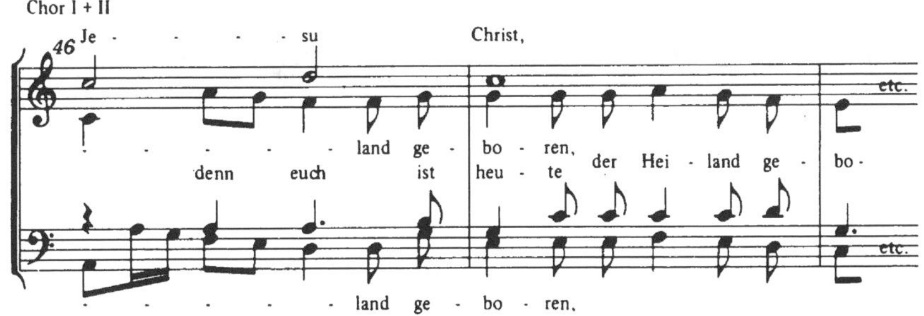

4. Seventeenth-century sacred (chorale) concerto from *Opella nova* (Leipzig, 1618) by Johann Hermann Schein (1586–1630). Each chorale line is prepared by the two soprano parts in *concertato* style and then delivered by the tenor in long note-values. All three voices unite in *concertato* texture for the last two chorale lines. The derivation of this type from the polychoral concerto is clear from a comparison with Ex. 3.

5
ge - lo - bet seist du, ge - lo - bet seist du,
seist du, ge - lo - bet seist du, ge - lo - bet
7
Je - - su Christ, seist du, Je - - - su Christ,
seist du, Je - - - su Christ, Je - - su Christ,
Ge - -
9
etc.
etc.
lo - bet seist du, Je - - su Christ,
etc.
etc.

5. Permutation fugue from Cantata 182, second movement, by Johann Sebastian Bach (1685–1750). The permutation scheme corresponds with that outlined above on p. 12. Each phase of the scheme is one bar long (from the second crotchet of one bar to the first crotchet of the next); the instruments are added from the fifth phase onwards.

1 = first subject, etc.
A = phase in *dux* form (tonic)
B = phase in *comes* form (dominant)

S.
A.
T.
B.
Bc.
- men_, sei will - kom - men, Him - - mels - kö - nig, sei will -
kö - nig_, sei_ will - kom - - - - - - men_, sei will -
Him - mels - kö - nig_, sei_ will -
A
V.
Va.
kom - - - - - - - men, Him - mels - kö - nig_, sei_ will -
kom - men, Him - mels - kö - nig, sei will - kom - - - - - - -
kom - - - - men, sei will - kom - men, Him - mels - kö - nig, sei will -
Him - mels - kö - nig_, sei_ will - kom - - - - men, sei will -
B
A

6
V.
Va.
Vc.
S.
kom - - - men, sei will-kom-men, Him-mels-kö-nig, sei will-
A.
men, Him-mels-kö-nig_, sei_ will-kom - - - - men, sei will-
T.
kom - - - - - - - men, Him-mels-kö-nig_, sei_ will-
B.
kom-men, Him-mels-kö-nig, sei will-kom - - - - - -
Bc.
B
A
8
kom - - - - - - - - - - - - -
kom - men, Him - mels - kö - nig, sei will -
kom - - - - - - - - men__, sei will -
men, Him - mels - kö - nig___, sei___ will -
B
etc.

6. Recitative (*secco* with arioso section) from Cantata 18, second movement, by J. S. Bach. It opens with free recitation, syllabically declaimed (i.e. one syllable to each note), with melismatic (i.e. a syllable slurred over several notes) adornment of the word 'feuchtet' ('moisten'). It changes to arioso in bar 5: fixed tempo ('andante'), active accompaniment, imitation between voice and continuo, and formation of distinctive motives (bb. 6–7).

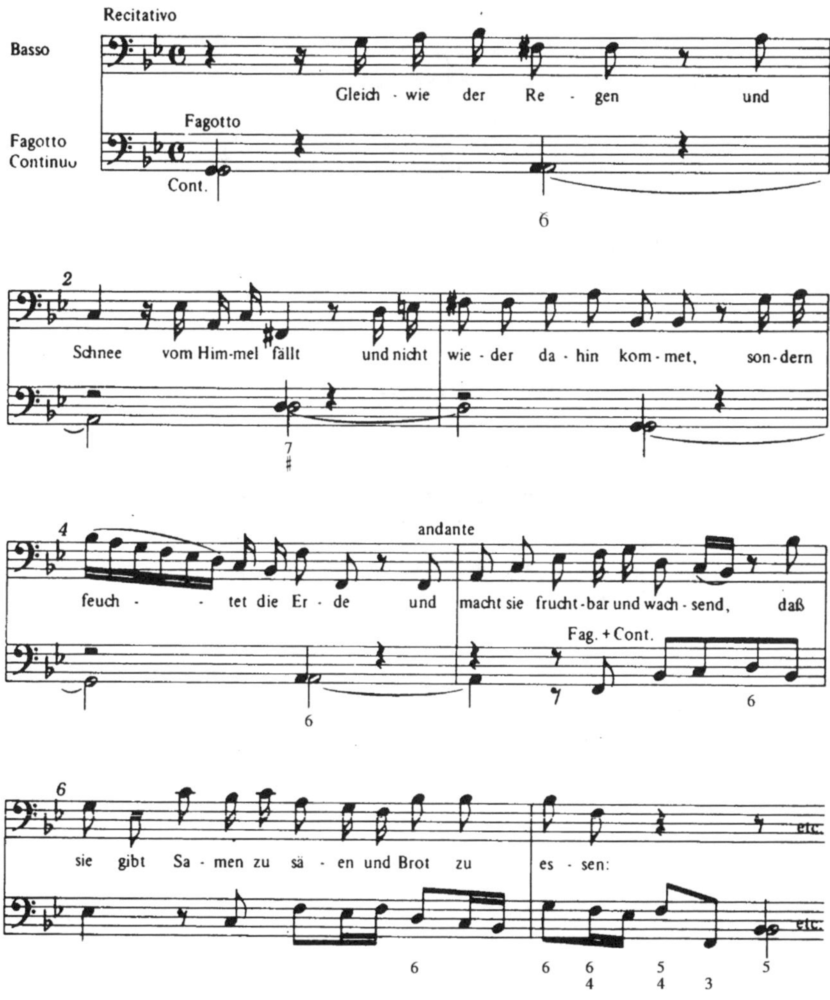

7. Recitative (motivically imprinted *accompagnato**) from Cantata 175, first movement (complete), by J. S. Bach. The scoring with three recorders serves to characterize the pastoral atmosphere.

8. Aria from Cantata 21, third movement (complete), by J. S. Bach. The introductory ritornello consists of two similar components *a* and *a*[1] (bars 1–5, 5–7), whose individual phrases, here numbered 1–7, recur so frequently in the following vocal section that altogether only 1 bars (half each of bars 10, 16, and 17) lack thematic material from the ritornello.

8
1
Seuf - zer, Trä - nen, Kum - mer, Not__, Seuf - zer,
Fine
10
2
3
6'
Trä - nen, ängst - lichs Seh - nen, Furcht und Tod__
12
4
na - gen mein_ be - klemm - tes Herz, ich_ emp - fin - de Jam - mer,
14
5
6
5'
6'
Schmerz. Seuf - zer, Trä - nen, Kum - mer, Not__, Kum - mer,

16
Not, ängst - lichs Seh - nen, Furcht und Tod ,
18
Seuf - zer, Trä - nen, Kum - mer, Not , Seuf - zer, Trä - nen, Kum-mer
20
Not na - gen mein be-klemm-tes Herz, ich emp-fin - de Jam - mer,
22
Schmerz. Seuf - zer, Trä - nen, Kum - mer, Kummer, Not.

Dal segno al fine

PART 2

Church Cantatas

I

Cantatas for the church year: Advent to Trinity

1.1 First Sunday in Advent

Epistle: Romans 13.11–14: 'The night is far spent; the day is at hand'.
Gospel: Matthew 21.1–9: Jesus's entry into Jerusalem.

Nun komm, der Heiden Heiland, BWV 61

NBA I/1, p. 3 BC A1 Duration: *c.* 18 mins

1. Ouverture SATB vln I,II vla I,II cello bsn bc a ¢ $\frac{3}{4}$ ¢

Nun komm, der Heiden Heiland,	**Now come, Saviour of the Gentiles,**
Der Jungfrauen Kind erkannt,	**Known as the Virgin's Child;**
Des sich wundert alle Welt,	**All the world marvels that**
Gott solch Geburt ihm bestellt.	**God has ordained for Him such a birth.**

2. Recitativo T bc C–C c

Der Heiland ist gekommen,	The Saviour has come;
Hat unser armes Fleisch und Blut	Our poor flesh and blood
An sich genommen	He has taken upon Himself
Und nimmet uns zu Blutsverwandten an.	And accepts us as blood relations.
O allerhöchstes Gut!	O supreme Good!
Was hast du nicht an uns getan?	What have You not done for us?
Was tust du nicht	What do You not do
Noch täglich an den Deinen?	Still daily for Your people?
Du kömmst und läßt dein Licht	You come and let Your Light
Mit vollem Segen scheinen.	Shine with full Blessing.

3. Aria T vlns + vlas bc C $\frac{9}{8}$

Komm, Jesu, komm zu deiner Kirche	Come, Jesus, come to Your Church
Und gib ein selig neues Jahr!	And grant us a blessed New Year!
Befördre deines Namens Ehre,	Promote the honour of Your name,
Erhalte die gesunde Lehre	Maintain sound doctrine,
Und segne Kanzel und Altar!	And bless pulpit and altar!

4. Recitativo B vln I,II vla I,II cello bc e–G c

'Siehe, ich stehe vor der Tür und klopfe an. So jemand meine Stimme hören wird und die Tür auftun, zu dem werde ich eingehen und das Abendmahl mit ihm halten und er mit mir.'	'See, I stand before the door and knock. If anyone hears my voice and opens the door, I will go in to him and have supper with him and he with me.'

5. ARIA S bc — G $\frac{3}{4}$ C $\frac{3}{4}$

Öffne dich, mein ganzes Herze,	Open, my whole heart:
Jesus kömmt und ziehet ein.	Jesus comes and moves in.
Bin ich gleich nur Staub und Erde,	Though I am but dust and earth,
Will er mich doch nicht verschmähn,	Yet He would not disdain
Seine Lust an mir zu sehn,	To find His pleasure in me,
Daß ich seine Wohnung werde.	So that I become His dwelling.
O wie selig werd ich sein!	Oh, how blessed I shall be!

6. [CHORALE] SATB vln I + II bc (+ other instrs) — G C

Amen, amen!	**Amen, amen!**
Komm, du schöne Freudenkrone, bleib nicht lange!	**Come, you fair crown of joy, do not delay for long!**
Deiner wart ich mit Verlangen.	**I await you with longing.**

The libretto of this cantata, by Erdmann Neumeister, opens with the first verse of the old church hymn *Veni redemptor gentium* in Martin Luther's German translation of 1524. For centuries this was the principal hymn of the Advent season in the Lutheran Church. The recitative 'Siehe, ich stehe vor der Tür' is a biblical passage from Revelation 3.20. And the text concludes with the *Abgesang** from the last verse of the hymn *Wie schön leuchtet der Morgenstern* by Philipp Nicolai (1599). In the freely versified movements Neumeister develops a sermon-like succession of ideas. The coming of the Saviour daily brings us new blessings (no. 2). This is linked to the prayer that Jesus will come to His Church and hence to His congregation (no. 3). After the biblical passage already mentioned, Jesus is asked to enter into the heart of the individual Christian and not to reject it, despite its sinfulness. As the theme of the libretto, then, general and individual prayers for the coming of the Saviour stand face to face in the two arias.

The score is dated in Bach's own hand '1714'. That year brought him the office of Concertmaster, with its attendant duty of composing monthly cantatas for the court chapel at Weimar. Later, as Thomascantor at Leipzig, Bach noted down the order of the Leipzig Advent service in the score of this cantata, which has sometimes led to the conjecture that the work was already composed for Leipzig in 1714, or at least performed there before 1723, and that Bach wanted to become acquainted with a liturgy that was new to him. This is neither substantiated, however, nor very likely—for the Advent cantata with the same opening lines, BWV 62 of 1724, contains a similar entry. In each case, then, Bach's note on the liturgy probably represents an overt emphasis on the start of a new church year.

The instrumentation, which includes two viola parts (as often in Bach's early cantatas), dispenses with independent wind instruments. However, we lack the original performing parts which might have shown whether, at least in a Leipzig revival, Bach reinforced the strings with doubling oboes, a procedure that experience tells us is not always marked in the score.

The opening movement is an ingenious combination of chorale arrangement and French Overture:* the overture inaugurates the church year. In French opera an overture was customarily played while the king entered his royal box. In this cantata too it serves to greet the entry of a King. The basic form of the *ouverture*, slow–fast (fugue*)–slow, is so combined with the four-line Lutheran chorale that the first two lines are assigned to the slow opening section and a line each to the two following sections. The orchestra begins with a quotation of the first chorale line in the instrumental bass, after which the same line is sung by all four voices in turn against the ceremonial dotted rhythms of the instruments. Line 2 follows in a chordal texture of voices, again embedded in the instrumental rhythms. In the quick fugato of line 3, the instruments double the choir in unison, but line 4, returning to the style of line 2, is heard chordally within the solemn instrumental texture.

The second movement begins as a *secco*; that is, a plainly declaimed recitative accompanied only by continuo chords; but after a few bars it turns into a structurally consolidated arioso,* with imitation* between tenor and continuo. In the third movement, unison violins and violas form a single obbligato* part. This, in conjunction with frequent recurrences of portions of the introductory ritornello within the vocal passages, lends the whole aria a rather pointedly strict and unified character.

The true high point of the work is the fourth movement. Plucked string chords here create the impression of knocking, and the voice likewise turns to pictorial representation at the words 'klopfe an' ('knock').The choice of bass for the voice part is deliberate: this is the 'vox Christi' of the liturgical singing of the Passion. The most expressive text-engendered declamation is here ingeniously melted down into a structure only ten bars long but of compelling musical logic.

The soprano aria no. 5 is accompanied only by continuo, allowing the voice all the greater opportunity for display. The rhythmically contrasted middle section ('adagio') underlines the personal character that distinguishes this aria from the first (no. 3), a contrast already prescribed in the text. Finally, the *Abgesang* of Nicolai's hymn is heard in a five-part figural* setting, in which the obbligato violins soar up to top g^3 at the close in Advent jubilation. That Neumeister was here content with only part of a hymn verse is surely a sign of incipient indifference to the chorale. We may safely assume that in later years Bach would not have adopted his textual model so uncritically and might have sought to avoid such mutilation.

Nun komm, der Heiden Heiland, BWV 62

NBA I/1, p. 77 BC A2 Duration: *c.* 22 mins

1. [Chorale] S + hn ATB ob I,II str bc b $\frac{6}{4}$

Nun komm, der Heiden Heiland,	**Now come, Saviour of the Gentiles,**
Der Jungfrauen Kind erkannt,	**Known as the Virgin's Child;**

Des sich wundert alle Welt,	**All the world marvels that**
Gott solch Geburt ihm bestellt.	**God has ordained for Him such a birth.**

2. Aria T ob I,II str bc — G 3/8

Bewundert, o Menschen, dies große Geheimnis:	Marvel, O people, at this great mystery:
Der höchste Beherrscher erscheinet der Welt.	The highest Ruler appears to the world.
Hier werden die Schätze des Himmels entdecket,	Here the treasures of heaven are disclosed;
Hier wird uns ein göttliches Manna bestellt,	Here a divine manna is for us ordained;
O Wunder! Die Keuschheit wird gar nicht beflecket.	O wonder! chastity is not at all blemished.

3. Recitativo B bc — D–A C

So geht aus Gottes Herrlichkeit und Thron	Thus from God's glory and throne
Sein eingeborner Sohn.	His only begotten Son proceeds.
Der Held aus Juda bricht herein,	The Hero from Judah breaks forth
Den Weg mit Freudigkeit zu laufen	To run His course with joyfulness
Und uns Gefallne zu erkaufen.	And to redeem us fallen ones.
O heller Glanz, o wunderbarer Segensschein!	O bright lustre, O wondrous light of Blessing!

4. Aria B bc + str 8va — D C

Streite, siege, starker Held!	Fight, conquer, strong Hero!
Sei vor uns im Fleische kräftig!	Be mighty for us in the flesh!
Sei geschäftig,	Be active in making
Das Vermögen in uns Schwachen	The capability of us weaklings
Stark zu machen!	Strong!

5. Recitativo [Duetto] SA str bc — A–b C

Wir ehren diese Herrlichkeit	We honour this glory
Und nahen nun zu deiner Krippen	And now approach Your crib
Und preisen mit erfreuten Lippen,	And praise with delighted lips
Was du uns zubereit';	What You have prepared for us;
Die Dunkelheit verstört uns nicht	Darkness did not disturb us
Und sahen dein unendlich Licht.	When we saw Your unending Light.

6. Choral SATB bc (+ instrs) — b C

Lob sei Gott dem Vater ton,	**Praise be given to God the Father,**
Lob sei Gott sein'm eingen Sohn,	**Praise be to God His only Son,**
Lob sei Gott dem Heilgen Geist	**Praise be to God the Holy Spirit**
Immer und in Ewigkeit!	**Always and in eternity!**

Unlike the cantata just discussed, which adopted only the opening verse of the chorale, the libretto of Cantata 62 is based exclusively on Martin Luther's hymn of 1524 and hence on its model, the Latin hymn *Veni redemptor gentium*. Of the eight verses of Luther's hymn, the first and last are preserved in their original wording; nos. 2 and 3 are very freely paraphrased in the first aria; and nos. 4 and 5 form the basis of the following recitative. The second aria (no. 4) is based on verse 6 and the duet recitative (no. 5) on verse 7. The author of this textual paraphrase is unknown.

Bach's setting was written for the First Sunday in Advent, 1724, as part of the cycle of chorale-cantatas. A horn is added to the usual ensemble (which includes two oboes), but it is merely allotted the role of doubling the soprano part in order to reinforce the chorale melody in the *cantus firmus** movements (nos. 1 and 6).

The most splendid movement in the cantata is undoubtedly the concerted opening chorus.* The chorale melody lies in the soprano (plus horn), but, as in Cantata 61, its first and last lines are already quoted in the instrumental prelude—in the continuo at the beginning and in the oboes at the end, now in free rhythmic diminution.* This introductory ritornello develops the independent thematic material of the movement (except for the chorale quotations just mentioned) in a concerto-like division between various instrumental groups. The oboes state the ritornello theme, while from the background of accompanying strings the first violin detaches itself with concertante* figuration and the continuo instruments intone the first chorale line. In various shortened forms, the ritornello recurs three times as an episode between the chorale lines, finally closing the movement in unabridged form. In the intervening choral passages, the soprano delivers the chorale melody line by line, supported by the other choral parts in fore-imitation* (lines 1 and 4), in very freely inverted chorale motives* (line 2), and in thematically independent imitation,* related to the ritornello (line 3), while the instruments develop their ritornello motives further. Thereby the following structure arises (normal type = voice parts; italics = instruments):

Ritornello (chorale quotation [lines 1 and 4] at beginning [bc] and end [oboes])
Line 1 (fore-imitation in lower parts + *ritornello motives*)
Ritornello, abridged (chorale quotation at the end [oboes])
Line 2 (inverted chorale motives in the lower parts + *ritornello motives*)
Ritornello, abridged
Line 3 (ritornello motives in lower parts + *ritornello motives*)
Ritornello, abridged (chorale quotation at the beginning [bc] and end [oboes])
Line 4 (expanded reprise of line 1 + *ritornello motives*)
Ritornello, in full

Bach's music—in 6/4 time, to which the long notes of the chorale melody have to be accommodated—sets up an opposition between the *concertato* brilliance of the instrumental writing and the reflective gravity with which the wonder of Christ's becoming man is celebrated in the chorale. Alongside the ideas of Luther's hymn, the image of the entry into Jerusalem from the Gospel,* read before the cantata performance, certainly had its effect on Bach's setting.

The same basic approach, albeit with more intimate scoring, is carried over into the joyfully soaring aria no. 2, characterized by its subdominant-related major key and, in particular, by the siciliano rhythm of its ritornello theme. A short *secco* recitative (no. 3) leads to the second aria (no. 4). Skilfully, the librettist has already incorporated effective contrasts, making the two arias carry the great paradoxes of Luther's hymn: the miracles of unblemished chastity and of the Saviour's 'victory in the flesh'. Bach's setting underlines their antithesis by means of different scoring (no. 2: string texture with oboes reinforcing the tuttis; no. 4: continuo texture), time signature, and choice of affect*—the tenderly soaring theme of the first aria is contrasted with the militant, tumultuous continuo theme of the second, played not only on continuo instruments but doubled at the upper octave by violins and violas, a rare but not entirely unknown effect at that time.

A duet recitative accompanied by strings, again quite tender and intimate, expresses the gratitude of Christendom and leads back to the mood of the first aria. It is followed by the final verse of Luther's hymn in a plain chorale setting.

Schwingt freudig euch empor, BWV 36

NBA I/1, pp. 19, 43 BC A3 Duration: *c.* 31 mins

1.	Chorus SATB ob d'am I + II str bc	D 3/4
	Schwingt freudig euch empor zu den erhabnen Sternen,	Soar joyfully up to the lofty stars,
	Ihr Zungen, die ihr itzt in Zion fröhlich seid!	You tongues, which are now cheerful in Zion!
	Doch haltet ein! Der Schall darf sich nicht weit entfernen,	But stop! the sound need not spread far,
	Es naht sich selbst zu euch der Herr der Herrlichkeit.	For He approaches you in person, the Lord of Glory.
2.	Choral S + ob d'am I A + ob d'am II bc	f♯ C
	Nun komm, der Heiden Heiland,	**Now come, Saviour of the Gentiles,**
	Der Jungfrauen Kind erkannt,	**Known as the Virgin's Child;**
	Des sich wundert alle Welt,	**All the world marvels that**
	Gott solch Geburt ihm bestellt.	**God has ordained for Him such a birth.**
3.	Aria T ob d'am I bc	b 3/8
	Die Liebe zieht mit sanften Schritten	Love with soft steps gradually
	Sein Treugeliebtes allgemach.	Draws his truly beloved.
	Gleichwie es eine Braut entzücket,	Just as a bride is enchanted
	Wenn sie den Bräutigam erblicket,	When she sees the bridegroom,
	So folgt ein Herz auch Jesu nach.	So too does a heart follow after Jesus.
4.	Chorale SATB bc (+ instrs)	D C
	Zwingt die Saiten in Cythara	**Compel the strings in Cythera**
	Und laßt die süße Musica	**And let the sweet music**
	Ganz freudenreich erschallen,	**Sound quite rich in joy,**

Daß ich möge mit Jesulein,
Dem wunderschönen Bräutgam mein,
In steter Liebe wallen!
Singet, springet,
Jubilieret, triumphieret,
Dankt dem Herren!
Groß ist der König der Ehren.

So that with my Jesus,
My wondrous fair Bridegroom,
I may simmer in constant love!
Sing, spring,
Exult, triumph,
Thank the Lord!
Great is the King of honour.

Secunda pars:

5. ARIA B str bc — D C

Willkommen, werter Schatz!
Die Lieb und Glaube machet Platz
Vor dich in meinem Herzen rein,
Zieh bei mir ein!

Welcome, dear treasure!
Love and Faith make room
For You in my pure heart;
Move in with me!

6. CHORALE T ob d'am I,II bc — b 3/4

Der du bist dem Vater gleich,
Führ hinaus den Sieg im Fleisch,
Daß dein ewig Gotts Gewalt
In uns das krank Fleisch enthalt.

You who are equal to the Father,
Bring forth victory in the flesh,
So that Your eternal divine power
Be contained in our ailing flesh.

7. ARIA S vln I solo bc — G 12/8

Auch mit gedämpften, schwachen Stimmen
Wird Gottes Majestät verehrt.
  Denn schallet nur der Geist darbei,
  So ist ihm solches ein Geschrei,
  Das er im Himmel selber hört.

Even with subdued, weak voices
God's majesty is honoured.
  For even if only the spirit sounds,
  It makes such a cry to Him
  As He Himself hears in heaven.

8. CHORALE SATB bc (+ instrs) — b C

Lob sei Gott dem Vater ton,
Lob sei Gott sein'm eingen Sohn,
Lob sei Gott dem Heilgen Geist
Immer und in Ewigkeit!

Praise be given to God the Father,
Praise be to God His only Son,
Praise be to God the Holy Spirit
Always and in eternity!

By the First Sunday in Advent 1731, when this cantata was heard for the first time in the version familiar to us today, some of its music already had a long history behind it. The opening chorus* and the arias go back to a secular cantata of the same name, BWV 36c, performed by Bach in early 1725 for the birthday of a teacher. This music was reused repeatedly in subsequent years: for the birthday of Princess Charlotte Friederike Wilhelmine of Anhalt-Cöthen on 30 November 1726[1] under the title *Steigt freudig in die Luft* (BWV 36a); in honour of a member

[1] According to the title of Picander's text, 'Bey der Ersten Geburts-Feyer . . . 1726', but since the nuptials of the royal pair took place on 21 June 1725, a performance date of 30 November 1725 would also come into consideration. See H.-J. Schulze, 'Neuerkenntnisse zu einigen Kantatentexten Bachs auf Grund neuer biographischer Daten', in M. Geck, ed., *Bach-Interpretationen* (Göttingen, 1969), 22–8, 208–10.

of the Leipzig Rivinus family of lawyers, as *Die Freude reget sich* (BWV 36b); and in a sacred paraphrase of the opening chorus and the arias, as a church cantata for the First Sunday in Advent. In this version only a final chorale was at first added to the movements adopted from the secular cantata (nos. 1, 3, 5 and 7 of the above text). The chorale was the last verse of the hymn *Wie schön leuchtet der Morgenstern* by Philipp Nicolai (1599), whose closing words 'Come, you fair crown of joy, do not delay for long! I await you with longing' (see Cantata 61/6 above) were clearly designed to reflect the Advent character of the newly assembled church cantata. However, Bach must have regarded this rather superficial adaptation as a half-way measure, for the new version of 1731, transmitted in a freshly written-out score with parts, is the product of radical remodelling.

The opening chorus and the arias were preserved in overall design but improved in numerous details. Placed between them, however, were not recitatives, as in most other cantatas (and as in the secular original), but chorale arrangements, all (except for no. 4, the movement transferred from the earlier version) based on Martin Luther's hymn *Nun komm, der Heiden Heiland*, the favourite Advent chorale of the time. The cantata was expanded into a two-part structure, and the former closing chorale placed at the end of the first half, which necessitated a change of text from verse 7 to verse 6 of Nicolai's hymn. The whole work closed with the last verse of Luther's hymn, in accordance with its new dominant role.

The form the cantata now took is unique in Bach's *oeuvre*. Chorus and arias are adopted from the then modern Neumeister type of cantata, but recitatives are abandoned in favour of chorale verses, largely drawn from one and the same hymn. Evidently, Bach here sought a new manner of synthesizing the 'modern' cantata with the chorale. And it is perhaps no mere chance that Cantata 140—not entirely dissimilar in form, uniting madrigalian* movements with a complete chorale—was performed only a week before.

The opening chorus is unable to conceal its secular origin. As an Advent movement, it is justified by the Gospel,* read beforehand, which tells of Jesus's entry into Jerusalem. Musically, it is determined by two figures heard together at the start of the introduction: the short upward-swinging triplet motive* in the strings and the more extended oboe melody. Formally, the movement is divided into two equivalent halves, each further subdivided into two contrasting passages, 'Schwingt freudig . . .' and 'Doch haltet ein!'.

In its fervour, the following chorale duet may be regarded as one of Bach's happiest inspirations. Although the link with the chorale is clearly audible, both in the two voice parts (doubled by oboes d'amore*) and in the continuo, the expressivity of each individual figure is enhanced to the utmost, as in the pleading leaps of a sixth on 'Nun komm', the syncopations on 'Des sich wundert alle Welt', or the chromatic* boldness of 'Gott solch Geburt ihm bestellt'. The tenor aria, no. 3, celebrates the entry of Jesus in the image—then current—of the Bridegroom of the Soul. The same image pervades the closing chorale of Part I, a plain four-part setting which, despite the change of text it had to undergo, fits in well at this point.

The joyful opening aria of Part II, whose character again betrays its origin in a congratulatory cantata, bids the Lord welcome, beseeching Him to enter into the heart of the Christian. The pre-existing music proves to be particularly well-suited to the jubilant cries of 'Welcome!' in the Advent text. The sixth movement forms a marked contrast: it is a chorale setting, with the unvaried *cantus firmus** in long notes in the tenor, accompanied by a lively figuration on two oboes d'amore, which seems to represent the battle and victory of God's Son over the 'ailing flesh' of mankind. Ostinato* figures in the continuo strengthen the impression of severity in this movement.

All the lovelier, by contrast, is the effect of the soprano aria (no. 7), with muted solo violin, whose text affirms that even the praise of sinful man is pleasing to the Creator. The words of the middle section, 'Denn schallet nur der Geist darbei' ('For even if only the spirit sounds'), give rise to charming echo effects between soprano and violin. As at the end of Part I, the closing chorale is a plain four-part setting, and it allows the individual's praise of God to merge into that of the whole Christian congregation.

1.2 Second Sunday in Advent

EPISTLE: Romans 15.4–13: the calling of the Gentiles.
GOSPEL: Luke 21.25–36: the Second Coming of Christ; 'be watchful, then, at all times and pray'.

Wachet! betet! betet! wachet!, BWV 70a

NBA I/1, Krit. Bericht BC [A4] Music lost

This cantata, composed at Weimar in 1716, survives only in its expanded Leipzig adaptation for the Twenty-sixth Sunday after Trinity (for further details, see under Cantata 70). Its original form can be reconstructed, however (with minor uncertainties), by taking into account only the relevant movements, which are:

1. CHORUS SATB str bc[2] C 𝄵

Wachet! betet! betet! wachet!	Watch, pray, pray, watch!
Seid bereit	Be prepared
Allezeit,	At all times

[2] Joshua Rifkin (*BJ* 1999, 127–32) concludes that the trumpet and oboe were added for the Leipzig version of 1723, BWV 70.

Bis der Herr der Herrlichkeit
Dieser Welt ein Ende machet.

Until the Lord of Glory
Makes an end of this world.

2. Aria 1 A bc — a 3/4

Wenn kömmt der Tag, an dem wir ziehen
Aus dem Ägypten dieser Welt?
Ach! laßt uns bald aus Sodom fliehen,
Eh uns das Feuer überfällt!
Wacht, Seelen, auf von Sicherheit,
Und glaubt, es ist die letzte Zeit!

When will the day come on which we move
Out of the Egypt of this world?
Ah! let us soon flee from Sodom
Before the fire overwhelms us!
Awake, O souls, out of complacency
And believe: it is the end of time!

3. Aria 2 S vln I + II vla bc — e c

Laßt der Spötter Zungen schmähen,
Es wird doch und muß geschehen,
Daß wir Jesum werden sehen
Auf den Wolken, in den Höhen.
Welt und Himmel mag vergehen,
Christi Wort muß fest bestehen.

Let mockers' tongues scorn,
Yet it will and must happen
That we will see Jesus
On the clouds, in the heights.
World and heaven may pass away;
Christ's Word must stand firm.

4. Aria 3 T str bc — G c

Hebt euer Haupt empor
Und seid getrost, ihr Frommen,
Zu euer Seelen Flor!
Ihr sollt in Eden grünen,
Gott ewiglich zu dienen.
Hebt euer Haupt empor
Und seid getrost, ihr Frommen!

Lift up your heads
And be of good cheer, you devout ones,
To the blossoming of your souls!
You shall flourish in Eden
To serve God for ever.
Lift up your heads
And be of good cheer, you devout ones!

5. Aria 4 B vln I + II vla bc — C 3/4

Seligster Erquickungstag,
Führe mich zu deinen Zimmern!
Schalle, knalle, letzter Schlag,
Welt und Himmel, geht zu Trümmern!
Jesus führet mich zur Stille,
An den Ort, da Lust die Fülle.

Most blessed day of refreshment,
Lead me to your chambers!
Sound, crack, last stroke!
World and heaven, go to ruins!
Jesus leads me to tranquillity
At that place where delight is in abundance.

6. Choral SATB str bc — C c

Nicht nach Welt, nach Himmel nicht
Meine Seele wünscht und sehnet,
Jesum wünsch ich und sein Licht,
Der mich hat mit Gott versöhnet,
Der mich freiet vom Gericht,
Meinen Jesum laß ich nicht.

Not for the world, not for heaven
Does my soul crave and long;
I desire Jesus and His Light,
He who has reconciled me with God,
Who frees me from judgement;
I will not let my Jesus go.

1.3 Third Sunday in Advent

Epistle: 1 Corinthians 4.1–5: the ministry of the true apostle.
Gospel: Matthew 11.2–10: John the Baptist in prison.

Ärgre dich, o Seele, nicht, BWV 186a

NBA I/1, Krit. Bericht BC [A5] Music lost

This cantata, composed at Weimar in 1716, survives only in its expanded Leipzig adaptation for the Seventh Sunday after Trinity (for further details, see under Cantata 186).Only a rough reconstruction of the original version is possible[3] by taking into account the relevant movements and restoring the following Advent text by Salomo Franck:

1. Chorus SATB str bc — g c

Ärgre dich, o Seele, nicht,	Do not be offended, O soul,
Daß das allerhöchste Licht,	That the most high Light,
Gottes Glanz und Ebenbild,	God's brightness and image,
Sich in Knechtsgestalt verhüllt.	Disguises Himself in a servant's form.
Ärgre dich, o Seele, nicht!	Do not be offended, O soul!

2. Aria 1 B bc — B♭ $\frac{3}{4}$

Bist du, der da kommen soll,	Is it You who shall come,
Seelenfreund im Kirchengarten?	Friend of souls, into the church's garden?
Mein Gemüt ist zweifelsvoll,	My mind is full of doubt:
Soll ich eines andern warten?	Should I await another?
Doch, o Seele, zweifle nicht.	Yet, do not doubt, O soul.
Laß Vernunft dich nicht verstricken,	Do not let reason ensnare you;
Deinen Schilo, Jakobs Licht,	Your Shiloh, Jacob's light,
Kannst du in der Schrift erblicken!	You can see in the Scriptures!

3. Aria 2 T vla? bc — d c

Messias läßt sich merken	The Messiah lets Himself be known
Aus seinen Gnadenwerken,	Through His deeds of Grace,
Unreine werden rein.	And lets the impure become pure.
Die geistlich Lahme gehen,	The spiritually lame walk,
Die geistlich Blinde sehen	The spiritually blind see
Den hellen Gnadenschein.	The bright appearance of Grace.

4. Aria 3 S vln I + II bc — g c

Die Armen will der Herr umarmen	The Lord will embrace the poor
Mit Gnaden hier und dort!	With Grace both here and there!
Er schenket ihnen aus Erbarmen	He gives them of His mercy
Den höchsten Schatz, des Lebens Wort!	The highest treasure, the Word of Life!

5. Aria 4 [Duetto] SA str bc — c $\frac{3}{8}$

Laß, Seele, kein Leiden	Let, O soul, no suffering
Von Jesu dich scheiden,	Separate you from Jesus;
Sei, Seele, getreu!	Be faithful, O soul!
Dir bleibet die Krone	A crown awaits you
Aus Gnaden zu Lohne,	As the reward of Grace
Wenn du von Banden des Leibes nun frei.	When you are free of the fetters of the body.

[3] A reconstruction for practical use, based on the later version, has been published by Diethard Hellmann (Stuttgart, 1963).

6. CHORAL[4] [scoring unknown] ? ?

Darum, ob ich schon dulde	**So although I already endure**
Hie Widerwärtigkeit,	**Adversity here,**
Wie ich auch wohl verschulde,	**Just as I, too, am no doubt guilty,**
Kommt doch die Ewigkeit,	**Yet eternity comes**
Ist aller Freuden voll,	**And is full of all joys;**
Dieselb ohn einigs Ende,	**This without any end—**
Dieweil ich Christum kenne,	**As long as I know Christ—**
Mir widerfahren soll.	**Shall befall me.**

1.4 Fourth Sunday in Advent

EPISTLE: Philippians 4.4–7: 'Rejoice in the Lord always'.
GOSPEL: John 1.19–28: the witness of John the Baptist.

Bereitet die Wege, bereitet die Bahn, BWV 132

NBA I/1, p. 101 BC A6 Duration: *c.* 22 mins

1. ARIA S ob str bsn bc A 6/8

Bereitet die Wege, bereitet die Bahn!	Prepare the ways, prepare the path!
Bereitet die Wege	Prepare the ways
Und machet die Stege	And make the footpaths,
Im Glauben und Leben	In faith and life,
Dem Höchsten ganz eben,	Quite smooth for the Highest:
Messias kömmt an!	The Messiah is coming!

2. RECITATIVO T bc A–A C

Willst du dich Gottes Kind und Christi Bruder nennen,	If you would call yourself God's child and Christ's brother,
So müssen Herz und Mund den Heiland frei bekennen.	Then heart and mouth must freely acknowledge the Saviour.
Ja, Mensch, dein ganzes Leben	Indeed, your whole life, O man,
Muß von dem Glauben Zeugnis geben!	Must bear witness to the Faith!
Soll Christi Wort und Lehre	Should Christ's word and teaching
Auch durch dein Blut versiegelt sein,	Even be sealed by your blood,
So gib dich willig drein!	Then give yourself to this willingly!
Denn dieses ist der Christen Kron und Ehre!	For this is the Christian's crown and honour!
Indes, mein Herz, bereite	Meanwhile, my heart, prepare
Noch heute	This very day
Dem Herrn die Glaubensbahn	The path of Faith for the Lord
Und räume weg die Hügel und die Höhen,	And clear away the hills and the heights
Die ihm entgegen stehen!	That stand in His way!

[4] Franck gives only the first two lines; the remainder has been supplied from a contemporary hymn-book (Weimar, 1713).

Wälz ab die schweren Sündensteine,
Nimm deinen Heiland an,
Daß er mit dir im Glauben sich vereine!

Roll away the heavy stones of sin;
Receive your Saviour,
So that He may be united with you in Faith!

3. ARIA B cello bc — E c

Wer bist du? Frage dein Gewissen,
Da wirst du sonder Heuchelei,
Ob du, o Mensch, falsch oder treu,
Dein rechtes Urteil hören müssen.
Wer bist du? Frage das Gesetze,
Das wird dir sagen, wer du bist:
Ein Kind des Zorns in Satans Netze,
Ein falsch- und heuchlerischer Christ.

Who are you? Ask your conscience,
Then you must hear without hypocrisy
Whether you, O man, are false or true
In your right judgement.
Who are you? Ask the Law:
It will tell you who you are—
A child of wrath in Satan's net,
A false and hypocritical Christian.

4. RECITATIVO A str bc — b–D c

Ich will, mein Gott, dir frei heraus bekennen,
Ich habe dich bisher nicht recht bekannt.
Ob Mund und Lippen gleich dich Herrn und Vater nennen,
Hat sich mein Herz doch von dir abgewandt.
Ich habe dich verleugnet mit dem Leben!
Wie kannst du mir ein gutes Zeugnis geben?
Als, Jesu, mich dein Geist und Wasserbad
Gereiniget von meiner Missetat,
Hab ich dir zwar stets feste Treu versprochen;
Ach! aber ach! der Taufbund ist gebrochen.
Die Untreu reuet mich!
Ach Gott, erbarme dich,
Ach hilf, daß ich mit unverwandter Treue
Den Gnadenbund im Glauben stets erneue!

I would freely confess to You, my God,
I have not rightly acknowledged You before.
Though mouth and lips call You Lord and Father,
Yet my heart has turned away from You.
I have denied You in my living!
How can You give me a good testimony?
When, Jesus, Your Spirit and baptismal water
Cleansed me of my misdeeds,
I did indeed promise to keep constant, firm faithfulness with You;
Ah, but alas! the baptismal covenant is broken.
I repent the unfaithfulness!
Ah God, have mercy on me;
Ah help me, that with unswerving loyalty
I may constantly renew in Faith the covenant of Grace!

5. ARIA A vln solo bc — b c

Christi Glieder, ach bedenket,
Was der Heiland euch geschenket
Durch der Taufe reines Bad!
Bei der Blut- und Wasserquelle
Werden eure Kleider helle,
Die befleckt von Missetat.

Members of Christ, ah consider
What the Saviour has given you
Through baptism's purifying bath!
With this blood- and water-fountain
Your garments become bright,
Which were stained with misdeeds.

Christus gab zum neuen Kleide
Roten Purpur, weiße Seide,
Diese sind der Christen Staat.

Christ gave you as new garments
Scarlet purple, white silk:
These are the Christians' splendour.

6. Choral [A C]

Ertöt uns durch dein Güte,
Erweck uns durch dein Gnad;
Den alten Menschen kränke,
Daß der neu leben mag
Wohl hie auf dieser Erden,
Den Sinn und all Begehrden
Und Gdanken habn zu dir.

Mortify us through Your goodness,
Awaken us through Your Grace;
Weaken the old man,
That the new may live
Even here on this earth,
That mind and all desires
And thoughts may be directed towards You.

This cantata, composed in Weimar, is dated '1715' in Bach's own hand. For the text, a libretto from Salomo Franck's cycle *Evangelisches Andachts-Opffer*, which had evidently been unavailable for the Advent period of the previous year, was now at his disposal. In substance, Franck's text follows the ideas of the Gospel.* Even the reference to Isaiah 40.3–4 ('Prepare the way for the Lord . . .'), whose paraphrase forms the content of the opening aria, is found in the reading for the day. The priests' and Levites' interrogation of John ('Who are you?'), the acknowledgement of Christ, the concept of baptism ('I baptize with water, but there is One among you whom you do not know'): all these things recur in the cantata libretto, but they are turned into personal, contemporary issues—the individual Christian and the 'members of Christ' are addressed directly.

Bach's setting makes use of the chamber-music scoring he favoured in 1715: four voices, strings, oboe and continuo (with bassoon). No closing chorale survives, though Franck prescribed for it the fifth verse of the hymn *Herr Christ, der einig Gotts Sohn* by Elisabeth Creutziger (1524). It is likely that, as in Cantata 163 composed four weeks before, a chorale 'in simplice stylo' was to end the work, and that it was notated on a loose scrap of paper (the three sheets of the score were full) which has since gone missing, along with the performing parts. For today's performances, then, the best course of action is to borrow the chorale with the same text from Cantata 164, transposing it into A major.

In his setting, Bach successfully captures the characteristic warmth of Franck's verse. The very first aria, with its buoyant rhythm, is of exceptional charm. The soloistic figure-work, the runs and trills of the oboe, are manifestly not far removed from the instrumental concerto; and the extended coloraturas* of the soprano make a virtuoso impact. Only in the middle section, where two regular countersubjects are combined with the initial motive,* exchanging places with one another, does the movement take on a more serious character, only to break out all the more jubilantly with the cry 'The Messiah is coming!'.

The following recitative, like most of those in Bach's early cantatas, contains extended arioso* passages. The tenor and continuo repeatedly interact in canon* or imitation,* which is to be understood as a symbol of the Imitation of Christ. Upon the words 'So that He may be united with you in faith!' the imitations change into unisons, which may also be understood as textual illustration.

The aria 'Wer bist du?' is set with continuo accompaniment only, but the cello frequently detaches itself from the continuo in a concertante* role (or should the figural* part be played by the bassoon also?). The probing repetitions of the initial motive, which dominate the whole movement and from which the vocal melody is also derived, seem to ask again and again, 'Who are you?'; but the question is here addressed not to John the Baptist but to the individual Christian, the listener. Perhaps the choice of bass for the voice part is not without significance: it is Christ who puts this question to mankind. Musically, the movement is full of audacities in voice-leading, chiefly because the voice often lies below the cello figuration, giving rise to harmonic relationships explained by Spitta in terms of an 'inverted pedal point':

In the second recitative (no. 4) Bach dispenses with arioso episodes, but it is scored with strings, whose held chords provide a background for the expressive declamation of the voice. The fifth movement, an alto aria with concertante solo violin, is characterized by virtuoso string passages, perhaps suggested by the words 'Christ gave you as new garments scarlet purple, white silk'. It has already been mentioned that a plain chorale setting was presumably to follow: it could hardly be assumed that Bach would have let his cantata end with a thin-textured aria of this kind.

Herz und Mund und Tat und Leben, BWV 147a

NBA I/1, Krit. Bericht BC A7 Music lost

This cantata, composed in Weimar in 1716, survives only in its expanded Leipzig adaptation for the Visitation of the Virgin Mary (for further details, see under Cantata 147). Among the three Advent cantatas of 1716—BWV 70a, 186a and 147a—the original version is in this case the most difficult to establish. A reconstruction of the work for practical use is indeed possible,[5] but there is a

[5] And has been attempted by Uwe Wolf (Stuttgart, 1996), who discusses the task in 'Eine "neue" Bach-Kantate zum 4. Advent: Zur Rekonstruktion der Weimarer Adventskantate "Herz und Mund und Tat und Leben" BWV 147a', *Musik und Kirche* 66 (1996), 351–5.

rather uncertain scholarly basis for it. The following movements, more or less radically remodelled in Leipzig, presumably belonged to the Weimar cantata BWV 147a:

1. CHORUS SATB tr str bc — C $\frac{6}{4}$

Herz und Mund und Tat und Leben	Heart and mouth and deed and life
Muß von Christo Zeugnis geben	Must bear witness of Christ—
Ohne Furcht und Heuchelei,	Without fear and hypocrisy—
Daß er Gott und Heiland sei.	That He is God and Saviour.

2. ARIA 1 A vla? bc — a $\frac{3}{4}$

Schäme dich, o Seele, nicht,	Do not be ashamed, O soul,
Deinen Heiland zu bekennen,	To acknowledge your Saviour,
Soll er seine Braut dich nennen	Should He call you His bride
Vor des Vaters Angesicht!	Before His Father's countenance!
Denn wer ihn auf dieser Erden	For he who on this earth
Zu verleugnen sich nicht scheut,	Does not shrink from denying Him
Soll von ihm verleugnet werden,	Shall be denied by Him
Wenn er kommt zur Herrlichkeit!	When He comes in glory!

3. ARIA 2 T bc — F $\frac{3}{4}$

Hilf, Jesu, hilf, daß ich auch dich bekenne	Help, Jesus, help me also to acknowledge You
In Wohl und Weh! in Freud und Leid!	In weal and woe! in joy and sorrow!
Daß ich dich meinen Heiland nenne	That I may call You my Saviour
In Glauben mit Gelassenheit.	In Faith with composure;
Daß stets mein Herz von deiner Liebe brenne!	That my heart may ever burn with Your Love!

4. ARIA 3 S vln solo bc — d c

Bereite dir, Jesu, noch heute die Bahn!	Prepare the way to You, Jesus, this very day!
Beziehe die Höhle	Occupy the cavern
Des Herzens, der Seele,	Of the heart, of the soul,
Und blicke mit Augen der Gnade mich an.	And look upon me with eyes of Grace!

5. ARIA 4 B tr str bc — C c

Laß mich der Rufer Stimme hören,	Let me hear the Voice of the Caller
Die mit Johanne treulich lehren,	That, with John, teaches faithfully;
Ich soll in dieser Gnadenzeit	I shall in this time of Grace
Von Finsternis und Dunkelheit	Become converted from darkness and gloom
Zum wahren Lichte mich bekehren.	To the true Light.

6. CHORAL[6] [scoring unknown] — ? ?

Dein Wort laß mich bekennen	**Let me acknowledge Your Word**
Für dieser argen Welt,	**Before this wicked world,**

[6] Franck gives only the first two lines; the remainder has been supplied from a contemporary hymn-book (Weimar, 1713).

Auch mich dein'n Diener nennen,
Nicht fürchten Gwalt noch Geld,
Das mich bald mög ableiten
Von deiner Wahrheit klar;
Wollst mich auch nicht abscheiden
Von der christlichen Schar.

And call myself Your servant,
Fearing neither power nor wealth,
Which might soon lead me away
From Your plain Truth;
Would You please not separate me
From the Christian host.

1.5 Christmas Day

Epistle: Titus 2.11–14: 'The healing Grace of God has appeared'; or Isaiah 9.2–7: 'A Child is born to us'.

Gospel: Luke 2.1–14: the Birth of Christ; the announcement to the shepherds; the angels' song of praise.

Christen, ätzet diesen Tag, BWV 63

NBA I/2, p. 3 BC A8 Duration: *c.* 30 mins

1. Chorus SATB tr I–IV timp ob I–III bsn str bc C 3/8

Christen, ätzet diesen Tag
In Metall und Marmorsteine!
Kommt und eilt mit mir zur Krippen
Und erweist mit frohen Lippen
Euren Dank und eure Pflicht;
Denn der Strahl, so da einbricht,
Zeigt sich euch zum Gnadenscheine.

Christians, etch this day
In metal and marble stones!
Come and hasten with me to the crib
And show with joyful lips
Your thanks and your duty;
For the ray that breaks in there proves to be
For you the appearance of Grace.

2. Recitativo A str bc C–a C

O selger Tag! o ungemeines Heute,
An dem das Heil der Welt,
Der Schilo, den Gott schon im Paradies
Dem menschlichen Geschlecht verhieß,
Nunmehro sich vollkommen dargestellt
Und suchet Israel von der Gefangenschaft und Sklavenketten
Des Satans zu erretten.
Du liebster Gott, was sind wir arme doch?
Ein abgefallnes Volk, so dich verlassen;
Und dennoch willst du uns nicht hassen;
Denn eh wir sollen noch nach dem Verdienst zu Boden liegen,
Eh muß die Gottheit sich bequemen,
Die menschliche Natur an sich zu nehmen
Und auf der Erden

O blessed day! O rare today,
On which the Salvation of the world,
The Shiloh that God already in Paradise
Promised to the human race,
Has now wholly represented Himself
And seeks to deliver Israel from the captivity and slave-chains
Of Satan.
You dearest God, what are we wretches, though?
An iniquitous people that forsake You;
And still You do not hate us;
For before we, according to our deserts, are laid low,
The Godhead must condescend
To take human nature upon Himself
And on the earth

Im Hirtenstall zu einem Kinde werden.
O unbegreifliches, doch seliges Verfügen!

In a shepherd's stall to become a child.
O inconceivable yet blessed disposition!

3. Aria [Duetto] SB ob I solo [later: obbl org] bc — a C

Gott, du hast es wohl gefüget,
Was uns itzo widerfährt.
Drum laßt uns auf ihn stets trauen
Und auf seine Gnade bauen,
Denn er hat uns dies beschert
Was uns ewig nun vergnüget.

O God, You have well disposed
What now befalls us.
Therefore let us ever trust Him
And build upon His Grace,
For He has bestowed upon us
What now delights us for ever.

4. Recitativo T bc — C–G C

So kehret sich nun heut
Das bange Leid,
Mit welchem Israel geängstet und beladen,
In lauter Heil und Gnaden.
Der Löw aus Davids Stamme ist erschienen,
Sein Bogen ist gespannt, das Schwert ist schon gewetzt,
Womit er uns in vor'ge Freiheit setzt.

Now today, then,
The alarming suffering
With which Israel is frightened and burdened
Is turned into pure Salvation and Grace.
The Lion from David's tribe has appeared,
His bow is bent, his sword already whetted
With which He restores our former freedom.

5. Aria [Duetto] AT str bc — G 3/8

Ruft und fleht den Himmel an,
Kommt, ihr Christen, kommt zum Reihen,
Ihr sollt euch ob dem erfreuen,
Was Gott hat anheut getan!
Da uns seine Huld verpfleget
Und mit so viel Heil beleget,
Daß man nicht g'nug danken kann.

Call and beseech heaven;
Come, you Christians, come to the dance;
You shall rejoice over that
Which God has done today!
For His favour takes care of us
And showers us with so much well-being
That we cannot thank Him enough.

6. Recitativo B ob I–III str bc — e–C C

Verdoppelt euch demnach, ihr heißen Andachtsflammen,
Und schlagt in Demut brünstiglich zusammen!
Steigt fröhlich himmelan
Und danket Gott vor dies, was er getan!

Redouble yourselves, then, you burning flames of devotion,
And ardently throb together in humility!
Climb joyfully to heaven
And thank God for what He has done!

7. Chorus [scoring as in no. 1] — C C

Höchster, schau in Gnaden an
Diese Glut gebückter Seelen!
Laß den Dank, den wir dir bringen,
Angenehme vor dir klingen,
Laß uns stets in Segen gehn,
Aber niemals nicht geschehn,
Daß uns Satan möge quälen!

Most High, look with Grace upon
These souls stooped in ardour!
Let the thanks we give You
Sound agreeable to You;
Let us ever walk in Blessing,
But never let it happen
That Satan might torment us!

This cantata, composed in Weimar for Christmas 1714,[7] was formerly thought to be based on a libretto by the Halle pastor Johann Michael Heineccius, though there is no solid evidence to connect him with the text. Without doubt the work has a decidedly festive character, but not one specifically associated with Christmas. All the pieces typical of Christmas music are absent: the music of the shepherds, the cradle song, the 'Glory be to God on high' of the angels, the Christmas hymns (indeed, there is no chorale at all). This could be mere chance—a whim of the librettist with which the composer concurred. Or perhaps we should conclude that the cantata originated as the parody* of a secular original, though further support for this rather vague hypothesis has not so far been found.

The structure of the work is remarkably symmetrical: around a central *secco* recitative, 'So kehret sich nun heut' (no. 4), are grouped two duets (nos. 3 and 5), two accompanied recitatives (nos. 2 and 6), and, as an outer frame, two *tutti* choruses* (nos. 1 and 7). And among the individual movements the similarly symmetrical da capo* structure predominates: nos. 1, 3 and 7 exhibit it in its pure form (ABA), whereas in no. 5 a free reprise of the opening section suffices (ABA′). Time and again the recitatives consolidate rhythmically and motivically into arioso,* in accordance with Bach's Weimar style.

Not quite so typical of Bach's early period is the large-scale design of the individual movements or of individual themes—for example, the oboe melody in the third movement. This represents a substantial departure from the small-scale articulation of Bach's earliest efforts. Yet the choruses, in particular, with their thematically independent middle sections, betray their origin in the sectional form of the motet,* for the unifying technique of choral insertion,* which Bach used in almost all his concertante* choruses from Advent 1716 onwards, is altogether absent.

Bach revived this cantata on several later occasions: at his first Christmas in Leipzig in 1723 and at least once more thereafter. At one of these later performances he replaced the obbligato* oboe of the third movement with obbligato organ, entering the music himself in the organ continuo part. This version differs materially from the oboe part only in certain altered ornaments and in its broader articulation, added to which it lacks any dynamic marks. It should hardly be regarded as a 'last will and testament', a replacement of the oboe version, but rather as an alternative solution. In accordance with the practice of the time, both scoring possibilities should, in any case, be considered available for today's performances.

[7] According to Y. Kobayashi, 'Quellenkundliche Überlegungen zur Chronologie der Weimarer Vokalwerke Bachs', in K. Heller and H.-J. Schulze, eds, *Das Frühwerk J. S. Bachs* [conference report, Rostock, 1990] (Cologne, 1995), 290–310.

Gelobet seist du, Jesu Christ, BWV 91

NBA I/2, p. 133 BC A9 Duration: *c.* 20 mins

1. [Chorale] SATB hn I,II timp ob I–III str bc — G 𝄴

Gelobet seist du, Jesu Christ,	**May You be praised, O Jesus Christ,**
Daß du Mensch geboren bist	**Since You were born a man**
Von einer Jungfrau, das ist wahr;	**From a Virgin—this is true;**
Des freuet sich der Engel Schar.	**At which the host of angels rejoices.**
Kyrie eleis!	**Lord, have mercy!**

2. Recitativo [+ Chorale] S bc — e–e 𝄴

Der Glanz der höchsten Herrlichkeit,	The radiance of the highest Glory,
Das Ebenbild von Gottes Wesen,	The image of God's nature,
Hat in bestimmter Zeit	Has at the appointed time
Sich einen Wohnplatz auserlesen.	Chosen for Himself a dwelling-place.
Des ewgen Vaters einigs Kind,	**The eternal Father's only Child,**
Das ewge Licht, von Licht geboren,	The eternal Light, born of Light,
Itzt man in der Krippe findt.	**Is now found in a crib.**
O Menschen, schauet an,	O Man, look at
Was hier der Liebe Kraft getan!	What the power of Love has done here!
In unser armes Fleisch und Blut	**In our poor flesh and blood**
(Und war denn dieses nicht verflucht, verdammt, verloren?)	(And was this not cursed, condemned, lost?)
Verkleidet sich das ewge Gut.	**The eternal Good is clothed.**
So wird es ja zum Segen auserkoren.	Thus it is indeed elected for Blessing.

3. Aria T ob I–III bc — a 3/4

Gott, dem der Erden Kreis zu klein,	God, for whom the earth's circle is too small,
Den weder Welt noch Himmel fassen,	Whom neither world nor heaven contains,
Will in der engen Krippe sein.	Would be in a narrow crib.
Erscheinet uns dies ewge Licht,	Since this eternal Light appears to us,
So wird hinfüro Gott uns nicht	God will henceforth not hate us,
Als dieses Lichtes Kinder hassen.	As we are now the children of this Light.

4. Recitativo B str bc — G–C 𝄴

O Christenheit!	O Christendom!
Wohlan, so mache dich bereit,	Well then, make yourself ready
Bei dir den Schöpfer zu empfangen.	To receive the Creator.
Der große Gottessohn	The great Son of God
Kömmt als ein Gast zu dir gegangen.	Comes to you as a guest.
Ach, laß dein Herz durch diese Liebe rühren;	Ah, let your heart be stirred by this Love;
Er kömmt zu dir, um dich vor seinen Thron	He comes to you to lead you before His throne
Durch dieses Jammertal zu führen.	Through this vale of tears.

5. ARIA [DUETTO] SA vln I + II bc e C

Die Armut, so Gott auf sich nimmt,	The poverty that God takes upon Himself
Hat uns ein ewig Heil bestimmt,	Has ordained for us an eternal Salvation,
Den Überfluß an Himmelsschätzen.	The abundance of heavenly treasures.
Sein menschlich Wesen machet euch	His human nature makes you
Den Engelsherrlichkeiten gleich,	Like the angels' splendours,
Euch zu der Engel Chor zu setzen.	Placing you in the angels' choir.

6. CHORAL SATB hn I,II timp bc [+ ww str] G C

Das hat er alles uns getan,	**He has done all this for us**
Sein groß Lieb zu zeigen an;	**To show His great Love;**
Des freu sich alle Christenheit	**For this may all Christendom rejoice**
Und dank ihm des in Ewigkeit.	**And thank Him for it in eternity.**
Kyrie eleis!	**Lord, have mercy!**

On Christmas Day, as on the First Sunday in Advent, Bach based his chorale cantata* of 1724 on the hymn by Luther (1524) which was then the principal hymn of the day. The first and last verses of the seven-verse hymn were, as usual, retained word-for-word. The same applies to verse 2 (without its 'Kyrie eleis'), which was, however, expanded by troping* passages of recitative. The other verses, nos. 3–6, were freely paraphrased, the third and fourth forming an aria (no. 3), the fifth a recitative (no. 4), and the sixth another aria (no. 5).

In accordance with the festive occasion, two horns and drums were added to the normal cantata ensemble, and the oboes increased to three. For the opening movement, the possibility thereby arises of juxtaposing choirs of horns, oboes, and strings as equal bodies of sound, to which the vocal choir is added as a fourth body. The design of this chorus* is related to that of the equivalent movement in Cantata 62. This time, however, no instrumental reference is made to the chorale (such references occur all the more abundantly in the second movement), the thematic material of the orchestra being completely independent of it. The opening and closing ritornello furnishes material both for episodes between the chorale lines and for accompanying motives* in the vocal passages. The thematic elements of this ritornello are manifold and may be combined in numerous different ways. The most important figures are scale-figure *a*, which enters at the outset, and its counterpoint* *b*, which descends in broken triads:

and also a circling horn figure *c* (not shown), which is likewise combined with counterpoint *b* and, though perhaps originally designed as a horn adaptation of scale-figure *a*, acquires its own separate function in the course of the movement.

In each chorale-line passage, the chorale is assigned to the soprano, and the lower parts provide counterpoints of various kinds:

Line 1 ('Gelobet . . .'): ritornello motive *a*, imitative*
Line 2 ('Daß du Mensch . . .'): ritornello motive *b*, chordal; *c*, freely polyphonic*
Line 3 ('Von einer Jungfrau . . .'): chorale-line opening, metrically diminished, imitative; chordal confirmatory postlude ('das ist wahr')
Line 4 ('Des freuet sich . . .'): ritornello motive *a*, imitative
Line 5 ('Kyrie eleis'): freely polyphonic, making use of *b*

The line sections are thus grouped symmetrically around line 3, the only line in which the lower parts participate in the substance of the chorale.

In the second movement, in which the soprano is accompanied only by continuo, recitative passages alternate with chorale quotations in accordance with the text. In each case Bach counterpoints these chorale passages with an ever-recurring quotation of line 1 in the continuo, in quaver diminution:*

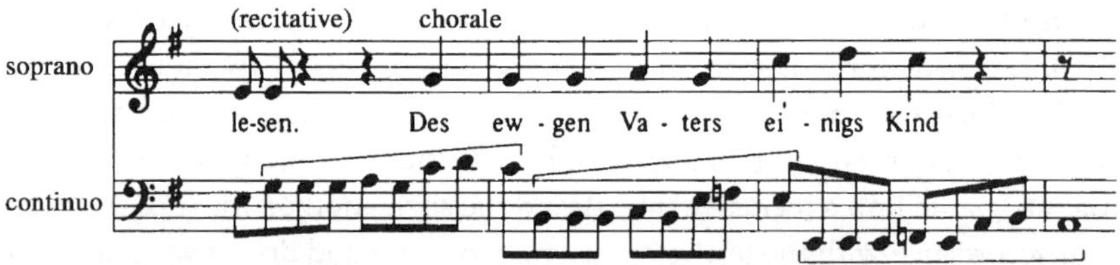

The chorale melody in the soprano is mostly unvaried, but at the line 'Itzt man in der Krippe findt' ('Is now found in a crib') it is expressively ornamented.

The tenor aria, no. 3, is accompanied by the particularly charming instrumental combination of three oboes, whose theme sets up marked rhythmic accents, perhaps to represent the Will of God, His initiative, and His power to deliver the human race. No. 4, a recitative accompanied by strings, develops into an impressive arioso*—with bold chromaticism* and a radiant final cadence—at its closing words, 'to lead you . . . through this vale of tears'. In the duet, no. 5, Bach treats the contrasts of the text—poverty/abundance, human nature/the angel choir—as an opportunity for musical differentiation. The contrasts of the main section are:

'Die Armut' ('poverty'): imitative suspensions
'Hat uns ein ewig Heil bestimmt' ('Has ordained for us an eternal Salvation'): homophonic* parallel voice-leading

Those of the middle section are:

'Sein menschlich Wesen' ('His human nature'): rising chromaticism
'Den Engelsherrlichkeiten gleich' ('Like the angels' splendours'): coloraturas,* triadic melody.

The symbolism of these antitheses is clear.

In the closing chorale, the horns have partially independent parts. This is partly due to the necessity of restricting them to the notes of the harmonic series. But it also gives rise to a spirited final cadence on the words 'Kyrie eleis', which distantly recalls the circling figure *c* from the opening movement and thereby describes an arc back to the beginning of the cantata.

Unser Mund sei voll Lachens, BVW 110

NBA I/2, p. 73 BC A10 Duration: c. 27 mins

1. [Chorus] SATB (+ SAT[B] rip) tr I–III timp fl I,II ob I–III bsn str bc — D ¢ 9/8 3/4 c

'Unser Mund sei voll Lachens und unsre Zunge voll Rühmens. Denn der Herr hat Großes an uns getan.'	'May our mouth be full of laughter and our tongue full of praise. For the Lord has done great things for us.'

2. Aria T fl I,II bc — b c

Ihr Gedanken und ihr Sinnen,	You thoughts and you senses,
Schwinget euch anitzt von hinnen,	Swing up now from here,
Steiget schleunig himmelan	Climb swiftly up to heaven
Und bedenkt, was Gott getan!	And consider what God has done!
Er wird Mensch, und dies allein,	He becomes man, and just for this:
Daß wir Himmels Kinder sein.	That we may be heaven's children.

3. Recitativo B str bc — f♯–A c

'Dir, Herr, ist niemand gleich. Du bist groß und dein Name ist groß und kannsts mit der Tat beweisen.'	'No one is like You, Lord. You are great and Your name is great, and You can prove it in deeds.'

4. Aria A ob d'am solo bc — f♯ 3/4

Ach Herr, was ist ein Menschenkind,	Ah Lord, what is a child of man,
Daß du sein Heil so schmerzlich suchest?	That You seek his Salvation so painfully?
Ein Wurm, den du verfluchest,	A worm that You curse
Wenn Höll und Satan um ihn sind;	When Hell and Satan are about him;
Doch auch dein Sohn, den Seel und Geist	Yet also Your Son, whom soul and spirit,
Aus Liebe seinen Erben heißt.	Out of love, call their inheritance.

5. Duetto ST bc — A 12/8

'Ehre sei Gott in der Höhe und Friede auf Erden und den Menschen ein Wohlgefallen!'	'Glory be to God on high and peace on earth and goodwill towards mankind!'

6. Aria B tr I str + ob I,II, ob da c bc — D c

Wacht auf, ihr Adern und ihr Glieder,	Wake up, you veins and you limbs,
Und singt dergleichen Freudenlieder,	And sing such joyful songs
Die unserm Gott gefällig sein.	As are pleasing to our God.
Und ihr, ihr andachtsvollen Saiten,	And you, you devout strings,
Sollt ihm ein solches Lob bereiten,	Shall prepare for Him such praise
Dabei sich Herz und Geist erfreun.	As delights heart and spirit.

7. Choral SATB (+ SAT[B] rip) bc (+ most instrs) b c

Alleluja! Gelobt sei Gott,	**Alleluia! Praised be God,**
Singen wir all aus unsers Herzens Grunde.	**We all sing from the bottom of our hearts.**
Denn Gott hat heut gemacht solch Freud,	**For God has today made such joy**
Die wir vergessen solln zu keiner Stunde.	**As we shall not forget at any time.**

This composition, written for Christmas Day 1725, belongs to Bach's third Leipzig cycle of cantatas. The libretto is drawn from the church-year cycle *Gottgefälliges Kirchen-Opffer* of 1711 by Georg Christian Lehms. As far as we know, it is the only text Bach drew from Lehms's morning cycle, which contains only biblical words, madrigalian* arias and chorales. Scriptural words and arias alternate three times, after which a chorale concludes the work. Freely versified recitatives are altogether absent. As a result, the following succession of chief textual types emerges in the Christmas Day cantatas for Bach's first three years in Leipzig:

1723 BWV 63: freely versified movements (no biblical words or chorale)
1724 BWV 91: chorale
1725 BWV 110: biblical words

The text, which thanks God for His act of redemption, avoids specific Christmas allusions in some of its movements; and for this reason it has sometimes been completely misunderstood, being interpreted as a reaction of Bach's to the political events of the day: the cantata's origin has been linked[8] to the turn of the War of the Polish Succession in Saxony's favour at the end of 1734. However, it would hardly have occurred to Bach to celebrate military victory in a Christmas service; and that date has, in fact, since been refuted both by the discovery of the printed text and by the diplomatic findings of the original sources.

The first movement is a paraphrase of Psalm 126.2–3, in which the psalmist expresses his hope that captive Zion will be delivered: 'Then will our mouth be full of laughter and our tongue full of praise'. In the following aria, the divine act that is commemorated today is seen as an occasion for joy. The second biblical passage, Jeremiah 10.6, praises the greatness of the Lord, which, in the next aria, is contrasted with the baseness of mankind, in accordance with another biblical text: 'What is man, that You think of him, and the child of man, that You accept him?' (Psalm 8.4). The third biblical passage (no. 5), the angels' song in praise of God, is drawn from the Christmas story itself (Luke 2.14); and the following aria encourages the Christian congregation, too, to sing songs of joy. This call is answered by the choir, acting on behalf of the congregation, in

[8] By Arnold Schering, 'Kleine Bachstudien', *BJ* 1933, 30–70.

the closing chorale, the fifth verse of the hymn *Wir Christenleut* by Caspar Füger (1592).

In his setting Bach had recourse to several of his earlier works. The opening chorus* is based on the Overture from the Orchestral Suite in D, BWV 1069, to which trumpets and drums were added for the cantata version,[9] in accordance with its festive occasion. Within this instrumental texture Bach interweaves the choir in masterly fashion. The form of the French Overture,* slow–quick (fugal)–slow, is so deployed that the slow sections form instrumental borders framing the quick choral section. This middle section, in which the 'laughter' of the text is often made quite graphically audible, was even as an instrumental piece very much geared towards the antiphonal use of separate instrumental groups. In a later performance of the cantata, Bach further emphasized this concertante* effect by augmenting the vocal ensemble with differentiated ripieno parts.

As an effective contrast to the display of splendour in the opening movement, the following aria, no. 2, requires two transverse flutes,* presumably as a reference to the lowly birth of God's Son. The piece is bipartite in form, renouncing the customary da capo*. The third movement is a jewel—a recitative on biblical words only five bars long, with expressive upward-pointing gestures in the strings against the pregnant declamation of the bass voice. The next movement, no. 4, an alto aria with obbligato* oboe d'amore,* is again bipartite: here this form is determined by the antithesis prescribed in the text between mankind cursed and mankind redeemed.

Whereas the introductory biblical passage was set as a chorus and the second as a recitative, the third (no. 5) takes the form of a duet with continuo accompaniment. The music is based on 'Virga Jesse floruit', the fourth Christmas interpolation in the original version of the Magnificat, BWV 243a, of 1723. The voice parts were substantially altered in order to assimilate them to the new text. Yet the essentially lyrical character of the piece, transferred to the angels' song of praise from its musical source, remains conspicuous.

If a quiet note was struck in the middle movements, the third aria (no. 6), with its full scoring for trumpet, oboes, and strings, demands all the more energetically, 'Wake up, you veins and you limbs, and sing such joyful songs as are pleasing to our God'. Dynamic nuance is achieved by the resting or re-entry of the oboe choir that doubles the strings. The triadic figure on the trumpet, also taken up by the bass voice, and the virtuoso trumpet passage-work make the aria seem like a counterpart to the opening chorus. Finally, a plain four-part chorale brings the work to a close.

[9] See H. Besseler and H. Grüss, KB, NBA VII/1 (1967), 88–91, and J. Rifkin, 'Klangpracht und Stilauffassung: zu den Trompeten der Ouvertüre BWV 1069', in M. Geck and K. Hofmann, eds, *Bach und die Stile* [conference report, Dortmund, 1998] (Dortmund, 1999), 255–89 (especially 271–6).

Ehre sei Gott in der Höhe, BWV 197a

NBA I/2, p. 65 BC A11 Transmitted incomplete

1. [Chorus? Lost]

'Ehre sei Gott in der Höhe, Friede auf Erden und den Menschen ein Wohlgefallen.'	'Glory be to God on high, peace on earth and goodwill towards mankind.'

2. Aria [lost]

Erzählet, ihr Himmel, die Ehre Gottes,
Ihr Feste, verkündiget seine Macht.
  Doch vergesset nicht dabei
  Seine Liebe, seine Treu,
  Die er an denen Verlornen vollbracht.
	Tell, you heavens, the Glory of God;
	You firmaments, proclaim His might.
	  Yet do not forget
	  His love, his faithfulness,
	  Which He shows to those who are lost.

3. [Recitative; lost]

O Liebe, der kein Lieben gleich! Der hochgelobte Gottessohn Verläßt sein Himmelreich; Ein Prinz verläßt den Königsthron Und wird ein Knecht Und als ein armer Mensch geboren, Damit das menschliche Geschlecht Nicht ewig sei verloren. Was wird denn dir, Mein treuer Jesu, nun dafür?	O Love, to which no love is equal! The highly praised Son of God Leaves His heavenly kingdom; A Prince leaves His royal throne And becomes a servant And is born as a poor man; Thereby the human race Is not forever lost. What will You have, then, My faithful Jesus, therefore?

4. Aria A fl I,II cello or bsn bc G c

O! du angenehmer Schatz,
  Hebe dich aus denen Krippen,
  Nimm dafür auf meinen Lippen
  Und in meinem Herzen Platz.
	O You delightful treasure!
	  Rise out of Your crib;
	  Take Your place instead on my lips
	  And in my heart.

5. Recitativo B bc e–A c

Das Kind ist mein, Und ich bin sein, Du bist mein alles unter allen, Und außer dir Soll mir Kein Gut, kein Kleinod wohlgefallen. In Mangel hab ich Überfluß, In Leide Hab ich Freude, Bin ich krank, so heilt er mich, Bin ich schwach, so trägt er mich, Bin ich verirrt, so sucht er mich, Und wenn ich falle, hält er mich, Ja, wenn ich endlich sterben muß,	The Child is mine And I am His; You are my all in all, And apart from You Shall no possession, No jewel please me. In want I have abundance, In sorrow I have joy; If I am ill, He heals me; If I am weak, He carries me; If I go astray, He seeks me; And when I fall, He upholds me; Indeed, when at last I must die,

So bringt er mich zum Himmelsleben.
Geliebter Schatz, durch dich
Wird mir noch auf der Welt der
Himmel selbst gegeben.

He will bring me to heavenly Life.
Beloved Treasure, through You
Even in the world, Heaven itself has been
given to me.

6. ARIA B ob d'am solo bc — D 6/8

Ich lasse dich nicht,
Ich schließe dich ein
Im Herzen durch Lieben und
Glauben.
Es soll dich, mein Licht,
Noch Marter, noch Pein,
Ja! selber die Hölle nicht rauben.

I will not let You go,
I enclose You
In my heart through Love and Faith.

Of You, my Light,
Neither torment nor pain,
Indeed, not even Hell itself shall rob
me!

7. CHORAL SATB bc (+ instrs?) — D C

Wohlan! so will ich mich
An dich, o Jesu, halten,
Und sollte gleich die Welt
In tausend Stücke spalten.
O Jesu, dir, nur dir,
Dir leb ich ganz allein,
Auf dich allein, auf dich,
O Jesu, schlaf ich ein.

Well, then! I would
Cling to you, O Jesus,
Even though the world should
Split into a thousand pieces.
O Jesus, for You, only for You,
Just for You alone do I live;
In You alone, in You,
O Jesus, will I fall asleep.

The libretto of this cantata is by Henrici (Picander), and the closing chorale is the fourth verse of the hymn *Ich freue mich in dir* by Caspar Ziegler (1697). The text was included in the cycle that Picander published in 1728, and therefore Bach might have set it for Christmas 1728, or perhaps a year or two later. Unfortunately, however, the music has come down to us in a fragmentary state. The sole surviving score is incomplete, lacking the opening of the work: it starts towards the end of the fourth movement and contains the complete nos. 5–7. Bach later reused the second and third arias (nos. 4 and 6) in a parodied and radically altered form in the wedding cantata *Gott ist unsre Zuversicht*, BWV 197—an exceptional case, since the transplantation of movements from compositions that could be performed regularly to occasional works happens less often than the reverse. With the help of BWV 197, it is possible to form an adequate impression of the fourth movement, despite the loss of all but the last few bars.[10] The first three movements, however, cannot be reconstructed. Nor do we know whether Bach preceded them with an instrumental sinfonia such as is transmitted in other cantatas from this cycle.

[10] An attempted reconstruction for practical use has been published by Diethard Hellmann (Stuttgart, 1963).

Jauchzet, frohlocket, auf, preiset die Tage

Weihnachts-Oratorium Christmas Oratorio, BWV 248, Part I

NBA II/6, p. 3 BC D7[I] Duration: *c.* 29 mins

1. CORO SATB tr I–III timp fl I,II ob I,II str bc — D $\frac{3}{8}$

Jauchzet, frohlocket, auf, preiset die Tage,	Shout for joy, exult, rise up, praise the day,
Rühmet, was heute der Höchste getan!	Extol what the Highest has done today!
Lasset das Zagen, verbannet die Klage,	Stop being faint-hearted, banish lamentation,
Stimmet voll Jauchzen und Fröhlichkeit an!	Strike up, full of rejoicing and exultation!
Dienet dem Höchsten mit herrlichen Chören,	Serve the Highest with splendid choirs;
Laßt uns den Namen des Herrschers verehren!	Let us revere the name of the Sovereign!

2. EVANGELISTA T bc — b–A C

'Es begab sich aber zu der Zeit, daß ein Gebot von dem Kaiser Augusto ausging, daß alle Welt geschätzet würde. Und jedermann ging, daß er sich schätzen ließe, ein jeglicher in seine Stadt. Da machte sich auch auf Joseph aus Galiläa, aus der Stadt Nazareth, in das jüdische Land zur Stadt David, die da heißet Bethlehem; darum, daß er von dem Hause und Geschlechte David war, auf daß er sich schätzen ließe mit Maria, seinem vertrauten Weibe, die war schwanger. Und als sie daselbst waren, kam die Zeit, daß sie gebären sollte.'	'The time came when a decree went out from Caesar Augustus that an assessment should be made of the whole world. And everyone went to be assessed, each to his own city. Then Joseph went up out of Galilee, from the city of Nazareth, into the land of Judea, to the city of David which is called Bethlehem—for he was of the house and lineage of David—to be assessed with his betrothed Mary, who was pregnant. And while they were there, the time came for her to give birth.'

3. [RECITATIVE] A ob d'am I,II bc — A–e C

Nun wird mein liebster Bräutigam,	Now my dearest Bridegroom,
Nun wird der Held aus Davids Stamm	Now the strong man of David's stock,
Zum Trost, zum Heil der Erden	For the comfort and Salvation of the earth,
Einmal geboren werden.	Shall at last be born.
Nun wird der Stern aus Jakob scheinen,	Now the Star out of Jacob shall shine;
Sein Strahl bricht schon hervor.	Its rays already break forth.
Auf, Zion, und verlasse nun das Weinen,	Rise up, Zion, and stop weeping now:
Dein Wohl steigt hoch empor!	Your welfare climbs on high!

4. ARIA A ob d'am I + vln I bc — a $\frac{3}{8}$

Bereite dich, Zion, mit zärtlichen Trieben,	Make ready, Zion, with tender desire

Den Schönsten, den Liebsten bald bei dir zu sehn!
Deine Wangen
Müssen heut viel schöner prangen,
Eile, den Bräutigam sehnlichst zu lieben!

To see the fairest, the dearest with you soon!
Your cheeks
Must today look much lovelier;
Hasten, to love the Bridegroom most longingly!

5. CHORAL SATB bc (+ ww str) e C

Wie soll ich dich empfangen?
Und wie begegn' ich dir?
O aller Welt Verlangen!
O meiner Seelen Zier!
O Jesu, Jesu, setze
Mir selbst die Fackel bei,
Damit, was dich ergötze,
Mir kund und wissend sei!

How should I receive You?
And how encounter You?
O longing of all the world!
O ornament of my soul!
O Jesus, Jesus, place
Your lamp by me Yourself,
So that whatever delights You
May be known and understood by me!

6. EVANGELISTA T bc e–G C

'Und sie gebar ihren ersten Sohn und wickelte ihn in Windeln und legte ihn in eine Krippen, denn sie hatten sonst keinen Raum in der Herberge.'

'And she gave birth to her first Son and wrapped Him in swaddling-clothes and laid Him in a manger, for otherwise they had no room in the lodgings.'

7. CHORAL + RECITATIVO SB ob d'am I,II bc G 3/4

Er ist auf Erden kommen arm,
Wer will die Liebe recht erhöhn,
Die unser Heiland vor uns hegt?
Daß er unser sich erbarm
Ja, wer vermag es einzusehen,
Wie ihn der Menschen Leid bewegt?
Und in dem Himmel mache reich
Des Höchsten Sohn kömmt in die Welt,
Weil ihm ihr Heil so wohl gefällt,
Und seinen lieben Engeln gleich.
So will er selbst als Mensch geboren werden.
Kyrieleis!

He has come on earth poor
Who would rightly extol the Love
That our Saviour feels for us?
To be merciful to us
Indeed, who is able to appreciate
How man's suffering moves Him?
And make us rich in heaven
The Highest's Son comes into the world
Because its Salvation pleases Him so well
And like His beloved angels.
That He Himself would be born as a man.
Lord, have mercy!

8. ARIA B tr I fl + str bc D 2/4

Großer Herr, o starker König,
Liebster Heiland, o wie wenig
Achtest du der Erden Pracht!
Der die ganze Welt erhält,
Ihre Pracht und Zier erschaffen,
Muß in harten Krippen schlafen.

Great Lord, O mighty King,
Dearest Saviour, oh how little
You respect earthly splendour!
He who preserves the whole world
And created its splendour and adornment
Must sleep in a hard crib.

9. CHORAL SATB tr I–III timp bc (+ ww str) D C

Ach mein herzliebes Jesulein,

Ah, my beloved Jesus,

Mach dir ein rein sanft Bettelein,	**Make Yourself a clean, soft bed,**
Zu ruhn in meines Herzens Schrein,	**To rest in my heart's shrine,**
Daß ich nimmer vergesse dein!	**So that I may never forget You!**

The original date of the *Christmas Oratorio* has been handed down to us with all the certainty one could desire: both Bach's autograph score and the printed text for the same performance, which for once survives, are dated '1734'. It is not known who wrote the text, though Picander is an obvious possibility, since the oratorio* contains numerous parodied movements, and Picander had elsewhere proved himself to be a master of the art of parody,* which demands musical knowledge as well as poetic ability.

Characteristic of the textual structure is the presence of freely versified recitative of a contemplative kind, familiar from the *St Matthew Passion*, above all, and often inserted between the Evangelist's recitative and an aria. Martin Dibelius has pointed out[11] that in the *St Matthew Passion* the order Evangelist—free recitative—aria corresponds to the functions of reading—meditation—prayer advocated by August Hermann Francke for correct Bible reading (similar demands are found in the works of other theologians). It should be added that a sequence of this kind as a rule concluded with a chorale in which the congregation said their 'Amen' to it, so to speak. Similar circumstances prevail in the *Christmas Oratorio*, as the following analysis shows. After an introductory chorus,* Part I consists of two halves, alike in structure, one for Advent and the other for Christmas:

Reading:	2. Es begab sich aber	6. Und sie gebar ihren ersten Sohn
Meditation:	3. Nun wird mein liebster Bräutigam	7. Er ist auf Erden kommen arm / Wer will die Liebe recht erhöhn
Prayer:	4. Bereite dich, Zion	8. Großer Herr, o starker König
Congregation:	5. Wie soll ich dich empfangen	9. Ach mein herzliebes Jesulein

Bach's setting—one of the pinnacles of world musical literature—is so well known that only a few features need to be pointed out here.[12]

The opening chorus and both arias are parodies, derived from the secular cantatas BWV 214 and 213. This is particularly evident in the opening chorus, where the instruments' order of entry—drums, trumpets, strings—was conditioned by the text of the congratulatory cantata BWV 214. The first two lines

[11] In 'Individualismus und Gemeindebewußtsein in Joh. Seb. Bachs Passionen', *Archiv für Reformationsgeschichte*, 41 (1948), 132–54.

[12] More detailed analyses of the whole oratorio have been published by A. Dürr, *J. S. Bach: Weihnachts-Oratorium BWV 248* (Munich, 1967), and W. Blankenburg, *Das Weihnachts-Oratorium von J. S. Bach* (Munich and Kassel etc., 1982).

of the secular text, 'Tönet, ihr Pauken! Erschallet, Trompeten! Klingende Saiten, erfüllet die Luft!' ('Sound, you drums! resound, trumpets! Resonant strings, fill the air!'), might easily have been adopted in the *Christmas Oratorio* too, preserving our comprehension of musical events.[13] Since Bach did *not* do this, we may assume that such external text imitation* was, in the last resort, not particularly important to him. It follows that, in our attempt to penetrate Bach's art, we should not ascribe exaggerated significance to the musical imitation of the words of the text. Even the affect* of a parody *vis-à-vis* its model can be altered within certain parameters, as a comparison of the aria 'Bereite dich, Zion' (no. 4) with its secular model 'Ich will dich nicht hören' (BWV 213/9) clearly indicates: Bach's music is incomparably well suited not only to the indignant cries of 'Ich will nicht, ich mag nicht' ('I will not, I may not') but also to the Advent jubilation of 'den Schönsten, den Liebsten' ('the fairest, the dearest').

Finally, attention should be drawn to the significant role played in the oratorio by the chorale. That the first and last chorales of the entire work, nos. 5 and 64, were sung to the same melody may have been intended by Bach as a form of thematic unification. Less likely is the theory that with this melody he wished to anticipate Christ's Passion. For the melody *Herzlich tut mich verlangen* was, at that time, not so closely connected with Paul Gerhardt's Passion hymn *O Haupt voll Blut und Wunden* in the consciousness of the congregation that this allusion would have been readily understood. Moreover, the tune was so commonly used in Leipzig for the hymn *Wie soll ich dich empfangen* that none of the listeners would have guessed that a special reference to the Passion lay behind it. Of the other two chorale arrangements in Part I of the oratorio, the combination in no. 7 of the hymn verse 'Er ist auf Erden kommen arm' ('He has come on earth poor') with freely versified recitative attracts special attention. Here the chorale is clearly assigned the function of lending emphasis to the decisive statement of the biblical narrative, 'And she gave birth to her first Son' (no. 6). Neither here nor in the closing chorale is Bach content merely with the usual four-part setting. Instead, with its obbligato* trumpet episodes, the finale forms a bridge back to the opening chorus.

Gloria in excelsis Deo, BWV 191

NBA I/2, p. 173 BC E16 Duration: *c.* 17 mins

1. [Chorus] S I,II ATB tr I–III timp fl + ob I fl + ob II str bc D $\frac{3}{8}$ C

'Gloria in excelsis Deo. Et in terra pax hominibus bonae voluntatis.'	'Glory be to God on high. And on earth peace to men of good will.'
Post orationem:	After the oration:

[13] Bach at first entered these opening words in the autograph score of the *Christmas Oratorio*. This was probably not intentional, however, but the result of mechanical copying as he transferred the music from its secular model.

2. [Duetto] ST fl I + II str bc — G C

Gloria Patri et Filio et Spiritui sancto.	Glory to the Father, Son and Holy Spirit.

3. [Chorus] S I,II ATB tr I–III timp fl I,II ob I,II str bc — D 3/4

Sicut erat in principio et nunc et semper et in saecula saeculorum, amen.	As it was in the beginning, is now and ever shall be, world without end. Amen.

We do not know for certain what occasioned the origin of this Latin Christmas music. A Latin cantata during the principal Leipzig service would have been so exceptional that we have to ask whether Bach might have written the work for a quite different occasion. Arnold Schering suggested that it might have been composed for a special Christmas celebration to mark a political event of some kind.[14] In 1992, Gregory Butler pinpointed the most likely occasion:[15] a special service of thanksgiving that took place in the Paulinerkirche, the Leipzig university church, on Christmas Day 1745 to mark the signing of a peace treaty in Dresden following the Prussian invasion of Saxony.

The text of the work consists solely of the Latin version of the song of the angels from Luke 2.14 ('Glory be to God on high . . .'), to which the shorter doxology* is appended ('Glory be to the Father and to the Son . . .'). These words are divided among three movements, the first of which was performed before an oration and the other two afterwards. The music itself is not new: all three movements were borrowed from the Missa of 1733, which later formed the Kyrie and Gloria of the B minor Mass, BWV 232[I]. Bach was able to adopt the opening movement, 'Gloria in excelsis Deo', virtually without change from the Gloria of the Missa. For the second movement, he selected the 'Domine Deus' in a slightly abridged form and furnished with a new text. The third movement was adapted in a similar fashion by fitting a new text to the 'Cum Sancto Spiritu'. Here, in order to accommodate the opening words, a slight lengthening of the original was necessary.[16]

1.6 Second Day of Christmas

Epistle: Titus 3.4–7: 'God's mercy has appeared in Christ'.
Gospel: Luke 2.15–20: the shepherds at the crib.

Also celebrated as a day of remembrance for the martyr Stephen:

Epistle: Acts 6.8–7.2a and 7.51–9: the martyrdom of Stephen.
Gospel: Matthew 23.34–9: 'Jerusalem, you that kill the prophets!'

[14] See A. Schering, *BJ* 1936, p. 6, note 1.

[15] In G. Butler, 'J. S. Bachs Gloria in excelsis Deo BWV 191: Musik für ein Leipziger Dankfest', *BJ* 1992, 65–71.

[16] Details of the relationship between original and parody are given by A. Dürr in KB, NBA I/2 (1957), 156 ff.

Darzu ist erschienen der Sohn Gottes, BWV 40

NBA I/3.1, p. 3 BC A12 Duration: *c.* 20 mins

1. [CHORUS] SATB hn I,II ob I,II str bc — F c

'Darzu ist erschienen der Sohn Gottes,
daß er die Werke des Teufels zerstöre.'

'For this the Son of God has appeared:
that He may destroy the works of the Devil.'

2. RECITATIVO T bc — F–B♭ c

Das Wort ward Fleisch und wohnet in der Welt,
Das Licht der Welt bestrahlt den Kreis der Erden,
Der große Gottessohn
Verläßt des Himmels Thron,
Und seiner Majestät gefällt,
Ein kleines Menschenkind zu werden.
Bedenkt doch diesen Tausch, wer nur gedenken kann;
Der König wird ein Untertan,
Der Herr erscheinet als ein Knecht
Und wird dem menschlichen Geschlecht
—O süßes Wort in aller Ohren!—
Zu Trost und Heil geboren.

The Word became flesh and dwells in the world;
The Light of the World irradiates the circle of the earth;
The great Son of God
Leaves His heavenly throne,
And it pleased His Majesty
To become a little human child.
Consider this exchange, whoever can but think:
The King becomes a subject,
The Lord appears as a servant
And is born to the human race
—O sweet word in all ears!—
For comfort and Salvation.

3. CHORAL SATB bc (+ hn I ww str) — g c

Die Sünd macht Leid;
Christus bringt Freud,
Weil er zu Trost in diese Welt ist kommen.
Mit uns ist Gott
Nun in der Not:
Wer ist, der uns als Christen kann verdammen?

Sin causes suffering;
Christ brings joy,
For He has come into this world for our comfort.
God is with us
Now in our need;
Who is there that can condemn us as Christians?

4. ARIA B ob I,II str bc — d 3/8

Höllische Schlange,
Wird dir nicht bange?
Der dir den Kopf als ein Sieger zerknickt,
Ist nun geboren,
Und die verloren,
Werden mit ewigem Frieden beglückt.

Hellish serpent,
Do you not become anxious?
He who as a victor crushes your head
Is now born,
And those who are lost
Are blessed with eternal peace.

5. RECITATIVO A str bc — B♭ c

Die Schlange, so im Paradies
Auf alle Adamskinder
Das Gift der Seelen fallen ließ,
Bringt uns nicht mehr Gefahr;
Des Weibes Samen stellt sich dar,

The serpent which in Paradise
On all Adam's children
Let the poison of souls fall
Brings us no more danger;
The woman's seed is manifest,

Der Heiland ist ins Fleisch gekommen
Und hat ihr allen Gift benommen.
Drum sei getrost! betrübter Sünder.

The Saviour has come in the flesh
And has taken away all its poison.
Then be comforted, troubled sinner!

6. CHORAL SATB bc (+ instrs as in no. 3) d c

Schüttle deinen Kopf und sprich:
Fleuch, du alte Schlange!
Was erneuerst du deinen Stich,
Machst mir angst und bange?
Ist dir doch der Kopf zerknickt,
Und ich bin durchs Leiden
Meines Heilands dir entrückt
In den Saal der Freuden.

Shake your head and say:
Flee, you old serpent!
Why do you renew your sting,
Making me fearful and anxious?
Your head is truly crushed,
And I am, through the suffering
Of my Saviour, carried off from you
Into the Hall of Joys.

7. ARIA T hn I,II ob I,II bc F $\frac{12}{8}$

Christenkinder, freuet euch!
Wütet schon das Höllenreich,
Will euch Satans Grimm erschrecken:
Jesus, der erretten kann,
Nimmt sich seiner Küchlein an
Und will sie mit Flügeln decken.

Christian children, rejoice!
Though Hell's kingdom rages,
Though Satan's fury would terrify you,
Jesus, who can rescue you,
Takes care of His chicks
And will cover them with His wings.

8. CHORAL SATB bc (+ instrs as in no. 3) f c

Jesu, nimm dich deiner Glieder
Ferner in Genaden an;
Schenke, was man bitten kann,
Zu erquicken deine Brüder;
Gib der ganzen Christenschar
Frieden und ein selges Jahr!
Freude, Freude über Freude!
Christus wehret allem Leide.
Wonne, Wonne über Wonne!
Er ist die Genadensonne.

O Jesus, take care of Your members
Henceforth in Your Grace;
Give whatever we can ask for
To refresh Your brothers;
Grant the entire Christian throng
Peace and a blessed year!
Joy, joy upon joy!
Christ curbs all sorrow.
Bliss, bliss upon bliss!
He is the Sun of Grace.

This cantata, which dates from 1723, Bach's first year in Leipzig, makes little reference to the readings of the day: it describes Jesus as destroyer of the sin brought into the world by Adam. The text is full of biblical allusions. The words of the first movement are drawn from the First Epistle of John 3.8; 'The Word became flesh and dwells in the world' (no. 2) from John 1.14; 'The serpent which in Paradise let the poison of souls fall on all Adam's children' (no. 5) refers to Genesis 3, the account of the Fall of Man, in which v. 15, 'I will put emnity between you and the woman and between your seed and her seed; it shall crush your head . . .', was interpreted, in the biblical exegesis of Bach's day, as a reference to the coming of Christ;[17] the image of the serpent whose head is

[17] For more details see H. Werthemann, *Die Bedeutung der alttestamentlichen Historien in J. S. Bachs Kirchenkantaten* (Tübingen, 1960), 16–18.

crushed by Christ is also employed in nos. 4 and 6; the phrase 'Jesus takes care of His chicks' in no. 7, on the other hand, uses an image from the Gospel* for St Stephen's Day (Matt. 23.37): 'How often would I have gathered your children together, as a hen gathers her chicks under her wings, and yet you would not have it'. This last allusion arouses the suspicion that the cantata was intended for St Stephen's Day, even though there are no other specific grounds for this conjecture.

It is also worth noting the presence of no fewer than three chorale verses, whereas the cantata revived on the previous day, no. 63, had contained not a single one. Two of the three chorale movements are based on Christmas hymns: the text of no. 3 is the third verse of the hymn *Wir Christenleut* by Caspar Füger (1592); that of no. 8, the fourth verse of the hymn *Freuet euch, ihr Christen alle* by Christian Keymann (1645). No. 6, the second verse of Paul Gerhardt's hymn *Schwing dich auf zu deinem Gott* (1653), was no doubt used here only on account of the specific content of this verse. Although it fits in well, it could have been added to the libretto subsequently (cf. the basic textual scheme of this group of cantatas above, p. 27).

The most impressive movement in the cantata, as often in Bach, is the ceremonial opening chorus,* which acquires a festive, joyful character through the participation of two horns. Bach later parodied it to form the finale, 'Cum Sancto Spiritu', of the Lutheran Missa in F, BWV 233. A signal-like, militant horn call,

opens the instrumental ritornello. Its repeat, transposed to the dominant, is followed by an antiphonal, sequential answering sentence. In musical substance, the first section of the movement is an expanded reprise of the instrumental prelude, whose opening is interrupted by homophonic* choral interjections and extended by repeats; and the answering sentence of the ritornello incorporates the choir by means of choral insertion.* The middle section is made up of an elaborate choral fugue.* With its new, highly singable subject,

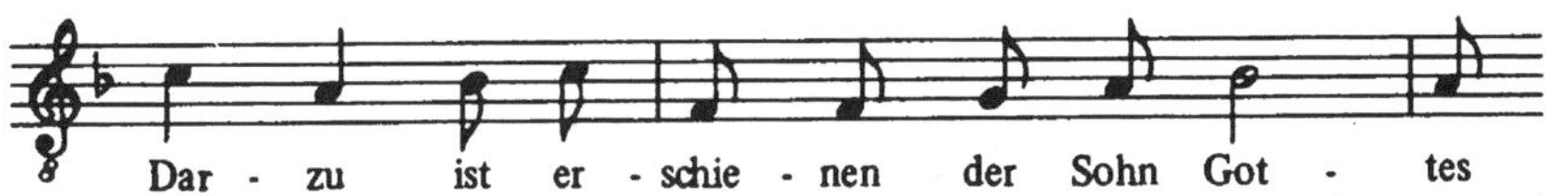

it allows the vocal principle to dominate by contrast with the concerted, instrumentally conceived first section. The first exposition* is delivered by the voice parts only, with continuo accompaniment; in the second, which includes the instruments (though with only semi-independent parts), a second subject is added at the words 'daß er die Werke des Teufels zerstöre' ('that He may destroy the works of the Devil'). And now a thick fabric of strettos* follows. The fugue ends in freely flowing polyphony,* leading back to a free reprise of the opening section.

The second movement, a plain *secco* recitative, refers to the marvel of God's becoming man; the third, a four-part chorale setting, returns to the main theme of the cantata, Christ as the conqueror of sin, not only in its text but in the chromaticism* that characterizes its harmony. The combative tone of the first movement is heard again in the bass aria, no. 4, a movement of full-blooded drama. In colourful, iridescent harmony, a picture is sketched of the 'hellish serpent'. But the movement also gains a triumphant character from its sharply dotted 3/8 rhythm and its clearly periodic phrasing, which is not far removed from dance: it is entirely based on the scheme (2 + 2) + 4 bars, which is only rarely expanded by doubling the first half, and only once broken by the insertion of one bar (b. 105) just before the end.

A motivically-imprinted string *accompagnato,** no. 5, serves to emphasize the words of the alto recitative, 'The serpent which in Paradise . . .': the prophecy has been fulfilled and Adam's sin annulled. Another four-part chorale, no. 6, is followed by the second aria, no. 7, which is still more suggestive of the opening chorus than the first aria, recalling the festive character of the introductory movement in its wind scoring, its triadic melody, and the subdominant twist of its vocal entry. Elaborate tenor coloraturas* on 'freuet' ('rejoice') contribute to the interpretation of the text, as do the faltering rests on 'erschrecken' ('terrify') in the middle section. A plain chorale setting ends the work.

Christum wir sollen loben schon, BWV 121

NBA I/3.1, p. 57 BC A13 Duration: *c.* 21 mins

1. [Chorale] SATB bc (+ cornett trb I–III ob d'am str) e–f♯ ¢

Christum wir sollen loben schon,[18]	**Christ we shall praise splendidly—**
Der reinen Magd Marien Sohn,	**Son of the pure maiden Mary—**
So weit die liebe Sonne leucht	**As far as the dear sun shines,**
Und an aller Welt Ende reicht.	**Reaching to all ends of the world.**

2. Aria T ob d'am bc b 3/4

O du von Gott erhöhte Kreatur,	O you creature exalted by God,
Begreife nicht, nein, nein, bewundre nur:	Do not comprehend, no, no, just marvel:
Gott will durch Fleisch des Fleisches Heil erwerben.	God would gain the Salvation of flesh through flesh—
Wie groß ist doch der Schöpfer aller Dinge,	How great indeed is the Creator of all things,

[18] 'schon' = 'schön'.

Und wie bist du verachtet und geringe,	And how despised and mean you are—
Um dich dadurch zu retten vom Verderben.	In order to save you from perdition.
3. RECITATIVO A bc	D–C c
Der Gnade unermeßlichs Wesen	The immeasurable essence of Grace
Hat sich den Himmel nicht	Has not chosen heaven
Zur Wohnstatt auserlesen,	For its dwelling-place,
Weil keine Grenze sie umschließt.	For no bounds enclose it.
Was Wunder, daß allhie Verstand und Witz gebricht,	What wonder that, in all this, understanding and wit break down
Ein solch Geheimnis zu ergründen,	In trying to fathom such a mystery,
Wenn sie sich in ein keusches Herze gießt.	As when Grace is poured into a pure heart.
Gott wählet sich den reinen Leib zu einem Tempel seiner Ehren,	God chooses Himself a pure body as a temple of His honour,
Um zu den Menschen sich mit wundervoller Art zu kehren.	So that He may turn to mankind in a wondrous manner.
4. ARIA B str bc	C c
Johannis freudenvolles Springen	John's joyful leaping
Erkannte dich, mein Jesu, schon.	Recognized You, my Jesus, already.
Nun da ein Glaubensarm dich hält,	Now as an arm of faith holds You,
So will mein Herze von der Welt	So would my heart ardently break through
Zu deiner Krippen brünstig dringen.	From the world to Your crib.
5. RECITATIVO S bc	G–b c
Doch wie erblickt es dich in deiner Krippen?	Yet how does it see You in Your crib?
Es seufzt mein Herz: Mit bebender und fast geschloßner Lippen	My heart sighs: with shaking and almost closed lips
Bringt es sein dankend Opfer dar.	It presents its grateful offering.
Gott, der so unermeßlich war,	God, who was so immeasurable,
Nimmt Knechtsgestalt und Armut an.	Takes on the form of a servant and poverty.
Und weil er dieses uns zugutgetan,	And because He has done this for our benefit,
So laß ich mit der Engel Chören	Then let me, with the angel choirs,
Ein jauchzend Lob- und Danklied hören!	Hear a jubilant song of praise and thanks!
6. CHORAL SATB bc (+ instrs as in no. 1)	e–f♯ c
Lob, Ehr und Dank sei dir gesagt,	**Praise, honour and thanks be to You,**
Christ, geborn von der reinen Magd,	**Christ, born of a pure maiden,**
Samt Vater und dem Heilgen Geist	**Together with the Father and Holy Spirit**
Von nun an bis in Ewigkeit.	**From now on until eternity.**

The German translation by Martin Luther (1524) of the old church hymn *A solis ortus cardine* forms the textual foundation of this chorale cantata,* composed for 26 December 1724. The anonymous librettist retained the first and last verses (nos. 1 and 8) literally, as usual, but adapted the middle verses, one for each of the two arias and two for each of the two recitatives. Thus verse 2 formed the second movement, verses 3–4 the third, verse 5 the fourth, and verses 6–7 the fifth. The text hardly exhibits a close connection with the readings of the day. Yet phrases such as 'So would my heart ardently break through . . . to Your crib' (no. 4) and 'Yet how does [my heart] see You in Your crib?' (no. 5) indicate that the day was probably celebrated that year not as St Stephen's Day but as the Second Day of Christmas, with its reading about the shepherds at the crib.

Bach's librettist divides up the ideas of the text more clearly than Luther's hymn translation, making a rhyming sermon out of an original oriented towards glorifying adoration. The first half (nos. 1–3) celebrates the unimaginable wonder of the Birth of God's Son; the second (nos. 4–6) gives the response of man, who approaches the crib in adoration. Though the hymn source had already referred to the leaping of John in his mother's womb (Luke 1.44), Bach's librettist expands on the hymn in the fourth movement: 'Now as an arm of faith holds You, so would my heart ardently break through from the world to Your crib'. The holding of Jesus on the arms of faith and the departure from this world refer, no doubt intentionally, to the words of the aged Simeon at the presentation of Christ in the temple (Luke 2.22–32), thereby going beyond Luther's hymn.

Even in Bach's day there must have been something archaic about the melody of the chosen chorale. Though a simplified version of the ancient hymn melody, it reproduces its obscure tonality: the beginning leads us to expect a Dorian melody, but it closes in the Phrygian mode. Bach's setting of the opening movement underlines this antiquated impression by taking the form of a chorale motet.* Each line is introduced imitatively* by the three lower voice parts over an independent continuo and then delivered by the soprano in doubled note-values. After each soprano entry, the lower parts have unthematic counterpoint* and the continuo is united with the choral bass, so that the movement never goes beyond a four-part texture. Its structure may be represented as follows (1 = line 1, I = line 1 augmented, etc.):

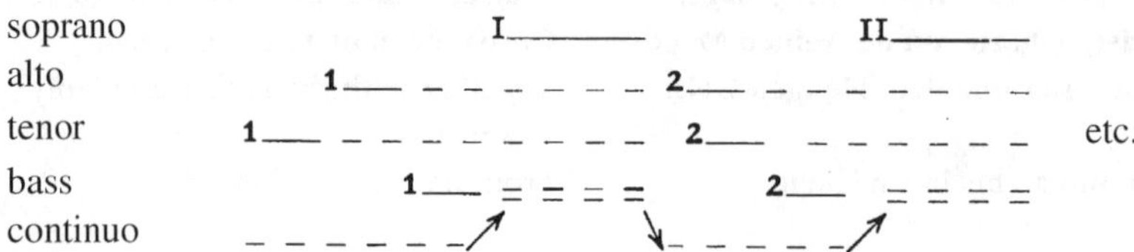

The unthematic, freely polyphonic* parts are nonetheless motivically bound by a figure derived from the opening of the first chorale line, which occurs for the first time in bar 2 of the continuo part:

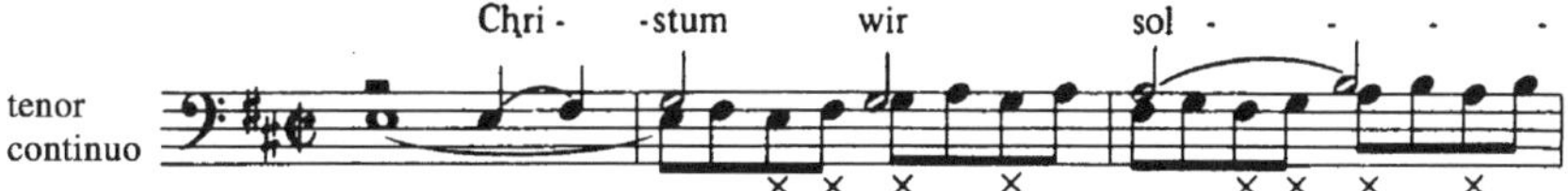

The voice parts are doubled *colla parte** by the entire instrumental ensemble, which contains not only strings and oboe d'amore* but a four-part choir of trombones (cornett—their usual treble instrument—and trombones I–III), which contributes to the antiquated impression made by the movement.

The second movement begins the 'modern' part of the cantata. Noteworthy here is the irregular periodic structure of the opening ritornello (3 + 3 + 2 + 2 + 2 bars) and its cadence in the relative major, D. In order to reach a conclusion in the home key of B minor, it has to be substantially modified when repeated at the end of the main section. This tendency towards the remodelling of thematic material is also noticeable elsewhere in the aria. It leads to a happy avoidance of the stereotype of pure da capo* form and lends the movement an unconventional character.

The third movement is set as *secco* and would require no special mention if Bach had not illustrated the closing words, 'So that He may turn to mankind in a wondrous manner', with an exceedingly bold and surprising harmonic twist: a sixth-chord of C ♯ major is followed not by the expected F ♯ minor but by an abrupt turn, via a diminished seventh, to C major. In Bach's instrumental works we hardly find unprepared progressions of this kind. Here it is justified by the text, which speaks of the 'wonder' of the Birth of Jesus.

The text of the fourth movement turns towards the human sphere, towards the spectator of the miracle, and this finds expression in Bach's setting too. It is a bass aria, fully scored for strings, and the most approachable piece in the whole cantata. Its uncomplicated diatonic melody and clear, simple harmony contribute to this impression, as does its method of joining together in a mosaic-like, oft-changing fashion parts of themes stated in the ritornello, so that throughout we repeatedly encounter what we have already heard. Despite its elaborate thematic material, built on frequent motivic imitations, the aria creates the impression of predominantly homophonic* euphony, distinguished by motion in thirds and sixths. The second recitative, no. 5, again a plain *secco*, is followed by the closing chorale, no. 6, in which Bach, with great skill, clothes the church-mode melody in the major-minor tonality of his day.

Selig ist der Mann (Dialogus), BWV 57

NBA I/3.1, p. 83 BC A14 Duration: *c.* 28 mins

1. Aria B ob I,II taille + str bc g 3/4

'Selig ist der Mann, der die Anfechtung erduldet; denn nachdem er bewähret ist, wird er die Krone des Lebens empfahen.'

'Blessed is the man who endures temptation; for after he is tested, he will receive the Crown of Life.'

2. Recitativo S bc E♭–c C

Ach! dieser süße Trost
Erquickt auch mir mein Herz,
Das sonst in Ach und Schmerz
Sein ewig Leiden findet
Und sich als wie ein Wurm in seinem Blute windet.
Ich muß als wie ein Schaf
Bei tausend rauhen Wölfen leben;
Ich bin ein recht verlaßnes Lamm
Und muß mich ihrer Wut
Und Grausamkeit ergeben.
Was Abeln dort betraf,
Erpresset mir
Auch diese Tränenflut.
Ach! Jesu, wüßt ich hier
Nicht Trost von dir,
So müßte Mut und Herze brechen,
Und voller Trauren sprechen:

Ah! this sweet comfort
Refreshes even my heart,
Which otherwise in grief and pain
Finds eternal suffering
And writhes in its own blood like a worm.
I have to live like a sheep
Among a thousand savage wolves;
I am a truly forsaken lamb
And have to surrender to their rage
And ferocity.
What there befell Abel
Extorts from me
Too this flood of tears.
Ah! Jesus, if I knew
No comfort from You here,
Then my courage and heart must break
And, full of sadness, say:

3. Aria S str bc c 3/4

Ich wünschte mir den Tod, den Tod,
Wenn du, mein Jesu, mich nicht liebtest.
  Ja wenn du mich annoch betrübtest,
  So hätt ich mehr als Höllennot.

I would wish upon myself death, death,
If You, my Jesus, did not love me.
  Indeed, if You still grieved me,
  I would have more than Hell's anguish.

4. Recitativo SB bc g–B♭ C

Jesus
Ich reiche dir die Hand
Und auch damit das Herze.
Seele
Ach! süßes Liebespfand,
Du kannst die Feinde stürzen
Und ihren Grimm verkürzen.

Jesus
I reach out my hand to you
And with it my heart.
Soul
Ah! sweet pledge of love,
You can overthrow my enemies
And curtail their fury.

5. Aria B str bc B♭ 3/4

Ja, ja, ich kann die Feinde schlagen,
Die dich nur stets bei mir verklagen,
Drum fasse dich, bedrängter Geist.

Yes, yes, I can strike the enemies
That constantly accuse you before Me;
Then compose yourself, harassed spirit.

Bedrängter Geist, hör auf zu weinen,
Die Sonne wird noch helle scheinen,
Die dir itzt Kummerwolken weist.

Harassed spirit, cease to weep;
The sun will shine brightly again,
Which now shows you clouds of woe.

6. Recitativo SB bc — E♭–d C

Jesus
In meiner Schoß liegt Ruh und Leben,
Dies will ich dir einst ewig geben.
Seele
Ach! Jesu, wär ich schon bei dir,
Ach striche mir
Der Wind schon über Gruft und Grab,
So könnt ich alle Not besiegen.
Wohl denen, die im Sarge liegen
Und auf den Schall der Engel hoffen!
Ach! Jesu, mache mir doch nur
Wie Stephano den Himmel offen!
Mein Herz ist schon bereit,
Zu dir hinaufzusteigen.
Komm, komm, vergnügte Zeit!
Du magst mir Gruft und Grab
Und meinen Jesum zeigen.

Jesus
In my bosom lies rest and life;
This will I give you one day for ever.
Soul
Ah! Jesus, would that I were already with You;
Ah, if the wind already swept
Over my tomb and grave,
Then I could overcome all affliction.
Blessed are those who lie in their coffin
And hope for the sound of the angels!
Ah! Jesus, make the heavens open for me
As they were for Stephen!
My heart is already prepared
To climb up to You.
Come, come, delightful time!
You may show me tomb and grave
As well as my Jesus.

7. Aria S vln solo bc — g–B♭ 3/8

Ich ende
Behende
Mein irdisches Leben.
Mit Freuden
Zu scheiden
Verlang ich itzt eben.
Mein Heiland, ich sterbe mit höchster Begier,
Hier hast du die Seele, was schenkest du mir?

I end
Swiftly
My earthly life.
Joyfully
I now long
Just to depart.
My Saviour, I die with the greatest eagerness;
Here You have my soul: what will You grant me?

8. Choral SATB bc (+ instrs) — B♭ 3/4

Richte dich, Liebste, nach meinem Gefallen und gläube,
Daß ich dein Seelenfreund immer und ewig verbleibe,
Der dich ergötzt
Und in den Himmel versetzt
Aus dem gemarterten Leibe.

Direct yourself, beloved, according to My pleasure, and believe
That I remain always and forever your soul's Friend,
Who delights you
And transfers you into heaven
From out of your tortured body.

Among Bach's cantatas for the Second Day of Christmas, this work, first performed on 26 December 1725, is the true St Stephen's Day cantata, for it makes no reference at all to the celebration of Christ's Birth and from the very beginning praises martyrdom. It is also the most personal cantata for the day, for, as we see at once in the second movement, its subject is not external temptation or persecution but rather the distress caused by the temptation of sin, over which Christ is celebrated as victor. This personal theme is reflected in Bach's setting: he himself designated the two characters of this dialogue cantata as 'Jesus' and 'Anima' (the Soul); and the dialogue form of the work is even carried over into the concluding four-part chorale.

The librettist, Georg Christian Lehms, refers to both Epistle* and Gospel* readings in the course of his reflections, enriching them with further biblical allusions.[19] A quotation from the Epistle of James (1.12) forms the text of the opening movement: whoever stands the test of temptation will receive the Crown (Greek: 'stephanos') of Life. In order to comprehend the following recitative, no. 2, we need to know that Abel, to whom reference is made in the Gospel (Matt. 23.35), is linked to Stephen in traditional Christian teaching, the one being the first martyr of the Old Covenant, the other of the New Covenant. Under the Old Covenant, the Soul has to live 'like a sheep among a thousand savage wolves', an image that recurs in Matt. 10.16. 'What there befell Abel extorts from me too this flood of tears'; and if Jesus did not love the Soul, she would have to wish for death (no. 3). With the fourth movement, the breakthrough—already prepared—into the world of the New Covenant takes place. Jesus reaches His hand out to the Soul. He can strike the enemies (no. 5), and therefore the Soul, like Stephen (Acts 7.55–6), can hope to find heaven open to her at the end of her life (no. 6). Death brings the desired union with Jesus (no. 7). Although Lehms had prescribed for the conclusion a chorale verse of contemplative substance—'Kurz ist dein irdisch Leben' ('Short is your earthly life') from the hymn *Gott lob, die Stund ist kommen* by Johann Heermann (1632)—Bach continues the dialogue in the closing chorale: upon the Soul's question, 'What will You grant me?', in no. 7, Jesus now promises her the Kingdom of Heaven in the words of the sixth verse of the hymn *Hast du denn, Jesu, dein Angesicht gänzlich verborgen*—described as a 'Seelengespräch mit Christo', a 'Conversation of the Soul with Christ'—by Ahasverus Fritsch (1668).

In accordance with the dialogue character of the text, the dramatic component is more clearly evident than in other church cantatas. This applies to Bach's setting no less than to the libretto. The recitatives are closer to their original function in opera, namely that of advancing the plot. Each is a plain *secco* that forms a transition to a new affect,* spaciously treated in the next aria. The scoring is restricted almost exclusively to two solo singers, soprano

[19] Here, in essentials, we follow the comments of H. Werthemann, *Die Bedeutung der alttestamentlichen Historien*, 56 ff.

and bass, plus strings and continuo. Only in the concluding chorale are four voices required; and in the outer movements, nos. 1 and 8, two oboes and taille* are added to the strings, not with independent parts but by way of reinforcement.

The opening movement occupies the intermediate territory between arioso* and aria. No doubt quite intentionally, the introductory ritornello lacks a firm thematic profile. And the three vocal sections that follow exhibit textual and musical correspondences that do not coincide but rather overlap:

Text:	1	2	2
Music:	A	A^1	B

The dominating impression, however, is made by the expressive voice part, with its broadly swinging melodic line and its long-held notes, whose falling or rising sequence creates the effect of repose ('blessed', 'crown') and enhancement ('tested') respectively.

In the third movement, to a greater extent than in the first, the contrasts inherent in the text are exploited for the thematic material of Bach's setting. In the string ritornello, two motives of divergent character may already be recognized. The first, characterized by an ascent followed by a large intervallic leap downwards, is later heard to the words 'I would wish upon myself death':

The second, an almost minuet-like figure, is later attached to the words 'If You, my Jesus, did not love me':

It is indicative of the aesthetics of Bach's time that the unreality of the statement—'I would . . . if not . . .'—is completely disregarded: Death (distance from Jesus) and Life (the love of Jesus) are the opposites from which the composer yields his thematic material.

The third aria, no. 5, shares its string scoring with the previous one, but in affect* they are fully contrasting. Repeated semiquavers, a radiant B ♭ major, rising and falling broken triads: all these things contribute to the praise of Christ as victor over his enemies. Only at the word 'accuse' and in the middle section do minor-mode disturbances remind us of the opening situation of the cantata.

The Soul, now comforted, declares her longing for heaven in a powerfully expressive recitative (no. 6). This love of the hereafter ('Blessed are those who lie in their coffin'), with which we can scarcely sympathize any longer today, also pervades the following aria, no. 7, whose words 'Swiftly I end my earthly life' are clothed by Bach in music of aching, passionate bliss. The first bars of the violin solo depict this 'end' as a wild gesture of letting oneself fall into the arms of Jesus:

In Bach's setting of the words 'Mein Heiland, ich sterbe' ('My Saviour, I die') from the second half of the aria, the mystical love of Jesus and of death finds a perfect artistic form such as it very seldom achieves. Logically, the aria lacks a da capo*, ending in the relative major, B♭, with the question 'What will You grant me?', to which the following four-part chorale, no. 8, gives the response: for the Christian, faith signifies deliverance from death.

Und es waren Hirten in derselben Gegend

Weihnachts-Oratorium Christmas Oratorio, BWV 248, Part II

NBA II/6, p. 57 BC D7[II] Duration: *c.* 29 mins

10. SINFONIA fl I,II ob d'am I,II ob da c I,II str bc — G 12/8

11. EVANGELISTA T bc — e–b C

'Und es waren Hirten in derselben Gegend auf dem Felde bei den Hürden, die hüteten des Nachts ihre Herde. Und siehe, des Herren Engel trat zu ihnen, und die Klarheit des Herren leuchtet um sie, und sie furchten sich sehr.'	'And there were shepherds in the same environs, in the field with their flocks. They kept watch over their flock by night. And see, the angel of the Lord came to them, and the brightness of the Lord shone around them, and they were very afraid.'

12. CHORAL SATB bc (+ instrs) — G C

Brich an, o schönes Morgenlicht, Und laß den Himmel tagen! Du Hirtenvolk, erschrecke nicht, Weil dir die Engel sagen, Daß dieses schwache Knäbelein Soll unser Trost und Freude sein, Dazu den Satan zwingen Und letztlich Friede bringen!	**Break out, O fair morning light, And let the heavens dawn! You shepherd folk, do not fear, For the angels tell you That this weak little boy Shall be our comfort and joy, Overcome Satan, And finally bring peace!**

13. EVANGELISTA TS str bc — D–b C

'Und der Engel sprach zu ihnen:' *Angelus*	'And the angel said to them:' *Angel*

'Fürchtet euch nicht, siehe, ich verkündige euch große Freude, die allem Volke widerfahren wird. Denn euch ist heute der Heiland geboren, welcher ist Christus, der Herr, in der Stadt David.'

'Do not be afraid; look, I bring you news of great joy, which shall come upon all the people. For today the Saviour is born to you, He who is Christ the Lord, in the city of David.'

14. RECITATIVO B ob d'am I,II ob da c I,II bc — G–e c

Was Gott dem Abraham verheißen,
Das läßt er nun dem Hirtenchor
Erfüllt erweisen.
Ein Hirt hat alles das zuvor
Von Gott erfahren müssen.
Und nun muß auch ein Hirt die Tat,
Was er damals versprochen hat,
Zuerst erfüllet wissen.

What God promised to Abraham,
He now lets it be shown to the choir of
Shepherds as fulfilled.
A shepherd had to learn it all
Beforehand from God.
And now too a shepherd must first know
The deed that He then promised
To be fulfilled.

15. ARIA T fl I bc — e $\frac{3}{8}$

Frohe Hirten, eilt, ach eilet,
Eh ihr euch zu lang verweilet,
Eilt, das holde Kind zu sehn!
Geht, die Freude heißt zu schön,
Sucht die Anmut zu gewinnen,
Geht und labet Herz und Sinnen!

Joyful shepherds, hurry, oh hurry,
In case you linger too long,
Hurry to see the lovely Child!
Go, the joy is too great,
Seek to gain that charm,
Go and comfort your hearts and minds!

16. EVANGELISTA T bc — G–a c

'Und das habt zum Zeichen: Ihr werdet finden das Kind in Windeln gewickelt und in einer Krippe liegen.'

'And this shall be a sign for you: you shall find the Child wrapped in swaddling-clothes and lying in a manger.'

17. CHORAL SATB bc (+ instrs) — C c

Schaut hin, dort liegt im finstern Stall,
Des Herrschaft gehet überall!
Da Speise vormals sucht ein Rind,
Da ruhet itzt der Jungfrau'n Kind.

Look, there lies in a dark stable
He who has dominion over all!
Where before an ox sought food
Now rests the Virgin's Child.

18. RECITATIVO B ob d'am I,II ob da c I,II bc — a–G c

So geht denn hin, ihr Hirten, geht,
Daß ihr das Wunder seht:
Und findet ihr des Höchsten Sohn
In einer harten Krippe liegen,
So singet ihm bei seiner Wiegen
Aus einem süßen Ton
Und mit gesamtem Chor
Dies Lied zur Ruhe vor!

Then go forth, you shepherds, go,
That you may see the marvel;
And if you find the Son of the Highest
Lying in a hard manger,
Then sing to Him at His cradle—
In a sweet tone
And with the whole choir—
This song as a lullaby:

19. ARIA A fl I ob d'am I,II ob da c I,II + str bc — G $\frac{2}{4}$

Schlafe, mein Liebster, genieße der Ruh,
Wache nach diesem vor aller Gedeihen!
Labe die Brust,

Sleep, my most beloved, enjoy Your rest,
Then awake, that all may increase!
Comfort the breast,

Empfinde die Lust,	Feel the pleasure
Wo wir unser Herz erfreuen!	With which we gladden our hearts!

20. EVANGELISTA T bc — D C

'Und alsobald war da bei dem Engel die Menge der himmlischen Heerscharen, die lobten Gott und sprachen:'	'And suddenly there with the angel was the multitude of the heavenly hosts, who praised God and said:'

21. CHORUS SATB fl I,II ob d'am I,II ob da c I,II str bc — G ¢

'Ehre sei Gott in der Höhe und Friede auf Erden und den Menschen ein Wohlgefallen.'	'Glory be to God on high and peace on earth and goodwill towards mankind.'

22. RECITATIVO B bc — G C

So recht, ihr Engel, jauchzt und singet,	Quite right, you angels, rejoice and sing
Daß es uns heut so schön gelinget!	That it has turned out so well for us today!
Auf denn! wir stimmen mit euch ein,	Rise, then! We will join in with you:
Uns kann es so wie euch erfreun.	It can gladden us as well as you.

23. CHORAL SATB fl I,II ob d'am I,II ob da c I,II bc (+ str) — G $\frac{12}{8}$

Wir singen dir in deinem Heer	**We sing to You within Your host,**
Aus aller Kraft Lob, Preis und Ehr,	**With all our power, 'Blessing, glory and honour',**
Daß du, o lang gewünschter Gast,	**For You, O long-desired Guest,**
Dich nunmehr eingestellet hast.	**Have now appeared.**

Part II of the oratorio* departs from the readings for the day, being concerned with the announcement of the Birth of Christ to the shepherds. This subject brings with it certain formal characteristics. Since the choir is assigned a significant role in the song of the angels, 'Glory be to God on high', it does not appear at the beginning. Instead, the work opens with an instrumental sinfonia, which is no doubt correctly interpreted (following Schweitzer) as the music-making of antiphonal choirs of angels (strings plus flutes) and shepherds (oboes). The sinfonia is tripartite (A A^1 A^2), with each section in turn subdivided into three according to the unvarying sequence strings (+ flutes)—oboes—tutti. Of the three main sections, the middle one is more freely formed, and the third a varied da capo* of the first, so that we may see in this piece a forerunner of the sonata form of a classical symphonic movement: exposition* (A), development (A^1), and recapitulation (A^2). To extend the analogy further, the string theme occupies the position of first subject, the oboe theme that of second subject, and the tutti that of closing group.

In the recitative, no. 13, the words of the angel are sung by a soprano. After a reference to the fulfilment of God's old promise (no. 14) and the shepherds' aria (no. 15), the continuation of the angel's words in no. 16 is sung by the Evangelist, which provides confirmation of the essentially undramatic conception of the oratorio. A further example is the aria 'Schlafe, mein Liebster', no. 19, and its preparatory accompanied recitative, no. 18. If importance were to be attached to the logical unfolding of events, we would have to follow Schweitzer's demand that this aria should be transferred to Part III of the oratorio, for at this stage we are still with the shepherds in the field. Yet this is not a case of a drama unfolding in temporal order, but rather of a sermon in music.

The most significant movement in Part II is the large-scale chorus,* no. 21, whose form is derived from the motet.* The texture is dominated by the choir, for the instruments have an accompanying function. The text is delivered in three sections: a) 'Ehre sei Gott in der Höhe'; b) 'und Friede auf Erden'; and c) 'und den Menschen ein Wohlgefallen'. Thereafter the entire complex is repeated in an abbreviated form. Each of the three sections is founded on a different musical principle, the structural framework being: a) a passacaglia-like continuo bass, heard three times at various pitches; b) a pedal point, likewise in the continuo; and c) an imitative* theme delivered by the voice parts, mostly in pairs. Thus the compositional principles out of which this chorus was developed are ground bass, pedal, and canon.*

As often in Bach's works, the overall form of Part II may either be conceived as bipartite (nos. 10–17 and 18–23) or else as organized symmetrically around a central point: the chorale, no. 17. The symmetry of the form is emphasized by the return of the themes from the introductory sinfonia in the closing chorale. At the centre lies the chorale verse 'Schaut hin, dort liegt im finstern Stall' ('Look, there lies in a dark stable . . .'), whose relatively low pitch (in the key of C major) acts as a symbol of God's abasement. At the end, the same melody is heard a fifth higher as a radiant glorification of God's act of salvation in the singing of angels and men.

1.7 Third Day of Christmas

EPISTLE: Hebrews 1.1–14: Christ is higher than the angels.
GOSPEL: John 1.1–14: prologue to St John's Gospel.

Also celebrated as a day of remembrance for the apostle John:

EPISTLE: 1 John 1.1–10: God is light; the Blood of Christ cleanses us from sin.
GOSPEL: John 21.20–4: Jesus's words to Peter concerning John.

Sehet, welch eine Liebe, BWV 64

NBA I/3.1, p. 113 BC A15 Duration: *c.* 25 mins

1. CHORUS SATB bc (+ cornettino trb I–III str) e C

'Sehet, welch eine Liebe hat uns der Vater erzeiget, daß wir Gottes Kinder heißen.'	'See what love the Father has shown to us, in that we are called God's Children.'

2. Choral SATB bc (+ instrs) G c

Das hat er alles uns getan,
Sein groß Lieb zu zeigen an.
Des freu sich alle Christenheit
Und dank ihm des in Ewigkeit.
Kyrieleis!

All this He has done for us
To show His great Love.
For this let all Christendom rejoice
And thank Him in eternity.
Lord, have mercy!

3. Recitativo A bc C–D c

Geh, Welt! behalte nur das Deine,
Ich will und mag nichts von dir haben,
Der Himmel ist nun meine,
An diesem soll sich meine Seele laben.
Dein Gold ist ein vergänglich Gut,
Dein Reichtum ist geborget,
Wer dies besitzt, der ist gar schlecht versorget.
Drum sag ich mit getrostem Mut:

Go, world! Keep but what is yours:
I would have nothing from you;
Heaven is now mine:
With this my soul shall refresh itself.
Your gold is a transient good,
Your wealth borrowed;
Whoever possesses it is indeed poorly cared for.
Therefore I say with confident spirit:

4. Choral SATB bc (+ instrs) D c

Was frag ich nach der Welt
Und allen ihren Schätzen,
Wenn ich mich nur an dir,
Mein Jesu, kann ergötzen.
Dich hab ich einzig mir
Zur Wollust fürgestellt:
Du, du bist meine Lust;
Was frag ich nach der Welt.

What do I ask of the world
And all its treasures,
When I can have joy
Only in You, my Jesus?
Only You have I imagined
For my pleasure;
You, you are my delight;
What do I ask of the world?

5. Aria S str bc b c

Was die Welt
In sich hält,
Muß als wie ein Rauch vergehen.
  Aber was mir Jesus gibt
  Und was meine Seele liebt,
  Bleibet fest und ewig stehen.

What the world
Contains within itself
Must fade away like smoke.
  But what Jesus gives me
  And what my soul loves
  Remains firm for ever.

6. Recitativo B bc G c

Der Himmel bleibet mir gewiß,
Und den besitz ich schon im Glauben.
Der Tod, die Welt und Sünde,
Ja selbst das ganze Höllenheer
Kann mir, als einem Gotteskinde,
Denselben nun und nimmermehr
Aus meiner Seele rauben.
Nur dies, nur einzig dies
Macht mir noch Kümmernis,
Daß ich noch länger soll auf dieser Welt verweilen;
Denn Jesus will den Himmel mit mir teilen,

Heaven remains certain for me,
And I possess it already through Faith.
Death, the world and sin,
Indeed the whole host of Hell itself,
Cannot—since I am a child of God—
Now or ever
Steal it from my soul.
Only this, this one thing only,
Still causes me grief:
That I shall abide still longer in this world;
For Jesus would share heaven with me,

Und darzu hat er mich erkoren,
Deswegen ist er Mensch geboren.

And for that He has chosen me,
For that He was born a man.

7. Aria A ob d'am bc G $\frac{6}{8}$

Von der Welt verlang ich nichts,
Wenn ich nur den Himmel erbe.
  Alles, alles geb ich hin,
  Weil ich genung versichert bin,
  Daß ich ewig nicht verderbe.

From the world I desire nothing,
If only I inherit heaven.
  All, all do I give up,
  For I am sufficiently assured
  That I shall not be forever destroyed.

8. Choral SATB bc (+ instrs) e C

Gute Nacht, o Wesen,
Das die Welt erlesen,
Mir gefällst du nicht.
Gute Nacht, ihr Sünden,
Bleibet weit dahinten,
Kommt nicht mehr ans Licht!
Gute Nacht, du Stolz und Pracht;
Dir sei ganz, du Lasterleben,
Gute Nacht gegeben.

Good night, O state
That the world has chosen:
You do not please me.
Good night, you sins:
Stay far behind,
Come to light no more!
Good night, you pride and splendour;
You life of vice, be wished
Good night altogether.

This cantata, composed during Bach's first year in Leipzig, and performed for the first time on 27 December 1723, makes hardly any reference to the details of the day's readings. Instead, it conlcudes from reflections on the love of God, as manifest in Christ's Birth, that the children of God should no longer care for worldly things, since they are assured of eternal life. Hard as it is for us to comprehend today, it is characteristic of the thinking and emotional character of the Baroque to link the most jubilant days of the church year with thoughts of the futility of the world, of death, and of longing for the afterlife.

The structure of this cantata is striking for its copious use of chorales. The anonymous librettist included no fewer than three chorale verses, of which only one is drawn from a Christmas hymn. The author may be the same person who supplied the text of Cantata 40 so abundantly with chorale verses. In any case, the libretto is unmistakably based on a text with the same opening, and for the same occasion, by Johann Knauer (Gotha, 1720).

For the introductory biblical passage, 1 John 3.1, Bach chose a four-part motet* texture with partly independent continuo, a compositional style not very often found in Bach's works. Strings and a choir of trombones (with cornettino as treble instrument) reinforce the voice parts, lending the movement a rather severe, archaic character as well as a distinctive tone colour.[20] The thematic material is entirely governed by the words, particularly the introductory, demonstrative 'Sehet' ('See'), which might be compared with the similarly

[20] It is curious that both in the opening movement and in the chorale movements nos. 2, 4, and 8 the original oboe d'amore part contains *tacet** indications. Perhaps the oboist was employed in a different capacity in these movements.

demonstrative 'Also' ('Thus') of the motet *Also hat Gott die Welt geliebt* from Heinrich Schütz's *Geistliche Chormusik* of 1648. With the aid of strettos* and frequent quotations of the theme's head-motive (without its continuation), Bach enhances this demonstrative character in the course of the movement.

The opening chorus* is followed by a chorale, the last verse of Luther's hymn *Gelobet seist du, Jesu Christ* (1524) in a plain four-part setting. In the recitative, no. 3, incessant scale figures in the continuo underline the words of the alto: 'Go, world! Keep but what is yours'. Thereby this movement, with its animated gestures, also acquires a highly descriptive character. It leads directly into the next chorale: the opening verse of the hymn *Was frag ich nach der Welt* by Georg Michael Pfefferkorn (1667), whose continuous bass motion recalls the preceding scale motive.*

No less vivid are the words of the following aria, no. 5, 'What the world contains within itself must fade away like smoke'. The text alludes to certain biblical passages, such as Psalm 37.20. The 'world' is represented by the gavotte-like character of the movement. After a few bars, however, the simple, periodic dance-step figures of the ritornello are loosened up into a livelier figuration in the first violin, in which the scale figure familiar from the recitative no. 3 once again plays an important role. One might find reflected in it not only the 'fading away like smoke', but also the renunciation of the world announced in the recitative. It follows that figures of this kind are absent from the textually contrasting middle section ('But what Jesus gives me . . . remains firm for ever').

A recitative (no. 6) leads to the second aria (no. 7), which, like the first, is concerned with the renunciation of the world. However, our attention is now turned towards the gifts of heaven, and both textually and musically the second aria strikes a more confident note. This is manifest not only in its tonality—being in G major, it takes the work into the major realm for the first time within the more extended movements—but also in its concertante* style of writing for obbligato* oboe d'amore* in a flowing 6/8 rhythm. In sum, then, the stylistic resources that pervade the most prominent movements in this cantata are those of the motet, dance, and concerto. A plain four-part setting of the fifth verse of the hymn *Jesu, meine Freude* by Johann Franck (1650) ends the work.

Ich freue mich in dir, BWV 133

NBA I/3.1, p. 135 BC A16 Duration: *c.* 20 mins

1. [Chorale] S + cornett ATB ob d'am I,II + str bc D ¢

Ich freue mich in dir	**I rejoice in You**
Und heiße dich willkommen,	**And bid You welcome,**
Mein liebes Jesulein.	**My dear little Jesus.**
Du hast dir vorgenommen,	**You have undertaken**
Mein Brüderlein zu sein.	**To be my little brother.**

Ach, wie ein süßer Ton!
Wie freundlich sieht er aus,
Der große Gottessohn!

Ah, what a sweet sound!
How friendly He looks,
The great Son of God!

2. Aria A ob d'am I,II bc — A ¢

Getrost! es faßt ein heilger Leib
Des Höchsten unbegreiflichs Wesen.
Ich habe Gott—wie wohl ist mir geschehen!—
Von Angesicht zu Angesicht gesehen.
Ach, meine Seele muß genesen.

Be of good cheer! A holy body encloses
The incomprehensible being of the Most High.
I have seen God—how blessed am I!—
Face to face.
Ah, my soul must be preserved.

3. Recitativo T bc — f♯–D C

Ein Adam mag sich voller Schrecken
Vor Gottes Angesicht im Paradies verstecken.
Der allerhöchste Gott
Kehrt selber bei uns ein.
Und so entsetzet sich mein Herze nicht;
Es kennet sein erbarmendes Gemüte.
Aus unermeßner Güte
Wird er ein kleines Kind
Und heißt mein Jesulein.

An Adam, full of terror, may hide
Before God's countenance in Paradise.
The Most High God
Himself lodges with us.
And so my heart does not take fright:
It knows His merciful cast of mind.
Out of immeasurable goodness
He becomes a little Child
And is called my Jesus.

4. Aria S str bc — b ¢ $\frac{12}{8}$ ¢

Wie lieblich klingt es in den Ohren,
Dies Wort: mein Jesus ist geboren,
Wie dringt es in das Herz hinein!
Wer Jesu Namen nicht versteht
Und wem es nicht durchs Herze geht,
Der muß ein harter Felsen sein.

How lovely they sound in my ears:
The words 'my Jesus is born',
How they penetrate my heart!
He who does not comprehend Jesus's Name
And it does not go to his heart
Must be as hard as a rock.

5. Recitativo B bc — b–D C

Wohlan! des Todes Furcht und Schmerz
Erwägt nicht mein getröstet Herz.
Will er vom Himmel sich
Bis zu der Erde lenken,
So wird er auch an mich
In meiner Gruft gedenken.
Wer Jesum recht erkennt,
Der stirbt nicht, wenn er stirbt,
Sobald er Jesum nennt.

Well, then! death's fear and pain
Are not considered by my comforted heart.
If He would make His way
From heaven to earth,
Then He will also remember me
In my tomb.
He who knows Jesus aright
Does not die when he dies
As soon as he calls 'Jesus'.

6. Choral SATB bc (+ instrs) — D C

Wohlan, so will ich mich
An dich, o Jesu, halten,
Und sollte gleich die Welt

Well then, I would
Cling to You, O Jesus,
Even though the world should

In tausend Stücken spalten.	**Split into a thousand pieces.**
O Jesu, dir, nur dir,	**O Jesus, for You, only for You,**
Dir leb ich ganz allein;	**Just for You alone do I live;**
Auf dich, allein auf dich,	**In You, in You alone,**
Mein Jesu, schlaf ich ein.	**My Jesus, will I fall asleep.**

When Bach composed his six-part Sanctus, BWV 232[III] for Christmas 1724—the Sanctus setting that he later incorporated in the B minor Mass—he notated at the bottom of the first page of the score a melody that was evidently new to him, and thus probably rare in Leipzig, for the hymn *Ich freue mich in dir.*[21] This melody forms the basis of his chorale cantata* for the Third Day of Christmas (27 December) 1724. The text of the hymn by Caspar Ziegler (1697) comprises four verses, of which the first and last are here retained literally. The two middle verses were divided up by the unknown author of the paraphrase, verse 2 forming the second and third movements and verse 3 the fourth and fifth. Several chorale lines, however, were preserved either word for word or approximately so, and in Bach's setting of the recitatives nos. 3 and 5 they are raised to prominence in the form of arioso.*

The text is not directly linked to the readings of the day. Instead, the ideas of the librettist—even where he makes his own additions—remain close to the chorale text, which extols the marvel of God's becoming brother of mankind. Even in the Old Testament, God appeared to Jacob, whose words 'I have seen God face to face, and my life is preserved' (Genesis 32.30) are in the second movement re-interpreted to apply to Christ's Birth. In the third movement, the librettist interweaves a further comparison with the Old Testament: Adam had to hide from the wrath of God (Gen. 3.8), but now God draws near to man as a friend, full of compassion. In the fifth movement, the librettist at last includes his own ideas: death has lost its power over the Christian, and therefore God will remember me when I lie in my grave. We thus observe that, as in other chorale cantatas, the poet enriches the contemplative, devotional chorale text with ideas of an interpretative, sermon-like nature, most noticeably by turning to the situation of the individual Christian in the fifth movement ('Then He will also remember me . . .').

Bach's setting exhibits certain features that we can probably connect with the circumstances of his Leipzig post. Performing forces could no longer be disposed very extensively on the last of three successive feast-days, and therefore Bach had to prove himself to be a master of limitation. In this he succeeds admirably. The instrumental ensemble is reduced to normal size, with two oboes d'amore* in addition to strings and continuo; only in the outer movements does a cornett

[21] The earliest known printed source of this melody dates from 1738, but Bach's copy may well be based on an earlier printed version which is no longer extant.

Entry in Bach's hand of the chorale *Ich freue mich in dir* on the first page of the score of the *Sanctus*, BWV 232[III]. Above the chorale is a preparatory sketch of the theme 'Pleni sunt coeli' from the same *Sanctus*; below it, a comment referring to the performing material of the *Sanctus*: 'NB. Die Parteyen sind in Böhmen bey Graff Sporck' ('NB. the parts are in Bohemia with Count Sporck'). (Staatsbibliothek zu Berlin, Preußischer Kulturbesitz, Mus. ms. Bach P 13).

help to emphasize the chorale melody in the soprano. Even in the concertante* opening movement, the choir sings the chorale in a plain, four-part setting, divided up into its individual lines. Only at the line-ends ('Ah, what a sweet sound' and 'The great Son of God') does it expand a little into polyphony.* The joyful excitement promised by the text is reflected chiefly in the orchestral texture: concertante string writing is developed out of the motive*

Exceptionally, the two oboes d'amore double the second violin and viola; together, these instruments form a lively complex of middle parts—whose very grouping affords contrast—between the continuo foundation and the wide-ranging, idiomatic, virtuoso figuration of the first violin. No less attractive is the two-bar echo repetition during the aforementioned extension of the line-end 'Ah, what a sweet sound!'.

The semiquaver motion of the opening chorus* spreads into the second movement, to some extent even with strikingly similar running figures, which are now adopted by the two obbligato* oboes d'amore. The head-motive, however, is entirely dictated by its text in the principal section, which calls out to the listener three times in succession the word 'Getrost!' ('Be of good cheer!'). The middle section is pervaded by a more confined, circling quaver figure to the words 'how blessed am I!'. This figure is derived from the oboe ritornello and, traced back to its origin, turns out to be none other than the continuo bass to the pervasive head-motive of the main section:

The *secco* recitative, no. 3, with its two arioso chorale insertions ('adagio'), is a relative of the trope,* though neither text nor melody of the chorale is very strictly preserved. The melody is recognizable only at the line 'Kehrt selber bei uns ein' ('Himself lodges with us'), whereas the other lines are restricted to thematic allusions. The second aria, no. 4, is an invention of graceful tenderness. Its string texture is dominated by the first violin, the middle parts receding into the background; and an oft-recurring ostinato* motive is conspicuous in the continuo. The middle section provides a contrast of time (12/8 instead of ¢), tempo ('largo') and scoring—the continuo is *tacet** and the second violin and viola unite to form the lowest part of a trio with soprano and first violin. In the main section, echo effects, *bariolage* (alternating stopped and open strings) and a solo violin *passaggio* all serve to interpret the text 'How lovely they sound in my ears . . .'.

The fifth movement is plainly a counterpart to the third, being set as *secco* recitative and closing with a chorale quotation in which the melody of the last three lines is radically transformed. It is followed by the final verse of the chorale in a plain four-part setting.

Süßer Trost, mein Jesus kömmt, BWV 151

NBA I/3.1, p. 169 BC A17 Duration: *c.* 18 mins

1. ARIA S fl ob d'am + str bc G 12/8 ¢ 12/8

Süßer Trost, mein Jesus kömmt,	Sweet comfort: my Jesus comes,
Jesus wird anitzt geboren.	Jesus is now born.

Herz und Seele freuet sich,
Denn mein liebster Gott hat mich
Nun zum Himmel auserkoren.

Heart and soul rejoice,
For my beloved God has
Now chosen me for heaven.

2. RECITATIVO B bc — D–e C

Erfreue dich, mein Herz,
Denn itzo weicht der Schmerz,
Der dich so lange Zeit gedrücket.
Gott hat den liebsten Sohn,
Den er so hoch und teuer hält,
Auf diese Welt geschicket.
Er läßt den Himmelsthron
Und will die ganze Welt
Aus ihren Sklavenketten
Und ihrer Dienstbarkeit erretten.
O wundervolle Tat!
Gott wird ein Mensch und will auf Erden
Noch niedriger als wir und noch viel ärmer werden.

Rejoice, my heart,
For now the pain vanishes
Which has for so long oppressed you.
God has sent His beloved Son,
Whom He holds so high and dear,
Into this world.
He leaves His heavenly throne
And would deliver the whole world
From its chains of slavery
And its servitude.
O wondrous deed!
God becomes a Man and would on earth
Become still lowlier than we and far poorer.

3. ARIA A ob d'am unis str bc — e ¢

In Jesu Demut kann ich Trost,
In seiner Armut Reichtum finden.
Mir macht desselben schlechter Stand
Nur lauter Heil und Wohl bekannt,
Ja, seine wundervolle Hand
Will mir nur Segenskränze winden.

In Jesus's humility I can find comfort,
In His poverty, wealth.
His poor station makes known to me
Just pure Salvation and well-being;
Indeed, His wonderful hand
Will twine for me just wreaths of blessing.

4. RECITATIVO T bc — b–G C

Du teurer Gottessohn,
Nun hast du mir
Den Himmel aufgemacht
Und durch dein Niedrigsein
Das Licht der Seligkeit zuwege bracht.
Weil du nun ganz allein
Des Vaters Burg und Thron
Aus Liebe gegen uns verlassen,
So wollen wir dich auch
Dafür in unser Herze fassen.

You precious Son of God,
Now for me You have
Opened up heaven,
And through Your lowliness
Brought about the Light of Salvation.
Since You have now, quite alone,
Left the Father's citadel and throne
Out of Love towards us,
We want to embrace You
For this in our heart.

5. CHORAL SATB bc (+ instrs) — G C

Heut schleußt er wieder auf die Tür
Zum schönen Paradeis;
Der Cherub steht nicht mehr dafür,
Gott sei Lob, Ehr und Preis.

Today He opens the door again
To fair Paradise;
The cherub stands before it no longer;
To God be glory, honour and praise.

Like the texts of all Bach's cantatas for the Third Day of Christmas, this libretto, by the Darmstadt poet Georg Christian Lehms, which was set to music in 1725, is not closely connected with the readings of the day. Instead, it gives very general expression to feelings of joy over the attainment of salvation through the coming of Jesus. Attention is repeatedly drawn to the paradox that the abasement of God exalts the human race. Finally, the closing chorale—the eighth verse of the hymn *Lobt Gott, ihr Christen, allzugleich* (Nikolaus Herman, 1560)—enlarges the prospect, leading back to the Fall of Man: paradise, from which Adam was driven out, is now open once more.

The chamber-music scoring of Bach's setting takes account of the heavy demands made on the pupils of the Thomasschule during the Christmas season. The four voices come together only in the closing chorale, and they are accompanied by just one flute, one oboe d'amore,* strings, and continuo. The intimate character of Bach's setting is well suited to the text, which almost invariably speaks in the first person, emphasizing the significance of God's act of salvation for the individual Christian.

The opening aria, the best-known movement in the cantata, is one of Bach's happiest inspirations. From the text he derives a contrast (relatively speaking) between comfort and joy, represented musically by the antithesis between a main section headed 'molt' adagio' and a middle section headed 'vivace'. Particularly remarkable are the extensive melodic arches which in the opening ritornello are developed out of the ornamental passages of the flute,[22] accompanied 'piano sempre' by oboe d'amore and strings. The soprano enters with a vocally simplified reprise of this opening melody. After two bars, however, the flute takes up the melody again, leading a reprise of the opening ritornello in expanded form, against the tranquil *cantabile* singing of the soprano, to its conclusion. Shortly before the end of the main section, the head-motive, previously given over to the soprano, is once more taken up by the flute itself. The instrumental transition to the middle section brings another statement of the opening ritornello, now reduced to half its length. The quick middle section is pervaded by its opening motive:*

At first it is sung by the soprano, but the instruments take it up repeatedly, interrupted by triplet melismas* from the voice on 'freuet sich' ('rejoice'), which are thereafter played on the flute in a similar concertante* fashion but in an

[22] For a later performance, *c.* 1727/31, Bach had the part written out again, but without stating whether a different instrument (solo violin?) was now intended. A unison of two instruments, conceivable on the basis of the source findings, is hardly plausible on musical grounds.

enhanced form. A literal da capo* of the principal section rounds off the movement.

All that follows is overshadowed by this exceptional aria. Two *secco* recitatives frame an aria in ¢ time, nonetheless marked 'andante', in which oboe d'amore, violins, and viola unite to form a single obbligato* part. Bach achieves nuances of timbre and dynamics through his requirement that during the vocal sections the obbligato part is played only by the oboe and first desk of Violin I, the remaining strings being silent. The work ends with a plain four-part setting of the closing chorale.

Herrscher des Himmels, erhöre das Lallen
Weihnachts-Oratorium Christmas Oratorio, BWV 248, Part III

NBA II/6, p. 109 BC D7[III] Duration: *c.* 26 mins

24. CORO SATB tr I–III timp fl I,II ob I,II str bc — D $\frac{3}{8}$

Herrscher des Himmels, erhöre das Lallen,	Ruler of heaven, hear our babble;
Laß dir die matten Gesänge gefallen,	Let our faint songs please You
Wenn dich dein Zion mit Psalmen erhöht!	When Your Zion exalts You with psalms!
Höre der Herzen frohlockendes Preisen,	Hear our hearts' jubilant praise
Wenn wir dir itzo die Ehrfurcht erweisen,	As we now show You reverence,
Weil unsre Wohlfahrt befestiget steht.	For our welfare is secured.

25. EVANGELISTA T bc — E–A C

'Und da die Engel von ihnen gen Himmel fuhren, sprachen die Hirten untereinander:'	'And as the angels went from them into heaven, the shepherds said to each other:'

26. CHORUS SATB fl I + II + vln I (+ ww vln II vla) bc — A–c♯ $\frac{3}{4}$

'Lasset uns nun gehen gen Bethlehem und die Geschichte sehen, die da geschehen ist, die uns der Herr kundgetan hat.'	'Let us now go to Bethlehem and see the event that has happened there, which the Lord has made known to us.'

27. RECITATIVO B fl I,II bc — c♯–A C

Er hat sein Volk getröst',	He has comforted His people,
Er hat sein Israel erlöst,	He has redeemed His Israel,
Die Hülf aus Zion hergesendet	Sent salvation out of Zion,
Und unser Leid geendet.	And ended our sorrow.
Seht, Hirten, dies hat er getan;	See, shepherds, this He has done;
Geht, dieses trefft ihr an!	Go, this is what you shall find!

28. CHORAL SATB bc (+ ww + str) — A C

Dies hat er alles uns getan,	**All this He has done for us**
Sein groß Lieb zu zeigen an;	**To show His great Love;**
Des freu sich alle Christenheit	**For which let all Christendom rejoice**
Und dank ihm des in Ewigkeit.	**And thank Him in eternity.**
Kyrieleis!	**Lord, have mercy!**

29. Aria Duetto SB ob d'am I,II bc — A 3/8

Herr, dein Mitleid, dein Erbarmen
Tröstet uns und macht uns frei.
Deine holde Gunst und Liebe,
Deine wundersamen Triebe
Machen deine Vatertreu
Wieder neu.

Lord, Your compassion, Your mercy
Comforts us and makes us free.
Your gracious favour and Love,
Your wondrous impulses
Make Your fatherly faithfulness
New again.

30. Evangelista T bc — f♯–b C

'Und sie kamen eilend und funden beide, Mariam und Joseph, dazu das Kind in der Krippe liegen. Da sie es aber gesehen hatten, breiteten sie das Wort aus, welches zu ihnen von diesem Kind gesaget war. Und alle, für die es kam, wunderten sich der Rede, die ihnen die Hirten gesaget hatten. Maria aber behielt alle diese Worte und bewegte sie in ihrem Herzen.'

'And they came in haste and found both Mary and Joseph, with the Child lying in the crib. But when they had seen it, they spread abroad the words that were spoken to them of this Child. And all those to whom it came wondered at the speech that the shepherds had delivered to them. But Mary kept all these words and set them astir in her heart.'

31. Aria A vln solo bc — b 2/4

Schließe, mein Herze, dies selige Wunder
Fest in deinem Glauben ein!
Lasse dies Wunder, die göttlichen Werke,
Immer zur Stärke
Deines schwachen Glaubens sein!

Enclose, my heart, this blessed miracle
Firmly within your Faith!
Let this miracle, these divine deeds
Ever serve to strengthen
Your weak Faith!

32. Recitativo A fl I,II bc — D–G C

Ja, ja, mein Herz soll es bewahren,
Was es an dieser holden Zeit
Zu seiner Seligkeit
Für sicheren Beweis erfahren.

Yes, yes, my heart shall preserve
What at this propitious time,
For its Salvation,
It has experienced as certain proof.

33. Choral SATB bc (+ ww + str) — G C

Ich will dich mit Fleiß bewahren,
Ich will dir
Leben hier,
Dir will ich abfahren,
Mit dir will ich endlich schweben
Voller Freud
Ohne Zeit
Dort im andern Leben.

I will diligently keep You in mind;
I will
Live here for You,
To You will I depart,
With You will I finally hover,
Full of joy,
Beyond time,
There in the other life.

34. Evangelista T bc — e–f♯ C

'Und die Hirten kehrten wieder um, preiseten und lobten Gott um alles, das sie gesehen und gehöret hatten, wie denn zu ihnen gesaget war.'

'And the shepherds retraced their steps, glorifying and praising God for all that they had seen and heard, as it had been said to them.'

35. Choral SATB bc (+ ww + str) f♯ c

Seid froh dieweil,	**Be glad, meanwhile,**
Daß euer Heil	**That your Salvation**
Ist hie ein Gott und auch ein Mensch geboren,	**Has here been born both as God and man,**
Der, welcher ist	**He who is**
Der Herr und Christ	**The Lord and Christ,**
In Davids Stadt, von vielen auserkoren.	**In David's city, chiefest among many.**

24. Coro [reprise of opening chorus] D $\frac{3}{8}$

The Third Part of the *Christmas Oratorio* concludes the first half of the work. Parts I–III are felt to belong together particularly closely on account of their tonality (D–G–D) and scoring (with flutes), the continuity of the Gospel* narrative, and their immediate succession on the three Christmas feast-days. This may explain why Bach concluded Part III not with a chorale, as in the other five parts, but with a reprise of the opening chorus* (no. 24). It is possible, however, that the concise simplicity of the movement, its plain bipartite form, its clearly perceptible periodic phrase structure, and its dance-like character would have given it too little weight on a single hearing, and Bach was therefore induced to repeat it. The second chorus from Part III, no. 26, is also brief in extent. Both its compositional type—a vocal texture with instruments that either double the voices or unite in an unthematic obbligato* part—and its bipartite form (imitative–freely polyphonic*) establish it as a derivative of the motet.*

The three chorales of Part III are less substantial than those of the preceding parts, since they are all set in a plain four-part texture. Our attention is therefore focused on the two arias, particularly on no. 31, which stands out as perhaps the only newly composed aria in the entire oratorio.* A first sketch of it was repeatedly altered and finally rejected; and even the draft of the new, definitive version, with its profusion of corrections, bears witness to Bach's self-critical engagement with its composition. The violin part, written out from the score, contains exceptionally conscientious articulation marks—a further indication of the care taken by the composer over this particular aria. Despite the almost virtuoso character of the violin part, Bach's art here seems much intensified. The solo scoring points to the personal content of the text; and the unison on the words 'Firmly within your Faith!' likewise serves the purpose of textual interpretation.

1.8 Sunday after Christmas

Epistle: Galatians 4.1–7: Through Christ we are come of age and free of the Law.
Gospel: Luke 2.33–40: The words of Simeon and of Anna to Mary.

Tritt auf die Glaubensbahn, BWV 152

NBA I/3.2, p. 3 BC A18 Duration: *c.* 21 mins

1. [Sinfonia] rec ob vla d'am vla da g bc e/g[23] C 3/8
2. Aria B ob bc e/g 3/4

Tritt auf die Glaubensbahn!	Walk on the path of Faith!
Gott hat den Stein geleget,	God has laid the Stone
Der Zion hält und träget,	That holds and carries Zion;
Mensch! stoße dich nicht dran!	O man, do not stumble against it!
Tritt auf die Glaubensbahn!	Walk on the path of Faith!

3. Recitativo B bc e–G/g–B♭ C

Der Heiland ist gesetzt	The Saviour is set
In Israel zum Fall und Auferstehen!	For the fall and rising again of many in Israel!
Der edle Stein ist sonder Schuld,	The noble Stone is without guilt,
Wenn sich die böse Welt so hart an ihm verletzt,	Even though the wicked world so badly wounds itself on it,
Ja, über ihn zur Höllen fällt,	Indeed, falls over it to Hell,
Weil sie boshaftig an ihn rennet	For it maliciously crashes against it
Und Gottes Huld und Gnade nicht erkennet!	And does not acknowledge God's favour and Grace!
Doch selig ist	Yet blessed is
Ein auserwählter Christ,	A chosen Christian
Der seinen Glaubensgrund auf diesen Eckstein leget,	Who lays the foundation of his Faith on this Cornerstone,
Weil er dadurch Heil und Erlösung findet.	For thereby he finds Salvation and Redemption.

4. Aria S rec vla d'am bc G/B♭ C

Stein, der über alle Schätze,	O Stone above all treasures,
Hilf, daß ich zu aller Zeit	Help me that at all times,
Durch den Glauben auf dich setze	Through Faith, I may set in You
Meinen Grund der Seligkeit	My ground of Salvation
Und mich nicht an dir verletze,	And not wound myself on You,
Stein, der über alle Schätze!	O Stone above all treasures!

5. Recitativo B bc e–G/g–B♭ C

Es ärgre sich die kluge Welt,	It is a stumbling block to the world's wisdom
Daß Gottes Sohn	That God's Son
Verläßt den hohen Ehrenthron,	Leaves His high throne of honour,
Daß er in Fleisch und Blut sich kleidet	That He clothes Himself in flesh and blood
Und in der Menschheit leidet.	And suffers as a human being.
Die größte Weisheit dieser Erden	The greatest wisdom of this earth
Muß vor des Höchsten Rat	Must, before the counsel of the Highest,

[23] The first specified key refers to *Chorton** ('choir pitch'), the second to *Kammerton* ('chamber pitch'); see W. Neumann, 'Zur Aufführungspraxis der Kantate 152', *BJ* 1949–50, 100–3.

Zur größten Torheit werden!
Was Gott beschlossen hat,
Kann die Vernunft doch nicht ergründen;
Die blinde Leiterin verführt die geistlich Blinden.

Become the greatest folly!
What God has decided
Reason cannot indeed fathom;
A blind leader, it seduces the spiritually blind.

6. [Duet] SB unis instrs bc e/g $\frac{6}{4}$

Seele
Wie soll ich dich, Liebster der Seelen, umfassen?
Jesus
Du mußt dich verleugnen und alles verlassen!
Seele
Wie soll ich erkennen das ewige Licht?
Jesus
Erkenne mich gläubig und ärgre dich nicht!
Seele
Komm! lehre mich, Heiland, die Erde verschmähen!
Jesus
Komm, Seele! durch Leiden zur Freude zu gehen.
Seele
Ach, ziehe mich, Liebster, so folg ich dir nach!
Jesus
Dir schenk ich die Krone nach Trübsal und Schmach!

Soul
How should I embrace You, beloved of souls?
Jesus
You must deny yourself and forsake all things!
Soul
How should I recognize the eternal Light?
Jesus
Acknowledge me in Faith and do not fret!
Soul
Come! Teach me, Saviour, to scorn the earth!
Jesus
Come, Soul! Through suffering attain joy.
Soul
Ah, draw me, Beloved, that I may follow You!
Jesus
I shall grant you a crown after affliction and shame!

In St Luke's Gospel, the reading for this Sunday immediately follows Simeon's song of praise, the Nunc dimittis* ('Lord, now let Your servant depart in peace'); and it contains his prophetic words 'See, this Child is set for the fall and rising again of many in Israel and as a sign that shall be contradicted . . . that the thoughts of many hearts may be revealed'. Salomo Franck, the author of the libretto (from his cycle *Evangelisches Andachts-Opffer* of 1714–15), adopts Simeon's words, from Luke 2.34, in the third movement, concluding that, since the appearance of the Saviour brings with it falling or rising again, contradiction or acceptance, it is necessary to stand on the side of those who accept Jesus in faith, to walk in the 'path of Faith', and to reject the wisdom of the world. The manner in which Luke's account is formulated clearly harks back to Isaiah 8.14–15: 'He shall thus be a sanctuary, but also a stone for stumbling against and a rock of vexation to both the houses of Israel, a trap and snare to the populace, so that many of them shall stumble . . .'; and in Psalm 118.22 we read: 'The stone that the builders rejected has become the cornerstone'. A knowledge of these associations[24] is assumed in Franck's text when, in the very first aria (no. 2), he alludes to the 'Stone'. The following recitative, no. 3, is also concerned with the stone metaphor; and in the next aria, no. 4, Jesus is addressed as the 'Stone above all treasures' and implored not to become a stumbling-block to the faithful Christian. Vexation over Christ is the concern of the 'wise' world, from which nothing is to be expected. The text ends with a dialogue between Jesus and the Soul, which once again calls upon the Christian to follow the Saviour and reject the world. It takes the form of a love duet, which is characteristic not only of Franck but of Lehms and other contemporaries.

Bach's setting was composed in Weimar for 30 December 1714. With its markedly chamber-music style of instrumentation for recorder, oboe, viola d'amore,* viola da gamba, and continuo, it is one of the few Bach cantatas that depart from the norm of full string scoring with reinforcing woodwind. Instead, four distinctive solo instruments are contrasted with each other. Even the vocal writing requires only two soloists, and the customary closing chorale is omitted. It is very likely that Bach here made a virtue out of necessity: the demands of Christmas on the Weimar court musicians may have made a reduction of resources seem expedient. Yet it is this unusual scoring that makes the cantata so delightful to us. Bach's choice concord of distinctive instruments creates an individual sound-world, well suited to Franck's poem, but far less evident in the representative works of the Leipzig period. For, in the course of his creative life, Bach increasingly departed from the ideal of the subjective, sensuous appeal of sound in favour of harmonic balance and a spiritualized, incorporeal beauty of line.

The cantata begins with an extended sinfonia, whose bipartite structure, with its contrast between slow introduction and quick fugue,* recalls the form of the French Overture*. The opening chorus* of Cantata 61, performed only four weeks earlier, had been designed as a French overture. Yet the four introductory bars of the sinfonia to Cantata 152, with their widely swung ornamental festoons, show little resemblance to the energetic overture rhythms of the French tradition. The fugue subject, on the other hand, has a far more rhythmic profile and is closely related to the subject of the Fugue in A, BWV 536/2, for organ:

24 Other biblical passages relevant in this context are Matt. 21.42, Rom. 9.33, and 1 Peter 2.6–8.

It is tempting to assume that the two works originated in close temporal proximity, especially since one cannot fail to be struck by the similar relationship between an organ fugue and Cantata 21 (q.v.), which was performed during the same year as the present cantata. The fugue of Cantata 152—one of the few purely instrumental fugues in Bach's cantatas—is designed according to the permutation principle. Unlike vocal permutation fugues, however, it includes modulatory episodes. These are few as far as the eighth entry of the combined subjects, but thereafter the form grows looser. At the end, the recorder and oboe state the subject in stretto* (at the eleventh entry) and in parallel sixths (at the twelfth) against unthematic counterpoints.*

The second movement, an aria with obbligato* oboe, seems to depict the 'path of Faith' in its numerous thematically determined scale figures. The following movement, no. 3, derives the musically contrasting forms of recitative and arioso* from the textual contrast between the wicked world and the blessed Christian. The striking downward leap of a tenth, from *f*♯ to *D*♯ (or from *a* to *F*♯ at Chamber Pitch*) on the words 'zum Fall' ('for the fall') has often attracted attention. In the arioso passage, the frequent imitation* between bass and continuo is probably to be interpreted as a symbol of the Imitation of Christ.

As a call to 'walk on the path of faith', the first aria was assigned to bass voice, the traditional *vox Christi*; but the prayer-like text of the second aria, no. 4, is now allotted to the soprano, who also takes the part of the 'Soul' in the closing duet. In its scoring for recorder, viola d'amore and continuo, this second aria is of quite exceptional charm. One almost regrets that it is cast in the relatively brief form of the early Bach cantata arias: the middle section is contracted to only four bars, and the da capo* abridged. A brief *secco* recitative leads to the closing duet, no. 6, whose form is singular: the dialogue text is divided up into separate passages, each of which takes the musical form of dialogue followed by canon.* The introductory instrumental ritornello is also disintegrated into fragments, which are then combined, one by one, with the duet. At the end of the movement—and thus of the whole cantata—there is a reprise of the complete instrumental ritornello.

Das neugeborne Kindelein, BWV 122

NBA I/3.2, p. 53   BC A19   Duration: *c.* 20 mins

1. [Chorale] SATB ob I,II, taille + str bc   g   3/8

Das neugeborne Kindelein,	**The newborn little Child,**	
Das herzeliebe Jesulein	**The darling little Jesus**	
Bringt abermal ein neues Jahr	**Brings once again a New Year**	
Der auserwählten Christenschar.	**To the chosen Christian throng.**	

2. Aria B bc   c   ¢

O Menschen, die ihr täglich sündigt,	O mortals, who sin daily,	

Ihr sollt der Engel Freude sein.
  Ihr jubilierendes Geschrei,
  Daß Gott mit euch versöhnet sei,
  Hat euch den süßen Trost verkündigt.

You shall be the angels' joy.
  Their exultant cry
  That God is reconciled with you
  Has proclaimed sweet comfort to you.

3. Recitativo S rec I–III bc — g c

Die Engel, welche sich zuvor
Vor euch als vor Verfluchten scheuen,
Erfüllen nun die Luft im höhern Chor,
Um über euer Heil sich zu erfreuen.
Gott, so euch aus dem Paradies
Aus englischer Gemeinschaft stieß,
Läßt euch nun wiederum auf Erden
Durch seine Gegenwart vollkommen selig werden:
So danket nun mit vollem Munde
Vor die gewünschte Zeit im neuen Bunde.

The angels, who formerly shrank away
From you, as from the damned,
Now fill the air in the lofty choir
To rejoice over your Salvation.
God, who cast you out of Paradise,
Out of the communion of angels,
Now lets you once more on earth
Become perfectly blessed through His presence:
Then be thankful now in full voice
For the desired age of the New Covenant.

4. Aria [+ Chorale] ST A + vln I + II + vla bc — d 6/8

Ist Gott versöhnt und unser Freund,
O wohl uns, die wir an ihn glauben,
Was kann uns tun der arge Feind?
Sein Grimm kann unsern Trost nicht rauben;
Trotz Teufel und der Höllen Pfort,
Ihr Wüten wird sie wenig nützen,
Das Jesulein ist unser Hort.
Gott ist mit uns und will uns schützen.

If God is reconciled and our friend,
Oh, blessed are we who believe in Him!
What can the wicked foe do to us?
His fury cannot rob us of our comfort;
In the face of the Devil and Hell's gates,
Their raging will do them little good;
Little Jesus is our refuge.
God is with us and will protect us.

5. Recitativo B str bc — B♭–g c

Dies ist ein Tag, den selbst der Herr gemacht,
Der seinen Sohn in diese Welt gebracht.
O selge Zeit, die nun erfüllt!
O gläubigs Warten, das nunmehr gestillt!
O Glaube, der sein Ende sieht!
O Liebe, die Gott zu sich zieht!
O Freudigkeit, so durch die Trübsal dringt!
Und Gott der Lippen Opfer bringt.

This is a day that the Lord Himself has made,
When He has brought His Son into this world.
O blessed time, now fulfilled!
O faithful waiting, now gratified!
O Faith, that sees its goal!
O Love, that God draws to Himself!
O joyfulness, that breaks through sorrow
And brings God the offering of our lips.

6. Choral SATB bc (+ instrs) — g 3/4

Es bringt das rechte Jubeljahr,
Was trauren wir denn immerdar?
Frisch auf! itzt ist es Singenszeit,
Das Jesulein wendt alles Leid.

The true Year of Jubilation arrives!
Why, then, are we sad any more?
Cheer up! Now is the time of singing;
Little Jesus reverses all suffering.

The train of ideas in this chorale cantata,* first performed on 31 December 1724, nowhere takes account of the readings of the day. The hymn on which it is based, by Cyriakus Schneegaß (1597), follows an old tradition in celebrating Christmas and the New Year at the same time. Even the text expansions by the anonymous librettist, which may have been occasioned by the brevity of the four-verse hymn, go their own way rather than referring to the substance of the day's readings. The chorale text is arranged as follows: movement no. 1 is verse 1 of the hymn, word for word; no. 2 is a free paraphrase of verse 2; no. 3 refers to verse 2 in its opening lines but then shifts its focus—as Christmas texts often do (cf., for example, Cantata 40 above)—to the Old Testament account of the Fall of Man, which has now been annulled by God's New Covenant; no. 4 includes verse 3 in full, expanded by a free text in trope-like fashion; no. 5 is a free insertion which, however, varies the content of the last verse, as the following comparison of keywords illustrates:

Movement no. 5	*Chorale verse 4*
Dies ist ein Tag	das rechte Jubeljahr
This is a day	The true Year of Jubilation
	Was trauren wir?
Freudigkeit, so durch die Trübsal dringt	Why are we sad?
Joyfulness that breaks through sorrow	Das Jesulein wendt alles Leid
	little Jesus reverses all suffering
der Lippen Opfer	Singenszeit
the offering of our lips	the time of singing

No. 6 is verse 4, word for word.

Not only are the verses few in number, but each individual verse is only four lines long. This explains why Bach's opening chorus* is strikingly brief and compact. The instrumental introduction, for strings reinforced by oboes, with its clear periodic phrasing and echo effects (pairs of bars are twice immediately repeated in varied form), evokes a dance-like impression, no doubt inspired by the joyful text. The chorale now enters with the chorale melody in the soprano, while the excited lower parts enter in turn with the opening of the chorale line in metrical diminution,* and the instruments develop further the independent thematic material of the opening ritornello. The four chorale lines are heard one at a time, separated by instrumental episodes based on modified ritornello motives.* The share of the accompanying vocal parts, which invariably enter imitatively,* in the thematic material of the chorale is constantly reduced, and in the fourth line it is no longer perceptible at all. At the same time, the motivic material of the instruments gradually detaches itself from its link with the ritornello, eventually blending in a temporary unison with the lower voice parts.

In the bass aria, no. 2, accompanied only by continuo, an impassioned, chromatically* tormented ritornello melody for the bass instruments is broken up into its constituent motives and, in this form, pervades the entire movement; even the vocal melody is derived from it. The minor mode (c), maintained in the intermediate cadences (f and g), contributes to the impression of the text, 'O mortals, who sin daily, you shall be the angels' joy', as closer to a penitential sermon than a message of joy. Why Bach treated it thus becomes clear in the third movement, a soprano recitative that incorporates the chorale melody in a homophonic* texture for three recorders.[25] The contrast enshrined in the opening words of these two movements—'O mortals' (no. 2) and 'The angels' (no. 3)—is reflected in their pitch and tone colour: no. 2 is for bass voice, in concertante* duet with continuo bass; no. 3, for soprano plus recorders (the highest instruments in Bach's orchestra), while the continuo resumes its usual accompanying role. The relationship between the two movements, however, is clearly not just one of contrast but of correspondence, as the first vocal entry of each movement illustrates:

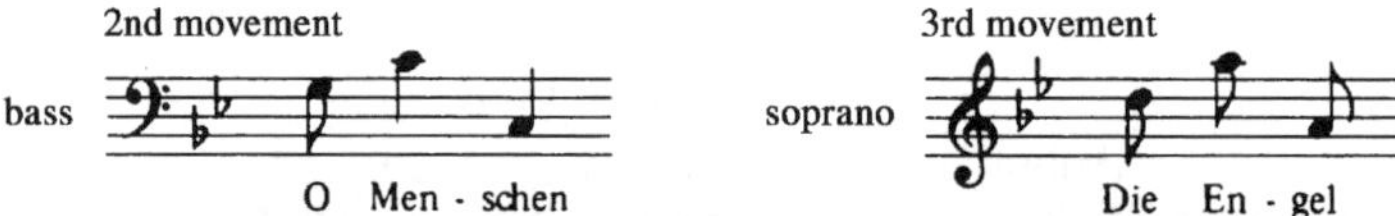

Perhaps Bach might have wanted to say that the opposing spheres of mankind and the angels become reconciled with one another.

It is perhaps no accident, then, that the terzetto 'Ist Gott versöhnt', no. 4, takes us into an intermediate realm of sound. A six-bar continuo ritornello in siciliano rhythm forms an ostinato* pattern (preserved rhythmically rather than melodically to make allowances for the *cantus firmus**), over which the soprano and tenor sing a duet on a freely composed text, while the alto sings the chorale melody, reinforced by unison violins and viola. After the end of the chorale verse, however, the alto (without the instruments) unites with the other two voices in an imitative texture, repeating the last line of the trope* text, 'God is with us and will protect us'.

The bass recitative, no. 5, accompanied by strings, contains no real arioso* writing throughout its fourteen bars, but it is constantly brought close to arioso by its vocal melismas* and by the liveliness of its string accompaniment: it is a type of setting suggested of its own accord by the strongly emotional text with its frequent exclamations. The concluding chorale, no. 6, is the fourth verse of the hymn in a plain four-part setting.

[25] In Bach's score their parts are notated an octave lower—evidently he originally envisaged them played by strings; see K. Hofmann, KB, NBA I/3.2 (2000), 44–5.

Looking back over the overall form of the cantata, we are struck by the predominance of the chorale *cantus firmus** and the subservient function of the instruments. Indeed, despite the brevity of the four-verse chorale, only two of the six movements are independent of it. Their disposition divides the cantata symmetrically as follows:

1. Chorale	2. Aria	3. Recitative	4. Terzetto	5. Recitative	6. Chorale
CF: S		*CF*: rec	*CF*: A + str		*CF*: S

In movements 1, 4, and 6 the preservation of the chorale melody was prompted by that of the chorale text; in no. 3, on the other hand, the chorale melody was added by the composer.

Gottlob! nun geht das Jahr zu Ende, BWV 28

NBA I/3.2, p. 75 BC A20 Duration: *c.* 20 mins

1. ARIA S ob I,II taille str bc a $\frac{3}{4}$

Gottlob! nun geht das Jahr zu Ende.	Praise God! Now the year comes to an end.
Das neue rücket schon heran.	The new one already draws near.
Gedenke, meine Seele, dran,	Consider this, my soul:
Wieviel dir deines Gottes Hände	How much good your God's hands
Im alten Jahre Guts getan!	Have done for you in the old year!
Stimm ihm ein frohes Danklied an.	Strike up a joyful song of thanks to Him.
So wird er ferner dein gedenken	Then He will remember you further
Und mehr zum neuen Jahre schenken.	And give you more in the new year.

2. CHORAL SATB bc (+ cornett trb I–III ww str) C ¢

Nun lob, mein Seel, den Herren,	**Now praise the Lord, my soul,**
Was in mir ist, den Namen sein.	**Whatever is in me, praise His Name.**
Sein Wohltat tut er mehren,	**His good deeds He increases,**
Vergiß es nicht, o Herze mein.	**Do not forget it, O my heart.**
Hat dir dein Sünd vergeben	**He has forgiven your sin**
Und heilt dein Schwachheit groß,	**And heals your great weakness,**
Errett' dein armes Leben,	**Saves your poor life,**
Nimmt dich in seinen Schoß,	**And takes you into His bosom,**
Mit reichem Trost beschüttet,	**Showered with rich comfort,**
Verjüngt, dem Adler gleich;	**Rejuvenated like the eagle;**
Der Kön'g schafft Recht, behütet,	**The King creates justice and protects**
Die leidn in seinem Reich.	**Those who suffer in His Kingdom.**

3. RECITATIVO ED ARIOSO B bc e C

'So spricht der Herr: Es soll mir eine Lust sein, daß ich ihnen Gutes tun soll, und ich will sie in diesem Lande pflanzen treulich, von ganzem Herzen und von ganzer Seele.'	'Thus says the Lord: it shall be a pleasure to me that I shall do good to them, and I will plant them in this land faithfully, with my whole heart and my whole soul.'

4. RECITATIVO T str bc — G–C c

Gott ist ein Quell, wo lauter Güte fleußt.	God is a fountain where pure goodness flows.
Gott ist ein Licht, wo lauter Gnade scheinet.	God is a Light where pure Grace shines.
Gott ist ein Schatz, der lauter Segen heißt.	God is a treasure that is called pure Blessing.
Gott ist ein Herr, ders treu und herzlich meinet.	God is a Lord whose intentions are faithful and heartfelt.
Wer ihn im Glauben liebt, in Liebe kindlich ehrt,	Whoever loves Him in Faith, honours Him in Love like a child,
Sein Wort von Herzen hört	Hears His Word from his heart,
Und sich von bösen Wegen kehrt,	And turns from evil ways,
Dem gibt er sich mit allen Gaben.	To him He gives Himself with all gifts.
Wer Gott hat, der muß alles haben.	Whoever has God must have everything.

5. ARIA DUETTO AT bc — C 6/8

Gott hat uns im heurigen Jahre gesegnet,	God has so blessed us in the present year
Daß Wohltun und Wohlsein einander begegnet.	That good deed and well-being have met together.
Wir loben ihn herzlich und bitten darneben:	We praise Him heartily and pray, moreover,
Er woll auch ein glückliches neues Jahr geben.	That He will also grant us a Happy New Year.
Wir hoffens von seiner beharrlichen Güte	We hope for this from His unwavering goodness
Und preisens im voraus mit dankbarm Gemüte.	And praise Him for it in anticipation with a grateful spirit.

6. CHORAL SATB bc (+ instrs) — a c

All solch dein Güt wir preisen,	**All such goodness of Yours we praise,**
Vater ins Himmels Thron,	**Father on heaven's throne,**
Die du uns tust beweisen	**As You show us**
Durch Christum, deinen Sohn,	**Through Christ, Your Son,**
Und bitten ferner dich:	**And we pray you further:**
Gib uns ein friedsam Jahre,	**Grant us a peaceful year,**
Für allem Leid bewahre	**Preserve us from all suffering,**
Und nähr uns mildiglich!	**And nourish us abundantly!**

Bach drew this text from the fourth cycle of cantatas by Erdmann Neumeister. Its substance is not connected with the readings of the day. Instead, like the previous year's cantata, BWV 122, it directs our thoughts to the change from one year to the next: it thanks God for good things received during the old year, praises Him, and finally prays that He will continue to bless His people in the coming year too.

Bach's composition, first performed on 30 December 1725, is distinguished by its exceptional wealth of forms: no one movement is remotely like another. The opening aria is a joyful, dance-like song of thanksgiving, whose themes exhibit clear, periodic articulation. This formal transparency is reinforced by the double-choir treatment of the instrumental ensemble, which consists of three oboes (of which the third is a taille,* or tenor oboe), strings and continuo. In the ritornellos, choirs of oboes and strings take the lead in alternation, while the trailing group (plus continuo) marks the cadences in tutti reinforcement. Even in the vocal passages this double-choral disposition is still heard throughout. The length of the text may explain why Bach dispenses with the usual da capo* form in favour of a tripartite sequence. Only the articulating instrumental ritornellos furnish an element of reprise. Their motives generate the vocal melody, which gradually unfolds with increasing freedom. Only at the admonitory calls of 'Gedenke' ('Consider') does it briefly take on a more tranquil mode of movement.

The call to strike up a song of thanksgiving is now accepted by the choir—acting on behalf of the assembled congregation—reinforced by doubling instruments, which now include cornett and trombones as well as woodwind and strings. In this motet-style chorale arrangement,[26] based on the first verse of the hymn by Johann Gramann of 1530—perhaps the best-known movement of the cantata—the chorale melody is stated by the top part in long notes, while the three lower parts (plus partly independent continuo) prepare and accompany each line in a livelier, imitative* texture. This distinctly archaizing type of chorale arrangement stands in palpable contrast to the fashionable, dance-like style of the preceding aria. In several of the chorale lines, Bach dispenses with imitative preparation of the next soprano entry, and instead chooses newly invented themes for imitation. An example is the chromatic* ascent on 'Hat dir dein Sünd vergeben' ('He has forgiven your sin'), which—provided that we understand it correctly—not only laments the sin in its chromaticism, but also discloses the source of forgiveness, namely the Passion of Christ. A parallel may be found in the chromaticism of the fugue* subject 'Denn ich habe dich erlöset' ('For I have redeemed you') from the motet* *Fürchte dich nicht*, BWV 228.

In the third movement, whose text is drawn from Jeremiah 32.41, the bass voice acts as the traditional *vox Christi*. Accompanied only by continuo, and introduced by a single bar of recitative ('Thus says the Lord:'), the piece takes the form of a song-like bass arioso* such as Bach frequently used for the setting

[26] Robert Marshall's theory (see his *The Compositional Process of J. S. Bach: a Study of the Autograph Scores of the Vocal Works*, 2 vols, Princeton, 1972, pp. 19 and 174), based on the relatively clean appearance of the score, that this movement is based on an earlier composition has been persuasively refuted by Klaus Hofmann, KB, NBA I/3.2, p. 73.

of biblical words. Whereas an aria is characterized by a theme, this movement is pervaded by a motive,* which occurs frequently in various modified forms in the continuo part. Such modifications are still more profuse in the vocal part, and with their aid the voice is able to follow all the nuances of the text in compelling declamation.

A tenor recitative accompanied by strings, no. 4, leads to the duet 'Gott hat uns im heurigen Jahre gesegnet', no. 5, for voices and continuo only. In compositional style it follows the Italian manner: each of its three sections begins with the two voice parts in imitative entries, which are thereafter partly continued in free polyphony* and partly combined in a plain note-against-note texture. The continuo ritornello recurs not only in the episodes but in the vocal passages in the form of a 'basso quasi ostinato'.* Moreover, it determines the vocal theme in the first of the three sections; the second then begins with a variant of this theme, and the third flows into a reprise of the first with interchanged parts, forming a free da capo. A plain four-part setting of the last verse of the New Year hymn *Helft mir Gotts Güte preisen* by Paul Eber (*c.* 1580) brings the work to a close.

1.9 New Year

Feast of the Circumcision of Christ

EPISTLE: Galatians 3.23–9: Through faith we are heirs by promise.
GOSPEL: Luke 2.21: The circumcision and naming of Jesus.

Singet dem Herrn ein neues Lied, BWV 190

NBA I/4, p. 3 BC A21 Duration: *c.* 19 mins

1. [CHORUS] Extant: SATB vln I,II — D $\frac{3}{4}$

'Singet dem Herrn ein neues Lied;	'Sing to the Lord a new song;
die Gemeine der Heiligen soll ihn loben!	the community of saints shall praise Him!
Lobet ihn mit Pauken und Reigen,	Praise Him with drums and dances,
lobet ihn mit Saiten und Pfeifen!	praise Him with strings and pipes!
Herr Gott, dich loben wir!	**Lord God, we praise You!**
Alles, was Odem hat, lobe den Herrn!	Let all that has breath praise the Lord!
Herr Gott, wir danken dir!	**Lord God, we thank you!**
Alleluja!'	Alleluia!'

2. CHORAL E RECITATIVO Extant: SATB vln I,II — b–A C

Herr Gott, dich loben wir!	**Lord God, we praise You!**
Baß	*Bass*
Daß du mit diesem neuen Jahr	That with this New Year

Uns neues Glück und neuen Segen schenkest
Und noch in Gnaden an uns denkest.
Herr Gott, wir danken dir!
Tenor
Daß deine Gütigkeit
In der vergangnen Zeit
Das ganze Land und unsre werte Stadt
Vor Teurung, Pestilenz und Krieg behütet hat.
Herr Gott, dich loben wir!
Alt
Denn deine Vatertreu
Hat noch kein Ende,
Sie wird bei uns noch alle Morgen neu.
Drum falten wir,
Barmherzger Gott, dafür
In Demut unsre Hände
Und sagen lebenslang
Mit Mund und Herzen Lob und Dank.

Herr Gott, wir danken dir!

3. ARIA A str bc
Lobe, Zion, deinen Gott,
Lobe deinen Gott mit Freuden,
Auf! erzähle dessen Ruhm,
Der in seinem Heiligtum
Fernerhin dich als dein Hirt,
Will auf grüner Auen weiden.

4. RECITATIVO B bc
Es wünsche sich die Welt,
Was Fleisch und Blute wohlgefällt;
Nur eins, eins bitt ich von dem Herrn,

Dies eine hätt ich gern,
Daß Jesus, meine Freude,
Mein treuer Hirt, mein Trost und Heil

Und meiner Seelen bestes Teil,
Mich als ein Schäflein seiner Weide

Auch dieses Jahr mit seinem Schutz umfasse
Und nimmermehr aus seinen Armen lasse.

You grant us new fortune and new blessings
And still think of us with Grace.
Lord God, we thank You!
Tenor
That Your goodness
In time past
Has protected the whole land
And our worthy city from famine, pestilence and war.
Lord God, we praise You!
Alto
For Your fatherly faithfulness
Still has no end;
It is renewed for us every morning.
For this, then,
Merciful God, we fold
Our hands in humility,
And all our lives exclaim
With mouth and heart our praise and thanks.
Lord God, we thank You!

A 3/4

Praise your God, O Zion,
Praise your God with joy;
Rise up! Tell the glory of Him
Who in His sanctuary
Henceforth, as your Shepherd,
Will feed you in green pastures.

f♯–A c

Let the world desire
What pleases flesh and blood;
Only one thing, just one, do I ask of the Lord,
This one thing would I like,
That Jesus, my joy,
My faithful Shepherd, my comfort and Salvation
And my soul's best portion,
Would embrace me as a little sheep of His pasture,
This year too, with His protection

And nevermore let me go from His arms.

Sein guter Geist,
Der mir den Weg zum Leben weist,
Regier und führe mich auf ebner Bahn,
So fang ich dieses Jahr in Jesu Namen an.

May His good Spirit,
Which shows me the way to Life,
Govern and lead me on a level path;
Thus I begin this year in Jesus's Name.

5. Aria [Duet] TB ob d'am or solo vln bc — D $\frac{6}{8}$

Jesus soll mein alles sein,
Jesus soll mein Anfang bleiben,
Jesus ist mein Freudenschein,
Jesu will ich mich verschreiben.
Jesus hilft mir durch sein Blut,
Jesus macht mein Ende gut.

Jesus shall be my all,
Jesus shall remain my starting-point,
Jesus is my light of joy,
To Jesus will I assign myself.
Jesus aids me through His Blood,
Jesus makes my end good.

6. Recitativo T str bc — b–A c

Nun, Jesus gebe,
Daß mit dem neuen Jahr auch sein Gesalbter lebe;
Er segne beides, Stamm und Zweige,
Auf daß ihr Glück bis an die Wolken steige.
Es segne Jesus Kirch und Schul,
Er segne alle treue Lehrer,
Er segne seines Wortes Hörer;
Er segne Rat und Richterstuhl;
Er gieß auch über jedes Haus
In unsrer Stadt die Segensquellen aus;
Er gebe, daß aufs neu
Sich Fried und Treu
In unsern Grenzen küssen mögen.
So leben wir dies ganze Jahr im Segen.

Now Jesus grant
That in the New Year His anointed one may live also;
May He bless both trunk and branches,
So that their fortune may climb to the clouds.
May Jesus bless church and school,
May He bless all faithful teachers,
May He bless those who hear His Word;
May He bless council and seat of judgement;
May He also pour out over every house
In our city His fount of blessing;
May He grant anew
That peace and fidelity
Might kiss within our borders.
Then we shall live this whole year in Blessing.

7. Choral SATB tr I–III timp ob I–III bc (+ str) — D c

Laß uns das Jahr vollbringen
Zu Lob dem Namen dein,
Daß wir demselben singen
In der Christen Gemein;
Wollst uns das Leben fristen
Durch dein allmächtig Hand,
Erhalt deine lieben Christen
Und unser Vaterland.
Dein Segen zu uns wende,
Gib Fried an allem Ende;
Gib unverfälscht im Lande
Dein seligmachend Wort.
Die Heuchler mach zuschanden
Hier und an allem Ort!

Let us complete the year
In praise of Your Name,
That we may sing of it
In the Christian community;
Let us make a bare living
Through Your almighty hand;
Preserve Your dear Christians
And our fatherland.
Turn Your Blessing towards us,
Grant peace in all quarters,
Grant us, uncorrupted in the land,
Your saving Word.
Bring hypocrites to ruin
Here and everywhere!

Bach's first Leipzig New Year cantata, composed for 1 January 1724, has unfortunately been handed down in an incomplete state. In the first two movements, only the voice and violin parts survive; the remainder have to be reconstructed. The reconstruction by Walther Reinhardt, though highly questionable in detail, skilfully restores the work for present-day performances.

The text, by an anonymous librettist, refers to the Gospel* reading only by allusion: at the end of the fourth movement, where 'Jesus's Name' is mentioned; and in the following aria, where the name 'Jesus' is used as an anaphora to introduce each line. For the rest, the text is concerned with praise and thanksgiving for past benefits and with prayers for future blessing.The dominant movement is the opening chorus,* whose text is assembled from various psalm verses (Psalms 149.1, 150.4, and 150.6) and from the beginning of Luther's German Te Deum of 1529. Musically, it is a tripartite structure in which the Te Deum quotations, sung to the liturgical melody in choral unison, form pivot points as follows:

A Concerted passage ('Singet dem Herrn . . .')
Te Deum ('Herr Gott, dich loben wir')
B Choral fugue* ('Alles, was Odem hat . . .')
Te Deum ('Herr Gott, wir danken dir')
A[1] Opening section, abridged ('Alleluia')

The opening lines of the German Te Deum are heard again in the second movement, this time in a plain four-part harmonization interrupted by 'troping' recitative insertions. Although we do not know the original scoring of this movement, any more than that of the first, we may assume, with Werner Neumann (NBA I/4) and contrary to Reinhardt's view, that it requires a smaller ensemble than its predecessor (SATB and continuo [plus strings]).

These two introductory movements are followed by an aria (no. 3) in a simple, dance-like melodic style. Its homophonic* string texture, articulated by echo dynamics, suggests a secular original, though no concrete evidence of this has come to light. A *secco* recitative then leads to the second aria (no. 5), a duet whose unspecified obbligato* part is probably intended for oboe d'amore,* though solo violin is another possibility. The vocal parts are mostly treated in imitation;* and, as in the first aria, the concise bipartite structure forgoes a da capo*. The prayers of the following recitative, no. 6, are accompanied by held string chords, giving them a sense of urgency. The work concludes with the second verse of the New Year hymn *Jesu, nun sei gepreiset* by Johannes Herman (1593), in which an obbligato trumpet choir marks the end of each line.

In 1730 Bach reused the work with a different text for the bicentenary of the Augsburg Confession, but the music of that version has not survived. It may have been this adaptation that led to the mutilation of the score of the New Year cantata.

Jesu, nun sei gepreiset, BWV 41

NBA I/4, p. 39 BC A22 Duration: *c.* 30 mins

1. [CHORALE] SATB tr I–III timp ob I–III str bc — C C 3/4 ¢ C

Jesu, nun sei gepreiset	**O Jesus, now be praised**
Zu diesem neuen Jahr	**At this New Year**
Für dein Güt, uns beweiset	**For Your goodness, shown to us**
In aller Not und Gefahr,	**In all distress and danger,**
Daß wir haben erlebet	**So that we have experienced**
Die neu fröhliche Zeit,	**The new gladsome time**
Die voller Gnaden schwebet	**Which hovers full of Grace**
Und ewger Seligkeit;	**And eternal Salvation;**
Daß wir in guter Stille	**So that in goodly stillness**
Das alt Jahr habn erfüllet.	**We have completed the old year.**
Wir wollen uns dir ergeben	**We want to give ourselves to You**
Itzund und immerdar,	**Now and for evermore;**
Behüt Leib, Seel und Leben	**Protect body, soul and life**
Hinfort durchs ganze Jahr!	**Henceforth throughout the whole year!**

2. ARIA S ob I–III bc — G 6/8

Laß uns, o höchster Gott, das Jahr vollbringen,	Let us, O highest God, so complete the year
Damit das Ende so wie dessen Anfang sei.	That the end may be like the beginning.
Es stehe deine Hand uns bei,	May Your hand be with us,
Daß künftig bei des Jahres Schluß	That in future at the year's end
Wir bei des Segens Überfluß	We may amidst the abundance of blessings,
Wie itzt ein Halleluja singen.	As now, sing an alleluia.

3. RECITATIVO A bc — a–e C

Ach! deine Hand, dein Segen muß allein	Ah! Your hand, Your Blessing alone
Das A und O, der Anfang und das Ende sein.	Must be the A and O, beginning and end.
Das Leben trägest du in deiner Hand,	Our life You carry in Your hand,
Und unsre Tage sind bei dir geschrieben;	And with You our days are written;
Dein Auge steht auf Stadt und Land;	Your eye looks upon city and country;
Du zählest unser Wohl und kennest unser Leiden,	You count our prosperity and know our misfortunes;
Ach! gib von beiden,	Ah! grant us of both
Was deine Weisheit will, worzu dich dein Erbarmen angetrieben.	Whatever Your Wisdom wills, wherever Your mercy impels You.

4. ARIA T cello picc bc — a C

Woferne du den edlen Frieden	Provided that You have granted a noble peace

Vor unsern Leib und Stand beschieden,	For our body and station,
So laß der Seele doch dein selig machend Wort.	Then allow our soul still Your saving Word.
Wenn uns dies Heil begegnet,	When we encounter this cure,
So sind wir hier gesegnet	We are blessed here on earth
Und Auserwählte dort!	And chosen ones there in heaven!

5\. Recitativo B bc (line 6: + SAT) C c

Doch weil der Feind bei Tag und Nacht	Yet since the Foe by day and night
Zu unserm Schaden wacht	Watches out to do us harm
Und unsre Ruhe will verstören,	And would disturb our repose,
So wollest du, o Herre Gott, erhören,	Then would You listen, O Lord God,
Wenn wir in heiliger Gemeine beten:	When we pray in the holy congregation:
Den Satan unter unsre Füße treten.	**Let Satan be trodden under our feet.**
So bleiben wir zu deinem Ruhm	Then we remain, to Your renown,
Dein auserwähltes Eigentum	Your chosen property
Und können auch nach Kreuz und Leiden	And can also, after cross and sorrow,
Zur Herrlichkeit von hinnen scheiden.	Depart from here into Glory.

6\. Choral SATB tr I–III timp ob I–III bc (+ str) C c $\frac{3}{4}$ c

Dein ist allein die Ehre,	**Yours alone is the honour,**
Dein ist allein der Ruhm;	**Yours alone is the renown;**
Geduld im Kreuz uns lehre,	**Teach us forbearance in cross-bearing,**
Regier all unser Tun,	**Govern all our deeds**
Bis wir fröhlich abscheiden	**Till we joyfully depart**
Ins ewig Himmelreich,	**Into the eternal Kingdom of Heaven,**
Zu wahrem Fried und Freude,	**To true peace and joy,**
Den Heilgen Gottes gleich.	**Like the saints of God.**
Indes machs mit uns allen	**Meanwhile, deal with us all**
Nach deinem Wohlgefallen:	**According to Your pleasure:**
Solchs singet heut ohn Scherzen	**This is sung today without jest**
Die christgläubige Schar	**By the host faithful to Christ,**
Und wünscht mit Mund und Herzen	**Wishing with mouth and heart**
Ein seligs neues Jahr.	**A blessed New Year.**

This work, first performed on 1 January 1725, is a chorale cantata* based on the three-verse New Year hymn by Johannes Herman of 1593. The first and last verses are preserved word for word in nos. 1 and 6, while a free paraphrase of the middle verse serves as the text of nos. 2–5. Although the anonymous librettist acted very freely and could not avoid making his own additions to fill out the cantata text, the fourteen-line second verse may nonetheless be recognized in all four inner movements of the cantata:

Cantata 41 *Movement*	*Chorale, verse 2* *Line*
2 Laß uns . . . das Jahr vollbringen	1 Laß uns das Jahr vollbringen
3 Ach! deine Hand, dein Segen . . .	9 Dein' Segen zu uns wende
4 Woferne du den edlen Frieden . . .	10 Gib Fried an allem Ende
So laß . . . dein selig machend Wort	12 Dein seligmachend Wort
5 Doch weil der Feind bei Tag und Nacht . . .	13 Die Teufel mach zuschanden
'Den Satan unter unsre Füße treten' (litany)	
2 Let us . . . complete the year	1 Let us complete the year
3 Ah! Your hand, Your blessing . . .	9 Turn Your blessing towards us
4 Provided that You have granted a noble peace	10 Grant peace in all quarters
Then allow . . . Your saving Word	12 Your saving Word
5 Yet since the Foe by day and night . . .	13 Bring the Devil to ruin
'Let Satan be trodden under our feet' (litany)	

On the other hand, nowhere do we discover a close link with the readings for the day.

Bach's compositional problem in the opening movement lay in the formal task of dividing up the exceptionally long hymn verse. The chorale seems to have been popular in Leipzig (or with Bach?), for Bach used it in three of his New Year cantatas (Nos. 190, 41, and 171) and in an additional chorale setting (BWV 362), despite the fact that its melody is not one of the strongest inspirations of early Protestantism and is hardly known at all today. In Leipzig, it was evidently sung with a repeat of the last two lines to a reprise of the beginning of the melody; in this form, at any rate, it is transmitted in all Bach's settings. The melody, thus expanded to sixteen lines, is in the first movement of Cantata 41 arranged in a series of four sections and sung throughout by the soprano in long notes, line-by-line, interrupted by episodes, as follows:

Lines 1–4 = 5–8: freely polyphonic* choral texture, incorporated in a thematically independent, concerted orchestral texture for three trumpets and drums, three oboes, strings and continuo.

Lines 9–10: slower ('adagio'), dynamically more subdued section ('in goodly stillness'); homophonic* choral texture with figurative accompanying orchestra.

Lines 11–12 = 13–14: quick ('presto') fugato in the three lower vocal parts, with the instruments *colla parte*.*

Lines 13–14: rounding-off with a repeat of the last two lines to the music of lines 1–2 = 5–6.

The display of splendour in the opening movement gives way to an introspective *cantabile* style in the following soprano aria, no. 2, whose 6/8 time and scoring with three oboes lend it a pastoral character. A brief *secco* recitative leads to the second aria, no. 4, which is characterized by wide-ranging gestures on its obbligato* instrument, the violoncello piccolo.* Here Bach evidently requires a five-string instrument with a range from *C* to b^1; and he well knows how to draw distinctive effects, based on agility and expansive melody, from this newly invented outsize viola.

In the bass *secco* recitative, no. 5, the librettist inserted a line from the German litany, which Bach sets 'allegro' in a four-part vocal texture. Here the congregation intervenes, as it were, in the prayer of the individual. The closing chorale, no. 6, clearly harks back to the opening movement, whose trumpet motive* is heard several times as an episode between the chorale lines. Again, the hymn verse is articulated in a striking manner: in lines 9–14 the trumpets are silent; lines 11–14 are set apart by their change of time (from **c** to 3/4); and the final fanfare on the trumpets closes the circle back to the opening lines.

Herr Gott, dich loben wir, BWV 16

NBA I/4, p. 105 BC A23 Duration: *c.* 21 mins

1. [CHORALE] S + hn ATB ob I,II + str bc		a–G **c**
Herr Gott, dich loben wir,	**Lord God, we praise You,**	
Herr Gott, wir danken dir:	**Lord God, we thank You:**	
Dich, Gott Vater in Ewigkeit,	**You, God the Father in eternity,**	
Ehret die Welt weit und breit.	**The world honours far and wide.**	
2. RECITATIVO B bc		C–G **c**
So stimmen wir	Thus we strike up	
Bei dieser frohen Zeit	At this glad time	
Mit heißer Andacht an	With ardent devotion	
Und legen dir,	And lay before You,	
O Gott, auf dieses neue Jahr	O God, at this New Year	
Das erste Herzensopfer dar.	The first offering of our hearts.	
Was hast du nicht von Ewigkeit	What have You not done from eternity	
Vor Heil an uns getan;	For our salvation?	
Und was muß unsre Brust	And what must our breast feel	
Noch jetzt vor Lieb und Treu verspüren?	Even now of Your Love and faithfulness?	
Dein Zion sieht vollkommne Ruh,	Your Zion sees perfect peace,	
Es fällt ihm Glück und Segen zu;	Good fortune and blessing befall it;	
Der Tempel schallt	The temple resounds	
Von Psaltern und von Harfen,	With psalteries and with harps,	
Und unsre Seele wallt,	And our soul warms up	
Wenn wir nur Andachtsglut in Herz und Munde führen.	If we but take the glow of devotion into our heart and mouth.	
O! sollte darum nicht	Oh! should not therefore	
Ein neues Lied erklingen	A new song be heard	
Und wir in heißer Liebe singen?	And should we not sing in ardent love?	
3. ARIA TUTTI SATB hn str + ob I,II bc		C **c**
Chor	*Choir*	
Laßt uns jauchzen, laßt uns freuen:	Let us exult, let us rejoice:	

Gottes Güt und Treu
Bleibet alle Morgen neu.
Baß
Krönt und segnet seine Hand,
Ach! so glaubt, daß unser Stand
Ewig, ewig glücklich sei.

God's goodness and faithfulness
Are new every morning.
Bass
Since His hand crowns and blesses,
Ah, then believe that our situation
May be fortunate for ever and ever.

4. RECITATIVO A bc — e–C c

Ach treuer Hort,
Beschütz auch fernerhin dein wertes Wort:
Beschütze Kirch und Schule,
So wird dein Reich vermehrt
Und Satans arge List gestört.
Erhalte nur den Frieden
Und die beliebte Ruh,
So ist uns schon genug beschieden,
Und uns fällt lauter Wohlsein zu.
Ach! Gott, du wirst das Land
Noch ferner wässern,
Du wirst es stets verbessern,
Du wirst es selbst mit deiner Hand
Und deinem Segen bauen.
Wohl uns, wenn wir
Dir für und für,
Mein Jesus und mein Heil, vertrauen.

Ah, faithful Refuge,
Protect also henceforth Your esteemed Word;
Protect church and school;
Then Your Kingdom will be augmented
And Satan's evil cunning vexed.
Preserve our peace
And beloved tranquillity;
Then enough has already been granted us
And pure welfare befalls us.
Ah, God! You will water the land
Still further,
You will constantly improve it,
You will, with Your own hand
And blessing, cultivate it.
Blessed are we if,
For ever and ever,
We trust in You, my Jesus and my Salvation.

5. ARIA T ob da c or violetta bc — F $\frac{3}{4}$

Geliebter Jesu, du allein
Sollst unser Seelen Reichtum sein.
Wir wollen dich vor allen Schätzen
In unser treues Herze setzen,
Ja, wenn das Lebensband zerreißt,
Stimmt unser gottvergnügter Geist
Noch mit den Lippen sehnlich ein:
Geliebter Jesu, du allein
Sollst unser Seelen Reichtum sein.

Beloved Jesus, You alone
Shall be our souls' wealth.
We would place You before all treasures
In our faithful hearts;
Indeed, when the bond of life tears,
Our God-contented spirit still
Chimes in longingly with our lips:
Beloved Jesus, You alone
Shall be our souls' wealth.

6. CHORAL SATB bc (+ instrs) — a c

**All solch dein Güt wir preisen,
Vater ins Himmels Thron,
Die du uns tust beweisen
Durch Christum, deinen Sohn,
Und bitten ferner dich,
Gib uns ein friedlich Jahre,
Vor allem Leid bewahre
Und nähr uns mildiglich.**

**All such goodness of Yours we praise,
Father on heaven's throne,
As You show us
Through Christ, Your Son,
And we pray You further:
Grant us a peaceful year,
Preserve us from all suffering,
And nourish us abundantly.**

Like the librettist of Cantata 41, Georg Christian Lehms conceived this New Year text, published in 1711, entirely in terms of praise and thanksgiving, without entering into the readings of the day. As in Cantata 190, the opening makes use of the first four lines of Martin Luther's German Te Deum. The two recitative-aria pairs that follow are so disposed that the first deals with thanksgiving for past benefits and the second with a prayer for future blessing. The last verse of the New Year hymn *Helft mir Gotts Güte preisen* by Paul Eber (*c.* 1580), which concludes the work, is an addition of Bach's: Lehms makes no provision for a concluding chorale.

Bach composed this cantata in Leipzig for the New Year's Day service in 1726. It opens with a concise *cantus firmus** movement based on the liturgical melody of the Te Deum (lines 1–4), which is stated by the soprano (plus horn), while the three lower parts, doubled by instruments, furnish lively counterpoint.* The role of the instruments, however, is not restricted to the reinforcement of the voice parts. The continuo, which is assigned a four-bar introduction, remains largely independent throughout the movement. Also independent are oboe I and violin I in unison: leaving the strengthening of the soprano part to the horn, they form a contrapuntal part of their own, whose character in no way differs from that of the vocal counterpoints. Indeed, if this part did not lie exceptionally high for the human voice, the movement might easily be converted into a piece for five voice parts with independent continuo.

A *secco* recitative, no. 2, now accounts for the jubilation: peace reigns ('Your Zion sees perfect peace') and God's praise is sung in church ('The temple resounds with psalteries and with harps'). The conclusion—'Oh! should not therefore a new song be heard, and should we not sing in ardent love?'—leads directly into the third movement's call of 'Let us exult', which for that reason is sung immediately by bass and tutti voices, without preceding ritornello. This third movement is quite exceptional in form, uniting features of aria and chorus.* It is a free da capo* structure, whose main section consists of a chorus from which the bass steps forward only occasionally. The bipartite middle section, on the other hand, consists of a bass solo with a central interruption from the choir. The various structural layers of this chorus-aria may be outlined in simplified form as follows:

A Choral opening sentence *a* ('Laßt uns jauchzen') with:
Orchestral answering phrase *b*
Choral fugue* on *a*—choral insertion* within *b*
Orchestral episode *b*

B Bass solo *c* ('Krönt und segnet seine Hand')
Choral interjection *a*
Bass solo c^1

A[1] Chorus *a* with orchestral answer *b*[1] (see above)
Choral fugue on *a* (varied)—choral insertion within *b*
Orchestral postlude *b*

The second recitative, no. 4, again a *secco*, brings prayers for future blessing. It is followed by the tenor aria, no. 5, whose obbligato* instrument in 1726 was an oboe da caccia;* for a later revival, perhaps in 1731, it was replaced by a 'violetta' which, according to Johann Gottfried Walther, could mean either viola or alto gamba. The alto pitch of this obbligato part—especially with the timbre of a string instrument—is extremely well suited to the heartfelt, intimate character of the aria. A plain four-part chorale setting concludes the work.

Gott, wie dein Name, so ist auch dein Ruhm, BWV 171

NBA I/4, p. 133 BC A24 Duration: *c.* 22 mins

1. [Chorus] SATB tr I–III timp ob I,II str bc — D 2

'Gott, wie dein Name, so ist auch dein Ruhm bis an der Welt Ende.'	'O God, as Your Name is, so also is Your renown to the ends of the world.'

2. Aria T vln I,II bc — A C

Herr, so weit die Wolken gehen,	Lord, as far as the clouds go
Gehet deines Namens Ruhm.	So goes Your Name's renown.
Alles, was die Lippen rührt,	All that stirs the lips,
Alles, was noch Odem führt,	All that yet draws breath
Wird dich in der Macht erhöhen.	Will exalt You in Your might.

3. Recitativo A bc — f♯–D C

Du süßer Jesus-Name du,	You sweet Name of Jesus, You,
In dir ist meine Ruh,	In You is my repose,
Du bist mein Trost auf Erden,	You are my comfort on earth;
Wie kann denn mir	How, then, can I become
Im Kreuze bange werden?	Afraid in cross-bearing?
Du bist mein festes Schloß und mein Panier,	Your are my strong fortress and my banner:
Da lauf ich hin,	There do I run
Wenn ich verfolget bin.	When I am pursued.
Du bist mein Leben und mein Licht,	Your are my Life and my Light,
Mein Ehre, meine Zuversicht,	My honour, my confidence,
Mein Beistand in Gefahr	My help in danger,
Und mein Geschenk zum neuen Jahr.	And my gift for the New Year.

4. Aria S vln solo bc — D 12/8

Jesus soll mein erstes Wort	'Jesus' shall be my first word
In dem neuen Jahre heißen.	In the New Year.
Fort und fort	On and on
Lacht sein Nam in meinem Munde,	Smiles His Name in my mouth,
Und in meiner letzten Stunde	And in my last hour
Ist Jesus auch mein letztes Wort.	'Jesus' shall also be my last word.

5. Recitativo B ob I,II bc G–b c $\frac{3}{8}$ c

Und da du, Herr, gesagt:
Bittet nur in meinem Namen,
So ist alles Ja! und Amen!
So flehen wir,
Du Heiland aller Welt, zu dir:
Verstoß uns ferner nicht,
Behüt uns dieses Jahr
Für Feuer, Pest und Kriegsgefahr!

Laß uns dein Wort, das helle Licht,
Noch rein und lauter brennen;
Gib unsrer Obrigkeit
Und dem gesamten Lande
Dein Heil des Segens zu erkennen;
Gib allezeit
Glück und Heil zu allem Stande.
Wir bitten, Herr, in deinem Namen,
Sprich: ja! darzu, sprich: Amen! amen!

And since You said, Lord:
'If you but ask in My Name',
Then all is 'Yes!' and 'Amen!'
Then we beseech You,
You Saviour of all the world:
Do not put us away further;
Protect us this year
From fire, pestilence, and the danger of war!

Let Your Word, that bright Light,
Still burn for us pure and clear;
Let our government
And the entire land
Acknowledge Your Salvation-Blessing;
Grant at all times
Good fortune and welfare to all stations.
We ask this, Lord, in Your Name:
Say 'Yes!' to it, say 'Amen! Amen!'

6. Choral SATB tr I–III timp bc (+ ww str) D c $\frac{3}{4}$ c

**Laß uns das Jahr vollbringen
Zu Lob dem Namen dein,
Daß wir demselben singen
In der Christen Gemein.
Wollst uns das Leben fristen
Durch dein allmächtig Hand,
Erhalt dein liebe Christen
Und unser Vaterland!
Dein Segen zu uns wende,
Gib Fried an allem Ende,
Gib unverfälscht im Lande
Dein seligmachend Wort,
Die Teufel mach zuschanden
Hier und an allem Ort!**

**Let us complete the year
In praise of Your Name,
That we may sing of it
In the Christian community.
Let us make a bare living
Through Your almighty hand;
Preserve Your dear Christians
And our fatherland!
Turn Your Blessing towards us,
Grant peace in all quarters,
Grant us, uncorrupted in the land,
Your saving Word;
Bring devils to ruin
Here and everywhere!**

The text of this cantata is drawn from Picander's cycle of 1728. It follows that Bach's setting might have been written for 1 January 1729, or perhaps a year or two later.[27] Picander adheres more closely than the librettists of most of Bach's other New Year cantatas (cf. BWV 190, 41, 16, and 143) to the New Year Gospel,* which is concerned with the naming of Jesus. In his interpretation, he tries to show the significance of Jesus's name for Christianity (see also the discussion of the *Christmas Oratorio*, Part IV, below). With this in mind, he first introduces a

[27] According to Kobayashi Chr, p. 39, an origin as late as *c.* 1736/7 is not impossible.

verse from the Psalms (Ps. 48.10): the entire world knows and praises the name of God. The aria, no. 2, takes up the same idea, but the recitative no. 3 strikes a more personal note, addressing Jesus Himself: called in times of persecution and adversity, Jesus's name gives comfort and protection; and, in a reference to the occasion of the work, it is 'my gift for the New Year'. The following aria no. 4 tells us that, just as Jesus's name is my first word at the beginning of this new year, so too it shall be my last word at the hour of my death. The last two movements have the character of prayers. In a reference to John 14.13—'Whatever you ask in my name, I will do it' (John 16.23 is similar)—God is asked to protect his people in the coming year too. Similar ideas are present in the closing chorale, the second verse of the hymn *Jesu, nun sei gepreiset* by Johannes Herman (1591), whose opening lines again refer to the name of Jesus. The text of this cantata thus moves through three stages: reading (biblical words), contemplation, and prayer.

Bach sets the introductory psalm words as a large-scale choral fugue* in which strings and oboes largely double the voice parts, lending it a somewhat archaic, motet-like character. The trumpets, on the other hand, have independent parts (the first trumpet is even thematic), and it is through this that the movement acquires its awe-inspiring radiance. The music is probably not new: an earlier vocal work that no longer survives apparently formed the common source of this opening chorus* and of the later adaptation of the same music to the words 'Patrem omnipotentem, factorem coeli et terrae, visibilium et invisibilium' ('Father Almighty, Maker of heaven and earth and of all things visible and invisible') in the Credo, or 'Symbolum Nicenum', of the B minor Mass, BWV 232^{II}. Here again, the underlying concept is the world-embracing almighty power of God.

The two obbligato* instruments of the following aria, no. 2, are unspecified in the sole surviving autograph score. Their range of *g*♯ to $e^3/c\sharp^3$ suggests that they are two violins. There is a certain contrapuntal severity about this movement also, with its richly imitative* texture in which voices and instruments participate on equal terms. Compared with the opening chorus, however, it is to a considerable degree loosened up by its wide-ranging, concertante* instrumental figures. A plain recitative accompanied only by continuo, no. 3, leads to the second aria, no. 4, in which the virtuoso element is more pronounced. Its music is drawn from the secular cantata *Zerreißet, zersprenget, zertrümmert die Gruft*, BWV 205, where the text, 'Angenehmer Zephyrus' ('Pleasant Zephyr'), sang the praises of that gentle wind. Now the elaborate violin figures are summoned to the praise of Jesus's name, a bold transference which is nonetheless a convincing success.

The following recitative, no. 5, is another masterpiece of its kind. An introductory arioso,* accompanied only by continuo, alludes to God's promise to hear prayers said in the name of Jesus. The prayers that follow are sung in recitative to an accompaniment of two oboes and continuo. The conclusion, 'Wir bitten, Herr . . .' ('We ask, Lord . . .'), again turns into arioso but maintains the oboes' *accompagnato*,* thereby surpassing the two previous sections. The closing chorale unites the entire instrumental ensemble: oboes and strings strengthen the choir, as in the first movement, while trumpets and drums interpose their own episodes. Bach borrowed the movement from his New Year cantata *Jesu, nun sei gepreiset*, BWV 41, where it is thematically linked with the opening chorus. And even in the later cantata, a link back to the first movement may easily be felt by virtue of the similar style of instrumental treatment.

Fallt mit Danken, fallt mit Loben
Weihnachts-Oratorium Christmas Oratorio, BWV 248, Part IV

NBA II/6, p. 145 BC D7^{IV} Duration: *c.* 27 mins

36. Chorus SATB hn I,II ob I,II str bc — F 3/8

Fallt mit Danken, fallt mit Loben
Vor des Höchsten Gnadenthron!
  Gottes Sohn
  Will der Erden
  Heiland und Erlöser werden,
  Gottes Sohn
  Dämpft der Feinde Wut und Toben.

Fall with thanks, fall with praise
Before the Highest's throne of Grace!
  God's Son
  Would become
  Saviour and Redeemer of the earth;
  God's Son
  Subdues the Foe's rage and fury.

37. Evangelista T bc — C–a c

'Und da acht Tage um waren, daß das Kind beschnitten würde, da ward sein Name genennet Jesus, welcher genennet war von dem Engel, ehe denn er im Mutterleibe empfangen ward.'

'And as eight days were up, when the Child would be circumcised, His Name was called Jesus, which He was called by the angel before He was conceived in the womb.'

38. Recitativo con Chorale SB str bc — d–C c

Immanuel, o süßes Wort!
Mein Jesus heißt mein Hort,
Mein Jesus heißt mein Leben,
Mein Jesus hat sich mir ergeben;
Mein Jesus soll mir immerfort
Vor meinen Augen schweben.
Mein Jesus heißet meine Lust,
Mein Jesus labet Herz und Brust.
  Jesu, du mein liebstes Leben,
  Meiner Seelen Bräutigam,
Komm! ich will dich mit Lust umfassen,
Mein Herze soll dich nimmer lassen,

Emmanuel, O sweet word!
My Jesus is my refuge,
My Jesus is my life,
My Jesus has submitted Himself to me;
My Jesus shall evermore
Hover before my eyes.
My Jesus is my delight,
My Jesus comforts heart and breast.
  Jesus, my dearest life,
  My soul's Bridegroom,
Come! I would embrace You with delight,
My heart shall never leave You,

Der du dich vor mich gegeben
An des bittern Kreuzes Stamm!
Ach! so nimm mich zu dir!
Auch in dem Sterben sollst du mir
Das Allerliebste sein;
In Not, Gefahr und Ungemach
Seh ich dir sehnlichst nach.
Was jagte mir zuletzt der Tod für Grauen ein?
Mein Jesus! Wenn ich sterbe,
So weiß ich, daß ich nicht verderbe.
Dein Name steht in mir geschrieben,
Der hat des Todes Furcht vertrieben.

Who gave Yourself for me
On the bitter Cross's stem!
Ah! then take me to You!
Even in dying You shall be
Dearest of all to me;
In need, danger, and affliction
I gaze after You longingly.
How at last should death strike terror in me?
My Jesus, when I die
I know that I shall not perish.
Your Name inscribed within me
Has driven away the fear of death.

39. Aria S Echo (S) ob I solo bc — C $\frac{6}{8}$

Flößt, mein Heiland, flößt dein Namen
Auch den allerkleinsten Samen
Jenes strengen Schreckens ein?
Nein, du sagst ja selber nein. Nein!
Sollt ich nun das Sterben scheuen?
Nein, dein süßes Wort ist da!
Oder sollt ich mich erfreuen?
Ja, du Heiland sprichst selbst ja. Ja!

My Saviour, does Your Name instil
Even the tiniest seed
Of that sharp fear?
No, You Yourself say no. No!
Should I now be afraid of dying?
No. Your sweet word is there!
Or should I rejoice?
Yes. You, O Saviour, say it Yourself. Yes!

40. Recitativo con Chorale SB str bc — C–F c

Wohlan, dein Name soll allein
In meinem Herzen sein!
Jesu, meine Freud und Wonne,
Meine Hoffnung, Schatz und Teil,
So will ich dich entzücket nennen,
Wenn Brust und Herz zu dir vor Liebe brennen.
Mein Erlösung, Schmuck und Heil,

Doch Liebster, sage mir:
Wie rühm ich dich? Wie dank ich dir?
Hirt und König, Licht und Sonne,
Ach! wie soll ich würdiglich,
Mein Herr Jesu, preisen dich?

Well then, Your Name alone
Shall be in my heart!
Jesus, my joy and gladness,
My hope, treasure, and portion,
This is what I shall call You, entranced,
When breast and heart burn with love for You.
My Redemption, ornament and Salvation,
Yet Beloved, tell me:
How can I praise You? how thank You?
Shepherd and King, Light and Sun,
Ah! how should I worthily
Praise You, my Lord Jesus?

41. Aria T vln I solo vln II solo bc — d c

Ich will nur dir zu Ehren leben,
Mein Heiland, gib mir Kraft und Mut,

Daß es mein Herz recht eifrig tut!
Stärke mich,
Deine Gnade würdiglich
Und mit Danken zu erheben!

I would live only for Your honour,
My Saviour, grant me strength and courage,
That my heart may do so with true zeal!
Strengthen me,
That I may extol Your Grace
Worthily and with thanksgiving!

42. CHORALE SATB hn I,II ob I,II str bc F $\frac{3}{4}$

Jesus richte mein Beginnen,	**Jesus, guide my beginning,**
Jesus bleibe stets bei mir,	**Jesus, remain with me always,**
Jesus zäume mir die Sinnen,	**Jesus, bridle my inclinations,**
Jesus sei nur mein Begier,	**Jesus, be my sole desire,**
Jesus sei mir in Gedanken,	**Jesus, be in my thoughts,**
Jesu, lasse mich nicht wanken!	**Jesus, let me not waver!**

Of the six parts of the *Christmas Oratorio*, Part IV is the most independent. The biblical narrative of the second movement, which is also the Gospel* reading for New Year's Day, forms a unity in itself. And with its F major key and its scoring for two horns, Bach's setting departs furthest from the brighter D major splendour—marked by trumpet sonorities—of the outer parts. The text is concerned only with the naming of Jesus and associated reflections; the new year is nowhere mentioned.

The opening chorus* and the two arias are parodied from the secular cantata *Hercules at the Crossroads*, BWV 213. In the chorus, contrasted caressing and alert figures, formerly associated respectively with 'caring for' and 'watching over' the infant Hercules, are now aptly applied to the gesture of kneeling before God 'mit Danken' (with thanks) and 'mit Loben' (with praise). In the echo aria, however, the part of 'faithful Echo', who in the secular cantata reinforced the young Hercules's enlightened choice between Pleasure and Virtue, proves rather less convincing when allotted to the Saviour in the soprano aria 'Flößt, mein Heiland' (no. 39). Similarly, the relationship between text and music suffers a little when the soaring duet violin parts of the tenor aria 'Ich will nur dir zu Ehren leben' (no. 41), which formerly depicted Virtue's wings hovering and climbing 'to the stars like an eagle', are associated merely with a generalized prayer for 'strength and courage'.

Nevertheless, the sacred work has its own distinctive qualities as a meditation on the naming of Jesus. The *name*, from the Old Testament to our fairy-tales (Rumpelstiltskin, for example!), is no chance attribute but, as it were, the key to its bearer. In this work it affords the occasion for a very personal conversation with Jesus. The echo aria, so far removed from our way of thinking, should thus be linked with the old practice of sacred dialogue composition and regarded as a 'Conversation between God and the Faithful Soul' ('Gespräch zwischen Gott und einer gläubigen Seele', Andreas Hammerschmidt, 1645). Bach's treatment of the chorale texts also exhibits very personal features. Verse 1 of the chorale *Jesu, du mein liebstes Leben* by Johann Rist (1642) is divided between nos. 38 and 40 and sung by solo soprano to a melody which is probably an original composition of Bach's. And even the closing chorale, no. 42, embedded in an impressive orchestral setting, is sung to an unknown melody, probably likewise composed by Bach himself.

Lobe den Herrn, meine Seele, BWV 143

NBA I/4, p. 167 BC T99 Duration: *c.* 14 mins

1. Coro SATB hn I–III timp bsn str bc — B♭ 3/4

'Lobe den Herrn, meine Seele.'	'Praise the Lord, O my soul.'

2. Choral S vln solo bc — B♭ C

Du Friedefürst, Herr Jesu Christ,	**You Prince of peace, Lord Jesus Christ,**
Wahr' Mensch und wahrer Gott,	**True man and true God,**
Ein starker Nothelfer du bist	**A strong helper in trouble are You,**
Im Leben und im Tod;	**In life and in death;**
Drum wir allein	**Therefore only**
Im Namen dein	**In Your Name**
Zu deinem Vater schreien.	**Do we cry to Your Father.**

3. Recitativo T bc — E♭–c C

'Wohl dem, des Hülfe der Gott Jakob ist, des Hoffnung auf dem Herrn, seinem Gotte, stehet.'	'Blessed is he whose help is the God of Jacob, whose hope is in the Lord, his God.'

4. Aria T str bc — c C

Tausendfaches Unglück, Schrecken,	A thousandfold misfortunes, fears,
Trübsal, Angst und schnellen Tod,	Tribulation, anguish, and sudden death,
Völker, die das Land bedecken,	Peoples who sweep over the land,
Sorgen und sonst noch mehr Not	Cares and still more adversities
Sehen andre Länder zwar,	Are indeed seen by other countries,
Aber wir ein Segensjahr.	But we see a year of blessings.

5. Aria B hn I–III timp bsn bc — B♭ 3/4

'Der Herr ist König ewiglich, dein Gott, Zion, für und für.'	'The Lord is King eternally, your God, O Zion, for ever and ever.'

6. Aria T bsn unis str bc — g C

Jesu, Retter deiner Herde,	O Jesus, deliverer of Your flock,
Bleibe ferner unser Hort,	Continue to be our refuge,
Daß dies Jahr uns glücklich werde,	That this year may be fortunate for us;
Halte Sakrament und Wort	Keep Your Sacrament and Word
Rein der ganzen Christenschar	Pure for the whole Christian host
Bis zu jenem neuen Jahr.	Until the next New Year.

7. Coro [+ Chorale] SATB hn I–III timp bsn str bc — B♭ 6/8

'Alleluja.'	'Alleluia.'
Gedenk, Herr, jetzund an dein Amt,	**Remember now, Lord, Your office,**
Daß du ein Friedfürst bist,	**That You are a Prince of peace,**
Und hilf uns gnädig allesamt	**And graciously help us altogether**
Jetzund zu dieser Frist;	**Now at this time;**
Laß uns hinfort	**Henceforth**
Dein göttlich Wort	**Let Your divine Word**
Im Fried noch länger schallen.	**Resound to us in peace still longer.**

The deficient transmission of this cantata, which survives only in a manuscript copy from the second half of the eighteenth century and its derivatives, leaves us with all sorts of puzzles; and doubts about its authenticity have been raised.[28] Its simple construction and the restriction of madrigalian* texts to two movements (nos. 4 and 6) both suggest that—presupposing its authenticity—it might be an early work from the period around 1708. The date proposed by Spitta and accepted by Schering for its first performance, namely New Year 1735, can, in any case, be ruled out on stylistic grounds, quite apart from the fact that on this occasion Part IV of the *Christmas Oratorio* was performed. Furthermore, it is doubtful whether we should really see in the text of the fourth movement—'A thousandfold misfortunes . . . are indeed seen by other countries, but we see a year of blessings'—an allusion to the dangers of war, as Spitta does, or whether such turns of phrase should not be counted among the armoury of homage formulas with which the prince of every realm was habitually honoured in the Baroque period, as long as the political situation did not all too convincingly prove the opposite.

The text, which reveals no connections with the readings of the day, consists largely of verses from Psalm 146, together with verses of the hymn *Du Friedefürst, Herr Jesu Christ* by Jakob Ebert (1601). Here is a summary:

No.	*Psalm 146*		*Du Friedefürst*		*Other*
1	v. 1				
2			v. 1		
3	v. 5				
4					free verse
5	v. 10a				
6			Instr. *CF*	+	free verse
7	v. 10b	+	v. 3		

Uniquely among the Bach works known to us, the instrumentation of the cantata includes three horns in addition to drums, strings, bassoon, and continuo. The work is perhaps a little colourless in invention, particularly the opening chorus* and the third movement; and the second movement displays little of the creative genius with which Bach was capable of embedding a soprano *cantus firmus** within instrumental figuration (as, for example, in Cantata 6). More exciting is the fourth movement, in which the 'misfortunes, fears, tribulation, anguish, and sudden death' of the text induce the composer to deploy some richer harmony. And the fifth movement delights by virtue of its scoring for

[28] By William H. Scheide in correspondence with the author and by Martin Geck, *Bach-Studien* 5 (Leipzig, 1975), p. 70, neither with detailed substantiation. On the basis of internal evidence and comparison with other Bach works, Klaus Hofmann concludes that such doubts are probably unfounded. See *BJ* 1997, 177–9, and K. Hofmann, 'Perfidia und Fanfare: zur Echtheit der Bach-Kantate "Lobe den Herrn, meine Seele" BWV 143', in B. Mohn and H. Ryschawy, eds, *Cari amici: Festschrift 25 Jahre Carus-Verlag* (Stuttgart, 1997), 34–43.

three horns and timpani, recalling 'Durch mächtige Kraft' from BWV 71, the Mühlhausen council election cantata of 1708 (which, however, has trumpets instead of horns), especially since the figure

which recurs several times (bb. 10, 27 and 29), resembles the setting of the opening words of that work, 'Gott ist mein König'.

The most charming movement, and the most characteristic of Bach, is no. 6, in which continuo and bassoon form a quasi-ostinato bass out of scale figures in complementary rhythms, over which the tenor sings his aria melody, while the chorale *Du Friedefürst, Herr Jesu Christ* is heard in unison strings. In the closing chorus, no. 7, verse 3 of the same chorale is sung by the soprano, while alto, tenor, and bass form a lively contrapuntal texture to the word 'Alleluia', surrounded and accompanied by instrumental figures. The instruments, however, neither participate in the substance of the chorale melody nor develop their own themes—a mode of composition that Bach scarcely used any more after 1714.

1.10 Sunday after New Year

Epistle: 1 Peter 4.12–19: The suffering of the Christian.
Gospel: Matthew 2.13–23: The flight into Egypt.

Schau, lieber Gott, wie meine Feind, BWV 153

NBA I/4, p. 201 BC A25 Duration: *c.* 15 mins

1. Choral SATB bc (+ str) a–e C

Schau, lieber Gott, wie meine Feind,	**See, dear God, how my enemies,**
Damit ich stets muß kämpfen,	**With whom I must constantly grapple,**
So listig und so mächtig seind,	**Are so cunning and so mighty**
Daß sie mich leichtlich dämpfen!	**That they easily subdue me!**
Herr, wo mich deine Gnad nicht hält,	**Lord, if Your grace does not hold me up,**
So kann der Teufel, Fleisch und Welt	**Devil, flesh, and world can**
Mich leicht in Unglück stürzen.	**Easily cast me into misfortune.**

2. Recitativo A bc a–b C

Mein liebster Gott, ach laß dichs doch erbarmen,	My beloved God, ah have mercy on me,

Ach hilf doch, hilf mir Armen!
Ich wohne hier bei lauter Löwen und bei Drachen,
Und diese wollen mir durch Wut und Grimmigkeit
In kurzer Zeit
Den Garaus völlig machen.

Ah, help, help poor me!
I dwell here among nothing but lions and dragons,
And these, through rage and ferocity,
In a short while,
Want to put an end to me completely.

3. Arioso B bc — e 3/8

'Fürchte dich nicht, ich bin mit dir.
Weiche nicht, ich bin dein Gott;
ich stärke dich, ich helfe dir auch durch
die rechte Hand meiner Gerechtigkeit.'

'Fear not, I am with you.
Do not yield, I am your God.
I will strengthen you; indeed, I will help you
with the right hand of my righteousness.'

4. Recitativo T bc — G–d C

Du sprichst zwar, lieber Gott, zu meiner Seelen Ruh
Mir einen Trost in meinen Leiden zu.
Ach, aber meine Plage
Vergrößert sich von Tag zu Tage,
Denn meiner Feinde sind so viel,
Mein Leben ist ihr Ziel,
Ihr Bogen wird auf mich gespannt,
Sie richten ihre Pfeile zum Verderben,
Ich soll von ihren Händen sterben;
Gott! meine Not ist dir bekannt,
Die ganze Welt wird mir zur Marterhöhle;
Hilf, Helfer, hilf! errette meine Seele!

True, You speak, dear God—for the peace of my soul—
A word of comfort to me in my suffering.
Ah, but my torment
Increases from day to day,
For my enemies are so many,
My life is their goal,
Their bows are bent,
They direct their arrows against me for destruction,
I shall die at their hands;
O God! my distress is known to You;
The whole world becomes to me a den of torture;
Help, O Helper, help! Deliver my soul!

5. Choral SATB bc (+ str) — e C

Und ob gleich alle Teufel
Dir wollten widerstehn,
So wird doch ohne Zweifel
Gott nicht zurücke gehn;
Was er ihm fürgenommen
Und was er haben will,
Das muß doch endlich kommen
Zu seinem Zweck und Ziel.

And though all the devils
Would resist you,
Yet without doubt
God will not retreat;
Whatever He has resolved
And whatever He would have
Must finally come
To His purpose and goal.

6. Aria T str bc — a C

Stürmt nur, stürmt, ihr Trübsalswetter,
Wallt, ihr Fluten, auf mich los!
Schlagt, ihr Unglücksflammen,
Über mich zusammen,
Stört, ihr Feinde, meine Ruh,

Storm then, storm, you whirlwind of tribulation!
Billow freely over me, you waterspouts!
Strike, you flames of misfortune,
Upon me altogether!
Disturb my repose, you enemies!

Spricht mir doch Gott tröstlich zu:	For God says to me comfortingly:
Ich bin dein Hort und Erretter.	I am your refuge and deliverer.
7. Recitativo B bc	F–C c
Getrost! mein Herz,	Be trusting, my heart!
Erdulde deinen Schmerz,	Endure your pain,
Laß dich dein Kreuz nicht unterdrücken!	Do not let your cross-bearing oppress you!
Gott wird dich schon	God will refresh you
Zu rechter Zeit erquicken;	At the proper time;
Muß doch sein lieber Sohn,	Indeed, His beloved Son,
Dein Jesus, in noch zarten Jahren	Your Jesus, when still of tender years,
Viel größre Not erfahren,	Had to undergo far greater woe
Da ihm der Wüterich Herodes	When the tyrant Herod threatened Him
Die äußerste Gefahr des Todes	With the utmost danger of death
Mit mörderischen Fäusten droht!	With his murderous fists!
Kaum kömmt er auf die Erden,	He had hardly come on earth
So muß er schon ein Flüchtling werden!	Before He had to become a fugitive!
Wohlan, mit Jesu tröste dich	Well then, comfort yourself with Jesus
Und glaube festiglich:	And believe firmly:
Denjenigen, die hier mit Christo leiden,	To those who suffer here with Christ
Will er das Himmelreich bescheiden.	He will grant the Kingdom of Heaven.
8. Aria A str bc	G $\frac{3}{4}$
Soll ich meinen Lebenslauf	Should I lead my life's course
Unter Kreuz und Trübsal führen,	Amidst cross-bearing and tribulation,
Hört es doch im Himmel auf.	It will nonetheless cease in heaven.
Da ist lauter Jubilieren,	There is pure jubilation;
Daselbsten verwechselt mein Jesus das Leiden	There my Jesus will exchange my suffering
Mit seliger Wonne, mit ewigen Freuden.	For blessed gladness, for eternal joys.
9. Choral SATB bc (+ str)	C $\frac{3}{4}$
Drum will ich, weil ich lebe noch,	**While I still live then, I will**
Das Kreuz dir fröhlich tragen nach;	**Gladly carry the cross, following You;**
Mein Gott, mach mich darzu bereit,	**My God, make me ready for it;**
Es dient zum Besten allezeit!	**It is for the best always!**
Hilf mir mein Sach recht greifen an,	**Help me to set about my affairs aright**
Daß ich mein' Lauf vollenden kann,	**So that I can complete the course of my life;**
Hilf mir auch zwingen Fleisch und Blut,	**Help me also to subdue flesh and blood;**
Für Sünd und Schanden mich behüt!	**Preserve me from sin and shame!**
Erhalt mein Herz im Glauben rein,	**Keep my heart pure in Faith**
So leb und sterb ich dir allein;	**So that I live and die to You alone;**
Jesu, mein Trost, hör mein Begier,	**Jesus, my comfort, hear my desire;**
O mein Heiland, wär ich bei dir!	**O my Saviour, would that I were with You!**

The anonymous librettist, whose text Bach set for 2 January 1724, takes the Gospel* reading about the flight into Egypt and Herod's Massacre of the Innocents as an opportunity to speak in general terms about the enemies of the Christian. In so doing, he draws near to the thinking of the Epistle.* The seventh movement contains direct references to the Gospel reading: whereas God's own Son already had to suffer 'when still of tender years', the Christian may confidently hope that his suffering will end one day and that God will open to him the Kingdom of Heaven. The text has in common with others of the same period (for example, those of Cantatas 40 and 64) its exceptionally large number of chorale verses. All these texts should probably be attributed to the same librettist.

The opening of Bach's setting is unorthodox: he begins not with one of his representative choruses* but with a plain four-part chorale, the first verse of the hymn by David Denicke of 1646. The cause of this is probably to be sought in external circumstances which may be readily explained. Since the Sunday after New Year in 1724 fell on 2 January, the pupils of the Thomasschule had had to sing Cantata 190 on the previous day, and this after their almost uninterrupted activity on the three Christmas feast-days. With the performance of Cantatas 63, 40, and 64, the Magnificat BWV 243a with its four Christmas insertions, and the Sanctus BWV 238 at the Thomascantor's first Christmas in his new post, the people of Leipzig were made familiar with a truly overwhelming wealth of new music, which imposed quite exceptional demands upon listeners and interpreters alike. On 2 January, however, Bach found it advisable to spare the productivity of the Thomasschule pupils, for in only four days' time, at Epiphany, they would have to perform Cantata 65, which opens with one of the most impressive choruses in Bach's entire output of cantatas.

In the present cantata, then, the choir is assigned only plain chorale settings, and the rest of the ensemble is restricted to three singers, strings, and continuo. The recitatives are throughout accompanied by continuo only, variety being introduced by the ariosos* that conclude the second and third (nos. 4 and 7). 'Arioso' is also the heading of the third movement, one of Bach's characteristic bass solos to biblical texts (here Isaiah 41.10), closely related to aria but seldom so called. The instrumental part, restricted to continuo as in the recitatives, begins with a short ritornello of eight bars, which not only frames the movement but is constantly heard as an accompaniment to the voice in various different transpositions (cadencing in e, e, b, D, e, and e).

The textual contrast between earthly suffering and heavenly comfort is most clearly reflected in the two arias. The image of our enemies charging in from all sides pervades the first aria, no. 6, which is marked by rapid violin passages and rushing unison strings, by taut dotted rhythms and bold harmonies. The second aria, on the other hand (no. 8), makes no pretence at being other than a minuet; indeed, it might have originated as the vocal version of a suite movement or as the parody* of a movement from a secular cantata. In the present context, however, it serves to describe the 'eternal joys' of the soul in heaven. As becomes a minuet, it is in binary dance form: each section is first stated by the instruments alone, after which the voice part is incorporated in its slightly expanded reprise. Only towards the end of the second reprise—at the words 'There my Jesus will exchange my suffering for blessed gladness, for eternal joys'—does a new 'allegro' theme enter, forming a spirited conclusion to the vocal part of the aria. Thereafter, the instruments take up the interrupted reprise once more, bringing it to an end in the form of a postlude.

Ach Gott, wie manches Herzeleid, BWV 58

NBA I/4, p. 219 BC A26 Duration: *c.* 17 mins

1. [Chorale + Aria] SB ob I,II taille str bc C $\frac{3}{4}$

Ach Gott, wie manches Herzeleid	**Ah God, how much heartbreak**
Nur Geduld, Geduld, mein Herze,	Just patience, patience, my heart,
Begegnet mir zu dieser Zeit!	**Do I encounter at this time!**
Es ist eine böse Zeit!	It is an evil time!
Der schmale Weg ist Trübsals voll,	**The narrow way is full of tribulation**
Doch der Gang zur Seligkeit	Yet the way of eternal Salvation
Den ich zum Himmel wandern soll.	**By which I must travel to heaven.**
Führt zur Freude nach dem Schmerze,	Leads to joy after pain;
Nur Geduld, Geduld, mein Herze,	Just patience, patience, my heart;
Es ist eine böse Zeit!	It is an evil time!

2. Recitativo B bc a–F c

Verfolgt dich gleich die arge Welt,	Though the evil world persecutes you,
So hast du dennoch Gott zum Freunde,	You nonetheless have God as your friend,
Der wider deine Feinde	Who against your enemies
Dir stets den Rücken hält.	Always holds the rear.
Und wenn der wütende Herodes	And though the furious Herod
Das Urteil eines schmähen Todes	Passes a sentence of ignominious death
Gleich über unsern Heiland fällt,	Upon our Saviour,
So kommt ein Engel in der Nacht,	An angel comes in the night,
Der lässet Joseph träumen,	Who lets Joseph dream
Daß er dem Würger soll entfliehen	That he should flee from the murderer
Und nach Ägypten ziehen.	And go to Egypt.
Gott hat ein Wort, das dich vertrauend macht.	God has a word that makes you trusting;
Er spricht: Wenn Berg und Hügel niedersinken,	He says: though mountain and hill sink down,
Wenn dich die Flut des Wassers will ertrinken,	Though flood waters would drown you,
So will ich dich doch nicht verlassen noch versäumen.	Yet I will surely neither leave nor forsake you.

3. ARIA S vln solo bc — d c

Ich bin vergnügt in meinem Leiden,	I am content with my suffering,
Denn Gott ist meine Zuversicht.	For God is my confidence.
Ich habe sichern Brief und Siegel,	I have it under secure hand and seal,
Und dieses ist der feste Riegel,	And this is a strengthened bar
Den bricht die Hölle selber nicht.	That even Hell cannot break.

4. RECITATIVO S bc — F–a c

Kann es die Welt nicht lassen,	Though the world cannot desist
Mich zu verfolgen und zu hassen,	From persecuting and hating me,
So weist mir Gottes Hand	Yet God's hand shows me
Ein andres Land.	Another land.
Ach! könnt es heute noch geschehen,	Ah! if only it could happen this very day
Daß ich mein Eden möchte sehen!	That I might see my Eden!

5. [CHORALE + ARIA] SB ob I,II taille str bc — C 2/4

Ich hab für mir ein schwere Reis	**I have a hard journey before me**
Nur getrost, getrost, ihr Herzen,	Just be of good cheer, you hearts,
Zu dir ins Himmels Paradeis,	**To You in heavenly Paradise;**
Hier ist Angst, dort Herrlichkeit!	Here is anguish, there glory!
Da ist mein rechtes Vaterland,	**There is my true fatherland,**
Und die Freude jener Zeit	And the joy of that time
Daran du dein Blut hast gewandt.	**On which You have spent Your Blood.**
Überwieget alle Schmerzen.	Outweighs all sorrows.
Nur getrost, getrost, ihr Herzen,	Just be of good cheer, you hearts:
Hier ist Angst, dort Herrlichkeit!	Here is anguish, there glory!

The anonymous libretto of this cantata adheres even more closely to the Sunday Gospel* than that of Cantata 153, composed a few years earlier. And since the Epistle* deals with the suffering of the Christian, it is natural that close connections in ideas are established with that reading also. As in the cantata considered above, temporal suffering is contrasted with heavenly joy. And in the second movement, the whole Gospel account of the flight into Egypt is briefly reiterated before becoming the subject of a topical re-interpretation in the fourth: even if the world hates me, God will one day lead me into another land, the land of eternal salvation. The two outer movements, nos. 1 and 5, correspond with one another: in both cases, a chorale verse—in no. 1, the first verse of the hymn *Ach Gott, wie manches Herzeleid* by Martin Moller (1587); in no. 5, the second verse of the hymn *O Jesu Christ, meins Lebens Licht* by Martin Behm (1610), both sung to the same melody—is combined with a freely versified text, which has the same strophic structure in each movement. Presumably, the librettist envisaged that both texts would be set to the same music, which is not the case in Bach's composition.

The cantata was probably composed for 5 January 1727. However, it survives only in a revised version of 1733 or 1734, whose main characteristics are the addition of three oboes (the third being a taille* or tenor oboe) to the outer movements and the complete replacement of the middle movement, no. 3. Of the original third movement only a continuo part survives, and therefore we do not know whether the existing text corresponds with the original text, or whether that, too, was changed. What induced Bach to rewrite the movement can only be conjectured. As in Cantata 153, written three years earlier, it seems to have been Bach's intention in the first version to ease the burden on musicians exhausted by festive demands, which would explain why he forgoes wind instruments, alto and tenor voices, and choral music. For the revival, conditions may have been somewhat more favourable. Here, the strings and the soprano *cantus firmus** are, in the outer movements, reinforced by oboes, which play or rest depending on the pitch of the part concerned; and it is possible that the newly composed soprano aria was designed to replace a simpler predecessor.

In the definitive ordering of his annual cycles of cantatas, Bach assigned this work to the chorale cantatas* (Cycle II), although it does not really belong to them: the texts of the inner movements are not hymn paraphrases, nor are the hymn verses of the outer movements drawn from the same chorale. Owing to the structure of these outer movements, however, the work acts as an adequate replacement for a *missing* chorale cantata.

The opening movement, which is marked 'adagio', takes the form of a chorale arrangement: the chorale melody lies in the soprano, reinforced by the third oboe or taille.* It is also a duet, however, for the bass delivers the freely versified text in the form of a concertante* counterpoint* to the chorale melody, and with his vocal part he links the four chorale lines in two pairs. The instrumental ritornello, whose three statements frame the two vocal passages, only distantly resembles the chorale melody. It is characterized by the dotted rhythms that pervade the entire movement and, no less significantly, by a chromatically* falling lament figure, heard at the outset in the continuo and later in the upper parts too:

A *secco* recitative leads to the soprano aria with obbligato* violin, no. 3—the movement that survives complete only in its later, substitute version. Here, the lively violin figures form a marked contrast to the predominantly *cantabile*, almost song-like soprano part. The following recitative, no. 4, flows, after only four bars, into an arioso*—'Ah! if only it could happen this very day!'—which, in compelling melodic style, gives expression to the yearning of the soul for redemption from the sufferings of this world.

The finale is an overtly concerto-like chorale arrangement, equivalent in form and scoring to the opening movement. The triadic fanfare at the beginning is reminiscent of the opening of Bach's E major Violin Concerto, BWV 1042. As in that work, it acts as an oft-recurring motive,* pervading the entire movement. At the beginning of the bass part it is set to the words 'Nur getrost' ('Just be of good cheer'):

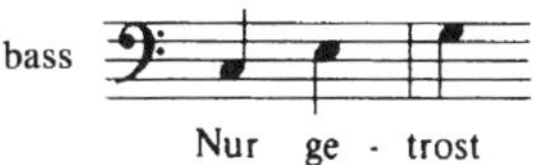

And, delivered by the continuo in syncopated form, it serves as bass to the concertante figuration of the oboe and first violin.

In his score, Bach at first assigned the free vocal part of the first movement to the alto. Only when writing out the parts did he give it instead to the bass, the traditional *vox Christi*. There can be no mistake, therefore, that this cantata is to be numbered among the successors of the seventeenth-century dialogue compositions as a 'Dialogue of the Faithful Soul with God'.

Ehre sei dir, Gott, gesungen
Weihnachts-Oratorium Christmas Oratorio, BWV 248, Part V

NBA II/6, p. 201 BC $D7^{V}$ Duration: *c.* 26 mins

43. Coro SATB ob d'am I,II str bc — A 3/4

Ehre sei dir, Gott, gesungen,	Let honour be sung to You, O God,
Dir sei Lob und Dank bereit'.	To You let praise and thanks be prepared.
Dich erhebet alle Welt,	All the world exalts You
Weil dir unser Wohl gefällt,	Because our welfare pleases You,
Weil anheut	Because this day
Unser aller Wunsch gelungen,	Our every wish has come true,
Weil uns dein Segen so herrlich erfreut.	Because Your Blessing so greatly delights us.

44. Evangelista T bc — f♯–b c

'Da Jesus geboren war zu Bethlehem im jüdischen Lande zur Zeit des Königes Herodis, siehe, da kamen die Weisen vom Morgenlande gen Jerusalem und sprachen:'	'When Jesus was born in Bethlehem in the Judaean land at the time of King Herod, see, there came Wise Men from the East to Jerusalem, saying:'

45. Chor + Recitativo SATB ob d'am I,II str bc — b–f♯ c

'Wo ist der neugeborne König der Jüden?'	'Where is the newborn King of the Jews?'

Alt
Sucht ihn in meiner Brust,
Hier wohnt er, mir und ihm zur Lust!
'Wir haben seinen Stern gesehen im Morgenlande und sind kommen, ihn anzubeten.'
Alt
Wohl euch, die ihr dies Licht gesehen,
Es ist zu eurem Heil geschehen!
Mein Heiland, du, du bist das Licht,
Das auch den Heiden scheinen sollen,
Und sie, sie kennen dich noch nicht,
Als sie dich schon verehren wollen.
Wie hell, wie klar muß nicht dein Schein,
Geliebter Jesu, sein!

Alto
Seek Him in my breast,
Here He dwells, to my delight and His!
'We have seen His Star in the East and have come to worship Him.'
Alto
Blessed are you who have seen this Light;
It has come about for your Salvation!
My Saviour, You, You are the Light
Which shall also shine on the Gentiles,
And they: they do not yet know You,
Though they would already worship You.
How bright, how clear must Your lustre be,
Beloved Jesus!

46. CHORAL SATB bc (+ instrs) — A C

Dein Glanz all Finsternis verzehrt,
Die trübe Nacht in Licht verkehrt.
Leit uns auf deinen Wegen,
Daß dein Gesicht
Und herrlichs Licht
Wir ewig schauen mögen!

Your radiance consumes all darkness
And turns gloomy night into Light.
Lead us in Your ways,
That Your Countenance
And splendid Light
May ever be seen by us!

47. ARIA B ob d'am I solo bc — f♯ $\frac{2}{4}$

Erleucht auch meine finstre Sinnen,
Erleuchte mein Herze
Durch der Strahlen klaren Schein!
Dein Wort soll mir die hellste Kerze
In allen meinen Werken sein;
Dies lässet die Seele nichts Böses beginnen.

Illuminate also my dark thoughts,
Illuminate my heart
Through the clear light of Your rays!
Your Word shall be the brightest candle
To me in all my deeds;
This lets the soul embark on nothing wicked.

48. EVANGELISTA T bc — A–c♯ C

'Da das der König Herodes hörte, erschrack er und mit ihm das ganze Jerusalem.'

'When King Herod heard this, he was afraid, and with him the whole of Jerusalem.'

49. RECITATIVO A str bc — c♯–E C

Warum wollt ihr erschrecken?
Kann meines Jesu Gegenwart
Euch solche Furcht erwecken?
O! solltet ihr euch nicht
Vielmehr darüber freuen,
Weil er dadurch verspricht,
Der Menschen Wohlfahrt zu verneuen.

Why are you afraid?
Can the presence of my Jesus
Arouse such fear in you?
Oh! should you not
Rather rejoice over it?
For He promises thereby
To restore the well-being of mankind.

50. EVANGELISTA T bc E–b c

'Und ließ versammlen alle Hohepriester und Schriftgelehrten unter dem Volk und erforschete von ihnen, wo Christus sollte geboren werden. Und sie sagten ihm: Zu Bethlehem im jüdischen Lande; denn also stehet geschrieben durch den Propheten: Und du Bethlehem im jüdischen Lande bist mitnichten die kleinest unter den Fürsten Juda; denn aus dir soll mir kommen der Herzog, der über mein Volk Israel ein Herr sei.'

'And he assembled all the high-priests and scribes among the people and demanded of them where Christ should be born. And they said to him: in Bethlehem in the Judaean land; for it is written thus by the prophet: and you, Bethlehem in the Judaean land, are not the least among the princes of Judah; for out of you shall come the Sovereign to me, who shall be a ruler over my people Israel.'

51. ARIA TERZETTO SAT vln I solo bc b 2/4

Ach, wenn wird die Zeit erscheinen?
Ach, wenn kömmt der Trost der
Seinen?
Schweigt: er ist schon würklich hier!
Jesu, ach! so komm zu mir!

Ah, when will the time appear?
Ah, when will His people's comfort
arrive?
Be silent: He is in truth already here!
Jesus, ah! then come to me!

52. RECITATIVO A ob d'am I,II bc f♯–A c

Mein Liebster herrschet schon.
Ein Herz, das seine Herrschaft liebet
Und sich ihm ganz zu eigen gibet,
Ist meines Jesu Thron.

My Beloved rules already.
A heart that loves His dominion
And gives itself to Him all as His own
Is my Jesus's throne.

53. CHORAL SATB bc (+ instrs) A c

Zwar ist solche Herzensstube
Wohl kein schöner Fürstensaal,
Sondern eine finstre Grube;
Doch, sobald dein Gnadenstrahl
In denselben nur wird blinken,
Wird es voller Sonnen dünken.

Indeed such a heart's chamber is
Certainly no fine prince's hall,
But rather a dark pit;
Yet as soon as Your beam of Grace
But gleams within it,
It will seem full of sunlight.

Whereas the two surviving cantatas for this Sunday, nos. 153 and 58, are closely modelled on the pericopes of the day, Part V of the *Christmas Oratorio* already anticipates the first half of the Epiphany Gospel.* For, since the six parts of the oratorio* are conceived as a cyclical whole, importance had to be attached to the correct order in the recounting of events. Thus the flight into Egypt—in so far as it was to be included in the oratorio—would have to be narrated after the adoration of the Wise Men from the East. The central focus of Part V is therefore the Star, the light 'which shall also shine on the Gentiles' and whose 'radiance consumes all darkness', together with the prayer that our own heart may also be illuminated, and finally the recognition that the awaited King of Israel has already entered upon His sovereignty.

Bach's renunciation of large-scale instrumentation—already observed in the cantatas for this Sunday—may also be seen in this part of the oratorio, though to a much lesser extent. Admittedly, the work includes a large-scale introductory chorus,* but brass and flutes are absent, and only two oboes (d'amore*) are required. As far as scoring is concerned, then, this part is the most modest in the whole oratorio.

Bach dropped his original plan of reusing an older composition for the opening chorus (the gavotte-like finale of Cantata 213) and, in its place, invented a new chorus with a captivating swing. Its thematic material grows out of a head-motive (expanded in antiphonal exchanges between oboes and strings) and its continuation, which unites concertante* string figuration with syncopated motives* in the oboes. This concertante opening chorus is contrasted with the motet-like chorus on biblical words, 'Wo ist der neugeborne König der Jüden?' ('Where is the newborn King of the Jews?'), no. 45, with its troping recitative insertions.

The two arias from Part V are probably both based on older compositions. The model of the first, no. 47, is known: it is the seventh movement of Cantata 215 in a radically revised form. The model of the second aria, the terzetto no. 51, is unknown, and our conjecture regarding its origin is founded solely on the distinctly fair-copy character of the piece in Bach's autograph score. Yet it is in this very movement that the text is most effectively set, for the syncopations in which the alto is heard on the repeated word 'Schweigt!' ('Be silent!') point to the Johannine understanding that Jesus has already long since entered upon His sovereignty—'He is in truth already here!'. The closing chorale (and here we may perhaps detect another frugal measure) is the only one in all six parts of the oratorio to be set simply as a plain four-part harmonization.

1.11 Epiphany

Epistle: Isaiah 60.1–6: The Gentiles shall be converted.
Gospel: Matthew 2.1–12: The Wise Men from the East.

Sie werden aus Saba alle kommen, BWV 65

NBA I/5, p. 3 BC A27 Duration: *c.* 18 mins

1. [Chorus] SATB hn I,II rec I,II ob da c I,II str bc — C $\frac{12}{8}$

'Sie werden aus Saba alle kommen, Gold und Weihrauch bringen und des Herren Lob verkündigen.'	'They will all come out of Sheba, bearing gold and incense and proclaiming the Lord's praise.'

2. Choral SATB bc (+ instrs) — a $\frac{3}{4}$

Die Kön'ge aus Saba kamen dar, **Gold, Weihrauch, Myrrhen brachten sie dar,** **Alleluja, alleluja!**	**The Kings came out of Sheba,** **Bringing gold, incense, and myrrh.** **Alleluia, alleluia!**

3. RECITATIVO B bc	F–G 𝄴
Was dort Jesaias vorhergesehn,	What Isaiah had there foreseen
Das ist zu Bethlehem geschehn.	Has happened in Bethlehem.
Hier stellen sich die Weisen	Here the Wise Men appear
Bei Jesu Krippen ein	At Jesus's crib
Und wollen ihn als ihren König preisen.	And would praise Him as their King.
Gold, Weihrauch, Myrrhen sind	Gold, incense and myrrh are
Die köstlichen Geschenke,	The costly gifts
Womit sie dieses Jesuskind	With which they honour this Child Jesus
Zu Bethlehem im Stall beehren.	At Bethlehem in the stable.
Mein Jesu, wenn ich itzt an meine Pflicht gedenke,	My Jesus, if I now remember my duty,
Muß ich mich auch zu deiner Krippen kehren	I too must turn to Your crib
Und gleichfalls dankbar sein:	And likewise be grateful,
Denn dieser Tag ist mir ein Tag der Freuden,	For today is to me a day of joy,
Da du, o Lebensfürst,	When You, O Prince of Life,
Das Licht der Heiden	Become the Light of the Gentiles
Und ihr Erlöser wirst.	And their Redeemer.
Was aber bring ich wohl, du Himmelskönig?	But what do I bring, You heavenly King?
Ist dir mein Herze nicht zuwenig,	If my heart is not too small for You,
So nimm es gnädig an,	Then accept it graciously,
Weil ich nichts Edlers bringen kann.	For I can bring nothing nobler.
4. ARIA B ob da c I,II bc	e 𝄴
Gold aus Ophir ist zu schlecht,	Gold from Ophir is too poor;
Weg, nur weg mit eitlen Gaben,	Away, away with idle gifts
Die ihr aus der Erde brecht!	Which you break out of the earth!
Jesus will das Herze haben.	Jesus would have your heart.
Schenke dies, o Christenschar,	Give this, O Christian host,
Jesu zu dem neuen Jahr!	To Jesus for the New Year!
5. RECITATIVO T bc	a–e 𝄴
Verschmähe nicht,	Do not disdain,
Du meiner Seele Licht,	You Light of my soul,
Mein Herz, das ich in Demut zu dir bringe.	My heart, which I bring You in humility.
Es schließt ja solche Dinge	It indeed includes such things—
In sich zugleich mit ein,	At the same time—
Die deines Geistes Früchte sein.	As are the fruits of Your Spirit.
Des Glaubens Gold, der Weihrauch des Gebets,	The gold of Faith, the incense of prayer,
Die Myrrhen der Geduld sind meine Gaben,	The myrrh of patience are my gifts,

Die sollst du, Jesu, für und für
Zum Eigentum und zum Geschenke haben.
Gib aber dich auch selber mir,
So machst du mich zum Reichsten auf der Erden;
Denn, hab ich dich, so muß
Des größten Reichtums Überfluß
Mir dermaleinst im Himmel werden.

Which You shall have, Jesus, for ever and ever
As Your property and gift.
But give Yourself to me too,
Then You will make me the richest on earth;
For if I have You, then
The greatest wealth's abundance
Must become mine hereafter in heaven.

6. [Aria] T hn I,II rec I,II ob da c I,II str bc — C $\frac{3}{8}$

Nimm mich dir zu eigen hin,
Nimm mein Herze zum Geschenke.
Alles, alles, was ich bin,
Was ich rede, tu und denke,
Soll, mein Heiland, nur allein
Dir zum Dienst gewidmet sein.

Accept me as Your own,
Accept my heart as a gift.
All, all that I am,
Whatever I say, do and think
Shall, my Saviour, be dedicated
To Your service alone.

7. Choral SATB bc (+ instrs) — a C

Ei nun, mein Gott, so fall ich dir
Getrost in deine Hände.
Nimm mich, und mach es so mit mir
Bis an mein letztes Ende,
Wie du wohl weißt, daß meinem Geist
Dadurch sein Nutz entstehe,
Und deine Ehr je mehr und mehr
Sich in mir selbst erhöhe.

Ah! now, then, my God, I fall
Confidently into Your hands.
Take me, and make it so with me,
Till my final end,
As You know best, so that my spirit
May derive profit therefrom,
And Your honour may more and more
Be exalted in me.

The unknown librettist of this cantata, who perhaps also wrote the texts for Cantatas 40, 64, and several others, combines ideas from the Epistle* and Gospel* for the Feast of the Epiphany. The opening words, 'They will all come out of Sheba', are drawn from the end of the Epistle (Isaiah 60.6); and the chorale that follows—the fourth verse of the German version of the hymn *Puer natus in Bethlehem* (1545)—reiterates the substance of the Gospel reading and also makes the Old Testament prophecy of the Epistle appear as fulfilled: the Kings come out of Sheba bearing gold, frankincense, and myrrh, just as Isaiah had foreseen. The first half of the following recitative clearly articulates this prophetic fulfilment, and the second half brings its application to the contemporary Christian: I too am obliged to turn to the crib and offer my heart as a gift to the Redeemer. This idea, first put forward as a reflection in the recitative, is then given in the form of a demand in the aria: gold from Ophir—the land from which Solomon once brought 420 talents of gold (1 Kings 9.28)—is too poor, and therefore Christians should give their hearts to the Saviour for the New Year. The following recitative brings compliance with this demand: faith is the gold, prayer the incense, and patience the myrrh that Jesus receives as a gift. Once again the reflection of the recitative is followed by a call in the aria, 'Accept me as Your own'. The closing chorale—transmitted without text, but probably intended as the tenth verse of the hymn *Ich hab in Gottes Herz und Sinn* by Paul Gerhardt (1647)—acts as a symbol of the unanimity in this wish of the whole of Christendom.

As a whole, then, the text exhibits a well thought-out structure: in pairs of movements, it first reiterates the underlying ideas of the reading in the form of prophecy and fulfilment (nos. 1 and 2), then in reflection and resolution demands that Jesus be given our heart (nos. 3 and 4), and finally offers this gift in reality in the form of a vow (nos. 5 and 6), which is confirmed when the whole Christian congregation subscribes to it (no. 7).

In its rich scoring, Bach's setting reflects the significance that was then attached to the Feast of the Epiphany. Once more, Bach lets us hear the splendour of the festive Christmas orchestra, and in the opening chorus* he paints an impressive picture of the crowds of Gentiles flocking past. Canonic and fugal devices keep bringing before the eyes of the listener the increasing size of the worshipping multitude. The movement is tripartite: an extended choral fugue* is framed by two outer sections in which elements of the opening instrumental introduction are subject to choral insertion.* This large-scale opening chorus is followed by a plain chorale for choir and instruments, no. 2, and a *secco* recitative, no. 3. The following bass aria, no. 4, is notable not only for its scoring with two obbligato* oboes da caccia,* but also for the constant repetition of its initial motive,* which gives the impression that the instruments (including continuo) keep saying to each other, 'Gold from Ophir is too poor'.

Another *secco* recitative, no. 5, leads to the second aria, no. 6, whose joyful prayer 'Accept me as Your own' is underlined by music of a distinctly dance-like character. As in the first aria, Bach forgoes conventional da capo* form and, disregarding the textual structure, produces two corresponding *Stollen**—A ('Nimm mich dir zu eigen hin') and A^1 ('Alles, alles, was ich bin')—so that the musically independent third section, textually a repeat of the second, is conceived as an *Abgesang.** The resulting *Bar* form* reinforces the song- and dance-like impression of the movement. A plain chorale setting, to the melody *Was mein Gott will, das g'scheh allzeit*, concludes the work.

Bach composed this cantata during his first year in Leipzig and performed it for the first time on 6 January 1724. A Christmas season herewith came to an end during which the Magnificat BWV 243a, the Sanctus in D, BWV 238, and six cantatas—almost all newly composed—were heard in Leipzig for the first time within a period of thirteen days. One wonders whether the people of Leipzig truly appreciated what riches had been unveiled before them.

Liebster Immanuel, Herzog der Frommen, BWV 123

NBA I/5, p. 49 BC A28 Duration: *c.* 22 mins

1. [Chorus] SATB fl I,II ob d'am I,II str bc b $\frac{9}{8}$

Liebster Immanuel, Herzog der Frommen,	**Beloved Emmanuel, Prince of the devout,**
Du, meiner Seelen Heil, komm, komm nur bald!	**You, my soul's Salvation, come, come soon!**
Du hast mir, höchster Schatz, mein Herz genommen,	**You, highest treasure, have ravished my heart,**
So ganz vor Liebe brennt und nach dir wallt.	**Which quite burns and throbs with love for You.**
Nichts kann auf Erden	**Nothing on earth can**
Mir liebers werden,	**Become dearer to me**
Als wenn ich meinen Jesum stets behalt.	**Than if I always keep my Jesus.**

2. Recitativo A bc f♯–A c

Die Himmelssüßigkeit, der Auserwählten Lust,	Heavenly sweetness, the delight of the chosen
Erfüllt auf Erden schon mein Herz und Brust,	Already on earth fills my heart and breast
Wenn ich den Jesusnamen nenne	When I call the Name of Jesus
Und sein verborgnes Manna kenne:	And know His hidden Manna:
Gleichwie der Tau ein dürres Land erquickt,	Just as the dew refreshes a dry land,
So ist mein Herz	So is my heart,
Auch bei Gefahr und Schmerz	Even in danger and pain,
In Freudigkeit durch Jesu Kraft entzückt.	Transported into joyfulness through Jesus's power.

3. Aria T ob d'am I,II bc f♯ c

Auch die harte Kreuzesreise	Even the hard journey of the cross
Und der Tränen bittre Speise	And the bitter food of tears
Schreckt mich nicht.	Do not frighten me.
Wenn die Ungewitter toben,	When storms rage
Sendet Jesus mir von oben	Jesus sends me from above
Heil und Licht.	Salvation and Light.

4. Recitativo B bc A–D c

Kein Höllenfeind kann mich verschlingen,	No Sheol enemy can swallow me,
Das schreiende Gewissen schweigt.	My crying conscience is silent.
Was sollte mich der Feinde Zahl umringen?	How should the enemy's numbers surround me?
Der Tod hat selbsten keine Macht,	Death itself has no power,
Mir aber ist der Sieg schon zugedacht,	But victory is already intended for me,
Weil sich mein Helfer mir, mein Jesus, zeigt.	For my Helper, my Jesus, shows Himself to me.

5. Aria B fl I solo bc — D C

Laß, o Welt, mich aus Verachtung
In betrübter Einsamkeit!
Jesus, der ins Fleisch gekommen
Und mein Opfer angenommen,
Bleibet bei mir allezeit.

Out of contempt, leave me, O world,
In distressed solitude!
Jesus, who has come in the flesh
And accepted my offering,
Remains with me always.

6. Choral SATB bc (+ instrs) — b $\frac{3}{2}$

Drum fahrt nur immer hin, ihr Eitelkeiten,
Du, Jesu, du bist mein, und ich bin dein;
Ich will mich von der Welt zu dir bereiten;
Du sollt in meinem Herz und Munde sein.
Mein ganzes Leben
Sei dir ergeben.
Bis man mich einsten legt ins Grab hinein.

Therefore depart for ever, you vanities;
You, Jesus, You are mine and I am Yours;
I will prepare to depart from the world to You;
You shall be in my heart and mouth.
May my entire life
Be surrendered to You,
Till one day I am laid in the grave.

This chorale cantata,* first performed on 6 January 1725, has only a very loose connection with the Feast of the Epiphany. As usual, the outer verses of the hymn (nos. 1 and 6), by Ahasverus Fritsch (1679), were retained literally, the inner verses being paraphrased to form a movement each. The inclusion of the word 'Jesusnamen' ('the Name of Jesus') in the second movement may have been a recollection of the Gospel* for New Year's Day. 'Heil und Licht' ('Salvation and Light') in the third movement—another addition to Fritsch's hymn—is reminiscent of the Epistle* for Epiphany. And 'Jesus, der ins Fleisch gekommen' ('Jesus, who has come in the flesh') from the fifth movement reminds us of the Christmas season which is now drawing to a close. But with this the *de tempore** references are exhausted. For the rest, the cantata text, like the hymn on which it is based, derives its substance from the World—Jesus contrast: the world's hostility and contempt cannot do me any harm, for Jesus stands at my side.

In the opening chorus,* the instruments assume the chief responsibility for thematic development. From the beginning of the first chorale line:

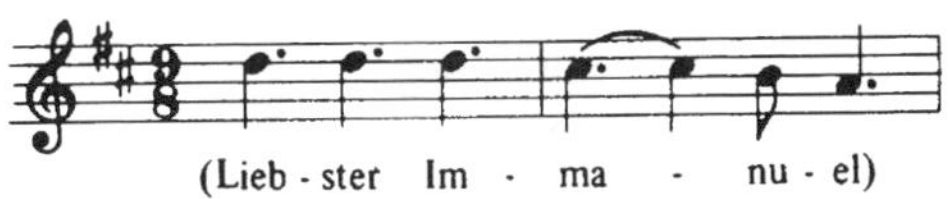

Bach derives a twenty-bar instrumental prelude (with a central section that lacks continuo, unison strings furnishing the bass-line) in which the instrumental groups constantly exchange the chorale motive.* Thereafter, the same motive pervades not only the episodes but the instrumental counterpoint* played against the voices in the choral passages. The choir delivers the chorale, line by line, in a remarkably homophonic* texture, only slightly breaking up into polyphony.* This plainness is discarded in only two places, one of which is repeated. First, on the final held note of line 4 of the soprano *cantus firmus*,* the words 'komm nur bald!' ('come soon!') are repeatedly and eloquently called out by the lower parts; a corresponding passage at the same place in the second *Stollen** seems less convincing, being set to the words 'und nach dir wallt' ('and throbs for You'). Second, the text of the last line is sung to the beginning of the first line of the melody, quoted above, first by the bass alone, and then by alto and tenor in counterpoint with the soprano *cantus firmus*, which establishes a unifying link between the first and last chorale lines. The entire opening chorus has a distinctively intimate and meditative character. Already perceptible in Fritsch's hymn, this can probably be traced back to early Pietist influences.

The two recitatives, nos. 2 and 4, set as *secco*, present no special features. More striking is the first aria, no. 3, whose text, which deals with the 'hard journey of the cross', gives rise to a powerfully chromatic* ritornello—interfused with augmented intervals—which constantly modulates within its brief extent of four bars and, with its motivic material, determines the character of the principal vocal section. The ritornello at the end of this section, perhaps motivated by the words 'Schreckt mich nicht' ('Do not frighten me'), has surprisingly calmer movement in the upper parts and a statement of the chromatic theme in the continuo. In the middle section, however, opposing forces are aroused: it contains internal contrasts, starting 'allegro' with new motives and rapid vocal passages at the words 'When storms rage', and then suddenly changing at the words 'Jesus sends me from above Salvation and Light' to an emphatically tranquil 'adagio' tempo. The appearance of the 'Light'—present in our thoughts at the Feast of the Epiphany—is thus made prominent more by musical than by textual means.

From a formal point of view, the second aria, no. 5, follows more conventional lines. The phrase 'In betrübter Einsamkeit' ('In distressed solitude'), however, provides the opportunity for some charming harmonic twists. The plain four-part closing chorale ends with an idiosyncrasy: unlike in the first movement, Bach repeats not only the *Stollen* but also the *Abgesang*,* sung ***p***, no doubt with the last line in mind, 'Till one day I am laid in the grave'. Such *piano* endings are not quite so rare in Bach's works as today's performances suggest: they are found not only in early cantatas such as BWV 106 and 71 but also in Cantata 68 of 1725.

Herr, wenn die stolzen Feinde schnauben
Weihnachts-Oratorium Christmas Oratorio, BWV 248, Part VI

NBA II/6, p. 245 BC $D7^{VI}$ Duration: *c.* 25 mins

54. CHORUS SATB tr I–III timp ob I,II str bc — D 3/8

Herr, wenn die stolzen Feinde schnauben,	Lord, when our insolent enemies snort,
So gib, daß wir im festen Glauben	Grant that in steadfast Faith
Nach deiner Macht und Hülfe sehn!	We may look to Your strength and help!
Wir wollen dir allein vertrauen,	We would trust You alone;
So können wir den scharfen Klauen	Then we can escape the sharp claws
Des Feindes unversehrt entgehn.	Of the enemy unhurt.

55. EVANGELISTA TB bc — A–D C

Evangelista	*Evangelist*
'Da berief Herodes die Weisen heimlich und erlernet mit Fleiß von ihnen, wenn der Stern erschienen wäre? Und weiset sie gen Bethlehem und sprach:'	'Then Herod summoned the Wise Men secretly and learnt from them diligently when the Star would have appeared. And he directed them to Bethlehem and said:'
Herodes	*Herod*
'Ziehet hin und forschet fleißig nach dem Kindlein, und wenn ihrs findet, sagt mirs wieder, daß ich auch komme und es anbete.'	'Go there and inquire diligently after the little Child, and when you find Him, bring me word, that I may come too and worship Him.'

56. RECITATIVO S str bc — b–A C

Du Falscher, suche nur den Herrn zu fällen,	False one, you seek only to bring the Lord down,
Nimm alle falsche List,	Use every false artifice
Dem Heiland nachzustellen;	To waylay the Saviour;
Der, dessen Kraft kein Mensch ermißt,	He whose power no man estimates
Bleibt doch in sichrer Hand.	Yet remains in safe hands.
Dein Herz, dein falsches Herz ist schon,	Your heart, your false heart,
Nebst aller seiner List, des Höchsten Sohn,	With all its cunning, is to the Highest's Son,
Den du zu stürzen suchst, sehr wohl bekannt.	Whom you seek to cast down, already very well known.

57. ARIA S ob d'am I str bc — A 3/4

Nur ein Wink von seinen Händen	Just a wave of His hands
Stürzt ohnmächtger Menschen Macht.	Casts down the powerless strength of man.
Hier wird alle Kraft verlacht!	Here all power is derided!
Spricht der Höchste nur ein Wort,	If the Highest says but one word
Seiner Feinde Stolz zu enden,	To end the pride of His enemies,
O, so müssen sich sofort	Oh, then at once must
Sterblicher Gedanken wenden.	Mortal men's thoughts change.

58. EVANGELISTA T bc — f♯–G c

'Als sie nun den König gehöret hatten, zogen sie hin. Und siehe, der Stern, den sie im Morgenlande gesehen hatten, ging für ihnen hin, bis daß er kam und stund oben über, da das Kindlein war. Da sie den Stern sahen, wurden sie hoch erfreuet und gingen in das Haus und funden das Kindlein mit Maria, seiner Mutter, und fielen nieder und beteten es an und täten ihre Schätze auf und schenkten ihm Gold, Weihrauch und Myrrhen.'	'When they had heard the king, they went away. And look, the Star, which they had seen in the East, went before them, till it came and stood over where the little Child was. When they saw the Star, they rejoiced greatly and went into the house and found the little Child with Mary, His mother, and fell down and worshipped Him and opened their treasures and gave Him gold, frankincense, and myrrh.'

59. CHORAL SATB bc (+ ww str) — G c

Ich steh an deiner Krippen hier, **O Jesulein, mein Leben!** **Ich komme, bring und schenke dir,** **Was du mir hast gegeben.** **Nimm hin! es ist mein Geist und Sinn,** **Herz, Seel und Mut, nimm alles hin,** **Und laß dirs wohlgefallen!**	**I stand here at Your crib,** **O little Jesus, my Life!** **I come, bring, and give You** **What You have given to me.** **Take it! It is my spirit and mind,** **Heart, soul, and courage: take it all** **And let it please You well!**

60. EVANGELISTA T bc — e–f♯ c

'Und Gott befahl ihnen im Traum, daß sie sich nicht sollten wieder zu Herodes lenken, und zogen durch einen andern Weg wieder in ihr Land.'	'And God commanded them in a dream that they should not return to Herod, and they departed by another route back to their own land.'

61. RECITATIVO T ob d'am I,II bc — f♯–b c

So geht! Genug, mein Schatz geht nicht von hier, Er bleibet da bei mir, Ich will ihn auch nicht von mir lassen. Sein Arm wird mich aus Lieb Mit sanftmutsvollem Trieb Und größter Zärtlichkeit umfassen; Er soll mein Bräutigam verbleiben, Ich will ihm Brust und Herz verschreiben. Ich weiß gewiß, er liebet mich, Mein Herz liebt ihn auch inniglich Und wird ihn ewig ehren. Was könnte mich nun für ein Feind Bei solchem Glück versehren! Du, Jesu, bist und bleibst mein Freund; Und werd ich ängstlich zu dir flehn: Herr, hilf!, so laß mich Hülfe sehn!	Go, then! Enough that my Treasure will not depart from here: He stays here with me; I too will not let Him leave me. His arm will embrace me out of Love With an impulse full of gentleness And with the greatest tenderness; He shall remain my Bridegroom: I will assign to Him my breast and heart. I know for certain that He loves me; My heart dearly loves Him too And will ever honour Him. How could an enemy harm me now, With such good fortune! You, Jesus, are and remain my Friend; And if I implore You anxiously: 'Lord, help!', then let me see Your help!

62. Aria T ob d'am I,II bc	b $\frac{2}{4}$
Nun mögt ihr stolzen Feinde schrecken;	Now you insolent enemies may terrify:
Was könnt ihr mir für Furcht erwecken?	How could you arouse any fear in me?
Mein Schatz, mein Hort ist hier bei mir.	My treasure, my refuge is here with me.
Ihr mögt euch noch so grimmig stellen,	Though you may appear ever so fierce
Droht nur, mich ganz und gar zu fällen,	And threaten to cast me down altogether,
Doch seht! mein Heiland wohnet hier.	Yet see! my Saviour dwells here.
63. Recitativo SATB bc	D c
Was will der Höllen Schrecken nun?	What will Hell's terror do now?
Was will uns Welt und Sünde tun,	What will the world and sin do to us,
Da wir in Jesu Händen ruhn?	Since we rest in Jesus's hands?
64. Choral [scoring as in no. 54]	D c
Nun seid ihr wohl gerochen	**Now you are well avenged**
An eurer Feinde Schar,	**On your enemy host,**
Denn Christus hat zerbrochen,	**For Christ has broken to pieces**
Was euch zuwider war.	**What was against you.**
Tod, Teufel, Sünd und Hölle	**Death, Devil, Sin, and Hell**
Sind ganz und gar geschwächt;	**Are utterly diminished;**
Bei Gott hat seine Stelle	**With God it has its place:**
Das menschliche Geschlecht.	**The human family.**

This last part of the oratorio* once more calls for a festive ensemble with trumpets and drums: only flutes are absent from the orchestra of Parts I and III. The text brings to its conclusion the account of the Wise Men from the East—the second half of the Gospel* reading for the Feast of the Epiphany. Its bearing on the assembled congregation is established in no. 59, the first verse of Paul Gerhardt's hymn *Ich steh an deiner Krippen hier* ('I stand here at Your crib'; 1653). The madrigalian* verse re-interprets the Christian triumph over the failure of Herod's plotting as an all-inclusive recognition: now that God has become man, hell can no longer do us any harm. The same idea is taken up once more in the closing chorale, the fourth verse of the hymn *Ihr Christen auserkoren* by Georg Werner (1648).

Except for the Evangelist's recitatives and the chorale *Ich steh an deiner Krippen hier*, Bach's composition is based on a church cantata of unknown text, composed shortly beforehand. Yet the recitatives in particular, and also the other vocal music, must have been remodelled in various ways.

The opening chorus* is a multi-sectional structure of imposing grandeur—closely related to fugue*—whose form may be outlined as follows:

Ritornello *a b c*

A Choral fugue on *a* ('Herr, wenn die stolzen Feinde schnauben')
Repeat to a new text ('So gib, daß wir im festen Glauben')
Imitative passage ('Nach deiner Macht und Hülfe sehn!')
Choral insertion* within ritornello section *b* ('So gib. . .')

B Free canon* at the 5th ('Wir wollen dir allein vertrauen')
Choral insertion within c^1 and b^1 ('So können wir. . .')

A^1 Choral fugue on *a* ('Herr, wenn . . . im festen Glauben')
Imitative passage ('Nach deiner Macht und Hülfe sehn!')
Choral insertion within b^1 and *c* ('So gib . . .')

Sections B and A^1 together take up 120 bars—exactly the same number as A. The polyphonic* structure of all its sections allows the chorus to be experienced by listeners as a single great fugue.

In stark contrast, the first aria, no. 57, is of a pronounced dance character with a clear, periodic phrase structure. Indeed, the ritornellos might easily be united to form an instrumental movement for strings and oboe d'amore* which, disregarding a short episode, would take the form A—BC—ABC. In the second aria, on the other hand (no. 62, which calls for two obbligato* oboes d'amore) the concerto-like element is strongly emphasized. Also notable is the closing chorale: as the conclusion of the entire oratorio, it surpasses all the preceding chorale movements in splendour and dimensions. The chorale, delivered line by line in the soprano part and supported by the three lower voice parts in a homophonic* texture, is incorporated in a splendid concertante* orchestral texture in which the first trumpet takes a pre-eminent role. Singularly, a Phrygian melody—*Herzlich tut mich verlangen*—is built into an orchestral texture in the purest and most radiant D major.

In the chief movements of Part VI of the oratorio, then, four basic elements of Bach's cantata composition are predominant: fugue (no. 54), dance (no. 57), concerto (no. 62), and chorale arrangement (no. 64).

1.12 First Sunday after Epiphany

EPISTLE: Romans 12.1–6: The duties of the Christian.
GOSPEL: Luke 2.41–52: The twelve-year-old Jesus in the temple.

Mein Liebster Jesus ist verloren, BWV 154

NBA I/5, p. 91 BC A29 Duration: *c.* 17 mins

1. ARIA T str bc b $\frac{3}{4}$

Mein liebster Jesus ist verloren:	My beloved Jesus is lost:
O Wort, das mir Verzweiflung bringt,	O words that bring me despair,

O Schwert, das durch die Seele dringt,
O Donnerwort in meinen Ohren.

O sword that pierces my soul,
O thunder-word in my ears!

2. Recitativo T bc — f♯–A c

Wo treff ich meinen Jesum an,
Wer zeiget mir die Bahn,
Wo meiner Seelen brünstiges Verlangen,
Mein Heiland, hingegangen?
Kein Unglück kann mich so empfindlich rühren,
Als wenn ich Jesum soll verlieren.

Where do I find my Jesus?
Who will show me the path
Where my soul's most ardent desire,
My Saviour, has gone?
No misfortune could stir me so intensely
As if I should lose Jesus.

3. Choral SATB bc (+ ob d'am I,II str) — A c

Jesu, mein Hort und Erretter,
Jesu, meine Zuversicht,
Jesu, starker Schlangentreter,
Jesu, meines Lebens Licht!
Wie verlanget meinem Herzen,
Jesulein, nach dir mit Schmerzen!
Komm, ach komm, ich warte dein,
Komm, o liebstes Jesulein!

Jesus, my refuge and deliverer,
Jesus, my confidence,
Jesus, strong serpent-crusher,
Jesus, my life's Light!
How grievously my heart longs
For You, little Jesus!
Come, oh come, I await You,
Come, O dearest little Jesus!

4. Aria A ob d'am I,II hpschd + str 8va — A 12/8

Jesu, laß dich finden,
Laß doch meine Sünden
Keine dicke Wolken sein,
Wo du dich zum Schrecken
Willst für mich verstecken,
Stelle dich bald wieder ein!

Jesus, let me find You,
Do not let my sins
Be a thick cloud
Where, to my terror,
You would hide from me;
Appear again soon!

5. Arioso B bc — f♯ c

'Wisset ihr nicht, daß ich sein muß in dem, das meines Vaters ist?'

'Do you not know that I must be about my Father's business?'

6. Recitativo T bc — D–f♯ c

Dies ist die Stimme meines Freundes,
Gott Lob und Dank!
Mein Jesus, mein getreuer Hort,
Läßt durch sein Wort
Sich wieder tröstlich hören;
Ich war vor Schmerzen krank,
Der Jammer wollte mir das Mark
In Beinen fast verzehren;
Nun aber wird mein Glaube wieder stark,
Nun bin ich höchst erfreut;
Denn ich erblicke meiner Seelen Wonne,
Den Heiland, meine Sonne,
Der nach betrübter Trauernacht
Durch seinen Glanz mein Herze fröhlich macht.

This is the voice of my Friend,
Praise and thank God!
My Jesus, my faithful refuge,
Through His Word makes Himself
Heard again comfortingly.
I was stricken with grief,
Woe would almost consume
The marrow in my bones;
But now my Faith grows strong again,
Now I am highly delighted,
For I see my soul's delight,
The Saviour, my sun,
Who, after a troubled night of sorrow,
Through His radiance makes my heart joyful.

Auf, Seele, mache dich bereit!
Du mußt zu ihm
In seines Vaters Haus, hin in den Tempel ziehn;
Da läßt er sich in seinem Wort erblicken,
Da will er dich im Sakrament erquicken;
Doch, willst du würdiglich sein Fleisch und Blut genießen,
So mußt du Jesum auch in Buß und Glauben küssen.

Rise up, O soul, make yourself ready!
You must go to Him
In His Father's house, in the temple;
There He may be seen through His Word,
There He will refresh you in the Sacrament;
Yet if you would worthily consume His Flesh and Blood,
Then you must also kiss Jesus in repentance and Faith.

7. Aria [Duetto] AT str + ob d'am I,II bc — D c $\frac{3}{8}$ c

Wohl mir, Jesus ist gefunden,
Nun bin ich nicht mehr betrübt.
Der, den meine Seele liebt,
Zeigt sich mir zur frohen Stunden.
Ich will dich, mein Jesu, nun nimmermehr lassen,
Ich will dich im Glauben beständig umfassen.

Blessed am I: Jesus is found;
Now I am no longer distressed.
He whom my soul loves
Appears to me at this glad time.
I will now leave You nevermore, my Jesus,
I will constantly embrace You in Faith.

8. Choral SATB bc (+ ww str) — D c

Meinen Jesum laß ich nicht,
Geh ihm ewig an der Seiten;
Christus läßt mich für und für
Zu den Lebensbächlein leiten.
Selig, wer mit mir so spricht:
Meinen Jesum laß ich nicht.

I will not let go of my Jesus,
I will go ever at His side;
Christ leads me for ever and ever
To the stream of life.
Blessed is he who says with me:
I will not let go of my Jesus.

Little is known about the origin of this cantata. It was performed on 9 January 1724 and revived at least once thereafter (*c.* 1736/7),[29] but its composition seems to date from an earlier period: perhaps from Bach's Weimar years. The anonymous librettist follows the Gospel* reading, but at the same time gives it a contemporary relevance. It is no longer Jesus's parents but rather man, imprisoned in sin, who has lost his Jesus, and despite anxious searching he is unable to find Him again. The chorale, no. 3, prays in the name of the entire congregation, and the aria (no. 4) in the name of the individual Christian, that Jesus might come back again. In the arioso,* no. 5, Jesus's reply is heard, sung by the bass—the *vox Christi*—in the words of a verse from the Sunday Gospel (Luke 2.49). And he who was searching realizes gratefully that, through faith, Jesus may be found in his Father's house (that is, in church) in sermon and sacrament (no. 6). Both the individual Christian (no. 7) and the assembled congregation

[29] Date of revival according to Kobayashi Chr, p. 39.

(no. 8) now vow gladly to leave Jesus nevermore, but rather to belong to Him in perpetuity.

Bach's setting is notable for its striking directness. The three arias pass through the underlying affects* of the text: despairing lamentation, ardent longing, and exuberant joy. Between them, we hear the solemn, eloquent rhetorical question of the bass arioso, and the recitatives, which are set as plain *secco*. The opening aria, with string accompaniment, is built on an ostinato* bass in the continuo. With its chromatically* falling opening, it may be recognized as a relative of the *lamento** basses that descend through a fourth which were often used at that time and are encountered several times in Bach—for example, in the 'Crucifixus' of the B minor Mass. Above this bass we hear an expressive lament, first played by Violin I, then sung by the tenor, and repeated numerous times by both in the course of the movement. The middle section is abruptly interrupted: at the words 'O sword that pierces my soul, O thunder-word in my ears!'[30] we hear a triadic fanfare, followed by a string tremolo whose bold harmonies depict the terror of man abandoned by God. A substantially abridged da capo* of the main section concludes the aria—a movement of pregnant concision.

A short *secco* recitative, no. 2, is followed by a plain chorale setting, no. 3: the second verse of the hymn *Jesu, meiner Seelen Wonne* by Martin Jahn (1661), sung to the melody *Werde munter, mein Gemüte*. The second aria, no. 4, is scored for two obbligato* oboes d'amore;* and its lower part (a so-called 'bassett'*) is played by unison violins and viola (organ and instrumental basses are *tacet**). For one of his performances (perhaps in 1724) Bach added a harpsichord part. The beatific thirds of the oboes and alto voice lend the aria a simple song-like character. The words 'Do not let my sins be a thick cloud' are the key to an understanding of the instrumentation: as in the aria 'Aus Liebe will mein Heiland sterben' from the *St Matthew Passion*, the absence of continuo bass serves as a symbol of innocence.

In the arioso, no. 5, the melodic line of the bass is entirely geared towards effective declamation. The imitation* of the voice in the continuo may probably be interpreted as a symbol of the imitation that Jesus owed to His heavenly Father. The following recitative borrows a phrase from the Song of Solomon 2.8: 'This is the voice of my friend'. Joy over the rediscovery of Jesus fills the duet, no. 7, which is largely homophonic* in the French duet style. Two thematically related sections, again often in beatific thirds and sixths, lead to a third and last section in which a poetic change to dactylic metre coincides with a musical change to canonic writing in 3/8 time. The homophonic conclusion of this passage is followed by a reprise of the introductory ritornello only. A

[30] An obvious reminiscence of Johann Rist's hymn 'O Ewigkeit, du Donnerwort, o Schwert, das durch die Seele bohrt' (1642) and, even more closely, of Luke 2.35.

plain chorale setting—the sixth verse of the hymn *Meinen Jesum laß ich nicht* by Christian Keymann (1658)—concludes the work. Here, it remains unclear whether the version of the opening line 'Meinen Jesum laß ich nicht', in place of 'Jesum laß ich nicht von mir' (note the rhyme scheme), is intentional or an error on the part of the composer.

Meinen Jesum laß ich nicht, BWV 124

NBA I/5, p. 117 BC A30 Duration: *c.* 17 mins

1. [Chorale] S + hn ATB conc ob d'am str bc — E 3/4

Meinen Jesum laß ich nicht,
Weil er sich für mich gegeben,
So erfordert meine Pflicht,
Klettenweis an ihm zu kleben.
Er ist meines Lebens Licht,
Meinen Jesum laß ich nicht.

I will not let my Jesus go,
For He has given Himself for me
And thus demands my duty
To stick to Him like a bur.
He is the Light of my life;
I will not let my Jesus go.

2. Recitativo T bc — A–c♯ C

Solange sich ein Tropfen Blut
In Herz und Adern reget,
Soll Jesus nur allein
Mein Leben und mein alles sein.
Mein Jesus, der an mir so große Dinge tut:
Ich kann ja nichts als meinen Leib und Leben
Ihm zum Geschenke geben.

As long as a drop of blood
Stirs in my heart and veins,
Jesus alone shall be
My life and my all.
My Jesus, who does such great things for me:
I can indeed give Him naught but my body and life
As a gift.

3. Aria T ob d'am str bc — f♯ 3/4

Und wenn der harte Todesschlag
Die Sinnen schwächt, die Glieder rühret,
Wenn der dem Fleisch verhaßte Tag
Nur Furcht und Schrecken mit sich führet,
Doch tröstet sich die Zuversicht:
Ich lasse meinen Jesum nicht.

And when the harsh stroke of death
Weakens the senses, stirs the limbs,
When the day hated by the flesh
Brings with it only fear and terror,
Yet this assurance comforts me:
I will not let my Jesus go.

4. Recitativo B bc — A C

Doch ach!
Welch schweres Ungemach
Empfindet noch allhier die Seele?
Wird nicht die hart gekränkte Brust
Zu einer Wüstenei und Marterhöhle
Bei Jesu schmerzlichstem Verlust?
Allein mein Geist sieht gläubig auf
Und an den Ort, wo Glaub und Hoffnung prangen,

Yet alas!
What hard adversity
The soul still experiences here!
Does not the severely ailing breast
Become a wilderness and den of torment
At the most grievous loss of Jesus?
However my spirit looks up, believing,
To the place where Faith and Hope shine forth,

Allwo ich nach vollbrachtem Lauf
Dich, Jesu, ewig soll umfangen.

Where, after my race is run,
I shall embrace You, Jesus, for evermore.

5. Aria Duetto SA bc — A $\frac{3}{8}$

Entziehe dich eilends, mein Herze, der Welt,
Du findest im Himmel dein wahres Vergnügen.
Wenn künftig dein Auge den Heiland erblickt,
So wird erst dein sehnendes Herze erquickt,
So wird es in Jesu zufriedengestellt.

Hide yourself in haste, my heart, from the world:
You will find in heaven your true contentment.
When in future your eye sees the Saviour,
Only then will your longing heart be refreshed,
Then it will be contented in Jesus.

6. Choral SATB bc (+ instrs) — E C

Jesum laß ich nicht von mir,
Geh ihm ewig an der Seiten;
Christus läßt mich für und für
Zu den Lebensbächlein leiten.
Selig, der mit mir so spricht:
Meinen Jesum laß ich nicht.

I will not let Jesus go from me,
I will go ever at His side;
Christ leads me for ever and ever
To the stream of life.
Blessed is he who says with me:
I will not let go of my Jesus.

As in the previous year (BWV 154), the text of this cantata, composed for 7 January 1725, refers to the Gospel* reading. The faithful Christian, like Jesus's parents at one time, desires not to lose Jesus but to follow Him in all circumstances. Thus far, the choice of the hymn by Christian Keymann of 1658 as the model of this chorale cantata* is comprehensible. Further on, however, the biblical account and the chorale text depart from each other considerably: the one tells of the rediscovery of Jesus in the temple; the other turns our thoughts to future life on earth (verse 2), to death (verse 3), to reunification with Jesus after death (verse 4), and to the futility of the world (verse 5). Moreover, the anonymous librettist, who adapts each of these verses to form a madrigalian* movement, has taken no steps to establish further links with the Sunday Gospel. Instead, he gives free rein to a truly baroque predilection for graphic descriptions of death and disdain for this world.

The opening chorus* follows the usual scheme: the choir sings the chorale line by line in a texture either homophonic* or lightly broken up into polyphony,* while the orchestra develops its own thematic material in the introduction, episodes, and accompanying passages. The initial theme has the character of a minuet, but soon the oboe d'amore* detaches itself from the instrumental body and takes the lead in concertante* passages. Alternately, it is supported by the strings, which simplify its figuration in the tuttis, or accompanied by continuo alone, as it repeats and varies the motive heard previously in an echo-like fashion. The line 'To stick to Him like a bur' is accorded a very striking interpretation: alto, tenor, and bass all unite on a long-held b^1 (or b) to the word 'kleben' ('stick').

A brief *secco* recitative is followed by the first aria, no. 3, whose words are set no less graphically. The strings add hints of a realized continuo accompaniment to the obbligato* of the oboe d'amore. Their rhythmic ostinato* figure, which pervades the entire movement apart from a few cadential bars, reflects the words 'fear and terror'

(compare the accompaniment to 'Warum wollt ihr erschrecken?' from the *Christmas Oratorio*, No. 49).

The second recitative, no. 4, is another *secco*: only on the word 'Lauf' ('run') does it forego its plain declamation in favour of a semiquaver octave scale figure. In the duet that follows, no. 5, dance-style genres are recalled still more obviously than in the opening movement. The voice parts—accompanied by continuo only—are canonic at every entry. Yet this imitation* is so completely subordinate to the clear, periodic four-bar phrase structure that linear polyphony recedes beneath the dance-like rhythms. The sixth verse of the hymn, in unaltered wording, concludes the work in a plain four-part chorale setting.

Liebster Jesu, mein Verlangen (Concerto in Dialogo), BWV 32

NBA I/5, p. 145 BC A31 Duration: *c.* 24 mins

1. Aria S ob str bc — e C

Liebster Jesu, mein Verlangen,	Dearest Jesus, my desire,
Sage mir, wo find ich dich?	Tell me, where do I find You?
Soll ich dich so bald verlieren	Shall I lose You so soon
Und nicht ferner bei mir spüren?	And no longer feel You with me?
Ach! mein Hort, erfreue mich,	Ah! my refuge, gladden me;
Laß dich höchst vergnügt umfangen.	Utterly contented, let me embrace You.

2. Recitativo B bc — b C

'Was ists, daß du mich gesuchet? Weißt du nicht, daß ich sein muß in dem, das meines Vaters ist?'	'Why is it that you sought Me? Did you not know that I must be about My Father's business?'

3. Aria B vln solo bc — G 3/8

Hier in meines Vaters Stätte,	Here in My Father's abode
Findt mich ein betrübter Geist.	A distressed spirit finds me.
Da kannst du mich sicher finden	Here you can surely find me
Und dein Herz mit mir verbinden,	And unite your heart with Me,
Weil dies meine Wohnung heißt.	For this is called my dwelling.

4. RECITATIVO SB str bc — b–G c

Seele	*Soul*
Ach! heiliger und großer Gott,	Ah! holy and great God,
So will ich mir	Then I will
Denn hier bei dir	Here with You
Beständig Trost und Hülfe suchen.	Constantly seek comfort and help.
Jesus	*Jesus*
Wirst du den Erdentand verfluchen	If you curse earthly trifles
Und nur in diese Wohnung gehn,	And just enter this dwelling,
So kannst du hier und dort bestehn.	Then you can endure both here and there.
Seele	*Soul*
Wie lieblich ist doch deine Wohnung,	How lovely is Your dwelling-place,
Herr, starker Zebaoth;	Lord of the mighty Sabaoth;
Mein Geist verlangt	My spirit longs
Nach dem, was nur in deinem Hofe prangt.	For what shines only in Your court.
Mein Leib und Seele freuet sich	My body and soul rejoice
In dem lebendgen Gott:	In the living God:
Ach! Jesu, meine Brust liebt dich nur ewiglich.	Ah! Jesus, my breast just loves You eternally.
Jesus	*Jesus*
So kannst du glücklich sein,	Then you can be happy,
Wenn Herz und Geist	When heart and spirit
Aus Liebe gegen mich entzündet heißt.	Are enkindled by love of Me.
Seele	*Soul*
Ach! dieses Wort, das itzo schon	Ah! this Word, which now already
Mein Herz aus Babels Grenzen reißt,	Tears my heart out of Babel's confines,
Faß ich mir andachtsvoll in meiner Seele ein.	Do I devoutly place in my soul.

5. ARIA DUETTO SB ob str bc — D c

beide	*both*
Nun verschwinden alle Plagen,	Now all torments vanish,
Nun verschwindet Ach und Schmerz.	Now grief and sorrow disappear.
Seele	*Soul*
Nun will ich nicht von dir lassen,	Now I will not part from You,
Jesus	*Jesus*
Und ich dich auch stets umfassen.	And I will constantly embrace you too.
Seele	*Soul*
Nun vergnüget sich mein Herz	Now my heart is contented
Jesus	*Jesus*
Und kann voller Freude sagen:	And, full of joy, can say:
beide	*both*
Nun verschwinden alle Plagen,	Now all torments vanish,
Nun verschwindet Ach und Schmerz!	Now grief and sorrow disappear!

6. CHORAL SATB bc (+ instrs) G c

Mein Gott, öffne mir die Pforten	**My God, open to me the gates**
Solcher Gnad und Gütigkeit,	**Of such grace and benevolence,**
Laß mich allzeit allerorten	**Let me at all times and places**
Schmecken deine Süßigkeit!	**Taste Your sweetness!**
Liebe mich und treib mich an,	**Love me and drive me on,**
Daß ich dich, so gut ich kann,	**So that as best I can**
Wiederum umfang und liebe	**In return I might embrace and love You**
Und ja nun nicht mehr betrübe.	**And indeed grieve You now no more.**

This cantata, performed for the first time on 13 January 1726, is one of Bach's settings of texts by the Darmstadt court poet Georg Christian Lehms. The succession of ideas in the libretto corresponds to a large extent with that of Cantata 154 and thus closly follows the Gospel* reading. As in Cantata 57, however, Lehms clothes the words in the form of a dialogue between the Soul and Jesus. This dialogue concludes with the duet 'Nun verschwinden alle Plagen', for the closing chorale is an addition of Bach's.

The work has sometimes been viewed as an adaptation of a lost cantata from Bach's Cöthen years; and indeed there is something to be said for this view. The duet structure recalls similar dialogue arias in Hunold's congratulatory cantata librettos. And in musical substance the opening movement resembles that of Cantata 202, a work of uncertain origin which nonetheless, in the opinion of some scholars, might belong to Bach's Cöthen years. The hypothesis of an adaptation, however, is contradicted not only by the recently recovered evidence of Lehms's printed text of 1711 but also by the draft character of the autograph score. At most, therefore, the possibility might be admitted that Bach adapted certain parts of the work, radically altering them in the process.

The most significant movement in Bach's composition is undoubtedly the opening aria. Over brief string chords, the oboe extends broadly sweeping, richly embellished melodic arches—subsequently taken up by the soprano—so that the overall impression arises of a concerto slow movement. The anxious questioning of the Soul is answered by Jesus in the second movement in the words of Luke 2.49 (with His interlocutor now in the singular). These words, also quoted in Cantata 154, are here set in plain *secco* recitative. In keeping with the unrealistic, allegorical character of the dialogue, the *vox Christi* is assigned to bass voice as in liturgical Passion settings, rather than to a voice of boys' pitch. Textually, the following movement, no. 3, provides confirmation of the preceding biblical words. Musically, it is a bass aria with obbligato* violin, which surrounds the voice with a lively, almost virtuoso figuration. Of special charm is the text-engendered overclouding in minor mode to the words 'betrübter Geist' ('distressed spirit').

At the heart of the fourth movement (a dialogue recitative with string accompaniment) lies another free biblical quotation: 'How lovely is Your dwelling-place' from Psalm 84.1–2. These words are set by Bach in enraptured arioso*—one of the high points in a cantata far from short of attractions. The dialogue action reaches its conclusion in the duet-aria, no. 5. Here, joy is expressed in almost frolicsome leaps of a sixth, derived from the ritornello theme, which pervade the entire movement. By contrast with the opening aria, the concertante* figures and rapid scale passages are now assigned to the first violin, while oboe and voices are content with a simplified version of the melody. After the unencumbered cheerfulness of this movement, greater depths are plumbed in the closing chorale added by Bach, the twelfth verse of the hymn *Weg, mein Herz, mit den Gedanken* by Paul Gerhardt (1647), sung to the melody *Freu dich sehr, o meine Seele*. Here the dialogue form is relinquished, and the Soul's prayer to be taken up into eternal bliss becomes the concern of the entire Christian congregation.

1.13 Second Sunday after Epiphany

Epistle: Romans 12.6–16: 'We have diverse gifts'; the rules of life.
Gospel: John 2.1–11: The Wedding at Cana.

Mein Gott, wie lang, ach lange, BWV 155

NBA I/5, p. 175 BC A32 Duration: *c.* 13 mins

1. Recitativo S str bc — d–a C

Mein Gott, wie lang, ach lange?	My God, how long, ah, how long?
Des Jammers ist zuviel!	My misery is too great!
Ich sehe gar kein Ziel	I see no end at all
Der Schmerzen und der Sorgen.	To pain and sorrow.
Dein süßer Gnadenblick	Your sweet glance of grace
Hat unter Nacht und Wolken sich verborgen,	Is hidden under night and clouds;
Die Liebeshand zieht sich, ach! ganz zurück!	Love's hand is, alas, fully withdrawn!
Um Trost ist mir sehr bange!	I am very anxious for comfort!
Ich finde, was mich Armen täglich kränket,	I find what daily grieves poor me:
Das Tränenmaß wird stets voll eingeschenket,	The cup of tears is always poured out in full,
Der Freudenwein gebricht;	Whereas the wine of joy is wanting;
Mir sinkt fast alle Zuversicht.	Almost all my confidence sinks.

2. Aria [Duetto] AT bsn bc — a C

Du mußt glauben, du mußt hoffen,	You must have faith, you must hope,

Du mußt Gott gelassen sein!	You must be serene in God!
Jesus weiß die rechten Stunden,	Jesus knows the right time
Dich mit Hülfe zu erfreun.	To delight you with His help.
Wenn die trübe Zeit verschwunden,	When the dismal time is over,
Steht sein ganzes Herz dir offen!	His whole Heart will be open to you!

3. Recitativo B bc — C–F c

So sei, o Seele! sei zufrieden!	Then be content, O Soul!
Wenn es vor deinen Augen scheint,	If it appears to your eyes
Als ob dein liebster Freund	As though your dearest Friend
Sich ganz von dir geschieden;	Has departed from you completely,
Wenn er dich kurze Zeit verläßt!	If He leaves you for a little while,
Herz! glaube fest,	O heart, keep firm faith!
Es wird ein Kleines sein,	It will only be a short while
Da er für bittre Zähren	Before, in place of bitter tears,
Den Trost- und Freudenwein	The wine of comfort and joy,
Und Honigseim für Wermut will gewähren!	And liquid honey in place of wormwood, will be granted to you!
Ach! denke nicht,	Ah! do not think
Daß er von Herzen dich betrübe;	That He grieves You from His Heart;
Er prüfet nur durch Leiden deine Liebe;	He merely tests your love through suffering;
Er machet, daß dein Herz bei trüben Stunden weine,	He makes your heart weep in troubled times
Damit sein Gnadenlicht	So that His Light of Grace
Dir desto lieblicher erscheine;	May appear all the lovelier to you;
Er hat, was dich ergötzt,	What delights you
Zuletzt	He has in the end
Zu deinem Trost dir vorbehalten;	Reserved for your comfort;
Drum laß ihn nur, o Herz, in allem walten!	Then let Him govern in all things, O heart!

4. Aria S str bc — F c

Wirf, mein Herze, wirf dich noch	Cast yourself, my heart,
In des Höchsten Liebesarme,	Into the loving arms of the Highest,
Daß er deiner sich erbarme.	That He may have mercy on you.
Lege deiner Sorgen Joch,	Lay your yoke of cares
Und was dich bisher beladen,	And whatever has laden you till now
Auf die Achseln seiner Gnaden.	Upon the shoulders of His grace.

5. Choral SATB bc (+ instrs) — F c

Ob sichs anließ, als wollt er nicht,	**Though it appears as if He is unwilling,**
Laß dich es nicht erschrecken,	**Do not let it frighten you,**
Denn wo er ist am besten mit,	**For where He is most with you**
Da will ers nicht entdecken.	**He would not disclose.**
Sein Wort laß dir gewisser sein,	**Let His Word be more certain for you,**
Und ob dein Herz spräch lauter Nein,	**And though your heart says plainly 'No',**
So laß doch dir nicht grauen.	**Do not let yourself shudder.**

This cantata, composed in Weimar for 19 January 1716, is based on a text from Salomo Franck's collection *Evangelisches Andachts-Opffer*. In essence, the poet has drawn from the Gospel* text a single idea: Jesus keeps Himself hidden, for His hour has not yet come, but the soul may hope that, at the right time, He will be at hand with His solace. Certain phrases, such as 'the wine of joy is wanting' (no. 1) or 'It will only be a short while before, in place of bitter tears, the wine of comfort and joy . . . will be granted to you!' (no. 3) allude to the Gospel account of the Wedding at Cana, which would have been read during the service before the cantata performance.

As in most of the cantatas from Franck's 1715 cycle, Bach requires only a small instrumental group: strings and continuo, plus in the second movement obbligato* bassoon, which is assigned one of the most virtuoso bassoon parts in Bach's entire output of cantatas. The singers required are one of each voice type, which come together only in the closing chorale. The music radiates that youthful freshness and sensuousness of sound that we love in the cantatas of the Weimar Bach.

The opening recitative engages our attention by virtue of its throbbing pedal *D*, heard for eleven-and-a-half bars, which forcefully underlines the impression of anxious waiting conveyed in the text. The voice, supported by brief string chords, declaims in expressive gestures until, at the words 'the wine of joy is wanting', everything is set astir, only to slacken again at the following words, 'Almost all my confidence sinks'. The duet 'Du mußt glauben, du mußt hoffen', no. 2, is probably one of the most original that Bach ever wrote. At the very outset the obbligato bassoon, supported by lightly touched continuo chords, covers the interval of a thirteenth:

And it continues this wide-ranging figuration throughout the aria, at times ornamenting it with rapid runs. The vocal duet parts sing in a largely homophonic* texture, only lightly broken up into polyphony,* and almost rapturously euphonious.

The following recitative, no. 3, brings comfort to the soul. It is no mere chance that Bach here chose the bass voice, the voice of Christ. Although the continuo part never assumes a firm structure for long, the proximity of the movement to arioso* is often much in evidence, particularly at the words 'So that His Light of Grace may appear all the lovelier to you'. Lively dotted rhythms in the strings, and later in the voice part too, characterize no. 4, the aria 'Wirf, mein Herze, wirf dich noch'. The continuo also takes up this rhythmic movement on several occasions against held string chords. The twelfth verse of the hymn *Es ist das*

Heil uns kommen her by Paul Speratus (1524) in a plain chorale setting concludes the work.

Ach Gott, wie manches Herzeleid, BWV 3

NBA I/5, p. 191 BC A33 Duration: *c.* 27 mins

1. [Chorale] SATB + trb ob d'am I,II str bc A C

Ach Gott, wie manches Herzeleid	**Ah God, how much heartbreak**
Begegnet mir zu dieser Zeit!	**Do I encounter at this time!**
Der schmale Weg ist trübsalvoll,	**The narrow way is full of tribulation**
Den ich zum Himmel wandern soll.	**By which I must travel to heaven.**

2. Recitativo [+ Chorale] SATB bc D–A C

Wie schwerlich läßt sich Fleisch und Blut	**How hard it is for flesh and blood**
Tenor	*Tenor*
So nur nach Irdischem und Eitlem trachtet	That minds only earthly and vain things
Und weder Gott noch Himmel achtet,	And values neither God nor Heaven,
Zwingen zu dem ewigen Gut.	**To be husbanded to the eternal Good.**
Alt	*Alto*
Da du, o Jesu, nun mein alles bist,	Since You, O Jesus, are now my all,
Und doch mein Fleisch so widerspenstig ist.	And yet my flesh is so oppositional.
Wo soll ich mich denn wenden hin?	**Where, then, shall I turn?**
Sopran	*Soprano*
Das Fleisch ist schwach, doch will der Geist;	The flesh is weak, yet the spirit is willing;
So hilf du mir, der du mein Herze weißt.	So help me, You who know my heart.
Zu dir, o Jesu, steht mein Sinn.	**To You, O Jesus, is my mind inclined.**
Baß	*Bass*
Wer deinem Rat und deiner Hülfe traut,	Whoever trusts Your counsel and Your help
Der hat wohl nie auf falschen Grund gebaut,	Has surely never built on false ground,
Da du der ganzen Welt zum Trost gekommen	For You have come for the comfort of the whole world
Und unser Fleisch an dich genommen,	And have taken our flesh upon Yourself;
So rettet uns dein Sterben	So Your Dying delivers us
Vom endlichen Verderben.	From final destruction.
Drum schmecke doch ein gläubiges Gemüte	Therefore a believing spirit does indeed taste
Des Heilands Freundlichkeit und Güte.	The Saviour's friendship and goodness.

3. Aria B bc f♯ 3/4

Empfind ich Höllenangst und Pein,	Though I feel Hell's anguish and pain,

Doch muß beständig in dem Herzen
Ein rechter Freudenhimmel sein.
Ich darf nur Jesu Namen nennen,
Der kann auch unermeßne Schmerzen
Als einen leichten Nebel trennen.

Yet there must be perpetually in my heart
A true heavenly joy.
I need only call on the Name of Jesus,
Who can dispel even immeasurable griefs
Like a light mist.

4. Recitativo T bc c♯–E C

Es mag mir Leib und Geist verschmachten,
Bist du, o Jesu, mein
Und ich bin dein,
Will ichs nicht achten.
Dein treuer Mund
Und dein unendlich Lieben,
Das unverändert stets geblieben,
Erhält mir noch dein' ersten Bund,
Der meine Brust mit Freudigkeit erfüllet
Und auch des Todes Furcht, des Grabes Schrecken stillet.
Fällt Not und Mangel gleich von allen Seiten ein,
Mein Jesus wird mein Schatz und Reichtum sein.

My body and spirit may fail,
But if You, O Jesus, are mine
And I am Yours,
I will pay no attention to it.
Your faithful mouth
And Your endless Love,
Which has always remained unchanged,
Still preserve for me Your first Covenant,
Which fills my breast with joyfulness
And also calms death's fear, the grave's terror.
Though need and want invade from all sides,
My Jesus will be my treasure and wealth.

5. Aria Duetto SA ob d'am I + II + vln I bc E C

Wenn Sorgen auf mich dringen,
Will ich in Freudigkeit
Zu meinem Jesu singen.
Mein Kreuz hilft Jesus tragen,
Drum will ich gläubig sagen:
Es dient zum besten allezeit.

When cares press upon me,
I will in joyfulness
Sing to my Jesus.
Jesus helps me to bear my cross,
Therefore I will say in faith:
It works for the best at all times.

6. Choral SATB bc (+ instrs) A C

Erhalt mein Herz im Glauben rein,
So leb und sterb ich dir allein.
Jesu, mein Trost, hör mein Begier,
O mein Heiland, wär ich bei dir.

Keep my heart pure in faith,
So that I live and die to You alone.
Jesus, my comfort, hear my desire;
O my Saviour, would that I were with You!

In this chorale cantata,* composed for 14 January 1725, the link with the Sunday Gospel* is still looser than in the other two cantatas for this Sunday. The work is based on the eighteen-verse hymn (based on the Latin *Jesu dulcis memoria*) by Martin Moller (1587), which sings of Jesus as our comforter and helper in need. In his paraphrase, the anonymous cantata librettist has taken no steps to accommodate more specific allusions to the biblical account of the Wedding at Cana, beyond this general connection, although his reliance on the chorale text is relatively slight. The second movement begins as a trope* of verse 2, retained word for word, and continues as a paraphrase of verses 3–5 in bass recitative. The third movement is based on verse 6, and the fourth on verses 7–14 which, however, are often merely touched upon allusively. Verses 15–16 are more clearly recognizable in the fifth movement, verse 17 is absent altogether, and verse 18 retained word for word in the last movement.

Bach sets the opening chorus* as a stirring elegy. In the introductory orchestral ritornello, the lead is taken by the two oboes d'amore* which, accompanied by a choir of strings, extend broad and expressive melodic arches in concertante* duet. Among the strings, the first violin is predominant, often accompanying the oboes with sigh figures, while the other strings form a background of quiescent or briefly interjected chords. The melodic framework of the oboes' theme, which pervades the whole movement, is a chromatic* scale figure falling through the interval of a fourth (identified by the sign + in the following music example):

Not only the instrumental music, however, but also the four choral passages, each of which contains a single chorale line, derive their thematic material from the above oboe melody: in each passage, the three upper voice parts enter contrapuntally with its head-motive; and even during the delivery of the chorale—sung by bass, reinforced by trombone, to the melody *O Jesu Christ, meins Lebens Licht*—the head-motive is heard repeatedly wherever it may be combined with the *cantus firmus*.* The movement is thus all of a piece: a grand, eloquent lament.

No less unified in effect is the second movement, a chorale troped by recitatives, which are interpolated between the chorale lines and sung in turn by tenor, alto, soprano, and bass. The integrating component is an ostinato* motive* in the continuo, derived from the first chorale line and often repeated in the course of the movement, not only as an introduction and accompaniment to the chorale lines (sung by four-part voices) but also as a means of bridging the caesuras in the rather more extended bass recitative that follows the chorale. The subsequent aria for bass and continuo, no. 3, is, like the first movement, much pervaded by chromaticism. To be more precise, each of its vocal passages (a a^1 b b^1 a a^1) reflects the textual contrast between 'Hell's anguish and pain' and 'true heavenly joy' (section a), or between 'immeasurable griefs' and 'a light mist' (section b), in its melodic line: a syllabic,* wide-ranging, highly chromatic opening, followed in each case by a melismatic,* figurative, diatonic conclusion.

A *secco* recitative leads to the duet, no. 5, whose obbligato* accompanying part is played by oboes and first violin combined. Again, it is notable for its unified thematicism. In the opening ritornello, in counterpoint* with rhythmic complementary figures in the continuo, we hear a highly distinctive melody whose gestures might perhaps be interpreted as cross figures, inspired by the words 'Jesus helps me to bear my cross' from the middle section. The same theme is then taken up by the voice parts, which enter in imitation.* A plain chorale setting draws to its conclusion a work particularly impressive for the quality of its invention.

Meine Seufzer, meine Tränen, BWV 13

NBA I/5, p. 231 BC A34 Duration: *c.* 21 mins

1. ARIA T rec I,II ob da c bc — d $\frac{12}{8}$

Meine Seufzer, meine Tränen
Können nicht zu zählen sein.
Wenn sich täglich Wehmut findet
Und der Jammer nicht verschwindet,
Ach! so muß uns diese Pein
Schon den Weg zum Tode bahnen.

My sighs, my tears
Cannot be counted.
If woefulness occurs daily
And misery does not vanish,
Ah, then this pain must already
Set before us the way of death.

2. RECITATIVO A bc — B♭–F C

Mein liebster Gott läßt mich
Annoch vergebens rufen
Und mir in meinem Weinen
Noch keinen Trost erscheinen.
Die Stunde lässet sich
Zwar wohl von ferne sehen,
Allein ich muß doch noch vergebens flehen.

My dearest God lets me
Hitherto call in vain
And to me in my weeping
Still lets no comfort appear.
The hour may indeed
Be seen afar off,
Only I still have to beseech in vain.

3. CHORAL A + rec I + II 8va + ob da c str bc — F C

Der Gott, der mir hat versprochen
Seinen Beistand jederzeit,
Der läßt sich vergebens suchen
Itzt in meiner Traurigkeit.
Ach! Will er denn für und für
Grausam zürnen über mir,
Kann und will er sich der Armen
Itzt nicht wie vorhin erbarmen?

God, who has promised me
His help at all times,
Lets Himself be sought in vain
Now in my sadness.
Ah! will He then be
Cruelly angry with me for ever?
Can and will He not have mercy on the poor
Now as before?

4. Recitativo S bc — B♭ c

Mein Kummer nimmet zu	My sorrow increases
Und raubt mir alle Ruh.	And robs me of all rest.
Mein Jammerkrug ist ganz	My cup of trouble is quite
Mit Tränen angefüllet,	Filled with tears,
Und diese Not wird nicht gestillet,	And this sorrow is not soothed,
So mich ganz unempfindlich macht.	Which makes me quite numbed.
Der Sorgen Kummernacht	The grievous night of sorrow
Drückt mein beklemmtes Herz darnieder,	Oppresses my heavy heart,
Drum sing ich lauter Jammerlieder.	Therefore I sing pure songs of woe.
Doch, Seele, nein,	Yet no, O soul,
Sei nur getrost in deiner Pein:	Be but hopeful in your pain:
Gott kann den Wermutsaft	God can turn the wormwood sap
Gar leicht in Freudenwein verkehren	Quite easily into wine of joy
Und dir alsdenn viel tausend Lust gewähren.	And thereupon grant you many thousand delights.

5. Aria B rec I + II + vln solo bc — g c

Ächzen und erbärmlich Weinen	Moaning and pitiful weeping
Hilft der Sorgen Krankheit nicht.	Do not aid the sickness of care.
Aber wer gen Himmel siehet	But whoever looks towards heaven
Und sich da um Trost bemühet,	And seeks comfort there,
Dem kann leicht ein Freudenlicht	To him a joyful light can easily
In der Trauerbrust erscheinen.	Appear in his sorrowful breast.

6. Choral SATB bc (+ instrs) — B♭ c

So sei nun, Seele, deine	**Then be true to yourself, O soul,**
Und traue dem alleine,	**And trust Him alone**
Der dich erschaffen hat.	**Who has created you.**
Es gehe, wie es gehe,	**Be it as it may,**
Dein Vater in der Höhe,	**Your Father on high**
Der weiß zu allen Sachen Rat.	**Knows the right counsel for all things.**

This work, which belongs to Bach's third cycle of cantatas, was performed for the first time on 20 January 1726. Its scoring is particularly charming, for, in addition to the usual strings and continuo, it employs two recorders and an oboe da caccia.* The choir comes together only in the closing chorale. The libretto is drawn from the Darmstadt cycle of 1711 by Georg Christian Lehms. Like Franck in Cantata 155, Lehms singles out from the Gospel* reading the phrase 'My hour has not yet come' (John 2.4), drawing from it the conclusion that, though God's help is not evident at present, I may nonetheless trust that He will send me His comfort. A specific reference to the biblical account of the Wedding at Cana is found in the fourth movement: 'God can turn the wormwood sap quite easily into wine of joy'.

In overall structure, the text may be divided into two parts, each made up of three movements. The first part describes the hopelessness of the soul that appears to be deserted by God; the second part, the confidence of the soul that hopes for God's assistance. Each part concludes with a chorale: the first part with verse 2 of Johann Heermann's hymn *Zion klagt mit Angst und Schmerzen* (1636), and the second with the last verse of Paul Fleming's *In allen meinen Taten* (1641). Whether this bipartite structure occasioned a division of the cantata into two parts in performance (in which case the sermon would have intervened between the two parts) is doubtful in view of the brevity of the work.

Bach's setting illustrates how the imagination of the baroque musician is especially enkindled by texts dealing with sighs and pain. The opening aria is a long drawn-out lament with obbligato* parts for two recorders and oboe da caccia. The recorders enter with the theme, but later on the leading role is often taken by the middle-pitched instrument, the oboe da caccia, which lends the movement a charming tone-colour. Formally, it is a pure da capo* aria, whose bipartite middle section gives a striking vocal portrayal of the 'way of death' by sinking down stepwise into the depths. The following recitative, a short *secco*, enters the sphere of chromatic* arioso* at the end with its expressive coloratura* on the word 'flehen' ('beseech'). In the chorale, no. 3, only the strings have independent parts: the woodwind double the chorale melody of the alto in plain, unadorned notes. The lively string figures in a joyful F major express our hope for God's promised help, even though the text tells us that so far no such help is forthcoming.

A recitative, no. 4, plain but exceptionally graphic in text illustration, leads to the second aria, no. 5, whose choice of obbligato instruments—unison of solo violin and two recorders—is no less original than that of the first. To the words of its opening section, 'Moaning and pitiful weeping', we hear a lament whose melodic style is characterized by the interval of an augmented second and its inversion, as well as by the diminished seventh and diminished fifth (even in the continuo). The introductory ritornello, however, already embodies contrasting affects:* the antecedent phrase develops the aforementioned lament melody; but the consequent, with its lively demisemiquaver passages and intervallic leaps, strikes a far more joyful note, which is then carried further in the middle section to the words 'But whoever looks towards heaven and seeks comfort there'. Just as the 'way of death' was represented by a descent in the first aria, so now do we hear, on the words 'gen Himmel' ('towards heaven'), a rising octave leap in the voice and an ascending scale in quick notes on the obbligato instruments. A free reprise of the opening section ends the aria, after which the cantata concludes with a chorale in a plain four-part setting.

1.14 Third Sunday after Epiphany

EPISTLE: Romans 12.17–21: The Christian rules of life.
GOSPEL: Matthew 8.1–13: The healing of a leper; the centurion of Capernaum.

Herr, wie du willt, so schicks mit mir, BVW 73

NBA I/6, p. 3 BC A35 Duration: *c.* 17 mins

1. [CHORALE + RECITATIVE] SATB obbl hn or org ob I,II str bc g C

Herr, wie du willt, so schicks mit mir
Im Leben und im Sterben!
Tenor
Ach! aber ach! wieviel
Läßt mich dein Wille leiden!
Mein Leben ist des Unglücks Ziel,
Da Jammer und Verdruß
Mich lebend foltern muß,
Und kaum will meine Not im Sterben von mir scheiden.
Allein zu dir steht mein Begier,
Herr, laß mich nicht verderben!
Baß
Du bist mein Helfer, Trost und Hort,
So der Betrübten Tränen zählet
Und ihre Zuversicht,
Das schwache Rohr, nicht gar zubricht;
Und weil du mich erwählet,
So sprich ein Trost- und Freudenwort:
Erhalt mich nur in deiner Huld,
Sonst wie du willt, gib mir Geduld,
Denn dein Will ist der beste.
Sopran
Dein Wille zwar ist ein versiegelt Buch,
Da Menschenweisheit nichts vernimmt;
Der Segen scheint uns oft ein Fluch,
Die Züchtigung ergrimmte Strafe,
Die Ruhe, so du in dem Todesschlafe
Uns einst bestimmt,
Ein Eingang zu der Hölle.
Doch macht dein Geist uns dieses Irrtums frei

Lord, as You will, so dispose things for me
In living and in dying!
Tenor
Ah, but alas! how much
Your Will lets me suffer!
My life is misfortune's goal,
Since woe and vexation
Must torture me in life
And my adversity will scarcely part from me in death.
In You alone lies my desire;
Lord, let me not perish!
Bass
You are my helper, comfort and refuge,
Who counts the tears of the distressed,
And their confidence—
That weak reed—does not quite break;
And since You have chosen me,
Say a word of comfort and joy:
Keep me in Your favour,
Otherwise as You will, grant me patience
For Your Will is the best.
Soprano
Your Will is indeed a sealed book
Where human wisdom understands nothing;
Blessing often seems to us a curse,
Instruction, angered reproof,
The rest that in death's sleep
You have one day ordained for us,
An entry into Hell.
Yet Your Spirit makes us free of this error

Und zeigt, daß uns dein Wille heilsam sei.	And shows that Your Will is beneficial to us.
Herr, wie du willt!	**Lord, as You will!**
2. Aria T ob I bc	E♭ C
Ach senke doch den Geist der Freuden	Ah, sink the spirit of joy
Dem Herzen ein!	Into my heart!
Es will oft bei mir geistlich Kranken	My spiritual sickness often makes
Die Freudigkeit und Hoffnung wanken	Joyfulness and hope waver
Und zaghaft sein.	And me faint-hearted.
3. Recitativo B bc	c C
Ach, unser Wille bleibt verkehrt,	Ah, our will remains perverse:
Bald trotzig, bald verzagt,	At times obstinate, at times despondent;
Des Sterbens will er nie gedenken.	It will never consider death.
Allein ein Christ, in Gottes Geist gelehrt,	Only a Christian, taught by God's Spirit,
Lernt sich in Gottes Willen senken	Learns to immerse himself in God's Will
Und sagt:	And says:
4. Aria B str bc	c 3/4
Herr, so du willt,	Lord, if You will,
So preßt, ihr Todesschmerzen,	Then press, you death-pains,
Die Seufzer aus dem Herzen,	The sighs out of my heart,
Wenn mein Gebet nur vor dir gilt.	If only my prayer is valid before You.
Herr, so du willt,	Lord, if You will,
So lege meine Glieder	Then lay my limbs
In Staub und Asche nieder,	Down in dust and ashes,
Dies höchst verderbte Sündenbild.	This most corrupted image of sin.
Herr, so du willt,	Lord, if You will,
So schlagt, ihr Leichenglocken,	Then strike, you funeral bells;
Ich folge unerschrocken,	I follow unperturbed,
Mein Jammer ist nunmehr gestillt,	My distress is now stilled,
Herr, so du willt.	Lord, if You will.
5. Choral SATB bc (+ instrs)	c C
Das ist des Vaters Wille,	**That is the Will of the Father,**
Der uns erschaffen hat;	**Who has created us;**
Sein Sohn hat Guts die Fülle	**His Son has inherited the fullness**
Erworben und Genad;	**Of Goodness and Grace;**
Auch Gott der Heilge Geist	**God the Holy Spirit also**
Im Glauben uns regieret,	**Governs us in Faith,**
Zum Reich des Himmels führet.	**Leads us to the Kingdom of Heaven.**
Ihm sei Lob, Ehr und Preis!	**To Him be glory, honour and praise!**

This work belongs to Bach's first Leipzig cycle of cantatas and received its first performance on 23 January 1724. The anonymous librettist based his ideas chiefly on the leper's words to Jesus (from the Sunday Gospel*), 'Lord, if You will, You can cleanse me'. These words embody the kernel of the biblical healing narrative, for the trust in Jesus shown by the leper and by the centurion of Capernaum teaches us faithfully to accept the Will of God. It is characteristic of the exegesis of the time, however, that the thoughts of the librettist on this basis do not have as their central focus Jesus's healing of the sick, but are instead directed towards death, praying for the joyful resignation of the 'spiritually sick' to the Will of God, even when the hour of death strikes.

On this textual basis Bach creates a cantata of the most striking individuality. The opening movement is based on the first verse of the hymn by Kaspar Bienemann (1582), sung to the melody *Wo Gott der Herr nicht bei uns hält* and expanded by troping recitative insertions. By musical means Bach closely unites the chorale setting and the recitative, for the entire movement is pervaded by a single motive,* derived from the initial notes of the chorale:

The favoured bearer of this motive is the horn, which in a subsequent revival (*c.* 1732/5) was replaced by obbligato* organ (*Rückpositiv*). The other instruments—two oboes, strings, and continuo—represent Bach's normal cantata ensemble.

The introductory ritornello is thematically independent, but in the caesuras of the theme (stated by the oboes with string accompaniment) the horn and strings twice interject the above motive. And in the last bars of the ritornello, the second half of chorale line 1 and the whole of line 2 are interpolated, again played on the horn. Next, the choir enters in a predominantly chordal texture, interrupted by instrumental episodes between the chorale lines—invariably including quotations of the 'Leitmotiv'—and by recitative insertions. These recitative passages are more closely integrated than in many similar Bach compositions into the thematic material of the movement as a whole. They are set as *accompagnato,** being accompanied by ritornello motives in the oboes; and further, the head-motive of the chorale is heard frequently at various pitches in horn-and-string interjections. In the final reprise of the ritornello, the whole choir breaks in with two quotations of the head-motive; it then does so a third time in an appended cadential conclusion, so that, despite its complex structure, the entire movement is literally pervaded by a single *Leitmotiv*, 'Herr, wie du willt' ('Lord, as You will').

The tenor aria, no. 2, is the only cheerfully relaxed movement in the cantata. The short introductory oboe ritornello, which is notable for its unsymmetrical phrase structure (1½ + 1½ + 1 bars)—text-engendered, as the following vocal passage shows—depicts in two falling melodic lines the 'sinking' of the spirit of joy into the heart. Bach employs the motives in these phrases in spirited play:

after the brief first vocal passage, the whole ritornello is heard again in free inversion; and in the course of the movement the initial motive and its inversion alternate on several occasions. Its frequent modifications are, in the middle section, linked with a shaking figure which represents the word 'wanken' ('waver').

The few bars of the third movement include, on the words 'Bald trotzig, bald verzagt' ('at times obstinate, at times despondent'; after Jeremiah 17.9), a bold harmonic progression that illustrates with incomparable vividness the rebellious will falling back on itself:

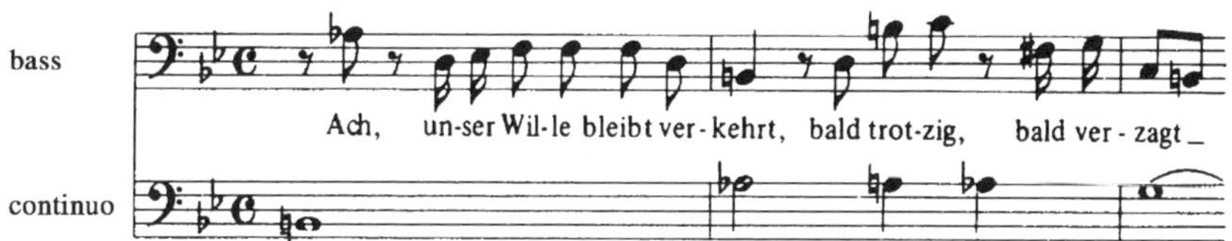

This recitative leads without a break into the following aria, no. 4, which opens without ritornello and, like the first movement, is built on a *Leitmotiv*. This motive, a setting of words from the Gospel reading (Matthew 8.2), is heard at the outset of the aria as a motto*:

Bach structures the movement according to the text, which is exceptional in that it consists of three four-line stanzas, each opening with the line 'Herr, so du willt' ('Lord, if You will'). Accordingly, Bach's setting is likewise strophic, though the individual stanzas are very freely varied, and the aria ends with a coda which—again by analogy with the first movement—yet once more reiterates the words 'Herr, so du willt'. The unorthodox form of the movement might be outlined as follows:

'Motto'—instrumental episode *a*
Verse 1 (head-motive—sigh motives)
Instrumental episode a^1
Verse 2 (varied head-motive—descending melodic lines)
Instrumental episode *b*
Verse 3 (varied head-motive—*pizzicato*:* 'funeral bells')
Instrumental episode *c* (bells motive)
Coda 'Herr, so du willt' (varied head-motive)
Instrumental postlude a^1

The various motives, whose profusion keeps opening up new perspectives, are of unique beauty and expressive power. The variant of the above head-motive (heard numerous times in various intervallic forms) is worth quoting:

as is the instrumental figure that occurs alongside the head-motive:

In the absence of an extended thematic ritornello, this movement—one of Bach's greatest inspirations—forms the impression of a spacious arioso.* It provides an example of how weighty Bach's creations often become when conceived within a fixed formal scheme. The cantata concludes with a plain chorale setting: the final verse of the hymn *Von Gott will ich nicht lassen* by Ludwig Helmbold (1563).

Was mein Gott will, das gscheh allzeit, BVW 111

NBA I/6, p. 27 BC A36 Duration: *c.* 22 mins

1. [Chorale] SATB ob I,II str bc a ¢

Was mein Gott will, das gscheh allzeit,	**Whatever my God wills, may that happen always;**
Sein Will, der ist der beste;	**His Will: that is best;**
Zu helfen den'n er ist bereit,	**He is ready to help those**
Die an ihn glauben feste.	**Who have firm faith in Him.**
Er hilft aus Not, der fromme Gott,	**He helps those in need, the righteous God,**
Und züchtiget mit Maßen:	**And corrects with just measure.**
Wer Gott vertraut, fest auf ihn baut,	**Whoever trusts God, builds firmly on Him,**
Den will er nicht verlassen.	**Will not be forsaken by Him.**

2. Aria B bc e C

Entsetze dich, mein Herze, nicht,	Do not be dismayed, my heart:
Gott ist dein Trost und Zuversicht	**God is your comfort and confidence**
Und deiner Seelen Leben.	And the life of your soul.
Ja, was sein weiser Rat bedacht,	Indeed, what His wise counsel
Dem kann die Welt und Menschenmacht	Has considered, the world and human might
Unmöglich widerstreben.	Cannot possibly counter.

3. Recitativo A bc	b C
O Törichter! der sich von Gott entzieht	O foolish one, who withdraws from God
Und wie ein Jonas dort	And like a Jonah there
Vor Gottes Angesichte flieht;	Flees before God's countenance;
Auch unser Denken ist ihm offenbar,	Even our thinking is plain to Him,
Und unsers Hauptes Haar	And the hair of our head
Hat er gezählet.	He has counted.
Wohl dem, der diesen Schutz erwählet	Blessed is he who chooses this protection
Im gläubigen Vertrauen,	In faithful trust,
Auf dessen Schluß und Wort	Looking to His decision and Word
Mit Hoffnung und Geduld zu schauen.	With hope and patience.
4. Aria [Duetto] AT str bc	G $\frac{3}{4}$
So geh ich mit beherzten Schritten,	Then I walk with spirited steps,
Auch wenn mich Gott zum Grabe führt.	Even when God leads me to the grave.
Gott hat die Tage aufgeschrieben,	God has recorded my days,
So wird, wenn seine Hand mich rührt,	So that when His Hand stirs me
Des Todes Bitterkeit vertrieben.	Death's bitterness shall be driven away.
5. Recitativo S ob I,II bc	F–a C
Drum wenn der Tod zuletzt den Geist	When at last, then, death powerfully
Noch mit Gewalt aus seinem Körper reißt,	Tears my spirit out of its body,
So nimm ihn, Gott, in treue Vaterhände!	Then take it, O God, in Your faithful, fatherly hands!
Wenn Teufel, Tod und Sünde mich bekriegt	When devil, death, and sin wage war on me
Und meine Sterbekissen	And my death-pillow
Ein Kampfplatz werden müssen,	Must become a battleground,
So hilf, damit in dir mein Glaube siegt!	Then help my Faith in You to be victorious!
O seliges, gewünschtes Ende!	O blessed, desirable end!
6. Chorale SATB bc (+ instrs)	a C
Noch eins, Herr, will ich bitten dich,	**One more thing, Lord, would I beg of You**
Du wirst mirs nicht versagen:	**—You will not refuse me—**
Wenn mich der böse Geist anficht,	**When the evil spirit tempts me,**
Laß mich doch nicht verzagen.	**Let me not lose heart.**
Hilf, steur und wehr, ach Gott, mein Herr,	**Help, steer, and defend, ah God, my Lord,**
Zu Ehren deinem Namen.	**To the honour of Your Name.**
Wer das begehrt, dem wird's gewährt;	**Whoever desires that, it will be granted him;**
Drauf sprech ich fröhlich: Amen.	**Therefore I say gladly 'Amen'.**

Bach composed this chorale cantata* for 21 January 1725. The four-verse hymn on which it is based comprises three verses by Duke Albrecht of Prussia

(1547), plus an extra verse added in the original edition of 1554. The outer verses are retained word for word in nos. 1 and 6; the second verse is paraphrased in nos. 2 and 3, and the third in nos. 4 and 5. Although correspondences in ideas, and even the literal adoption of certain phrases, are easily recognizable, as a whole the paraphrase is nonetheless very free, owing to the brevity of the original hymn. It is worth noting that material from the Sunday Gospel* was not used to fill out the text; instead, the anonymous librettist drew upon other biblical passages. Thus at the hymn words 'Wenns ihm gefällt, will ich ihm halten stille' ('If it pleases Him, I will hold Him calmly') he adduces the example of Jonah, who in vain sought to withdraw from the Lord (no. 3; cf. Jonah 1.3); and the phrase 'Death's bitterness shall be driven away' (no. 4) is found, albeit in a different context, in 1 Samuel 15.32. Accordingly, the link with the Sunday Gospel rests exclusively—still more so than in the cantata of the previous year, BWV 73—on the idea that the Christian has to submit to God's Will.

The large-scale introductory movement exhibits the form typical of numerous chorale cantatas from this cycle. The chorale melody is delivered by the soprano in long notes, line by line, supported by the other voices which prepare imitatively* for each soprano entry. On several occasions, the individual chorale lines are sung again by the lower parts in crotchets underneath the long-held last note of the soprano *cantus firmus*.* This thematically unified texture is embedded in instrumental surroundings with their own thematic material, which is developed in the introductory ritornello, repeated in the episodes, and often played during the choral passages. In it two oboes alternate with the strings, and even the continuo sometimes takes a thematic role.

The second movement, an aria for bass and continuo only, contains frequent quasi-ostinato* recurrences of the continuo ritornello. The lines 'God is your comfort and confidence | And the life of your soul' are similar to the opening lines of the second hymn verse and, accordingly, are set to the corresponding phrases of the chorale melody. In keeping with the subjective character of an aria, the chorale is here broken up ornamentally, yet it remains unmistakable. The third movement, a plain *secco* recitative, is followed by a sonorous, dance-like duet, no. 4, whose extended string ritornello, with its dotted rhythms and calm continuo pedal-points, illustrates the 'spirited steps' of the text. Occasional harmonic overclouding on words such as 'zum Grabe' ('to the grave') or 'des Todes Bitterkeit' ('death's bitterness') are swiftly dissolved again and serve only to strengthen the impression of joyful determination. By contrast, the fifth movement turns our attention towards death as the 'blessed, desirable end'. Bach sets it as an accompanied recitative, scored for two oboes and continuo, with arioso* conclusion. It is followed by the concluding verse of the hymn in a plain four-part setting.

Alles nur nach Gottes Willen, BWV 72

NBA I/6, p. 59 BC A37 Duration: *c.* 20 mins

1. [CHORUS] SATB ob I,II str bc — a $\frac{3}{4}$

Alles nur nach Gottes Willen,	All just according to God's Will,
So bei Lust als Traurigkeit,	In both pleasure and sorrow,
So bei gut- als böser Zeit.	In both good and bad times.
Gottes Wille soll mich stillen	God's Will shall calm me
Bei Gewölk und Sonnenschein!	In cloud and sunshine!
Alles nur nach Gottes Willen!	All just according to God's Will!
Dies soll meine Losung sein.	This shall be my motto.

2. RECITATIVO A bc — C–d C

O selger Christ,	O blessed Christian,
Der allzeit seinen Willen	Who always sinks his will
In Gottes Willen senkt,	In God's Will,
Es gehe wie es gehe,	Be it as it may,
Bei Wohl und Wehe!	In weal or woe!
Herr, so du willt, so muß sich alles fügen!	Lord, if You will, all must fall into place!
Herr, so du willt, so kannst du mich vergnügen!	Lord, if You will, You can content me!
Herr, so du willt, verschwindet meine Pein!	Lord, if You will, my pain vanishes!
Herr, so du willt, werd ich gesund und rein!	Lord, if You will, I grow healthy and pure!
Herr, so du willt, wird Traurigkeit zur Freude!	Lord, if You will, sorrow shall turn into joy!
Herr, so du willt, find ich auf Dornen Weide!	Lord, if You will, I find pasture among thorns!
Herr, so du willt, werd ich einst selig sein!	Lord, if You will, I shall one day be blessed!
Herr, so du willt,—laß mich dies Wort im Glauben fassen	Lord, if You will—let me grasp these words in Faith
Und meine Seele stillen!—	And calm my soul!—
Herr, so du willt, so sterb ich nicht,	Lord, if You will, I shall not die,
Ob Leib und Leben mich verlassen,	Even though life and limb forsake me,
Wenn mir dein Geist dies Wort ins Herze spricht!	If Your Spirit says these words in my heart!

3. ARIA A vln I,II bc — d C

Mit allem, was ich hab und bin,	With all that I have and am
Will ich mich Jesu lassen,	I will leave myself to Jesus,
Kann gleich mein schwacher Geist und Sinn	Though my weak spirit and mind
Des Höchsten Rat nicht fassen;	Cannot grasp the Highest's counsel;

Er führe mich nur immer hin
Auf Dorn- und Rosenstraßen!

May He lead me ever forth
On paths of thorns and roses!

4. Recitativo B bc — a–G C

So glaube nun!
Dein Heiland saget: ich wills tun!
Er pflegt die Gnadenhand
Noch willigst auszustrecken,
Wenn Kreuz und Leiden dich erschrecken,
Er kennet deine Not und löst dein Kreuzesband!
Er stärkt, was schwach!
Und will das niedre Dach
Der armen Herzen nicht verschmähen,
Darunter gnädig einzugehen!

Then have Faith now!
Your Saviour says: I will do it!
He is wont to stretch out
His hand of Grace most willingly
When cross and suffering terrify you;
He knows your need and loosens your cross's bond!
He strengthens what is weak!
And under the lowly roof
Of poor hearts He will not scorn
Graciously to enter!

5. Aria S ob I str bc — C $\frac{3}{4}$

Mein Jesus will es tun! Er will dein Kreuz versüßen.
Obgleich dein Herze liegt in viel Bekümmernissen,
Soll es doch sanft und still in seinen Armen ruhn,
Wenn ihn der Glaube faßt! Mein Jesus will es tun!

My Jesus will do it! He will sweeten your cross.
Although your heart lies amidst many afflictions,
It shall nonetheless rest gently and quietly in His arms
Whenever Faith takes hold of it! My Jesus will do it!

6. Choral SATB bc (+ instrs) — a C

Was mein Gott will, das gscheh allzeit,
Sein Will, der ist der beste,
Zu helfen den'n er ist bereit,
Die an ihn glauben feste.
Er hilft aus Not, der fromme Gott,
Und züchtiget mit Maßen.
Wer Gott vertraut, fest auf ihn baut,
Den will er nicht verlassen.

Whatever my God wills, may that happen always;
His Will: that is best;
He is ready to help those
Who have firm Faith in Him.
He helps those in need, the righteous God,
And corrects with just measure.
Whoever trusts God, builds firmly on Him,
Will not be forsaken by Him.

Bach drew the text of this cantata from the cycle *Evangelisches Andachts-Opffer* of 1715 by Salomo Franck, which suggests that it might have originated during Bach's Weimar period. In its transmitted form, however, it was composed in Leipzig for 27 January 1726; and if Bach did compose a Weimar cantata to this text, it must have had little in common with the present work.

The Franck text adheres closely to the Gospel and, moreover, exhibits a striking similarity with that of Cantata 73, which may have been modelled on it. Franck also interprets the Sunday Gospel from the standpoint that the Christian must resign himself to the Will of God 'in both good and bad times'. The ideas that follow from this, however, are not so exclusively concerned with death as in the other texts for this Sunday. Instead, the Gospel account of the healing of the sick is treated as an occasion for trusting Jesus's promise that 'He will sweeten your cross'. Looking at the text in detail, we find several verbal parallels with the Gospel reading. The words 'Herr, so du willt' ('Lord, if You will') from Matthew 8.2, for example, are (as in Cantata 73) reiterated nine times as an anaphora within the first recitative, no. 2. Likewise, the second recitative, no. 4, draws upon Matthew 8.3, in which the leper entreats Jesus to heal him, upon which 'Jesus stretched out His hand, touched him, and said, "I will do it" '. Franck applies this text to the present: 'Then have Faith now! Your Saviour says: I will do it! He is wont to stretch out His hand of Grace most willingly . . .'. In the fifth movement, Franck again reverts to this same biblical passage in the words 'Mein Jesus will es tun!' ('My Jesus will do it!'). Finally, Franck's words from the recitative no. 4, 'Und will das niedre Dach der armen Herzen nicht verschmähen, darunter gnädig einzugehen!' ('And He will not scorn graciously to enter under the lowly roof of poor hearts'), refer to the words of the centurion of Capernaum, 'Lord, I am not worthy that You should enter under my roof' (Matthew 8.8).

In place of the aria prescribed by Franck (for Weimar, 1715), Bach's setting begins with an introductory chorus,* which after 1735 was adapted to form the Gloria of the Missa in G minor, BWV 235. The thematic material is stated in the opening concertante* ritornello. Among the instruments (two oboes, strings and continuo) the violins are predominant with their semiquaver figuration, which towards the end of the introduction shifts to the continuo too. At the beginning of the vocal section, the choir takes the lead at first, only to yield it gradually to the instruments again, for the framing sections of the movement—designed in free da capo* form—each end with choral insertion* within a complete reprise of the opening ritornello. The short middle section comprises a canonic fabric of voices—'God's Will shall calm me'—to the accompaniment of the orchestra.

After six bars of recitative, the second movement, which is accompanied only by continuo, turns into arioso for the lines beginning 'Herr, so du willt' ('Lord, if You will'). The setting of these much repeated words is not unlike that of Cantata 73: its basic form, often varied, is:

The following aria, no. 3, begins without ritornello, the alto voice entering immediately with the first two lines of text. Here again, the fourth movement of

Cantata 73—composed two years earlier—served as a model. The adjoining of recitative and aria may be derived from the text, for the recitative closes with the words:

Herr, so du willt, so sterb ich nicht,	Lord, if You will, I shall not die,
Ob Leib und Leben mich verlassen,	Even though life and limb forsake me,
Wenn mir dein Geist dies Wort ins Herze spricht!	If Your Spirit says these words in my heart!

'These words', inspired within me by the Spirit of God, probably refer to the ninefold repeated 'Lord, if You will', but Bach may have taken them to refer to the words of the following aria, which therefore follow without a break:

Mit allem, was ich hab und bin	With all that I have and am
Will ich mich Jesu lassen.	I will leave myself to Jesus.

Only after this motto* do we hear the ritornello. The instrumental passage that serves this function is one of the relatively few Bach aria ritornellos constructed as a fugal exposition.* Two obbligato* violins and continuo, which has an accompanying role at first, enter in turn with a running semiquaver theme, after which the ritornello concludes with an epilogue. We then hear the main section of the aria, which consists of a reprise of the motto followed by vocal insertion* within the fugal exposition. This entire complex of motto—ritornello—main section is now repeated to the two following lines of text before a thematically freer middle section and an abridged da capo of the main section. The aria as a whole, then, only pays lip service to da capo form: in reality it is constructed in *Bar* form* (A A B A^1, the so-called 'reprise *Bar*').

A *secco* recitative leads to the second aria, no. 5, which is accompanied by oboe and strings. By contrast with the previous aria, it has a song- and dance-like character and gives ample scope for purely instrumental music: after the motto 'Mein Jesus will es tun!' ('My Jesus will do it!'), the sixteen-bar ritornello is repeated in full. Only then does the main section begin, and it includes yet another ritornello reprise, this time freer and involving vocal insertion. The second section is more closely text-related, with its minor-mode over-clouding on the words 'Although your heart lies amidst many afflictions' and its long-held notes on 'rest . . . quietly in His arms'. At the very end of the final ritornello we hear a 'closing motto', a repeat of the words 'Mein Jesus will es tun!' by the soprano, and here we are reminded for a third time of Cantata 73 (first movement). A plain four-part setting of the first verse of the hymn *Was mein Gott will, das gscheh allzeit*, which had formed the basis of a chorale cantata* on the same Sunday in the previous year (BWV 111), concludes the work.

Ich steh mit einem Fuß im Grabe, BWV 156

NBA I/6, p. 91 BC A38 Duration: *c.* 17 mins

1. Sinfonia ob str bc — F–C c

2. Aria [+ Chorale] ST unis str bc — F 3/4

Ich steh mit einem Fuß im Grabe,
Machs mit mir, Gott, nach deiner Güt,
Bald fällt der kranke Leib hinein,
Hilf mir in meinen Leiden,
Komm, lieber Gott, wenn dirs gefällt,
Was ich dich bitt, versag mir nicht.
Ich habe schon mein Haus bestellt.
Wenn sich mein Seel soll scheiden,
So nimm sie, Herr, in deine Händ.
Nur laß mein Ende selig sein!
Ist alles gut, wenn gut das End.

I stand with one foot in the grave,
Deal with me, O God, according to Your loving kindness,
Soon the sick body slumps,
Help me in my suffering,
Come, dear God, when it pleases You,
What I ask of You do not refuse me.
I have already set my house in order.
When my soul must depart,
Take it, Lord, in Your hands.
Just let my end be blessed!
All is well that ends well.

3. Recitativo B bc — d c

Mein Angst und Not,
Mein Leben und mein Tod
Steht, liebster Gott, in deinen Händen;
So wirst du auch auf mich
Dein gnädig Auge wenden.
Willst du mich meiner Sünden wegen
Ins Krankenbette legen,
Mein Gott, so bitt ich dich,
Laß deine Güte größer sein
Als die Gerechtigkeit;
Doch hast du mich darzu versehn,
Daß mich mein Leiden soll verzehren,
Ich bin bereit:
Dein Wille soll an mir geschehn;
Verschone nicht und fahre fort,
Laß meine Not nicht lange währen,
Je länger hier, je später dort.

My fear and distress,
My life and my death
Lie, dearest God, in Your hands;
Then will You turn on me
Your gracious eye.
If, on account of my sins, You would
Lay me on my sick-bed,
My God, then I beg You,
Let Your loving kindness be greater
Than Your righteousness.
Yet if You have ordained for me
That my suffering should consume me,
I am prepared:
Your Will shall be done to me;
Do not spare me and proceed,
Do not let my misery last long:
The longer here, the later there.[31]

4. Aria A ob vln I + II (or solo vln?) bc — B♭ c

Herr, was du willt, soll mir gefallen,
Weil doch dein Rat am besten gilt.
In der Freude,
In dem Leide,
Im Sterben, in Bitten und Flehn
Laß mir allemal geschehn,
Herr, wie du willt.

Lord, what You will shall please me,
For Your counsel counts as the best.
In joy,
In suffering,
In dying, in prayer and supplication,
Let it always happen to me,
Lord, as You will.

[31] i.e. 'the longer I am here on earth, the later I will arrive there in heaven'.

5. RECITATIVO B bc g–a c

Und willst du, daß ich nicht soll kranken,	And if You will that I should not be sick,
So werd ich dir von Herzen danken.	Then I shall thank You from my heart.
Doch aber gib mir auch dabei,	Yet grant me also
Daß auch in meinem frischen Leibe	That in my healthy body
Die Seele sonder Krankheit sei	My soul too may be without sickness
Und allezeit gesund verbleibe.	And ever remain healthy.
Nimm sie durch Geist und Wort in acht,	Take heed of it through Spirit and Word,
Denn dieses ist mein Heil,	For this is my Salvation,
Und wenn mir Leib und Seel verschmacht,	And when my body and soul fail,
So bist du, Gott, mein Trost und meines Herzens Teil!	Then You, my God, are my comfort and my heart's portion!

6. CHORAL SATB bc (+ instrs) C c

Herr, wie du willt, so schicks mit mir	**Lord, as You will, so dispose things for me**
Im Leben und im Sterben;	**In living and in dying;**
Allein zu dir steht mein Begier,	**In You alone lies my desire;**
Herr, laß mich nicht verderben!	**Lord, let me not perish!**
Erhalt mich nur in deiner Huld,	**Keep me in Your favour,**
Sonst wie du willt, gib mir Geduld,	**Otherwise as You will, grant me patience;**
Dein Will, der ist der beste.	**Your Will: it is the best.**

The fourth and latest of Bach's surviving cantatas for the Third Sunday after Epiphany was composed to a text from Picander's 1728 cycle and probably first performed on 23 January 1729. Like the librettists of the other three cantatas, Picander based his text upon the Gospel. Jesus's healing of the sick is to him an allusion to the infirmity of man who, in confronting his end, leaves his future to the Will of God. The words of the leper, 'Lord, if You will, You can make me clean', are taken by him—as they were by the librettists of Cantatas 73 and 72—as the key words of the biblical narrative. Accordingly, he begins and ends the second aria, no. 4, with the lines 'Herr, was du willt . . . Herr, wie du willt' ('Lord, what You will . . . Lord, as You will') and, for the concluding chorale, chooses the first verse of the hymn *Herr, wie du willt, so schicks mit mir* ('Lord, as You will, so dispose things for me') by Kaspar Bienemann (1582), which had already been set by Bach in 1724 within the opening movement of Cantata 73.

Picander's text is strikingly brief, containing only two arias and two recitatives, and Bach prefaces it with an introduction in the form of an Adagio for concertante* oboe with an unobtrusive string accompaniment, a piece known to us in its later version as the slow movement of the Harpsichord Concerto in F minor, BWV 1056. Even the cantata version, however, was probably not a new composition, but rather a borrowing from a still older instrumental concerto.[32] At the end, after a full-close in the tonic, the *cantabile* oboe melody suddenly moves towards the dominant C, ending the movement, as it were, with a question.

The second movement is an aria with chorale—a type with which we are familiar from Bach's early cantatas. The theme, engendered purely by the text, is stated in the introductory ritornello for unison violins and viola, and then taken up by the tenor voice in the vocal section. The long-held f^1 represents 'standing', the sinking of the counterpoints* (*catabasis*) reveals the deceptiveness of this stance, and the descent of the melodic line on 'im Grabe' ('in the grave') speaks for itself. Here is the beginning of the vocal section:

The tenor's singing of the aria is combined with the soprano's delivery of the first verse of the hymn *Machs mit mir, Gott, nach deiner Güt* by Johann Hermann Schein (1628).

The third movement, a *secco* recitative, concludes with a short arioso* passage on the words 'Je länger hier, je später dort' ('The longer here [on earth], the later there [in heaven]'). In the second aria, no. 4, obbligato* oboe and unison violins,[33] together with continuo, form an instrumental trio texture, which becomes a quartet when the voice part is added. The head-motive with which the upper parts enter one after another proves to be the most significant theme, pervading the entire movement. It is heard with text at the beginning of the vocal section:

The joyfully excited mood of the aria is only temporarily disturbed in the middle section, where the rhythmic motion is reduced at the words 'im Sterben' ('in dying'). The second recitative, no. 5, is, like the first, a plain *secco*, and even the

[32] See J. Rifkin, 'Ein langsamer Konzertsatz J. S. Bachs', *BJ* 1978, 140–7.

[33] According to the sole surviving manuscript copy, which dates from a later period. Solo violin scoring is more likely, however.

reference to Psalm 73.26 with which it closes—'And when my body and soul fail, then You, my God, are my comfort and my heart's portion!'—receives no special emphasis in its musical setting. The work ends in the usual manner with a plain chorale setting.

1.15 Fourth Sunday after Epiphany

EPISTLE: Romans 13.8–10: So Love is now the fulfilment of the Law.
GOSPEL: Matthew 8.23–7: Jesus, sleeping in the boat, is awakened and calms the storm.

Jesus schläft, was soll ich hoffen, BWV 81

NBA I/6, p. 111 BC A39 Duration: *c.* 19 mins

1. ARIA A rec I,II str bc		e C
Jesus schläft, was soll ich hoffen?	Jesus sleeps: what hope have I?	
Seh ich nicht	Do I not see,	
Mit erblaßtem Angesicht	With face turned pale,	
Schon des Todes Abgrund offen?	Death's abyss open already?	
2. RECITATIVO T bc		a–G C
Herr! warum trittest du so ferne?	Lord, why do You stand so far off?	
Warum verbirgst du dich zur Zeit der Not,	Why do You hide Yourself in times of trouble,	
Da alles mir ein kläglich Ende droht?	When for me all threatens a woeful end?	
Ach, wird dein Auge nicht durch meine Not beweget,	Ah, does my distress not move Your eye,	
So sonsten nie zu schlummern pfleget?	Otherwise never wont to slumber?	
Du wiesest ja mit einem Sterne	Once with a Star You did indeed make wise	
Vordem den neubekehrten Weisen,	The Wise Men, neophytes in Christ,	
Den rechten Weg zu reisen.	As to the right(eous) way to travel.	
Ach leite mich durch deiner Augen Licht,	Ah, lead me by the Light of Your eyes,	
Weil dieser Weg nichts als Gefahr verspricht.	For this way promises nothing but danger.	
3. ARIA T str bc		G $\frac{3}{8}$
Die schäumenden Wellen von Belials Bächen	The foaming waves of Belial's waters	
Verdoppeln die Wut.	Redouble their rage.	
Ein Christ soll zwar wie Wellen stehn,	A Christian should indeed stand like a rock[34]	

[34] The translation is here based on the conjectural reading 'wie Felsen' recommended by Wustmann, p. 48. The printed text in St Petersburg, however, reads 'wie Wellen' ('like waves').

Wenn Trübsalswinde um ihn gehn,
Doch suchet die stürmende Flut
Die Kräfte des Glaubens zu schwächen.

When affliction's winds go round him,
Yet the storming torrent seeks
To weaken the strength of Faith.

4. Arioso B bc — b c

'Ihr Kleingläubigen, warum seid ihr so furchtsam?'

'You of little faith, why are you so fearful?'

5. Aria B ob d'am I,II str bc — e c

Schweig, aufgetürmtes Meer!
Verstumme, Sturm und Wind!
Dir sei dein Ziel gesetzet,
Damit mein auserwähltes Kind
Kein Unfall je verletzet.

Peace, towering sea!
Be still, storm and wind!
May your time be so determined
That My chosen child
Is not injured by any incident.

6. Recitativo A bc — G–b c

Wohl mir, mein Jesus spricht ein Wort,
Mein Helfer ist erwacht,
So muß der Wellen Sturm, des Unglücks Nacht
Und aller Kummer fort.

Blessed am I: my Jesus speaks the Word,
My Helper has awoken;
Then the waves' storm, misfortune's night,
And all sorrow must be gone.

7. Choral SATB bc (+ ob d'am I,II str) — e c

Unter deinen Schirmen
Bin ich für den Stürmen
Aller Feinde frei.
Laß den Satan wittern,
Laß den Feind erbittern,
Mir steht Jesus bei.
Ob es itzt gleich kracht und blitzt,
Ob gleich Sünd und Hölle schrecken,
Jesus will mich decken.

Under Your shadow
I am free from the storms
Of all enemies.
Let Satan nose about,
Let the enemy be exasperated:
Jesus stands by me.
Though it now crashes and flashes,
Though sin and hell terrify me,
Jesus will cover me.

This work, which belongs to Bach's first Leipzig cycle of cantatas, was composed for 30 January 1724. The anonymous librettist relies closely on the Gospel* text and—like the librettists of the cantatas for the First Sunday after Epiphany—draws his material from the contrast between Jesus hidden (sleeping) and Jesus manifest (actively intervening). Here again, the biblical account is reinterpreted to refer directly to the present situation of the Christian. Confronted by death, I see no help from Jesus (no. 1). The anxious questioning of no. 2, 'Lord, why do You stand so far off? Why do You hide Yourself in times of trouble?', is drawn almost word for word from the first verse of Psalm 10. No. 3, meanwhile, compares the predicament of the Christian, overwhelmed by the godless, with the waves of a storm at sea, as recounted in the Gospel for the day. No. 4, a literal quotation from the Gospel reading (Matt. 8.26), brings the turning-point: Christ is only apparently distant, and by means of his absolute command (no. 5) the Christian is saved (no. 6). The concluding chorale—the second verse of the hymn *Jesu, meine Freude* by Johann Franck (1653)—involves the entire congregation, as it were, in an avowal of trust in God.

Bach's setting is remarkably dramatic, closely resembling the cantatas conceived as a dialogue between the Soul and Jesus. The choir comes together only in the final chorale. The instrumental ensemble includes not only strings and continuo but, in the first movement, two recorders to characterize the 'sleeping' Jesus. In no. 5 their place is taken by two oboes d'amore,* which would have been played by the same musicians: the mastery of several instruments was, for the musician of Bach's day, an essential professional qualification.

The opening aria employs the typical resources of the time to depict the sleeping Jesus: strings in low register, doubled at the octave by recorders, throbbing pedal notes in the continuo, and low held notes sung by the alto (similar expressive means are employed by Bach in the aria 'Sanfte soll mein Todeskummer' from the *Easter Oratorio*, BWV 249). But the cantata aria is not only a lullaby: it is also a lament, as revealed by its numerous diminished intervals and augmented or chromatic* seconds. And its text frames an anxious question, hence the singer's not coming to rest on the tonic but closing, with voice raised in pitch, on the second degree in a dominant context.

The tenor recitative, no. 2, also begins with several reproachful questions, which are repeatedly turned upwards by the voice at the cadence. The second half of the movement includes a prayer to be guided upon the right path and harks back to the Feast of the Epiphany in the words 'Once with a Star You did indeed make wise the Wise Men, neophytes in Christ, as to the right(eous) way to travel'. The phrase 'Ah, lead me by the Light of Your eyes', represented by a descending scale figure, alludes to Exodus 33.14: 'My countenance shall go before you, therewith shall I lead you'.

The third movement—an aria with strings in an amplified trio texture, led by the first violin—with its striking depiction of a storm, borders closely on the operatic musical literature of the day. In the opening ritornello, the waves piling upon themselves and their torrential descent may be clearly discerned:

In the middle section, at the words 'A Christian should indeed stand like a rock when affliction's winds go round him', a sudden calm (marked 'adagio') intervenes three times, but then the storm breaks out anew.

The arioso* 'Ihr Kleingläubigen', no. 4, for bass voice—the *vox Christi*—and continuo, employs thematic material of such homogeneity that it virtually turns into a two-part fugue* or invention; in fact, the biblical text could easily be added to the continuo part too. What emerges is a 'speech' movement of the most compelling effectiveness. Like the opening movement, it ends with a question: its Phrygian cadence* enables the following aria, no. 5, in which Jesus commands the waves to be at peace, to appear to be a direct outcome of it. Here again, we encounter a storm aria, but this time the 'allegro' raging unison runs of the strings are contrasted with the more tranquil motion of the two oboes d'amore. The short alto recitative, no. 6, announces restored calm. And the plain closing chorale lends the cantata's world of feeling—so far decidedly subjective in character—a more general significance.

Finally, it is worth drawing attention to the formal symmetry that distinguishes this cantata. The substance of the text divides the work into two parts: life without Jesus (nos. 1–3) and life with Jesus (nos. 5–7). At the centre is the biblical-text movement, no. 4, in which mankind is addressed by Jesus Himself. This middle movement is surrounded by two storm arias, whereas in the outer movements relative calm prevails, albeit the contrasting calm of distance from God (no. 1) and security in God (no. 7). This symmetry is emphasized by Bach's choice of key: at the centre lies the dominant B minor; the tonic E minor and the relative major G prevail in the other movements; and, in addition, the subdominant (A minor) and dominant (B minor) are touched upon in the recitatives.

Wär Gott nicht mit uns diese Zeit, BWV 14

NBA I/6, p. 139 BC A40 Duration: *c.* 18 mins

1. [Chorale] SATB hn + ob I + II str bc — g $\frac{3}{8}$

Wär Gott nicht mit uns diese Zeit,	**Were God not with us at this time,**
So soll Israel sagen,	**So shall Israel say,**
Wär Gott nicht mit uns diese Zeit,	**Were God not with us at this time,**
Wir hätten müssen verzagen,	**We should have had to be dismayed,**
Die so ein armes Häuflein sind,	**We who are such a wretched little band,**
Veracht' von so viel Menschenkind,	**Despised by so many children of men,**
Die an uns setzen alle.	**Who all set upon us.**

2. Aria S tr or hn[35] str bc — B♭ $\frac{3}{4}$

Unsre Stärke heißt zu schwach,	Our strength is too weak
Unserm Feind zu widerstehen.	To withstand our enemy.
Stünd uns nicht der Höchste bei,	If the Highest did not stand by us,
Würd uns ihre Tyrannei	Their tyranny would
Bald bis an das Leben gehen.	Soon threaten our life.

[35] A high B♭ instrument designated 'tromba' in the autograph score, but in the original performing material the part is included in the horn's copy; see P. Wollny, KB, NBA I/6 (1996), 149–50.

3. RECITATIVO T bc	g–d c
Ja, hätt es Gott nur zugegeben,	Yes, had God but allowed it,
Wir wären längst nicht mehr am Leben,	We would long have been alive no more;
Sie rissen uns aus Rachgier hin,	They would tear us away out of thirst for revenge,
So zornig ist auf uns ihr Sinn.	So angry with us is their disposition.
Es hätt uns ihre Wut	Their rage,
Wie eine wilde Flut	Like a wild torrent
Und als beschäumte Wasser überschwemmet,	And like foaming water, would have swamped us,
Und niemand hätte die Gewalt gehemmet.	And no one would have impeded their force.
4. ARIA B ob I,II bc	g c
Gott, bei deinem starken Schützen	O God, by Your powerful protection
Sind wir vor den Feinden frei.	We are free of enemies.
Wenn sie sich als wilde Wellen	When, like wild waves, they
Uns aus Grimm entgegenstellen,	Set themselves against us in fury,
Stehn uns deine Hände bei.	Your hands assist us.
5. CHORAL SATB bc (+ instrs)	g c
Gott Lob und Dank, der nicht zugab,	**Praise and thank God, who did not allow**
Daß ihr Schlund uns möcht fangen.	**Their jaws to trap us.**
Wie ein Vogel des Stricks kömmt ab,	**As a bird gets away from the snare,**
Ist unsre Seel entgangen:	**Our soul has escaped:**
Strick ist entzwei, und wir sind frei;	**The snare is asunder and we are free;**
Des Herren Name steht uns bei,	**The Lord's Name stands by us,**
Des Gottes Himmels und Erden.	**The God of heaven and earth.**

This chorale cantata* does not belong to the cycle of 1724–5, for Easter was so early in 1725 (1 April) that there was no Fourth Sunday after Epiphany. Consequently Bach composed Cantata 14 at a later date when he required a chorale cantata for this Sunday. According to the dated autograph, that happened in 1735, a few weeks after the first performance of the *Christmas Oratorio*.

The hymn that forms the basis of the text is Martin Luther's adaptation of Psalm 124 (1524), whose first and third verses are retained literally in the outer movements, nos. 1 and 5, while the second verse is paraphrased in the tenor recitative no. 3. The two arias lack specific links with Luther's hymn and are at most indebted to it in general substance. From the Sunday Gospel,* the anonymous librettist chiefly draws a general moral: that our life is guided by God's help, without which we are lost. A certain connection with the Gospel narrative of the storm at sea is already found in the original psalm: the image of streams of water which, according to the psalmist, would drown our soul if the Lord were not with us (vv. 4–5) recurs both in Luther's hymn and in the cantata libretto (at the end of no. 3 and in the middle section of no. 4).

In Bach's setting, the opening chorus* arouses particular interest, since it does not accord with the form predominantly used by Bach, with concertante* ritornellos and the chorale melody sung by the choir. Instead, it resembles the chorale-motet type, in which each line is first prepared in an imitative* texture and then delivered by a single part in long note-values. The *specific* properties of this movement, however, render it unique in all Bach. Its foundation is a four-part vocal texture, reinforced by doubling strings, in which the continuo is partly independent and partly doubles the vocal bass. This homogeneous, motet-like vocal texture states each chorale line in turn in the form of a counter-fugue;* that is, every subject entry is answered by its inversion. The opening may be quoted here:

In addition, each chorale line, after its fugal exposition* in four voice parts, is stated again in augmentation* (dotted crotchets) by unison horn and oboes, giving rise to a real five-part polyphony.* This exceptionally elaborate, contrapuntal mode of writing has only one approximate parallel within the Bach cantata choruses known to us: the opening movement of Cantata 80, which, however, lacks the inversion of the chorale lines (though on the other hand, their augmentation is there given in canon*).

Compared with this remarkable opening chorus, the other movements are of a more conventional character. The aria 'Unsre Stärke heißt zu schwach' (no. 2) acquires particular sonic charm from the trumpet (or horn?) added to the string orchestra. The third movement, a *secco* recitative, almost has the character of an arioso* due to the rapid continuo passages that form the background to words like 'Rachgier' ('thirst for revenge'), 'Wut' ('rage'), 'Flut' ('torrent'), and 'überschwemmet' ('swamped'), alongside other, less affect-laden* words.

The second aria (no. 4), in which two obbligato* oboes (and continuo) form a concertante texture in conjunction with the bass voice, is song-like but grave in character. The middle section brings greater excitement, with its powerful octave leaps and downward-shooting scales on 'Wellen' ('waves') and 'entgegenstellen' ('set against'). Like the first aria, it is designed in free da capo* form. A four-part chorale setting, plain but considerably broken up into quaver motion in the inner parts, closes a work that counts as one of the latest surviving original church cantatas by Bach.

1.16 Septuagesima (Third Sunday before Lent)

Epistle: 1 Corinthians 9.24–10.5: The sprint to victory.
Gospel: Matthew 20.1–16: The parable of the labourers in the vineyard.

Nimm, was dein ist, und gehe hin, BWV 144

NBA I/7, p. 3 BC A41 Duration: *c.* 16 mins

	German	English	Key	Time
1.	[Chorus] SATB bc (+ str + ob I,II)		b	¢
	'Nimm, was dein ist, und gehe hin!'	'Take what is yours and go your way!'		
2.	Aria A str (+ ob I,II?) bc		e	3/4
	Murre nicht, Lieber Christ, Wenn was nicht nach Wunsch geschicht; Sondern sei mit dem zufrieden, Was dir dein Gott hat beschieden, Er weiß, was dir nützlich ist.	Do not murmur, Dear Christian, If what happens accords not with your wishes; Rather be content with that Which Your God has destined for you: He knows what is beneficial to you.		
3.	Choral SATB bc (+ str)		G	c
	Was Gott tut, das ist wohlgetan, **Es bleibt gerecht sein Wille;** **Wie er fängt meine Sachen an,** **Will ich ihm halten stille.** **Er ist mein Gott,** **Der in der Not** **Mich wohl weiß zu erhalten:** **Drum laß ich ihn nur walten.**	**Whatever God deals is dealt bountifully:** **His Will remains just;** **However He runs my affairs,** **I will hold still before Him.** **He is my God,** **Who in time of trouble** **Well knows how to uphold me:** **Therefore I will just let Him rule.**		
4.	Recitativo T bc		e–b	c
	Wo die Genügsamkeit regiert Und überall das Ruder führt, Da ist der Mensch vergnügt Mit dem, wie es Gott fügt.	Where contentment governs And everywhere takes the helm, There man is satisfied With that which God ordains.		

Dagegen, wo die Ungenügsamkeit das Urteil spricht,
Da stellt sich Gram und Kummer ein,
Das Herz will nicht zufrieden sein,
Und man gedenket nicht daran:
Was Gott tut, das ist wohlgetan.

On the other hand, where discontent pronounces judgement,
There grief and sorrow arise,
The heart will not be satisfied,
And people do not remember that
Whatever God deals is dealt bountifully.

5. ARIA S ob d'am solo bc b c

Genügsamkeit
Ist ein Schatz in diesem Leben,
Welcher kann Vergnügung geben
In der größten Traurigkeit,
Denn es lässet sich in allen
Gottes Fügung wohl gefallen
Genügsamkeit.

Contentment
Is a treasure in this life
That can give pleasure
Amidst the greatest sorrow,
For it lets itself be well pleased
With all God's dispensation:
Contentment.

6. CHORAL SATB bc (+ instrs) b c

Was mein Gott will, das gscheh allzeit,
Sein Will, der ist der beste.
Zu helfen den'n er ist bereit,
Die an ihn gläuben feste.
Er hilft aus Not, der fromme Gott,
Er züchtiget mit Maßen.
Wer Gott vertraut, fest auf ihn baut,
Den will er nicht verlassen.

Whatever my God wills, may that happen always;
His Will: that is best.
He is ready to help those
Who have firm Faith in Him.
He helps those in need, the righteous God,
He corrects with just measure.
Whoever trusts God, builds firmly on Him
Will not be forsaken by Him.

This cantata originated during Bach's first year in Leipzig and received its first performance on 6 February 1724. Its authenticity has on occasion been doubted—incorrectly, however, for the original source material establishes Bach's authorship without ambiguity. The anonymous librettist refers to the Gospel* reading, from which the text of the opening movement is drawn (Matt. 20.14). He concludes from it, however, only the rather superficial moral (as it may seem to some modern listeners) that one should cultivate contentment, be satisfied with one's lot, and resign oneself to the Will of God.

Bach's setting largely renounces the concertante* element, which may have nourished the aforementioned doubts about its authenticity. The opening movement is a motet-fugue with *colla parte** instruments (two oboes and strings) and partly independent continuo. Friedrich Wilhelm Marpurg admired the 'splendid declamation which the composer has applied to the main section and to a special little play on the words "gehe hin" ':[36]

[36] The 'vortreffliche Deklamation' which 'der Componist im Hauptsatze und in einem kleinen besonderen Spiele mit dem *gehe hin* angebracht hatte'; *Kritische Briefe über die Tonkunst*, I (Berlin, 1760), 381.

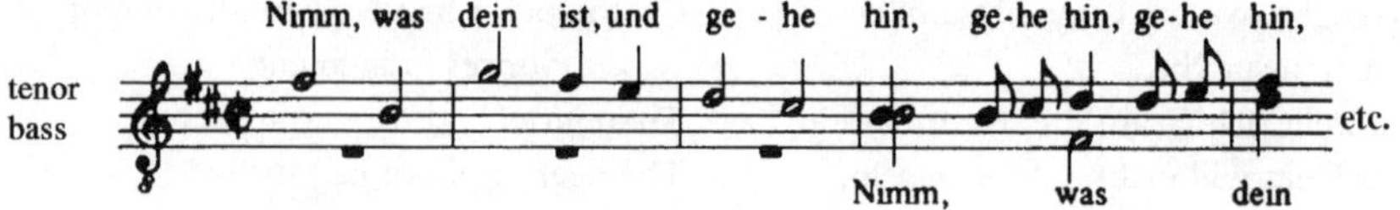

In the course of the movement, the countersubject (bar 4, tenor) undergoes an episode-like development which brings still more clearly to the listener's consciousness the admired text declamation.

By contrast, the following aria (no. 2) has a markedly homophonic* character and is close to dance (the minuet) in its down-beat phrase structure. Repeated quavers in the accompanying parts depict the 'murmuring' of the text—based on 1 Corinthians 10.10, which in turn echoes Numbers 14.27. The opening ritornello is divided into two eight-bar halves, the theme of the second being a free inversion of that of the first. The bipartite main section employs the same structure, and here the text also undergoes an 'inversion' ('lieber Christ, murre nicht'), so that the words 'murre nicht' ('do not murmur') occur on low notes as before and 'lieber Christ' ('dear Christian') on high notes. A plain chorale—the first verse of the hymn *Was Gott tut, das ist wohlgetan* by Samuel Rodigast (1675)—has an articulating function as the conclusion of the first half of the work. In view of the cantata's brevity, however, it is doubtful whether Bach availed himself of the opportunity of performing one half before the sermon and the other half afterwards.

The fourth movement is a *secco* recitative, whose closing words, 'Was Gott tut, das ist wohlgetan' ('Whatever God deals is dealt bountifully'), are set as arioso* but without employing the chorale melody. This is followed by a soprano aria with obbligato* oboe d'amore* (no. 5) in which the concertante principle comes into its own. We are struck by its form: in place of the expected da capo*, the third and longest section contains a restatement of the entire text, but without literal reprise of the music, so that the movement acquires the character of a very free sequence of variations rather than a da capo aria. A plain chorale setting of the first verse of the hymn *Was mein Gott will, das gscheh allzeit* by Duke Albrecht of Prussia (1547) concludes the cantata.

Ich hab in Gottes Herz und Sinn, BWV 92

NBA I/7, p. 43 BC A42 Duration: *c.* 33 mins

1. [CHORALE] SATB ob d'am I,II str bc b $\frac{6}{8}$

Ich hab in Gottes Herz und Sinn	**I have to God's heart and mind**
Mein Herz und Sinn ergeben,	**Yielded my own heart and mind;**
Was böse scheint, ist mein Gewinn,	**What seems bad is my gain:**
Der Tod selbst ist mein Leben.	**Death itself is my Life.**
Ich bin ein Sohn	**I am a son**

Des, der den Thron
Des Himmels aufgezogen;
Ob er gleich schlägt
Und Kreuz auflegt,
Bleibt doch sein Herz gewogen.

Of Him who has been raised
To the Throne of Heaven;
Though He should strike me
And impose a cross upon me,
Yet His heart remains well-disposed to me.

2. RECITATIVO [+ CHORALE] B bc e C

Es kann mir fehlen nimmermehr!
Es müssen eh'r,
Wie selbst der treue Zeuge spricht,
Mit Prasseln und mit grausem Knallen
Die Berge und die Hügel fallen:
Mein Heiland aber trüget nicht,
Mein Vater muß mich lieben.
Durch Jesu rotes Blut bin ich in seine Hand geschrieben;
Er schützt mich doch!
Wenn er mich auch gleich wirft ins Meer,
So lebt der Herr auf großen Wassern noch,
Der hat mir selbst mein Leben zugeteilt,
Drum werden sie mich nicht ersäufen.
Wenn mich die Wellen schon ergreifen
Und ihre Wut mit mir zum Abgrund eilt,
So will er mich nur üben,
Ob ich an Jonam werde denken,
Ob ich den Sinn mit Petro auf ihn werde lenken.
Er will mich stark im Glauben machen,
Er will vor meine Seele wachen
Und mein Gemüt,
Das immer wankt und weicht,
In seiner Güt,
Der an Beständigkeit nichts gleicht,
Gewöhnen fest zu stehen.
Mein Fuß soll fest
Bis an der Tage letzten Rest
Sich hier auf diesen Felsen gründen.
Halt ich denn Stand
Und lasse mich in felsenfestem Glauben finden,
Weiß seine Hand,

It can fail me nevermore!
It must happen soon,
As the faithful witness himself says,
That with crackles and fierce cracks
The mountains and the hills fall;
But my Saviour does not deceive,
My Father must love me.
In Jesus's red Blood I am written upon His hand;
He protects me indeed!
Even if He should cast me straight into the sea,
The Lord lives in great waters too,
He who has assigned to me my life itself,
Therefore it will not drown me.
Even if the waves should seize me
And their rage rush with me into the abyss,
He would only be training me,
To see whether I will think of Jonah,
Or whether, with Peter, I will direct my mind towards Him.
He will make me strong in Faith,
He will watch over my soul
And accustom my spirit,
Which always wavers and yields,
In His goodness,
Which nothing equals for constancy,
To stand firm.
My foot shall firmly—
Till the last remnant of my days—
Be grounded here upon this Rock.
If I keep firm
And am found to be rock-firm in Faith,
Then His hand,

Die er mir schon vom Himmel beut,

Zu rechter Zeit
Mich wieder zu erhöhen.

Which He already holds out to me from heaven,
At the right time
Knows how to exalt me again.

3. Aria T str bc — b C

Seht, seht! wie reißt, wie bricht, wie fällt,
Was Gottes starker Arm nicht hält.

Seht aber fest und unbeweglich prangen,
Was unser Held mit seiner Macht umfangen.
Laßt Satan wüten, rasen, krachen,
Der starke Gott wird uns unüberwindlich machen.

See, see! How it tears, breaks and falls,
Whatever God's strong arm does not hold.
But see it shine forth firmly and steadfastly,
Whatever our Hero has embraced with His might.
Let Satan rage, storm, and crash:
The powerful God will make us invincible.

4. Choral A ob d'am I,II bc — f♯ C

Zudem ist Weisheit und Verstand
Bei ihm ohn alle Maßen,
Zeit, Ort und Stund ist ihm bekannt,

Zu tun und auch zu lassen.
Er weiß, wenn Freud,
Er weiß, wenn Leid
Uns, seinen Kindern, diene,
Und was er tut,
Ist alles gut,
Ob's noch so traurig schiene.

Moreover, wisdom and understanding
With Him are beyond all measure;
Time, place, and hour are known to Him,
Whether to do or to leave undone.
He knows when joy,
He knows when suffering
Will serve us, His children,
And whatever He does
Is all good,
However sad it seems.

5. Recitativo T bc — D–b C

Wir wollen nun nicht länger zagen
Und uns mit Fleisch und Blut,
Weil wir in Gottes Hut,
So furchtsam wie bisher befragen.
Ich denke dran,
Wie Jesus nicht gefürcht' das tausendfache Leiden;
Er sah es an
Als eine Quelle ewger Freuden.
Und dir, mein Christ,
Wird deine Angst und Qual, dein bitter Kreuz und Pein
Um Jesu willen Heil und Zucker sein.

Vertraue Gottes Huld
Und merke noch, was nötig ist:
Geduld! Geduld!

We would now no longer be dismayed,
And with our flesh and blood—
Since we are in God's care—
No longer consult as fearfully as before.
I think of this:
How Jesus did not fear a thousandfold suffering;
He saw it
As a source of eternal joy.
And for you, my Christian,
Your fear and torment, your bitter cross and pain
For Jesus's sake shall be Salvation and sweetness.
Trust God's favour
And note what is needed:
Patience, patience!

6. Aria B bc

Das Brausen/Stürmen von den rauhen Winden
Macht, daß wir volle Ähren finden.
Des Kreuzes Ungestüm schafft bei den Christen Frucht,
Drum laßt uns alle unser Leben
Dem weisen Herrscher ganz ergeben.
Küßt seines Sohnes Hand, verehrt die treue Zucht.

D 3/4

The blustering/storming of the rough winds
Makes us find full ears of corn.
The Cross's violence bears fruit in the Christian,
Therefore let us all our life
Yield fully to the wise Ruler.
Kiss His Son's hand, honour His loyal discipline.

7. [Chorale +] Recitativo SATB bc

Ei nun, mein Gott, so fall ich dir
Getrost in deine Hände.
Baß
So spricht der Gott gelaßne Geist,
Wenn er des Heilands Brudersinn
Und Gottes Treue gläubig preist.

Nimm mich, und mache es mit mir
Bis an mein letztes Ende.
Tenor
Ich weiß gewiß,
Daß ich ohnfehlbar selig bin,
Wenn meine Not und mein Bekümmernis
Von dir so wird geendigt werden:
Wie du wohl weißt,
Daß meinem Geist
Dadurch sein Nutz entstehe,
Alt
Daß schon auf dieser Erden,
Dem Satan zum Verdruß,
Dein Himmelreich sich in mir zeigen muß
Und deine Ehr
Je mehr und mehr
Sich in ihr selbst erhöhe.
Sopran
So kann mein Herz nach deinem Willen
Sich, o mein Jesu, selig stillen,
Und ich kann bei gedämpften Saiten
Dem Friedensfürst ein neues Lied bereiten.

b–D c

Ah now, my God, then I fall
Confidently into Your hands.
Bass
So says the spirit entrusted to God
When in Faith it praises the Saviour's
Brotherly disposition and God's faithfulness.
Take me and manage me
Until my final end.
Tenor
I know for certain
That I shall be unfailingly blessed
When my distress and my affliction
Are thus ended by You:
As You well know,
That for my spirit
Thereby its benefit may arise,
Alto
So that already on this earth,
To Satan's vexation,
Your heavenly Kingdom must come to light within me
And Your honour
Ever more and more
May be exalted in the earth.
Soprano
Then can my heart, according to Your Will,
O my Jesus, be blessedly assured,
And I can with muted strings
Prepare a new song for the Prince of Peace.

8. Aria S ob d'am 1 str bc senza org D $\frac{3}{8}$

Meinem Hirten bleib ich treu.	To my Shepherd I remain loyal.
Will er mir den Kreuzkelch füllen,	If He would fill me the cross's cup,
Ruh ich ganz in seinem Willen,	I should rest wholly in His Will:
Er steht mir im Leiden bei.	He stands by me in suffering.
Es wird dennoch nach dem Weinen	After weeping nonetheless
Jesu Sonne wieder scheinen.	Jesus's sun shall shine again.
Meinem Hirten bleib ich treu.	To my Shepherd I remain loyal.
Jesu leb ich, der wird walten,	I live for Jesus, who shall rule;
Freu dich, Herz, du sollst erkalten,	Rejoice, heart, you shall grow cold through dying;
Jesus hat genug getan.	Jesus has done enough.
Amen: Vater, nimm mich an!	Amen: Father, accept me into heaven!

9. Choral SATB bc (+ instrs) b C

Soll ich denn auch des Todes Weg	**Should I, then, travel on the way of death**
Und finstre Straße reisen,	**And on dark streets?**
Wohlan! ich tret auf Bahn und Steg,	**Well, then! I step on the road and path**
Den mir dein Augen weisen.	**That Your eyes point out to me.**
Du bist mein Hirt,	**You are my Shepherd,**
Der alles wird	**Who shall turn all**
Zu solchem Ende kehren,	**To such an end**
Daß ich einmal	**That one day**
In deinem Saal	**In Your hall**
Dich ewig möge ehren.	**I may honour You for ever.**

This chorale cantata,* composed for 28 January 1725, is based on Paul Gerhardt's twelve-verse hymn of 1647. The extensive libretto may explain why the cantata is also exceptionally long, especially since the anonymous librettist, instead of merging the verses wherever possible, has retained a considerable number of them in their original wording, even adding 'trope'* texts on two occasions (verses 2 and 10). Thus, in addition to the outer verses in nos. 1 and 9, the second (in no. 2), the fifth (in no. 4), and the tenth (in no. 7) are adopted literally. The freely paraphrased movements adhere only very loosely to the substance of the other verses, passing over many details. The third movement proves to be a paraphrase of verse 4 (verse 3 is omitted); the fifth movement includes phrases from verses 6 and 8, but without following their content in detail; the sixth movement is more firmly based on verse 9, and the eighth loosely on verse 11.

From the readings for the day no specific ideas are adopted, but only the general admonition to acquiesce in whatever God sends in the way of joy or suffering. References to other biblical passages are included, however, especially in the second movement. Thus the following lines:

Es müssen eh'r,	It must happen soon,
Wie selbst der treue Zeuge spricht,	As the faithful witness himself says,
Mit Prasseln und mit grausem Knallen	That with crackles and fierce cracks
Die Berge und die Hügel fallen.	The mountains and the hills fall.

allude to Isaiah 54.10, and the words 'Durch Jesu rotes Blut bin ich in seine Hand geschrieben' ('In Jesus's red Blood I am written upon His hand') to Isaiah 49.16. Deliverance by the Lord from 'great waters' (also in no. 2) is celebrated in several of the Psalms (18.16, 77.19 and 144.7); and the prophet Jonah and the disciple Peter, both named in the second movement, were alike saved by the Lord from dangerous waters (Jonah 2; Matt. 14.29–31). It has been surmised that the lines 'And I can with muted strings/Prepare a new song for the Prince of Peace' at the end of the seventh movement were added by Bach as a reference to the *pizzicato** accompaniment of the following aria. Yet the *pizzicato* might just as well have been occasioned by the text of the aria.

The large-scale opening movement begins with two oboes d'amore* and strings in alternation. Their thematic material is independent of the chorale melody (*Was mein Gott will, das gscheh allzeit*), which is delivered by the soprano in long notes, line by line, after the introductory ritornello. The other voice parts take no share in the chorale theme, but instead join with the strings in an imitative,* thematically unified texture. In the vocal passages, then, the participants are assigned the following roles:

Soprano: chorale melody in long notes, line by line
Oboe I and II: partly resting, partly with independent instrumental themes
Violin I, II + alto, viola + tenor, continuo + bass: imitative* texture, instrumental themes

Thus, once a dubious hunt for vague allusions is abandoned, one finds that the chorale imparts none of its melodic material to the surrounding texture.

The second movement is polymorphous. It begins with a continuo ritornello, which, in a suitably modifed form, serves as the accompaniment for each chorale line—sung in a lightly ornamented fashion by the bass—during the course of the movement. The inserted recitative passages, by virtue of their continuo accompaniment (which often moves in a very lively manner), have a strong tendency towards arioso.* No. 3, a passionate tenor aria with strings, has as its theme the futility of the world, whose collapse is illustrated by rapid violin passages and energetic dotted rhythms.

The fifth chorale verse is delivered by the alto, line by line, in a quasi-aria (no. 4) to an accompaniment of two oboes d'amore* and continuo, which develop their own thematic material in the episodes. This movement, with its more objectively representational stance (the chorale melody is unvaried and stated without ornament), forms a surely intentional contrast with the preceding one. Yet the minor-mode overclouding on 'er weiß, wenn Leid' ('He knows when suffering') is unmistakable; and, still more strikingly, the words 'Ob's noch so traurig schiene' ('however sad it seems') at the close are interpreted by a chromatically* falling line in the oboes.

A syllabically* declaimed *secco* recitative, no. 5, in which only the last bar—'Geduld! Geduld!' ('Patience! patience!')—is set as arioso, leads to the second aria, no. 6, for bass and continuo only, whose agitation in no way resembles that of the first aria. In place of strongly marked rhythms, Bach now uses running semiquaver passages and extended melismas* on 'Brausen' ('blustering') to characterize the fruit-bearing 'violence' of the text. The second chorale movement with recitative insertions, no. 7, differs from the first in that the chorale is now delivered in four-part texture and the recitative singer changes in rising order of pitch from bass to soprano.

The soprano aria 'Meinem Hirten bleib ich treu', no. 8, scored with obbligato* oboe d'amore and a plucked string accompaniment, without organ, stands out from the two preceding arias by virtue of its dance-like stepping motion. Whereas they were pervaded with passionate energy, here we find cheerful, peaceful serenity, culminating in the incomparably set words 'Amen: Vater, nimm mich an!' ('Amen: Father, accept me [into heaven]'). The last verse of the hymn follows in a plain four-part setting.

Ich bin vergnügt mit meinem Glücke, BWV 84

NBA I/7, p. 23 BC A43 Duration: *c.* 16 mins

1. ARIA S ob str bc — e $\frac{3}{4}$

Ich bin vergnügt mit meinem Glücke,	I am content with my fortune,
Das mir der liebe Gott beschert.	Which our dear God has allotted me.
Soll ich nicht reiche Fülle haben,	Should I not have riches to the full,
So dank ich ihm vor kleine Gaben	Then I thank Him for small gifts,
Und bin auch nicht derselben wert.	And am not even worthy of them.

2. RECITATIVO S bc — b–d C

Gott ist mir ja nichts schuldig,	God indeed owes me nothing,
Und wenn er mir was gibt,	And when He gives me something,
So zeigt er mir, daß er mich liebt;	He shows me that He loves me;
Ich kann mir nichts bei ihm verdienen,	I can earn nothing from Him,
Denn was ich tu, ist meine Pflicht.	For whatever I do is my duty.
Ja! wenn mein Tun gleich noch so gut geschienen,	Yes! though my deeds appeared ever so good,
So hab ich doch nichts Rechtes ausgericht'.	I have nonetheless accomplished nothing righteous.
Doch ist der Mensch so ungeduldig,	Yet man is so impatient
Daß er sich oft betrübt,	That he is often distressed
Wenn ihm der liebe Gott nicht überflüssig gibt.	If our dear God does not lavish him to overflowing.

Hat er uns nicht so lange Zeit
Umsonst ernähret und gekleidt
Und will uns einsten seliglich
In seine Herrlichkeit erhöhn?
Es ist genug vor mich,
Daß ich nicht hungrig darf zu Bette
gehn.

Has He not for such a long time
Fed and clothed us for nothing?
And will He not one day lift us up
Blessedly into His glory?
It is enough for me
That I need not go hungry to bed.

3. ARIA S ob vln I solo bc — G $\frac{3}{8}$

Ich esse mit Freuden mein weniges
Brot
Und gönne dem Nächsten von Herzen
das Seine.
Ein ruhig Gewissen, ein fröhlicher
Geist,
Ein dankbares Herze, das lobet und
preist,
Vermehret den Segen, verzuckert
die Not.

I eat with joy my scanty bread
And from my heart do not begrudge my
neighbour what is his.
A calm conscience, a joyful spirit,
A grateful heart that glorifies and
praises
Increase blessing, sweeten distress.

4. RECITATIVO S str bc — e–f♯ c

Im Schweiße meines Angesichts
Will ich indes mein Brot genießen,
Und wenn mein Lebenslauf,
Mein Lebensabend wird beschließen,
So teilt mir Gott den Groschen aus,
Da steht der Himmel drauf.
O! wenn ich diese Gabe
Zu meinem Gnadenlohne habe,
So brauch ich weiter nichts.

Amidst the sweat of my brow
I will meanwhile take my bread,
And when the course of my life,
My life's evening comes to an end,
God will distribute my pennies to me,
As sure as heaven stands.
Oh! if I have this gift
As my reward reckoned of Grace,
Then I need nothing further.

5. CHORAL SATB bc (+ instrs) — b c

Ich leb indes in dir vergnüget
Und sterb ohn alle Kümmernis,
Mir gnüget, wie es mein Gott füget,
Ich glaub und bin es ganz gewiß:
Durch deine Gnad und Christi Blut
Machst du's mit meinem Ende gut.

I live meanwhile contented in You
And die without any grief;
I am satisfied with how God ordains it;
I believe and am quite persuaded of it:
Through Your grace and Christ's
Blood,
With my end You bring good to pass.

As in the two cantatas just discussed, the reference to the Parable of the Labourers in the Vineyard is here unmistakable (see no. 4: 'God will distribute my pennies to me'). Yet the kernel of the parable is overlaid by a more rational and practically oriented interpretation: I content myself with what God has apportioned to me and am not envious when others have more than I. In all probability Bach set this text for 9 February 1727. Although the librettist is unknown, a text from Picander's 1728 cycle, *Ich bin vergnügt mit meinem Stande*, corresponds so closely with the present text in its succession of ideas, and partly even in wording, that some relationship between the two must be assumed. On the other hand, the differences between the two are so far-reaching that in the adaptation, to quote Wustmann, 'no stone is left standing on another'.[37] Today it is impossible to say whether both librettos stem from Picander, whether Picander followed the model of another writer, or whether, on the contrary, Picander's text already existed when this cantata was composed but was completely reworked, possibly by Bach himself.

Bach's setting, for a single solo voice, augmented to four voices only in the concluding chorale, bears the designation 'Cantata', otherwise seldom used by Bach. Some have wanted to conclude from this solo scoring, in conjunction with the aforementioned textual adaptation, that the work is no more than a piece of domestic sacred music, perhaps written for Bach's second wife Anna Magdalena. This is surely incorrect, however, as we gather from the assignment of the work to Septuagesima: as mentioned above, the text allows for the fact that the Gospel* (the Parable of the Labourers in the Vineyard) had been read out immediately before the cantata performance. Bach employs the restricted means required—one oboe, strings, and continuo, in addition to the solo soprano—with careful thought for the possibilities of variety they offer. The opening aria demands the full instrumental ensemble, but the second (no. 3) only two solo instruments; and the first recitative (no. 2) is accompanied only by continuo, the second (no. 4) by strings also. The movements also vary in character: a slow, solemn opening aria and a plainly declaimed recitative are followed by an animated, dance-like aria; the subsequent recitative, with its held string chords, returns to the solemnity of the opening, after which the chorale forms a full-textured conclusion.

The first movement, with its broadly swung oboe coloraturas,* creates the impression of the slow movement of an oboe concerto. The triple time, constantly audible in the calmly regular chord strokes of the accompanying parts, and adorned on the oboe with rich embellishments, syncopations, and runs (as it is later in the voice part too), aptly characterizes the equanimity of the person contented with the fate ordained for him or her by God. Formally, the aria is tripartite, with a varied da capo*. The subdivision of the middle section into two halves makes it particularly wide-ranging in effect. All the plainer by contrast is the following recitative, no. 2, which lacks any melismatic* adornment or expansion into arioso.*

The aria 'Ich esse mit Freuden mein weniges Brot', no. 3, with its spirited, song-like melody, illustrates not only the 'joy' of the text but, still more, the words of the middle section, 'a joyful spirit, a grateful heart that glorifies and praises'. Particularly charming is the treatment of the obbligato* instruments,

[37] '. . . kein Stein auf dem anderen blieb'.

oboe and solo violin, which play together in unison at the beginning—with the lively violin figuration simplified in the oboe part—but are then separated, only to come together again later, so that a constant interplay arises between one and two parts. The following recitative, no. 4, acquires special textual and formal emphasis, as a counterbalance to the opening aria, from its string scoring. As in the first recitative, however, arioso insertions are altogether absent. A plain four-part chorale—the twelfth verse of the hymn *Wer weiß, wie nahe mir mein Ende* by Ämilie Juliane of Schwarzburg-Rudolstadt (1686), sung to the melody of *Wer nur den lieben Gott läßt walten*—concludes the cantata.

1.17 Sexagesima (Second Sunday before Lent)

EPISTLE: 2 Corinthians 11.19–12.9: God's power is mighty in the weak.
GOSPEL: Luke 8.4–15: The Parable of the Sower.

Gleichwie der Regen und Schnee vom Himmel fällt, BWV 18

NBA I/7, pp. 83, 109 BC A44 Duration: *c.* 21 mins

1. SINFONIA vla I–IV (+ rec I,II 8va) bsn cello bc — g/a[38] 6/4
2. RECITATIVO B bc — g/a C

'Gleichwie der Regen und Schnee vom Himmel fällt und nicht wieder dahin kommet, sondern feuchtet die Erde und macht sie fruchtbar und wachsend, daß sie gibt Samen zu säen und Brot zu essen: Also soll das Wort, so aus meinem Munde gehet, auch sein; es soll nicht wieder zu mir leer kommen, sondern tun, das mir gefället, und soll ihm gelingen, dazu ichs sende.'	'Just as the rain and snow fall from heaven and do not return again, but rather moisten the earth and make it fruitful and fertile, so that it gives seeds to sow and bread to eat: so too shall be the Word that goes out of My mouth; it shall not return to Me empty, but rather do what pleases Me, and it shall succeed in the purpose for which I send it.'

3. RECITATIVO [+ LITANY] SATB vla I–IV (+ rec I,II 8va) bc — E♭–c/F–d C

Tenor	*Tenor*
Mein Gott, hier wird mein Herze sein:	My God, here shall my heart be:
Ich öffne dirs in meines Jesu Namen;	I open it to You in my Jesus's Name;
So streue deinen Samen	Then scatter Your seeds in it
Als in ein gutes Land hinein.	As if on good ground.
Mein Gott, hier wird mein Herze sein:	My God, here shall my heart be:
Laß solches Frucht, und hundertfältig, bringen.	Let it bring forth fruit a hundredfold.
O Herr, Herr, hilf! o Herr, laß wohlgelingen!	O Lord, Lord, help! O Lord, let it succeed well!

38 The first specified key refers to *Chorton** (Weimar version), the second to *Kammerton* (Leipzig version).

Du wollest deinen Geist und Kraft zum Worte geben.	**May You grant Your Spirit and power to the Word.**
Erhör uns, lieber Herre Gott!	**Hear us, dear Lord God!**
Baß	*Bass*
Nur wehre, treuer Vater, wehre,	But forbid, faithful Father, forbid
Daß mich und keinen Christen nicht	That I or any Christian
Des Teufels Trug verkehre.	Be perverted by the devil's deceit.
Sein Sinn ist ganz dahin gericht',	His mind is entirely set on
Uns deines Wortes zu berauben	Robbing us of Your Word
Mit aller Seligkeit.	Together with all Salvation.
Den Satan unter unsre Füße treten.	**Bruise Satan under our feet.**
Erhör uns, lieber Herre Gott!	**Hear us, dear Lord God!**
Tenor	*Tenor*
Ach! viel' verleugnen Wort und Glauben	Ah! many deny Word and Faith
Und fallen ab wie faules Obst,	And fall away like rotten fruit
Wenn sie Verfolgung sollen leiden.	When they have to suffer persecution.
So stürzen sie in ewig Herzeleid,	Then they fall into eternal affliction,
Da sie ein zeitlich Weh vermeiden.	Since they avoid a temporal pain.
Und uns für des Türken und des Papsts grausamen Mord und Lästerungen, Wüten und Toben väterlich behüten.	**And from the Turk's and the Pope's cruel murder and blasphemies, rages and storms, preserve us like a father.**
Erhör uns, lieber Herre Gott!	**Hear us, dear Lord God!**
Baß	*Bass*
Ein andrer sorgt nur für den Bauch;	Another cares only for his belly;
Inzwischen wird der Seele ganz vergessen.	Meanwhile his soul is quite forgotten.
Der Mammon auch	Mammon also
Hat vieler Herz besessen.	Has taken possession of many hearts.
So kann das Wort zu keiner Kraft gelangen.	Then the Word can achieve no power.
Und wieviel Seelen hält	And how many souls does
Die Wollust nicht gefangen?	Pleasure not hold captive?
So sehr verführet sie die Welt!	So greatly does the world lead them astray!
Die Welt, die ihnen muß anstatt des Himmels stehen,	The world, which for them must stand in place of heaven,
Darüber sie vom Himmel irregehen!	Over which they have erred from heaven!
Alle Irrige und Verführte wiederbringen.	**All those who err and are led astray, bring back.**
Erhör uns, lieber Herre Gott.	**Hear us, dear Lord God.**

4. Aria S vla I–IV unis. (+ rec I,II 8va) bc — E♭/F **c**

Mein Seelenschatz ist Gottes Wort.	My soul's treasure is God's Word.
Außer dem sind alle Schätze	Otherwise all treasures are

Solche Netze,	Such webs
Welche Welt und Satan stricken,	As the world and Satan spin
Schnöde Seelen zu berücken.	To bewitch base souls.
Fort mit allen, fort, nur fort!	Away with them all, away, away!
Mein Seelenschatz ist Gottes Wort.	My soul's treasure is God's Word.

5. CHORAL SATB bc (+ instrs; rec I,II 8va) g/a C

Ich bitt, o Herr, aus Herzens Grund,	**I pray, O Lord, from the depth of my heart**
Du wollst nicht von mir nehmen	**That You will not take**
Dein heilges Wort aus meinem Mund;	**Your Holy Word out of my mouth;**
So wird mich nicht beschämen	**Then I will not be ashamed**
Mein Sünd und Schuld,	**Of my sin and guilt,**
Denn in dein Huld	**For in Your favour**
Setz ich all mein Vertrauen.	**I place all my trust.**
Wer sich nur fest	**Whoever firmly**
Darauf verläßt,	**Relies upon it**
Der wird den Tod nicht schauen.	**Will not see death.**

This cantata originated during Bach's Weimar years, most likely in 1713 (for 19 February),[39] or possibly a year or two later. Bach drew the text from Erdmann Neumeister's third cycle of cantatas (1711), which had been written for the Eisenach court and set to music by Telemann. Referring to the Parable of the Sower, which had been read out beforehand as the Gospel,* the text considers the efficacy of God's Word in the world. The point of departure is an Old Testament passage, Isaiah 55.10–11, after which a recitative describes, in the manner of a sermon, the dangers that threaten the Word of God from Satan, interweaving four prayers from the Litany. Finally, in aria and chorale, the individual Christian and the whole congregation in turn acknowledge the treasure of God's Word and pray to God that He will preserve it for them.

Bach's setting survives in two different versions, essentially due to the differing performance practice in Weimar and Leipzig. The instrumental ensemble of the Weimar version is just four violas and continuo. The key was G minor, but tuned at Choir Pitch*—about a tone to a tone-and-a-half higher than Chamber Pitch.* Bach's performance in A minor at Leipzig would thus correspond roughly with the cantata's Weimar pitch. Apparently the viola players did not receive new parts in Leipzig: they simply tuned their instruments a tone higher than the Chamber Pitch that was otherwise customary there. Newly added to the A minor Leipzig version were two recorders, which doubled the first and second viola parts at the upper octave. This version has become standard in present-day performances. However, inadequate understanding of the work's

[39] According to Y. Kobayashi, 'Quellenkundliche Überlegungen'.

transmission has often led to performances in G minor Chamber Pitch (with recorders)—too low to correspond with any authentic pitch.

At the beginning of a work quite restricted in its use of the voice (it contains only a single aria) Bach places an introductory Sinfonia, which is akin to a concerto movement. Within an overall da capo* form, it is structured as a free chaconne, whose theme is stated in the first four bars. A gradual descent from higher to lower tessitura is apparent within all three sections, A A^1 A, each of which is framed by the original theme. The biblical text of no. 2 is significantly assigned to the bass as *vox Christi*. This movement, a *secco* recitative accompanied only by continuo, nonetheless contains several arioso* passages—a characteristic of Bach's early recitatives (see the partial reproduction in the Introduction, Music Example No. 6).

In order to form a contrast between two consecutive recitatives, the violas (plus recorders in the Leipzig version) enter in no. 3, filling out the harmony. This extended movement is articulated into four sections, each opening with recitative and flowing into a quotation from the Litany. Each litany quotation begins with a prayer, sung by soprano with continuo accompaniment, to which the choir, with *cantus firmus** in the soprano and with reinforcing instruments, responds in the words 'Hear us, dear Lord God!' Especially noteworthy are the vividly text-engendered instrumental figures on the words 'berauben' ('rob'), 'Verfolgung' ('persecution'), 'Mord und Lästerungen, Wüten und Toben' ('murder and blasphemies, rages and storms'), and 'irregehen' ('err'), which are at times combined with rich coloratura* figures in the voice part. These passages are not linked by shared thematic material: such composing in small units in accordance with the text is, again, typical of early Bach.

The only aria, no. 4, is bipartite and, at 42 bars, surprisingly brief—another characteristic of Bach's early works—but of great warmth and tenderness. The four violas (plus two recorders at the higher octave in the Leipzig version) unite to play a lively, flowing unison obbligato* part. In the first section, the soprano provides a melodious contrast to the instruments, but in the second, obbligato, soprano, and continuo twice share a thematically unified, imitative* texture in an antecedent phrase—'Away with them all, away, away!'—whose consequent, 'My soul's treasure is God's Word', is then modelled on the first section in text, style and thematic material. The concluding chorale is a plain four-part setting of the eighth verse of the hymn *Durch Adams Fall ist ganz verderbt* by Lazarus Spengler (1524).

Leichtgesinnte Flattergeister, BWV 181

NBA I/7, p. 135 BC A45 Duration: *c.* 14 mins

1. Aria B str bc (+ fl, ob ad lib.) e C
Leichtgesinnte Flattergeister — Frivolous flutter-spirits

Rauben sich des Wortes Kraft.
Belial mit seinen Kindern
Suchet ohnedem zu hindern,
Daß es keinen Nutzen schafft.

Rob themselves of the Word's power.
Belial with his children
Seeks, at any rate, to hamper it
So that it achieves nothing beneficial.

2. Recitativo A bc — e–b C

O unglückselger Stand verkehrter Seelen,
So gleichsam an dem Wege sind;
Und wer will doch
Des Satans List erzählen,
Wenn er das Wort dem Herzen raubt,
Das, am Verstande blind,
Den Schaden nicht versteht noch glaubt.
Es werden Felsenherzen,
So boshaft widerstehn,
Ihr eigen Heil verscherzen
Und einst zu Trümmern/zugrunde gehn.
Es wirkt ja Christi letztes Wort,
Daß Felsen selbst zerspringen;
Des Engels Hand bewegt des Grabes Stein,
Ja Mosis Stab kann dort
Aus einem Berge Wasser bringen.
Willst du, o Herz, noch härter sein?

Oh, unhappy state of perverted souls,
Who are, as it were, by the wayside.
And who would indeed
Recount Satan's cunning,
When he steals the Word from the heart,
Which, blind in understanding,
Neither comprehends nor believes its harm?
Hearts of stone
That maliciously resist
Will forfeit their own Salvation
And one day go to pieces/ruin.
Christ's last Word indeed caused
Rocks themselves to shatter;
The angel's hand moved the grave's stone;
Indeed, Moses's rod could once
Bring water out of a mountain.
Would you, O heart, be yet harder?

3. Aria T vln I solo (?) bc — b 3/8

Der schädlichen Dornen unendliche Zahl,
Die Sorgen der Wollust, die Schätze zu mehren,
Die werden das Feuer der höllischen Qual
In Ewigkeit nähren.

The infinite number of harmful thorns,
The concern of pleasure to increase one's treasures:
These shall feed the fire of hellish torment
In eternity.

4. Recitativo S bc — D C

Von diesen wird die Kraft erstickt,
Der edle Same liegt vergebens,
Wer sich nicht recht im Geiste schickt,
Sein Herz beizeiten
Zum guten Lande zu bereiten,
Daß unser Herz die Süßigkeiten schmecket,
So uns dies Wort entdecket,
Die Kräfte dieses und des künftgen Lebens.

From these the Word's power will choke;
The precious seed lies useless
For whoever is not rightly fitted in spirit
To prepare his heart in season
For good ground
So that our heart may taste the sweetnesses
That this Word discloses to us,
The powers of this and of the future life.

5. CHORUS SATB tr str bc (+ fl, ob ad lib) D C

Laß, Höchster, uns zu allen Zeiten	Grant us, O Highest, at all times
Des Herzens Trost, dein heilig Wort.	Our heart's comfort: Your holy Word.
Du kannst nach deiner Allmachtshand	You can by Your almighty hand
Allein ein fruchtbar gutes Land	Alone prepare good, fruitful ground
In unsern Herzen zubereiten.	In our hearts.

This cantata was first performed on 13 February 1724, perhaps alongside the revival of Cantata 18—one before the sermon and the other afterwards, or else in two different churches. It seems that no woodwind instruments participated at that time, for the flute and oboe parts that survive today belong to a much later revival (*c.* 1743/6).[40] Moreover, we must assume that at least the closing chorus* and perhaps other movements also are parodies whose musical substance is derived from an earlier work—probably a secular cantata. So far, however, it has not proved possible to ascertain any further details.

The text adheres closely to the Sunday Gospel,* reproducing the various events in the Parable of the Sower and in Jesus's interpretation thereof. Indeed, the opening lines of the second movement, 'Oh, unhappy state of perverted souls, / Who are, as it were, by the wayside', are fully comprehensible only when we recall Luke 8.12: 'But those by the wayside are the ones who hear [the Word of God], but then the devil comes and takes the Word from their hearts, lest they might believe and be blessed'. And the following lines, which are concerned with the 'hearts of stone'—reflecting that once an angel rolled away the stone from Jesus's grave (Matt. 28.2) and that Moses was able to strike water from a rock (Exodus 17.6)—refer to Luke 8.13: 'But those on the rock are the ones who . . .'. The tenor aria, which deals with 'harmful thorns', alludes to the next verse of the Gospel, Luke 8.14: 'But that which fell among thorns . . .'; and the soprano recitative follows on without a conceptual pause. The work concludes with a prayer that, in our case, God's Word may fall on fruitful ground.

With its nimble staccatos, the opening aria gives a graphic depiction of the 'frivolous flutter-spirits' of the text. The introductory instrumental motive,* to which the opening words are later set, pervades the entire movement:

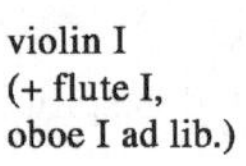

In the B section, the name 'Belial' is sung with fine effect within the caesuras of the instrumental theme. The overall form is not tripartite, as in most arias, but

[40] The late revival is so dated in Kobayashi Chr, p. 52.

in two halves with the B section also repeated: A B | A^1 B^1. The following *secco* recitative, no. 2, includes extended arioso* passages that lend special emphasis to the prophecy that 'hearts of stone . . . will forfeit their own Salvation'.

The tenor aria no. 3 survives in an incomplete state: in all probability, as demonstrated in the *Bach-Jahrbuch* for 1960 (pp. 32–6), it lacks a solo violin part. It would no doubt be possible to write a replacement in order to restore the movement for present-day performances, but the result could not be expected to accord even approximately with Bach's intentions, since the clues found in the existing instrumental themes are too meagre. A short *secco* recitative, no. 4, leads to the closing chorus, no. 5, the only movement that unites the entire instrumental ensemble—trumpet, strings and continuo, plus flute and oboe reinforcing the first violin in the late revival. The joyously straightforward character of the movement points to a secular origin, as noted above, though the middle section was subjected to extensive alterations.

Erhalt uns, Herr, bei deinem Wort, BWV 126

NBA I/7, p. 157 BC A46 Duration: *c.* 22 mins

1. [Chorale] SATB tr ob I,II str bc — a C

Erhalt uns, Herr, bei deinem Wort	**Uphold us, Lord, by Your Word**
Und steur des Papsts und Türken Mord,	**And ward off the murderousness of Pope and Turk,**
Die Jesum Christum, deinen Sohn,	**Who would cast Jesus Christ,**
Stürzen wollen von seinem Thron.	**Your Son, from His throne.**

2. Aria T ob I,II bc — e C

Sende deine Macht von oben,	Send Your might from above,
Herr der Herren, starker Gott!	Lord of Lords, mighty God!
Deine Kirche zu erfreuen	To delight Your Church
Und der Feinde bittern Spott	And the enemy's bitter mockery
Augenblicklich zu zerstreuen.	Instantly to dispel.

3. Recitativo [+ Chorale] AT bc — a–e C

Alt	*Alto*
Der Menschen Gunst und Macht wird wenig nützen,	Man's favour and might would be of little use
Wenn du nicht willt das arme Häuflein schützen,	If You would not protect this poor little band of men,
beide	*Both*
Gott Heilger Geist, du Tröster wert,	**God the Holy Spirit, You dear Comforter,**
Tenor	*Tenor*
Du weißt, daß die verfolgte Gottesstadt	You know that the persecuted City of God
Den ärgsten Feind nur in sich selber hat	Has within it the most wicked enemy

Durch die Gefährlichkeit der falschen Brüder.	In the peril of false brethren.
beide	*Both*
Gib deinm Volk einerlei Sinn auf Erd,	**Grant Your people one mind on earth,**
Alt	*Alto*
Daß wir, an Christi Leibe Glieder,	That we, the members of Christ's Body,
Im Glauben eins, im Leben einig sei'n.	May be one in Faith, united in life.
beide	*Both*
Steh bei uns in der letzten Not!	**Stand by us in our last agony!**
Tenor	*Tenor*
Es bricht alsdann der letzte Feind herein	The last enemy then breaks in on us
Und will den Trost von unsern Herzen trennen;	And would remove the comfort from our hearts;
Doch laß dich da als unsern Helfer kennen.	But let Yourself be known then as our Helper.
beide	*Both*
G'leit uns ins Leben aus dem Tod!	**Escort us out of death into Life!**

4. Aria B bc — C 3/8

Stürze zu Boden schwülstige Stolze!	Cast to the ground bombastic pride!
Mache zunichte, was sie erdacht!	Bring to desolation what it has devised!
Laß sie den Abgrund plötzlich verschlingen,	Let the abyss suddenly devour it;
Wehre dem Toben feindlicher Macht,	Curb the raving of hostile might,
Laßt ihr Verlangen nimmer gelingen!	Let its desires never succeed!

5. Recitativo T bc — a–d c

So wird dein Wort und Wahrheit offenbar	Thus Your Word and Truth will be manifest
Und stellet sich im höchsten Glanze dar,	And present itself in the highest splendour,
Daß du vor deine Kirche wachst,	So that You watch over Your Church,
Daß du des heilgen Wortes Lehren	So that You make the teachings of the holy Word
Zum Segen fruchtbar machst;	Fruitful in blessing;
Und willst du dich als Helfer zu uns kehren,	And if You would turn to us as Helper,
So wird uns denn in Frieden	Then in peace will
Des Segens Überfluß beschieden.	Blessing's abundance be granted to us.

6. Choral SATB bc (+ instrs) — a c

Verleih uns Frieden gnädiglich,	**Grant us peace graciously,**
Herr Gott, zu unsern Zeiten;	**Lord God, in our times;**
Es ist doch ja kein andrer nicht,	**There is indeed none other**
Der für uns könnte streiten,	**Who could fight for us**
Denn du, unser Gott, alleine.	**Than You, our God, alone.**
Gib unsern Fürstn und aller Obrigkeit	**Grant our princes and all in authority**

Fried und gut Regiment,	**Peace and good government,**
Daß wir unter ihnen	**That we under them**
Ein geruh'g und stilles Leben führen mögen	**May lead a peaceable and quiet life**
In aller Gottseligkeit und Ehrbarkeit.	**In all godliness and honesty.**
Amen.	**Amen.**

Bach composed this chorale cantata* for 4 February 1725. Its text is a heterogeneous structure which, in the hymnbooks of Bach's day, was often assembled to form a seven-verse hymn as follows:
Martin Luther's hymn of 1542:

1. Erhalt uns, Herr, bei deinem Wort
2. Beweis dein Macht, Herr Jesu Christ
3. Gott heilger Geist, du Tröster wert

Two additional verses by Justus Jonas:

4. Ihr' Anschläg, Herr, zunichte mach
5. So werden sie erkennen doch

Martin Luther's German translation of the antiphon *Da pacem domine* (1531):

6. Verleih uns Frieden gnädiglich

Johann Walter's additional verse after 1 Timothy 2.2 (1566):

7. Gib unsern Fürsten und aller Obrigkeit

Bach's anonymous text editor retained verses 1, 3, 6, and 7 word for word, made 'troped'* recitative insertions in verse 3, and paraphrased verses 2, 4, and 5 to form the corresponding cantata movements. There is a straightforward connection with the Sunday Gospel,* though the librettist has taken no steps to make this link emerge more clearly in the form of specific references. The essence of the text is a prayer to God to uphold His congregation through His Word, to protect them from His enemies, and to keep the peace for them.

In the opening chorus* Bach adds a trumpet in D to the conventional instrumental ensemble of two oboes, strings, and continuo. Clearly he had a skilled player at his disposal, for the trumpeter is accorded the rather difficult task—his range of notes being restricted by the natural overtone series—of taking a leading role in a movement in A minor. In form, the movement follows the scheme favoured by Bach: the chorale melody is delivered by the soprano one line at a time, underpinned by an imitative* and freely polyphonic* texture in the lower parts, which lacks a strong thematic link with the chorale or the instrumental theme, but attaches graphic emphasis to significant words such as 'Mord' ('murderousness') or 'stürzen' ('cast down') by means of intensified motion in a downward direction. This chorale texture is incorporated in a thematically independent orchestral setting which includes ritornellos and episodes. Only the introductory trumpet fanfare, which often recurs subsequently, anticipates the opening of the chorale melody in its first three notes:

The first of the two arias, no. 2, has the character of an insistent prayer, whose gestures are underscored by the two obbligato* oboes. In the middle section, however, there is an unexpected change to rapid demisemiquaver motion in the tenor part on the words 'erfreuen' ('delight') and 'zerstreuen' ('dispel'). The second aria, no. 4, is inherently more dramatic: the prayer that the Lord will cast the proud down to the ground is supported by raging descending scale passages in the continuo. A truly Old Testament zeal against the enemies of the things of God prevents the continuo—the sole accompaniment of the bass singer—from coming to rest throughout the entire movement, which results in an aria of genuinely baroque dramatic force.

The first of the two recitatives, no. 3, is especially noteworthy in that it unites chorale melody and trope in a curious way: the recitative passages are sung solo (with continuo), and the chorale lines in alto-tenor duet. The chorale melody, judiciously ornamented, invariably lies in the part that enters afresh, which then proceeds alone with the following passage of recitative:

Alto:	recitative —	accompanying part		chorale line 2
Tenor:		chorale line 1	— recitative —	accompanying part etc.

The second recitative, no. 5, on the other hand, is a plain *secco*. It is followed by the concluding chorale, no. 6, in a plain four-part setting.

1.18 Quinquagesima (Estomihi; Sunday before Lent)

EPISTLE: 1 Corinthians 13.1–13: In praise of Love.
GOSPEL: Luke 18.31–43: Jesus and the twelve disciples go to Jerusalem; the healing of a blind man.

Du wahrer Gott und Davids Sohn, BWV 23

NBA I/8.1, pp. 35, 71 BC A47 Duration: *c.* 20 mins

1. ARIA DUETTO SA ob (d'am) I,II bc c/b[41] C

Du wahrer Gott und Davids Sohn,	O true God and Son of David,

[41] The first specified key refers to the version originally planned but not performed till *c.* 1728/31 (with oboes), the second to the version of 1723–4 (with oboes d'amore and later also a choir of trombones).

Der du von Ewigkeit in der Entfernung schon
Mein Herzeleid und meine Leibespein
Umständlich angesehn, erbarm dich mein!
Und laß durch deine Wunderhand,
Die so viel Böses abgewandt,
Mir gleichfalls Hülf und Trost geschehen.

Who from eternity at a distance already
Looked closely upon my affliction
And my bodily pain, have mercy on me!
And through Your wondrous hand,
Which has averted so much evil,
Let help and comfort befall me likewise.

2. Recitativo T str + ob (d'am) I + II bc — A♭–E♭/G–D c

Ach! gehe nicht vorüber;
Du aller Menschen Heil,
Bist ja erschienen,
Die Kranken und nicht die Gesunden zu bedienen.
Drum nehm ich ebenfalls an deiner Allmacht teil;
Ich sehe dich auf diesen Wegen,
Worauf man
Mich hat wollen legen,
Auch in der Blindheit an.
Ich fasse mich
Und lasse dich
Nicht ohne deinen Segen.

Ah! do not pass by;
You, the Salvation of all mankind,
Have indeed appeared
To serve the sick and not the healthy.
Therefore I too partake of Your almighty power;
I see You on these paths
Where they
Have seen fit to lay me
Even in my blindness.
I compose myself
And do not let You go
Without Your Blessing.

3. Chor SATB ob (d'am) I,II str bc — E♭/D 3/4

Aller Augen warten, Herr,
Du allmächtger Gott, auf dich,
Und die meinen sonderlich.
Gib denselben Kraft und Licht,
Laß sie nicht
Immerdar in Fünsternüssen!
Künftig soll dein Wink allein
Der geliebte Mittelpunkt
Aller ihrer Werke sein,
Bis du sie einst durch den Tod
Wiederum gedenkst zu schließen.

The eyes of all wait upon You, Lord,
You almighty God,
And mine in particular.
Grant them strength and light;
Do not leave them
Forever in darkness!
In future Your signal alone
Shall be the beloved focus
Of all their activity,
Till one day through death
You decide to close them again.

4. Choral SATB ob (d'am) I,II str bc (+ cornett, trb I–III) — g–c/f♯–b c

Christe, du Lamm Gottes,
Der du trägst die Sünd der Welt,
Erbarm dich unser!
Christe, du Lamm Gottes,
Der du trägst die Sünd der Welt,
Erbarm dich unser!
Christe, du Lamm Gottes,
Der du trägst die Sünd der Welt,
Gib uns dein'n Frieden. Amen.

Christ, You Lamb of God,
Who bears the sin of the world,
Have mercy upon us!
Christ, You Lamb of God,
Who bears the sin of the world,
Have mercy upon us!
Christ, You Lamb of God,
Who bears the sin of the world,
Give us Your peace. Amen.

The Gospel* for Quinquagesima Sunday includes two distinct narratives: Jesus's announcement that He is about to go up to Jerusalem, where His Passion will be accomplished; and the healing of a blind man, who stands by the wayside calling out, 'Jesus, You Son of David, have mercy upon me!' In its madrigalian* movements, nos. 1–3, this cantata refers only to the healing of the blind man; not until the closing chorale (and also in the textless quotation of the same chorale melody in no. 2) does it refer to the announcement of the Passion and thus anticipate Good Friday, forming a bridge over the Lenten period, during which figural* music in Leipzig customarily ceased.

Jesus's words to the blind man, 'your faith has saved you' (Luke 18.42), should evidently be taken to mean that the blind man's call of 'You Son of David' embodies an implicit acknowledgement of the Christ. For it was then regarded as quite certain that the Messiah was to be a descendant of David. The anonymous librettist of the cantata text applies these ideas to the present day: 'O true God and Son of David . . . have mercy on me! And . . . let help and comfort befall me likewise' (no. 1). The next two movements again repeatedly apply various aspects of the Gospel account to the present-day Christian, while simultaneously interweaving allusions to other biblical passages. Thus the words 'You . . . have indeed appeared to serve the sick and not the healthy' (no. 2) recall Mark 2.17; the closing words of the same movement, 'I . . . do not let You go without Your Blessing' refer to Genesis 32.26; and the opening of the following chorus,* no. 3, refers to Psalm 145.15 in its assertion that not only the eyes of the blind but those of all, and therefore mine too, wait upon the Lord.

Bach evidently composed the first three movements of this cantata in Cöthen, with a view to performing them as the trial-piece in his application for the post of cantor at St Thomas's, Leipzig, on 7 February 1723. After his arrival in Leipzig, he rearranged the work, adding a closing chorale (presumably an older composition) and transposing the whole cantata down from C minor to B minor. The strings must have been tuned a semitone lower; the oboes were replaced by oboes d'amore;* and the organ, tuned at Choir Pitch,* received a part in A minor.[42] A year later, on 20 February 1724,[43] Bach apparently revived the work, reinforcing the choral parts of the concluding chorale with cornett and trombones.[44] An additional performance (in C minor, without trombones, and with oboes in place of oboes d'amore) is documented for the period *c.* 1728/31.

[42] For details see C. Wolff, 'Bach's Audition for the St Thomas Cantorate', in *Bach: Essays on his Life and Music* (Cambridge, Mass., 1991), 128–40.

[43] A surviving printed text indicates that its companion cantata BWV 22 was revived on that date; see Wolff, 'Bach's Audition for the St Thomas Cantorate', p. 135.

[44] See Kobayashi Chr, p. 7, note 4.

In Bach's Cöthen score, then, there was no concluding chorale. Perhaps there was no provision for it in the libretto, which indeed deals only with the healing of the blind. On the other hand, the chorale's repeated line 'Erbarm dich unser!' (Have mercy upon us!') unites in an ideal fashion the blind man's appeal to Jesus with the announcement of the Passion that opens the Gospel reading. The chorale was thus chosen with great care. In addition, the textless quotation of this melody in the second movement suggests that, as in several of his Weimar cantatas, Bach wanted to anticipate the closing chorale in a previous instrumental statement and thus conceived the plan of closing with this chorale during composition at the latest. On Good Friday 1725, the same chorale setting served as the conclusion of the second version of the *St John Passion*; but it was subsequently removed from that context, whereas it retained its place in the present cantata.

Bach's setting is of great intensity. In the opening duet, two oboes (or oboes d'amore) and continuo form a trio texture which, with the addition of the voice parts, is expanded to a quintet. With striking effect Bach makes the more or less strictly canonic vocal parts climb chromatically* on the words 'mein Herzeleid' ('my affliction'), whereas on 'erbarm dich mein!' ('have mercy on me!') we hear sigh figures—similarly chromatic, but now falling—in one of the voice parts against a held note in the other. In the accompanied recitative, no. 2, the top instrumental part, played by two oboes and first violin in unison, delivers in long-held notes the first verse of the hymn *Christe, du Lamm Gottes*. In the words 'Ah! do not pass by', a picture is here conjured up of the blind man at the wayside. And by means of the chorale his appeal to Jesus as He approaches Jerusalem is elevated to a prayer for mercy from the whole of Christendom. Here the unique art of Bach, which so far surpasses that of his contemporaries, is revealed in full.

With its rondeau structure and homophonic* texture, the following chorus, no. 3, is akin to a measured dance movement and closely resembles the choruses from the secular cantatas of the Cöthen period. The episodes, or *couplets*, are invariably designed as tenor-bass duets, another feature that has models in that period. Yet how ingeniously these stylistic means are made to serve the present purpose! The declamation in the refrain bars, especially in the upper parts, is faultless:

Perhaps it is no accident that the opening of the continuo part (and later that of the bass part) is suggestive of the chorale *Christe, du Lamm Gottes*.

The concluding chorale, a setting of the German Agnus Dei (Brunswick, 1528), is of sublime intensity. Oboes and strings form an independent structure which incorporates a prelude and interludes. In order to counterbalance them, the vocal parts were in 1724 reinforced by a choir of trombones (with cornett as treble instrument, in accordance with contemporary practice), which make their first entry in this movement. The chorale setting is through-composed; in other words, each of the three verses is set differently as follows:

Verse 1 ('adagio'): motivically independent instrumental texture (though developed out of the chorale melody); the chorale, with the melody in the soprano, is delivered line by line in a texture either chordal or lightly broken up into polyphony.*

Verse 2 ('andante'): chorale *cantus firmus** in three-part canon*, for soprano, oboes, and violin I, with polyphonic subsidiary parts; the oboes are independent in the episodes. The strings not involved in the canon double the voice parts.

Verse 3: chorale melody delivered line by line in the soprano, with a polyphonic substructure. The oboes unite in an independent part, rich in syncopations. The strings accompany the oboes in the episodes and double the voices in the vocal passages.

Thus, in compelling solemnity, this uniquely splendid chorale movement points forward to the time when we commemorate the Passion of Christ.

Jesus nahm zu sich die Zwölfe, BWV 22

NBA I/8.1, p. 3 BC A48 Duration: *c.* 20 mins

1. [Arioso + Chorus] SATB ob str bc g C

Tenor	*Tenor*
'Jesus nahm zu sich die Zwölfe und sprach:'	'Jesus took the Twelve to Him and said:'
Baß	*Bass*
'Sehet, wir gehn hinauf gen Jerusalem, und es wird alles vollendet werden, das geschrieben ist von des Menschen Sohn.'	'Look, we are going up to Jerusalem, and what is written of the Son of Man shall all be accomplished.'
Chor	*Choir*
'Sie aber vernahmen der keines und wußten nicht, was das gesaget war.'	'But they understood nothing of this and did not know what was said.'

2. Aria A ob solo bc c 9/8

Mein Jesu, ziehe mich nach dir, Ich bin bereit, ich will von hier	My Jesus, draw me to You: I am ready, I will go from here

Und nach Jerusalem zu deinen Leiden gehn.	And into Jerusalem to Your Passion.
Wohl mir, wenn ich die Wichtigkeit	Blessed am I if the importance
Von dieser Leid- und Sterbenszeit	Of this time of suffering and dying
Zu meinem Troste kann durchgehends wohl verstehn!	For my consolation can be thoroughly understood by me!
3. Recitativo B str bc	E♭–B♭ C
Mein Jesu, ziehe mich, so werd ich laufen,	My Jesus, draw me to You, then I will run,
Denn Fleisch und Blut verstehet ganz und gar,	For flesh and blood quite fail to understand—
Nebst deinen Jüngern nicht, was das gesaget war.	With Your disciples—what was said.
Es sehnt sich nach der Welt und nach dem größten Haufen.	They yearn for the world and for the biggest crowd.
Sie wollen beiderseits, wenn du verkläret bist,	They would both, when You are transfigured,
Zwar eine feste Burg auf Tabors Berge bauen;	Build a strong citadel on Tabor's mountain;
Hingegen Golgatha, so voller Leiden ist,	Whereas Golgatha is so full of suffering
In deiner Niedrigkeit mit keinem Auge schauen.	That they avert their eyes from Your abasement.
Ach! kreuzige bei mir in der verderbten Brust	Ah! crucify in me, in my corrupted breast
Zuvörderst diese Welt und die verbotne Lust,	First of all the world and its forbidden pleasure,
So werd ich, was du sagst, vollkommen wohl verstehen	Then I shall understand what You say perfectly
Und nach Jerusalem mit tausend Freuden gehen.	And go to Jerusalem with a thousand joys.
4. Aria T str bc	B♭ 3/8
Mein alles in allem, mein ewiges Gut,	My all-in-all, my eternal Good,
Verbeßre das Herze, verändre den Mut,	Improve my heart, transform my spirit,
Schlag alles darnieder,	Strike down everything that runs contrary
Was dieser Entsagung des Fleisches zuwider!	To this renunciation of the flesh!
Doch wenn ich nun geistlich ertötet da bin,	Yet when I am spritually mortified,
So ziehe mich nach dir in Friede dahin!	Then draw me towards You into peace!
5. Chorale SATB str + ob bc	B♭ C
Ertöt uns durch dein Güte,	**Mortify us through Your goodness,**
Erweck uns durch dein Gnad;	**Awaken us through Your grace;**
Den alten Menschen kränke,	**Disable the old man**
Daß der neu' leben mag	**That the new may live**

Wohl hie auf dieser Erden,	**Even here on this earth,**
Den Sinn und all Begehren	**That our minds and all desires**
Und Gdanken habn zu dir.	**And thoughts may be directed towards You.**

A score of this cantata in the hand of Bach's industrious copyist Johann Andreas Kuhnau, dating from 1723, bears the inscription 'Dies ist das Probestück in Leipzig' ('This is the Leipzig trial-piece'). We may conclude that at his audition for the post of Thomascantor on 7 February 1723, Bach, like Christoph Graupner before him, performed two cantatas—BWV 22 and 23—one before and the other after the sermon. An additional performance of Cantata 22 at Quinquagesima (20 February) 1724 is attested by the printed libretto, now in St Petersburg.

The text, by an anonymous librettist, to some extent complements that of Cantata 23, for while both are connected with the Sunday Gospel,* BWV 23 deals with the healing of the blind man and BWV 22 with the journey to Jerusalem. Two verses from the Gospel, Luke 18.31 and 34, preface the text like a heading: they are concerned with the announcement of the Passion and the incomprehension of the disciples (no. 1). The following movements reinterpret this text in order to make it relevant to the present-day Christian, whom Jesus is also willing to take with Him on His bitter path to the Cross, so that he might grasp the event and find comfort in it (no. 2). For the Christian is in the same plight as Jesus's disciples, who are unable to comprehend His Passion and would rather participate in His Transfiguration on Mount Tabor, a reference to Matthew 17.1–9 (no. 3). The libretto ends with the prayer that heart and spirit might be made capable of the 'renunciation of the flesh', so that Jesus might draw the Christian to Him after his death (no. 4). The concluding chorale—the fifth verse of the hymn *Herr Christ, der einig Gotts Sohn* by Elisabeth Creutziger (1524)—allows the whole congregation, as it were, to unite in this prayer.

The first half of the bipartite opening movement is a setting of Luke 18.31. After an orchestral ritornello for oboe, strings, and continuo, the tenor enters as Evangelist and reports that 'Jesus took the Twelve to Him and said:', whereupon the bass—the voice of Christ—announces the Passion. Musically, this announcement takes the form of vocal insertion* within several more or less exact restatements of the orchestral ritornello, or sections thereof. A full instrumental reprise of the ritornello closes the first half of the movement. The continuation of the Gospel narrative—'But they understood nothing of this . . .' (Luke 18.34)—is no longer sung by the Evangelist but as a choral fugue,* at first accompanied only by continuo (solo choir) but then reinforced by doubling instruments (tutti choir), and concluding with a short instrumental postlude.

The first of the two arias, no. 2, requires an obbligato* oboe whose expressive gestures underline the prayer of the text. It is charming to note how Bach represents the words 'I will go from here and into Jerusalem to Your Passion' by rising scale figures at first, but then on 'Leiden' ('Passion') with a C ♭ major chord at the interval of a third from the prevailing tonic, at which point the motion of the upper parts comes to a standstill. The second aria, no. 4, is a dance-like piece for strings that brings to mind the Cöthen rather than the Leipzig Bach. Two passages are especially noteworthy—one in the middle section and the other in the freely varied da capo*—in which the tenor soloist sings a held note on 'Friede' ('peace') or 'ewiges' ('eternal') while the motion in the orchestra continues and the theme of the aria is heard (in the second case, in the continuo bass).

The two arias are linked by a bass recitative accompanied by strings, no. 3, whose song-like declamation and lively accompaniment on several occasions, particularly towards the end, brings it close to arioso.* The concluding chorale is more richly decked out than usual: a plain four-part setting of the hymn is incorporated line by line in an independent instrumental texture dominated by the running semiquaver motion of the oboe and first violin.

Herr Jesu Christ, wahr' Mensch und Gott, BWV 127

NBA I/8.1, p. 107 BC A49 Duration: *c.* 21 mins

1. [Chorale] S (+ tr?) ATB rec I,II ob I,II str bc F C

Herr Jesu Christ, wahr' Mensch und Gott,	**Lord Jesus Christ, true man and God,**
Der du littst Marter, Angst und Spott,	**Who suffered torment, fear and mockery**
Für mich am Kreuz auch endlich starbst	**And finally died for me on the Cross**
Und mir deins Vaters Huld erwarbst,	**And earned for me Your Father's favour,**
Ich bitt durchs bittre Leiden dein:	**I pray through Your bitter Passion**
Du wollst mir Sünder gnädig sein.	**That You would be gracious to me, a sinner.**

2. Recitativo T bc B♭–F C

Wenn alles sich zur letzten Zeit entsetzet,	When in the last days everything takes fright,
Und wenn ein kalter Todesschweiß	And when a cold death-sweat
Die schon erstarrten Glieder netzet,	Moistens my already numbed limbs,
Wenn meine Zunge nichts, als nur durch Seufzer spricht	When my tongue says nothing except through sighs
Und dieses Herze bricht:	And this heart breaks:
Genung, daß da der Glaube weiß,	Enough that Faith then knows
Daß Jesus bei mir steht,	That Jesus stands by me,
Der mit Geduld zu seinem Leiden geht	He who with patience goes to His Passion

Und diesen schweren Weg auch mich geleitet
Und mir die Ruhe zubereitet.

And on this hard path leads me also
And prepares repose for me.

3. Aria S rec I,II ob I str bc — c C

Die Seele ruht in Jesu Händen,
Wenn Erde diesen Leib bedeckt.
Ach ruft mich bald, ihr Sterbeglocken,
Ich bin zum Sterben unerschrocken,
Weil mich mein Jesus wieder weckt.

My soul rests in Jesus's hands
When earth covers this body.
Ah, call me soon, you death-bells:
I am not afraid of dying,
For my Jesus shall rouse me again.

4. Recitativo + Aria B tr str bc — C C

Wenn einstens die Posaunen schallen,
Und wenn der Bau der Welt
Nebst denen Himmelsfesten
Zerschmettert wird zerfallen,
So denke mein, mein Gott, im besten;
Wenn sich dein Knecht einst vors Gerichte stellt,
Da die Gedanken sich verklagen,
So wollest du allein,
O Jesu, mein Fürsprecher sein
Und meiner Seele tröstlich sagen:

When one day the trumpets sound
And when the structure of the world
Alongside that of the firmament
Collapses, dashed to pieces,
Then remember me, my God, for good;
When Your servant one day stands before Judgement,
Where his thoughts accuse him,
Then would You alone,
O Jesus, be my advocate
And to my soul say comfortingly:

Fürwahr, fürwahr, euch sage ich:
Wenn Himmel und Erde im Feuer vergehen,
So soll doch ein Gläubiger ewig bestehen.
Er wird nicht kommen ins Gericht
Und den Tod ewig schmecken nicht.
Nur halte dich,
Mein Kind, an mich:
Ich breche mit starker und helfender Hand
Des Todes gewaltig geschlossenes Band.

Truly, truly I say to you:
When heaven and earth pass away in fire,
A believer shall nonetheless last for ever.
He shall not come under judgement
And shall not taste everlasting death.
Just cling,
My child, to Me:
I break, with strong and helping hand,
Death's powerful, tight snare.

5. Choral SATB bc (+ tr? rec I,II 8va ob I,II str) — F C

Ach, Herr, vergib all unser Schuld;
Hilf, daß wir warten mit Geduld,
Bis unser Stündlein kömmt herbei,
Auch unser Glaub stets wacker sei,
Dein'm Wort zu trauen festiglich,
Bis wir einschlafen seliglich.

Ah, Lord, forgive all our debts;
Help us to wait with patience
Till our hour of death arrives,
And may our Faith be ever bolder
To trust Your Word firmly,
Till we blessedly fall into death's sleep.

This chorale cantata* was heard for the first time on 11 February 1725. The text is based on the eight-verse hymn by Paul Eber (1562), whose first and last verses were adopted word for word, whereas the other six were adapted to form recitatives and arias. Specifically, verses 2 and 3 were paraphrased to form the first recitative (no. 2), verse 4 for the first aria (no. 3), verse 5 for the second recitative (no. 4, first part), and verses 6–7 for the second aria (no. 4, second part). It is not known who was responsible for this textual adaptation.

Though a funeral hymn, Eber's poem was not unsuited to Quinquagesima, for the opening verse, with its reference to Jesus's Passion and Death on the Cross, ties in with the Gospel* announcement of the Passion; and the last line of this verse, 'That You would be gracious to me, a sinner', is reminiscent of the blind man's call for mercy (Luke 18.38–9). The other verses then proceed freely with reflections on death: Jesus is asked that, when our own death comes, He will prove to be a deliverer by saving the faithful from judgement—a theme that recurs again and again in baroque poetry. The link between this theme and the Sunday Gospel is established in the first recitative (no. 2): 'Faith then knows that Jesus stands by me, He who with patience goes to His Passion and on this hard path leads me also'. In other words, in making his journey to Jerusalem Jesus begins to fulfil His work of Salvation and therewith our own hope for a blessed end.

Bach's setting attempts to clarify still further the connections pointed out here between the chorale and the Sunday Gospel. The introductory sinfonia and episodes of the large-scale opening chorus,* which is based on the first verse of the chorale, combine the chorale's opening line—constantly interchanged between the various instrumental groups in a rhythmically diminished form—with the melody *Christe, du Lamm Gottes*, the German Agnus Dei, which is delivered in long notes, first by the strings and later by the oboes and recorders. This melody is significant in a double sense: first, as a reference to Christ's Passion, and secondly as the prayer for mercy called out by the blind man in the Gospel text. In addition, the scoring with recorders and the invariable dotted rhythms evoke the impression of submissive, beseeching gestures.

A plain recitative leads to the first aria, no. 3, whose chosen instrumentation may be encountered nowhere else in Bach: an obbligato* part is played by solo oboe against a background of staccato chords for recorders. At the keyword 'death-bells' in the middle section, plucked strings enter with an imitation of bells. The following movement, no. 4, paints a graphic picture of the Judgement of the World. The string choir is joined by a trumpet—the characteristic instrument for the depiction of the Last Day—which enters on the words 'When one day the trumpets sound'. The form is exceptional: an accompanied recitative leads directly into an aria, which lacks the customary ritornello and approximates to rondeau form in its constant alternation between continuo-accompanied and fully scored passages. The formal shaping of this aria may have been stimulated by the textual contrast between the annihilation of heaven and earth and the certainty of the faithful at the end of time. At the lines 'Truly, truly I say to you' and 'He shall not come under judgement', adopted literally from Eber's hymn, we hear melodic quotations of the chorale, which are to be understood as a symbol of the Church founded by Christ and as a witness to the certainty of the faithful.

The cantata ends with a plain four-part chorale. Yet even in this simple movement Bach shows himself to be a master of characterization, for example when the line 'And may our Faith be ever bolder' is marked out by special mobility in the accompanying parts, or when the words 'Till we blessedly fall into death's sleep' are made prominent by means of elaborate harmonization.

Sehet, wir gehn hinauf gen Jerusalem, BWV 159

NBA I/8.1, p. 153 BC A50 Duration: *c.* 17 mins

1. Arioso + Recitativo AB str bc — c 𝄴

'Sehet!'	'See!'
Komm, schaue doch, mein Sinn,	Come, behold, my soul,
Wo geht dein Jesus hin?	Where is your Jesus going?
'Wir gehn hinauf'	'We are going up'
O harter Gang! hinauf?	Oh, what hard going! Up?
O ungeheurer Berg, den meine Sünden zeigen!	Oh, what a monstrous mountain my sins display!
Wie sauer wirst du müssen steigen!	How tryingly You have to climb!
'Gen Jerusalem.'	'To Jerusalem.'
Ach, gehe nicht!	Ah, do not go!
Dein Kreuz ist dir schon zugericht',	Your Cross is already prepared for You,
Wo du dich sollt zu Tode bluten;	Where You shall bleed to death;
Hier sucht man Geißeln vor, dort bindt man Ruten;	Here they seek whips, there they bind whipping-rods;
Die Bande warten dein;	Bonds abide You;
Ach! gehe selber nicht hinein!	Ah! do not go there Yourself!
Doch bliebest du zurücke stehen,	Yet if You would remain behind,
So müßt ich selbst nicht nach Jerusalem,	I myself would have to go not up to the heavenly Jerusalem,
Ach! leider in die Hölle gehen.	But alas down to Hell.

2. Aria Duetto [+Chorale] S + ob A bc — E♭ $\frac{6}{8}$

Ich folge dir nach	I follow after You
Ich will hier bei dir stehen,	**I will here stand by You,**
Verachte mich doch nicht!	**Do not despise me!**
Durch Speichel und Schmach;	Through spitting and insult;
Am Kreuz will ich dich noch umfangen,	I will still embrace You on the Cross,
Von dir will ich nicht gehen,	**I will not go away from You**

Bis dir dein Herze bricht.
Dich laß ich nicht aus meiner Brust,
Wenn dein Haupt wird erblassen
Im letzten Todesstoß,
Und wenn du endlich scheiden mußt,
Alsdenn will ich dich fassen,
Sollst du dein Grab in mir erlangen.
In meinen Arm und Schoß.

Until Your Heart breaks.
I do not let You go from my breast;
When Your Head will turn pale
In the last stroke of death,
And when You must finally depart,
Even then I will embrace You,
You shall find Your grave in me.
In my arm and bosom.

3. Recitativo T bc — B♭ 𝄴

Nun will ich mich,
Mein Jesu, über dich
In meinem Winkel grämen;
Die Welt mag immerhin
Den Gift der Wollust zu sich nehmen,
Ich labe mich an meinen Tränen
Und will mich eher nicht
Nach einer Freude sehnen,
Bis dich mein Angesicht
Wird in der Herrlichkeit erblicken,
Bis ich durch dich erlöset bin;
Da will ich mich mit dir erquicken.

I will now,
My Jesus,
Grieve over You in my corner;
The world may ever take to itself
The poison of hedonism;
I comfort myself with my tears
And would sooner not
Yearn for any joy
Until my countenance
Shall see You in glory,
Until I have been redeemed by You;
Then I will be refreshed with You.

4. Aria B ob str bc — B♭ 𝄴

Es ist vollbracht,
Das Leid ist alle,
Wir sind von unserm Sündenfalle
In Gott gerecht gemacht.
Es ist vollbracht,
Nun will ich eilen
Und meinem Jesu Dank erteilen,
Welt, gute Nacht!
Es ist vollbracht!

It is accomplished,
Suffering is over;
From our sinful Fall we have been
Justified in God.
It is accomplished,
Now I will hasten
To give thanks to my Jesus;
World, good night!
It is accomplished!

5. Choral SATB bc (+ instrs) — E♭ 𝄴

Jesu, deine Passion
Ist mir lauter Freude,
Deine Wunden, Kron und Hohn
Meines Herzens Weide;
Meine Seel auf Rosen geht,
Wenn ich dran gedenke,
In dem Himmel eine Stätt
Mir deswegen schenke.

Jesus, Your Passion
Is to me pure joy;
Your wounds, crown, and disgrace
Are my heart's pasture;
My soul walks on roses
When I consider that, on account of this,
A place in heaven
Is given to me.

The libretto of this cantata is drawn from Picander's cycle of 1728; and although we cannot determine the precise date of Bach's setting, it is reasonable to place its first performance in close temporal proximity to the publication of the text—thus perhaps 27 February 1729. If this date is correct, it is intriguing to reflect that the work, whose libretto points forward more clearly than any of the other Quinquagesima texts to the approaching Passiontide of Christ, would have been Bach's last cantata before the performance of the *St Matthew Passion* on Good Friday 1729; for during the intervening Lenten period there was no figural* music in Leipzig.

The text extracts from the Sunday Gospel* only Jesus's decision to go to Jerusalem, where His Passion will be accomplished, a decision at first felt to be monstrous (no. 1), then as an incentive to follow Him (no. 2), as the motive for departing from the joys of this world (no. 3), and finally as an occasion for thanksgiving (nos. 4 and 5). The anticipated words from the Cross in the fourth movement, 'It is accomplished' (John 19.30), in fact refer to Jesus's words in the Sunday Gospel, 'And everything that is written by the prophets shall be accomplished' (Luke 18.31).

The opening movement is a dialogue of exceptional dramatic power and stirring descriptiveness, a conversation between Jesus and the faithful Soul. Bach distinguishes between speech and reply by setting Jesus's words as arioso* with continuo accompaniment and the words of the Soul as recitative accompanied by strings—the reverse of his procedure in the *St Matthew Passion*. The arioso reveals Bach's highest mastery in its eloquent text declamation. After a long drawn-out melisma* on 'Sehet!' ('See!'), the anxious questioning of the alto is answered by an ascending scale figure in rising sequence on 'wir gehn hinauf' ('we are going up'); and after a further interruption from the alto, the cadence fixes the goal, namely 'to Jerusalem'. A repeat of the text then brings variations in the setting of individual words in order to deepen the listener's grasp of the weighty significance of the movement. The principle of monody,* invented long before in Italy, here reaches its highest degree of perfection.

The second movement, similarly wide-ranging and powerfully expressive in melodic style, combines the words of the alto, 'I follow after You', with the sixth verse of Paul Gerhardt's hymn *O Haupt voll Blut und Wunden* (1656), the one text providing a gloss on the other. But the true high point of the cantata, introduced by a plain *secco* recitative (no. 3), is the second aria (no. 4). Here the concertante* oboe spans the broad arches of a mellow, consoling melody over a string fabric that fills out the harmony, underpinned by a calm, pedal-like continuo part. The head-motive as antecedent phrase and its immediate inversion as consequent; the Mixolydian a^1 flat and its return to a^1 natural, turning harmonically towards the subdominant and then back to the tonic: all these things conjure up for the listener an image of what is well-balanced, poised and complete in itself, without any addition. The same melody at the entry of the voice forms an inimitable setting of the words 'Es ist vollbracht' ('It is accomplished'):

In the second half of the aria, the style of setting changes: at the words 'Now I will hasten . . .' semiquaver motion increases and violin I joins the oboe and bass voice in an imitative* texture. At the final words 'Welt, gute Nacht!' ('World, good night!') a brief quasi-da capo* is initiated by the resumption of the opening motive.[45] A plain four-part setting of the thirty-third verse of the hymn *Jesu Leiden, Pein und Tod* by Paul Stockmann (1633) brings the work to an end.

1.19 Third Sunday in Lent (Oculi)

EPISTLE: Ephesians 5.1–9: An appeal for pure conduct of life.
GOSPEL: Luke 11.14–28: 'He casts out devils through Beelzebub'.

Widerstehe doch der Sünde, BWV 54

NBA I/18, p. 3 BC A51 Duration: *c.* 14 mins

1. ARIA A vln I,II vla I,II bc — E♭[46] **C**

Widerstehe doch der Sünde,	Resist sin indeed,
Sonst ergreifet dich ihr Gift.	Or else its poison takes hold upon you.
Laß dich nicht den Satan blenden;	Do not let Satan delude you;
Denn die Gottes Ehre schänden,	For whoever abuses God's honour
Trifft ein Fluch, der tödlich ist.	Is stricken by a curse that is deadly.

2. RECITATIVO A bc — c–A♭ **C**

Die Art verruchter Sünden	The nature of wicked sin
Ist zwar von außen wunderschön;	Is indeed from without wonderfully fair;
Allein man muß	But one must
Hernach mit Kummer und Verdruß	Afterwards, with grief and vexation,
Viel Ungemach empfinden.	Experience much adversity.
Von außen ist sie Gold;	From outside it is gold;
Doch will man weiter gehn,	Yet if one would go further,
So zeigt sich nur ein leerer Schatten	It is found to be but an empty shadow
Und übertünchtes Grab.	And a whited sepulchre.
Sie ist den Sodomsäpfeln gleich,	It is like Sodom's apples,
Und die sich mit derselben gatten,	And those who consort with them
Gelangen nicht in Gottes Reich.	Do not reach the Kingdom of God.
Sie ist als wie ein scharfes Schwert,	It is like a sharp sword
Das uns durch Leib und Seele fährt.	That pierces through our body and soul.

[45] After this aria, a recitative, 'Herr Jesu, dein verdienstlich Leiden', intervenes before the final chorale in Picander's text. Since Bach's cantata survives only in a posthumous MS copy, it is uncertain whether he set the missing movement.

[46] The specified keys refer to *Chorton** ('choir pitch').

3. [Aria] A vln I + II vla I + II bc E♭ ¢

Wer Sünde tut, der ist vom Teufel,	He who commits sin is of the Devil,
Denn dieser hat sie aufgebracht.	For the Devil has brought it about.
Doch wenn man ihren schnöden Banden	Yet if its vile bonds are
Mit rechter Andacht widerstanden,	Resisted with true devotion,
Hat sie sich gleich davon gemacht.	It immediately makes off.

The text of this cantata is drawn from the cycle *Gottgefälliges Kirchen-Opffer* of 1711 by the Darmstadt court librarian Georg Christian Lehms. There it is assigned to the Third Sunday in Lent, though the content is of a very general nature, and the sources of the cantata include no reference to a specific liturgical occasion. Nor is there general agreement among scholars as to its date of origin, beyond the general fact that it clearly originated during Bach's Weimar years. Various possible dates have been put forward in recent years:[47] 1713, perhaps for use 'in ogni tempo' (on any occasion), like most of Bach's pre-Weimar cantatas; 1714, more likely in the summer or autumn than in Lent; and 1715, for the Third Sunday in Lent (24 March).

The text of this brief cantata essentially makes a single point: it warns against sin as an endowment of the devil, outwardly attractive but deadly within, which, with 'true devotion', can be resisted so that the tempter takes flight. Here and there, Lehms interweaves biblical allusions: the 'whited sepulchre' (no. 2) is quoted from Matthew 23.27, a saying of Jesus's in which we also find (as also elsewhere in the Bible) the outward–inward contrast that provides the basic idea of the second movement; and the opening line of the third—'He who commits sin is of the Devil'—is taken word for word from the First Epistle of John 3.8. The phrase 'It is like Sodom's apples' (no. 2) alludes to a tradition reported by Flavius Josephus, according to which such apples—the fruit of *calotropis procera*—outwardly resemble edible fruits, but when picked dissolve into ash and vapour. The text thus has links with the Epistles* for the Third Sunday in Lent and the Seventh Sunday after Trinity, but is only very loosely connected with the Gospel* reading for either occasion.[48]

It used to be thought that this cantata survives in an incomplete state, but since the discovery of the printed text we know that this is not the case. The work is a true 'cantata' for a single voice, an alto soloist, and is laid out according to the simplest standard scheme of this genre, grouping two arias around a single recitative. The instrumental ensemble is made up only of strings, with divided violas, and continuo. Within this restricted scope, the composer had to create a field of tension that would be sufficiently arresting for the listener. For

[47] By C. Wolff, KB, NBA I/8.1–2 (1998), 89–90, Dürr St 2, 66, and 170 f., and K. Hofmann, 'Neue Überlegungen zu Bachs Weimarer Kantaten-Kalender', *BJ* 1993, 9–29, respectively.

[48] The most likely connection is that of the third movement with the account of the casting out of a devil in the Gospel reading for the 3rd Sunday in Lent.

this Bach found the necessary motive in the double character of sin disclosed in the recitative: it is described as 'from without wonderfully fair' but inwardly deadly and the work of the devil.

The opening aria, with its ingratiating suspensions, depicts the tempting beauty of sin;[49] but the initial dissonance (a dominant-seventh chord against a tonic pedal-point) already calls for resistance. This harshly dissonant opening has on occasion been viewed as a unique stroke of genius. Around the same time, however, Bach used the same chord to open the recitative 'Siehe, ich stehe vor der Tür und klopfe an' from the Advent cantata BWV 61, and here again it represents an awakening out of security and indifference. The middle section of the aria 'Widerstehe doch' is also full of harmonic audacities, among which the repeated deceptive cadence is unfailingly effective as a description of the 'curse that is deadly'.[50] The recitative, no. 2, is again boldly descriptive. The phrase 'an empty shadow and a whited sepulchre' has an immediately graphic effect with its lurid harmony. And the arioso* conclusion—a feature of numerous recitatives by the young Bach—here draws its significance from the quick, text-engendered continuo runs, which portray the 'sharp sword that pierces through our body and soul'.

In the second aria, no. 3, the deceptive beauty of sin is exposed as truly reprehensible, but also susceptible to defeat. Bach here unites the violins and violas to form a single part each, so that with the addition of alto voice and continuo a fugue-like quartet texture arises. With its regular subject and countersubjects, the movement is oriented towards the permutation principle. Even the seemingly unthematic opening continuo part, with its stepping quavers, is later sung by the alto to the words 'Denn dieser hat sie aufgebracht' ('For [the Devil] has brought it about'), thereby disclosing its function as the second regular countersubject. The middle section is more freely structured, but only in its vocal passages, for the instrumental epilogue that follows each of them even treats the main theme in stretto.* A free da capo* of the main section concludes the aria and therewith the whole cantata.

Alles, was von Gott geboren, BWV 80a

NBA I/8, Krit. Bericht BC [A52] Music lost

This cantata is lost apart from the text, which was written in 1715 by Salomo Franck for performance in the Weimar court chapel and published in his

[49] Dr Elke Axmacher has pointed out to the author that in the semiquaver melody of this movement the serpent might be represented as a symbol of sin (see Genesis 3).

[50] 'Trifft ein Fluch, der tödlich ist'. Lehms's precise words were 'Trifft ein Fluch, der tödlich trifft' ('strikes a curse that strikes mortally'), so that 'trifft' rhymed with 'Gift'. Either Bach wanted to avoid the doubling of the word 'trifft' by using the weaker 'tödlich ist', or else, perhaps more plausibly, this reading results from faulty transmission (the work survives only in MS copies). In the latter case, the appreciably more powerful 'tödlich trifft' should be sung at the dissonant interrupted cadences of Bach's cantata.

collection *Evangelisches Andachts-Opffer*. That Bach did indeed set the text to music—either for 24 March 1715 or for 15 March 1716[51]—is clear from the work's surviving adaptation as the Leipzig chorale cantata* *Ein feste Burg ist unser Gott*, BWV 80 (see the account of that work for details of the music). This was occasioned by the absence of figural* music in Leipzig during Lent, which meant that Bach had no further use for a cantata written for the Third Sunday in Lent.

Although Cantata 80a can no longer be reconstructed accurately, it may be roughly restored for performance purposes by selecting the relevant movements from BWV 80, omitting the soprano from the opening aria, employing BWV 303 as the concluding chorale, and altering the text to Franck's version which relates to the Third Sunday in Lent (the following details of scoring, key, and metre are added in accordance with BWV 80 for practical use).

1. ARIA B ob unis str bc — D C

Alles, was von Gott geboren,	Whatsoever is born of God
Ist zum Siegen auserkoren.	Is elected for victory.
Was bei Christi Blutpanier	What to Christ's Blood-standard
In der Taufe Treu geschworen,	Has in baptism sworn fidelity
Siegt in Christo für und für.	Is victorious in Christ for ever and ever.
Alles, was von Gott geboren,	Whatsoever is born of God
Ist zum Siegen auserkoren.	Is elected for victory.

2. RECITATIVO B bc — b–f♯ C

Erwäge doch,	Consider well,
Kind Gottes, die so große Liebe,	Child of God, what great Love
Da Jesus sich	In that Jesus pledged Himself
Mit seinem Blute dir verschriebe,	To you with His Blood;
Wormit er dich	By which,
Zum Kriege wider Satans Heer	For the war against Satan's host
Und wider Welt und Sünde	And against the world and sin,
Geworben hat!	He enlisted you!
Gib nicht in deiner Seele	Do not grant a place in your soul
Dem Satan und den Lastern statt!	For Satan and vices!
Laß nicht dein Herz,	Do not let your heart—
Den Himmel Gottes auf der Erden,	God's heaven on earth—
Zur Wüste werden!	Become desolate!
Bereue deine Schuld mit Schmerz,	Bewail your guilt with anguish,
Daß Christi Geist mit dir sich fest verbinde!	That the Spirit of Christ may be firmly united with you!

3. ARIA S bc — b $\frac{12}{8}$

Komm in mein Herzenshaus,	Come into my heart's house,
Herr Jesu, mein Verlangen!	Lord Jesus, my desire!

[51] The first date is that of Dürr St 2, the second has been proposed more recently by K. Hofmann, 'Neue Überlegungen'.

Treib Welt und Satan aus
Und laß dein Bild in mir erneuet prangen!
Weg! schnöder Sündengraus!

Cast out the world and Satan
And let Your Image shine forth from a renewed me!
Away! vile horror of sin!

4. RECITATIVO T bc — b–D c

So stehe denn
Bei Christi blutgefärbten Fahne
O Seele, fest!
Und glaube, daß dein Haupt dich nicht verläßt,
Ja, daß sein Sieg
Auch dir den Weg zu deiner Krone bahne!
Tritt freudig an den Krieg!
Wirst du nur Gottes Wort
So hören als bewahren,
So wird der Feind
Gezwungen auszufahren.
Dein Heiland bleibt dein Hort!

Then stand fast
By Christ's blood-stained banner,
O soul!
And believe that your Head does not forsake you,
Indeed, that His victory
Paves the way for your crown too!

Tread joyfully into battle!
If only God's Word
Is both heard and kept by you,
Then the Enemy will be
Forcibly cast out.
Your Saviour remains your protector!

5. ARIA [DUETTO] AT vln vla? bc — G $\frac{3}{4}$

Wie selig ist der Leib, der, Jesu, dich getragen?
Doch selger ist das Herz, das dich im Glauben trägt!
Es bleibet unbesiegt und kann die Feinde schlagen
Und wird zuletzt gekrönt, wenn es den Tod erlegt.

How blessed is the body that bore You, O Jesus!
Yet still more blessed is the heart that bears You in Faith!
It remains unvanquished and can strike its enemies,
And will at last be crowned when it defeats death.

6. CHORAL[52] SATB bc (+ instrs) — D c

Mit unser Macht ist nichts getan,
Wir sind gar bald verloren.
Es streit' vor uns der rechte Mann,
Den Gott selbst hat erkoren.
Fragst du, wer er ist?
Er heißt Jesus Christ,
Der Herre Zebaoth,
Und ist kein andrer Gott,
Das Feld muß er behalten.

With our might nothing is done:
We are very soon lost.
The right Man shall fight for us,
Whom God Himself has chosen.
Do you ask who He is?
He is called Jesus Christ,
The Lord of Sabaoth,
And there is no other God:
He must hold the field.

[52] Franck gives only the first two lines; the remainder is drawn from BWV 80.

1.20 Palm Sunday

EPISTLE: Philippians 2.5–11: Let everyone be of the mind of Christ.
Or 1 Corinthians 11.23–32: Of Holy Communion.
GOSPEL: Matthew 21.1–9: Jesus's entry into Jerusalem.

Himmelskönig, sei willkommen, BWV 182

NBA I/8.2, pp. 3,43 BC A53 Duration: *c.* 30 mins

1. SONATA rec vln conc vln rip vla I,II bc — G/B♭[53] C

2. CHORUS SATB rec vln vla I,II vc bc — G/B♭ C

Himmelskönig, sei willkommen,	Heavenly King, welcome!
Laß auch uns dein Zion sein!	Let us be Your Zion too!
Komm herein!	Come in!
Du hast uns das Herz genommen.	You have ravished our heart.

3. RECITATIVO B bc — C/E♭ C

'Siehe, ich komme, im Buch ist von mir geschrieben. Deinen Willen, mein Gott, tu ich gerne.'	'See, I come; in the Book it is written of me. I delight to do Your Will, my God.'

4. ARIA B vln vla I,II bc — C/E♭ C

Starkes Lieben,	What strong Love
Das dich, großer Gottessohn,	That drove You, great Son of God,
Von dem Thron	From the throne
Deiner Herrlichkeit getrieben!	Of Your glory!
Starkes Lieben,	What strong Love,
Daß du dich zum Heil der Welt	That for the Salvation of the world
Als ein Opfer fürgestellt,	You set Yourself forth as a Sacrifice,
Daß du dich mit Blut verschrieben.	That You assigned Yourself with Blood.

5. ARIA A rec bc — e/g C

Leget euch dem Heiland unter,	Lay yourselves down before the Saviour,
Herzen, die ihr christlich seid!	O hearts that are Christian!
Tragt ein unbeflecktes Kleid	Wear an unblemished garment
Eures Glaubens ihm entgegen,	Of your Faith to meet Him;
Leib und Leben und Vermögen	May your life and limb and possessions
Sei dem König itzt geweiht.	Now be consecrated to the King.

6. ARIA T bc — b/d 3/4

Jesu, laß durch Wohl und Weh	O Jesus, through weal and woe
Mich auch mit dir ziehen!	Let me too go with You!
Schreit die Welt nur 'Kreuzige!',	Though the world cry only 'Crucify!',
So laß mich nicht fliehen,	Do not let me flee,
Herr, von deinem Kreuzpanier;	Lord, from Your Cross's banner:
Kron und Palmen find ich hier.	Here I find both crown and palms.

[53] The first specified key refers to the Weimar performance at *Chorton** (in Leipzig, *Kammerton*), the second to the *Kammerton* of the Weimar performance.

7. CHORALE SATB bc (+ instrs, rec 8[va]) G/B♭ c

Jesu, deine Passion	**Jesus, Your Passion**
Ist mir lauter Freude,	**Is to me pure joy;**
Deine Wunden, Kron und Hohn	**Your wounds, crown, and disgrace**
Meines Herzens Weide;	**Are my heart's pasture;**
Meine Seel auf Rosen geht,	**My soul walks on roses**
Wenn ich dran gedenke,	**When I consider that, on account of this,**
In dem Himmel eine Stätt	**A place in heaven**
Uns deswegen schenke.	**Is given to us.**

8. CHORUS SATB rec vln vla I,II vc bc G/B♭ $\frac{3}{8}$

So lasset uns gehen in Salem der Freuden,	Then let us go into the Salem of Joy
Begleitet den König in Lieben und Leiden.	Accompanying the King in good times and bad.
Er gehet voran	He goes before us
Und öffnet die Bahn.	And opens up the way.

This is probably Bach's first cantata after his appointment as Concertmeister at the Weimar court, which carried with it the duty of monthly composition of new cantatas. The appointment was announced on 2 March 1714, and three weeks later, on 25 March, Bach carried out his new duty for the first time by performing the present work. The text is probably by Salomo Franck, for although it cannot be found among his printed works, Franck was then in-house poet at the Weimar court; and even if he did not come into consideration on that account, the poetic style undoubtedly points to his authorship, as Spitta rightly acknowledged. The text exhibits the transitional form between the old and new cantata type—characterized by the absence of freely versified recitative—which has so far been found only in Franck's librettos. It is possible that the cantata was originally designed to end with a repeat of the opening chorus* after the last aria, for a da capo* indication to that effect is found in several performing parts. Yet there is no doubt that the last two movements were already included in the original Weimar performance. The Leipzig performing parts indicate that there Bach omitted the chorale no. 7.

The content of the text is linked with the Gospel* for Palm Sunday. The opening chorus states the theme in accordance with the old style of sermon: Christ's entry into Jerusalem should also be His entry into our own hearts. This idea is thereafter expounded, first from the viewpoint of Christ Himself: strong love has driven the Son of God to fulfil the will of His Father and sacrifice Himself for the salvation of the world (nos. 3–4). The individual Christian is then summoned to lay his heart at the feet of the Saviour—as the people of Jerusalem once laid their garments—as an unblemished witness of faith (no. 5) and not to depart from Jesus even in times of persecution (no. 6). The two choruses that close the work refer to the heavenly reward that has been bestowed upon the Christian through the Passion of Christ. The 'Salem of Joy' (Jerusalem) into which Jesus leads the faithful is now no longer the earthly city, in which the Crucifixion will shortly take place, but the heavenly Jerusalem, the City of God, which the heavenly King enters in order to take possession of His Sovereignty, and where a place will be granted for us too. The entire text has a mystical, enraptured character, which is manifest not only in the choice of words—'Heavenly King', 'You have ravished our heart', 'Lay yourselves down before the Saviour'—but in the interpretation of the biblical text: entry into Jerusalem, into one's own heart, into the City of God. These characteristics indicate how close even non-Pietistic Lutheran verse often was to Pietism; and they may also have been in keeping with the disposition of the youthful composer, who found here plentiful stimulation for some richly expressive music.

The scoring of the original Weimar version is typical of early Bach in that, contrary to early baroque practice of orchestration in choirs of instruments, individual solo instruments are pitted against one another. Bach's gain from his engagement with modern Italian genres—the da capo aria and the Vivaldian instrumental concerto—is clearly perceptible. The small space available in the Weimar court chapel may have been better suited to writing in few parts than to lavishly scored music. In any case, up to 1715 Bach shows a marked preference for small-scale, select scoring, as in the present cantata. The only woodwind instrument, largely treated as soloist, is the recorder, which in the fully scored movements is joined by solo violin, stepping forward in a concertante* role from a string group in which it plays alongside *ripieno* violins (but no second violin), first and second violas, and an occasionally independent cello. The work was gradually transformed from this chamber-music conception into a richly scored Leipzig cantata. *Ripieno* violins took over the entire violin part, and finally the violins were doubled throughout by oboe, the recorder was largely doubled by a new violin part, and a violone added to the continuo group.[54]

The recorder part poses several problems for today's performance practice. Bach's instrument—in Chamber Pitch* (probably Deep Chamber Pitch)—was a third lower than the organ, to which the Weimar strings were accustomed to tune their instruments. Thus the recorder playing in B♭ would sound the same as the G major of the other instruments. When Bach revived the cantata in Leipzig—in G major at Chamber Pitch—he had to raise the lowest passages of the recorder part in the aria no. 5, since they lie unplayably low in G major. Today we have the choice of following Bach in this respect or performing the

[54] Details of the various Weimar and Leipzig performances and their occasion and scoring (in so far as these things can be established) are given by C. Wolff in KB, NBA I/8.2 (1998), 116–23; see also the review-article 'The Bach Compendium' by J. Rifkin in *Early Music* 17 (1989), 79–88 (especially 84).

work at a higher pitch: perhaps in A major with E recorders. For, played with their original compass, the expressive recorder figures give a more striking portrayal of the 'laying down' of the text, and the voice parts gain in brightness from a higher pitch.

The introductory Sonata depicts the approach of the heavenly King as He enters Jerusalem. Its ceremonial dotted rhythms have associations with the French *ouverture*, during which the king was accustomed to enter his royal box (this association is still more evident in Cantata 61 for the First Sunday in Advent, when the same Gospel account was read: its first movement literally takes the form of a French overture*). The strings accompany *pizzicato*,* changing to long bowed notes shortly before the end of the movement. The impression is thereby formed of a gradual enhancement, which continues in the successive entries of the parts in the following chorus, no. 2, right up to the fully scored greeting salutation. The formal structure of this chorus is exceptionally clear: the two identical outer sections of its ABA da capo form begin with a permutation fugue* on 'Himmelskönig, sei willkommen' (see the partial reproduction in the introduction, Music Example No. 5), which then—via a texture of canonic imitation* on 'Laß auch uns dein Zion sein!'—reaches a homophonic* conclusion. The middle section is made up of two similar canonic complexes on 'Du hast uns das Herz genommen'.

The following biblical words are no longer set as a chorus, in the old style, but as a recitative (no. 3), perhaps to compensate for the absence of freely versified recitative in Franck's text. After a short introduction, however, the recitative changes into arioso*—a characteristic of the youthful Bach that survives even up to his first Leipzig cantatas. The scoring of the three arias that follow reflects the changing perspective of the text from Christendom as a whole to the individual Christian. The third aria (no. 6), in particular, is full of expressive gestures that must have seemed extravagant at the time. The chorale 'Jesu, deine Passion', no. 7, whose words and melody are identical with those of BWV 159/5, belongs to the so-called Pachelbel type of chorale arrangement: each line is prepared imitatively before its delivery by the soprano in long notes. It breaks out of the traditional mould, however, by virtue of the individual shaping of the chorale lines in the accompanying parts. Note, for example, the lively motion on 'Freude' ('joy') or 'Weide' ('pasture') and the syncopations on 'Meine Seel auf Rosen geht' ('My soul walks on roses'). The last chorus, no. 8, is designed as a counterpart to the first. Here again we are struck by incidental illustrative strokes, particularly the minor-mode overclouding on 'Leiden' ('misfortunes'). These compensate the listener for the lack of the lengthy phrases and extensive forms of the mature Leipzig period. Instead, we are offered a youthful, tender shaping of even the smallest motive,* an instrumental scoring chosen with careful consideration, and an inexhaustible abundance of inspiration.

1.21 Easter Sunday

EPISTLE: 1 Corinthians 5.6–8: Christ is our Easter Lamb.
GOSPEL: Mark 16.1–8: The Resurrection of Christ.

Christ lag in Todes Banden, BWV 4

NBA I/9, p. 3 BC A54 Duration: *c.* 22 mins

1. SINFONIA vln I,II vla I,II bc — e C
2. VERSUS 1 SATB (+ cornett trb I–III) vln I,II vla I,II bc — e C

Christ lag in Todes Banden	**Christ lay in the snares of death**
Für unsre Sünd gegeben,	**And has given Himself for our sins;**
Er ist wieder erstanden	**He is risen again**
Und hat uns bracht das Leben;	**And has brought us Life;**
Des wir sollen fröhlich sein,	**For this we should be joyful,**
Gott loben und ihm dankbar sein	**Praise God and be grateful to Him,**
Und singen halleluja,	**And sing 'Alleluia'.**
Halleluja.	**Alleluia!**

3. VERSUS 2 S + cornett A + trb I bc — e C

Den Tod niemand zwingen kunnt	**Death no one could subdue**
Bei allen Menschenkindern;	**Among all the children of men;**
Das macht alles unsre Sünd,	**That was all caused by our sin:**
Kein Unschuld war zu finden.	**No innocence was to be found.**
Davon kam der Tod so bald	**Therefore soon came Death**
Und nahm über uns Gewalt,	**And took power over us,**
Hielt uns in seinem Reich gefangen.	**Holding us captive in its kingdom.**
Halleluja.	**Alleluia!**

4. VERSUS 3 T vln I + II bc — e C

Jesus Christus, Gottes Sohn,	**Jesus Christ, God's Son,**
An unser Statt ist kommen	**Has come in our place**
Und hat die Sünde weggetan,	**And has abolished our sin,**
Damit dem Tod genommen	**Thereby removing from Death**
All sein Recht und sein Gewalt;	**All its right and its power;**
Da bleibet nichts denn Tods Gestalt,	**Nothing remains but Death's form:**
Den Stachel hat er verloren.	**It has lost its sting.**
Halleluja.	**Alleluia!**

5. VERSUS 4 SATB bc — e C

Es war ein wunderlicher Krieg,	**There was a marvellous battle**
Da Tod und Leben rungen,	**When Death and Life struggled;**
Das Leben behielt den Sieg,	**Life won the victory:**
Es hat den Tod verschlungen.	**It has swallowed up Death.**
Die Schrift hat verkündigt das,	**Scripture has proclaimed this:**
Wie ein Tod den andern fraß,	**How one Death devoured another;**
Ein Spott aus dem Tod ist worden.	**A mockery has been made of Death.**
Halleluja.	**Alleluia!**

6. Versus 5 B vln I,II vla I,II bc e 3/4

Hie ist das rechte Osterlamm,	**Here is the true Easter Lamb,**
Davon Gott hat geboten,	**As God has commanded,**
Das ist hoch an des Kreuzes Stamm	**High on the Cross's beam it has**
In heißer Lieb gebraten,	**Roasted in burning Love.**
Das Blut zeichnet unser Tür,	**Its Blood marks our door,**
Das hält der Glaub dem Tode für,	**Faith holds it up to Death:**
Der Würger kann uns nicht mehr schaden.	**The murderer can harm us no more.**
Halleluja.	**Alleluia!**

7. Versus 6 ST bc e C

So feiern wir das hohe Fest	**Then we celebrate this high feast**
Mit Herzensfreud und Wonne,	**With heartfelt joy and delight,**
Das uns der Herr erscheinen läßt.	**Which the Lord makes manifest to us.**
Er ist selber die Sonne,	**He Himself is the Sun,**
Der durch seiner Gnaden Glanz	**Who through the radiance of His grace**
Erleuchtet unsre Herzen ganz,	**Wholly illuminates our hearts;**
Der Sünden Nacht ist verschwunden.	**The night of sin has vanished.**
Halleluja.	**Alleluia!**

8. Versus 7 SATB bc (+ instrs) e C

Wir essen und leben wohl	**We eat and live well**
In rechten Osterfladen,	**On true Easter Bread:**
Der alte Sauerteig nicht soll	**The old leaven ought not to abide**
Sein bei dem Wort der Gnaden,	**With the Word of Grace;**
Christus will die Koste sein	**Christ would be our sustenance**
Und speisen die Seel allein,	**And alone nourish the soul:**
Der Glaub will keins andern leben.	**Faith would live on nothing else.**
Halleluja.	**Alleluia!**

In the history of Protestant church music, Easter Sunday—strictly speaking, the central feast of Christianity—is often accorded less significance than Good Friday. We possess a rich store of Passion music, but relatively few outstanding pieces of Easter music. Such a disproportion is also perceptible in Bach's output. Settings of the Passion apparently laid such a strong claim on his creative power that no original Easter Sunday music survives from his mature years. We must be all the more grateful that a truly outstanding early work has been handed down to us in the form of the cantata *Christ lag in Todes Banden*, which has to compensate for the many Easter works of later years that were either never composed or perhaps have not survived.

Ever since William H. Scheide established that Cantata 15, *Denn du wirst meine Seele nicht in der Hölle lassen*, is not by Johann Sebastian Bach but by his cousin Johann Ludwig Bach, Cantata 4 has generally been considered not only Bach's earliest Easter work but one of his earliest cantatas altogether. On the other hand, in a pure chorale cantata* such as this, the absence of all traces of

Neumeister's 'modern' cantata form cannot be regarded as relevant to its dating, and an origin in Bach's early Weimar years (1708–13) cannot be discounted.[55] It has to be admitted that we have no definite information about the original version of the work, for its earliest source is a set of Leipzig performing parts which dates from 1724 and 1725. The possibility must therefore be taken into account that the earliest version differed in detail from the version we know today. Yet the alterations cannot have been very extensive, for the extant version exhibits too clearly the stamp of a youthful work.

The text is made up entirely of Martin Luther's Easter hymn of 1524, which freely paraphrases the Latin sequence *Victimae paschali laudes* and is modelled on the old hymn *Christ ist erstanden*. All of the verses of Luther's hymn are preserved by Bach in the usual textual version of the day. Luther's language is rich in images and often makes reference to biblical ideas, particularly to the Easter Epistle,* with its metaphor of Christ as the Easter Lamb (verse 5) and its call to sweep out the old leaven (verse 7). The words 'It has lost its sting' (verse 3) recall 1 Corinthians 15.55; and the sacrificial blood that 'marks our door' and wards off the murderer (verse 5) refers to the Old Testament account of the Israelite exodus from Egypt (Exodus 12).

Bach's setting adopts the seventeenth-century technique of chorale variations *per omnes versus*. In other words, the chorale melody—after an introductory instrumental sinfonia, in which we hear its first line—is retained throughout all seven verses and subjected to different kinds of variation. Bach's immediate model might have been Johann Pachelbel's Easter cantata of the same name, which is likewise based on all the verses of Luther's hymn. Pachelbel's setting exhibits striking parallels with Bach's, though it dispenses with the chorale melody in several of the verses. If we compare Bach's work with his later cantatas, we are struck by the total absence of all stylistic elements derived from the Neapolitan school or from the instrumental concerto—recitatives, da capo* arias, thematic ritornellos, concertante* introductory sinfonias—in short, the lack of all movement types introduced since Neumeister. In form, the work corresponds with the chorale concerto* as it had evolved by the end of the seventeenth century. The instrumental ensemble is based on the traditional full five-part string sonority (with two viola parts) and lacks oboes or flutes. The choir of trombones that doubles the voices was apparently added for the revival in 1725.

The sinfonia forgoes concertante treatment of a single theme; instead, it joins together short chordal passages, or sometimes passages lightly broken up into polyphony,* in the style of the Venetian opera sinfonia. The first line of the

[55] Armin Schneiderheinze has proposed 1713 as a possible year of origin; see his 'Christ lag in Todes Banden: Überlegungen zur Datierung von BWV 4', in K. Heller and H.-J. Schulze, eds, *Das Frühwerk J. S. Bachs* [conference report, Rostock, 1990](Cologne, 1995), 267–79.

chorale melody—after two false starts in Georg Böhm's style of chorale treatment—is played in the top part in a lightly decorated form. Thereafter Bach's setting of the chorale verses is designed symmetrically as follows:

Verse:	1	2	3	4	5	6	7
Setting:	chorus	duet	solo	chorus	solo	duet	chorus

We cannot entirely rule out the possibility that the oldest version ended with an exact reprise of the opening chorus* to the text of verse 7, in place of the present plain chorale setting. Even the instrumental treatment is antiquated. The complementary rhythm of the violin figures in the opening chorus

is borrowed from the technique of the clavier or organ partita (i.e. variation), just as many of the bass figures are clearly inspired by organ pedal technique. The style of chorale treatment within the individual verses may be characterized as follows:

Verse 1: chorale melody in long notes in the soprano, with imitations* of it in the lower parts and free figuration in the instruments. The last line, 'Hallelujah', is expanded into a motet-like passage with an increase of tempo.

Verse 2: soprano-alto duet over an ostinato* continuo figuration; chorale melody in the soprano, lightly varied and prepared by fore-imitation.*

Verse 3: trio for unison violins, tenor, and continuo; chorale melody in the tenor, almost unvaried until the last line, which is treated freely. Lively motivic (though unthematic) figuration in the violins. Text-engendered retardation on 'nichts denn Tods Gestalt' ('nothing but death's form'; 'adagio').

Verse 4: motet-like four-part chorale setting with continuo but no other instruments; chorale melody in slow notes in the alto, transposed to the dominant, b-Dorian, with fore-imitation and lively counterpoints* in the other parts.

Verse 5: for solo bass, strings, and continuo; each chorale line stated twice in succession, first in solo bass and then (sometimes transposed to the dominant) in violin I in counterpoint with the bass voice; the last line, 'Hallelujah', treated freely.

Verse 6: soprano-tenor duet over an ostinato continuo figuration; the chorale melody lightly varied and divided between the two voices.

Verse 7: plain four-part chorale setting with the instruments *colla parte*.*

What makes Bach's music so full of life, despite its antiquated character, is the highly expressive manner in which he sets each phrase of the text. The concluding 'Hallelujah', for example, is invariably set in a particularly lively fashion—through acceleration of the beat or shorter note-values—often involving a different compositional technique from that of its surroundings. Other figurative means of expression employed for specific parts of the text are as follows:

'gefangen' ('captive', verse 2): low pitch, soprano part crossing under the alto
'Gewalt' ('power', verse 3): multiple stops on the violin, semiquaver figuration in the continuo (pedal-like bass—an image of treading underfoot?)
'nichts' ('nothing', verse 3): rest in all parts
'Wie ein Tod den andern fraß' ('How one death devoured another', verse 4): canonic writing at the closest possible distance between entries
'des Kreuzes Stamm' ('the Cross's beam', verse 5): cross figure in the voice part
'dem Tode' ('to death', verse 5): downward leap from *b* to *E*♯ (diminished 12th) in the voice part
'Der Würger' ('The murderer', verse 5): lively figuration in violin I
'Wonne', 'Sonne', 'Gnaden', 'Herzen' ('delight', 'sun', 'grace', 'hearts', verse 6): lively triplet figuration in the voice parts

Christ lag in Todes Banden is thus a masterpiece of baroque textual interpretation and one of the most remarkable of all pre-Neumeister cantatas. Bach's preservation of the chorale text in unaltered form elevates the work poetically above the fashionable, mediocre products of the eighteenth century and also anticipates Bach's late chorale cantatas,* which are likewise based on the pure chorale text. The style of setting was, of course, substantially modified during the intervening period.

Der Himmel lacht! Die Erde jubilieret, BWV 31

NBA I/9, p. 43 BC A55 Duration: *c.* 24 mins

1. SONATA tr I–III timp ob I–III taille bsn vln I,II vla I,II rip vc bc — C/E♭[56] $\frac{6}{8}$
2. CORO S I,II ATB (instrs as in no. 1) — C/E♭ 𝄴

Der Himmel lacht! Die Erde jubilieret	Heaven laughs! the earth rejoices,
Und was sie trägt in ihrem Schoß!	And what it carries in its bosom!
Der Schöpfer lebt! Der Höchste triumphieret	The Creator lives! the Highest triumphs
Und ist von Todesbanden los.	And is free from the snares of death.
Der sich das Grab zur Ruh erlesen,	He who chose the grave for rest, the Holiest,
Der Heiligste kann nicht verwesen!	Will not be able to see corruption!

3. RECITATIVO B bc — C–e/E♭–g 𝄴

Erwünschter Tag! Sei, Seele, wieder froh!	Welcome Day! Be joyful again, O soul!

[56] The first specified key refers to the Weimar performance at *Chorton** (= the Leipzig performance at *Kammerton*), the second to the Weimar performance at *Kammerton*.

Das A und O,
Der erst und auch der letzte,
Den unsre schwere Schuld
In Todeskerker setzte,
Ist nun gerissen aus der Not!
Der Herr war tot,
Und sieh, er lebet wieder!
Lebt unser Haupt, so leben auch die
 Glieder!
Der Herr hat in der Hand
Des Todes und der Höllen Schlüssel!
Der sein Gewand
Blutrot besprützt in seinem bittern
 Leiden,
Will heute sich mit Schmuck und
 Ehren kleiden.

The Alpha and Omega,
The first and also the last,
Whom our heavy debt
Placed in death's prison,
Has now been torn free of misery!
The Lord was dead,
And see, He lives again!
If our Head lives, His members live
 too!
The Lord has in His hand
The keys of death and of hell!
He whose garment was
Bespattered blood-red in His bitter
 Passion
Will today be clothed in glory and
 honour.

4. ARIA B bc — C/E♭ c

Fürst des Lebens! starker Streiter,
Hochgelobter Gottessohn!
 Hebet dich des Kreuzes Leiter
 Auf den höchsten Ehrenthron?
 Wird, was dich zuvor gebunden,
 Nun dein Schmuck und Edelstein?
 Müssen deine Purpurwunden
 Deiner Klarheit Strahlen sein?

Prince of Life! strong champion,
Highly praised Son of God!
 Does the ladder of the Cross lift You
 Up to the highest throne of honour?
 Does what once bound You become
 Now Your decoration and precious
  stone?
 Must Your purple wounds be
 The rays of Your bright light?

5. RECITATIVO T bc — a–G/c–B♭ c

So stehe dann, du gottergebne Seele,
Mit Christo geistlich auf!
Tritt an den neuen Lebenslauf!
Auf! von den toten Werken!
Laß, daß dein Heiland in dir lebt,
An deinem Leben merken!
Der Weinstock, der jetzt blüht,
Trägt keine tote Reben!
Der Lebensbaum läßt seine Zweige
 leben!
Ein Christe flieht
Ganz eilend von dem Grabe!
Er läßt den Stein,
Er läßt das Tuch der Sünden
Dahinten
Und will mit Christo lebend sein!

Rise up, then, you God-devoted soul,
Spiritually with Christ!
Set out on a new course of life!
Rise up from dead works!
Let your Saviour live in you,
To be felt in your life!
The Vine that now blooms
Bears no dead branches!
The Tree of Life lets its boughs live!
A Christian flees
With great haste from the grave!
He leaves the stone,
He leaves the fabric of sins
Behind
And wishes to be alive with Christ!

6. ARIA T vln I,II vla I,II rip vc bc — G/B♭ c

Adam muß in uns verwesen,

Adam must decay within us

Soll der neue Mensch genesen,	If the new man is to be saved,
Der nach Gott geschaffen ist!	Who is created in God's Image!
Du mußt geistlich auferstehen	You must be resurrected in spirit
Und aus Sündengräbern gehen,	And leave the graves of sin
Wenn du Christi Gliedmaß bist.	If you are a member of Christ.

7. Recitativo S bc — e–C/g–E♭ c

Weil dann das Haupt sein Glied	For as the head
Natürlich nach sich zieht,	Naturally draws its limb with it,
So kann mich nichts von Jesu scheiden.	So nothing can separate me from Jesus.
Muß ich mit Christo leiden,	Though I must suffer with Christ,
So werd ich auch nach dieser Zeit	After this time I shall
Mit Christo wieder auferstehen	Rise up again with Christ
Zur Ehr und Herrlichkeit	To honour and glory
Und Gott in meinem Fleische sehen!	And in my flesh see God!

8. Aria S ob I vlns + vlas bc — C/E♭ 3/4

Letzte Stunde, brich herein,	Last hour, break forth
Mir die Augen zuzudrücken!	And close my eyes!
Laß mich Jesu Freudenschein	Let me see Jesus's gleam of joy
Und sein helles Licht erblicken!	And His bright Light!
Laß mich Engeln ähnlich sein!	Let me be like the angels!
Letzte Stunde, brich herein!	Last hour, break forth!

9. Choral S I,II ATB tr I + vln I bc (+ ww, other str) — C/E♭ c

So fahr ich hin zu Jesu Christ,	**Then I go forth to Jesus Christ,**
Mein Arm tu ich ausstrecken;	**My arm do I outstretch;**
So schlaf ich ein und ruhe fein;	**Then I fall asleep and rest well;**
Kein Mensch kann mich aufwecken	**No mortal can awaken me,**
Denn Jesus Christus, Gottes Sohn,	**For Jesus Christ, God's Son,**
Der wird die Himmelstür auftun,	**Who will open heaven's door,**
Mich führn zum ewgen Leben.	**Will lead me to life everlasting.**

Bach composed this cantata within his four-weekly cycle at Weimar for 21 April 1715. It is based on a text from the cycle *Evangelisches Andachts-Opffer* by Salomo Franck, who refers to the Easter Gospel* but thereafter pursues his own ideas. Movements 2–4 celebrate the Resurrection of Christ and the newly liberated human creature. In no. 5 the poet turns to the individual Christian: he too must be resurrected in spirit and must lay aside the old man (no. 6). The poet's thoughts take a new turn in no. 7: the Christian, who follows Jesus, must also suffer with Him in order to enter with Him into His glory. This idea gives rise to the longing for death with which the work ends: the 'last hour' signifies not only death but also the restoration of life through Christ (no. 8). This thought is confirmed in the closing chorale, an additional verse (Bonn, 1575) to Nikolaus Herman's hymn *Wenn mein Stündlein vorhanden ist.*

Thus, at the end of the cantata, the joyous Easter jubilation of the opening gives way to a mystical longing for death. Franck's text includes many literal references to biblical passages; for example, 'The Holiest will not be able to see corruption' (no. 2; Psalm 16.10), 'The Alpha and Omega' (no. 3; Revelation 1.8), 'The Lord has in His hand the keys of death and of hell' (no. 3; Rev. 1.18), 'He whose garment was bespattered blood-red' (no. 3; Isaiah 63.2), 'Rise up from dead works' (no. 5; Hebrews 9.14), 'Adam must decay within us if the new man is to be saved, who is created in God's Image!' (no. 6; Ephesians 4.24; cf. 1 Corinthians 15.42 ff.), and 'I shall . . . in my flesh see God' (no. 7; Job 19.26).

The full feast-day scoring of this cantata underwent numerous changes for Bach's repeated performances. His first draft seems to have required an oboe in no. 8 only, being restricted elsewhere to trumpet choir, string choir, and five-part voices. While still resident in Weimar—and probably for the original 1715 performance—Bach added a five-part choir of reed instruments (three oboes, taille,* and bassoon) in nos. 1, 2, and 9. Although they almost invariably double the string or voice parts, they nonetheless lend the work a distinctive lustre.

The work was originally conceived in C major at Choir Pitch,* but for the Leipzig revivals—documented for 1724, 1731, and probably also 1735—Bach performed it in C major at Chamber Pitch* and, as a result, found himself confronted with the pitch problem described above in connection with Cantata 182. Consequently he omitted most of the woodwind, retaining only the first oboe part in 1724 (its player read from music in C major but must have played at least no. 8 on the oboe d'amore*) and adding the second oboe part in 1731—now played on the oboe d'amore (in E♭, sounding in C). The bassoonist may have played from one of the C major continuo parts. As in Cantata 182, however, this procedure was only a temporary expedient. The work would best recapture its original pitch and brilliance from an upward transposition to D major. An autograph title-page, perhaps from 1735, suggests that in Leipzig Bach may have reduced the five-part vocal writing of the cantata to four parts (simply by omitting the second soprano part?), but such a version does not survive.

In contrast to the restrained opening of Cantata 4, full Easter rejoicing breaks out at once in the introductory *concertato* Sonata. A fanfare-like unison theme gives way to a more figurative theme, after which the two are combined. Finally, they are recapitulated in reverse order to round off the movement. The opening chorus,* no. 2, sustains the jubilant mood of the Sonata. Its overall form is that of the *Bar** with reprise, but the relative independence of its individual sections points to the series principle of the motet,* which was never wholly abandoned as a means of textual interpretation. The formal scheme that arises is thus as follows:

A Choral fugue* with freely polyphonic* epilogue (text-lines 1–2)
A Reprise of the choral fugue to lines 3–4
B 'Adagio' homophonic* choral passage, partly loosened up into polyphony (lines 5–6)
C 'Allegro' canonic texture (line 6)
A[1] Reprise of bars 1–8 (instruments only)

The instruments are independent only in part, but in the vocal passages they never have the upper hand.

The recitatives are accompanied only by continuo throughout. No. 5 is set largely as a syllabically* declaimed *secco*, with melismatic* scale figures on 'flieht . . . eilend' ('flees with great haste'); and only at the end does no. 7 turn into arioso.* No. 3, on the other hand, alternates frequently between mostly short recitative passages ('adagio'), rolling scale figures ('allegro') on 'sei wieder froh' ('be joyful again'), and canonic formations ('andante') whose interpretative function on the words 'If our Head lives, His members live too!' is immediately evident.

The first of the three arias, no. 4, is also accompanied by continuo only, so that the fully scored introductory movements (nos. 1–2) are followed by three continuo movements in succession (nos. 3–5). No. 4, marked 'molto adagio', draws its thematic material from a four-bar continuo ritornello which recurs constantly thereafter in the form of a slightly varied ostinato.* Inherently more melodious is the aria 'Adam muß in uns verwesen', no. 6, whose string ritornello, with its rising and falling melodic lines, might perhaps signify the conversion of mankind, for the melody of bars 3–4 is derived by free inversion from that of bars 1–2. In addition, the overall structure of this bipartite aria reveals a symmetrical ordering of its individual members, which might also be intended as a form of textual interpretation.

The third and last aria, 'Letzte Stunde, brich herein', no. 8, includes, within a vocal movement for soprano and obbligato* oboe, a rendition of the chorale *Wenn mein Stündlein vorhanden ist* on unison strings. Here, in contrast with the warmth and fullness of string sonority that characterizes the preceding aria, a mystically enraptured, other-wordly atmosphere prevails, aided not only by the distinction between the high soprano pitch and the low-lying chorale melody, but also by the motivic character of the writing, with the wide-ranging fourths of its melodic material. The listener is now prepared to encounter the same hymn melody again in the concluding chorale, now in the form of a plain choral setting. Added to it, however, is a high-pitched obbligato part for first trumpet and first violin in unison, which again lends the movement a transfigured atmosphere—a halo, as it were—recalling the words of the preceding aria 'Let me be like the angels'.

Kommt, eilet und laufet *Oster-Oratorium* *Easter Oratorio*, BWV 249

NBA II/7, p. 3 BC D8 Duration: *c.* 47 mins

	German	English	Key	Time
1.	SINFONIA tr I–III timp ob I,II str bsn bc		D	3/8
2.	ADAGIO fl or ob I str bc		b	3/4
3.	CHORUS SATB tr I–III timp ob I,II str bc		D	3/8
	Kommt, eilet und laufet, ihr flüchtigen Füße,	Come, hasten and run, you fugitive feet,		
	Erreichet die Höhle, die Jesum bedeckt!	Reach the cave that hides Jesus!		
	Lachen und Scherzen	Laughing and jesting		
	Begleitet die Herzen,	Accompany our hearts,		
	Denn unser Heil ist auferweckt.	For our Salvation has arisen!		
4.	RECITATIVO SATB bc		b	c
	Maria Magdalena	*Mary Magdalene*		
	O kalter Männer Sinn!	O cold heart of men!		
	Wo ist die Liebe hin,	Where has the love gone		
	Die ihr dem Heiland schuldig seid?	That you owe to the Saviour?		
	Maria Jacobi	*Mary, Mother of James*		
	Ein schwaches Weib muß euch beschämen!	A weak woman must put you to shame!		
	Petrus	*Peter*		
	Ach, ein betrübtes Grämen	Ah, a distressed grieving		
	Johannes	*John*		
	Und banges Herzeleid	And anxious sorrow		
	Petrus, Johannes	*Peter, John*		
	Hat mit gesalznen Tränen	Has with salted tears		
	Und wehmutsvollem Sehnen	And melancholy longing		
	Ihm eine Salbung zugedacht,	Planned an anointing for Him,		
	Maria Jacobi, Maria Magdalena	*Mary, Mother of James, Mary Magdalene*		
	Die ihr, wie wir, umsonst gemacht.	Which you, like us, have prepared in vain.		
5.	ARIA S fl bc		b	3/4
	Maria Jacobi	*Mary, Mother of James*		
	Seele, deine Spezereien	O soul, your spices		
	Sollen nicht mehr Myrrhen sein.	Shall no longer be myrrh.		
	Denn allein	For only		
	Mit dem Lorbeerkranze prangen,	To adorn with laurel wreath		
	Stillt dein ängstliches Verlangen.	Will still your anxious longing.		
6.	RECITATIVO ATB bc		D–b	c
	Petrus	*Peter*		
	Hier ist die Gruft	Here is the tomb		
	Johannes	*John*		
	Und hier der Stein,	And here the stone		
	Der solche zugedeckt;	That covered it;		
	Wo aber wird mein Heiland sein?	But where is my Saviour gone?		

Maria Magdalena
Er ist vom Tode auferweckt!
Wir trafen einen Engel an,
Der hat uns solches kundgetan.
Petrus
Hier seh ich mit Vergnügen
Das Schweißtuch abgewickelt liegen.

Mary Magdalene
He is arisen from death!
We met an angel
Who told us this.
Peter
Here I see with delight
The napkin lying unwound.

7. Aria T vln I,II + rec I,II 8va bc — G c

Petrus
Sanfte soll mein Todeskummer
Nur ein Schlummer,
Jesu, durch dein Schweißtuch sein.
Ja, das wird mich dort erfrischen
Und die Zähren meiner Pein
Von den Wangen tröstlich wischen.

Peter
Gently shall my death-agony be
But a slumber,
O Jesus, through Your napkin.
Indeed, it will there refresh me
And wipe the tears of my pain
Comfortingly from my cheeks.

8. Recitativo SA bc — b–A c

Maria Jacobi, Maria Magdalena
Indessen seufzen wir
Mit brennender Begier:
Ach, könnt es doch nur bald geschehen,
Den Heiland selbst zu sehen!

Mary, Mother of James, Mary Magdalene
Meanwhile we sigh
With burning desire:
Ah, if only it could happen soon
That we might see the Saviour Himself!

9. Aria A ob d'am str bc — A c

Maria Magdalena
Saget, saget mir geschwinde,
Saget, wo ich Jesum finde,
Welchen meine Seele liebt!
Komm doch, komm, umfasse mich,
Denn mein Herz ist ohne dich
Ganz verwaiset und betrübt.

Mary Magdalene
Tell me, tell me quickly,
Tell me where I find Jesus,
Whom my soul loves!
Come now, come and embrace me,
For my heart is, without You,
Quite orphaned and distressed.

10. Recitativo B bc — G–A c

Johannes
Wir sind erfreut,
Daß unser Jesus wieder lebt,
Und unser Herz,
So erst in Traurigkeit zerflossen und geschwebt,
Vergißt den Schmerz
Und sinnt auf Freudenlieder;
Denn unser Heiland lebet wieder.

John
We are overjoyed
That our Jesus lives again,
And our heart,
At first dissolved and suspended in sorrow,
Forgets its pain
And devises songs of joy;
For our Saviour lives again.

11. Chorus SATB tr I–III timp ob I,II str bc — D c 3/8

Preis und Dank
Bleibe, Herr, dein Lobgesang!
Höll und Teufel sind bezwungen,

Let glory and thanks
Remain, O Lord, Your song of praise!
Hell and Devil have been overcome

Ihre Pforten sind zerstört;	And their gates destroyed;
Jauchzet, ihr erlösten Zungen,	Exult, you redeemed tongues,
Daß man es im Himmel hört!	That it may be heard in heaven!
Eröffnet, ihr Himmel, die prächtigen Bogen,	Open, you heavens, Your splendid arches:
Der Löwe von Juda kömmt siegend gezogen!	The Lion of Judah comes, drawn victoriously!

This work differs from all other pieces of church music by Bach in that it is based on a sung plot rather than one narrated by an Evangelist. Peter (tenor) and John (bass) hasten to Jesus's grave (no. 3). Mary, mother of James, and Mary Magdalene (soprano and alto) are already there, having discovered that their plan of anointing the body is in vain (no. 4) and that, instead of the intended spices, only the victor's laurel wreath is appropriate (no. 5). Peter and John gather from Mary Magdalene that an angel has told them the good news of the Resurrection (no. 6). Peter finds Jesus's napkin and concludes—curiously enough—that his own death will be nothing more than a slumber now that he has evidence of Jesus's Resurrection in his hands in the form of this napkin (no. 7).[57] The two women now wish to see the Saviour again soon (no. 8), for without Him—so Mary Magdalene tells us in no. 9—they feel 'quite orphaned and distressed'. John calls for joy over Jesus's Resurrection (no. 10), and finally all join together in singing a song of thanksgiving to the Lord (no. 11).

Bach performed this work for the first time on 1 April 1725 as the Easter cantata *Kommt, gehet und eilet* (the first line originally read 'Kommt, fliehet und eilet', but it was probably altered before the first performance). It was first described as an 'Oratorium' when performed in a revised version (with the opening line as we know it today) around 1738. Still later, around 1743/6, Bach made further alterations, rearranging the duet 'Kommt, eilet und laufet', no. 3, for four-part choir.[58]

The history of the work becomes comprehensible only when we take account of its origin as a sacred parody* of the pastoral cantata *Entfliehet, verschwindet, entweichet, ihr Sorgen*, BWV 249a, composed in 1725 for the court of Weißenfels. The sacred paraphrase, for which Picander might have been responsible, being the librettist of the pastoral cantata, follows its model so closely that the arias and the closing chorus* could be adopted in the same order, and only the recitatives had to be composed afresh. The shepherds and

[57] Lothar and Renate Steiger (*Musik und Kirche* 53, 1983, p. 194) believe that my formulation 'exposes' the text 'to ridicule'. Yet one cannot dispose of a poetic awkwardness by elucidating the theological background of its underlying thought processes.

[58] Dates from Kobayashi Chr, pp. 41 and 53. The usual practice today of starting the movement as a duet and ending it as a chorus is based on a pure misunderstanding which originated with Wilhelm Rust. In the BG edition (21/3, 1874) he united the two versions, but only to avoid printing the work twice, not to establish an unauthorized version for our use.

shepherdesses who congratulated Duke Christian on his birthday now become the disciples who hasten to Jesus's grave. This transformation was perhaps facilitated by the old custom of scenic representation of the Easter story. In any case, we would do well to conceive the plot as an 'Easter play' and not to question its theological substance. Even the arbitrary addition of a concluding chorale, which is found in one modern edition, does not allow the work to be converted into a church cantata. Instead, it reveals still more clearly the differences between this and a cantata of the conventional type.

The work is introduced by two concerto-like movements, formerly considered remnants of a lost instrumental work from the Cöthen period, of which the third movement of the oratorio* was thought to have formed the finale. This view has recently been rejected, however, on the grounds that the internal structure of the three movements concerned is quite unlike that of Bach's concertos.[59] In 'Kommt, eilet und laufet', no. 3, the rising scale figures that accompany the vocal parts seem to portray clearly the running of the disciples' 'fugitive feet'. The middle section remains a duet even in the later choral version of the movement. The other movements are probably not very different from their equivalents in the lost (but reconstructable) pastoral cantata, to whose discussion the reader is referred (see p. 805). Most impressive is the expansion at the end of the middle section of no. 9, which takes the form of an 'adagio' appendix, giving striking musical expression to the words 'quite orphaned and distressed'. The bipartite structure of the notably brief closing chorus is modelled on that of the Sanctus, BWV 232^{III}, composed shortly beforehand (Christmas 1724) and later incorporated in the B minor Mass.

1.22 Easter Monday

EPISTLE: Acts 10.34–43: Peter's sermon on Christ.
GOSPEL: Luke 24.13–35: The disciples' journey to Emmaus.

Erfreut euch, ihr Herzen, BWV 66

NBA I/10, p. 3 BC A56 Duration: *c.* 32 mins

1. [CHORUS] SATB tr ad lib ob I,II bsn str bc — D $\frac{3}{8}$

Erfreut euch, ihr Herzen,	Rejoice, you hearts;
Entweichet, ihr Schmerzen,	Vanish, you sorrows:
Es lebet der Heiland und herrschet in euch.	The Saviour lives and reigns among you.

[59] See J. Rifkin, 'Verlorene Quellen, verlorene Werke: Miszellen zu Bachs Instrumentalkomposition', in M. Geck and W. Breig, eds, *Bachs Orchesterwerke* [conference report, Dortmund, 1996](Witten, 1997), 59–75 (specifically 74, note 57). See also the more recent discussion in S. Rampe and D. Sackmann, *Bachs Orchestermusik: Entstehung – Klangwelt – Interpretation* (Kassel, 2000), 466, note 2.

Ihr könnet verjagen
Das Trauren, das Fürchten, das ängstliche Zagen,
Der Heiland erquicket sein geistliches Reich.

You can drive away
Sorrow, fear, anxious dismay:
The Saviour refreshes His spiritual Kingdom.

2. RECITATIVO B str bc b–A c

Es bricht das Grab und damit unsre Not,
Der Mund verkündigt Gottes Taten;
Der Heiland lebt, so ist in Not und Tod
Den Gläubigen vollkommen wohl geraten.

The grave is broken and therewith our distress;
My mouth shall show forth God's deeds;
The Saviour lives, so in distress and death
All turns out perfectly well for the people of faith.

3. ARIA B ob I,II bsn str bc D 3/8

Lasset dem Höchsten ein Danklied erschallen
Vor sein Erbarmen und ewige Treu.
Jesus erscheinet, uns Friede zu geben,
Jesus berufet uns, mit ihm zu leben,
Täglich wird seine Barmherzigkeit neu.

Let a song of thanks to the Highest be heard
For His mercy and everlasting faithfulness.
Jesus appears, to give us peace,
Jesus calls us to live with Him;
His compassion is new every day.

4. RECITATIVO a 2 AT bc G–D–A c

Hoffnung
Bei Jesu Leben freudig sein
Ist unsrer Brust ein heller Sonnenschein.
Mit Trost erfüllt auf seinen Heiland schauen
Und in sich selbst ein Himmelreich erbauen,
Ist wahrer Christen Eigentum.
Doch! weil ich hier ein himmlisch Labsal habe,
So sucht mein Geist hier seine Lust und Ruh,
Mein Heiland ruft mir kräftig zu:
'Mein Grab und Sterben bringt euch Leben,
Mein Auferstehn ist euer Trost'.
Mein Mund will zwar ein Opfer geben,
Mein Heiland! doch wie klein,
Wie wenig, wie so gar geringe

Hope
To be joyful over Jesus's Life
Is bright sunshine to our breast.
To look upon their Saviour, filled with comfort
And to build a heavenly kingdom among themselves
Is the property of true Christians.
Yet! since I have heavenly refreshment here,
My spirit seeks here its delight and repose;
My Saviour calls to me forcibly:
'My Grave and Death bring you life,
My Resurrection is your comfort'.
My mouth would indeed give You an offering,
My Saviour! yet how small,
How paltry, how very insignificant

Wird es vor dir, o großer Sieger, sein,
Wenn ich vor dich ein Sieg- und Danklied bringe?
Hoffnung/Furcht
Mein/Kein Auge sieht den Heiland auferweckt,
Es hält ihn nicht/noch der Tod in Banden.
Hoffnung
Wie? darf noch Furcht in einer Brust entstehn?
Furcht
Läßt wohl das Grab die Toten aus?
Hoffnung
Wenn Gott in einem Grabe lieget,
So halten Grab und Tod ihn nicht.
Furcht
Ach Gott! der du den Tod besieget,
Dir weicht des Grabes Stein, das Siegel bricht,
Ich glaube, aber hilf mir Schwachen,
Du kannst mich stärker machen.
Besiege mich und meinen Zweifelmut,
Der Gott, der Wunder tut,
Hat meinen Geist durch Trostes Kraft gestärket,
Daß er den auferstandnen Jesum merket.

It will be to You, O great Victor,
When I bring You a song of victory and thanksgiving!
Hope/Fear
My/No eye sees the Saviour arisen:
Death holds Him not/still in its snares.
Hope
What? may Fear still arise in any breast?
Fear
Does the grave indeed let the dead out?
Hope
If God lies in a grave,
Grave and Death do not hold Him.
Fear
Ah God! You who conquer Death,
For You the grave's stone yields, the seal breaks;
I believe, but help my weakness:
You can make me stronger.
Conquer me and my spirit of doubt;
God, who does wonders,
Has strengthened my spirit through the power of comfort
So that it takes heed of the risen Jesus.

5. ARIA [DUETTO] AT vln solo bc — A $\frac{12}{8}$

Furcht/Hoffnung
Ich furchte zwar/furchte nicht des Grabes Finsternissen
Und klagete,/hoffete, mein Heil sei nun/nicht entrissen.
à 2
Nun ist mein Herze voller Trost,
Und wenn sich auch ein Feind erbost,
Will ich in Gott zu siegen wissen.

Fear/Hope
I feared indeed/did not fear the grave's darkness
And lamented/hoped that my Salvation was now/not snatched away.
a 2
Now my heart is full of comfort,
And though an enemy should be angry,
I will know how to triumph in God.

6. [CHORALE] SATB bc (+ instrs) — f♯ **c**

Alleluja! Alleluja! Alleluja!
Des solln wir alle froh sein,
Christus will unser Trost sein.
Kyrie eleis.

Alleluia! Alleluia! Alleluia!
We shall all be glad of this:
Christ will be our comfort.
Lord, have mercy.

Performances of this cantata on 10 April 1724 and 26 March 1731 are attested by the evidence of printed texts, but the surviving version seems to have originated a few years later (1735?). Friedrich Smend has established, however, that the work is a sacred parody* of a Cöthen congratulatory cantata, BWV 66a of 1718. Its history can probably be envisaged by analogy with that of Cantata 134: in 1724 Bach was able to undertake only a superficial adaptation of the secular model to the sacred text; but later, recognizing the inadequacy of the parodied work, he undertook a radical revision during the process of copying out a new score, which is the only version that survives.

The anonymous librettist, confronted with the task of inventing a cantata text for Easter Monday to fit an existing piece of music, acquitted himself with considerable skill. The original finale was transferred to the opening of the work and replaced with a concluding chorale. The substance of this opening chorus* and of the two movements that follow is jubilation and gratitude over the Resurrection of Christ. The next movement is a duet recitative with arioso* insertion, no. 4, in which the singers are characterized as 'Schwachheit' ('Weakness'; alto) and 'Zuversicht' ('Confidence'; tenor) in 1724, becoming in 1731 'Furcht' ('Fear') and 'Hoffnung' ('Hope'). This corresponds to the dialogue between 'Glückseligkeit Anhalts' ('The Felicity of Anhalt') and 'Fama' ('Fame') in the secular original. Rudolf Wustmann has pointed out that the allegorical characters in the Easter Monday cantata were chosen with reference to the Gospel* reading: 'But we *hoped* that He would redeem Israel' (Luke 24.21) and 'Certain women have *frightened* us' (Luke 24.22). Yet this does not suffice to establish a close connection with the readings for Easter Monday.

The work opens with an extended chorus in da capo* form with a concertante* orchestral ritornello. Two contrasting instrumental groups alternate with one another: strings, with continuo accompaniment, and a woodwind trio of two oboes and bassoon. An optional trumpet—evidently a subsequent addition—mostly reinforces the highest melodic line only on account of its range. The choral texture, part chordal and part freely polyphonic,* is from time to time built into the dominant orchestral texture. Numerous duet passages—for example, at the very opening of the vocal section on 'Erfreut euch, ihr Herzen', answered by 'Entweichet, ihr Schmerzen'—were in the secular original sung by 'Glückseligkeit Anhalts' and 'Fama', and should no doubt be sung by soloists in the Easter cantata too. The middle section, by comparison with the outer ones, brings a reduction not only in sonority but in tempo ('andante'). After the initial entry of a new chromatic* vocal melody, however, it is linked to the main sections by the unvarying thematic material of the instrumental parts.

A short recitative accompanied by strings, no. 2, is followed by a splendid bass aria, no. 3, whose dance-like vitality is derived from its secular model. The first oboe and first violin at times emerge from the united woodwind-and-string texture to form a concertante duet. The fourth movement, which opens the dialogue between Fear and Hope, is a multi-layered structure for alto, tenor, and continuo that takes the form of recitative–duet–recitative. The first recitative, however, incorporates an arioso passage at the Saviour's words 'My Grave and Death bring you life . . .'; and the duet is itself bipartite, since an extended imitative passage is followed by its abridged reprise (A A^1). The text retains the partial splitting of the secular original, which is typical of Hunold's Cöthen cantata texts:

> *Furcht/Hoffnung*
> Kein/Mein Auge sieht den Heiland auferweckt
> *Fear/Hope*
> No/My eye sees the Saviour arisen

In contrast to the duet section of no. 4, which relies on the imitative* principle, the duet texture of the following aria, no. 5, is essentially homophonic.* After a brief head-motive, the obbligato* solo violin turns to concertante figuration and, as a result, makes notably little contribution to thematic development. The charm of the movement lies in its vocal themes: though similar in the two voice parts, they nonetheless reflect musically the distinctions in character that arise from their partially split text:

The cantata concludes with a plain four-part chorale setting of the third verse of the medieval Easter hymn *Christ ist erstanden.*

Bleib bei uns, denn es will Abend werden, BWV 6

NBA I/10, p. 45 BC A57 Duration: *c.* 26 mins

1. [Chorus] SATB ob I,II ob da c str bc — c 3/4 ¢ 3/4

'Bleib bei uns, denn es will Abend werden, und der Tag hat sich geneiget.'	'Remain with us, for it is towards evening and the day has drawn to a close.'

2. Aria A ob da c or vla bc — E♭ 3/8

Hochgelobter Gottessohn,	Highly praised Son of God,
Laß es dir nicht sein entgegen,	Let it not be unwelcome to You
Daß wir itzt vor deinem Thron	That now before Your throne
Eine Bitte niederlegen:	We lay down a prayer:
Bleib, ach bleibe unser Licht,	Remain, oh remain our Light,
Weil die Finsternis einbricht.	For darkness falls.

3. Choral S vc picc bc B♭ C

**Ach bleib bei uns, Herr Jesu Christ,
Weil es nun Abend worden ist,
Dein göttlich Wort, das helle Licht,
Laß ja bei uns auslöschen nicht.**

**In dieser letztn betrübten Zeit
Verleih uns, Herr, Beständigkeit,
Daß wir dein Wort und Sakrament
Rein bhalten bis an unser End.**

**Ah remain with us, Lord Jesus Christ,
For it has now become evening;
Your divine Word, that bright Light,
Let it indeed not be extinguished.**

**In this final, troubled time
Lend us, Lord, steadfastness, that we
May hold Your Word and Sacrament
Pure until our end.**

4. Recitativo B bc d–g C

Es hat die Dunkelheit
An vielen Orten überhand genommen.
Woher ist aber dieses kommen?
Bloß daher, weil sowohl die Kleinen als die Großen
Nicht in Gerechtigkeit
Vor dir, o Gott, gewandelt
Und wider ihre Christenpflicht gehandelt.
Drum hast du auch den Leuchter umgestoßen.

Darkness has gained
The upper hand in many places.
But how has this come about?
Simply thus: because both small and great
Without righteousness
Have walked before You, O God,
And acted contrary to their Christian duty.
Therefore You have knocked over their candlesticks.

5. Aria T str bc g ¢

Jesu, laß uns auf dich sehen,
Daß wir nicht
Auf den Sündenwegen gehen.
Laß das Licht
Deines Worts uns helle scheinen
Und dich jederzeit treu meinen.

O Jesus, let us look unto You
So that we do not
Walk in the way of sinners.
Let the Light
Of Your Word shine brightly for us
And may You at all times have faithful intentions.

6. Choral SATB bc (+ instrs) g C

**Beweis dein Macht, Herr Jesu Christ,
Der du Herr aller Herren bist;
Beschirm dein arme Christenheit,
Daß sie dich lob in Ewigkeit.**

**Declare Your strength, Lord Jesus Christ,
Who are Lord of all lords;
Shield Your poor Christendom,
That it may praise You in eternity.**

The text of the opening movement, Luke 24.29 (about the journey to Emmaus), is drawn from the Gospel* for Easter Monday. Following widespread tradition, the anonymous librettist interprets the departing light, night closing in, and the disciples' plea to the stranger to come into the house with them (interpreted out of context, however, as a plea not to be left alone in the dark themselves) as a generally valid symbol of the Christian experience of faith. Without going further into the Emmaus story, the librettist celebrates Jesus as the Light in the sinful darkness of the world. The drily didactic quality of the text and the reference to Revelation 2.5, skilfully woven into the end of the fourth movement ('Therefore You have knocked over their candlesticks'), suggest that the librettist might have been a theologian. The work is divided up by the two chorale movements. The first part closes with the German version of *Vespera iam venit* by Philipp Melanchthon (1579), plus the additional verse by Nikolaus Selnecker (1572), and the second part with verse 2 of Luther's hymn *Erhalt uns, Herr, bei deinem Wort* (1542). Nevertheless, there are no indications that Bach performed the two parts separately, one before and one after the sermon.

Hard though it may be to find poetic qualitites in the text, Bach's music—written for performance on 2 April 1725—is incomparable. The opening chorus* is of imposing grandeur. A choir of oboes (two oboes plus oboe da caccia*), accompanied by strings and continuo, deliver a theme of speech-like gestures, which is immediately repeated by the choir to the opening words of the text. Choir, oboes, and strings take the lead alternately in homophonic* choral passages and instrumental episodes. A kind of choral fugue* on four subjects then forms a middle section, accompanied at first by continuo only (solo choir?) but later by doubling instruments too (ripieno choir?). The marking 'andante' and the *alla breve* notation clearly indicate an acceleration *vis-à-vis* the outer sections, which lack tempo mark. An abridged reprise of the first section closes the movement.

The second movement has occasionally been regarded—surely in error—as the parody* of a secular movement. That this is not the case is indicated both by the draft character of the autograph score and by the graphic upward gesture of the opening of the theme, which addresses the '*Hoch*gelobter Gottessohn', the '*highly* praised Son of God'. In the second part of the aria, 'darkness' falling is illustrated in an inimitable fashion by falling whole-tone steps. Exceptional (and on that account, of special charm) is the choice of alto pitch for both voice and obbligato* instrument, the oboe da caccia, which was replaced by viola at a subsequent revival. The following chorale, no. 3—well known in its organ transcription as one of the Schübler Chorales, BWV 649—now requires an obbligato instrument at tenor pitch, the violoncello piccolo,* whose virtuoso figurations surround the chorale, sung unvaried by the soprano. A short *secco*, the only recitative in the cantata, leads to the tenor aria, no. 5, whose head-motive, stated first in the strings and then by the voice, is surely designed to represent the Cross:

A plain chorale setting closes this impressive work.

Ich bin ein Pilgrim auf der Welt, BWV Anh. I 190

See NBA I/33, Critical Report, pp. 58–9 BC A58 Music almost all lost

1. [RECITATIVE] Ich bin ein Pilgrim auf der Welt
2. ARIA Lebe wohl, du Sündenwüste
3. [RECITATIVE] Was sollt ich mich noch lange sehnen
4. ARIA B bc Wenn ich nicht soll Jesum haben D (?) 3/4
5. [RECITATIVE] Bei Jesu bin ich auch nicht fremde
6. CHORAL O süßer Herre Jesu Christ

This cantata, based on a text from Picander's cycle of 1728, was probably composed for performance on 18 April 1729. All that survives, however, is a brief fragment of the fourth movement: the close of the middle section, which is in D major and 3/4 time. In addition, the concluding chorale is probably transmitted within C. P. E. Bach's collection of his father's four-part chorales (BWV 342). However, this material does not suffice to give even a rough idea of the original character of the cantata.

1.23 Easter Tuesday

EPISTLE: Acts 13.26–33: Paul preaches in Antioch.
GOSPEL: Luke 24.36–47: Jesus appears to the disciples in Jerusalem.

Ein Herz, das seinen Jesum lebend weiß, BWV 134

NBA I/10, p.71 BC A59 Duration: *c.* 20 mins

1. RECITATIVO AT bc B♭ C

Tenor	*Tenor*
Ein Herz, das seinen Jesum lebend weiß,	A heart that knows its Jesus to be alive
Empfindet Jesu neue Güte	Feels Jesus's goodness afresh
Und dichtet nur auf seines Heilands Preis.	And is inditing only to its Saviour's praise.
Alt	*Alto*
Wie freuet sich ein gläubiges Gemüte?	How the believing mind rejoices!

2. ARIA T ob I,II str bc B♭ 3/8

Auf! Gläubige, singet die lieblichen Lieder,	Rise up, believers! sing lovely songs;
Euch scheinet ein herrlich verneuetes Licht.	A splendid renewed Light shines in you.
Der lebende Heiland gibt selige Zeiten,	The living Saviour causes blessed times;
Auf! Seelen, ihr müsset ein Opfer bereiten,	Rise, souls! you must prepare an offering,

Bezahlet dem Höchsten mit Danken die Pflicht.	Pay your duty to the Most High with thanksgiving.

3. Recitativo AT bc — g–E♭ **c**

Tenor	*Tenor*
Wohl dir! Gott hat an dich gedacht,	Blessed are you! God has remembered you,
O Gott geweihtes Eigentum!	O possession consecrated by God!
Der Heiland lebt und siegt mit Macht.	The Saviour lives and conquers with might.
Zu deinem Heil, zu seinem Ruhm	For your salvation, to His praise
Muß hier der Satan furchtsam zittern	Satan must here tremble fearfully
Und sich die Hölle selbst erschüttern.	And Hell itself be shaken.
Es stirbt der Heiland dir zugut	The Saviour dies for your benefit
Und fähret vor dich zu der Höllen,	And for you journeys to Hell;
Sogar vergießet er sein kostbar Blut,	He even sheds His precious Blood
Daß du in seinem Blute siegst,	So that by His Blood you conquer,
Denn dieses kann die Feinde fällen,	For it can fell your enemies,
Und wenn der Streit dir an die Seele dringt,	So that when strife pierces your soul
Daß du alsdann nicht überwunden liegst.	You do not then lie overcome.
Alt	*Alto*
Der Liebe Kraft ist vor mich ein Panier	Love's power is for me a banner
Zum Heldenmut, zur Stärke in den Streiten:	For a hero's courage, for strength in battle:
Mir Siegeskronen zu bereiten,	To prepare my victor's crown
Nahmst du die Dornenkrone dir,	You accepted the Crown of Thorns,
Mein Herr, mein Gott, mein auferstandnes Heil,	My Lord, my God, my risen Salvation;
So hat kein Feind an mir zum Schaden teil.	Thus no enemy partakes in my harm.
Tenor	*Tenor*
Die Feinde zwar sind nicht zu zählen.	Our enemies indeed cannot be counted.
Alt	*Alto*
Gott schützt die ihm getreuen Seelen.	God protects souls faithful to Him.
Tenor	*Tenor*
Der letzte Feind ist Grab und Tod.	The last enemy is the grave and death.
Alt	*Alto*
Gott macht auch den zum Ende unsrer Not.	God makes that indeed the end of our misery.

4. Aria [Duetto] AT str bc — E♭ ¢

Wir danken und preisen dein brünstiges Lieben	We thank and praise Your ardent Love
Und bringen ein Opfer der Lippen vor dich.	And bring You an offering from our lips.

Der Sieger erwecket die freudigen Lieder,
Der Heiland erscheinet und tröstet uns wieder
Und stärket die streitende Kirche durch sich.

The Victor arouses joyful songs,
The Saviour appears and comforts us again
And through Himself strengthens the Church Militant.

5. Recitativo AT bc — c–B♭ C

Tenor

Doch würke selbst den Dank in unserm Munde,
Indem er allzu irdisch ist;
Ja schaffe, daß zu keiner Stunde
Dich und dein Werk kein menschlich Herz vergißt;
Ja, laß in dir das Labsal unsrer Brust
Und aller Herzen Trost und Lust,
Die unter deiner Gnade trauen,
Vollkommen und unendlich sein.
Es schließe deine Hand uns ein,
Daß wir die Würkung kräftig schauen,
Was uns dein Tod und Sieg erwirbt,
Und daß man nun nach deinem Auferstehen
Nicht stirbt, wenn man gleich zeitlich stirbt,
Und wir dadurch zu deiner Herrlichkeit eingehen.

Alt

Was in uns ist, erhebt dich, großer Gott,
Und preiset deine Huld und Treu.
Dein Auferstehen macht sie wieder neu,
Dein großer Sieg macht uns von Feinden los
Und bringet uns zum Leben;
Drum sei dir Preis und Dank gegeben.

Tenor

Yet Yourself fashion the thanks in our mouths,
Since they are too worldly;
Yes, cause that at no time are
You and Your Work forgotten by any human heart;
Yes, let the refreshment of our breast
And the comfort and delight of all hearts
That trust in Your grace
Be complete and unending.
May Your hand enclose us,
That we may see clearly the effect
That Your Death and Victory gain for us,
And that now after Your Resurrection we do
Not die, even though we die temporally,
But enter thereby into Your glory.

Alto

Whatever is in us exalts You, great God,
And praises Your favour and faithfulness.
Your Resurrection makes them new again,
Your great Victory makes us free of enemies
And brings us to Life;
Therefore praise and thanks be given to You.

6. Chorus SATB ob I,II str bc — B♭ 3/8

Erschallet, ihr Himmel, erfreue dich, Erde,
Lobsinge dem Höchsten, du glaubende Schar!
Es schauet und schmecket ein jedes Gemüte

Resound, you heavens; rejoice, O earth;
Sing praises to the Highest, you believing throng!
Every spirit tastes and sees

Des lebenden Heilands unendliche Güte,	The living Saviour's unending goodness;
Er tröstet und stellet als Sieger sich dar.	He comforts us and presents Himself as Victor.

Like BWV 66, this cantata is a sacred parody* of a Cöthen congratulatory cantata, BWV 134a. In this case, however, the sources survive in greater numbers, which enables us to follow more clearly the history of the work's origin. Its secular model originated as a New Year cantata for 1 January 1719. During his first year in Leipzig, on 11 April 1724, Bach took the opportunity of performing the Cöthen music (without its fifth and sixth movements) to a sacred text during divine service. Essentially, the necessary alterations involved the adaptation of the vocal parts to the newly written text. Therefore Bach first had the vocal parts of the congratulatory cantata (except for the excluded movements) copied out without text. He then entered the new text himself, while at the same time making the necessary alterations to the music. The instrumental parts of the secular work could be reused (they were merely supplemented by duplicates), and Bach did not even need to write out a score: with a few cues* added, the score of the New Year cantata provided the composer with an adequate tool for directing the performance (probably due to shortage of time, the effort to produce a new score did not extend beyond the copying out of the first sheet).

It is evident that, in the long run, such a superficial adaptation of a secular work into a church cantata could not satisfy the composer. In particular, the almost note-for-note taking over of the recitatives with new text must have seemed to him inadequate. Therefore, for a later performance—probably that which, according to a printed libretto, took place on 27 March 1731—Bach composed the recitatives nos. 1, 3, and 5 afresh, covering the old sheets among the performing parts with replacements. Finally, Bach seems to have wanted to enshrine the work, together with the improvements made to it in the interim, within a new score. Accordingly, after 1731 (perhaps for 12 April 1735) an autograph fair copy came into being which contained a new version: not only did it include the newly composed recitatives, but the arias and the closing chorus* underwent numerous improvements. These changes are mostly unimportant in themselves, but taken together they yield a fundamentally revised version of the cantata. This version alone is of interest to present-day performers, and the alterations represent genuine improvements throughout.

Although, in the course of its history, this work became a festive church cantata of high quality, it is nonetheless unable to conceal its secular origin. Particularly striking is the absence of biblical text and chorale. For, unlike in Cantata 66, Bach retained the choral finale instead of replacing it with a chorale.The text makes no reference at all to the readings of the day. It brings to mind the Resurrection of Christ, stirs us to songs of thanksgiving, recalls Christ's Passion and descent into hell, mentions the comfort felt by the Church Militant and by each individual till the very end of his life due to Christ's Resurrection, and closes with a chorus of thanksgiving to Christ as victor. The frequent dialogue character of Bach's setting recalls the interaction of the allegorical characters 'Time' and 'Divine Providence' in the secular original. This applies to all three recitatives and especially to the closing chorus, whose duet passages—as in the opening chorus of Cantata 66—should no doubt be conceived in terms of solo singing.

Ich lebe, mein Herze, BWV 145

NBA I/10, pp. 113, 141 BC A60 Duration: *c.* 19 mins

Choral SATB bc (+ instrs) D c

Auf, mein Herz, des Herren Tag	**Rise up, my heart; the Lord's day**
Hat die Nacht der Furcht vertrieben:	**Has driven away the night of fear:**
Christus, der im Grabe lag,	**Christ, who lay in the grave,**
Ist im Tode nicht geblieben.	**Has not abided in death.**
Nunmehr bin ich recht getröst',	**Now I am truly comforted:**
Jesus hat die Welt erlöst.	**Jesus has redeemed the world.**

Coro SATB tr str + ob I,II bc D 3/4

'So du mit deinem Munde bekennest Jesum, daß er der Herr sei, und gläubest in deinem Herzen, daß ihn Gott von den Toten auferwecket hat, so wirst du selig.'	'If you acknowledge Jesus with your mouth, that He is the Lord, and believe in your heart that God has raised Him from the dead, then you shall be blessed.'

1. Aria Duetto ST vln I solo bc D 2/4

Jesus	*Jesus*
Ich lebe, mein Herze, zu deinem Ergötzen,	I live, my heart, to your delight;
Mein Leben erhebet dein Leben empor.	My Life raises your life on high.
Seele	*Soul*
Du lebest, mein Jesu, zu meinem Ergötzen,	You live, my Jesus, to my delight;
Dein Leben erhebet mein Leben empor.	Your Life raises my life on high.
beide	*both*
Die klagende Handschrift ist völlig zerrissen,	The plaintiff handwriting of ordinances is completely torn up;
Der Friede verschaffet ein ruhig Gewissen	Peace procures a calm conscience
Und öffnet den Sündern das himmlische Tor.	And opens to sinners the heavenly gate.

2. Recitativo T bc — b C

Nun fordre, Moses, wie du willt,	Now demand, Moses, as you will,
Das dräuende Gesetz zu üben,	That we practise the threatening Law:
Ich habe meine Quittung hier	I have my receipt here,
Mit Jesu Blut und Wunden unterschrieben.	Signed with Jesus's Blood and Wounds.
Dieselbe gilt;	This holds force;
Ich bin erlöst, ich bin befreit	I am redeemed, I am freed
Und lebe nun mit Gott in Fried und Einigkeit;	And live now with God in peace and unity;
Der Kläger wird an mir zuschanden,	The plaintiff is in me confounded,
Denn Gott ist auferstanden.	For God is arisen.
Mein Herz, das merke dir!	My heart, take note of that!

3. Aria B tr fl ob d'am I,II vln I,II bc — D 3/8

Merke, mein Herze, beständig nur dies,	Mark, my heart, constantly just this,
Wenn du alles sonst vergißt,	Though you forget all else,
Daß dein Heiland lebend ist!	That your Saviour is alive!
Lasse dieses deinem Gläuben	Let that continue to be in your Faith
Einen Grund und Feste bleiben,	Grounded and settled;
Auf solche besteht er gewiß.	On that it rests secure.
Merke, meine Herze, merke nur dies!	Mark, my heart, mark just this!

4. Recitativo S bc — A–f♯ C

Mein Jesus lebt!	My Jesus lives!
Das soll mir niemand nehmen,	That no one shall take from me,
Drum sterb ich sonder Grämen.	Therefore I shall die without grieving.
Ich bin gewiß	I am certain
Und habe das Vertrauen,	And have trust
Daß mich des Grabes Finsternis	That the grave's darkness
Zur Himmelsherrlichkeit erhebt.	Raises me to heavenly glory.
Mein Jesus lebt!	My Jesus lives!
Ich habe nun genug,	I now have enough;
Mein Herz und Sinn	My heart and mind
Will heute noch zum Himmel hin,	Would this very day go up to heaven
Selbst den Erlöser anzuschauen.	To see the Redeemer Himself.

5. Choral SATB bc (+ instrs) — f♯ 3/4

Drum wir auch billig fröhlich sein,	**Therefore we are justly cheerful,**
Singen das Halleluja fein,	**Sing Alleluia finely,**
Und loben dich, Herr Jesu Christ;	**And praise You, Lord Jesus Christ;**
Zu Trost du uns erstanden bist.	**For our comfort You are arisen.**
Halleluja!	**Alleluia!**

Since this work is transmitted only in a nineteenth-century manuscript copy plus derivatives, its origin cannot be reconstructed with certainty. The text of nos. 1–5 is drawn from Picander's cycle of 1728, and Bach probably set it a year or two later—perhaps for performance on 19 April 1729. In this form the work is, of course, very brief; and it is conceivable that—as in other cantatas of the same cycle, such as BWV 174 and 188—Bach prefaced it with a concerto movement as introductory sinfonia. However, the surviving sources reveal nothing of this kind. Instead, the work is prefaced by two movements whose rightful place in the cantata remains questionable: a plain chorale setting of the first verse of the hymn *Auf, mein Herz, des Herren Tag* by Caspar Neumann (*c.* 1700), for which Bach was no doubt responsible; and the chorus* 'So du mit deinem Munde bekennest Jesum' from Georg Philipp Telemann's cantata of that title (though in the present context it forms the second movement, its opening lines serve as the title in the surviving manuscript copy). It remains unclear whether the inclusion of Telemann's chorus goes back to Bach and what was the function of the chorale movement. In any event, it is evident that these additions were associated with a change of occasion: the text was originally written for Easter Tuesday, but in its expanded form the cantata is assigned, in its surviving manuscript copy, to Easter Sunday.

The chorus 'So du mit deinem Munde bekennest Jesum' (based on Romans 10.9), which in Telemann's cantata is preceded by an instrumental sinfonia on the same theme, displays a bipartite form characteristic of its composer. The first part is a duet for soprano and alto concertists,* accompanied by continuo; the second part ('so wirst du selig'), a four-part choral fugue* reinforced by oboes and strings, together with a partially independent trumpet part. Though the banal opening theme has an awkward effect in the neighbourhood of Bach's music, there is no doubt that Telemann knew how to make effective use of his ideas.

Picander's text, like that of Cantata 134, does not enter closely into the readings for Easter Tuesday. The opening consists of a soprano-alto duet with obbligato* solo violin, whose characteristic splitting-up of the text—

Jesus: Ich lebe, mein Herze, zu deinem Ergötzen
Soul: Du lebest, mein Jesu, zu meinem Ergötzen

—recalls Hunold's Cöthen congratulatory cantatas and thus arouses the suspicion that the movement might be a sacred parody* of one of Bach's Cöthen works, a conjecture that can neither be confirmed nor refuted. Nevertheless, all the characteristics of a secular-cantata duet are present here, notably the euphonious parallel writing for the voices and the clearly periodic phrase-structure, to which even the imitative* passages are readily subordinate.

The text of the following *secco* recitative, no. 2, points out that Jesus's sacrificial death has set its seal on our peace with God. It ends with an arioso* passage, 'My heart, take note of that!', which gives the cue* to the following aria. This bass aria, no. 3, requires the largest instrumental ensemble in the whole cantata: trumpet, flute, two oboes d'amore* (which, however, may easily be replaced by oboes), two violins (but, surprisingly, no violas), and continuo.

The movement is, again, very close in character to Bach's secular compositions and could be a parody. It is not only the dance-like style, the periodic phrase-structure of the themes, and the extended opening ritornello that point in this direction, but also the discrepancies within the text: the opening line, 'Merke, mein Herze, beständig nur dies', is reproduced in the da capo* as 'Merke, mein Herze, merke nur dies'. However, the work's transmission gives rise to so many questionable features that it remains unclear which peculiarities in this movement should be ascribed to its origin and which to the unreliability of the copyist. A recitative, no. 4, expresses the conviction that now even death is only the beginning of heavenly joy. And the cantata ends with a plain four-part setting of the fourteenth verse of the Easter hymn *Erschienen ist der herrlich Tag* by Nikolaus Herman (1560).

Der Friede sei mit dir, BWV 158

NBA I/10, p. 131 BC A61 Duration: *c.* 12 mins

1. Recitativo B bc	D–G c
Der Friede sei mit dir,	Peace be with you,
Du ängstliches Gewissen!	You uneasy conscience!
Dein Mittler stehet hier,	Your Mediator stands here,
Der hat dein Schuldenbuch	By whom your book of debts
Und des Gesetzes Fluch	And the Law's curse
Verglichen und zerrissen.	Have been settled and torn up.
Der Friede sei mit dir,	Peace be with you:
Der Fürste dieser Welt,	The prince of this world,
Der deiner Seele nachgestellt,	Who laid snares for your soul,
Ist durch des Lammes Blut bezwungen und gefällt.	Is through the Lamb's Blood overcome and laid low.
Mein Herz, was bist du so betrübt,	My heart, why are you so troubled
Da dich doch Gott durch Christum liebt?	When God loves you through Christ?
Er selber spricht zu mir:	He Himself says to me:
Der Friede sei mit dir!	Peace be with you!
2. Aria con Corale S + ob B vln solo bc	G c
Welt, ade, ich bin dein müde,	World, farewell, I am weary of you:
Salems Hütten stehn mir an,	Salem's refuge suits me;
Welt, ade! ich bin dein müde,	**World, farewell! I am weary of you:**
Ich will nach dem Himmel zu,	**I would go to heaven,**
Wo ich Gott in Ruh und Friede	Where in rest and peace,
Ewig selig schauen kann.	Ever blessed, I can see God.
Da wird sein der rechte Friede	**There will be true peace**
Und die ewig stolze Ruh.	**And eternal, glorious rest.**
Da bleib ich, da hab ich Vergnügen zu wohnen,	There I remain, there I delight to dwell;

Welt, bei dir ist Krieg und Streit,
Nichts denn lauter Eitelkeit;
Da prang ich gezieret mit himmlischen Kronen.
In dem Himmel allezeit
Friede, Freud und Seligkeit.

World, in you is war and fighting,
Nothing but pure vanity;
There I shine forth, adorned with a heavenly crown.
In Heaven there is at all times
Peace, joy and salvation.

3. RECITATIVO B bc — e C

Nun Herr, regiere meinen Sinn,
Damit ich auf der Welt,
So lang es dir mich hier zu lassen noch gefällt,
Ein Kind des Friedens bin,
Und laß mich zu dir aus meinen Leiden
Wie Simeon in Frieden scheiden!
Da bleib ich, da hab ich Vergnügen zu wohnen,
Da prang ich gezieret mit himmlischen Kronen.

Now Lord, rule my thoughts,
So that in the world,
As long as it pleases You to leave me here,
I may be a child of peace;
And let me come to You from my suffering,
Like Simeon departing in peace!
There I remain, there I delight to dwell,
There I shine forth, adorned with a heavenly crown.

4. CHORAL SATB bc (+ instrs) — e C

Hier ist das rechte Osterlamm,
Davon Gott hat geboten;
Das ist hoch an des Kreuzes Stamm
In heißer Lieb gebraten.
Des Blut zeichnet unsre Tür,
Das hält der Glaub dem Tode für;
Der Würger kann uns nicht rühren.
Alleluja!

Here is the true Easter Lamb,
As God has commanded;
High on the Cross's beam it has
Roasted in burning Love.
Its Blood marks our door,
Faith holds it up to Death;
The murderer cannot touch us.
Alleluia!

On account of its defective source transmission, this work leaves us with no fewer puzzles than the cantata just discussed. Neither its librettist nor its date of origin is known; and, unless we are altogether deceived, the version transmitted is a fragment made up of several originally independent parts, from which only very inadequate conclusions may be drawn as to the original character of the work. With Philipp Spitta[60] we must assume that the aria and the second recitative, nos. 2 and 3, are the oldest parts. Their text, which deals with the yearning for death and for heavenly life, is clearly not an Easter poem, but seems to have been intended for the Feast of the Purification (the title on the wrapper of the work, which is transmitted only in manuscript copies, names as its occasion both Easter Tuesday and the Purification), for the third movement expressly refers to Simeon, whose words 'Lord, now let your

[60] Spitta II, 785 f.; Eng. version II, 687 ff.

servant depart in peace' belong to the Gospel* for that occasion. When these two middle movements originated is uncertain. Spitta believed that they stem from Bach's Weimar period and wanted to ascribe the libretto to Salomo Franck, but no real confirmation of this may be found. If it were so, at the very least a radical revision of these movements must have been undertaken in Leipzig.

The scoring of the aria, no. 2, evidently has a pre-history that has not so far been clarified. This movement is the centre-piece of the cantata and a masterwork of Bach's art. A bass aria with obbligato* solo violin—handled in a truly virtuoso fashion—is combined with the first verse of the hymn *Welt, ade, ich bin dein müde* by Johann Georg Albinus (1649) to the melody by Johann Rosenmüller, which is stated by soprano and oboe in unison. It is odd, however, that the violin never goes down below d^1, so that the G-string remains unused; indeed, at one point an expected $c^1\sharp$ is evidently avoided. Was the obbligato instrument originally (or temporarily) transverse flute?* No less doubtful, it seems to me, is whether the chorale melody was from the outset assigned to soprano *and* oboe, especially since the oboe has no further role in the other movements. Perhaps the *cantus firmus** was originally just instrumental and only later furnished with a text and sung; such, at any rate, was Bach's procedure when revising several of his Weimar cantatas (BWV 80a and possibly 161). The third movement begins as a plain *secco*, but then changes into an arioso,* whose text—and, by allusion, its music too—refers back to the second movement, a phenomenon that we encounter in several Bach cantatas that originated around 1726: for example, in the Kreuzstab Cantata BWV 56.

It seems likely, then, that movements 2–3 are a torso, torn out of their original context, that nos. 1 and 4 were added subsequently to give the fragment a new outer frame, and that the whole work was now intended for performance on Easter Tuesday. This follows from the choice of concluding chorale—the fifth verse of Luther's hymn *Christ lag in Todes Banden* (1524)—as well as from the reference to the 'Lamb's Blood' in the first movement and from its closing words, 'He Himself says to me: Peace be with you', for although the Purification Gospel is also concerned with peace (see above), only in the Gospel for Easter Tuesday does Jesus Himself utter the words 'Peace be with you'. Though accompanied only by continuo, this opening movement is ingeniously shaped in musical terms around three arioso passages, each on the text 'Peace be with you': at the outset, in the course of the recitative, and—most extensively—at the close.

Despite all the open questions that remain concerning this cantata and its limited dimensions, it is nonetheless a work of high artistic rank that makes considerable demands upon its vocal and instrumental soloists. We should therefore be grateful that, at least in its present state, it has survived.

1.24 First Sunday after Easter (Quasimodogeniti)

Epistle: 1 John 5.4–10: Our faith is the victory that has overcome the world.
Gospel: John 20.19–31: Jesus appears to the disciples; doubting Thomas.

Halt im Gedächtnis Jesum Christ, BWV 67

NBA I/11.1, p. 3 BC A62 Duration: *c.* 17 mins

1. [Chorus] SATB cor da t fl ob d'am I,II str bc — A ¢

'Halt im Gedächtnis Jesum Christ, der auferstanden ist von den Toten.'	'Keep in remembrance Jesus Christ, who is arisen from the dead.'

2. Aria T fl + ob d'am str bc — E C

Mein Jesus ist erstanden!	My Jesus is arisen!
Allein, was schreckt mich noch?	But what still frightens me?
Mein Glaube kennt des Heilands Sieg,	My Faith knows the Saviour's victory,
Doch fühlt mein Herze Streit und Krieg,	Yet my heart feels war and fighting;
Mein Heil, erscheine doch!	My Salvation, appear then!

3. Recitativo A bc — c♯–F♯ C

Mein Jesu, heißest du des Todes Gift	My Jesus, are You called death's poison
Und eine Pestilenz der Hölle,	And a pestilence for Hell,
Ach, daß mich noch Gefahr und Schrecken trifft?	Alas, only to find that danger and fear still strike me?
Du legtest selbst auf unsre Zungen	You laid on our very tongues
Ein Loblied, welches wir gesungen:	A song of praise that we sang:

4. Choral SATB bc (+ instrs) — f♯ 3/4

Erschienen ist der herrlich Tag,	**The glorious day has appeared**
Dran sich niemand gnug freuen mag:	**When no one may rejoice enough:**
Christ, unser Herr, heut triumphiert,	**Christ, our Lord, today triumphs;**
All sein Feind er gefangen führt.	**All His enemies He leads captive.**
Alleluja!	**Alleluia!**

5. Recitativo A bc — c♯–A C

Doch scheinet fast,	Yet it seems almost
Daß mich der Feinde Rest,	That the remaining enemies,
Den ich zu groß und allzu schrecklich finde,	Whom I find too great and far too fearful,
Nicht ruhig bleiben läßt.	Do not let me stay calm.
Doch, wenn du mir den Sieg erworben hast,	Yet, if You have won the victory for me,
So streite selbst mit mir,	Then fight even with me,
Mit deinem Kinde:	With Your child:
Ja, ja, wir spüren schon im Glauben,	Yes, yes, we feel already in Faith
Daß du, o Friedefürst,	That You, O Prince of Peace,
Dein Wort und Werk an uns erfüllen wirst.	Will fulfil in us Your Word and Work.

6. Aria [+ Chorus] SATB fl ob d'am I,II str bc A C 3/4

Baß	*Bass*
'Friede sei mit euch!'	'Peace be with you!'
Sopran, Alt, Tenor	*Soprano, Alto, Tenor*
Wohl uns! Jesus hilft uns kämpfen	Blessed are we! Jesus helps us fight
Und die Wut der Feinde dämpfen,	And subdue the rage of the Enemy;
Hölle, Satan, weich!	Hell, Satan, yield!
Baß	*Bass*
'Friede sei mit euch!'	'Peace be with you!'
Sopran, Alt, Tenor	*Soprano, Alto, Tenor*
Jesus holet uns zum Frieden	Jesus summons us to peace
Und erquicket in uns Müden	And refreshes in us weary ones
Geist und Leib zugleich.	Spirit and body at once.
Baß	*Bass*
'Friede sei mit euch!'	'Peace be with you!'
Sopran, Alt, Tenor	*Soprano, Alto, Tenor*
O! Herr, hilf und laß gelingen,	O Lord! help us and let us succeed
Durch den Tod hindurchzudringen	In passing from death through
In dein Ehrenreich!	To Your glorious Kingdom!
Baß	*Bass*
'Friede sei mit euch!'	'Peace be with you!'

7. Choral SATB bc (+ instrs) A C

Du Friedefürst, Herr Jesu Christ,	**You Prince of Peace, Lord Jesus Christ,**
Wahr' Mensch und wahrer Gott,	**True Man and true God,**
Ein starker Nothelfer du bist	**A strong Helper in trouble are You,**
Im Leben und im Tod:	**In life and in death:**
Drum wir allein	**Therefore only**
Im Namen dein	**In Your Name**
Zu deinem Vater schreien.	**Do we cry to Your Father.**

Bach composed this cantata during his first year in Leipzig and performed it for the first time on 16 April 1724. In a biblical passage, 2 Timothy 2.8, the anonymous librettist brings to mind the Resurrection of Christ (no. 1). In the following aria, no. 2, however, he confesses that, despite all his faith, his heart has no peace. Thereafter, it becomes increasingly clear that the Christian assailed by doubts is symbolized by Doubting Thomas. Although Jesus is 'death's poison and a pestilence for hell' (a reference to Hosea 13.14), and although we have rejoiced in Christ's Resurrection in the words of the Easter hymn *Erschienen ist der herrlich Tag* (no. 4), the Enemy would harass us still further if Jesus did not fight for us without interruption (no. 5). The high point of the cantata is no. 6: as He once did to His disciples, so this very day Jesus appears to His Christian Church with a helping hand and with the words of greeting 'Peace be with you!' (John 20.19). These words, quoted four times, frame the three stanzas of a poem. Finally, in the hymn *Du Friedefürst, Herr Jesu Christ* (Jakob Ebert, 1601) the assembled congregation, represented by the choir, declare their faith in Christ as bringer of peace.

In its purposeful structure and its mounting contrast between doubt and confidence, leading up to the high point of the words 'Peace be with you!', this text is infused with exceptional dramatic power, which any composer would inevitably experience as a truly worthwhile incentive for musical setting. Out of it Bach fashioned one of his greatest and most original cantatas. The two main themes of the first movement form a striking portrayal of a) 'keeping in remembrance' and b) the Resurrection:

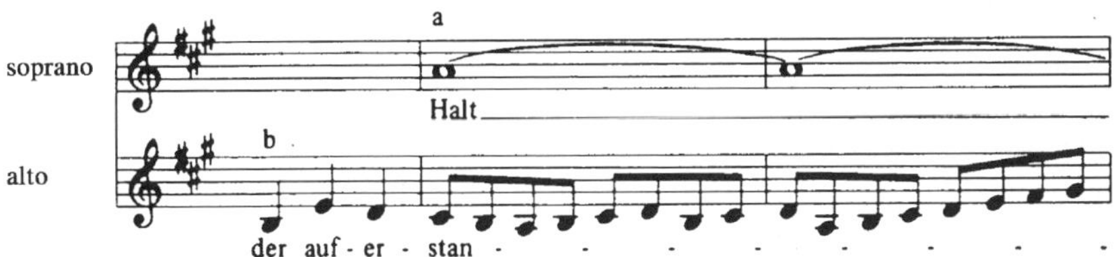

Perhaps it is no accident that theme a) recalls the chorale melody *O Lamm Gottes, unschuldig*: He who is arisen had been crucified for our sins, and it is this that deserves to be remembered. Formally, this opening movement is an elaborate and symmetrical structure. In its instrumental introduction for horn, flute, two oboes d'amore,* strings, and continuo, we already hear theme *a* on the horn, and later in the continuo. The chorus* itself is made up of two similar sections, each of which begins with block chords (theme *a* plus choral interjections on 'Halt'), continues with a permutation fugue* employing themes *a* and *b*, and closes with freely polyphonic* choral insertion* within a reprise of the opening sinfonia. In the following schema, italics denote instrumental writing:

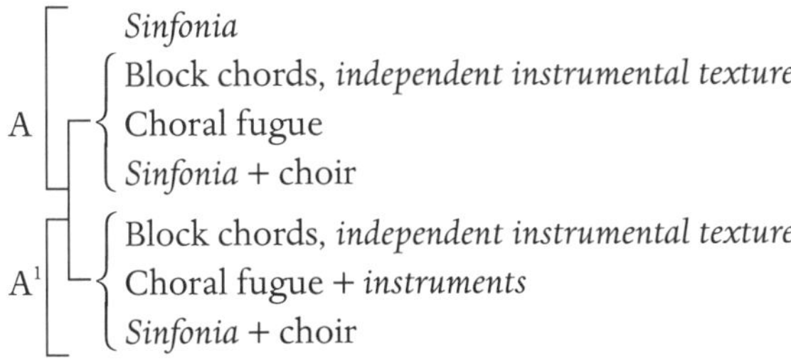

No less pictorial is the theme of the second movement, within which we recognize in turn the certainty of its assertion, the Resurrection, fear, and finally the framing of a question (in the lifting of the voice). This theme, first stated by the strings in the opening ritornello, is then taken up by the tenor in the principal section:

The next three movements form a unity: *secco* recitatives for the alto (nos. 3 and 5) surround a plain chorale setting (no. 4), the first verse of the Easter hymn by Nikolaus Herman (1560).

Though designated an aria by Bach, the sixth movement is in reality a complex structure: a chorus in strophic form, with each of its three stanzas framed by the bass solo 'Friede sei mit dir!' ('Peace be with you!'). It opens with a string sinfonia, whose violent motion depicts the attack of the Enemy. After this has subsided, we hear a bass solo of speech-like eloquence, with a dancing woodwind accompaniment of gently dotted rhythms. The words 'Friede sei mit dir!', sung three times, are followed by the first stanza of the poem sung by the other three voice parts (soprano, alto, and tenor) and incorporated in a reprise of the tumultuous string passage. The other two stanzas follow, alternating with the bass solo and with some slight modification of their thematic material. At the last bass solo, the strings join in the dance-like theme of the woodwind: the Enemy is vanquished and peace reigns. The overall form of the movement is thus as follows:

A *String passage*
  B Bass solo + *woodwind*
A^1 *String passage* + choir, stanza 1
  B^1 Bass solo + *woodwind*
A^2 *String passage* + choir, stanza 2
  B^2 Bass solo + *woodwind*
A^3 *String passage* + choir, stanza 3 + bass solo
  B^3 Bass solo + *woodwind* + *strings*

The contrasting content of A and B—mankind under attack as against Christ the bringer of peace—is underlined by musical means: motion/repose, choir/solo, high voices/low voice (the *vox Christi*), strings/woodwind, and square/triple time. Around 1738, Bach adapted this remarkable movement to form the Gloria of the Lutheran Missa in A, BWV 234. The cantata concludes with a plain four-part setting of the first verse of the hymn *Du Friedefürst, Herr Jesu Christ*.

Am Abend aber desselbigen Sabbats, BWV 42

NBA I/11.1, p. 63 BC A63 Duration: *c.* 33 mins

1. SINFONIA ob I,II bsn str bc — D C

2. RECITATIVO T bc bsn org — b C

'Am Abend aber desselbigen Sabbats, da die Jünger versammlet und die Türen verschlossen waren aus Furcht für den Jüden, kam Jesus und trat mitten ein.'

'But in the evening of the same Sabbath, when the disciples were assembled and the doors closed for fear of the Jews, Jesus came and stood in their midst.'

3. ARIA A ob I,II bsn str bc — G C $\frac{12}{8}$ C

Wo zwei und drei versammlet sind
In Jesu teurem Namen,
Da stellt sich Jesus mitten ein
Und spricht darzu das Amen.
Denn was aus Lieb und Not geschicht,
Das bricht des Höchsten Ordnung nicht.

Where two or three are gathered together
In Jesus's precious Name,
There Jesus appears in their midst
And says to them 'Amen'.
For what happens out of love and need
Breaks not the Highest's dispensation.

4. CHORAL DUETTO ST bsn + vc bc — b $\frac{3}{4}$

Verzage nicht, o Häuflein klein,
Obschon die Feinde willens sein,
Dich gänzlich zu verstören,
Und suchen deinen Untergang,
Davon dir wird recht angst und bang:
Es wird nicht lange währen.

Do not be faint-hearted, O little band,
Although your enemies are of the will
To upset you completely
And seek your downfall, of which
You are most distressed and perplexed:
It will not last long.

5. RECITATIVO B bc — G–a C

Man kann hiervon ein schön Exempel sehen
An dem, was zu Jerusalem geschehen;
Denn da die Jünger sich versammlet hatten
Im finstern Schatten,
Aus Furcht für denen Jüden,
So trat mein Heiland mitten ein
Zum Zeugnis, daß er seiner Kirchen Schutz will sein.
Drum laßt die Feinde wüten!

One can see a fine example
In what happened at Jerusalem;
For when the disciples had gathered together
In dark shadows
For fear of those Jews,
My Saviour entered in their midst
As a witness that He will be the defence of His Church.
Therefore let the enemies rage!

6. ARIA B vln I div bc — A ¢

Jesus ist ein Schild der Seinen,
Wenn sie die Verfolgung trifft.
Ihnen muß die Sonne scheinen
Mit der güldnen Überschrift:
Jesus ist ein Schild der Seinen,
Wenn sie die Verfolgung trifft.

Jesus is a shield of His own people
When persecution strikes them.
For them the sun must shine
With the gilt heading:
Jesus is a shield of His own people
When persecution strikes them.

7. CHORAL SATB bc (+ instrs) f♯ c

Verleih uns Frieden gnädiglich,	**Grant us peace graciously,**
Herr Gott, zu unsern Zeiten;	**Lord God, in our times;**
Es ist doch ja kein andrer nicht,	**There is indeed none other**
Der für uns könnte streiten,	**Who could fight for us**
Denn du, unsr Gott, alleine.	**Than You, our God, alone.**
Gib unserm Fürsten und allr Obrigkeit	**Grant our princes and all in authority**
Fried und gut Regiment,	**Peace and good government,**
Daß wir unter ihnen	**That we under them**
Ein geruhig und stilles Leben führen mögen	**May lead a peaceable and quiet life**
In aller Gottseligkeit und Ehrbarkeit.	**In all godliness and honesty.**
Amen.	**Amen.**

Bach composed this cantata for performance on 8 April 1725. The structure of the text and its dry, learned character suggest that it was written by the same librettist as the text of Cantata 6, which had been performed only six days before. It opens with a literal quotation of the first verse of the Sunday Gospel,* which alone provides the theme of the free verse that follows. The third movement quotes Jesus's promise that 'Where two or three are gathered together in my Name, there am I in the midst of them' (Matthew 18.20). And the following chorale—the first verse of the hymn by Jacob Fabricius (1632)—gives the fearful Christian further encouragement to trust in God. The recitative, no. 5, gives a 'fine example' as evidence of Jesus's promise: as He then appeared to His disciples, so He will always remain a shield to His own people when persecution strikes them (no. 6). In the concluding chorale, the congregation prays for God's peace in the words of Luther's hymn *Verleih uns Frieden gnädiglich* (see above, p. 239).

The introductory sinfonia perhaps originally opened a lost secular vocal work from the Cöthen period, the serenata* *Der Himmel dacht auf Anhalts Ruhm und Glück*, BWV 66a, for the birthday of Prince Leopold of Anhalt-Cöthen on 10 December 1718.[61] *Ripieno* strings are set against a *concertino* of two oboes and bassoon. At first, the two groups each state their own theme (though the two themes are related), but later on they often play independently, exchange themes, or else join together. A startling effect occurs at the beginning of the middle section: the first oboe and bassoon (later, second oboe and bassoon) enter with a new, highly melodious theme—Bach himself labelled it 'cantabile'—while the strings provide a figurative accompaniment. The passage remains a brief episode, however: long before the da capo* of the principal section, both groups have resumed their initial themes.

[61] See Rifkin, 'Verlorene Quellen, verlorene Werke', 65–7.

The biblical passage (no. 2) that prefaces the madrigalian* text (no. 3) is set as *secco* recitative over throbbing continuo semiquavers, which are no doubt designed to depict the disciples' fear of 'the Jews'. In stark contrast, the third movement unfolds a supraterrestrial calm. Over held string chords and pulsating quavers on the bassoon, the two oboes play an 'adagio' duet in broad melodic arches, interrupted by triplet scrolls. This aria seems to be a parody,* drawn from the same lost secular cantata as the sinfonia, BWV 66a;[62] there it would have formed the sixth movement, whose text opens with the lines:

> Beglücktes Land von süßer Ruh und Stille,
> In deiner Brust wallt nur ein Freudenmeer.
>
> Fortunate land of sweet calm and quiet,
> In your breast flows but a sea of joys.

The extended bipartite principal section of the aria is followed by a middle section accompanied only by continuo (plus bassoon)—marked 'un poco andante' and in a different metre—after which there is a literal da capo of the principal section.

The fourth movement, despite its hymn text, is set as a duet largely free of references to the chorale melody, accompanied only by continuo but with figurative embellishment in bassoon and cello. With a little care, fragments of the associated melody, *Kommt her zu mir, spricht Gottes Sohn*, may certainly be discovered, but they are overlaid by the vocal themes, which change from line to line. The bass recitative, no. 5—a *secco* with arioso* conclusion ('Therefore let the enemies rage!')—leads to the second aria, which is scored for divided first violins and continuo (which often comes to the fore motivically). Like the sixth movement of Cantata 67, though with different means, this aria derives its themes from the conceptual antithesis between the unrest of the world and peace with Jesus. The lively semiquaver motion of the instruments, with their tumult motives,* is contrasted with the calm vocal theme of the bass, which changes to a more consistent semiquaver figuration only on the word 'Verfolgung' ('persecution'). As in Cantata 6, performed six days before, the figure

appears to be a musical representation of the Cross. A plain chorale setting concludes the work.

[62] See Rifkin, 'Verlorene Quellen, verlorene Werke', 65–7.

1.25 Second Sunday after Easter (Misericordias Domini)

EPISTLE: 1 Peter 2.21–5: Christ as our model; 'be converted to the shepherd and bishop of your souls'.

GOSPEL: John 10.12–16: 'I am the Good Shepherd'.

Du Hirte Israel, höre, BWV 104

NBA I/11.1, p. 115 BC A65 Duration: *c.* 23 mins

1. [CHORUS] SATB ob I,II taille str bc — G $\frac{3}{4}$

'Du Hirte Israel, höre, der du Joseph	'You Shepherd of Israel, give ear, You
hütest wie der Schafe, erscheine,	who lead Joseph like sheep; shine forth,
der du sitzest über Cherubim.'	You who are enthroned upon the Cherubim.'

2. RECITATIVO T bc — e–b C

Der höchste Hirte sorgt vor mich,	The highest Shepherd cares for me:
Was nützen meine Sorgen?	What use are my cares?
Es wird ja alle Morgen	Indeed, every morning
Des Hirtens Güte neu.	The Shepherd's loving kindnesses are new.
Mein Herz, so fasse dich,	My heart, then compose yourself:
Gott ist getreu.	God is faithful.

3. ARIA T ob d'am I,II bc — b C

Verbirgt mein Hirte sich zu lange,	If my Shepherd is hidden too long,
Macht mir die Wüste allzu bange,	If the wilderness makes me too anxious,
Mein schwacher Schritt eilt dennoch fort.	Still my weak step hurries on.
Mein Mund schreit nach dir,	My mouth cries to You,
Und du, mein Hirte, würkst in mir	And You, my Shepherd, work in me
Ein gläubig Abba durch dein Wort.	A believing 'Abba' through Your Word.

4. RECITATIVO B bc — D C

Ja dieses Wort ist meiner Seelen Speise,	Yes, this Word is my soul's nourishment,
Ein Labsal meiner Brust,	A refreshment to my breast,
Die Weide, die ich meine Lust,	The pasture that I call my delight,
Des Himmels Vorschmack, ja mein alles heiße.	A foretaste of heaven, indeed my all.
Ach! sammle nur, o guter Hirte,	Ah! gather up, O Good Shepherd,
Uns Arme und Verirrte,	Us poor and straying ones;
Ach laß den Weg nur bald geendet sein	Ah, let the path be ended soon
Und führe uns in deinen Schafstall ein!	And lead us into Your sheepfold!

5. ARIA B str + ob I bc — D $\frac{12}{8}$

Beglückte Herde, Jesu Schafe,	Happy flock, Jesus's sheep,
Die Welt ist euch ein Himmelreich.	The world is to you a heavenly kingdom.

Hier schmeckt ihr Jesu Güte schon	Here you already taste Jesus's goodness
Und hoffet noch des Glaubens Lohn	And still hope for faith's reward
Nach einem sanften Todesschlafe.	After a sweet sleep of death.

6. CHORAL SATB bc (+ instrs) A c

Der Herr ist mein getreuer Hirt,	**The Lord is my faithful Shepherd**
Dem ich mich ganz vertraue,	**To whom I fully entrust myself;**
Zur Weid er mich, sein Schäflein, führt,	**To a meadow He leads me, His little sheep,**
Auf schöner grünen Aue,	**On fair green pasture,**
Zum frischen Wasser leit' er mich,	**To cool water He leads me**
Mein Seel zu laben kräftiglich	**To refresh my soul thoroughly**
Durchs selig Wort der Gnaden.	**Through the blessed Word of Grace.**

Whether in painting, poetry, or music, baroque art took special delight in the representation of rural life, and particularly the pastoral setting, which seemed calm and peaceful, far from the despotism and intrigues of absolutist princes, and a valuable aid to the realization of ideal feelings, such as love, faith, innocence, friendship, and so on. It therefore comes as no surprise that the Christian faith of the age was enkindled with special ardour by the image of Jesus as the Good Shepherd. The music of the shepherds—the pastorale—could be directly understood as a symbol of the community watched over by Christ. And a phrase like 'Lead us into Your sheepfold!' (no. 4) could be taken into this world-view without reflection, nor with that touch of the comic which might be felt in it by the modern listener.

The text of this cantata begins with a passage from the Psalms (80.1), from which the following recitative, no. 2—with the aid of other biblical texts, such as Lamentations 3.23 ('His compassion . . . is new every morning') and 1 Corinthians 10.13 ('God is faithful')—derives the insight that God, 'the highest Shepherd', faithfully cares for me. At times, however, the 'wilderness makes me too anxious', and therefore I cry 'a believing Abba' to God (no. 3; cf. Romans 8.15 and Galatians 4.6). That I may call to God is a foretaste of heaven, we are told in the following recitative (no. 4), and therefore I pray that my earthly path might soon come to an end and that the Good Shepherd will lead me into His sheepfold. The following aria (no. 5) elaborates on the same ideas: if Jesus is my Shepherd, so that I experience His goodness here already, how much happier shall I be later, 'after a sweet sleep of death'. The work concludes with the first verse of Psalm 23 in the paraphrase by Cornelius Becker of 1598.

Bach composed this cantata during his first year in Leipzig for performance on 23 April 1724. The opening movement skilfully unites the pastoral atmosphere with the prayer for comfort of the psalm text. The extended introductory sinfonia is composed in the style of a pastorale: triplets and broad pedal-points provide the rural colouring. In the vocal section, the choir enters with imploring, beseeching cries of 'höre!' ('give ear!') and 'erscheine!' ('shine forth!'). From these block-chordal cries, a choral fugue,* on the words 'der du Joseph hütest wie der Schafe' ('You who lead Joseph like sheep'), twice detaches itself, so that altogether the movement aquires the form: sinfonia–chorus–fugue–chorus–fugue–chorus. 'Chorus'* here for the most part indicates homophonic* choral passages brought about by choral insertion.* The parts for two oboes and taille* (tenor oboe), which contribute so much to the pastoral colouring of the movement, were nonetheless evidently added as an afterthought.[63]

A short *secco* recitative (no. 2), with arioso* conclusion to the words 'Gott ist getreu' ('God is faithful', a biblical quotation), leads to the first aria, no. 3, with its two obbligato* oboes d'amore.* Here, the words 'allzu bange' ('too anxious') are strongly emphasized, both harmonically and thematically, as is the word 'schreit' ('cries') in the middle section, either by octave leaps or by rising scale motion. A plainly declaimed *secco*, no. 4, is followed by another pastorale, no. 5, an aria of overwhelming beauty. The triplet motion (here notated in 12/8) and the pedal-points establish a clear connection with the opening movement. In substance, however, the two movements stand in the relation of entreaty to fulfilment, of Old Testament to New: now that Christ has appeared, we can be certain that God will not forsake His flock. Particularly remarkable is the emphasis on the passage 'after a sweet sleep of death' in the middle section, with the aid of the Neapolitan-sixth chord.* This passage is brought into relation with the rest of the movement by the continuity of the instrumental themes, a circumstance which might be construed thus: even in death's state of withdrawal, Jesus remains my Good Shepherd. The work concludes with a plain chorale setting to the melody *Allein Gott in der Höh sei Ehr*.

Ich bin ein guter Hirt, BWV 85

NBA I/11.1, p. 159 BC A66 Duration: *c.* 20 mins

1. [Bass Solo] B ob str bc c C

'Ich bin ein guter Hirt, ein guter	'I am a good shepherd; a good shepherd
Hirt läßt sein Leben für die Schafe.'	gives up his life for his sheep.'

2. Aria A vc picc bc g C

Jesus ist ein guter Hirt;	Jesus is a good shepherd;
Denn er hat bereits sein Leben	For He has already given His Life
Für die Schafe hingegeben,	For His sheep,
Die ihm niemand rauben wird.	Which no one shall steal from Him.
Jesus ist ein guter Hirt.	Jesus is a good shepherd.

[63] See R. Emans, 'Überlegungen zur Genese der Kantate *Du Hirte Israel, höre* (BWV 104)', in K. Beißwenger *et al.*, eds, *Acht kleine Präludien und Studien über Bach* (Wiesbaden, 1992), 44–50. Emans also raises the possibility that the opening chorus and the bass aria, no. 5, might have been parodied from the lost graduation cantata *Siehe, der Hüter Israel*, BWV Anh. I 15.

3. CHORAL S ob I,II bc — B♭ $\frac{3}{4}$

Der Herr ist mein getreuer Hirt,
Dem ich mich ganz vertraue,
Zur Weid er mich, sein Schäflein, führt
Auf schöner grünen Aue,
Zum frischen Wasser leit er mich,
Mein Seel zu laben kräftiglich
Durchs selig Wort der Gnaden.

The Lord is my faithful Shepherd
To whom I fully entrust myself;
To a meadow He leads me, His little sheep,
On fair green pasture,
To cool water He leads me
To refresh my soul thoroughly
Through the blessed Word of Grace.

4. RECITATIVO T str bc — E♭–A♭ C

Wenn die Mietlinge schlafen,
Da wachet dieser Hirt bei seinen Schafen,
So daß ein jedes in gewünschter Ruh
Die Trüft und Weide kann genießen,
In welcher Lebensströme fließen.
Denn sucht der Höllenwolf gleich einzudringen,
Die Schafe zu verschlingen,
So hält ihm dieser Hirt doch seinen Rachen zu.

While hirelings sleep,
This Shepherd watches over His sheep,
So that each in welcome repose
Can partake of the meadow and pasture
In which shall flow living streams.
For though hell's wolf should seek to break in
And devour the sheep,
This Shepherd keeps its mouth closed.

5. ARIA T vlns + vla bc — E♭ $\frac{9}{8}$

Seht, was die Liebe tut.
  Mein Jesus hält in guter Hut
  Die Seinen feste eingeschlossen
  Und hat am Kreuzesstamm vergossen
  Für sie sein teures Blut.

See what Love works.
  My Jesus keeps in good hands
  His own, shut up tightly,
  And on the Cross's beam has shed
  For them His precious Blood.

6. CHORAL SATB bc (+ instrs) — c C

Ist Gott mein Schutz und treuer Hirt,
Kein Unglück mich berühren wird:
Weicht, alle meine Feinde,
Die ihr mir stiftet Angst und Pein,
Es wird zu eurem Schaden sein,
Ich habe Gott zum Freunde.

If God is my defence and faithful Shepherd,
No misfortune shall touch me:
Depart, all my enemies,
Who cause me fear and pain:
It will be to your harm—
I have God as my friend.

The text of this cantata follows the Sunday Gospel* still more closely than that of the cantata just discussed, and the opening movement is drawn from it word for word (John 10.11). The second movement points out that these words—the words of Jesus Himself—come true in His Passion. After the first verse of the German version of Psalm 23 by Cornelius Becker (1598) in no. 3, the anonymous librettist again reverts to the Gospel reading in no. 4: 'The hireling, however . . . sees the wolf coming and leaves the sheep' (John 10.12). Departing from the reading, the librettist says that while hirelings sleep the Good Shepherd watches over us and keeps the mouth of 'hell's wolf' closed. For through the sacrifice of His death on the Cross, Jesus has revealed His love for us and proved Himself to be the true Shepherd (no. 5). The work concludes with the fourth verse of the hymn *Ist Gott mein Schild und Helfersmann* by Ernst Christoph Homburg (1658).

Bach set this text for performance on 15 April 1725. The scoring, for two oboes, strings, and continuo, plus four voices, keeps within the usual bounds. The four voices come together only in the concluding chorale. The opening movement is one of those settings of Jesus's words for bass voice whose form lies somewhere betweeen aria and arioso.* Framed and articulated by a six-bar instrumental ritornello, this dictum is heard in two corresponding vocal sections, A and A[1]. The vocal head-motive has already been quoted four times by the continuo during the ritornello before it is taken up by the bass as a 'motto':*

As a counterpoint* to this motive* we hear descending semiquaver runs, which, however, do not consolidate thematically to the same extent. The oboe repeatedly comes to the fore in concertante* style, so that at times the movement resembles the middle movement of an oboe concerto.

The second movement is characterized by richly figurative motion in its obbligato* part for violoncello piccolo.* Unusually, the alto delivers the complete text three times over, giving a full statement of it in each of the three vocal sections, A, A[1], and A[2]. The following chorale verse, no. 3, is sung by the soprano in a lightly ornamented form to the melody *Allein Gott in der Höh sei Ehr*, surrounded by instrumental ritornellos for the two oboes on a theme derived from the first line of the chorale. The sole recitative, no. 4, in substance a synoptic sermon, is enhanced in significance by virtue of its string accompaniment. On several occasions, where the instruments bridge the caesuras of the voice part, certain phrases of text are interpreted by string motives.

The fifth movement, with its moderate compound-triple time, is a true pastorale and the only movement that underlines musically the pastoral theme of the text (unless we regard the use of oboes in nos. 1 and 3 as an emphasis on the pastoral element). The instrumental texture radiates a powerful warmth and intimacy, which is achieved by frequent parallel thirds and sixths between the obbligato part (for unison violins and violas) and the continuo, by the deep pitch of the string part, and by the simple harmony, which on several occasions touches upon the subdominant. The highly text-engendered singing of the tenor stands out against this instrumental background. Not only does the tenor enter with its threefold cry of 'Seht!' ('See!') at a relatively high pitch, but thereafter it often lies above the instruments, becoming the highest part. Furthermore, in contrast to the more meditative instrumental texture, it is the bearer of a highly eloquent and animated melodic line. In the middle section, at the words 'Und hat am Kreuzesstamm vergossen' ('And on the Cross's beam has shed'), it even reaches top b^1 flat. The movement is one of the most impressive arias in all Bach's cantatas. A plain chorale setting, using the little-known melody of the hymn *Ist Gott mein Schild und Helfersmann*, concludes the cantata.

Der Herr ist mein getreuer Hirt, BWV 112

NBA I/11.1, p. 181 BC A67 Duration: *c.* 15 mins

Versus 1 [Chorale] SATB hn I,II str + ob d'am I,II bc G ¢

Der Herr ist mein getreuer Hirt,	**The Lord is my faithful Shepherd,**
Hält mich in seiner Hute,	**Who keeps me in His care;**
Darin mir gar nichts mangeln wird	**Therein I shall not lack**
Irgend an einem Gute,	**Any good thing;**
Er weidet mich ohn Unterlaß,	**He feeds me without ceasing**
Darauf wächst das wohlschmeckend Gras	**From where the tasty grass grows**
Seines heilsamen Wortes.	**Of His sound Word.**

Versus 2 Aria A ob d'am I solo bc e $\frac{6}{8}$

Zum reinen Wasser er mich weist,	**He leads me to pure water,**
Das mich erquicken tue.	**Which refreshes me.**
Das ist sein fronheiliger Geist,	**It is His Holy Spirit**
Der macht mich wohlgemute.	**That makes me cheerful.**
Er führet mich auf rechter Straß	**He leads me on the true path**
Seiner Geboten ohn Ablaß	**Of His Commandments incessantly**
Von wegen seines Namens willen.	**For His Name's sake.**

Versus 3 Recitativo B str bc C–G c

Und ob ich wandert im finstern Tal,	**And though I wander in a dark valley,**
Fürcht ich kein Ungelücke	**I fear no misfortune**
In Verfolgung, Leiden, Trübsal	**In persecution, suffering, tribulation**
Und dieser Welte Tücke:	**And this world's malice:**
Denn du bist bei mir stetiglich,	**For You are with me constantly,**
Dein Stab und Stecken trösten mich,	**Your staff and rod comfort me;**
Auf dein Wort ich mich lasse.	**I devote myself to Your Word.**

Versus 4 [Duetto] ST str bc D 2

Du bereitest für mir einen Tisch	**You prepare for me a table**
Für mein' Feinden allenthalben,	**Before my enemies everywhere,**
Machst mein Herze unverzagt und frisch,	**You make my heart intrepid and fresh;**
Mein Haupt tust du mir salben	**My head You anoint**
Mit deinem Geist, der Freuden Öl,	**With Your Spirit, the oil of joy,**
Und schenkest voll ein meiner Seel	**And fill my soul full**
Deiner geistlichen Freuden.	**Of Your spiritual joys.**

VERSUS 5 [CHORALE] SATB bc (+ instrs; hn II independent) G c

Gutes und die Barmherzigkeit	**Goodness and compassion**
Folgen mir nach im Leben,	**Follow me in life,**
Und ich werd bleiben allezeit	**And I will remain always**
Im Haus des Herren eben,	**In the House of the Lord,**
Auf Erd in christlicher Gemein	**On earth in the Christian community,**
Und nach dem Tod da werd ich sein	**And after death I shall be there**
Bei Christo, meinem Herren.	**With Christ, my Lord.**

Bach composed this work for 8 April 1731, though it is possible that he made use of an earlier composition for the opening chorus.* His text is the paraphrase of Psalm 23 by Wolfgang Meuslin (?), published in Augsburg in 1530 (not to be confused with the hymn by Cornelius Becker with the same opening line and verse structure, which Bach had used in Cantatas 104 and 85), in unaltered wording. The work is thus a chorale cantata,* retrospectively assigned to the chorale-cantata cycle of 1724–5, which in its original form lasted only until the Feast of the Annunciation. The textual link with the Sunday Gospel* is clear. It was, of course, impossible to insert specific references to it, since the text was an established psalm paraphrase, set in its original form. But this was in any case unnecessary, for the reinterpretation of Psalm 23 to refer to Jesus is a commonplace of general Christian thought.

The introductory chorale-chorus follows the form favoured by Bach for such movements. Embedded in a concertante* orchestral texture for two horns, two oboes d'amore,* strings, and continuo, the chorale melody is stated by the soprano one line at a time, supported by an imitative* texture in the three lower voice parts. The orchestral music takes the opening of the first chorale line as its head-motive (the melody is *Allein Gott in der Höh sei Ehr*), and the continuo also enters (in bar 2) with this line-opening. But the remaining thematic material of the instruments is largely independent, pitting the two horns against the strings (reinforced by oboes) in *concertato* style. More obviously influenced by the chorale theme is the imitative voice texture that serves as substructure to the *cantus firmus*.* Its imitative themes, evidently derived throughout from the beginning of the first line, nonetheless often peter out into free reminiscences that can easily be linked with most of the other chorale lines.

The second movement, an aria with obbligato* oboe d'amore, is based on a new minor-mode theme, which may nonetheless (if value is attached to such thematic links) be construed as an inversion of the opening of the chorale. Formally, the aria unites the two *Stollen** of the hymn verse to form the first vocal section and fashions a second section—related to the first—out of the *Abgesang*.* Its bipartite design, A A^1, thus follows neither the textual scheme nor the da capo* form then so popular in aria composition.

Formally the most original movement within the cantata, however, is no. 3, which is made up of two heterogeneous sections, the first being a thematically-imprinted arioso* with continuo accompaniment. The theme, no doubt inspired by the image of 'wandering', is taken up now and again by either voice or continuo, perhaps as an illustration of the text, which tells us that the wanderer is not left alone in the 'dark valley'. The second part of the movement is a recitative with string accompaniment, whose free declamation returns at the close to the metrically fixed form of arioso, though here the writing remains unthematic throughout.

The fourth movement gives free rein to our jubilation over God's care. The theme was perhaps suggested by the words 'You make my heart intrepid and fresh'. With its accessible melodic style and its clear, periodic phrase structure, the movement gives the impression of a joyous dance, of a *bourrée*. Even the canonic entry of the voice parts, as of the violins previously, is not at all 'learned' in effect because the sequence of entries is subordinate to the movement's four-bar phrase-structure. The theme—a slightly simplified vocal form of the ritornello melody—is more clearly derived from the chorale melody than that of the previous aria:

The form of the aria (*Bar** with reprise) follows that of the chorale. Due to the threefold statement of the A section (the third time, transposed to the subdominant in order to conclude in the tonic), the form is particularly easy to grasp: A A B A. A plain chorale setting, in which the second horn has an independent part due to its limited range of notes, concludes the cantata.

1.26 Third Sunday after Easter (Jubilate)

EPISTLE: 1 Peter 2.11–20: Be subject to every human ordinance.
GOSPEL: John 16.16–23: Jesus's valedictory address: 'your sorrow shall be turned into joy'.

Weinen, Klagen, Sorgen, Zagen, BWV 12

NBA I/11.2, p. 3 BC A68 Duration: *c.* 28 mins

1. SINFONIA ob vln I,II vla I,II bc f/g[64] **c**

[64] The first specified key refers to *Chorton*,* the presumed pitch of the Weimar performance, the second to the *Kammerton* of the Leipzig performance.

2. [Chorus] SATB vln I,II vla I,II bsn bc — f/g $\frac{3}{2}$

Weinen, Klagen,
Sorgen, Zagen,
Angst und Not
Sind der Christen Tränenbrot,
Die das Zeichen Jesu tragen.

Weeping, lamenting,
Grieving, trembling,
Anguish and distress
Are the Christian's bread of tears:
They who bear the mark of Jesus.

3. Recitativo A vln I,II vla I,II bc — c/d C

'Wir müssen durch viel Trübsal in das Reich Gottes eingehen.'

'Through much tribulation must we enter into the Kingdom of God.'

4. Aria A ob bc — c/d C

Kreuz und Kronen sind verbunden,
Kampf und Kleinod sind vereint.
Christen haben alle Stunden
Ihre Qual und ihren Feind,
Doch ihr Trost sind Christi Wunden.

Cross and crowns are bound together,
Contest and prize medal are united.
Christians have at every hour
Their torment and their enemy,
Yet Christ's wounds are their comfort.

5. Aria B vln I,II bc — E♭/F C

Ich folge Christo nach,
Von ihm will ich nicht lassen
Im Wohl und Ungemach,
Im Leben und Erblassen.
Ich küsse Christi Schmach,
Ich will sein Kreuz umfassen.
Ich folge Christo nach,
Von ihm will ich nicht lassen.

I follow after Christ,
I will not let go of Him
In prosperity or affliction,
In living or dying.
I kiss the reproach of Christ,
I will embrace His Cross.
I follow after Christ,
I will not let go of Him.

6. Aria T tr bc — g/a $\frac{3}{4}$

Sei getreu, alle Pein
Wird doch nur ein Kleines sein.
Nach dem Regen
Blüht der Segen,
Alles Wetter geht vorbei.
Sei getreu, sei getreu!

Be faithful: all pain
Will be but a little while.
After rain
Blessing blooms:
All bad weather passes.
Be faithful, be faithful!

7. Choral SATB vln I (?) bc (+ other instrs) — B♭/C C

Was Gott tut, das ist wohlgetan,
Dabei will ich verbleiben,
Es mag mich auf die rauhe Bahn
Not, Tod und Elend treiben,
So wird Gott mich
Ganz väterlich
In seinen Armen halten:
Drüm laß ich ihn nur walten.

Whatever God deals is dealt bountifully:
I will abide by that;
Though I may be driven on a rough road
By need, death, and misery,
God will hold me
Quite fatherly
In His arms:
Therefore I let only Him rule.

This cantata is probably the second work in which, after his appointment as *Concertmeister* at Weimar, Bach fulfilled his obligation to provide new cantatas monthly for the court chapel service. It was first heard on 22 April 1714 and revived in Leipzig ten years later, on 30 April 1724. The text is probably by Salomo Franck, who follows the ideas of the Sunday Gospel* in detail, developing his basic plan from the contrast set forth there between joy and sorrow. The opening movement recalls Christ's words 'You shall weep and lament' (John 16.20); and the following biblical quotation, 'Through much tribulation must we enter into the Kingdom of God' (Acts 14.22), reminds us that Christ's words relating to the sorrow that shall be turned into joy, once addressed to the disciples, also apply to every Christian today. In the three arias that follow, the suffering Christian is first brought face to face with the Passion of Christ as a form of comfort (no. 4);[65] and this leads to the resolution to take suffering upon oneself in imitation of Christ (no. 5) and, finally, to the consolation (again, in accordance with a passage from the Gospel) that it 'will be but a little while' before all sorrow passes away (no. 6). The admonition to 'be faithful' is a reference to Revelation 2.10, already alluded to in no. 4 (see note 65). The cantata concludes with the final verse of the hymn *Was Gott tut, das ist wohlgetan* by Samuel Rodigast (1675).

In Bach's setting, the text is prefaced with an instrumental movement, as in Cantata 182, performed four weeks before. This Sinfonia, marked 'adagio assai', has the character of a concerto slow movement. The intensity of movement of the individual parts is graded from top to bottom: the solo oboe plays in broadly swung demisemiquaver garlands, free of all thematic ties; an accompanying ostinato* semiquaver motive* is assigned to the two violins; the two viola parts—a characteristic of Bach's earlier cantatas—fill out the texture in quavers; and the continuo marks the half bars.

The principal section of the chorus* 'Weinen, Klagen', no. 2, which is designed in pure da capo* form, consists of a chaconne over a chromatic* instrumental bass, played twelve times: a lapidary adaptation of those seventeenth-century *lamento** themes that descend through the interval of a fourth:

The upper parts have a moving song of lamentation, with bold harmony, in a loosely fugal, imitative texture which coalesces into chordal writing in the

[65] The words in this aria linked by alliteration likewise refer to biblical ideas: 'Kreuz und Kronen' ('cross and crowns') to Rev. 2.10 ('Be faithful unto death, then I will give you the crown of life'), and 'Kampf und Kleinod' ('contest and prize') to 1 Cor. 9.24 ('those who run in a race, they all run but only one receives the prize').

middle statements of the theme, nos. 7–8. The last statement, no. 12, is purely instrumental. In the last decade of his life, Bach adapted the music of this main section to form the Crucifixus of the B minor Mass. The middle section—'un poco allegro'—is motet-like, lacking independent instrumental parts (presumably the instruments should not be *tacet*,* as most modern editions prescribe, but rather double the voice parts). The texture is part polyphonic* and part chordal, with imitation* in the outer parts.

The biblical-text movement that follows, no. 3, is set as an accompanied recitative (with strings). The entry into the Kingdom of God, to which the text refers, is represented doubly: as a C major scale from c^2 to c^3 in the long-held harmony notes of the first violin; and as a C minor scale from d^1 to c^2 in the alto part, to the words 'in das Reich Gottes ein(gehen)'.

The three arias, which succeed one another without intervening recitative, differ in form, scoring, and character. The first, a slow piece of immense gravity in pure da capo form, is characterized by the expressive, wide-ranging figures of the obbligato* oboe. In the second aria, no. 5, it is the text—which is concerned with the imitation of Christ—that provides the stimulus for its compositional style: the canonically treated head-motive is first stated by the two obbligato violins and continuo, then taken up by the bass in the first vocal section, and closes the movement suggestively—with a brief hint of da capo—in the form of a rising vocal scale of a ninth (*A*♭ to *b*♭): the imitation of Christ also signifies entry into the Kingdom of God (cf. the rising scale in no. 3).

The third aria, no. 6, is introduced by a brief ostinato-like ritornello in the continuo. Immediately after the tenor's entry, however, the trumpet starts to quote a lightly varied form of the chorale melody *Jesu, meine Freude*. If Bach had in mind a particular verse, over and above the general content of the hymn, it might have been the last, 'Weicht, ihr Trauergeister' ('Retreat, you spectres of sorrow'), which is most closely linked both to the substance of Franck's poem ('all pain will be but a little while') and to the Gospel* reading, with its reference to the sorrow that shall be turned into joy. The form of the aria is accommodated to the *Bar** form (A A B) of the hymn.

In the concluding chorale, the usual plain four-part vocal texture is joined by an instrumental obbligato part—probably to be played by first violin (cf. Cantatas 172, 31, and 185)—which lends the setting a special lustre. The chorale melody has a particular significance in the context of this cantata: as now becomes clear, it was anticipated by the imitative theme of no. 5, which is itself thematically related to no. 3 (see above). Thus the thematic contrast between chromatic descent (no. 2) and diatonic ascent (nos. 3, 5, and 7, and also by allusion in the continuo steps of no. 1) pervades the entire cantata.

Ihr werdet weinen und heulen, BWV 103

NBA I/11.2, p. 27 BC A69 Duration: *c.* 18 mins

1. Chorus SATB fl picc ob d'am I,II str bc — b 3/4 C 3/4

Chor	*Choir*
'Ihr werdet weinen und heulen, aber die Welt wird sich freuen.'	'You shall weep and lament, but the world shall rejoice.'
Baß	*Bass*
'Ihr aber werdet traurig sein.'	'Now you shall be sorrowful.'
Chor	*Choir*
'Doch eure Traurigkeit soll in Freude verkehret werden.'	'Yet your sorrow shall be turned into joy.'

2. Recitativo T bc — f♯–c♯ C

Wer sollte nicht in Klagen untergehn,	Who would not sink into lamentation
Wenn uns der Liebste wird entrissen?	When our Beloved is snatched away from us?
Der Seelen Heil, die Zuflucht kranker Herzen	Ours souls' Salvation, refuge of sick hearts,
Acht nicht auf unsre Schmerzen.	Pays no heed to our sorrows.

3. Aria A fl picc bc — f♯ 6/8

Kein Arzt ist außer dir zu finden,	No physician is to be found other than You,
Ich suche durch ganz Gilead;	Though I search through all Gilead;
Wer heilt die Wunden meiner Sünden?	Who will heal the wounds of my sins?
Weil man hier keinen Balsam hat.	For they have no balsam here.
Verbirgst du dich, so muß ich sterben.	If You hide Yourself, I must die.
Erbarme dich, ach! höre doch!	Have mercy, ah! do listen!
Du suchest ja nicht mein Verderben,	You do not indeed seek my ruin:
Wohlan, so hofft mein Herze noch.	Well then, my heart still trusts in You.

4. Recitativo A bc — b–D C

Du wirst mich nach der Angst auch wiederum erquicken;	You will revive me again after my trouble;
So will ich mich zu deiner Ankunft schicken,	Then I will make myself fit for Your coming;
Ich traue dem Verheißungswort,	I trust Your promised Word
Daß meine Traurigkeit	That my sorrow
In Freude soll verkehret werden.	Shall be turned into joy.

5. Aria T tr str + ob d'am I + II bc — D C

Erholet euch, betrübte Sinnen,	Recover, distressed minds:
Ihr tut euch selber allzu Weh.	You cause yourselves too much woe.
Laßt von dem traurigen Beginnen,	Leave off your sorrowful beginnings;
Eh ich in Tränen untergeh,	Before I collapse into tears,
Mein Jesus läßt sich wieder sehen,	My Jesus lets Himself be seen again:
O Freude, der nichts gleichen kann!	O joy, to which nothing can compare!
Wie wohl ist mir dadurch geschehen!	What good has thereby come upon me!

Nimm, nimm mein Herz zum Opfer an.	Accept, accept my heart as a sacrifice.

6. Choral SATB bc (+ instrs) b c

Ich hab dich einen Augenblick,	**I have for a moment,**
O liebes Kind, verlassen;	**O dear child, forsaken you;**
Sieh aber, sieh, mit großem Glück	**But see, see, with great good fortune**
Und Trost ohn alle Maßen	**And comfort beyond all measure,**
Will ich dir schon die Freudenkron	**I will set the crown of joy**
Aufsetzen und verehren;	**Upon you and honour you;**
Dein kurzes Leid soll sich in Freud	**Your brief suffering shall be turned into joy**
Und ewig Wohl verkehren.	**And everlasting welfare.**

This cantata, composed for 22 April 1725, inaugurates Bach's series of nine compositions on texts by the poet Mariane von Ziegler. He did not adopt the text unaltered, however: especially in the fourth movement, he substantially abridged it without regard for the rhyme scheme. It opens with a passage from the Sunday Gospel* (John 16.20), whose weeping–joy antithesis is of decisive significance for the substance of the following movements. The first recitative-aria pair bewails the loss of Jesus, without whom the soul cannot be saved (the mention of Gilead, celebrated for its wealth of balsam, refers to Jeremiah 8.22). The second pair, however (nos. 4–5), recalls Jesus's 'promised Word', calls for confidence, and offers the heart as a sacrifice of thanksgiving. The concluding chorale—the ninth verse of the hymn *Barmherzger Vater, höchster Gott* by Paul Gerhardt (1653)—is a judicious choice: the preceding aria had announced that 'My Jesus lets Himself be seen again', and now Jesus Himself speaks words of comfort to His people.

In the instrumental ensemble of the opening chorus* and the first aria, Bach requires a 'flauto piccolo'*—not the modern small transverse flute* but a soprano recorder in *d*²—from which he demands concertante* figuration and a considerable range. For a later performance, on 15 April 1731, the part was rewritten for solo violin or transverse flute: at that time Bach evidently had no suitable player (or instrument) for the original part at his disposal.

In form, the opening movement is very elaborately constructed. After the introductory concertante instrumental sinfonia, the voices enter with a fugal exposition* on a completely new theme, which uses chromatic* and augmented intervallic steps to interpret the words 'You shall weep and lament'. We then hear—as choral insertion* within the first part of the instrumental sinfonia—the text 'but the world shall rejoice'. The same sequence is now repeated on a larger scale: the second fugue* (like the first, constructed as a permutation fugue) gives the impression of double fugue through combination with the text 'aber die Welt wird sich freuen' ('but the world shall rejoice') to a theme derived from the sinfonia; and the choral insertion passage now brings with it a complete reprise of the introductory sinfonia. The chorus then suddenly breaks off to make way for an eight-bar, fully scored bass recitative, marked 'adagio', to the words 'Now you shall be sorrowful'. The choir now enters again, and the remainder of the text is sung to a literal, but transposed, reprise of the second fugue plus the choral insertion passage. Altogether, then, the following form arises (italics denote instrumental passages):

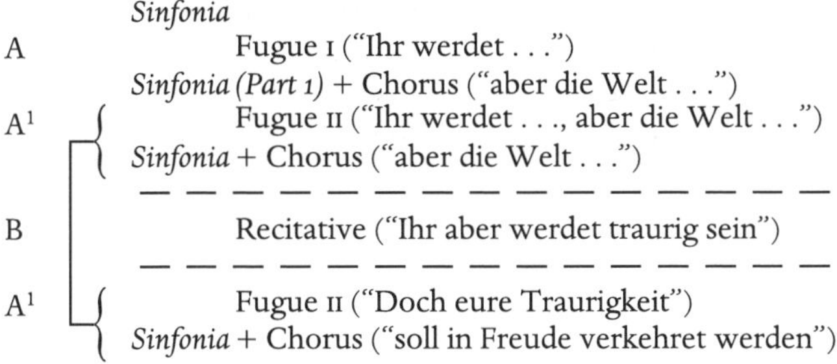

This form represents a fascinating attempt to unite the old principle of the motet*—a sequence of separate, text-engendered passages—with the large form of the more modern concertante* movement.

The two arias, like the recitatives that precede them, are attuned to the sorrow–joy contrast prescribed in the text. Whereas the first recitative, no. 2, ends with arioso* chromaticism on the word 'Schmerzen' ('sorrows'), the second, no. 4, brings the breakthrough to hope, with its extended coloratura* on 'Freude' ('joy'). The first aria, no. 3, with its elaborate flauto piccolo part and its yearning mood, stamped by a very individual mode of chromaticism, contrasts with the joyful, almost dance-like theme of the second aria, no. 5. Here, trumpet and strings together form a concertante texture, and the triadic motives,* only temporarily disturbed by dissonances, give expression to our joy over Jesus's promise. A plain chorale setting, to the melody *Was mein Gott will, das gscheh allzeit*, concludes the work.

Wir müssen durch viel Trübsal, BWV 146

NBA I/11.2, p. 67 BC A70 Duration: *c.* 40 mins

1. [SINFONIA] ob I,II taille str bc obbl org — d C
2. [CHORUS] SATB str bc obbl org — g 3/4

'Wir müssen durch viel Trübsal in das Reich Gottes eingehen.'	'We must through much tribulation enter into the Kingdom of God.'

3. ARIA A obbl org? (vln?) bc — B♭ C

Ich will nach dem Himmel zu,	I would go to heaven;
Schnödes Sodom, ich und du	Vile Sodom, you and I
Sind nunmehr geschieden.	Are now separated.

Meines Bleibens ist nicht hier,	My continuing city is not here,
Denn ich lebe doch bei dir	For I will indeed live with you
Nimmermehr in Frieden.	Never again in idleness.
4. [Recitative] S str bc	g–d C
Ach! wer doch schon im Himmel wär!	Ah! would that I were already in heaven!
Wie drängt mich nicht die böse Welt!	How the wicked world oppresses me!
Mit Weinen steh ich auf,	With weeping I get up,
Mit Weinen leg ich mich zu Bette,	With weeping I lay myself in bed;
Wie trüglich wird mir nachgestellt!	How treacherously I am ensnared!
Herr! merke, schaue drauf,	Lord! take note, look at it:
Sie hassen mich, und ohne Schuld,	They hate me, and without cause,
Als wenn die Welt die Macht,	As if the world had the might
Mich gar zu töten hätte;	Even to kill me;
Und leb ich denn mit Seufzen und Geduld	And though I live with sighs and forbearance,
Verlassen und veracht',	Forsaken and despised,
So hat sie noch an meinem Leide	Yet in my suffering it takes
Die größte Freude.	The greatest delight.
Mein Gott, das fällt mir schwer.	My God, that is hard for me!
Ach! wenn ich doch,	Ah! if only,
Mein Jesu, heute noch	My Jesus, this very day
Bei dir im Himmel wär!	I were with You in heaven!
5. Aria S fl ob d'am I,II bc	d C
Ich säe meine Zähren	I sow my tears
Mit bangem Herzen aus.	With an anxious heart.
Jedoch mein Herzeleid	Yet my heart's suffering
Wird mir die Herrlichkeit	Shall reap glory for me
Am Tage der seligen Ernte gebären.	On the day of the blessed harvest.
6. Recitativo T bc	a C
Ich bin bereit,	I am ready
Mein Kreuz geduldig zu ertragen.	To carry my cross patiently.
Ich weiß, daß alle meine Plagen	I know that all my torments
Nicht wert der Herrlichkeit,	Are not worthy to be compared with the glory
Die Gott an den erwählten Scharen	That God will reveal to His chosen hosts
Und auch an mir wird offenbaren.	And also to me.
Itzt wein ich, da das Weltgetümmel	Now I weep, as the world's hurly-burly
Bei meinem Jammer fröhlich scheint:	Seems joyful at my affliction;
Bald kommt die Zeit,	Soon the time will come
Da sich mein Herz erfreut,	When my heart shall rejoice and when one day
Und da die Welt einst ohne Tröster weint.	The world shall weep without a comforter.
Wer mit dem Feinde ringt und schlägt,	He who wrestles and fights with the enemy,

Dem wird die Krone beigelegt;	For him the crown of righteousness is laid up;
Denn Gott trägt keinen nicht mit Händen in den Himmel.	For God bears everyone with angels' hands into heaven.
7. Duetto TB ob I,II str bc	F $\frac{3}{8}$
Wie will ich mich freuen, wie will ich mich laben,	How I will rejoice, how I will refresh myself,
Wenn alle vergängliche Trübsal vorbei!	When all passing tribulation is gone!
Da glänz ich wie Sterne und leuchte wie Sonne,	Then I shall glitter like stars and shine like the sun,
Da störet die himmlische selige Wonne	Then heavenly, blessed delight shall be disturbed
Kein Trauren, Heulen und Geschrei.	By no sadness, howling, or crying.
8. Choral SATB bc (+ instrs)	F c
[**Denn wer selig dahin fähret,**	[**For the blessed one who goes there,**
Da kein Tod mehr klopfet an,	**Where death no longer knocks,**
Dem ist alles wohl gewähret,	**To him all is indeed granted**
Was er ihm nur wünschen kann.	**That he could ever wish.**
Er ist in der festen Stadt,	**He is in the secure City**
Da Gott seine Wohnung hat;	**Where God has His dwelling;**
Er ist in das Schloß geführet,	**He is led into the mansion**
Das kein Unglück nie berühret.]	**That no misfortune ever touches.**]

As in the other two cantatas for this Sunday, the sorrow–joy antithesis of the Gospel* for the day forms the basis of the text. A biblical passage from Acts 14.22—the same text that Franck had used in Cantata 12—prefaces the libretto as a motto.* In the three movements that follow (nos. 3–5), the anonymous librettist bewails the sufferings that the Christian, harassed by the world, has to endure in mortal life. The last three movements (nos. 6–8), on the other hand, are oriented towards joyful hope for a future life in the Kingdom of God.

However, the general validity assigned to the words once spoken to the disciples about the sorrow that shall be turned into joy involves a shift of emphasis which is carried out with greater intensity than in the other two cantatas: the impending Easter and Pentecost joy of the disciples now becomes the joy of the present-day Christian over his or her union with God, and thus turns into a longing for death. This pervades the entire cantata. The aria 'Ich säe meine Zähren', no. 5, paraphrases Psalm 126.5: 'Those who sow in tears shall reap in joy'; and the recitative no. 6 alludes to Romans 8.18: 'For I reckon that the sufferings of the present time are not worthy to be compared with the glory that shall be revealed in us'. The concluding chorale is transmitted without text: Wustmann recommends the ninth verse of the hymn *Lasset ab von euren Tränen* by Gregorius Richter (1658), and Petzoldt the first verse of *Freu dich sehr, o meine Seele* (Freiberg, 1620).[66]

Bach's cantata is transmitted not in the original sources but only in manuscript copies of later date, which has given scholars the opportunity to cast doubts on its authenticity—incorrectly, in our view. Not only would it be hard to find another composer capable of writing such music, but the reuse in nos. 1 and 2 of the first two movements of an earlier instrumental concerto (and of the third movement of the same concerto in Cantata 188) has a striking parallel in Cantatas 169 and 49, whose authenticity is beyond doubt. The date of the cantata under consideration is not known, but it was unquestionably composed after Bach's move to Leipzig in 1723. Since we know the cantatas for the Third Sunday after Easter in 1724 and 1725 (BWV 12 and 103), the earliest possible date is 12 May 1726; and, in fact, several factors (which we cannot go into here) point to this date, though the next two years are also possible. However, since Cantata 188, which contains the third movement of the concerto mentioned above, probably originated in 1728 or a little later, we might place the use of the previous two movements—and thus the origin of Cantata 146—no later than 1728.

The work whose first and second movements were reused in this cantata was originally a violin concerto (a reconstruction is published in NBA VII/7). Only its later version survives, however—as the Harpsichord Concerto in D minor, BWV 1052. Doubts have been cast on the authenticity of this concerto, too—surely incorrectly, though it is scarcely possible to reconstruct its pre-history. In the cantata, it becomes an organ concerto (with the top part played on octave lower at four-foot pitch for reasons of keyboard compass), in which the original string tutti is enriched by woodwind. The first movement of the concerto now becomes a powerful, almost oversized introductory sinfonia, and its second movement provides the instrumental music of the following chorus.* Here again, the solo part is assigned to the organ, and the choral texture is worked into the existing composition (which, on this occasion, lacks added woodwind). The result is satisfying only if one takes into account the small number of singers at Bach's disposal: performance by one of the massed choirs customary today overwhelms not only the graceful filigree of the organ part but even the string tutti.

The alto aria with obbligato* organ,[67] no. 3, turns away from the world and

[66] See M. Petzoldt, 'Schlußchoräle ohne Textmarken in der Überlieferung von Kantaten J. S. Bachs', *Musik und Kirche* 59 (1989), 235–40. The hymn verse recommended by Neumann in BT, 'Ach, ich habe schon erblicket', has one syllable too many or too few in lines 5, 6, and 7 and therefore cannot be the verse intended. Yet even in the other possible texts at least one alteration (the splitting of the last note) is unavoidable.

[67] Another MS calls for violin, but only in a later hand. Evidently Bach left the stave unspecified in his score.

towards heaven in mystic zeal; and the following recitative, no. 4, breaks out into agitated lamentation over the persecution of the 'wicked world', with held string chords accompanying the voice's declamation. The musical high point of the cantata, however, is doubtless the soprano aria 'Ich säe meine Zähren', no. 5. The agitated figurations of an obbligato flute, plus two oboes d'amore,* surround and accompany a vocal part in two sections, of which the first depicts the 'sowing with tears' with the greatest eloquence, while the second—with little alteration to the thematic material but with jubilant sounds—celebrates the day of the blessed harvest. It is hard to imagine who other than Bach could have accomplished such a work of art.

A *secco* recitative, no. 6, leads to a duet of joyous excitement, no. 7, which might possibly have been parodied from a lost secular composition. Except for insignificant passages of imitation,* the tenor and bass move in rich parallel thirds and sixths. The instruments surround the main section with a full-textured, dance-like ritornello, but are silent in the middle section, which is accompanied only by continuo. The plain concluding chorale is based on the melody *Werde munter, mein Gemüte*.

1.27 Fourth Sunday after Easter (Cantate)

Epistle: James 1.17–21: Every good gift comes from the Father of Light.
Gospel: John 16.5–15: Jesus's valedictory address: 'If I did not go away, the Comforter would not come to you'.

Leb ich oder leb ich nicht, BWV Anh. I 191

This text by Salomo Franck was possibly set to music by Bach in Weimar for 19 May 1715. The music is lost.[68]

Wo gehest du hin, BWV 166

NBA I/12, p. 3 BC A71 Duration: *c.* 17 mins

1. [Bass Solo] B ob str bc — B♭ $\frac{3}{8}$

'Wo gehest du hin?'	'Where are you going?'		

2. Aria T ob vln solo bc — g C

Ich will an den Himmel denken	I will think of heaven
Und der Welt mein Herz nicht schenken.	And not give the world my heart.
Denn ich gehe oder stehe,	For whether I go or stay,
So liegt mir die Frag im Sinn:	The question is in my mind:
Mensch, ach Mensch, wo gehst du hin?	Man, ah man, where are you going?

[68] See Dürr St 2, 67, and 244 f.

3. Choral S unis str bc — c **C**

Ich bitte dich, Herr Jesu Christ,	**I pray You, Lord Jesus Christ,**
Halt mich bei den Gedanken	**Hold me to these thoughts**
Und laß mich ja zu keiner Frist	**And indeed let me at no time**
Von dieser Meinung wanken,	**Waver from this intention,**
Sondern dabei verharren fest,	**But rather hold firmly to it**
Bis daß die Seel aus ihrem Nest	**Until my soul comes out of its nest**
Wird in den Himmel kommen.	**Into heaven.**

4. Recitativo B bc — g–d **C**

Gleichwie die Regenwasser bald verfließen	Just as the rainwater soon flows away
Und manche Farben leicht verschießen,	And many colours easily fade,
So geht es auch der Freude in der Welt,	So it is with joy in the world,
Auf welche mancher Mensch so viele Stücken hält;	Which many people hold in such high regard;
Denn ob man gleich zuweilen sieht,	For though one sometimes sees
Daß sein gewünschtes Glücke blüht,	That his desired fortune blooms,
So kann doch wohl in besten Tagen	Yet in the best days
Ganz unvermut' die letzte Stunde schlagen.	Quite unexpectedly the last hour can strike.

5. Aria A str + ob bc — B♭ 3/4

Man nehme sich in acht,	May one take care
Wenn das Gelücke lacht.	When good fortune laughs.
Denn es kann leicht auf Erden	For on earth it can easily
Vor abends anders werden,	Turn out differently before evening
Als man am Morgen nicht gedacht.	From how one thought in the morning.

6. Choral SATB bc (+ instrs) — g **C**

Wer weiß, wie nahe mir mein Ende!	**Who knows how near is my end!**
Hin geht die Zeit, her kommt der Tod;	**There goes time, here comes death;**
Ach wie geschwinde und behende	**Ah, how quickly and swiftly**
Kann kommen meine Todesnot.	**My death agony can come!**
Mein Gott, ich bitt durch Christi Blut:	**My God, I pray by Christ's Blood:**
Machs nur mit meinem Ende gut!	**Just make my end be good!**

This cantata originated during Bach's first year in Leipzig and was first performed on 7 May 1724. The anonymous librettist refers to the Sunday Gospel,* which opens with the words 'But now I go to Him who sent me, and none of you asks me, "Where are you going?" '. The librettist takes up this question, attaching personal significance to it. Thus whereas the opening movement could be understood simply as a biblical quotation, in the following aria we hear, 'Man . . . where are you going?' Here, the question 'Where?' is no longer put to

Jesus but rather to each individual Christian. The other movements are also associated with these ideas. A chorale—the third verse of the hymn *Herr Jesu Christ, ich weiß gar wohl* by Bartholomäus Ringwaldt (1582)—prays for true faith; the following recitative-aria pair warns against the joys of the world; and the concluding chorale—the first verse of the hymn *Wer weiß, wie nahe mir mein Ende* by Ämilie Juliane of Schwarzburg-Rudolstadt (1686)—prays to God for His support at the end of life's earthly path.

Bach's composition underlines the ideas of the librettist through his style of setting in the opening movement. The words 'Where are you going?' are assigned to the bass voice, which from of old served as the *vox Christi*, so that the movement is heard not just as a quotation from the Sunday Gospel, but as Jesus's questioning of his people and of each individual. Formally, the movement belongs to a group that lies somewhere between aria and arioso;* and, no doubt for good reason, Bach gave it no classificatory designation.

The second movement, whose complete scoring for oboe, solo violin, and continuo was first reconstructed in the *Neue Bach-Ausgabe* (I/12, 1960) is of exceptional beauty. In the middle section, Bach strikingly depicts 'going' and 'staying' by means of rising scale figures and long-held notes respectively. In the following chorale, no. 3, the hymn melody, sung in unadorned long notes by the soprano, is surrounded by a vigorous unison of violins and violas. The whole movement thereby acquires a somewhat severe quality in accordance with the character of the text.

By contrast, the following recitative and aria, nos. 4–5, especially the latter, strike an essentially more cheerful note, regardless of the fact that they are supposed to warn *against* the joy of the world. The aria, whose dance character is unmistakable, doubtless portrays in its shaking figures the laughter of good fortune, which is also to be heard in the long coloraturas* and trills of the voice. With the typical indifference of the baroque musician, Bach here takes advantage of all possibilities for pictorial representation of the 'affects',* even though they are contradicted or dismissed by the text. A broad contrast is thereby achieved between the opening movements and the second half of the work: their opposing affects correspond with the textual opposition between heaven and earth. After this dance-like aria, the solemnity of the concluding chorale, with its prayer 'Just make my end be good', is all the more striking.

Es ist euch gut, daß ich hingehe, BWV 108

NBA I/12, p. 19 BC A72 Duration: *c.* 20 mins

1. [Bass Solo] B ob d'am I str bc A C

'Es ist euch gut, daß ich hingehe; denn so ich nicht hingehe, kömmt der Tröster nicht zu euch. So ich aber gehe, will ich ihn zu euch senden.'	'It is good for you that I go away; for if I do not go away, the Comforter will not come to you. But if I go, I will send Him to you.'

2. ARIA T vln I solo bc f♯ 3/4

Mich kann kein Zweifel stören,	No doubt can disturb me
Auf dein Wort, Herr, zu hören.	From heeding Your Word, Lord.
Ich glaube, gehst du fort,	I believe that if You depart
So kann ich mich getrösten,	I can be confident
Daß ich zu den Erlösten	That along with the ransomed I will
Komm an gewünschten Port.	Come to the desired haven.

3. RECITATIVO T bc b–A c

Dein Geist wird mich also regieren,	Your Spirit will so lead me
Daß ich auf rechter Bahne geh;	That I walk on the upright path;
Durch deinen Hingang kommt er ja zu mir,	Through Your departure He comes to me indeed;
Ich frage sorgensvoll: Ach, ist er nicht schon hier?	I ask anxiously: ah, is He not already here?

4. CHORUS SATB bc (+ instrs) D ¢

'Wenn aber jener, der Geist der Wahrheit, kommen wird, der wird euch in alle Wahrheit leiten. Denn er wird nicht von ihm selber reden, sondern was er hören wird, das wird er reden; und was zukünftig ist, wird er verkündigen.'	'But when He, the Spirit of Truth, comes, He will guide you into all truth. For He shall not speak of Himself, but whatever He hears, He shall say; and He will foretell what is to come.'

5. ARIA A str bc b 6/8

Was mein Herz von dir begehrt,	What my heart desires of You,
Ach! das wird mir wohl gewährt.	Ah! that will indeed be fulfilled.
Überschütte mich mit Segen,	Shower me with blessing,
Führe mich auf deinen Wegen,	Lead me on Your paths,
Daß ich in der Ewigkeit	That in eternity
Schaue deine Herrlichkeit!	I may see Your glory!

6. CHORAL SATB bc (+ instrs) b c

Dein Geist, den Gott vom Himmel gibt,	**Your Spirit, whom God grants from heaven**
Der leitet alles, was ihn liebt,	**Leads all those who love Him**
Auf wohl gebähntem Wege.	**On well-laid paths.**
Er setzt und richtet unsren Fuß,	**He places and guides our foot,**
Daß er nicht anders treten muß,	**So that it has to tread**
Als wo man findt den Segen.	**Only where one finds blessing.**

The text of this cantata, composed for 29 April 1725, was supplied by Christiane Mariane von Ziegler. As in the cantata for the previous week, however (BWV 103), Bach shortened the recitative text without regard for rhyme. The opening of the work, like that of the cantata for the same Sunday in the previous year, BWV 166, consists of a quotation from the Gospel* reading, John 16.7. But whereas the librettist of Cantata 166 extracted the biblical words from their context and reinterpreted them to refer to the present-day Christian, the poet here places the emphasis on Jesus's promise to send the Holy Spirit and on the certainty of salvation that derives from it. This certainty prevails in the second and third movements. In the fourth, Jesus Himself returns with a statement of the Word as handed down in the Gospel reading (John 16.13). The following aria turns our attention to the future and prays for guidance on the right path till death. Finally, the tenth verse of the hymn *Gott Vater, sende deinen Geist* by Paul Gerhardt (1653) expresses confidence in God's right guidance in the name of the assembled congregation.

As in the cantata of the previous year, Bach's setting begins with a bass solo which in form lies somewhere between aria and arioso,* and—as often in solo movements on biblical words—lacks designation. The oboe d'amore* is assigned an obbligato* part which contains extensive melodic arches of exceptional beauty. The string accompaniment, though mostly chordal and homophonic,* is motivically imprinted. The following aria, no. 2, with its energetic, wide-ranging figures on solo violin over an ostinato* continuo motive,* expresses the affect* of confidence. Particuarly striking for its musical characterization of the text is the second half, whose first words 'I believe that if You depart . . .' are interpreted by a held note on 'believe' and a rising scale on 'depart'.

A short *secco* recitative leads to the second of the two biblical-text movements, nó. 4, this time set as a chorus.* This movement represents one of many attempts made during Bach's Leipzig period to unite the text-related serial form of the motet* with the high baroque ideal of closed (arch) form. The extensive text is divided into three sections, each of which is set as a choral fugue.* The subject of the third fugue, however, is derived from that of the first by assimilating it to the new text, so that overall a free da capo* form arises:

A 'Wenn aber jener, der Geist der Wahrheit, kommen wird . . .'
B 'Denn er wird nicht von ihm selber reden . . .'
A^1 'Und was zukünftig ist, wird er verkündigen.'

The first fugue begins in unorthodox fashion with two subject entries (bass and tenor) in *comes** form: at the opening, one really expects a threefold *d* rather than *e*; and in fact, Bach seems to have wavered for some time before deciding upon the reading generally reproduced in modern edtions.

The alto aria, no. 5, is scored for full string ensemble. The first violin is again, nonetheless, assigned a leading role, so that a certain virtuoso element is present throughout the whole cantata. A plain chorale, to the melody *Kommt her zu mir, spricht Gottes Sohn*, concludes the work.

1.28 Fifth Sunday after Easter (Rogate; Rogation Sunday)

Epistle: James 1.22–7: 'Be doers of the Word and not hearers only'.
Gospel: John 16.23–30: Jesus's valedictory address: 'If you ask something of the Father in my Name, He will grant it to you'.

Wahrlich, wahrlich, ich sage euch, BWV 86

NBA I/12, p. 47 BC A73 Duration: *c.* 18 mins

1. [Bass Solo] B str + ob d'am I,II bc — E ¢

'Wahrlich, wahrlich, ich sage euch, so ihr den Vater etwas bitten werdet in meinem Namen, so wird ers euch geben.'

'Truly, truly I say to you, if you ask something of the Father in my Name, He will grant it to you.'

2. Aria A vln solo bc — A $\frac{3}{4}$

Ich will doch wohl Rosen brechen,
Wenn mich gleich die Dornen stechen.
Denn ich bin der Zuversicht,
Daß mein Bitten und mein Flehen
Gott gewiß zu Herzen gehen,
Weil es mir sein Wort verspricht.

I would indeed gather roses,
Even though the thorns should prick me.
For I have confidence
That my prayer and supplication
Certainly go to God's heart,
For His Word promises it to me.

3. Choral S ob d'am I,II bc — f♯ $\frac{6}{8}$

Und was der ewig gütig Gott
In seinem Wort versprochen hat,
Geschworn bei seinem Namen,
Das hält und gibt er gewiß fürwahr.
Der helf uns zu der Engel Schar
Durch Jesum Christum, amen!

And what the eternally good God
Has promised in His Word,
Sworn by His Name,
In truth He certainly keeps and grants.
May He help us to join the angel host,
Through Jesus Christ, Amen!

4. Recitativo T bc — b–E c

Gott macht es nicht gleichwie die Welt,
Die viel verspricht und wenig hält;
Denn was er zusagt, muß geschehen,
Daß man daran kann seine Lust und Freude sehen.

God does not behave like the world,
Which makes many promises and keeps few;
For what He promises must come to pass,
So that therein one can see His delight and joy.

5. Aria T str bc — E c

Gott hilft gewiß;
Wird gleich die Hülfe aufgeschoben,
Wird sie doch drum nicht aufgehoben.
Denn Gottes Wort bezeiget dies:
Gott hilft gewiß!

God's help is secure;
Though His help be delayed,
It is not on that account nullified.
For God's Word testifies to this:
God's help is secure!

6. Choral SATB bc (+ instrs) — E c

Die Hoffnung wart' der rechten Zeit,

Hope awaits the right time

Was Gottes Wort zusaget;	**For what God's Word promises;**
Wenn das geschehen soll zur Freud,	**When, to our joy, that shall happen**
Setzt Gott kein gwisse Tage.	**God sets no certain day.**
Er weiß wohl, wenns am besten ist,	**He well knows when it is best,**
Und braucht an uns kein arge List;	**And uses no wicked cunning on us;**
Des solln wir ihm vertrauen.	**Therefore we should trust Him.**

The anonymous librettist of this cantata takes the opening of the Gospel* reading (no. 1) as an opportunity for exploring, albeit circumspectly, the question of how these words of Jesus are compatible with our experience of life. Even though thorns should prick me now, says the poet, I may still trust in God's promise (no. 2), for God keeps His promises (nos. 3–4), even if His help is delayed (no. 5); He alone knows the right time for His help (no. 6).

Bach composed this cantata during his first year in Leipzig for performance on 14 May 1724. The first movement—one of those typical arioso*-style bass solos in which we are addressed by the *vox Christi*—is nonetheless exceptional in its compositional make-up. All parts, not only the bass but also the strings (which are probably to be reinforced with oboes), are decidedly vocal in conception. In fact, if the instruments adhered to the range of the human voice, it would be easy to sing the entire movement as a four-part motet with continuo accompaniment. The instrumental introduction states the distinctive motives* to which the text is later sung by the bass. Here is the uppermost part of the texture, with the first subject in *comes** form:

The motives marked with the sign ⌐ are adopted literally by the voice, with the last one in modified form, as indicated by square brackets in the text. The movement is structured as a free fugue.* The instrumental prelude is followed by three similar vocal sections, A A^1 A^2, within each of which the text is delivered in full.

The alto aria, no. 2, is also exceptional in that its obbligato* violin part contains a minimum of thematic writing and a maximum of virtuoso figuration, possibly in order to represent heavenly radiance and the lively hope of the person who relies upon God's promise. The third movement—an arrangement of the sixteenth verse of the hymn *Kommt her zu mir, spricht Gottes Sohn* by Georg Grünwald (1530)—returns to strict part-writing. Two oboes d'amore* and continuo form an instrumental trio texture with imitative* upper parts; within it the chorale melody is incorporated, sung one line at a time by the soprano in an unadorned form.

A short *secco* recitative leads to the tenor aria, no. 5, whose full string texture is dominated by the first violin. The entire movement is pervaded by the opening motive, which is adopted by the tenor in the vocal section—

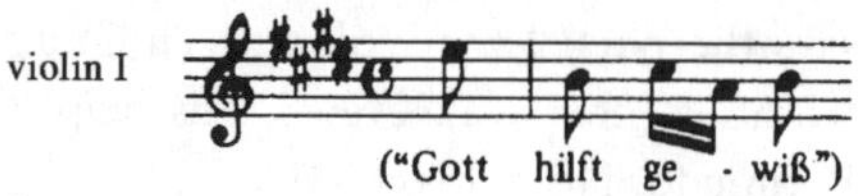

—and thus seems to call out these words repeatedly to the listener. A plain chorale setting of the eleventh verse of the hymn *Es ist das Heil uns kommen her* by Paul Speratus (1523) concludes the work.

Bisher habt ihr nichts gebeten in meinem Namen, BWV 87

NBA I/12, p. 63 BC A74 Duration: *c.* 22 mins

1. [Bass Solo] B str + ob I,II, ob da c bc	d C
'Bisher habt ihr nichts gebeten in meinem Namen.'	'Hitherto you have asked nothing in my Name.'
2. Recitativo A bc	a–g C
O Wort! das Geist und Seel erschreckt.	O Word that terrifies spirit and soul!
Ihr Menschen, merkt den Zuruf, was dahinter steckt!	You people, mark His call, what lies behind it!
Ihr habt Gesetz und Evangelium vorsätzlich übertreten,	You have deliberately transgressed Law and Gospel,
Und diesfalls möcht' ihr ungesäumt in Buß und Andacht beten.	And therefore you should pray immediately in penitence and devotion.
3. Aria A ob da c I,II bc	g C
Vergib, o Vater! unsre Schuld,	Forgive, O Father, our guilt
Und habe noch mit uns Geduld,	And still have patience with us
Wenn wir in Andacht beten	When we pray in devotion
Und sagen, Herr, auf dein Geheiß:	And say, Lord, at Your behest:
Ach rede nicht mehr sprüchwortsweis,	Ah, speak no more in proverbs,
Hilf uns vielmehr vertreten!	Rather help us to intercede!
4. Recitativo T str bc	d–c C
Wenn unsre Schuld bis an den Himmel steigt,	When our trespass has grown up to the heavens,
Du siehst und kennest ja mein Herz, das nichts vor dir verschweigt;	You indeed see and know my heart, which hides nothing from You;
Drum suche mich zu trösten!	Therefore seek to comfort me!

5. [Bass Solo] B bc — c 3/8

'In der Welt habt ihr Angst; aber seid getrost, ich habe die Welt überwunden.'	'In the world you will have tribulation; but be of good cheer: I have overcome the world.'

6. Aria T str bc — B♭ 12/8

Ich will leiden, ich will schweigen, Jesus wird mir Hülf erzeigen, Denn er tröst' mich nach dem Schmerz.	I would suffer, I would be dumb: Jesus will show me His help, For He comforts me after pain.
Weicht, ihr Sorgen, Trauer, Klagen! Denn warum sollt ich verzagen? Fasse dich, betrübtes Herz!	Retreat, you cares, sadness, laments! For why should I give up hope? Compose yourself, my faint heart!

7. Choral SATB bc (+ instrs) — d C

Muß ich sein betrübet? So mich Jesus liebet, Ist mir aller Schmerz Über Honig süße, Tausend Zuckerküsse Drücket er ans Herz. Wenn die Pein sich stellet ein, Seine Liebe macht zur Freuden Auch das bittre Leiden.	**Must I be downcast? If Jesus loves me, All pain is to me Sweeter than honey; A thousand sweet kisses He presses on my heart. When pain occurs, His Love turns Even bitter suffering into joy.**

This cantata, based on a text by Mariane von Ziegler, was composed for performance on 6 May 1725. The poet chooses to open with some words of Jesus's from the Sunday Gospel*, John 16.24, which she takes as a threatening reproach: despite their obvious guilt, mortals have not prayed to God for forgiveness (nos. 2–3). The penultimate line of the aria, no. 3, 'Ah, speak no more in proverbs', likewise refers to a passage from the Gospel (John 16.25): 'But the time comes when I shall no longer speak to you in proverbs but shall tell you freely of my Father'. The short second recitative, no. 4, which prays for comfort, is absent from Ziegler's printed text and might have been written by Bach to render less abrupt the transition to the following 'comfortable words' of Jesus (John 16.33), and also, perhaps, to diversify a succession of similar movements (nos. 3, 5, and 6: aria–arioso*–aria). The consoling biblical passage leads to the decision to endure the suffering God has ordained by relying upon Jesus's help. The conclusion is formed by the ninth verse of the hymn *Selig ist die Seele* by Heinrich Müller (1659): if Jesus loves me, even my suffering will be turned into joy.

The opening movement is, in many respects, similar to the equivalent movement in the cantata for the same Sunday in the previous year, BWV 86, though it in no way achieves the vocal character of that piece. Again the instruments (strings reinforced by oboes) are handled in a strikingly polyphonic* manner, with imitative* entries in the two upper parts; and again the instrumental theme is taken up by the bass almost without alteration so that, with all its freedom of structure, the movement resembles a fugue.*

A *secco* recitative leads to the alto aria, no. 3, whose scoring with two oboes da caccia* lends it an unusual colouring, characterized by its concentration of sound in the middle register. An upward-striving ostinato* figure in the continuo has the effect of a beseeching gesture, while the frequent sigh figures of the oboes' theme, which moves largely in parallel motion, seem to articulate no less persistently the word 'vergib' ('forgive'). The immediate and compelling effect of the movement owes much to these manifestly speech-like gestures within its instrumental motives.* The second recitative, no. 4, is, unlike the first, accompanied by strings. After a brief opening in recitative style, it flows into an expressive arioso* on the words 'Therefore seek to comfort me'.

The fifth movement—another of those very aria-like bass ariosos to the words of Christ—is of unexpected severity. This impression is at once conveyed by its restriction to bass voice and continuo; and, in addition, the eight-bar opening theme pervades the entire movement with its ostinato-like but freely varied recurrences. The second half, 'but be of good cheer', begins with a relative-major version of the theme, but at its continuation, 'I have overcome the world', the original minor form (at first in the dominant, then in the tonic), with its painful diminished seventh, returns as if to say that this comfort was achieved at no smaller price than the Passion of Christ.

The sixth movement—a siciliano for tenor, strings, and continuo of overwhelming beauty—brings the joyful affirmation that in our suffering we can rely upon Jesus's comfort. Over lengthy pedal points, the first violin unfolds a highly expressive melody, accompanied by tranquil chords or homophonic* chord sequences on the second violin and viola. The tenor at first takes over the violin theme, but in the second half, 'Retreat, you cares . . .', he develops his own melody. The cantata concludes with a plain chorale setting to the melody *Jesu, meine Freude*.

1.29 Ascension

EPISTLE: Acts 1.1–11: Prologue; Jesus's last promise; His Ascension.
GOSPEL: Mark 16.14–20: The injunction to undertake mission and baptism; the Ascension.

Wer da gläubet und getauft wird, BWV 37

NBA I/12, p. 81 BC A75 Duration: *c.* 21 mins

1. [CHORUS] SATB ob d'am I,II str bc — A $\frac{3}{2}$

'Wer da gläubet und getauft wird, der wird selig werden.'	'Whoever believes and is baptized, he shall be saved.'

2. ARIA T vln solo (?) bc — A c

Der Glaube ist das Pfand der Liebe,	Faith is the pledge of the Love
Die Jesus für die Seinen hegt.	That Jesus has for His own people.
Drum hat er bloß aus Liebestriebe,	Therefore purely out of a loving impulse,
Da er ins Lebensbuch mich schriebe,	When He inscribed me in the Book of Life,
Mir dieses Kleinod beigelegt.	He bestowed upon me this prize medal.

3. CHORALE SA bc — D $\frac{12}{8}(\frac{4}{4})$

Herr Gott Vater, mein starker Held!	**Lord God the Father, my mighty Hero!**
Du hast mich ewig vor der Welt	**You have ever loved me, before the world,**
In deinem Sohn geliebet.	**In Your Son.**
Dein Sohn hat mich ihm selbst vertraut,	**Your Son has betrothed Himself to me,**
Er ist mein Schatz, ich bin sein Braut,	**He is my treasure, I am His bride,**
Sehr hoch in ihm erfreuet.	**Most highly delighted in Him.**
Eia, eia!	**Eia, eia!**
Himmlisch Leben wird er geben mir dort oben;	**Heavenly Life shall He give me there above;**
Ewig soll mein Herz ihn loben.	**Forever shall my heart praise Him.**

4. RECITATIVO B str bc — b c

Ihr Sterblichen, verlanget ihr,	You mortals, do you desire,
Mit mir	With me,
Das Antlitz Gottes anzuschauen?	To behold the face of God?
So dürft ihr nicht auf gute Werke bauen;	Then you should not build upon good works;
Denn ob sich wohl ein Christ	For although a Christian
Muß in den guten Werken üben,	Must indeed practise good works,
Weil es der ernste Wille Gottes ist,	Since it is the severe Will of God,
So macht der Glaube doch allein,	Yet Faith alone ensures
Daß wir vor Gott gerecht und selig sein.	That before God we are justified and saved.

5. ARIA B str + ob d'am I bc — b c

Der Glaube schafft der Seele Flügel,	Faith gives the soul wings
Daß sie sich in den Himmel schwingt,	To soar up into the heavens;
Die Taufe ist das Gnadensiegel,	Baptism is the seal of grace
Das uns den Segen Gottes bringt;	That brings us the blessing of God;
Und daher heißt ein selger Christ,	And therefore he is called a saved Christian:
Wer gläubet und getaufet ist.	Whoever believes and is baptized.

6. CHORALE SATB bc (+ instrs) — A c

Den Glauben mir verleihe	**Grant me faith**

An dein' Sohn Jesum Christ,	**In Your Son Jesus Christ;**
Mein Sünd mir auch verzeihe	**Cleanse me, too, from my sin**
Allhier zu dieser Frist.	**Here at this time.**
Du wirst mir nicht versagen,	**You will not deny me**
Was du verheißen hast,	**What You have promised,**
Daß er mein Sünd tu tragen	**That He does take away my sins**
Und lös mich von der Last.	**And frees me of their burden.**

This cantata was written for Ascension (18 May) 1724. The Gospel* for the day first tells of Jesus's injunction to undertake mission and baptism, and then of His Ascension. Bach's cantatas for this feast-day refer to either one or the other of these narratives. Accordingly, in the present cantata the account of the Ascension remains unmentioned. Its theme is faith and the Christian's justification by faith. The anonymous librettist is no doubt identical with that of a number of other cantata texts for the period between Easter and Whit 1724. Despite its concise form, which surely induced Bach to perform it without intermission, the cantata is bipartite: each half concludes with a chorale setting.

The opening chorus* sets the theme by quoting Mark 16.16 from the Gospel read out beforehand. The following aria, no. 2, celebrates faith as the sign of Jesus's love for His own people; and the chorale no. 3—the fifth verse of the hymn *Wie schön leuchtet der Morgenstern* by Philipp Nicolai (1599)—is a prayer of thanksgiving by the Christian for the love shown him in Jesus. In a manner reminiscent of the structure of a sermon, the recitative that introduces the second part, no. 4, now brings a refutation of the false view that a Christian could be saved by good works alone. With reference to Romans 3.28, the librettist emphasizes that faith alone justifies man before God. The following aria, no. 5, recapitulates: faith is the pre-condition, and baptism the confirmation, that the Christian is saved. Like the chorale no. 3, the concluding chorale no. 6—the fourth verse of the hymn *Ich dank dir, lieber Herre* by Johann Kolrose (*c.* 1535)—takes the form of a prayer.

For a feast-day cantata, Bach's setting is modest in its requirements: apart from four voices, strings, and continuo, it requires only two oboes d'amore.* Bach nonetheless knew how to achieve exceptionally attractive effects from this scoring, and in the nineteenth century the cantata already enjoyed a relatively large circulation and popularity. The extended introductory sinfonia of the first movement develops three melodic lines, which are stated simultaneously. The first of these, played on the oboes, later forms the opening theme of the chorus, to the words 'Wer da gläubet'; the second, assigned to the violins, recalls Luther's chorale *Dies sind die heilgen zehn Gebot*, though it is doubtful whether the allusion to this melody (originally of secular origin) was intentional. Finally, in the continuo we hear a descending note sequence that recurs in the third movement as the last line of the chorale *Wie schön leuchtet der Morgenstern*, though here again we are not obliged to hear a conscious allusion of Bach's to the chorale melody:

The chorus itself proves to be largely a combination of vocal writing with parts of the introductory sinfonia. Each of its two large sections contains an almost complete reprise of the sinfonia (partly transposed) with choral insertion,* interrupted by brief passages in which the lead is taken by the choir, which adopt the oboes' theme and later occasionally the string theme.

The second movement is unfortunately incomplete, lacking a solo violin part, as was first established in the *Neue Bach-Ausgabe*. However, with the aid of thematic material developed in the tenor and continuo parts, it may be reconstructed well enough for no breach of style to be apparent and without the overall impression suffering from its failings. In the third movement, Bach, by contrast with his contemporaries who showed little interest in the chorale, takes up an older form: the modestly scored chorale concerto* as cultivated in the seventeenth century, for example by Johann Hermann Schein (*Opella nova*; see the Introduction, Music Example No. 4). A more modern feature, however, is the greater flexibility of Bach's texture, especially the lively and motivically structured lead taken by the continuo—the sole instrumental accompaniment of the two voice parts. According to the substance of the text, the chorale melody undergoes various expressive modifications, particularly on the words 'dort oben' ('there above') and 'loben' ('praise').

A recitative accompanied by strings, no. 4, leads to the second aria, no. 5, in which Bach achieves charming sound effects through the full string accompaniment and the alternation between the playing and resting of the oboe. The concluding chorale, no. 6, is set in the usual plain four-part texture. In the first *Stollen** of its melody, we hear the change to the minor mode that was probably usual at the time, whereas the corresponding passage in the second *Stollen*—now on the word 'verzeihe' ('cleanse')—is, surely on textual grounds, in the major instead.

Auf Christi Himmelfahrt allein, BWV 128

NBA I/12, p. 103 BC A76 Duration: *c.* 22 mins

1. [Chorale] SATB hn I,II str + ob, ob d'am, ob da c bc		G c
Auf Christi Himmelfahrt allein	**On Christ's Ascension alone**	
Ich meine Nachfahrt gründe	**I base my following journey,**	
Und allen Zweifel, Angst und Pein	**And all doubt, tribulation, and pain**	
Hiermit stets überwinde;	**Herewith always overcome;**	
Denn weil das Haupt im Himmel ist,	**For since the Head is in heaven,**	
Wird seine Glieder Jesus Christ	**Jesus Christ will fetch its members**	
Zu rechter Zeit nachholen.	**Afterwards, in due season.**	
2. Recitativo T bc		e–b c
Ich bin bereit, komm, hole mich!	I am ready, come, fetch me!	
Hier in der Welt	Here in the world	
Ist Jammer, Angst und Pein;	Is woe, tribulation, and pain;	
Hingegen dort in Salems Zelt	But there in Salem's tabernacle	
Werd ich verkläret sein.	I shall be changed.	
Da seh ich Gott von Angesicht zu Angesicht,	There I shall see God face to face,	
Wie mir sein heilig Wort verspricht.	As His holy Word promises me.	
3. Aria + Recitativo B tr str bc		D 3/4 c 3/4
Auf, auf, mit hellem Schall	Up, up! with bright sound	
Verkündigt überall:	Proclaim everywhere:	
Mein Jesus sitzt zur Rechten!	My Jesus sits at God's right hand!	
Wer sucht mich anzufechten?	Who would seek to tempt me?	
Ist er von mir genommen,	Though He is taken up from me,	
Ich werd einst dahin kommen,	I shall one day come there,	
Wo mein Erlöser lebt.	Where my Redeemer lives.	
Mein Augen werden ihn in größter Klarheit schauen.	My eyes shall behold Him in the greatest clarity.	
O könnt ich im voraus mir eine Hütte bauen!	Oh, if only I could build myself a tabernacle in advance!	

Wohin? Vergebner Wunsch!	Where? Vain wish!
Er wohnet nicht auf Berg und Tal,	He dwells not on hill and vale,
Sein Allmacht zeigt sich überall;	His omnipotence appears everywhere;
So schweig, verwegner Mund,	So be dumb, audacious mouth,
Und suche nicht dieselbe zu ergründen!	And do not seek to fathom this!
4. ARIA [DUETTO] AT ob d'am I bc	b 6/8
Sein Allmacht zu ergründen,	To fathom His omnipotence
Wird sich kein Mensche finden,	No one will be found:
Mein Mund verstummt und schweigt.	My mouth grows dumb and silent.
Ich sehe durch die Sterne,	I see through the stars
Daß er sich schon von ferne	Already from afar
Zur Rechten Gottes zeigt.	That He appears at God's right hand.
5. CHORAL SATB (+ ww + str) hn I,II bc	G C
Alsdenn so wirst du mich	**Thereupon You shall set me**
Zu deiner Rechten stellen	**At Your right hand,**
Und mir als deinem Kind	**And on me, as Your child,**
Ein gnädig Urteil fällen,	**Pass a merciful sentence,**
Mich bringen zu der Lust,	**Bringing me to that delight**
Wo deine Herrlichkeit	**Wherein Your glory**
Ich werde schauen an	**I shall behold**
In alle Ewigkeit.	**In all eternity.**

The text of this cantata, by Christiane Mariane von Ziegler, was set to music by Bach for 10 May 1725. Bach later assigned most of the cantatas with texts by Ziegler to the third Leipzig cycle, but he seems to have made exceptions of this and BWV 68, classifying them among the chorale cantatas,* with which they belong in terms of their date of origin. Perhaps he considered this justified by the large-scale chorale choruses* that open both cantatas, though the essential characteristic of the chorale cantata—the adoption of a single chorale in its entirety within the text—is not here applicable.

The author drew the theme of her libretto from the introductory chorale, the first verse of the hymn by Ernst Sonnemann (1661; after Josua Wegelin, 1636): now that Christ has ascended into heaven, nothing has the power to keep me in the world, for I have God's promise that I shall one day see Him 'face to face' (no. 2; cf. 1 Corinthians 13.12). Joy over Jesus's seat at the right hand of God is followed by the 'vain wish' that 'if only I could build myself a tabernacle in advance!', an allusion to the account of Christ's Transfiguration (Matthew 17.4). Yet Jesus's almighty power does not inhabit a particular place but is found everywhere and cannot be fathomed (no. 3). I am resigned to that, and yet I see 'through the stars, already from afar, that He appears at God's right hand' (no. 4; cf. Acts 7.55). So too will Jesus one day place me at *His* right hand (cf. Matt. 25.33) and 'pass a merciful sentence' on me. With this text—the fourth verse of the hymn *O Jesu, meine Lust* by Matthäus Avenarius (1673)—the cantata ends.

For his setting Bach made a number of alterations to the text. The most significant is that the aria 'Auf, auf, mit hellem Schall' and the following recitative are combined to form a single movement (no. 3) by the interpolation of the connecting line 'Wo mein Erlöser lebt' ('Where my Redeemer lives'). Bach also linked the substance of this complex with that of the following aria, no. 4, by adding to the third movement the last two lines of recitative, 'So schweig, verwegner Mund, / Und suche nicht dieselbe zu ergründen!' ('So be dumb, audacious mouth, / And do not seek to fathom this!'). It is, of course, conceivable that these lines were already present in Ziegler's manuscript and were simply omitted from her edition of 1728. But since all three additional lines lack rhyme (which, though permitted, is not the rule in madrigalian* verse) it is more likely that they were added by Bach. By linking and relating the middle movements in this way, Bach achieves an exceptionally tight overall form, in which the salient structure of the opening chorus,* modelled on the chorale cantatas,* dominates all the more powerfully.

This opening movement, like many others, is made up of a concertante* orchestral texture with chorale passages inserted, in which the hymn—to the melody *Allein Gott in der Höh sei Ehr*—is delivered by the soprano in long note-values, line by line, supported by an imitative* texture in the lower parts. On this occasion, however, the thematic material of the instrumental parts is derived more obviously than usual from the chorale melody. After a head-motive heard three times—

—and transferred from the strings, reinforced by oboes, to the two horns, we hear a concertante instrumental fugue* on the following subject:

The entire first chorale line is contained within this subject, as indicated by the sign × in the above music example. In addition, significance is attached to a running semiquaver motive* whose derivation from the beginning of the chorale is likewise unmistakable. This thematic material forms the basis of the ensuing instrumental texture in the episodes and, as far as possible, in the choral passages. Consequently, a chorale arrangement emerges which, though differentiated in texture (instruments *concertato*, voices imitative) is nonetheless unified in thematic material.

A brief *secco* recitative is followed by two arias which contrast markedly in scoring, metre, tempo, and sonority—in short, in overall character. Indeed, it is possible that the inclusion of the second recitative within the first aria, no. 3, arose from the intention of making the contrast between the two arias as conspicuous as possible by means of direct juxtaposition. The scoring of the third movement—with trumpet added to strings and continuo—signifies that Christ has now entered upon His sovereignty. An extended ritornello of radiant brilliance is then reiterated in the principal section, partly in vocal form but for the most part instrumentally with vocal insertion.* A freer second section does not lead back to the expected da capo* of the principal section, but changes abruptly to a recitative with string accompaniment on the words 'Wo mein Erlöser lebt . . .'. The final reprise of the instrumental ritornello then follows, giving rise to the overall form:

ritornello—vocal section A—vocal section B—recitative—ritornello

The pure jubilation of this movement gives way to a duet of decidedly reticent, intimate character, whose ritornello theme, incidentally, formed the basis of Max Reger's Bach Variations, Op. 81. Bach's score prescribes 'organo' as the obbligato* instrument, but in the original performing parts the obbligato is assigned not to organ but to first oboe. The part does not specify oboe d'amore* but, according to the required compass, only this instrument comes into consideration. Since at no point does the part exceed the range of the oboe d'amore—an unnecessary limitation for an obbligato organ part—we may assume that during composition itself Bach altered his original plan of scoring for organ in favour of oboe d'amore, but without making a written note of it. The possibility cannot be excluded that the word 'organo' in the score was a subsequent addition (of Bach's?), but the source findings give no definite information on this point. Despite the imitative texture of the duet parts, the structure is in essentials predominantly homophonic,* since the imitation is largely subordinate to the periodic articulation of the movement. On account of its unabridged da capo form, it is very extensive. The concluding chorale is a plain setting to the melody *O Gott, du frommer Gott*. Among the instruments, only the horns have independent parts on account of the limited range of notes at their disposal.

Gott fähret auf mit Jauchzen, BWV 43

NBA I/12, p. 135 BC A77 Duration: *c.* 25 mins

1. [Chorus] SATB tr I–III timp str + ob I,II bc C 𝄴 𝄵

'Gott fähret auf mit Jauchzen und der Herr mit heller Posaunen. Lobsinget, lobsinget Gott! lobsinget, lobsinget unserm Könige!'	'God is gone up with jubilation, and the Lord with ringing trumpets. Sing praises, sing praises to God! Sing praises, sing praises to our King!'

2. Recitativo T bc — a–G c

Es will der Höchste sich ein Siegsgepräng bereiten,
Da die Gefängnisse er selbst gefangen führt.
Wer jauchzt ihm zu? Wer ists, der die Posaunen rührt?
Wer gehet ihm zur Seiten?
Ist es nicht Gottes Heer,
Das seines Namens Ehr,
Heil, Preis, Reich, Kraft und Macht mit lauter Stimme singet
Und ihm nun ewiglich ein Hallelujah bringet.

The Highest would prepare for Himself a victory parade,
For He leads captivity itself captive.
Who acclaims Him? Who is it that sounds the trumpets?
Who goes at His side?
Is it not God's host
That sings of His Name's honour,
Salvation, praise, kingdom, power, and might with loud voice
And now brings Him an Alleluia for ever.

3. Aria T vln I + II bc — G 3/8

Ja tausendmal tausend begleiten den Wagen,
Dem König der Kön'ge lobsingend zu sagen,
Daß Erde und Himmel sich unter ihm schmiegt
Und was er bezwungen, nun gänzlich erliegt.

Yes, a thousand times a thousand attend the chariot,
Singing praises to the King of kings, saying
That earth and heaven bow down beneath Him,
And what He has subdued now entirely succumbs.

4. Recitativo S bc — e c

'Und der Herr, nachdem er mit ihnen geredet hatte, ward er aufgehaben gen Himmel und sitzet zur rechten Hand Gottes.'

'And the Lord, after He had spoken with them, was lifted up into heaven, and sits at the right hand of God.'

5. Aria S str + ob I,II bc — e c

Mein Jesus hat nunmehr
Das Heilandwerk vollendet
Und nimmt die Wiederkehr
Zu dem, der ihn gesendet.
Er schließt der Erde Lauf,
Ihr Himmel! öffnet euch und nehmt ihn wieder auf!

My Jesus has now finished
His work of Salvation
And makes His return
To Him who sent Him.
He closes His earthly journey:
You heavens! open and take Him back up!

II. Teil — *Part II*

6. Recitativo B str bc — C c

Es kommt der Helden Held,
Des Satans Fürst und Schrecken,
Der selbst den Tod gefällt,
Getilgt der Sünden Flecken,
Zerstreut der Feinde Hauf.
Ihr Kräfte! eilt herbei und holt den Sieger auf.

The Hero of heroes comes,
Satan's Prince and terror,
Who felled Death itself,
Blotted out the stains of transgression,
And scattered the crowd of enemies.
You Powers! come quickly and hand up the Victor.

7. ARIA B tr I solo or vln I bc — C C

Er ists, der ganz allein
Die Kelter hat getreten
Voll Schmerzen, Qual und Pein,
Verlorne zu erretten
Durch einen teuren Kauf.
Ihr Thronen! mühet euch und setzt ihm Kränze auf!

It is He who, quite alone,
Has trodden the winepress,
Full of anguish, torment, and pain,
To save the lost
At a costly price.
You Thrones! stir yourselves and place garlands on Him!

8. RECITATIVO A bc — a C

Der Vater hat ihm ja
Ein ewig Reich bestimmet;
Nun ist die Stunde nah,
Da er die Krone nimmet
Vor tausend Ungemach.
Ich stehe hier am Weg und schau ihm freudig nach.

The Father has indeed ordained
For Him an eternal Kingdom;
Now the hour is at hand
When He receives the Crown
For enduring a thousand adversities.
I stand here at the wayside and gaze after Him joyfully.

9. ARIA A ob I,II bc — a $\frac{3}{4}$

Ich sehe schon im Geist,
Wie er zu Gottes Rechten
Auf seine Feinde schmeißt,
Zu helfen seinen Knechten
Aus Jammer, Not und Schmach.
Ich stehe hier am Weg und schau ihm sehnlich nach.

I see already, in the spirit,
How at God's right hand
He dashes His enemies to pieces
To help His servants
From distress, need, and dishonour.
I stand here at the wayside and gaze after Him longingly.

10. RECITATIVO S bc — G–e C

Er will mir neben sich
Die Wohnung zubereiten,
Damit ich ewiglich
Ihm stehe an der Seiten,
Befreit von Weh und Ach!
Ich stehe hier am Weg und ruf ihm dankbar nach.

He will prepare for me
A mansion next to Him,
That I may eternally
Stand at His side,
Freed from grief and woe!
I stand here at the wayside and call after Him gratefully.

11. CHORAL SATB bc (+ instrs) — G $\frac{3}{4}$

Du Lebensfürst, Herr Jesu Christ,
Der du bist aufgenommen
Gen Himmel, da dein Vater ist
Und die Gemein der Frommen,
Wie soll ich deinen großen Sieg,
Den du durch einen schweren Krieg
Erworben hast, recht preisen
Und dir gnug Ehr erweisen?

Zieh uns dir nach, so laufen wir,
Gib uns des Glaubens Flügel!
Hilf, daß wir fliehen weit von hier

You Prince of Life, Lord Jesus Christ,
Who have been taken up
Into heaven, where Your Father is
And the congregation of the upright,
How shall I justly praise Your great victory,
Which through a hard war
You have achieved,
And show You honour enough?

Draw us to You, and we shall run,
Grant us the wings of Faith!
Help us to flee far from here

Auf Israelis Hügel!	**On to Israel's hills!**
Mein Gott! wenn fahr ich doch dahin,	**My God! when do I go there,**
Woselbst ich ewig fröhlich bin?	**Where I shall be happy for ever?**
Wenn werd ich vor dir stehen,	**When shall I stand before You**
Dein Angesicht zu sehen?	**To behold Your countenance?**

The text of this cantata is unorthodox in form, for it consists largely of a poem in six strophes (nos. 5–10). The explanation for this has been uncovered by the American Bach scholar William H. Scheide. It was already known that in 1726 Bach performed several cantatas by his cousin Johann Ludwig Bach, and Scheide has established that the texts of several Bach cantatas of that year are identical in form to those of his Meiningen cousin. Among them is the text of the present cantata, which exhibits the following scheme:

> biblical passage (OT)—recitative—aria—biblical passage (NT)—strophic poem—chorale.

In accordance with an old Christian tradition, the Old Testament words (Psalm 47.5–6) are interpreted as a reference to Christ's Ascension. The two madrigalian* movements that follow celebrate Jesus's victory, referring to Psalm 68.18 and its quotation in Ephesians 4.8 ('You have ascended on high and taken captivity captive'), to Daniel 7.10 ('a thousand times a thousand ministered to Him'), and probably also to Psalm 68.17 ('the chariots of God are many thousand times a thousand'). The New Testament words, Mark 16.19, are drawn from the Gospel* for Ascension Day, and the following strophic poem praises the completion of Christ's work of salvation and the defeat of Satan, leading to the hope that the Saviour will prepare for me, too, a dwelling in heaven. Again several references are found here to biblical passages, such as Isaiah 63.3 ('I have trodden the winepress alone'), while the words 'I see already, in the spirit, how at God's right hand He dashes His enemies to pieces' in the fifth strophe (no. 9), as in Cantata 128, no doubt allude to the vision of Stephen (Acts 7.56): 'I see the heavens open and the Son of Man standing at the right hand of God'. The work concludes with the first and thirteenth verses of the hymn *Du Lebensfürst, Herr Jesu Christ* by Johann Rist (1641).

Bach's composition was written for 30 May 1726. In its festive scoring for three trumpets and drums, two oboes, strings, and continuo, it is exceeded a little only by the *Ascension Oratorio* among Bach's works for this occasion. The dominant movement is the splendid opening chorus,* which begins with a six-bar 'adagio' introduction for strings, supported by oboes. This is followed by an *alla breve* fugue* which, after two instrumental entries of the subject, is taken over by the choir, with the choral subject entries—as often in Bach—masked by homophonic* block chords. The first exposition* ends with a crowning subject entry on the first trumpet. This is followed directly by a second exposition, which touches on related minor keys and cadences in the dominant G. Now the second half of the text begins, 'Lobsinget Gott . . .', first in homophony (modelled motivically on the above-mentioned block chords) then as a third exposition of the fugue (to a new text) with a homophonic coda. The movement as a whole may thus be represented as follows:

Instrumental prelude:
  introduction (adagio)—two fugal entries (*alla breve*)

Chorus:
  lst fugal exposition ('Gott fähret auf . . .') with thematic first trumpet
  2nd fugal exposition ('Gott fähret auf . . .')
  homophonic passage ('Lobsinget . . .'), instrumental episode
  3rd fugal exposition ('Lobsinget . . .')
  homophonic coda

A syllabically* declaimed *secco* recitative (no. 2) is followed by a tenor aria (no. 3) in which the violins are united in a vigorous obbligato* part. Here, each of the three different vocal passages includes the entire text. Whereas the Old Testament passage was set in a wide-ranging opening chorus, the New Testament words are set merely in a brief, plainly declaimed *secco* recitative (no. 4), which is curiously assigned not to the tenor—the traditional Evangelist—but to the soprano. The series of strophic texts begins with a soprano aria (no. 5) with strings reinforced by oboes, probably the most attractive piece among the arias of this cantata. In its A section, syllabic delivery predominates, but in the B section the contrasting melismatic* motion on the words 'Er schließt der Erde Lauf' ('He closes His earthly journey'; rising) and its repeat (falling) is of special charm.

Part II of the cantata, probably performed after the sermon, begins with the sixth movement, an accompanied recitative with strings in which powerful triadic fanfares and *p* tremolos alternate with each other. The drama of this movement is carried over into the next, a bass aria with obbligato trumpet (no. 7). The extreme difficulty of the trumpet part may explain why at a later performance Bach had the part played on the violin. The continuo figuration may have been suggested by the image of treading the winepress, for it represents a typical organ pedal figure. The words 'Full of anguish, torment, and pain' are emphasized both harmonically and by means of slower movement. The eighth movement is another brief *secco* recitative, in which the coloratura* towards the end on the word 'schau (ihm freudig nach)' ('gaze (after Him joyfully)'), in its rising motion, strikingly portrays the turning of our gaze towards heaven.

The text 'I see already, in the spirit, how . . . He dashes His enemies to pieces' (no. 9) is notably undramatic compared with the earlier movements nos. 6 and 7, and Bach sets it almost meditatively, in a dance-like style with two oboes in thirds. Perhaps he was here guided by the Johannine conception that Christ's victory over His enemies was achieved long ago and only needed to be made manifest. Hence, despite its expressive chromaticism* on 'Jammer, Not und Schmach' ('distress, need, and dishonour') and 'sehnlich' ('longingly'), the movement reflects a vision of achieved victory in blessed joy rather than the destruction of Christ's enemies. The last strophe of the poem (no. 10), again set as a *secco* recitative, is followed by two verses of a hymn: a plain chorale setting to the melody *Ermuntre dich, mein schwacher Geist*.

This cantata leaves behind a somewhat mixed impression. The extensive text may explain a certain brevity—even scantiness—in its setting, which is reflected in the short arias and no fewer than four plain *secco* recitatives. Only the opening chorus forms an exception. The thematic invention itself is at times a trifle stereotyped in effect, with its preference for triadic or scale-based melody. Without doubt the work is a genuine and unmistakable creation of Bach's, but perhaps Johann Sebastian here modelled himself consciously on a work by his cousin Johann Ludwig.

Lobet Gott in seinen Reichen
Himmelfahrts-Oratorium *Ascension Oratorio*, BWV 11

NBA II/8, p. 3 BC D9 Duration: *c.* 32 mins

1. Chorus SATB tr I–III timp fl I,II ob I,II str bc — D $\frac{2}{4}$

Lobet Gott in seinen Reichen,	Laud God in His kingdoms,
Preiset ihn in seinen Ehren,	Praise Him in His honours,
Rühmet ihn in seiner Pracht!	Glorify Him in His splendour!
Sucht sein Lob recht zu vergleichen,	Seek rightly to liken His praise,
Wenn ihr mit gesamten Chören	When with whole choirs
Ihm ein Lied zu Ehren macht!	You make a song in His honour!

2. Evangelista T bc — b–A c

'Der Herr Jesus hub seine Hände auf und segnete seine Jünger, und es geschah, da er sie segnete, schied er von ihnen.'	'The Lord Jesus lifted up His hands and blest His disciples; and it came to pass that, as He blest them, He departed from them.'

3. Recitativo B fl I,II bc — f♯–a c

Ach, Jesu, ist dein Abschied schon so nah?	Ah Jesus, is Your departure already so near?
Ach, ist denn schon die Stunde da,	Ah, has the hour already come
Da wir dich von uns lassen sollen?	When we should let You part from us?
Ach, siehe, wie die heißen Tränen	Ah, see how hot tears
Von unsern blassen Wangen rollen,	Roll down our pale cheeks:
Wie wir uns nach dir sehnen,	How we yearn for You!

Wie uns fast aller Trost gebricht.
Ach, weiche doch noch nicht!

How almost all our comfort is lost!
Ah, do not leave us yet!

4. Aria A vln I + II bc — a C

Ach, bleibe doch, mein liebstes Leben,
Ach fliehe nicht so bald von mir!
Dein Abschied und dein frühes Scheiden
Bringt mir das allergrößte Leiden,
Ach ja, so bleibe doch noch hier;
Sonst werd ich ganz von Schmerz umgeben.

Ah do stay, my dearest Life,
Ah, do not flee so soon from me!
Your departure and Your early parting
Cause me the greatest suffering of all;
Ah yes, then do stay here yet;
Otherwise I shall be quite enveloped in grief.

5. Evangelista T bc — e–f♯ C

'Und ward aufgehaben zusehends und fuhr auf gen Himmel, eine Wolke nahm ihn weg vor ihren Augen, und er sitzet zur rechten Hand Gottes.'

'And He was visibly lifted up and went up to heaven, and a cloud took Him away before their eyes, and He sits at the right hand of God.'

6. Choral SATB bc (+ ww str) — D 3/4

Nun lieget alles unter dir,
Dich selbst nur ausgenommen;
Die Engel müssen für und für
Dir aufzuwarten kommen.
Die Fürsten stehn auch auf der Bahn
Und sind dir willig untertan;
Luft, Wasser, Feuer, Erden
Muß dir zu Dienste werden.

Now all lies under You,
You Yourself only excepted;
The angels must for ever and ever
Come to wait upon You.
Princes, too, stand on the way
And are willingly subject to You;
Air, water, fire, earth
Must be at Your service.

7a. Evangelista TB bc — D C

Tenor
'Und da sie ihm nachsahen gen Himmel fahren, siehe, da stunden bei ihnen zwei Männer in weißen Kleidern, welche auch sagten:'
beide
'Ihr Männer von Galiläa, was stehet ihr und sehet gen Himmel? Dieser Jesus, welcher von euch ist aufgenommen gen Himmel, wird kommen, wie ihr ihn gesehen habt gen Himmel fahren.'

Tenor
'And as they watched Him going up to heaven, look! there stood by them two men in white garments, who said:'
both
'You men of Galilee, why do you stand there looking up towards heaven? This Jesus, who has been taken up from you into heaven, shall come, just as you have seen Him go to heaven.'

7b. Recitativo A fl I,II bc — G–b [C]

Ach ja! so komme bald zurück:
Tilg einst mein trauriges Gebärden,
Sonst wird mir jeder Augenblick
Verhaßt und Jahren ähnlich werden.

Ah yes! then come back soon:
Cut off one day my sad looks,
Otherwise for me every moment
Shall be hated and become like years.

7c. Evangelista T bc D–G c

'Sie aber beteten ihn an, wandten um gen Jerusalem von dem Berge, der da heißet der Ölberg, welcher ist nahe bei Jerusalem und liegt einen Sabbater-Weg davon, und sie kehreten wieder gen Jerusalem mit großer Freude.'

'But they worshipped Him and turned towards Jerusalem from the mountain which is called the Mount of Olives, which is near Jerusalem, lying a Sabbath's journey away, and they returned again to Jerusalem with great joy.'

8. Aria S fl I + II ob I unis str G 3/8

Jesu, deine Gnadenblicke
Kann ich doch beständig sehn.
Deine Liebe bleibt zurücke,
Daß ich mich hier in der Zeit
An der künftgen Herrlichkeit
Schon voraus im Geist erquicke,
Wenn wir einst dort vor dir stehn.

Jesus, Your glances of grace
I can indeed see constantly.
Your Love stays behind
So that, here at this time,
In that future glory
I may refresh my spirit in advance,
When one day we stand there before You.

9. Choral [scoring as in no. 1] D 6/4

Wenn soll es doch geschehen,
Wenn kömmt die liebe Zeit,
Daß ich ihn werde sehen
In seiner Herrlichkeit?
Du Tag, wenn wirst du sein,
Daß wir den Heiland grüßen,
Daß wir den Heiland küssen?
Komm, stelle dich doch ein!

When shall it come about,
When will the beloved time come
When I shall see Him
In His glory?
O day, when will you be,
When we greet the Saviour,
When we kiss the Saviour?
Come, do appear!

The *Ascension Oratorio* was probably written for 19 May 1735—during the same church year as the *Christmas Oratorio*. Not all of the music was new, however: the opening chorus* and the two arias were drawn from older works: the chorus from the cantata *Froher Tag, verlangte Stunden*, BWV Anh. I 18, for the consecration of the rebuilt Thomasschule in 1732; and the two arias from the wedding cantata *Auf! süß entzückende Gewalt*, BWV Anh. I 196, composed in 1725 to a text by Gottsched.

The librettist of the oratorio* is unknown. As in the case of the *Christmas Oratorio*, Picander might be considered a possible candidate, since he is known to have been skilled in parody,* though this text is likewise missing from the five-volume edition of his verse. The framework of the libretto is the biblical account of the Ascension as transmitted in Luke, Acts (the Epistle* for the day) and Mark (the Gospel* for the day). Accordingly, the text of no. 2 is drawn from Luke 24.50–1, no. 5 from Acts 1.9 and Mark 16.19, no. 7a from Acts 1.10–11, and no. 7c from Luke 24.52a, Acts 1.12 and Luke 24.52b. Whereas the biblical texts concentrate on the essentials in concise narration, the interwoven madrigalian* verse adds contemplation in the freely versified recitatives and prayer in the arias. Hence the recitative no. 3 asks in distress—although Jesus has already taken His departure from His disciples—'Ah Jesus, is Your departure already so near?', while the aria, no. 4, prays to Jesus that He will stay longer. The announcement of the two men in white garments that, just as Jesus has gone to heaven, so He will return (no. 7a) is joined to a prayer for His speedy return (no. 7b); and the final biblical narrative of no. 7c is followed by the comforting thought that Jesus's love remains behind as a sign of the hope for our ultimate union with Him. Of the two chorales, no. 6 is the fourth verse of the hymn *Du Lebensfürst, Herr Jesu Christ* by Johann Rist (1641), and no. 9 the seventh verse of *Gott fähret auf gen Himmel* by Gottfried Wilhelm Sacer (1697), which makes the hope for the day of Christ's Second Coming into the concern of the entire congregation.

In its general laudatory content, the festive chorus from the Thomasschule cantata of 1732 is particularly well suited to form the opening movement of the oratorio. Trumpets, flutes, oboes, strings, and continuo open with a concerted prelude. The choir then enters homophonically* with its own thematic material, but in the course of the movement it repeatedly becomes subordinate to the orchestra in a freely polyphonic* texture as a result of choral insertion.* A new syncopated theme predominates in the bipartite middle section which, though leading to related minor keys, nonetheless retains the prevailing jubilant tone. A free da capo* of the principal section concludes the movement.

According to an old tradition, the Gospel narrative is assigned to the tenor voice and set as *secco* recitative. The only exception to this is the direct speech of the two men in white (no. 7a), which is sung by tenor and bass and set as arioso,* first in homophony ('Ihr Männer von Galiläa . . .') and then in canon* ('Dieser Jesus . . .'). As in the *Christmas Oratorio*, the freely versified recitatives, nos. 3 and 7b, are set as *accompagnato*.* The accompanying instruments in both cases are transverse flutes,* which partly harmonize the declamation with held chords and partly bridge over the cadences with figuration or illustrate the text ('Ah, see how hot tears roll down our pale cheeks').

The music of the first of the two arias, no. 4, is well known from the Agnus Dei of the B minor Mass. However, the oratorio aria is not the original of the mass movement, as was formerly assumed, but rather both are derived independently from the aforementioned wedding cantata. Yet the imploring gesture is so clearly stamped on the thematic material, the adaptation so perfect, that only knowledge of the origin of the movement makes us conscious of its nature as a parody. The second aria, no. 8, is of exceptional charm. Two transverse flutes in unison, oboe, and a bassett* of unison violins and viola form a trio texture, which is expanded to a quartet by the addition of the soprano in the vocal passages. Since the participating instruments and the voice are all of high or middle pitch, the aria creates the impression of an upward gaze, with all earthly weight seemingly eradicated. Music once invented to characterize

'Innocence, the gem of pure souls' ('Unschuld, Kleinod reiner Seelen') thus here acquires a new and no less meaningful significance.

Whereas the first of the two chorales, no. 6, is a plain four-part choral setting, the concluding chorale, no. 9, is presented in the garb of a splendid concertante* orchestral texture, similar to that of the equivalent movement in the *Christmas Oratorio*, BWV 248/64. In both cases, a chorale melody in a foreign key is incorporated in a radiant D major setting, which allows the whole work to end on a note of jubilation. Here, the chorale melody, *Von Gott will ich nicht lassen*, is assigned to the soprano and reinforced by oboes, flutes, and strings in alternation. The remaining choral parts support the chorale melody in a freely polyphonic,* or at times imitative,* texture.

1.30 Sunday after Ascension (Exaudi)

Epistle: 1 Peter 4.8–11: Minister to one another, each according to the gift he has received.

Gospel: John 15.26–16.4: Jesus's valedictory address: the spirit of truth shall come; the disciples will be persecuted.

Sie werden euch in den Bann tun, BWV 44

NBA I/12, p. 167 BC A78 Duration: *c.* 22 mins

1. [Duetto] TB ob I,II bc — g 3/4

'Sie werden euch in den Bann tun.'

'They will place you under a ban.'

2. [Chorus] SATB str + ob I,II bc — g ¢

'Es kömmt aber die Zeit, daß, wer
euch tötet, wird meinen, er tue
Gott einen Dienst daran.'

'But the time will come when whoever
kills you shall think he does God a service
thereby.'

3. Aria A ob I solo bc — c 3/4

Christen müssen auf der Erden
Christi wahre Jünger sein.
  Auf sie warten alle Stunden,
  Bis sie selig überwunden,
  Marter, Bann und schwere Pein.

Christians must on earth
Be Christ's true disciples.
  For them at every hour—
  Until, blessed, they overcome—
  Await torment, ban, and severe pain.

4. Choral T bc — E♭ c

Ach Gott, wie manches Herzeleid
Begegnet mir zu dieser Zeit.
Der schmale Weg ist trübsalvoll,
Den ich zum Himmel wandern soll.

Ah God, how much heartbreak
Confronts me at this time.
The narrow way is full of tribulation,
That I have to take to heaven.

5. Recitativo B bc — g–d c

Es sucht der Antichrist,
Das große Ungeheuer,
Mit Schwert und Feuer

The Antichrist,
That great monster,
With sword and fire

Die Glieder Christi zu verfolgen,
Weil ihre Lehre ihm zuwider ist.
Er bildet sich dabei wohl ein,
Es müsse sein Tun Gott gefällig sein.
Allein, es gleichen Christen denen Palmenzweigen,
Die durch die Last nur desto höher steigen.

Seeks to persecute the members of Christ
Because their teaching is offensive to him.
He probably imagines that
His deeds must be pleasing to God.
However, Christians resemble palm branches,
Which through their burden just climb all the higher.

6. ARIA S str + ob I,II bc — B♭ c

Es ist und bleibt der Christen Trost,
Daß Gott vor seine Kirche wacht.
Denn wenn sich gleich die Wetter türmen,
So hat doch nach den Trübsalstürmen
Die Freudensonne bald gelacht.

It is and remains the Christian's comfort
That God watches over His Church.
For when the whirlwinds suddenly pile up,
Yet after the storms of tribulation
The sun of joy soon laughs.

7. CHORAL SATB bc (+ instrs) — B♭ c

So sei nun, Seele, deine
Und traue dem alleine,
Der dich erschaffen hat.
Es gehe, wie es gehe,
Dein Vater in der Höhe,
Der weiß zu allen Sachen Rat.

Then be true to yourself, O soul,
And trust Him alone
Who has created you.
Be it as it may,
Your Father on high
Knows the right counsel for all things.

Since they share the same opening lines, Cantatas 44 and 183 are often called *Sie werden euch in den Bann tun* I and II. Yet apart from the Sunday for which they were written, they have in common only their introductory biblical text: there are no further textual, let alone musical, connections between them. The present cantata, BWV 44, originated during Bach's first year in Leipzig, for performance on 21 May 1724. The anonymous librettist, who also supplied other texts for this part of the church year, quotes a verse from the Gospel* for the day, John 16.2, which prophecies the persecution of Jesus's disciples (nos. 1 and 2). The following madrigalian* verse (no. 3) takes up the same idea, which is then confirmed in the chorale no. 4, the first verse of the hymn by Martin Moller (1587): until this world is overcome, the Christian has to bear suffering. The recitative, no. 5, gives the explanation: the teaching of Jesus is offensive to the Antichrist, who even believes that he renders God a service by persecuting Christ's followers. In sermon-like style, the refutation of false teaching—a central concept in the homiletics of the day—now begins, with the aid of an image drawn from the popular symbolism of the baroque age:[69] the enemies of

[69] See A. Schöne, *Emblematik und Drama im Zeitalter des Barock* (Munich, 1964; 2nd edn Munich, 1968), where illustrations of weighted palms may be found on p. 72 and after p. 128.

Christ are in error, for just as palms are hung with weights so that they may grow all the straighter and more upright, so too the Christian will not collapse under the burden of suffering, but will enter into heaven with all the greater certainty. In the next movement, no. 6, we are told that God watches over His Church, and if it is threatened by persecution and suffering, Christendom may confidently pin its hopes on God's help. The concluding chorale, no. 7, is the last verse of the hymn *In allen meinen Taten* by Paul Fleming (1642).

For his setting of the introductory biblical words, Bach chooses a form seldom found in his cantatas but often in those of Telemann. As often happens elsewhere, the attempt is made not to abandon the traditional serial form of the motet,* but rather to preserve its superior aptitude for the musical illustration of sectional prose texts, and at the same time unite it with the concertante* forms of the late baroque. The biblical text is so divided that its opening is sung by two voices (no. 1) and its continuation by the full vocal ensemble (no. 2)—the same form that we observed in Telemann's cantata movement 'So du mit deinem Munde bekennest Jesum' in the above commentary on Cantata 145.

Bach's concertante opening movement is of exceptional beauty. It is an expressive lament, introduced by an instrumental ritornello in which two oboes, accompanied by continuo, state the theme in an imitative* texture before it is taken up by tenor and bass duet. With the entry of the voices, the texture is expanded to five parts. The vocal duet flows into a complete reprise of the introductory ritornello, in which the opening sentence is now assigned to the voices, with instrumental accompaniment, whereas the more instrumentally figurative continuation is played on the oboes, accompanied by vocal insertion.* A short instrumental postlude gives a single reminder of the theme in the continuo and then leads without a break into the entry of the choir, which is accompanied by a change of time and an acceleration of tempo. This second movement is concise and lucid in form:

A Predominantly homophonic* texture with independent instrumental parts
- a) two equivalent chordal blocks ('Es kömmt aber die Zeit')
- b) chromatic* block, played *p* ('daß, wer euch tötet')
- c) chordal conclusion, in part more loosely textured, with imitation in the outer voices ('wird meinen, er tue Gott einen Dienst daran')

A^1 a–c) in free transposed reprise, with *Stimmtausch** in section c)

B^A Predominantly imitative texture with the instruments *colla parte*;* rounding-off at the close with recourse to A (A^1):
- d) imitative texture ('Es kömmt aber die Zeit, daß . . .')
- c) free transposed reprise of the conclusion of A/A^1 ('wird meinen . . .')

The overall form of the chorus* thus resembles the *Bar** with reprise.

The third movement, with its calm triple time, its few parts, and its scoring for obbligato* oboe, returns to the mood of the opening duet. The words 'torment, ban, and severe pain' in the middle section are illustrated by chromaticism, regardless of the fact that the text speaks of their blessed overcoming. The chorale *Ach Gott, wie manches Herzeleid*, no. 4, is accompanied only by continuo. The tenor sings the virtually unadorned chorale melody to an ostinato* accompanying figure in the continuo, which is developed out of the first chorale line but chromatically modified for interpretative reasons.

In content, the fifth movement, a syllabically* declaimed *secco* recitative, represents the turning-point of the cantata. For the soprano aria that follows (no. 6, with strings reinforced by oboes) is in a consoling B flat major, free of heaped-up chromaticism, and with lively gestures of an almost dance-like cheerfulness. Even the building up of the storm—represented graphically in the middle section by sequences of 6–3 and 6–4 chords (chords in first and second inversion respectively)—does not seriously disturb the mood, and is followed by the laughter of the 'sun of joy' in lively soprano coloraturas.* A plain chorale setting, to the melody *O Welt, ich muß dich lassen*, concludes the cantata.

Sie werden euch in den Bann tun, BWV 183

NBA I/12, p. 189 BC A79 Duration: *c.* 15 mins

1.	RECITATIVO B ob d'am I,II ob da c I,II bc	a–e **c**
	'Sie werden euch in den Bann tun, es kömmt aber die Zeit, daß, wer euch tötet, wird meinen, er tue Gott einen Dienst daran.'	'They will place you under a ban, but the time will come when whoever kills you will think he does God a service thereby.'
2.	ARIA T vc picc solo bc	e **c**
	Ich fürchte nicht des Todes Schrecken, Ich scheue ganz kein Ungemach. Denn Jesus' Schutzarm wird mich decken, Ich folge gern und willig nach. Wollt ihr nicht meines Lebens schonen Und glaubt, Gott einen Dienst zu tun, Er soll euch selben noch belohnen, Wohlan! es mag dabei beruhn.	I do not fear death's terror, I shy away from no adversity at all. For Jesus's protecting arm will cover me; I follow Him gladly and willingly. If you would not spare my life And believe that you do God a service And He shall yet reward you for it, Well, then, let it be so!
3.	RECITATIVO A ob d'am I,II ob da c I,II str bc	G–C **c**
	Ich bin bereit, mein Blut und armes Leben Vor dich, mein Heiland, hinzugeben,	I am ready to give my blood and my poor life For You, my Saviour.

Mein ganzer Mensch soll dir gewidmet sein;	My entire being shall be dedicated to You;
Ich tröste mich, dein Geist wird bei mir stehen,	I comfort myself that Your Spirit will stand by me
Gesetzt, es sollte mir vielleicht zuviel geschehen.	In the event that it should perhaps become too much for me.

4. ARIA S ob da c I + II str bc — C 3/8

Höchster Tröster, Heilger Geist,	Highest Comforter, Holy Spirit,
Der du mir die Wege weist,	Who teach me the ways
Darauf ich wandeln soll,	Whereby I am to walk,
Hilf meine Schwachheit mit vertreten,	Help my infirmity with Your intercession,
Denn von mir selber kann ich nicht beten,	For of myself I cannot pray;
Ich weiß, du sorgest vor mein Wohl!	I know You care for my well-being!

5. CHORAL SATB bc (+ instrs) — a C

Du bist ein Geist, der lehret,	**You are a Spirit who teaches**
Wie man recht beten soll;	**How one should pray aright;**
Dein Beten wird erhöret,	**Your praying is heard,**
Dein Singen klinget wohl.	**Your singing sounds well.**
Es steigt zum Himmel an,	**It climbs up to heaven,**
Es steigt und läßt nicht abe,	**It climbs and does not cease**
Bis der geholfen habe,	**Till He has helped**
Der allein helfen kann.	**Who alone can help.**

This cantata, composed for 13 May 1725, makes use of a text by the poet Christiane Mariane von Ziegler, though not without a few alterations such as may also be found in Bach's other cantatas to Ziegler texts. Yet the extent of this intervention is here slighter than in the cantatas of the preceding weeks. As in the cantata for the same Sunday in 1724, the text opens with Christ's words from the Gospel* reading, John 16.2. On this occasion, however, the thoughts that follow emphasize not so much suffering itself as the fearlessness with which the Christian can await this suffering in his reliance upon 'Jesus's protecting arm' (no. 2). It is clear from nos. 3 and 4 that the poet also refers to the previous verse of the Gospel, which announces the sending of the Spirit of Truth: this Spirit will intercede for me, since I cannot pray of my own accord (cf. Romans 8.26). The cantata ends with the fifth verse of the hymn *Zeuch ein zu deinen Toren* by Paul Gerhardt (1653).

Bach's setting is notable for its unusual scoring: in addition to strings and continuo, it requires no fewer than four oboes—two oboes d'amore* and two oboes da caccia*—as well as a violoncello piccolo* in the second movement. In marked contrast to the setting of the same text in Cantata 44, with its complex, elaborate structure, the introductory biblical text is here set as a plain five-bar recitative. The bass—the *vox Christi*—declaims syllabically, for the most part, against the background of held chords in the four oboes.

The two arias reveal that Bach's demands on his musicians increased with time. Considerable facility is demanded not only of the singers but of the instrumentalists too. From the running semiquaver figuration of the violoncello piccolo, the second movement acquires a decidedly severe, almost inexorable character. Presumably the contrast between the motoric character of the instrumental part and the elaborate, ornamental tenor part was consciously designed by Bach as a means of textual illustration. Only in the middle section does the violoncello piccolo join the continuo part, not just for a few notes but for several bars, causing a relaxation of the background instrumental movement. An unchanged da capo* of the principal section follows.

The second recitative (no. 3), like the first, is set as an *accompagnato*,* this time accompanied by the entire instrumental ensemble. While the strings provide the harmonic background, with their held chords, the pairs of oboes d'amore and oboes da caccia play in alternation a motive* whose constant repetition pervades the whole movement, which thus takes on the character of a 'motivically imprinted' *accompagnato*. This motive is none other than the opening figure of the alto part—

—whose words are thus, as it were, repeated by the instruments throughout.

The second aria, no. 4, requires not only strings but two unison oboes da caccia, which extend their obbligato* part over lengthy stretches of music, accompanied by short, often motivic interjections from the strings. This unusual scoring is all the more remarkable in that both arias in this cantata involve obbligato instruments in the middle register (tenor or alto pitch). The triple time and the motivic repetition within the opening phrase create a relaxed, almost dance-like impression, in marked contrast to the severity of the first aria. The four-part concluding chorale is based on the melody *Helft mir Gotts Güte preisen*.

1.31 Whit Sunday

Epistle: Acts 2.1–13: The descent of the Holy Spirit.

Gospel: John 14.23–31: Jesus's valedictory address: 'the Holy Spirit shall instruct you in all things'.

Erschallet, ihr Lieder, BWV 172

NBA I/13, pp. 3, 35 BC A81 Duration: *c.* 25 mins

1. Coro SATB tr I–III timp vln I (+ fl ob), II vla I,II bc — C/D[70] $\frac{3}{8}$

Erschallet, ihr Lieder, erklinget, ihr Saiten!	Resound, you songs; ring out, you strings!
O seligste Zeiten!	O most blessed times!
Gott will sich die Seelen zu Tempeln bereiten.	God would prepare our souls to be His temples.

2. Recitativo B bc — a–C/b–D c

'Wer mich liebet, der wird mein Wort halten, und mein Vater wird ihn lieben, und wir werden zu ihm kommen und Wohnung bei ihm machen.'	'Whoever loves me will keep my Word, and my Father will love him, and we will come to him and make our abode with him.'

3. Aria B tr I–III timp bc — C/D c

Heiligste Dreieinigkeit,	Most Holy Trinity,
Großer Gott der Ehren,	Great God of honour,
Komm doch, in der Gnadenzeit	Come in this time of grace
Bei uns einzukehren;	And stay with us;
Komm doch in die Herzenshütten,	Come into the tabernacles of our hearts,
Sind sie gleich gering und klein;	Though they be slight and small;
Komm und laß dich doch erbitten,	Come and let us beg You,
Komm und kehre bei uns ein!	Come and stay with us!

4. Aria T vln I + II + vla I + II (+ fl 8va) bc — a/b $\frac{3}{4}$

O Seelenparadies,	O souls' paradise
Das Gottes Geist durchwehet,	That God's Spirit wafts through,
Der bei der Schöpfung blies,	As it breathed at the Creation,
Der Geist, der nie vergehet.	The Spirit that never passes away.
Auf, auf, bereite dich,	Rise up, make ready:
Der Tröster nahet sich!	The Comforter approaches!

5. Aria [Duetto] SA ob (d'am) vc obbl or SA org obbl — F/G c

Anima	*Soul*
Komm, laß mich nicht länger warten,	Come, let me wait no longer,
Komm, du sanfter Himmelswind,	Come, you gentle wind of heaven,
Wehe durch den Herzensgarten!	Waft through the garden of the heart!
Spiritus Sanctus	*Holy Spirit*
Ich erquicke dich, mein Kind.	I will refresh you, my child.
Anima	*Soul*
Liebste Liebe, die so süße,	Dearest Love, who are so sweet,
Aller Wollust Überfluß!	The abundance of all delight!

[70] The first specified key refers to *Chorton** (in Leipzig performances, *Kammerton*), the second to *Kammerton*.

Ich vergeh, wenn ich dich misse.	I shall die if I am without You.
Spiritus Sanctus	*Holy Spirit*
Nimm von mir den Gnadenkuß.	Take from me the kiss of grace.
Anima	*Soul*
Sei im Glauben mir willkommen,	I welcome You in Faith,
Höchste Liebe, komm herein!	Highest Love, come within!
Du hast mir das Herz genommen.	You have ravished my heart.
Spiritus Sanctus	*Holy Spirit*
Ich bin dein, und du bist mein!	I am yours and you are Mine!

6. CHORALE SATB vln I (+ fl) bc (+ other ww str) F/G c

Von Gott kömmt mir ein Freudenschein,	**From God a light of joy comes to me**
Wenn du mit deinen Äugelein	**When with Your lovely eyes**
Mich freundlich tust anblicken.	**You cast a friendly eye on me.**
O Herr Jesu, mein trautes Gut,	**O Lord Jesus, my beloved treasure,**
Dein Wort, dein Geist, dein Leib und Blut	**Your Word, Spirit, Body and Blood**
Mich innerlich erquicken:	**Refresh me within:**
Nimm mich freundlich	**Take me like a friend**
In deine Arme, daß ich warme werd von Gnaden:	**In Your arms, that I may grow warm through grace:**
Auf dein Wort komm ich geladen.	**At Your Word I come invited.**

7. CHORUS REPETATUR AB INITIO (repeat of no. 1; omitted in late revivals)

This cantata, written in Weimar for 20 May 1714, is probably the third in the series of sacred works that Bach was obliged to compose and perform after his appointment as Concermaster on 2 March 1714. Although the libretto is not included in Salomo Franck's printed collections of verse, his authorship is revealed with sufficient certainty in a number of stylistic idiosyncracies. From a formal standpoint, this type of Franck text is characterized by a succession of several arias and by the absence of freely versified recitative. Though Franck cannot be classified as a Pietist, the substance of the libretto is nonetheless close to pietistic modes of thought. This is generally manifest in a certain exuberance of feeling ('O most blessed times!') and, more specifically, in the mystical demeanour of the duet between the Soul and the Holy Spirit that forms the third aria ('. . . I am yours and you are mine!'). In addition, the concluding chorale—the fourth verse of the hymn *Wie schön leuchtet der Morgenstern* by Philipp Nicolai (1599)—is an early example of the mystical frame of mind, with its emphasis on feeling, out of which Pietism emerged.

In his setting, Bach seeks to emphasize the festive character of the Pentecost text. As a result, the work acquires a notably 'secular' character, particularly in the opening chorus:* indeed, it is not wholly unthinkable that this chorus might be drawn from a lost congratulatory cantata. On the other hand, it might have been Bach's desire to exhibit the full diversity of his stylistic resources, as well as his own capabilities, that induced him to employ a different compositional principle in each of the opening choruses of a series of cantatas begun in 1714, not excluding the festive concerto movement as illustrated here. In this opening chorus, cast in pure da capo* form, the trumpets, with drums as their bass instrument, and the strings plus oboe form antiphonal choirs of instruments, to which the vocal choir is added as a third participant after the introductory ritornello. The texture is predominantly chordal or freely polyphonic,* changing in the middle section to imitative* polyphony sung by the choir, doubled by strings (the trumpets are here silent). In this bipartite, motet-like middle section, it is charming to observe how Bach first builds the imitative texture upwards from the bass, only to lead it downwards again from the soprano in the second half.

The following biblical-text recitative, no. 2, reiterates an extract from the Gospel* read out beforehand (John 14.23) and also provides a theme for exegesis in the madrigalian* movements. Later on, during his Leipzig period, Bach tends to place such biblical texts at the beginning of a work, preferring to set them as large-scale choruses (as in his setting of the same text in Cantata 74, for example). In 1714, however, he preferred the persuasive, declamatory form of recitative, which is here elevated in significance by the rhythmically fixed, arioso* style of the closing bars. For the aria 'Heiligste Dreieinigkeit', no. 3, Bach chooses the rare scoring of trumpets, drums, and continuo as concertante* counterpart to the vocal bass—a choice of special consequence at the time, since the trumpet, then considered a specifically 'courtly' instrument, is here included to symbolize the sovereign power of God.

It is evident that the display of splendour in the opening chorus and the first aria has to be followed by a substantial contrast. This is supplied, in the aria no. 4, by violins and violas in unison (supported by flute an octave higher at a later performance), playing a flowing melody that represents the wafting of the divine Spirit. This, in conjunction with the chosen triple time, conveys the impression of release from all earthly gravity. Only in the second half of the middle section does vigorous triadic melody come to the fore at the words 'Rise up, make ready'.

The design of the fifth movement is most ingenious: Bach combines the three-verse poem of the duet with the chorale melody *Komm, Heiliger Geist, Herre Gott*, which—in a scarcely recognizable form on account of its extremely rich ornamentation—is played line by line on the oboe (or, in a later performance, on obbligato* organ) as an accompaniment to the vocal duet. In the introductory ritornello, the chorale melody is already implied in the top notes of the cello ostinato* figures. At the vocal entry, the texture is expanded to a quartet, made up of soprano (the Soul), alto (the Holy Spirit), oboe (the chorale) and cello (continuo)—a texture of admirable, filigree-like polyphony.

In the concluding chorale, as often in Bach's early cantatas, an independent fifth part for violin I is added to the plain four-part choral texture, doubled by instruments. At least in some of Bach's performances, this was followed by a reprise of the opening chorus to round off the work. Bach revived the cantata several times in Leipzig,[71] making various alterations for this purpose. For the key of the work, he sometimes chose D major, which would have corresponded roughly with Choir-Pitch* C in Weimar, and sometimes C major. All the various changes he made show how much trouble Bach took over a work which—as the number of documented performances (at least four) suggests—he seems to have particularly loved.

Wer mich liebet, der wird mein Wort halten, BWV 59

NBA I/13, p. 67 BC A82 Duration: *c.* 14 mins

1. DUETTO SB tr I,II timp str bc — C 𝄴

'Wer mich liebet, der wird mein Wort halten, und mein Vater wird ihn lieben, und wir werden zu ihm kommen und Wohnung bei ihm machen.'	'Whoever loves me will keep my Word, and my Father will love him, and we will come to him and make our abode with him.'

2. RECITATIVO S str bc — a–G 𝄴

O, was sind das vor Ehren,	Oh, what are those honours
Worzu uns Jesus setzt?	To which Jesus leads us?
Der uns so würdig schätzt,	He who values us so highly
Daß er verheißt,	That He promises,
Samt Vater und dem heilgen Geist	Together with Father and Holy Spirit,
In unsern Herzen einzukehren.	To dwell in our hearts.
O! was sind das vor Ehren?	Oh! what are those honours?
Der Mensch ist Staub,	Mankind is dust,
Der Eitelkeit ihr Raub,	The spoils of vanity,
Der Müh und Arbeit Trauerspiel	The tragic stage play of sorrow and labour,
Und alles Elends Zweck und Ziel.	And purpose and goal of all misery.
Wie nun? Der Allerhöchste spricht:	What, then? The Almighty says:
Er will in unsern Seelen	He will in our souls
Die Wohnung sich erwählen?	Choose His dwelling-place.
Ach, was tut Gottes Liebe nicht?	Ah, what does God's Love not do?
Ach, daß doch, wie er wollte,	Ah, would that, as He wished,
Ihn auch ein jeder lieben sollte!	Everyone should love Him too!

3. CHORALE SATB str bc — G 𝄴

Komm, Heiliger Geist, Herre Gott,	**Come, Holy Spirit, Lord God,**
Erfüll mit deiner Gnaden Gut	**Fill with the goodness of Your grace**

[71] Details of the various performances are given by D. Kilian in KB, NBA I/13 (1960), 35 ff.

Deiner Gläubigen Herz, Mut und Sinn.	**The heart, will, and mind of Your believers.**
Dein brünstig Lieb entzünd in ihn'.	**Enkindle Your burning Love within them.**
O Herr, durch deines Lichtes Glanz	**O Lord, through the radiance of Your Light**
Zu dem Glauben versammlet hast	**You have assembled in the Faith**
Das Volk aus aller Welt Zungen;	**People of all the world's tongues;**
Das sei dir, Herr, zu Lob gesungen.	**May that be sung, Lord, to Your praise.**
Alleluja, alleluja!	**Alleluia, alleluia!**

4. Aria B vln solo bc C c

Die Welt mit allen Königreichen,	The world with all its kingdoms,
Die Welt mit aller Herrlichkeit	The world with all its glory
Kann dieser Herrlichkeit nicht gleichen,	Cannot compare with this glory
Womit uns unser Gott erfreut:	With which our God delights us:
Daß er in unsern Herzen thronet	That He is enthroned in our hearts
Und wie in einem Himmel wohnet.	And dwells as in a heaven.
Ach! Gott, wie selig sind wir doch!	Ah! God, how blessed we are indeed!
Wie selig werden wir erst noch,	How blessed shall we yet become
Wenn wir nach dieser Zeit der Erden	When after this time on earth
Bei dir im Himmel wohnen werden?	We shall dwell with you in heaven!

The origin of this little work is not altogether clear. The autograph score was written for Whit (16 May) 1723 at the latest, but the surviving original performing parts not till the following year, for 28 May 1724. From the choice of text it follows that the composition must have originated in reduced circumstances, for Bach set the libretto—from Erdmann Neumeister's fourth cycle of 1714—only in part.[72] In addition, the work makes only moderate demands on the capability of the performers. And the instrumentation, though decidedly festive with its two trumpets and drums, plus the usual strings and continuo, nonetheless lacks a third trumpet, which is otherwise invariably required in Bach's festive orchestra, and includes no woodwind instruments at all. The vocal ensemble is restricted to soprano and bass, which are joined by alto and tenor only in the plain chorale, no. 3. All these observations justify Arnold Schering's conjecture[73] that Bach composed the cantata for a Leipzig University service. But it remains unclear whether it was performed in 1723, in which case the original performing materials must be lost, or whether Bach postponed its first performance till the following year, as the extant performing parts suggest. Finally, there remains

[72] The missing movements are nos. 5–7: the chorale 'Gott heiliger Geist, du Tröster wert' (verse 3 of *Erhalt uns, Herr, bei deinem Wort*), the biblical quotation 'Gott der Hoffnung erfülle euch . . .' (Rom. 15.13), and the aria 'Ich bin der Seligkeit gewiß'.

[73] *BJ* 1938, 75 ff.

the possibility that the work originated still earlier for an unknown purpose, though that does not affect the performance verified for 1724.

The text begins with a quotation from the Gospel* reading—the same passage that Franck quoted in his text for Cantata 172 (John 14.23). In the other movements set by Bach, the librettist first praises the inordinate love of God for the frail human race (no. 2), then prays for the coming of the Holy Spirit (no. 3) in the words of Martin Luther—from the first verse of his Pentecost hymn of 1524—and finally points out, in a truly baroque manner, how much happier the Christian will be in heaven.

In his setting, Bach proves himself to be a master even in limitation. The opening duet begins with a short instrumental prelude, whose head-motive then serves as the opening of all the vocal passages:

The duet itself is divided into five sections, each of which presents the entire text: the first four canonic, though with frequent intervallic alteration, in the keys C–G, C–a, a–d and F–C, and the fifth homophonic,* in parallel sixths, in the key of C. The fourth section is, except in the instruments, a subdominant transposition of the first, which gives the impression of an implied reprise, and the fifth section follows by way of coda. The instrumental accompaniment is independent and—apart from the frequent repetition of the head-motive—unthematic. The answering phrase of the instrumental prelude acquires no significance at all during the movement, and the postlude is even given a new answering phrase, which likewise displays no thematic connection with what precedes it.

The following recitative with string accompaniment, no. 2, ends with the sentence 'Ah, would that, as He wished, everyone should love Him too!', whose last phrase, as often in Bach's earlier works, is set as arioso,* accompanied only by continuo. The chorale, no. 3, is a plain choral setting, but the second violin and viola have partly independent parts, which makes the movement sound particularly full in texture, even though no real six-part writing is heard.

The last movement is a bass aria with an obbligato* part for solo violin. The relatively long text is set in two parts, of which the first (in itself articulated musically according to the scheme A A B) derives its thematic material strictly from the opening ritornello, whereas the second is more freely structured. Scholars have puzzled greatly over the question whether the cantata should end with this aria, whether Neumeister's fifth movement should have followed as a closing chorale, or whether nos. 3 and 4 should be performed in the reverse order. Nothing of this sort may be concluded from the autograph score, and the puzzling inscription 'Chorale segue' at the end of the original bass part leaves us without any definite information as to what is required. Perhaps a concluding chorale was played by reading from the performing parts of another work. In any event, a definitive explanation is possible only in the unlikely event of a new discovery.

Wer mich liebet, der wird mein Wort halten, BWV 74

NBA I/13, p. 85 BC A83 Duration: *c.* 24 mins

1. [Chorus] SATB tr I–III timp ob I,II ob da c str bc		C c
'Wer mich liebet, der wird mein Wort halten, und mein Vater wird ihn lieben, und wir werden zu ihm kommen und Wohnung bei ihm machen.'	'Whoever loves me will keep my Word, and my Father will love him, and we will come to him and make our abode with him.'	
2. Aria S ob da c bc		F c
Komm, komm, mein Herze steht dir offen, Ach, laß es deine Wohnung sein! Ich liebe dich, so muß ich hoffen: Dein Wort trifft itzo bei mir ein; Denn wer dich sucht, fürcht', liebt und ehret, Dem ist der Vater zugetan. Ich zweifle nicht, ich bin erhöret, Daß ich mich dein getrösten kann.	Come, come, my heart is open to You: Ah, let it be Your dwelling-place! I love You, so I must hope that Your Word will now come true in me; For whoever seeks, fears, loves, and honours You, To him the Father is attached. I do not doubt that I have been heard, So that I can have confidence in You.	
3. Recitativo A bc		d–a c
Die Wohnung ist bereit. Du findst ein Herz, das dir allein ergeben, Drum laß mich nicht erleben, Daß du gedenkst, von mir zu gehn. Das laß ich nimmermehr, ach, nimmermehr geschehen!	Your dwelling is ready. You find a heart that is devoted to You alone, Therefore do not let me experience That You consider going away from me. I will let that happen nevermore, ah, nevermore!	
4. Aria B bc		e c
'Ich gehe hin und komme wieder zu euch. Hättet ihr mich lieb, so würdet ihr euch freuen.'	'I go away and come back to you again. If you loved Me, you would rejoice.'	
5. Aria T str bc		G c
Kommt, eilet, stimmet Sait und Lieder In muntern und erfreuten Ton! Geht er gleich weg, so kömmt er wieder, Der hochgelobte Gottessohn.	Come, hasten, voice strings and songs In a lively and delighted sound! Though He goes away, He comes back again, The highly praised Son of God.	

Der Satan wird indes versuchen,	Satan will meanwhile attempt
Den Deinigen gar sehr zu fluchen.	Greatly to curse those who follow You.
Er ist mir hinderlich,	He is a hindrance to me,
So glaub ich, Herr, an dich.	So I have faith, Lord, in You.

6. RECITATIVO B ob I,II ob da c bc — e–C 𝄴

'Es ist nichts Verdammliches an denen, die in Christo Jesu sind.'	'There is no condemnation for those who are in Christ Jesus.'

7. ARIA A ob I,II ob da c vln I solo other str bc — C $\frac{3}{8}$

Nichts kann mich erretten	Nothing can deliver me
Von höllischen Ketten	From hellish chains
Als, Jesu, dein Blut.	Other than Your Blood, O Jesus.
Dein Leiden, dein Sterben	Your Passion, Your dying
Macht mich ja zum Erben:	Indeed make me an heir:
Ich lache der Wut.	I laugh at hell's rage.

8. CHORALE SATB bc (+ most instrs) — a 𝄴

Kein Menschenkind hier auf der Erd	**No child of man here on earth**
Ist dieser edlen Gabe wert,	**Is worthy of this noble gift:**
Bei uns ist kein Verdienen;	**In us there is no merit;**
Hier gilt gar nichts als Lieb und Gnad,	**Here nothing counts but love and grace,**
Die Christus uns verdienet hat	**Which Christ has earned for us**
Mit Büßen und Versühnen.	**By atonement and expiation.**

Bach wrote this cantata for 20 May 1725 to a text by the poet Christiane Mariane von Ziegler. For at least two of the movements he made use of earlier music: nos. 1 and 2 are drawn from Cantata 59 (nos. 1 and 4), with which, in its existing form, the composer was no doubt dissatisfied in the long run. It is not known whether the other movements also include parodies: if so, their model is lost. With Picander, Bach was accustomed to reach agreement on parody* schemes that suited the metre of the original, but this was apparently not the case with Mariane von Ziegler. Although Bach made several alterations to the wording, as in the other Ziegler texts, neither he nor Ziegler made any attempt to assimilate the verse structure of the second movement to that of its parody model, Cantata 59, no. 4.

As in Cantata 59, the freely versified text is prefaced by a passage from the Gospel* for Whit Sunday (John 14.23). To this the faithful Christian adds the prayer that Jesus will make His dwelling in his heart, too, and nevermore depart from him (nos. 2 and 3). Christ answers this prayer with another passage from the Gospel reading (no. 4): 'I go away and come back to you again. If you loved Me, you would rejoice' (John 14.28); and the following aria, no. 5, celebrates in joyful sounds this promise of the Second Coming of Christ. Meanwhile, we are told in the middle section of the aria that many temptations from Satan are to be withstood in faith. A third biblical passage, Romans 8.1, dispels this reflection also: 'There is no condemnation for those who are in Christ Jesus' (no. 6). Even 'hellish chains' can no longer harm the Christian, who is appointed heir of heaven through Jesus's Blood (no. 7). The cantata concludes with the second verse of Paul Gerhardt's hymn *Gott Vater, sende deinen Geist* (1653).

The opening chorus* is a skilful expansion of the opening duet from Cantata 59. The instrumental texture is enriched by a third trumpet and a three-part choir of oboes (two oboes and oboe da caccia*); and the music that was formerly assigned to strings only is effectively divided between strings and oboes, which sometimes play independently of each other and elsewhere together. The structure of the model, together with its length in number of bars, is essentially maintained. Even the expansion of the five vocal duet passages in terms of four-part choir is done without altering the basic scheme, as is clear from the longer duet passages which are simply transferred to the new version. Nevertheless, Bach succeeds in enriching the voice parts in various ways: by vocalizing former instrumental parts, by transferring formerly independent bass passages to the alto or making the new bass part double the continuo, and by adding newly composed parts.

It also proved possible to adopt the second movement from Cantata 59, no. 4, without making radical alterations. The transposition to F major goes hand in hand with the replacement of solo violin by oboe da caccia and of bass voice by soprano, but the overall number of bars and formal structure remain unaltered. A short *secco* recitative leads to the fourth movement, a bass solo of the kind that Bach often chose for the setting of Jesus's words. The continuo accompaniment consists of a *basso quasi ostinato*,* whose basic form, stated at the outset, musically enacts the 'going away' and 'coming back again' of the text in its rising and falling motion. The second section, 'If you loved Me . . .', is shaped more freely and characterized by text-engendered coloraturas* on 'freuen' ('rejoice'). The last vocal passage is combined with a literal reprise of the second half of the continuo ritornello, after which the entire ritornello is heard once more as an instrumental postlude.

If the monodic, declamatory principle comes to the fore in the fourth movement, in the fifth it is the concertante* principle. The string texture is here dominated by the first violin, while the other instruments for the most part merely provide harmonic support. The generally joyful tone of the text is reflected in the extended coloraturas of the voice and in the lively instrumental parts.

Whereas the first biblical passage was set as a concerted chorus and the second as a bass solo over a continuo ostinato, the third, no. 6, is an oboe-accompanied recitative of only five bars with plain, syllabic* declamation. It is followed by the last aria, no. 7: a lively, dance-like piece in which woodwind and string choirs engage in antiphonal exchanges. Also present is a solo violin, whose virtuoso broken-chordal figurations, like the repeated semiquavers of the other instruments, were perhaps stimulated by imagining the clanking of the 'hellish chains'. The plain concluding chorale is based on the melody *Kommt her zu mir, spricht Gottes Sohn*.

O ewiges Feuer, o Ursprung der Liebe, BWV 34

NBA I/13, p. 131 BC A84 Duration: *c.* 21 mins

1.	[CHORUS] SATB tr I–III timp ob I,II str bc	D 3/4
	O ewiges Feuer, o Ursprung der Liebe, Entzünde die Herzen und weihe sie ein. Laß himmlische Flammen durchdringen und wallen, Wir wünschen, o Höchster, dein Tempel zu sein, Ach, laß dir die Seelen im Glauben gefallen!	O eternal Fire, O source of Love, Enkindle our hearts and consecrate them. Let heavenly flames penetrate and well up; We desire, O most High, to be Your temple; Ah, let our souls please You in faith!
2.	RECITATIVO T bc	b–f♯ c
	Herr, unsre Herzen halten dir Dein Wort der Wahrheit für: Du willst bei Menschen gerne sein, Drum sei das Herze dein; Herr, ziehe gnädig ein. Ein solch erwähltes Heiligtum Hat selbst den größten Ruhm.	Lord, our hearts hold out to You Your Word of Truth: You would gladly be with man, Therefore may my heart be Yours; Lord, graciously enter it. Such a chosen sanctuary Itself has the greatest renown.
3.	ARIA A str + fl I,II 8va bc	A c
	Wohl euch, ihr auserwählten Seelen, Die Gott zur Wohnung ausersehn! Wer kann ein größer Heil erwählen? Wer kann des Segens Menge zählen? Und dieses ist vom Herrn geschehn.	Blessed are you, you chosen souls, Whom God has selected for His dwelling! Who could choose a grander salvation? Who count the multitude of blessings? And this is the Lord's doing.
4.	RECITATIVO B bc	f♯–A c
	Erwählt sich Gott die heilgen Hütten, Die er mit Heil bewohnt, So muß er auch den Segen auf sie schütten, So wird der Sitz des Heiligtums belohnt. Der Herr ruft über sein geweihtes Haus Das Wort des Segens aus:	If God chooses the holy tabernacles, Which He inhabits with salvation, Then He must also pour blessing on them, Then the seat of the sanctuary is rewarded. The Lord calls out over His consecrated house These words of blessing:
5.	TUTTI SATB tr I–III timp str + ob I,II bc	D c ¢
	'Friede über Israel!'	'Peace upon Israel!'

Dankt den höchsten Wunderhänden,	Thank the wondrous hands of the Highest,
Dankt, Gott hat an euch gedacht!	Be thankful: God has been mindful of you!
Ja, sein Segen wirkt mit Macht,	Yes, His Blessing works mightily
Friede über Israel,	To send peace upon Israel,
Friede über euch zu senden.	Peace upon you.

This cantata is an exceptionally late work, dating from around 1746/7. In all essentials, however, it is based on a wedding cantata with the same opening line (BWV 34a) which dates from 1726. Bach may have been stimulated to reuse it for Whit Sunday by the image of 'heavenly flames' that determines both the text and music of the opening chorus.* The anonymous librettist was assigned the task of modelling the opening and closing choruses and the aria sufficiently closely on the existing wedding cantata that the music at hand might be reused with the fewest possible alterations. Although the connection with Whit Sunday often finds expression only in general turns of phrase, the librettist carried out his task with considerable skill. The opening words, which even in the wedding cantata had evoked the aid of the Holy Spirit, already establish a link with the 'cloven tongues as if of fire' of the Epistle* reading (Acts 2.3). The Gospel* for the day culminates in two sayings of Jesus: 'Whoever loves me will keep my word, and my Father will love him, and we will come to him and make our abode with him' (John 14.23) and 'Peace I leave with you, my peace I give to you' (John 14.27). The newly written recitatives refer to the first saying, no. 2 in its reference to the 'Word of Truth' and its prayer that the Lord will enter into our heart, and no. 4 in its mention of the 'holy tabernacles' inhabited by God. The aria paraphrase, no. 3, also alludes to Jesus's first saying in its exaltation of the 'chosen souls whom God has selected for His dwelling' (the last line, 'And this is the Lord's doing', is a quotation from Psalm 118.23). The psalm text of the closing chorus, on the other hand, 'Peace upon Israel!' (Psalm 128.6—probably once sung at the wedding of a minister) refers to the second saying of Jesus.

The music that Bach set aside for this libretto is of bewitching charm. The lively figuration of the opening chorus, inspired by the image of licking flames, is interlaced with long-held notes, first on the trumpet and later in the voice parts, to illustrate the word 'ewiges' ('eternal'). Despite its resplendent scoring, this movement, designed in pure da capo* form, makes a transparent and elated effect throughout. A short recitative leads to the only aria in the cantata, whose pastoral character is comprehensible in the light of its original text, 'Blessed are you, you chosen sheep': the minister-bridegroom was formerly honoured here as shepherd of his congregation. The scoring is rare: muted violins doubled at the octave by flutes, with repeated pedal notes in the bass, lend the music an unearthly calm. The aria is rightly regarded as one of Bach's happiest inspirations. No less impressive is the concluding chorus, into which the intervening bars of recitative directly flow. It is introduced by two solemn, chordal Adagio bars—'Peace upon Israel!'—and then launches into a lively bipartite structure in which each section is heard twice, first on the instruments alone and then again with the addition of the choir.

1.32 Whit Monday

EPISTLE: Acts 10.42–8: The end of Peter's sermon before Cornelius; the baptism of the Gentiles.

GOSPEL: John 3.16–21: 'God so loved the world . . .'.

Erhöhtes Fleisch und Blut, BWV 173

NBA I/14, p. 3 BC A85 Duration: *c.* 17 mins

1. RECITATIVO T str bc — D C

Erhöhtes Fleisch und Blut,	Raised flesh and blood,
Das Gott selbst an sich nimmt,	Which God takes upon Himself,
Dem er schon hier auf Erden	For which already here on earth
Ein himmlisch Heil bestimmt,	He ordains a heavenly salvation,
Des Höchsten Kind zu werden,	To become a child of the most High;
Erhöhtes Fleisch und Blut!	Raised flesh and blood!

2. ARIA T str + fl I + II bc — D C

Ein geheiligtes Gemüte	A sanctified disposition
Sieht und schmecket Gottes Güte.	Sees and tastes God's goodness.
Rühmet, singet, stimmt die Saiten,	Praise, sing, tune the strings
Gottes Treue auszubreiten!	To spread God's faithfulness!

3. [ALTO SOLO] A str bc — b C

Gott will, o! ihr Menschenkinder,	God will, O you children of men,
An euch große Dinge tun.	Do great things to you.
Mund und Herze, Ohr und Blicke	Mouth and heart, ear and sight
Können nicht bei diesem Glücke	Cannot rest amidst this fortune
Und so heilger Freude ruhn.	And such holy joy.

4. ARIA [DUETTO] SB fl I,II str bc — G–D–A $\frac{3}{4}$

Baß	*Bass*
So hat Gott die Welt geliebt,	God has so loved the world—
Sein Erbarmen	His mercy
Hilft uns Armen,	Helps us poor ones—
Daß er seinen Sohn uns gibt,	That He gives us His Son,
Gnadengaben zu genießen,	To partake of the gifts of grace
Die wie reiche Ströme fließen.	That flow like rich streams.
Sopran	*Soprano*
Sein verneuter Gnadenbund	His renewed Covenant of Grace
Ist geschäftig	Is effective
Und wird kräftig	And grows powerful

In der Menschen Herz und Mund,	In the human heart and mouth,
Daß sein Geist zu seiner Ehre	So that His Spirit, to His honour,
Gläubig zu ihm rufen lehre.	Teaches them to cry out to Him in faith.
beide	*both*
Nun wir lassen unsre Pflicht	Now we let our duty
Opfer bringen,	Bring an offering,
Dankend singen,	Sing gratefully,
Da sein offenbartes Licht	For His manifested Light
Sich zu seinen Kindern neiget	Inclines to His children
Und sich ihnen kräftig zeiget.	And appears mightily to them.
5. Recitativo [Duetto] ST bc	f♯–b c
Unendlichster, den man doch Vater nennt,	Everlasting One, whom we nonetheless call Father,
Wir wollen dann das Herz zum Opfer bringen,	We would bring, then, our heart as an offering
Aus unsrer Brust, die ganz vor Andacht brennt,	From out of our breast, which quite burns with devotion;
Soll sich der Seufzer Glut zum Himmel schwingen.	The ardour of our sighs shall soar up to heaven.
6. Chorus SATB fl I + II str bc	D $\frac{3}{4}$
Rühre, Höchster, unsern Geist,	Stir, O Most High, our spirit,
Daß des höchsten Geistes Gaben	That the gifts of the highest Spirit
Ihre Würkung in uns haben!	May have their effect in us!
Da dein Sohn uns beten heißt,	Since Your Son bids us pray,
Wird es durch die Wolken dringen	Our prayer will pierce the clouds
Und Erhörung auf uns bringen.	And give us a hearing.

This work, which is based on the Cöthen congratulatory cantata BWV 173a, was, in all probability, first performed as a church cantata on 29 May 1724. No sources for that performance have been transmitted, however, and we can only conjecture that the version then performed might have been, in many respects, still closer to its secular model than the version we know. The work did not acquire its present form till about 1728 (or 1727?) or, at the latest, 1731—a performance that year is testified by a printed libretto. The unknown author of the sacred paraphrase closely parodied not only the arias and the closing chorus* but also the two recitatives, nos. 1 and 5: evidently the music for all the movements of the new cantata was to be adopted from the secular model. The content of the text is formulated in very general terms, thanking God and praising Him for the great things He does for mankind. Only in the first movement and, above all, in the first strophe of the fourth, are closer connections established with the Gospel* for Whit Monday.

Despite many alterations of detail, the music of the cantata often betrays its secular origin. The two vocal parts are increased to four; two movements from the secular work are omitted (BWV 173a/6 and 7, of which the second recurs as

BWV 175/4); and, particularly in the opening recitative, the vocal writing is adapted to suit the new text. Yet the instrumental writing throughout remains essentially the same as before. In so far as the music of Cantata 173a was adopted unchanged, the reader is referred to the discussion of that work. Here, then, it will suffice to point out the special features of the sacred version BWV 173.

As already mentioned, despite its character as a recitative, the first movement is a textual parody* of the equivalent movement in Cantata 173a. Even the return of the opening line at the close is maintained. Bach assigned the parody to tenor in place of soprano and substantially altered the melodic line of the voice part, entering these alterations in the secular score—an exceptional procedure within the source material known to us. The accompaniment, however, and hence the harmonic shape of the movement too, remains untouched.

Apart from the adaptation of the voice parts to the parody text and various exchanges in the pitch of parts, nos. 2–5 show no essential alterations. The fully scored dance-like aria no. 2, the short, aria-like but unthematic third movement, the three-strophe fourth movement (quite exceptionally conceived in variation form, with a gradual enhancement of scoring and rhythmic movement), indeed even the duet-recitative, no. 5, which changes to arioso* after 4 bars: all these movements recur in the sacred version. They are followed by the final chorus of the secular version as no. 6, with its vocal parts increased from two to four, though in keeping with the compositional structure—choral insertion* within an instrumental dance movement—the four-part vocal texture is restricted to plain homophony. The imitative* duet passages occasionally recall the original version of the movement. Its binary form, with choral insertion within the reprise of each half (A A + choir B B + choir) remains unchanged.

Also hat Gott die Welt geliebt, BWV 68

NBA I/14, p. 33 BC A86 Duration: *c.* 20 mins

1. CHORAL S + hn ATB str + ob I,II + taille bc d $\frac{12}{8}$

Also hat Gott die Welt geliebt,	**God so loved the world**
Daß er uns seinen Sohn gegeben.	**That He gave us His Son.**
Wer sich im Glauben ihm ergibt,	**Whoever submits to Him in faith**
Der soll dort ewig bei ihm leben.	**Shall live with Him there for ever.**
Wer glaubt, daß Jesus ihm geboren,	**Whoever believes Jesus was born for him**
Der bleibet ewig unverloren,	**Remains forever unforlorn;**
Und ist kein Leid, das den betrübt,	**And there is no trouble that vexes him**
Den Gott und auch sein Jesus liebt.	**Whom God and likewise His Jesus love.**

2. ARIA S vc picc bc + RITORNELLO ob I vln I vc picc bc F ¢

Mein gläubiges Herze,	My believing heart,
Frohlocke, sing, scherze,	Exult, sing, jest,

Dein Jesus ist da!
  Weg Jammer, weg Klagen,
  Ich will euch nur sagen:
  Mein Jesus ist nah.
	Your Jesus is here!
	  Away with distress and lamentation;
	  I will say to you only:
	  My Jesus is near.

3. Recitativo B bc — d–G 𝄴

Ich bin mit Petro nicht vermessen,
Was mich getrost und freudig macht,
Daß mich mein Jesus nicht vergessen.
Er kam nicht nur, die Welt zu richten,
Nein, nein, er wollte Sünd und Schuld
Als Mittler zwischen Gott und Mensch
  vor diesmal schlichten.
	With Peter, I am not presumptuous,
	Which makes me confident and joyful
	That my Jesus does not forget me.
	He came not only to judge the world,
	No, no, He wished to straighten out
	Sin and guilt once and for all as mediator
	  between God and man.

4. Aria B ob I,II taille bc — C 𝄴

Du bist geboren mir zugute,
Das glaub ich, mir ist wohl zumute,
Weil du vor mich genung getan.
  Das Rund der Erden mag gleich
    brechen,
  Will mir der Satan widersprechen,
  So bet ich dich, mein Heiland, an.
	You have been born for my benefit:
	That I believe; I am in good heart,
	Since You have done enough for me.
	  Though the earth's sphere might
	    break,
	  And Satan would oppose me,
	  Yet I would pray to You, my Saviour.

5. Chorus SATB (+ ctt trb I–III + ww + str) bc — a–d 𝄵

'Wer an ihn gläubet, der wird nicht gerichtet; wer aber nicht gläubet, der ist schon gerichtet; denn er gläubet nicht an den Namen des eingebornen Sohnes Gottes,'	'Whoever believes in Him is not condemned; but whoever does not believe is condemned already, for he does not believe in the Name of the only begotten Son of God.'

This cantata, composed for 21 May 1725, belongs among the nine compositions to texts by the poet Christiane Mariane von Ziegler with which Bach ended his second Leipzig cycle of 1724–5, a cycle mostly devoted to chorale cantatas.* Later, Bach removed most of the non-chorale-based cantatas from the cycle, retaining only Cantatas 128 and 68. Those two are not genuine chorale cantatas, of course, but they open with a concerted chorale movement and are therefore related to the chorale cantata.

The text refers to the Gospel* for Whit Monday, which had been read out before the performance. The first words of the reading are taken up again in the opening chorale—the first verse of the hymn by Salomo Liscow (1675). In the recitative, no. 3, reference is again made to words from the Gospel: 'God sent His Son into the world not to condemn the world but so that the world might be saved through Him' (John 3.17); and the concluding chorus* is a literal quotation from John 3.18. The recitative words 'With Peter, I am not presumptuous' (no. 3) clearly allude to the Epistle* reading for the day. They have been linked with Peter's words to Cornelius (which precede the reading), 'Stand up, I too am a man' (Acts 10.26). Yet they might also apply to the closing words of the reading, in which Peter pacifies those Jewish followers of Jesus who were outraged that the Holy Spirit descended on the Gentiles too: 'May anyone forbid water, that these should not be baptized, who have received the Holy Spirit just as we have?' (Acts 10.47). This would signify that the Spirit blows where it will—even Gentile sinners against God's commandments will partake of Him—and I am unassuming and grateful that the Saviour has not forgotten me, an idea linked to the words 'all who believe in Him' shall have eternal life, and taken up again in the following aria 'Du bist geboren mir zugute'.

In the large-scale opening chorus, Bach adopts the melody by Gottfried Vopelius (1682) that belongs to the hymn, stating it in the soprano (supported by horn) and reshaping it in a remarkably expressive manner, with the result that—particularly to the modern listener who no longer knows the original melody—it hardly seems like a chorale any more. The introduction and episodes for strings, supported by oboes, develop a theme in siciliano rhythm which is independent of the chorale; and even the lower vocal parts—chordal or lightly broken up into polyphony*—are largely unrelated to the chorale melody. In this way a cheerfully relaxed and amiably buoyant movement (despite the minor mode of the chorale melody) emerges that gives expression to our joy over the Pentecost miracle. As a chorale arrangement, it probably belongs among the freest that Bach ever wrote.

Ever since the earliest years of the Bach renaissance, the aria 'Mein gläubiges Herze' (no. 2) has enjoyed quite exceptional popularity. It is adapted from the aria 'Weil die wollenreichen Herden' from the 'Hunt' Cantata, BWV 208 (no. 13). The ostinato* theme, originally in the continuo, is now entrusted to the violoncello piccolo,* and the continuo is given a new bass part made up largely of supporting notes. The most radically altered part, however, is that of the soprano: the original, simple song-like melody turns into an extremely lively part characterized by wide intervallic leaps and embellished by numerous small melismas.* Finally, Bach appends to the aria a 'ritornello' in which the violoncello piccolo is joined by oboe and violin, and supported by continuo, in a spirited terzetto based on the instrumental theme of the aria. This ritornello was also present in the score of the Hunt Cantata as an independent instrumental piece.

The second aria, no. 4, separated from the first by a brief *secco* recitative, is likewise drawn from the 'Hunt' Cantata (no. 7), where it was assigned to Pan, the god of woods and shepherds, hence its scoring for three instruments of the oboe family (two oboes and taille*). As in the first aria, no attempt is made to assimilate the verse structure of the text to that of its model. Consequently Bach was obliged to undertake a far-reaching musical adaptation, though no such radical melodic changes as those of the soprano aria proved necessary.

The work concludes with a motet-like chorus* in which the voices are reinforced not only by the strings and oboes used beforehand but also by a choir of trombones, with the cornett as their treble instrument. It takes the form of a double fugue,* opening with the first subject on 'Wer an ihn gläubet, der wird nicht gerichtet', after which, sixteen bars later, we hear the former countersubject as an independent second subject to the words 'wer aber nicht gläubet, der ist schon gerichtet'; the two subjects are then combined. Finally, in the last bars of the movement, the first subject is sung to a new text, 'denn er gläubet nicht an den Namen des eingebornen Sohnes Gottes'. Like many early cantatas or cantata movements by Bach, the chorus ends *piano*, according to Bach's explicit instruction. This gives rise to an echo effect which for us, after the age of Beethoven, Bruckner, and Reger, does not quite match up to our own self-made Bach image. Nevertheless, if we attempt to enter into the spirit of it, it is found to possess a certain charm.

Ich liebe den Höchsten von ganzem Gemüte, BWV 174

NBA I/14, p. 65 BC A87 Duration: *c.* 23 mins

1. SINFONIA hn I,II ob I,II taille + rip str conc vln I–III conc vla I–III conc vc I–III bc — G C

2. ARIA A ob I,II bc — D $\frac{6}{8}$

Ich liebe den Höchsten von ganzem Gemüte,	I love the Most High with all my mind;
Er hat mich auch am höchsten lieb.	He has loved me too in the highest degree.
Gott allein	God alone
Soll der Schatz der Seelen sein.	Shall be the treasure of souls.
Da hab ich die ewige Quelle der Güte.	There I have the eternal source of goodness.

3. RECITATIVO T conc vln I + II + III conc vla I + II + III bc — b C

O! Liebe, welcher keine gleich!	O Love beyond compare!
O! unschätzbares Lösegeld!	O priceless ransom!
Der Vater hat des Kindes Leben	The Father has given His Child's Life
Vor Sünder in den Tod gegeben	In death for sinners,
Und alle, die das Himmelreich	And all who trifled with and lost
Verscherzet und verloren,	The heavenly Kingdom
Zur Seligkeit erkoren.	He has elected for Salvation.
Also hat Gott die Welt geliebt!	God so loved the world!
Mein Herz, das merke dir,	My heart, take note of that,
Und stärke dich mit diesen Worten;	And strengthen yourself with these words;
Vor diesem mächtigen Panier	Before this mighty standard
Erzittern selbst die Höllenpforten.	Even hell's gates tremble.

4. ARIA B vlns + vlas bc — G ¢

Greifet zu!	Stretch out your hand!
Faßt das Heil, ihr Glaubenshände!	Grasp your salvation, you hands of faith!
Jesus gibt sein Himmelreich	Jesus gives His heavenly Kingdom

Und verlangt nur das von euch:
Gläubt getreu bis an das Ende!

And demands only this of you:
Believe faithfully to the end!

5. Choral SATB bc (+ ww str) D c

Herzlich lieb hab ich dich, o Herr!
Ich bitt, wollst sein von mir nicht fern
Mit deiner Hülf und Gnaden.
Die ganze Welt erfreut mich nicht,
Nach Himmel und Erden frag ich nicht,
Wenn ich dich nur kann haben.
Und wenn mir gleich mein Herz zerbricht,
So bist du doch mein Zuversicht,
Mein Heil und meines Herzens Trost,
Der mich durch sein Blut hat erlöst.
Herr Jesu Christ,
Mein Gott und Herr, mein Gott und Herr,
In Schanden laß mich nimmermehr!

Heartily will I love You, O Lord!
I pray that You will not be far from me
With Your help and grace.
The whole world delights me not,
I do not inquire after heaven and earth,
If only I can have You.
And though my heart breaks,
You are yet my confidence,
My salvation and my heart's comfort,
Who has redeemed me by His Blood.
Lord Jesus Christ,
My God and Lord, my God and Lord,
Let me never be ashamed!

This cantata is based on a text from Picander's cycle of 1728; and, as we know from a copyist's note in the original parts, Bach's setting was composed at the earliest possible opportunity thereafter, namely for performance on 6 June 1729. Evidently it belonged to a comprehensive series of settings of these Picander texts, of which only a few fragments survive today.

The content of the libretto relies entirely on the introductory words of the Gospel* reading, 'God so loved the world . . .'. On this basis, according to the first aria, the Christian's love of God rests; the recitative, no. 3, includes a meditation on these words, in which they are quoted literally; and the second aria, no. 4, is addressed to the assembled congregation, who are invited to lay hold of the salvation manifest in God's love so that they may be included among those who believe in Him and gain eternal life. The concluding chorale—the first verse of the hymn by Martin Schalling (1569)—returns to the ideas of the opening aria in the words 'Heartily will I love you, O Lord'.

As in various other cantatas of the period around 1726–9, Bach prefaces the text with a sinfonia drawn from a concerto of earlier origin: here the first movement of Brandenburg Concerto No. 3 in G, BWV 1048, which perhaps originated during Bach's earlier Weimar years. In his cantata transcription, Bach altered none of its musical substance; indeed, he simply let a copyist transfer much of it into the new score. But its instrumental clothing was enriched and its texture thereby enriched in a characteristic fashion. Whereas the original had required nine solo strings (three each of violins, violas, and cellos) plus continuo, the cantata version adds two horns, with newly composed parts, and a ripieno choir of oboes and strings (oboe I + violin I, oboe II + violin II, and oboe da caccia* + viola), whose three parts were also newly composed, but largely as a reinforcement of existing parts. As a result, the string ensemble, which formerly functioned as a single group, now becomes a *concertino* set against a *ripieno* body of horns, oboes, and strings, a structural modification that replaces the original concept of nine instruments on equal terms with something fundamentally different.

The scale of this opening movement disrupts the proportions of the cantata: it is followed only by a pair of arias, divided by a recitative, and the concluding chorale. In the arias, polyphonic* writing in few parts is contrasted with the full concertante* texture of the opening movement. The first aria, no. 2, employs two obbligato* oboes in an extensive imitative* texture; and since the alto part begins with a vocal version of the opening sentence of the ritornello, what emerges is a homogeneous upper-part complex with continuo accompaniment. In the second aria, no. 4, violins and violas are united to form a single obbligato part; and although here again the beginning of the vocal section is achieved by transferring the opening sentence of the ritornello to the voice, the obbligato part is altogether more instrumental in style and livelier in character than the voice part, and lengthy vocal passages are incorporated by means of vocal insertion* within ritornello extracts in the obbligato part. A plain four-part chorale setting concludes the work.

1.33 Whit Tuesday

EPISTLE: Acts 8.14–17: The dissemination of the Holy Spirit in Samaria.
GOSPEL: John 10.1–11: Jesus as the true shepherd.

Erwünschtes Freudenlicht, BWV 184

NBA I/14, p. 121 BC A88 Duration: *c.* 25 mins

1. RECITATIVO T fl I,II bc — G C

Erwünschtes Freudenlicht,
Das mit dem neuen Bund anbricht
Durch Jesum, unsern Hirten!
Wir, die wir sonst in Todes Tälern irrten,
Empfinden reichlich nun,
Wie Gott zu uns den längst erwünschten Hirten sendet,
Der unsre Seele speist
Und unsern Gang durch Wort und Geist

Desired Light of Joy
That dawns with the New Covenant
Through Jesus, our Shepherd!
We, who formerly strayed in death's valleys,
Now feel abundantly
How God sends to us the long-awaited Shepherd,
Who nourishes our soul
And through Word and Spirit

Zum rechten Wege wendet.	Turns our steps to the right ways.
Wir, sein erwähltes Volk,	We, His chosen people,
Empfinden seine Kraft;	Sense His power;
In seiner Hand allein	In His hand alone
Ist, was uns Labsal schafft,	Is what gives us refreshment,
Was unser Herze kräftig stärket.	What vigorously strengthens our heart.
Er liebt uns, seine Herde,	He loves us, His flock,
Die seinen Trost und Beistand merket.	Who feel His comfort and support.
Er ziehet sie vom Eitlen, von der Erde,	He draws them from vanities, from the earth
Auf ihn zu schauen	To look upon Him
Und jederzeit auf seine Huld zu trauen.	And at all times to trust His favour.
O Hirte! so sich vor die Herde gibt,	O Shepherd! who gives Himself for His flock,
Der bis ins Grab und bis in Tod sie liebt.	He loves them to the grave and to death.
Sein Arm kann denen Feinden wehren,	His arm can repel their enemies,
Sein Sorgen kann uns Schafe geistlich nähren,	His care can spiritually nourish us sheep;
Ja! kömmt die Zeit, durchs finstre Tal zu gehen,	Yes! when the time comes to go through the Dark Vale,
So hilft und tröstet uns sein sanfter Stab.	Then His gentle staff helps and comforts us.
Drum folgen wir mit Freuden bis ins Grab.	Therefore we follow Him with joy to the grave
Auf! Eilt zu ihm, verklärt vor ihm zu stehen.	Rise up! Hasten to Him, to stand before Him transfigured.
2. ARIA [DUETTO] SA fl I,II str bc	G $\frac{3}{8}$
Gesegnete Christen, glückselige Herde,	Blessed Christians, blissful flock,
Kommt, stellt euch bei Jesu mit Dankbarkeit ein!	Come, appear alongside Jesus with gratitude!
Verachtet das Locken der schmeichlenden Erde,	Despise the lure of the flattering earth,
Daß euer Vergnügen vollkommen kann sein!	So that your contentment can be complete!
3. RECITATIVO T bc	C–D C
So freuet euch, ihr auserwählten Seelen!	Then rejoice, you chosen souls!
Die Freude gründet sich in Jesu Herz.	Joy is founded in Jesus's heart.
Dies Labsal kann kein Mensch erzählen.	This refreshment no man can recount.
Die Freude steigt auch unterwärts	This joy also climbs downwards

Zu denen, die in Sündenbanden lagen,
Die hat der Held aus Juda schon zuschlagen.
Ein David steht uns bei.
Ein Heldenarm macht uns von Feinden frei.
Wenn Gott mit Kraft die Herde schützt,
Wenn er im Zorn auf ihre Feinde blitzt,
Wenn er den bittern Kreuzestod
Vor sie nicht scheuet,
So trifft sie ferner keine Not,
So lebet sie in ihrem Gott
Erfreuet.
Hier schmecket sie die edle Weide
Und hoffet dort vollkommne Himmelsfreude.

To those who lay in the bonds of sin,
Which the Hero from Judah has already burst.
A David stands by us!
A Hero's arm makes us free of enemies.
When God protects His flock with might,
When He flashes His wrath on its enemies,
When He does not shrink from bitter Death
On the Cross for it,
Then no adversity strikes it further,
Then it lives in its God,
Delighted.
Here it tastes noble pasture
And there hopes for perfect heavenly joy.

4\. Aria T vln I solo bc — b $\frac{3}{4}$

Glück und Segen sind bereit,
Die geweihte Schar zu krönen.
Jesus bringt die güldne Zeit,
Welche sich zu ihm gewöhnen.

Fortune and blessing are ready
To crown the dedicated throng.
Jesus brings the golden age
To those who adapt themselves to Him.

5\. Choral SATB bc (+ instrs) — D C

**Herr, ich hoff je, du werdest die
In keiner Not verlassen,
Die dein Wort recht als treue Knecht
Im Herzn und Glauben fassen;
Gibst ihn' bereit die Seligkeit
Und läßt sie nicht verderben.
O Herr, durch dich bitt ich, laß mich
Fröhlich und willig sterben.**

**Lord, I hope that You will not
Leave in any distress
Those who, as faithful servants,
Embrace Your Word in heart and faith;
Grant them Salvation already
And let them not decay.
O Lord, through You I pray, let me
Die joyfully and willingly.**

6\. Chorus SATB fl I + II str bc — G 2

Guter Hirte, Trost der Deinen,
Laß uns nur dein heilig Wort!
Laß dein gnädig Antlitz scheinen,
Bleibe unser Gott und Hort,
Der durch allmachtsvolle Hände
Unsern Gang zum Leben wende!

Good Shepherd, comfort of Your own people,
Leave us only Your Holy Word!
Let Your gracious countenance shine,
Remain our God and refuge,
Who by Your almighty hands
Turns our path to Life!

This cantata is evidently a sister-work to Cantata 173. Both are based on secular works from the Cöthen period, both were remodelled as Whit cantatas during

Bach's first year at Leipzig, and both were revived at Whit 1731, as the surviving printed texts prove. The source transmission of the two works is, so to speak, complementary: roughly speaking, what we know for certain about the one we can only guess about the other, and vice versa. Thus the secular model of Cantata 173 survives complete (BWV 173a), but that of Cantata 184 (BWV 184a) is largely lost: vocal parts, score, and text are missing, and only a few instrumental parts survive. In the case of Cantata 173, we lack the sources of the 1724 performance and only a later, revised version of the score has been transmitted; in the case of Cantata 184, on the other hand, only the performing parts of 1724 survive and not the original score. We know for certain, therefore, that the present work was performed for the first time as a church cantata on 30 May 1724 in the form of a very hasty revision of its secular model. But we do not know whether Bach, who can hardly have been satisfied with this version in the long run, later undertook a fundamental revision of it, as he did, for example, in the case of BWV 66, 134, 249, and probably also 173. Consequently, it is unreasonable to make a critical comparison between these works without being conscious of the differences in their source transmission.

The anonymous author of the parody* follows the ideas of the Gospel* reading in praising Jesus as the Shepherd of Christendom and describing Christians as His 'blissful flock' (nos. 1–2). The third movement points out that through Jesus's Death on the Cross even sinners have been included in this flock, closing with a glimpse of the 'perfect heavenly joy' which is anticipated after death. The theme of the tenor aria, no. 4, and the chorale, no. 5—the eighth verse of the hymn *O Herre Gott, dein göttlich Wort* by Anarg von Wildenfels (1526)—is Jesus as bringer of the 'golden age'. Finally, the concluding chorus* addresses the 'Good Shepherd', praying for His future clemency and for His 'Holy Word'.

The source findings described above explain why even the recitatives nos. 1 and 3 are transmitted without any essential alterations to the secular original. This also probably explains the rather curious wording of the opening, 'Erwünschtes Freudenlicht' ('Desired Light of Joy'). These words were perhaps transferred from the secular (New Year?) text: they must have been hard to alter, since the two flutes with which the first movement (a motivically-imprinted *accompagnato**) is scored constantly repeat a figure that illustrates this 'light' flaring up. In the context of a Whit cantata, this flute figure may be heard as a depiction of the fiery tongues of the Pentecost miracle, though nothing is done to facilitate this interpretation in the parody text.

The second movement was, from the outset, probably conceived as a pastorale and is therefore well suited to the sacred text. The mainly song-like, homophonic* writing for the voices and the considerable extent of the instrumental episodes also strengthen the impression of a shepherds' dance. The third movement is set as a *secco* recitative, but, as in numerous recitatives from Bach's pre-Leipzig period, it changes at the end into an arioso.* It is followed by an aria with obbligato* violin, no. 4, which, at least with its new text, forms rather a colourless impression. The fifth movement, a new composition in place of an excluded recitative from the secular model, is a plain chorale setting which, however, does not end the cantata: it is followed by a chorus in the style of a gavotte, whose extended duet passages—as in the equivalent movement from Cantata 173—betray its origin in a finale with two voice parts. The secular original of this movement underwent an essentially more radical adaptation in later years when it was reused as the finale of the Hercules Cantata, BWV 213.

Er rufet seinen Schafen mit Namen, BWV 175

NBA I/14, p. 149 BC A89 Duration: *c.* 18 mins

1. Recitativo T rec I–III bc — G C

'Er rufet seinen Schafen mit Namen und führet sie hinaus.'	'He calls His sheep by name and leads them out.'

2. Aria A rec I–III bc — e 12/8

Komm, leite mich,	Come, lead me,
Es sehnet sich	My spirit longs
Mein Geist auf grüner Weide!	For green pasture!
Mein Herze schmacht',	My heart languishes,
Ächzt Tag und Nacht,	It groans day and night,
Mein Hirte, meine Freude.	My Shepherd, my joy.

3. Recitativo T bc — a–C C

Wo find ich dich?	Where do I find You?
Ach! wo bist du verborgen?	Ah! where are you hidden?
O! Zeige dich mir bald!	Oh! appear to me soon!
Ich sehne mich.	I am languishing.
Brich an, erwünschter Morgen!	Dawn, O longed-for day!

4. Aria T vc picc solo bc — C ¢

Es dünket mich, ich seh dich kommen,	It seems to me that I see You coming:
Du gehst zur rechten Türe ein.	You enter in through the right door.
Du wirst im Glauben aufgenommen	You have been received in faith
Und mußt der wahre Hirte sein.	And must be the True Shepherd.
Ich kenne deine holde Stimme,	I know Your kind voice,
Die voller Lieb und Sanftmut ist,	Which is full of love and meekness,
Daß ich im Geist darob ergrimme,	So that I groan in spirit over
Wer zweifelt, daß du Heiland seist.	Whoever doubts that You are Saviour.

5. Recitativo AB str bc — a–D C

Alt	*Alto*
'Sie vernahmen aber nicht, was es war, das er zu ihnen gesaget hatte.'	'But they did not understand what it was that He had said to them.'
Baß	*Bass*
Ach ja! Wir Menschen sind oftmals den Tauben zu vergleichen:	Ah yes! we men are often to be compared with the deaf:

Wenn die verblendete Vernunft nicht weiß, was er gesaget hatte.
O! Törin, merke doch, wenn Jesus mit dir spricht,
Daß es zu deinem Heil geschicht.

When deluded reason does not know what He has said.
O fool! note when Jesus speaks to you
That it concerns your Salvation.

6. Aria B tr I,II bc — D 6/8

Öffnet euch, ihr beiden Ohren,
Jesus hat euch zugeschworen,
Daß er Teufel, Tod erlegt.
Gnade, Gnüge, volles Leben
Will er allen Christen geben,
Wer ihm folgt, sein Kreuz nachträgt.

Open up, you two ears:
Jesus has sworn to you
That He destroys Devil and Death.
Grace, plenty, full life
He would give to every Christian who
Follows Him and carries his cross after Him.

7. Chorale SATB rec I–III bc (+ str) — G C

Nun, werter Geist, ich folge dir;
Hilf, daß ich suche für und für
Nach deinem Wort ein ander Leben,
Das du mir willt aus Gnaden geben.
Dein Wort ist ja der Morgenstern,
Der herrlich leuchtet nah und fern.
Drum will ich, die mich anders lehren,
In Ewigkeit, mein Gott, nicht hören.
Alleluja, alleluja!

Now, worthy Spirit, I follow You;
Help me to seek for ever and ever,
According to Your Word, another life,
Which You would grant me through grace.
Your Word is indeed the Morning Star
That shines gloriously near and far.
Therefore I will not ever listen to those
Who would teach me otherwise, my God.
Alleluia, alleluia!

Bach composed this cantata for 22 May 1725 to a text by Christiane Mariane von Ziegler. As in most of the texts drawn from this poet, however, he made several cuts and alterations. The following lines, for example—

Ach ja! Wir Menschen seynd gar offt,
Den Tauben zu vergleichen,
Wenn die verblendete Vernunfft nicht kan erreichen,
Was sein geheilgter Mund gesagt.

Ah yes! We men are often
To be compared with the deaf,
When deluded reason cannot get at
What His sanctified mouth says.

—are reproduced in the following abbreviated form, without regard for rhyme:

Ach ja! Wir Menschen sind oftmals den Tauben zu vergleichen:
Wenn die verblendete Vernunft nicht weiß, was er gesaget hatte.

Ah yes! we men are often to be compared with the deaf:
When deluded reason does not know what He has said.

The succession of ideas in the text is closely connected with the Gospel* reading, which tells of the Good Shepherd and His sheep. The sheep know the voice of the true Shepherd and follow Him; they do not, however, follow a thief and murderer, who does not enter through the door of the sheepfold and whose voice they do not recognize. When Jesus is not understood by His listeners, He explains the parable to them: 'I am the door for the sheep; all those who came before me are thieves and murderers' (John 10.7–8). The text is divided clearly into two parts, nos. 1–4 and 5–7, both of which are introduced by a literal quotation from the Gospel. The first part describes Jesus as the true Shepherd, and phrases such as 'You enter in through the right door' and 'I know Your kind voice' repeatedly establish links with the reading. The second part deals with the incomprehension of Jesus's listeners, giving it an interpretation that was highly topical in Bach's day but in no way prescribed in the Gospel: it is 'deluded reason' that makes men deaf to Jesus's words. Here we note how Lutheranism wards off the incipient age of the Enlightenment and the atheism that followed in its train. The cantata concludes with the ninth verse of the hymn *O Gottes Geist, mein Trost und Rat* by Johann Rist (1651).

Bach's setting derives its distinctive colour from his chosen instrumentation with three recorders, which are heard in nos. 1 and 2 as an attribute of the Good Shepherd. The aria 'Komm, leite mich', no. 2, with its continuous 12/8 rhythm, is a pure pastorale whose dense triadic sequences—probably derived from the image of 'leading'—exert a very special kind of charm on the listener. In the middle section, chromatic* sigh figures depict the pining for the Shepherd expressed in the text. Not only in the first two movements but thereafter as well the usual pre-eminence of violins is almost wholly renounced. The second aria, no. 4, calls for obbligato* violoncello piccolo* to characterize the joyful expectation with which the faithful Christian awaits the approach of his Saviour and Shepherd. This movement is a parody* of the aria 'Dein Name gleich der Sonnen geh' from the secular cantata BWV 173a, though the substantial differences between the verse schemes of the two texts led to numerous compositional alterations; evidently Bach's intention of resorting to parody had not been discussed with the poet in advance.

The following recitative—the only movement with full string accompaniment—makes the injunction not to close one's ears to Jesus's words seem all the more imperative by virtue of its arioso* conclusion. The same demand is presented to the listener most graphically in the bass aria, no. 6, by two trumpets, which celebrate Jesus as the victor over death and the devil. With good reason, the trumpets are silent in the middle section, which tells of the gifts of the Saviour. This aria might be derived from an earlier work, like no. 4, though no model for it survives. The concluding chorale—an arrangement of the melody *Komm, Heiliger Geist, Herre Gott* in seven-part texture—is drawn from an earlier Whit cantata, BWV 59, though the string parts are here replaced by recorders. This chorale, with its obbligato recorder parts, harks back to the opening pair of movements and brings the music of this Whit feast-day to a splendid, full-textured conclusion.

1.34 Trinity

EPISTLE: Romans 11.33–6: 'What depth of the riches of the wisdom and knowledge of God!'
GOSPEL: John 3.1–15: Jesus's conversation with Nicodemus.

O Heilges Geist- und Wasserbad, BWV 165

NBA I/15, p. 3 BC A90 Duration: *c.* 15 mins

1. [ARIA] S str bc G C

O heilges Geist- und Wasserbad,	O holy washing of spirit and water
Das Gottes Reich uns einverleibet	That embodies God's Kingdom for us
Und uns ins Buch des Lebens schreibet!	And writes us in the Book of Life!
O Flut! die alle Missetat	O flood! that drowns all iniquity
Durch ihre Wunderkraft ertränket	Through its miraculous power
Und uns das neue Leben schenket.	And gives us the New Life.
O heilges Geist und Wasserbad!	O holy washing of spirit and water!

2. RECITATIVO B bc e–a C

Die sündige Geburt verdammter Adamserben	The sinful birth of damned Adam's legacy
Gebieret Gottes Zorn,	Bears God's wrath,
Den Tod und das Verderben.	Death and destruction.
Denn was vom Fleisch geboren ist,	For what is born of the flesh
Ist nichts als Fleisch, von Sünden angestecket,	Is nothing but flesh, infected by sin,
Vergiftet und beflecket.	Poisoned and defiled.
Wie selig ist ein Christ!	How blessed is the Christian!
Er wird im Geist- und Wasserbade	In the washing of spirit and water he becomes
Ein Kind der Seligkeit und Gnade.	A child of salvation and grace.
Er ziehet Christum an	He puts on Christ
Und seiner Unschuld weiße Seide!	And His fine linen of innocence!
Er wird mit Christi Blut, der Ehren Purpurkleide,	He is attired in Christ's Blood, the purple robe of honour,
Im Taufbad angetan.	In the baptismal washing.

3. ARIA A bc e $\frac{12}{8}$

Jesu, der aus großer Liebe	Jesus, who out of great Love
In der Taufe mir verschriebe	Prescribed for me in baptism
Leben, Heil und Seligkeit,	Life, salvation, and blessedness,
Hilf, daß ich mich dessen freue	Help me to rejoice over this

Und den Gnadenbund erneue	And renew the Covenant of Grace
In der ganzen Lebenszeit.	Throughout my whole lifetime.
4. RECITATIVO B str bc	b–G c
Ich habe ja, mein Seelenbräutigam,	I have indeed, my soul's Bridegroom,
Da du mich neu geboren,	Since You have given me new birth,
Dir ewig treu zu sein geschworen!	Sworn ever to be true to You,
Hochheilges Gotteslamm;	Most Holy Lamb of God;
Doch hab ich, ach! den Taufbund oft gebrochen	Yet I have, alas, often broken the baptismal covenant
Und nicht erfüllt, was ich versprochen!	And not carried out what I promised!
Erbarme, Jesu, dich	Have mercy on me, Jesus,
Aus Gnaden über mich!	In Your grace!
Vergib mir die begangne Sünde,	Forgive me the sins I have committed;
Du weißt, mein Gott, wie schmerzlich ich empfinde	You know, my God, how painfully I feel
Der alten Schlangen Stich!	The old serpent's bruise!
Das Sündengift verderbt mir Leib und Seele!	Sin's poison corrupts my body and soul!
Hilf! daß ich gläubig dich erwähle,	Help me to choose You in faith,
Blutrotes Schlangenbild,	Blood-red serpent's image,
Das an dem Kreuz erhöhet,	Lifted up on the Cross,
Das alle Schmerzen stillt	Who soothes all pains
Und mich erquickt, wenn alle Kraft vergehet.	And revives me when all strength departs.
5. ARIA T vln I + II bc	G c
Jesu, meines Todes Tod,	Jesus, my death's death,
Laß in meinem Leben	In my life
Und in meiner letzten Not	And in my last agony
Mir für Augen schweben,	Let it hover before my eyes
Daß du mein Heilschlänglein seist	That You are my serpent of salvation
Vor das Gift der Sünde!	In place of the poison of sin!
Heile, Jesu, Seel und Geist,	Heal, Jesus, my soul and spirit,
Daß ich Leben finde!	That I may find Life!
6. CHORALE SATB bc (+ instrs)	G c
Sein Wort, sein Tauf, sein Nachtmahl	**His Word, His Baptism, His Supper**
Dient wider allen Unfall,	**Serve to protect us against all disaster;**
Der Heilge Geist im Glauben	**May the Holy Spirit teach us**
Lehr uns darauf vertrauen.	**To rely upon this in faith.**

The uncertain source transmission of this cantata allows us to give only a qualified account of its origin. We may assume with some certainty, however, that it was composed in Weimar for 16 June 1715 and revived with minor alterations during Bach's first year in Leipzig (for Trinity 1724?). The text, drawn from

Salomo Franck's Weimar cycle of texts for the church year 1715, *Evangelisches Andachts-Opffer*, is closely associated with the Gospel* reading. The rebirth from the spirit which Jesus discusses with Nicodemus is granted to the Christian in baptism (no. 1). It nullifies the 'sinful birth of damned Adam's legacy' and puts Christians into a state of grace (no. 2). Yet the covenant of grace needs to be renewed throughout my whole lifetime (no. 3). For the 'old serpent's bruise'—that is, Adam's Fall—means that even the pledged baptismal covenant keeps being broken and the Christian constantly requires renewed forgiveness (no. 4). The freely versified text closes with a prayer for the realization that Christ's Death on the Cross has brought us salvation (nos. 4 and 5). The fifth verse of the hymn *Nun laßt uns Gott dem Herren* by Ludwig Helmbold (1575) then follows as a confirmatory concluding chorale.

The formal structure of the text is clear and visible at a glance. Of the outer movements, no. 1 sets the theme and no. 6 unites what has been expounded and refers back to the opening. In the inner movements, reflection in a recitative is twice followed by prayer in the form of an aria. The first of these sequences, nos. 2–3, deals with baptism as the salvation of the Christian, the second, nos. 4–5, with the consecration of the baptized Christian until death. Several phrases in Franck's text refer directly to the Gospel reading: for example, 'What is born of the flesh is nothing but flesh' (no. 2; cf. John 3.6) and 'Blood-red serpent's image, lifted up on the Cross' (no. 4), which, together with 'my serpent of salvation' (no. 5), may be understood with reference to John 3.14–15: 'As Moses lifted up the serpent in the wilderness, even so must the Son of Man be lifted up'.

Bach's setting employs only modest means: four voices, strings and continuo. It is all the more remarkable how the composer was nonetheless capable of producing a succession of movements full of diversity and rich in contrasts. The opening aria is emphatically polyphonic* in its mode of construction. The string ritornello at the outset comprises a fugal exposition,* plus a redundant entry of the first violin, and even the instrumental episodes are each made up of a four-part fugal exposition. The vocal passages, on the other hand, are set as an imitative* duo for soprano and first violin over continuo, based on the same thematic material. These five vocal passages, which deliver the text in succession (no. 5 is a reprise of no. 1, the opening line) are set symmetrically according to the formal scheme A B C B^1 A^1, where B is derived from the inverted subject of A. Section C is based on a new theme, derived from the second bar of the ritornello, which is then reused in the violin part of B^1, again by inversion. The prominent use made of formal schemes based on the principles of symmetry and inversion is in all probability intentional, serving as a symbol of the inner inversion of mankind—his rebirth in baptism.

The second movement is set as a *secco* recitative, though like many recitatives from the earlier cantatas, it contains several passages that approach arioso* in their expressive melodic shaping. The second aria, no. 3, is accompanied only by continuo, whose brief ritornello theme, powerfully expressive in shape due to its leap of a rising sixth, pervades the entire movement. It is taken up by the voice and, when reiterated by the continuo in each of the four vocal passages, serves as the basis of vocal insertion.*

With its full string accompaniment, the second recitative, no. 4, is still closer to arioso than the first. Not only does the voice part contain numerous melismas,* but the instruments accompany the words 'Hochheilges Gotteslamm' ('Most Holy Lamb of God') motivically at an 'adagio' tempo, and their held notes are so often broken up into melody that the threshold between free recitation and metrically regular delivery is constantly transgressed. The third aria, no. 5, unites the violins in an obbligato* part whose theme is evidently inspired by the phrase 'Daß du mein Heilschlänglein seist' ('That You are my serpent of salvation'): the ritornello is formulated in continuous semiquaver motion, and numerous leaps of a third or fourth, together with rising or falling movement, convey the impression of a coiling serpent. The overall form of the aria—no less unusual than that of the first movement—originates in the uninterrupted sentence structure of the aria text, which virtually excludes the possibility of intervening episodes. Bach therefore divides the text into four passages of two lines each which follow one another without intervening ritornellos. By way of compensation, each passage is prefaced by the first line as a motto* and then by an instrumental episode. The number of bars and their allocation are identical in all four passages:

	Motto	Episode	Text passage	
Bars:	1	1	5	= 7

Moreover, since the first and second passages are musically identical and the third and fourth similar, an exceedingly rational overall form emerges of 8 + (4 × 7) + 8 bars:

Ritornello A A B B¹ Ritornello.

The cantata concludes with a plain chorale setting.

Höchsterwünschtes Freudenfest, BWV 194 (BC A91)

See pp. 715–20.

Es ist ein trotzig und verzagt Ding, BWV 176

NBA I/15, p. 19 BC A92 Duration: *c.* 13 mins

1. [Chorus] SATB (+ ob I,II ob da c) str bc c C

'Es ist ein trotzig und verzagt Ding um aller Menschen Herze.'	'There is something perverse and desperate about all human hearts.'

2. RECITATIVO A bc	g c
Ich meine, recht verzagt,	I think that, truly desperate,
Daß Nikodemus sich bei Tage nicht,	Nicodemus ventured to meet Jesus
Bei Nacht zu Jesu wagt.	Not by day but by night.
Die Sonne mußte dort bei Josua so lange stille stehn,	There the sun had to stand still so long for Joshua,
So lange bis der Sieg vollkommen war geschehn;	So long until the victory was fully accomplished;
Hier aber wünschet Nikodem: O säh ich sie zu Rüste gehn!	But here Nicodemus wishes: 'Oh, if only I saw it setting!'
3. ARIA S str bc	B♭ ¢
Dein sonst hell beliebter Schein	Your otherwise bright beloved light
Soll vor mich umnebelt sein,	Shall be befogged for me,
Weil ich nach dem Meister frage,	Since I ask for the Master,
Denn ich scheue mich bei Tage.	For I am afraid by day.
Niemand kann die Wunder tun,	No one can do such miracles,
Denn sein Allmacht und sein Wesen,	For His almighty power and His essence,
Scheint, ist göttlich auserlesen,	It seems, are divinely chosen:
Gottes Geist muß auf ihm ruhn.	God's Spirit must rest on Him.
4. RECITATIVO B bc	F–g c
So wundre dich, o Meister, nicht,	So marvel not, O Master,
Warum ich dich bei Nacht ausfrage!	Why I question You by night!
Ich fürchte, daß bei Tage	I fear that by day
Mein Ohnmacht nicht bestehen kann.	My powerlessness cannot endure.
Doch tröst ich mich, du nimmst mein Herz und Geist	Yet I comfort myself: You take up and accept my heart and spirit
Zum Leben auf und an,	Into Life,
Weil alle, die nur an dich glauben, nicht verloren werden.	For all who but believe in You shall not be lost.
5. ARIA A ob I + II + ob da c bc	E♭ 3/8
Ermuntert euch, furchtsam und schüchterne Sinne,	Rouse yourselves, fearful and diffident spirits,
Erholet euch, höret, was Jesus verspricht:	Recover, hear what Jesus promises:
Daß ich durch den Glauben den Himmel gewinne.	That I gain heaven through faith.
Wenn die Verheißung erfüllend geschicht,	When the promise is fulfilled,
Werd ich dort oben	I shall there above
Mit Danken und Loben	With thanks and praise
Vater, Sohn und Heilgen Geist	Glorify Father, Son, and Holy Spirit,
Preisen, der dreieinig heißt.	Which are called triune.
6. CHORAL SATB bc (+ instrs)	f–c c
Auf daß wir also allzugleich	**Thus all at once**

Zur Himmelspforten dringen	**We break through to heaven's gates**
Und dermaleinst in deinem Reich	**And some day in Your Kingdom**
Ohn alles Ende singen,	**Sing without end**
Daß du alleine König seist,	**That You alone are King,**
Hoch über alle Götter,	**High above all gods:**
Gott Vater, Sohn und Heilger Geist,	**God the Father, Son, and Holy Spirit,**
Der Frommen Schutz und Retter,	**Protector and deliverer of the devout,**
Ein Wesen, drei Personen.	**One Essence, three Persons.**

When the poet Christiane Mariane von Ziegler wrote this cantata text, which was set by Bach for 27 May 1725, she was particularly intrigued by the thought that Nicodemus, a 'ruler of the Jews' (John 3.1), risked meeting Jesus only by night. Here she finds a general human characteristic: 'The heart is a perverse and desperate thing; who can fathom it?', says the prophet Jeremiah (17.9), and the poet prefaces her text with these words—slightly modified—as a motto.* Unlike in the days of Joshua, when the sun stood still at Gibeon till the hoards of the Amorites had been vanquished (Joshua 10.12 f.), Nicodemus longs for night to come (no. 2). The following aria first takes up the same ideas and then proceeds with the words of Nicodemus: no one could do the signs that Jesus does unless God were with him. The second recitative-aria pair gives an indication of the comfort that the fearful Christian derives from faith in Jesus. Bach himself lends still greater weight to this reflection by adding to the recitative words of the poet a paraphrase of John 3.16: 'For all who but believe in You shall not be lost'. With praise and thanks for this promise, the aria leads to the concluding chorale, the eighth verse of the hymn *Was alle Weisheit in der Welt* by Paul Gerhardt (1653).

Bach's opening chorus* to words from Jeremiah is concise and pithy. A single great choral fugue*—with the strings independent but unthematic and the oboes doubling the voice parts—takes up the entire movement. There is no instrumental prelude or postlude at all, and the inner dynamic of the movement is achieved not, as often in Bach, by concerto-like solo–tutti or group contrasts, but by the text-engendered dynamic of the fugue subject itself and by the string accompaniment that underpins its character. The fugue subject, which enters in the bass—

—characterizes the textual distinction between the 'perverse' and 'desperate' sides of the human heart by means of rising triadic and scale motion on the one hand and sinking chromaticism* on the other, with the strings accompanying the opening part of the theme *f* and its continuation *p*. Once the fugue has achieved full texture with the entry of all four voice parts, it maintains it without change to the end, forming a unique musical monolith—like an erratic block left by a retreating glacier—whose overall character gives expression to defiance rather than despair.

The aria 'Dein sonst hell beliebter Schein' (no. 3), which is prefaced by a brief, contemplative recitative, forms a palpable contrast to this powerful introduction. Here again, the composer was essentially guided by a single image from a libretto rich in ideas, namely the bright light with which Jesus the Master, upon whom God's Spirit rests, confronts the timorous hearts of men. Consequently, the aria takes the form of a spirited gavotte whose relaxed triplet figuration does not cease even when the soprano holds a long note on the word 'ruhn' ('rest'). The second recitative, no. 4, though brief, is extended by an *andante* arioso* for the paraphrase of John 3.16 appended by Bach, which is longer than the preceding recitative altogether. This arioso is made up of two similar passages of highly expressive melody, which derive their impulse from an ostinato* figure.

Like the first aria, the second, no. 5, is somewhat dance-like, a quality that now emerges more self-evidently from the comforting words of the text. As in the opening fugue, the theme is a direct product of the text, as is clear from its upward surge on 'ermuntert euch' ('rouse yourselves') and its narrow, semitone steps on 'furchtsam und schüchterne' ('fearful and diffident'). The passages that follow also prove to be text-engendered: note the calling leaps of a seventh on 'höret' ('hear') and the coloraturas* on 'Loben' and 'preisen' ('praise' and 'glorify'). In the instrumental obbligato* part, Bach unites all three instruments of the oboe family—two oboes and oboe da caccia*—in unison, forming dynamic contrasts by requiring that two of them rest during the vocal passages.

The melody of the plain four-part concluding chorale originally belonged to Luther's hymn *Christ unser Herr zum Jordan kam*. Bach's harmonization reveals how the tension between church-tone melody and 'modern' major–minor tonality was endured and overcome on yet one more occasion before a rationalistic belief in progress allowed this insight into the art of chorale treatment to dwindle.

Gelobet sei der Herr, mein Gott, BWV 129

NBA I/15, p. 39 BC A93 Duration: *c.* 24 mins

1. Chorus [Versus 1] SATB tr I–III timp fl ob I,II str bc D 𝄵

Gelobet sei der Herr,	**Praised be the Lord,**
Mein Gott, mein Licht, mein Leben,	**My God, my Light, my Life,**

Mein Schöpfer, der mir hat	**My Creator, who has given me**
Mein' Leib und Seel gegeben,	**My flesh and heart,**
Mein Vater, der mich schützt	**My Father, who protects me**
Von Mutterleibe an,	**From the womb onwards,**
Der alle Augenblick	**Who every moment**
Viel Guts an mir getan.	**Has dealt me many good things.**

2. ARIA VERSUS 2 B bc — A 3/8

Gelobet sei der Herr,	**Praised be the Lord,**
Mein Gott, mein Heil, mein Leben,	**My God, my Salvation, my Life,**
Des Vaters liebster Sohn,	**The Father's dearest Son,**
Der sich für mich gegeben,	**Who gave Himself for me,**
Der mich erlöset hat	**Who has redeemed me**
Mit seinem teuren Blut,	**With His precious Blood,**
Der mir im Glauben schenkt	**Who in Faith gives me**
Sich selbst, das höchste Gut.	**Himself, the highest Good.**

3. ARIA VERSUS 3 S fl vln I solo bc — e ¢

Gelobet sei der Herr,	**Praised be the Lord,**
Mein Gott, mein Trost, mein Leben,	**My God, my Comfort, my Life,**
Des Vaters werter Geist,	**The Father's worthy Spirit,**
Den mir der Sohn gegeben,	**Whom the Son gave me,**
Der mir mein Herz erquickt,	**Who refreshes my heart,**
Der mir gibt neue Kraft,	**Who gives me new strength,**
Der mir in aller Not	**Who in all distress gives me**
Rat, Trost und Hülfe schafft.	**Counsel, comfort, and help.**

4. ARIA VERSUS 4 A ob d'am bc — G 6/8

Gelobet sei der Herr,	**Praised be the Lord,**
Mein Gott, der ewig lebet,	**My God, who lives for ever,**
Den alles lobet, was	**Whom everything praises that**
In allen Lüften schwebet;	**Hovers in all the skies;**
Gelobet sei der Herr,	**Praised be the Lord,**
Des Name heilig heißt,	**Whose Name is called Holy,**
Gott Vater, Gott der Sohn	**God the Father, God the Son**
Und Gott der Heilge Geist.	**And God the Holy Spirit.**

5. CHORALE VERSUS 5 [Scoring as in no. 1] — D c

Dem wir das Heilig itzt	**To whom we now let 'Holy'**
Mit Freuden lassen klingen	**Be heard with joy,**
Und mit der Engel Schar	**And with the angel host**
Das Heilig, Heilig singen,	**Sing 'Holy, Holy',**
Den herzlich lobt und preist	**Who is heartily glorified and praised**
Die ganze Christenheit:	**By the whole of Christendom:**
Gelobet sei mein Gott	**Praised be my God**
In alle Ewigkeit!	**In all eternity!**

This work belongs among the chorale cantatas* that Bach composed retrospectively for the cycle of 1724–5 in order to replace non-chorale-based compositions—in this case BWV 176. Its date of origin may be determined only roughly: Bach probably wrote it for Trinity 1726 (16 June), though the possibility that it was written for another suitable occasion around 1726 cannot be altogether discounted. For the text, the five-verse hymn by Johann Olearius (1665) is adopted, word for word. Its content is well suited to the Feast of the Trinity, for it is a song of praise to the triune God: verse 1 praises the Creator, God Himself, verse 2 the Son, verse 3 the Holy Spirit, and verses 4 and 5, which are united in substance, the Trinity. However, specific references to the readings for the day are absent, and since he set the text unaltered Bach made no attempt to introduce any.

With its orchestra of three trumpets and drums, flute, two oboes, strings, and continuo, the cantata is decked out in a positively festive manner. The opening chorus at once unfolds a lively *concertato* of strings and woodwind, with interjections from the trumpet choir. The *cantus firmus**—the melody *O Gott, du frommer Gott*—is delivered by the soprano one line at a time and supported by an imitative,* freely polyphonic,* or chordal substructure in the other voice parts. Not only does the orchestra develop independent thematic material, but the vocal counter-parts also lack a thematic connection with the chorale melody. Yet what the movement might lack in deep-seated thematic unity and learned counterpoint* it makes up for in the immediate effectiveness of its concertante* themes and their treatment.

Three arias in succession now follow without intervening recitatives. The first, no. 2, being accompanied only by continuo, gives the voice the opportunity for the most highly expressive melody:

It is surely no mere chance that this very aria is devoted to God the Son, who becomes man and sacrifices Himself 'for me'. In the second aria, no. 3, transverse flute* and solo violin, together with soprano and continuo, form a quartet texture of measured solemnity which, however, is constantly enlivened by an oft-recurring semiquaver motive* in the instruments:

Finally, in the third aria, no. 4, a relaxed and song-like—almost dance-like—joyfulness prevails. Since the alto part adopts the ritornello theme stated by the obbligato* oboe d'amore*—

—a homogeneous texture emerges in which even the continuo participates with occasional imitative motives.

The finale is of exceptional splendour. The trumpets, which in the opening chorus merely marked the cadences rather than carrying themes, here lead the six-bar ritornello and play a substantial role in the episodes between the lines of the chorale, which is delivered by the choir (plus flute) in a plain, homophonic* texture. The striking, joyfully excited theme of the orchestral music, which is again unrelated to the chorale melody, surrounds its lines in the same fashion as in the concluding chorales of the *Christmas* and *Ascension Oratorios*. In its concertante style, this chorale setting harks back to the opening chorus, so that the three inner verses, which are set for a few parts only, are framed by festive, full-textured outer movements.

2

Cantatas for the church year: First to Twenty-seventh Sunday after Trinity

2.1 First Sunday after Trinity

Epistle: 1 John 4.16–21: God is Love.
Gospel: Luke 16.19–31: The parable of the rich man and the poor Lazarus.

Die Elenden sollen essen, BWV 75

NBA I/15, p. 87 BC A94 Duration: *c.* 40 mins

1. [Chorus] SATB ob I,II str bc — e 3/4 C

'Die Elenden sollen essen, daß sie satt werden, und die nach dem Herrn fragen, werden ihn preisen. Euer Herz soll ewiglich leben.'

'The poor shall eat so that they shall be satisfied, and those that ask after the Lord shall praise Him. Your heart shall live for ever.'

2. Recitativo B str bc — b–e C

Was hilft des Purpurs Majestät,
Da sie vergeht?
Was hilft der größte Überfluß,
Weil alles, so wir sehen,
Verschwinden muß?
Was hilft der Kützel eitler Sinnen,
Denn unser Leib muß selbst von hinnen?
Ach, wie geschwind ist es geschehen,
Daß Reichtum, Wollust, Pracht
Den Geist zur Hölle macht!

What good is purple's majesty,
Since it fades?
What good is the greatest abundance,
Since all that we see
Must vanish?
What good is the tickle of vain sensations?
For our body itself must depart.
Ah, how swiftly does it happen
That wealth, voluptuousness, and luxury
Make one's spirit over to hell!

3. [Aria] T ob I str bc — G 3/4

Mein Jesus soll mein alles sein!
  Mein Purpur ist sein teures Blut,
  Er selbst mein allerhöchstes Gut,
  Und seines Geistes Liebesglut
  Mein allersüß'ster Freudenwein.

My Jesus shall be my all!
  My purple is His precious Blood,
  He Himself my highest good,
  And His Spirit's coals of love
  My sweetest wine of joy.

4. Recitativo T bc — a–C C

Gott stürzet und erhöhet
In Zeit und Ewigkeit.
Wer in der Welt den Himmel sucht,
Wird dort verflucht.
Wer aber hier die Hölle überstehet,
Wird dort erfreut.

God casts down and raises up
In time and eternity.
Whoever seeks heaven in the world
Shall yonder be accursed.
But whoever overcomes hell here
Shall yonder rejoice.

5. [Aria] S ob d'am bc — a 3/8

Ich nehme mein Leiden mit Freuden auf mich.
Wer Lazarus' Plagen
Geduldig ertragen,
Den nehmen die Engel zu sich.

I take my suffering upon myself with joy.
Whoever has endured Lazarus's torments
Patiently
Shall be taken to heaven by the angels.

6. Recitativo S bc — G C

Indes schenkt Gott ein gut Gewissen,
Dabei ein Christe kann
Ein kleines Gut mit großer Lust genießen.
Ja, führt er auch durch lange Not
Zum Tod,
So ist es doch am Ende wohlgetan.

Meanwhile God gives us a good conscience,
With which a Christian can
Enjoy a small good thing with great pleasure.
Yes, though He leads us through long misery
To death,
It is in the end dealt bountifully.

7. Chorale SATB str + ob I,II bc — G C

Was Gott tut, das ist wohlgetan;
Muß ich den Kelch gleich schmecken,
Der bitter ist nach meinem Wahn,
Laß ich mich doch nicht schrecken,
Weil doch zuletzt
Ich werd ergötzt
Mit süßem Trost im Herzen;
Da weichen alle Schmerzen.

Whatever God deals is dealt bountifully;
Though I must taste the cup
That is bitter according to my delusion,
Yet I do not let myself fear,
For nonetheless in the end
I shall be delighted
By sweet comfort in the heart;
There all pains recede.

Seconda parte — *Second part*

8. Sinfonia tr str (+ ww?) bc — G ¢

9. Recitativo A str bc — e–G C

Nur eines kränkt
Ein christliches Gemüte:
Wenn es an seines Geistes Armut denkt.
Es gläubt zwar Gottes Güte,
Die alles neu erschafft;

Only one thing grieves
A Christian mind:
When it thinks of its poverty in spirit.
It indeed believes in God's goodness,
Which makes all things new;

Doch mangelt ihm die Kraft,
Dem überirdschen Leben
Das Wachstum und die Frucht zu
geben.

Yet it lacks the strength
For metaphysical life
To grow and bear fruit.

10. [Aria] A unis vlns bc — e $\frac{3}{8}$

Jesus macht mich geistlich reich.
Kann ich seinen Geist empfangen,
Will ich weiter nichts verlangen;
Denn mein Leben wächst zugleich.
Jesus macht mich geistlich reich.

Jesus makes me spiritually rich.
If I can receive His Spirit,
I will long for nothing further;
For my life grows at the same time.
Jesus makes me spiritually rich.

11. Recitativo B bc — D–C c

Wer nur in Jesu bleibt,
Die Selbstverleugnung treibt,
Daß er in Gottes Liebe
Sich gläubig übe,
Hat, wenn das Irdische
verschwunden,
Sich selbst und Gott gefunden.

Whoever just abides in Jesus
And practises self-denial,
So that in God's Love
He exercises himself in faith,
Has, when earthly things have vanished,
Found himself and God.

12. [Aria] B tr str bc — C c

Mein Herze glaubt und liebt.
Denn Jesu süße Flammen,
Aus den' die meinen stammen,
Gehn über mich zusammen,
Weil er sich mir ergibt.

My heart believes and loves.
For Jesus's sweet flames,
From which my own come,
Envelop me altogether,
Since He devotes Himself to me.

13. Recitativo T bc — a–G c

O Armut, der kein Reichtum gleicht!
Wenn aus dem Herzen
Die ganze Welt entweicht
Und Jesus nur allein regiert.
So wird ein Christ zu Gott geführt!
Gib, Gott, daß wir es nicht
verscherzen!

O poverty that no wealth equals!
When from the heart
The whole world escapes
And Jesus alone rules.
Thus a Christian is led to God!
Grant, O God, that we do not forfeit it!

14. Choral [Scoring as in no. 7] — G c

Was Gott tut, das ist wohlgetan,
Dabei will ich verbleiben.
Es mag mich auf die rauhe Bahn
Not, Tod und Elend treiben;
So wird Gott mich
Ganz väterlich
In seinen Armen halten;
Drum laß ich ihn nur walten.

Whatever God deals is dealt
bountifully,
I will stand by that.
Though I be driven on a rough road
By want, death, and misery,
Yet God will
In a quite fatherly manner
Hold me in His arms;
Therefore I let Him alone rule.

A Leipzig chronicle, the *Acta Lipsiensium academica*, reports, among the events of May 1723, that:

Den 30. dito als am 1. Sonnt. nach Trinit. führte der neue Cantor u. Collegii Musici Direct. Hr. Joh. Sebastian Bach, so von dem Fürstl. Hofe zu Cöthen hieher kommen, mit guten applausu seine erste Music auf.

On the 30th of the same, the First Sunday after Trinity, the new Cantor and Director of the *Collegium musicum* Mr. Johann Sebastian Bach, who has come here from the princely court at Cöthen, performed his first music, with good applause.

From this formulation we gather that Bach's first music in the Leipzig town church was not regarded solely as the concern of the community's religious life: it was also for them a social event. How well the new cantor performed seemed significant enough for a report to be made that, at least for the present, people were content with him—yet not so important that mistakes were avoided in the coverage: 'Collegii Musici' should read 'Chori Musici', for Bach did not take over the Collegium musicum till 1729. 'Mit guten applausu' (in a metaphorical sense, since there was obviously no clapping) does not sound exactly rapturous, but it is likely that the expectations of the Leipzig people were nonetheless not disappointed. Most Leipzigers were probably united in the belief that they had acquired no star of the first magnitude, no one of the rank of a Telemann, say, and to this they had to resign themselves. Nevertheless, voices had also been raised in support of Bach, notably that of the mayor, Gottfried Lange: 'If Bach were chosen, one could forget Telemann'.

Such was perhaps the frame of mind in which the people of Leipzig listened to Bach's first church music there, Cantata 75. Like many works of the Trinity period in 1723, it is bipartite and of considerable dimensions. The anonymous librettist based its substance upon the Gospel* reading about the rich man and the poor Lazarus. The wealth–poverty antithesis becomes the fundamental idea of the entire text. The warning of the impermanence of earthly wealth in no. 2 is likewise derived from the Gospel reading. The recognition that God casts down and raises up (no. 4) explains the choice of the introductory biblical passage, Psalm 22.26: 'The poor shall eat so that they shall be satisfied . . .'. A Christian therefore joyfully takes upon himself the suffering of the world and, as Lazarus once did, endures its torments patiently (no. 5). For his true wealth is Jesus (no. 3), and therefore even misfortune proves beneficial in the end (no. 6). Following meaningfully from this as the conclusion of Part I is the fifth verse of the hymn *Was Gott tut, das ist wohlgetan* by Samuel Rodigast (1675). In Part II, the librettist attaches a metaphorical meaning to the concepts of poverty and wealth: the Christian is also poor in spirit, and it is only Jesus who makes him rich, for whoever clings firmly to Jesus in faith and thereby overcomes the world is truly wealthy. This reflection is finally endorsed in the last verse of Rodigast's above-named hymn.

The opening chorus* is the first of the great choruses on biblical words of the Leipzig years, for which the composer now had at his disposal the first cantorate of the celebrated choir of St Thomas's—the choir to which Heinrich Schütz had dedicated his *Geistliche Chormusik*. The bipartite structure, with its contrast between a slow, solemn, sharply rhythmic opening and a quick fugal continuation, recalls the form of the French Overture* (a year later, Bach chose this form to inaugurate his cycle of chorale cantatas*). It may also be interpreted, however, as a transference to the vocal sphere of the instrumental prelude-and-fugue pairing. The first section is in itself bipartite: each portion of text acquires its own thematic material after the manner of a motet.* The two sub-sections are, however, united by the independent, rhythmically profiled instrumental theme which is first stated in a ten-bar orchestral introduction. The fugal section that follows is divided by instrumental episodes into three sub-sections. The overall structure of the movement may therefore be represented schematically as follows (italics indicate instrumental passages without choir):

A 'Prelude', bipartite:
Instrumental introduction
(a)'Die Elenden sollen essen . . .': imitative* and freely polyphonic* choral texture with independent instrumental parts and some choral insertion*
Brief episode
(b)'und die nach dem Herrn fragen . . .': canon* at the fifth, with a freely polyphonic continuation; the instruments at first *colla parte** but then again independent
Reprise of the introduction

B Fugue* 'Euer Herz soll ewiglich leben':
(c)First exposition*: solo choir accompanied by continuo, then stretto* entries on the oboes
Episode, oboes and continuo
(c^1)Second exposition: tutti choir + strings; the oboes independent and, at the end, thematic
Episode, complete instrumental ensemble
(c^2)Coda: freely polyphonic choral texture, with the instruments largely *colla parte*; two complete subject entries, in soprano and bass

The recitatives are mostly set as *secco* (nos. 4, 6, 11, and 13), though nos. 2 and 9 are accompanied by strings. Arioso* passages are altogether absent, and plain syllabic* declamation is predominant. In the arias, by comparison with those of later works, it is notable that the virtuoso concertante* element retreats in favour of *cantabile* writing. Thus in all four arias the thematic material of the introductory ritornello also forms the basis of the first vocal passage. This is carried out in a particularly charming manner in the third movement, an aria with strings and oboe in which the tenor enters at first with an unthematic and decidedly vocal 'motto':*

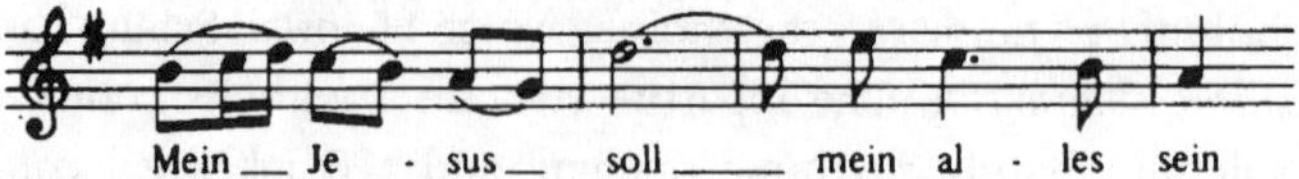

Thereafter the second half of the ritornello is repeated, and only then does the tenor enter with the ritornello's opening phrase, whose six bars he adopts literally:

It can hardly escape notice that, in character, the arias have a certain affinity with dance. The tenor aria just mentioned, no. 3, might be viewed as a polonaise, the soprano aria 'Ich nehme mein Leiden mit Freuden auf mich' with obbligato* oboe d'amore* (no. 5) as a minuet, and the alto aria 'Jesus macht mich geistlich reich' (no. 10), with an obbligato part for unison violins, as a quasi-passepied. The least dance-like aria, and the most strongly influenced by the concerto, is the last, no. 12. The trumpet, which takes no part in the opening movement and otherwise plays only the *cantus firmus** in the sinfonia that opens Part II (see below), is here, in the antepenultimate movement, assigned an unexpectedly significant role. It opens the movement thematically, with the support of the string orchestra, and thereafter comes to the fore with its virtuoso figuration. The bass timbre of the voice part, its wide and powerful intervals, and the radiant brilliance of the trumpet: all these things unite to give a most vivid illustration of the words 'My heart believes and loves . . .'.

It is evident that Bach's setting assigns a more significant role to the chorale than the text provides for it. Hence the concluding chorale of each part (the two movements are musically identical) is not set in the ordinary way as a plain four-part arrangement with doubling instruments. Instead, the vocal texture—chordal in principle but much loosened up into polyphony—is incorporated, one section at a time, within an independent orchestral texture whose theme is derived from the first line of the chorale. The lead is taken by the unison of oboe I and violin I, while the other instruments provide an accompaniment. Bach's use of the chorale in this cantata does not end here, however: exceptionally even for him, the introductory sinfonia to Part II (no. 8) is composed as a chorale arrangement on the basis of the same melody. The *cantus firmus*, here played on the trumpet, is again incorporated line by line within a string texture (plus oboes?) which, however, consists not of obbligato and accompaniment as in the concluding chorale of each part, but of polyphony, though it is not strictly fugal. The theme—

—is subject to frequent motivic transformation: both the first three notes and the semiquaver group later acquire their own significance, independent of the theme, the first as a bell motive* and the second as a sequential pattern.

Whoever was capable of listening with insight could learn decisive things about the new Thomascantor from his first cantata performance. Cantata 75 shows him to be a forward-looking musician, not afraid to incorporate new, even fashionable elements in his composition, not as alien features but as purposeful components within the fundamental structure of the work. Above all, however, this cantata shows him to be a master of chorale treatment. Indeed the chorale *Was Gott tut, das ist wohlgetan* ('Whatever God deals is dealt bountifully') proves to be the very programme of the work and thus a direct product of the exegesis of the Sunday Gospel. Perhaps Bach also had in mind here his own new field of responsibilities, of which seven years later he wrote: '. . . so fügte es Gott, daß zu hiesigem Directore Musices u. Cantore an der Thomas Schule vociret wurde.' ('. . . thus God ordained that I should receive the calling to be *Director Musices* and Cantor here at the St Thomas School.').

O Ewigkeit, du Donnerwort, BWV 20

NBA I/15, p. 135 BC A95 Duration: *c.* 31 mins

1. [Chorale] S + tr da t ATB ob I–III str bc — F C $\frac{3}{4}$ C

O Ewigkeit, du Donnerwort,	**O Eternity, you thunder-word!**
O Schwert, das durch die Seele bohrt,	**O sword that bores through the soul!**
O Anfang sonder Ende!	**O beginning without end!**
O Ewigkeit, Zeit ohne Zeit,	**O Eternity, time without time!**
Ich weiß vor großer Traurigkeit	**I know not, from great sorrow,**
Nicht, wo ich mich hinwende.	**Where to turn.**
Mein ganz erschrocken Herz erbebt,	**My quite terrified heart trembles, so that**
Daß mir die Zung am Gaumen klebt.	**My tongue cleaves to the roof of my mouth.**

2. Recitativo T bc — a–c C

Kein Unglück ist in aller Welt zu finden,	No misfortune is to be found in all the world
Das ewig dauernd sei:	That lasts for ever:
Es muß doch endlich mit der Zeit einmal verschwinden.	It must vanish in the end with time.
Ach! aber ach! die Pein der Ewigkeit hat nur kein Ziel;	Ah! but alas! the pain of eternity has no end;

Sie treibet fort und fort ihr Marterspiel,	It drives on and on its play of torment;
Ja, wie selbst Jesus spricht,	Yes, as Jesus Himself says,
Aus ihr ist kein Erlösung nicht.	**From it there is no redemption.**
3. ARIA T str bc	c $\frac{3}{4}$
Ewigkeit, du machst mir bange,	**Eternity, you make me alarmed:**
Ewig, ewig ist zu lange!	**Eternal, eternal is too long!**
Ach, **hier gilt fürwahr kein Scherz.**	Ah, **this is really no jest.**
Flammen, die auf ewig brennen,	Flames that burn for ever
Ist kein Feuer gleich zu nennen;	Are like no fire that can be named.
Es erschrickt und bebt mein Herz,	It terrifies my heart and makes it tremble
Wenn ich diese Pein bedenke	When I consider this pain
Und den Sinn zur Höllen lenke.	And turn my thoughts to hell.
4. RECITATIVO B bc	g–d C
Gesetzt, es dau'rte der Verdammten Qual	Granted that the torment of the damned lasted
So viele Jahr, als an der Zahl	As many years as in the number
Auf Erden Gras, am Himmel Sterne wären;	Of blades of grass on earth or stars in heaven;
Gesetzt, es sei die Pein so weit hinausgestellt,	Granted that the pain was as widespread
Als Menschen in der Welt	As mankind in the world
Von Anbeginn gewesen,	Has been from the very beginning,
So wäre doch zuletzt	Yet at last
Derselben Ziel und Maß gesetzt:	Its time would be determined and measure laid:
Sie müßte doch einmal aufhören.	It would have to cease one day.
Nun aber, wenn du die Gefahr,	**But now, when the danger,**
Verdammter! tausend Millionen Jahr	O damned one, for a thousand million years,
Mit allen Teufeln ausgestanden,	With all the devils, has been endured,
So ist doch nie der Schluß vorhanden;	Yet the end is never at hand;
Die Zeit, so niemand zählen kann,	**Time, which no one can count,**
Fängt jeden Augenblick	Begins at every moment—
Zu deiner Seelen ewgem Ungelück	To the eternal misfortune of your soul—
Sich stets von neuem an.	Ever anew.
5. ARIA B ob I–III bc	B♭ C
Gott ist gerecht in seinen Werken:	God is just in His deeds:
Auf kurze Sünden dieser Welt	**For the short-term sins of this world**
Hat er **so lange Pein bestellt;**	He has **ordained such long pain;**
Ach wollte doch die Welt dies merken!	Ah, would that the world might heed this!
Kurz ist die Zeit, der Tod geschwind,	**The time is short, death swift;**
Bedenke dies, o Menschenkind!	Consider this, O child of man!

6. ARIA A str bc	d 3/4
O Mensch, errette deine Seele, Entfliehe Satans Sklaverei Und mache dich von Sünden frei, Damit in jener Schwefelhöhle Der Tod, so die Verdammten plagt, Nicht deine Seele ewig nagt. O Mensch, errette deine Seele!	O man, deliver your soul, Flee from Satan's slavery And make yourself free of sins, So that in that cavern of brimstone Death, which torments the damned, Does not for ever gnaw your soul. O man, deliver your soul!
7. CHORAL SATB bc (+ instrs)	F c
Solang ein Gott im Himmel lebt Und über alle Wolken schwebt, Wird solche Marter währen: Es wird sie plagen Kält und Hitz, Angst, Hunger, Schrecken, Feur und Blitz Und sie doch nicht verzehren. Denn wird sich enden diese Pein, Wenn Gott nicht mehr wird ewig sein.	**As long as a God lives in heaven And hovers over all the clouds Will such torments last: They will be plagued by cold and heat, Anguish, hunger, fear, fire, and lightning, And yet not consumed by them. For this pain will end When God is no longer to be eternal.**
Seconda parte	*Second part*
8. ARIA B tr str + ob I–III bc	C c
Wacht auf, wacht auf, verlornen Schafe, Ermuntert euch vom Sündenschlafe Und bessert euer Leben bald! Wacht auf, eh die Posaune schallt, Die euch mit Schrecken aus der Gruft Zum Richter aller Welt vor das Gerichte ruft!	Wake up, wake up, lost sheep, Rouse yourselves from the sleep of sin And improve your life soon! Wake up before the trumpet sounds That calls you in terror from the tomb To the Judge of all the earth for judgement!
9. RECITATIVO A bc	a c
Verlaß, o Mensch, die Wollust dieser Welt, **Pracht, Hoffart, Reichtum, Ehr und Geld;**	Forsake, O man, the pleasure of this world, **Pomp, pride, wealth, honour, and gold;**
Bedenke doch In dieser Zeit annoch, Da dir der Baum des Lebens grünet, Was dir zu deinem Friede dienet! **Vielleicht ist dies der letzte Tag,** Kein Mensch weiß, wenn er sterben mag.	Do consider At this day already— When your Tree of Life grows verdant— The things that serve for your peace! **Perhaps this is the Last Day:** No man knows when he may die.
Wie leicht, wie bald Ist mancher tod und kalt! Man kann noch diese Nacht Den Sarg vor deine Türe bringen. Drum sei vor allen Dingen Auf deiner Seelen Heil bedacht!	How easily, how soon Is many a one dead and cold! Someone could this very night Bring the coffin to your door. Therefore be, before all things, Mindful of your soul's salvation!

10. DUETTO ARIA AT bc a $\frac{3}{4}$

O Menschenkind,	O child of man,
Hör auf geschwind,	Cease promptly
Die Sünd und Welt zu lieben,	To love sin and the world,
Daß nicht die Pein,	So that the pain,
Wo Heulen und Zähnklappen sein,	Where weeping and gnashing of teeth are,
Dich ewig mag betrüben!	May not distress you for ever!
Ach spiegle dich am reichen Mann,	Ah, see your reflection in the rich man
Der in der Qual	Who in his torment
Auch nicht einmal	Cannot have so much as
Ein Tröpflein Wasser haben kann!	A little drop of water!

11. CHORAL SATB bc (+ instrs) F C

O Ewigkeit, du Donnerwort,	**O Eternity, you thunder-word!**
O Schwert, das durch die Seele bohrt,	**O sword that bores through the soul!**
O Anfang sonder Ende!	**O beginning without end!**
O Ewigkeit, Zeit ohne Zeit,	**O Eternity, time without time!**
Ich weiß vor großer Traurigkeit	**I know not, from great sorrow,**
Nicht, wo ich mich hinwende.	**Where to turn.**
Nimm du mich, wenn es dir gefällt,	**Take me, if it pleases You,**
Herr Jesu, in dein Freudenzelt!	**Lord Jesus, into Your tabernacle of joy!**

With this composition Bach inaugurated his cycle of chorale cantatas* on 11 June 1724. The anonymous librettist based his text upon the well-known hymn by Johann Rist of 1642, which is ideally suited to the interpretation of the Gospel* account of the rich man and the poor Lazarus. Moreover, the tenth movement includes a direct reference to the parable, which had been read out beforehand. In the Leipzig hymn books of Bach's day, Rist's hymn was mostly printed with sixteen verses. However, a version shortened to twelve verses, such as that which Gottfried Vopelius, for example, published in his hymn book of 1682, served as the basis of this cantata. Verses 1, 8, and 12 were retained literally in movements 1, 7, and 11, and the other verses paraphrased in turn to form a cantata movement each, except that the fourth movement contains two verses (4 and 5) and the last lines of verse 9—'Vielleicht ist heut der letzte Tag, wer weiß noch, wie man sterben mag'—were adopted in a slightly modified form in the ninth movement, which is otherwise based on verse 10. Overall, the adaptation remains very close to the original—a particular characteristic of the first cantatas of this cycle.

The focal point of Bach's setting is the elaborate opening chorus,* which, as the first movement of his new cantata cycle, Bach significantly casts in the form of a French Overture.* The chorale melody lies in the soprano, reinforced by a slide trumpet. Lines 1–3 are assigned to the slow introductory section, lines 4–6 to the 'vivace' middle section, and lines 7–8 to the slow concluding section, with the result that the musical arch form A B A[1] is superimposed on the *Bar** form, A A B, of the text. Perhaps considerations of textual interpretation contributed to this, for the increase of tempo takes place at the line 'O Ewigkeit, Zeit ohne Zeit' ('O Eternity, time without time'). The chorale melody is underpinned by a predominantly chordal, occasionally freely polyphonic,* texture in the lower voices parts, which remain unthematic throughout. Consequently thematic development takes place entirely in the orchestra. The principal motive* of the slow introductory section is derived from the beginning of the chorale, as the following comparison illustrates:

On the other hand, the theme of the quick middle section, together with its chromatic* counterpoint,* is unrelated to the chorale:

This middle section is not a regular 'school fugue';* indeed, it cannot even be called a fugato, since the intervals of its thematic components are frequently altered. This freedom of compositional technique in the treatment of the vocal and orchestral parts contrasts with a close adherence to the text, which is manifest in a search for striking musical illustrations thereof. Here are some examples:

'Ewigkeit' ('Eternity'): long notes in the vocal substructure and in the strings

'Donnerwort' ('thunder-word'): sudden change to short note-values, with a melismatic* figure in the bass

'Traurigkeit' ('sorrow'): the falling chromatic line from the instrumental counter-subject of the middle section (see above) penetrates into the voice parts

'erschrocken' ('terrified'): jerking rhythms interrupted by rests, first in the orchestra and then in the lower voice parts too.

'klebt' ('cleaves'): held note f^1/f in the voice parts (the instruments have harmonic filling only).

The musical shaping of the recitatives exhibits the characteristics of Bach's mature style: the declamation has become more passionate but also more concise, since the arioso* passages of his early period are largely absent. Only in the ninth movement, at the words 'Pracht, Hoffart, Reichtum, Ehr und Geld' ('Pomp, pride, wealth, honour, and gold'), drawn verbatim from verse 10, is the recitative style enriched by a motivically treated continuo figure. For the rest, *secco* accompanied by continuo is predominant.

As a result, there is a greater contrast between the recitatives and the arias, which interpret both the affect* of the text and its individual turns of phrase. In the tenor aria, no. 3, the held notes on 'Ewigkeit' ('eternity'), 'ewig' ('eternal'), and 'lange' ('long'), and the chromaticism on 'bange' ('alarmed') are already foreshadowed in the ritornello theme, as are the large, powerful, and decisive intervallic leaps on 'Gott ist gerecht' ('God is just') in the bass aria, no. 5. The warning of the alto aria, no. 6, is particularly urgent in effect on account of its repeated change from 3/4 time to an implied 3/2:

Vigorous trumpet calls and rapid scale figures characterize the words 'Wacht auf' ('Wake up!') in the second bass aria, no. 8, turning our thoughts to the trumpet that announces the Last Judgement. Finally, the speech-like continuo motive at the beginning of the duet (no. 10) should not go unmentioned: after the entry of the voice parts, it betokens for the listener a constant warning call of 'O Menschenkind' ('O child of man').

Only in the concluding chorale of each part, identical in musical setting, does Bach's impassioned musical diction give way to a more objective mode of representation. In these plainly set hymn verses, the composer turns into the spokesman of the congregation, who at the end pray that they might be taken up into Jesus's 'tabernacle of joy'.

Brich dem Hungrigen dein Brot, BWV 39

NBA I/15, p. 181 BC A96 Duration: *c.* 24 mins

1. [Chorus] SATB rec I,II ob I,II str bc — g 3/4 C 3/8

'Brich dem Hungrigen dein Brot und die, so im Elend sind, führe ins Haus! So du einen nacket siehest, so kleide ihn und entzeuch dich nicht von deinem Fleisch.

'Break your bread with the hungry, and bring those who are in distress into your house! If you see someone naked, then clothe him, and do not avoid your own kin.

Alsdenn wird dein Licht herfürbrechen wie die Morgenröte, und deine Besserung wird schnell wachsen, und deine Gerechtigkeit wird für dir hergehen, und die Herrlichkeit des Herrn wird dich zu sich nehmen.'

Then your light shall break forth like the dawn and your improvement shall grow swiftly, and your righteousness shall go before you, and the glory of the Lord shall take you to His own home.'

2. RECITATIVO B bc — B♭–a C

Der reiche Gott wirft seinen Überfluß
Auf uns, die wir ohn ihn auch nicht den Odem haben.
Sein ist es, was wir sind; er gibt nur den Genuß,
Doch nicht, daß uns allein nur seine Schätze laben.
Sie sind der Probestein, wodurch er macht bekannt,
Daß er der Armut auch die Notdurft ausgespendet,
Als er mit milder Hand,
Was jener nötig ist, uns reichlich zugewendet.
Wir sollen ihm für sein gelehntes Gut
Die Zinse nicht in seine Scheuren bringen;
Barmherzigkeit, die auf dem Nächsten ruht,
Kann mehr als alle Gab ihm an das Herze dringen.

The bounteous God casts His abundance
Upon us, who without Him do not even have breath.
We are His, that is what we are; He gives us but enjoyment,
Yet not so that His treasures should bless us alone.
They are the touchstone whereby He makes known
That He has dealt out the necessaries of life to poverty also,
When with abundant hand
He bequeathes lavishly to us what is necessary for them.
We should not, for His possessions lent to us,
Bring the tributes into His barns;
Mercy that rests on one's neighbour,
Can, more than all gifts, go straight to His heart.

3. ARIA A ob I vln I solo bc — F 3/8

Seinem Schöpfer noch auf Erden
Nur im Schatten ähnlich werden,
Ist im Vorschmack selig sein.
Sein Erbarmen nachzuahmen,
Streuet hier des Segens Samen,
Den wir dorten bringen ein.

To become like one's Creator still on earth,
Though only as a pale imitation,
Is a foretaste of eternal bliss.
To follow the example of His mercy
Scatters seeds of blessing here
Which we will harvest there.

Seconda parte

Second part

4. [BASS SOLO] B bc — d ¢

'Wohlzutun und mitzuteilen vergesset nicht; denn solche Opfer gefallen Gott wohl.'

'Do not forget to do good and to share; for God is well pleased with such offerings.'

5. ARIA S rec I + II bc — B♭ 6/8

Höchster, was ich habe,
Ist nur deine Gabe.

O Highest One, whatever I have
Is only Your gift.

Wenn vor deinem Angesicht Ich schon mit dem Deinen Dankbar wollt erscheinen, Willt du doch kein Opfer nicht.	If before Your Countenance I should, with whatever is yet Yours, Want to appear thankful, You still want no offering.

6. RECITATIVO A str bc — E♭–g c

Wie soll ich dich, o Herr! denn sattsamlich vergelten,	How then, O Lord, should I repay You sufficiently
Was du an Leib und Seel mir hast zugut getan?	For what You have done for the benefit of my body and soul,
Ja, was ich noch empfang, und solches gar nicht selten,	Indeed, for what I still receive, and that not at all seldom,
Weil ich mich jede Stund noch deiner rühmen kann?	Since every hour I can still boast of You?
Ich hab nichts als den Geist, dir eigen zu ergeben,	To You as Your own I have nothing but my spirit to surrender,
Dem Nächsten die Begierd, daß ich ihm dienstbar werd,	To my neighbour, the desire to be of service,
Der Armut, was du mir gegönnt in diesem Leben,	To the poor, what You have granted me in this life,
Und, wenn es dir gefällt, den schwachen Leib der Erd.	And to the earth, when it pleases You, my weak body.
Ich bringe, was ich kann, Herr! laß es dir behagen,	I bring what I can, Lord! Let it please You,
Daß ich, was du versprichst, auch einst davon mög tragen.	So that what You promised I may one day yield from it.

7. CHORAL SATB bc (+ instrs, rec I + II 8va) — B♭ c

Selig sind, die aus Erbarmen **Sich annehmen fremder Not,** **Sind mitleidig mit den Armen,** **Bitten treulich für sie Gott.** **Die behülflich sind mit Rat,** **Auch, wo möglich, mit der Tat,** **Werden wieder Hülf empfangen** **Und Barmherzigkeit erlangen.**	**Blessed are they who out of mercy** **Attend to the affliction of strangers,** **Are compassionate with the poor,** **And pray faithfully for them to God.** **Those who are helpful in counsel** **And, where possible, in deed** **Shall in return receive help** **And obtain mercy.**

It is sometimes maintained that Bach composed his so-called 'Refugee Cantata' in 1732 for a service to celebrate the banished Protestants of Salzburg. This is no more than an agreeable legend, however, for research has established that the work was in fact written for 23 June 1726. It is, of course, possible that at a repeat performance six years later the cantata found a new purpose which had been anticipated by neither librettist nor composer, but whether this really happened we do not know.

The text is associated with the Sunday Gospel.* The librettists of earlier cantatas for this Sunday placed the poverty–wealth antithesis (BWV 75) or the call for repentance in the face of eternity (BWV 20) in the centre of their deliberations. The librettist of this text, however, sees in the parable of the rich man and the poor Lazarus a demand for active help on behalf of one's fellow human beings and gratitude for God's gifts. The libretto is drawn from the recently rediscovered cycle—largely uniform in formal layout—whose texts were set on a number of occasions both by Bach and by his Meiningen cousin Johann Ludwig Bach. Both parts of the work are introduced by a biblical text. The Old Testament words that open Part I, Isaiah 58.7–8, are attached to the injunction to love one's neighbour (nos. 2–3), the New Testament words of Part II, Hebrews 13.16 (no. 4), to an expression of gratitude for gifts received (no. 5), to the vow to cultivate love of one's neighbour, and to the prayer that one day I myself will be received with compassion by God (no. 6). The concluding chorale—the sixth verse of the hymn *Kommt, laßt euch den Herren lehren* by David Denicke (1648)—brings all these ideas together once more.

Bach's music shows the composer at the height of his powers. This applies, in particular, to the large-scale opening chorus,* whose 218 bars sum up the entire range of compositional means that Bach had acquired and developed further, methods that he now employed with perfect mastery. From the motet* Bach adopts the principle of a series of distinct passages for the various portions of the text: each grammatic sentence receives its own appropriate setting. This takes place within three large complexes, each of which is richly articulated in itself; we shall call them A, B, and C. The middle section B is relatively brief and predominantly chordal, taking on a mediating function within the overall structure. This is clear from its harmony: it modulates from the dominant D minor to the subdominant C minor and thereby allows the two surrounding complexes to be equivalent in key structure, each modulating to the dominant of its initial key (g–d and c–g). These two outer complexes are complementary in structure: in section A, two similar, mainly chordal passages surround a fugal section; in section C, two fugal passages based on the same subject surround a more chordal section. The overall structure of the movement may therefore be represented as follows (italics denote instrumental passages):

Introductory sinfonia: antiphonal exchanges between recorders, oboes and strings

A 'Brich dem Hungrigen dein Brot . . .', g–d $\frac{3}{4}$

- a Choral insertion* within the *introductory sinfonia, slightly expanded*
- b Fugal exposition* with *instrumental accompaniment figures*
- a Reprise of the first passage, transposed to the dominant

B 'So du einen nacket siehest . . .', d–c **C**

- c Imitative-chordal texture with *instrumental accompaniment figures*

C 'Alsdenn wird dein Licht herfürbrechen . . .', c–g $\frac{3}{8}$

- d Fugal exposition with *instruments partly colla parte,* partly accompanying* e Two brief, largely homophonic* choral passages ('und deine Besserung . . .' and 'und deine Gerechtigkeit . . .') with *instruments as in* d

d' Free reprise of d to new text ('und die Herrlichkeit des Herrn . . .') followed by brief chordal coda

The introductory sinfonia, with its block-chordal sequences interspersed with rests, passed between the various instrumental groups, unmistakably depicts the gesture of breaking bread. The fugue* subjects in sections d and d' are, in essence, identical despite their apparent differences, as the following comparison shows:

The movements based on madrigalian* verse are grouped symmetrically around the New Testament passage.The outer components, the recitatives nos. 2 and 6, are both couched in plain syllabic* declamation, lacking arioso* insertions—if we disregard the closing notes of no. 2, to the words 'an das Herze dringen' ('go straight to His heart'). But whereas the first recitative is a *secco* with continuo accompaniment, the second is fully scored for strings and by this means the question and prayer therein addressed to God are raised to prominence. The arias nos. 3 and 5 are set for a small number of parts only, no doubt in deliberate contrast to the fullness of sound of the opening chorus: no. 3 requires two obbligato* instruments, oboe and solo violin, and no. 5 unites the two recorders in a single obbligato part. The two arias are also similar in formal structure: both are bipartite, dispensing with the traditional da capo* of the opening vocal section in favour of a ritornello frame. In both cases, moreover, concertante* writing for the obbligato instruments contrasts with a *cantabile* voice part, especially in no. 5, which has a simple-song-like character.

The setting of the New Testament words in continuo texture in no. 4 forms another conspicuous contrast with the tutti of the introductory movement. There, the fullness of texture brought before one's very eyes, as it were, the general validity of the commandment of mercy. Here, on the other hand, it is as if we hear Christ Himself speaking (note the bass voice) with stirring insistency. The movement is one of those bass solos, formally situated between arioso and aria, that Bach chose on several occasions for the setting of biblical words. Although the entire continuo accompaniment is shaped out of motives* from the opening ritornello, forming a *basso quasi ostinato,** we nonetheless admire the inexhaustible richness of inspiration with which Bach sets the individual passages of text in ever-renewed urgency, placing strong emphasis first on one word and then on another ('. . . gefallen Gott *wohl* . . . gefallen *Gott* wohl'). The concluding chorale is a plain choral setting to the melody *Freu dich sehr, o meine Seele*.

2.2 Second Sunday after Trinity

EPISTLE: 1 John 3.13–18: 'Whoever does not love abides in death'.
GOSPEL: Luke 14.16–24: The parable of the great supper.

Die Himmel erzählen die Ehre Gottes, BWV 76

NBA I/16, p. 3 BC A97 Duration: *c.* 35 mins

1. [CHORUS] SATB + SA[TB] rip tr ob I,II str bc	C 3/4
'Die Himmel erzählen die Ehre Gottes, und die Feste verkündiget seiner Hände Werk. Es ist keine Sprache noch Rede, da man nicht ihre Stimme höre.'	'The heavens declare the honour of God, and the firmament proclaims His handiwork. There is no speech nor language where their voice is not heard.'
2. RECITATIVO T str bc	a–e C
So läßt sich Gott nicht unbezeuget!	So God has not left Himself without witness!
Natur und Gnade redt alle Menschen an:	Nature and Grace address all mankind:
Dies alles hat ja Gott getan, Daß sich die Himmel regen Und Geist und Körper sich bewegen. Gott selbst hat sich zu euch geneiget Und ruft durch Boten ohne Zahl: Auf! kommt zu meinem Liebesmahl!	All this God has indeed done So that the heavens move And spirit and body stir. God Himself has inclined to you And calls through countless messengers: Rise up! come to my love-feast!
3. ARIA S vln solo bc	G C
Hört, ihr Völker, Gottes Stimme, Eilt zu seinem Gnadenthron!	Hear God's voice, you peoples, Hasten to His throne of grace!

Aller Dinge Grund und Ende
Ist sein eingeborner Sohn,
Daß sich alles zu ihm wende.

The ground and end of all things
Is His only begotten Son,
So that all things turn to Him.

4. Recitativo B bc — e–C c

Wer aber hört,
Da sich der größte Haufen
Zu andern Göttern kehrt?
Der älteste Götze eigner Lust
Beherrscht der Menschen Brust.
Die Weisen brüten Torheit aus,
Und Belial sitzt wohl in Gottes Haus,
Weil auch die Christen selbst von Christo laufen.

But who hears,
Since the greatest multitude
Turn to other gods?
The oldest idol of his own pleasure
Dominates man's breast.
The wise hatch foolishness,
And Belial sits in God's House,
For even Christians themselves run away from Christ.

5. Aria B tr str + ob I,II bc — C c

Fahr hin, abgöttische Zunft!
Sollt sich die Welt gleich verkehren,
Will ich doch Christum verehren,
Er ist das Licht der Vernunft.

Go away, idolatrous gang!
Through the world should be perverted,
I would still honour Christ;
He is the Light of Reason.

6. Recitativo A bc — e c

Du hast uns, Herr, von allen Straßen
Zu dir geruft,
Als wir im Finsternis der Heiden saßen,
Und, wie das Licht die Luft
Belebet und erquickt,
Uns auch erleuchtet und belebet,
Ja mit dir selbst gespeiset und getränket
Und deinen Geist geschenket,
Der stets in unserm Geiste schwebet.
Drum sei dir dies Gebet demütigst zugeschickt:

From all the highways, Lord,
You have called us to You,
When we sat in the darkness of the Gentiles;
And, as light enlivens
And invigorates the air,
So too You have lightened and enlivened us,
Indeed, provided us with Yourself as meat and drink
And given us Your Spirit,
Which constantly moves in our spirit.
Therefore may this prayer be sent to You most humbly:

7. Choral SATB + SA[TB] rip tr str + ob I,II bc — e c

Es woll uns Gott genädig sein
Und seinen Segen geben;
Sein Antlitz uns mit hellem Schein
Erleucht zum ewgen Leben,
Daß wir erkennen seine Werk
Und was ihm lieb auf Erden,
Und Jesus Christus Heil und Stärk
Bekannt den Heiden werden
Und sie zu Gott bekehren.

May God be gracious to us
And give us His blessing;
May His face with bright shining
Lighten us to eternal life,
So that we recognize His work
And what is dear to Him on earth,
And Jesus Christ's salvation and power
Become known to the nations
And they will turn to God.

German	English	Key	Time
Seconda parte	*Second part*		
8. SINFONIA ob d'am vla da g bc		e	C
9. RECITATIVO B str bc		b–a	C
Gott segne noch die treue Schar,	God bless the faithful throng,		
Damit sie seine Ehre	So that His honour,		
Durch Glauben, Liebe, Heiligkeit	Through faith, love, and sanctity,		
Erweise und vermehre.	May be displayed and augmented.		
Sie ist der Himmel auf der Erden	This throng is heaven on earth,		
Und muß durch steten Streit	And through constant struggle		
Mit Haß und mit Gefahr	With hatred and with danger		
In dieser Welt gereinigt werden.	In this world, it must be purified.		
10. ARIA T bc		a	3/4
Hasse nur, hasse mich recht,	Hate then, hate me truly,		
Feindlichs Geschlecht!	You hostile generation!		
Christum gläubig zu umfassen,	To embrace Christ in faith		
Will ich alle Freude lassen.	I would forgo all joy.		
11. RECITATIVO A bc		F–C	C
Ich fühle schon im Geist	I feel already in spirit		
Wie Christus mir	How Christ shows me		
Der Liebe Süßigkeit erweist	The sweetness of love		
Und mich mit Manna speist,	And feeds me with manna,		
Damit sich unter uns allhier	So that among us here		
Die brüderliche Treue	Brotherly faithfulness		
Stets stärke und verneue.	May ever be strengthened and renewed.		
12. ARIA A ob d'am vla da g bc		e	9/8
Liebt, ihr Christen, in der Tat!	Love, you Christians, in your deeds!		
Jesus stirbet für die Brüder,	Jesus died for the brothers,		
Und sie sterben für sich wieder,	And they in turn die for each other,		
Weil er sich verbunden hat.	For He has made common cause with them.		
13. RECITATIVO T bc		C–e	C
So soll die Christenheit	Thus shall Christendom		
Die Liebe Gottes preisen	Extol the Love of God		
Und sie an sich erweisen:	And exhibit it in itself,		
Bis in die Ewigkeit	Until in eternity		
Die Himmel frommer Seelen	The devout souls of the heavens		
Gott und sein Lob erzählen.	Declare God and His praise.		
14. CHORAL [Scoring as in no. 7]		e	C
Es danke, Gott, und lobe dich	**Let the people praise and thank You,**		
Das Volk in guten Taten;	**O God, in good deeds;**		
Das Land bringt Frucht und bessert sich,	**The land brings forth fruit and improves,**		
Dein Wort ist wohlgeraten.	**Your Word prospers.**		
Uns segne Vater und der Sohn,	**May the Father and the Son bless us,**		
Uns segne Gott, der Heilge Geist,	**May God the Holy Spirit bless us,**		

Dem alle Welt die Ehre tu,	**May the whole world honour Him,**
Für ihm sich fürchte allermeist	**Fear Him most of all,**
Und sprech von Herzen: Amen!	**And say from the heart 'Amen!'**

Die Himmel erzählen die Ehre Gottes, the second cantata that Bach wrote as the newly appointed Thomascantor in Leipzig, received its first performance in the Thomaskirche on 6 June 1723. In form it is clearly recognizable as a sister-work to the first Leipzig cantata, No. 75; and the zeal with which Bach devoted himself to his new responsibilities is demonstrated by the considerable dimensions of both works. They have in common their two-part design, and in both cases Part II opens with an instrumental sinfonia.

The anonymous librettist refers to the Sunday Gospel,* choosing as his theme God's invitation to mankind to turn to Him. The words from the Psalms (19.1 and 3) that preface the work are to be understood thus: the entire cosmos is one great glorification of the splendid works of God, and therefore mankind is called upon to honour Him (nos. 1–3). In accordance with the parable from the Sunday Gospel, nos. 4 and 5 express indignation over the fact that the 'greatest multitude' reject God's call and turn to other gods. Therefore God has called the Gentiles to Himself 'from all the highways' (cf. Luke 14.23) and enlightened them (no. 6). The first verse of Martin Luther's paraphrase of Psalm 67 (1523) concludes Part I with a prayer for God's blessing. Part II deals with the task of the 'faithful throng' who have accepted God's invitation (no. 9) and consequently find themselves exposed to the hatred of the world (nos. 9 and 10). It is their duty to bestow upon their brothers in the world the love of Christ that has been shown to them (nos. 11–13), a demand that is encountered in the Sunday Epistle.* The work concludes with the third verse of Luther's psalm paraphrase. The libretto—exceptionally fine both poetically and in content—on account of its very general train of thought, allowed the cantata to be reused on other occasions. Accordingly, Bach seems to have performed at least Part I at the Reformation Festival, for this occasion was mentioned when the work was offered for sale by the Leipzig firm Breitkopf in 1761.

A distinctive feature of Bach's setting is its variety of relatively brief movements. The most important movement is the large-scale opening chorus,* whose instrumental scoring demands trumpet as well as oboes, strings, and continuo, while its vocal parts—in accordance with typical baroque practice—are to be sung with and without ripieno doubling. Formally, it is bipartite: a vocal transference, as it were, of the instrumental form of prelude and fugue. The prelude-like section A, in contrast with older examples of its kind, is uniformly structured by virtue of its independent orchestral parts, whose thematic material is stated in the introductory sinfonia and maintained after the entry of the voice parts. The B section that follows, which is based on a new theme, takes the form of a permutation fugue.* In a splendid process of enhancement, it begins with solo choir and continues with tutti choir, plus woodwind and strings, up to the crowning thematic entry of the trumpet. The coda consists of a canonic complex based on a modified version of the fugue subject, followed unexpectedly by the last four bars of the introductory sinfonia with choral insertion.*

The recitative that forms the second movement is given special musical weight by its string accompaniment and its extended middle section, in which motivic violin figures lend particular emphasis to the declamation of the voice as it devoutly contemplates the great works of God. The well-known aria 'Hört, ihr Völker, Gottes Stimme', no. 3, is stamped by a brief motive*—by contrast with Bach's numerous very extensive aria themes—which again and again seems to call out the words 'Hört, ihr Völker' ('Hear, you peoples!'); it is nonetheless rounded out via speech-like rests into a large melodic line. A brief recitative, no. 4, leads to another aria, no. 5, which contrasts with the first not only in text but in its full scoring (for trumpet and strings doubled by oboes) and in the deep pitch of its voice part (bass). Speech-like motives and rests are again conspicuous in the melody of the instrumental ritornello, but the voice part also contains extended coloraturas.*

The next two movements, nos. 6 and 7, merge into one another, proceeding from free *secco* recitative, via arioso* with continuo accompaniment, to chorale with independent instrumental parts. Bach here enriches the standard plain four-part chorale not only with the obbligato* of the first violin but with inter-line episodes in which the trumpet anticipates, in whole or in part, the melody of the chorale line that follows. In addition, we hear in the continuo an ostinato* bass motive which is derived from a lightly decorated version of the opening line of the chorale. This ostinato figure is another of those speech-like motives interspersed with rests in which this cantata is particularly rich.

In Part II, surely in recollection of the post of Cöthen Capellmeister that he had just quitted, Bach introduces a chamber-music sonority. His favoured instruments are oboe d'amore* and viola da gamba which, alongside the continuo, introduce the second part of the cantata with a sinfonia, no. 8. This piece, whose *adagio–vivace* sequence resembles that of a French Overture,* was later reused by Bach, with unimportant changes, in his organ trio sonata BWV 528. A brief recitative accompanied by strings, no. 9, leads to an aria over an ostinato bass, no. 10, whose impassioned affect* recalls no. 5 (the aria 'Fahr hin, abgöttische Zunft!'). On this occasion, however, no doubt in view of the personal statement of the text, Bach adopts the minimum texture of continuo accompaniment.[1] With the order of Part I reversed, we now hear a mediating

[1] Here it is necessary to contradict a widespread misinterpretation. As the sources reveal, the participation of viola da gamba in the continuo is to be understood not as a replacement but as a complement to the other continuo instruments. The sharply biting impulse of the movement should not be misconstrued as a tender gamba solo!

recitative, mostly in the form of arioso, followed by a lovely aria (no. 12, a special gem of this cantata) in the choice scoring of the sinfonia to Part II—that is, with oboe d'amore and viola da gamba as obbligato instruments. After a brief recitative, no. 13, the chorale returns to end the cantata, with its text altered to the last verse of the hymn.

Ach Gott, vom Himmel sieh darein, BWV 2

NBA I/16, p. 83 BC A98 Duration: *c.* 20 mins

1. Choral SATB (+ trb I–IV ob I,II str) bc	d ¢
Ach Gott, vom Himmel sieh darein	**Ah God, look down from heaven**
Und laß dichs doch erbarmen!	**And take pity on us!**
Wie wenig sind der Heilgen dein,	**How few are Your saints,**
Verlassen sind wir Armen.	**We wretches are abandoned.**
Dein Wort man nicht läßt haben wahr,	**Your Word is not believed**
Der Glaub ist auch verloschen gar	**And the Faith is quite extinguished**
Bei allen Menschenkindern.	**Among all the children of men.**
2. Recitativo T bc	c–d C
Sie lehren eitel falsche List,	**They teach idle, false cunning,**
Was wider Gott und seine Wahrheit ist;	Which is against God and His Truth;
Und was der eigen Witz erdenket	And what their own wit devises
—O Jammer! der die Kirche schmerzlich kränket—	—O misery that grievously infects the Church!—
Das muß anstatt der Bibel stehn.	That has to stand in place of the Bible.
Der eine wählet dies, der andre das,	The one chooses this, the other that;
Die törichte Vernunft ist ihr Kompaß;	Foolish reason is their compass;
Sie gleichen denen Totengräbern,	They resemble the graves of the dead
Die, ob sie zwar von außen schön,	Which, though fine from without,
Nur Stank und Moder in sich fassen	Contain only stench and rot
Und lauter Unflat sehen lassen.	And exhibit nothing but filth.
3. Aria A vln I solo bc	B♭ 3/4
Tilg, o Gott, die Lehren,	Strike out, O God, the teachings
So dein Wort verkehren!	That pervert Your Word!
Wehre doch der Ketzerei	Resist heresy
Und allen Rottengeistern;	And all the spirit-rabble;
Denn sie sprechen ohne Scheu:	For they say without reserve:
Trotz dem, der uns will meistern!	Defy Him who would master us!
4. Recitativo B str bc	E♭–g C
Die Armen sind verstört,	**The poor are oppressed;**
Ihr seufzend Ach! ihr ängstlich Klagen	Their sighing 'Ah!', their anxious complaints
Bei soviel Kreuz und Not,	At so much cross-bearing and distress,

Wodurch die Feinde fromme Seelen plagen,	With which enemies plague pious souls,
Dringt in das Gnadenohr des Allerhöchsten ein.	Penetrate the gracious ear of the Most High.
Darum spricht Gott: Ich muß ihr Helfer sein!	Therefore God says: I must be their helper!
Ich hab ihr Flehn erhört,	**I have heard their entreaty;**
Der Hilfe Morgenrot,	The dawn of help,
Der reinen Wahrheit heller Sonnenschein	The bright sunshine of pure Truth
Soll sie mit neuer Kraft,	Shall, with new strength
Die Trost und Leben schafft,	That brings comfort and life,
Erquicken und erfreun.	Refresh and delight them.
Ich will mich ihrer Not erbarmen,	I will have mercy on their distress;
Mein heilsam Wort	My wholesome Word
Soll sein die Kraft der Armen.	**Shall be the strength of the poor.**
5. Aria T vln I + ob I + II vln II vla bc	g c
Durchs Feuer wird das Silber rein,	Through fire is silver purified,
Durchs Kreuz das Wort bewährt erfunden.	Through the Cross is the Word proven.
Drum soll ein Christ zu allen Stunden	Therefore a Christian should at all times
Im Kreuz und Not geduldig sein.	Be patient in cross-bearing and distress.
6. Choral SATB bc (+ instrs)	d c
Das wollst du, Gott, bewahren rein	**Would You keep it pure, O God,**
Für diesem arg'n Geschlechte;	**From this wicked generation;**
Und laß uns dir befohlen sein,	**And let us be commended to You,**
Daß sichs in uns nicht flechte.	**So that they do not mix with us.**
Der gottlos Hauf sich umher findt,	**The godless mob is found here and there,**
Wo solche lose Leute sind	**Where such vile folk are**
In deinem Volk erhaben.	**Exalted among Your people.**

This chorale cantata *is based on Martin Luther's adaptation of Psalm 12 (1524), which laments that mankind turns away from God and is led astray into godless living by heretical teaching. The first and last verses are retained word for word (nos. 1 and 6), but each of the inner verses is paraphrased to form a recitative or aria (nos. 2–5). Several lines from verses 2 and 4, however, are adopted literally, or almost so, in the second and fourth movements. In general, the anonymous text editor follows Luther's hymn very accurately. The image of the graves that 'Contain only stench and rot' in the second movement is drawn from Matthew 23.27; but specific allusions to the Sunday Gospel* are nowhere to be found. However, the fundamental concept of Luther's hymn is in itself an adequate exegesis of the Sunday Gospel with its account of the absence of the guests invited for supper.

Bach's composition, the second of the cycle of chorale cantatas, was written for 18 June 1724. A contributory factor in the shaping of the opening chorus* was Bach's intention of marking the start of the cycle by varying the character of the opening movements. This particular first movement is the *locus classicus* of the *cantus firmus** motet:* the chorale melody is delivered by the alto in long notes, with each line first prepared by fugal treatment of its melody in the other voices. The constant change in the number of parts that thereby arises, with its progressive increase in each line up to the entry of the alto, lends the movement a special structurally conditioned dynamic. On the other hand, due to the lack of obbligato* instrumental parts, the chorus evokes an antiquated, archaic impression: only the continuo is at times given an independent part; the other instruments simply double the voices.

The second movement is composed as a *secco* recitative accompanied by continuo, but the two chorale-based lines are set as 'adagio' arioso,* with their associated melody (that of lines 1 and 5) not only adopted in the voice but even taken up canonically in the continuo. In the aria 'Tilg, o Gott, die Lehren', no. 3, the 'modern' concertante* style comes into its own, witness the lively figurations of the obbligato solo violin. In the middle section, Bach again avails himself of the opportunity to quote the chorale melody in the alto at the last line of verse 3, which is preserved almost word for word: 'Trotz dem, der uns will meistern!' ('Defy Him who would master us!'; Luther has 'Wer ist, der uns sollt meistern').

The recitative 'Die Armen sind verstört', no. 4, accompanied by strings, changes into arioso for the middle section which speaks of God's hearing our entreaty. In the outer sections, the relatively lively part-writing for the accompanying strings demands correspondingly strict rhythmic declamation in the voice, so that even the make-up of the recitative passages approaches arioso. The aria 'Durchs Feuer wird das Silber rein', no. 5, is supported by a decidedly chordal and periodically articulated instrumental texture for two oboes and strings. It is possible that the constantly recurring, counter-rotating melodic lines—admittedly more striking to the eye than to the ear—are intended to signify the conversion of the Christian, who is purified by the Cross:

In the middle section, the orchestra is at first silent (except for the continuo), re-entering only towards the end, after which two Adagio bars—'Im Kreuz und Not geduldig sein' ('Be patient in cross-bearing and distress')—lead back to the da capo*. The final chorale verse takes the form of a plain choral setting with doubling instruments.

2.3 Third Sunday after Trinity

Epistle: 1 Peter 5.6–11: 'Cast all your cares upon Him, for He cares for you'.
Gospel: Luke 15.1–10: The parables of the lost sheep and the lost coin.

Ich hatte viel Bekümmernis, BWV 21

NBA I/16, p. 111 BC A99 Duration: *c.* 44 mins

1. Sinfonia ob str bc — c/d[2] C
2. Chorus SATB ob str bsn bc — c/d C

'Ich hatte viel Bekümmernis in meinem Herzen; aber deine Tröstungen erquicken meine Seele.'	'I had much grief in my heart; but Your consolations revive my soul.'

3. Aria S ob bc — c/d 12/8

Seufzer, Tränen, Kummer, Not,	Sighs, tears, grief, distress,
Ängstlichs Sehnen, Furcht und Tod	Anxious yearning, fear and death
Nagen mein beklemmtes Herz,	Gnaw at my heavy heart;
Ich empfinde Jammer, Schmerz.	I feel misery, sorrow.

4. Recitativo T str bc — c–f/d–g C

Wie hast du dich, mein Gott,	Why, then, my God,
In meiner Not,	In my distress,
In meiner Furcht und Zagen	In my fear and dismay,
Denn ganz von mir gewandt?	Have You quite turned away from me?
Ach! kennst du nicht dein Kind?	Ah! do You not know Your child?
Ach! hörst du nicht das Klagen	Ah! do You not hear the lamentation
Von denen, die dir sind	Of those who are linked to You

[2] The first specified key refers to *Chorton** or 'choir pitch' (in Leipzig, *Kammerton* or 'chamber pitch'), the second to *Kammerton*.

Mit Bund und Treu verwandt?
Du warest meine Lust
Und bist mir grausam worden:
Ich suche dich an allen Orten;
Ich ruf und schrei dir nach,
Allein mein Weh und Ach!
Scheint itzt, als sei es dir ganz
 unbewußt.

By covenant and faithfulness?
You were my delight
And have become cruel to me;
I seek You on all sides;
I call and cry to You;
However, my woe and lament seem
Now as if You were quite unaware of
 them.

5. ARIA T str bsn bc — f/g C

Bäche von gesalznen Zähren,
Fluten rauschen stets einher.
 Sturm und Wellen mich versehren,
 Und dies trübsalsvolle Meer
 Will mir Geist und Leben
  schwächen,
 Mast und Anker wollen brechen,
 Hier versink ich in den Grund,
 Dort seh in der Hölle Schlund.

Streams of salty tears,
Floods rush along continually.
 Storm and waves destroy me,
 And this sea full of tribulation
 Would weaken my spirit and life,
 Mast and anchor would break;
 Here I sink into the ground,
 There I look into the jaws of hell.

6. CHORUS SATB (+ SATB rip) ob str bsn bc — f–c/g–d 3/4 C

'Was betrübst du dich, meine Seele,
und bist so unruhig in mir? Harre
auf Gott! Denn ich werde ihm noch
danken, daß er meines Angesichtes
Hilfe und mein Gott ist.'

'Why are you cast down, O my soul,
and why are you so disquieted within
me? Wait upon God! For I shall yet thank
Him for being the help of my
countenance and my God.'

Nach der Predigt / *After the sermon*

7. RECITATIVO SB str bc — E♭–B♭/F–C C

Seele
Ach Jesu, meine Ruh,
Mein Licht, wo bleibest du?
Jesus
O Seele, sieh! Ich bin bei dir.
Seele
Bei mir?
Hier ist ja lauter Nacht.
Jesus
Ich bin dein treuer Freund,
Der auch im Dunkeln wacht,
Wo lauter Schalken seind.
Seele
Brich doch mit deinem Glanz und
 Licht des Trostes ein!
Jesus
Die Stunde kömmet schon,
Da deines Kampfes Kron
Dir wird ein süßes Labsal sein.

Soul
Ah Jesus, my repose,
My light, where are you?
Jesus
O soul, see! I am with you.
Soul
With me?
Here is indeed nothing but night.
Jesus
I am your faithful Friend
Who watches over you even in darkness,
Where plain rascals are.
Soul
Break in, then, with the radiance and
 light of Your comfort!
Jesus
The hour already arrives
When your strife's crown
Shall be a sweet refreshment for you.

8. ARIA DUETTO SB bc — E♭/F C $\frac{3}{8}$ C

Seele	*Soul*
Jesus	*Jesus*
Komm, mein Jesu, und erquicke	Come, my Jesus, and replenish me
Ja, ich komme und erquicke	Yes, I come and replenish you
Und erfreu mit deinem Blicke!	And delight me with Your glance!
Dich mit meinem Gnadenblicke.	With My gracious glance.
Diese Seele,	This soul
Deine Seele,	Your soul
Die soll sterben	Shall die
Die soll leben	Shall live
Und nicht leben	And not live
Und nicht sterben,	And not die;
Und in ihrer Unglückshöhle	And in its cavern of misfortune
Hier aus dieser Wundenhöhle	Here from this cavern of wounds
Ganz verderben.	Completely perish.
Sollt du erben	You shall inherit
Ich muß stets in Kummer schweben,	I must constantly hover in affliction;
Heil durch diesen Saft der Reben.	Salvation from this juice of vines.
Ja, ach ja, ich bin verloren,	Yes, ah yes, I am lost,
Nein, ach nein, du bist erkoren,	No, ah no, you have been chosen,
Nein, ach nein, du hassest mich.	No, ah no, You hate me.
Ja, ach ja, ich liebe dich.	Yes, ah yes, I love you.
Ach, Jesu, durchsüße mir Seele und Herze!	Ah, Jesus, sweeten my soul and heart!
Entweichet, ihr Sorgen, verschwinde, du Schmerze!	Depart, you cares; vanish, you pains!
Komm, mein Jesu, und erquicke	Come, my Jesus, and replenish
Ja, ich komme und erquicke	Yes, I come and replenish
Mich mit deinem Gnadenblicke.	Me with Your gracious glance.
Dich mit meinem Gnadenblicke.	You with My gracious glance.

9. CHORUS [+ CHORALE] SATB (+ SATB rip) bc (strophe 2: + trb I–IV + ob + str) — g/a $\frac{3}{4}$

'Sei nun wieder zufrieden, meine Seele, denn der Herr tut dir Guts.'	'Now be content once more, my soul, for the Lord does you good.'
Was helfen uns die schweren Sorgen,	**What good are heavy cares?**
Was hilft uns unser Weh und Ach?	**What good are our woes and laments?**
Was hilft es, daß wir alle Morgen	**What good is it that every morning**
Beseufzen unser Ungemach?	**We bemoan our affliction?**
Wir machen unser Kreuz und Leid	**We make our cross-bearing and suffering**
Nur größer durch die Traurigkeit.	**But greater through sorrow.**

Denk nicht in deiner Drangsalshitze,	**Think not in the the heat of your ordeal**
Daß du von Gott verlassen seist,	**That you are forsaken by God**
Und daß Gott der im Schoße sitze,	**And that God places in His bosom**
Der sich mit stetem Glücke speist.	**Him who feeds on constant good fortune.**
Die folgend Zeit verändert viel	**The coming time will alter much**
Und setzet jeglichem sein Ziel.	**And appoint to each his goal.**

10. Aria T bc — F/G 3/8

Erfreue dich, Seele, erfreue dich, Herze,	Rejoice, O soul; rejoice, O heart;
Entweiche nun, Kummer, verschwinde, du Schmerze!	Depart now, grief; vanish, sorrow!
Verwandle dich, Weinen, in lauteren Wein!	Transform yourself, whining, into pure wine!
Es wird nun mein Ächzen ein Jauchzen mir sein.	My moaning will now become a singing to me.
Es brennet und flammet die reineste Kerze	There now burns and flames the purest candle
Der Liebe, des Trostes in Seele und Brust,	Of love, of comfort in my soul and breast,
Weil Jesus mich tröstet mit himmlischer Lust.	For Jesus consoles me with heavenly delight.

11. Chorus SATB (+ SATB rip) tr I–III timp ob str bsn bc — C/D C

'Das Lamm, das erwürget ist, ist würdig zu nehmen Kraft und Reichtum und Weisheit und Stärke und Ehre und Preis und Lob.	'The Lamb that was slain is worthy to receive power and riches and wisdom and strength and honour and praise and glory.
Lob und Ehre und Preis und Gewalt sei unserm Gott von Ewigkeit zu Ewigkeit. Amen, alleluja!'	Glory and honour and praise and power be to our God from eternity to eternity. Amen, alleluia!'

The origin of this cantata is largely obscure.[3] The earliest version, of which only traces survive, was possibly a dialogue cantata for soprano and bass,[4] with interspersed choral psalm quotations, in nine movements (nos. 1–9), perhaps for the Third Sunday after Trinity (1713?). Bach subsequently expanded the work, drawing an additional aria and chorus* (nos. 10 and 11) from elsewhere, which entailed the addition of trumpets and timpani to the instrumental ensemble. He also transferred the soprano solos to tenor and described the work as 'per ogni tempo' ('for any occasion') on the wrapper of the performing parts, the sole surviving original sources. According to a no longer verifiable

[3] The following attempted reconstruction of its history is based largely on the work of Paul Brainard (KB, NBA I/16, 1984), though modified by more recent scholarship.

[4] See Christoph Wolff, ' "Die betrübte und wieder getröstete Seele": Zum Dialog-Charakter der Kantate "Ich hatte viel Bekümmernis" BWV 21', *BJ* 1996, 139–45.

tradition, Bach performed the work thus expanded—in C minor at *Kammerton* or 'chamber pitch'*—at his audition for the post of organist at the Liebfrauenkirche, Halle, in December 1713.[5] Moreover, an autograph inscription on the title-page informs us that he performed it—now evidently in C minor at *Chorton** or choir pitch, which corresponds with D minor at *Kammerton*—on the Third Sunday after Trinity (17 June) 1714 in Weimar.

Of the numerous subsequent revivals, one can be dated, on the documentary evidence of the original parts, within Bach's Cöthen period (1717–23). Since the well-known Hamburg writer on music Johann Mattheson knew and criticized the work, Bach's visit to Hamburg to apply for the post of organist at the Jacobikirche in November 1720 presents itself as a possible occasion. This time Bach returned to the original soprano–bass dialogue structure and performed the work in D minor at *Kammerton*. A further revival took place in Leipzig on the Third Sunday after Trinity (13 June) 1723—the third cantata performance after Bach took up his Leipzig post. The work was now given in C minor at *Kammerton*, the solo soprano part divided between soprano and tenor, four trombones added to reinforce the vocal parts of the ninth movement, a four-part ripieno group added to the vocal ensemble, and the oboe part doubled in the four choruses (nos. 2, 6, 9, and 11).[6] Today's performances (and the above details) are based upon this last-transmitted, Leipzig version, which may have been heard several times during Bach's cantorship at St Thomas's.

By comparison with Bach's other cantata texts of 1714, the libretto, with its many interspersed biblical movements, seems decidedly antiquated: no. 2 is drawn from Psalm 94.19, no. 6 from Psalm 42.11, no. 9 from Psalm 116.7, and no. 11 from Revelation 5.12–13. The madrigalian* movements, on the other hand, correspond in style with the poems of Salomo Franck, to whom we have also ascribed the texts of the three preceding cantatas of 1714, BWV 182, 12, and 172. In particular, dialogues between Jesus and the Soul of the kind found in nos. 7 and 8 occur repeatedly in Franck's poems. The content of the text refers not so much to the Gospel* for the Third Sunday after Trinity as to the Epistle,* with its injunction to 'cast every care upon Jesus'. In its grief and distress (nos. 2–3) the soul feels forsaken by God (no. 4) and beset by the powers of hell (no. 5). Upon the ensuing call to wait upon God, who will provide help (no. 6), the soul turns to Jesus, who promises support and refreshment (nos. 7–8). Having thus cast its care upon Jesus, the soul is 'content once more' (no. 9), its sorrow vanishes (no. 10), and a song in praise of the 'Lamb that was slain' (no. 11) concludes the work. References to the Epistle are perhaps most clearly evident in the ninth movement, in which the following parallels may be drawn:

[5] This assertion was first made in print by Friedrich Chrysander, whose authority is not known. It has recently been dismissed by Petzoldt (*BJ* 1993, 31–46) and Wollny (*BJ* 1994, 25–39), but the question is left open by Dürr (*BJ* 1995, 183–4).

[6] See Joshua Rifkin, 'From Weimar to Leipzig: Concertists and Ripienists in Bach's *Ich hatte viel Bekümmernis*', *Early Music* 24 (1996), 583–603.

BWV 21/9	*1 Peter 5.7*
What good are our heavy cares?	Cast all your cares upon Him.
For the Lord does you good.	For He cares for you.

This is also the only movement that contains a chorale—verses 2 and 5 of the hymn *Wer nur den lieben Gott läßt walten* by Georg Neumark (1641)—and, as noted above, it is thought that an earlier and shorter version of the cantata came to an end at this point.

Bach prefaces the opening chorus with a thematically independent sinfonia, which is closely related in style to the sinfonia of Cantata 12. Since that work originated eight weeks before the 1714 performance, the sinfonia of Cantata 21 might have been composed for this occasion. Like its predecessor, it forms the impression of the slow, middle movement of a concerto, with oboe and first violin as soloists and second violin and viola providing harmonic support. Less characteristic of 1714 is the dominant role assigned to biblical words in the following movements and their exclusive setting as choruses, for the other cantatas of this period, in so far as they contain biblical words at all, set them only as recitative (see Cantatas 18, 182, 12, and 172). If these choruses in fact originated no earlier than 1714, we would have to regard them as the latest in an intentional series of forms: after the choral fugue* of Cantata 182, the passacaglia of Cantata 12, and the concerto movement of Cantata 172, Bach would now, in Cantata 21, endeavour to accord central place to the motet* principle.

The first chorus, no. 2, which was criticized by Mattheson for its frequent word repetition ('Ich, ich, ich . . .'), is bipartite. It opens with a fugue-like choral section, which is prefaced by introductory block chords and based on a popular subject that Bach perhaps adopted from Vivaldi's Concerto in D minor, Op. 3 No. 11 (Bach's organ transcription of this concerto, BWV 596, must have originated during the same period). This subject recurs in a slightly different form in the organ Fugue in G, BWV 541; and it is perhaps no coincidence that at the end of the year 1714 we encounter a similar relationship between cantata and organ fugue in BWV 152 and 536 respectively. Returning to the first chorus of Cantata 21, a lapidary, block-chordal 'aber' ('but') is followed by the 'vivace' second section to the words 'deine Tröstungen erquicken meine Seele' ('Your consolations revive my soul'), which is set in free polyphony* with mostly paired imitative* entries. With a broadening of tempo to 'andante', this impressive chorus comes to an end.

Let us now consider the other choruses. The second, no. 6, proves to be still more indebted than the first to the series principle of the motet. Its overall form may be characterized as 'fantasia and fugue': the second section is a permutation fugue of remarkably logical structure, gradually enhanced by virtue of the following order of entries: choir (single voices); instruments; choir with ripieno doubling (Leipzig version) plus strings; oboe, with the crowning entry of the subject. In the first section, on the other hand, one passage follows another in an antiquated succession of small units:

'Was betrübst du dich, meine Seele' ('Why are you cast down, O my soul?'): two homophonic* choral blocks; solo–tutti contrast
'und bist so unruhig' ('and are so disquieted'): canonic texture, 'spirituoso', syncopation
'in mir' ('within me'): two chords, 'adagio'
'Harre auf Gott' ('Wait upon God'): imitative succession of entries, instrumental episode
'Denn ich werde ihm noch danken' ('For I shall yet thank Him'): homophonic* choral texture

Thereafter, the permutation fugue described above begins on the words 'daß er meines Angesichtes Hilfc und mein Gott ist'.

The combination of biblical words ('Sei nun wieder zufrieden . . .') and chorale in the third chorus, no. 9, also belongs to the old motet tradition. The unified thematic shaping of the parts that deliver the biblical text might be felt as a 'modern' element: the whole texture is built upon a scale theme, to which the tenor part adds the first of the two chorale verses, and then the soprano part the second of them. The two sections are further differentiated by the assignment of the biblical-text parts in the first verse to solo voices with continuo accompaniment: the second verse is marked not only by the entry of the instruments used in previous movements—oboe and strings—but also (in the Leipzig version) by ripieno doubling of the voices and by the reinforcement of a choir of trombones. Finally, the concluding chorus no. 11, which includes additional parts for three trumpets and timpani (but none for trombones), consists of a short homophonic choral passage, with accompanying instruments disposed in antiphonal choirs, followed by an extended permutation fugue to the words 'Lob und Ehre und Preis und Gewalt . . .', which is again built on the principle of gradual enhancement and crowned by a pair of subject entries on the first trumpet.

In contrast with these antiquated choruses, the arias and recitatives embody the 'modern' principle. The third movement, an aria with obbligato* oboe, is remarkably concise and almost entirely developed out of the melodic stock of its seven-bar introductory ritornello. It is, moreover, of such overwhelming expressive power that it might be considered one of the most moving arias that Bach ever wrote (see the complete reproduction in the Introduction, Music Example No. 8). The second aria, no. 5, which is introduced by a string-accompanied recitative, is more superficial in conception. The thematic material is drawn from the image of flowing floods of tears, and in the middle section the composer avails himself of the opportunity to represent musically the 'storm and waves' of the text and the soul's 'sinking into the ground'.

The dialogue between the Soul and Jesus that opens Part II is unexpected, for it is neither anticipated nor carried through to the end of the cantata. Dialogues of this kind are not infrequent in Protestant church music from the seventeenth century onwards, but the drama with which this dialogue is handled here in recitative and duet may have been novel. At the opening of the recitative, no. 7, the light–dark contrast of the text is illustrated by means of a rising scale in the accompanying strings (similar to that of Cantata 12/3 eight weeks before the 1714 performance) and a sudden drop of a twelfth. In its passionate warmth, the duet, no. 8, differs little from the secular love duets of contemporary opera. In the tenth movement, Bach returns to the solo aria, now accompanied only by continuo. In its mood of spirited, excited abandon, it reflects the joy of the soul now freed from affliction.

Ich hatte viel Bekümmernis became well known early in the nineteenth century. As in the *Actus tragicus*, BWV 106, it may have been the very lack of concertante* brilliance and the predominance of biblical texts that elicited a response from listeners. Within Bach's output of cantatas, the work stands like an erratic block, and we would be glad to know what specific event occasioned its origin in the grand form in which it has come down to us. Reinhold Jauernig tried to account for it as a farewell cantata for the seventeen-year-old Prince Johann Ernst, a highly gifted pupil of Bach's who left Weimar in 1714. Already ill at that time, he died in Frankfurt a year later without returning to Weimar. The notion that Bach composed this music for the departure of his princely pupil, with whom he was linked by a common interest in concertos of the Vivaldian type, is attractive, but for the time being it remains no more than a hypothesis.

Ach Herr, mich armen Sünder, BWV 135

NBA I/16, p. 199 BC A100 Duration: *c.* 17 mins

1. [Chorale] SATB ob I,II str bc + trb e 3/4

Ach Herr, mich armen Sünder	**Ah Lord, do not rebuke me,**
Straf nicht in deinem Zorn,	**A poor sinner, in Your anger**
Dein' ernsten Grimm doch linder,	**But soften Your grave displeasure,**
Sonst ist mit mir verlorn.	**Otherwise all is lost with me.**
Ach Herr, wollst mir vergeben	**Ah Lord, would You forgive**
Mein Sünd und gnädig sein,	**My sin and be gracious,**
Daß ich mag ewig leben,	**That I may live for ever**
Entfliehn der Höllenpein.	**And escape the pain of hell.**

2. Recitativo T bc d–C C

Ach heile mich, du Arzt der Seelen,	Ah heal me, You Physician of Souls,
Ich bin sehr krank und schwach;	I am very sick and weak;
Man möchte die Gebeine zählen,	One might count my bones,
So jämmerlich hat mich mein Ungemach,	So deplorably has my adversity,

Mein Kreuz und Leiden zugericht';	My cross and suffering damaged me;
Das Angesicht	My face
Ist ganz von Tränen aufgeschwollen,	Is quite swollen up with tears,
Die, schnellen Fluten gleich, von Wangen abwärts rollen.	Which, like swift floods, roll down my cheeks.
Der Seelen ist von Schrecken angst und bange;	My soul is alarmed and anxious from vexation;
Ach, du Herr, wie so lange?	**Ah, You Lord, why so long?**
3. ARIA T ob I,II bc	C $\frac{3}{4}$
Tröste mir, Jesu, mein Gemüte,	Comfort my mind, O Jesus,
Sonst versink ich in den Tod,	Otherwise I sink into death;
Hilf mir, hilf durch deine Güte	Help me, through Your goodness,
Aus der großen Seelennot!	Out of my great spiritual trouble!
Denn **im Tod ist alles stille,**	For **in death all is still:**
Da gedenkt man deiner nicht.	**There one has no remembrance of You.**
Liebster Jesu, ists dein Wille,	Dearest Jesus, if it is Your Will,
So erfreu mein Angesicht!	Then delight my countenance!
4. RECITATIVO A bc	g–a C
Ich bin von Seufzen müde,	**I am weary with my sighing,**
Mein Geist hat weder Kraft noch Macht,	My spirit has neither strength nor might,
Weil ich die ganze Nacht	For all the night,
Oft ohne Seelenruh und Friede	Often without rest to the soul or peace,
In großem Schweiß und Tränen liege.	I lie in great sweat and tears.
Ich gräme mich fast tot und bin vor Trauren alt;	I fret myself almost to death and am old because of grief;
Denn meine Angst ist mannigfalt.	For my fear is manifold.
5. ARIA B str bc	a ¢
Weicht, all ihr Übeltäter,	**Depart, all you workers of iniquity!**
Mein Jesus tröstet mich!	My Jesus consoles me.
Er läßt nach Tränen und nach Weinen	After tears and weeping He lets
Die Freudensonne wieder scheinen.	The sun of joy shine again.
Das Trübsalswetter ändert sich,	The storm of affliction changes,
Die Feinde müssen plötzlich fallen	My enemies must suddenly fall
Und ihre Pfeile rückwärts prallen.	And their arrows rebound on them.
6. CHORAL SATB bc (+ ctt + ww + str)	e C
Ehr sei ins Himmels Throne	**Honour in the heavenly throne,**
Mit hohem Ruhm und Preis	**With high renown and praise,**
Dem Vater und dem Sohne	**Be to the Father and the Son**
Und auch zu gleicher Weis	**And also in like manner**
Dem Heilgen Geist mit Ehren	**To the Holy Spirit, with honour**
In alle Ewigkeit.	**In all eternity.**
Der woll uns alln bescheren	**He would bestow upon us all**
Die ewge Seligkeit.	**Eternal Salvation.**

This chorale cantata,* which was performed for the first time on 25 June 1724, is based on the hymn with the same opening line by Cyriakus Schneegaß (1597), a free paraphrase of Psalm 6. The text is only loosely related to the Sunday readings. The reflection that the Lord comforts us (no. 3) and will strike down our enemies (no. 5) is linked to the Epistle.* The most important theme, however—the one that led to the choice of this hymn—is to be found at the end of the Gospel* reading: 'Thus I say to you that there shall be joy before the angels of God over a single sinner who repents' (Luke 15.10). Thus the repentance of the sinner is the subject of the chorale and accordingly of Bach's cantata too. The anonymous author who was responsible for the cantata text retained verses 1 and 6 of the hymn word for word in the first and last movements and paraphrased the four middle verses to form an equal number of recitatives (nos. 2 and 4) and arias (nos. 3 and 5).

In his setting, Bach had to observe the scheme he had devised himself, according to which the opening movement of this fourth chorale cantata of the cycle would have the chorale melody in the bass and would differ in structure from the three that preceded it. Bach chose a type probably best described as 'chorale fantasia', which differs from the concertante* type (with independent, thematic instrumental parts) favoured by him elsewhere in respect of its contrapuntal structure. This allows all parts, both vocal and instrumental, to share in the chorale theme. All eight chorale lines are treated in like manner in an instrumental fore-structure and an ensuing vocal section, which exhibit the following characteristics:

Instrumental fore-structure: three parts (without continuo): oboe I, II and unison strings. Chorale-line melody in long notes (essentially minims and crotchets) in the strings; counterpoints* in the oboes, largely constructed out of the opening line in diminished note-values (quavers), which is retained as countersubject throughout all the lines. Afterwards (before the last line) this countersubject figure is taken over by the strings.

Vocal section: four parts, with the oboes resting and the other instruments doubling the voices. Towards the end, enhancement by the addition of the oboes and temporary expansion of the texture to six parts. Chorale melody in long notes in the bass, reinforced by continuo and trombone. Again, diminution* of the first chorale line as countersubject.

Some aspects of this scheme are modified in the various line sections as and where necessary. For example, the melody of the penultimate chorale line in the bass, to the words 'Daß ich mag ewig leben' ('That I may live for ever'), is augmented to dotted minims—an alteration no doubt motivated by the text. In addition, the instrumental fore-structure and the vocal section are often not sharply demarcated. But altogether the underlying structure is clearly perceptible. From it the movement acquires motet-like characteristics and also a latent antiphony through the stark contrast between the high pitch of the instrumental fore-structure and the markedly low pitch of the vocal section, with its bass *cantus firmus** reinforced by trombone.

The second movement is a *secco* recitative which gains dramatic force from its striking figurative portrayal of rapid floods, running tears, and vexation. The aria 'Tröste mir, Jesu, mein Gemüte', no. 3, is one of Bach's most charming inspirations. The melody of the two obbligato* oboes is reminiscent of a dance; and the vocal melody depicts sinking into death, the stillness of death, and the delighted countenance of the text. At the end, to the words 'So erfreu mein Angesicht!' ('Then delight my countenance!'), we hear the embellished last line of the chorale. Again in the following recitative, no. 4, Bach sets the opening words 'Ich bin von Seufzen müde' ('I am weary with my sighing', a quotation from the fourth verse) to an expressive transformation of the first chorale line, which is then followed by plain *secco*. The second aria, 'Weicht, all ihr Übeltäter', no. 5, is a most impassioned piece, whose bass melody, accompanied by strings, is characterized by rolling passage-work and large intervallic leaps. A plain chorale setting concludes the work.

As a whole, this cantata captivates not so much by brilliant concertante* writing as by its intensive textual interpretation. Whoever penetrates deeply into the beauties of the composition will learn to love it for this very reason.

2.4 Fourth Sunday after Trinity

Epistle: Romans 8.18–23: 'All nature cries out for the manifestation of the children of God'.

Gospel: Luke 6.36–42: From the Sermon on the Mount: be compassionate; do not judge.

Barmherziges Herze der ewigen Liebe, BWV 185

NBA I/17.1, p. 3 BC A101 Duration: *c.* 16 mins

1. Aria Duetto ST ob or tr bc f ♯/a (g)[7] 6/4

Barmherziges Herze der ewigen Liebe,	Compassionate heart of eternal love,
Errege, bewege mein Herze durch dich,	Arouse, move my heart through You,
Damit ich Erbarmen und Gütigkeit übe,	That I may show mercy and goodness;
O Flamme der Liebe, zerschmelze du mich!	A flame of love, melt me away!

[7] The first specified key refers to the *Chorton*, the second to the *Kammerton*, of the Weimar version. The bracketed key is that of *Chorton* in another Weimar performance, or perhaps in the first after hasty rearrangement; it is also the key of *Kammerton* in the Leipzig version.

2. RECITATIVO A str bc A–E/C–G (B♭–F) c

Ihr Herzen, die ihr euch
In Stein und Fels verkehret,
Zerfließt und werdet weich!
Erwägt, was euch der Heiland lehret;
Übt, übt Barmherzigkeit
Und sucht noch auf der Erden
Dem Vater gleich zu werden!
Ach! greifet nicht
Durch das verbotne Richten
Dem Allerhöchsten ins Gericht,
Sonst wird sein Eifer euch zernichten!
Vergebt, so wird euch auch vergeben!
Gebt, gebt in diesem Leben!
Macht euch ein Kapital,
Das dort einmal
Gott wiederzahlt mit reichen Interessen
Denn wie ihr meßt, wird man euch wieder messen!

You hearts that have turned yourselves
Into stone and rock,
Melt and grow soft!
Consider what the Saviour teaches you;
Show mercy
And seek while still on earth
To become like the Father!
Ah! do not,
Through that forbidden sentence,
Engage the Most High in judgement,
Otherwise His zeal will destroy you!
Forgive, then you too will be forgiven!
Give, give in this life!
Put by some capital,
Which there above one day
God will repay with ample interest,
For the way you measure will be measured to you again!

3. ARIA A ob str bc A/C (B♭) c

Sei bemüht in dieser Zeit,
Seele, reichlich auszustreuen,
Soll die Ernte dich erfreuen
In der reichen Ewigkeit,
Wo, wer Gutes ausgesäet,
Fröhlich nach den Garben gehet.

Endeavour at this time,
O soul, to scatter abundantly,
If the harvest is to gladden you
In the abundance of eternity,
Where whoever has sown good things
Joyfully gathers the sheaves.

4. RECITATIVO B bc D–b/F–d (E♭–c) c

Die Eigenliebe schmeichelt sich!
Bestrebe dich,
Erst deinen Balken auszuziehen;
Denn magst du dich üm Splitter auch bemühen,
Die in des Nächsten Augen sein!
Ist gleich dein Nächster nicht vollkommen rein,
So wisse, daß auch du kein Engel,
Verbeßre deine Mängel!
Wie kann ein Blinder mit dem andern
Doch recht und richtig wandern?
Wie, fallen sie zu ihrem Leide
Nicht in die Gruben alle beide?

Self-love flatters itself!
Endeavour first to cast out
The beam from your own eye;
Then you may trouble yourself over the motes
That are in your neighbours' eyes!
Though your neighbour is not perfectly pure,
Know that you too are no angel;
Rectify your lacks!
How can one blind person walk
Rightly and properly with another?
What? will they not, to their sorrow,
Both fall into the ditch?

5. ARIA B bc (+ str 8va) b/d (c) c

Das ist der Christen Kunst!
Nur Gott und sich erkennen,

This is the art of the Christian!
To know only God and oneself,

Von wahrer Liebe brennen,	To burn with true love,
Nicht unzulässig richten,	Not to judge unduly,
Noch fremdes Tun vernichten,	Nor nullify another's deeds,
Das Nächsten nicht vergessen,	Not to forget one's neighbour,
Mit reichem Maße messen!	And to mete out ample measure!
Das macht bei Gott und Menschen Gunst,	This finds favour with God and man,
Das ist der Christen Kunst!	This is the art of the Christian!

6. Chorale SATB vln I bc (+ tr ob vln II vla) f ♯/a (g) C

Ich ruf zu dir, Herr Jesu Christ,	**I call upon You, Lord Jesus Christ,**
Ich bitt, erhör mein Klagen,	**I pray You, hear my complaint;**
Verleih mir Gnad zu dieser Frist,	**Grant me mercy at this time,**
Laß mich doch nicht verzagen;	**Let me not despair;**
Den rechten Weg, o Herr, ich mein,	**The right way, O Lord, I mean,**
Den wollest du mir geben,	**You would give me that:**
Dir zu leben,	**To live for You,**
Mein'n Nächsten nütz zu sein,	**To be of use to my neighbour,**
Dein Wort zu halten eben.	**And to abide by Your Word.**

Bach composed this cantata as concertmaster at Weimar and added the date '1715' to the manuscript in his own hand. It was thus performed for the first time on 14 July that year. Possibly another Weimar performance took place, this time in G minor at *Chorton** pitch, or else the first performance was rearranged at short notice. For the revival of the work in Leipzig on 20 June 1723 (and again around 1746–7) Bach made several alterations: in particular, although it was written for performance at Weimar *Chorton* pitch, he transposed it once and for all into G minor *Kammerton**, since F sharp minor would have been too low.

The text is drawn from the cycle *Evangelisches Andachts-Opffer* by Salomo Franck and was thus specifically written for the 1715 performance. Franck closely follows the text of the Gospel.* The call to cultivate compassion, the injunction not to judge, the warning 'The way you measure will be measured to you again' (Luke 6.38), and the two concluding parables—of the mote and the beam and of the blind leading the blind—all these things are reproduced; and the final aria unites them under the motto 'This is the art of the Christian'. The cantata concludes with the first verse of the hymn *Ich ruf zu dir, Herr Jesu Christ* by Johann Agricola (*c.* 1530).

Bach's Weimar composition requires four voices, one oboe, strings, and continuo. The opening movement is a duet, accompanied by a continuo part which is at times thematic but for the most part moves swiftly in quavers. The melody of the concluding chorale is here anticipated line by line in an instrumental quotation on the oboe (which was altered to trumpet in the Leipzig version). The falling third of the voice and continuo theme also refers, no doubt intentionally, to the opening of the chorale. The mirror version of the opening theme is also its counterpoint,* probably in order to represent the 'reflection' of the text—the stirring of human compassion through its divine counterpart:

The recitative, no. 2, accompanied by strings, changes towards the end into an arioso* accompanied only by continuo, whose imitative* texture again serves the purpose of textual interpretation: 'For the way you measure will be measured to you again!' The complete instrumental forces are first deployed in the central aria, no. 3, where the oboe—at times treated as a soloist—is assigned some rich figure-work.

A plain *secco* recitative, no. 4, leads to the third aria, no. 5, for bass voice with a continuo part which in the Leipzig version is reinforced by all the strings at the octave above. The text, with its uninterrupted enumeration of all the injunctions in the Gospel reading, allows no room for episodes and is therefore most unsuitable for aria composition.[8] However, Bach knew how to organize it skilfully, repeating the introductory line 'Das ist der Christen Kunst' ('This is the art of the Christian') at the beginning and end of each section. Taking up the head-motive to which these words are set, even the continuo seems to interject the phrase repeatedly in the course of the musical flow. The concluding chorale, sung in four parts, is expanded to five-part texture by an independent violin part that lies above the soprano.

Ein ungefärbt Gemüte, BWV 24

NBA I/17.1, p. 49 BC A102 Duration: *c.* 21 mins

1. Aria A unis str bc F $\frac{3}{4}$

Ein ungefärbt Gemüte	An unvarnished spirit
An deutscher Treu und Güte	Of German faithfulness and goodness

[8] Elsewhere, too, Franck takes little account of this problem: cf., for instance, what has been said of BWV 165/5 and 208/7.

Macht uns vor Gott und Menschen schön.	Makes us fine before God and man.
Der Christen Tun und Handel,	Christians' deeds and business,
Ihr ganzer Lebenswandel	The whole course of their life
Soll auf dergleichen Fuße stehn.	Should be on this footing.
2. Recitativo T bc	B♭ **C**
Die Redlichkeit	Honesty
Ist eine von den Gottesgaben.	Is one of God's gifts.
Daß sie bei unsrer Zeit	That in our time
So wenig Menschen haben,	So few men have it
Das macht, sie bitten Gott nicht drum.	Is because they do not ask God for it.
Denn von Natur geht unsers Herzens Dichten	For by nature our heart's imaginings
Mit lauter Bösem ümb.	Are given over to nothing but evil.
Solls seinen Weg auf etwas Gutes richten,	Should its path be directed to something good,
So muß es Gott durch seinen Geist regieren	Then God must govern it through His Spirit
Und auf der Bahn der Tugend führen.	And lead it on the path of virtue.
Verlangst du Gott zum Freunde,	If you desire God as your friend,
So mache dir den Nächsten nicht zum Feinde	Then do not make an enemy of your neighbour
Durch Falschheit, Trug und List!	Through falsity, deceit and cunning!
Ein Christ	A Christian
Soll sich der Tauben Art bestreben	Should strive for the nature of a dove
Und ohne Falsch und Tücke leben.	And live harmless and without malice.
Mach aus dir selbst ein solches Bild,	Make of yourself such a figure
Wie du den Nächsten haben willt!	As you would want your neighbour to be!
3. Tutti SATB tr str + ob I,II bc	g $\frac{3}{4}$
'Alles nun, das ihr wollet, daß euch die Leute tun sollen, das tut ihr ihnen.'	'Everything that you would that people should do to you, you do to them.'
4. Recitativo B str bc	F–C **C**
Die Heuchelei	Hypocrisy
Ist eine Brut, die Belial gehecket:	Is a brood that Belial hatches:
Wer sich in ihre Larve stecket,	Whoever puts on its mask
Der trägt des Teufels Liberei.	Wears the devil's livery.
Wie? lassen sich denn Christen	What? do Christians let themselves
Dergleichen auch gelüsten?	Lust after such things?
Gott seis geklagt! die Redlichkeit ist teuer.	God forbid! Honesty is precious.
Manch teuflisch Ungeheuer	Many a devilish monster
Sieht wie ein Engel aus.	Looks like an angel.
Man kehrt den Wolf hinein,	If the wolf is turned within,

Den Schafspelz kehrt man raus.	The sheep's pelt is turned outwards.
Wie könnt es ärger sein?	How could it be worse?
Verleumden, Schmähn und Richten,	Slander, abuse, and blame,
Verdammen und Vernichten	Condemnation and annihilation
Ist überall gemein.	Are general everywhere.
So geht es dort, so geht es hier.	It is so here, there, and everywhere.
Der liebe Gott behüte mich dafür!	Dear God protect me from them!

5. ARIA T ob d'am I,II bc — a C

Treu und Wahrheit sei der Grund	May faithfulness and truth be the foundation
Aller deiner Sinnen.	Of all your thoughts.
Wie von außen Wort und Mund,	Like word and mouth from without
Sei das Herz von innen.	May the heart be from within.
Gütig sein und tugendreich	To be kind and rich in virtue
Macht uns Gott und Engeln gleich.	Makes us like God and the angels.

6. CHORAL SATB tr str + ob I + II bc — F C

O Gott, du frommer Gott,	**O God, you upright God,**
Du Brunnquell aller Gaben,	**You fountain-head of all gifts,**
Ohn den nichts ist, was ist,	**Without whom nothing is that is,**
Von dem wir alles haben,	**From whom we have everything,**
Gesunden Leib gib mir,	**Grant me a healthy body**
Und daß in solchem Leib	**And grant that in this body**
Ein unverletzte Seel	**There remains a soul intact**
Und rein Gewissen bleib.	**And a pure conscience.**

This cantata was first performed on 20 June 1723, apparently during the same service as the Leipzig version of Cantata 185. Presumably the modest dimensions of that work were regarded as inadequate by the new Thomascantor, who had introduced himself, on each of the three preceding Sundays, with a large two-part cantata (Nos. 75, 76, and 21). By placing the newly composed Cantata 24 alongside Cantata 185, he created a double work of which the first part was to be performed before the sermon and 'Part II', as it were, afterwards. In later years, he may have performed the two cantatas independently.

Cantata 24 is based on a libretto by Erdmann Neumeister, which was published as early as 1714. Perhaps Bach had still not found a suitable librettist for his Leipzig church music. The content is not so closely linked to the Gospel* as Franck's text for Cantata 185, and lacks its warmth. It is striking for its typically baroque exaggeration of Jesus's original injunctions: an Orthodox preacher here fulminates against the lack of virtue of his congregation. At the centre of the work (no. 3) are Jesus's words from Matthew's equivalent to the Sunday Gospel: 'Everything that you would that people should do to you, you do to them' (Matt. 7.12). This movement is flanked by two recitatives whose opening lines—'Die Redlichkeit' ('Honesty') and 'Die Heuchelei' ('Hypocrisy')—establish a clear link between them. These recitatives are in turn flanked by two arias. The first verse of the hymn *O Gott, du frommer Gott* by Johann Heermann (1630) forms the concluding chorale.

Bach's setting underlines the central position of the biblical-text chorus,* no. 3, by scoring the surrounding solo movements for a few parts only. The obbligato* part in the opening aria is played by unison violins and viola. Vocal and instrumental melodies are here assimilated to such an extent that strings, alto, and continuo blend into a unified trio texture. The first recitative, no. 2, a *secco* with arioso* conclusion, contains a striking musical and textual parallel with Cantata 185. Both cantatas include the injunction to treat our neighbours as we would wish to be treated by them—here in the words 'Make of yourself such a figure as you would want your neighbour to be'—and in both cases Bach chooses arioso and an imitative* texture of voice and continuo for the musical illustration of this reciprocal relationship.

The central chorus, no. 3, is bipartite: the entire text is first sung in a free choral setting and then again as a fugue*—a transference to the vocal domain, so to speak, of the instrumental form of prelude and fugue. The movement requires not only strings and continuo but two oboes, which reinforce the string parts, and an independent trumpet.[9] The opening prelude-like section begins and ends with antiphonal exchanges between choir and orchestra, but in the middle it is broken up into imitation, with the accompanying instruments partly *colla parte** and partly figurative. The second section begins as a double fugue sung only by the concertists* with continuo accompaniment, after which the ripienists* and the instruments, with the trumpet independent and the others *colla parte*, join them. The high point is the subject entry on the trumpet, which expands the number of thematic parts from four to five. At the end, the fugue merges into a more freely structured, sequential passage.

A recitative with string accompaniment, no. 4, again with arioso ending accompanied only by continuo, leads to the second aria, no. 5, a quartet for two oboes d'amore,* tenor, and continuo. Although the voice and instruments do not blend into the same kind of homogeneity as in the first aria, they are nonetheless united by a motive*—

[9] Designated 'Clarino' but best suited to a horn in F. See Thomas G. MacCracken, 'Die Verwendung der Blechblasinstrumente bei J. S. Bach unter besonderer Berücksichtigung der Tromba da tirarsi', *BJ* 1984, 59–89 (especially p. 82); and Kirsten Beißwenger and Uwe Wolf, 'Tromba, Tromba da tirarsi oder Corno? Zur Clarinostimme der Kantate "Ein ungefärbt Gemüte" BWV 24', *BJ* 1993, 91–101.

—which not only ranges through all the instrumental parts in the opening ritornello but also opens the vocal section, prefacing it as a 'motto'.* The concluding chorale is more richly decked out than usual. Independent orchestral parts, which provide episodes between the chorale lines and accompany the choir, contrast with the plain choral texture.

Ich ruf zu dir, Herr Jesu Christ, BWV 177

NBA I/17.1, p. 79 BC A103 Duration: *c.* 28 mins

1. Chorus [Versus 1] SATB ob I,II vln solo str bc — g 3/8

Ich ruf zu dir, Herr Jesu Christ,	**I call upon You, Lord Jesus Christ,**
Ich bitt, erhör mein Klagen,	**I pray You, hear my complaint;**
Verleih mir Gnad zu dieser Frist,	**Grant me mercy at this time,**
Laß mich doch nicht verzagen;	**Let me not despair;**
Den rechten Glauben, Herr, ich mein,	**The true Faith, O Lord, I mean,**
Den wollest du mir geben,	**You would give me that:**
Dir zu leben,	**To live for You,**
Mein'm Nächsten nütz zu sein,	**To be of use to my neighbour,**
Dein Wort zu halten eben.	**And to abide by Your Word.**

2. Versus 2 A bc — c C

Ich bitt noch mehr, o Herre Gott,	**I ask yet further, O Lord God—**
Du kannst es mir wohl geben:	**You can no doubt grant it to me—**
Daß ich werd nimmermehr zu Spott,	**That I nevermore be brought into derision;**
Die Hoffnung gib darneben,	**Grant me also the hope, in advance,**
Voraus, wenn ich muß hier davon,	**That when I must depart from here**
Daß ich dir mög vertrauen	**I may trust in You**
Und nicht bauen	**And not build**
Auf alles mein Tun,	**On all my deeds,**
Sonst wird michs ewig reuen.	**Otherwise I will regret it for ever.**

3. Versus 3 S ob da c bc — E♭ 6/8

Verleih, daß ich aus Herzensgrund	**Grant that from the bottom of my heart**
Mein' Feinden mög vergeben,	**I may forgive my enemies;**
Verzeih mir auch zu dieser Stund,	**Pardon me too at this hour,**
Gib mir ein neues Leben;	**Give me a new life;**
Dein Wort mein Speis laß allweg sein,	**Let Your Word always be my food**
Damit mein Seel zu nähren,	**With which to nourish my soul,**
Mich zu wehren,	**To defend me**
Wenn Unglück geht daher,	**When misfortune comes near,**
Das mich bald möcht abkehren.	**Which might soon turn me away.**

4. Versus 4 T vln solo bsn solo bc — B♭ C

Laß mich kein Lust noch Furcht von dir	**Let neither pleasure nor fear turn me**
In dieser Welt abwenden.	**Away from You in this world.**
Beständigsein ans End gib mir,	**Grant me constancy to the end:**

Du hasts allein in Händen;	**You alone have it in Your hands;**
Und wem dus gibst, der hats umsonst:	**And he to whom You give it has it freely:**
Es kann niemand ererben	**No one can inherit**
Noch erwerben	**Or acquire**
Durch Werke deine Gnad,	**Through deeds Your grace,**
Die uns errett' vom Sterben.	**Which delivers us from death.**
5. VERSUS 5 SATB bc (+ instrs)	g C
Ich lieg im Streit und widerstreb,	**I lie amid strife and resist:**
Hilf, o Herr Christ, dem Schwachen!	**Help me, a weak one, O Lord Christ!**
An deiner Gnad allein ich kleb,	**To Your grace alone I cleave:**
Du kannst mich stärker machen.	**You can make me stronger.**
Kömmt nun Anfechtung, Herr, so wehr,	**If temptation comes, Lord, then prevent it**
Daß sie mich nicht umstoßen.	**From casting me down.**
Du kannst maßen,	**You can judge**
Daß mirs nicht bring Gefahr;	**That it does not bring danger to me;**
Ich weiß, du wirsts nicht lassen.	**I know You will not let it.**

In 1724, when Bach began to compose his cycle of chorale cantatas,* the Fourth Sunday after Trinity took place on 2 July, the Feast of the Visitation. For that occasion Bach composed Cantata 10, *Meine Seel erhebt den Herren*, and only very much later did he write a cantata for the Fourth Sunday after Trinity in order to fill the gap in the cycle. The cantata concerned was composed in 1732—the score, clearly a draft manuscript, bears this date in Bach's own hand—and must have received its first performance on 6 July that year. For its libretto, Bach used the unchanged text of the hymn by Johann Agricola (*c.* 1530). One of the principal hymns for this Sunday, it had already played an important role in the Weimar cantata BWV 185. Its essential gist, particularly in the third verse, is closely connected with the content of the Gospel* for the day. The outer verses of the five-verse hymn are set as choruses* and the three inner verses as arias: recitatives are altogether absent.

The opening chorus displays the form familiar from most of the chorale cantatas: the chorale is delivered by the choir, line by line, with the melody in the soprano part. This chorale texture is incorporated in a thematically independent orchestral setting for two oboes (which otherwise reinforce the soprano *cantus firmus**), strings, and continuo plus concertante* solo violin. The motivic material of the orchestral parts is essentially made up of a figure tossed from solo violin to tutti strings and back, which is often varied but always recognizable, at least in rhythm:

In addition, a held note prefaced by a rising leap on the upbeat as heard at the outset on first oboe—

—plays an important part. It recurs in various modified forms and reveals its significance when heard vocally to the words 'Ich ruf' ('I call'). Bass, alto, and tenor enter with this motive before the soprano delivers the first line of the chorale. Like this line, most of the other chorale lines are introduced and accompanied by chorale-free motivic writing in the lower parts; only in line 6, 'Den wollest du mir geben', is the fore-imitation* based on the chorale melody itself, and the last two lines, nos. 8 and 9, are unprepared—the lower parts here enter at the same time as the chorale line itself.

In the three arias, the instrumental scoring undergoes a process of gradual enhancement from continuo texture (verse 2), via a trio with oboe da caccia* (verse 3), to a quartet with violin and bassoon (verse 4), a scoring charming for its rarity. At the same time, the thematic material increasingly departs from the chorale melody. In verse 2, the opening line of the chorale is still clearly audible, not so much in the 'motto'* that prefaces the first vocal section as in its true beginning at bars 9–10:

In verses 3 and 4, on the other hand, only the falling leap of a third with which both ritornello and vocal section begin remains from the opening of the chorale melody.

In addition, the musical structure of the arias gradually departs from the *Bar* form* (A A B) of the text. In verse 2, the musical and textual forms correspond with each other. The frequent recurrence of the continuo ritornello in various modifications, in whole or in part—even in the vocal sections as a *basso quasi continuo**—conveys a unified overall impression. In verse 3, the two *Stollen** of the text are united to form a single musical section and the text of the *Abgesang** is repeated, so that the setting acquires the form A B B^1. This aria, which for the first time introduces a major key to the work, sounds full of comfort and propitiation on account of its singing melody and the warm alto pitch of its obbligato* instrument, the oboe da caccia. Finally, verse 4 unites the form of the two preceding arias, since not only do the two *Stollen* of the text correspond musically but the *Abgesang* is repeated, leading to the extended form A A^1 B B^1. Here, solo violin and bassoon surround the voice in joyful abandon, which is disturbed temporarily—and, on that account, all the more impressively—only at the words 'vom Sterben' ('from death').

Within the limitations of its type, the concluding chorale—a plain four-part setting—is loosened up in part-writing and enhanced in expressive power with the aid of passing-notes and ornaments (see the above music example).

2.5 Fifth Sunday after Trinity

EPISTLE: 1 Peter 3.8–15: 'Sanctify Christ in your hearts'.
GOSPEL: Luke 5.1–11: Peter's great catch of fish.

Wer nur den lieben Gott läßt walten, BWV 93

NBA I/17.2, p. 3 BC A104 Duration: *c.* 23 mins

1. CHORUS SATB ob I,II str bc	c 12/8
Wer nur den lieben Gott läßt walten	**Whoever just lets our dear God govern**
Und hoffet auf ihn allezeit,	**And hopes in Him at all times**
Den wird er wunderlich erhalten	**Will be wonderfully supported by Him**
In allem Kreuz und Traurigkeit.	**In all cross-bearing and sorrow.**
Wer Gott, dem Allerhöchsten, traut,	**Whoever trusts in God, the Most High,**
Der hat auf keinen Sand gebaut.	**Has not built on sand.**
2. RECITATIVO [+ CHORALE] B bc	g C
Was helfen uns die schweren Sorgen?	**What good are our heavy cares?**
Sie drücken nur das Herz	They only oppress our heart
Mit Zentnerpein,	With a hundredweight of pain,
Mit tausend Angst und Schmerz.	With a thousand fears and agonies.
Was hilft uns unser Weh und Ach?	**What good is our woe and lament?**
Es bringt nur bittres Ungemach.	It only brings bitter adversity.
Was hilft es? daß wir alle Morgen	**What good is it that every morning**
Mit Seufzen von dem Schlaf aufstehn	We rise from sleep with sighs
Und mit beträntem Angesicht	And with tearful countenance
Des Nachts zu Bette gehn?	Go to bed at night?
Wir machen unser Kreuz und Leid	**We make our cross-bearing and suffering**
Durch bange Traurigkeit nur größer.	Only the greater through anxious sorrow.
Drum tut ein Christ viel besser,	Therefore a Christian does far better:
Er trägt sein Kreuz	He carries his cross
Mit christlicher Gelassenheit.	With Christ-like composure.
3. ARIA T str bc	E♭ 3/8
Man halte nur ein wenig stille,	**One should just keep still a little**

Wenn sich die Kreuzesstunde naht,	When the hour of cross-bearing approaches,
Denn unsres Gottes Gnadenwille	**For our God's gracious Will**
Verläßt uns nie mit Rat und Tat.	Never forsakes us in counsel or deed.
Gott, der die Auserwählten kennt,	God, who knows the elect,
Gott, der sich uns ein Vater nennt,	God, who calls Himself our Father,
Wird endlich allen Kummer wenden	Will finally turn away all affliction
Und seinen Kindern Hilfe senden.	And send His children help.
4. ARIA DUETTO SA unis str bc	c **C**
Er kennt die rechten Freudenstunden,	**He knows the right times for joy,**
Er weiß wohl, wenn es nützlich sei;	**He well knows when it may be beneficial;**
Wenn er uns nur hat treu erfunden	**If He has but found us faithful**
Und merket keine Heuchelei,	**And notes no hypocrisy,**
So kömmt Gott, eh wir uns versehn,	**Then God comes before we are aware of it**
Und lässet uns viel Guts geschehn.	**And lets much good happen to us.**
5. RECITATIVO [+ CHORALE] T bc	e ♭–g **C**
Denk nicht in deiner Drangsalshitze,	**Think not in the heat of your ordeal,**
Wenn Blitz und Donner kracht	When lightning and thunder crash
Und dir ein schwüles Wetter bange macht,	And a sultry storm makes you anxious,
Daß du von Gott verlassen seist.	**That you are forsaken by God.**
Gott bleibt auch in der größten Not,	God, even in the greatest distress,
Ja gar bis in den Tod	Yea even unto death,
Mit seiner Gnade bei den Seinen.	With His grace, abides with His own.
Du darfst nicht meinen,	You should not imagine
Daß dieser Gott im Schoße sitze,	**That this God places in His bosom**
Der täglich wie der reiche Mann	One who daily, like the rich man,
In Lust und Freuden leben kann.	Can live in pleasure and joy.
Der sich mit stetem Glücke speist,	**He who feeds on constant good fortune,**
Bei lauter guten Tagen,	With nothing but good days,
Muß oft zuletzt,	Must often at last,
Nachdem er sich an eitler Lust ergötzt,	After taking delight in idle pleasure,
'Der Tod in Töpfen!' sagen.	Say, 'There is death in the pots!'
Die Folgezeit verändert viel!	**The coming time will alter much!**
Hat Petrus gleich die ganze Nacht	Though Peter spent the whole night
Mit leerer Arbeit zugebracht	On fruitless toil
Und nichts gefangen:	And caught nothing,
Auf Jesu Wort kann er noch einen Zug erlangen.	At Jesus's Word he could still make a catch.
Drum traue nur in Armut, Kreuz und Pein	Therefore in poverty, cross-bearing, and pain
Auf deines Jesu Güte	Just trust in your Jesus's goodness

Mit gläubigem Gemüte.
Nach Regen gibt er Sonnenschein
Und setzet jeglichem sein Ziel.

With faithful spirit.
After rain He gives sunshine
And appoints to each his goal.

6. ARIA S ob I bc — g C

Ich will auf den Herren schaun
Und stets meinem Gott vertraun.
Er ist der rechte Wundersmann.
Der die Reichen arm und bloß
Und die Armen reich und groß
Nach seinem Willen machen kann.

I will look to the Lord
And constantly trust in my God.
He is the true miracle-worker.
He can make the rich poor and bare
And the poor rich and great
According to His Will.

7. CHORAL SATB bc (+ instrs) — c C

Sing, bet und geh auf Gottes Wegen,
Verricht das Deine nur getreu
Und trau des Himmels reichem Segen,
So wird er bei dir werden neu;
Denn welcher seine Zuversicht
Auf Gott setzt, den verläßt er nicht.

Sing, pray, and walk in God's ways;
Just perform your own tasks faithfully
And trust heaven's rich blessing,
Then it will be renewed for you;
For whoever places his confidence
In God is not forsaken by Him.

This chorale cantata* was performed for the first time on 9 July 1724. All that survives of the original performing material is a continuo fragment containing the first four movements. The remaining sources stem from a revival of about 1732–3, when the work may have been refashioned into the version we know today. It is also possible, however, that the original performing material was on this occasion reused without alteration.

With regard to its textual form, the cantata is a good example of how the anonymous librettist of the chorale-cantata cycle was wont to treat a chorale text. Of the seven verses of the hymn *Wer nur den lieben Gott läßt walten* by Georg Neumark (1641), he preserves the first, middle, and last word for word (nos. 1, 4, and 7), expands the second and fifth by inserting freely versified recitative (nos. 2 and 5), and paraphrases the third and sixth to form arias, retaining certain lines in unaltered form (nos. 3 and 6). The resulting libretto is beautifully symmetrical: around the central axis of the unaltered verse 4 are two pairs of movements, each consisting of recitative (expanded hymn verse) and aria (paraphrased hymn verse), while unaltered hymn verses form the outer frame.

The use of this chorale for the principal music on this Sunday is occasioned by the Gospel* narrative that was read out before the cantata performance. In the course of a whole night's fishing, Peter had caught nothing, but on Jesus's advice he casts his net once more and catches such a huge quantity of fish that his net and boat could hardly contain them all. The librettist draws the general conclusion that man should rely upon God's direction. In the freely-versified recitative inserted in no. 5, he refers directly to the biblical account: 'Though Peter spent the whole night on fruitless toil and caught nothing, at Jesus's Word he could still make a catch'. Thus the librettist directly links the substance of the chorale with the Gospel reading. The Sunday Epistle* also contains exhortations to the Christian virtues and to patience in suffering—general ideas entirely in line with those of the cantata text, though no direct references to the Epistle are made. The allusion to 2 Kings 4.40 in the fifth movement would have been more familiar to the congregation of 1724, acquainted as they were with the Bible, than it is to us today: the prophet Elisha has a dish cooked in time of dearth which is at first rejected as inedible with the words 'There is death in the pots!', but is then rendered edible by the prophet. More readily comprehensible is the 'rich man' of the same movement—an allusion to the parable of the rich man and the poor Lazarus (Luke 16.19–31).

Bach designed the work in close accordance with the text. A central axis is formed by the graceful duet, no. 4, in which the chorale melody is stated by unison violins and viola. Bach later arranged the movement for organ and had it published among his so-called 'Schübler Chorales' (BWV 647). The cantata opens with an extended chorus* which is introduced by, and interspersed with, thematically unified instrumental ritornellos (independent of the chorale) in which the two oboes often take a leading role. Each chorale line is also introduced by a concertante* vocal passage, sung by soprano and alto in the first *Stollen*,* by tenor and bass in the second, and by all four voices in the *Abgesang*.* These soloistic introductory passages are then followed by the chorale line itself with the unaltered melody in the soprano. The three lower voices at first accompany it in plain chords, but during the long-held last note of each line the supporting texture is broken up into polyphony.* To this vocal edifice the instruments add their thematic material from the ritornello. As a whole, the movement makes a concertante impression throughout but with ever-shifting focus of interest: in the ritornellos it centres on the instrumental ensemble, in the preparation of the chorale lines on the concertante vocal parts, in the chorale lines themselves on the soprano part, and during the long-held closing note of each line on the three lower voice parts.

The two chorale-recitatives nos. 2 and 5 are alike in structure. A lightly embellished chorale line, sung by the voice with continuo accompaniment, is followed by a few bars of *secco* recitative, which in turn lead to the next chorale line, and so forth. Bach here makes use of the principle of 'trope'.* Alongside biblical words, the Protestant chorale has to some extent an authoritative character for Bach. Yet he avails himself of it with true Protestant freedom: in any particular case he might vary, ornament, expand or abridge it in accordance with his specific intentions.

This freedom of Bach's in relation to the chorale becomes still clearer in the two arias, nos. 3 and 6. The first presents a major-mode version of the opening of the chorale melody, developing from it a joyful, minuet-like movement which no doubt expresses a child-like trust that, according to 'our God's gracious Will',

He will certainly 'send His children help'. The opening of the ritornello, which at the vocal entry is taken over by the tenor, was apparently conceived in terms of the text, for the rests that articulate the two-bar melodic phrases are clearly designed to represent keeping still and listening to what God's Will has to say to us:

Not only are two of the chorale lines preserved in their original form, but the structure of the movement recalls the original chorale: the reprise of the first section gives rise to a *Bar* form* which is not prescribed by the paraphrased text.

The second aria, no. 6, contains hardly any hints of the chorale melody in its opening theme. Instead it quotes the two lines of the *Abgesang* in the voice, literally at the words 'Er ist der rechte Wundersmann' ('He is the true miracle-worker', an unaltered chorale line) and in a lightly embellished form on 'Nach seinem Willen machen kann' ('Can make according to His Will', a freely paraphrased chorale line). The work concludes with a plain four-part chorale setting in Bach's usual style.

Siehe, ich will viel Fischer aussenden, BWV 88

NBA I/17.2, p. 33 BC A105 Duration: *c.* 22 mins

Parte prima	*First part*
1. BASSO SOLO B hn I,II str + ob d'am I,II taille bc	D–G 6/8 ¢
'Siehe, ich will viel Fischer aussenden, spricht der Herr, die sollen sie fischen. Und darnach will ich viel Jäger aussenden, die sollen sie fahen auf allen Bergen und auf allen Hügeln und in allen Steinritzen.'	'Behold, I will send out many fishermen, says the Lord, and they shall fish them. And thereafter I will send out many hunters, and they shall hunt them on all the mountains and on all the hills and in all the crevices in the rocks.'
2. RECITATIVO T bc	b–e c
Wie leichtlich könnte doch der Höchste uns entbehren Und seine Gnade von uns kehren, Wenn der verkehrte Sinn sich böslich von ihm trennt Und mit verstocktem Mut In sein Verderben rennt. Was aber tut Sein vatertreu Gemüte?	How easily could the Most High dispense with us And turn His grace from us When the reprobate mind wickedly separates from Him And with hardened spirit Rushes towards its ruin. But what does His paternally faithful Spirit do?

Tritt er mit seiner Güte
Von uns, gleich so wie wir von ihm, zurück,
Und überläßt er uns der Feinde List und Tück?

Does He with His goodness
Withdraw from us, just as we do from Him,
And abandon us to the enemy's cunning and malice?

3. ARIA T ob d'am I bc + RITORNELLO ob d'am I str + ob d'am II bc — e $\frac{3}{8}$

Nein, nein!
Gott ist allezeit geflissen,
Uns auf gutem Weg zu wissen
Unter seiner Gnaden Schein.
Ja, wenn wir verirret sein
Und die rechte Bahn verlassen,
Will er uns gar suchen lassen.

No, no!
It is God's purpose at all times
To know that we are on the good way
Under the light of His grace.
Yes, when we have gone astray
And left the true path
He would even have us sought out.

Parte seconda / *Second part*

4. ARIOSO TB str bc — G–D C $\frac{3}{4}$

Tenor
'Jesus sprach zu Simon:'
Baß
'Fürchte dich nicht; denn von nun an wirst du Menschen fahen.'

Tenor
'Jesus said to Simon:'
Bass
'Fear not, for from now on you will catch men.'

5. ARIA DUETTO SA ob d'am I + II + vln I + II bc — A ¢

Beruft Gott selbst, so muß der Segen
Auf allem unsern Tun
Im Übermaße ruhn,
Stünd uns gleich Furcht und Sorg entgegen.
Das Pfund, so er uns ausgetan,
Will er mit Wucher wieder haben;
Wenn wir es nur nicht selbst vergraben,
So hilft er gern, damit es fruchten kann.

If God Himself calls, then His blessing
Must rest on all our doings
In abundance,
Even though fear and care stand against us.
The pound that He has given us
He would have back with interest;
If only we do not bury it ourselves,
He gladly helps us so that it can bear fruit.

6. RECITATIVO S bc — f♯–b C

Was kann dich denn in deinem Wandel schrecken,
Wenn dir, mein Herz! Gott selbst die Hände reicht?
Vor dessen bloßem Wink schon alles Unglück weicht,
Und der dich mächtiglich kann schützen und bedecken.
Kommt Mühe, Überlast, Neid, Plag und Falschheit her
Und trachtet, was du tust, zu stören und zu hindern,

What can frighten you, then, in the course of your life
When to you, my heart, God Himself reaches out His hands?
Before His very wink all misfortune retreats,
And He can mightily protect and shelter you.
If trouble, burden, envy, torment, and falsehood come
And strive to disturb and hinder what you do,

Laß kurzes Ungemach den Vorsatz nicht vermindern!
Das Werk, so er bestimmt, wird keinem je zu schwer.
Geh allzeit freudig fort, du wirst am Ende sehen,
Daß, was dich eh gequält, dir sei zu Nutz geschehen!

Let not brief hardship diminish your purpose!
The work that He ordains will be too hard for no one.
Go forth joyfully at all times: you will see in the end
That what tormented you before happened for your benefit!

7. Choral SATB bc (+ ww str) b c

Sing, bet und geh auf Gottes Wegen,
Verricht das Deine nur getreu
Und trau des Himmels reichem Segen,
So wird er bei dir werden neu;
Denn welcher seine Zuversicht
Auf Gott setzt, den verläßt er nicht.

Sing, pray, and walk in God's ways;
Just perform your own tasks faithfully
And trust heaven's rich blessing,
Then it will be renewed for you;
For whoever places his confidence
In God is not forsaken by Him.

This cantata, which was performed for the first time on 21 July 1726, is one of the seven works whose texts were drawn from the same cycle as the cantatas by Johann Ludwig Bach that his cousin Johann Sebastian performed. Its content is connected with the Sunday Gospel* reading and takes the account of the calling of Peter as evidence for God's concern for the human race. The fourth movement not only stands midway but is accorded central significance in content, for it contains Jesus's words to Peter, 'Fear not, for from now on you will catch men' (Luke 5.10). A related passage from the Old Testament, Jeremiah 16.16, is placed at the outset of the work. Originally relevant to Israel's restoration from the Babylonian captivity, it announces that the Lord will send out fishermen and hunters to gather together His scattered people. In the madrigalian* verse of Part I, the poet reflects that, although the Almighty could easily dispense with mankind, He is nonetheless concerned for our salvation. Consequently, God's blessing rests upon us, the librettist concludes in Part II, even though 'brief hardship' renders this far from obvious. The text concludes with the last verse of the hymn *Wer nur den lieben Gott läßt walten* by Georg Neumark (1641), a hymn that had already been linked to the Gospel for this Sunday in the chorale cantata* BWV 93 of 1724.

The opening movement forms the focal point of Bach's setting. Though set not as a chorus* but as a bass solo (probably due to the direct speech of God in the singular) it is nonetheless of considerable extent and of unorthodox form. Its text-engendered bipartite form shows it to be related to the motet* and the sacred concerto*, hence Bach's avoidance of the designation 'aria'. The musical invention is based on the two central words 'fishermen' and 'hunters'. The first part is a pastorale, a 'scene at the lake', in which wave-like figures surge up and down over calm or gently moving pedal points. The text is oft-repeated in constantly varied, and thus all the more forceful, declamation. Then all of a sudden the scene changes into a hunt, 'allegro quasi presto', with two horns added to the strings and oboes. Again, one admires the effectiveness of the declamation which holds the listener captive to the very end.

The following recitative, no. 2, ends with a question, to which the aria, no. 3, gives the reply, and this explains why the latter movement begins not with the usual instrumental ritornello but with the voice answering spontaneously with its passionate 'No, no!' This aria is again characterized by its forceful delivery of the text, particularly when the initial 'no' is countered in the second part by a no less emphatic 'yes'. Only at the end is the obbligato* oboe d'amore* joined by the strings (with oboe d'amore II doubling the first violin), and here a ritornello compensates for the absence of an introduction and, more clearly than the vocal portion, reveals the true dance character of the movement: the clear pairing of bars brings to mind the minuet. The clarity of the periodic structure is here probably an image of the 'true path' by which God will lead us.

The fourth movement forms the centre of the work in content as well as in position, for the image of the fishermen and hunters here receives its interpretation. After a short introductory 'Evangelist's' recitative, sung by the tenor with string accompaniment, the words of Christ are, as usual, assigned to the bass. Here, for the third time in this cantata, we have occasion to admire Bach's compelling speech-melody in an arioso over a *basso quasi ostinato*.* As often in movements of this kind, its charm lies in the tension between the relatively strict, motivically imprinted continuo part and the eloquent and relatively free bass part. By contrast, an imitative* texture prevails in the following duet, no. 5. The voices in turn adopt the theme stated in the opening ritornello by unison oboes d'amore and violins, and the continuo on several occasions takes up the head-motive of this theme in imitation. Even the theme of section B is derived from the opening theme, giving rise to an A B B^1 structure of striking homogeneity. A *secco* recitative with continuo accompaniment, no. 6, is followed by the concluding chorale in a plain four-part texture.

What was already evident in our consideration of the individual movements proves to be characteristic of the entire cantata: a retreat of the concertante* style in favour of the monodic, declamatory principle and a renunciation of brilliant passage-work, founded in the joy of virtuoso playing, in favour of graphic textual interpretation. For the period around 1726 this is by no means characteristic: we need only recall the extended introductory sinfonias to Cantatas 35, 169, 49, and 52. It is all the more likely that the features concerned are intentional, peculiar to this cantata, and stimulated by the text.

2.6 Sixth Sunday after Trinity

EPISTLE: Romans 6.3–11: Through Christ's Death we are dead to sin.

GOSPEL: Matthew 5.20–6: From the Sermon on the Mount: the superior righteousness of the Christian, as opposed to the lesser fulfilment of the Law by the scribes and Pharisees.

Vergnügte Ruh, beliebte Seelenlust, BWV 170

NBA I/17.2, p. 61 BC A106 Duration: *c.* 24 mins

1. [ARIA] A str + ob d'am bc	D 12/8
Vergnügte Ruh! beliebte Seelenlust!	Contented rest! beloved pleasure of the soul!
Dich kann man nicht bei Höllensünden,	You cannot be found in hell's sins
Wohl aber Himmelseintracht finden;	But rather in heavenly concord;
Du stärkst allein die schwache Brust,	You alone strengthen the weak breast,
Vergnügte Ruh! beliebte Seelenlust!	Contented rest! beloved pleasure of the soul!
Drum sollen lauter Tugendgaben	Therefore nothing but virtue's gifts
In meinem Herzen Wohnung haben.	Shall have their dwelling in my heart.
2. RECITATIVO A bc	b–f♯ c
Die Welt, das Sündenhaus,	The world, that house of sin,
Bricht nur in Höllenlieder aus	Breaks out only into hellish songs
Und sucht durch Haß und Neid	And seeks through hate and envy
Des Satans Bild an sich zu tragen.	To bear Satan's image.
Ihr Mund ist voller Ottergift,	Its mouth is full of the poison of asps,
Der oft die Unschuld tödlich trifft,	Which often strikes innocence mortally
Und will allein von Racha! Racha! sagen.	And would only say, 'Raca! Raca!'
Gerechter Gott, wie weit	Righteous God, how far
Ist doch der Mensch von dir entfernet;	Man is alienated from You;
Du liebst, jedoch sein Mund	You love, yet his mouth
Macht Fluch und Feindschaft kund	Spreads curses and enmity
Und will den Nächsten nur mit Füßen treten.	And he would trample his neighbour underfoot.
Ach! diese Schuld ist schwerlich zu verbeten.	Ah! this guilt is hard to stand for!
3. ARIA A obbl org unis str	f♯ c
Wie jammern mich doch die verkehrten Herzen,	How I surely pity the perverted hearts
Die dir, mein Gott, so sehr zuwider sein:	That are so very contrary to You, my God!
Ich zittre recht und fühle tausend Schmerzen,	I quite tremble and feel a thousand pains

Wenn sie sich nur an Rach und Haß erfreun!	When they just rejoice in vengeance and hatred!
Gerechter Gott, was magst du doch gedenken,	Righteous God, what may you think
Wenn sie allein mit rechten Satansränken	When with true Satanic guiles
Dein scharfes Strafgebot so frech verlacht!	They so impudently deride Your strict command for punishment!
Ach! ohne Zweifel hast du so gedacht:	Ah! without doubt You have thought:
Wie jammern mich doch die verkehrten Herzen!	How I surely pity these perverted hearts!

4. Recitativo A str bc — D c

Wer sollte sich demnach	Who should therefore
Wohl hier zu leben wünschen,	Wish to live here,
Wenn man nur Haß und Ungemach	When one sees only hatred and adversity
Vor seine Liebe sieht.	In return for His Love?
Doch, weil ich auch den Feind	Yet since I too should love my enemy
Wie meinen besten Freund	Like my best friend
Nach Gottes Vorschrift lieben soll,	According to God's instruction,
So flieht	My heart flees
Mein Herze Zorn und Groll	From anger and resentment
Und wünscht allein bei Gott zu leben,	And wishes only to live with God,
Der selbst die Liebe heißt.	Who is Himself called Love.
Ach! eintrachtvoller Geist,	Ah! spirit full of concord,
Wenn wird er dir doch nur	When will He indeed give you
Sein Himmelszion geben?	His heavenly Zion?

5. Aria A obbl org or fl str + ob d'am bc — D c

Mir ekelt mehr zu leben,	I loathe to live longer,
Drum nimm mich, Jesu, hin!	Therefore take me, Jesus, hence!
Mir graut vor allen Sünden,	I shudder at all my sins;
Laß mich dies Wohnhaus finden,	Let me find this dwelling-place
Woselbst ich ruhig bin.	Where I may be at peace.

This cantata dates from 1726 and was performed for the first time that year on 28 July. With its brevity and economical scoring, it is not easily associated with the big two-part neighbouring works of the same year—it was preceded by Cantatas 39 and 88 and followed by Cantatas 187, 45, and 102. Yet there is a reasonable explanation: at the same service Bach probably performed a cantata by his Meiningen cousin Johann Ludwig Bach, *Ich will meinen Geist in euch geben*. As in earlier years (for example, on the Fourth Sunday after Trinity, 1723) the two cantatas were evidently united to form an overall work in two parts. Since he was unable, on this occasion, to set a libretto from the same cycle as his cousin, Bach fell back on the cycle of 1711 by Georg Christian Lehms.

Lehms interprets the ideas from the Sermon on the Mount, read out in the

Sunday Gospel,* in a truly baroque fashion. Since Jesus exposes the righteousness of the scribes and Pharisees as being only a seeming righteousness, the world proves to be a 'house of sin', according to Lehms, and only in heavenly thoughts does the soul find rest from it (nos. 1–2). Lehms further suggests that the Christian, confronted with 'perverted hearts' that are contrary to God (no. 3), can have only one wish, namely to end his life as soon as possible in order to be received by Jesus (nos. 4–5). A specific reference to the reading of the day is found only in the second movement: the world 'would only say, "Raca! Raca!" ' (an obscure term of abuse; see Matthew 5.22).

Bach's setting is a genuine cantata: it contains exclusively madrigalian* verse and requires an alto soloist only—a choir is not even needed for a concluding chorale. Bach probably had at his disposal a capable alto singer who six weeks later had to sing Cantata 35, and twelve weeks later, Cantata 169. The instrumental ensemble includes not only oboe d'amore,* strings, and continuo but obbligato* organ which, however (unlike in other Bach cantatas of that period) does not participate in a concertante* introductory sinfonia but plays only the obbligato accompaniment to two arias (the double performance mentioned above probably meant that limited time was available).

The opening aria is pastoral and contemplative. Repeated quavers in the strings (with the first violin doubled by oboe d'amore) over a bass figure descending in deliberate strides, form the instrumental framework within which the alto voice unfolds its expansive melody. A *secco* recitative leads to the second aria, no. 3, which is unorthodox in scoring. The continuo is silent, and the lowest part—designated 'bassett'* in such cases—is played by unison violins and violas, while two obbligato upper parts are each assigned to a different manual of the organ. In order to realize Bach's intention we must bear in mind the function of the thoroughbass at that time: it was the foundation, the reliable support of all music. As a rule, its omission by Bach has a symbolic character and refers either to someone who does not need this support[10] or else to someone who has lost it, who no longer has the ground under his feet and has withdrawn from God.[11] In the present aria, then, the absence of thoroughbass characterizes the 'perverted hearts that are so very contrary to You, my God!' The melodic material is pervaded by sharp suspended dissonances.

Our attention is now directed away from the world and towards God. This change is emphasized by the string accompaniment of the fourth movement, which mostly consists of held chords, though livelier motion underlines the words 'to live with God, who is Himself called Love'. The concluding aria is a

[10] Cf., for instance, the aria 'Aus Liebe will mein Heiland sterben' from the *St Matthew Passion* or 'Unschuld, Kleinod reiner Seelen' from the cantata *Auf! süß entzückende Gewalt*, BWV Anh. I 196.

[11] As, for example, in the aria 'Wie zittern und wanken der Sünder Gedanken' from Cantata 105.

triumphant song of renunciation of the world and longing for heaven, surrounded by the figurations of the obbligato organ,[12] which was replaced by obbligato flute in a performance that took place during the last years of Bach's life (around 1746/7). When taken up by the alto, the pregnant theme of the opening ritornello proves to be text-engendered, with its tritone interval—normally avoided as 'unsingable'—on 'mir ekelt' ('I loathe'). In the vocal version of this theme, a rising scale figure is included as an image of the Christian's rising up to Jesus:

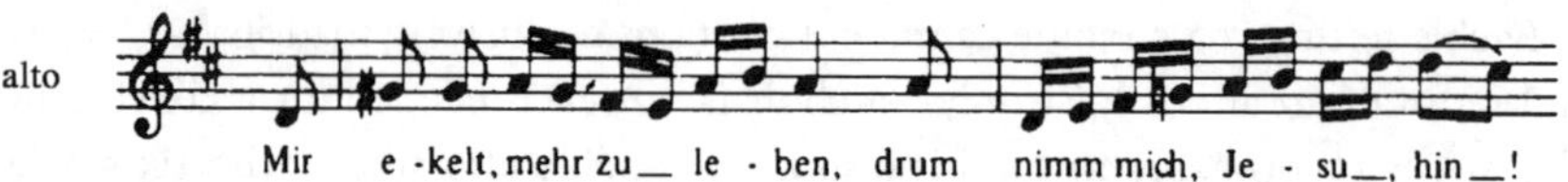

Es ist das Heil uns kommen her, BWV 9

NBA I/17.2, p. 93   BC A107   Duration: *c.* 28 mins

1. [Chorale] SATB fl ob d'am str bc — E $\frac{3}{4}$

Es ist das Heil uns kommen her	**Salvation has come to us**
Von Gnad und lauter Güte.	**From grace and pure goodness.**
Die Werk, die helfen nimmermehr,	**Good deeds no longer help us:**
Sie mögen nicht behüten.	**They cannot protect us.**
Der Glaub sieht Jesum Christum an,	**Faith looks to Jesus Christ,**
Der hat gnug für uns all getan,	**Who has done enough for us all:**
Er ist der Mittler worden.	**He has become the Mediator.**

2. Recitativo B bc — c♯–b C

Gott gab uns ein Gesetz, doch waren wir zu schwach,	God gave us a Law, yet we were too weak
Daß wir es hätten halten können.	To be able to keep it.
Wir gingen nur den Sünden nach,	We went after sin only:
Kein Mensch war fromm zu nennen;	No one could be called devout;
Der Geist blieb an dem Fleische kleben	The spirit adhered to the flesh
Und wagte nicht zu widerstreben.	And did not venture to resist.
Wir sollten im Gesetze gehn	We should have gone by the Law
Und dort als wie in einem Spiegel sehn,	And seen there as in a mirror
Wie unsere Natur unartig sei:	How rude our nature is;
Und dennoch blieben wir dabei.	And yet we persisted in it.
Aus eigner Kraft war niemand fähig,	From his own strength no one was capable
Der Sünden Unart zu verlassen,	Of giving up sin's rudeness,
Er mocht auch alle Kraft zusammenfassen.	Even though he summoned up all his strength.

[12] The part was perhaps originally conceived for a melody instrument (oboe d'amore?) but adapted for organ in time for the first performance. See Reinmar Emans, KB, NBA I/17.2 (1993).

3. ARIA T vln[13] bc — e 12/16

Wir waren schon zu tief gesunken,
Der Abgrund schluckt uns völlig ein,
  Die Tiefe drohte schon den Tod,
  Und dennoch konnt in solcher Not
  Uns keine Hand behülflich sein.

We were already sunk too deep,
The abyss swallowed us up completely,
  The depths already threatened death,
  And still in such distress
  No one could lend us a helping hand.

4. RECITATIVO B bc — b–A C

Doch mußte das Gesetz erfüllet werden;
Deswegen kam das Heil der Erden,
Des Höchsten Sohn, der hat es selbst erfüllt
Und seines Vaters Zorn gestillt.
Durch sein unschuldig Sterben
Ließ er uns Hülf erwerben.
Wer nun demselben traut,
Wer auf sein Leiden baut,
Der gehet nicht verloren.
Der Himmel ist vor den erkoren,
Der wahren Glauben mit sich bringt
Und fest um Jesu Arme schlingt.

Yet the Law had to be fulfilled;
Therefore came the Salvation of the earth,
The Son of the Highest, who has fulfilled it Himself
And stilled His Father's wrath.
Through His innocent Death
He let us purchase help.
Whoever now trusts Him,
Whoever builds on His Passion
Shall not be lost.
Heaven is chosen for him
Who brings true faith with him
And flings his arms round Jesus.

5. ARIA [DUETTO] SA fl ob d'am bc — A 2/4

Herr, du siehst statt guter Werke
Auf des Herzens Glaubensstärke,
Nur den Glauben nimmst du an.
  Nur der Glaube macht gerecht,
  Alles andre scheint zu schlecht,
  Als daß es uns helfen kann.

Lord, rather than at good deeds, You look
At the heart's strength of faith:
Only faith is acceptable to You.
  Only faith justifies us,
  All else shines forth too poorly
  To be able to help us.

6. RECITATIVO B bc — f♯–E C

Wenn wir die Sünd aus dem Gesetz erkennen,
So schlägt es das Gewissen nieder;
Doch ist das unser Trost zu nennen,
Daß wir im Evangelio
Gleich wieder froh
Und freudig werden;
Dies stärket unsern Glauben wieder.
Drauf hoffen wir der Zeit,
Die Gottes Gütigkeit
Uns zugesaget hat,
Doch aber auch aus weisem Rat
Die Stunden uns verschwiegen.

When we recognize sin from the Law
It strikes our conscience;
Yet this may be called our comfort:
That in the Gospel
We again become glad
And joyful;
This strengthens our faith again.
Therefore we look with hope to the time
That God's goodness
Has promised us,
But of which out of wise counsel
He has concealed the hour from us.

[13] 'Violini unisoni' in the autograph score was subsequently altered by Bach to 'Violino solo', but this change is not reflected in the original performing parts. See Emans, KB, NBA I/17.2.

Jedoch, wir lassen uns begnügen,
Er weiß es, wenn es nötig ist,
Und brauchet keine List
An uns: Wir dürfen auf ihn bauen
Und ihm allein vertrauen.

However we may be content:
He knows when it is necessary
And practises no deceit
On us: we may build on Him
And trust Him alone.

7. Choral SATB bc (+ fl 8va ob d'am str) E c

Ob sichs anließ, als wollt er nicht,
Laß dich es nicht erschrecken;
Denn wo er ist am besten mit,
Da will ers nicht entdecken.
Sein Wort laß dir gewisser sein,
Und ob dein Herz spräch lauter Nein,
So laß doch dir nicht grauen.

Though it appears as if He were unwilling,
Do not let it frighten you;
For where He is most with you
He would not reveal it.
Let His Word be more secure for you,
And though your heart should say but 'no',
Then still do not let yourself shudder!

This work is a chorale cantata* which, according to type—the hymn text is retained in the outer movements and paraphrased in the inner ones—belongs to the cycle of 1724–5. As the original sources prove, however, the cantata dates from as late as 1732–5, for on the Sixth Sunday after Trinity in 1724 (16 July), Bach and his wife were staying in Cöthen, where they 'gave performances',[14] so he seems to have laid aside the text provided for this Sunday, intending to set it at a later opportunity.

The work is based on the hymn by Paul Speratus (1523)—one of the principal hymns for this Sunday—which deals with justification by faith alone. The text editor was faced with the rather difficult task of condensing the fourteen-verse hymn into a suitable number of cantata movements. He omitted the last two verses, which are complete in themselves, being a rhyming version of the Paternoster, retained verses 1 and 12 literally in movements 1 and 7, condensed verses 2–4 in the first recitative (no. 2), verses 5–7 in the second recitative (no. 4), and verses 9–11 in the third recitative (no. 6),[15] and paraphrased verse 8 in the aria 'Herr, du siehst statt guter Werke', no. 5. The previous aria, no. 3, is not modelled on any particular verse; instead, it freely reiterates the closing reflections of the preceding recitative, which are derived from the first half of verse 4.

The opening chorus* is constructed according to Bach's favoured design: the chorale melody, delivered line by line in the soprano part and supported by an imitative* texture in the three lower voices, is embedded within an instrumental texture whose thematic material makes no obvious reference to the chorale.

[14] 'So sich hören lassen'; see Smend Kö, p. 20 (Eng. version, p. 36), Dok II, No. 184, p. 144, and NBR, No. 117, p. 117.

[15] Verse 10, 'Die Werke kommn gewißlich her', is admittedly only hinted at in the recitative line 'Dies stärket unsern Glauben wieder' ('This strengthens our faith again'), which is partly based on verse 9.

The aural charm of the movement results from its scoring with single transverse flute* and oboe d'amore,* which at times assume a concertante* role in relation to the string ensemble and elsewhere include the first violin in their concertino* group. This, together with the occasional occurrence of thematic motives* in the continuo, gives rise to a highly spirited movement of multifarious motivic allusions. In the two *Stollen** of the chorale, the imitative motives of the accompanying voice parts are derived from the orchestral texture (bar 3 of the flute part), but the accompanying vocal texture of the *Abgesang** is substantially looser in motivic structure.

Due to the compressed text of the recitatives (see above), the contrasting content of recitative and aria is, in this cantata, particularly marked. Bach stresses the contemplative, almost narrative character of the recitatives by assigning all three to the same voice, namely the bass, so that the impression almost arises of a continuous 'sermon', interrupted at two points by a meditative aria. All three recitatives are set as *secco*; only the end of the fourth movement consolidates into arioso* at its last line of text.

The aria 'Wir waren schon zu tief gesunken', no. 3, is a fine example of graphic textual interpretation. Falling violin figures and syncopated rhythms depict a giddy descent into the abyss of sin. The second aria, no. 5, is quite different, for here the two voices, flute, oboe d'amore, and continuo form a charming quintet on a canonic basis. Above a continuo part restricted to supporting notes, the two obbligato* instruments open the ritornello in canon* at the lower fifth, led by the flute; the continuation in the second half of the ritornello then takes the form of a canon at the upper fourth with reversed order of entries. The voices now take up the theme in a simplified vocal form, and after eight bars the obbligato instruments are added, likewise canonic, giving rise to a vocal and instrumental double canon. A second portion of the principal section, A, proceeds in like manner, after which the return of the ritornello leads into the middle section, B. This is also designed canonically, but here the instruments double the voices, providing occasional figurative decoration of their melodic lines. A da capo* of the principal section A ends this ingenious movement, whose playful, relaxed melodic style gives hardly any idea of its inherent strictness, let alone revealing it directly to the unalerted listener. The work concludes in the usual way with a plain chorale setting, whose lower parts are nonetheless considerably loosened up into polyphony.*

2.7 Seventh Sunday after Trinity

EPISTLE: Romans 6.19–23: 'The wages of sin is death; but the gift of God is eternal life'.

GOSPEL: Mark 8.1–9: The feeding of the four thousand.

Ärgre dich, o Seele, nicht, BWV 186

NBA I/18, p. 17 BC A108 Duration: *c.* 40 mins

1. CHORUS SATB str + ob I,II taille bc — g c

Ärgre dich, o Seele, nicht,	Do not be offended, O soul,
Daß das allerhöchste Licht,	That the Most High Light,
Gottes Glanz und Ebenbild,	God's brightness and image,
Sich in Knechtsgestalt verhüllt,	Disguises Himself in a servant's form;
Ärgre dich, o Seele, nicht!	Do not be offended, O soul!

2. RECITATIVO B bc — c–g c

Die Knechtsgestalt, die Not, der Mangel	A servant's form, need and want
Trifft Christi Glieder nicht allein,	Affect not only Christ's members:
Es will ihr Haupt selbst arm und elend sein.	Even their Head Himself would be poor and needy.
Und ist nicht Reichtum, ist nicht Überfluß	And is not wealth, is not excess
Des Satans Angel,	The hook of Satan
So man mit Sorgfalt meiden muß?	Which one must avoid with care?
Wird dir im Gegenteil	If on the contrary
Die Last zu viel zu tragen,	The burden is too great for you to bear,
Wenn Armut dich beschwert,	When poverty weighs you down,
Wenn Hunger dich verzehrt,	When hunger consumes you,
Und willst sogleich verzagen,	And you would despair forthwith,
So denkst du nicht an Jesum, an dein Heil.	Then you do not think of Jesus, your Salvation.
Hast du wie jenes Volk nicht bald zu essen,	If you do not eat soon like those folk,
So seufzest du: Ach Herr, wie lange willst du mein vergessen?	Then you sigh: Ah Lord, how long will You forget me?

3. ARIA B bc — B♭ 3/4

Bist du, der mir helfen soll,	If it is You who shall help me,
Eilst du nicht, mir beizustehen?	Do You not make haste to help me?
Mein Gemüt ist zweifelsvoll,	My mind is full of doubt:
Du verwirfst vielleicht mein Flehen;	Perhaps You reject my plea;
Doch, o Seele, zweifle nicht,	Yet do not doubt, O soul,
Laß Vernunft dich nicht bestricken!	Do not let reason ensnare you!
Deinen Helfer, Jakobs Licht,	Your Helper, Jacob's Light,
Kannst du in der Schrift erblicken.	You can see in the Scriptures.

4. RECITATIVO T bc — g–B♭ c

Ach, daß ein Christ so sehr	Alas, that a Christian should take
Vor seinen Körper sorgt!	Such care over his body!
Was ist er mehr?	What more is he
Ein Bau von Erden,	Than a building of dust
Der wieder muß zur Erde werden,	That must return to dust,

Ein Kleid, so nur geborgt.
Er könnte ja das beste Teil erwählen,
So seine Hoffnung nie betrügt:
Das Heil der Seelen,
So in Jesu liegt.
O selig! wer ihn in der Schrift erblickt,

Wie er durch seine Lehren
Auf alle, die ihn hören,
Ein geistlich Manna schickt!
Drum, wenn der Kummer gleich das Herze nagt und frißt,
So schmeckt und sehet doch, wie freundlich Jesus ist!

A garment that is just borrowed.
He could indeed choose the best part,
Which would never deceive his hope:
The Salvation of souls
That lies in Jesus.
Oh! blessed is he who sees in the Scriptures
How through His teachings
For all those who hear Him
He sends a spiritual manna!
Therefore when affliction gnaws and devours your heart,
Then taste and see how friendly Jesus is!

5. ARIA T ob I + vln I + II bc — d c

Mein Heiland läßt sich merken
In seinen Gnadenwerken.
Da er sich kräftig weist,
Den schwachen Geist zu lehren,
Den matten Leib zu nähren,
Dies sättigt Leib und Geist.

My Saviour lets Himself be known
In His deeds of grace.
Since He shows Himself heartily
Teaching the weak spirit,
Nourishing the feeble body,
This fills body and soul.

6. CHORAL SATB ob I,II str bc — F c

Ob sichs anließ, als wollt er nicht,

Laß dich es nicht erschrecken;
Denn wo er ist am besten mit,
Da will ers nicht entdecken.
Sein Wort laß dir gewisser sein,
Und ob dein Herz spräch lauter Nein,
So laß dir doch nicht grauen!

Though it appears as if He were unwilling,
Do not let it frighten you;
For where He is most with you
He would not reveal it.
Let His Word be more secure for you,
And though your heart should say but 'no',
Then still do not let yourself shudder.

Nach der Predigt / *After the Sermon*

7. RECITATIVO B str bc — E♭–B♭ c

Es ist die Welt die große Wüstenei;
Der Himmel wird zu Erz, die Erde wird zu Eisen,
Wenn Christen durch den Glauben weisen,
Daß Christi Wort ihr größter Reichtum sei;
Der Nahrungssegen scheint
Von ihnen fast zu fliehen,
Ein steter Mangel wird beweint,
Damit sie nur der Welt sich desto mehr entziehen;

The world is a great wilderness;
The heavens will turn to brass, the earth to iron
When Christians show through faith

That Christ's Word is their greatest wealth;
The blessing of nourishment seems
Almost to flee from them,
A constant want is bewailed,
Which causes them all the more to withdraw from the world;

Da findet erst des Heilands Wort,
Der höchste Schatz,
In ihren Herzen Platz:
Ja, jammert ihn des Volkes dort,

So muß auch hier sein Herze brechen
Und über sie den Segen sprechen.

Then the Saviour's Word,
The highest treasure,
At last finds a place in their hearts:
Indeed, if He had compassion on the people there,
Then here too His heart must break
And pronounce blessing upon them.

8. Aria S vln I + II bc — g C

Die Armen will der Herr umarmen
Mit Gnaden hier und dort;
Er schenket ihnen aus Erbarmen
Den höchsten Schatz, das Lebenswort.

The Lord will embrace the poor
With grace both here and there;
He gives them of His mercy
The highest treasure, the Word of Life.

9. Recitativo A bc — c–E♭ C

Nun mag die Welt mit ihrer Lust vergehen;
Bricht gleich der Mangel ein,
Doch kann die Seele freudig sein.
Wird durch dies Jammertal der Gang
Zu schwer, zu lang,
In Jesu Wort liegt Heil und Segen.

Es ist ihres Fußes Leuchte und ein Licht auf ihren Wegen.
Wer gläubig durch die Wüste reist,

Wird durch dies Wort getränkt, gespeist;
Der Heiland öffnet selbst, nach diesem Worte,
Ihm einst des Paradieses Pforte,
Und nach vollbrachtem Lauf
Setzt er den Gläubigen die Krone auf.

Now the world and the lust thereof may pass away;
Though want breaks out,
Yet the soul can be joyful.
If the way through this vale of tears
Becomes too hard, too long,
In Jesus's Word lies salvation and blessing.
It is a lamp for their feet and a light on their paths.
Whoever walks in faith through the wilderness
Is watered and fed by this Word;

According to this Word, the Saviour Himself opens
For him one day the gates of Paradise,
And after their course is finished,
He places a crown on those who have faith.

10. Aria [Duetto] SA str + ww bc — c 3/8

Laß, Seele, kein Leiden
Von Jesu dich scheiden,
Sei, Seele, getreu!
Dir bleibet die Krone
Aus Gnaden zu Lohne,
Wenn du von Banden des Leibes nun frei.

Let, O soul, no suffering
Separate you from Jesus;
Be faithful, O soul!
A crown awaits you
As the reward of grace
When you are free of the fetters of the body.

11. Choral SATB ob I,II str bc — F C

Die Hoffnung wart' der rechten Zeit,
Was Gottes Wort zusaget.
Wenn das geschehen soll zur Freud,

Hope awaits the right time
That God's Word promises.
When, to our joy, that shall happen

Setzt Gott kein gewisse Tage.	**God sets no certain day.**
Er weiß wohl, wenns am besten ist,	**He well knows when it is best**
Und braucht an uns kein arge List,	**And uses no wicked cunning on us,**
Des solln wir ihm vertrauen.	**Therefore we should trust Him.**

This work is an expanded version of the Weimar cantata BWV 186a, which had been composed for the Third Sunday in Advent 1716 on the basis of a text by Salomo Franck. Since no cantatas were performed in Leipzig from the Second to the Fourth Sunday in Advent, Bach was unable to make use of the Weimar work without altering it. Consequently, he adapted it for the Seventh Sunday after Trinity by inserting recitatives and making alterations to the text of the arias wherever it seemed necessary. As a result, a work in two parts was made out of the original single composition; and, in place of the original concluding chorale, both parts now ended with a verse of the hymn *Es ist das Heil uns kommen her* by Paul Speratus (1523; verses 12 and 11 respectively).

The reinterpretation of the Advent text to refer to the Gospel* for this Sunday was, in the first place, the function of the newly composed recitatives in which the feeding of the four thousand is repeatedly hinted at in the words 'Mangel' ('want', nos. 2, 7, and 9), 'Hunger' (no. 2), 'schmeckt und sehet doch, wie freundlich Jesus ist' ('taste and see how friendly Jesus is', no. 4; cf. Psalm 34.8), and even in a direct allusion to Mark 8.2: 'Ja, jammert ihn des Volkes dort . . .' ('Indeed, if He had compassion on the people there . . .', no.7). The want–excess antithesis thus becomes the fundamental idea of the revised version; and the words from the Advent Gospel which in Franck refer to Jesus's taking the form of a servant, 'Blessed is he who is not offended in me' (Matthew 11.6; cf. no. 1), are now reinterpreted to refer to the salvation of the Christian, who is here in distress but in heaven shall receive a crown.

As the date in the newly prepared score attests, the revised version of the cantata originated during the first year of Bach's Leipzig appointment, receiving its first performance on 11 July 1723. The opening chorus* is in rondeau form—A B A B A—with line 1 of Franck's four-line text assigned to section A and lines 2–4 to section B. Section B is conceived as *a cappella** and predominantly homophonic,* though with imitation in the outer parts. Section A, on the other hand, represents an interesting combination of vocal and instrumental principles of composition. An eight-bar instrumental sinfonia is followed by a brief motto-* like fore-structure, first vocal and then instrumental, which in turn leads to the main part of section A: a fugal texture for the choir built into partial returns of the instrumental sinfonia. Here the principal theme remains instrumental, whereas the counter-theme (a quasi-fugue subject) is assigned to the choir. At its second and third statements, section A is heard in an increasingly abbreviated form, especially as regards its instrumental introduction and motto-like fore-structure: on the third occasion they are absent altogether.

A progressive enhancement in scoring characterizes the four arias (which, in the Weimar version, followed each other without a break), ranging from continuo accompaniment (no. 3), via trio texture (nos. 5 and 8), to orchestral texture with vocal duet (no. 10). The stages were originally still clearer: the fifth movement formerly required a solo obbligato* instrument, an oboe da caccia,* and only later did Bach choose to score the part for unison violins and first oboe, with the result that it was transposed up an octave.[16] In structure, the third movement exhibits a type particularly favoured in Bach's earlier cantatas, namely the continuo movement over a *basso quasi ostinato*.* In the fifth and eighth movements, on the other hand, the concertante* element comes to the fore—it is significant that the vocal and instrumental themes are here different. Finally, the tenth movement exhibits a dance-like (gigue) character. The vocal duet parts here move predominantly in parallel motion, and where imitation* occurs it is largely accommodated within the periodic structure of a dance movement.

The four inserted recitatives, with their sometimes very extended arioso* sections, betray their close proximity in time to Bach's Weimar and Cöthen periods: there is not a single recitative in this cantata that does not show, at least at the end, a rhythmic consolidation into arioso. Lastly, the newly composed chorale, nos. 6 and 11 (which are musically identical; the original chorale is unknown to us), is particularly charming, for Bach incorporates the individual chorale lines within an instrumental texture of considerable extent which has its own thematic material. Furthermore, the chorale texture itself is not plainly chordal in the usual way; instead, occasionally imitative quaver motion in the lower parts is placed in counterpoint* with the stepping crotchets of the soprano *cantus firmus*.* For a concluding chorale, the structure that emerges is highly differentiated.

Was willst du dich betrüben, BWV 107

NBA I/18, p. 57 BC A109 Duration: *c.* 20 mins

1. [CHORALE] S + hn ATB fl I,II ob d'am I,II str bc — b C

Was willst du dich betrüben,	**Why would you grieve,**
O meine liebe Seel?	**O my dear soul?**
Ergib dich, den zu lieben,	**Devote yourself to loving Him**
Der heißt Immanuel!	**Who is called Emmanuel!**
Vertraue ihm allein,	**Trust Him alone:**
Er wird gut alles machen	**He will make all things good**
Und fördern deine Sachen,	**And so further your affairs**
Wie dirs wird selig sein!	**As will be a blessing to you!**

[16] For details see Dürr St, KB, NBA I/1, 89 ff., and KB, NBA I/18, 38, and 43 f.

2. Recitativo B ob d'am I,II bc — f♯ c

Denn Gott verlässet keinen,
Der sich auf ihn verläßt,
Er bleibt getreu den Seinen,
Die ihm vertrauen fest.
Läßt sichs an wunderlich,
So laß dir doch nicht grauen!
Mit Freuden wirst du schauen,
Wie Gott wird retten dich.

For God forsakes no one
Who trusts in Him;
He remains faithful to His own
Who trust Him firmly.
If things seem strange,
Yet do not be afraid!
With joy you will see
How God will deliver you.

3. Aria B str bc — A c

Auf ihn magst du es wagen
Mit unerschrocknem Mut,
Du wirst mit ihm erjagen,
Was dir ist nütz und gut.
Was Gott beschlossen hat,
Das kann niemand hindern
Aus allen Menschenkindern;
Es geht nach seinem Rat.

You may stake your life on Him
With fearless courage;
With Him you will hunt
For what is useful and good for you.
What God has purposed
No one can hinder
Among all the children of men;
Things go according to His counsel.

4. Aria T bc — e $\frac{3}{4}$

Wenn auch gleich aus der Höllen
Der Satan wollte sich
Dir selbst entgegenstellen
Und toben wider dich,
So muß er doch mit Spott
Von seinen Ränken lassen,
Damit er dich will fassen;
Denn dein Werk fördert Gott.

Though from hell
Satan would
Himself confront you
And rage against you,
Yet with scorn he must
Leave off his intrigues
With which he would catch you;
For God establishes the work of your hand.

5. Aria S ob d'am I,II bc — b $\frac{12}{8}$

Er richts zu seinen Ehren
Und deiner Seligkeit;
Solls sein, kein Mensch kanns wehren,
Und wärs ihm noch so leid.
Wills denn Gott haben nicht,
So kanns niemand forttreiben,
Es muß zurücke bleiben,
Was Gott will, das geschicht.

He disposes things to His honour
And to your salvation;
If it is to be, no man can stay this,
Even if he might regret it.
But what God would not have
No one can carry through:
It must remain undone;
What God wills, that is done.

6. Aria T fl I + II + vln I bc — D c

Drum ich mich ihm ergebe,
Ihm sei es heimgestellt;
Nach nichts ich sonst mehr strebe,
Denn nur was ihm gefällt.
Drauf wart ich und bin still,
Sein Will der ist der beste,

Therefore I surrender myself to Him:
On Him may reliance be placed;
I no longer strive after anything
Other than what pleases Him.
I await that and am calm;
His Will: it is best,

Das glaub ich steif und feste,	**That I believe rigidly and steadfastly;**
Gott mach es, wie er will!	**May God act as He wills!**

7. [Chorale] S + hn ATB str + ww bc b $\frac{6}{8}$

Herr, gib, daß ich dein Ehre	**Lord, grant that I promote Your honour**
Ja all mein Leben lang	**Indeed as long as I live**
Von Herzengrund vermehre,	**From the bottom of my heart,**
Dir sage Lob und Dank!	**And say praise and thanks to You!**
O Vater, Sohn und Geist,	**O Father, Son, and Spirit,**
Der du aus lauter Gnaden	**Who out of pure grace**
Abwendest Not und Schaden,	**Avert distress and harm,**
Sei immerdar gepreist!	**Evermore be praised!**

This work is a chorale cantata* whose first known performance took place on 23 July 1724. In the light of the Sunday Gospel,* the choice of the hymn by Johann Heermann (1630) requires no detailed explanation. The substance of the hymn—trust in God, even if Satan appears to gain the upper hand—is an obvious doctrinal interpretation of the account of the feeding of the four thousand. The form of the text, however, is strange and cannot be explained on the basis of the transmitted source material. It is the only work from the cycle of 1724–5 in which Bach retained the hymn text literally throughout (that is, without paraphrasing the middle verses, which are nonetheless treated as modern recitative and arias), a procedure characteristic only of Bach's later chorale cantatas. We do not know the grounds for this exception to the rule: it is idle to ponder whether the librettist supplied no text, whether for some reason Bach found the text supplied unusable, or whether the cantata is of earlier origin. We simply do not know the answer to these questions. On musical, stylistic grounds, at any rate, there is no reason to date the work any earlier than 1724, and the source findings unambiguously testify against a later dating.

The opening chorus* corresponds to the type that occurs most frequently in Bach's chorale cantatas. The chorale, to the melody *Von Gott will ich nicht lassen*, is delivered by the soprano doubled by horn, supported by the lower voice parts, and incorporated within an orchestral texture with its own themes, which is influenced by the chorale melody only to the extent of insignificant allusions. There are a number of idiosyncracies, however. In the instrumental texture, we are struck by the relatively rich woodwind scoring for two flutes and two oboes d'amore,* which was evidently not differentiated until the process of writing out the parts was already under way. In several places, the flutes, violins, and viola are singled out to form a kind of concertino* group, without continuo. The oboes d'amore reinforce the strings in the instrumental passages (as do the flutes, for the most part), but in the choral passages they strengthen the chorale melody in the soprano. The chorale itself is not in plain form throughout but at times expressively ornamented. Nor is the melody consistently embedded line by line within the orchestral texture in the usual way; instead, several lines are joined together thus: nos. 1 + 2 (first *Stollen**), 3 + 4 (second *Stollen*), and 5, 6–8 (*Abgesang**). The impression thereby arises of a concise and compressed structure, especially since the lower voice parts never prepare the chorale entries. Instead, they follow them in a gently agitated, broken-up texture, often closer to chordal writing than to thoroughgoing polyphony.*

The only recitative, no. 2, presented the composer with a special task. The symmetry of the chorale lines, each of which takes up exactly one bar, carries with it the danger of a stereotyped and constrained style of declamation. Bach counters this danger by scoring the movement with two oboes d'amore—which bridge over the caesuras of the voice part—and also by prolonging the last two lines: the penultimate line includes a melisma* on 'Freuden' ('joy'), and the last line is delivered 'a tempo'* (in other words, as arioso*) and includes another extended melisma on 'retten' ('deliver').

Verses 3–6 are set as four successive arias, each of which is unmistakably influenced by the textual structure of the chorale. Not a single aria follows the usual da capo* form; instead, they all contain a very marked caesura between *Stollen* and *Abgesang*, with the result that bipartite structure is predominant. Further subdivisions arise from the specific sentence structure of the text. In the third movement, a suggestion of *Bar* form* arises; in the fourth, the last line, 'Denn dein Werk fördert Gott' ('For God establishes the work of your hand'), acquires special significance; and in the sixth movement, the first line of the *Abgesang*, 'Drauf wart ich und bin still' ('I await that and am calm'), is set apart from those that follow. The outer arias, nos. 3 and 6, correspond in character: in their major mode, they depart furthest from the chorale melody, and their melodic style is song-like and even dance-like.

Turning to the two middle arias, the fourth movement is accompanied only by continuo and exhibits the kind of structure favoured by Bach in movements of this kind. Over the ostinato* formations of the continuo, the voice unfolds a much freer melodic line, interspersed with text-engendered coloraturas.* Only in a few places—all the more conspicuous for their rarity—does the voice partake of the continuo theme. At the outset of the first vocal section, the continuo enters with the ritornello theme while the tenor freely inverts it, which no doubt characterizes Satan's confrontation with the Will of God:

Logically, the head-motive is also heard in the voice part in its original ascending form only at the closing line, to the words 'Denn dein Werk fördert Gott' ('For God establishes the work of your hand'):

The fifth movement, a soprano aria with two obbligato* oboes d'amore, draws nearest to the chorale melody in its thematic material. Suggestions of the chorale's opening may already be heard in the instrumental ritornello, and it becomes still more clearly recognizable at the entry of the voice. The last chorale line, unveiled in its original form, is heard at the end of the aria to the words 'Was Gott will, das geschicht' ('What God wills, that is done').

The concluding chorale is richly decked out. The vocal texture is plainly chordal and, as in the first movement, unites several chorale lines within each section. However, it is embedded in a rich orchestral texture for strings and woodwind (the horn again reinforces the soprano), whose florid siciliano rhythm constantly preserves its independence, even in the chorale passages.

Liebster Gott, vergißt du mich, BWV Anh. I 209

1. [Recitative] Liebster Gott, vergißt du mich
2. [Aria] Liebster Gott, vergißt du mich
3. [Recitative + Aria] Bei diesen Worten muß ein Schwert durch meine Seele gehen/ Es ist genung, Herr Jesu, laß mich sterben
4. [Chorale] **Warum betrübst du dich, mein Herz**
5. [Recitative] Mein Geist erholt sich wieder
6. [Aria] Hör auf zu winseln und zu klagen

The music to this cantata is lost. Klaus Hofmann has argued plausibly that the text, drawn from Georg Christian Lehms's collection *Gottgefälliges Kirchen-Opffer* of 1711, was indeed set to music by Bach. The date of composition is 1725 at the latest, but Hofmann suggests that the work might have been written in Weimar for performance on 15 July 1714.[17]

[17] See K. Hofmann, 'Bachs Kantate "Ich lasse dich nicht, du segnest mich denn" BWV 157: Überlegungen zu Entstehung, Bestimmung und originaler Werkgestalt', *BJ* 1982, 51–80 (especially 62–5).

Es wartet alles auf dich, BWV 187

NBA I/18, p. 93 BC A110 Duration: *c.* 25 mins

1. [Chorus] SATB ob I,II str bc — g C

'Es wartet alles auf dich, daß du ihnen Speise gebest zu seiner Zeit. Wenn du ihnen gibest, so sammlen sie; wenn du deine Hand auftust, so werden sie mit Güte gesättiget.'

'These wait all upon You, that You may give them nourishment in due season. When You give it to them, they gather it; when You open Your hand, they are filled with good things.'

2. Recitativo B bc — B♭–g C

Was Kreaturen hält das große Rund der Welt!
Schau doch die Berge an, da sie bei tausend gehen;
Was zeuget nicht die Flut? Es wimmeln Ström und Seen.

Der Vögel großes Heer zieht durch die Luft zu Feld.
Wer nähret solche Zahl,
Und wer vermag ihr wohl die Notdurft abzugeben?
Kann irgendein Monarch nach solcher Ehre streben?
Zahlt aller Erden Gold ihr wohl ein einig Mahl?

What creatures does the great globe of the world contain!
Just look at the mountains as they roll out to the thousands!
What does the torrent not bring forth? The rivers and seas swarm with living things.
The great flock of birds moves through the air to the field.
Who feeds such a great number,
And who has the power to supply them with their needs?
Can any monarch strive after such an honour?
Would all the gold on earth buy them a single meal?

3. Aria A ob I + vln I vln II vla bc — B♭ $\frac{3}{8}$

Du Herr, du krönst allein das Jahr mit deinem Gut.
Es träufet Fett und Segen
Auf deines Fußes Wegen,
Und deine Gnade ists, die allen Gutes tut.

You, Lord, You alone crown the year with Your goodness.
Savoury richness and blessing drip
Upon the paths of Your feet,
And it is Your grace that does all good things.

Parte 2 / *Part 2*

4. [Bass Solo] B vln I + II bc — g C

'Darum sollt ihr nicht sorgen noch sagen: Was werden wir essen? was werden wir trinken? womit werden wir uns kleiden? Nach solchem allen trachten die Heiden. Denn euer himmlischer Vater weiß, daß ihr dies alles bedürfet.'

'Therefore you should not worry or say: what shall we eat? what shall we drink? with what shall we clothe ourselves? For after all such things the Gentiles seek. For your heavenly Father knows that you have need of all these things.'

5. Aria S ob I solo bc — E♭ C $\frac{3}{8}$ C

Gott versorget alles Leben,
Was hienieden Odem hegt.

God takes care of all life
That has breath here below.

Sollt er mir allein nicht geben,
Was er allen zugesagt?
Weicht, ihr Sorgen! Seine Treue
Ist auch meiner eingedenk
Und wird ob mir täglich neue
Durch manch Vaterliebs-Geschenk.

Would He not give me alone
What He has promised to all?
Retreat, you cares! His faithfulness
Is mindful of me too
And is daily renewed for me
Through many a gift of fatherly love.

6. Recitativo S str bc — c–B♭ C

Halt ich nur fest an ihm mit kindlichem Vertrauen
Und nehm mit Dankbarkeit, was er mir zugedacht,
So werd ich mich nie ohne Hülfe schauen,
Und wie er auch vor mich die Rechnung hab gemacht.
Das Grämen nützet nicht, die Mühe ist verloren,
Die das verzagte Herz um seine Notdurft nimmt;
Der ewig reiche Gott hat sich die Sorge auserkoren;
So weiß ich, daß er mir auch meinen Teil bestimmt.

If only I hold fast to Him with childlike confidence
And take with thanksgiving what He has intended for me,
Then I shall never see myself helpless
And shall see how He has taken account of me.
Worrying is useless, the trouble wasted
That the fearful heart takes over its need;
The ever-abundant God has chosen these cares for Himself;
Thus I know that He has determined my lot too.

7. Choral SATB bc (+ instrs) — g 3

Gott hat die Erde zugericht',
Läßts an Nahrung mangeln nicht;
Berg und Tal, die macht er naß,
Daß dem Vieh auch wächst sein Gras;
Aus der Erden Wein und Brot
Schaffet Gott und gibts uns satt,
Daß der Mensch sein Leben hat.

Wir danken sehr und bitten ihn,
Daß er uns geb des Geistes Sinn,
Daß wir solches recht verstehn,
Stets in sein' Geboten gehn,
Seinen Namen machen groß
In Christo ohn Unterlaß:
So singn wir recht das Gratias.

God has established the earth,
He allows no lack of nourishment;
Hill and dale He makes moist
So that grass may grow for the cattle;
Out of the earth, wine and bread
He makes and gives us plenty,
That man may have his life.

We thank Him greatly and pray
That He will grant us the Spirit's mind,
That we may truly understand such things,
Ever walk in His Commandments,
Make His Name great
In Christ without ceasing:
Thus we rightly sing the Gratias.

This work, composed for 4 August 1726, belongs to the group of cantatas whose texts were drawn from the same cycle as those of Johann Ludwig Bach. In Bach's later Leipzig years, the opening chorus* and all three arias (nos. 3–5) were parodied in the Lutheran Missa in G minor, BWV 235. The substance of the text is linked with the account of the feeding of the four thousand in the Sunday Gospel.* In Part I God is praised as the dispenser of all nourishment. The text of the first movement is drawn from Psalm 104.27–8, and the following recitative also speaks in the language of the psalms: again the librettist would have had Psalm 104 in mind, among other psalms, when he asks, 'What does the torrent not bring forth? The rivers and seas swarm [with living things]' (cf. Psalm 104.25: 'The sea, which is so great and wide, where things teem without number'), or when he talks of the 'great flock of birds' (cf. Psalm 104.17: 'Where the birds make their nests and the storks dwell in the fir-trees'). Finally, the text of the aria, no. 3, makes an unmistakable allusion to a passage from the psalms (cf. Psalm 65.11: 'You crown the year with Your goodness, and your footsteps drip with fat').

Part II, with its more personal words, turns to the Christian congregation. The introductory words of Jesus in the fourth movement (Matthew 6.31–2) are drawn from the Sermon on the Mount; their truth, the librettist wants to say, is revealed in the feeding of the four thousand. It follows that each individual Christian (the poet now significantly chooses the first person) may, 'with childlike confidence', let God care for him. The cantata concludes with verses 4 and 6 of the hymn *Singen wir aus Herzensgrund* by Hans Vogel (1563).

The opening chorus shows the composer at the height of his powers. The wide-ranging introductory sinfonia furnishes the thematic material, whose frequent occurrence in the course of the movement has a unifying effect. Extended parts of it are at times heard as a framework for choral insertion,* and elsewhere individual motives* are extracted as accompaniment figures to the independent vocal parts. In the vocal passages, the text is delivered in sections according to the old motet* style, but in the last vocal section it is repeated in its entirety. The following formal scheme thereby arises (italics denote instrumental passages):

Introductory sinfonia (28 bars)

A Freely polyphonic* choral texture with canonic formations and choral insertion

1. 'Es wartet alles auf dich'. Canonic or freely polyphonic choral complex (a); *instrumental accompaniment largely independent*
2. 'Es wartet . . .' and 'daß du ihnen Speise gebest . . .'. Dual-thematic, canonic or freely polyphonic choral complex (a + b); *instruments largely colla parte**
3. Choral insertion within the *sinfonia, bars 6–13*

Sinfonia, varied and abridged (17 bars)

B Choral fugue*; *instruments at first colla parte, then independent (based on sinfonia motives)*

Subject: 'Wenn du ihnen gibest . . .'; countersubject: 'wenn du deine Hand auftust . . .'

C Choral insertion (with allusions to A and B)—to the complete text—within the *sinfonia, bars (12) 16–28 (dovetailing with section B)*

This structure is characteristic of the biblical-text choruses from Bach's mature Leipzig period. The series principle of motet style guarantees a text-related shaping of the individual vocal passages, while the superimposed concerto principle effects the unification of the movement as a whole. The reprise of the text, in conjunction with allusions to section A within C, creates the overall impression of a very freely treated da capo* form.

A plain *secco* recitative leads to the first aria, no. 3, in which, with almost Handelian splendour, God is praised as the preserver of life. Its 3/8 time, underlined by the small-scale articulation of its motives,* creates the impression of a solemn dance. Its charm is enhanced by the syncopated rhythm which leads to irregular phrasing in the instrumental ritornello: in place of the two-, four-, and eight-bar groups favoured elsewhere, we find here a grouping of (3 + 3) + (4 + 4 + 4) bars.

The biblical passage that introduces Part II is assigned to solo bass as *vox Christi*. As in the opening chorus, the instruments, with their constant reiteration of supple motives,* take care of the unity of the movement. The following aria, no. 5, is designed in two contrasting sections. Ceremonial dotted rhythms and an extensive and elaborate melody for solo oboe characterize the first section, but at the words 'Weicht, ihr Sorgen!' ('Retreat, you cares!') the melody reverts to a dance-like style (in 3/8 time, marked *un poco allegro*). At the end, a reprise of the instrumental ritornello effects a return to the solemnity of the first section.

The choice of instrumentation in the arias and choruses is perhaps not without design: in the sequence tutti–strings + oboe I–unison violins–solo oboe, it is conceivable that Bach sought to reflect the change from general to particular in the succession of ideas within the text. If so, it is tempting to regard the string accompaniment of the recitative (no. 6) as a symbol of the security of the individual in God's love and within the Christian community. Similarly, the concluding chorale, which unites all participants in a general four-part texture, is sung in the name of the assembled congregation and on their behalf.

Gesegnet ist die Zuversicht, BWV Anh. I 1

A cantata of this title under Bach's name was in 1770 offered for sale by the music dealers Breitkopf in Leipzig, but the music has not survived. Possibly this was a case of confusion with a work of the same name by Georg Philipp Telemann; see the Critical Report to NBA I/18, pp. 118 f.

2.8 Eighth Sunday after Trinity

EPISTLE: Romans 8.12–17: 'Those who are driven by the Spirit of God: they are the children of God'.

GOSPEL: Matthew 7.15–23: From the Sermon on the Mount: a warning against false prophets; 'by their fruits you shall know them'.

Erforsche mich, Gott, und erfahre mein Herz, BWV 136

NBA I/18, p. 131 BC A111 Duration: *c.* 21 mins

1. [CHORUS] SATB hn ob I ob II d'am str bc — A 12/8

'Erforsche mich, Gott, und erfahre
mein Herz; prüfe mich und erfahre,
wie ichs meine!'

'Search me, O God, and know my heart;
try me and know my thoughts!'

2. RECITATIVO T bc — b–c♯ C

Ach, daß der Fluch, so dort die Erde schlägt,
Auch derer Menschen Herz getroffen!
Wer kann auf gute Früchte hoffen,
Da dieser Fluch bis in die Seele dringet,
So daß sie Sündendornen bringet
Und Lasterdisteln trägt.
Doch wollen sich oftmals die Kinder der Höllen
In Engel des Lichtes verstellen;
Man soll bei dem verderbten Wesen
Von diesen Dornen Trauben lesen.
Ein Wolf will sich mit reiner Wolle decken,
Doch bricht ein Tag herein,
Der wird, ihr Heuchler, euch ein Schrecken,
Ja unerträglich sein.

Alas, that the curse that there strikes the earth
Has also struck the heart of man!
Who can hope for good fruit
When this curse penetrates as far as the soul,
So that it brings the thorns of sin
And bears the thistles of vice.
Yet the children of hell would often disguise themselves
As the angels of light;
With our corrupted nature we should
Gather grapes from these thorns.
A wolf would cover himself in pure wool,
Yet a day dawns,
You hypocrites, when a terror
Will indeed be unbearable for you.

3. ARIA A ob d'am I bc — f♯ C 12/8 C

Es kömmt ein Tag,
So das Verborgne richtet,
Vor dem die Heuchelei erzittern mag.
  Denn seines Eifers Grimm vernichtet,
  Was Heuchelei und List erdichtet.

A day is coming
That will judge the secrets of men,
Before which hypocrisy may tremble.
  For the wrath of His jealousy annihilates
  What hypocrisy and cunning contrive.

4. RECITATIVO B bc — b C

Die Himmel selber sind nicht rein,

The heavens themselves are not clean:

Wie soll es nun ein Mensch vor diesem Richter sein?	How then shall it be for a man before this Judge?
Doch wer durch Jesu Blut gereinigt,	Yet he who is cleansed by Jesus's Blood
Im Glauben sich mit ihm vereinigt,	And united with Him in faith
Weiß, daß er ihm kein hartes Urteil spricht.	Knows that He will pronounce no harsh judgement upon him.
Kränkt ihn die Sünde noch,	Though sin still afflicts him—
Der Mangel seiner Werke,	The deficiency of his deeds—
Er hat in Christo doch	Yet he has in Christ
Gerechtigkeit und Stärke.	Righteousness and strength.

5. Aria [Duetto] TB vln I + II bc — b 12/8

Uns treffen zwar der Sünden Flecken,	We are indeed struck by spots of sin
So Adams Fall auf uns gebracht.	That Adam's Fall brought upon us.
Allein, wer sich zu Jesu Wunden,	But whoever has found Jesus's Wounds
Dem großen Strom voll Blut gefunden,	For himself—that great stream full of Blood—
Wird dadurch wieder rein gemacht.	Is thereby made clean again.

6. Choral SATB vln I bc (+ hn ww vln II vla) — b C

Dein Blut, der edle Saft,	**Your Blood, that noble sap,**
Hat solche Stärk und Kraft,	**Has such strength and power**
Daß auch ein Tröpflein kleine	**That even a little tiny drop**
Die ganze Welt kann reine,	**Can cleanse the entire world,**
Ja, gar aus Teufels Rachen	**Indeed from the Devil's jaws themselves**
Frei, los und ledig machen.	**Make us free, at liberty and discharged.**

In its present form, this work belongs to Bach's first Leipzig cycle of cantatas and was first performed on 18 July 1723. There are various indications in the sources, however, that Bach might have made use of music composed at an earlier date. Only the 12/8 section of the third movement and the final chorale are incontestably ad hoc compositions. It is tempting to imagine that the remainder might have originated in a secular work, or possibly in a church cantata for another occasion (and hence with a different concluding chorale). As yet, however, it has not proved possible to establish any further particulars.

Also unknown is the writer of the text, whose ideas closely follow the Sunday Gospel*—an observation that might perhaps militate against the suspicion of parody* entertained above. In the opening movement, the Gospel warning against false prophets leads to a prayer for true faith in the words of Psalm 139.23. The second movement establishes a connection with the original Fall of Man: Jesus's rhetorical question, 'Can one gather grapes from thorns or figs from thistles?' recalls Genesis 3.17–18 ('Cursed be the ground on your account . . . thorns and thistles shall it bring forth for you') to which the opening of the recitative refers in the words 'Alas, that the curse that there strikes the earth . . .'. In the third movement, the closing words of the Gospel, 'Not everyone who says to me, "Lord, Lord!" shall enter into the Kingdom of Heaven', serve as the occasion for a warning against hypocrisy. And now the true significance of the reference to the curse of Adam for an understanding of the whole text is revealed. The two recitative-aria pairs, nos. 2–3 and 4–5, are built upon the contrast between Adam's Fall and Jesus's atoning Death, an antithesis that occurs several times in Paul (Jesus as the new Adam: see, for example, Romans 5.14 or 1 Corinthians 15.22 and 45). The fourth movement, which is introduced by an allusion to Job 15.15 ('. . . the heavens are not clean in his sight') brings the turning-point: whoever accepts in faith Jesus's sacrifice is justified, despite 'the deficiency of his deeds'. The same point is made in the fifth movement and again in the concluding chorale, the ninth verse of the hymn *Wo soll ich fliehen hin* by Johann Heermann (1630).

The opening chorus* was later (around 1738) adapted to form the finale of the Lutheran Missa in A, BWV 234. It takes the form of an extensive fugue,* which nonetheless exhibits a certain lack of purposefulness in its development: the entire text is set from the very beginning, and only in the second half do a few held notes and homophonic* calls of 'prüfe mich' ('try me') gain some significance as a rudimentary form of textual interpretation. In addition, the fugue subject in its literal form—

—occurs considerably more often in the outer than in the inner parts, possibly due to the origin of the movement (it suggests an original in fewer parts). Curious, too, are the framing instrumental ritornellos, more concertante* than fugal in character, and the prefacing of the vocal section with a motto* which is followed by a bar-and-a-half of extra instrumental music before the fugue really begins. Finally, the instruments are assigned very different roles. The two oboes (ordinary oboe and oboe d'amore*) lack independent parts, simply doubling the two violins in the ritornellos and the soprano in the vocal passages. Among the strings, the first violin is predominant, with its almost continuous but unthematic, figurative semiquaver motion, whereas the second violin mostly proceeds in calmer quaver motion, as do the viola and continuo almost throughout. A horn presents the main theme (see the above music example) at the start of the ritornello and is also given an independent part thereafter. In form, the movement is constructed in two halves, A and A^1, which are choral-fugue complexes based on the same theme, surrounded and separated by instrumental passages.

A *secco* recitative leads to the first aria, no. 3, whose obbligato* oboe d'amore, with its expressive figuration, is well suited to the cautionary text, even though this might be of secondary origin. The contrasting 'presto' middle section ('For the wrath of His jealousy annihilates . . .') is, as mentioned above, an ad hoc addition. The second recitative, no. 4, is also *secco*, with a hint of arioso* in the closing bars only. It is followed by a duet with an obbligato part for unison violins. With its part-imitative and part-homophonic writing for the voices, this movement closely resembles the secular duets of the Cöthen years. On the other hand, it is admirably accommodated to the text: note, for example, the interjection 'Allein' ('But'), the modulatory side-stepping on the words 'Jesu Wunden' ('Jesus's Wounds'), and the sequential passage on 'Strom' ('stream').

The plain concluding chorale, based on the melody *Auf meinen lieben Gott*, is expanded to five-part texture by the addition of an independent first violin part. It seems possible that in this revaluation of the final chorale Bach wanted to counteract the indifferent quality—perhaps conditioned by parody—of the opening movement.

Wo Gott der Herr nicht bei uns hält, BWV 178

NBA I/18, p. 161 BC A112 Duration: *c.* 23 mins

1. [Chorale] S + hn ATB ob I,II str bc — a C

Wo Gott der Herr nicht bei uns hält,	**If God the Lord does not remain on our side**
Wenn unsre Feinde toben,	**When our enemies rage,**
Und er unser Sach nicht zufällt	**And if He does not support our cause**
Im Himmel hoch dort oben,	**In heaven there, high above,**
Wo er Israel Schutz nicht ist	**If He is not Israel's protection and does not**
Und selber bricht der Feinde List,	**Himself destroy the enemy's cunning,**
So ists mit uns verloren.	**Then all is lost with us.**

2. Recitativo [+ Chorale] A bc — C–e C

Was Menschenkraft und -witz anfäht,	**What human strength and wit contrive**
Soll uns billig nicht schrecken;	**Should not by rights terrify us;**
Denn Gott der Höchste steht uns bei	For God the Highest stands by us
Und machet uns von ihren Stricken frei.	And makes us free of their snares.
Er sitzet an der höchsten Stätt,	**He sits in the highest place;**
Er wird ihrn Rat aufdecken.	**He will expose their counsel.**
Die Gott im Glauben fest umfassen,	Those who embrace God firmly in faith
Will er niemals versäumen noch verlassen;	He will never leave nor forsake;
Er stürzet der Verkehrten Rat	He overturns the counsel of the perverted
Und hindert ihre böse Tat.	And hinders their evil deeds.

Wenn sies aufs klügste greifen an,
Auf Schlangenlist und falsche Ränke sinnen,
Der Bosheit Endzweck zu gewinnen;
So geht doch Gott ein ander Bahn:
Er führt die Seinigen mit starker Hand
Durchs Kreuzesmeer in das gelobte Land,
Da wird er alles Unglück wenden.
Es steht in seinen Händen.

When they attack most cleverly,
Plotting with a serpent's subtlety and with false intrigues
To gain their evil purpose,
Then God pursues another course:
He leads His own with mighty hand
Through the sea of the cross into the Promised Land;
There He will divert all misfortune.
It is in His hands.

3. ARIA B vln I + II bc — G $\frac{9}{8}$

Gleichwie die wilden Meereswellen
Mit Ungestüm ein Schiff zerschellen,
So raset auch der Feinde Wut
Und raubt das beste Seelengut.
Sie wollen Satans Reich erweitern,
Und Christi Schifflein soll zerscheitern.

Just as the wild waves of the sea
Tempestuously smash a ship to pieces,
So the enemies' fury rages
And steals the best possession of the soul.
They would extend Satan's kingdom,
And Christ's little ship would be wrecked.

4. CHORAL T ob d'am I,II bc — b c

Sie stellen uns wie Ketzern nach,
Nach unserm Blut sie trachten;
Noch rühmen sie sich Christen auch,
Die Gott allein groß achten.
Ach Gott, der teure Name dein
Muß ihrer Schalkheit Deckel sein,
Du wirst einmal aufwachen.

They persecute us as heretics:
They are out for our blood;
Still they are proud to call themselves Christians
Who greatly esteem God alone.
Ah God, that precious Name of Yours
Must be a cloak for their villainy:
One day You will wake up to it.

5. CHORAL ET RECITATIVO SATB bc — b c

Auf sperren sie den Rachen weit,
Baß
Nach Löwenart mit brüllendem Getöne;
Sie fletschen ihre Mörderzähne
Und wollen uns verschlingen.
Tenor
Jedoch,
Lob und Dank sei Gott allezeit;
Tenor
Der Held aus Juda schützt uns noch,
Es wird ihn' nicht gelingen.
Alt
Sie werden wie die Spreu vergehn,
Wenn seine Gläubigen wie grüne Bäume stehn.

They gaped their jaws
Bass
Like a lion with roaring sounds;
They bare their murderous teeth
And would swallow us up.
Tenor
However,
Blessing and thanks be to God always;
Tenor
The Hero out of Judah protects us still,
They will not succeed.
Alto
They will perish like chaff,
While His faithful stand like green trees.

Er wird ihrn Strick zerreißen gar
Und stürzen ihre falsche Lahr.

He will break their snares altogether
And overturn their false doctrine.

Baß
Gott wird die törichten Propheten
Mit Feuer seines Zornes töten
Und ihre Ketzerei verstören.
Sie werdens Gott nicht wehren.

Bass
God will kill the foolish prophets
With the fire of His wrath
And utterly destroy their heresy.
They will not restrain God.

6. ARIA T str bc — e C

Schweig, schweig nur, taumelnde Vernunft!
Sprich nicht: Die Frommen sind verlorn,
Das Kreuz hat sie nur neu geborn.

Denn denen, die auf Jesum hoffen,
Steht stets die Tür der Gnaden offen;
Und wenn sie Kreuz und Trübsal drückt,
So werden sie mit Trost erquickt.

Be silent, be silent, tottering reason!
Do not say: the devout are lost;
The Cross has just given them new birth.
For to those who hope in Jesus
The door of grace stands ever open;
And when cross and affliction oppress them
They shall be refreshed with comfort.

7. CHORAL SATB bc (+ instrs) — a C

Die Feind sind all in deiner Hand.
Darzu all ihr Gedanken;
Ihr Anschläg sind dir, Herr, bekannt,
Hilf nur, daß wir nicht wanken.
Vernunft wider den Glauben ficht,
Aufs Künftge will sie trauen nicht,
Da du wirst selber trösten.

Den Himmel und auch die Erden
Hast du, Herr Gott, gegründet;
Dein Licht laß uns helle werden,
Das Herz uns werd entzündet
In rechter Lieb des Glaubens dein,
Bis an das End beständig sein.
Die Welt laß immer murren.

Our enemies are all in Your hands,
Together with all their thoughts;
Their plots are known to You, Lord;
Help us, that we do not waver.
Reason struggles against Faith:
In future it will not be trusted,
For You Yourself will comfort us.

Both heaven and earth
You, Lord God, have founded;
Let Your Light become bright for us,
And our heart enkindled
In true love of Your Faith,
Remaining constant to the end.
Let the world ever murmur.

This chorale cantata,* first performed on 30 July 1724, is based on the paraphrase of Psalm 124 by Justus Jonas (1524). As a warning against the enemies of Christ, this hymn is easy to relate to the Sunday Gospel.* In particular, the words 'Ah God, that precious Name of Yours must be a cloak for their villainy' from the fourth movement correspond to Jesus's prophecy that not all who say to Him, 'Lord, Lord!' shall enter into the Kingdom of Heaven.

Half a century later, when the Göttingen music scholar Johann Nikolaus Forkel hired out Bach's chorale cantatas from Wilhelm Friedemann Bach for two louis d'or, he took the opportunity to copy out two cantatas that particularly pleased him. The works he chose were *Es ist das Heil uns kommen her*, BWV 9, and the cantata under discussion. It is not easy to say why these two works in particular took his fancy. In Cantata 178, the dramatic style of the two arias might have attracted him, as well as the prominence of chorale arrangements: the unknown arranger of the text retained as many as six verses from the eight-verse hymn (1, 2, 4, 5, 7, and 8), expanding verses 2 and 5 by means of troping recitative insertions. Only verses 3 and 6 were paraphrased, each forming an aria. In the trope* text of the fifth movement, the librettist took the opportunity to refer specifically to the Sunday Gospel, with its warning against false prophets: 'God will kill the foolish prophets with the fire of His wrath'.

The first movement embodies the type of introductory chorale chorus* that Bach particularly favoured. The chorale, sung by the choir, is incorporated line by line within a thematically independent orchestral texture. The chorale melody is in the soprano, reinforced by horn, and it is supported by the lower voice parts in a texture that is part chordal and part freely polyphonic,* with an occasional tendency to imitation.* The content of the first two lines clearly stimulated Bach to set them in a contrasting style: 'Wo Gott der Herr nicht bei uns hält' ('If God the Lord does not remain on our side'): plain homophony, long-held chord on 'hält' ('remain'); and 'Wenn unsre Feinde toben' ('When our enemies rage'): polyphony, dotted rhythms, and semiquaver runs. Yet he used the same setting for the second *Stollen** too, regardless of the fact that its text ('And if He does not support our cause/In heaven there, high above') gives no opportunity for contrasting treatment of the lines. The orchestral writing for two oboes, strings, and continuo, with its agitated semiquaver figuration and, still more, its tense dotted rhythms, seems to be inspired chiefly by the image of raging enemies. The maintenance of the opening thematic material in the instrumental parts—over and above the contrast heard in the handling of the vocal parts—lends the entire movement a grand consistency.

The troped chorale, no. 2, is a contrapuntal masterpiece. While the recitative insertions are set as *secco*, the chorale lines are sung throughout in minims in counterpoint* with their quaver diminution* in the continuo:

The bass aria, no. 3, is inspired by the image of the 'wild waves of the sea', whose rising and falling undulations are reflected in the melodic lines of the obbligato* string part, a unison of first and second violins, as well as in the voice and continuo. Vast coloraturas* are required of the bass on the words 'Meereswellen' ('waves of the sea'), 'erweitern' ('extend'), and in particular 'zerscheitern' ('wreck'). In the fourth movement, the faithful preservation of the unembellished chorale melody in the tenor corresponds with the literal retention of hymn verse 4. The chorale melody is here embedded in a homogeneous, motivic instrumental texture for two oboes d'amore* and a continuo part that remains on equal terms with them.

Like the second movement, the fifth is a troped chorale verse, though the two settings differ substantially from one another. The previous one was assigned throughout to a single singer, but Bach now differentiates: the chorale lines are heard in a plain four-part texture—only at the words 'und stürzen' ('and overturn') does Bach seize the opportunity to insert a text-related semiquaver figure in the bass—and the recitative insertions are assigned to bass, tenor, and alto in turn, and then once more to bass. The continuo, which remains independent in both chorale and recitative, is pervaded throughout by a triadic motive,* which lends the entire movement a unified character and demands a metrically strict vocal delivery of the recitative passages.

The tenor aria, no. 6, is not only among the most attractive movements in the work, it is also in substance the most topically significant for Bach's day, arguing against 'tottering reason'. The model of the hymn, Psalm 124, makes no mention of reason at all. Justus Jonas's chorale admittedly asserts that God's grace is incomprehensible to reason, but that is by no means the main point of the verse concerned, whose function is rather to give the Old Testament psalm a Gospel connotation. In the version of Bach's day, the verse reads:

Ach Herr Gott! wie reich trös test du,	Ah Lord God! how richly You comfort
Die gänzlich sind verlassen;	Those who are utterly forsaken;
Die Gnadentür steht nimmer zu,	The door of grace is never shut;
Vernunft kann das nicht fassen,	Reason cannot grasp that:
Sie spricht: 'Es ist nun alls verlorn',	It says: 'Now all is lost';
Da doch das Kreuz hat neu geborn,	Yet the Cross has born anew
Die deiner Hülf erwarten.	Those who await Your help.

For the century of the Enlightenment, the apologetics against rationalism were a major concern. Hence not only does Bach's librettist command reason to be silent at the opening of the aria, but Bach himself designs the string ritornello, with its syncopations and shaking figures, to reflect the image of the 'tottering' of reason. Meanwhile, time and again we hear the emphatic chordal cry of 'Schweig!' ('Be silent!'). Only the middle section of this highly dramatic aria comes to rest temporarily at the words 'They shall be refreshed with comfort' (fermata, 'adagio') before the free da capo* of the principal section. The seventh movement, a plain four-part chorale setting, concludes the cantata.

Es ist dir gesagt, Mensch, was gut ist, BWV 45

NBA I/18, p. 199 BC A113 Duration: *c.* 23 mins

1. [Chorus] SATB fl I,II ob I ob II d'am str bc — E ¢

'Es ist dir gesagt, Mensch, was gut ist und was der Herr von dir fordert, nämlich: Gottes Wort halten und Liebe üben und demütig sein vor deinem Gott.'	'You have been told, O man, what is good and what the Lord requires of you, namely: to keep God's Word, to cultivate love, and to be humble before your God.'

2. Recitativo T bc — B–g♯ c

Der Höchste läßt mich seinen Willen wissen	The Highest lets me know His Will
Und was ihm wohlgefällt;	And what pleases Him well;
Er hat sein Wort zur Richtschnur dargestellt,	He has presented His Word as a plumb-line
Wornach mein Fuß soll sein geflissen	By which my foot shall be intent
Allzeit einherzugehn	At all times to proceed
Mit Furcht, mit Demut und mit Liebe	With fear, with humility, and with love,
Als Proben des Gehorsams, den ich übe,	As tests of the obedience I practise,
Um als ein treuer Knecht dereinsten zu bestehn.	So that in future I prove to be a faithful servant.

3. Aria T str bc — c♯ 3/8

Weiß ich Gottes Rechte,	If I know God's justice,
Was ists das mir helfen kann,	What is there that can help me
Wenn er mir als seinem Knechte	When He demands of me, as His servant,
Fordert scharfe Rechnung an?	A strict account?
Seele! denke dich zu retten,	Soul! think to save yourself:
Auf Gehorsam folget Lohn;	Upon obedience follows reward;
Qual und Hohn	Torment and scorn
Drohet deinem Übertreten!	Threaten your transgression!

Parte seconda / *Second part*

4. Arioso B str bc — A c

'Es werden viele zu mir sagen an jenem Tage: Herr, Herr! haben wir nicht in deinem Namen geweissaget, haben wir nicht in deinem Namen Teufel ausgetrieben? Haben wir nicht in deinem Namen viel Taten getan?	'There will be many who say to me on that day: Lord, Lord! have we not prophesied in Your Name? Have we not in Your Name cast out devils? Have we not in Your Name done many deeds?
Denn werde ich ihnen bekennen: Ich habe euch noch nie erkannt, weichet alle von mir, ihr Übeltäter!'	Then I will acknowledge to them: I have never known you; depart from me, all you evil-doers!'

5. Aria A fl I bc — f♯ c

Wer Gott bekennt	Whoever acknowledges God

Aus wahrem Herzensgrund,	From the very bottom of his heart
Den will er auch bekennen.	Will be acknowledged by Him.
Denn der muß ewig brennen,	For he must burn for ever
Der einzig mit dem Mund	Who merely with his mouth
Ihn Herren nennt.	Calls Him Lord.

6. Recitativo A bc — E c

So wird denn Herz und Mund selbst von mir Richter sein,	Then heart and mouth themselves will be my judge,
Und Gott will mir den Lohn nach meinem Sinn erteilen;	And God will allot the reward to me according to my state of mind;
Trifft nun mein Wandel nicht nach seinen Worten ein,	Were my behaviour not to accord with His Words,
Wer will hernach der Seelen Schaden heilen?	Who would thereafter redeem the loss of my soul?
Was mach ich mir denn selber Hindernis?	Why then do I make a hindrance of myself?
Des Herren Wille muß geschehen;	The Will of the Lord must be done;
Doch ist sein Beistand auch gewiß,	Yet His assistance is also certain,
Daß er sein Werk durch mich mög wohl vollendet sehen.	So that He may see His workmanship well accomplished through me.

7. Choral SATB bc (+ instrs) — E c

Gib, daß ich tu mit Fleiß,	**Grant that I do with diligence**
Was mir zu tun gebühret,	**What is becoming for me to do,**
Worzu mich dein Befehl	**To which Your command leads me**
In meinem Stande führet!	**In my situation.**
Gib, daß ichs tue bald,	**Grant that I do it soon,**
Zu der Zeit, da ich soll;	**At the time when I should;**
Und wenn ichs tu, so gib,	**And when I do it, then grant**
Daß es gerate wohl!	**That it prospers!**

This cantata, written for 11 August 1726, belongs to a group of works whose texts were drawn from the same cycle as those of the cantatas by the Meiningen Capellmeister Johann Ludwig Bach. Even in the music of the two cousins, certain affinities may be observed. In the opening movement of Cantata 45, the anonymous librettist associates a saying of the prophet Micah (6.8) with Jesus's words from the Sunday Gospel* 'By their fruits you shall know them' and '. . . but he who does the will of my Father in heaven'. This idea, that God makes His will known to man and demands its fulfilment, is pursued in the madrigalian* verse. Here, the librettist draws upon the biblical image of the servant who knows his master's will (Luke 12.42 ff., especially v. 47) and of the steward who has to give an account of himself (Luke 16.1–9). Part II begins with a literal quotation of the concluding words of the Sunday Gospel. Again, other biblical references are associated with it: the following aria is a paraphrase of Jesus's words 'He who acknowledges me before men, him will I acknowledge before my heavenly Father' (Matthew 10.32). The libretto continues with the comforting assurance that God not only demands the fulfilment of His will but has promised His assistance in carrying it out. It ends with the second verse of the hymn *O Gott, du frommer Gott* by Johann Heermann (1630).

The opening chorus* is a splendid example of those complex choruses by the mature Bach which are nonetheless developed out of a single theme. The complexity here results from a structural alternation between the threefold imitative* passage with which the choral parts enter ('Es ist dir gesagt'), the sung fugal exposition* that follows, and choral insertion* within the partial reprise of the introductory instrumental sinfonia. The repeated return of various passages—only the fugal exposition does not recur—leads to an alternation between fugal and concertante* principles, in which sometimes the choir and at other times the instruments are ascendant. Hence Bach achieves the variety within thematic unity that is characteristic of his large-scale Leipzig choruses to biblical words.

Two arias and two recitatives are grouped symetrically around the New Testament words (no. 4), which simultaneously form the centrepiece of the work and the opening of Part II. The recitatives, set as plain *secco* accompanied only by continuo, are entirely geared towards compelling delivery of the text. The first of the two arias, no. 3, which requires a full string accompaniment, is strongly accented in rhythm and exhibits a clear periodic phrase-structure—two attributes that point to the close proximity of dance. Formally, it is bipartite, lacking a da capo*.

Solo bass—to be regarded as the *vox Christi*—opens Part II with the words of Christ. Again, the strings provide an accompaniment, this time in a lively semiquaver motion that lends passionate emphasis to the threatening words. Designated 'arioso'* by Bach, the movement is largely determined in musical content by the instrumental introduction, which recurs four times in various transpositions (A, E, f sharp, and A) during the vocal passages, mostly with only small changes, though the third statement is a mere allusion. This instrumental passage serves as a prescribed framework for the solo bass, whose melody is characterized by bold intervallic leaps and rich coloraturas.*

Something of the excitement of the arioso seems to spill over into the semiquaver figures of the ensuing aria, no. 5. Yet the lean-textured scoring for solo flute, alto voice, and continuo forms a considerable contrast with the preceding movements, which is underlined by the consolatory character of the text. The process of elucidation is taken still further in the largely clear major-mode harmonies of the following recitative and of the concluding chorale, which provides the 'severe' second part of the cantata with a relaxed termination.

2.9 Ninth Sunday after Trinity

EPISTLE: 1 Corinthians 10.6–13: A warning against idolatry and false security; comfort in temptation.

GOSPEL: Luke 16.1–9: The parable of the unjust steward.

Herr, gehe nicht ins Gericht, BWV 105

NBA I/19, p. 3 BC A114 Duration: *c.* 25 mins

1. [CHORUS] SATB str + hn ob I,II bc g c ¢

'Herr, gehe nicht ins Gericht mit deinem Knecht! Denn vor dir wird kein Lebendiger gerecht.'

'Lord, do not enter into judgement with Your servant! For before You no man living shall be justified.'

2. RECITATIVO A bc c–B♭ c

Mein Gott, verwirf mich nicht,
Indem ich mich in Demut vor dir beuge,
Von deinem Angesicht.
Ich weiß, wie groß dein Zorn und mein Verbrechen ist,
Daß du zugleich ein schneller Zeuge
Und ein gerechter Richter bist.
Ich lege dir ein frei Bekenntnis dar
Und stürze mich nicht in Gefahr,
Die Fehler meiner Seelen
Zu leugnen, zu verhehlen!

My God, do not cast me away—
As I bow down before You in humility—
From Your countenance.
I know how great is Your fury and my offence,
That You are at once a swift witness
And a righteous Judge.
I make a free acknowledgement to You
And do not fall into this danger:
The failings of my soul
To deny, to hide!

3. ARIA S ob str (senza bc) E♭ 3/4

Wie zittern und wanken
Der Sünder Gedanken,
Indem sie sich untereinander verklagen
Und wiederum sich zu entschuldigen wagen.
So wird ein geängstigt Gewissen
Durch eigene Folter zerrissen.

How they tremble and waver,
The thoughts of sinners,
As they accuse one another
And again dare to excuse themselves.
Thus a frightened conscience
Is torn on its own rack.

4. RECITATIVO B str bc B♭–E♭ c

Wohl aber dem, der seinen Bürgen weiß,
Der alle Schuld ersetzet,
So wird die Handschrift ausgetan,
Wenn Jesus sie mit Blute netzet.
Er heftet sie ans Kreuze selber an,
Er wird von deinen Gütern, Leib und Leben,

But happy is he who knows his Guarantor:
That makes amends for all his guilt; thus
The handwriting of ordinances is blotted out
When Jesus sprinkles it with His Blood.
He Himself nails it to the Cross;
The account of your possessions, body and life,

Wenn deine Sterbestunde schlägt,	When the hour of your death strikes,
Dem Vater selbst die Rechnung übergeben.	He Himself will deliver to the Father.
So mag man deinen Leib, den man zum Grabe trägt,	Thus when they carry your body to the grave,
Mit Sand und Staub beschütten,	Let them cover it with sand and dust,
Dein Heiland öffnet dir die ewgen Hütten.	For the Saviour opens up for you the everlasting habitations.
5. Aria T hn str bc	B♭ C
Kann ich nur Jesum mir zum Freunde machen,	If only I can make Jesus my friend,
So gilt der Mammon nichts bei mir.	Mammon will be worth nothing to me.
Ich finde kein Vergnügen hier	I find no pleasure here
Bei dieser eitlen Welt und irdschen Sachen.	In this idle world and among earthly things.
6. Choral SATB str bc (+ hn ob I,II)	g C/12/8
Nun, ich weiß, du wirst mir stillen	**Now I know that You will still**
Mein Gewissen, das mich plagt.	**My conscience that torments me.**
Es wird deine Treu erfüllen,	**Your faithfulness will fulfil**
Was du selber hast gesagt:	**What You Yourself have said:**
Daß auf dieser weiten Erden	**That on this wide earth**
Keiner soll verloren werden,	**No one shall be lost**
Sondern ewig leben soll,	**But shall live for ever,**
Wenn er nur ist Glaubens voll.	**If he be but full of faith.**

This cantata belongs to Bach's first Leipzig cycle and was written for performance on 25 July 1723. From the parable of the Sunday Gospel* the anonymous librettist draws the thought that mankind cannot survive before God's judgement, and also the advice 'Make friends with the mammon of unrighteousness' (Luke 16.9), which is applied to Jesus Himself; for since His sacrificial Death wipes out our guilt (no.4), we should make friends with Him alone (no. 5).

Psalm 143.2 serves as the opening dictum, and in the movements that follow a picture is drawn of guilt-laden man by allusion to various other biblical passages: the beginning of the second movement is based on Psalm 51.11—'Do not cast me away from Your sight'—and the words 'swift witness' in the same movement are found in Malachi 3.5: 'I shall come to you and punish you, and shall be a swift witness against sorcerers and adulterers . . .'. The soprano aria, no. 3, borrows an image from Romans 2.15: 'the thoughts that accuse or excuse one another'. And the image in the fourth movement of Jesus blotting out the handwriting of ordinances and nailing it to the Cross is also drawn from one of Paul's Epistles* (Colossians 2.14). The concluding chorale is the eleventh verse of the hymn *Jesu, der du meine Seele* by Johann Rist (1641).

Bach structures the opening chorus* in two sections, thereby following the grammatic structure of the text after the manner of a motet.* The first section ('Herr, gehe nicht ins Gericht mit deinem Knecht') embodies a quasi-prelude headed 'adagio' and introduced by eight instrumental bars. It unites freely polyphonic* choral writing with an independent orchestral texture and ends with choral insertion* within a complete reprise of the instrumental introduction. An orchestral episode on a pedal *D* is followed by the second section, a choral fugue* ('Denn vor dir wird kein Lebendiger gerecht') with *colla parte** instruments, which serves as an example of permutation fugue. In both 'prelude' and fugue the choir is at first accompanied only by continuo, with the other instruments added in a second choral passage. We may therefore assume that, as in several earlier cantatas from this cycle, Bach divided his singers into concertists* and ripienists* and that the latter group entered subsequently with the instruments.

A simple but expressive *secco* recitative is followed by one of Bach's most original and impressive arias (no. 3). The instability of the sinner, the trembling and wavering of his thoughts, their constant 'accusing' of one another—all these things are described in musical terms. The continuo is silent, so that the firm basis of music—a symbol of that of human existence—is absent. Instead, the viola, with its repeated quavers, takes over the lowest part. The two violins, filling in the harmony with a semiquaver tremolo, depict the trembling described in the text. Against this background, the eloquent gestures of the obbligato* oboe paint a picture of the aimlessly vascillating sinful conscience. Seventh chords, heaped up and ever changing, depict its tormented hopelessness. After the instrumental ritornello, the voice takes up the oboe theme and develops it further. To the text 'indem sie sich untereinander verklagen . . .' ('as they accuse one another . . .'), new canonic figures, which have not been anticipated in the ritornello, emerge in the soprano and oboe parts, and their chasing after one another illustrates the thoughts that accuse and excuse each other. A free reprise of this main section, A, leads to a shorter B section whose thematic material is freer, though likewise determined by the substance of the ritornello. A reprise of the instrumental ritornello closes this imposing movement.

The second recitative (no. 4), accompanied by strings, is moulded by Bach into a motivically imprinted *accompagnato** in order to lend emphasis to the text. For this movement brings the decisive turning-point: a reference to Jesus's standing surety for the sinner through His sacrificial death on the Cross. The second aria, no. 5, forms the greatest imaginable contrast with the first. The string ensemble is joined by a horn, whose part is constantly surrounded by the rapid figuration of the first violin. The melody is song-like, almost like that of a dance, and the rhythm and harmony are relaxed, allowing the structural divisions to be clearly perceived.

In the finale, the chorale melody, sung by the choir line by line in homophonic* texture, is embedded in an orchestral setting which once again takes up the tremolo that stamped its character on the aria 'Wie zittern und wanken', having already been heard allusively in the throbbing continuo quavers of the first movement. Now this tremolo characterizes the words 'You will still my conscience that torments me' through gradual retardation as the trembling conscience comes to rest. Beginning with semiquaver reiterations, the motion gradually subsides in triplet quavers (notated in 12/8), then in ordinary quavers, then triplet crotchet-plus-quavers (again notated in 12/8), until it reaches crotchets and minims, with which the cantata ends in a conciliatory mood. Thus ends a work that might well be numbered among the most sublime descriptions of the soul in baroque and Christian art.

Was frag ich nach der Welt, BWV 94

NBA I/19, p. 45 BC A115 Duration: *c.* 23 mins

1. [Chorale] SATB fl ob I,II str bc — D C

Was frag ich nach der Welt	**What do I ask from the world**
Und allen ihren Schätzen,	**And all its treasures,**
Wenn ich mich nur an dir,	**When I can have joy**
Mein Jesu, kann ergötzen!	**Only of You, my Jesus!**
Dich hab ich einzig mir	**You alone have I imagined**
Zur Wollust fürgestellt,	**For my pleasure;**
Du, du bist meine Ruh:	**You, You are my repose:**
Was frag ich nach der Welt!	**What do I ask from the world!**

2. Aria B bc — b C

Die Welt ist wie ein Rauch und Schatten,	The world is like smoke or a shadow
Der bald verschwindet und vergeht,	That soon vanishes and passes away,
Weil sie nur kurze Zeit besteht.	For it lasts only a short time.
Wenn aber alles fällt und bricht,	But when all falls and breaks,
Bleibt Jesus meine Zuversicht,	Jesus remains my confidence,
An dem sich meine Seele hält.	To whom my soul adheres.
Darum: was frag ich nach der Welt!	Therefore what do I ask from the world!

3. Recitativo [+ Chorale] T ob d'am I,II bc — G 3/8 C

Die Welt sucht Ehr und Ruhm	**The world seeks honour and renown**
Bei hocherhabnen Leuten.	**Among highly exalted people.**
Ein Stolzer baut die prächtigsten Paläste,	A proud man builds the most splendid palaces,
Er sucht das höchste Ehrenamt,	He seeks the highest post of honour,
Er kleidet sich aufs beste	He clothes himself of the best
In Purpur, Gold, in Silber, Seid und Samt.	In purple, gold, in silver, fine linen, and velvet.
Sein Name soll für allen	His name has to resound for all

In jedem Teil der Welt erschallen.
Sein Hochmuts-Turm
Soll durch die Luft bis an die Wolken dringen,
Er trachtet nur nach hohen Dingen
Und denkt nicht einmal dran,
Wie bald doch diese gleiten.
Oft bläst uns eine schale Luft
Den stolzen Leib auf einmal in die Gruft,
Und da verschwindet alle Pracht,
Wormit der arme Erdenwurm
Hier in der Welt so großen Staat gemacht.
Ach! solcher eitler Tand
Wird weit von mir aus meiner Brust verbannt.
Dies aber, was mein Herz
Vor anderm rühmlich hält,
Was Christen wahren Ruhm und wahre Ehre gibet
Und was mein Geist,
Der sich der Eitelkeit entreißt,
Anstatt der Pracht und Hoffart liebet,
Ist Jesus nur allein,
Und dieser solls auch ewig sein.
Gesetzt, daß mich die Welt
Darum vor töricht hält:
Was frag ich nach der Welt!

In every part of the world.
His Babel-like tower of arrogance
Has to penetrate through the air up to the clouds;
He minds only high things
And not once does he consider
How soon these things slip away.
Often a stale air all of a sudden
Blows the proud body into the grave,
And then all the splendour vanishes
With which this poor earthworm
Here in the world made such a great display.
Ah! such idle trifles
Are far from me, banished from my breast.
This, however, which my heart
Holds praiseworthy before all else,
Which gives Christians true renown and true honour
And which my spirit,
Tearing itself away from vanity, loves
In place of splendour and inordinate pride,
Is but Jesus alone,
And He it shall be for ever.
Granted that the world
Therefore regards me as foolish:
What do I ask from the world!

4. ARIA A fl solo bc — e c

Betörte Welt, betörte Welt!
Auch dein Reichtum, Gut und Geld
Ist Betrug und falscher Schein.
Du magst den eitlen Mammon zählen,
Ich will davor mir Jesum wählen;
Jesus, Jesus soll allein
Meiner Seelen Reichtum sein.
Betörte Welt, betörte Welt!

Deluded world, deluded world!
Even your riches, wealth, and gold
Are deceit and false appearances.
You may count vain mammon;
I will instead choose Jesus;
Jesus, Jesus alone
Shall be my soul's wealth.
Deluded world, deluded world!

5. RECITATIVO [+ CHORALE] B bc — D c

Die Welt bekümmert sich.
Was muß doch wohl der Kummer sein?
O Torheit! dieses macht ihr Pein:

The world is distressed.
But what must that distress be?
O folly! This causes its pain:

Im Fall sie wird verachtet.
Welt, schäme dich!
Gott hat dich ja so sehr geliebet,
Daß er sein eingebornes Kind
Vor deine Sünd
Zur größten Schmach um deine Ehre gibet,
Und du willst nicht um Jesu willen leiden?
Die Traurigkeit der Welt ist niemals größer,
Als wenn man ihr mit List
Nach ihren Ehren trachtet.
Es ist ja besser,
Ich trage Christi Schmach,
Solang es ihm gefällt.
Es ist ja nur ein Leiden dieser Zeit,
Ich weiß gewiß, daß mich die Ewigkeit
Dafür mit Preis und Ehren krönet;
Ob mich die Welt
Verspottet und verhöhnet,
Ob sie mich gleich verächtlich hält,
Wenn mich mein Jesus ehrt:
Was frag ich nach der Welt!

In case it is despised.
World, shame on you!
God has indeed loved you so very much
That He gave His only begotten Child,
For your sin,
To the greatest reproach for your honour,
And would you not suffer for Jesus's sake?
The sorrow of the world is never greater
Than when one strives with cunning
For its honours.
It is indeed better
That I suffer reproach for Christ
As long as it pleases Him.
It is indeed only a suffering of the present time;
I know for certain that eternity will crown me
For it with praise and honour;
Though the world
Scorns and derides me,
Though it regards me as contemptible,
If my Jesus honours me,
What do I ask from the world!

6. Aria T str bc — A C 12/8

Die Welt kann ihre Lust und Freud,
Das Blendwerk schnöder Eitelkeit,
Nicht hoch genug erhöhen.
  Sie wühlt, nur gelben Kot zu finden,
  Gleich einem Maulwurf in den Gründen
  Und läßt dafür den Himmel stehen.

The world's pleasure and joy—
The deception of contemptible vanity—
It cannot exalt highly enough.
  It digs, only to find yellow excrement,
  Like a mole in its burrows,
  And for that leaves heaven alone.

7. Aria S ob d'am I solo bc — f♯ C

Es halt es mit der blinden Welt,
Wer nichts auf seine Seele hält,
Mir ekelt vor der Erden.
  Ich will nur meinen Jesum lieben
  Und mich in Buß und Glauben üben,
  So kann ich reich und selig werden.

Let him keep to the blind world
Who cares nothing for his soul;
I am disgusted with the earth.
  I will but love my Jesus
  And exercise repentance and belief;
  Then I can become rich and blessed.

8. Choral SATB bc (+ instrs) — D C

Was frag ich nach der Welt!
Im Hui muß sie verschwinden,

What do I ask from the world!
In a trice it must vanish,

Ihr Ansehn kann durchaus	**Its authority can in no way**
Den blassen Tod nicht binden.	**Bind pale death.**
Die Güter müssen fort,	**Its goods must be gone**
Und alle Lust verfällt;	**And all its pleasure decay;**
Bleibt Jesus nur bei mir:	**If only Jesus abides with me,**
Was frag ich nach der Welt!	**What do I ask from the world!**
Was frag ich nach der Welt!	**What do I ask from the world!**
Mein Jesus ist mein Leben,	**My Jesus is my life,**
Mein Schatz, mein Eigentum,	**My treasure, my property,**
Dem ich mich ganz ergeben,	**To whom I have quite surrendered myself,**
Mein ganzes Himmelreich,	**My entire heavenly kingdom,**
Und was mir sonst gefällt.	**And whatever else pleases me.**
Drum sag ich noch einmal:	**Therefore I say once again:**
Was frag ich nach der Welt!	**What do I ask from the world!**

This chorale cantata,* composed for 6 August 1724, is based on the eight-verse hymn by Balthasar Kindermann (1664). The hymn was remodelled as a cantata text by an anonymous librettist, who retained verses 1, 3, 5, 7, and 8 word for word (expanding verses 3 and 5 by means of troping recitative insertions) and paraphrased verses 2, 4, and 6 to form arias. Verses 1–5 each correspond with a cantata movement, verse 6 forms the basis of a pair of arias (nos. 6 and 7),[18] and the last two verses are assigned to the concluding chorale, no. 8. The relationship between the text and the Sunday readings is relatively distant. The Epistle* does indeed warn against idolatry, and certain passages in the Gospel,* such as 'the children of this world are wiser than the children of light' or 'the mammon of unrighteousness' (Luke 16.8 and 9), emphasize the antithesis between the world and Jesus that dominates both hymn and cantata text. But the connections do not go beyond general ideas of this kind.

[18] The view of Wustmann (p. 187), followed by Arnold Schering (*BJ* 1933, pp. 67 and 70) and others, that BWV 94/7 consists of freely versified text is incorrect, as the following comparison reveals:

BWV 94/7	**Hymn verse 6, lines 5–8**
Es halt es mit der blinden Welt,	Ein andrer hälts mit ihr,
Wer nichts auf seine Seele hält,	Der von sich selbst nichts hält,
Mir ekelt vor der Erden.	
Ich will nur meinen Jesum lieben	Ich liebe meinen Gott,
Und mich in Buß und Glauben üben,	Was frag ich nach der Welt?
So kann ich reich und selig werden.	
Let him keep to the blind world	Another keeps to it,
Who cares nothing for his soul;	Who of himself keeps nothing;
I am disgusted with the earth.	
I will but love my Jesus	I love my God,
And exercise repentance and belief;	What do I ask from the world?
Then I can become rich and blessed.	

In setting this text, Bach seems to have felt an exceptionally strong sympathy with it; and nowadays the impression might arise that a world that produces such splendid compositions should not be disdained so unreservedly as the baroque poet would have us believe. External circumstances also seem to have had an effect on the composition. In his earlier Leipzig cantatas, Bach only seldom made use of the transverse flute,* entrusting it with moderately straightforward tasks. But here and in some of the later cantatas from the same cycle he assigns it a pre-eminent role: clearly he now had a gifted player at his disposal.

Immediately in the opening chorus,* the string orchestra (reinforced by oboes) is set against a concertante* flute, whose lively semiquaver figuration almost creates the impression of a flute concerto. The chorale melody, which moves mainly in crotchets, is, as usual, entrusted to the soprano. It is supported, however, by a relatively uncharacteristic homophonic* or lightly imitative* substructure, predominantly in quavers, in the other voice parts. The chorale, thus sung, is incorporated line by line within an orchestral texture whose thematic material, stated in a twelve-bar introductory ritornello, shows a clear affinity with the substance of the chorale melody—a contrast with many otherwise similar chorale-choruses by Bach. This material is chiefly characterized by two motives,* of which the first, *a*, is assigned to the flute, opens and closes the ritornello, and is present throughout in various modified forms:

The second motive, *b*, is heard at the top of a four-part tutti texture for the strings (plus two oboes):

Its derivation from the opening line of the chorale melody (*O Gott, du frommer Gott*) is clear:

But it is also related to lines 5 and 6:

Once this has been recognized, it does not seem impossible that the upper notes of the flute theme *a*, quoted above, represent a conscious derivation from the seventh chorale line:

It is less easy to point out connections between the character of the movement and its text. Perhaps Bach intended to illustrate the bustle of the world through the lively excitement of the chorus, especially of motive *a*, as a contrast to the calm offered by Jesus. For, in his textual interpretation, the baroque composer did not as a rule shrink from using a state of affairs denied or rejected in the text as a stimulus for his musical invention. We shall have occasion to return to this issue in due course.

The second movement, an aria with continuo accompaniment, contains ostinato* formations characteristic of movements of this kind. Falling motives (bars 1 and 2) and scale figures depict the transience of the world, while held notes on 'bleibt' ('remains') and 'hält' ('adheres') characterize the steadfastness of those who are faithful to Jesus but also—on 'besteht' ('lasts')—the continued existence of the world, though the text actually speaks of its transience ('For it lasts only a short time'). This confirms what was said above: a single idea alone is set to music, not the context of thought in which it occurs.

In the third movement, the chorale melody, sung by the tenor in a much embellished form, is introduced and accompanied by two oboes and continuo, which gives rise to an attractive trio or quartet texture. The movement may be regarded as a forerunner of 'Er ist auf Erden kommen arm' from the *Christmas Oratorio* (part I, no. 7), especially since both include recitative insertions accompanied by short chords on the oboes. The fourth movement, the aria 'Betörte Welt', with obbligato* flute, displays a remarkable bitter beauty. Frequent diminished or augmented intervals and false relations* characterize the 'deceit' and 'false appearances' of the world. Only the middle section brings a temporarily brighter mood. This section is in itself bipartite: an *allegro* passage contrasts with its surroundings in tempo, more fluid harmony and frequent parallel thirds and sixths, but after only seven bars it changes into an *adagio* (to be understood as *tempo primo*) which is thematically related to the principal section. An abridged da capo* concludes the movement.

The fifth movement corresponds with the third in textual structure—both take the form of a chorale-trope*—and its setting also shows similarities, for the chorale melody is again profusely embellished and assigned to solo voice (here bass). On this occasion, however, the voice is accompanied only by continuo, which constantly places unthematic chromatic-scale* motion in counterpoint* with the chorale lines, illustrating the affliction of the despised world. The recitative insertions are set as *secco*. The two arias that follow are more song-like, relaxed, and periodic in articulation than the previous ones. The tenor aria, no. 6, with its pronouncedly chordal string texture, is dance-like in character, resembling a pastorale; and the soprano aria, no. 7, is clearly a bourrée—at least, this is the impression formed by the ritornello for solo oboe d'amore* and continuo and by the opening of the vocal section, for the continuation takes on a more elaborate, less lapidary style. The cantata concludes with a plain choral setting of the last two verses of the hymn.

Arnold Schering devoted a spirited study to the soprano aria, no. 7,[19] pointing out the difficulty that arises for the present-day listener when a composition so obviously 'secular' in style is based on a text showing disgust for the world:

> Here is a case that reaches out beyond the frontiers of music and its capabilities. Two eternally irreconcilable elements come together: the essence of music, at all times positive, affirmative, close to life, only ever accessible as pure reality; and discursive thought, reckoning with assumptions, conditions, limitations, and poly-syllogisms of all kinds.

Though we may not concur with Schering in every detail—is a 'play on the figure of irony', as he describes it, really present here?—the difficulties are unmistakable. As in the cases noted above, Bach's music characterizes only individual concepts (such as 'world'), not what is asserted about them in the text. This is probably best understood if we consider that in Bach's day such concepts, together with the musical *inventio* correlated with them, were to a large extent rationalized and typified. What the music here responds to is the type 'world', not its specific characteristics such as blindness, wickedness, and so forth. And no psychological role is demanded of the music, such as seeking to evoke in the listener a disgust for the world. Movements like this aria should caution us against conceiving Bach's music too much as 'exegesis' of the text and against evaluating his art for its textual representation rather than for its purely aesthetic, musical value.

Tue Rechnung! Donnerwort, BWV 168

NBA I/19, p. 89 BC A116 Duration: *c.* 17 mins

1. ARIA B str bc b C

Tue Rechnung! Donnerwort,	Give an account! Thunder-word
Das die Felsen selbst zerspaltet,	That splits the very rocks!

[19] *BJ* 1933, 66–70.

Wort, wovon mein Blut erkaltet!	Word that makes my blood run cold!
Tue Rechnung! Seele, fort!	Give an account! Soul, away!
Ach! du mußt Gott wiedergeben	Ah! you must restore to God
Seine Güter, Leib und Leben!	Goods, body, and life!
Tue Rechnung! Donnerwort!	Give an account! Thunder-word!
2. Recitativo T ob d'am I,II bc	f♯–c♯ C
Es ist nur fremdes Gut,	It is only borrowed things
Was ich in diesem Leben habe;	That I have in this life;
Geist, Leben, Mut und Blut	Spirit, life, courage, and blood
Und Amt und Stand ist meines Gottes Gabe,	And function and caste are my God's gifts
Es ist mir zum Verwalten	For me to administer
Und treulich damit hauszuhalten	And manage faithfully,
Von hohen Händen anvertraut!	Entrusted to me by high hands!
Ach! aber ach! mir graut,	Ah! but alas! I am afraid
Wenn ich in mein Gewissen gehe	When I look into my conscience
Und meine Rechnungen so voll Defekte sehe!	And see my accounts so full of defects!
Ich habe Tag und Nacht	Day and night
Die Güter, die mir Gott verliehen,	The good things that God has bestowed on me
Kaltsinnig durchgebracht!	I have callously squandered!
Wie kann ich dir, gerechter Gott, entfliehen?	How can I escape from You, righteous God?
Ich rufe flehentlich:	I call earnestly:
Ihr Berge, fallt! ihr Hügel, decket mich	You mountains, fall! You hills, cover me
Vor Gottes Zorngerichte	From God's wrathful Judgement
Und vor dem Blitz von seinem Angesichte!	And from the lightning of His countenance!
3. Aria T ob d'am I + II bc	f♯ 3/8
Kapital und Interessen,	Principal and interest,
Meine Schulden groß und klein	My debts great and small
Müssen einst verrechnet sein!	Must one day be reckoned up!
Alles, was ich schuldig blieben,	All that I still owe
Ist in Gottes Buch geschrieben	Is written in God's book
Als mit Stahl und Demantstein!	As with steel and diamond!
4. Recitativo B bc	b–G C
Jedoch, erschrocknes Herz, leb und verzage nicht!	Yet, terrified heart, live and do not despair!
Tritt freudig vor Gericht!	Step joyfully before your judgement!
Und überführt dich dein Gewissen,	And if your conscience convicts you,
Du werdest hier verstummen müssen,	You must become speechless here;
So schau den Bürgen an,	See the Guarantor
Der alle Schulden abgetan!	Who disposes of all debts!

Es ist bezahlt und völlig abgeführt,	It is paid and fully discharged,
Was du, o Mensch, in Rechnung schuldig blieben;	What you, O man, still owed on account;
Des Lammes Blut, o großes Lieben!	The Lamb's Blood—O great Love!—
Hat deine Schuld durchstrichen	Has cancelled out your debt
Und dich mit Gott verglichen!	And settled you with God!
Es ist bezahlt, du bist quittiert!	It is paid, you are acquitted!
Indessen, weil du weißt,	Meanwhile, since you know
Daß du Haushalter seist,	That you are a steward,
So sei bemüht und unvergessen,	Take trouble and do not forget
Den Mammon klüglich anzuwenden,	To use mammon wisely,
Den Armen wohlzutun,	To do good to the poor;
So wirst du, wenn sich Zeit und Leben enden,	Then, when time and life end,
In Himmelshütten sicher ruhn!	You will rest securely in heavenly habitations!

5. Aria [Duetto] SA bc — e $\frac{6}{8}$

Herz, zerreiß des Mammons Kette!	O heart, break mammon's chain!
Hände! streuet Gutes aus!	O hands, disperse good things!
Machet sanft mein Sterbebette,	Make my death-bed soft,
Bauet mir ein festes Haus,	Build me a secure house
Das im Himmel ewig bleibet,	That ever remains in heaven
Wenn der Erden Gut zerstäubet.	When earthly goods turn to dust.

6. Choral SATB bc (+ instrs) — b **C**

Stärk mich mit deinem Freudengeist,	**Strengthen me with Your spirit of joy,**
Heil mich mit deinen Wunden,	**Heal me with Your Wounds,**
Wasch mich mit deinem Todesschweiß	**Wash me with Your death-sweat**
In meiner letzten Stunden;	**In my last hours;**
Und nimm mich einst, wenn dirs gefällt,	**And take me one day, when it pleases You,**
In wahrem Glauben von der Welt	**In true faith out of the world**
Zu deinen Auserwählten!	**To Your chosen ones!**

The text of this cantata is drawn from Salomo Franck's cycle *Evangelisches Andachts-Opffer* of 1715, which might suggest that the work should be dated to Bach's Weimar period. However, the autograph score, whose draft character is beyond doubt, is quite unambiguously of Leipzig origin. We must assume, therefore, that Bach earmarked the text for setting in Weimar, but that only in Leipzig did he carry out his intention. If a Weimar cantata to this text ever existed, it must have differed from the Leipzig version so much that it would amount to an altogether different composition.

The substance of the text adheres closely to the Sunday Gospel,* from which the first words of the opening aria are drawn (Luke 16.2). The situation of the unjust steward is conceived simply as that of mankind, of whom God will one day demand an account, with the result that man will then wish—according to Luke 23.30—that the mountains and hills might fall on him and cover him. The baroque poet Franck is not deterred from using detailed metaphors whose realism, to our way of thinking today, exceeds the bounds of poetic possibilities: for example, 'When I . . . see my accounts so full of defects' or 'principal and interest . . .'. As in Cantata 105, the fourth movement brings the decisive turning-point, with its reference to Jesus's sacrificial Death, which has 'cancelled out your debt'. Franck, however, develops this idea still further: it is now necessary to reflect upon the proper duties of the steward, namely 'to use mammon wisely' (cf. Luke 16.8–9) and 'to do good to the poor', with the result that death loses its terror (nos. 4 and 5). The concluding chorale—the eighth verse of the hymn *Herr Jesu Christ, du höchstes Gut* by Bartholomäus Ringwaldt (1588)—returns to thoughts of Jesus's Sacrifice and of our own death.

Bach's setting was probably written for performance on 29 July 1725. The scoring keeps within the bounds of chamber music: a choir is used only in the concluding chorale, and the only instruments required beyond strings and continuo are two oboes d'amore.* The ritornello of the opening aria begins with dotted-rhythm string chords (to be assimilated to the triplets) over semiquaver triplets in the continuo:

In the course of the movement, the continuo triplets prove to be the true thematic kernel: they are heard on unison strings at the end of the ritornello; they are taken up by the voice in the form of a coloratura* on 'Donnerwort' ('thunder-word'); and they often occur elsewhere in the continuo part without their chordal superstructure. In the principal section, Bach constructs large expanses of the voice part by means of vocal insertion* within partial restatements of the ritornello. The middle section, accompanied only by continuo, is more freely structured, but the almost incessant triplet figuration of the continuo links it with the thematic substance of the ritornello. The movement concludes with an abridged da capo*.

The recitative, no. 2, is accompanied by two oboes d'amore, which at first provide a harmonic background to the recitation of the voice in held notes only, but at the end they employ suitable figures to underline the words 'Ihr Berge, fallt!' ('You mountains, fall!') and 'Blitz' ('lightning'), thus forming an arioso* conclusion. By comparison with the first aria, the second and third exhibit a progressive reduction in scoring: the third movement is a tenor aria with obbligato* unison oboes d'amore, and the fifth (following a plain *secco* recitative) a duet accompanied by continuo, with largely canonic voice parts over a quasi-ostinato continuo bass, whose hurling demisemiquaver figures graphically depict the breaking of the chain of mammon. A plain four-part chorale movement ends the cantata.

2.10 Tenth Sunday after Trinity

EPISTLE: 1 Corinthians 12.1–11: 'There are many different gifts, but there is only one Spirit'.

GOSPEL: Luke 19.41–8: Jesus prophesies the destruction of Jerusalem and drives the traders out of the temple.

Schauet doch und sehet, ob irgend ein Schmerz sei, BWV 46

NBA I/19, p. 111 BC A117 Duration: *c.* 20 mins

1. [CHORUS] SATB tr o cor da t rec I,II ob da c I,II str bc d 3/4

'Schauet doch und sehet, ob irgendein Schmerz sei wie mein Schmerz, der mich troffen hat. Denn der Herr hat mich voll Jammers gemacht am Tage seines grimmigen Zorns.'	'Behold and see if there be any sorrow like my sorrow, which has been inflicted on me. For the Lord has made me full of misery on the day of His fierce anger.'

2. RECITATIVO T rec I,II str bc g C

So klage, du zustörte Gottesstadt,	Lament, then, you ruined city of God,
Du armer Stein- und Aschenhaufen!	You wretched heap of stone and ashes!
Laß ganze Bäche Tränen laufen,	Let whole rivers of tears flow,
Weil dich betroffen hat	For there has befallen you
Ein unersetzlicher Verlust	An irreplaceable loss
Der allerhöchsten Huld,	Of the highest favour,
So du entbehren mußt	Something you must do without
Durch deine Schuld.	Through your guilt.
Du wurdest wie Gomorra zugerichtet,	You were handled like Gomorrah,
Wiewohl nicht gar vernichtet.	Though not quite annihilated.
O besser wärest du in Grund verstört,	Oh, better that you were razed to the ground
Als daß man Christi Feind jetzt in dir lästern hört.	Than that one should now hear Christ's enemy blaspheme in you.
Du achtest Jesu Tränen nicht,	You do not heed Jesus's tears;
So achte nun des Eifers Wasserwogen,	Heed now, then, the tidal waves of zeal
Die du selbst über dich gezogen,	That you have drawn upon yourself
Da Gott, nach viel Geduld,	When God, after much forbearance,

Den Stab zum Urteil bricht!

Cuts asunder the Shepherd's staff in Judgement!

3. Aria B tr str bc — B♭ $\frac{3}{4}$

Dein Wetter zog sich auf von weiten,
Doch dessen Strahl bricht endlich ein
Und muß dir unerträglich sein,
Da überhäufte Sünden
Der Rache Blitz entzünden
Und dir den Untergang bereiten.

Your storm brewed from afar,
Yet its flash at last breaks out
And must be unbearable for you,
For sins great in number
Enkindle the lightning of vengeance
And prepare your downfall.

4. Recitativo A bc — F–c C

Doch bildet euch, o Sünder, ja nicht ein,
Es sei Jerusalem allein
Vor andern Sünden voll gewesen!
Man kann bereits von euch dies Urteil lesen:
Weil ihr euch nicht bessert
Und täglich die Sünden vergrößert,
So müsset ihr alle so schrecklich umkommen.

Yet do not imagine, O sinner,
That Jerusalem alone, above other places,
Was full of sins!
From you one can already read this judgement:
Since you do not repent,
But daily increase your sins,
You may all likewise horribly have to perish.

5. Aria A rec I,II ob da c I,II (senza bc) — g C

Doch Jesus will auch bei der Strafe
Der Frommen Schild und Beistand sein,
Er sammlet sie als seine Schafe,
Als seine Küchlein liebreich ein.
Wenn Wetter der Rache die Sünder belohnen,
Hilft er, daß Fromme sicher wohnen.

Yet Jesus would be, even in chastisement,
Shield and support of the devout;
He gathers them in like His sheep,
Like His chicks, lovingly.
While storms of vengeance reward sinners,
He helps the devout to dwell in safety.

6. Choral S + hn ATB rec I,II str bc — g C

O großer Gott von Treu,
Weil vor dir niemand gilt
Als dein Sohn Jesus Christ,
Der deinen Zorn gestillt,
So sieh doch an die Wunden sein,
Sein Marter, Angst und schwere Pein;
Um seinetwillen schone,
Uns nicht nach Sünden lohne.

O great God of faithfulness,
Since before You none is worthy
Save Your Son Jesus Christ,
Who has calmed Your Wrath,
Then behold His Wounds,
His torment, anguish, and harsh pain;
On His account spare us
And reward us not according to our sins.

To the baroque artist, inclined as he was to graphic representation, the Gospel* for this Sunday must have seemed particularly attractive. The anonymous librettist of this cantata refers to the first part of the Gospel reading, which proclaims a fearful judgement upon unrepentant sinners, and he fills his text with remonstrances, exhortations, and warnings. His starting point is a verse from the Lamentations of Jeremiah (1.12), 'Behold and see if there be any sorrow like my sorrow . . .', which is here reinterpreted to refer to Jesus's sorrow over Jerusalem. The following recitative clarifies the cause of this lamentation: Jerusalem's own guilt has brought down upon it the Judgement of God. Since Jesus's tears could not bring about repentance, the 'tidal waves of zeal'—in other words, a new deluge—will now annihilate sinners (note the typically baroque progression from 'tears' to 'tidal waves'). The aria that follows, no. 3, is also concerned with God's Judgement, comparing it with a storm that gradually gathers 'from afar' over the persistently unrepentant sinner, only to break out in a sudden flash of lightning. In the next movement, the recitative no. 4, the librettist turns to the present congregation, applying what has been said to them: it is not only the inhabitants of Jerusalem in Christ's time who are sinners but you yourselves, and if you do not repent you are doomed to destruction—an allusion to Luke 13.5: 'If you do not repent, you shall all likewise perish'. As the following aria, no. 5, promises consolingly, however, the devout will be secure under Jesus (compare Matthew 23.37: 'How often would I have gathered your children together, as a hen gathers her chickens under her wings . . .'). The concluding chorale—the ninth verse of the hymn *O großer Gott von Macht* by Johann Matthäus Meyfart (1633)—asks God to spare us for the sake of Christ's Passion.

Bach composed this cantata during the first year of his Leipzig appointment, performing it for the first time on 1 August 1723. The opening chorus* is a large-scale lament, which combines motet*-style and concertante* elements of form. To the motet style belongs the close link between the music and the sung text: in accordance with the sentence structure of the biblical text, the entire chorus is divided into two large sections: a freely polyphonic* setting of 'Schauet doch und sehet . . .' and a fugue* to the words 'Denn der Herr hat mich voll Jammers gemacht . . .'. Even the thematic invention is strikingly text-engendered, with its elevation of emphatic words, such as 'Schauet' ('Behold') and 'sehet' ('see'), and its dissonant semitonal steps on 'Schmerz' ('sorrow') and 'Jammers' ('misery'). No less motet-like in principle is the second section, the choral fugue, in which the instruments mostly double the voice parts, though the recorders have a fugal part of their own on an equal basis. Only towards the end do the other instruments again become independent. Concerto-like elements are chiefly present in the first section of the movement, with its introductory instrumental sinfonia (which is bipartite, *a* and *b*) and its independently functioning instruments during the following vocal section. This section exhibits a rondeau-like structure, alternating between canon* at the fifth (in the scheme below, subsection c) and choral insertion.* The overall form of the movement may therefore be represented as follows (italics denote instrumental passages):

A *Sinfonia: a b*
Canon at the 5th c with *motivic accompanying figures*
Sinfonia a + choral insertion
Canon at the 5th c^1 with *motivic accompanying figures*
Sinfonia a b + choral insertion (transposed to the dominant)

B Choral fugue, with *recorders thematic, other instruments colla parte,** and freely polyphonic coda with *instruments independent*

The instrumentation is notably rich for an ordinary Sunday in the church year, comprising two recorders, a slide trumpet that reinforces the soprano,[20] and two oboes da caccia* that double the alto and tenor, and this contributes to the compelling effect of the movement. That Bach himself valued it highly is attested by his reuse of the opening section to the words 'Qui tollis peccata mundi' in the Gloria of the B minor Mass, BWV 232^{I}/9 (1733).

The recitative 'So klage, du zustörte Gottesstadt' ('Lament, then, you ruined city of God'), no. 2, is given special prominence by its instrumentation. While string chords fill in the harmony, the two recorders play ostinato* semiquaver figures, probably to represent the 'rivers of tears' of the text. The following aria, no. 3, with its baroque-style graphic representation, is the dramatic high point of the cantata. The string ensemble is here joined by a trumpet as a symbol of divine sovereignty. Dotted rhythms represent the menace of the rising storm; falling scale figures, the breaking out of the flash of vengeance. In the notes of the bass part, too, Bach vividly depicts the gradual brewing of the storm—tranquil motion followed by the sudden tension of the major seventh—and its outbreak, which is characterized by metrical diminution*: the figure 'doch dessen Strahl' ('yet its flash') is repeated at double speed on the words 'bricht endlich ein' ('at last breaks out'). In addition, words such as 'unerträglich' ('unbearable') are set with the entire wealth of dissonance of Bach's tonal language.

A brief *secco* recitative leads to the second aria no. 5, which is designed to contrast in every respect with the aria just discussed. The first aria is dominated by trumpet, the second by recorders; the first was assigned to bass voice, which conjured up the image of a prophet announcing vengeance, whereas the second is assigned to a voice of middle range, the alto. A particularly distinctive feature of the second aria is its lack of instrumental bass: the continuo is replaced by two unison oboes da caccia, a procedure then known as 'bassett'.* Bach invariably made use of it with a special purpose in mind, and here it characterizes the innocence of the devout, whom Jesus will protect from the flash of divine vengeance. Only in the third section ('While storms of vengeance reward

[20] There is no structural reason for highlighting the soprano part; evidently Bach did not wish to leave the trumpeter of the third movement unoccupied.

sinners') do we encounter once more the image of divine wrath heard in the preceding aria, yet only to emphasize the contrary ('He helps the devout to dwell in safety') all the more forcibly by contrast.

The concluding chorale is not merely set in a plain four-part texture in the usual manner; instead, it is decked out by two obbligato* recorder parts,[21] which provide episodes between the chorale lines. Bach thereby gives the movement a musical weight equivalent to that of its text. For, although almost the whole cantata deals exclusively with the vengeance that will strike unrepentant souls, the concluding chorale, with its reference to the expiatory Death of Jesus, for the first time explains why even the sinner may hope for God's mercy. At the same time, the episodes between the lines serve as a musical reminder of similar figures in the opening movement; and this clear motivic resemblance between the outer movements creates an overall impression of exceptional formal integration.

Nimm von uns, Herr, du treuer Gott, BWV 101

NBA I/19, p. 175 BC A118 Duration: *c.* 25 mins

1. CHOR SATB (+ fl 8va ctt trb I–III) ob I,II taille str bc d ¢

Nimm von uns, Herr, du treuer Gott,	**Take from us, Lord, You faithful God,**
Die schwere Straf und große Not,	**The severe punishment and great distress**
Die wir mit Sünden ohne Zahl	**That we with countless sins**
Verdienet haben allzumal.	**Have altogether deserved.**
Behüt für Krieg und teurer Zeit,	**Preserve us from war and times of famine,**
Für Seuchen, Feur und großem Leid.	**From epidemics, fire, and great harm.**

2. ARIA T vln solo (or fl solo) bc g $\frac{3}{4}$

Handle nicht nach deinen Rechten	Do not deal according to Your rights
Mit uns bösen Sündenknechten,	With us wicked servants of sin;
Laß das Schwert der Feinde ruhn!	Let the sword of our enemies rest!
Höchster, höre unser Flehen,	Highest One, hear our supplication,
Daß wir nicht durch sündlich Tun	So that through sinful deeds
Wie Jerusalem vergehen!	We do not perish like Jerusalem!

3. RECITATIVO [+ CHORALE] S bc d $\frac{3}{4}$/C

Ach! Herr Gott, durch die Treue dein	**Ah! Lord God, through Your faithfulness**
Wird unser Land in Fried und Ruhe sein.	Our land will be in peace and repose.
Wenn uns ein Unglückswetter droht,	When a storm of misfortune threatens us,
So rufen wir,	Then we call,

[21] Each part is doubled: the oboe da caccia players here take up recorders instead.

Barmherzger Gott, zu dir
In solcher Not:
Mit Trost und Rettung uns erschein!

Du kannst dem feindlichen Zerstören
Durch deine Macht und Hülfe wehren.
Beweis an uns deine große Gnad
Und straf uns nicht auf frischer Tat,
Wenn unsre Füße wanken wollten
Und wir aus Schwachheit straucheln sollten.
Wohn uns mit deiner Güte bei
Und gib, daß wir
Nur nach dem Guten streben,
Damit allhier
Und auch in jenem Leben
Dein Zorn und Grimm fern von uns sei!

Merciful God, to You
In this distress:
Appear to us with comfort and deliverance!

You can repel the enemy's destruction
Through Your might and help.
Show in us Your great mercy
And do not punish us in the very act,
If our feet would totter
And we should stumble out of weakness.

Assist us with Your goodness
And grant that we
Strive only after good,
So that both here
And in the life to come
Your anger and fury may be far from us!

4. ARIA B ob I,II taille bc — a ¢

Warum willst du so zornig sein?
Es schlagen deines Eifers Flammen
Schon über unserm Haupt zusammen.
Ach, stelle doch die Strafen ein
Und trag aus väterlicher Huld
Mit unserm schwachen Fleisch Geduld!

Why would You be so angry?
The flames of Your zeal already
Strike together over our heads.
Ah, leave off Your punishments
And out of paternal favour deal
Patiently with our weak flesh!

5. RECITATIVO [+ CHORALE] T bc — d c

Die Sünd hat uns verderbet sehr.
So müssen auch die Frömmsten sagen
Und mit beträhnten Augen klagen:
Der Teufel plagt uns noch viel mehr.
Ja, dieser böse Geist,
Der schon von Anbeginn ein Mörder heißt,
Sucht uns um unser Heil zu bringen
Und als ein Löwe zu verschlingen.
Die Welt, auch unser Fleisch und Blut
Uns allezeit verführen tut.
Wir treffen hier auf dieser schmalen Bahn
Sehr viele Hindernis im Guten an.
Solch Elend kennst du, Herr, allein:
Hilf, Helfer, hilf uns Schwachen,
Du kannst uns stärker machen!
Ach, laß uns dir befohlen sein!

Sin has greatly corrupted us.
Thus even the most devout must say
And lament with tearful eyes:
The devil torments us much more still.
Yes, this evil spirit,
Who already from the outset was called a murderer,
Seeks to deprive us of our Salvation
And to devour us like a lion.
The world and even our flesh and blood
Lead us astray at all times.
We encounter here on this narrow path
Very many hindrances to goodness.
Such misery You alone know, Lord:
Help, O Helper, help us in our weakness:
You can make us stronger!
Ah, let us be commended to You!

6. Aria [Duetto] SA fl ob da c bc — d 12/8

Gedenk an Jesu bittern Tod!	**Remember Jesus's bitter Death!**
Nimm, Vater, deines Sohnes Schmerzen	Take, O Father, Your Son's sorrows
Und seiner Wunden Pein zu Herzen!	And His wounds' pain to heart!
Die sind ja für die ganze Welt	**They are indeed for the whole world**
Die Zahlung und das Lösegeld;	**Payment and ransom;**
Erzeig auch mir zu aller Zeit,	Show me too at all times,
Barmherzger Gott, Barmherzigkeit!	Merciful God, compassion!
Ich seufze stets in meiner Not:	I sigh constantly in my distress:
Gedenk an Jesu bittern Tod!	**Remember Jesus's bitter Death!**

7. Choral SATB bc (+ fl 8va & other instrs) — d c

Leit uns mit deiner rechten Hand	**Lead us with Your right hand**
Und segne unser Stadt und Land;	**And bless our city and land;**
Gib uns allzeit dein heilges Wort,	**Grant us at all times Your Holy Word,**
Behüt fürs Teufels List und Mord;	**Protect us from the Devil's cunning and murder;**
Verleih ein selges Stündelein,	**Bestow on us a blessed hour of death,**
Auf daß wir ewig bei dir sein.	**So that we may be with You for ever.**

This chorale cantata,* first performed on 13 August 1724, is based on the hymn by Martin Moller, which was written—after the Latin *Aufer immensam* (Wittenberg, 1541)—during a plague in 1584. In Leipzig, it was one of the principal hymns for this Sunday, having a clear conceptual relationship with the Sunday Gospel.* The anonymous librettist of the cantata text retained verses 1, 3, 5, and 7 word for word, making trope-like recitative insertions in verses 3 and 5. Verses 2, 4, and 6 were each paraphrased to form an aria. Thus each movement of the cantata corresponds with a verse of the hymn. The librettist occasionally took the opportunity to insert direct references to the Gospel reading, most obviously in the second movement ('So that through sinful deeds we do not perish like Jerusalem') but also in the third movement where it speaks of the 'enemy's destruction'. Allusions to other biblical passages are also made, for example to John 8.44 in the fifth movement (the devil 'who already from the outset was called a murderer') or to 1 Peter 5.8 in the same movement ('Your adversary the devil strolls about like a roaring lion looking for someone to devour'). Even in the madrigalian* verse, it may be noted, chorale lines were adopted either literally or in a slightly adapted form, as in the fourth movement ('Why would You be so angry?') or the sixth: 'Remember Jesus's bitter Death!' (Moller's original reads: 'Gedenk an deins Sohns bittern Tod!') and 'They are indeed for the whole world payment and ransom'. The second movement is the only one in the entire cantata that is free of literal chorale quotations.

Still more striking is the extent to which Bach repeatedly oriented his setting around the chorale melody. In music as well as text, the second movement alone lacks any obvious reference to the chorale. One reason why Bach's composition is so closely linked with the chorale may be that Moller's hymn was sung to the melody of Martin Luther's *Vater unser im Himmelreich*, the German version of the Lord's Prayer, which in Bach's day certainly still belonged to the familiar inheritance of the Reformation, though with its Dorian modality it may have been heard with a certain respectful aloofness. With a melody of more modern character, the composer might have felt justified in adopting a more unhampered mode of treatment.

In form, the opening chorus* hardly differs from the normal first-movement type of the chorale cantatas. The chorale melody lies in the soprano, prepared and supported line by line in the lower voice parts and incorporated in a thematically independent orchestral texture for two oboes, taille*, strings, and continuo. Nevertheless, the movement has certain characteristics that give the vocal element a commanding position in relation to its instrumental counterpart. Thus almost all traces of concertante* style are absent from the orchestral writing. Virtually without change, the introductory instrumental sinfonia in *alla breve* time could be furnished with a text and performed by voices. Its predominant theme is heard on woodwind and strings in alternation:

Another motive,* already heard in the introduction, first acquires significance as an accompanying figure to the voices and takes various intervallic forms as follows:

Significantly, the orchestral accompaniment to the voices is, over large expanses (though not throughout), motivically imprinted rather than thematic, and consequently it retreats more than usual in favour of the choir. The choral writing, on the other hand, is highlighted: the voice parts are reinforced by a choir of trombones (whose top part is, as usual, taken by a cornett), and the soprano *cantus firmus** is doubled at the upper octave by transverse flute.* Each chorale line, prior to its delivery in semibreves in the soprano part, is prepared by fore-imitation* in the lower voice parts (in minims and smaller note-values); it is then accompanied in free polyphony,* with occasional use of the instrumental themes quoted above. Thus the whole movement is essentially a large-scale *cantus firmus* motet,* whose distinctiveness lies in the participation of thematically independent instrumental parts, a property it shares with Bach's motet *O Jesu Christ, meins Lebens Licht*, BWV 118.

The second movement, whose original obbligato* instrument, the flute, was later replaced by solo violin, now brings the concertante element into its own. Bach has plentiful scope here for textual interpretation, witness the held notes on 'ruhn' ('rest'), the rising motives on 'Höchster' ('Highest'), the sigh motives on 'Flehen' ('supplication'), and the falling melodic line on 'vergehen' ('perish'). In the first of the two chorale-trope* movements, no. 3, the lavishly embellished chorale melody, altered to 3/4 time, is provided with an ostinato* continuo accompaniment, itself derived from the chorale. Passages of *secco* recitative are inserted between the chorale lines.

The second aria, no. 4, is quite exceptional in form owing to Bach's attempt to unite a passionately dramatic concertante aria ('vivace') with a part-vocal and part-instrumental quotation of every chorale line ('andante'). After the instrumental ritornello, played by three oboes and continuo, the bass enters with the first line of the chorale, whose text is set at times in the form of *cantus firmus* quotations and elsewhere in aria style. Section A, sung thus, is followed by a contrasting B section in which the entire chorale melody is delivered line by line at an 'andante' tempo in a four-part instrumental texture, combined with a free voice part. Only at the close of section B, shortly before the final ritornello, is the quick opening tempo taken up again. The instruments here quote thematic material from the ritornello, resulting in a kind of false da capo* which, at least by allusion, formally rounds off the movement. The second chorale-trope, no. 5, is similar to the first but in common time throughout. Again, the ostinato accompanying figure in the continuo is developed out of the chorale melody.

The duet with obbligato* flute and oboe da caccia,* no. 6, is probably the musical high point of the cantata. The frequent use of the transverse flute* in the first version of the work strengthens the suspicion that in 1724 Bach had a capable player at his disposal. The eloquent beseeching theme in siciliano rhythm, heard at the outset on the flute, also forms a counterpoint* to the first chorale line—here quoted on the oboe da caccia. The two themes, which are immediately repeated with interchanged parts, are heard not only at the opening of the instrumental ritornello: augmented by a vocal counterpoint, they form the essential thematic material of all three vocal sections (A B^{A} A^{1}). Chorale lines 1, 3, and 4, whose text is retained almost word for word, are also preserved melodically: the first section, A, begins with the first chorale line, entering imitatively* in the two voice parts; the second, B^{A}, opens with lines 3 and 4 (followed by an instrumental quotation of line 1); and the third, A^{1}, in accordance with its text, runs into a reprise of line 1, forming the impression of an abridged da capo*. The final verse of the hymn follows in a plain four-part setting.

Herr, deine Augen sehen nach dem Glauben, BWV 102

NBA I/19, p. 231 BC A119 Duration: *c.* 24 mins

1. [Chorus] SATB ob I,II str bc — g C

'Herr, deine Augen sehen nach dem Glauben! Du schlägest sie, aber sie fühlens nicht; du plagest sie, aber sie bessern sich nicht. Sie haben ein härter Angesicht denn ein Fels und wollen sich nicht bekehren.'

'Lord, Your eyes look for faith! You strike them, but they do not feel it; You torment them, but they do not better themselves. They have a harder countenance than a rock and will not convert.'

2. Recitativo B bc — B♭ C

Wo ist das Ebenbild, das Gott uns eingepräget,
Wenn der verkehrte Will sich ihm zuwider leget?
Wo ist die Kraft von seinem Wort,
Wenn alle Besserung weicht aus dem Herzen fort?
Der Höchste suchet uns durch Sanftmut zwar zu zähmen,
Ob der verirrte Geist sich wollte noch bequemen;
Doch, fährt er fort in dem verstockten Sinn,
So gibt er ihn ins Herzens Dünkel hin.

Where is the image God has imprinted in us,
If the perverted will sets itself against Him?
Where is the power of His Word,
If all improvement retreats from the heart?
The Highest indeed seeks to tame us through gentleness,
In case the misguided spirit would yet comply;
Yet if it persists in its obstinate mind,
Then He gives it over to the heart's darkness.

3. Aria A ob I bc — f C

Weh der Seele, die den Schaden
Nicht mehr kennt
Und, die Straf auf sich zu laden,
Störrig rennt!
Ja von ihres Gottes Gnaden
Selbst sich trennt!

Woe to the soul that no longer
Recognizes its lostness
And, to burden itself with punishment,
Rushes wilfully!
Indeed, even from its God's grace
Cuts itself off!

4. Arioso B str bc — E♭ 3/8

'Verachtest du den Reichtum seiner Gnade, Geduld und Langmütigkeit? Weißest du nicht, daß dich Gottes Güte zur Buße locket? Du aber nach deinem verstockten und unbußfertigen Herzen häufest dir selbst den Zorn auf den Tag des Zorns und der Offenbarung des gerechten Gerichts Gottes.'

'Do you despise the riches of His grace, forbearance, and long-suffering? Do you not know that God's goodness entices you to repentance? But, according to your obstinate and impenitent heart, you heap upon yourself wrath on the day of wrath and of the revelation of the righteous Judgement of God.'

Parte seconda

Second part

5. Aria T fl or vln picc solo bc — g 3/4

Erschrecke doch,
Du allzu sichre Seele!
Denk, was dich würdig zähle
Der Sünden Joch.
Die Gotteslangmut geht auf einem Fuß von Blei,
Damit der Zorn hernach dir desto schwerer sei.

Fear then,
You all too secure soul!
Think what counts as worthy
Of sin's yoke.
Divine forbearance walks on leaden foot,
So that hereafter its Wrath will be all the heavier against you.

6. Recitativo A ob I,II bc — c–G C

Bei Warten ist Gefahr;
Willt du die Zeit verlieren?
Der Gott, der ehmal gnädig war,
Kann leichtlich dich vor seinen Richtstuhl führen.
Wo bleibt sodann die Buß? Es ist ein Augenblick,
Der Zeit und Ewigkeit, der Leib und Seele scheidet.
Verblendter Sinn! ach kehre doch zurück,
Daß dich dieselbe Stund nicht finde unbereitet!

In waiting there is danger;
Would you lose the chance?
God, who was formerly gracious,
Can easily lead you before His judgement seat.
Where is your repentance then? It is but the twinkling of an eye
That divides time and eternity, body and soul.
Blinded mind! Ah, turn back,
So that this hour does not find you unprepared!

7. Choral SATB bc (+ fl 8va ob I,II str) — c C

Heut lebst du, heut bekehre dich,
Eh morgen kömmt, kanns ändern sich.
Wer heut ist frisch, gesund und rot,
Ist morgen krank, ja wohl gar tot.
So du nun stirbest ohne Buß,
Dein Leib und Seel dort brennen muß.

Hilf, o Herr Jesu, hilf du mir,
Daß ich noch heute komm zu dir
Und Buße tu den Augenblick,
Eh mich der schnelle Tod hinrück,
Auf daß ich heut und jederzeit
Zu meiner Heimfahrt sei bereit.

Today you live, today convert;
Before tomorrow comes things can change.
He who today is fresh, healthy, and ruddy
Is tomorrow ill or, yes indeed, even dead.
If you die now without repentance,
Your body and soul must there burn.

Save, O Lord Jesus, save me,
That this very day I may come to You
And do penance in the twinkling of an eye,
Before swift death catches up with me,
So that today and at all times
I may be ready for my homeward journey.

This cantata, composed for 25 August 1726, is one of those whose texts were drawn from the same cycle as the cantatas of Johann Ludwig Bach that were performed by his cousin Johann Sebastian. It is curious that on this occasion

Bach opened Part II with the fifth movement rather than the fourth, thus foregoing the equivalence caused by introducing both parts with a biblical passage. The opening chorus* was later adapted to form the Kyrie of the Missa in G minor, BWV 235, and the two arias, nos. 3 and 5, to form the 'Qui tollis' and the 'Quoniam' of the Missa in F, BWV 233.

The text refers to the Sunday Gospel* but without going into details, merely drawing from it the warning to do penance at the proper time. Part I describes the dangers that threaten the impenitent soul; and in Part II the poet endeavours to shake the soul into wakefulness and call upon it to convert. The expected reference here to God's offer of grace, sealed by Christ's Death on the Cross, such as we find in Cantata 46, for example, is absent on this occasion, for 'severe gravity prevails here to the last'.[22] The text of the first movement is drawn from Jeremiah 5.3 and that of the fourth from Romans 2.4–5. The concluding chorale comprises verses 6 and 7 of the hymn *So wahr ich lebe, spricht dein Gott* by Johann Heermann (1630).

The opening chorus, one of the great achievements of the mature Bach, exhibits, in its formal complexity, a constant alternation between the dominance of the orchestra, which involves frequent choral insertion,* and that of the choir, with its original, text-engendered thematic material—notable for its fine declamation. The movement is introduced by an instrumental sinfonia, scored for two oboes, strings, and continuo, which serves as an exposition* of the thematic material employed in the orchestra. The overall form of the movement may be represented as follows (italics denote instrumental passages):

Introductory sinfonia a b

A 'Herr, deine Augen . . .':

Concertante* fore-structure, soloistic, chordal; *sinfonia themes*

Sinfonia a + choral insertion

'Du schlägest sie . . .':

Fugal exposition with freely polyphonic* conclusion, *accompaniment figures*

'Herr, deine Augen . . .' (textual overlap):

Sinfonia b + choral insertion

B 'Sie haben ein härter Angesicht . . .':

Choral fugue,* *instruments partly colla parte,* partly independent*

A¹ 'Herr, deine Augen . . .' (textual overlap):

Sinfonia a b + choral insertion

It is curious how Bach veils the formal structure of the movement by textual overlapping. The entry of the reprise A¹, in particular, may be exactly fixed only by the analytic eye, scarcely by the impartial listening ear.

[22] 'Der strenge Ernst herrscht hier bis zuletzt' (Wustmann).

A plain *secco* recitative is followed by the third movement, an aria whose gestures could hardly be surpassed for compelling effect. Entering with a long-held dissonant d^2 flat, the obbligato* oboe seems to call out 'Woe!' over the impenitent soul. The entire melodic line of the movement, with its false relations* and extraordinary intervals, is a single highly graphic portrayal of the soul that 'cuts itself off from God's grace'. The New Testament passage (no. 4) is sung by the bass in the type of movement that Bach tends to label imprecisely 'Basso solo'. On this occasion it is given the heading 'Arioso',* though with its abridged da capo* it almost constitutes an aria. Major mode and lively triple time create a contrast with the preceding aria that is musically expedient rather than conditioned by the text; and the declamation of the voice ('Vérachtest', 'Géduld', with the stress on the wrong syllable) may be justified at best by the dubious explanation that Bach wanted to render contempt for God's grace allegorically by showing contempt for correct declamation. The middle section strikingly illustrates the stubbornness of the heart by fourfold motivic repetition, a procedure justified exclusively—according to the aesthetics of Bach's day—by the intention of clarifying musically a state of affairs presented in the text:

The aria 'Erschrecke doch' (no. 5), which introduces Part II, seeks to shake the sinner awake. The musical means employed are wide-ranging melody—especially in the obbligato flute part but also in the voice—and lively movement. Contrast in rhythmic movement is text-engendered, for it is based on the rather unpoetic metaphor (derived from the preceding biblical words), that 'Divine forbearance walks on leaden foot' (represented by held notes) 'So that hereafter its Wrath will be all the heavier against you' (represented by quavers and, in the flute, semiquavers).

The following recitative, no. 6, also stresses the urgency of repentance. The injunction is underlined by its musical structure as a motivically-imprinted *accompagnato*,* with its accompanying motive* played on two oboes. A two-verse plain chorale setting, to the melody *Vater unser im Himmelreich*, ends the cantata.

2.11 Eleventh Sunday after Trinity

EPISTLE: 1 Corinthians 15.1–10: Paul on the Gospel of Christ and on his calling as an apostle.

Gospel: Luke 18.9–14: The parable of the Pharisee and the publican.

Mein Herze schwimmt im Blut, BWV 199

NBA I/20, pp. 3, 25 BC A120 Duration: *c.* 26 mins

1. Recitativo S str bc — c/d[23] C

Mein Herze schwimmt im Blut,
Weil mich der Sünden Brut
In Gottes heilgen Augen
Zum Ungeheuer macht;
Und mein Gewissen fühlet Pein,
Weil mir die Sünden nichts als Höllenhenker sein.
Verhaßte Lasternacht,
Du, du allein
Hast mich in solche Not gebracht!
Und du, du böser Adamssamen,
Raubst meiner Seelen alle Ruh
Und schließest ihr den Himmel zu!
Ach! unerhörter Schmerz!
Mein ausgedorrtes Herz
Will ferner mehr kein Trost befeuchten;
Und ich muß mich vor dem verstecken,
Vor dem die Engel selbst ihr Angesicht verdecken.

My heart swims in blood,
For sin's brood
In God's holy eyes
Turns me into a monster;
And my conscience feels pain,
Since my sins are nothing but hell's executioner.
Detested night of vice,
You, you alone
Have brought me into such misery!
And you, you evil seed of Adam,
Rob my soul of all repose
And shut up the heavens to it!
Ah! unheard-of pain!
My dried-up heart
No solace will moisten any longer;
And I must hide myself from Him
Before whom even the angels cover their faces.

2. Aria S ob solo bc — c/d C

Stumme Seufzer, stille Klagen,
Ihr mögt meine Schmerzen sagen,
Weil der Mund geschlossen ist.
  Und ihr nassen Tränenquellen
  Könnt ein sichres Zeugnis stellen,
  Wie mein sündlich Herz gebüßt.
  Recitativo
  Mein Herz ist itzt ein Tränenbrunn,
  Die Augen heiße Quellen.
  Ach Gott! wer wird dich doch zufriedenstellen?

Silent sighs, quiet laments,
You may express my sorrows,
For my mouth is closed.
  And you watery fountains of tears
  Could be a certain witness
  Of how my sinful heart repents.

  My heart is now a well of tears,
  My eyes hot fountains.
  Ah God! who then will satisfy You?

3. Recitativo S str bc — B♭/C C

Doch Gott muß mir genädig sein,
Weil ich das Haupt mit Asche,
Das Angesicht mit Tränen wasche,

Yet God must be gracious to me,
For I bathe my head in ashes,
My face in tears,

[23] The first specified key refers to *Chorton*,* the second to *Kammerton*.

Mein Herz in Reu und Leid zerschlage
Und voller Wehmut sage:
'Gott sei mir Sünder gnädig!'
Ach ja! sein Herze bricht,
Und meine Seele spricht:

Batter my heart with remorse and sorrow,
And, full of melancholy, say:
'God be gracious to me, a sinner!'
Ah yes! His heart breaks,
And my soul says:

4. Aria S str bc — E♭/F 3/4

Tief gebückt und voller Reue
Lieg ich, liebster Gott, vor dir.
  Ich bekenne meine Schuld,
  Aber habe doch Geduld,
  Habe doch Geduld mit mir!

Bent low and full of remorse
I lie before You, dearest God.
  I confess my guilt,
  But yet have patience,
  Yet have patience with me!

5. Recitativo S bc — c–g/d–a C

Auf diese Schmerzensreu
Fällt mir alsdenn dies Trostwort bei:

In this sorrowful remorse
These words of comfort then come to me:

6. Corale S vla or vc or vla da g or vc picc bc — F/G C

Ich, dein betrübtes Kind,
Werf alle meine Sünd,
So viel ihr' in mir stecken
Und mich so heftig schrecken,
In deine tiefe Wunden,
Da ich stets Heil gefunden.

I, Your distressed child,
Cast all my sins—
As many as are hidden in me
And so severely frighten me—
Within Your deep Wounds,
Where I have always found Salvation.

7. Recitativo S str bc — E♭–B♭/F–C C

Ich lege mich in diese Wunden
Als in den rechten Felsenstein;
Die sollen meine Ruhstatt sein.
In diese will ich mich im Glauben schwingen
Und drauf vergnügt und fröhlich singen:

I lie in these Wounds
As in a veritable rock;
They shall be my resting-place.
In these I will soar in Faith
And, thereby contented and joyful, sing:

8. Aria S ob str (or vln, vla, vla da g) bc — B♭/C 12/8

Wie freudig ist mein Herz,
Da Gott versöhnet ist
  Und mir auf Reu und Leid
  Nicht mehr die Seligkeit
  Noch auch sein Herz verschließt.

How joyful is my heart,
Since God is reconciled,
  And upon my repentance and suffering
  No longer excludes me from eternal
  Blessedness, nor from His heart.

This cantata dates from Bach's Weimar period and was probably first performed on 27 August 1713, or at the latest the following year (12 August 1714). The text, which had already been set in 1712 by Johann Christoph Graupner, court Capellmeister at Darmstadt, was drawn from the cycle *Gottgefälliges Kirchen-Opffer* by the Darmstadt court librarian Georg Christian Lehms.

The libretto is based on the Sunday Gospel.* In a typically baroque graphic manner, the poet portrays mankind tormented by his consciousness of sin. The prayer of the publican, 'God be gracious to me, a sinner!' (Luke 18.13), is quoted word for word from the Gospel in the third movement. In the second half of the work, the remorseful sinner finds comfort in reflecting upon Christ's Death on the Cross, which has reconciled God so that, 'upon my repentance and suffering', He no longer withdraws His heart from the sinner.

Bach's setting exhibits all the richness of invention of the youthful composer, who endeavours to obtain a variety of effects from the modest means of solo soprano, oboe, strings, and continuo. Evidently no choir was at Bach's disposal, even for a plain chorale movement, or else he dispensed with it deliberately in order to create a pure 'cantata'. Consequently, a different kind of solution had to be found for setting the chorale included in the text. And by varying his instrumentation and forms, Bach tried to compensate for the invariable use of the soprano voice. In almost all the recitatives he chose an accompaniment not just of continuo but of strings too. By this means, particularly in the first movement, the drama of the text relating to the contrite and helpless heart in its consciousness of sin is emphasized in an exceptionally compelling fashion.

The second movement, an aria with obbligato* oboe, impresses by virtue of its wide-ranging melody; and perhaps it is not mistaken to hear in the large intervallic leaps of the oboe part, constantly changing direction, the hopelessness felt by the soul in its awareness of sin. From a technical, compositional viewpoint, it is interesting to note Bach's attempt to fill large expanses of the aria with the ritornello theme stated at the outset on the oboe: hardly a bar is to be found in the whole movement in which it does not occur. It is also worth noting a certain formal idiosyncrasy: following the librettist's intention, Bach inserts a few recitative bars with continuo accompaniment before the start of the usual da capo*.

The following recitative, no. 3, is differentiated from the recitative insertion in the aria by its string accompaniment. It leads directly into the second aria, no. 4, again scored for strings, whose broad solemnity and accessible melody are strongly reminiscent of Handel. It differs considerably in character from the previous aria: after confession of guilt, the hopelessness and despair of the sinner give way to calm repose, which is reflected in a change from minor to major mode and from a distinctive solo instrument (the oboe) to a full string sonority. The da capo is again preceded by a caesura: the middle section ends with a few cadential *adagio* bars, lending special emphasis to the prayer 'Yet have patience with me!'

A brief recitative of three bars, no. 5, leads into the only chorale, no. 6, the third verse of the hymn *Wo soll ich fliehen hin* by Johann Heermann (1630). Its melody, which is no longer in use today but was then evidently familiar, particularly to Thuringians, is sung by the soprano line by line against a lively figuration in the obbligato viola, whose thematic material is derived from the head-motive of the chorale. Indeed, the entire opening ritornello is a musical paraphrase of a chorale verse.[24] The recitative that follows, no. 7, is already fully attuned to the cheerful mood of the concluding aria. This becomes particularly clear in the extended coloratura* on the word 'fröhlich' ('joyful'), where the first violin joins in with the lively motion of the soprano part. The concluding aria, no. 8, is framed in the dance rhythm of a gigue to such an extent that a purely instrumental version of it might well form the finale of a suite. Its tripartite da capo form lacks a closing ritornello, bringing the cantata to an end with striking brevity.

After 1714 Bach revived the work on several occasions—notably during the Cöthen period, 1717–23, and in Leipzig on 8 August 1723—at times in reduced circumstances and with the viola of the chorale arrangement (no. 6) replaced by viola da gamba,[25] cello, or violoncello piccolo;* and this may be taken as an indication of the esteem in which the work was held by its composer.

Siehe zu, daß deine Gottesfurcht nicht Heuchelei sei, BWV 179

NBA I/20, p. 57 BC A121 Duration: *c.* 19 mins

1. Chorus SATB bc (+ str) G ¢

'Siehe zu, daß deine Gottesfurcht nicht Heuchelei sei, und diene Gott nicht mit falschem Herzen!'

'See to it that your fear of God be not hypocrisy, and do not serve God with a false heart!'

2. Recitativo T bc e–b c

Das heutge Christentum
Ist leider schlecht bestellt:
Die meisten Christen in der Welt
Sind laulichte Laodizäer
Und aufgeblasne Pharisäer,
Die sich von außen fromm bezeigen
Und wie ein Schilf den Kopf zur Erde beugen;
Im Herzen aber steckt ein stolzer Eigenruhm
Sie gehen zwar in Gottes Haus
Und tun daselbst die äußerlichen Pflichten;
Macht aber dies wohl einen Christen aus?
Nein! Heuchler könnens auch verrichten!

Today's Christianity
Is sadly in a sorry state:
Most Christians in the world
Are lukewarm Laodiceans
Or puffed-up Pharisees,
Who appear pious from without
And like a reed bow their head to the earth;
But in their heart is hidden a proud self-glorification.
They do indeed go into God's house
And there perform their outward duties;
But does this make a Christian?
No! hypocrites can do that too!

3. Aria T vln I + ob I + II vln II vla bc e c

Falscher Heuchler Ebenbild
Können Sodomsäpfel heißen,

The image of false hypocrites
Could be called 'Sodom's apples',

[24] See Dürr St 2, p. 165.

[25] See Dürr St 2, p. 30, and KB, NBA I/20 (1985).

Die mit Unflat angefüllt
Und von außen herrlich gleißen.
Heuchler, die von außen schön,
Können nicht vor Gott bestehn.

Which are filled with filth
But from without gleam splendidly.
Hypocrites, who are outwardly fine,
Cannot endure before God.

4. Recitativo B bc — G–C C

Wer so von innen wie von außen ist,
Der heißt ein wahrer Christ.
So war der Zöllner in dem Tempel:
Der schlug in Demut an die Brust,
Er legte sich nicht selbst ein heilig Wesen bei;
Und diesen stelle dir,
O Mensch, zum rühmlichen Exempel
In deiner Buße für!
Bist du kein Räuber, Ehebrecher,
Kein ungerechter Ehrenschwächer:
Ach, bilde dir doch ja nicht ein,
Du seist deswegen engelrein!
Bekenne Gott in Demut deine Sünden,
So kannst du Gnad und Hülfe finden!

He who is the same inside and out
Is called a true Christian.
Thus was the publican in the temple:
He beat his breast in humility,
He did not attribute to himself a pious character;
And set this before you,
O man, as a laudable example
In your penance!
Though you are no robber or adulterer,
No unjust slanderer,
Ah, do not then fancy that
You are on that account angel-pure!
Acknowledge your sins to God in humility,
Then you can find grace and help!

5. Aria S ob da c I,II bc — a 3/4

Liebster Gott, erbarme dich:
Laß mir Trost und Gnad erscheinen!
  Meine Sünden kränken mich
  Als ein Eiter in Gebeinen,
  Hilf mir, Jesu, Gottes Lamm,
  Ich versink in tiefen Schlamm!

Dearest God, have mercy:
Let comfort and grace appear to me!
  My sins afflict me
  Like rottenness in the bones;
  Help me Jesus, God's Lamb,
  I sink in a deep mire!

6. Choral SATB bc (+ instrs) — a C

Ich armer Mensch, ich armer Sünder
Steh hier vor Gottes Angesicht.
Ach Gott, ach Gott, verfahr gelinder
Und geh nicht mit mir ins Gericht!
Erbarme dich, erbarme dich,
Gott, mein Erbarmer, über mich!

I, poor man, poor sinner,
Stand here before God's countenance.
Ah God, ah God, deal more leniently
And enter not into judgement with me!
Have mercy, have mercy,
God, my Merciful One, upon me!

This cantata originated during Bach's first year in Leipzig and was first heard on 8 August 1723, probably in a two-part performance alongside Cantata 199. Towards the end of the 1730s, Bach adapted the opening chorus* and the two arias, nos. 1, 3, and 5, to form the Kyrie and 'Quoniam' of the Lutheran Missa in G, BWV 236, and the 'Qui tollis' of the Missa in A, BWV 234.

The text, by an anonymous librettist, relies closely on the Gospel* reading, preaching in the zealous tone of a pulpit orator against the hypocrisy that was widespread in contemporary Christianity. A saying from Ecclesiasticus 1.34 forms the opening text. The following moral sermon indulges in learned allusions, such as 'lukewarm Laodiceans' (cf. Revelation 3.14–16: 'To the congregation at Laodicea write: . . . but since you are lukewarm, and neither hot nor cold, I will spit you out'), 'puffed-up Pharisees' (cf. the Sunday Gospel), and 'Sodom's apples' (see p. 254). In the fourth movement, a direct reference is made to the 'example' of the Pharisee and the publican in Jesus's parable; and the fifth follows logically with a prayer similar to that of the publican, though here again an extraneous biblical allusion (to Habakkuk 3.16: 'Rottenness enters my bones'), more learned than poetic, is interwoven. The cantata concludes with the first verse of the hymn *Ich armer Mensch, ich armer Sünder* by Christoph Tietze (1663).

For the opening movement, Bach chose the form of the motet-fugue: the instruments double the voices, only the continuo being partly independent. The chorus opens with a counter-fugue (each new subject entry is the inversion of its predecessor), strictly periodic in its phrase-structure, in which the two phrases of the text are separated as subject ('Siehe zu . . .') and countersubject ('und diene Gott . . .'):

The conclusion of the fugue—a connecting link to the second, more freely structured half of the movement—consists of a brief canon* at the fifth on a new theme for the second phrase of the text (observe the chromaticism* that arises each time on the word 'falschem' ('false'):

In the second half of the movement, various sorts of thematic combination and stretto* take place.

A *secco* recitative with continuo accompaniment leads to the first aria, no. 3, whose top instrumental part—clearly differentiated in rhythm—is assigned to unison oboes and first violin, while the second violin and viola merely fill out the harmony. In the first vocal passage, the tenor takes up the ritornello theme, whose rich syncopation is probably designed to conjure up the dissembling of the hypocrite. In the second section, the voice part is more freely structured. In the absence of a da capo*, the movement is formally rounded off only by a concluding ritornello.

The second recitative (no. 4), like the first, is designed largely as *secco*, only the closing words, 'Then you can find grace and help', being set as arioso* in order to give them greater emphasis. The most powerfully expressive movement is the second aria, no. 5. In the ritornello, two oboes da caccia* unfold a compelling theme, marked by imploring gestures, which is then largely maintained in the vocal passages as an instrumental background for vocal insertion.* It nonetheless leaves the voice plenty of scope for a melodic line rich in gestures and characterized by large intervals such as sixths and sevenths.

The concluding chorale, to the melody *Wer nur den lieben Gott läßt walten*, though a plain choral setting, is nonetheless designed with a notably strong rhythmic differentiation of the accompanying parts, which once again lends powerful emphasis to the prayer for mercy.

Herr Jesu Christ, du höchstes Gut, BWV 113

NBA I/20, p. 81 BC A122 Duration: *c.* 30 mins

1\. [CHORALE] SATB ob d'am I,II str bc — b $\frac{3}{4}$

Herr Jesu Christ, du höchstes Gut,	**Lord Jesus Christ, You highest good,**
Du Brunnquell aller Gnaden,	**You fountain of all grace,**
Sieh doch, wie ich in meinem Mut	**See how in my spirit**
Mit Schmerzen bin beladen	**I am burdened with sorrows**
Und in mir hab der Pfeile viel,	**And have many arrows in me**
Die im Gewissen ohne Ziel	**That in my conscience, without end,**
Mich armen Sünder drücken.	**Oppress me, a poor sinner.**

2\. [CHORALE] A vln bc — f♯ C

Erbarm dich mein in solcher Last,	**Have mercy on me with such a burden,**
Nimm sie aus meinem Herzen,	**Remove it from my heart,**
Dieweil du sie gebüßet hast	**Since You have atoned for it**
Am Holz mit Todesschmerzen,	**On the Tree with the pains of death,**
Auf daß ich nicht für großem Weh	**So that I do not, from great woe,**
In meinen Sünden untergeh,	**Perish in my sins**
Noch ewiglich verzage.	**Nor forever despair.**

3\. ARIA B ob d'am I,II bc — A $\frac{12}{8}$

Fürwahr, wenn mir das kömmet ein,	**In truth, when it occurs to me**
Daß ich nicht recht vor Gott gewandelt	That I have not walked rightly before God

Und täglich wider ihn mißhandelt,
So quält mich Zittern, Furcht und Pein.
Ich weiß, daß mir das Herz zerbräche,
Wenn mir dein Wort nicht Trost verspräche.

And have daily trespassed against Him,
Then trembling, fear, and pain torment me.
I know that my heart would break
If Your Word did not promise me comfort.

4. RECITATIVO [+ CHORALE] B bc — e c

Jedoch dein heilsam Wort, das macht
Mit seinem süßen Singen,
Daß meine Brust,
Der vormals lauter Angst bewußt,
Sich wieder kräftig kann erquicken.
Das jammervolle Herz
Empfindet nun nach tränenreichem Schmerz
Den hellen Schein von Jesu Gnadenblicken;
Sein Wort hat mir so vielen Trost gebracht,
Daß mir das Herze wieder lacht,
Als wenns beginnt zu springen.
Wie wohl ist meiner Seelen!
Das nagende Gewissen kann mich nicht länger quälen,
Dieweil Gott alle Gnad verheißt,
Hiernächst die Gläubigen und Frommen
Mit Himmelsmanna speist,
Wenn wir nur mit zerknirschtem Geist
Zu unserm Jesu kommen.

Yet Your healing Word
With its sweet singing
Enables my breast,
Formerly knowing nothing but anguish,
To revive itself again powerfully.
My miserable heart
Now feels, after pain rich in tears,
The bright gleam of Jesus's gracious glances;
His Word has brought me so much comfort
That my heart laughs again
As if it starts to leap.
How blessed is my soul!
A gnawing conscience can no longer torment me,
Since God promises all His grace
And afterwards feeds the faithful and devout
With heavenly manna,
If only with broken spirit
We come to our Jesus.

5. ARIA T fl bc — D c

Jesus nimmt die Sünder an:
Süßes Wort voll Trost und Leben!
Er schenkt die wahre Seelenruh
Und rufet jedem tröstlich zu:
Dein Sünd ist dir vergeben!

Jesus receives sinners:
Sweet words full of comfort and life!
He gives true rest to the soul
And calls to everyone consolingly:
Your sin is forgiven you!

6. RECITATIVO T str bc — G–e c

Der Heiland nimmt die Sünder an:
Wie lieblich klingt das Wort in meinen Ohren!
Er ruft: Kommt her zu mir,
Die ihr mühselig und beladen,
Kommt her zum Brunnquell aller Gnaden,

The Saviour receives sinners:
How lovely these words sound in my ears!
He calls: Come here to me,
All you who labour and are heavy-laden,
Come here to the fount of all grace:

Ich hab euch mir zu Freunden auserkoren!	I have chosen you to be my friends!
Auf dieses Wort will ich zu dir	At these words I will come to You
Wie der bußfertge Zöllner treten	Like the penitent publican
Und mit demütgem Geist: Gott sei mir gnädig! beten.	And pray with humble spirit: 'God be gracious to me!'
Ach, tröste meinen blöden Mut	Ah, comfort my weak spirit
Und mache mich durch dein vergoßnes Blut	And make me, through Your shed Blood,
Von allen Sünden rein,	Cleansed of all sin;
So werd ich auch wie David und Manasse,	Then I too, like David and Manasseh—
Wenn ich dabei	If I also
Dich stets in Lieb und Treu	Constantly embrace You in love and loyalty
Mit meinem Glaubensarm umfasse,	With my arm of faith—
Hinfort ein Kind des Himmels sein.	Shall henceforth be a child of heaven.

7. ARIA [DUETTO] SA bc — e $\frac{3}{4}$

Ach Herr, mein Gott, vergib mirs doch,	**Ah Lord, my God, forgive me**
Wormit ich deinen Zorn erreget,	For what has aroused Your anger,
Zerbrich das schwere Sündenjoch,	Break the heavy yoke of sin
Das mir der Satan auferleget,	That Satan has laid upon me,
Daß sich mein Herz zufriedengebe	That my heart may be content
Und dir zum Preis und Ruhm hinfort	And henceforth, to Your praise and glory,
Nach deinem Wort	Live according to Your Word
In kindlichem Gehorsam lebe.	In child-like obedience.

8. CHORAL SATB bc (+ instrs) — b C

Stärk mich mit deinem Freudengeist,	**Strengthen me with Your spirit of joy,**
Heil mich mit deinen Wunden,	**Heal me with Your Wounds,**
Wasch mich mit deinem Todesschweiß	**Wash me with Your death-sweat**
In meiner letzten Stunden;	**In my last hours;**
Und nimm mich einst, wenn dirs gefällt,	**And take me one day, when it pleases You,**
In wahrem Glauben von der Welt	**In true faith out of the world**
Zu deinen Auserwählten!	**To Your chosen ones!**

This chorale cantata,* written for 20 August 1724, is based on the penitential hymn by Bartholomäus Ringwaldt (1588). In relation to the Sunday Gospel,* this hymn may be regarded as a paraphrase, as it were, of the publican's words 'God be gracious to me, a sinner'. The anonymous librettist adopted verses 1, 2, 4, and 8 literally in the movements so numbered, expanding verse 4 with recitative insertions. The other verses are freely paraphrased, though in the arias nos. 3 and 7 the opening line of the verse concerned is quoted. Verses 5 and 6 are the most freely treated: they are only distantly recalled in the corresponding cantata movements. The phrase 'like David and Manasseh', for example—an allusion to 2 Samuel 12.13 and to 2 Chronicles 33.12f.—is drawn from the fifth verse but taken up only at the end of the sixth movement. In movements 5 and 6, the librettist instead goes more deeply into the ideas of the Gospel reading. Forgiveness—for which Ringwaldt's hymn only prays—is here granted to the penitent Christian. It is these movements that give the text its sermon-like character. Not only is mention made of the 'penitent publican' of the parable and his prayer 'God be gracious to me' (no. 6) but a series of other biblical passages are adduced to testify that the sinner may be justified in hoping for Jesus's grace:

'Jesus receives sinners' (no. 5)	Luke 15.2
'The Saviour receives sinners' (no. 6)	Luke 15.2
'Your sin is forgiven you!' (no. 5)	Matthew 9.2, Luke 7.48
'Come here to me, all you who labour and are heavy-laden' (no. 6)	Matthew 11.28

The opening chorus* largely corresponds with the normal design of Bach's introductory chorale-choruses. The melody is assigned to the soprano, while the lower parts accompany in a plain vocal texture. Independent orchestral music surrounds the separate lines of the chorale. Among the instrumental ensemble of two oboes d'amore,* strings, and continuo, the first violin comes to the fore with an almost incessantly agitated, concertante* semiquaver figuration, which persists in the vocal passages even when the other instruments (except continuo) are silent. More clearly than in many similar movements, the theme of the instrumental ritornello reveals its derivation from the first chorale line:

No less exceptional is the contrast between the calm, chordal accompanying vocal texture and the somewhat decorated chorale melody in the soprano. Evidently it is the gesture of the sinner pleading for grace that Bach seeks to evoke through this mode of chorale treatment.

The second movement is rather more severe: it is a chorale trio for violin, alto, and continuo, similar in kind to the movements that Bach later transcribed for organ as the so-called Schübler Chorales. Here, the alto sings verse 2 of the chorale without any embellishment. The instrumental ritornello theme, with its many falling scale figures, was perhaps suggested by the image of the sinner oppressed by his burden, or possibly by the end of the Gospel reading: 'He who humbles himself . . .'. The first aria, no. 3, is in a hovering 12/8 rhythm, accompanied by two oboes d'amore and continuo, and again distantly reminiscent of the chorale melody, though now transformed into a consoling major mode. It is one of the most charming and accessible of Bach's inventions. The voice part takes up the same theme, but almost immediately it begins to imitate musically the images of the text, as in the extended coloratura* on 'gewandelt' ('walked') or the chromatic* movement later on to the words '[das Herz] zerbräche' ('[my heart] would break').

In the fourth movement—a chorale with troping* recitative insertions—the chorale melody, sung by the bass, is accompanied by an ostinato* continuo figure, whereas the intervening recitative passages are set as plain *secco*. Since the chorale melody remains virtually unadorned, the embellishment in the last line on the word 'Jesu' is felt as a concluding enhancement. The second aria, no. 5, which requires obbligato* flute, falls not far short of the first in giving expression to a joyfully relaxed mood. The flowing melody and hovering compound time of the first aria here give way to a more richly articulated ritornello in common time. Over extended passages, however, this common time becomes a latent 3/2, as we hear at the very outset, and here lies its charm:

A peculiarity already noted by Spitta is that the concluding line of the aria, 'Your sin is forgiven you!', though not drawn from the chorale, is nonetheless sung to the melismatically* adorned melody of the last chorale line.

The 'comfortable words' of the following recitative, no. 6, are emphasized by its string accompaniment. The high point of the movement is the phrase 'God be gracious to me!', in which the penitent Christian echoes the publican. The duet with continuo accompaniment, no. 7 (which lacks an introductory ritornello or episodes, containing only three instrumental bars by way of conclusion), proves to be related to the seventeenth-century chorale concerto* in a few parts. Although only the first line of text is a literal chorale quotation, Bach preserves the melody not only of this line but of lines 3, 5, and 7 in an embellished form, uniting it (as in the fifth movement) with free madrigalian* verse. Indeed, even a different number of syllables caused no hindrance, being accommodated by melismas and melodic extensions. The work concludes with the final verse of the chorale in a plain four-part setting.

2.12 Twelfth Sunday after Trinity

EPISTLE: 2 Corinthians 3.4–11: The splendour of the Spirit.
GOSPEL: Mark 7.31–7: The healing of a deaf-mute.

Lobe den Herrn, meine Seele, BWV 69a

NBA I/20, p. 119 BC A123 Duration: *c*. 27 mins

1. [CHORUS] SATB tr I–III timp ob I–III bsn str bc — D 3/4

'Lobe den Herrn, meine Seele, und vergiß nicht, was er dir Gutes getan!'

'Praise the Lord, O my soul, and do not forget what good He has done for you!'

2. RECITATIVO S bc — b–e C

Ach, daß ich tausend Zungen hätte!
Ach wäre doch mein Mund
Von eitlen Worten leer!
Ach, daß ich gar nichts redte,
Als was zu Gottes Lob gerichtet wär!
So machte ich des Höchsten Güte kund;
Denn er hat lebenslang so viel an mir getan,
Daß ich in Ewigkeit ihm nicht verdanken kann.

Ah, would that I had a thousand tongues!
Ah, would that my mouth were
Empty of idle words!
Ah, would that I said nothing other
Than what was geared to God's praise!
Then I would proclaim the Highest's goodness,
For all my life he has done so much for me
That I cannot thank Him in all eternity.

3. ARIA T rec ob da c bc — C 9/8

Meine Seele
Auf, erzähle,
Was dir Gott erwiesen hat!
  Rühme seine Wundertat,
  Laß ein gottgefällig Singen
  Durch die frohen Lippen dringen!

My soul,
Rise up, declare
What God has shown you!
  Praise His marvellous deeds,
  Let singing that pleases God
  Pass through your joyful lips!

4. RECITATIVO A bc — e–G C

Gedenk ich nur zurück,
Was du, mein Gott, von zarter Jugend an
Bis diesen Augenblick
An mir getan,
So kann ich deine Wunder, Herr,
So wenig als die Sterne zählen.
Vor deine Huld, die du an meiner Seelen
Noch alle Stunden tust,
Indem du nur von deiner Liebe ruhst,
Vermag ich nicht vollkommen Dank zu weihn.

If I but remember
What You, my God, from tender youth
Up to this moment,
Have done for me,
I cannot count Your wonders, Lord,
Any more than the stars.
For the favour that You bestow on my soul
Still at all hours—
Since You rest only out of Your Love—
I am unable to consecrate to You complete thanks.

Mein Mund ist schwach, die Zunge stumm	My mouth is weak, my tongue dumb
Zu deinem Preis und Ruhm.	For Your praise and glory.
Ach sei mir nah	Ah, be near me
Und sprich dein kräftig Hephata,	And say Your powerful 'Ephphatha',
So wird mein Mund voll Dankens sein!	Then my mouth will be full of thanks!
5. Aria B ob d'am str bc	b $\frac{3}{4}$
Mein Erlöser und Erhalter,	My Redeemer and Preserver,
Nimm mich stets in Hut und Wacht!	Keep me always in Your care and guard!
Steh mir bei in Kreuz und Leiden,	Stand by me in cross-bearing and suffering;
Alsdenn singt mein Mund mit Freuden:	Thereupon my mouth sings with joy:
Gott hat alles wohlgemacht!	God has done all things well!
6. Choral SATB bc (+ tr I ww str)	G c
Was Gott tut, das ist wohlgetan,	**Whatever God deals is dealt bountifully,**
Darbei will ich verbleiben.	**I will stand by that.**
Es mag mich auf die rauhe Bahn	**I may be driven on a rough path**
Not, Tod und Elend treiben:	**By need, death, and misery:**
So wird Gott mich	**Then God will**
Ganz väterlich	**In a quite fatherly manner**
In seinen Armen halten.	**Hold me in His arms.**
Drum laß ich ihn nur walten.	**Therefore I let Him alone govern me.**

This cantata was written for 15 August 1723 and later revived several times with various alterations. Thus around 1727 Bach adapted the tenor aria 'Meine Seele, auf, erzähle' (no. 3) to form an alto aria in G scored with oboe and violin in place of recorder and oboe da caccia.[26] And in the last years of his life he remodelled the work as a council election cantata, BWV 69.

The text refers to the Gospel* for the day, taking Jesus's miracle as a symbol of God's constant activity on behalf of man, who is therefore enjoined to praise Him in the words of Psalm 103.2 (no. 1). The following movements heed this demand. The special emphasis laid on the *declaration* of God's good deeds (no. 3) with 'a thousand tongues' (no. 2) should be understood as an allusion to the healing of the deaf-mute. Similarly, the words of the fourth movement, 'My mouth is weak, my tongue dumb . . . say Your powerful Ephphatha' are clarified only by the Gospel that had been read out beforehand. The fifth movement

[26] See KB, NBA I/20, p. 122. Christine Fröde (KB, NBA I/32.2) raises the possibility that Bach revised the work for a performance on 31 August 1727, which, however, did not take place owing to the last illness of Christiane Eberhardine, Electress of Saxony, for in these circumstances the performance of a festive work would have been considered improper. The Electress died five days later (5 September) and mourning began on the following Sunday (7 September); see Dürr Chr 2, p. 96.

prays to God our 'Preserver' for future protection and refers to the reading once more in the words 'God has done all things well!' (cf. Mark 7.37). The concluding chorale pursues the same line of thought in the words of the sixth verse of the well-known hymn by Samuel Rodigast (1675). The anonymous librettist took as his model for this cantata a text with the same opening and for the same occasion by Johann Knauer (Gotha, 1720).

In accordance with the laudatory character of the text, Bach's setting of the opening chorus,* which might have been adapted from an earlier composition,[27] calls for an instrumental ensemble that was exceptionally festive for an ordinary Sunday. The high point of the movement is the central, large-scale double fugue,* whose thematic duality is derived from its text: 'Praise the Lord . . . and do not forget . . .'. The two subjects are first stated singly and then combined within a bipartite structure in which each half employs the sequence choir–instruments–tutti. The first half is wholly occupied with the first subject; the second half opens with the second subject, but its tutti section presents the combination of the two subjects, so that the overall double-fugue structure is marked by a process of gradual enhancement accomplished in several phases. The exposition* of the first subject is designed as a permutation fugue, but its continuation and the expositions of the second subject are more freely structured. The whole fugue is framed by freely polyphonic* and chordal passages which in part take the form of choral insertion;* and these are in turn framed by the instrumental sinfonia, with the result that the movement as a whole exhibits a beautifully symmetrical structure: sinfonia–chorus–double fugue (bipartite)—chorus—sinfonia.

A *secco* recitative is followed by the aria 'Meine Seele, auf, erzähle', no. 3, in which the oboe da caccia* part had to be taken by the first oboist and the recorder part by the second oboist—an example of the versatility that Bach could expect of his instrumentalists. It is possible that the revision of around 1727, mentioned above, was due to the lack of the same skills in the players for that performance; or else Bach might have made use of the aria in a different context, outside the cantata. In any event, there is no reason to assume that Bach made the alteration out of an aesthetic dislike of the original wind scoring, which is so characteristic of the baroque ideal of sound. Musically, the movement belongs to the pastorale type, reflecting a mood of joyful abandon in its hovering compound-triple time.

Another *secco* recitative, enhanced to arioso* towards the end, leads to the second aria, no. 5, which is again in triple time but now powerfully and energetically rhythmical. In the second section, we admire the representation, within a confined space, of the suffering–joy antithesis given in the text by means of chromatic* (falling in the first passage, rising in the second) or lively

[27] See KB, NBA I/20, pp. 125–6.

bass coloraturas,* which flow into the jubilant cry of 'God has done all things well!' Bach borrowed the concluding chorale from Cantata 12, omitting the obbligato* top part of the original, although he could easily have managed it with the forces available. What might have induced him to do this it is no longer possible to say.

Lobe den Herren, den mächtigen König der Ehren, BWV 137

NBA I/20, p. 173 BC A124 Duration: *c.* 18 mins

1. Chorus SATB tr I–III timp ob I,II str bc C $\frac{3}{4}$

Lobe den Herren, den mächtigen König der Ehren,	**Praise the Lord, the mighty King of honour,**
Meine geliebete Seele, das ist mein Begehren.	**My dear soul, that is my desire.**
Kommet zu Hauf,	**Gather yourselves together;**
Psalter und Harfen, wacht auf!	**Awake, psaltery and harps!**
Lasset die Musicam hören!	**Let the music be heard!**

2. Aria [Chorale] A vln I solo bc G $\frac{9}{8}$ $\frac{3}{4}$

Lobe den Herren, der alles so herrlich regieret,	**Praise the Lord, who governs all things so excellently,**
Der dich auf Adelers Fittichen sicher geführet,	**Who bears you securely on eagle's wings,**
Der dich erhält,	**Who preserves you**
Wie es dir selber gefällt;	**As you yourself wish;**
Hast du nicht dieses verspüret?	**Have you not perceived this?**

3. Aria [Duetto] SB ob I,II bc e $\frac{3}{4}$

Lobe den Herren, der künstlich und fein dich bereitet,	**Praise the Lord, who adorns you artfully and finely,**
Der dir Gesundheit verliehen, dich freundlich geleitet;	**Who has granted you good health and guides you like a friend;**
In wieviel Not	**In how much adversity**
Hat nicht der gnädige Gott	**Has not the gracious God**
Über dir Flügel gebreitet!	**Spread His wings over you!**

4. Aria T tr I or ob I bc a $\frac{3}{4}$

Lobe den Herren, der deinen Stand sichtbar gesegnet,	**Praise the Lord, who has visibly blessed your caste,**
Der aus dem Himmel mit Strömen der Liebe geregnet;	**Who has rained down from heaven with streams of Love;**
Denke dran,	**Consider**
Was der Allmächtige kann,	**What the Almighty can do,**
Der dir mit Liebe begegnet.	**Who treats you with Love.**

5. Choral SATB tr I–III timp bc (+ ww str) C $\frac{3}{4}$

Lobe den Herren, was in mir ist, lobe den Namen!	**Praise the Lord, all that is in me, praise His Name!**

Alles, was Odem hat, lobe mit Abrahams Samen!	**Let everything that has breath, together with Abraham's seed, praise Him!**
Er ist dein Licht, Seele, vergiß es ja nicht; Lobende, schließe mit Amen!	**He is Your Light, O soul, do not indeed forget it; Those praising Him, conclude with Amen!**

Though designed as a chorale cantata,* this work did not originate within the well-known cycle of chorale cantatas (we do not know what cantata Bach performed on the Twelfth Sunday after Trinity 1724) but evidently the following year, on 19 August 1725.[28] Moreover, it lacks a characteristic property of the cycle of 1724–5, namely the madrigalian* paraphrase of the inner verses. Instead, Bach retains in unaltered wording all five verses of the hymn by Joachim Neander (1680).

Bach's setting also revolves around the chorale more fully than most comparable cantatas. Its melody is audible in all movements, being sung by the soprano in the first and last and by the alto in the second; in the third, its two opening bars are heard as a head-motive in the vocal duet parts; and in the fourth, a tenor aria, it is heard complete again on trumpet or oboe. Bach thereby creates a symmetrical five-movement structure in which the given melody takes on increasingly individual characteristics towards the middle: in the outer movements, it is heard in full texture, sung by the choir; in the intermediate movements, in *concertato* settings for a few parts only; but in the centre, it is expressively remodelled and recognizable only in allusions.

The opening chorus* unfolds a radiant splendour in its concertante* exchanges between trumpets, oboes, and strings. The chorale melody is heard in the soprano part of a vocal texture broken up into polyphony,* whose lower parts prepare the entries of the chorale lines in fugato writing based on the independent instrumental theme. Only at the words 'Kommet zu Hauf, Psalter und Harfen, wacht auf!' ('Gather yourselves together; awake, psaltery and harps!') do these vocal parts thicken to form a compact, chordal texture.

In charming figure-work, a concertante violin plays around the lightly ornamented second chorale verse, sung by the alto. Bach later arranged this joyful movement for organ (BWV 650) among the *Sechs Choräle* engraved by Schübler, assigning to it the text of the Advent hymn *Kommst du nun, Jesu, vom Himmel herunter auf Erden* by Kaspar Friedrich Nachtenhöfer (1667). In the third verse, a duet with two obbligato* oboes, the entry of the voice parts makes it clear that the oboe melody of the opening ritornello is also formed out of the substance

[28] On the unfounded assertion that the work also served as a council election cantata, see below, pp. 740–1.

of the chorale: the rise of a fifth and the fall in thirds are maintained, though in a minor-mode adaptation:

The form of this duet is exceptional in that all four vocal passages are to a large extent alike. Not only is the second passage—the second *Stollen** of the text—a reprise of the first, which is to be expected since it conforms with the *Bar* form* of the chorale, but the third and fourth passages, each of which gives the complete text of the *Abgesang*,* simply restate the first two in a slightly varied form, prefaced by a few chromatic* bars on the words 'In wieviel Not . . .' ('In how much adversity . . .').

The fourth verse is also set in the minor mode, but it has a special harmonic charm, for the chorale melody, played on trumpet (or oboe) alongside the singing of the tenor, with continuo accompaniment, is in the relative major C. Still more often than in the preceding duet, allusions to the chorale melody are woven into the voice part. A notable feature of the text is the metrically altered, energetic 'Denke dran', as opposed to Neander's 'Denke daran'. The plain concluding chorale is enhanced to a splendid seven-part texture by the independent treatment of the trumpets.

Geist und Seele wird verwirret, BWV 35

NBA I/20, p. 217 BC A125 Duration: *c.* 31 mins

1. CONCERTO ob I,II taille str obbl org bc — d C
2. ARIA A ob I,II taille str obbl org bc — a 6/8

Geist und Seele wird verwirret,	Spirit and soul are bewildered
Wenn sie dich, mein Gott, betracht'.	When they consider You, my God.
Denn die Wunder, so sie kennet	For the miracles they know,
Und das Volk mit Jauchzen nennet,	That people name with joyful shouts,
Hat sie taub und stumm gemacht.	Have made them deaf and dumb.

3. RECITATIVO A bc — F–g C

Ich wundre mich;	I am amazed,
Denn alles, was man sieht,	For all one sees
Muß uns Verwundrung geben.	Must cause us astonishment.
Betracht ich dich,	If I consider You,
Du teurer Gottessohn,	You dear Son of God,

So flieht
Vernunft und auch Verstand davon.
Du machst es eben,
Daß sonst ein Wunderwerk von dir
was Schlechtes ist.
Du bist
Dem Namen, Tun und Amte nach
Erst wunderreich;
Dir ist kein Wunderding auf dieser
Erde gleich.
Den Tauben gibst du das Gehör,
Den Stummen ihre Sprache wieder;
Ja, was noch mehr,
Du öffnest auf ein Wort die blinden
Augenlider.
Dies, dies sind Wunderwerke,
Und ihre Stärke
Ist auch der Engel Chor nicht mächtig
auszusprechen.

4. Aria A obbl org bc
Gott hat alles wohlgemacht!
Seine Liebe, seine Treu
Wird uns alle Tage neu.
Wenn uns Angst und Kummer
drücket,
Hat er reichen Trost geschicket,
Weil er täglich für uns wacht.
Gott hat alles wohlgemacht!

Seconda parte

5. Sinfonia [scoring as in no. 1]

6. Recitativo A bc
Ach, starker Gott, laß mich
Doch dieses stets bedenken,
So kann ich dich
Vergnügt in meine Seele senken.
Laß mir dein süßes Hephata
Das ganz verstockte Herz erweichen;
Ach, lege nur
Den Gnadenfinger in die Ohren,
Sonst bin ich gleich verloren.
Rühr auch das Zungenband
Mit deiner starken Hand,
Damit ich diese Wunderzeichen
In heilger Andacht preise
Und mich als Erb und Kind erweise.

Then I am deserted
By reason and understanding too.
You cause
What would otherwise be a miracle from
you to be something common.
You are,
In name, deed, and office,
Most wonderful;
There is no wondrous thing on this earth
like You.
To the deaf You give hearing,
To the dumb, restore their speech;
Indeed, what is more,
You open at a Word the eyelids of the
blind.
These, these are miracles,
And their power
Even the angels' choir is not mighty
enough to express.

F c

God has done all things well!
His Love, His faithfulness
Are renewed for us every day.
When fear and grief oppress us,

He has sent us sumptuous comfort,
For He watches over us daily.
God has done all things well!

Second part

d $\frac{3}{8}$

B♭–a c

Ah, mighty God, let me
Consider this constantly;
Then I can
Contentedly sink You into my soul.
Let Your sweet 'Hephphatha'
Soften my quite hardened heart;
Ah, put
Your finger of grace into my ears,
Otherwise I am quite lost.
Touch, too, the ligament of my tongue
With Your mighty hand,
That I may praise these wondrous signs
In sacred devotion
And prove myself Your heir and child.

7. Aria A ob I,II taille str obbl org bc C $\frac{3}{8}$

Ich wünsche nur bei Gott zu leben,
Ach! wäre doch die Zeit schon da,

Ein fröhliches Halleluja
Mit allen Engeln anzuheben!
Mein liebster Jesu, löse doch
Das jammerreiche Schmerzensjoch
Und laß mich bald in deinen Händen
Mein martervolles Leben enden!

I wish only to live with God;
Ah! would that the time were already here
To raise up a joyous Alleluia
With all the angels!
My dearest Jesus, loosen
The yoke of pain, rich in woe,
And let me soon in Your hands
End my torment-filled life!

The text of this cantata, by the Darmstadt court librarian Georg Christian Lehms, closely follows the Sunday Gospel.* The miracles of God, of which the people speak 'with joyful shouts', are so great—so we are told in the first aria—that when they consider them, their spirits and souls grow dumb in bewilderment. The following recitative mentions the healing of the deaf and dumb, recorded in the Gospel reading, still more directly: 'To the deaf You give hearing, to the dumb, restore their speech'. The conclusion of the biblical narrative forms the basis of the second aria—'God has done all things well!'—and the text of this movement continues with a reference to Lamentations 3.23: 'His Love, His faithfulness are renewed for us every day'. Part II, probably performed after the sermon, opens with a sinfonia, followed by the recitative 'Ach, starker Gott' which presents the *applicatio**: it applies the text to the Christians of the assembled congregation, for whom likewise God may open their ears and loosen their tongues so that they may praise Him and prove themselves to be His children and heirs. This inheritance of God's Kingdom is the true goal of Christian life, and accordingly the libretto ends with an expression of the wish to be freed very soon from the 'yoke of pain, rich in woe' of this earth in order to sing a 'joyous Alleluia' to God with all the angels.

Lehms's libretto of 1711 is a genuine 'cantata' in the terminology of the time, since it eschews biblical words and chorale in favour of madrigalian* verse throughout. In his setting, written for 8 September 1726, Bach follows his textual model, dispensing with a choir and assigning all the vocal music to one alto singer—that year he evidently had an exceptionally able alto at his disposal. In the absence of a choir, the role of the orchestra is all the more significant. As in various other cantatas of that year, Bach here reused an existing concerto, probably composed at Cöthen. Indeed, the cantata is a particularly valuable piece of evidence for that work, since the original, probably a concerto for oboe and strings, is lost, surviving only in the form of a nine-bar fragment from an unfinished arrangement as a harpsichord concerto (BWV 1059). In the cantata, obbligato* organ takes the place of the original solo instrument. Part I opens with the first movement of the concerto, and Part II with what is believed to be its finale. Whether the aria 'Geist und Seele wird verwirret', no. 2, should be considered an arrangement of the slow middle movement is uncertain but not impossible. Since the original concerto is lost, the extent of the alterations made in the movements concerned cannot be established with any certainty. However, the reinforcement of the strings by two oboes and taille,* which allows one or other of the instrumental groups to rest occasionally, may well be new in the cantata version (the unfinished harpsichord transcription requires only one oboe).

The introductory concerto movement is followed by the aria which, as already mentioned, should perhaps be regarded as the middle movement of the lost concerto. Yet caution is required here. Bach's autograph score is more heavily corrected than in the preceding movement, and the instrumental groups—woodwind and strings—are often treated independently. Both these observations might support the view that the movement was newly composed, or at least radically altered. In any case, the aria achieves admirably what was required of a composer of the time in the setting of such a text. For the ornamental figuration of the obbligato organ, combined with a most expressive siciliano melody for the other instruments, can easily be understood as a symbol for the miracles of God; and perhaps the rests that separate the phrases of the siciliano theme might even be conceived as a metaphor for growing dumb before such miracles.

The recitative no. 3 that follows the two concerto-like movements has a plain, syllabically* declaimed voice part accompanied only by continuo. In the aria 'Gott hat alles wohlgemacht!', no. 4, the cantata for the first time enters clear major-mode territory. The obbligato organ on this occasion accompanies the voice unaided save by continuo. In place of the rich, figurative embellishment of the previous aria, we now hear a simple, more triadic melody with sequential continuation and a largely motoric rhythm, which together impart a joyfully excited character to the movement and thus to the conclusion of Part I.

Part II opens with a 'presto' sinfonia in which the obbligato organ takes the lead from the outset, first in dialogue with the orchestra and thereafter as a soloist accompanied by the other instruments. The second section of the movement, which is designed in binary form with repeats, is dominated still more exclusively by the organ, and accordingly the opening theme no longer recurs here in full; its initial bar, however—

—pervades the entire movement as its driving force.

The second recitative, no. 6, is, like the first, designed as a syllabically declaimed *secco*. The concluding aria, no. 7, 'Ich wünsche nur bei Gott zu leben'

('I wish only to live with God'), is significantly dance-like in character. Moreover, being in C major, it avoids a return to the initial key of the cantata. Only its second section is temporarily overclouded by the minor mode in accordance with the text. Again, the obbligato organ takes a prominent role and thus proves to be the one and only solo instrument of the cantata. After only five bars, it initiates a triplet figuration that remains a determining factor not only for the remainder of the ritornello but for the accompaniment of the vocal passages. This figuration even shifts to the voice at the words 'Ein fröhliches Halleluja' ('a joyous Alleluia') and '[Mein martervolles Leben] enden' ('End [my torment-filled life]').

It is hard for us to understand today that in this work of art Bach can say, as it were, 'Yes' to life at the opening, by praising the healing miracles of Jesus, and a still more emphatic 'Yes' to death at the close in a prayer for a speedy end to life. Yet it is possible to account for this attitude not only by recalling the ever-present dangers of war and pestilence, nor just with reference to theological commonplaces such as our 'earthly vale of tears', however widespread they might have been, but also, surely, in the light of the biblical notion that here we see the activities of God only 'in a mirror', but one day we shall see Him 'face to face'.

2.13 Thirteenth Sunday after Trinity

EPISTLE: Galatians 3.15–22: Law and Promise.
GOSPEL: Luke 10.23–37: The parable of the Good Samaritan.

Du sollt Gott, deinen Herren, lieben, BWV 77

NBA I/21, p. 3 BC A126 Duration: *c.* 17 mins

1.	[CHORUS] SATB tr da t str bc	C 𝄴
	'Du sollt Gott, deinen Herren, lieben von ganzem Herzen, von ganzer Seele, von allen Kräften und von ganzem Gemüte und deinen Nächsten als dich selbst.'	'You shall love God, Your Lord, with all your heart, with all your soul, with all your strength and with all you mind, and your neighbour as yourself.'
2.	RECITATIVO B bc	C 𝄴
	So muß es sein!	It must be so!
	Gott will das Herz vor sich alleine haben.	God would have our heart for Himself alone.
	Man muß den Herrn von ganzer Seelen	We must choose the Lord with all our soul
	Zu seiner Lust erwählen	For our delight
	Und sich nicht mehr erfreun,	And never be more gladdened
	Als wenn er das Gemüte	Than when He enkindles the mind
	Durch seinen Geist entzündt,	Through His Spirit,

Weil wir nur seiner Huld und Güte	For only then are we truly assured
Alsdenn erst recht versichert sind.	Of His favour and goodness.
3. Aria S ob I,II bc	a C
Mein Gott, ich liebe dich von Herzen,	My God, I love You with all my heart:
Mein ganzes Leben hangt dir an.	My whole life follows hard after You.
Laß mich doch dein Gebot erkennen	Let me know Your Commandment
Und in Liebe so entbrennen,	And be so inflamed with love
Daß ich dich ewig lieben kann!	That I can love You for ever!
4. Recitativo T str bc	e–G C
Gib mir dabei, mein Gott! ein Samariterherz,	Grant me besides, my God, the heart of a Samaritan,
Daß ich zugleich den Nächsten liebe	That I may also love my neighbour
Und mich bei seinem Schmerz	And in his pain
Auch über ihn betrübe,	Be distressed over him,
Damit ich nicht bei ihm vorübergeh	So that I do not pass him by
Und ihn in seiner Not nicht lasse.	And leave him in his need.
Gib, daß ich Eigenliebe hasse,	Grant that I may hate self-love,
So wirst du mir dereinst das Freudenleben	Then You will one day grant me the life of joy
Nach meinem Wunsch, jedoch aus Gnaden geben.	According to my wish, yet out of grace.
5. [Aria] A tr bc	d 3/4
Ach, es bleibt in meiner Liebe	Ah, there remains in my love
Lauter Unvollkommenheit!	Nothing but imperfection!
Hab ich oftmals gleich den Willen,	Though the will may be quite present in me
Was Gott saget, zu erfüllen,	To fulfil what God says,
Fehlt mirs doch an Möglichkeit.	Yet I lack the ability.
6. Choral SATB bc (+ instrs)	g–D C
[Herr, durch den Glauben wohn in mir,	**[Lord, dwell in me through Faith;**
Laß ihn sich immer stärken,	**Let it ever strengthen,**
Daß er sei fruchtbar für und für	**That it may be fruitful for ever and ever**
Und reich in guten Werken;	**And abounding in good works;**
Daß er sei tätig durch die Lieb,	**That it may be working through Love**
Mit Freuden und Geduld sich üb,	**And with joy and forbearance**
Dem Nächsten fort zu dienen.]	**Continue to serve my neighbour.]**

This cantata, from Bach's first Leipzig cycle, received its first performance on 22 August 1723. The anonymous librettist used as his model the second part of a cantata text for the same occasion by Johann Knauer (Gotha, 1720). The libretto adheres closely to the Sunday Gospel,* making particularly abundant use of the background to the parable, which is included in the reading, namely the lawyer's question, 'What must I do to inherit eternal life?' and the reply that Jesus, referring to the Law, elicits from the lawyer himself, 'You shall love the

Lord your God . . . and your neighbour as yourself'. These words preface the cantata as an opening dictum, and their conceptual duality determines the textual structure of the madrigalian* verse that follows: a recitative-aria pair each deals with the love of God and the love of our neighbour, which (so we are told in the second aria) remains imperfect, however good our intentions. The concluding chorale is transmitted without text. Here, the resolution to obey the commandment of love and the prayer for God's blessing upon this resolution were no doubt confirmed in the name of the assembled congregation. Karl Friedrich Zelter suggested the eighth verse of the hymn *Wenn einer alle Ding verstünd* by David Denicke (1657); but Werner Neumann, pointing out the musically unsatisfactory connection between this text and the Bach chorale, recommended the eighth verse of *O Gottes Sohn, Herr Jesu Christ*, also by Denicke (1657).

The weightiest movement is the opening chorus,* a chorale arrangement which, on account of its profound symbolism, has acquired considerable celebrity in the Bach literature, though unfortunately not in present-day performance. Bach recalls the equivalent passage in Matthew's Gospel (22.34–40) in which Jesus is asked what is the 'first Commandment in the Law' and replies—virtually in the words of this opening chorus—that the commandments of loving God and one's neighbour are of equal rank, adding, 'On these two Commandments hang all the Law and the Prophets'. Consequently, Bach seeks to comment upon and underline the significance of these two commandments with all the resources at his disposal. He bases the movement on the chorale melody *Dies sind die heilgen zehn Gebot* ('These are the holy Ten Commandments') in order to show that the entire Law is contained within the commandment of love. The chorale melody is heard in canon,* a symbol of the Law, at the highest (trumpet) and lowest pitch (continuo) to clarify the all-embracing character ('all the Law and the Prophets') of the love commandment. Moreover, this canon at the lower fifth is an augmentation* canon: the basic note-values are crotchet (trumpet) and minim (continuo), with the result that the trumpet has several opportunities to repeat the chorale lines, and at the end it repeats the entire chorale. This augmentation canon signifies that the love-commandment is the pre-eminent one. This is also indicated by the line repetitions, by the manifold presence of the chorale. As a result of these repetitions, Bach also contrives to give the trumpet precisely ten entries (following rests), which is clearly to be conceived as an allusion to the *ten* commandments.

The chorus, introduced by an eight-bar instrumental prelude and then interrupted only once, by seven instrumental bars (which help to make the chorale melody audible), is fugal, or to be more precise imitative,* since the specific characteristic of fugue*—the subject answer at the fifth—is absent. The subject, already heard in the instrumental prelude, is not a direct quotation from the chorale but a derivative of it:

Its note repetitions recall the first line of the chorale—

—and its first eight notes, marked above with a square bracket, might be construed as a retrograde inversion of this chorale line. Even without this complicated derivation, however, upon hearing the movement the relationship of the theme to the beginning of the chorale is unmistakable.

A plain, syllabic* *secco* recitative leads to the first aria, whose intimate character is due to the voice-leading in parallel thirds of the two obbligato* oboes. The second recitative is accompanied by strings, first with held chords and then at the end in livelier motion. This scoring underlines the prayerful character of the movement, lending special musical emphasis to the soul's pleading for the 'heart of a Samaritan' and for eternal life. Curiously, the second aria, no. 5, is scored with obbligato trumpet, which seems ill-suited to the text's lament over personal inadequacy. Perhaps there was an external cause for this,[29] of which we know nothing. The work concludes with a plain chorale setting (transmitted without text) to the melody *Ach Gott, vom Himmel sieh darein.*

Allein zu dir, Herr Jesu Christ, BWV 33

NBA I/21, p. 25 BC A127 Duration: *c.* 27 mins

1. [Chorale] SATB ob I,II str bc a $\frac{3}{4}$

Allein zu dir, Herr Jesu Christ,	**In You alone, Lord Jesus Christ,**
Mein Hoffnung steht auf Erden;	**My hope is placed on earth;**
Ich weiß, daß du mein Tröster bist,	**I know that You are my Comforter:**
Kein Trost mag mir sonst werden.	**There may be no solace for me otherwise.**
Von Anbeginn ist nichts erkorn,	**From the beginning nothing was ordained,**
Auf Erden war kein Mensch geborn,	**On earth no man was born**

[29] Or an internal symbolism? The text refers to love ('in meiner Liebe'), and the trumpet is the instrument of the love commandment from the first movement. In addition, a difficult minor-mode obbligato* for the baroque (slide) trumpet might be particularly effective in capturing the sense of imperfection; see Michael Marissen, *The Social and Religious Designs of J. S. Bach's Brandenburg Concertos* (Princeton: Princeton University Press, 1995), 3–4.

Der mir aus Nöten helfen kann.	**Who could help me out of my distress.**
Ich ruf dich an,	**I call upon You,**
Zu dem ich mein Vertrauen hab.	**In whom I have my trust.**
2. Recitativo B bc	e–G 𝄴
Mein Gott und Richter, willst du mich aus dem Gesetze fragen,	My God and Judge, if You would question me from the Law,
So kann ich nicht,	Then I could not—
Weil mein Gewissen widerspricht,	Since my conscience contradicts me—
Auf tausend eines sagen.	Answer one in a thousand.
An Seelenkräften arm und an der Liebe bloß,	I am poor in strength of soul and empty of love
Und **meine Sünd ist schwer und übergroß;**	And **my sin is heavy and very great;**
Doch weil sie mich von Herzen reuen,	Yet because I regret it from my heart,
Wirst du, mein Gott und Hort,	You, my God and refuge,
Durch ein Vergebungswort	With a Word of forgiveness
Mich wiederum erfreuen.	Will again delight me.
3. Aria A str bc	C 𝄴
Wie furchtsam wankten meine Schritte,	How fearfully my steps wavered,
Doch Jesus hört auf meine Bitte	Yet Jesus hears my prayer
Und zeigt mich seinem Vater an.	And shows me to His Father.
Mich drückten Sündenlasten nieder,	Sin's burden weighed me down,
Doch hilft mir Jesu Trostwort wieder,	Yet Jesus's Word of Comfort reassures me
Daß er für mich genung getan.	That He has done enough for me.
4. Recitativo T bc	a 𝄴
Mein Gott, verwirf mich nicht,	My God, cast me not away—
Wiewohl ich dein Gebot noch täglich übertrete,	Though I still daily transgress Your Commandment—
Von deinem Angesicht!	From Your Presence!
Das kleinste ist mir schon zu halten viel zu schwer;	Even the smallest one is too hard for me to keep;
Doch, wenn ich um nichts mehr	Yet if I pray for nothing more
Als Jesu Beistand bete,	Than Jesus's support,
So wird mich kein Gewissensstreit	Then no dispute of conscience
Der Zuversicht berauben;	Will rob me of confidence;
Gib mir nur aus Barmherzigkeit	**Just grant me of Your mercy**
Den wahren Christenglauben!	**True Christian Faith!**
So stellt er sich mit guten Früchten ein	Then it will show itself in good fruits
Und wird durch Liebe tätig sein.	And will be working through Love.
5. Aria [Duetto] TB ob I,II bc	e $\frac{3}{4}$
Gott, der du die Liebe heißt,	O God, You who are called Love,
Ach, entzünde meinen Geist,	Ah, enkindle my spirit;
Laß zu dir vor allen Dingen	To You above all things

Meine Liebe kräftig dringen!
Gib, daß ich aus reinem Triebe
Als mich selbst den Nächsten liebe;
Stören Feinde meine Ruh,
Sende du mir Hülfe zu!

Let my love powerfully break through!
Grant that out of pure impulse
I love my neighbour as myself;
Should enemies disturb my rest,
May You send help to me!

6. Choral SATB bc (+ instrs) a C

Ehr sei Gott in dem höchsten Thron,
Dem Vater aller Güte,
Und Jesu Christ, sein'm liebsten Sohn,
Der uns allzeit behüte,
Und Gott dem Heiligen Geiste,
Der uns sein Hülf allzeit leiste,
Damit wir ihm gefällig sein,
Hier in dieser Zeit
Und folgends in der Ewigkeit.

Honour be to God on the highest throne,
To the Father of all goodness,
And to Jesus Christ, His dearest Son,
Who always keep us,
And to God the Holy Spirit,
Who gives us His help at all times;
That we may be pleasing to Him
Here at this time
And hereafter in eternity.

This cantata originated during Bach's second year in Leipzig within the cycle of chorale cantatas, receiving its first performance on 3 September 1724. It is based on the hymn by Konrad Hubert (1540; verse 4: Nuremberg, 1540), of which the anonymous librettist retained the first and last (fourth) verses literally, paraphrasing the two middle verses to form a recitative-aria pair each (thus verse 2 = nos. 2–3, verse 3 = nos. 4–5). Although the connection between paraphrase and hymn is unmistakable due to the numerous correspondences of substance and the literal adoption of whole phrases, the expansion by two movements and the consequent lengthening of the text resulted in a freer paraphrase of the hymn than in the cantatas for the preceding Sundays.

In general, the relationship between Hubert's hymn—which asks Jesus for release from the oppressive burden of sin—and the Sunday readings is not very close. The main reason for its use was probably the phrase 'Above all, love You and my neighbour as myself' from the third verse, a reference to Luke 10.27 paraphrased in the fifth movement. In movements 2–4, however, the librettist does nothing substantial to establish a closer link with the readings. Instead, he interweaves a number of additional biblical references: in no. 2 to Job 9.3 (the man who rails against God can answer Him 'not one in a thousand') and in no. 4 to Psalm 51.11 ('Cast me not away from Your Presence') and to Galatians 5.6 ('In Christ Jesus avails . . . faith that works through love').

The opening chorus* corresponds to the type used most frequently for Bach's introductory chorale movements. The chorale melody is assigned to the soprano and supported by the other voices, which accompany in a plain chordal or imitative* texture and are at times rhythmically accentuated, as on the words 'Ich ruf dich an' ('I call upon You'). This chorale texture is embedded line by line within a thematically independent orchestral texture, which is nonetheless loosely connected with the beginning of the chorale through its initial, imitative semiquaver motive.*

The second movement, a *secco* recitative accompanied by continuo, has an arioso* conclusion whose text, 'Mich wiederum erfreuen' ('Will again delight me'), is effectively differentiated from the preceding plainly declaimed text by means of a lively coloratura.* The scoring of the following aria no. 3 is particularly charming: in its string texture, the muted first violin prevails as bearer of the melody, while second violin, viola, and continuo accompany *pizzicato*.* The first violin part, with its melodic wavering up and down, its chromatic* false relations, and its syncopated rhythm, unmistakably portrays the fearful, wavering footsteps of the text. These features, which obtain throughout virtually the whole movement, are significantly absent in the middle section at the words 'Yet Jesus's Word of Comfort reassures me that He has done enough for me'.

The fourth movement is another plain *secco* recitative, with a single, text-engendered lengthening on the word 'halten' ('keep'). The first two lines of hymn verse 3, adopted almost word for word—'Gib mir nur aus [Hubert: "nach deinr"] Barmherzigkeit/Den wahren Christenglauben!' ('Just grant me out of [Hubert: "according to Your"] mercy/True Christian Faith!'—are not emphasized in Bach's setting, nor set to their chorale melody, as often happens elsewhere. In the following duet, no. 5, we might almost believe that Bach allowed himself to be inspired by the soprano aria from the previous year's cantata, BWV 77/3. In both cases, the subject is our love of God, the obbligato* instruments are two oboes, and the theme (or at least its head-motive) is characterized by parallel sixths or thirds, which in the present case, since it is a duet, are present in the voice parts too. Although the continuation of the theme is on this occasion more polyphonic,* the impression of tender intimacy holds true in both cases. Generally speaking, there are grounds for the assumption that the listener of Bach's day was more inclined to associate oboe tone with inspired singing than we are today: the tendency nowadays is to assign the instrument a more coquettish, pert character. A distinctive feature of this movement is that the melody of the two oboes is so similar to that of the voices that the movement might be rewritten without any great difficulty as a vocal quartet for soprano and alto (playing the oboe parts), tenor and bass. The cantata concludes with the last verse of the hymn in a plain choral setting.

Ihr, die ihr euch von Christo nennet, BWV 164

NBA I/21, p. 59 BC A128 Duration: *c.* 17 mins

1. [Aria] T str bc — g $\frac{9}{8}$

Ihr, die ihr euch von Christo nennet,	You who call yourselves after Christ,
Wo bleibet die Barmherzigkeit,	Where is the mercy

Daran man Christi Glieder kennet?	By which one recognizes Christ's members?
Sie ist von euch, ach! allzu weit!	It is, alas, too far removed from you!
Die Herzen sollten liebreich sein,	Your hearts should be rich in love,
So sind sie härter als ein Stein.	But they are harder than a stone.

2. Recitativo B bc — c–a C

Wir hören zwar, was selbst die Liebe spricht:	We indeed hear what Love itself says:
Die mit Barmherzigkeit den Nächsten hier umfangen,	Those who here embrace their neighbour with mercy
Die sollen vor Gericht	Shall for judgement
Barmherzigkeit erlangen!	Receive mercy!
Jedoch, wir achten solches nicht!	Yet we do not heed this!
Wir hören noch des Nächsten Seufzer an!	We still listen to our neighbour's sighs!
Er klopft an unser Herz; doch wirds nicht aufgetan!	He knocks on our heart; yet it will not open!
Wir sehen zwar sein Händeringen,	We indeed see his hand-wringing,
Sein Auge, das von Tränen fleußt;	His eye that runs with tears;
Doch läßt das Herz sich nicht zur Liebe zwingen!	Yet our heart is not driven to love!
Der Priester und Levit,	The priest and Levite,
Der hier zur Seite tritt,	Who here step aside,
Sind ja ein Bild liebloser Christen;	Are indeed an image of loveless Christians;
Sie tun, als wenn sie nichts von fremdem Elend wüßten,	They act as if they knew nothing of another's misery;
Sie gießen weder Öl noch Wein	They pour neither oil nor wine
Ins Nächsten Wunden ein!	Into their neighbour's wounds!

3. Aria A fl I,II bc — d C

Nur durch Lieb und durch Erbarmen	Only through love and through mercy
Werden wir Gott selber gleich!	Do we become equal with God Himself!
Samaritergleiche Herzen	Samaritan-like hearts
Lassen fremden Schmerz sich schmerzen	Let themselves feel pain at another's pain
Und sind an Erbarmung reich.	And are rich in mercy.

4. Recitativo T str bc — E♭–g C

Ach! schmelze doch durch deinen Liebesstrahl	Ah! melt with Your ray of Love
Des kalten Herzens Stahl!	The cold heart's steel!
Daß ich dir wahre Christenliebe,	So that true Christian Love, my Saviour,
Mein Heiland, täglich übe,	May daily be cultivated by me,
Daß meines Nächsten Wehe,	So that my neighbour's woe,
Er sei auch, wer er ist,	Whoever he is,
Freund oder Feind, Heid oder Christ,	Friend or foe, heathen or Christian,

Mir als mein eignes Leid zu Herzen allzeit gehe!
Mein Herz sei liebreich, sanft und mild,
So wird in mir verklärt dein Ebenbild.

May ever go to my heart like my own suffering!
May my heart be rich in love, gentle and mild,
Then Your Image will be transfigured in me.

5. Aria [Duetto] SB fls + obs + vlns in unis bc g ¢

Händen, die sich nicht verschließen,
Wird der Himmel aufgetan!
Augen, die mitleidend fließen,
Sieht der Heiland gnädig an.
Herzen, die nach Liebe streben,
Will Gott selbst sein Herze geben.

To hands that do not shut
Heaven will be open!
Eyes that run compassionately
Are regarded graciously by the Saviour.
To hearts that pursue charity
God Himself will give His Heart.

6. Choral SATB bc (+ instrs) B♭ c

Ertöt uns durch dein Güte,
Erweck uns durch dein Gnad!
Den alten Menschen kränke,
Daß der neu' leben mag
Wohl hier auf dieser Erden,
Den Sinn und all Begehrden
Und Gdanken habn zu dir.

Mortify us through Your goodness,
Awaken us through Your grace!
Weaken the old man,
That the new man may live
Even here on this earth,
And that the mind and all desires
And thoughts may be directed towards You.

The text of this cantata is drawn from the cycle *Evangelisches Andachts-Opffer* of 1715 by Salomo Franck. Nevertheless, Bach's setting dates from as late as 26 August 1725; or, to put it more cautiously, if a Weimar setting of this text by Bach ever existed, it must have differed so much from the setting we know that it would practically amount to a different composition. This is clearly apparent from the draft character of the autograph score of 1725. The circumstances are thus similar to those of Cantata 168.

In his libretto, Franck adheres closely to the Sunday Gospel,* relying chiefly on its second half, in contrast to the librettists whose texts Bach had set in the two previous years. Thus man's love of God ('You shall love the Lord your God . . .') is not mentioned, but mercy towards one's neighbour ('. . . and your neighbour as yourself') is strongly urged and its absence among Christians bitterly lamented. There are several references to the parable from the Sunday reading: priest and Levite 'are indeed an image of loveless Christians' (no. 2), whereas 'Samaritan-like hearts . . . are rich in mercy' (no. 3). Certain sayings from the Sermon on the Mount (Matthew 5.7 and 7.7) are recalled in the second movement. The work concludes with the fifth and last verse of the hymn *Herr Christ, der einig Gotts Sohn* by Elisabeth Creutziger (1524).

In its scoring for a few parts only, Bach's setting corresponds with the chamber-music style that he had already largely employed for Franck's cantata texts in 1715. The four voices come together only in the concluding chorale; and although the instrumentation (two flutes, two oboes, strings, and continuo) is quite rich, Bach avoids pitting the instruments against one another in concertante* exchange. Instead, they enter as soloists, in a unison of a few parts, or in a string texture without independent wind parts. The opening aria, then, though full-textured, is scored only for strings. The theme, which opens with a striking downward leap of a fifth, largely dominates the vocal and instrumental material; and the vocal passages in this A B A[1] B[1] structure contain frequent vocal insertion* within returns of the instrumental ritornello.

In the second movement, a *secco* recitative, the paraphrase from the Sermon on the Mount ('Those who here embrace their neighbour with mercy shall for judgement receive mercy') is made prominent through its setting as arioso.* The hymn-like melody of this passage has led to the conjecture that Bach here introduced a chorale quotation in a freely adorned form. However, no chorale melody that might come under consideration has so far been discovered. The following alto aria, no. 3, scored with two obbligato* flutes, is of exceptional charm. Its sighing melody is designed to symbolize the love and mercy of the text. Like the first aria, it does not fall into the usual da capo* form; instead, its second section is freely recapitulated, forming the structure A B B[1], the so-called *Gegenbar.**

A recitative, given emphasis by its string accompaniment, leads to the third aria, no. 5, a duet that unites flutes, oboes, and violins in a unison obbligato part. As in the first movement, the themes and, indeed, the entire melodic make-up of the vocal and instrumental parts are assimilated to such an extent that a homogeneous quartet texture arises of instrumental top part, soprano, bass, and continuo. The structure of the movement is highly elaborate. The thematic inversion in the opening ritornello is probably designed to represent the reciprocal relationship mentioned in the text between human and divine mercy. The four vocal passages are still more elaborate in design. The text is divided between the first three of them, after which the fourth (musically a free reprise of the first) gives the entire text once more. Each vocal passage opens with canonic writing but continues and concludes with free polyphony.* The third and most extended passage contains two such canons,* resulting in the following symmetrical arrangement:

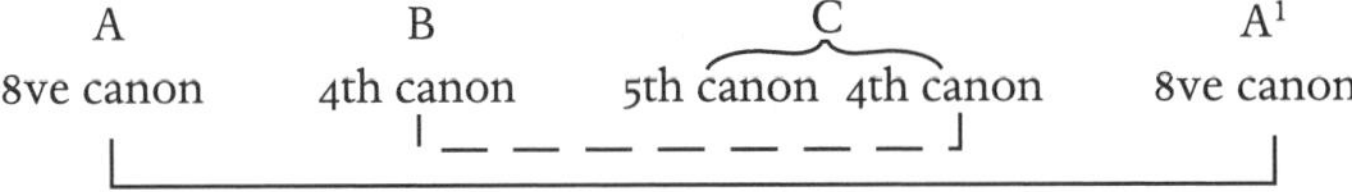

The conclusion of section A[1] is made up of vocal insertion within a complete reprise of the opening ritornello, which is nonetheless heard immediately afterwards as an instrumental postlude. A plain chorale movement ends the work.

2.14 Fourteenth Sunday after Trinity

Epistle: Galatians 5.16–24: The works of the flesh and the fruits of the spirit.
Gospel: Luke 17.11–19: The healing of the ten lepers.

Es ist nichts Gesundes an meinem Leibe, BWV 25

NBA I/21, p. 81   BC A129   Duration: *c.* 16 mins

1. [Chorus] SATB ctt trb I–III rec I–III in unis str + ob I,II bc   e   c

'Es ist nichts Gesundes an meinem
Leibe vor deinem Dräuen und ist
kein Friede in meinen Gebeinen vor
meiner Sünde.'

'There is nothing sound in my body
because of Your threats, nor is there any
peace in my bones because of my sin.'

2. Recitativo T bc   d   c

Die ganze Welt ist nur ein Hospital,
Wo Menschen von unzählbar großer Zahl
Und auch die Kinder in der Wiegen
An Krankheit hart darniederliegen.
Den einen quälet in der Brust
Ein hitzges Fieber böser Lust;
Der andre lieget krank
An eigner Ehre häßlichem Gestank;
Den dritten zehrt die Geldsucht ab
Und stürzt ihn vor der Zeit ins Grab.
Der erste Fall hat jedermann beflecket
Und mit dem Sündenaussatz angestecket.
Ach! dieses Gift durchwühlt auch meine Glieder.
Wo find ich Armer Arzenei?
Wer stehet mir in meinem Elend bei?
Wer ist mein Arzt, wer hilft mir wieder?

The whole world is but a hospital
Where men in countless numbers
And even children in the cradle
Are lying down severely ill.
One is tormented in his breast
By a raging fever of wicked pleasure;
Another lies sick
From the hateful stench of his own honour;
A third is consumed by lust for wealth,
Which hurls him into the grave before his time.
The Fall of Man has stained everyone
And infected him with sin's leprosy.
Ah! this poison stirs my limbs too.
Where do I, poor wretch, find medicine?
Who stands by me in my misery?
Who is my physician? Who will restore me?

3. Aria B bc   d   c

Ach, wo hol ich Armer Rat?
Meinen Aussatz, meine Beulen
Kann kein Kraut noch Pflaster heilen
Als die Salb aus Gilead.
Du, mein Arzt, Herr Jesu, nur
Weißt die beste Seelenkur.

Ah, poor me! Where do I seek advice?
My leprosy, my boils
Neither herb nor plaster can heal,
Only the balm of Gilead.
Only You, Lord Jesus, my Physician,
Know the best cure of the soul.

4. Recitativo S bc   a–C   c

O Jesu, lieber Meister,
Zu dir flieh ich;

O Jesus, dear Master,
To You I flee;

Ach, stärke die geschwächten Lebensgeister!	Ah, strengthen my weakened vital spirits!
Erbarme dich,	Have mercy,
Du Arzt und Helfer aller Kranken,	You Physician and Helper of all the sick,
Verstoß mich nicht	Cast me not out
Von deinem Angesicht!	From Your Presence!
Mein Heiland, mache mich von Sündenaussatz rein,	My Saviour, make me clean from the leprosy of sin,
So will ich dir	Then I will
Mein ganzes Herz dafür	Consecrate my whole heart to You in return
Zum steten Opfer weihn	As a constant offering
Und lebenslang vor deine Hülfe danken.	And all my life thank You for Your help.
5. Aria S rec I–III str + ob I,II bc	C 3/8
Öffne meinen schlechten Liedern,	Open to my poor songs,
Jesu, dein Genadenohr!	O Jesus, Your ear of grace!
Wenn ich dort im höhern Chor	When there in the choir on high
Werde mit den Engeln singen,	I shall sing with the angels,
Soll mein Danklied besser klingen.	My song of thanks shall sound better.
6. Choral SATB bc (+ instrs)	C 𝄴
Ich will alle meine Tage	**I would all my days**
Rühmen deine starke Hand,	**Glorify Your strong hand**
Daß du meine Plag und Klage	**With which my torment and complaint**
Hast so herzlich abgewandt.	**Have been so fully averted.**
Nicht nur in der Sterblichkeit	**Not only in mortality**
Soll dein Ruhm sein ausgebreit':	**Shall Your glory be spread abroad:**
Ich wills auch hernach erweisen	**I will also show it hereafter**
Und dort ewiglich dich preisen.	**And praise You there for ever.**

This cantata, from Bach's first Leipzig cycle, was composed for 29 August 1723. The text, whose graphic baroque metaphors seem to us today barely tolerable and anything but poetic, refers to the Sunday Gospel,* applying its account of the healing of the lepers to the situation of mankind as a whole. Since Adam's original sin—'The Fall of Man has stained everyone' (no. 2)—the whole world is 'but a hospital', for sin has made man sick. This notion is initially expressed in the words of Psalm 38.3 (no. 1) and then treated fully in the second and third movements. The phrase 'balm of Gilead' (no. 3) alludes to Jeremiah 8.22 and 46.11: Gilead, the heartland east of the Jordan, was rich in balsam. At the end of the third movement, Jesus becomes the focus of attention. He alone can heal the soul and is therefore asked in the fourth and fifth movements for purification from the 'leprosy of sin', curiously without the reference to His sacrificial Death on the Cross which is to be expected here according to Christian theology. As a result, despite all the graphic realism of the text, Jesus here appears a trifle pale as an almighty miracle-worker rather than as the oblation for our sins. The most successful movement poetically is perhaps the second aria, no. 5, with its prayer that 'my poor songs' might be heard and its hope that one day it might be possible to sing a better song of thanksgiving in the choir of the angels. The twelfth and last verse of the hymn *Treuer Gott, ich muß dir klagen* by Johann Heermann (1630) utters similar sentiments (praise and thanks to God, both here and in eternity) rendering them the concern of the assembled congregation.

In this work, as in Cantata 77 performed a week earlier, Bach took particular care over the composition of the opening chorus.* Again, it is designed as a chorale arrangement whose basis is a complete instrumental chorale quotation: here, the melody *Herzlich tut mich verlangen nach einem selgen End* ('Heartily do I long for a blessed end'). Perhaps it is not this text that is meant, however, but rather the hymn *Ach Herr, mich armen Sünder* ('Ah Lord, [do not punish] me, a poor sinner') on which Cantata 135 was based—a paraphrase of Psalm 6 likewise universally known in Bach's day and sung to the same melody. Not only is the entire content of this hymn closer to the cantata text than that of the hymn previously mentioned, but the opening of its second verse—'Heil du mich, lieber Herre, denn ich bin krank und schwach' ('Heal me, dear Lord, for I am sick and weak')—would establish a direct connection with the text of the present movement.

The formal layout of this Phrygian-mode movement is most elaborate. It is introduced by a quotation of the first chorale line in long notes in the continuo, in counterpoint* with a motivic quaver figuration in the string ensemble, reinforced by oboes. The vocal choir then enters with a double fugue* based on its own subjects, to which a choir of trombones (with cornett on the top part as usual) adds the chorale line by line in four-part texture. When he wrote out the parts, Bach doubled the chorale melody at the upper octave on three recorders. The overall structure of the movement may be represented as follows:

	Voice Parts	*Strings + oboes*	*Trombones + recorders*
A		Prelude: independent motivic figuration against first chorale line in continuo	
	Choral fugue *a* ('Es ist nichts . . .')	Independent motivic figuration	Chorale, first Stollen*
A^1		Prelude as above	
	Choral fugue *a*^{1} (with exchanged parts)	As above	Chorale, second Stollen
B	Choral fugue *b* ('und ist kein Friede . . .')	Silent at first, then colla parte*	Chorale, Abgesang*, part 1
C	Combination of choral fugue subjects a + b	colla parte	Chorale, Abgesang, part 2

A syllabically* declaimed *secco* recitative is followed by the first aria, no. 3, accompanied only by continuo, whose ostinato-like ritornello motive,* repeated throughout in various modified forms, strikingly illustrates the helplessness described in the text. The second recitative, no. 4, is also accompanied only by continuo and is plainly syllabic, with the exception of a few melismas*—on 'flieh' ('flee') and 'lebenslang' ('all my life'). Thus three continuo movements in succession follow the richly scored opening movement. Not until the second aria, no. 5, do the woodwind and strings come together once more: here the choir of three recorders is antiphonally—in echo fashion, as it were—pitted against the string choir (reinforced by oboes). After all the agonizing helplessness described in the text up to this point, after the elaborately constructed opening chorus and the three scantily scored intervening movements, the dancing, minuet-like melody of this movement opens up a new perspective. The music has a tender, song-like, ethereal sound. One is reminded of baroque representations of angels playing music—not least, of course, because they are mentioned in the text. The cantata, following its meditative beginning, is brought to a conciliatory conclusion in a plain chorale setting to the melody *Freu dich sehr, o meine Seele*.

Jesu, der du meine Seele, BWV 78

NBA I/21, p. 117 BC A130 Duration: *c.* 25 mins

1. [Chorale] S + hn ATB fl ob I,II str bc — g 3/4

Jesu, der du meine Seele	**Jesus, by whom my soul,**
Hast durch deinen bittern Tod	**Through Your bitter Death,**
Aus des Teufels finstern Höhle	**From the devil's dark cave**
Und der schweren Seelennot	**And heavy affliction of the soul,**
Kräftiglich herausgerissen	**Has been forcibly torn out,**
Und mich solches lassen wissen	**And You have let me know this**
Durch dein angenehmes Wort,	**Through Your agreeable Word,**
Sei doch itzt, o Gott, mein Hort!	**Be even now, O God, my refuge!**

2. Aria Duetto SA vne bc — B♭ C

Wir eilen mit schwachen, doch emsigen Schritten,	We hasten with weak yet eager steps,
O Jesu, o Meister zu helfen, zu dir.	O Jesus, O Master, for help to You.
Du suchest die Kranken und Irrenden treulich.	You faithfully seek the sick and straying.
Ach höre, wie wir	Ah, hear how we
Die Stimme erheben, um Hülfe zu bitten!	Lift up our voices to pray for help!
Es sei uns dein gnädiges Antlitz erfreulich!	May Your gracious countenance be gratifying to us!

3. Recitativo T bc — d–c C

Ach! ich bin ein Kind der Sünden,	**Ah! I am a child of sin;**

Ach! ich irre weit und breit.	**Ah! I stray far and wide.**
Der Sünden Aussatz, so an mir zu finden,	Sin's leprosy, which is found in me,
Verläßt mich nicht in dieser Sterblichkeit.	Will not leave me in this mortal life.
Mein Wille trachtet nur nach Bösen.	My will strives only after evil.
Der Geist zwar spricht: ach! wer wird mich erlösen?	My spirit indeed says: ah! who will deliver me?
Aber Fleisch und Blut zu zwingen	**But to subdue flesh and blood**
Und das Gute zu vollbringen,	**And to perform that which is good**
Ist über alle meine Kraft.	Is beyond all my strength.
Will ich den Schaden nicht verhehlen,	If I would not conceal the harm done,
So kann ich nicht, wie oft ich fehle, zählen.	Then I could not count how often I err.
Drum nehm ich nun der Sünden Schmerz und Pein	Therefore I now take up sin's sorrow and pain
Und meiner Sorgen Bürde,	And the burden of my cares,
So mir sonst unerträglich würde,	Otherwise grievous for me to bear,
Ich liefre sie dir, Jesu, seufzend ein.	And, sighing, give them over to You, Jesus.
Rechne nicht die Missetat,	**Do not count the misdeeds**
Die dich, Herr, erzürnet hat!	**That have angered You, Lord!**
4. ARIA T fl bc	g $\frac{6}{8}$
Das Blut, so meine Schuld durchstreicht,	The Blood that cancels out my guilt
Macht mir das Herze wieder leicht	Makes my heart light again
Und spricht mich frei.	And pronounces me free.
Ruft mich der Höllen Heer zum Streite,	If hell's host calls me to battle,
So stehet Jesus mir zur Seite,	Then Jesus stands at my side
Daß ich beherzt und sieghaft sei.	So that I am heartened and victorious.
5. RECITATIVO B str bc	E♭–f C
Die Wunden, Nägel, Kron und Grab,	The wounds, nails, crown, and grave,
Die Schläge, so man dort dem Heiland gab,	The blows they gave the Saviour there
Sind ihm nunmehro Siegeszeichen	Are now His signs of victory
Und können mir verneute Kräfte reichen.	And can give me renewed powers.
Wenn ein erschreckliches Gericht	When a fearful judgement
Den Fluch vor die Verdammten spricht,	Pronounces a curse on the damned,
So kehrst du ihn in Segen.	You change it into a blessing.
Mich kann kein Schmerz und keine Pein bewegen,	Neither sorrow nor pain can move me
Weil sie mein Heiland kennt;	Because my Saviour knows them;

Und da dein Herz vor mich in Liebe brennt,
So lege ich hinwieder
Das meine vor dich nieder.
Dies mein Herz, mit Leid vermenget,
So dein teures Blut besprenget,
So am Kreuz vergossen ist,
Geb ich dir, Herr Jesu Christ.

And since Your Heart burns with Love for me,
I will lay down in return
Whatever is mine before You.
This my heart, mingled with grief,
Sprinkled with Your precious Blood,
Which was shed on the Cross,
I give to You, Lord Jesus Christ.

6. Aria B ob I str bc — c C

Nun du wirst mein Gewissen stillen,
So wider mich um Rache schreit,
Ja, deine Treue wirds erfüllen,
Weil mir dein Wort die Hoffnung beut.
Wenn Christen an dich glauben,
Wird sie kein Feind in Ewigkeit
Aus deinen Händen rauben.

Now You will still my conscience
That cries against me for vengeance;
Yes, Your faithfulness will fulfil it,
For Your Word give me hope.
If Christians believe in You,
No enemy in all eternity
Will steal them out of Your hands.

7. Choral SATB bc (+ instrs, fl 8va) — g C

Herr, ich glaube, hilf mir Schwachen,
Laß mich ja verzagen nicht;
Du, du kannst mich stärker machen,
Wenn mich Sünd und Tod anficht.
Deiner Güte will ich trauen,
Bis ich fröhlich werde schauen
Dich, Herr Jesu, nach dem Streit
In der süßen Ewigkeit.

Lord, I believe; help me in my weakness:
Let me indeed not lose heart;
You, You can make me stronger
When sin and death attack me.
I will trust Your goodness
Till joyfully I see You,
Lord Jesus, after the strife
In sweet eternity.

This cantata was first performed on 10 September 1724 in the context of Bach's cycle of chorale cantatas.* At a revival, perhaps in the late 1730s,[30] Bach required the flute to play in the chorale movements nos. 1 and 7 (while apparently omitting the horn) and added the violone part to the duet, no. 2.

The cantata is based on the twelve-verse hymn of 1641 by Johann Rist. The anonymous librettist retained the first and last verses word for word and paraphrased the others into madrigalian* verse, quoting several chorale lines literally in the recitatives as follows:

verse 3, lines 1–2: beginning of 3rd movement
verse 4, lines 5–6: middle of 3rd movement
verse 5, lines 7–8: end of 3rd movement
verse 10, lines 5–8: end of 5th movement

The paraphrase is handled strictly in content but often very freely in form, which necessarily follows from the large number of verses in the hymn. Thus

[30] According to Kobayashi Chr, p. 36.

only the second and sixth movements are based on a single verse each (verses 2 and 11 respectively); the third is based on verses 3–5, the fourth on verses 6–7, and the fifth on verses 8–10.

The choice of hymn in no way follows conclusively from the Sunday readings. In complete contrast to the cantata text of the previous year (BWV 25), the healing of the sick is barely mentioned and understood in an exclusively symbolic way. The core of the hymn, and therefore of the cantata, is the thought of Christ's Passion, which has healed the faithful and stilled the conscience. Only in a few places does the librettist enter more closely into the Gospel* reading than the hymn text ('You seek the sick . . .'; 'Sin's leprosy'). The entire second half of the cantata goes beyond the text of the Sunday Gospel, expanding and interpreting it; and here the libretto's affinity with a sermon is clearly evident.

Bach's setting is remarkable for its immediate impact and its wealth of forms. It is striking that movements particularly strict in formal structure often achieve the maximum expressive power. This applies, above all, to the opening chorus,* which takes the form of a passacaglia. Altogether, the passacaglia theme enters twenty-seven times, including two statements in inversion and several transferred to the top part or transposed to other keys (subdominant, dominant, relative major and its dominant). But even when bars are occasionally inserted that appear to be thematically free, the connection with the theme is maintained: it is either represented by a distinctive counterpoint,* already known from several presentations of the theme, or else its head-motive moves through the voice parts in stretto.* A certain restraint is imposed on the instruments by the passacaglia structure: concertante* opposition and collaboration are replaced by varied succession; but as a result, the role assigned to the voices is all the more significant. The three lower voice parts do not merely accompany the soprano chorale melody in a plain or lightly polyphonic* texture, as often happens elsewhere. Instead, they prepare each chorale-line entry with different themes in an imitative* texture and accompany the lines with expressive polyphony. Their function is to mediate between passacaglia and chorale. With all its polyphony, the texture of the lower voice parts belongs to the variational framework, with which it is thematically linked. On the other hand, it is also assigned the role of interpreting the sung chorale text, so that for each line Bach strives to invent a distinctive, illustrative theme for imitation.

The passacaglia theme, one of the most lapidary themes in musical history, may be traced back a long time before Bach. It fills the interval of a chromatically* descending fourth from a note normally to be understood as tonic to a concluding dominant, which then leads back to the tonic (the starting-point of the thematic repetition). Bach himself quoted the theme briefly for the first time in Cantata 4, *Christ lag in Todes Banden* (before 1714), Versus 5 ('Hier ist das rechte Osterlamm'), then again in Cantata 12, *Weinen, Klagen* (1714), whose second movement in its late adaptation as the 'Crucifixus' of the B minor Mass was to become the best-known example of its type. In the present cantata, the first presentation of the theme reads:

It is remarkable how Bach manages to unite the forms of passacaglia and chorale while imparting individual expression to various phrases of the text within the chorale lines. For example, 'forcibly torn out' is illustrated by rising imitative themes, marked rhythm, and a modulation to F major.

The duet, no. 2, is exceptionally charming and therefore widely known. The chromatically descending figure of the first movement is here replaced by a diatonically ascending figure as a symbol of hastening towards Jesus. The continuo instruments, partly by nimble movement (cellos) and partly by marking the bass notes (violone), depict in a most telling fashion the 'weak yet eager steps' with which the faithful hasten towards their Master. The canonic opening of the vocal duet parts, being a symbol of the Imitation of Christ, also has its justification in the text, as do the many reiterations of the words 'O Jesu' and 'zu dir' ('to You') and the coloraturas* on 'erfreulich' ('gratifying').

The following recitative, no. 3, is conspicuous for its large intervallic leaps, which portray the despair of the sinner. Bach does not take the opportunity of setting the numerous literal hymn quotations to their chorale melody. The closing quotation from the fifth verse, however, he sets as arioso* in the most expressive melodic style, thereby making it stand out from the *secco* of the rest of the movement. In the aria that follows, no. 4, the first reference is made to the annulment of our guilt through the Passion of Christ. It is thought that in the flute passages we can hear the 'cancelling out' of our guilt (scale figure) as well as the relieved leaping of the heart (staccato figures).

The second recitative, no. 5, is most elaborately designed. The pathos-laden recitation of the bass part and the string *accompagnato** recall similar movements in the Bach Passions. Sudden changes of tempo ('vivace', 'adagio', 'andante') and the performance indication 'con ardore' (in the *vivace* passage) heighten the dramatic effect. As in the previous recitative, wide intervallic leaps in the voice part (the second bar contains an augmented eleventh) serve as a means of expressive enhancement. The hymn quotation at the end is, on this occasion, set to the *Abgesang** of the chorale melody, which, however, is so elaborately paraphrased that several hearings are required to recognize it. This must surely be one of the most subjective and eloquent elaborations of a *cantus firmus** ever written for the human voice.

The last aria, no. 6, again opens up a new prospect. It is designed almost like a miniature concerto for solo oboe and bass voice with tutti interjections from the strings. The movement is, in fact, built out of a constant alternation between a tutti opening phrase *a*, a solo continuation *b* on the oboe, and, as point of departure or arrival, a tutti cadence *c*. The eight-bar opening ritornello is assembled thus (surprisingly, the irregular lengths of the individual phrases add up to an apparently regular eight bars for the introduction altogether):

	Tutti	Solo	Tutti	Solo	Tutti
Form:	*a*	*b*	*a*	b^1	*c*
Bars:	I	$2\frac{1}{2}$	I	$2\frac{1}{2}$	I

This structure is maintained throughout the entire A section (amounting to thirty-two bars), being varied only by the solo bass's replacing the tutti *a* by vocal insertion* in the solo passages, and by dominant transposition. The B section, inclined to the subdominant, is rather more freely structured, although the basic theme remains recognizable, and its close is even designed as a pseudo da capo*: the voice part is built into an almost unvaried, complete reprise of the ritornello before an instrumental ritornello statement brings the movement to a close. A plain four-part chorale at the end of the work leads us back again to the original hymn text and its associated melody.

Wer Dank opfert, der preiset mich, BWV 17

NBA I/21, p. 149 BC A131 Duration: *c.* 19 mins

1. [CHORUS] SATB ob I,II str bc	A $\frac{3}{4}$
'Wer Dank opfert, der preiset mich, und das ist der Weg, daß ich ihm zeige das Heil Gottes.'	'Whoever offers thanks praises Me, and that is the way by which I will show him the Salvation of God.'
2. RECITATIVO A bc	f♯–c♯ **c**
Es muß die ganze Welt ein stummer Zeuge werden Von Gottes hoher Majestät, Luft, Wasser, Firmament und Erden, Wenn ihre Ordnung als in Schnuren geht. Ihn preiset die Natur mit ungezählten Gaben, Die er ihr in den Schoß gelegt, Und was den Odem hegt, will noch mehr Anteil an ihm haben, Wenn es zu seinem Ruhm so Zung als Fittich regt.	The whole world must become a silent witness To God's high majesty: Air, water, firmament, and earth, When they are ordered in lines, as it were. Nature praises Him with countless gifts, Which He has laid in her bosom, And whatever has breath shall have a still greater share in Him When it stirs both tongue and wing to praise Him.
3. ARIA S vln I,II bc	E **c**
Herr! deine Güte reicht, so weit der Himmel ist,	Lord! Your goodness reaches as far as heaven,

Und deine Wahrheit langt, so weit die Wolken gehen.
Wüßt ich gleich sonsten nicht, wie herrlich groß du bist,
So könnt ich es gar leicht aus deinen Werken sehen.
Wie sollt man dich mit Dank davor nicht stetig preisen?
Da du uns willt den Weg des Heils hingegen weisen.

And Your truth extends as far as the clouds go.
Though I might not otherwise know how wonderfully great You are,
I could quite easily see it from Your works.
How should one not praise You constantly for them with thanksgiving?
You, on the other hand, would show us the Way of Salvation.

Parte seconda / *Second part*

4. Recitativo T bc — c♯–f♯ C

'Einer aber unter ihnen, da er sahe, daß er gesund worden war, kehrete um und preisete Gott mit lauter Stimme und fiel auf sein Angesicht zu seinen Füßen und dankete ihm; und das war ein Samariter.'

'But one of them, when he saw that he had become healthy, turned round and praised God with a loud voice and fell on his face and thanked Him; and he was a Samaritan.'

5. Aria T str bc — D C

Welch Übermaß der Güte
Schenkst du mir!
Doch was gibt mein Gemüte
Dir dafür?
Herr! ich weiß sonst nichts zu bringen,
Als dir Dank und Lob zu singen.

What excess of goodness
You give me!
Yet what does my spirit give
You in return?
Lord! I do not know what else to bring
Other than to sing You thanks and praise.

6. Recitativo B bc — b–c♯ C

Sieh meinen Willen an; kenne, was ich bin:
Leib, Leben und Verstand, Gesundheit, Kraft und Sinn,
Der' du mich läßt mit frohem Mund genießen,
Sind Ströme deiner Gnad, die du auf mich läßt fließen.
Lieb, Fried, Gerechtigkeit und Freud in deinem Geist
Sind Schätz, dadurch du mir schon hier ein Vorbild weist,
Was Gutes du gedenkst mir dorten zuzuteilen
Und mich an Leib und Seel vollkommentlich zu heilen.

Look at my will; know what I am:
Body, life, and understanding, health, strength, and mind,
Which You let me enjoy with cheerful mouth,
Are streams of Your grace, which You let flow on me.
Love, peace, righteousness, and joy in Your Spirit
Are treasures by which here already You show me an example
Of what good You intend to grant me there,
To heal me perfectly in body and soul.

7. Choral SATB bc (+ instrs) — A $\frac{3}{4}$

Wie sich ein Vatr erbarmet

As a father takes pity

Übr seine junge Kindlein klein:	**On his small young children:**
So tut der Herr uns Armen,	**So does the Lord on us wretches,**
So wir ihn kindlich fürchten rein.	**If we fear Him purely like a child.**
Er kennt das arme Gemächte,	**He knows His poor creature:**
Gott weiß, wir sind nur Staub.	**God knows we are but dust.**
Gleich wie das Gras vom Rechen,	**Just like grass from the rake,**
Ein Blum und fallendes Laub,	**A flower and falling leaf:**
Der Wind nur drüber wehet,	**The wind but blows over it**
So ist es nimmer da:	**And it is no longer there:**
Also der Mensch vergehet,	**So too does man pass away;**
Sein End, das ist ihm nah.	**His end is near.**

This cantata, composed for 22 September 1726, forms part of the series of works based on the same cycle of texts as the cantatas of Johann Ludwig Bach. The substance of the text is linked with the Sunday Gospel* reading, emphasizing mankind's debt of gratitude for the benefits conferred by God. Part I tells chiefly of the world-embracing goodness of God, whose beneficent deeds are everywhere in evidence; and Part II deals with the duty of the Christian to thank God for them. These good deeds, however (so we are told in the final recitative), are merely images of the still richer treasures that we are one day to expect in heaven.

In the text all sorts of biblical passages are interwoven. The first movement is drawn from Psalm 50.23. The words 'When they are ordered in lines, as it were' from the first recitative (no. 2) allude to Psalm 19.4 ('their line goes out into all lands'), and the beginning of the following aria, no. 3, is modelled on Psalm 36.5 ('Lord, Your goodness reaches as far as heaven, and Your truth as far as the clouds go'). The recitative that introduces Part II, no. 4, is drawn from the Sunday Gospel itself (Luke 17.15–16). And in the words 'peace, righteousness and joy in Your Spirit', the last recitative (no. 6) paraphrases a passage from Romans 14.17: 'the Kingdom of God is . . . righteousness and peace and joy in the Holy Spirit'. These many allusions reveal in the librettist a profound knowledge of the Bible, though from a Christian standpoint his praises remain partial in their restriction to the first article of faith. The concluding chorale is the third verse of the hymn *Nun lob, mein Seel, den Herren* by Johann Gramann (1530).

The music bears those unmistakable touches of uniqueness that make Bach's works stand out from the common wares of his contemporaries, including Johann Ludwig Bach. The twenty-seven-bar introductory sinfonia to the first movement is itself an impressively bold conception in structure. The chorus* that follows, which was adapted to form the finale of the Missa in G, BWV 236 in around 1738–9, is divided into two similar halves, each of which is itself bipartite. Thus the following overall form emerges (italics denote instrumental passages):

Introductory sinfonia a a[1] *b*

A Fugal exposition* x, *instruments gradually added*
Sinfonia a[1] *b* + choral insertion*
Transition, vocal-*instrumental*

A[1] Fugal exposition x^1, *instruments partly independent, partly colla parte**
Sinfonia a b + choral insertion

Such a thematically unified architectonic structure over an extensive area in Bach's mature vocal works is the product of a purposeful development from the multi-sectional form of the motet* towards a coherent large form.

A plain *secco* recitative forms a connecting link to the first aria, no. 3, whose vocal section, probably due to the length of the text, dispenses with a da capo* and is tripartite in form. A formal rounding-off is achieved, however, by combining the end of the third vocal passage with the return of the ritornello in such a way that the ritornello is assigned partly to the soprano as well as the instruments, after which just a few instrumental bars close the movement.

Part II, to be performed after the sermon, begins (in accordance with this type of libretto) with a passage from the New Testament: not, on this occasion, the words of Jesus set as a bass solo but a brief narrative which, as such, is assigned to the tenor as a plain 'Evangelist's' recitative. This brief *secco* forms, as it were, the introduction to the second aria, no. 5, which is again for tenor voice but now accompanied by the full string ensemble. In a hymn-like melodic style, it gives expression to mankind's debt of gratitude to God, stressing words such as 'Dank' ('thanks') and 'Lob' ('praise') by means of extended coloraturas.* Here again, Bach renounces a regular da capo on textual grounds, though he lets the third section be heard as a clear reminiscence of the first. Another *secco* recitative, no. 6 (arioso* passages are altogether absent from this cantata), leads to the concluding chorale, which, for all its simplicity, illustrates Bach's inventive gifts—for example, in the seemingly autumnal sounds on the words 'The wind but blows over it'.

2.15 Fifteenth Sunday after Trinity

EPISTLE: Galatians 5.25–6.10: An injunction to walk in the spirit.
GOSPEL: Matthew 6.24–34: From the Sermon on the Mount: a call not to worry or be of little faith but to strive after the Kingdom of God.

Warum betrübst du dich, mein Herz, BWV 138

NBA I/22, p. 3 BC A132 Duration: *c.* 20 mins

1. [CHORALE + RECITATIVE] SATB ob d'am I,II str bc b C

Warum betrübst du dich, mein Herz?	**Why are you distressed, my heart?**

Bekümmerst dich und trägest Schmerz	**Are you grieved and sorrowful**
Nur um das zeitliche Gut?	**Over a mere temporal matter?**
Alt	*Alto*
Ach, ich bin arm,	Ah, I am wretched,
Mich drücken schwere Sorgen.	Heavy cares oppress me.
Vom Abend bis zum Morgen	From evening till morning
Währt meine liebe Not.	This distress of mine lasts.
Daß Gott erbarm!	God have mercy!
Wer wird mich noch erlösen	Who shall deliver me
Vom Leibe dieser bösen	From the body of this wicked
Und argen Welt?	And evil world?
Wie elend ists um mich bestellt!	What a miserable plight I am in!
Ach! wär ich doch nur tot!	Ah! would that I were dead!
Vertrau du deinem Herren Gott,	**Trust your Lord God,**
Der alle Ding erschaffen hat.	**Who has created all things.**
2. Recitativo B bc	e C
Ich bin veracht',	I am despised;
Der Herr hat mich zum Leiden	The Lord has made me suffer
Am Tage seines Zorns gemacht;	On the day of His wrath;
Der Vorrat, hauszuhalten,	My stock of goods laid up to keep house
Ist ziemlich klein;	Is fairly small;
Man schenkt mir vor den Wein der Freuden	They have filled for me, in place of the wine of joy,
Den bittern Kelch der Tränen ein.	The bitter cup of tears.
Wie kann ich nun mein Amt mit Ruh verwalten,	How can I now carry out my duty in peace
Wenn Seufzer meine Speise und Tränen das Getränke sein?	When sighs are my food and tears my drink?
3. [Chorale + Recitative Scoring as in no. 1]	b C
Er kann und will dich lassen nicht,	**He cannot and will not leave you;**
Er weiß gar wohl, was dir gebricht,	**He knows full well what you lack:**
Himmel und Erd ist sein!	**Heaven and earth are His!**
Sopran	*Soprano*
Ach, wie?	Ah, what?
Gott sorget freilich vor das Vieh,	God indeed cares for the cattle,
Er gibt den Vögeln seine Speise,	He gives the birds their food,
Er sättiget die jungen Raben,	He satisfies the young ravens;
Nur ich, ich weiß nicht, auf was Weise	Only I, I do not know in what way
Ich armes Kind	I, poor child,
Mein bißchen Brot soll haben;	Shall have my little bit of bread;
Wo ist jemand, der sich zu meiner Rettung findt?	Where can anyone be found to deliver me?

Dein Vater und dein Herre Gott,
Der dir beisteht in aller Not.

Alt
Ich bin verlassen,
Es scheint,
Als wollte mich auch Gott bei meiner Armut hassen,
Da ers doch immer gut mit mir gemeint.
Ach Sorgen,
Werdet ihr denn alle Morgen
Und alle Tage wieder neu?
So klag ich immerfort;
Ach! Armut! hartes Wort,
Wer steht mir denn in meinem Kummer bei?
Dein Vater und dein Herre Gott,
Der steht dir bei in aller Not.

Your Father and your Lord God,
Who stands by you in all distress.

Alto
I am forsaken;
It seems
As though even God would hate me in my poverty,
When He always means well by me.

Ah, cares,
Are you renewed, then, every morning
And every day?
Then I shall lament for ever;
Ah, poverty! harsh word!
Who, then, will stand by me in my grief?

Your Father and your Lord God,
Who stands by you in all distress.

4. Recitativo T bc

G–D C

Ach süßer Trost! Wenn Gott mich nicht verlassen
Und nicht versäumen will,
So kann ich in der Still
Und in Geduld mich fassen.
Die Welt mag immerhin mich hassen,
So werf ich meine Sorgen
Mit Freuden auf den Herrn,
Und hilft er heute nicht, so hilft er mir doch morgen.
Nun leg ich herzlich gern
Die Sorgen unters Kissen
Und mag nichts mehr als dies zu meinem Troste wissen:

Ah, sweet comfort! If God would neither leave
Nor forsake me,
Then I can compose myself
In patience and tranquillity.
The world may still hate me,
Yet I will cast my cares
With joy upon the Lord,
And if He does not help today, then He will nonetheless help me tomorrow.
Now I am heartily glad to lay
My cares under my pillow
And wish to know nothing more than this for my comfort:

5. Aria B str bc

D 3/4

Auf Gott steht meine Zuversicht,
Mein Glaube läßt ihn walten.
  Nun kann mich keine Sorge nagen,
  Nun kann mich auch kein Armut plagen.
  Auch mitten in dem größten Leide
  Bleibt er mein Vater, meine Freude,
  Er will mich wunderlich erhalten.

In God lies my confidence,
My faith lets Him rule.
  Now no care can gnaw at me,
  Now no poverty can plague me.

  Even amidst the greatest suffering
  He remains my Father, my joy;
  He will marvellously uphold me.

6. Recitativo A bc

b C

Ei nun!
So will ich auch recht sanfte ruhn.

Why now!
Then I will rest quite peacefully.

Euch, Sorgen! sei der Scheidebrief gegeben.
Nun kann ich wie im Himmel leben.

To you, O cares, may a bill of divorce be given.
Now I can live as if in heaven.

7. [Chorale] SATB ob d'am I,II str bc b $\frac{6}{8}$

Weil du mein Gott und Vater bist,
Dein Kind wirst du verlassen nicht,
Du väterliches Herz!
Ich bin ein armer Erdenkloß,
Auf Erden weiß ich keinen Trost.

Since You are my God and Father,
You will not leave Your child,
You fatherly Heart!
I am wretched dust of the earth;
On earth I know no comfort.

This work in many ways resembles a chorale cantata,* although it was first performed on 5 September 1723—about a year before the cycle of chorale cantatas—and it does not follow their characteristic textual scheme. Thus of the fourteen-verse hymn only the first three verses are used, and the remainder of the text in no way corresponds with the other verses. On the other hand, it is a single hymn (Nuremberg, 1561; sometimes ascribed to Hans Sachs) whose first three verses are quoted in full in the first, third, and seventh movements. Due to its close link with the substance of the Gospel* reading, this hymn had been used from of old for this particular Sunday (as well as for the Seventh Sunday after Trinity).

With some skill, the anonymous librettist enriched this chorale framework with a dramatic element: the hymn to trust in God is contrasted with the individual voice of doubting care, and the regular strophic structure of the hymn with the madrigalian* freedom of recitative verse (which includes a remarkable number of short lines). Thus the first three movements form a great complex in which the lines of the chorale are constantly interrupted by contrasting recitative insertions. The turning-point occurs in the fourth movement, where the call for trust in God is accepted. At this point a place is found for the only aria in a libretto so rich in recitatives. Yet another short recitative then leads to the concluding chorale, verse 3 of the hymn.

The substance of the libretto repeatedly borrows from the Sunday Gospel, as for example in the words 'God indeed cares for the cattle' in the third movement. In addition, the librettist has not omitted to interweave various other biblical passages, ranging from vague reminiscences to clearly recognizable quotations. Compare, for example, 'Who shall deliver me from the body of this . . . world?' (no. 1) with Romans 7.24; 'When sighs are my food and tears my drink' (no. 2) with Psalm 42.3; 'He gives the birds their food, He satisfies the young ravens' (no. 3) with Psalm 147.9; and finally 'If God would neither leave nor forsake me' (no. 4) with Hebrews 13.5.

Bach's setting is as unorthodox as the structure of the text. The great opening complex, with its constant alternation of chorale lines and recitative, is designed not as a single scheme but as a free succession. The text structure prompted the composition of the opening as a dialogue—perhaps between Fear (recitative) and Hope (chorale)—similar to that of Cantatas 60 and 66/4–5. However, by assigning the recitatives variously to alto (no. 1), bass (no. 2), and soprano and finally alto again (no. 3), Bach renounces a dramatic confrontation between a single soloist and the chorale chorus.* Nor do the chorale passages form a unified contrast with the solo recitative sections; instead, each chorale insertion is differently structured. If the first three movements are conceived as a single overall complex, alternating between chorale and recitative, the following structure emerges (disregarding more detailed formal correspondences, the chorale passages are designated A, A[1], etc. and the recitative passages B, B[1], etc.):

First movement

A Hymn verse 1, lines 1–3. Each line in the order:
- Independently thematic string introduction (+ continuo) *a*
- Addition of 2 oboes d'amore,* the first with the chorale line *b*, the second with a chromatically* descending lament motive* *c*
- Entry of tenor with chorale text as arioso;* theme *a* in tenor and oboes with accompanying strings
- Entry of choir with chorale line; chorale melody sung by soprano in plain, full texture; theme *c* in the rather more agitated vocal bass

B Alto recitative accompanied by strings, with the caesuras bridged by oboe figuration

A[1] Hymn verse 1, lines 4–5, in plain, full texture with rather more lively bass; no lament theme (see text)

Second movement

B[1] Bass recitative (*secco*) accompanied by continuo

Third movement

A[2] Hymn verse 2, lines 1–3, in plain 4-part texture (choir + strings) with brief episodes between the lines (oboes + strings)

B[2] Soprano recitative accompanied by strings

A[3] Hymn verse 2, lines 4–5, in imitative* choral texture (+ instruments) based on theme of 4th chorale line; 5-part texture (violin I independent)

B[3] Alto recitative (*secco*) accompanied by continuo

A[3] Reprise of hymn verse 2, lines 4–5 (as above)

The fourth and fifth movements are also performed without a break: a *secco* recitative is followed immediately by a hymnic, dance-like bass aria (later adapted to the words 'Gratias agimus tibi' in the Missa in G, BWV 236) whose string accompaniment is dominated by the semiquaver figuration of the first violin. The text-engendered contrast with the previous complex of movements is clearly apparent. A few *secco* recitative bars then lead to the concluding chorale, whose plain choral texture, lightly broken up into polyphony,* is incorporated line by line within an independently thematic orchestral texture.

Was Gott tut, das ist wohlgetan, BWV 99

NBA I/22, p. 43 BC A133 Duration: *c.* 21 mins

1. [Chorale] S + hn ATB fl ob d'am str bc — G C

Was Gott tut, das ist wohlgetan,	**What God deals is dealt bountifully,**
Es bleibt gerecht sein Wille;	**His Will remains just;**
Wie er fängt meine Sachen an,	**However He runs my affairs,**
Will ich ihm halten stille.	**I will hold still before Him.**
Er ist mein Gott,	**He is my God,**
Der in der Not	**Who in time of trouble**
Mich wohl weiß zu erhalten;	**Well knows how to uphold me;**
Drum laß ich ihn nur walten.	**Therefore I will just let Him rule.**

2. Recitativo B bc — b C

Sein Wort der Wahrheit stehet fest	His Word of Truth stands sure
Und wird mich nicht betrügen,	**And will not deceive me,**
Weil es die Gläubigen nicht fallen noch verderben läßt.	For it lets the faithful neither fall nor perish.
Ja, weil es mich den Weg zum Leben führet,	Indeed, since it leads me on the path of Life,
So faßt mein Herze sich und lässet sich begnügen	My heart is composed and satisfied with God's
An Gottes Vatertreu und Huld	Fatherly faithfulness and favour,
Und hat Geduld,	**And has patience**
Wenn mich ein Unfall rühret.	When an incident upsets me.
Gott kann mit seinen Allmachtshänden	God can with His almighty hands
Mein Unglück wenden.	Turn round my misfortune.

3. Aria T fl bc — e 3/8

Erschüttre dich nur nicht, verzagte Seele,	Do not shake, despondent soul,
Wenn dir der Kreuzeskelch so bitter schmeckt!	When the cross's cup tastes so bitter to you!
Gott ist dein weiser Arzt und Wundermann,	God is your wise physician and miracle-man,
So dir kein tödlich Gift einschenken kann,	Who can pour you out no deadly poison,
Obgleich die Süßigkeit verborgen steckt.	Although the sweetness lies hidden.

4. Recitativo A bc — b–D C

Nun, der von Ewigkeit geschloßne Bund	Now, the covenant contracted from eternity
Bleibt meines Glaubens Grund.	Remains the ground of my faith.

Er spricht mit Zuversicht	It says with confidence
Im Tod und Leben:	In death and life:
Gott ist mein Licht,	God is my Light,
Ihm will ich mich ergeben.	**To Him will I submit.**
Und haben alle Tage	And though every day
Gleich ihre eigne Plage,	Has its own torments,
Doch auf das überstandne Leid,	Yet upon suffering withstood,
Wenn man genug geweinet,	When one has wept enough,
Kömmt endlich die Errettungszeit,	Comes at last the time of deliverance,
Da Gottes treuer Sinn erscheinet.	When God's faithful disposition appears.
5. ARIA DUETTO SA fl ob d'am bc	b c
Wenn des Kreuzes Bitterkeiten	When the bitternesses of the cross
Mit des Fleisches Schwachheit streiten,	Struggle with the weakness of the flesh,
Ist es dennoch wohlgetan.	It is nonetheless beneficial.
Wer das Kreuz durch falschen Wahn	Whoever through false opinion
Sich vor unerträglich schätzet,	Regards the cross as unbearable
Wird auch künftig nicht ergötzet.	Will not find delight in the future.
6. CHORAL SATB bc (+ instrs, fl 8va)	G c
Was Gott tut, das ist wohlgetan,	**What God deals is dealt bountifully,**
Dabei will ich verbleiben.	**I will abide by that.**
Es mag mich auf die rauhe Bahn	**Though I am driven upon a rough road**
Not, Tod und Elend treiben,	**By need, death and misery,**
So wird Gott mich	**Yet God will**
Ganz väterlich	**In a quite fatherly manner**
In seinen Armen halten;	**Hold me in His arms;**
Drum laß ich ihn nur walten.	**Therefore I let Him alone govern me.**

Bach wrote this chorale cantata* for performance on 17 September 1724. It is based on the well-known hymn by Samuel Rodigast (1674), which (like *Warum betrübst du dich* from the previous year) is easy to relate to the injunctions of the Sermon on the Mount from the Sunday Gospel.* The outer verses (nos. 1 and 6) are retained as usual, whereas the four inner verses are each paraphrased to form a madrigalian* cantata movement. In the fourth movement, the anonymous librettist alludes directly to the Sunday Gospel in the words 'And though every day has its own torments' (cf. Matthew 6.34). For the rest, he follows the succession of ideas in the hymn verses quite faithfully, even preserving almost all of the rhymes in the second movement. It is curious that he repeatedly interweaves references to the 'cross' that God imposes on man: 'When the cross's cup tastes so bitter to you' (no. 3), 'the bitternesses of the cross' and 'Whoever . . . regards the cross as unbearable' (both in no. 5). With still more emphasis than the Gospel reading or the hymn, then, the libretto refers to the sufferings imposed on the Christian in this world, as they once were on Christ Himself.

The opening chorus* is distinctly concerto-like in character. The strings state an independent theme, which is nonetheless derived from the opening of the chorale. After a cadence in bar 16, a concertino* group made up of flute, oboe d'amore,* and first violin with continuo accompaniment, enters with a reprise of the theme's head-motive on the oboe, in counterpoint* with a semiquaver figuration on the flute. After three bars, this is joined by the choir, in which the soprano, doubled by horn, delivers the chorale melody line by line in long notes—essentially minims—while the three lower voice parts accompany in a more agitated, though largely chordal texture in crotchets and quavers. The following episode for the first time brings together strings and woodwind in antiphonal groups. This entire complex for the first *Stollen** of the hymn is repeated for the second, but the *Abgesang** introduces new groupings. Passages assigned a tutti function are no longer played by strings alone but by strings and woodwind—a true instrumental tutti—and the flute occasionally yields its figurative concertante* role to the oboe. Consequently, the instrumental postlude is not identical with the opening ritornello, as it is in most cases: the tutti–solo succession is abandoned and the concertino passages are instead incorporated within the tutti complex.

The second movement, a plain *secco* recitative with continuo accompaniment, nonetheless ends with an extensive arioso* coloratura* on the word 'wenden' ('turn round'). The following aria, no. 3, nourishes afresh our suspicion that towards the end of 1724 Bach had at his disposal a particularly capable flautist. The shaping of the theme in the opening ritornello is already clearly determined by the text: although its continuation runs on in figurative demisemiquaver motion, the opening phrase strikingly depicts the shaking of the despondent soul with its shaking motive* and chromatic* descent. It thus gives a faithful representation of the affect* of the text, regardless of the injunction 'Do *not* shake, despondent soul':

It is also worth noting the down-beat opening, which at the vocal entry leads to the accentuation 'érschüttre'—contrary to the rules, but apparently intended as a means of textual interpretation.

The fourth movement is evidently designed to correspond with the second: again, it is a *secco* accompanied by continuo, ending with arioso on the word 'erscheinet' ('appears'). Bach's partiality for the flute in this cantata is clearly apparent. After its concertante role in the opening chorus and its obbligato* use in the tenor aria, it is now once more assigned a solo part, alongside the oboe d'amore, in the duet, no. 5. The strings, on the other hand, are required only in the outer movements. In the duet, Bach at first forms a trio texture for the ritornello out of the two woodwind parts with accompanying continuo. At the entry of the voice parts, which have the same theme, the texture is expanded to a quintet. As in many of Bach's duets, something of the sectional structure of the motet* is still maintained. The duets of Agostino Steffani, regarded as classics in Bach's day, were constructed according to the same principle. The B section of Bach's duet carries a new theme; and since a da capo* is not prescribed, formal rounding-off is achieved by an instrumental quotation from A within B, followed by a concluding reprise of the introductory instrumental ritornello. A plain chorale—a setting of the sixth verse of the hymn—ends the cantata.

Jauchzet Gott in allen Landen, BWV 51

NBA I/22, p. 79 BC A134 Duration: *c.* 20 mins

1. [Aria] S tr str bc	C ¢
Jauchzet Gott in allen Landen!	Shout for joy to God in all lands!
Was der Himmel und die Welt	Whatever creatures heaven and earth
An Geschöpfen in sich hält,	Contain
Müssen dessen Ruhm erhöhen,	Must exalt His glory,
Und wir wollen unserm Gott	And we too would now bring
Gleichfalls itzt ein Opfer bringen,	An offering to our God,
Daß er uns in Kreuz und Not	For in cross-bearing and distress
Allezeit hat beigestanden.	He has at all times stood by us.
2. Recitativo S str bc	a ¢
Wir beten zu dem Tempel an,	We worship towards the Temple
Da Gottes Ehre wohnet,	Where God's honour dwells,
Da dessen Treu	Where His faithfulness,
So täglich neu,	Daily renewed,
Mit lauter Segen lohnet.	Rewards us with pure blessing.
Wir preisen, was er an uns hat getan.	We praise what He has done for us.
Muß gleich der schwache Mund von seinen Wundern lallen,	Though our weak mouths must babble about His marvels,
So kann ein schlechtes Lob ihm dennoch wohlgefallen.	Yet wretched praise can nonetheless please Him.
3. Aria S bc	a $\frac{12}{8}$
Höchster, mache deine Güte	O Highest One, make Your goodness
Ferner alle Morgen neu.	Henceforth new every morning.
So soll vor die Vatertreu	Then for Your fatherly faithfulness
Auch ein dankbares Gemüte	A grateful spirit in return
Durch ein frommes Leben weisen,	Shall show through its devout life
Daß wir deine Kinder heißen.	That we are called Your children.
4. Chorale S vln I,II bc	C $\frac{3}{4}$
Sei Lob und Preis mit Ehren	**Blessing and praise with honour be to**
Gott Vater, Sohn, Heiligem Geist!	**God the Father, Son, and Holy Spirit!**
Der woll in uns vermehren,	**Who would increase in us**

Was er uns aus Gnaden verheißt,	**What He promises us out of grace,**
Daß wir ihm fest vertrauen,	**That we hold fast our confidence in Him,**
Gänzlich uns lassn auf ihn,	**Fully rely on Him,**
Von Herzen auf ihn bauen,	**Build on Him from our hearts,**
Daß unsr Herz, Mut und Sinn	**That our heart, courage, and mind**
Ihm festiglich anhangen;	**Cleave firmly to Him;**
Drauf singen wir zur Stund:	**Of this we sing at this hour:**
Amen, wir werdns erlangen,	**Amen, we will obtain it**
Glaubn wir zu aller Stund.	**If we have faith at all times.**

5. [FINALE] S tr str bc C $\frac{2}{4}$

Alleluja!	Alleluia!

The autograph score of this cantata, whose fair copy character (except in the concluding chorale and alleluia, nos. 4–5) suggests that Bach might have been adapting an existing composition,[31] dates from the period 1727–31. On the wrapper of the Leipzig performing parts, prepared between late 1729 and 1731,[32] Bach at first stated the occasion as 'In ogni tempo' ('at any time'). Only later did he add the postscript 'Dominica 15 post Trinitatis',[33] which surely explains why it is hard to find connections between the libretto and the readings for that Sunday. The splendid concertante* trumpet part points to a festive occasion; and the solo soprano part, which exceeds in range and technical demands all others in Bach's Leipzig church music, might have been conceived in the first place for female coloratura* soprano rather than boy treble. It is possible, therefore, that the cantata originated as an occasional work somewhere other than Leipzig: the court of Weißenfels and the Duke's birthday on 23 February (1729?) have been put forward[34] as a plausible venue and occasion. Thus if the work really was performed in Leipzig on the Fifteenth Sunday after Trinity (17 September) 1730, as was formerly thought,[35] then that would no doubt have been a revival rather than the original performance.

There are in the text a few, presumably fortuitous, links with the Gospel* reading for this Sunday. The words 'For in cross-bearing and distress He has at all times stood by us' (no. 1), for example, might have been chosen with Matthew 6.30 in mind ('Shall He not do it all the more for you, O you of little faith?'), and 'Make Your goodness henceforth new every morning' (no. 3) might allude to Matt. 6.34 ('Tomorrow shall take care of itself'). All told, however, the text is a jubilant song of praise and thanks for God's support, coupled with a prayer for

[31] See M. Wendt, KB, NBA I/22 (1988), p. 85.

[32] Dates of the score and parts from Dürr Chr 2, p. 101.

[33] This was pointed out by Klaus Hofmann, *BJ* 1989, 43–54 (see p.44, note 7).

[34] By Hofmann, *BJ* 1989. Uwe Wolf, however (*BJ* 1997, 145–50), has found no archival evidence in support of this hypothesis.

[35] This occasion was proposed by Dürr Chr 2.

His future faithfulness. The words 'We worship towards the Temple where God's honour dwells' (no. 2) allude to Psalms 138.2 and 26.8; and the assertion that God's faithfulness or goodness is 'daily renewed' (no. 2) and the prayer that it may be made 'new every morning' (no. 3) refer to Lamentations 3.22–3 ('The goodness of the Lord . . . is new every morning, and great is His faithfulness'). The work concludes with the additional verse (Königsberg, 1549) to Johann Gramann's hymn *Nun lob, mein Seel, den Herren* (1530), to which an alleluia is appended.

Bach's setting is so well known that it hardly requires an exhaustive commentary. As a genuine 'cantata', it demands a single voice throughout (solo soprano) and the only instruments used are trumpet (an arrangement by W. F. Bach added a second trumpet and drums), strings, and continuo. This scoring is unique in Bach's cantatas, but it occurs frequently in the works of Italian masters such as Alessandro Scarlatti. The soprano part is truly virtuosic and astonishingly high, reaching top c^3: for the Leipzig performance Bach must have had an extremely able singer at his disposal (one can hardly entertain the notion of a female soprano in conservative Leipzig). Considerable skill is also demanded of the trumpeter, whose part was certainly in good hands in Leipzig: it would have been played by the senior member of the town musicians Gottfried Reiche (1667–1734). An inclusion of virtuoso elements of this kind is characteristic of Bach's later cantatas.

The opening movement displays an unmistakable resemblance to the form of the instrumental concerto. The soloists—soprano, trumpet, and on occcasion first violin—launch into extensive coloraturas but are repeatedly interrupted or accompanied by motivic tutti interjections from the ritornello, whose head-motive, a triadic broken chord, is heard not only in the tonic C but in the related keys of G, a, e, and B (dominant of e). Despite the extent of its text (eight lines, of which seven are assigned to the middle section) the movement as a whole thereby acquires outstanding thematic unity.

The only recitative, no. 2, is in two sections. It opens as an *accompagnato** with strings (A), but the last two lines of text ('Muß gleich der schwache Mund . . .') are expanded to form a second section of their own, an arioso* accompanied by continuo only, which itself falls into two halves (B, B^1). The second aria, no. 3—like the preceding arioso,* accompanied by continuo only—is characterized by quasi-ostinato bass figures over which the soprano expands in expressive coloraturas. Despite its free-ranging vocal melody, the movement is, like the first aria, unified by its unchanging instrumental theme.

The concluding chorale is not sung in the usual way in a plain four-part setting. Instead, the chorale melody, sung unadorned by the soprano, is incorporated within an instrumental trio for two violins and continuo. A fugal 'Alleluia' follows, whose virtuoso treatment of the voice brings the cantata to a stirring final climax. So ends a work that, with all its formal concision, nonetheless unites five characteristic compositional principles of baroque music: concerto (no. 1), monody* (no. 2), ostinato* variation (no. 3), chorale arrangement (no. 4), and fugue* (no. 5).

2.16 Sixteenth Sunday after Trinity

EPISTLE: Ephesians 3.13–21: Paul prays that the community in Ephesus may be strengthened in faith.

GOSPEL: Luke 7.11–17: The raising from the dead of the youth at Nain.

Komm, du süße Todesstunde, BWV 161

NBA I/23, pp. 3, 35 BC A135 Duration: *c.* 19 mins

1. ARIA A rec I,II org (or fl I,II + vln I,II S) bc C/E♭[36] 𝄴

Komm, du süße Todesstunde,	Come, you sweet hour of death,
Da mein Geist	When my spirit
Honig speist	Shall feed on honey
Aus des Löwens Munde.	From out of the lion's mouth.
Mache meinen Abschied süße,	Make my departure sweet;
Säume nicht,	Do not linger,
Letztes Licht,	Last light,
Daß ich meinen Heiland küsse.	So that I may kiss my Saviour.
[And in 'Leipzig version'[37] only (S):]	
Herzlich tut mich verlangen	**Heartily do I long**
Nach einem selgen End,	**For a blessed end,**
Weil ich hie bin umfangen	**For I am here surrounded**
Mit Trübsal und Elend.	**By tribulation and misery.**
Ich hab Lust abzuscheiden	**I have a desire to depart**
Von dieser bösen Welt,	**From this wicked world;**
Sehn mich nach himmlschen Freuden,	**I yearn for heavenly joys:**
O Jesu, komm nur bald!	**O Jesus, do come soon!**

2. RECITATIVO T bc a–C/c–E♭ 𝄴

Welt! deine Lust ist Last!	World! your pleasure is a burden!
Dein Zucker ist mir als ein Gift verhaßt!	Your sugar is loathsome to me like poison!
Dein Freudenlicht	Your joyful light
Ist mein Komete,	Is my comet,
Und wo man deine Rosen bricht,	And where your roses are picked
Sind Dornen ohne Zahl	There are thorns without number

[36] The first specified key refers to *Chorton** (in Leipzig, *Kammerton*), the second to the *Kammerton* of the Weimar performance.

[37] In view of the deficient transmission of the work, it is unclear whether the so-called 'Leipzig version' is really by Bach or only an arrangement by someone else.

Zu meiner Seelen Qual!
Der blasse Tod ist meine Morgenröte,
Mit solcher geht mir auf die Sonne
Der Herrlichkeit und Himmelswonne.
Drum seufz ich recht von Herzensgrunde
Nur nach der letzten Todesstunde!
Ich habe Lust, bei Christo bald zu weiden,
Ich habe Lust, von dieser Welt zu scheiden.

To the anguish of my soul!
Pale death is my sunrise:
With it arises for me the sun
Of glory and heavenly bliss.
So I sigh from the very bottom of my heart
Only for the final hour of death!
I have a desire to pasture soon with Christ,
I have a desire to depart from this world.

3. ARIA T str bc — a/c $\frac{3}{4}$

Mein Verlangen
Ist, den Heiland zu umfangen
Und bei Christo bald zu sein!
Ob ich sterblich' Asch und Erde
Durch den Tod zermalmet werde,
Wird der Seele reiner Schein
Dennoch gleich den Engeln prangen.

My longing
Is to embrace the Saviour
And soon to be with Christ!
Though as mortal ash and dust
I will be crushed by death,
My soul's pure light will
Nonetheless shine forth equal to the angels.

4. RECITATIVO A rec I,II (or fl I,II) str bc — C/E♭ c

Der Schluß ist schon gemacht:
Welt, gute Nacht!
Und kann ich nur den Trost erwerben,
In Jesu Armen bald zu sterben:
Er ist mein sanfter Schlaf!
Das kühle Grab wird mich mit Rosen decken,
Bis Jesus mich wird auferwecken,
Bis er sein Schaf
Führt auf die süße Himmelsweide,
Daß mich der Tod von ihm nicht scheide!
So brich herein, du froher Todestag!
So schlage doch, du letzter Stundenschlag!

The decision is already made:
World, good night!
And if only I can gain the consolation
Of dying soon in Jesus's arms!
It is my sweet sleep!
The cool grave will cover me with roses,
Till Jesus restores me to life,
Till He leads His sheep
To that sweet heavenly pasture,
So that death may not part me from Him!
Then dawn, you joyful day of death!
Then strike, you stroke of the last hour!

5. CHOR SATB rec I,II (or fl I,II) str bc — C/E♭ $\frac{3}{8}$

Wenn es meines Gottes Wille,
Wünsch ich, daß des Leibes Last
Heute noch die Erde fülle
Und der Geist, des Leibes Gast,
Mit Unsterblichkeit sich kleide
In der süßen Himmelsfreude.
Jesu, komm und nimm mich fort!
Dieses sei mein letztes Wort.

If it is my God's Will,
I wish that the burden of the body
May fill the earth this very day,
And the spirit, the body's guest,
May be clothed with immortality
In sweet heavenly joy.
Jesus, come and take me away!
May this be my last word.

6. Choral [Scoring as in no. 5] e/g c

Der Leib zwar in der Erden	**The body will indeed in the earth**
Von Würmen wird verzehrt,	**Be consumed by worms,**
Doch auferweckt soll werden,	**Yet it shall rise again**
Durch Christum schön verklärt,	**Through Christ, beautifully transfigured,**
Wird leuchten als die Sonne	**Will shine like the sun**
Und leben ohne Not	**And live without distress**
In himmlscher Freud und Wonne.	**In heavenly joy and gladness.**
Was schadt mir denn der Tod?	**How, then, can death hurt me?**

Bach's Cantata 161 was written in Weimar and probably performed for the first time on 27 September 1716. The text is by Salomo Franck, whose cantata cycle *Evangelisches Andachts-Opffer* was actually intended for the 1715 church music at the Weimar court chapel. That year, however, owing to the public mourning that had been decreed, the cycle could only be performed in an incomplete state.

In the exegesis of Bach's day, the Gospel* reading about the youth of Nain often served as an opportunity to express the most fervent longing for death. The resurrection of a dead man by Jesus was not unthinkingly interpreted as an affirmation of life, but rather understood as a parable: Jesus will one day restore me to life, too, and therefore I can wish for myself nothing better than an early death, which will bring me closer to the desired resurrection. It is not only this basic idea that strikes today's listener as strange, but also various individual features of the libretto, regardless of its high poetic quality, towering far above the common wares of the day. A parade of learning, characteristic of the sermons of that epoch, also found its way into sacred verse. And when, in the opening aria, Franck employs the image of the spirit 'feeding on honey from out of the lion's mouth', the listener well-versed in the Bible is expected to recall Judges 14, in which Samson kills a lion and, a few days later, discovers that a swarm of bees have nested in the carcass, whereupon he eats the honey. Just as sweet nourishment comes out of the dead lion, Franck wants to say, so in truth my death will turn out to be sweet and life-giving. The end of the second movement contains an allusion to Philippians 1.23: 'I have a desire to depart and to be with Christ', a sentiment that recurs in the next movement. A play on words such as 'deine Lust ist Last' ('your pleasure is a burden', no. 2) is characteristic of Franck, as is the delight shown in antithesis: for example, 'Your joyful light is my comet' (a comet being a symbol of calamity) or 'where your roses are picked there are thorns without number', both in the second movement. All told, Franck's poem is a deeply felt, personal confession of longing for Jesus, furnishing evidence of the arousal of piety—in the wake of Pietism—even in those who did not consider themselves out-and-out Pietists.

Bach's composition is of indescribable charm. As in the *Actus Tragicus*, the sound of two recorders characterizes the peaceful, spiritualized tone that prevails. Here, the recorders are joined by a complete string ensemble. Bach unites the work, like Cantatas 80a and 185 from the same cycle, in an arch form by having the melody of the concluding chorale—the fourth verse of the hymn *Herzlich tut mich verlangen* by Christoph Knoll (1611)—played on the organ in the opening aria alongside the alto melody (in the doubtfully authentic 'Leipzig version', the first verse of the hymn sung by soprano replaced the textless instrumental quotation). Indeed, even the thematic invention of the first and third movements, and by allusion that of the fifth too, proves to be derived from the chorale melody, which thereby becomes the governing theme of the entire cantata. The first five movements become progressively further and further removed from the original form of the chorale melody, in the manner of variations, but it is then heard unaltered once more in the sixth and last movement. Compare the first thematic entry of each movement:

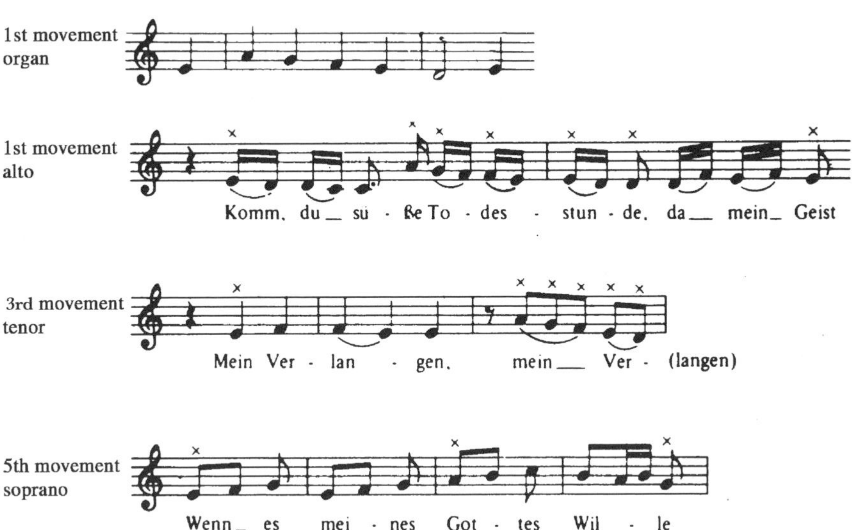

The opening aria begins with a ritornello for the two recorders (transverse flutes* in the 'Leipzig version'),[38] which move largely in parallel motion, accompanied by continuo. With the entry of the alto soloist and later the organ *cantus firmus*,* the texture is augmented from a trio to an elaborate five parts, whose internal contrast—the 'subjectively' shaped vocal melody set against the 'objective' form of the prescribed chorale melody—anticipates something of

[38] Assuming that this later version is authentic, but see above under note 37.

the impression made on the listener by the opening chorus* of the *St Matthew Passion* over a decade later.

The tenor recitative, no. 2, exhibits a form widely typical of early Bach: the *secco* with arioso* conclusion. In this particular case, it seems to be motivated by the text, which flows into the aforementioned biblical paraphrase. The third movement, a tenor aria with full string accompaniment, returns to the affect* of the opening aria: longing for death and yearning for union with Christ. Its rhythmic impulse, however, contrasts with the flowing melody of the first movement. The agitation of its triple time, at first dammed up in syncopation ('my longing'), then flowing along freely in quavers ('to embrace the Saviour'), proves to be text-engendered. The middle section, accompanied in the main by continuo only, is overshadowed by the surrounding main section, though the 'longing' head-motive recurs here also in the form of string interjections.

Bach took particular care over the composition of the following alto recitative. The accompaniment, for the full ensemble of recorders and strings, portrays in turn the prominent textual images: gentle sleep (falling scale motion in the alto, continuo, and recorders, against held notes in the strings), the raising from the dead by Jesus (semiquaver motion), and finally the striking of small death-bells on recorders and of deeper bells on *pizzicato** violins and violas, mostly on open strings.

The fifth movement, designated an aria by Franck, is set by Bach as a four-part chorus, perhaps for four singers only. The instrumental ritornello, with its falling sigh figures on the recorders, is clearly derived from the theme of the introductory aria—now, however, transformed into a triple-time version that expresses lively joy over the forthcoming union with Jesus. Arnold Schering has drawn attention to the increasing rapture as this homophonic,* song-like movement proceeds. The final line of text, 'May this be my last word', precludes a textual da capo*: the relatively long text (eight lines), set with several repetitions but without returning to previous lines, is overlaid by the musical form A B B^1 A^1.

The plain concluding chorale is augmented to five parts by an independent unison part for the two recorders, whose lively counterpoint* superimposes an unexpected highlight on the solemn old Phrygian melody: a symbol of the transfigured radiance of the resurrected body described in the text.

Christus, der ist mein Leben, BWV 95

NBA I/23, p. 67 BC A136 Duration: *c.* 21 mins

1. [Chorale + Recitative] SATB hn ob d'am I,II str bc G G–g g $\frac{3}{4}$/C ¢

Christus, der ist mein Leben,	**Christ, He is my Life,**
Sterben ist mein Gewinn;	**To die is my gain;**
Dem tu ich mich ergeben,	**To it do I surrender myself,**
Mit Freud fahr ich dahin.	**With joy do I go to that place.**

Tenor
Mit Freuden,
Ja mit Herzenslust
Will ich von hinnen scheiden.
Und hieß es heute noch: Du mußt!
So bin ich willig und bereit,
Den armen Leib, die abgezehrten Glieder,
Das Kleid der Sterblichkeit
Der Erde wieder
In ihren Schoß zu bringen.
Mein Sterbelied ist schon gemacht;
Ach, dürft ichs heute singen!
Mit Fried und Freud ich fahr dahin
Nach Gottes Willen,
Getrost ist mir mein Herz und Sinn,
Sanft und stille.
Wie Gott mir verheißen hat:
Der Tod ist mein Schlaf worden.

Tenor
With joy,
Yes, with delight of the heart
Would I depart from this place.
And were it said this very day, 'You must!',
Then I am willing and ready
To bring my poor body, my wasted limbs,
The garb of mortality,
Back to earth,
Into its bosom.
My funeral dirge is already arranged;
Ah, would that I might sing it today!
With peace and joy I go to that place,
According to the Will of God;
Established is my heart and mind,
Meek and quiet.
As God has promised me:
Death has become my sleep.

2. Recitativo S bc — d–b c

Nun, falsche Welt!
Nun hab ich weiter nichts mit dir zu tun;
Mein Haus ist schon bestellt,
Ich kann weit sanfter ruhn,
Als da ich sonst bei dir,
An deines Babels Flüssen,
Das Wollustsalz verschlucken müssen,
Wenn ich an deinem Lustrevier
Nur Sodomsäpfel konnte brechen.
Nein, nein! nun kann ich mit gelaßnerm Mute sprechen:

Now, false world!
Now I have nothing further to do with you;
My house is already in order;
I can rest far more calmly
Than I might normally with you,
Where by your rivers of Babylon
I have to swallow the salt of voluptuousness,
When in your pleasure district
I could gather only Sodom's apples.
No, no! now with a more composed spirit I can say:

3. Chorale S ob d'am I + II bc — D $\frac{3}{4}$

Valet will ich dir geben,
Du arge, falsche Welt,
Dein sündlich böses Leben
Durchaus mir nicht gefällt.
Im Himmel ist gut wohnen,
Hinauf steht mein Begier.
Da wird Gott ewig lohnen
Dem, der ihm dient allhier.

I would bid you farewell,
You evil, false world;
Your sinful, wicked life
Thoroughly displeases me.
In heaven it is good to dwell,
Above is my desire.
There God will ever reward
Him who serves Him here.

4. Recitativo T bc — b–A c

Ach könnte mir doch bald so wohl geschehn,

Ah, if only it could soon turn out so well for me

Daß ich den Tod,
Das Ende aller Not,
In meinen Gliedern könnte sehn;
Ich wollte ihn zu meinem Leibgedinge wählen
Und alle Stunden nach ihm zählen.

That I could see death,
The end of all adversity,
In my limbs;
I would choose it for my annuity
And count all the hours by it.

5. Aria T ob d'am I,II str bc — D $\frac{3}{4}$

Ach, schlage doch bald, selge Stunde,
Den allerletzten Glockenschlag!
Komm, komm, ich reiche dir die Hände,
Komm, mache meiner Not ein Ende,
Du längst erseufzter Sterbenstag!

Ah, strike soon, blessed hour,
The very last bell-stroke!
Come, come, I reach out my hands to you,
Come, make an end of my distress,
You long sighed-for day of death!

6. Recitativo B bc — b–G c

Denn ich weiß dies
Und glaub es ganz gewiß,
Daß ich aus meinem Grabe
Ganz einen sichern Zugang zu dem Vater habe.
Mein Tod ist nur ein Schlaf,
Dadurch der Leib, der hier von Sorgen abgenommen,
Zur Ruhe kommen.
Sucht nun ein Hirte sein verlornes Schaf,
Wie sollte Jesus mich nicht wieder finden,
Da er mein Haupt und ich sein Gliedmaß bin!
So kann ich nun mit frohen Sinnen
Mein selig Auferstehn auf meinen Heiland gründen.

For I know this
And believe it is quite certain
That from out of my grave
I have quite secure access to the Father.
My death is but a sleep,
By which the body, which here wastes away from cares,
Comes to rest.
If a shepherd seeks his lost sheep,
How should Jesus not find me again,
Since He is my Head and I am His member!
So I can now with a joyful mind
Found my blessed resurrection upon my Saviour.

7. Choral SATB vln I bc (+ other instrs) — G c

Weil du vom Tod erstanden bist,
Werd ich im Grab nicht bleiben;
Dein letztes Wort mein Auffahrt ist,
Todsfurcht kannst du vertreiben.
Denn wo du bist, da komm ich hin,
Daß ich stets bei dir leb und bin;
Drum fahr ich hin mit Freuden.

Since You are risen from the dead,
I will not remain in the grave;
Your last Word is my ascension,
Death's fear You can drive away.
For where You are, there do I come,
That I may always live and be with You;
Therefore I depart with joy.

This cantata dates from Bach's first year in Leipzig and received its first performance on 12 September 1723. Like Salomo Franck in Cantata 161, the anonymous librettist takes the Gospel* reading as an opportunity to express a yearning for death and contempt for the world. Although, like Franck, he does not explicitly refer to the youth of Nain, the last recitative, no. 6, which gives the motivation for the death wish, nonetheless makes the connection sufficiently clear: 'For I know . . . that from out of my grave I have quite secure access to the Father . . . so I can now with a joyful mind found my blessed resurrection upon my Saviour'. What the poet means here is that, just as Jesus once raised the youth of Nain from the dead, so too He will one day raise me.

The number of chorale verses interwoven in the text is curious and, in their present disposition, exceptional. As in Cantata 138, first performed only a week before, the first three movements form a closely connected complex of three chorale settings joined together by recitative transitions. On this occasion, however, the librettist chose not several verses of the same hymn but the first verse of three different hymns: *Christus, der ist mein Leben* (Jena, 1609), *Mit Fried und Freud ich fahr dahin* (Martin Luther, 1524; after the Nunc dimittis,* Luke 2.29–32), and *Valet will ich dir geben* (Valerius Herberger, 1613). The cantata concludes with the fourth verse of the hymn *Wenn mein Stündlein vorhanden ist* by Nikolaus Herman (1560), so that altogether it contains no fewer than four chorale verses.

The first movement begins with a ritornello for the orchestra (two oboes d'amore,* strings, and continuo) in which the thematic material of the opening section, unrelated to the chorale, is stated, an intimate melody of yearning for death, rhythmically syncopated and rich in thirds and sixths. Within this orchestral framework a plain four-part chorale is incorporated, sung by the choir and reinforced by a horn. The expansion of the line 'Sterben ist mein Gewinn' ('To die is my gain') appears to go back to an old Leipzig tradition, for a similar procedure is noted in an entry ascribed to Johann Hermann Schein in his Leipziger Cantional (1627) for singers of the hymn *Ich hab mein Sach Gott heimgestellt*: 'When they come to the tenth verse, there they sing *adagio* with a very slow pulse, because in this verse *verba emphatica* are present, namely "S t e r b n i s t m e i n G w i n n" ["To die is my gain"]'.[39] The following tenor solo, which alternates between arioso* and *secco* recitative, is united with the opening chorale through thematic interjections on the instruments. Thereafter, the second chorale enters abruptly, 'allegro', with thematic fore-imitation* of each line on the horn (the widespread view that it should be a cornett is based on a misreading) and oboes, followed by a plain choral setting, expanded to five parts by the independent voice-leading of the first violin (the other instruments double the voices). Another *secco* recitative follows, no. 2, this time accompanied only by continuo and without arioso insertions. This flows into the third chorale, no. 3, whose unadorned melody is sung by the soprano alone. The first line is accompanied only by continuo, which has an ostinato* motive,* but

[39] 'Wenn sie nun auf den 10. Versicul . . . kommen, da singen sie adagio mit einem sehr langsamen Tactu, weiln in solchen versiculis verba emphatica enthalten, nemlich S t e r b n i s t m e i n G w i n n.'

thereafter unison oboes d'amore enter with an obbligato* melody that lends the movement the character of an aria.

After this opening complex we hear, surrounded by *secco* recitatives, the only aria in the cantata, no. 5, a movement of affecting beauty. The instrumental lead is taken by the oboes d'amore, while accompanying figures on plucked strings imitate the striking of funeral bells. The curious contrast between the calm oboe melody, with its echo effects, and the lively voice part lends the aria the charm of the unusual, which is heightened by the tension-filled harmony. Like *Mit Fried und Freud* from the first movement, the plain concluding chorale is augmented to five parts by the addition of an obbligato part for the first violin, which hovers high above the rest of the texture—a symbol of the yearning for Jesus that pervades the entire work.

Liebster Gott, wenn werd ich sterben, BWV 8

NBA I/23, pp. 107, 165 BC A137 Duration: *c.* 23 mins

1. [Chorale] S + hn ATB fl picc or fl ob d'am I,II str bc — E 12/8
SATB (+ ob d'am I,II taille) fl vln conc I,II str bc — D[40]

Liebster Gott, wenn werd ich sterben?	**Dearest God, when shall I die?**
Meine Zeit läuft immer hin,	**My time keeps running on,**
Und des alten Adams Erben,	**And old Adam's heirs,**
Unter denen ich auch bin,	**Among whom I also belong,**
Haben dies zum Vaterteil,	**Have this as patrimony:**
Daß sie eine kleine Weil	**That they are for a little while**
Arm und elend sein auf Erden	**Poor and miserable on earth**
Und denn selber Erde werden.	**And then become earth themselves.**

2. Aria T ob d'am I bc — c♯ 3/4
T vln conc I bc — b

Was willst du dich, mein Geist, entsetzen,	Why would you be so afraid, my spirit,
Wenn meine letzte Stunde schlägt?	When my last hour strikes?
Mein Leib neigt täglich sich zur Erden,	My body daily inclines itself towards earth,
Und da muß seine Ruhstatt werden,	And there its resting-place must be,
Wohin man soviel tausend trägt.	Whither so many thousands are carried.

3. Recitativo A str bc — g♯–A C
A str bc — f♯–G

Zwar fühlt mein schwaches Herz	My weak heart indeed feels
Furcht, Sorge, Schmerz:	Fear, care, pain:
Wo wird mein Leib die Ruhe finden?	Where shall my body find rest?
Wer wird die Seele doch	By whom shall my soul
Vom aufgelegten Sündenjoch	From the yoke of sin put on it

[40] The details of scoring and key given first refer to the original version of 1724, the second ones to a revival of *c.* 1746/7.

Befreien und entbinden?	Be freed and released?
Das Meine wird zerstreut,	What is mine shall be dispersed,
Und wohin werden meine Lieben	And whither shall my loved ones
In ihrer Traurigkeit	In their sorrow,
Zertrennt, vertrieben?	Separated, be driven?
4. ARIA B fl picc or fl str bc	A $\frac{12}{8}$
B fl ob d'am I str bc	G
Doch weichet, ihr tollen, vergeblichen Sorgen!	Yet retreat, you mad, vain cares!
Mich rufet mein Jesus, wer sollte nicht gehn?	My Jesus calls me, who would not go?
Nichts, was mir gefällt,	Nothing that pleases me
Besitzet die Welt.	Does the world possess.
Erscheine mir, seliger, fröhlicher Morgen,	Appear to me, blessed, joyful morning,
Verkläret und herrlich vor Jesu zu stehn.	To stand before Jesus, transfigured and glorious.
5. RECITATIVO S bc	f♯–g♯ C
S bc	e–f♯
Behalte nur, o Welt, das Meine!	Keep then, O world, what is mine!
Du nimmst ja selbst mein Fleisch und mein Gebeine;	You indeed take even my flesh and my bones;
So nimm auch meine Armut hin!	Then take my poverty too!
Genug, daß mir aus Gottes Überfluß	Enough that out of God's abundance
Das höchste Gut noch werden muß;	The highest good must yet befall me;
Genug, daß ich dort reich und selig bin.	Enough that I shall there be rich and blessed.
Was aber ist von mir zu erben	But what is there for me to inherit
Als meines Gottes Vatertreu?	Other than my God's paternal faithfulness?
Die wird ja alle Morgen neu	It is indeed new every morning
Und kann nicht sterben.	And cannot die.
6. CHORAL SATB bc (+ instrs, fl picc or fl 8va)	E C
SATB bc (+ instrs, fl 8va)	D
Herrscher über Tod und Leben,	**Ruler over death and life,**
Mach einmal mein Ende gut,	**Make my end good one day,**
Lehre mich den Geist aufgeben	**Teach me to give up the ghost**
Mit recht wohlgefaßtem Mut!	**With a truly well-composed spirit!**
Hilf, daß ich ein ehrlich Grab	**Help me to have an honourable grave**
Neben frommen Christen hab	**Next to devout Christians,**
Und auch endlich in der Erde	**And finally in the earth**
Nimmermehr zuschanden werde!	**Nevermore to be ashamed!**

Like all Bach's cantatas for this Sunday, *Liebster Gott, wenn werd ich sterben* takes the Gospel* account of the raising to life of the youth at Nain as an occasion for thoughts about one's own death. Unlike the earlier works discussed above

(BWV 161 and 95), however, the cantata begins not with the desire for an early union with Jesus but rather with anxious questioning about death, which for the Christian, as one of 'old Adam's heirs', brings with it a consciousness of sin (nos. 1–3). All cares are dismissed, however, with reference to Jesus (no. 4) and to God's faithfulness, which is 'new every morning' (no. 5), one of many references in Bach's cantatas to Lamentations 3.23.

The anonymous librettist used the hymn by Caspar Neumann (before 1697) as the basis of his text, retaining the outer verses (1 and 5) word for word in movements 1 and 6. The second and third verses were paraphrased to form nos. 2 and 3; the opening lines of the fourth verse served as the model of no. 4, and the rest of this verse as that of no. 5. Although the librettist had to eke out the text with his own additions, particularly in nos. 4 and 5, he nonetheless adhered almost entirely to the hymn's train of thought. The words 'My Jesus calls me, who would not go?' in the fourth movement—in place of Neumann's 'Should I not go to Jesus?' ('Sollt ich nicht zu Jesu gehn?')—may be regarded as a reference to Jesus's words in the Gospel reading for the day, 'I say to you, arise' (Luke 7.14).

In its E major version, Bach's composition was first performed on 24 September 1724 and thus belongs to the cycle of chorale cantatas.* For a revival around 1746–7,[41] Bach transposed the work to D major. The opening chorus* presents the listener with a sublime vision of the hour of death. Within the instrumental ensemble, the two oboes d'amore,* whose expressive melody underscores the anxious questioning about the hour of death, are responsible for their own thematic development, while the other instruments imitate the sound of death-bells in a naturalistic manner, with string broken chords at low pitch and transverse flute* (originally envisaged as 'flauto piccolo'* or high recorder) at very high pitch. The chorale melody is sung by the soprano, line by line, reinforced by doubling horn and supported by the other voice parts in a chordal or lightly polyphonic texture. The melody, by Daniel Vetter, organist of the Nicolaikirche in Leipzig, had been commissioned for the burial of the Cantor Jakob Wilisius, and was no doubt especially well known in Leipzig. Bach might have borrowed it from Vetter's chorale book *Kirch- und Haus-Ergötzlichkeit*, Part II (Leipzig, 1713). Its expressiveness, which bears witness to the spread of Pietism at that time, distinguishes it clearly from the core hymns of Luther's time and of Orthodox Lutheranism, which are otherwise chiefly used in the chorale cantatas.

The four madrigalian* middle movements are divided according to textual content and musical affect* into two contrasting aria-recitative pairs. The first

[41] The late revival in D major is dated thus in Kobayashi Chr, p. 55. BG 1 gives a conflation of the two versions, and not until 1982 (NBA I/23) were they published separately. The present commentary refers to the E major version, for in many respects the D major is unable to conceal its makeshift character.

pair expresses anxious concern over death; the second pair, comfort derived from the certainty of God's faithfulness.

The death-bells of the opening movement linger in the plucked continuo notes of the tenor aria, against which the obbligato* oboe d'amore unfolds an eloquent melody. Upon its repeat in bar 2, and again by allusion in bar 3, the head-motive of the first bar is metrically diminished, which captures graphically the growing uneasiness that befalls the spirit in its thoughts of death:

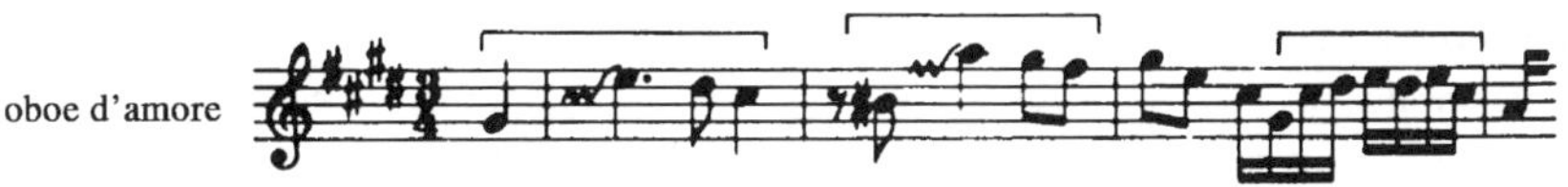

The following alto recitative, accompanied by strings, also contains anxious questions, hence the two Phrygian cadences:* this cadence, with a rising top part, was favoured by Bach as a question formula due to its dominant or half-close effect within the tonal system.

The bass aria, no. 4 strikes a quite different note. The fear of death is now overcome, and the ritornello, clearly articulated and in a joyful gigue rhythm, unfolds its theme in a homophonic* string texture together with a virtuoso concertante* flute part. This extended aria is followed by a brief *secco* recitative, after which all participants unite in the concluding chorale—borrowed from Daniel Vetter, albeit with radical alterations.

Wer weiß, wie nahe mir mein Ende, BWV 27

NBA I/23, p. 223 BC A138 Duration: *c.* 19 mins

1. [Chorale +] Recitativo S + hn ATB ob I,II str bc c $\frac{3}{4}$

Wer weiß, wie nahe mir mein Ende?	**Who knows how near is my end?**
Sopran	*Soprano*
Das weiß der liebe Gott allein,	Dear God alone knows
Ob meine Wallfahrt auf der Erden	Whether my pigrimage on earth
Kurz oder länger möge sein.	May be short or longer.
Hin geht die Zeit, her kommt der Tod.	**There goes time, here comes death.**
Alt	*Alto*
Und endlich kommt es doch so weit,	And at last it will come so far
Daß sie zusammentreffen werden.	That they will meet together.
Ach, wie geschwinde und behende	**Ah, how swiftly and nimbly**
Kann kommen meine Todesnot!	**My throes of death can come!**
Tenor	*Tenor*
Wer weiß, ob heute nicht	Who knows whether or not today
Mein Mund die letzten Worte spricht!	My mouth will say its last words!
Drum bet ich alle Zeit:	Therefore I pray always:

Mein Gott, ich bitt durch Christi Blut,	**My God, I pray by the Blood of Christ,**
Machs nur mit meinem Ende gut!	**Make all well at my end!**

2. Recitativo T bc — g–c C

Mein Leben hat kein ander Ziel,	My life has no other goal
Als daß ich möge selig sterben	Than that I may die blessed
Und meines Glaubens Anteil erben;	And inherit my faith's share;
Drum leb ich allezeit	Therefore I live always
Zum Grabe fertig und bereit,	Ready and prepared for the grave;
Und was das Werk der Hände tut,	And what the work of my hands does
Ist gleichsam, ob ich sicher wüßte,	Is as though I knew for certain
Daß ich noch heute sterben müßte;	That I had to die this very day;
Denn: Ende gut, macht alles gut!	For all is well that ends well!

3. Aria A ob da c obbl hpschd or org bc — E♭ C

Willkommen! will ich sagen,	'Welcome!', I will say
Wenn der Tod ans Bette tritt.	When death comes to my bed.
Fröhlich will ich folgen, wenn er ruft,	Gladly will I follow, when he calls,
In die Gruft.	Into the tomb.
Alle meine Plagen	All my plagues
Nehm ich mit.	I take with me.

4. Recitativo S str bc — c C

Ach, wer doch schon im Himmel wär!	Ah, would that one were already in heaven!
Ich habe Lust zu scheiden	I have a desire to depart
Und mit dem Lamm,	And with the Lamb,
Das aller Frommen Bräutigam,	The Bridegroom of all the devout,
Mich in der Seligkeit zu weiden.	To revel in Salvation.
Flügel her!	Come, wings!
Ach, wer doch schon im Himmel wär!	Ah, would that one were already in heaven!

5. Aria B str bc — g 3/4

Gute Nacht, du Weltgetümmel!	Good night, you worldly tumult!
Jetzt mach ich mit dir Beschluß;	Now I make an end with you;
Ich steh schon mit einem Fuß	I stand already with one foot
Bei dem lieben Gott im Himmel.	With our dear God in heaven.

6. Choral S I,II ATB bc (+ instrs) — B♭ C 3/4

Welt, ade! ich bin dein müde,	**World, adieu! I am weary of you,**
Ich will nach dem Himmel zu,	**I would go to heaven:**
Da wird sein der rechte Friede	**There will be true peace**
Und die ewge, stolze Ruh.	**And eternal, splendid repose.**
Welt, bei dir ist Krieg und Streit,	**World, with you is war and fighting,**
Nichts denn lauter Eitelkeit,	**Nothing but pure vanity;**
In dem Himmel allezeit	**In heaven at all times,**
Friede, Freud und Seligkeit.	**Peace, joy, and salvation.**

The anonymous librettist of this cantata, first performed on 6 October 1726, in his ideas largely accords with the text of Cantata 8. Again, the Gospel* reading provides the opportunity to ponder one's own death with cares and anxieties and to acknowledge it as the goal of life (nos. 1 and 2). At this point, however, the mood suddenly changes for no apparent reason. Death is welcomed (no. 3) and—in an allusion to Philippians 1.23—even desired (no. 4). The last two movements, nos. 5 and 6, seal the Christian's departure from this world. Here, then, the underlying concept of the Gospel reading—the raising from the dead of the youth at Nain as a symbolic anticipation of the raising of all the dead and thus a guarantee of our own resurrection—is only presupposed and not given as an interpretation (perhaps the initial exegesis was given in the sermon). This is the unspoken cause of the reversal in the meditations on death from anxiety to hope, from fear of death to a yearning for it and to contempt for this world.

This slight lack of self-sufficiency in the text (whether due to conscious dependence on outside models or out of regard for the content of the sermon, or neither) is reflected in two other, quite concrete observations. The first two lines of the third movement are modelled on an aria text by Erdmann Neumeister, from his first cantata cycle of 1700 (First Sunday after Trinity); and Bach himself borrowed a composition by Johann Rosenmüller for the concluding chorale. For this reason, Bach has been regarded as his own librettist, but beyond mere suspicion there are no solid grounds for this view. The first verse of the hymn *Wer weiß, wie nahe mir mein Ende* by Ämilie Juliane of Schwarzburg-Rudolstadt (1686) serves as the chorale in the opening movement, and the work concludes with the first verse of the hymn *Welt, ade! ich bin dein müde* by Johann Georg Albinus (1649).

The opening chorus* is related to the first movements of the chorale cantatas.* A plain chorale setting is incorporated, one line at a time, within a thematically independent orchestral texture. The chorale is, however, three times interrupted by troping recitative insertions, first after one line, then after two, sung in turn by soprano, alto, and tenor. The cohesion of this complex structure is guaranteed by the instrumental texture, whose thematic material is stated in a twelve-bar introduction. Here, two concertante* oboes play a thoughtful, anxiously questioning melody over a motivic accompanying string texture. The entry of the first oboe exhibits a distant relationship with the chorale melody, *Wer nur den lieben Gott läßt walten*, which is afterwards stated by soprano and horn:

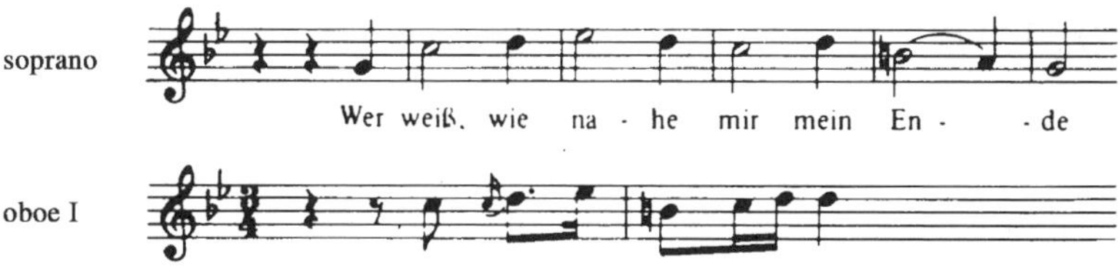

The choral texture is predominantly homophonic;* only a few ends of lines are expanded by text repetition beneath prolonged last notes in the soprano, and the last line opens with a brief passage of fore-imitation* in the lower parts. The unity of the movement relies, above all, on the motivic accompaniment figure in the strings, which temporarily migrates to the continuo but seldom ceases, being maintained even during the recitative insertions. These insertions are the only example in Bach of recitative in triple time.

A *secco* recitative, no. 2, leads to the alto aria, no. 3, with its unusual scoring for oboe da caccia* and obbligato* harpsichord with continuo. The aria is also transmitted with obbligato organ in place of harpsichord, and it is impossible to say with certainty whether the organ replaced the harpsichord at a later revival or as early as the first performance. The song-like, accessible melody enhances the charm of the unusual instrumentation.

The string accompaniment of the following recitative, no. 4, in general consists of held chords, but the repeated call of 'Flügel her!' ('Come, wings!') is each time illustrated in an unmistakable fashion by a rising scale figure on the first violin. It is also worth noting that the words 'Ah, would that one were already in heaven!' are set at the outset as an exclamation, but at the end with a Phrygian cadence* and a rising melodic line as if in a question: the end of the movement, like that of life itself, remains open.

In the introductory string ritornello of the bass aria, no. 5, the thematic material is developed out of the contrasting ideas present in the first line of text: 'Good night' gives rise to a tranquil opening phrase and 'you worldly tumult' to an agitated continuation. Only in the middle section do the interspersed tumult motives* give way to an expansive calm, after which there is an abridged da capo* of the principal section.

The charm of this cantata lies in a certain simplicity, almost innocence, which—surely by design—stands in marked contrast to the earnest theme of death. This is already implicit in the text when in the first movement, and again in the fifth, the Deity is referred to as 'our dear God'. And the music reinforces this impression through the simplicity of the two chorale movements (the second of which is borrowed from Rosenmüller), the song-like quality of the alto aria, and the serenity of Bach's setting of 'Gute Nacht' ('good night') in the bass aria.

2.17 Seventeenth Sunday after Trinity

EPISTLE: Ephesians 4.1–6: An injunction to keep the unity of the spirit.

GOSPEL: Luke 14.1–11: The healing of a man with dropsy on the Sabbath; a call for modesty.

Bringet dem Herrn Ehre seines Namens, BWV 148

NBA I/23, p. 255 BC A140 Duration: *c.* 23 mins

1. [Chorus] SATB tr str (+ ob I,II?) bc — D ¢

'Bringet dem Herrn Ehre seines Namens, betet an den Herrn im heiligen Schmuck!'

'Bring to the Lord the honour of His Name; worship the Lord in holy adornment!'

2. [Aria] T vln solo bc — b 6/8

Ich eile, die Lehren
Des Lebens zu hören,
Und suche mit Freuden das heilige Haus.
  Wie rufen so schöne
  Das frohe Getöne
  Zum Lobe des Höchsten die Seligen aus!

I hasten to hear
The testimonies of life,
And seek with joy that holy house.
  How beautifully
  That joyful ringing
  Summons the blessed to praise the Highest!

3. [Recitativo] A str bc — G c

So, wie der Hirsch nach frischem Wasser schreit,
So schrei ich, Gott, zu dir.
Denn alle meine Ruh
Ist niemand außer du.
Wie heilig und wie teuer
Ist, Höchster, deine Sabbatsfeier!
Da preis ich deine Macht
In der Gemeine der Gerechten.
O! wenn die Kinder dieser Nacht
Die Lieblichkeit bedächten!
Denn Gott wohnt selbst in mir.

Then as the hart cries out for fresh water,
So do I cry out to You, O God.
For all my repose
Is no one but You.
How holy and how precious,
Most High, is Your Sabbath feast!
There I praise Your might
In the congregation of the righteous.
Oh, if only the children of the present darkness
Might consider that loveliness!
For God Himself dwells in me.

4. [Aria] A ob d'am I,II ob da c bc — G c

Mund und Herze steht dir offen,
Höchster, senke dich hinein!
  Ich in dich, und du in mich;
  Glaube, Liebe, Dulden, Hoffen
  Soll mein Ruhebette sein.

Mouth and heart are open to You,
Most High, sink Yourself therein!
  I in You and You in me;
  Faith, love, endurance, hope
  Shall be my bed of peace.

5. Recitativo T bc — e–f♯ c

Bleib auch, mein Gott, in mir
Und gib mir deinen Geist,
Der mich nach deinem Wort regiere,
Daß ich so einen Wandel führe,
Der dir gefällig heißt,
Damit ich nach der Zeit
In deiner Herrlichkeit,
Mein lieber Gott, mit dir
Den großen Sabbat möge halten!

Abide also, my God, in me
And grant me Your Spirit;
May it direct me according to Your Word,
That I may lead such a life
As is pleasing to You,
So that after the present time,
In Your Glory,
My dear God, with You I may keep
That Sabbath of complete rest!

6. [Chorale] SATB bc (+ instrs) f♯ c

[Amen zu aller Stund	**['Amen' at every hour**
Sprech ich aus Herzensgrund;	**I say from the bottom of my heart;**
Du wollest uns tun leiten,	**We pray that You would lead us,**
Herr Christ, zu allen Zeiten,	**Lord Christ, at all times,**
Auf daß wir deinen Namen	**So that we may praise Your Name**
Ewiglich preisen. Amen.]	**For ever. Amen.]**

The text of this cantata is a very free adaptation of a six-strophe poem, *Weg, ihr irdischen Geschäfte* ('Away, you worldly affairs!'), published by Picander under the Seventeenth Sunday after Trinity in his first sacred work, *Erbauliche Gedanken* of 1725. There are a few indications in the sources of the cantata, however, that might point to a performance as early as 19 September, 1723. Is so, we might assume that Picander himself adapted his so far unpublished poem, or even that the cantata text was the original poem. However, since source criticism furnishes no incontestable proofs (indeed, nothing beyond conjecture), the possibility must also be considered that Bach's composition originated a few years later.

The libretto refers to the first part of the Gospel* reading, which deals with healing on the Sabbath. It is not concerned with the question raised in the biblical account (whether good deeds may be done on the Sabbath, contrary to the commandment of rest) but rather with the opposite: the inviolability of the feast day and the duty of man to honour God on it. The text thus begins with Psalm 29.2 and then celebrates joy in the Sabbath (no. 2) and longing for God (no. 3). The Highest One is asked to enter into the heart of the faithful (no. 4) and to bestow His Spirit upon them so that one day, 'after the present time', they may be allowed to celebrate 'that Sabbath of complete rest' with God in heaven (no. 5). The concluding chorale, sung to the melody *Auf meinen lieben Gott*, is transmitted without text. Erk, Wustmann and (following him) Neumann choose as text the sixth verse (see above, no. 6) of the well-known hymn associated with that melody (Lübeck, before 1603), but Spitta and the *Bach-Gesellschaft* preferred the closing verse—'Führ auch mein Herz und Sinn' ('Lead also my heart and mind')—of the hymn *Wo soll ich fliehen hin* by Johann Heermann (1630), which in Leipzig was sung to the same melody.[42]

Bach's composition requires an unexpectedly festive instrumental ensemble for an ordinary Sunday (trumpet, three oboes, strings, and continuo) clearly in order to add instrumental lustre to the laudatory text. The opening chorus,* in which the entire instrumental ensemble presumably participates (the meagre source transmission gives no indication of oboes, which, however, should no doubt double the strings), exhibits in essentials the following structure:

[42] Martin Petzoldt (*Musik und Kirche* 59 (1989), 235–40) suggests 'Da denn all unser Leid', verse 20 of the anonymous hymn *Frisch auf, mein Seel, in Not.*

A Instrumental sinfonia: exposition* of thematic material.

A[1] Choral fugue,* prefaced by a brief homophonic* choral block. Includes two fugal expositions on different subjects, both augmented to five-part texture by an independent trumpet part:

a 'Bringet dem Herrn Ehre seines Namens'

b 'betet an den Herrn im heiligen Schmuck'

A Choral insertion* within a reprise of the introductory sinfonia.

The main section A[1] is articulated by instrumental episodes. It is worth noting that the fugal opening is veiled by a four-bar, full-textured choral passage,[43] from which the soprano and alto, entering with the subject, detach themselves; the tenor and bass then follow. Such disguises of the underlying form are not infrequent elsewhere in Bach: a comparable case is the opening of the choral fugue 'Fecit potentiam' from the *Magnificat*, BWV 243. Bach achieves a powerful unification of the entire movement by developing both fugue subjects, *a* and *b*, out of the opening of the instrumental sinfonia, as the following comparison illustrates:

[43] This choral passage is *not* identical with the brief homophonic choral block mentioned under A[1], which precedes the fugue and is separated from it by intervening instrumental bars.

In the second movement, Bach uses a lively, figurative obbligato* part for solo violin to delineate not only the joy of the Lord's day but also the Christian's 'hastening to hear the testimonies of life'. The whole movement is pervaded by a radiant, but never frolicsome, joyfulness. By contrast, the alto recitative with string accompaniment, no. 3, strikes an almost mystical note. The eloquent declamation of the voice culminates in the words 'For God Himself dwells in me'. The mystical sinking of the soul in God, and of God in the soul, forms the content of the following aria, no. 4, which is accompanied by three oboes (probably two oboes d'amore* and an oboe da caccia*). It is curious that the continuo is on several occasions silent at the entry of the voice. According to our knowledge of the symbolism of Bach's *senza continuo* movements, this may be a symbolic representation of the self-release of the soul from earthly gravity and its unification with God. A *secco* recitative leads to the plain four-part concluding chorale, whose problematic text is discussed above.

Ach, lieben Christen, seid getrost, BWV 114

NBA I/23, p. 289 BC A139 Duration: *c.* 26 mins

1. [Chorale] S + hn ATB ob I,II str bc — g $\frac{6}{4}$

Ach, lieben Christen, seid getrost,	**Ah, dear Christians, be of good courage!**
Wie tut ihr so verzagen!	**How you despair!**
Weil uns der Herr heimsuchen tut,	**Since the Lord afflicts us,**
Laßt uns von Herzen sagen:	**Let us say from our heart:**
Die Straf wir wohl verdienet han,	**Punishment we have well deserved,**
Solchs muß bekennen jedermann,	**This everyone must acknowledge,**
Niemand darf sich ausschließen.	**No one may exclude himself.**

2. Aria T fl solo bc — d $\frac{3}{4}$ $\frac{12}{8}$ $\frac{3}{4}$

Wo wird in diesem Jammertale	Where in this vale of tears
Vor meinen Geist die Zuflucht sein?	Will there be a refuge for my spirit?
Allein zu Jesu Vaterhänden	To Jesus's fatherly hands alone
Will ich mich in der Schwachheit wenden,	I will turn in my weakness,
Sonst weiß ich weder aus noch ein.	Otherwise I know not where to turn.

3. Recitativo B bc — g–d C

O Sünder, trage mit Geduld,	O sinner, bear with longsuffering
Was du durch deine Schuld	What through your guilt
Dir selber zugezogen!	You have brought upon yourself!
Das Unrecht säufst du ja	Iniquity you do indeed drink
Wie Wasser in dich ein,	Like water,
Und diese Sünden-Wassersucht	And this sinful dropsy
Ist zum Verderben da	Is there for your ruin
Und wird dir tödlich sein.	And will be deadly for you.

Der Hochmut aß vordem von der
verbotnen Frucht,
Gott gleich zu werden;
Wie oft erhebst du dich mit
schwülstigen Gebärden,
Daß du erniedrigt werden mußt.
Wohlan, bereite deine Brust,
Daß sie den Tod und Grab nicht
scheut,
So kömmst du durch ein selig Sterben

Aus diesem sündlichen Verderben
Zur Unschuld und zur Herrlichkeit.

Pride once ate of the forbidden fruit

To become like God;
How often do you exalt yourself with
grandiloquent gestures,
So that you have to be abased.
Well then, prepare your breast
So that it shuns not death and grave;

Then, through a blessed death, you will
come
Out of this sinful corruption
Into innocence and into glory.

4. CHORAL S bc — g c

Kein Frucht das Weizenkörnlein
bringt,
Es fall denn in die Erden;
So muß auch unser irdscher Leib
Zu Staub und Aschen werden,
Eh er kömmt zu der Herrlichkeit,
Die du, Herr Christ, uns hast bereit'
Durch deinen Gang zum Vater.

A little grain of wheat brings forth no
fruit
Unless it falls into the earth;
So too must our earthly body
Turn to dust and ashes
Before it comes to the glory that
You, Lord Christ, have prepared for us
By going to the Father.

5. ARIA A ob I str bc — B♭ c

Du machst, o Tod, mir nun nicht
ferner bange,
Wenn ich durch dich die Freiheit nur
erlange,
Es muß ja so einmal gestorben sein.
Mit Simeon will ich in Friede fahren,
Mein Heiland will mich in der Gruft
bewahren
Und ruft mich einst zu sich verklärt
und rein.

You do not now make me anxious, O
death, any longer;
If I do but attain freedom through you,

Then I must indeed die one day.
With Simeon I will depart in peace;
My Saviour will preserve me in the
tomb
And one day call me to Himself,
transfigured and pure.

6. RECITATIVO T bc — g c

Indes bedenke deine Seele
Und stelle sie dem Heiland dar;
Gib deinen Leib und deine Glieder
Gott, der sie dir gegeben, wieder.
Er sorgt und wacht,
Und so wird seiner Liebe Macht
Im Tod und Leben offenbar.

Meanwhile consider your soul
And present it to the Saviour;
Yield your body and your members
Back to God who gave you them.
He cares and watches,
And thus His Love's might will be
Manifest in death and life.

7. CHORAL SATB bc (+ instrs) — g c

Wir wachen oder schlafen ein,
So sind wir doch des Herren;
Auf Christum wir getaufet sein,

Whether we wake or sleep,
We are the Lord's;
In Christ we are baptized,

Der kann dem Satan wehren.	**He can restrain Satan.**
Durch Adam auf uns kömmt der Tod,	**Through Adam death comes upon us,**
Christus hilft uns aus aller Not.	**Christ helps us out of all distress.**
Drum loben wir den Herren.	**Therefore we praise the Lord.**

The hymn by Johannes Gigas (1561) on which this chorale cantata* is based is, at first sight, not easy to connect with the readings for this Sunday. It is a penitential hymn, announcing that Christendom has well deserved the present visitation of the Lord, and that if soul and body are preserved by God's angels, the Christian will be transported through a blessed death from affliction into joy. Specific links with the Gospel* reading are made in the paraphrase by the anonymous librettist, who leaves verses 1, 3, and 6 untouched as movements 1, 4, and 7, and derives the second and third movements from verse 2 and the fifth and sixth from verses 4 and 5. The hymn source is clearly recognizable in movements 2, 5, and 6, but the third movement departs appreciably from the scanty three lines of its model and elaborates on the question of guilt over God's visitation: 'Iniquity you do indeed drink like water, and this sinful dropsy is there for your ruin and will be deadly for you'. Here, the librettist concludes that, just as Jesus healed the man with dropsy in the Gospel account, so too He has healed my sins, another form of dropsy, 'by going to the Father'. The third movement also contains another allusion to the Gospel: 'Pride once ate of the forbidden fruit to become like God; how often do you exalt yourself with grandiloquent gestures, so that you have to be abased'. Here, Jesus's warning against pride—'Whoever exalts himself shall be abased' (Luke 14.11)—is related to Adam's Fall, man's Original Sin, and at the same time applied to the present congregation. Thus understood, the following chorale ('A little grain of wheat brings forth no fruit unless it falls into the earth') and the subsequent movements, with their reference to blessedness after death, form a single great interpretation of the above words of Jesus that close the Gospel reading.

Bach's composition was written for 1 October 1724 within the context of the cycle of chorale cantatas. For the instrumental ensemble, Bach essentially adheres to the norm of two oboes, strings, and continuo, but he adds a horn to reinforce the *cantus firmus** in the outer movements and a transverse flute* in the second movement. The player of this instrument was apparently used in a different capacity in the other movements—or at least in the fully scored ones (for example, he might have played the horn in nos. 1 and 7)—for not without necessity would Bach have had 'Chorus tacet' written in the flute part of the first movement.

The opening chorus,* headed 'vivace', is constructed according to the form generally favoured by Bach for the first movements of the chorale cantatas. The lines of the hymn, sung by the choir with the melody (*Wo Gott der Herr nicht bei uns hält*) in the soprano and horn, are individually incorporated within an independent orchestral texture. Despite its thematic independence, this instrumental texture is motivically derived from the opening of the chorale, for the characteristic degrees of the scale on which it is based—third, tonic, and fifth—are heard in the first bar, both in the top part and in the continuo:

While the instrumental texture forms a consistently motivic or thematic background, almost ostinato-like in character, the choral texture of the individual chorale lines is heavily dependent upon the text. In the first two lines, the words 'getrost' ('of good courage') and 'verzagen' ('despair') immediately establish a striking contrast:

Line 1 ('getrost'): lively, chordal, homorhythmic texture
Line 2 ('verzagen'): held notes, polyphonic texture, successive quasi-imitative entries

The style of setting of the other chorale lines ranges between these two possibilities. It is also worth noting that the penultimate, sixth line adopts the opening of the continuo part (see the above music example) in a simplified vocal form as an imitative* motive* in the lower parts.

The textual contrast between dejection and consolation is also woven into the second movement. This aria, one of a series of cantata movements that require a highly skilled obbligato* flute player, incorporates a contrasting middle section. A wide-ranging flute melody in the principal section characterizes the anxious questioning as to where the spirit can find refuge in 'this vale of tears'. The middle section, with its *vivace* flowing flute figuration, then provides the answer: 'To Jesus's fatherly hands alone I will turn in my weakness'. The subsequent reprise of the principal section is hard to justify in terms of content and was no doubt included for structural reasons (da capo* form).

The third movement begins as a *secco* recitative, but it consolidates into arioso* in the middle section in order to give expressive prominence to the words 'erhebst' ('exalt') and 'erniedrigt' ('abased') which refer to the Gospel reading. In the fourth movement, the third verse of the hymn is set in continuo texture. Over a quasi-ostinato instrumental bass, the soprano sings the separate lines of the chorale in a plain, virtually unadorned fashion.

The alto aria 'Du machst, o Tod, mir nun nicht ferner bange' ('You do not now make me anxious, O death, any longer'), scored for oboe and strings, brings a joyful, confident tone into the cantata. It is the only movement in a major key, though it is repeatedly overclouded by the minor, with particularly impressive effect at the words 'Then I must indeed die one day', which were adopted almost word for word from the hymn. A brief *secco* recitative then leads swiftly to the plain four-part concluding chorale.

Wer sich selbst erhöhet, der soll erniedriget werden, BWV 47

NBA I/23, p. 321 BC A141 Duration: *c.* 24 mins

1. [Chorus] SATB ob I,II str bc	g ¢
'Wer sich selbst erhöhet, der soll erniedriget werden, und wer sich selbst erniedriget, der soll erhöhet werden.'	'Whoever exalts himself shall be abased, and whoever humbles himself shall be exalted.'
2. Aria S vln solo or org obbl bc	d 3/8
Wer ein wahrer Christ will heißen,	Whoever would be called a true Christian
Muß der Demut sich befleißen.	Must study humility.
Demut stammt aus Jesu Reich.	Humility comes from Jesus's Kingdom.
Hoffart ist dem Teufel gleich.	Haughtiness is like the Devil.
Gott pflegt alle die zu hassen,	God cultivates hatred for all those
So den Stolz nicht fahren lassen.	Who do not abandon haughtiness.
3. Recitativo B str bc	g–E♭ c
Der Mensch ist Kot, Stank, Asch und Erde;	Man is excrement, stench, ashes, and earth;
Ist's möglich, daß vom Übermut,	Is it possible that by arrogance,
Als einer Teufelsbrut,	Like a devil's brood,
Er noch bezaubert werde?	He will still be bewitched?
Ach Jesus, Gottes Sohn,	Ah Jesus, God's Son,
Der Schöpfer aller Dinge,	The Creator of all things,
Ward unsertwegen niedrig und geringe;	Became for our sake lowly and small;
Er duldte Schmach und Hohn;	He endured disgrace and mockery;
Und du, du armer Wurm, suchst dich zu brüsten?	And do you, you poor worm, seek to put on airs?
Gehört sich das vor einen Christen?	Is that fit for a Christian?
Geh, schäme dich, du stolze Kreatur,	Go, shame on you, you proud creature,
Tu Buß und folge Christi Spur;	Do penance and follow Christ's footsteps;
Wirf dich vor Gott im Geiste gläubig nieder!	Throw yourself down before God in a faithful spirit!
Zu seiner Zeit erhöht er dich auch wieder.	In due time He will exalt you again.
4. Aria B ob vln bc	E♭ c
Jesu, beuge doch mein Herze	Jesus, bow down my heart
Unter deine starke Hand,	Under Your mighty hand,

Daß ich nicht mein Heil verscherze	So that I do not trifle away my salvation,
Wie der erste Höllenbrand.	As did that first Hell-hound.
Laß mich deine Demut suchen	Let me seek Your humility
Und den Hochmut ganz verfluchen.	And wholly curse arrogance.
Gib mir einen niedern Sinn,	Grant me a lowly mind,
Daß ich dir gefällig bin!	That I may be pleasing to You!

5. CHORAL SATB bc (+ instrs) g c

Der zeitlichen Ehrn will ich gern entbehrn,	**Temporal honours I would gladly forgo,**
Du wollst mir nur das Ewge gewährn,	**If You would but grant me what is eternal,**
Das du erworben hast	**Which You have purchased**
Durch deinen herben, bittern Tod.	**With Your harsh, bitter Death.**
Das bitt ich dich, mein Herr und Gott.	**This I ask of You, my Lord and God.**

In 1720, the government secretary Johann Friedrich Helbig published a cycle of cantata librettos under the title *Auffmunterung zur Andacht* for the use of the ducal chapel at Eisenach. Most of Helbig's texts were set by Georg Philipp Telemann, the out-of-house Capellmeister. On just one occasion, as far as we know, Bach set to music a text from this cycle. Perhaps the rather meagre verse made him disinclined to undertake further settings. Or perhaps he became acquainted with the text not from Helbig's edition but from Telemann's setting. From the publication date of the printed text it was formerly concluded that Bach composed the work in 1720 while he was Capellmeister at Cöthen, during his stay at Carlsbad with the prince, in order to have a new composition ready for his intended journey to Hamburg. However, studies of the source material, no less than the mature style of the work, contradict this theory. There can be no doubt, then, about the origin of the work in Leipzig: it was written for performance on 13 October 1726.

The text refers to Jesus's warning against pride, recounted in the second part of the Sunday Gospel* reading. The opening movement quotes the last verse of this reading, Luke 14.11, word for word. This is followed by a truly Draconian sermon against pride in the second and third movements, which flows into a prayer for humility and for eternal blessedness in the second aria and the concluding chorale, nos. 4 and 5. The phrase 'So that I do not trifle away my salvation, as did that first Hell-hound' in the fourth movement alludes to a legend widespread in popular Christian belief according to which Lucifer, originally an angel, was hurled down into hell on account of his pride (in accordance with Luke 10.18). The eleventh verse of the hymn *Warum betrübst du dich, mein Herz* (anonymous, 1561) serves as the concluding chorale.

The focal point of Bach's composition is the powerful opening chorus* of 228 bars. At first hearing, the impression is formed of a stupendous choral fugue,* accompanied instrumentally and introduced by an extended, non-fugal instrumental sinfonia. Upon closer consideration, however, the movement proves to be a considerably more differentiated structure. The instrumental sinfonia—in the normal scoring of two oboes, strings, and continuo—first states an earnest theme *a*, whose homophonic* opening phrase, with its alternation between strings and wind, turns out to be derived from old polychoral practice. Quite by way of parenthesis, we then hear in the continuation (first on the oboes, in bars 12–14) the sequence that will later form the kernel of the fugue subject, depicting 'exalting oneself':

The continuo takes up this sequential motive* for two bars, and then, after a dominant cadence, an expanded and varied reprise of this first ritornello section brings about the return to the tonic. Only now, after forty-four bars, does the choir (of concertists* only?) enter with an extended fugal exposition,* whose subject, with its ascending and descending melodic line, graphically represents the first half of the text ('exalted'—'abased'). Meanwhile, the first countersubject, maintained thereafter (on which account Spitta speaks of a double fugue), illustrates the second half of the text ('humbled'—'exalted') in a melodic line that runs in contrary motion. A short, more homophonic conclusion follows, sung twice and surrounded by instrumental bars. And now the entire fugal complex (this time with ripienists?*) plus conclusion is freely recapitulated, leading to choral insertion* within a complete reprise of the instrumental sinfonia, a quasi da capo* of the introduction. A schematic representation of the movement yields a symmetrical arch form as follows (italics denote instrumental passages):

A *Sinfonia a a^1*
B Choral fugue b (solo?), *instruments part motivic (a), part silent, oboes finally thematic (5th subject entry)*
Homophonic conclusion c c
B^1 Choral fugue b^1 (tutti?), *instruments from 2nd subject entry colla parte,* oboes finally thematic (as above)*
Homophonic conclusion c c^1
A *Sinfonia a a^1* + choral insertion

The soprano aria, no. 2, has posed many problems to scholarship with regard to the scoring of its highly virtuoso instrumental obbligato* part. Today we can assert that, in all probability, the original version of 1726 required obbligato organ. In this respect, the aria proves to be a relative of 'Ich geh und suche mit Verlangen' from Cantata 49, first performed three weeks later. Not until the revival of the work in the late 1730s did Bach rethink the part, now clearly intending it for obbligato violin, as Spitta correctly recognized. Musically, the movement reflects the humility–pride antithesis of the text. The main section, which deals with humility, is characterized by a flowing and (especially in the instrumental part) elaborately figurative melody. The middle section, which is concerned with pride, is by contrast marked by an obstinate rhythm in the voice, accompanied by double-stops in the obbligato part, which is also rhythmically accentuated, while the continuo takes up the theme of the main section, thereby ensuring the formal unity of the movement.

A recitative fully scored for strings, though declaimed in a plain syllabic* style, leads to the second aria, no. 4. Here, the two obbligato instruments, oboe and violin, together with the continuo form a trio in an imitative* texture, which, with the entry of the voice, is expanded into a quartet. Since the solo bass part is assimilated to the instrumental obbligato parts both in thematic material and in rhythmic movement, a homogeneous texture emerges. The relatively long, eight-line text induced Bach to frame the aria in tripartite form without vocal da capo. In the B section, the humility–pride antithesis of the text is again strikingly illustrated using methods similar to those of the first aria: on the one hand, flowing rhythm and stepwise melody, and on the other, speech-like rests and large intervals. The work concludes with a curiously plain chorale setting.

2.18 Eighteenth Sunday after Trinity

EPISTLE: 1 Corinthians 1.4–9: Paul gives thanks for the blessing of the Gospel at Corinth.

GOSPEL: Matthew 22.34–46: Jesus names the first commandment as the love of God and of one's neighbour; he questions the Pharisees over the Christ, who is called both David's Son and David's Lord.

Herr Christ, der einge Gottessohn, BWV 96

NBA I/24, p. 3 BC A142 Duration: *c.* 17 mins

1. [CHORALE] S A + hn or trb TB fl picc ob I,II str bc F $\frac{9}{8}$

Herr Christ, der einge Gottessohn,	**Lord Christ, the only Son of God,**
Vaters in Ewigkeit,	**Of the Father in eternity,**
Aus seinem Herzn entsprossen,	**Originating from His Heart,**
Gleichwie geschrieben steht.	**As it is written.**
Er ist der Morgensterne,	**He is the Morning Star:**

Sein' Glanz streckt er so ferne
Vor andern Sternen klar.

His brightness He extends so far
That it is clear beyond all other stars.

2. Recitativo A bc — B♭–F c

O Wunderkraft der Liebe,
Wenn Gott an sein Geschöpfe denket,
Wenn sich die Herrlichkeit
Im letzten Teil der Zeit
Zur Erde senket.
O unbegreifliche, geheime Macht!
Es trägt ein auserwählter Leib
Den großen Gottessohn,
Den David schon
Im Geist als seinen Herrn verehrte,
Da dies gebenedeite Weib
In unverletzter Keuschheit bliebe.
O reiche Segenskraft! so sich auf uns ergossen,
Da er den Himmel auf, die Hölle zugeschlossen.

O wondrous power of Love!
When God considers His creatures,
When His Glory
In the final portion of time
Sinks to earth.
O incomprehensible, hidden might!
A chosen womb bears
The great Son of God,
Whom David already
In spirit honoured as his Lord;
For this woman, blessed among women,
Remained in unspotted chastity.
O rich power of blessing, poured out on us!
For He has opened heaven and shut hell.

3. Aria T fl solo bc — C c

Ach, ziehe die Seele mit Seilen der Liebe,
O Jesu, ach zeige dich kräftig in ihr!
  Erleuchte sie, daß sie dich gläubig erkenne,
  Gib, daß sie mit heiligen Flammen entbrenne,
  Ach würke ein gläubiges Dürsten nach dir!

Ah, draw my soul with bands of love,
O Jesus, ah, show Yourself powerfully therein!
  Give it light, that it may know You in faith,
  Grant that it may burn with sacred flames,
  Ah, create a thirst for faith in You!

4. Recitativo S bc — F c

Ach, führe mich, o Gott, zum rechten Wege,
Mich, der ich unerleuchtet bin,
Der ich nach meines Fleisches Sinn
So oft zu irren pflege;
Jedoch gehst du nur mir zur Seiten,
Willst du mich nur mit deinen Augen leiten,
So gehet meine Bahn
Gewiß zum Himmel an.

Ah lead me, O God, onto the path of righteousness,
I who am unenlightened,
Who in my carnal mindedness
Am so often wont to stray;
Yet if only You walk at my side,
If only You would guide me with Your eyes,
Then my path will
Certainly lead to heaven.

5. Aria B ob I,II str bc — d $\frac{3}{4}$

Bald zur Rechten, bald zur Linken
Lenkt sich mein verirrter Schritt.
Gehe doch, mein Heiland, mit,

Now to the right, now to the left
My straying steps turn.
Walk with me, my Saviour,

Laß mich in Gefahr nicht sinken,
Laß mich ja dein weises Führen
Bis zur Himmelspforte spüren!

Let me not sink into danger,
Let me indeed feel Your wise guidance
To the gates of heaven!

6. CHORAL SATB bc (+ hn obs str) F c

Ertöt uns durch dein Güte,
Erweck uns durch dein Gnad;
Den alten Menschen kränke,
Daß er neu Leben hab
Wohl hier auf dieser Erden,
Den Sinn und all Begierden
Und Gdanken habn zu dir.

Mortify us through Your goodness,
Awaken us through Your Grace;
Weaken the old man,
That he may have new life
Even here on this earth,
That our minds and all desires
And thoughts be turned to You.

This chorale cantata* is based upon the five-verse hymn by Elisabeth Creutziger (1524), which praises Christ—the true Son of God—as the Morning Star and prays for love and knowledge so that the old man may die and the new, who strives only after God, may come alive. The anonymous librettist retains the outer verses as usual, and so paraphrases the middle ones that verses 2 and 3 each become the like-numbered cantata movement and verse 4 serves as the model of movements 4 and 5. As one might expect, in these two movements the paraphrase is particularly free. Although the hymn is today mostly assigned to the Epiphany period, it had of old been associated with the Eighteenth Sunday after Trinity. The link occurs in the second part of the Gospel* reading, where Jesus questions the Pharisees concerning Christ, the Messiah, and poses them a dilemma by pointing out that in the Scriptures He is called both David's son (2 Samuel 7.12–14) and David's lord (Psalm 110.1). The reply of the faithful Christian—which might also have been made in the sermons of Bach's day—is given at the beginning of the hymn: Christ, of David's line according to ancient prophecy, is also the only Son of God; and, as the libretto states still more clearly than the hymn, 'David already in spirit honoured [Him] as his Lord' (no. 2). The second half of the cantata (and of the hymn) speaks on behalf of the assembled congregation, praying to the Lord, who is acknowledged as their Saviour, for future guidance upon the path of righeousness.

Bach's composition, written for 8 October 1724, departs in certain details from the favoured scheme of the chorale cantatas. In the opening chorus,* the chorale *cantus firmus*,* delivered in long note-values, lies in the alto rather than the more usual soprano, reinforced by horn (or trombone in a later revival, probably on 1 October 1747) in order to render it more audible. Moreover, the instrumental ensemble includes not only the usual two oboes, strings, and continuo but a 'flauto piccolo'* (a sopranino recorder in F) whose figuration is doubtless intended to portray the radiant twinkling of the morning star. For a subsequent performance, probably on 24 October 1734, Bach replaced the sopranino recorder with a 'violino piccolo', probably out of necessity. The thematically independent orchestral texture, in which the chorale lines are incorporated one at a time, influences the choral writing. For the voice parts in counterpoint* with the chorale (soprano, tenor, and bass) are not restricted to plain chordal accompaniment but develop a polyphonic, imitative* texture of countersubjects, whose thematic material is in part directly borrowed from the instrumental music and in part more distantly related to it.

A *secco* recitative, no. 2, leads to the aria 'Ach, ziehe die Seele mit Seilen der Liebe' ('Ah, draw my soul with bands of Love'), an image borrowed from Hosea 11.4. As often in this cantata cycle, Bach here gives the flautist (no doubt the recorder player from the first movement) the opportunity to display his artistry. The second recitative, no. 4, also a plain *secco*, is followed by an aria with a full accompaniment of oboes and strings, no. 5, in which the wavering of straying steps to the right and left is graphically illustrated in unmistakable figures, as well as in the alternation between strings and woodwind. In the middle section, at the words 'Walk with me, my Saviour', the predominant motive* changes: the wavering figures give way to simple, chordal step motives. The third part of the aria, which is designed according to the scheme A B C^{A}, brings a synthesis of the two motives and musically interprets the words 'Let me not sink into danger' and 'To the gates of heaven' in turn by falling and climbing melodic lines. A concluding chorale in plain four-part texture ends the work.

Gott soll allein mein Herze haben, BWV 169

NBA I/24, p. 61 BC A143 Duration: *c.* 27 mins

1. Sinfonia ob d'am I,II taille str obbl org bc — D c
2. Arioso A bc — D–f♯ 3/8/C

Gott soll allein mein Herze haben.	God alone shall have my heart.
Zwar merk ich an der Welt,	Indeed I remark of the world—
Die ihren Kot unschätzbar hält,	Which regards its muck as priceless—
Weil sie so freundlich mit mir tut,	Since it is so friendly to me,
Sie wollte gern allein	That it alone would gladly be
Das Liebste meiner Seelen sein.	The beloved of my soul.
Doch nein; Gott soll allein mein Herze haben:	But no; God alone shall have my heart:
Ich find in ihm das höchste Gut.	I find in Him the highest good.
Wir sehen zwar	We see indeed
Auf Erden hier und dar	On earth here and there
Ein Bächlein der Zufriedenheit,	A brooklet of contentment
Das von des Höchsten Güte quillet;	That swells from the goodness of the Highest;
Gott aber ist der Quell, mit Strömen angefüllet,	But God is the source, filled with streams,
Da schöpf ich, was mich allezeit	Where I draw what can at all times

Kann sattsam und wahrhaftig laben:
Gott soll allein mein Herze haben.

Sufficiently and truly refresh me:
God alone shall have my heart.

3. Aria A obbl org bc — D c

Gott soll allein mein Herze haben,
Ich find in ihm das höchste Gut.
Er liebt mich in der bösen Zeit
Und will mich in der Seligkeit
Mit Gütern seines Hauses laben.

God alone shall have my heart:
I find in Him the highest good.
He loves me in this evil time
And will in the blessed hereafter
Refresh me with the goods of His house.

4. Recitativo A bc — G–f♯ c

Was ist die Liebe Gottes?
Des Geistes Ruh,
Der Sinnen Lustgenieß,
Der Seele Paradies.
Sie schließt die Hölle zu,
Den Himmel aber auf;
Sie ist Elias Wagen,
Da werden wir im Himmel nauf
In Abrams Schoß getragen.

What is the Love of God?
The spirit's repose,
The delight of the senses,
The soul's paradise.
It shuts up hell
But opens out heaven;
It is Elijah's chariot,
Where we shall be carried up to heaven
Into Abraham's bosom.

5. Aria A str obbl org bc — b 12/8

Stirb in mir,
Welt und alle deine Liebe,
Daß die Brust
Sich auf Erden für und für
In der Liebe Gottes übe;
Stirb in mir,
Hoffart, Reichtum, Augenlust,
Ihr verworfnen Fleischestriebe!

Die in me,
World and all your love,
That my breast
May on earth for ever and ever
Cultivate the love of God;
Die in me,
Pride, wealth, lust of the eyes,
You depraved inclinations of the flesh!

6. Recitativo A bc — D–A c

Doch meint es auch dabei
Mit eurem Nächsten treu!
Denn so steht in der Schrift geschrieben:
Du sollst Gott und den Nächsten lieben.

But this also means
Be true to your neighbour!
For thus it is written in the Scriptures:
You shall love God and your neighbour.

7. Choral SATB bc (+ instrs) — A c

Du süße Liebe, schenk uns deine Gunst,
Laß uns empfinden der Liebe Brunst,
Daß wir uns von Herzen einander lieben
Und in Friede auf einem Sinn bleiben.
Kyrie eleis.

You sweet Love, grant us Your favour,
Let us feel the fervency of Your Love,
That we love each other from our hearts
And remain in peace, of the same mind.
Lord, have mercy.

Bach composed this cantata for performance on 20 October 1726. Its scoring is unusual: except for the undemanding final chorale, the vocal music is throughout assigned to solo alto, but this vocal restriction is set against a rich instrumental ensemble made up of three oboes (oboe d'amore* I and II plus taille*), strings, obbligato* organ, and continuo. Among the instruments, the obbligato organ is predominant, as in several other cantatas from this period.

The librettist is unknown. In substance, the text is linked to the first part of the Sunday Gospel.* Asked which is the greatest commandment of the Law, Jesus replies, 'You shall love the Lord your God with all your heart, with all your soul, and will all your mind. This is the first and greatest commandment; and the second is alike, namely: you shall love your neighbour as yourself'. Hence movements 2–5 are concerned with the love of God and movements 6–7 with the love of one's neighbour. The librettist ingeniously links the introductory arioso-cum-recitative, no. 2, with the aria that follows by prefacing each part of the bipartite recitative with a line of text from the aria. Each portion of the recitative text thus forms an interpretation of the motto that precedes it, and it also ends with the opening line of the aria. Thus the aria no. 3 opens with the lines:

Gott soll allein mein Herze haben,	God alone shall have my heart:
Ich find in ihm das höchste Gut.	I find in Him the highest good.

And the preceding recitative is articulated as follows:

Gott soll allein mein Herze haben.
. . . *(interpretation)* . . .
Gott soll allein mein Herze haben:
Ich find in ihm das höchste Gut.
. . . *(interpretation)* . . .
Gott soll allein mein Herze haben.

An allusion to 2 Kings 2.11 is found in the second recitative, no. 4. According to Old Testament tradition, the prophet Elijah did not die but was carried off to heaven alive in a fiery chariot. Love for God, the poet wants to say, conquers death itself and lets us partake of God's Kingdom even here on earth. The second aria, no. 5, is a paraphrase of 1 John 2.15–16: 'Do not love the world, nor what is in the world. If anyone loves the world, the Love of the Father is not in him. For everything that is in the world—the lust of the flesh, the lust of the eyes, and the life of pride—is not of the Father but of the world'. The concluding chorale is the third verse of Martin Luther's hymn *Nun bitten wir den Heiligen Geist* (1524).

In his composition, Bach made use of an earlier instrumental concerto for two of the movements. We know it as the Harpsichord Concerto in E, BWV 1053, but in its lost original form it was probably intended for a different solo instrument, possibly oboe or flute. The first movement is here employed as the introductory sinfonia, in the key of D and with the organ as obbligato instrument. The tutti instruments are strings, continuo, and (added afresh for the cantata) three oboes. This extended introductory movement in pure da capo* form gives the opening of the cantata exceptional weight. However, the following movements are also most elaborately designed. The second movement several times alternates between arioso and recitative. The motto lines quoted from the following aria, as shown above, are set as arioso, the intervening interpretative passages as recitative. Finally, the opening line is repeated once more at the close, this time in the form of recitative.

The following aria, no. 3, in which the alto is accompanied only by obbligato organ and continuo, gives the opening 'motto' line, 'God alone shall have my heart', a setting that distantly suggests an inversion of the arioso melody, but essentially it constitutes a new invention. These words were clearly conceived by the composer, as well as the librettist, as the essence of the whole cantata, and the entire art of Bach as preacher is manifest in the constantly new light in which they occur in arioso, recitative, and aria. The truly virtuoso organ part of the aria also helps to emphasize their significance.

A plain recitative, no. 4, leads to the second aria, no. 5, 'Stirb in mir, Welt und alle deine Liebe' ('Die in me, world and all your love'), which is also drawn from the instrumental concerto mentioned above. The organ is again assigned the function of obbligato instrument, and the alto voice part is most ingeniously woven into the existing movement. This aria ought to count as one of the most striking proofs of how a piece can gain rather than lose from its adaptation in the context of a new work. The revised version, grown far beyond the original concerto movement, is undoubtedly one of the most inspired vocal pieces that Bach ever wrote. In the E major Harpsichord Concerto, the movement is designated 'Siciliano'; in the cantata, it is probably conceived as a dirge for the delights of this world. But what a dirge! Here, celebrated by earthly means, is a passionate submersion in heavenly love.

Whereas the call to love God here acquires an exceptionally rich form, even for Bach, the call to love one's neighbour follows in a brief recitative, no. 6, which leads directly to the concluding chorale. Here, the personally uttered decision of the individual Christian to love only God and one's neighbour is joined by the prayer of the entire congregation that the Holy Spirit may assist them in this love.

2.19 Nineteenth Sunday after Trinity

Epistle: Ephesians 4.22–8: Put on the new man, who is created after God.
Gospel: Matthew 9.1–8: The healing of a man sick of the palsy.

Ich elender Mensch, wer wird mich erlösen, BWV 48

NBA I/24, p. 107 BC A144 Duration: *c.* 16 mins

1. [Chorus] SATB tr or hn ob I + II str bc — g $\frac{3}{4}$

'Ich elender Mensch, wer wird mich erlösen vom Leibe dieses Todes?'

'Wretched man that I am, who shall redeem me from the body of this death?'

2. Recitativo A str bc — E♭–B♭ c

O Schmerz, o Elend, so mich trifft,
Indem der Sünden Gift
Bei mir in Brust und Adern wütet:
Die Welt wird mir ein Siech- und Sterbehaus,
Der Leib muß seine Plagen
Bis zu dem Grabe mit sich tragen.
Allein die Seele fühlet
Den stärksten Gift,
Damit sie angestecket;
Drum, wenn der Schmerz den Leib des Todes trifft,
Wenn ihr der Kreuzkelch bitter schmecket,
So treibt er ihr ein brünstig Seufzen aus.

O pain, O misery that afflicts me,
As sin's poison
Rages in my breast and veins:
The world becomes for me a house of sickness and death,
The body must carry its torments
With it to the grave.
But the soul feels
The strongest poison,
With which it is infected;
Therefore when pain strikes this body of death,
When the cross's cup tastes bitter to the soul,
This cup drives from the soul a fervent sigh.

3. Choral SATB bc (+ instrs) — B♭ c

Solls ja so sein,
Daß Straf und Pein
Auf Sünde folgen müssen,
So fahr hie fort
Und schone dort
Und laß mich hie wohl büßen.

Should it indeed be so
That punishment and pain
Must follow sin,
Then carry on here
And spare me there,
And let me here truly repent.

4. Aria A ob solo bc — E♭ $\frac{3}{8}$

Ach lege das Sodom der sündlichen Glieder,
Wofern es dein Wille, zustöret darnieder!
Nur schone der Seele und mache sie rein,
Um vor dir ein heiliges Zion zu sein.

Ah, lay down the Sodom of my sinful members,
If it is Your Will, destroyed!
Only spare my soul and make it pure,
So that it may be a sacred Zion for You.

5. Recitativo T bc — B♭ c

Hier aber tut des Heilands Hand	But here the Saviour's hand works
Auch unter denen Toten Wunder.	Wonders even among the dead.
Scheint deine Seele gleich erstorben,	Though your soul seems to have died,
Der Leib geschwächt und ganz verdorben,	Your body weakened and quite ruined,
Doch wird uns Jesu Kraft bekannt:	Yet Jesus's power is made known to us:
Er weiß im geistlich Schwachen	In the spiritually weak He knows how
Den Leib gesund, die Seele stark zu machen.	To make the body healthy, the soul strong.

6. Aria T str + ob I + II bc — g 3/4

Vergibt mir Jesus meine Sünden,	Forgive me, O Jesus, my sins,
So wird mir Leib und Seel gesund.	Then my body and soul shall be healthy.
Er kann die Toten lebend machen	He can make the dead alive
Und zeigt sich kräftig in den Schwachen,	And shows His power in the weak;
Er hält den längst geschloßnen Bund,	He keeps the long-contracted Covenant,
Daß wir im Glauben Hilfe finden.	So that in faith we find salvation.

7. Choral SATB bc (+ instrs) — g c

Herr Jesu Christ, einiger Trost,	**Lord Jesus Christ, my only comfort,**
Zu dir will ich mich wenden;	**To You I will turn;**
Mein Herzleid ist dir wohl bewußt,	**My affliction is well known to You:**
Du kannst und wirst es enden.	**You can and will end it.**
In deinen Willen seis gestellt,	**On Your Will may it all depend;**
Machs lieber Gott, wie dirs gefällt:	**Let it be done, dear God, as You please:**
Dein bin und will ich bleiben.	**Yours I am and will remain.**

The text of this cantata (the work of an anonymous librettist) is related to the Sunday Gospel.* Jesus's words to the man sick with the palsy, 'Your sins are forgiven you', turn our thoughts to our own sinfulness, which is in need of forgiveness. The starting point is a saying of Paul's from Romans 7.24 (no. 1). The following recitative compares sin with a poison that leads to death: though the body ends in death under torment, the death of the soul in sin is still more ruinous. Therefore the poet prays to God that the Christian might be spared, if not in the body, then at least in the soul. This prayer is first uttered in the words of the fourth verse of the hymn *Ach Gott und Herr* by Martin Rutilius (1604), then again in the following aria, no. 4. Now, however, the poet finds consolation in the Gospel story, for since Jesus 'works wonders even among the dead' (cf. Psalm 88.10) and 'shows His power in the weak' (cf. 2 Corinthians 12.9), He will also—contrary to all appearances—'make the body healthy, the soul strong' (nos. 5 and 6). The cantata ends confidently with the twelfth verse of the hymn *Herr Jesu Christ, ich schrei zu dir* (Freiberg, 1620).

Bach's composition belongs to his first Leipzig cycle of cantatas and was first performed on 3 October 1723. It shares with several other cantatas of that year an instrumentally quoted chorale melody in the opening movement. In Bach's day, this melody was mostly associated with the hymn *Herr Jesu Christ, du höchstes Gut*, and, judging by its content, it is quite conceivable that this is the hymn to which Bach refers. However, since the hymn *Herr Jesu Christ, ich schrei zu dir* was sung to the same melody, Bach was here able to establish a connection with the concluding chorale, whose first verse can just as well be linked with the instrumental quotation. In structure, the opening movement is three-layered. The introduction, played by strings and continuo, is thematically independent. Its opening phrase also forms a counterpoint* to the vocal theme, which is developed after twelve bars in an imitative* texture. This theme, which opens with a striking leap of a sixth, pervades the entire movement in manifold exchanges of parts and canonic formations. Alongside it, the trumpet[44] and unison oboes deliver the chorale melody line by line in canon* at the lower fourth.

The alto recitative, no. 2, is also characterized by wide intervallic leaps, whose effect is all the more expressive against the background of held string chords. It is unexpectedly followed by a plain four-part chorale, no. 3, whose rich harmonization (especially in the closing line, 'And let me here truly repent') nonetheless in its own way maintains the expressive weight of the preceding movements. The following aria, no. 4, takes us aback with its melodic charm. No threatening sentence of punishment, no contrition is uttered here, but rather a childlike meekness in the prayer that at least the soul should be spared. The obbligato* oboe melody, with its almost dance-like swing, is also taken over by the voice, so that alto and oboe form a homogeneous duet over an unthematic continuo part.

The second aria, no. 6, separated from the first only by a brief *secco* recitative, resembles it in its rhythmic swing, which is here still more perceptible in the constant alternation between hemiola* 3/4 (a disguised form of 3/2) and standard 3/4 time. The compact string texture (with oboe I doubling violin I) lends the aria a confident character that accords with the text and stands out in relief against the tenderness of the previous aria.

Wo soll ich fliehen hin, BWV 5

NBA I/24, p. 135 BC A145 Duration: *c.* 23 mins

1. [Chorale] S + tr da t ATB ob I,II str bc g C

Wo soll ich fliehen hin,	**Where shall I flee?**
Weil ich beschweret bin	**For I am burdened**

[44] It is not altogether clear what *cantus firmus* instrument is intended in nos. 1, 3, and 7. The title-page has 'Corno', the score (in no. 1) 'Tromba', and the part 'Clarino'.

Mit viel und großen Sünden?	**With many great sins.**
Wo soll ich Rettung finden?	**Where shall I find deliverance?**
Wenn alle Welt herkäme,	**If all the world came here,**
Mein Angst sie nicht wegnähme.	**It would not take away my distress.**
2. RECITATIVO B bc	d–g C
Der Sünden Wust hat mich nicht nur befleckt,	Sin's filth has not only defiled me,
Er hat vielmehr den ganzen Geist bedeckt,	It has covered my whole spirit;
Gott müßte mich als unrein von sich treiben;	God would have to drive me away from Him as unclean;
Doch weil ein Tropfen heilges Blut	Yet since a drop of sacred Blood
So große Wunder tut,	Does such great marvels,
Kann ich noch unverstoßen bleiben.	I can still remain unrejected.
Die Wunden sind ein offnes Meer,	His Wounds are an open sea
Dahin ich meine Sünden senke,	Wherein I sink my sins,
Und wenn ich mich zu diesem Strome lenke,	And when I go to these waters,
So macht er mich von meinen Flecken leer.	He makes me without blemish.
3. ARIA T vla (vln? vln picc?) solo bc	E♭ $\frac{3}{4}$
Ergieße dich reichlich, du göttliche Quelle,	Gush forth abundantly, you divine spring,
Ach, walle mit blutigen Strömen auf mich!	Ah, well up with streams of Blood on me!
Es fühlet mein Herze die tröstliche Stunde,	My heart feels the comforting hour:
Nun sinken die drückenden Lasten zu Grunde,	Now the oppressing burdens sink to the bottom,
Es wäschet die sündlichen Flecken von sich.	The sinful blemishes are washed away.
4. RECITATIVO A ob I bc	c C
Mein treuer Heiland tröstet mich,	My faithful Saviour comforts me;
Es sei verscharrt in seinem Grabe,	Let them be buried in His grave,
Was ich gesündigt habe;	**Whatever sins I have committed;**
Ist mein Verbrechen noch so groß,	However great my offence,
Er macht mich frei und los.	He makes me free and liberated.
Wenn Gläubige die Zuflucht bei ihm finden,	When the Faithful find refuge with Him,
Muß Angst und Pein	Anguish and pain must
Nicht mehr gefährlich sein	No longer be perilous
Und alsobald verschwinden;	And presently disappear;
Ihr Seelenschatz, ihr höchstes Gut	Their souls' treasure, their highest good
Ist Jesu unschätzbares Blut;	Is Jesus's priceless Blood;

Es ist ihr Schutz vor Teufel, Tod und Sünden,	It is their protection against devil, death, and sins,
In dem sie überwinden.	Through which they overcome.
5. Aria B tr str + ob I + II bc	B♭ c
Verstumme, Höllenheer,	Be silent, host of hell,
Du machst mich nicht verzagt!	You do not make me despair!
Ich darf dies Blut dir zeigen,	I ought to show you this Blood,
So mußt du plötzlich schweigen,	Then you must suddenly be quiet;
Es ist in Gott gewagt.	It is ventured in God's Name.
6. Recitativo S bc	g c
Ich bin ja nur das kleinste Teil der Welt,	I am indeed only the smallest part of the world,
Und da des Blutes edler Saft	And since Your Blood's noble sap
Unendlich große Kraft	Contains infinitely great power
Bewährt erhält,	Preserved within it,
Daß jeder Tropfen, so auch noch so klein,	So that every drop, however small,
Die ganze Welt kann rein	Can make the whole world pure
Von Sünden machen,	Of sin,
So laß dein Blut	Then do not let Your Blood
Ja nicht an mir verderben,	Indeed be wasted on me;
Es komme mir zugut,	May it be for my benefit,
Daß ich den Himmel kann ererben.	So that I can inherit heaven.
7. Choral SATB bc (+ instrs)	g c
Führ auch mein Herz und Sinn	**Lead my heart and mind**
Durch deinen Geist dahin,	**There through Your Spirit,**
Daß ich mög alles meiden,	**That I may avoid everything**
Was mich und dich kann scheiden,	**That can separate me and You,**
Und ich an deinem Leibe	**And of Your Body**
Ein Gliedmaß ewig bleibe.	**Ever remain a member.**

This work is a chorale cantata,* written for performance on 15 October 1724. It is based on the eleven-verse hymn by Johann Heermann (1630), whose first and last verses are retained unaltered, whereas the inner verses are very freely paraphrased by the anonymous librettist (verses 2–3 in movement no. 2, verse 4 in no. 3, verses 5–7 in no. 4, verse 8 in no. 5, and verses 9–10 in no. 6).

As in the cantata for the previous year, BWV 48, the starting-point is the phrase 'Your sins are forgiven you' from the Sunday Gospel,* spoken by Jesus to the man sick of the palsy. These words arouse our own consciousness of sin and lead to the assurance that Jesus has not only healed the palsied man but, through the sacrifice of His life, has taken away the sins of all mankind. The first three movements gradually draw our attention away from the hopeless situation of the sinner and towards the expiatory death of Jesus. The fourth movement brings the turning-point towards a more confident attitude. The sinner now finds the strength to rebel against Satan (no. 5) and prays to God that Christ's death may bring him the redemption for which he longs (nos. 6 and 7).

From among the many verses of the hymn, the librettist must have endeavoured to find powerful images for the two arias in order to furnish the composer in each case with the basis of a distinctive *inventio* that would allow sufficient contrast between them. For the third movement, his choice fell on the image of the 'divine spring', full of Christ's Blood, which washes away the blemishes of sin—an image truly baroque in its graphic character, but suggested by numerous biblical passages, such as Psalm 51.2 and 7 or Revelation 1.5 and 7.14. For the fifth movement, the librettist chose the image of the raging 'host of hell', whose tumult must cease all of a sudden at the bidding of the faithful Christian when he shows them Jesus's Blood.

In his setting, Bach takes a further step. By setting the recitatives nos. 2 and 6 as plain *secco* but combining the recitative no. 4 with the chorale *cantus firmus** on the oboe, he emphasizes the movement that brings the decisive turning-point from despair to consolation and also creates a formal centre around which the other movements (in outward order: aria, recitative, and chorale) are symmetrically grouped.

The opening movement follows the customary form. The individual chorale lines are sung by the soprano, with trumpet reinforcement, and supported by the other choral parts within an independent orchestral texture for two oboes, strings, and continuo. As in Cantata 114, first performed a fortnight earlier, the thematic material of the orchestra, though independent and developed autonomously, is nonetheless derived from the chorale melody, as revealed by a comparison between the opening of the introductory sinfonia and the soprano *cantus firmus*:

As early as bar 3, an inversion of this instrumental theme occurs which might be construed as a derivative of the second chorale line, itself a free inversion of the first:

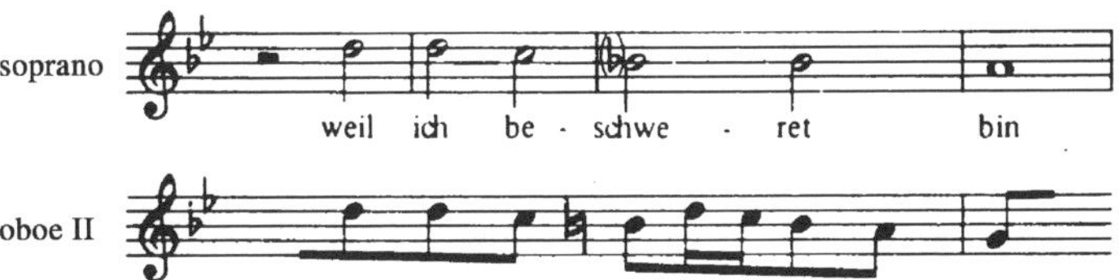

This theme, together with its inversion, pervades the entire opening chorus,* dominating not only the instrumental texture but even the vocal substructure of the chorale melody, which is mostly imitative,* less often chordal, in texture. In addition, three- and four-note scale figures, both ascending and descending, occur frequently in the orchestra. These may be linked with the other thematic material, if not as derivatives of the theme, then at least in their general affinity with the opening of the chorale.

Although the two arias have many features in common, their musical design reflects their contrasting textual content. The third movement is scored for a few parts only,[45] whereas the fifth is fully scored. The third, in accordance with its text, is pervaded by a flowing melody in running semiquavers on the viola, the fifth by briefly articulated, sharply accentuated rhythms interspersed with 'speaking' rests. Here, the introductory three-quaver motive,* which often recurs later, seems to anticipate the opening of the text, 'Verstumme' ('Be silent'). A certain resemblance between the two arias is revealed in their use of instrumental figures. In the third movement, this figurative element, in conjunction with a four-note falling scale, is used to characterize the abundantly flowing spring. And when in the fifth movement similar figures are heard in the first violin (doubled by oboes), an element of textual interpretation may be detected therein, for it is this very spring that causes the 'host of hell' to be silent. The concluding chorale takes the usual form of a plain four-part setting reinforced by instruments.

Ich will den Kreuzstab gerne tragen, BWV 56

NBA I/24, p. 175 BC A146 Duration: *c.* 21 mins

1. ARIA B ob I,II taille str bc — g 3/4

Ich will den Kreuzstab gerne tragen,	I would gladly carry the Cross-beam:
Es kömmt von Gottes lieber Hand,	It comes from God's dear hand,
Der führet mich nach meinen Plagen	It leads me after my torments
Zu Gott in das gelobte Land.	To God in the Promised Land.
Da leg ich den Kummer auf einmal ins Grab,	There I lay my sorrows all at once in the grave,
Da wischt mir die Tränen mein Heiland selbst ab.	There my Saviour Himself wipes away my tears.

2. RECITATIVO B vc bc — B♭ C

Mein Wandel auf der Welt	My life in the world
Ist einer Schiffahrt gleich:	Is like a voyage:
Betrübnis, Kreuz und Not	Sorrow, affliction, and distress
Sind Wellen, welche mich bedecken	Are waves that cover me
Und auf den Tod	And with death

[45] The obbligato instrument is not specified. Viola and perhaps also Violin I come under consideration, and even violoncello piccolo is not unlikely.

Mich täglich schrecken;
Mein Anker aber, der mich hält,
Ist die Barmherzigkeit,
Womit mein Gott mich oft erfreut.

Der rufet so zu mir:
Ich bin bei dir,
Ich will dich nicht verlassen noch versäumen!
Und wenn das wütenvolle Schäumen
Sein Ende hat,
So tret ich aus dem Schiff in meine Stadt,
Die ist das Himmelreich,
Wohin ich mit den Frommen
Aus vielem Trübsal werde kommen.

Daily terrify me;
But my anchor that holds me
Is the mercy
With which my God often gladdens me.
He calls to me thus:
I am with you,
I will neither leave nor forsake you!

And when the stormy foaming
Comes to an end,
I shall disembark from the ship into my city,
Which is the Kingdom of Heaven,
Wherein with the devout
I shall come out of much tribulation.

3. Aria B ob I solo bc — B♭ C

Endlich, endlich wird mein Joch
Wieder von mir weichen müssen.
Da krieg ich in dem Herren Kraft,
Da hab ich Adlers Eigenschaft,
Da fahr ich auf von dieser Erden
Und laufe sonder matt zu werden.
O gescheh es heute noch!

Finally, finally, my yoke
Must be removed from me again.
Then I shall gain strength in the Lord,
Then I shall be as an eagle,
Then I shall mount up from this earth
And run without growing weary.
Oh, may it happen this very day!

4. Recitativo B str bc — g–c C $\frac{3}{4}$

Ich stehe fertig und bereit,
Das Erbe meiner Seligkeit
Mit Sehnen und Verlangen
Von Jesus' Händen zu empfangen.
Wie wohl wird mir geschehn,
Wenn ich den Port der Ruhe werde sehn.
Da leg ich den Kummer auf einmal ins Grab,
Da wischt mir die Tränen mein Heiland selbst ab.

I stand ready and prepared
To receive my inheritance of salvation
With longing and yearning
From Jesus's hands.
How good it will be for me
When I shall see the harbour of rest!

There I lay my sorrows all at once in the grave,
There my Saviour Himself wipes away my tears.

5. Choral SATB bc (+ instrs) — c C

Komm, o Tod, du Schlafes Bruder,
Komm und führe mich nur fort;
Löse meines Schiffleins Ruder,
Bringe mich an sichern Port!
Es mag, wer da will, dich scheuen,
Du kannst mich vielmehr erfreuen;
Denn durch dich komm ich herein
Zu dem schönsten Jesulein.

Come, O Death, you brother of sleep,
Come and lead me forth;
Loosen my little ship's rudder,
Bring me to a secure harbour!
Let whoever so wishes shun you:
You can rather delight me;
For through you I come therein
To the most lovely Jesus.

The unknown poet of this exceptionally well-written text evidently relied on the libretto *Ich will den Kreuzweg gerne gehen* for the Twenty-first Sunday after Trinity from Erdmann Neumeister's first cycle of cantatas. Bach's librettist may be the one who, three weeks earlier in Cantata 27, had paraphrased some lines by Neumeister from the same cycle. Once again, the starting-point of the present text is the Sunday Gospel.* Though the healing of the man sick with the palsy is not expressly mentioned, it is he who is represented by the follower of Christ who takes His Cross-beam upon himself and goes his way under torment until the prophecy of Revelation 7.17 comes true, namely that 'God shall wipe away the tears from their eyes' (no. 1), for, as the Gospel reading tells us, Jesus has forgiven the sins of the palsied man.

The image of the second movement is also borrowed from the Gospel reading, which opened with the words: 'There He went on board a ship and passed over and came into His own city' (Matthew 9.1). In this movement, our whole life is conceived as a voyage whose goal is our native city, the Kingdom of Heaven. A few biblical allusions again help to embellish this image. It was in the words 'I will neither leave nor forsake you' that the writer of the Epistle to the Hebrews (13.5) quoted God's promise to Joshua (1.5); and the image of him who shall come 'out of much tribulation' is drawn from Revelation 7.14.

The third movement is full of joy over the anticipated union with the Saviour. Its text is based on the well-known words of Isaiah 40.31: 'Those who wait upon the Lord shall gain new strength so that they mount up with wings like an eagle, so that they run and do not grow weary'. At the same time, a longing for death is aroused: 'Oh, may it happen this very day'. This longing permeates the fourth movement and the concluding chorale, which is the sixth verse of the hymn *Du, o schönes Weltgebäude* by Johann Franck (1653). Before this chorale, however, two lines from the opening movement recur, a peculiarity that we observe on several occasions within the librettos of Bach's third cycle of cantatas.

Bach set this text to music for performance on 27 October 1726, titling the autograph score 'Cantata à Voce Sola e Stromenti'; for with the exception of the four-part concluding chorale, the vocal writing is throughout assigned to solo bass. It is thus one of the few Bach cantatas that bear the designation 'cantata' in the original source.

In the opening aria, scored for the entire instrumental ensemble, Bach chose an unconventional tripartite form with the scheme A A^1 B, probably out of regard for the length of the text. This may be construed as a free *Bar* form* (with the first *Stollen** cadencing in the dominant, the second in the subdominant) in accordance with the rhyme scheme of the text, *ab ab cc*. Section A draws its thematic material from the opening ritornello, whose head-motive* (which recurs in the continuo at the close of each ritornello and of vocal sections A and A^1), with its augmented second, unmistakably symbolizes the Cross-beam, while the stepwise falling sigh figures that follow represent the action of carrying it. Bach's instrumental introductions are not always as patently invented with a view to the ensuing textual underlay as this one is:

The second section, A^1, largely corresponds with the first, but its opening is significantly varied on account of the new text, 'It leads me after my torments . . .'. The third section, the *Abgesang** of the *Bar* form, brings with it an entirely new and highly declamatory vocal theme in triplets to the words 'There I lay my sorrows all at once in the grave'. Only the instruments refer to the A-sections by quoting the sigh figures mentioned above in the caesuras of the voice part, and this also establishes a connection with the concluding ritornello statement.

The second movement depicts the waves of the sea in its cello accompaniment figures. As soon as the text reaches the words 'I shall disembark from the ship, this accompanying motion comes to rest. The second aria, no. 3, with its joyful atmosphere, forms an emphatic contrast with the first. Solo oboe and bass unite in a concertante* duet full of extended figurations and coloraturas.* Unlike the opening movement, this aria follows the customary da capo* form. The fourth movement begins as a recitative with string accompaniment, but after only seven bars it flows into a slightly varied version of the second half of the *Abgesang* from the opening aria. Even the sigh figures of the strings recur in their aforementioned function as a bridge over the vocal caesuras, giving the work a pronounced formal rounding-off seldom encountered in Bach.

Despite its plain four-part style, the concluding chorale is an exceptional masterpiece. The choice of text is itself felicitous, since the wish to be united with Jesus through death is associated with the image of the ship moored in a 'secure harbour', a return to the metaphor of life as a voyage in the second movement. In Bach's setting, the alteration of the opening of Crüger's melody (Leipzig, 1649) from two minims–𝅗𝅥 𝅗𝅥–to the form 𝄾𝅗𝅥 ♩, with its emphatic syncopation on the word 'Komm', is truly inspired. So, too, is the setting of the penultimate line where, in the resolution of a diminished seventh onto a G major chord, we seem able to perceive directly the soul passing through the pain of death into glory:

[Untexted Fragment] BWV Anh. I 2 BC A147

The autograph of the motet* *Der Geist hilft unser Schwachheit auf*, composed for the funeral of Johann Heinrich Ernesti, Rector of the Thomasschule, on 24 October 1729, contains on its reverse side a six-bar fragment:

J. J. Concerto Dominica 19 post Trinitatis à 4 Voci. 1 Violino Conc: 2 Violini/ Viola e Cont. di Bach.

Evidently this is the opening of a cantata; and since the Nineteenth Sunday after Trinity took place that year on 23 October, the day before the performance of the motet, we may confidently date the fragment 1729. The composition of this cantata was probably interrupted by the intervening death and at least temporarily discontinued. It is questionable whether the sketch may be linked with Picander's text for this Sunday from his cycle of 1728–9, *Gott, du Richter der Gedanken*, for that text already existed in 1728 and could therefore have been set during the previous year.

2.20 Twentieth Sunday after Trinity

EPISTLE: Ephesians 5.15–21: 'Walk circumspectly . . . be filled with the spirit'.
GOSPEL: Matthew 22.1–14: The parable of the royal wedding feast.

Ach! ich sehe, itzt, da ich zur Hochzeit gehe, BWV 162

NBA I/25, pp. 3, 23 BC A148 Duration: *c.* 18 mins

1. ARIA B str bc (+ cor da t in Leipzig version only) a/b[46] c

Ach! ich sehe,	Ah! I see
Itzt, da ich zur Hochzeit gehe,	Now, as I go to the wedding,
Wohl und Wehe!	Weal and woe!
Seelengift und Lebensbrot,	Poison of the soul and Bread of Life,
Himmel, Hölle, Leben, Tod!	Heaven and hell, life and death!
Himmelsglanz und Höllenflammen	Brightness of heaven and flames of hell
Sind beisammen!	Are together!
Jesu, hilf, daß ich bestehe!	Jesus, help me to endure it!

2. RECITATIVO T bc C–d/D–e c

O großes Hochzeitsfest,	O great wedding feast,
Darzu der Himmelskönig	To which the King of Heaven
Die Menschen rufen läßt!	Lets mankind be called!
Ist denn die arme Braut,	Is the poor bride, then—
Die menschliche Natur, nicht viel zu schlecht und wenig,	Human nature—not far too low and insignificant
Daß sich mit ihr der Sohn des Höchsten traut?	For the Son of the Highest to marry her?
O großes Hochzeitsfest,	O great wedding feast,
Wie ist das Fleisch zu solcher Ehre kommen,	How has human flesh come to such honour
Daß Gottes Sohn	That God's Son
Es hat auf ewig angenommen?	Has for ever taken it upon Himself?
Der Himmel ist sein Thron,	Heaven is His throne,
Die Erde dient zum Schemel seinen Füßen,	The earth serves as His footstool,

[46] The first specified key refers to the *Chorton** of the Weimar performance, the second to the Leipzig revival in *Kammerton*.

Noch will er diese Welt
Als Braut und Liebste küssen!
Das Hochzeitmahl ist angestellt!
Das Mastvieh ist geschlachtet;
Wie herrlich ist doch alles zubereitet!
Wie selig ist, den hier der Glaube leitet,
Und wie verflucht ist doch, der dieses Mahl verachtet!

Yet He would kiss this world
As His bride and beloved!
The wedding supper is ready!
The fattened cattle are slaughtered;
How grandly is everything prepared!
How blessed is he whom Faith leads here,
And how cursed is he who makes light of this meal!

3. Aria [extant:] S bc — d/e 12/8

Jesu, Brunnquell aller Gnaden,
Labe mich elenden Gast,
Weil du mich berufen hast!
Ich bin matt, schwach und beladen,
Ach! erquicke meine Seele,
Ach! wie hungert mich nach dir!
Lebensbrot, das ich erwähle,
Komm! vereine dich mit mir!

Jesus, fountain of all Grace,
Refresh me, your wretched guest,
For You have called me!
I am dull, weak, and heavy laden;
Ah! refresh my soul;
Ah! how I hunger for You!
Bread of Life that I have chosen,
Come! unite with me!

4. Recitativo A bc — a–C/b–D C

Mein Jesu, laß mich nicht
Zur Hochzeit unbekleidet kommen,
Daß mich nicht treffe dein Gericht!

Mit Schrecken hab ich ja vernommen,
Wie du den kühnen Hochzeitgast,
Der ohne Kleid erschienen,
Verworfen und verdammet hast!
Ich weiß auch mein Unwürdigkeit:
Ach! schenke mir des Glaubens Hochzeitkleid;
Laß dein Verdienst zu meinem Schmucke dienen!
Gib mir zum Hochzeitkleide
Den Rock des Heils, der Unschuld weiße Seide!
Ach! laß dein Blut, den hohen Purpur, decken
Den alten Adamsrock und seine Lasterflecken,
So werd ich schön und rein
Und dir willkommen sein,
So werd ich würdiglich das Mahl des Lammes schmecken.

My Jesus, let me not come
To the wedding improperly dressed,
So that Your Judgement may not fall on me!
With terror I have indeed learnt
How that rash wedding guest,
Who appeared without proper attire,
Was cast out and condemned by You!
I know my own unworthiness:
Ah! give me the wedding-dress of Faith;
Let Your merit serve as my adornment!
Grant me as wedding garment
The robe of Salvation, the white linen of innocence!
Ah! let Your Blood, that high purple, cover
The old cloak of Adam and its blemishes of vice;
Then I shall be fair and pure
And welcome to You;
Then I shall worthily taste the Supper of the Lamb.

5. ARIA DUETTO AT bc C/D $\frac{3}{4}$

In meinem Gott bin ich erfreut!	In my God I am delighted!
Die Liebesmacht hat ihn bewogen,	Love's power has stirred Him,
Daß er mir in der Gnadenzeit	So that in this time of Grace,
Aus lauter Huld hat angezogen	Out of pure benevolence, He has dressed me
Die Kleider der Gerechtigkeit.	In the garments of righteousness.
Ich weiß, er wird nach diesem Leben	I know that after this life
Der Ehren weißes Kleid	The white robe of honour
Mir auch im Himmel geben.	Will He give me in heaven.

6. CHORAL SATB bc (+ instrs) a/b C

Ach, ich habe schon erblicket	**Ah, I have already glimpsed**
Diese große Herrlichkeit.	**This great glory.**
Itzund werd ich schön geschmücket	**Now I shall be beautifully adorned**
Mit dem weißen Himmelskleid;	**In the white robe of heaven;**
Mit der güldnen Ehrenkrone	**In the golden crown of honour**
Steh ich da für Gottes Throne,	**I shall stand there before God's throne**
Schaue solche Freude an,	**And see such joy**
Die kein Ende nehmen kann.	**As can have no end.**

This cantata was written in Weimar and probably first performed on 25 October 1716, a month after Cantata 161. Bach drew the text from the cycle *Evangelisches Andachts-Opffer* by Salomo Franck. As the title of this collection indicates, the libretto relates to the Sunday Gospel.* Explicit reference is made to this reading, which preceded the cantata performance, in the fourth movement: 'With terror I have indeed learnt how that rash wedding guest, who appeared without proper attire, was cast out and condemned by You'. The poet is alarmed by the great crisis that mankind has brought upon himself: he is in a position to accept or reject God's invitation—a situation characterized by Jesus's closing words in the Gospel reading, 'Many are called but few are chosen'.

After an introductory reference to the decisive significance of God's invitation—'weal or woe' hangs upon my reply—the text considers God's great Love which is made manifest in this invitation (no. 2), asks Jesus for the refreshing Bread of Life (no. 3) and to help the guest to prove worthy of the invitation (no. 4), and ends with the joyful hope that, 'after this life' in heaven, God will grant a robe of honour to the sinner, whom He has made righteous through Jesus's death (no. 5). The same reflections are taken up again in the concluding chorale, the seventh verse of the hymn *Alle Menschen müssen sterben* by Johann Rosenmüller (1652).

Franck's language is often emphatic, even enraptured, culminating in the mystical, yearning call to Christ, 'Come! unite with me'. A favourite stylistic resource of Franck's—the formation of poetic compounds, such as 'Seelengift und Lebensbrot' or 'Himmelsglanz und Höllenflammen'—is everywhere in evidence, alongside the use of biblical images such as 'Heaven is His throne, the earth serves as His footstool' (after Isaiah 66.1), 'Then I shall worthily taste the Supper of the Lamb' (after Revelation 19.9), or 'He has dressed me in the garments of righteousness' (after Isaiah 61.10). All in all, Franck once more turns out to be the most original and, from a poetic standpoint, probably the most powerful of the poets whose texts Bach set for this Sunday.

Bach revived this composition during his first year in Leipzig, on 10 October 1723, and for that purpose he made a few alterations. A part for corno da tirarsi (slide trumpet) was evidently added for this performance. Furthermore, the *Kammerton** tuning of Bach's Leipzig performances had to be taken into account by upward transposition, which meant that the instrumental parts had to be written out afresh. Although we possess two sets of parts, this performing material appears to be incomplete. At all events, it is most unlikely that the soprano aria, no. 3, is to be performed as transmitted, with the accompaniment of continuo only, which is on its own in the ritornellos and lacks sufficient substance for this purpose. Since Bach's score is lost, however, we lack any clear indication as to what part or parts should be added (possibly oboe?).[47]

The cantata begins with a bass aria accompanied, so far as we can tell, by the entire instrumental ensemble. In places, after the entry of the voice, the imitative,* polyphonic texture of the three upper parts (violin I, II, and viola, supported by slide trumpet) grows into a highly sonorous, dense web of sound through which the head-motive—

—is repeatedly heard. The two recitatives, nos. 2 and 4, composed as *secco*, surround an aria, no. 3, which, as already mentioned, is incomplete.

The alto-tenor duet, no. 5, is again accompanied only by continuo, which incidentally supports the theory of a missing obbligato* part in no. 3: otherwise, four successive continuo movements would, exceptionally, be found within a six-movement cantata. In this duet, however, nothing appears to be missing. The quasi-ostinato continuo part is characterized by broad, vigorous intervallic leaps. The multi-sectional form of Bach's duets—here A B B C A C—often reveals a clear relationship with the series form of the motet.*

The plain concluding chorale employs for the hymn *Alle Menschen müssen sterben* a melody that was evidently most unusual, since Johannes Zahn (*Die Melodien der deutschen evangelischen Kirchenlieder*, No. 6783) was unable to trace it

[47] Winfried Radeke has published in keyboard score a reconstruction for practical use with two violins (Wiesbaden, n.d.).

elsewhere. It is also found, however, in a chorale arrangement (*DdT* 26/7, p. 32) by the Weimar town organist Johann Gottfried Walther, a distant cousin of Bach's, and thus seems to have been known at that time in Weimar.

Schmücke dich, o liebe Seele, BWV 180

NBA I/25, p. 43 BC A149 Duration: *c.* 28 mins

1. [CHORALE] SATB rec I,II ob taille str bc F $\frac{12}{8}$

Schmücke dich, o liebe Seele,	**Adorn yourself, O dear soul,**
Laß die dunkle Sündenhöhle,	**Leave the dark cave of sin,**
Komm ans helle Licht gegangen,	**Come into the bright light,**
Fange herrlich an zu prangen;	**Begin to shine gloriously;**
Denn der Herr voll Heil und Gnaden	**For the Lord, full of Salvation and Grace,**
Läßt dich itzt zu Gaste laden.	**Lets you be invited now as His guest.**
Der den Himmel kann verwalten,	**He who can conduct the affairs of heaven**
Will selbst Herberg in dir halten.	**Would Himself take lodgings within you.**

2. ARIA T fl bc C c

Ermuntre dich: dein Heiland klopft,	Stir yourself: your Saviour knocks;
Ach, öffne bald die Herzenspforte!	Ah, open soon the door of your heart!
Ob du gleich in entzückter Lust	Even though in enraptured delight
Nur halb gebrochne Freudenworte	Only half-broken words of joy
Zu deinem Jesu sagen mußt.	Must you say to your Jesus.

3. RECITATIVO [+ CHORALE] S vc picc bc a–F c

Wie teuer sind des heilgen Mahles Gaben!	How precious are the gifts of the sacred meal!
Sie finden ihresgleichen nicht.	Their like is not to be found.
Was sonst die Welt	Whatever else the world
Vor kostbar hält,	Regards as valuable
Sind Tand und Eitelkeiten;	Are trifles and vanities;
Ein Gotteskind wünscht diesen Schatz zu haben	A child of God wishes to have this treasure
Und spricht:	And says:
Ach wie hungert mein Gemüte,	**Ah, how my spirit hungers,**
Menschenfreund, nach deiner Güte!	**Friend of man, for Your goodness!**
Ach, wie pfleg ich oft mit Tränen	**Ah, how often with tears am I wont**
Mich nach dieser Kost zu sehnen!	**To pine for this food!**
Ach, wie pfleget mich zu dürsten	**Ah, how I am wont to thirst**
Nach dem Trank des Lebensfürsten!	**For the drink of the Prince of Life!**
Wünsche stets, daß mein Gebeine	**Wishing ever that my bones**
Mich durch Gott mit Gott vereine.	**May be united through God with God.**

4. RECITATIVO A rec I,II bc B♭ c

Mein Herz fühlt in sich Furcht und Freude;	My heart feels within fear and joy;

Es wird die Furcht erregt,
Wenn es die Hoheit überlegt,
Wenn es sich nicht in das Geheimnis findet,
Noch durch Vernunft dies hohe Werk ergründet.
Nur Gottes Geist kann durch sein Wort uns lehren,
Wie sich allhier die Seelen nähren,
Die sich im Glauben zugeschickt.
Die Freude aber wird gestärket,
Wenn sie des Heilands Herz erblickt
Und seiner Liebe Größe merket.

Fear is aroused
When it considers His majesty,
When it finds no way into the mystery,
Nor through reason fathoms this high deed.
Only God's Spirit can teach us through His Word
How souls are nourished here
Who array themselves in faith.
Joy is strengthened, however,
When it sees the Saviour's Heart
And marks the greatness of His Love.

5. ARIA S rec I,II ob taille str bc — B♭ 3/4

Lebens Sonne, Licht der Sinnen,
Herr, der du mein alles bist!
Du wirst meine Treue sehen
Und den Glauben nicht verschmähen
Der noch schwach und furchtsam ist.

Sun of life, Light of the senses,
Lord, You who are my all!
You will see my faithfulness
And not scorn faith
That is still weak and fearful.

6. RECITATIVO B bc — F c

Herr, laß an mir dein treues Lieben,
So dich vom Himmel abgetrieben,
Ja nicht vergeblich sein!
Entzünde du in Liebe meinen Geist,
Daß er sich nur nach dem, was himmlisch heißt
Im Glauben lenke
Und deiner Liebe stets gedenke.

Lord, to me let Your faithful Love,
Which brought You down from heaven,
Indeed not be in vain!
Enkindle my spirit in love,
So that only to what is called heavenly
May it turn in faith
And ever be mindful of Your Love.

7. CHORAL SATB bc (+ instrs) — F c

Jesu, wahres Brot des Lebens,
Hilf, daß ich doch nicht vergebens
Oder mir vielleicht zum Schaden
Sei zu deinem Tisch geladen.
Laß mich durch dies Seelenessen
Deine Liebe recht ermessen,
Daß ich auch, wie itzt auf Erden,
Mög ein Gast im Himmel werden.

Jesus, true Bread of Life,
Help me not to be invited in vain,
Or perhaps to my harm,
To Your table.
Let me through this souls' meal
Estimate Your Love aright,
That, as now on earth, I may also
Become a guest in heaven.

The Gospel* reading for this Sunday can easily be associated with Holy Communion. Indeed, the equivalent passage in Luke (14.16–24) speaks explicitly of a 'great supper' rather than the wedding feast mentioned by Matthew. Accordingly, the anonymous librettist of this chorale cantata* bases his text upon Johann Franck's communion hymn of 1649. He retains the outer verses, nos. 1 and 9, literally as well as verse 4 but so paraphrases the others that verses 2 and 7 become the arias, nos. 2 and 5, and verses 3, 5–6, and 8 the recitatives, nos. 3, 4, and 6. The paraphrase accurately reflects the succession of ideas in the hymn, sometimes even reproducing its wording; and the librettist did not find it necessary to go beyond the hymn's general connection with the Gospel reading and introduce specific points of reference.

Bach's composition, written for 22 October 1724, exhibits in almost all its movements a celebratory, almost hymnic character. It is clear that at the heart of the work lies not the critical situation of man as to whether to accept or reject God's invitation, as in Franck's text for Cantata 162, but rather the wedding feast itself and the love of God for man that is made manifest in His invitation to it. The opening chorus* and the two arias are dance-like in character: though not real dances, the first movement resembles a gigue, the second a bourrée, and the fifth a polonaise.

The opening movement follows the customary form of the chorale cantata introductions. The chorale melody in the soprano, supported by the other voices, is incorporated line by line within a thematically self-sufficient orchestral texture. The distinctive features of this movement are the complete independence of the orchestral themes from the chorale melody, a concertante* alternation between instrumental groups, and the constant maintenance of imitative* texture in the accompanying voice parts. Like the instrumental themes, the imitative motives* of the accompanying vocal texture are mostly unrelated to the chorale *cantus firmus** and developed out of a single motive—

—except in the melodically identical chorale-lines 5 and 6 ('For the Lord, full of Salvation and Grace, lets you be invited now as His guest'), in which the accompanying voice parts are derived from the chorale melody—in this way, Bach perhaps wanted to emphasize musically God's invitation and its significance for mankind.

The obbligato* flute in the second movement enters with a reveille and with rhythmic sequential figures, perhaps intended to represent the 'knocking' of the Saviour; and the tenor, with his vigorous calls of 'Ach, öffne, öffne bald' ('Ah, open, open soon'), helps to reinforce the 'rousing' character of the aria. This movement adds support to our conjecture that in the autumn of 1724 Bach had at his disposal a most able transverse flute* player. The third movement, after only a few bars of *secco* recitative, flows into the fourth verse of the hymn. This is sung by the soprano to an expressive, but not over-adorned, elaboration of the chorale melody, which is embedded line by line within a figurative, motivically-imprinted obbligato part for violoncello piccolo.* The following movement, no. 4, is another recitative, but Bach skilfully avoids the danger of monotony by filling out the texture with two recorders, which at first accompany with held notes, but then gradually in a more lively fashion: in the second half, the caesuras of the voice part are bridged over by quaver and semiquaver motion in the recorders, and the conclusion approaches arioso.*

Full homophonic* sonority characterizes the second aria, no. 5. Only occasionally in the vocal passages do the strings and woodwind split up into separate groups, as in the first movement. For the most part, the woodwind instruments serve to strengthen the upper string parts. This full sonority lends the movement a rather radiant, hymnic quality, especially in the outer sections; the middle section, in accordance with its text, inclines to a more minimal texture. The sixth movement, a brief *secco* recitative, concludes with arioso on the words 'and ever by mindful of Your Love'. The concluding chorale has the usual form of a plain, instrumentally reinforced four-part choral setting.

Ich geh und suche mit Verlangen, BWV 49

NBA I/25, p. 109 BC A150 Duration: *c.* 29 mins

1. SINFONIA ob d'am str obbl org bc — E 3/8
2. ARIA B obbl org bc — c♯ 3/8

Ich geh und suche mit Verlangen	I go and seek you with longing,
Dich, meine Taube, schönste Braut.	My dove, fairest bride.
Sag an, wo bist du hingegangen,	Tell me, where have you gone,
Daß dich mein Auge nicht mehr schaut?	So that my eye no longer sees you?

3. RECITATIVO SB str bc — A C/3/8

Baß	*Bass*
Mein Mahl ist zubereit'	My dinner is prepared
Und meine Hochzeittafel fertig,	And my wedding table ready;
Nur meine Braut ist noch nicht gegenwärtig.	Only my bride is still not present.
Sopran	*Soprano*
Mein Jesus redt von mir;	My Jesus speaks of me;
O Stimme, welche mich erfreut!	O voice that delights me!
Baß	*Bass*
Ich geh und suche mit Verlangen	I go and seek you with longing,
Dich, meine Taube, schönste Braut.	My dove, fairest bride.
Sopran	*Soprano*
Mein Bräutigam, ich falle dir zu Füßen.	My Bridegroom, I fall at Your feet.
Sopran	*Soprano*
Baß	*Bass*
Komm, Schönster, komm und laß dich küssen,	Come, fairest One, come and let me kiss You,

Komm, Schönste, komm und laß dich küssen,
Laß mich dein fettes Mahl genießen.
Du sollst mein fettes Mahl genießen.
Mein Bräutigam, ich eile nun,
Komm, liebe Braut, und eile nun,
beide
Die Hochzeitkleider anzutun.

Come, fairest one, come and let me kiss you.
Let me enjoy Your feast of fat things.
You shall enjoy my feast of fat things.
My Bridegroom, I hasten now
Come, dear bride, and hasten now
both
To put on the wedding garments.

4. ARIA S ob d'am vc picc bc — A c

Ich bin herrlich, ich bin schön,
Meinen Heiland zu entzünden.
  Seines Heils Gerechtigkeit
  Ist mein Schmuck und Ehrenkleid;
  Und damit will ich bestehn,
  Wenn ich werd im Himmel gehn.

I am glorious, I am fair
To inflame my Saviour.
  The righteousness of His Salvation
  Is my adornment and robe of honour;
  And with these I shall pass through
  When I am bound for heaven.

5. RECITATIVO SB bc — f♯–E c

Sopran
Mein Glaube hat mich selbst so angezogen.
Baß
So bleibt mein Herze dir gewogen,
So will ich mich mit dir
In Ewigkeit vertrauen und verloben.
Sopran
Wie wohl ist mir!
Der Himmel ist mir aufgehoben:
Die Majestät ruft selbst und sendet ihre Knechte,
Daß das gefallene Geschlechte
Im Himmelssaal
Bei dem Erlösungsmahl
Zu Gaste möge sein,
Hier komm ich, Jesu, laß mich ein!
Baß
Sei bis im Tod getreu,
So leg ich dir die Lebenskrone bei.

Soprano
My faith itself has thus clothed me.
Bass
Thus my heart remains well-disposed to you,
Thus to you will I entrust
And betrothe myself in eternity.
Soprano
How blessed am I!
Heaven is reserved for me:
His Majesty Himself calls and send His servants
So that the fallen race
In the heavenly chamber
At the Meal of Redemption
May be His guests;
Here I come, Jesus, let me in!
Bass
Be faithful unto death,
Then I will set upon you the Crown of Life.

6. ARIA [+ CHORALE] SB str + ob d'am obbl org bc — E 2/4

Dich hab ich je und je geliebet,
  Wie bin ich doch so herzlich froh,
  Daß mein Schatz ist das A und O,
  Der Anfang und das Ende.
Und darum zieh ich dich zu mir.
  Er wird mich doch zu seinem Preis

I have loved you for ever and ever,
  How heartily glad am I that
  My treasure is the Alpha and Omega,
  The beginning and the end.
And therefore I draw you to Me.
  He will indeed—praise be to Him!—

Aufnehmen in das Paradeis;	**Take me up into Paradise,**
Des klopf ich in die Hände.	**For which I clap my hands.**
Ich komme bald,	I come soon,
Amen! Amen!	**Amen! Amen!**
Ich stehe vor der Tür,	I stand before the door,
Komm, du schöne Freudenkrone, bleib nicht lange!	**Come, you fair Crown of Joy, do not delay for long!**
Mach auf, mein Aufenthalt!	Open up, my place of residence!
Deiner wart ich mit Verlangen.	**I await you with longing.**
Dich hab ich je und je geliebet,	I have loved you for ever and ever,
Und darum zieh ich dich zu mir.	And therefore I draw you to me.

This cantata is expressly designated 'Dialogus', and it turns out to be a later derivative of the sacred dialogue compositions of the seventeenth century. This genre, which began with the setting of biblical dialogues, later favoured the dialogue partners Jesus and the Faithful Soul, thereby removing the dialogue from the sphere of narrative into that of personal feeling. The individual Christian now finds himself confronted with Jesus Himself as his conversational partner. This explains why the biblical text for such dialogues was sought above all in the Song of Songs, a love poem which, according to old church tradition, was re-interpreted as a dialogue between Christ as bridegroom and the Soul (or the Church) as bride. Hence, the cantata *Ich geh und suche mit Verlangen* draws its imagery chiefly from this Old Testament book, though reference is also made to other scriptural passages.

The anonymous librettist finds his inducement for the choice of this material in the Sunday Gospel* reading (the parable of the royal wedding feast) from which, however, he extracts certain features only. Jesus Himself is the bridegroom and the Soul His bride. She is invited to the wedding and honoured by Jesus on account of her faith. The invitation of the King is thus made once, rather than twice as in the parable, the refusal of the guests first invited is left unmentioned, and the unworthiness of those invited in their place is merely alluded to: 'His Majesty Himself calls and sends His servants so that the fallen race may be His guests in the heavenly chamber at the Meal of Redemption'. Moreover, the story appended to the parable about the guest being thrown into darkness because he has no wedding robe seems to be used, if at all, only in a positive sense: the Soul chosen by Jesus as bride says of herself, 'I am glorious, I am fair . . . the righteousness of His Salvation is my adornment and robe of honour'.[48]

[48] The middle section of this aria (no. 4) is derived almost word for word from a chorale verse (Leipzig, 1638):

Christi Blut und Gerechtigkeit	Christ's Blood and righteousness,
Das ist mein Schmuck und Ehrenkleid,	That is my adornment and robe of honour,
Damit will ich vor Gott bestehn,	With these shall I come through before God
Wenn ich zum Himmel werd eingehn.	When I am bound for heaven.

Numerous other biblical images are included, such as that of the dove with which the bride is compared (Song of Songs 5.2, 6.9), the feast of fat things which the Lord has prepared for His peoples (Isaiah 25.6), the covenant made by the Lord with Israel (Hosea 2.19: 'I will betrothe myself to you in eternity'), the faithfulness unto death that wins the Crown of Life (Revelation 2.10), and the Lord standing before the door and knocking (Rev. 3.20). Finally, the opening of the last aria recalls the words of Jeremiah 31.3: 'I have loved you for ever and ever; therefore I have drawn you to me out of pure loving kindness'.

Bach set this text in 1726 and performed the work for the first time that year on 3 November. The text is prefaced by a large-scale sinfonia with obbligato* organ, which originally formed the finale of a three-movement concerto, perhaps from Bach's Cöthen period. The other two movements of this concerto (the original model of the Harpsichord Concerto in E, BWV 1053) had already been adopted by Bach in Cantata 169, *Gott soll allein mein Herze haben*, which had been performed only a fortnight earlier. Cantatas thus expanded by large-scale concerto movements have a decidedly virtuoso and decorative character which is of its very nature foreign to the cantata as 'sermon music'. Perhaps Bach wanted to compensate in this way for the absence of a choir. In the present cantata, moreover, he creates the impression of wedding music, which helps to illustrate the following words of the bridegroom, 'My dinner is prepared and my wedding table ready'. Not least, however, this concertante* character bears witness to the freedom of Lutheranism, which sees in the exercise of the role ordained by God—here that of the skilled musician—a legitimate form of divine service.

The following movements are also markedly virtuoso in character due to their abundant use of obbligato organ. After the sinfonia, we hear the aria 'Ich geh und suche mit Verlangen' in a contrasting C sharp minor, accompanied only by obbligato organ and continuo. The wide intervallic leaps of the opening ritornello, sometimes ascending and elsewhere descending, may be construed as the zealous searching of the bridegroom for his bride. In form, the aria is closer to the rondeau[49] structure of a concerto movement than to the clear, tripartite form of the da capo* aria. The dialogue recitative that follows, no. 3, is decidedly dramatic in character. Even its opening is elevated above the level of plain *secco* recitative by the accompanying strings; and at the words 'Come, fairest one, come and let me kiss you', we hear, in a dance-like triple time, a true love duet such as might have done credit to any opera.

The following soprano aria, no. 4, with its choice scoring for oboe d'amore* and violoncello piccolo,* is a masterpiece of Bach's art of characterization.

[49] Though to modern eyes the French spelling 'rondeau' suggests a medieval chanson rather than the later instrumental form, it was the spelling Bach used—since he was familiar with the French tradition of the form rather than the Italian—and hence is used here.

Perhaps we are not reading too much into it if, in the complementary figures that the obbligato instruments toss to one another, we see the spinning and turning of the bride adorned by her hoop-skirt, taking pleasure in her own beauty. The metaphor of the wedding garment as the justification of the sinner in the middle section gives a clear indication as to where the text's train of thought is leading; and the application of the parable is clearly expressed in the following recitative, no. 5: it is through faith in Christ that the fallen human race is invited to the heavenly Meal of Redemption.

The concluding duet, no. 6, is among the richest in artistry of all Bach's cantata movements. He was faced with the formal task of so weaving the chorale into the texture that the impression is formed of a finale, despite the lack of choir. At the same time, in the interests of a balanced overall form, the aria has to form a counterpart to the concertante virtuosity of the opening movements. Bach achieves both these aims with brilliant success. The chorale—the seventh verse of the hymn *Wie schön leuchtet der Morgenstern* by Philipp Nicolai (1599)—is heard in long notes in the soprano. Thereby the symbolic nature of the dialogue is conclusively made manifest: the bride, as the individual soul, also stands for the Church founded by Christ, the fellowship of those elected for God. The instruments, including the obbligato organ, and the solo bass also have a share in the substance of the chorale, for the rising fifth and falling thirds of its opening are clearly perceptible both in the ritornello and in the bass melody:

The simultaneous double text of soprano and bass crowns the dialogue character of the work. This is particularly clear in the *Abgesang*,* where we hear at the same time the words 'I come soon . . . open up my place of residence!' (bass) and 'Amen! Amen! Come, you fair Crown of Joy!' (soprano). The overall form is determined by the *Bar* form* of the chorale. An instrumental ritornello serves as a frame, with the bass part, reiterating the opening words of the movement, incorporated within its closing reprise—a technique doubly effective as a concluding enhancement and as a hint of da capo form.

This cantata is one of those works whose full content is not immediately revealed upon superficial acquaintance. One might object to it that Bach musically conjures away the negative aspects of the parable in a rich display of musical beauties—following the librettist, who had already high-mindedly disregarded whatever alarming features the parable contains. As a rejoinder, it should be pointed out that not only the wedding joy expressed in this music but also the fear of death found in other Bach cantatas were then felt much more immediately than they are today, the one invariably forming the necessary complement to the other. Whoever could sing, 'Last hour, draw on!' in an Easter cantata, without doing violence to the significance of the feast, could also delight in the 'worldliness' of the present cantata without eliminating thoughts of darkness and death, as our compartmentalized world does today.

2.21 Twenty-first Sunday after Trinity

Epistle: Ephesians 6.10–17: 'Lay hold of the armour of God so that when the evil day comes you may hold the field'.

Gospel: John 4.46–54: The healing of a nobleman's son after his father shows faith in Jesus.

Ich glaube, lieber Herr, hilf meinem Unglauben, BWV 109

NBA I/25, p. 159 BC A151 Duration: *c.* 25 mins

1. [Chorus] SATB hn ob I,II str bc — d C

'Ich glaube, lieber Herr, hilf meinem Unglauben!'	'I believe, dear Lord, help my unbelief!'

2. Recitativo T bc — B♭–e C

Des Herren Hand ist ja noch nicht verkürzt,	The Lord's hand has indeed not yet waxed short:
Mir kann geholfen werden.	I can be saved.
Ach nein, ich sinke schon zur Erden	Ah no, I already sink to the earth
Vor Sorge, daß sie mich zu Boden stürzt.	From worry, which casts me down to destruction.
Der Höchste will, sein Vaterherze bricht.	The Highest is willing; His fatherly heart breaks.
Ach nein! er hört die Sünder nicht.	Ah no! He does not hear sinners.
Er wird, er muß dir bald zu helfen eilen,	He will, He must soon hasten to help you
Um deine Not zu heilen.	In order to cure your distress.
Ach nein, es bleibet mir um Trost sehr bange.	Ah no, I remain very anxious for comfort.

Ach Herr, wie lange?	Ah Lord, how long?
3. Aria T str bc	e C
Wie zweifelhaftig ist mein Hoffen, Wie wanket mein geängstigt Herz! Des Glaubens Docht glimmt kaum hervor, Es bricht dies fast zustoßne Rohr, Die Furcht macht stetig neuen Schmerz.	How full of doubt is my hope, How my anxious heart wavers! The wick of belief scarcely glimmers forth, This bruised reed almost breaks, Fear creates ever-new pain.
4. Recitativo A bc	C–d C
O fasse dich, du zweifelhafter Mut, Weil Jesus itzt noch Wunder tut! Die Glaubensaugen werden schauen Das Heil des Herrn; Scheint die Erfüllung allzufern, So kannst du doch auf die Verheißung bauen.	Take hold of yourself, O doubt-filled spirit, For Jesus even now does miracles! Eyes of faith shall behold The Salvation of the Lord; If its fulfilment seems too distant, You can nonetheless build on the promise.
5. Aria A ob I,II bc	F 3/4
Der Heiland kennet ja die Seinen, Wenn ihre Hoffnung hülflos liegt. Wenn Fleisch und Geist in ihnen streiten, So steht er ihnen selbst zur Seiten, Damit zuletzt der Glaube siegt.	The Saviour indeed knows them that are His When their hope lies helpless. When flesh and spirit struggle within them, He Himself stands at their side So that at last faith is victorious.
6. Choral S + hn ATB ob I,II str bc	d–a C
Wer hofft in Gott und dem vertraut, Der wird nimmer zuschanden; Denn wer auf diesen Felsen baut, Ob ihm gleich geht zuhanden Viel Unfalls hie, hab ich doch nie Den Menschen sehen fallen, Der sich verläßt auf Gottes Trost; Er hilft sein'n Gläubgen allen.	**Whoever hopes in God and trusts in Him Will never be put to shame; For whoever builds on this rock, Even though many accidents might Befall him here, I have yet Never seen that person fall Who relies upon God's comfort; For He helps all those of His in the Faith.**

The Gospel* reading for this Sunday deals with the question of belief, for which the healing of the sick merely provides a pretext. Jesus says, 'If you do not see signs and wonders, you do not believe'. Yet the nobleman believes when Jesus says to him, 'Go your way, your son lives', and the Gospel implies that, because he believes, his call for help is answered. The anonymous librettist prefaces the text with words from a similar account (Mark 9.24) in which Jesus is addressed by the father of a man possessed. These words, like no others, characterize the situation of mankind torn between doubt and belief. The following movements form a kind of dialogue between Fear and Hope, such as Bach set three weeks later in Cantata 60, or in this case perhaps between Doubt and Belief. The second movement might easily be imagined as a dialogue, wavering constantly between confidence and dejection. It is followed by an aria for Doubt, no. 3, who is then corrected by Belief in nos. 4 and 5. Of course, it remains uncertain whether the librettist really had in mind something of this kind (and if so, why Bach did not set the second movement as a dialogue).

As in many other cantata texts, not only does the language of the libretto in general approximate closely to biblical language, it also contains a number of clear biblical references, particularly in the second movement, whose opening lines 'The Lord's hand has indeed not yet waxed short: I can be saved' allude not only to Numbers 11.23 ('Is the hand of the Lord waxed short?') but to Isaiah 59.1 ('The Lord's hand is not so short that it cannot save'). In the same movement, the phrase 'His fatherly heart breaks' refers to Jeremiah 31.20, 'I remain very anxious for comfort' to Isaiah 38.17, and the concluding question, 'Ah Lord, how long?', to Psalm 6.3. Underneath the doubts of the following aria, no. 3 ('The wick of belief scarcely glimmers forth, this bruised reed almost breaks') we hear the hopeful promise of Isaiah 42.3: 'The bruised reed He shall not break and the glimmering wick He shall not quench'. The turning-point comes in the fourth movement. Just as Jesus once worked miracles, so too He will this very day save those who believe in Him, even if the fulfilment of this redemption seems far distant, for 'The Saviour indeed knows them that are His' (no. 5; see 2 Timothy 2.19 and cf. John 10.14 and 27). The work concludes with the seventh verse of the hymn *Durch Adams Fall ist ganz verderbt* by Lazarus Spengler (1524).

Bach's composition was first performed on 17 October 1723 within the context of his first Leipzig cycle of cantatas. As in the revived Weimar cantata BWV 162 on the previous Sunday, Bach subsequently wrote an extra part for 'corne du Chasse', which is not included in the score. It mostly reinforces violin I in the first movement and the soprano chorale melody in the sixth. The range of the part indicates that the instrument required is the corno da tirarsi (slide trumpet), for it is unplayable on natural horn.

The opening movement is strikingly loose in construction and contains marked concertante* elements both in the orchestral and the choral parts. Noteworthy is the thematic independence between the vocal and the instrumental parts. The extended introductory ritornello for the orchestra alternates between tuttis and solo passages in which oboe I and solo violin I play concertante duets. The ritornello is developed out of a motive* later heard repeatedly on the instruments during the vocal passages. Despite its speech-like gesture, this motive proves to be unsuited to the vocal text and is therefore substantially remodelled to form the opening theme of the vocal section, as the following juxtaposition shows:

In this comparison, the displacement of accent in the vocal adaptation is clear. The vocal section, like the ritornello, continues with frequent alternation between a single part, a duet and full four-part choral passages against independent orchestral parts, which dominate in choral-insertion* passages and elsewhere recede behind the vocal parts in an accompanying role. In addition, *Stimmtausch** (exchange of parts) plays an important role in the construction of this movement. All these factors may be accorded either a text-interpretative significance (reflecting the alternation between belief and doubt), or else a constructive purpose, reflecting the extreme brevity of the sung text.

In the following *secco* recitative no. 2, confident and doubting assertions are set off from one another by *forte* and *piano* indications in the voice part. The concluding question (after Psalm 6.3) is set as an arioso* ending. The third movement, fully scored for strings but with the first violin predominant, uses marked rhythms and wide intervals to characterize the wavering between fear and hope of the text. In addition, the frequent alternation between string and continuo accompaniment in the vocal passages may have a programmatic purpose as a depiction of mood changes.

The 'belief' part of the work begins with the fourth movement, a short *secco* recitative sung by solo alto, who also sings the following aria, no. 5. This movement resembles a saraband in its dance rhythm (note the second-beat stress) and its clear periodic phrase structure. The calm regularity of the opening gives way to increasing animation in the middle section, stimulated by the word 'streiten' ('struggle'). This B section then ends *adagio* with the words 'faith is victorious', after which we hear an unaltered recapitulation of the A section. The concluding chorale does not follow the usual pattern of a plain homophonic* setting with *colla parte** instruments. Instead, the chorale melody is delivered by the soprano (plus horn) in minims line by line, articulated by episodes, while the chordal substructure of the lower voices takes a livelier form (in crotchets and quavers). The chorale thus sung is embedded within an extended, figurative orchestral texture.

Aus tiefer Not schrei ich zu dir, BWV 38

NBA I/25, p. 219 BC A152 Duration: *c.* 21 mins

1. CHORAL SATB bc (+ trb I–IV ob I + II str) e ¢

Aus tiefer Not schrei ich zu dir,
Herr Gott, erhör mein Rufen;
Dein gnädig Ohr' neig her zu mir
Und meiner Bitt sie öffne!
Denn so du willt das sehen an,
Was Sünd und Unrecht ist getan,

Wer kann, Herr, vor dir bleiben?

Out of deep distress I cry to You,
Lord God, hear my calling;
Incline Your gracious ear to me
And open it to my prayer!
For if You would regard
Whatever sin and injustice has been done,
Who, Lord, could abide before You?

2. RECITATIVO A bc C–a c

In Jesu Gnade wird allein
Der Trost vor uns und die Vergebung sein,
Weil durch des Satans Trug und List
Der Menschen ganzes Leben
Vor Gott ein Sündengreuel ist.
Was könnte nun
Die Geistesfreudigkeit zu unserm Beten geben,
Wo Jesu Geist und Wort nicht neue Wunder tun?

In Jesus's Grace alone
Will there be comfort and forgiveness for us,
For through Satan's deceit and cunning
The whole life of man is
Before God an abomination of sin.
What, then,
Could give the spirit of joyfulness to our prayer
If Jesus's Spirit and Word did not work new wonders?

3. ARIA T ob I,II bc a c

Ich höre mitten in den Leiden
Ein Trostwort, so mein Jesus spricht.

Drum, o geängstigtes Gemüte,
Vertraue deines Gottes Güte,
Sein Wort besteht und fehlet nicht,
Sein Trost wird niemals von dir scheiden!

I hear amidst my sufferings
A Word of comfort spoken by my Jesus.
Therefore, O anguished spirit,
Trust Your God's goodness:
His Word prevails and does not fail,
His comfort will never depart from you!

4. RECITATIVO S bc d c

Ach!
Daß mein Glaube noch so schwach,
Und daß ich mein Vertrauen
Auf feuchtem Grunde muß erbauen!
Wie ofte müssen neue Zeichen
Mein Herz erweichen?
Wie? kennst du deinen Helfer nicht,
Der nur ein einzig Trostwort spricht,

Und gleich erscheint,
Eh deine Schwachheit es vermeint,
Die Rettungsstunde.

Alas!
That my faith is still so weak
And that I have to build my confidence
On damp ground!
How often must new signs
Soften my heart?
What? Do you not know your Helper,
Who says but a single Word of comfort,
And at once there appears,
Before your weakness imagines it,
The hour of deliverance.

Vertraue nur der Allmachtshand und seiner Wahrheit Munde!	Just trust the hand of the Almighty and the truth of His mouth!

5. Terzetto SAB bc — d ¢

Wenn meine Trübsal als mit Ketten	When my tribulation as with chains
Ein Unglück an den andern hält,	Binds one misfortune to another,
So wird mich doch mein Heil erretten,	My Salvation shall nonetheless deliver me
Daß alles plötzlich von mir fällt.	So that everything suddenly falls off me.
Wie bald erscheint des Trostes Morgen	How soon the morning of comfort appears
Auf diese Nacht der Not und Sorgen!	After this night of distress and cares!

6. Choral SATB bc (+ instrs) — e c

Ob bei uns ist der Sünden viel,	**Though in us sins are many,**
Bei Gott ist viel mehr Gnade;	**In God there is much more Grace;**
Sein Hand zu helfen hat kein Ziel,	**His helping hand has no bounds,**
Wie groß auch sei der Schade.	**However great the harm.**
Er ist allein der gute Hirt,	**He alone is the Good Shepherd,**
Der Israel erlösen wird	**Who will redeem Israel**
Aus seinen Sünden allen.	**From all its sins.**

This chorale cantata,* written for 29 October 1724, is based on Martin Luther's hymn of 1524, a paraphrase of Psalm 130. In Leipzig, the hymn was assigned to this Sunday from of old, since it reflects the principal themes of the Sunday Gospel* reading: the nobleman's call for help in time of need and the life that arises from faith and forgiveness. The anonymous librettist lays still greater emphasis on these associations. The outer verses, nos. 1 and 5, are as usual retained word for word and the inner ones freely paraphrased, verses 2 and 3 forming the like-numbered movements, and verse 4 the fifth movement. The fourth movement has no direct connection with Luther's hymn; it follows up threads from verses 3 and 4 and establishes most clearly the relationship of the text with the Sunday Gospel. Its opening might be thought to reflect Luther's lines 'Therefore I will place my hopes in God and not depend on what I deserve'.[50] Much clearer than the link with Luther's hymn, however, is the reference to Jesus's words in the Gospel reading, 'If you do not see signs and wonders, you do not believe' (John 4.48). The words of Luther '. . . His precious Word, that is my comfort and faithful refuge' are taken up repeatedly in the cantata text. The word 'Trost' ('comfort') occurs altogether three times, and 'Trostwort' ('word of comfort') twice. For 'this single Word of comfort spoken by Jesus' is again found in the Gospel reading ('Go your way: your son lives'), and these words are felt as a guarantee that even today 'Jesus's Spirit and Word'

[50] 'Darum auf Gott will hoffen ich, auf mein Verdienst nicht bauen . . .'.

will work 'new wonders' and that for me, too, the 'hour of deliverance' will therefore arrive. Luther's hymn and the Sunday Gospel are thus interwoven in this libretto in many different ways.

In the opening chorus,* as in that of Cantata 2, *Ach Gott, vom Himmel sieh darein*, performed a few months earlier, Bach integrates the time-honoured Phrygian melody of Luther's hymn, not in a concertante* orchestral setting as in most of the other chorale cantatas, but in the tradition-bound form of the motet-style chorale arrangement. All instruments double the voice parts in unison, only the continuo becoming temporarily independent of the bass. Each chorale line is delivered in the same fashion. Prepared imitatively* by the three lower voices in the manner of a fugal exposition,* it is then heard in doubled note-values in the soprano. A distinctive feature of this movement is that the counterpoint* to each chorale line, developed in the lower parts, acquires special significance. This counterpoint, after its fugal function has been fulfilled in the passages of fore-imitation,* is detached from the theme of the chorale line in the accompaniment to the soprano *cantus firmus** and takes on a thematic life of its own. Each chorale line begins afresh with only a few parts and then grows to full texture. Bach avoids opening each section with one part, however, by the independence of the continuo and sometimes by the immediate entry of the counterpoint to the chorale line. In line 6 ('Whatever sin and injustice has been done') the counterpoint is chromatic* and at times inverted as an illustration of the words. The entire movement forms a severe and antiquated impression. Nevertheless, it bears the stamp of Bach's unmistakable personal style. This finds expression, above all, in the powerful chromaticism of line 6, already mentioned, and in the highly declamatory counterpoints to the words 'Lord God, hear my calling' (line 2) and 'Who, Lord, could abide before You?' (line 7). Fourteen years later, Bach employed a similar style when he arranged the same chorale melody for the organ in Part III of the *Clavierübung*. A comparison between the two movements shows the direction in which Bach had developed in the interim. The outstanding feature of the later piece is the still more flowing and more linear part-writing. On the other hand, the chief characteristic of the earlier, vocal movement—the varied character of each line-section in accordance with its textual content—recedes in the organ chorale.[51]

The second movement, a plain but forcefully declaimed *secco* recitative, is followed by the tenor aria, no. 3, which is scored with two obbligato* oboes moving in largely parallel motion. Curiously, the movement opens in an apparent 3/2 time; only later does the listener become aware of its regular metre. The syncopated rhythm—♪ ♩ ♩ ♩—which is present from the outset,

[51] See C. Wolff, *Der stile antico in der Musik J. S. Bachs: Studien zu Bachs Spätwerk* (Wiesbaden, 1968), 69 f.

pervades the entire movement, lending it a joyfully animated character suggestive of the 'Word of comfort' of the text. As we have seen, the fourth movement departs furthest in its text from Luther's hymn and refers directly to the Gospel reading. Perhaps by way of compensation, Bach forges a close link with the hymn by placing the chorale melody in the continuo part and having the recitative sung *a battuta*, or in fixed rhythm. After the first *Stollen*,* the chorale melody is transposed from Phrygian a to Phrygian d, but otherwise it remains unaltered (if we disregard the sharpening of the third degree of the scale, which was optional at that time). Nevertheless, it hardly dawns on the listener that this is a *cantus firmus** movement, so skilfully does Bach combine the voice part—that is, the interpreter of the text—with the given substructure.

In place of a second aria the cantata contains a terzetto with continuo accompaniment, no. 5. The two sections of its bipartite form, A B, create a contrast which is characterized textually by the words 'Trübsal' ('tribulation') and 'Trost' ('comfort'). However, Bach's setting also aims at unifying the two sections and forming a reciprocal relationship between them, since parts of the first recur in the second. After a continuo ritornello, whose sequential figures reveal a clear two-bar phrase structure (a a^1 a^2 a^3) and lead us to expect some kind of passacaglia form, the voice parts unexpectedly enter with a new chromatic theme in an imitative* texture—a style that recalls the first movement. This material pervades the A section, and only at the very end of it are ritornello motives* once more allowed to emerge. The continuo ritornello follows, transposed to the dominant, as an articulating episode. Section B then introduces a new theme ('How soon the morning of comfort appears'), whose sequel ('After this night of distress and cares'), however, flows into the material of section A, within which ritornello allusions are further developed. As if this were not enough, in an expanded conclusion section B introduces the complete ritornello in bass and continuo before the end of the vocal section, and a purely instrumental reprise of the continuo ritornello closes the movement. The work ends with a plain chorale setting.

Was Gott tut, das ist wohlgetan, BWV 98

NBA I/25, p. 243 BC A153 Duration: *c.* 17 mins

1. [Chorale] S + ob I A + ob II T + taille B str bc — B♭ $\frac{3}{4}$

Was Gott tut, das ist wohlgetan,	**Whatever God deals is dealt bountifully;**
Es bleibt gerecht sein Wille;	**His Will remains just;**
Wie er fängt meine Sachen an,	**However He runs my affairs,**
Will ich ihm halten stille.	**I will hold still before Him.**
Er ist mein Gott,	**He is my God,**
Der in der Not	**Who in time of trouble**
Mich wohl weiß zu erhalten;	**Well knows how to uphold me;**
Drum laß ich ihn nur walten.	**Therefore I will just let Him rule.**

2. Recitativo T bc — g–E♭ C

Ach Gott! wenn wirst du mich einmal
Von meiner Leidensqual,
Von meiner Angst befreien?
Wie lange soll ich Tag und Nacht
Um Hülfe schreien?
Und ist kein Retter da!
Der Herr ist denen allen nah,
Die seiner Macht
Und seiner Huld vertrauen.
Drum will ich meine Zuversicht
Auf Gott alleine bauen,
Denn er verläßt die Seinen nicht.

Ah God! When at last will You free me
From my torment of suffering,
From my anguish?
How long shall I day and night
Cry for help?
And no deliverer is there!
The Lord is near all those
Who trust His might
And His favour.
Therefore I will build my confidence
On God alone,
For He does not forsake His own people.

3. Aria S ob I bc — c $\frac{3}{8}$

Hört, ihr Augen, auf zu weinen!
Trag ich doch
Mit Geduld mein schweres Joch.
Gott, der Vater, lebet noch,
Von den Seinen
Läßt er keinen.
Hört, ihr Augen, auf zu weinen!

Cease, you eyes, to weep!
Indeed I bear
My heavy yoke with patience.
God, the Father, still lives;
Of His own people
He abandons none.
Cease, you eyes, to weep!

4. Recitativo A bc — g–d C

Gott hat ein Herz, das des Erbarmens Überfluß;
Und wenn der Mund vor seinen Ohren klagt
Und ihm des Kreuzes Schmerz
Im Glauben und Vertrauen sagt,
So bricht in ihm das Herz,
Daß er sich über uns erbarmen muß.
Er hält sein Wort;
Er saget: Klopfet an,
So wird euch aufgetan!
Drum laßt uns alsofort,
Wenn wir in höchsten Nöten schweben,
Das Herz zu Gott allein erheben!

God has a Heart that abounds in mercy;
And when our mouth laments before His ears
And tells Him of the cross's pain
In faith and trust,
Then His Heart breaks within Him
So that He must have mercy on us.
He keeps His Word;
He says: knock
And it will be opened to you!
Therefore let us from now on,
When we hover in the greatest distress,
Raise our hearts to God alone!

5. Aria B vln I + II bc — B♭ ¢

Meinen Jesum laß ich nicht,
Bis mich erst sein Angesicht
Wird erhören oder segnen.
  Er allein
  Soll mein Schutz in allem sein,
  Was mir Übels kann begegnen.

I will not let go of my Jesus
Till His Countenance
Hears or blesses me.
  He alone
  Shall be my defence in all
  The evil that can befall me.

Unlike the other two works with the same opening lines, BWV 99 and 100, this is not a chorale cantata* but a setting of a formally unorthodox text: a chorale opens the work but it lacks the usual concluding chorale. The content of the libretto (by an unknown author) is related to the Sunday Gospel* but does not go into details. The faithful soul may trust that his prayer for deliverance will find a hearing, and this is confirmed in the words of the Sermon on the Mount, 'Knock, and it shall be opened to you' (Matthew 7.7; fourth movement). Therefore, so we are told in the fifth movement in an allusion to Genesis 32.26 ('I will not let you go unless you bless me'), I do not part from Jesus and I place my trust in His protection.

Bach composed the work for performance on 10 November 1726. According to date of origin, it is thus the second of the three cantatas with the same opening lines (BWV 99: 1724; BWV 100: *c.* 1734–5). And of all three cantatas (in so far as it is worth comparing works that by chance begin with the same text) it is the most intimate in character: not only the shortest but the nearest to a chamber-music sonority.

This character is particularly clear in the opening chorus.* In form, it is not dissimilar to the opening movements of the chorale cantatas. The choral texture, with the hymn melody in the soprano, is incorporated one line at a time within an independent instrumental texture. The instrumental music, however, is radically reduced in significance: it is played only by the strings, while the oboes (oboe I, II, and taille) double the voice parts. And even within the strings, the first violin is predominant to such an extent that the texture amounts to little more than obbligato* violin I plus instrumentally realized continuo—something very different from the chorale cantatas, in which such a prominent part is played by concertante* instrumental exchanges. In addition, the choral texture is predominantly chordal and homophonic;* only in the last line does it become freely polyphonic* and more extended, continuing beneath the long-held last note of the chorale melody. The charm of the movement lies, above all, in the almost speech-like violin theme, in which Bach seems to have depicted musically the wavering of the soul between doubt and trust in God. An additional feature reinforces this almost dramatic character: during both *Stollen** of the hymn, the strings and choir become prominent in alternation, uniting together only in the *Abgesang*.*

Two recitative-aria pairs now follow, in which the recitative is in each case set as plain *secco*. The arias are alike in texture: both have a single obbligato instrument, in the first case (no. 3) played by solo oboe, and in the second (no. 5) by unison violins. In order to underline the 'finale' character of the second aria, and to compensate for the absence of a concluding chorale, Bach has its opening line, 'Meinen Jesum laß ich nicht' ('I will not let go of my Jesus'), sung to the lightly varied melody of the chorale of that name by Christian Keymann (1658):

The aria thereby acquires a double function: as a personal expression of the individual Christian—as reflected in the aria form, in solo singing, in the first person of the text, and in the expressive adornment of the chorale—and as an expression of the assembled congregation, as reflected in the introduction of the chorale as a symbol of the Church founded by Christ.

Ich habe meine Zuversicht, BWV 188

NBA I/25, p. 267 BC A154 Duration: *c.* 29 mins

1. [Sinfonia] ob I,II taille str obbl org bc — d [3/4]
2. Aria T ob I str bc — F 3/4

Ich habe meine Zuversicht	I have placed my confidence
Auf den getreuen Gott gericht',	In our faithful God;
Da ruhet meine Hoffnung feste.	There my hope rests steadfastly.
Wenn alles bricht, wenn alles fällt,	When all breaks, when all falls,
Wenn niemand Treu und Glauben hält,	When no one holds up loyalty or faith,
So ist doch Gott der allerbeste.	God is indeed best of all.

3. Recitativo B bc — C c 6/8

Gott meint es gut mit jedermann	God means well with everyone,
Auch in den allergrößten Nöten.	Even in the greatest afflictions of all.
Verbirget er gleich seine Liebe,	Though He hides His Love,
So denkt sein Herz doch heimlich dran,	His Heart nonetheless recalls it secretly,
Das kann er niemals nicht entziehn;	And He can never withdraw it;
Und wollte mich der Herr auch töten,	And even if the Lord wanted to kill me,
So hoff ich doch auf ihn.	My hope would rest in Him.
Denn sein erzürntes Angesicht	For His wrathful face
Ist anders nicht	Is nothing other
Als eine Wolke trübe,	Than a dark cloud;
Sie hindert nur den Sonnenschein,	It only hinders the sunshine
Damit durch einen sanften Regen	So that through a gentle shower
Der Himmelssegen	Heavenly blessings
Um so viel reicher möge sein.	May be all the richer.
Der Herr verwandelt sich in einen grausamen,	The Lord changes into a cruel Lord

Um desto tröstlicher zu scheinen;
Er will, er kanns nicht böse meinen.

In order to seem all the more comforting;
He neither would nor could mean us harm.

Drum laß ich ihn nicht, er segne mich denn.

Therefore I will not let Him go unless He blesses me.

4. Aria A obbl org vc — e C

Unerforschlich ist die Weise,
Wie der Herr die Seinen führt.
  Selber unser Kreuz und Pein
  Muß zu unserm Besten sein
  Und zu seines Namens Preise.

Unsearchable is the way in which
The Lord leads His own people.
  Even our cross and pain
  Must be for the best
  And to His Name's praise.

5. Recitativo S str bc — C–a C

Die Macht der Welt verlieret sich.
Wer kann auf Stand und Hoheit bauen?
Gott aber bleibet ewiglich,
Wohl allen, die auf ihn vertrauen!

The might of the world dies away.
Who can build on station and high rank?
God, however, shall endure for ever;
Blessed are all they that put their trust in Him!

6. Choral SATB bc (+ instrs) — a C

Auf meinen lieben Gott
Trau ich in Angst und Not;
Er kann mich allzeit retten
Aus Trübsal, Angst und Nöten;
Mein Unglück kann er wenden,
Steht alls in seinen Händen.

In my dear God
I trust in fear and distress;
He can always deliver me
From tribulation, fear, and distress;
He can turn round my misfortune;
It is all in His hands.

This cantata belongs to the cycle whose texts were published in 1728–9 by Bach's favoured Leipzig poet Picander. Its composition therefore probably dates from 1728 (for performance on 17 October) or soon afterwards. Like the other surviving cantatas of this cycle, it is imperfectly transmitted. In this particular case, posterity's whole shameful want of judgement is manifest in a particularly crass form. Whether out of greed (in order to fetch higher prices upon sale) or because the owner wanted to present to as many friends as possible a relic of the 'great Sebastian', Bach's autograph score was cut up into numerous small strips, which are today scattered among libraries in Berlin, Eisenach, Paris, Washington, and Vienna, as well as among various private owners. A substantial portion of the score, however, including almost the entire sinfonia, is probably lost for ever. The other movements can be completed from later manuscript copies, but all we know of the sinfonia is that it corresponded musically with the third movement of the work known today as the Harpsichord Concerto in D minor, BWV 1052 (whose original version as a violin concerto is likewise lost),[52] that it

[52] A reconstruction of this violin concerto is given in NBA VII/7, pp. 3 ff.

required obbligato* organ, and that three oboes (oboe I, II and taille) were added—whose parts have not survived, however, apart from the closing bars. Today, therefore, the cantata is usually performed without its introductory sinfonia.

In his text, Picander establishes a very loose connection with the Sunday Gospel,* drawing from it only the general message that trust in God will be rewarded, even though it may seem, for the time being, as though God is cruel. Like the anonymous librettist of Cantata 98 of 1726, Picander interweaves at the end of the first recitative (no. 3) a reference to Genesis 32.26: 'I will not let You go unless You bless me'. The work concludes with the first verse of the hymn *Auf meinen lieben Gott* (Lübeck, before 1603).

The composition itself is notable for a certain simplicity, which has led many scholars to doubt its authenticity. This appears to be unjustified, however, for not only do we possess the autograph score, albeit in a fragmentary state, but the objection that Bach might have copied out another composer's work may be countered by pointing out the draft character of the handwriting as well as features of Bach's personal style. Typical compositional traits such as the frequent reuse of ritornello extracts in the vocal sections of the arias argue in favour of Bach's authorship. Not least, Picander's announcement in the preface to the printed edition of the cycle may serve as evidence: here, it is expressly stated that compensation for any deficiencies in the texts may be found in the 'beauty of the incomparable Herr Capellmeister Bach's music'.[53] At most, the question might be left open as to whether this or that movement might have originated during tuition as a combined effort of pupil and teacher. Yet there is no evidence of this whatsoever.

The concerto movement with obbligato organ, largely lost in its cantata version, is followed by the first aria, a full-textured piece for strings with an oboe part that in places doubles the first violin and elsewhere achieves independence as a soloist. The introductory ritornello is dance-like in effect, resembling the Polonaise from the sixth French Suite. Its phrase structure fluctuates between two- and three-bar groups (twice 2 + 2 + 3 bars), which creates a hovering, relaxed impression. The tenor takes up the opening theme in the A section, sometimes indeed singing it in octaves with the top instrumental part, which causes an easy, unproblematic effect. The relatively brief middle section brings a sudden change of mood at the words 'When all breaks, when all falls, when no one holds up loyalty or faith'. Here, lively string figuration and falling oboe motives* illustrate the text; and, significantly, only at the closing line of this section, 'God is indeed best of all', does the thematic material of the principal section return.

[53] '. . . durch die Lieblichkeit des unvergleichlichen Herrn Capell-Meisters, Bachs.'

A plain *secco* recitative follows (no. 3), which flows into arioso* (with a change of time signature) for the closing paraphrase of Genesis 32.26. The second aria, no. 4—probably the most significant piece in the cantata—is scored for alto voice, obbligato organ, and cello, which doubles the organ bass line in continuo style. Like the first aria, this movement has a hovering rhythm, here caused by the syncopated opening theme and the clustered figure-work of the upper organ part which is rhythmically articulated in multifarious ways. The brief recitative that precedes the plain concluding chorale is scored with strings, which depict in concise but graphic figures the waning of earthly might (tremolos) and the eternity of God (held notes and ongoing accompaniment figures).

2.22 Twenty-second Sunday after Trinity

EPISTLE: Philippians 1.3–11: Paul thanks God and prays for the community at Philippi.
GOSPEL: Matthew 18.23–35: The parable of the unfaithful steward.

Was soll ich aus dir machen, Ephraim, BWV 89

NBA I/26, p. 3   BC A155   Duration: *c.* 14 mins

1. ARIA B hn ob I,II str bc   c C

'Was soll ich aus dir machen, Ephraim?
Soll ich dich schützen, Israel? Soll
ich nicht billig ein Adama aus dir
machen und dich wie Zeboim
zurichten? Aber mein Herz ist
anders Sinnes, meine Barmherzigkeit
ist zu brünstig.'

'What am I to make of you, Ephraim?
Shall I protect you, Israel? Shall I not
simply make an Admah out of you and
treat you like Zeboim? But my heart is
otherwise inclined, my mercy too
passionate.'

2. RECITATIVO A bc   g–d C

Ja, freilich sollte Gott
Ein Wort zum Urteil sprechen
Und seines Namens Spott
An seinen Feinden rächen.
Unzählbar ist die Rechnung deiner
Sünden,
Und hätte Gott auch gleich Geduld,
Verwirft doch dein feindseliges
Gemüte
Die angebotne Güte
Und drückt den Nächsten um die
Schuld;
So muß die Rache sich entzünden.

Yes, of course God should
Utter a Word of Judgement
And avenge the mockery of His Name
On His enemies.
Countless is the sum of your sins,
And even though God had forbearance,
Your hostile disposition would
nonetheless reject
The kindness offered
And press your neighbour over his debt;
Thus vengeance must be enkindled.

3. Aria A bc — d c

Ein unbarmherziges Gerichte
Wird über dich gewiß ergehn.
Die Rache fängt bei denen an,
Die nicht Barmherzigkeit getan,
Und machet sie wie Sodom ganz zunichte.

A judgement without mercy
Will surely be pronounced upon you.
Vengeance begins with those
Who have shown no mercy
And brings them, like Sodom, to nought.

4. Recitativo S bc — F–B♭ c

Wohlan! mein Herze legt Zorn, Zank und Zwietracht hin;
Es ist bereit, dem Nächsten zu vergeben.
Allein, wie schrecket mich mein sündenvolles Leben,
Daß ich vor Gott in Schulden bin!
Doch Jesu Blut
Macht diese Rechnung gut,
Wenn ich zu ihm, als des Gesetzes Ende,
Mich gläubig wende.

Well, then! my heart lays aside wrath, sedition, and strife;
It is prepared to forgive my neighbour.
Yet how my sinful life terrifies me,
In that I am before God in my trespasses!
But Jesus's Blood
Makes good this account,
If to Him, as the end of the Law,
I turn in belief.

5. Aria S ob I bc — B♭ $\frac{6}{8}$

Gerechter Gott, ach, rechnest du?
So werde ich zum Heil der Seelen
Die Tropfen Blut von Jesu zählen.
Ach! rechne mir die Summe zu!
Ja, weil sie niemand kann ergründen,
Bedeckt sie meine Schuld und Sünden.

Righteous God, ah, do You take reckoning?
Then for the salvation of my soul
I will count the drops of the Blood of Jesus.
Ah! credit that sum to my account!
Indeed, since no one can fathom them,
They cover my debt and sins.

6. Choral SATB bc (+ instrs) — g c

Mir mangelt zwar sehr viel,
Doch, was ich haben will,
Ist alles mir zugute
Erlangt mit deinem Blute,
Damit ich überwinde
Tod, Teufel, Höll und Sünde.

I am indeed very deficient,
Yet what I would have
Is all, for my benefit,
Achieved by Your Blood,
So that I overcome
Death, devil, hell, and sin.

The text of this cantata refers to the Sunday Gospel* and to the antithesis brought to light within it between human guilt and divine grace. The work opens with biblical words of related content, Hosea 11.8. Of the four freely versified movements that follow, the first recitative-aria pair deals with the unpardonable sinfulness of man, who is himself not prepared to forgive (nos. 2–3), and the second with the divine Love manifest in Jesus's sacrificial Death, which disposes of all guilt (nos. 4–5). The concluding chorale summarizes this contrast between human imperfection and divine grace in the words of the seventh verse of the hymn *Wo soll ich fliehen hin* by Johann Heermann (1630). The anonymous librettist further interweaves a series of biblical allusions into his text. The third movement proves to be, in the main, a paraphrase of James 2.13: 'A judgement without mercy will be pronounced on him who has shown no mercy'. The passage in the fourth movement that refers to Jesus as 'the end of the Law' is drawn from a well-known verse in Romans (10.4). And repeated allusions are made to the Gospel reading itself, for example in the second movement: '. . . And press your neighbour over his debt'.

Bach composed this cantata during his first year in Leipzig, perhaps on the basis of older, Weimar material (the alto aria, no. 3, was transposed from E minor to D minor);[54] he performed it for the first time on 24 October 1723. The instrumental ensemble includes not only two oboes, strings, and continuo but also, as in the two previous cantatas (BWV 162 and 109) a horn ('corne du chasse'), evidently added after the preparation of the parts. In the first movement, this instrument is given an insignificant filling-in part, and in the finale it reinforces the chorale melody in the soprano. Clearly Bach had at his disposal during those weeks a brass player whose participation he welcomed, though without being able to entrust him with anything more than straightforward assignments.

The opening movement is one of those bass solos to biblical words which formally lie somewhere between arioso* and aria. In this case, it is impossible to say whether the heading 'aria', found in a few *tacet** indications in parts written out by Bach's copyists, is authorized by the composer. The thematically imprinted ritornello, portions of which recur in the vocal section as the basis of vocal insertion,* points to a relationship with aria. The formal structure, on the other hand, is closer to arioso, since the individual portions of text are delivered in succession and without da capo*. Hence a rounding-off is achieved only by the insertion of the last vocal passage within a complete ritornello statement, followed by a purely instrumental da capo of the ritornello. Within this ritornello, special significance is accorded to a motive* which is perhaps intended to represent the irresolution of the text's open question, since something similar is heard in the chorus* 'Lasset uns den nicht zerteilen' from the *St John Passion* to the word 'losen' ('cast lots'). It occurs in the continuo at the beginning of the cantata movement thus:

[54] See Andreas Glöckner, KB, NBA I/26 (1995).

The other movements are notably light in scoring: three continuo movements in succession (nos. 2–4) are followed by an aria with obbligato* oboe, and the complete ensemble is not required again till the plain concluding chorale. In the centre of the three continuo movements, surrounded on both sides by recitative, is the alto aria 'Ein unbarmherziges Gerichte' (no. 3), whose expressive theme is first stated in a continuo ritornello and then taken up by the alto voice. The middle section introduces lively, impassioned coloraturas,* and a highly modified da capo forms the conclusion. Of the two flanking recitatives, the first (no. 2) is a plain *secco*, and the second (no. 4) begins as such but flows into an arioso conclusion which raises the turning-point in content to prominence—from the threat of judgement to comfort, which now forms the subject of the fifth movement. In this aria, as in the previous one, the ritornello melody, here played on the oboe, is taken over by the voice, albeit in a simplified vocal form. The song-like simplicity of this relaxed, almost dance-like movement forms an effective contrast with the elaborate expressiveness of the first aria. A plain chorale setting concludes the work.

Mache dich, mein Geist, bereit, BWV 115

NBA I/26, p. 23 BC A156 Duration: *c.* 22 mins

1. Choral S + hn ATB fl ob d'am unis str bc — G 6/4

Mache dich, mein Geist, bereit,	**Make ready, my spirit,**
Wache, fleh und bete,	**Watch, supplicate, and pray**
Daß dich nicht die böse Zeit	**That the evil time does not**
Unverhofft betrete;	**Unexpectedly come upon you;**
Denn es ist	**For it is**
Satans List	**Satan's subtlety**
Über viele Frommen	**That comes upon many devout souls**
Zur Versuchung kommen.	**In temptation.**

2. Aria A ob d'am str bc — e 3/8

Ach schläfrige Seele, wie? ruhest du noch?	Ah, slumbering soul, what? do you still rest?
Ermuntre dich doch!	Rouse yourself!
Es möchte die Strafe dich plötzlich erwecken	Punishment may suddenly wake you up
Und, wo du nicht wachest,	And, if you are not awake,
Im Schlafe des ewigen Todes bedecken.	Cover you in the sleep of eternal death.

3. Recitativo B bc — G–b C

Gott, so vor deine Seele wacht,	God, who watches over your soul,
Hat Abscheu an der Sünden Nacht;	Has a horror of the night of sin;
Er sendet dir sein Gnadenlicht	He sends you His Light of Grace,
Und will vor diese Gaben,	And for these gifts,
Die er so reichlich dir verspricht,	Which He so abundantly promises you,

Nur offne Geistesaugen haben.	Would but have from you open spiritual eyes.
Des Satans List ist ohne Grund,	Satan's subtlety is: without cause
Die Sünder zu bestricken;	To ensnare sinners;
Brichst du nun selbst den Gnadenbund,	If you now break the Covenant of Grace,
Wirst du die Hülfe nie erblicken.	You will never see salvation.
Die ganze Welt und ihre Glieder	The whole world and its members
Sind nichts als falsche Brüder;	Are nothing but false brothers;
Doch macht dein Fleisch und Blut hiebei	Yet your flesh and blood see in them
Sich lauter Schmeichelei.	Pure flattery.
4. ARIA S fl vc picc bc	b C
Bete aber auch dabei	**But pray too, even**
Mitten in dem Wachen!	**Amidst your watch!**
Bitte bei der großen Schuld	In your great guilt, ask
Deinen Richter um Geduld,	Your Judge for forbearance,
Soll er dich von Sünden frei	If He is to make you free of sin
Und gereinigt machen!	And purified!
5. RECITATIVO T bc	b–G C
Er sehnet sich nach unserm Schreien,	He longs for our crying,
Er neigt sein gnädig Ohr hierauf;	He bows down His gracious ear to it;
Wenn Feinde sich auf unsern Schaden freuen,	When enemies rejoice in our harm,
So siegen wir in seiner Kraft:	We are victorious through His strength:
Indem sein Sohn, in dem wir beten,	Since His Son, in whom we pray,
Uns Mut und Kräfte schafft	Gives us courage and strength
Und will als Helfer zu uns treten.	And will come to us as Saviour.
6. CHORAL SATB bc (+ instrs)	G C
Drum so laßt uns immerdar	**Therefore let us forever**
Wachen, flehen, beten,	**Watch, supplicate, pray,**
Weil die Angst, Not und Gefahr	**Since fear, distress, and danger**
Immer näher treten;	**Come ever nearer;**
Denn die Zeit	**For the time**
Ist nicht weit,	**Is not far**
Da uns Gott wird richten	**When God will judge us**
Und die Welt vernichten.	**And destroy the world.**

Bach composed this chorale cantata* for performance on 5 November 1724. The text is based on the ten-verse hymn of 1695 by Johann Burchard Freystein, whose theme—a warning to be vigilant and to pray—is only loosely connected with the Sunday Gospel.* It is not the kernel of the parable (the contrast between God's Grace and man's lack of mercy) that lies at the heart of this cantata text but rather a certain aspect of it: the king's demand for settlement catches the unfaithful servant unawares, which teaches us to be prepared when the Lord comes and demands settlement of us. Some such passage as Luke 21.36 perhaps suggested the choice of hymn for this Sunday: 'Thus watch and pray now always so that you may be accounted worthy of escaping all these things that shall come to pass . . .'. The anonymous librettist retained the first and last verses of Freystein's hymn literally and paraphrased the remainder so that movement no. 2 is derived from verse 2, no. 3 from verses 3–6, no. 4 from verse 7, and no. 5 from verses 8–9. The first two lines of verse 7 are quoted word for word in the principal section of the second aria, no. 4. The first aria-recitative pair (nos. 2–3) is concerned with the call to watch, the second pair (nos. 4–5) with the call to pray.

The opening chorus* follows Bach's favoured form. The chorale melody, *Straf mich nicht in deinem Zorn*, lies in the soprano, reinforced by horn and supported by the other voice parts in a part-imitative and part-homophonic* texture. This vocal structure is incorporated line by line within an independent orchestral setting. A special feature of this movement is that violins I, II, and viola are combined in unison and set against the woodwind, with the result that the instruments form a quartet texture made up of transverse flute,* oboe d'amore,* upper strings, and continuo. In the course of the movement, this texture undergoes several modifications. The ritornello opens in a two-part texture, for the woodwind are added only in its second half. Thus the introduction is divided into a six-bar duo section *a* and a five-bar quartet section *b*. These two sections have in common only the initial motive,* which continues to play an important role thereafter, although it shows no relationship with the chorale melody:

Shortened to quavers, it also provides the motivic material for the imitative* texture of the vocal substructure in chorale-lines 1, 3, and 7. In the episode after line 7, the structure of the instrumental music is altered, perhaps in order to represent graphically the dominance of Satan. Here, the two woodwind instruments unite in a unison statement of the six opening bars *a*, transposed to the dominant, and the strings expand the texture from its original two parts to three by introducing a new tumult motive in a lively semiquaver figuration. The last line of the chorale is now sung by the choir, after which a reverse da capo* of the introduction acts as concluding ritornello—*b a*, in which *a*, enriched not only by the tumult motive (now on the flute) but by an extra oboe part and thus augmented to four parts, forms a full-textured conclusion.

The second movement, an aria for alto voice, strings, and oboe d'amore, which in part doubles the first violin and in part takes a prominent concertante* role, is conceived in vividly text-related terms. The principal section is a melancholy siciliano, marked 'adagio'—apparently a lullaby of the 'slumbering soul'. The middle section contains an internal contrast: an *allegro* passage warns of sudden punishment, and then a return to the original *adagio* tempo reflects the 'sleep of eternal death'. A *secco* recitative, no. 3, leads to the second aria, no. 4, which, like the first, is slow in tempo: it is marked *molto adagio*. The compact texture of the first aria, however, now gives way to a transparent quartet texture made up of two obbligato* instruments (transverse flute and violoncello piccolo*), soprano voice, and simple supporting bass notes in the continuo. The eloquent instrumental theme *a* and its no less expressive counterpoint* *b* are present throughout the entire movement:

The soprano also takes possession of theme *a*. In this movement, Bach does not avail himself of the opportunity—as he frequently does in such cases elsewhere—of having the chorale melody sung, or at least suggested, at the hymn quotation 'Bete aber auch dabei mitten in dem Wachen!' ('But pray too, even amidst your watch!'). Among Bach's arias, this movement, with its rare instrumentation and its exploitation of a wide range of pitch—from the highest (flute) via treble (voice) and tenor (violoncello piccolo) to bass (continuo)—exercises an exceptional fascination on the listener.

Only very rarely in this cantata does a consoling encouragement of the congregation come to the fore. It is found, however, at the close of the recitative, no. 5, and is raised to special prominence by means of an arioso* expansion upon the words 'And will come to us as Saviour'. The plain concluding chorale setting, with its bass part broken up into quavers, finally returns to the underlying theme of the whole cantata, 'Watch, supplicate, pray'.

Ich armer Mensch, ich Sündenknecht, BWV 55

NBA I/26, p. 57 BC A157 Duration: *c.* 15 mins

1. Aria T fl ob d'am vln I,II bc — g $\frac{6}{8}$

Ich armer Mensch, ich Sündenknecht,	I, poor man, servant of sin,
Ich geh vor Gottes Angesichte	I go before God's Presence
Mit Furcht und Zittern zum Gerichte.	For judgement with fear and trembling.
Er ist gerecht, ich ungerecht.	He is just, I unjust.
Ich armer Mensch, ich Sündenknecht!	I, poor man, servant of sin!

2\. Recitativo T bc

c–d C

Ich habe wider Gott gehandelt
Und bin demselben Pfad,
Den er mir vorgeschrieben hat,
Nicht nachgewandelt.
Wohin? soll ich der Morgenröte Flügel
Zu meiner Flucht erkiesen,
Die mich zum letzten Meere wiesen,
So wird mich doch die Hand des Allerhöchsten finden
Und mir die Sündenrute binden.
Ach ja!
Wenn gleich die Höll ein Bette
Vor mich und meine Sünden hätte,
So wäre doch der Grimm des Höchsten da.
Die Erde schützt mich nicht,
Sie droht mich Scheusal zu verschlingen;
Und will ich mich zum Himmel schwingen,
Da wohnet Gott, der mir das Urteil spricht.

I have acted against God,
And that path
Which he prescribed for me
I have not followed.
Where now? Shall I choose the wings of the morning
For my flight,
Which would take me to the uttermost sea?
Then the hand of the Most High would still find me
And chastise me with the rods of sin.
Ah yes!
Even if hell had a bed
For me and my sins,
The wrath of the Highest would still be there.
The earth does not protect me:
It threatens to devour me, an object of horror;
And if I would leap up to heaven,
There dwells God, who pronounces judgement on me.

3\. Aria T fl bc

d C

Erbarme dich!
Laß die Tränen dich erweichen,
Laß sie dir zu Herzen reichen;
Laß um Jesu Christi willen
Deinen Zorn des Eifers stillen!
Erbarme dich!

Have mercy!
Let my tears soften You,
Let them reach Your Heart;
For Jesus Christ's sake,
Let Your jealous fury be stilled!
Have mercy!

4\. Recitativo T str bc

B♭ C

Erbarme dich!
Jedoch nun tröst ich mich,
Ich will nicht für Gerichte stehen
Und lieber vor dem Gnadenthron
Zu meinem frommen Vater gehen.
Ich halt ihm seinen Sohn,
Sein Leiden, sein Erlösen für,
Wie er für meine Schuld
Bezahlet und genug getan,
Und bitt ihn um Geduld,
Hinfüro will ichs nicht mehr tun.

Have mercy!
Yet now I console myself:
I will not stand for trial
But rather go before the Throne of Grace,
To my righteous Father.
I hold before Him His Son—
His Passion, His Redemption,
How He has paid for my wrongs
And done enough—
And beg Him for forbearance;
Henceforth I will no longer commit them.

So nimmt mich Gott zu Gnaden wieder an.

Then God will again receive me into Grace.

5. CHORAL SATB bc (+ instrs) B♭ C

Bin ich gleich von dir gewichen,
Stell ich mich doch wieder ein;
Hat uns doch dein Sohn verglichen
Durch sein Angst und Todespein.
Ich verleugne nicht die Schuld,
Aber deine Gnad und Huld
Ist viel größer als die Sünde,
Die ich stets bei mir befinde.

Though I have turned away from You,
I have nonetheless come back again;
Your Son has indeed reconciled us
Through His anguish and death's pain.
I do not deny my wrongs,
But Your grace and favour
Are far greater than my sin,
Which I continually find within me.

With the exception of the concluding chorale, this work is written for solo tenor (plus instrumental ensemble and continuo) only. Alongside a series of other solo cantatas by Bach, it originated in 1726, receiving its first performance that year on 17 November. Evidently, only the first two movements were then newly composed, however; movements 3–5 were adapted from an older, lost composition—possibly a Passiontide cantata or the lost Weimar Passion of 1717 (BC [D1]).[55]

The anonymous librettist refers directly to the Sunday Gospel's* account of the unfaithful steward. The distinctive antithesis of this parable—the mercy of God as opposed to the hard-heartedness of man—recurs in the words of the opening aria, 'He is just, I unjust'. And the overall structure of the libretto is stamped with this contrast: two movements each deal with the sinfulness of man (nos. 1–2) and the mercy of God (nos. 3–4). In his description of the omnipresence of God in the second movement, the poet draws upon images from Psalm 139.7–10. The third and fourth movements are interlinked by their common opening line, 'Erbarme dich!' ('Have mercy!'). These words and the chorale that follows—the sixth verse of the hymn *Werde munter, mein Gemüte* by Johann Rist (1642)—anticipate the movements with related text in the *St Matthew Passion*, which originated not long afterwards.

Bach's setting conspicuously favours woodwind instruments. In the opening aria, obbligato* flute and oboe d'amore* play together as a pair with frequent parallel thirds and sixths, as do the first and second violins. Together with the continuo, a five-part texture thus emerges, which is expanded to six parts upon the entry of the tenor voice. The polyphonic* web of parts, in conjunction with a preference for treble pitch (there is no viola part) and the exposed high tessitura of much of the tenor part, not only results in an extraordinarily rich texture, it also conjures up an impression of the writhing sinner who in vain revolts against his burden of sin, since he is unable to free himself from it. Note,

[55] See Glöckner, KB, NBA I/26, and the same author's 'Neue Spuren zu Bachs "Weimarer" Passion, *Leipziger Beiträge zur Bach-Forschung* 1 (1995), 33–46.

for example, the setting of the words 'Ich Sündenknecht' ('I, servant of sin'), of which two forms emerge in particular, transposed to various pitches:

A *secco* recitative, no. 2, is followed by the aria 'Erbarme dich' ('Have mercy') with obbligato flute, no. 3, which is comparable with the opening aria in richness of expression. Here, however, in place of the image of the writhing sinner, we find the gesture of beseeching, which is musically represented by a rising leap of a sixth and then a falling step of a second, by expressive, virtuoso flute passage-work, and by frequent use of the Neapolitan-sixth chord.* The manifold, ever-changing melodic garb of the words 'Erbarme dich' extends into the following recitative, no. 4, whose held string chords now bring the repose found by the sinner in his remembrance of Christ's Passion. This solace also radiates from the four-part concluding chorale, which is nonetheless more restrained in expression than the setting of the same verse in the *St Matthew Passion*.

2.23 Twenty-third Sunday after Trinity

EPISTLE: Philippians 3.17–21: Our citizenship is in heaven.
GOSPEL: Matthew 22.15–22: The Pharisees' trick question to Jesus: is it right to pay tribute to Caesar?

Nur jedem das Seine, BWV 163

NBA I/26, p. 79 BC A158 Duration: *c.* 18 mins

1. ARIA T str[56] bc — b C

Nur jedem das Seine!	Only to each his own!
Muß obrigkeit haben	If the authorities must have
Zoll, Steuern und Gaben,	Duties, taxes, and gratuities,
Man weigre sich nicht	Let no one refuse
Der schuldigen Pflicht!	His due obligation!
Doch bleibet das Herze dem Höchsten alleine.	Yet the heart remains for the Highest alone.

2. RECITATIVO B bc — G–a C

Du bist, mein Gott, der Geber aller Gaben;	You are, my God, the giver of all gifts;
Wir haben, was wir haben,	We have what we have

[56] The oboe d'amore specified in BG 33 is erroneous.

Allein von deiner Hand!	Solely from Your hand!
Du, du hast uns gegeben	You, You have given us
Geist, Seele, Leib und Leben	Spirit, soul, body, and life
Und Hab und Gut und Ehr und Stand!	And property, goods, honour, and standing!
Was sollen wir	What should we
Denn dir	Then pay You
Zur Dankbarkeit dafür erlegen,	In gratitude for this,
Da unser ganz Vermögen	Since our entire means
Nur dein und gar nicht unser ist?	Are only Yours and not ours at all?
Doch ist noch eins, das dir, Gott, wohlgefällt!	Yet there is still one thing, O God, that pleases You well!
Das Herze soll allein,	The heart alone,
Herr, deine Zinsemünze sein!	Lord, shall be Your coin of tribute!
Ach! aber ach! ist das nicht schlechtes Geld?	Ah! but alas! Is that not worthless money?
Der Satan hat dein Bild daran verletzet,	Satan has damaged Your Image on it:
Die falsche Münz ist abgesetzet.	This false coin is written off.
3. ARIA B vc obbl I,II bc	e c
Laß mein Herz die Münze sein,	Let my heart be the coin
Die ich dir, mein Jesu, steure!	That I pay You as tax, my Jesus!
Ist sie gleich nicht allzu rein;	Though it is not too clean,
Ach! so komm doch und erneure,	Ah! then come and restore,
Herr, den schönen Glanz bei ihr!	Lord, the lovely shine on it!
Komm! arbeite, schmelz und präge,	Come! work, refine, and stamp it,
Daß dein Ebenbild bei mir	That Your Image in me
Ganz erneuert glänzen möge.	May shine forth, quite renewed.
4. RECITATIVO [DUETTO] SA bc	b–D c
Ich wollte dir,	I would gladly,
O Gott, das Herze gerne geben!	O God, give You my heart!
Der Will ist zwar bei mir;	I have indeed the will;
Doch Fleisch und Blut will immer widerstreben,	Yet flesh and blood are always warring,
Dieweil die Welt	Since the world
Das Herz gefangen hält;	Holds my heart captive;
So will sie sich den Raub nicht nehmen lassen;	Thus it will not let the spoils be taken from it;
Jedoch ich muß sie hassen,	Yet I must hate the world
Wenn ich dich lieben soll!	If I am to love You!
So mache doch mein Herz mit deiner Gnade voll,	Then make my heart full of Your grace,
Leer es ganz aus von Welt und allen Lüsten	Empty it altogether of the world and all lusts,
Und mache mich zu einem rechten Christen.	And turn me into a true Christian.

5. ARIA [DUETTO] SA unis str bc D $\frac{3}{4}$

Nimm mich mir	Take me from myself
Und gib mich dir,	And give me to You,
nimm mich mir und meinem Willen,	Take my from myself and my will
Deinen Willen zu erfüllen!	To fulfil Your Will!
Gib dich mir mit deiner Güte,	Give Yourself to me with Your goodness,
Daß mein Herz und mein Gemüte	That my heart and my spirit
In dir bleibe für und für,	May abide in You for ever;
Nimm mich mir und gib mich dir!	Take me from myself and give me to You!

6. CHORAL [only bc extant] D C

Führ auch mein Herz und Sinn	**Lead my heart and mind**
Durch deinen Geist dahin,	**There through Your Spirit,**
Daß ich mög alles meiden,	**That I may avoid everything**
Was mich und dich kann scheiden,	**That can separate me and You,**
Und ich an deinem Leibe	**And of Your Body**
Ein Gliedmaß ewig bleibe.	**Ever remain a member.**

The text of this cantata is drawn from Salomo Franck's cycle *Evangelisches Andachts-Opffer* of 1715, and the work was performed for the first time that year on 24 November. The content is closely linked with the Gospel* reading. The opening aria paraphrases Jesus's reply to the Pharisees, and on this the poet's reflections in the following movements are based. The tribute money that we owe God is our heart. Unfortunately, however, it is often not God but a false image that is stamped on the coin, and this devalues it (no. 2). God is therefore asked to stamp His image on the heart anew (no. 3). This didactic metaphor is abandoned in the next two movements. In accordance with Paul's words in Romans 7.15, the Christian acknowledges that he cannot do the good that he wishes to do (no. 4); he therefore prays that he may be able to fulfil God's Will (no. 5). The prayer of the concluding chorale—the last verse of the hymn *Wo soll ich fliehen hin* by Johann Heermann (1630)—is on similar lines.

Bach's composition continues the chamber-music style that, in particular, characterizes the Weimar cantatas of the year 1715. The instrumental ensemble is restricted to strings and continuo (doubling woodwind might have been prescribed in the lost original parts but are nowhere used independently) and a choir is heard only in the concluding chorale. In the opening aria, the first line of text in the vocal A section is anticipated as a 'motto'*—

—a motive* heard not only in the vocal section but at the very opening of the instrumental ritornello, first in the continuo part and then in the first violin. It recurs in the same instrumental sequence in the middle of the ritornello and then proceeds to pervade the entire movement. Even the instruments constantly quote the catch-phrase of the whole cantata 'Nur jedem das Seine!' ('Only to each his own!').

A *secco* recitative (no. 2) leads to the second aria, whose scoring for bass voice, two cellos, and continuo is probably unique within Bach's output of arias: a quartet texture entirely restricted to bass pitch. The lively figuration of the two cellos lends the movement an excited, almost restless character, perhaps stimulated by the phrase 'Come! work, refine, and stamp it'. The rather lengthy text (as often in Franck) suggested to Bach a tripartite design without vocal da capo*.

The delight Bach took in experimentation in his younger years is no less in evidence in the following recitative, no. 4, which takes the form of a duet. The texture is throughout imitative and at times displays the rigour of a canon;* only seldom do brief homophonic* interjections occur. Although freedom of time in delivery is excluded in such a structure, Bach nonetheless achieves a marked contrast between the syllabically* declaimed opening and an increasingly melismatic* second half—a contrast that corresponds with the form of *secco* with arioso* conclusion favoured by Bach in other Weimar works. This recitative acts as a mere prelude to the duet-aria that follows, no. 5, whose text contains the prayer that emerges from the preceding reflections. Bach enriches the movement musically by introducing the chorale melody *Meinen Jesum laß ich nicht*, which is quoted line by line in unison strings alongside the continuo-accompanied vocal dialogue. By this means the imitative,* polyphonic* texture is enhanced beyond the level of the similarly textured recitative-arioso that precedes it.

For the finale, Bach notated only the continuo bass in the sole surviving score, together with the direction 'Chorale in semplice stylo'. The lost performing parts no doubt contained a full realization, presumably in the usual plain four-part texture. With the aid of the figured bass, a movement in the style of Bach's concluding chorales may easily be reconstructed. The melody usually sung in Weimar to the hymn *Wo soll ich fliehen hin* (elsewhere mostly sung to the tune *Auf meinen lieben Gott*) is known to us from the sixth movement of Cantata 199, *Mein Herze schwimmt im Blut*.

Bach no doubt revived this cantata on several occasions in Leipzig, though in view of the loss of the original performing material we cannot prove that he did. A peculiarity of the score is that it requires of the singers a higher tessitura than the other Weimar cantatas (the soprano part goes up to top b^2). Presumably the original performance took place not at the *Chorton* pitch* otherwise used in Weimar but at *Kammerton* pitch,* which was also customary in Leipzig.

Wohl dem, der sich auf seinen Gott, BWV 139

NBA I/26, p. 99 BC A159 Duration: *c.* 23 mins

1. CHORUS [CHORALE] SATB ob d'am I,II str bc E C

Wohl dem, der sich auf seinen Gott	**Blessed is he who can trust in his God**
Recht kindlich kann verlassen!	**Quite in the spirit of adoption!**
Den mag gleich Sünde, Welt und Tod	**Though sin, world, and death**
Und alle Teufel hassen,	**And all devils may hate him,**
So bleibt er dennoch wohlvergnügt,	**Yet he remains well contented**
Wenn er nur Gott zum Freunde kriegt.	**If only he obtains God as his friend.**

2. ARIA T vln conc I,II bc A $\frac{3}{4}$

Gott ist mein Freund; was hilft das Toben,	God is my friend; what use is that raging
So wider mich ein Feind erhoben!	Which the enemy has inflicted on me!
Ich bin getrost bei Neid und Haß.	I am confident amidst envy and hatred.
Ja, redet nur die Wahrheit spärlich,	Indeed, speak the truth but sparsely,
Seid immer falsch, was tut mir das?	Be ever false: what is that to me?
Ihr Spötter seid mir ungefährlich.	You mockers are harmless to me.

3. RECITATIVO A bc f♯ C

Der Heiland sendet ja die Seinen	The Saviour indeed sends His own people
Recht mitten in der Wölfe Wut.	Right into the midst of the wolf's fury.
Um ihn hat sich der Bösen Rotte	Around Him the assembly of the wicked,
Zum Schaden und zum Spotte	For harm and for mockery,
Mit List gestellt;	Have enclosed themselves with cunning;
Doch da sein Mund so weisen Ausspruch tut,	Yet since His mouth makes such a wise pronouncement,
So schützt er mich auch vor der Welt.	He protects me ever from the world.

4. ARIA B ob d'am I + II vln bc f♯ C/$\frac{6}{8}$

Das Unglück schlägt auf allen Seiten	Misfortune throws around me on all sides
Um mich ein zentnerschweres Band.	A hundred-weight bond.
Doch plötzlich erscheinet die helfende Hand.	Yet suddenly the helping hand appears.
Mir scheint des Trostes Licht von weiten;	Comfort's Light shines for me from afar;
Da lern ich erst, daß Gott allein	**Then I first learn that God alone**
Der Menschen bester Freund muß sein.	**Must be man's best friend.**

5. RECITATIVO S str bc c♯–E C

Ja, trag ich gleich den größten Feind in mir,	Yes, though I bear the greatest enemy within,
Die schwere Last der Sünden,	The heavy burden of iniquities,

Mein Heiland läßt mich Ruhe finden.	My Saviour lets me find rest.
Ich gebe Gott, was Gottes ist,	I give God what is God's,
Das Innerste der Seelen.	The innermost part of the soul.
Will er sie nun erwählen,	If He would now choose it,
So weicht der Sünden Schuld, so fällt des Satans List.	Then sin's guilt would retreat, then Satan's cunning would collapse.

6. Choral SATB bc (+ instrs) E c

Dahero Trotz der Höllen Heer!	**Therefore defy the host of hell!**
Trotz auch des Todes Rachen!	**Defy too the jaws of death!**
Trotz aller Welt! mich kann nicht mehr	**Defy all the world! I can no longer be made**
Ihr Pochen traurig machen!	**Sorrowful by its battering!**
Gott ist mein Schutz, mein Hilf und Rat;	**God is my defence, my help and counsel;**
Wohl dem, der Gott zum Freunde hat!	**Blessed is he who has God as his friend!**

This chorale cantata,* written for performance on 12 November 1724, is based on the five-verse hymn with the same opening line by Johann Christoph Rube (1692). As usual, the anonymous librettist retains the first and last verses word for word. The inner verses are each paraphrased to form a cantata movement (nos. 2, 4, and 5). The third movement, however, is a free insertion that establishes a link with the Sunday Gospel.* This takes place—by way of digression, as it were—at the very point where the hymn draws closest in content to the biblical narrative. Trust in God, says Rube's hymn, protects us in all things (verse 1): against the wickedness of the world (verse 2), against all misfortune (verse 3), from my burden of iniquities (verse 4), and finally from the fear of death (verse 5). After verse 2 (the wickedness of the world), the librettist adduces the biblical narrative as an example: the biblically depicted malice of the Pharisees is but another manifestation of the wickedness of the world, into which the Saviour sends His own people as among wolves (cf. Matthew 10.16). Yet even here Jesus protects me, since His mouth makes such a wise pronouncement—the reference here is to His reply to the Pharisees, 'Give to Caesar what is Caesar's and to God what is God's'. With this pronouncement the cunning attack of the world is staved off.

Bach's composition is transmitted only in a slightly incomplete set of performing parts: it lacks the second obbligato* part in the aria, no. 2, which was presumably for a second solo violin.[57] For the fourth movement, we possess (in addition to the other parts; see below) a violin part prepared for a revival around

[57] Dürr (*BJ* 1960, pp. 41 f.) and Scheide (*Bach-Studien* 5, pp. 123 ff.) established that the part was missing and concluded that it was probably for violin.

1744–7 by Bach's pupil and eventual son-in-law Johann Christoph Altnickol, who was resident in Leipzig from 1744 to 1748. Thus in 1724 the movement seems to have required a second obbligato instrument other than violin—perhaps a violoncello piccolo.*

The opening movement follows the design especially favoured by Bach. The chorale, sung by the choir with the melody in the soprano, is incorporated line by line within a concertante* orchestral texture. A distinctive feature of this particular movement is the clear reference made to the chorale in all parts. Even the theme of the introductory instrumental ritornello is derived from the chorale melody, *Machs mit mir, Gott, nach deiner Güt*:

This theme is maintained both in the instrumental episodes and in the postlude, a reprise of the opening ritornello. In the choral passages, all parts, when they are not resting, share in the theme of whichever chorale line is being sung. The soprano delivers the chorale line in minims, while the other voices, the two oboes d'amore,* and the continuo accompany it in an imitative texture with the chorale line diminished to quavers. At the beginning of each vocal passage the strings rest (probably to make the *cantus firmus** more audible) entering only towards the end of each chorale line. They too are thematic, provided that sufficient time remains for thematic treatment (in lines 1 and 3 they have only a brief cadence). Thematic imitation,* which in the 'normal' chorale-cantata first movement is restricted to the preparatory texture before the entry of the chorale *cantus firmus*, is thus here maintained throughout the whole chorale line. It even drives out the independent concertante texture of the instruments, which here finds scope only in the episodes.

In the aria 'Gott ist mein Freund', no. 2, Bach derives his thematic material from the textual contrast between the 'raging' of the enemy and the confident tranquillity of the Christian who is secure in the friendship of God. Voice and instruments have the same theme. In the opening ritornello, the two solo instruments and the continuo alternate between calm and excited passages, and in the vocal section the 'raging' is illustrated by lively violin figures. Even the middle section of the movement, which is designed in pure da capo* form, brings no relaxation.

Only eight bars of *secco* recitative separate the first aria from the second, no. 4, which again requires two obbligato instruments—in its transmitted form, unison oboes d'amore and violin. The flowing figuration and symmetrical form of the first aria here give way to oft-changing rhythms and a text-engendered multi-sectional form that might be construed as a complex variant of da capo form: a b c c a b^1 a^1 b^2. In the first aria textual antithesis was largely developed as a simultaneous contrast between calmer and more agitated parts; now it takes the form of successive contrast:

a 'Das Unglück schlägt . . .' ('Misfortune throws . . .'): dotted rhythms, 'poc' allegro'

b 'Doch plötzlich erscheinet . . .' ('Yet suddenly appears . . .'): triadic melody, compound duple time, 'vivace'

c 'Mir scheint des Trostes Licht . . .' ('Comfort's Light shines for me . . .'): flowing *cantabile*, continuo texture (the obbligato instruments resting), 'andante'

The last two lines of text ('Da lern ich erst . . .') are quoted from the third verse of the hymn, but in his setting Bach makes no reference at all to the chorale melody. The second recitative, no. 5, is accompanied by strings, which lends musical prominence to the admission that the 'greatest enemy' lies 'within me'. The line 'I give God what is God's' refers to Jesus's words in the Gospel* reading. A plain chorale setting ends the cantata.

Falsche Welt, dir trau ich nicht, BWV 52

NBA I/26, p. 133 BC A160 Duration: *c.* 18 mins

1. SINFONIA hn I,II ob I–III bsn str bc — F C
2. RECITATIVO S bc — d–a C

Falsche Welt, dir trau ich nicht!	False world, I do not trust you!
Hier muß ich unter Skorpionen	Here I must dwell among scorpions
Und unter falschen Schlangen wohnen.	And among false serpents.
Dein Angesicht,	Your countenance,
Das noch so freundlich ist,	Which is yet so friendly,
Sinnt auf ein heimliches Verderben:	Plans a secret destruction:
Wenn Joab küßt,	When Joab kisses,
So muß ein frommer Abner sterben.	Devout Abner must die.
Die Redlichkeit ist aus der Welt verbannt,	Honesty is banned from the world,
Die Falschheit hat sie fortgetrieben,	Falsehood has driven it away;
Nun ist die Heuchelei	Now hypocrisy
An ihrer Stelle blieben.	Remains in its place.
Der beste Freund ist ungetreu,	One's best friend is disloyal;
O jämmerlicher Stand!	Oh, what a lamentable situation!

3. ARIA S vln I,II bc — d C

Immerhin, immerhin,	After all, after all,

Wenn ich gleich verstoßen bin!	Even though I am cut off from Your sight,
Ist die falsche Welt mein Feind,	Though the false world is my enemy,
O so bleibt doch Gott mein Freund,	Oh, yet God remains my friend,
Der es redlich mit mir meint.	Who means to be honest with me.

4. RECITATIVO S bc — B♭–F C

Gott ist getreu!	God is faithful!
Er wird, er kann mich nicht verlassen;	He will not, He cannot forsake me;
Will mich die Welt und ihre Raserei	Even though the world and its frenzy
In ihre Schlingen fassen,	Would ensnare me,
So steht mir seine Hülfe bei.	His Salvation helps me.
Gott ist getreu!	God is faithful!
Auf seine Freundschaft will ich bauen	On His friendship I will build
Und meine Seele, Geist und Sinn	And my soul, spirit, and mind
Und alles, was ich bin,	And all that I am
Ihm anvertrauen.	I will commit to Him.
Gott ist getreu!	God is faithful!

5. ARIA S ob I–III bc — B♭ 3/4

Ich halt es mit dem lieben Gott,	I side with our dear God:
Die Welt mag nur alleine bleiben.	The world may be left alone.
Gott mit mir, und ich mit Gott,	God with me and I with God:
Also kann ich selber Spott	Thus I myself can cast derision
Mit den falschen Zungen treiben.	On false tongues.

6. CHORAL SATB bc (+ instrs; hn II independent) — F C

In dich hab ich gehoffet, Herr,	**In You I have placed my hope, Lord,**
Hilf, daß ich nicht zuschanden werd,	**Help me not to be put to shame**
Noch ewiglich zu Spotte!	**Nor eternally reproached!**
Das bitt ich dich,	**This I pray You,**
Erhalte mich	**Uphold me**
In deiner Treu, Herr Gotte!	**In Your faithfulness, Lord God!**

Whereas the librettist of Cantata 163, Salomo Franck, used the biblical account of the tribute money to create a very sturdy analogy between the coin and the heart of the Christian, here the wrath of the anonymous librettist is aroused exclusively by the cunning of the Pharisees who attempt to catch Jesus in a trap. The librettist, being a true child of his time, concludes that the Christian has no choice other than to turn his back on the world with all its falsehood and focus his mind on God alone. The murder of Abner by Joab (2 Samuel 3.27) is adduced as an example of worldly cunning. The four freely versified movements are ordered in clear antithesis: a recitative-aria pair each deals with the falsehood of the world (nos. 2–3) and the faithfulness of God (nos. 4–5). The cantata concludes with the first verse of the hymn *In dich hab ich gehoffet, Herr* by Adam Reusner (1533).

Bach's composition was written for performance on 24 November 1726. With the exception of the four-part concluding chorale, the vocal music is throughout for solo soprano only. All the richer by contrast is the instrumentation, which employs two horns, three oboes, strings, and continuo. As in several other cantatas of that year, Bach used an instrumental movement from his pre-Leipzig period as introductory sinfonia, in this case the first movement of the first Brandenburg Concerto in its early version without violino piccolo, BWV 1046a.

The vocal portion of the cantata opens with a *secco* recitative, no. 2, which leads to the first aria, no. 3, scored for soprano, two violins, and continuo. The instrumental motives* and, above all, the brief interjections of 'Immerhin' ('after all') from the soprano strikingly illustrate the Christian's disdainful contempt for a world that is of no consequence to him. Even in the middle section, where we are told that 'God remains my friend' and the soprano develops a sustained melody rich in coloraturas,* the violins nonetheless constantly reiterate their opening motive.

The two movements that follow are concerned with the faithfulness of God. The brief *secco* recitative no. 4, with its repeated statement of the words 'Gott ist getreu' ('God is faithful'), reaches the borders of arioso.* The following aria, no. 5, is relaxed and dance-like on account of its scoring for three oboes and continuo, its decidedly chordal texture, its triple time, and the clearly periodic phrase structure of its melody. This dance character apparently reflects not the 'world', as is often the case elsewhere, but rather the joy of those who know themselves to be secure in God. In the plain concluding chorale, a pair of horns—otherwise used only in the introductory sinfonia—are added to the instrumental ensemble. Horn I reinforces the chorale melody in the soprano, while horn II has an independent part due to its restriction to the notes of the natural harmonic series.

2.24 Twenty-fourth Sunday after Trinity

EPISTLE: Colossians 1.9–14: Paul prays for the Colossians.
GOSPEL: Matthew 9.18–26: The raising from the dead of Jairus's daughter.

O Ewigkeit, du Donnerwort, BWV 60

NBA I/27, p. 3 BC A161 Duration: *c.* 20 mins

1. ARIA A + hn T ob d'am I,II str bc — D C

Furcht	*Fear*
O Ewigkeit, du Donnerwort,	**O Eternity, you word of thunder!**
O Schwert, das durch die Seele bohrt,	**O sword that bores through the soul!**
O Anfang sonder Ende!	**O beginning without end!**
O Ewigkeit, Zeit ohne Zeit,	**O Eternity, time without time!**

Ich weiß vor großer Traurigkeit	**I know not, from great sorrow,**
Nicht, wo ich mich hinwende;	**Where to turn;**
Mein ganz erschrocknes Herze bebt,	**My quite terrified heart trembles**
Daß mir die Zung am Gaumen klebt.	**So that my tongue cleaves to my palate.**
Hoffnung	*Hope*
'Herr, ich warte auf dein Heil.'	'Lord, I wait for Your Salvation.'
2. RECITATIVO AT bc	b–G c
Furcht	*Fear*
O schwerer Gang zum letzten Kampf und Streite!	A hard road to the last battle and strife!
Hoffnung	*Hope*
Mein Beistand ist schon da,	My Helper is already there:
Mein Heiland steht mir ja	My Saviour indeed stands
Mit Trost zur Seite.	At my side with comfort.
Furcht	*Fear*
Die Todesangst, der letzte Schmerz	Fear of death, that last agony,
Ereilt und überfällt mein Herz	Overtakes and surprises my heart
Und martert diese Glieder.	And tortures my limbs.
Hoffnung	*Hope*
Ich lege diesen Leib vor Gott zum Opfer nieder.	I lay down this body before God as a sacrifice.
Ist gleich der Trübsal Feuer heiß,	Though the furnace of adversity is hot,
Genung, es reinigt mich zu Gottes Preis.	Enough: it purifies me to God's praise.
Furcht	*Fear*
Doch nun wird sich der Sünden große Schuld	Yet now my sins' great guilt
Vor mein Gesichte stellen.	Will appear before my countenance.
Hoffnung	*Hope*
Gott wird deswegen doch kein Todesurteil fällen.	Nonetheless God will not on that account sentence you to death.
Er gibt ein Ende den Versuchungsplagen,	He provides a way of escape from the torments
Daß man sie kann ertragen.	Of temptation, so that one will be able to bear them.
3. ARIA [DUETTO] AT ob d'am I vln I solo bc	b $\frac{3}{4}$
Furcht	*Fear*
Mein letztes Lager will mich schrecken,	My last bed will terrify me,
Hoffnung	*Hope*
Mich wird des Heilands Hand bedecken,	My Saviour's hand will hide me,
Furcht	*Fear*
Des Glaubens Schwachheit sinket fast,	Faith's weakness almost sinks,

Hoffnung
Mein Jesus trägt mit mir die Last.
Furcht
Das offne Grab sieht greulich aus,
Hoffnung
Es wird mir doch ein Friedenshaus.

Hope
My Jesus bears the burden with me.
Fear
The open sepulchre looks dreadful,
Hope
Yet it will be for me a peaceable habitation.

4. Recitativo AB bc e–D c

Furcht
Der Tod bleibt doch der menschlichen Natur verhaßt
Und reißet fast
Die Hoffnung ganz zu Boden.
Baß
'Selig sind die Toten;'
Furcht
Ach! aber ach, wieviel Gefahr
Stellt sich der Seele dar,
Den Sterbeweg zu gehen!
Vielleicht wird ihr der Höllenrachen
Den Tod erschrecklich machen,
Wenn er sie zu verschlingen sucht;
Vielleicht ist sie bereits verflucht
Zum ewigen Verderben.
Baß
'Selig sind die Toten, die in dem
Herren sterben;'
Furcht
Wenn ich im Herren sterbe,
Ist denn die Seligkeit mein Teil und Erbe?
Der Leib wird ja der Würmer Speise!

Ja, werden meine Glieder
Zu Staub und Erde wieder,
Da ich ein Kind des Todes heiße,
So schein ich ja im Grabe zu verderben.
Baß
'Selig sind die Toten, die in dem
Herren sterben, von nun an.'
Furcht
Wohlan!
Soll ich von nun an selig sein:
So stelle dich, o Hoffnung, wieder ein!

Fear
Yet death remains hateful to human nature
And almost pulls
Hope right down to the ground.
Bass
'Blessed are the dead;'
Fear
Ah! but alas, how much danger
Presents itself to the soul
In walking on the path of death!
Perhaps the jaws of hell will make
Death terrifying to my soul
When they seek to devour it;
Perhaps it is already condemned
To everlasting destruction.
Bass
'Blessed are the dead who die in the
Lord;'
Fear
If I die in the Lord,
Is then Salvation my portion and inheritance?
The body indeed becomes the food of worms!
Indeed, my limbs will return
To dust and earth;
As I am called a child of death,
Indeed I seem to decay in the grave.

Bass
'Blessed are the dead who die in the Lord
from henceforth.'
Fear
Well, then!
If I am to be blessed from henceforth:
Then appear again, O Hope!

Mein Leib mag ohne Furcht im Schlafe ruhn,	My body may rest in sleep without fear,
Der Geist kann einen Blick in jene Freude tun.	My spirit can catch a glimpse of the joy hereafter.

5. CHORALE SATB bc (+ instrs) A c

Es ist genung;	**It is enough;**
Herr, wenn es dir gefällt,	**Lord, if it pleases You,**
So spanne mich doch aus!	**Then do unharness me!**
Mein Jesus kömmt;	**My Jesus comes;**
Nun gute Nacht, o Welt!	**Now good night, O world!**
Ich fahr ins Himmelshaus,	**I am going into my heavenly frame,**
Ich fahre sicher hin mit Frieden,	**I go there securely in peace;**
Mein großer Jammer bleibt danieden.	**My great woe remains down below.**
Es ist genung.	**It is enough.**

This cantata originated during Bach's first year in Leipzig and was performed for the first time on 7 November 1723. The anonymous librettist refers to the Sunday Gospel* read out before the cantata performance. As in the cantatas for the Sixteenth Sunday after Trinity, the raising of the dead by Jesus is felt as a symbol of our own resurrection, which the person confronting death awaits with doubt and hope. This wavering between despair and confidence forms the theme of the cantata, which is fashioned as a 'Dialogue between Fear and Hope'. In these two allegorical figures the divided soul of man is reflected.

The text displays a systematic and symmetrical structure. It is framed by two chorales: the first verse of Johann Rist's hymn *O Ewigkeit, du Donnerwort* (1642) and the fifth verse of the hymn *Es ist genung, so nimm, Herr, meinen Geist* by Franz Joachim Burmeister (1662). Two biblical passages also function as a frame: 'Lord, I wait for Your Salvation' (Genesis 49.18) is the response of Hope to the chorale sung by Fear in the first movement; and 'Blessed are the dead . . .' (Revelation 14.13) in the penultimate movement is another response to the objections of Fear who, on the strength of it, casts aside his anxieties once and for all. Thus the first biblical text follows from the opening chorale, and the concluding chorale from the second biblical text. The middle movements are freely versified. At the centre is a duet-aria, around which are grouped two recitatives (of which the second alternates with biblical words, as noted above).

With the exception of the concluding chorale, the entire work is set as a dialogue; solo vocal movements are altogether absent. In the fourth movement, however, there is a change of dialogue partners. Previously the alto took the part of Fear and the tenor that of Hope, but now the alto of Fear is joined by the bass, the *vox Christi*, for it is not Hope—part of the divided soul of man—who announces the blessedness of the dead 'who die in the Lord' but rather the authority of God. Only thus do we understand when, at the end of the movement, Fear sings, 'Then appear again, O Hope!'; the bass cannot be meant by this, since only three bars earlier he was engaged in a duet with Fear!

The opening movement takes the form of a chorale arrangement for solo alto with framing ritornellos and interspersed orchestral episodes. From the second *Stollen** onwards the tenor, in counterpoint* with the chorale and the ritornello theme, sings biblical words in a freely moving arioso* made up of extensive melodic arches, occasionally including ritornello motives.* The orchestral ritornello, whose theme holds this multi-layered movement together, consists of a lamenting duet for two oboes d'amore* against the background of an ostinato-like tremolo motive for strings and continuo which pervades the entire movement. If the oboe duet might be construed as the yearning wait for the Lord's Salvation, the tremolo motive would then depict the trembling of Fear. This motive is derived from the chorale melody (the second half of line 1)—

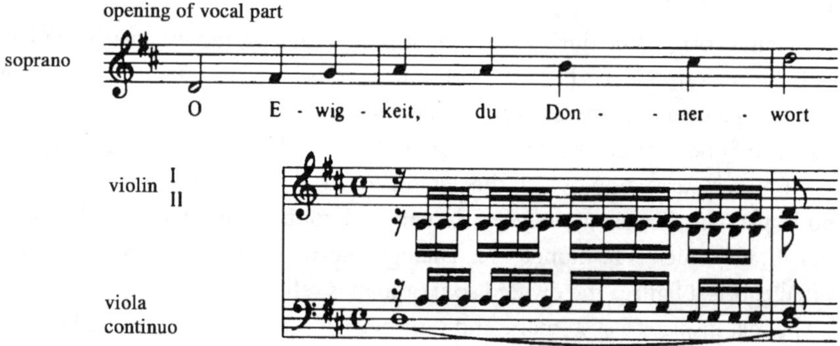

—and by allusion it also anticipates the first line of the concluding chorale (see below).

The following dialogue-recitative begins as *secco*, but in two places it changes into arioso: at the word 'martert' ('tortures'), where we hear a chromatic* melisma* with brief supporting chords; and at the close on 'ertragen' ('bear'), which is sung to a wide-ranging melisma accompanied by complementary figures in the continuo. The first arioso passage is assigned to Fear, the second to Hope.

The central movement, the duet-aria, acquires its dramatic style from the dialogue character of the work as a whole. Only the instrumental ritornellos ensure formal coherence, for the three vocal sections, A B C, lack clearly perceptible thematic links between each other. Each section, however, pursues the same course, beginning with the reflections of Fear, to which Hope responds, after which the two sing together as a duet, Hope having the last word. Each section thus comprises the threefold sequence solo–duet–solo. The clearly text-engendered nature of the melodic material prevents the two voices from sharing the same theme, but their themes are interrelated. The theme of Fear is remodelled in a characteristic manner in the reply of Hope, for example in section A:

or in section C:

The dialogue character of the movement extends to the instrumental themes, though not in the form of alternating entries but rather that of simultaneous contrast. Thus the oboe d'amore and continuo have, for the most part, an emphatically rhythmic motive made up of dotted rhythms, while the solo violin intersperses flowing scale passages. In form, then, the movement is closer to the open form of the motet* than to the closed form of the aria. Its course is directional rather than symmetrical and its melodic writing motivically rather than thematically imprinted.

A directional course is also taken by the following recitative, no. 4, in which the *secco* of Fear is three times interrupted by bass arioso. As in the central chorus* of the *Actus tragicus*, BWV 106, the repetition serves the purpose of intensification, increasing awareness and final catharsis. While the *secco* of Fear, of its very nature, remains thematically free as its text very gradually falls in with that of the bass, the bass arioso takes the form of variations. Each portion of arioso text is longer than the previous one, according to the scheme a ab abc. Musically, the second arioso section is a repeat of the first, transposed up a tone, and the third a much expanded variant of those that precede it. The overall scheme is thus A A A^1. The fascination of these ariosos lies in their memorable and eloquent melodic line which presents the text in heightened speech but without the dependence on the text fettering the musical flow. Here we encounter a late, ripe fruit of continuo-accompanied monody* or sacred solo concerto* at a time when text-engendered declamation and musically finished form had, in general, long since come to separate fruition in recitative and aria respectively.

The finale comprises Burmeister's hymn to the melody by Johann Rudolf Ahle, father of Johann Georg Ahle, both of whom were Bach's predecessors as organist of the Blasiuskirche, Mühlhausen. The opening, with its sequence of three whole tones, forming a tritone (the so-called 'Diabolus in musica') might have been felt as outrageous in Ahle's time, only justified as a musical figure depicting the soul's crossing over from life into death:

This image becomes still clearer within Bach's composition if we compare it with the initial motive of the whole work, derived from the chorale *O Ewigkeit, du Donnerwort*: the opening figure a-b-c^1 sharp-d^1 becomes in the finale a^1-b^1-c^2 sharp-d^2 sharp. This whole-tone sequence fascinated Alban Berg, who wove this very Bach chorale into his Violin Concerto. No doubt he would have been no less fascinated by Bach's setting itself, whose harmonization and loosening-up into polyphony* allows the text to become, as it were, transparent—something that not even Bach always achieved. Here, for example, is the sixth line of the chorale:

Ach wie flüchtig, ach wie nichtig, BWV 26

NBA I/27, p. 31 BC A162 Duration: *c.* 19 mins

1. [Chorale] S + hn ATB ob I–III + fl str bc a C

Ach wie flüchtig, ach wie nichtig	**Ah how fleeting, ah how empty**
Ist der Menschen Leben!	**Is the life of man!**
Wie ein Nebel bald entstehet	**As a mist soon arises**
Und auch wieder bald vergehet,	**And soon passes away again,**
So ist unser Leben, sehet!	**So too is our life, see!**

2. Aria T fl solo vln I solo bc — C 6/8

So schnell ein rauschend Wasser schießt,
So eilen unser Lebenstage.
Die Zeit vergeht, die Stunden eilen,
Wie sich die Tropfen plötzlich teilen,
Wenn alles in den Abgrund schießt.

As swiftly as rushing water shoots forth
Do the days of our life run by.
Time passes away, hours run by
Just as the drops suddenly divide
When everything shoots into the depths.

3. Recitativo A bc — C–e c

Die Freude wird zur Traurigkeit,
Die Schönheit fällt als eine Blume,
Die größte Stärke wird geschwächt,
Es ändert sich das Glücke mit der Zeit,
Bald ist es aus mit Ehr und Ruhme,
Die Wissenschaft und was ein Mensche dichtet,
Wird endlich durch das Grab vernichtet.

Joy turns to heaviness,
Beauty withers like a flower,
The greatest strength is weakened,
Good fortune changes with time,
Soon it is over with honour and renown,
Knowledge and whatever man imagines
Are finally destroyed by the grave.

4. Aria B ob I–III bc — e ¢

An irdische Schätze das Herze zu hängen,
Ist eine Verführung der törichten Welt.
Wie leichtlich entstehen verzehrende Gluten,
Wie rauschen und reißen die wallenden Fluten,
Bis alles zerschmettert in Trümmern zerfällt.

To set one's heart on earthly treasures
Is a seduction of the foolish world.
How easily consuming blazes arise,
How the foaming floods rush and tear
Till everything collapses, dashed to pieces.

5. Recitativo S bc — G–a c

Die höchste Herrlichkeit und Pracht
Umhüllt zuletzt des Todes Nacht.
Wer gleichsam als ein Gott gesessen,
Entgeht dem Staub und Asche nicht,
Und wenn die letzte Stunde schläget,
Daß man ihn zu der Erde träget,
Und seiner Hoheit Grund zerbricht,
Wird seiner ganz vergessen.

The highest glory and splendour
Is at last enveloped in death's night.
Whoever sat, as it were, like a god
Does not escape dust and ashes,
And when his last hour strikes
And he is carried to the earth
And the foundation of his dignity is shattered,
He will be quite forgotten.

6. Choral SATB bc (+ instrs) — a c

Ach wie flüchtig, ach wie nichtig
Sind der Menschen Sachen!
Alles, alles, was wir sehen,
Das muß fallen und vergehen.
Wer Gott fürcht', bleibt ewig stehen.

Ah how fleeting, ah how empty
Are the affairs of man!
All, all that we see
Must fall and perish.
Whoever fears God shall endure for ever.

This work belongs to Bach's cycle of chorale cantatas* and was written for performance on 19 November 1724. It is based on the thirteen-verse hymn by Michael Franck (1652), whose first and last verses were adopted literally in the outer movements, whereas the remainder were so paraphrased by the anonymous librettist that a large number of hymn verses could be condensed into only a few cantata movements. Since the substance of the chorale is an enumeration of transitory things, it is easy to follow the use of the various verses in the paraphrase: the keywords in both hymn and paraphrase are 'days' (verse 2, movement 2), 'joy', 'beauty', 'strength', 'good fortune', 'honour', 'knowledge', 'imaginings' (verses 3–9, movement 3), 'treasures' (verse 10, movement 4), 'glory' and 'splendour' (verses 11–12, movement 5). Although the hymn is clearly related to the Sunday Gospel* account of the raising from the dead, it nonetheless restricts itself to a general statement of the theme without going into details. Indeed, even the contradiction revealed therein—that Jesus brings the dead back to this 'ah so empty' life—remains undiscussed.

The opening movement follows Bach's favoured design for the first chorus* of his chorale cantatas. Embedded within a thematically independent orchestral texture, the chorale is delivered by the soprano (reinforced by horn) line by line, supported by the three lower voices, whose chordal yet swiftly moving texture (in quavers) illustrates the fleeting nature of life. Each chorale line ends with a unison quotation of the first two half-lines of the chorale melody ('Ah how fleeting, ah how empty') in quaver motion, with changing text, in the three lower voice parts. The orchestral theme depicts the fleeting nature of earthly life still more vividly. Flute, three oboes, and strings are united in chordal rising and falling semiquaver scales. Even the continuo takes up these scale figures, whose spectral showers refuse to come to rest throughout the entire movement.

The scale figures even extend into the tenor aria (no. 2), now in a more flowing form—the text tells of the swiftness of rushing waters—but no less lively for all that. The two obbligato* instruments, transverse flute* and solo violin, keep changing function. At times both run in unison, with temporary resting of the violin part, suggestive of echo effects; elsewhere, violin and continuo adopt an accompanying role; and in still other places, flute and violin run in thirds or else unite in some other kind of concertante* duet. Even the tenor voice takes up the markedly instrumental-style scale theme of the obbligato parts, uniting with them in a homogeneous quartet texture. Only in the middle section, at the words 'Just as the drops suddenly divide', do triadic motives* temporarily supplant the running scales.

In the third movement, the rhythmic motion of the cantata calms down for the first time, after an introductory coloratura* on 'Freude' ('joy'), subsiding in plain *secco* declamation. In the following aria (no. 4), however, the weird death-dance mood is newly awakened when three oboes and continuo strike up in a genuine bourrée. Again, the singer takes up the instrumental theme, here designed to characterize the 'earthly treasures' with which we are seduced. Due to the minor mode, coupled with the oboe sonority, the atmosphere conjured up is not one of liberating joyfulness but rather of macabre fear: Death strikes up and men have to dance to his shawm. The following recitative, no. 5, like the previous one, is composed as plain *secco*. Only the last line of the concluding chorale, 'Whoever fears God shall endure for ever', brings a suggestion of comfort.

In verbal content this cantata may have little in common with what a preacher of our time would have to say about the Gospel reading. Yet in its imposing display of pregnant images it creates a stirring impression, it accords well with the general themes of the close of the church year, and from a musical standpoint, above all, it is an unrivalled masterpiece.

2.25 Twenty-fifth Sunday after Trinity

EPISTLE: 1 Thessalonians 4.13–18: The Second Coming of Christ.
GOSPEL: Matthew 24.15–28: Temptations at the end of the world.

Es reißet euch ein schrecklich Ende, BWV 90

NBA I/27, p. 61 BC A163 Duration: *c.* 14 mins

1. [ARIA] T str bc	d 3/8
Es reißet[58] euch ein schrecklich Ende,	A terrifying end sweeps you away,
Ihr sündlichen Verächter, hin.	You sinful despisers!
Der Sünden Maß ist voll gemessen,	The measure of your sin is full,
Doch euer ganz verstockter Sinn	Yet your quite hardened mind
Hat seines Richters ganz vergessen.	Has altogether forgotten its Judge.
2. RECITATIVO A bc	B♭–d c
Des Höchsten Güte wird von Tag zu Tag neu,	The Highest's goodness is new from day to day,
Der Undank aber sündigt stets auf Gnade.	But ingratitude constantly sins against Grace.
O, ein verzweifelt böser Schade,	Oh, what a desperately malignant bruise
So dich in dein Verderben führt.	That leads you to your destruction!
Ach! wird dein Herze nicht gerührt?	Ah! is your heart not moved,
Daß Gottes Güte dich	So that God's goodness leads you
Zur wahren Buße leitet?	To true repentance?
Sein treues Herze lässet sich	His faithful Heart reveals itself
Zu ungezählter Wohltat schauen:	In countless good deeds:
Bald läßt er Tempel auferbauen,	Now He has the Temple built,
Bald wird die Aue zubereitet,	Now the pasture is prepared

[58] The version 'reifet' is a misreading found in older editions.

Auf die des Wortes Manna fällt,	On which the Word's Manna falls
So dich erhält.	That upholds you.
Jedoch, o! Bosheit dieses Lebens,	Yet, oh! the wickedness of this life:
Die Wohltat ist an dir vergebens.	Good deeds are for you of no avail.

3. Aria B tr str bc — B♭ C

So löschet im Eifer der rächende Richter	Thus the avenging Judge in His jealousy
Den Leuchter des Wortes zur Strafe doch aus.	Will extinguish the candlestick of the Word for punishment.
Ihr müsset, o Sünder, durch euer Verschulden	Through your guilt, O sinners, you must endure
Den Greuel an heiliger Stätte erdulden,	The abomination in the holy place;
Ihr machet aus Tempeln ein mörderisch Haus.	You make a murderous house out of temples.

4. Recitativo T bc — g–d C

Doch Gottes Auge sieht auf uns als Auserwählte:	Yet God's eye looks upon us as the elect;
Und wenn kein Mensch der Feinde Menge zählte,	And though no one could count the number of his enemies,
So schützt uns doch der Held in Israel,	Yet the Hero in Israel protects us,
Es hemmt sein Arm der Feinde Lauf	His Arm impedes the enemy's movement
Und hilft uns auf;	And helps us up;
Des Wortes Kraft wird in Gefahr	In peril the Word's power
Um so viel mehr erkannt und offenbar.	Is all the more recognized and revealed.

5. Choral SATB bc (+ instrs) — d C

Leit uns mit deiner rechten Hand	**Lead us with Your right hand**
Und segne unser Stadt und Land;	**And bless our city and land;**
Gib uns allzeit dein heilges Wort,	**Grant us always Your Holy Word,**
Behüt fürs Teufels List und Mord;	**Guard us from the devil's cunning and murder;**
Verleih ein selges Stündelein,	**Grant us a blessed hour of death**
Auf daß wir ewig bei dir sein!	**So that we are with You for ever!**

The anonymous librettist of this cantata draws from the Sunday Gospel* reading the threat of the 'abomination of desolation' which will lead the human race into temptation before the Last Day. Towards the end, in the fourth movement, the poet alludes to the consoling prophecy that 'for the sake of the elect those days shall be shortened' (Matthew 24.22). The text contains an exceptionally large number of biblical allusions:

Second movement

The Highest's goodness is new from day to day	Lamentations 3.22f.
But ingratitude constantly sins against Grace	Romans 6.1

Ah! is your heart not moved,	
So that God's goodness leads you	
To true repentance?	Romans 2.4
Now He has the Temple built	Zechariah 6.12–15
Now the pasture is prepared	Psalm 23.2
Third movement	
Thus the avenging Judge in His jealousy	
Will extinguish the candlestick of the Word for punishment	Nahum 1.2 and Revelation 2.5
You make a murderous house out of temples	Matthew 21.13 (and elsewhere)
Fourth movement	
Yet God's eye looks upon us as the elect	Matthew 24.22 (see above)

The seventh verse of the hymn *Nimm von uns, Herr, du treuer Gott* by Martin Moller (1584) serves as the concluding chorale.

Bach set this text to music for performance on 14 November 1723. Unfortunately, the autograph score (the sole surviving original source) gives no information whatsoever as to the scoring required. The participation of voices, strings, and continuo, of course, follows directly from the appearance of the score. And for the obbligato* instrument in the third movement only the trumpet (or possibly horn) comes into consideration. However, we remain in the dark as to whether, in certain movements (nos. 1 and 5; perhaps no. 3 also), the strings are to be reinforced by oboes, as they usually are in Bach's cantata orchestra.

The opening movement is an impassioned tenor aria, rich in coloraturas,* in which the lively figuration and rapid scale passages of the first violin (the second violin and viola have an accompanying function) illustrate the threat of punishment for sinners. In the middle section, however, continuo texture is predominant: the strings are here restricted to episodes and occasional interjections.

The two recitatives are set as plain *secco*, but the second aria (no. 3) again requires full string accompaniment, together with a trumpet (or possibly horn; see above), which competes with the strings not only in its signal-like triadic melody but in its rapid passage-work. The aria recalls its predecessor in ardour, but the vocal coloraturas of that movement here give way to the *reveille* character of syllabic* triad motives.* The preference for continuo texture in the middle section also recalls the structure of the first movement. On this occasion, however, the freely formed da capo* allows the inclusion of a coda-like passage in continuo texture before the arrival of the concluding instrumental ritornello. The concluding chorale is a plain four-part setting to the melody *Vater unser im Himmelreich*.

Du Friedefürst, Herr Jesu Christ, BWV 116

NBA I/27, p. 81 BC A164 Duration: *c.* 21 mins

1. [Chorale] S + hn ATB ob d'am I,II str bc — A ¢

Du Friedefürst, Herr Jesu Christ,
Wahr' Mensch und wahrer Gott,
Ein starker Nothelfer du bist
Im Leben und im Tod.
Drum wir allein
Im Namen dein
Zu deinem Vater schreien.

You Prince of Peace, Lord Jesus Christ,
True Man and true God,
A strong Helper in distress are You,
In life and in death.
Therefore
In Your Name alone
Do we cry to Your Father.

2. Aria A ob d'am I solo bc — f♯ 3/4

Ach, unaussprechlich ist die Not
Und des erzürnten Richters Dräuen!
Kaum, daß wir noch in dieser Angst,
Wie du, o Jesu, selbst verlangst,
Zu Gott in deinem Namen schreien.

Ah, unspeakable is the distress
And the incensed Judge's threats!
In this anguish we can scarcely—
As You Yourself, O Jesus, demand—
Cry to God in Your Name.

3. Recitativo T bc — A–E c

Gedenke doch,
O Jesu, daß du noch
Ein Fürst des Friedens heißest!
Aus Liebe wolltest du dein Wort uns senden.
Will sich dein Herz auf einmal von uns wenden,
Der du so große Hülfe sonst beweisest?

Remember,
O Jesus, that You are still
Called a Prince of Peace!
Out of Love You would send us Your Word.
Would You all of a sudden turn Your Heart away from us,
You who have otherwise shown us such great help?

4. Terzetto STB bc — E 3/4

Ach, wir bekennen unsre Schuld
Und bitten nichts als um Geduld
Und um dein unermeßlich Lieben.
Es brach ja dein erbarmend Herz,
Als der Gefallnen Schmerz
Dich zu uns in die Welt getrieben.

Ah, we acknowledge our debt
And pray for nothing but patience
And for Your immeasurable Love.
Your merciful Heart indeed broke
When the pain of the fallen
Drove You to us in the world.

5. Recitativo A str bc — c♯–A c

Ach, laß uns durch die scharfen Ruten
Nicht allzu heftig bluten!
O Gott, der du ein Gott der Ordnung bist,
Du weißt, was bei der Feinde Grimm
Vor Grausamkeit und Unrecht ist.
Wohlan, so strecke deine Hand
Auf ein erschreckt geplagtes Land,
Die kann der Feinde Macht bezwingen
Und uns beständig Friede bringen!

Ah, from the sharp lashes
Let us not bleed too heavily!
O God, You who are a God of order,
In the enemy's fury You know
What cruelty and wrong there is.
Well then, stretch out Your hand
On a terrified, plagued land;
It can conquer the enemy's might
And bring us lasting peace!

6. CHORAL SATB bc (+ instrs) A C

Erleucht auch unser Sinn und Herz	**And illuminate our mind and heart**
Durch den Geist deiner Gnad,	**Through the Spirit of Your Grace,**
Daß wir nicht treiben draus ein Scherz,	**So that we do not make a jest out of it**
Der unsrer Seelen Schad.	**To the loss of our souls.**
O Jesu Christ,	**O Jesus Christ,**
Allein du bist,	**You alone are the One**
Der solchs wohl kann ausrichten.	**Who can indeed do this.**

This chorale cantata,* from the cycle of 1724–5, was written for performance on 26 November 1724. It is based on the seven-verse hymn by Jakob Ebert (1601), of which the first and last verses were retained literally, while the inner verses were paraphrased so that verses 2–4 became the like-numbered cantata movements and verses 5–6 the fifth movement.[59] The author of this paraphrase is unknown. The text of the chosen hymn bewails the deserved misfortune that has befallen mankind and prays for forgiveness and for deliverance from all dangers, among which the misery of war is named as the greatest. The cantata paraphrase largely follows the text of the hymn. Although the general connection with the Sunday Gospel* and its announcement of the Abomination of Desolation is clear, the cantata librettist has hardly taken the trouble to interweave specific allusions to the reading.

The opening movement follows the formal scheme favoured by Bach for his large-scale chorale choruses. The chorale melody, sung by the soprano (reinforced by horn) line by line in long notes (mainly minims), is incorporated within a thematically independent orchestral texture which includes surrounding ritornellos and episodes between the lines of the chorale. Within the instrumental ensemble, which is made up of two oboes d'amore,* strings, and continuo, the first violin, with its lively concertante* figuration, is predominant. The treatment of the vocal substructure that accompanies the chorale melody varies. In the outer lines it is relatively plain, but in the second half it becomes more independent (italics denote instrumental passages):

1st Stollen:*

Lines 1 and 2: homogeneous, chordal accompanying texture in the same basic note-values as the chorale melody (minims); *instruments independent*

2nd Stollen:

Lines 3 and 4: more lively, imitative* texture, making use of the ritornello theme; *instruments partly colla parte**

[59] The former assumption that the cantata contained freely-versified interpolations referring to the danger of war in 1744 (or 1745?) was refuted by A. Dürr in KB, NBA I/27 (1968), pp. 91 ff.

Abgesang:*

Lines 5–6 (joined together): chordal texture, whose short note-values contrast with the cantus firmus*; *instruments independent*

Line 7: analogous to lines 1 and 2

In lines 1, 2, and 7 the lower voice parts merge into a unity with the chorale melody. In lines 3 and 4, on the other hand, they unite with the instrumental texture. They achieve the greatest independence, in the interests of textual illustration, in lines 5–6. In none of the lines, however, do the lower voice parts take a thematic share in the chorale melody.

If the opening chorus* seems like a modified concerto movement, due to its figurative treatment of the first violin, the second movement is an expressive solo song with obbligato* oboe d'amore. The speech-like character of this movement, which has an immediate effect on the listener, is achieved by the use of the same theme in the solo alto and *cantabile* oboe parts, by the alternating prominence of the two thematic parts (the continuo accompaniment is unthematic), and by the renunciation of a figurative, concertante style. It would be possible to adapt the movement as a vocal duet with continuo simply by providing the oboe part with a text (and occasionally transposing it downwards).

The following ten-bar recitative, no. 3, is set as *secco*, but the words 'Remember, O Jesus, that You are still called a Prince of Peace', no doubt because they relate to the substance of the hymn, are surrounded by quotations of the first line of the chorale in the continuo. As in Cantata 38, performed four weeks earlier, the next movement is a terzetto accompanied by continuo, whose motivically imprinted ritornello contains the thematic kernel of the main vocal section. In its richness of expression, this movement is not inferior to the alto aria, no. 2. The recitative, no. 5, being a prayer for an end to torments and for a lasting peace, is decked out with string accompaniment and with an arioso*-style conclusion. It is followed by the concluding chorale in a plain four-part setting.

2.26 Twenty-sixth Sunday after Trinity

EPISTLE: 2 Peter 3.3–13: We await a new heaven and a new earth.
GOSPEL: Matthew 25.31–46: The Judgement of the world.

Wachet! betet! betet! wachet!, BWV 70
NBA I/27, p. 109 BC A165 Duration: *c.* 26 mins

1. CORO SATB tr ob str bc C 𝄵

Wachet! betet! betet! wachet!	Watch! pray! pray! watch!
Seid bereit	Be prepared
Allezeit,	At all times

Bis der Herr der Herrlichkeit
Dieser Welt ein Ende machet.

Until the Lord of Glory
Makes an end of this world.

2. Recitativo B tr ob str bc — F–a c

Erschrecket, ihr verstockten Sünder!
Ein Tag bricht an,
Vor dem sich niemand bergen kann:
Er eilt mit dir zum strengen Rechte,
O! sündliches Geschlechte,
Zum ewgen Herzeleide.
Doch euch, erwählte Gotteskinder,
Ist er ein Anfang wahrer Freude.
Der Heiland holet euch, wenn alles fällt und bricht,
Vor sein erhöhtes Angesicht;
Drum zaget nicht!

Tremble, you obdurate sinners!
A day dawns
From which no one can hide:
It hastens with you to severe Justice,
O sinful race,
To everlasting woe!
Yet to you, chosen children of God,
It is the beginning of true joy.
The Saviour fetches you, when all falls and breaks,
Before His exalted countenance;
Therefore do not despair!

3. Aria A vc or org bc — a $\frac{3}{4}$

Wenn kömmt der Tag, an dem wir ziehen
Aus dem Ägypten dieser Welt?
Ach! laßt uns bald aus Sodom fliehen,
Eh uns das Feuer überfällt!
Wacht, Seelen, auf von Sicherheit,
Und glaubt, es ist die letzte Zeit!

When will the day come on which we move
Out of the Egypt of this world?
Ah! let us soon flee from Sodom
Before the fire overwhelms us!
Awake, O souls, out of complacency
And believe: it is the end of time!

4. Recitativo T bc — d–b c

Auch bei dem himmlischen Verlangen
Hält unser Leib den Geist gefangen;
Es legt die Welt durch ihre Tücke
Den Frommen Netz und Stricke.
Der Geist ist willig, doch das Fleisch ist schwach;
Dies preßt uns aus ein jammervolles Ach!

Even in heavenly longing
Our body holds the spirit captive;
In its malice the world lays
Snares and traps for the devout.
The spirit is willing, yet the flesh is weak;
This forces out of us a woeful 'alas!'

5. Aria S vln I vln II + vla bc — e c

Laßt der Spötter Zungen schmähen,
Es wird doch und muß geschehen,
Daß wir Jesum werden sehen
Auf den Wolken, in den Höhen.
Welt und Himmel mag vergehen,
Christi Wort muß fest bestehen.

Let mockers' tongues scorn,
Yet it will and must happen
That we will see Jesus
On the clouds, in the heights.
World and heaven may pass away;
Christ's Word must stand firm.

6. Recitativo T bc — D–G c

Jedoch bei dem unartigen Geschlechte
Denkt Gott an seine Knechte,
Daß diese böse Art
Sie ferner nicht verletzet,

Yet among this untoward species
God thinks of His servants,
So that this evil generation
Will not offend Him further,

	Indem er sie in seiner Hand bewahrt Und in ein himmlisch Eden setzet.	For He keeps them in His hand And puts them in a heavenly Eden.
7.	CHORAL SATB bc (+ instrs)	G 3/4
	Freu dich sehr, o meine Seele, Und vergiß all Not und Qual, Weil dich nun Christus, dein Herre, Ruft aus diesem Jammertal! Seine Freud und Herrlichkeit Sollt du sehn in Ewigkeit, Mit den Engeln jubilieren, In Ewigkeit triumphieren.	**Rejoice greatly, O my soul, And forget all misery and torment, For Christ Your Lord now calls you Out of this vale of tears! His joy and glory You shall behold in eternity, When you exult with the angels And eternally triumph.**
	Pars 2	*Part 2*
8.	ARIA T str + ob bc	G c
	Hebt euer Haupt empor Und seid getrost, ihr Frommen, Zu eurer Seelen Flor! Ihr sollt in Eden grünen, Gott ewiglich zu dienen. Hebt euer Haupt empor Und seid getrost, ihr Frommen!	Lift up your heads And be of good cheer, you devout ones, To the blossoming of your souls! You shall flourish in Eden To serve God for ever. Lift up your heads And be of good cheer, you devout ones!
9.	RECITATIVO B tr str bc	e–C c
	Ach, soll nicht dieser große Tag, Der Welt Verfall Und der Posaunen Schall, Der unerhörte letzte Schlag, Des Richters ausgesprochne Worte, Des Höllenrachens offne Pforte In meinem Sinn Viel Zweifel, Furcht und Schrecken, Der ich ein Kind der Sünden bin, Erwecken? Jedoch, es gehet meiner Seelen Ein Freudenschein, ein Licht des Trostes auf. Der Heiland kann sein Herze nicht verhehlen, So vor Erbarmen bricht, Sein Gnadenarm verläßt mich nicht. Wohlan, so ende ich mit Freuden meinen Lauf.	Ah, should not this great day— The ruin of the world And the trumpet's sound, The unheard-of last stroke, The Judge's pronounced sentence, The open gates of hell's jaws— Awaken Much doubt, fear and dread— Since I am a child of sin— In my mind? However, there arises in my soul A gleam of joy, a light of comfort. The Saviour cannot conceal His Heart, Which breaks out of mercy; His gracious arm does not forsake me. Well then, I end my life's course with joy!
10.	ARIA B tr vln I + II vla bc	C 3/4
	Seligster Erquickungstag, Führe mich zu deinen Zimmern! Schalle, knalle, letzter Schlag,	Most blessed day of refreshment, Lead me to your chambers! Sound, crack, last stroke!

Welt und Himmel, geht zu Trümmern!	World and heaven, go to ruins!
Jesus führet mich zur Stille,	Jesus leads me to tranquillity
An den Ort, da Lust die Fülle.	At that place where delight is in abundance.

11. CHORAL S + tr + ob ATB str bc C 𝄵

Nicht nach Welt, nach Himmel nicht	**Not for the world, not for heaven**
Meine Seele wünscht und sehnet,	**Does my soul desire and yearn;**
Jesum wünsch ich und sein Licht,	**I desire Jesus and His Light,**
Der mich hat mit Gott versöhnet,	**He who has reconciled me with God,**
Der mich freiet vom Gericht,	**Who frees me from judgement;**
Meinen Jesum laß ich nicht.	**I will not let my Jesus go.**

In the form in which it is transmitted to us, this cantata was first performed on 21 November 1723. It is, however, an adaptation of the Weimar cantata BWV 70a for the Second Sunday in Advent—in Leipzig cantatas could be performed during the Advent period only on the First Sunday. It was not hard to adapt the work for the Twenty-sixth Sunday after Trinity, for on both occasions the readings deal with the end of time and the expectation of the Second Coming of Christ. Salomo Franck's text could be preserved without change. The work was expanded, however—by the introduction of recitatives (there are none in Franck's text) and an additional chorale—into a two-part structure; and trumpet and oboe were evidently added to the original instrumental ensemble of strings and continuo.

The author of the recitative texts is unknown. The obvious conjecture that Bach himself might have been responsible for them can neither be substantiated nor refuted. In so far as it was still necessary to establish a closer link with the Sunday Gospel,* the recitatives perform that function, hence the reference to the 'Judge's pronounced sentence' (no. 9; cf. Matthew 25.34–6 and 41–3) or to the opposite significance of the Last Day for 'obdurate sinners' and the 'chosen children of God' respectively (no. 2; cf. also nos. 6 and 9). Thus expanded, of course, the text lacks the consistent exposition* of a single idea. It vacillates constantly between the fear of being inadequately prepared for the end of the world and the hope of one day being numbered among the elect, for whom the Last Day will be 'the beginning of true joy' (no. 2).

Bach's composition unites the youthful freshness, originality, and richness of invention of his Weimar years with that tendency to large form which is perceptible for the first time in the Advent cantatas of 1716 and still more evident in the expansion of 1723. In the opening chorus,* Bach tries out on a large scale for the first time (as far as we can tell from his surviving works) the compositional technique of 'choral insertion'* within the reprise of extended portions of the orchestral ritornello. This gives rise to a form of alternation, rich in tension, in which either the choir (with accompanying orchestra) or the orchestra (with built-in choir) comes to the fore. The overall design of the movement in abridged da capo* form is related to the aria—a consequence of the setting of a madrigalian* text as a chorus, since choruses on biblical words are mostly closer to the series form of the motet* than to cyclical aria form. The structure of the opening chorus may be represented schematically as follows (italics denote instrumental passages):

Introductory sinfonia, bipartite: a b
A Main section ('Wachet! betet! . . .'):
Sinfonia a + chorus
Imitative choral passage, *instrumentally accompanied*
Sinfonia a b + chorus
B Middle section ('Seid bereit . . .'):
Bipartite imitative*-chordal choral passage; *instruments rest or accompany*
A[1] Main section, abridged ('Wachet! betet! . . .'):
Sinfonia a b + chorus

The instrumentation acquires its distinctive tone colour from the participation of a trumpet (in addition to oboe, strings, and continuo), whose signal-like *reveille* initiates lively figural* movement in the other instruments and in the choir. Moreover, brief calls of 'Wachet!' ('Watch!') and long-held chords on 'betet!' ('pray!') are heard in the choral-insertion passages, which allow Franck's text to be experienced in graphic, vivid, and indeed thrilling immediacy.

In the second movement, an *accompagnato** performed by the entire instrumental ensemble, Bach depicts in succession the terror of the sinner, the calm of the elect and their joy (lively coloraturas*), the destruction of the universe, and finally the fear of those called before Christ's countenance, for whom the text announces consolation. The aria, no. 3, is accompanied by continuo only, but its instrumental bass is split up into a calm, supporting fundamental part and an additional part that figuratively breaks up the bass line. This obbligato* part was in 1723 played on the organ (with cello?), but in a 1731 revival by cello only, with organ, bassoon, and violone on the fundamental part. Ostinato* effects arise from manifold repetitions in the instrumental parts. The voice takes up the instrumental head-motive and assimilates itself in rhythmic movement to the obbligato instrumental part. Livelier motion in the alto emphasizes individual words, such as 'fliehen' ('flee') or 'Feuer' ('fire').

A *secco* recitative forms a bridge to the second aria, no. 5, in which violins and violas are united in a common obbligato part, though with constant dynamic changes brought about by the resting and re-entry of violin II and viola, an effect which in this particular form can scarcely be found elsewhere in Bach's works. Ritornello and voice part are again thematically alike, though the instrumental part exceeds the voice part in agility, especially on account of the rapid scale figures of violin I. A brief *secco* leads to the plain four-part chorale that concludes Part I, the last verse of the hymn *Freu dich sehr, o meine Seele* (Freiberg, 1620).

Part II opens with an aria, no. 8, in which the strings no longer play together in unison as in the previous aria (no. 5) but instead form a full instrumental texture, though with violin I (reinforced by oboe) clearly predominant. The other strings have an accompanying function, which results in a fully harmonized trio texture. The opening of the ritornello, later taken up by the solo tenor, recalls one of the melodies to the hymn *O Gott, du frommer Gott* (Darmstadt, 1698). At the same time, its rising opening illustrates the call to 'lift up your heads' (after Luke 21.28). It is not very likely that Bach here consciously wished to allude to the hymn mentioned. If anything, the hymn *Was frag ich nach der Welt*, which was sung to the same melody, might rather have been intended.

The last recitative and aria, nos. 9 and 10, bring an unexpected dramatic enhancement. The two aspects of the Last Day with which this cantata is concerned—terror and joy—are here placed in immediate juxtaposition. For this purpose, the complete instrumental ensemble is required (in alternation with monody* accompanied by continuo only) which means that the instrumentation of the cantata's four arias is progressively increased. The recitative begins with a *furioso* depicting the 'unheard-of last stroke', while the trumpet intones the chorale *Es ist gewißlich an der Zeit*. Thereafter, a very gradual calming process takes place up to the arioso* conclusion, with its extended melisma* on the words 'Well then, I end my life's course with joy!' The aria 'Seligster Erquickungstag' ('Most blessed day of refreshment') follows unheralded and without ritornello, performed 'molt' adagio' and with continuo accompaniment only. It is an otherworldly, transfigured bass solo, closer to arioso than to the more structured form of aria. An immense contrast follows with the 'presto' middle section, 'Schalle, knalle, letzter Schlag' ('Sound, crack, last stroke!'), which once again depicts the collapse of the cosmic system. Afterwards, in a change no less sudden than before, the opening arioso returns in a quasi-da capo* to the words 'Jesus leads me to tranquillity at that place where delight is in abundance'.

After this vivid tone picture has quietly died away, we hear in hymnic grandeur the seven-part concluding chorale—the fifth verse of the hymn *Meinen Jesum laß ich nicht* by Christian Keymann (1658). The joy of the Christian who, on the Last Day, knows that he is safe through Jesus's intercession wins through in the end!

2.27 Twenty-seventh Sunday after Trinity

EPISTLE: 1 Thessalonians 5.1–11: Being prepared for the Last Day.
GOSPEL: Matthew 25.1–13: The parable of the ten virgins.

Wachet auf, ruft uns die Stimme, BWV 140

NBA I/27, p. 151 BC A166 Duration: *c.* 31 mins

1. CHORALE S + hn ATB ob I,II taille str + vln picc bc — E♭ 3/4

Wachet auf, ruft uns die Stimme	**'Awake!', we are called by the voice of**
Der Wächter sehr hoch auf der Zinne,	**The watchmen very high on the battlement,**
Wach auf, du Stadt Jerusalem!	**'Awake, you city of Jerusalem!'**
Mitternacht heißt diese Stunde;	**The hour is midnight;**
Sie rufen uns mit hellem Munde:	**They call us with a clear voice:**
Wo seid ihr klugen Jungfrauen?	**Where are you, you wise virgins?**
Wohl auf, der Bräutgam kömmt;	**Rise up, the Bridegroom comes;**
Steht auf, die Lampen nehmt!	**Stand up, take your lamps!**
Alleluja!	**Alleluia!**
Macht euch bereit	**Get ready**
Zu der Hochzeit,	**For the wedding;**
Ihr müsset ihm entgegen gehn!	**You must go out to meet Him!**

2. RECITATIVO T bc — c C

Er kommt, er kommt,	He comes, He comes,
Der Bräutgam kommt!	The Bridegroom comes!
Ihr Töchter Zions, kommt heraus,	You daughters of Zion, come forth:
Sein Ausgang eilet aus der Höhe	His going forth hastens from on high
In euer Mutter Haus.	Into your mother's house.
Der Bräutgam kommt, der einem Rehe	The Bridegroom comes, who like a roe,
Und jungen Hirsche gleich	Like a young hart,
Auf denen Hügeln springt	Skips upon the hills
Und euch das Mahl der Hochzeit bringt.	And brings you the wedding feast.
Wacht auf, ermuntert euch!	Awake, stir yourselves
Den Bräutgam zu empfangen!	To receive the Bridegroom!
Dort, sehet, kommt er hergegangen.	There, see, he is approaching!

3. ARIA DUETTO SB vln picc bc — c 6/8

Sopran	*Soprano*
Wenn kömmst du, mein Heil?	When are You coming, my Salvation?
Baß	*Bass*
Ich komme, dein Teil.	I am coming, your portion.
Sopran	*Soprano*
Ich warte mit brennendem Öle.	I am waiting with burning oil.

Sopran
Baß
Eröffne den Saal
Ich öffne den Saal
beide
Zum himmlischen Mahl.
sopran
Komm, Jesu!
Baß
Komm, liebliche Seele!

Soprano
Bass
Open the hall
I open the hall
both
For the heavenly feast.
soprano
Come, Jesus!
Bass
Come, lovely soul!

4. CHORALE T unis str bc — E♭ c

Zion hört die Wächter singen,
Das Herz tut ihr vor Freuden springen,
Sie wachet und steht eilend auf.
Ihr Freund kommt vom Himmel prächtig,
Von Gnaden stark, von Wahrheit mächtig,
Ihr Licht wird hell, ihr Stern geht auf.
Nun komm, du werte Kron,
Herr Jesu, Gottes Sohn!
Hosianna!
Wir folgen all
Zum Freudensaal
Und halten mit das Abendmahl.

Zion hears the watchmen singing,
Her heart leaps for joy,
She watches and rises up in haste.
Her Beloved comes from heaven in splendour,
Strong in grace, mighty in truth;
Her Light is bright, her Star ascends.
Now come, You precious Crown,
Lord Jesus, God's Son!
Hosanna!
We all follow
To the hall of joy
And join in Communion.

5. RECITATIVO B str + vln picc bc — E♭–B♭ c

So geh herein zu mir,
Du mir erwählte Braut!
Ich habe mich mit dir
Von Ewigkeit vertraut.
Dich will ich auf mein Herz,
Auf meinen Arm gleich wie ein Siegel setzen
Und dein betrübtes Aug ergötzen.
Vergiß, o Seele, nun
Die Angst, den Schmerz,
Den du erdulden müssen;
Auf meiner Linken sollst du ruhn,
Und meine Rechte soll dich küssen.

Then come in to me,
You, my chosen Bride!
I have betrothed myself to you
From eternity.
Upon my heart,
Upon my arm I will set you as a seal
And delight your troubled eye.
Forget now, O soul,
The fear, the pain
That you have had to endure;
Upon my left hand you shall rest,
And my right hand shall kiss you.

6. ARIA DUETTO SB ob I solo bc — B♭ c

Sopran
Mein Freund ist mein,

Soprano
My Beloved is mine,

Baß	*Bass*
Und ich bin sein,	And I am his,[60]
beide	*both*
Die Liebe soll nichts scheiden.	Nothing shall separate our Love.
Sopran	*Soprano*
Baß	*Bass*
Ich will mit dir in Himmels Rosen weiden,	I will feed with You among heaven's roses;
Du sollst mit mir in Himmels Rosen weiden,	You shall feed with Me among heaven's roses;
beide	*both*
Da Freude die Fülle, da Wonne wird sein.	There shall be the fullness of joy and gladness.

7. Choral SATB bc (+ instrs) E♭ C

Gloria sei dir gesungen	**Glory be sung to You**
Mit Menschen- und englischen Zungen,	**In the tongues of men and of angels,**
Mit Harfen und mit Zimbeln schon.	**With harps and with cymbals.**
Von zwölf Perlen sind die Pforten,	**Of twelve pearls are the gates;**
An deiner Stadt sind wir Konsorten	**In Your City we are the consorts**
Der Engel hoch um deinen Thron.	**Of the angels high about Your throne.**
Kein Aug hat je gespürt,	**No eye has ever seen,**
Kein Ohr hat je gehört	**No ear has ever heard**
Solche Freude.	**Such joy.**
Des sind wir froh,	**Whereof we are glad,**
Io, io!	**Io, io!**
Ewig in dulci jubilo.	**For ever *in dulci jubilo*.**

The calendar of the church year contains a Twenty-seventh Sunday after Trinity only when Easter takes place before 27 March (between 22 and 26 March). This very seldom happens. During his Leipzig period, Bach experienced it only in 1731 and 1742, and before that (leaving aside his childhood: 1690 and 1693) only once: in 1704, when, as organist at Arnstadt, he was reproached that 'hitherto no concerted music had been performed'.[61] The dating of the only Bach cantata that survives for this Sunday therefore presents no difficulties. Cantata 140 was written for performance on 25 November 1731 and may have been revived in 1742. Bach thus took the opportunity to supplement his cycle of chorale cantatas* with an additional work, albeit one that does not fully accord with the type he favoured in 1724–5. For the three-verse hymn by Philipp Nicolai (1599), with its single inner verse, offers too few possibilities for madrigalian* paraphrase and consequently had to be enriched with freely versified insertions. Accordingly, the anonymous librettist retained all three hymn verses word for word—they

[60] This problematic line is discussed in the commentary.

[61] '. . . bißher gar nichts musiciret worden'; see Dok II, p. 20, and NBR, p. 46.

mark the beginning, middle, and end of the cantata (nos. 1, 4, and 7)—and inserted as interludes two pairs of movements, both made up of solo recitative followed by a duet-aria.

The text derives from the Sunday Gospel,* carrying further the idea of the bridegroom coming to meet his bride. The bridegroom is Jesus Himself, and His bride the Soul of the faithful Christian. The libretto includes a rich crop of biblical allusions, chiefly drawn from the Song of Songs:

2nd Movement	
He comes, He comes,	
The Bridegroom comes!	Matthew 25.6
You daughters of Zion, come forth	Song of Songs 3.11
His going forth hastens from on high	Luke 1.78
Into your mother's house	Song of Songs 3.4, 8.2
The Bridegroom comes, who like a roe,	
Like a young hart	Song of Songs 2.9, 2.17, 8.14
Skips upon the hills	Song of Songs 2.8
3rd Movement	
When are You coming, my Salvation?	Isaiah 62.11
I am waiting with burning oil	Genesis 49.18, Matthew 25.4
5th Movement	
I have betrothed myself to you	
From eternity	Hosea 2.19
Upon my heart,	
Upon my arm I will set you as a seal	Song of Songs 8.6
Upon my left hand you shall rest,	
And my right hand shall kiss you.	Song of Songs 2.6
6th Movement	
My Beloved is mine, and I am his	Song of Songs 2.16, 6.3
. . . feed . . . among heaven's roses	Song of Songs 6.3
There shall be the fullness of joy and gladness	Psalm 16.11, Isaiah 35.10

The division of the opening words of the sixth movement between the two dialogue partners of Bach's duet—'Mein Freund ist mein'/'Und ich bin sein' ('My Beloved is mine'/'And I am his')—is strictly speaking incorrect. Nor is it rectified by altering the second clause to 'und ich bin dein' ('and I am yours'), as in older editions of the cantata (perhaps it would be correct to say, 'und du bist mein', 'and you are mine'). Evidently, Bach's concern was not with a realistic dialogue but with keeping the biblical quotation intact and disregarding dramatic secondary intentions.

The large-scale opening movement follows Bach's favoured type of chorale chorus.* The chorale melody, sung by the soprano (reinforced by horn), is incorporated line by line within an independent orchestral texture. Although it possesses its own theme, this instrumental music is nonetheless by no means devoid of suggestions of the chorale melody; compare, for example, bars 5 f. of the introductory ritornello with the chorale opening in the soprano:

The orchestral music, scored for three oboes (oboe I, II, and taille), strings (including violino piccolo), and continuo, begins with block chords in dotted rhythm, alternating between strings and oboes, out of which the melody quoted above emerges in a dialogue between violin I (plus violino piccolo) and oboe I. These instruments are then united in the final cadence of the introductory ritornello. Perhaps in this introduction Bach already wanted to draw attention to the dialogue structure of the work as a whole. The independent orchestral themes are maintained during the vocal passages. The three lower voices accompany the chorale melody (which is stated in long notes) in a livelier, mostly imitative* texture without reference to the chorale theme. At times, the lower parts are condensed into brief chordal shouts of 'Wach auf' ('Awake!') or 'Macht euch bereit!' ('Get ready!'). The ninth chorale-line, 'Alleluja', alone acquires a more extended, fugal substructure, derived thematically from the orchestral ritornello. Though the shortest line of text, it is thereby extended to double the length of the other line-passages.

The three solo singers of the cantata have clearly defined roles: the tenor as narrator, the soprano as the Soul, and the bass as Jesus. A joyfully excited *secco* recitative, no. 2, announces the approach of the Bridegroom and, accordingly, leads to the first duet between Jesus and the Soul, no. 3. Here the obbligato* instrument prescribed by Bach is the violino piccolo, a violin of smaller dimensions than usual, with its strings tuned to *b flat*, f^1, c^2, and g^2—a minor third higher than a normal violin. As a result, the lively and decidedly virtuoso figuration of this solo part sounds especially bright and silvery, perhaps depicting the radiant brilliance of the bride, who awaits her beloved 'with burning oil'. The yearning, sensuous character of the vocal dialogue, developed thematically out of the opening of the ritornello, arouses mystical impressions, for heavenly and earthly love are here blended into a unity. Musically, the movement belongs among the most beautiful love duets in the musical literature of the world.

The central chorale (verse 2 of the hymn) is set as a trio, by contrast with the two chorale-based outer movements. The chorale melody, sung by the tenor in a slightly embellished form, is incorporated line by line within a thematically independent instrumental texture in which violins and violas unite in a powerful unison over an unthematic continuo part. The accessible instrumental melody has rendered this chorale arrangement extremely popular. Bach himself later transcribed it for organ as the first of the six so-called Schübler Chorales (BWV 645).

Now the Bridegroom takes the Soul as His bride. The string accompaniment of the recitative, no. 5, highlights the significance of this moment for the Christian and also serves the purpose of textual illustration, as in the unusual harmonic sequences on the words 'And delight your troubled eye'. The following duet, no. 6, gives expression to the joy of the united pair. Like the third movement, it is a pure love duet, cheerful and dance-like, yet so deeply felt in musical terms and of such consummate artistry that its relaxed mood brings with it no lowering of artistic intensity. Here again, earthly happiness in love and heavenly bliss are blended into a unity. In any account of Christian mysticism in great art this cantata should not go unmentioned.

Bach wrote the plain four-part concluding chorale in antiquated minim notation. With the high pitch of the chorale melody in the soprano and its octave doubling in the violino piccolo, this setting uses earthly means in an inimitable manner to give symbolic shape once more to the bliss anticipated by the Christian in the heavenly Jerusalem.

3

The Marian Feasts

3.1 The Feast of the Purification (Candlemas; 2 February)

Epistle: Malachi 3.1–4: The Lord shall come to His temple.
Gospel: Luke 2.22–32: The presentation of Jesus in the temple.

Erfreute Zeit im neuen Bunde, BWV 83

NBA I/28.1, p. 3 BC A167 Duration: *c.* 20 mins

1. Aria A hn I,II ob I,II vln solo str bc — F C

Erfreute Zeit im neuen Bunde,	Glad time of the New Covenant,
Da unser Glaube Jesum hält:	When our Faith holds Jesus:
Wie freudig wird zur letzten Stunde	How joyfully at the last hour
Die Ruhestatt, das Grab bestellt!	Will our resting-place, the grave, be disposed!

2. Aria [Chorale + Recitative] B unis str bc — B♭ 6/8/C

'Herr, nun lässest du deinen Diener in Friede fahren, wie du gesaget hast.'	'Lord, now let Your servant depart in peace, as You have said.'
Was uns als Menschen schrecklich scheint,	What appears fearful to us as men
Ist uns ein Eingang zu dem Leben.	Is for us an entry into Life.
Es ist der Tod	Death is an end
Ein Ende dieser Zeit und Not,	To this time and trouble,
Ein Pfand, so uns der Herr gegeben	A pledge that the Lord gave us
Zum Zeichen, daß ers herzlich meint	As a sign that He means well
Und uns will nach vollbrachtem Ringen	And after the struggle is over
Zum Friede bringen.	Will bring us to peace.
Und weil der Heiland nun	And since the Saviour is now
Der Augen Trost, des Herzens Labsal ist,	The eyes' consolation, the heart's refreshment,

Was Wunder, daß mein Herz des Todes Furcht vergißt?
Es kann erfreut den Ausspruch tun:

'Denn meine Augen haben deinen Heiland gesehen, welchen du bereitet hast für allen Völkern.'

What wonder that my heart forgets the terror of death?
It can joyfully make the utterance:

'For my eyes have seen Your Saviour, whom You have prepared before all peoples.'

3. Aria T vln solo str bc — F c

Eile, Herz, voll Freudigkeit
Vor den Gnadenstuhl zu treten!
Du sollt deinen Trost empfangen
Und Barmherzigkeit erlangen,
Ja, bei kummervoller Zeit
Stark am Geiste kräftig beten.

Hasten, O heart, full of joyfulness,
To step before the Throne of Grace!
You shall receive your consolation
And obtain mercy;
Indeed, at sorrowful times,
Pray vigorously, strong in spirit.

4. Recitativo A bc — d–a c

Ja, merkt dein Glaube noch viel Finsternis,
Dein Heiland kann
Der Zweifel Schatten trennen;
Ja, wenn des Grabes Nacht
Die letzte Stunde schrecklich macht,
So wirst du doch gewiß
Sein helles Licht
Im Tode selbst erkennen.

Yes, though your faith is still aware of much darkness,
Your Saviour can
Disperse the shadows of doubt;
Yes, when the grave's night
Makes the last hour fearful,
You shall certainly
Recognize His bright Light
In death itself.

5. Choral SATB bc (+ hn I ww str) — d c

Er ist das Heil und selig Licht
Für die Heiden,
Zu erleuchten, die dich kennen nicht,
Und zu weiden.
Er ist deins Volks Israel
Der Preis, Ehr, Freud und Wonne.

He is the Salvation and blessed Light
For the Gentiles,
To enlighten those who do not know You
And to shepherd them.
He is the praise, honour, joy, and gladness
Of Your people Israel.

The Gospel* reading for the Feast of the Purification gives only a brief account of the ceremony of Mary's purification but a much fuller account of Simeon, of whom it had been prophesied that he would not die before he had seen the Messiah. The baroque period in verse and sermon, united in this, invariably turned its thoughts on this day to the death of the individual. Thus, in the very opening aria of this cantata, the anonymous librettist directly juxtaposes the 'glad time' with the 'last hour'. And only the person who has heard the Gospel reading beforehand knows that Simeon's saying is here applied to the whole of Christendom: now that the Saviour has appeared, the faithful Christian can die confidently, for death has lost its terror. In the second movement, a sermon-like exegesis of this idea is framed by Simeon's own words from Luke 2.29–31, the

Nunc dimittis.* The third movement is exceptional in that its entire text constitutes a biblical paraphrase, as follows:

3rd Movement	*Hebrews 4.16*
Hasten, O heart, full of joyfulness	Therefore let us
To step before the Throne of Grace!	step up to the Throne of Grace with joyfulness,
You shall receive your consolation	that we may obtain mercy
And obtain mercy;	and find grace
Indeed, at sorrowful times,	at the time when
Pray vigorously, strong in spirit.	we are in need of help.

The recitative that concludes the madrigalian* verse, no. 4, unites the reflections of the previous movements with the last verse of the Gospel reading: even though much darkness still surrounds us today, the Saviour Himself will nonetheless turn out to be a 'bright Light' at our death. The same biblical verse as paraphrased by Martin Luther in the fourth verse of the hymn *Mit Fried und Freud ich fahr dahin* (1524) forms the concluding chorale.

Bach's composition was written for performance on 2 February 1724 and probably revived on the same occasion in 1727. The vocal scoring is largely restricted to solo rendition, for the four vocal parts join together only in the concluding chorale. Yet the opening movement is festively scored: two horns and concertante* violin are added to the normal instrumental ensemble of two oboes, strings, and continuo. The textual antithesis 'glad time'/'last hour' influences the contrasting compositional structure of the outer and inner sections of this da capo* form movement. The principal section is derived from thematic material stated in the introductory ritornello, with its threefold contrast between chordal tutti (head-motive), antiphonal motivic treatment, and virtuoso figuration for solo violin. The head-motive also forms the opening of the vocal section:

Due to frequent use of vocal insertion,* the instrumental music is clearly predominant in this bipartite principal section. The middle section, however, is organized quite differently. Here, the ritornello themes are heard only in a brief articulating episode and in the following two-bar passage of vocal insertion. Otherwise, largely new, text-engendered themes are developed. In addition, the solo violin has idiomatic *bariolage* figures, an alternation of stopped and open strings (first on a^1, then on d^1, and in the second half of the middle section twice in an enhanced form on e^2), here without doubt intended as an imitation of tolling bells, indicating death:

Both halves of the middle section end with expressive chromaticism.*

A parallel to the second movement is scarcely to be found within Bach's entire corpus of cantatas. The literally quoted biblical passage on which it is based is the opening of Simeon's canticle, the Nunc dimittis, one of three psalm-like poems in the New Testament which in the Christian Church formed a fixed liturgical component of the day-hours and were sung to one of the nine psalm-tones. The musical form of the movement essentially accords with its text structure: canticle verse 1—recitative—canticle verses 2–3. The recitative is set as *secco* accompanied by continuo, the canticle as a chorale arrangement based on the eighth psalm-tone. The psalmody of the bass voice is framed by a passage of free two-part canon* for unison strings and continuo. The canonic theme, unrelated to the chorale, is stated in a six-bar prelude and thereafter repeated at ever-changing pitch. In addition, fragments of it serve at two points to mark the caesuras of the recitative, so that the following overall form arises (italics denote instrumental passages):

A verse 1: *canonic texture* + psalm-tone VIII (bass)
B recitative—*canon*—recitative—*canon*—recitative
A^1 verses 2 + 3: *canonic texture* + psalm-tone VIII (bass)

The tenor aria for concertante violin solo and strings, no. 3, with its constantly running triplets, is stamped by the image of 'hastening' drawn from the text. The voice participates in the triplet runs in the form of extensive coloratura* festoons. The movement is to a large extent pervaded by vocal insertion within the return of extracts of the ritornello played by the instrumental ensemble. A brief *secco* recitative leads to the plain four-part concluding chorale.

Mit Fried und Freud ich fahr dahin, BWV 125

NBA I/28.1, p. 33 BC A168 Duration: *c.* 24 mins

1. [Chorale] S + hn ATB fl ob str bc e $^{12}_{8}$

Mit Fried und Freud ich fahr dahin	**In peace and joy I go to that place**
In Gottes Willen;	**According to the Will of God;**
Getrost ist mir mein Herz und Sinn,	**Established is my heart and mind,**
Sanft und stille;	**Meek and quiet;**
Wie Gott mir verheißen hat,	**As God has promised me,**
Der Tod ist mein Schlaf worden.	**Death has become my sleep.**

2. Aria A fl ob d'am bc — b 3/4

Ich will auch mit gebrochnen Augen	I will, even with feeble eyes,
Nach dir, mein treuer Heiland, sehn.	Look to You, my faithful Saviour.
Wenngleich des Leibes Bau zerfällt [zerbricht]	Though the body's frame collapses,
Doch fällt mein Herz und Hoffen nicht.	Yet my heart and hope do not fail.
Mein Jesus sieht auf mich im Sterben	My Jesus looks upon me in dying
Und lässet mir kein Leid geschehn.	And lets no hurt befall me.

3. Recitativo [+ Chorale] B str bc — a–b c

O Wunder, daß ein Herz	O wonder, that a heart,
Vor der dem Fleisch verhaßten Gruft	Before the tomb, hated by the flesh,
Und gar des Todes Schmerz	And even the pain of death,
Sich nicht entsetzet!	Should not be frightened!
Das macht Christus, wahr' Gottes Sohn,	**This is caused by Christ, true Son of God,**
Der treue Heiland,	**The faithful Saviour,**
Der auf dem Sterbebette schon	Who on one's deathbed already
Mit Himmelssüßigkeit den Geist ergötzet,	Delights the spirit with heavenly sweetness,
Den du mich, Herr, hast sehen lan,	**He whom You, Lord, have let me see**
Da in erfüllter Zeit	When in the fullness of time
Ein Glaubensarm das Heil des Herrn umfinge;	An arm of faith embraced the Salvation of the Lord;
Und machst bekannt	**And have made it known**
Von dem erhabnen Gott, dem Schöpfer aller Dinge,	From the exalted God, the Creator of all things,
Daß er sei das Leben und Heil,	**That He is the Life and Salvation,**
Der Menschen Trost und Teil,	The comfort and portion of men,
Ihr Retter vom Verderben	Their deliverer from destruction
Im Tod und auch im Sterben.	**In death and also in dying.**

4. Aria Duetto TB vln I,II bc — G c

Ein unbegreiflich Licht erfüllt	An incomprehensible Light fills
Den ganzen Kreis der Erden.	The entire circle of the earth.
Es schallet kräftig fort und fort	There goes on and on sounding powerfully
Ein höchst erwünscht Verheißungswort:	A most highly desired word of promise:
Wer glaubt, soll selig werden.	Whoever believes shall be saved.

5. Recitativo A bc — e c

O unerschöpfter Schatz der Güte,	O unexhausted treasure chest of goodness,
So sich uns Menschen aufgetan:	Opened to us men:

Es wird der Welt,
So Zorn und Fluch auf sich geladen,
Ein Stuhl der Gnaden
Und Siegeszeichen aufgestellt,
Und jedes gläubige Gemüte
Wird in sein Gnadenreich geladen.

For the world,
Which has invited wrath and curse upon itself,
A seat of Grace
And sign of victory is set up,
And every believing spirit
Is invited into His Kingdom of Grace.

6. Choral SATB bc (+ instrs) e C

Er ist das Heil und selig Licht
Für die Heiden,
Zu erleuchten, die dich kennen nicht,
Und zu weiden.
Er ist deins Volks Israel
Der Preis, Ehr, Freud und Wonne.

He is the Salvation and blessed Light
For the Gentiles,
To enlighten those who do not know You
And to shepherd them.
He is the praise, honour, joy, and gladness
Of Your people Israel.

This work, a chorale cantata* from the cycle of 1724–5, written for performance on 2 February 1725, is based on Martin Luther's German translation (1524) of the Nunc dimittis,* the canticle of Simeon (Luke 2.29–32). This canticle not only forms a fixed liturgical element in Compline, the last of the canonical day-hours, which was said at the end of the day, but it also forms part of the Gospel* reading for the Feast of the Purification. Luther turns each verse of the biblical canticle into the verse of a hymn. Bach's anonymous librettist had to expand this hymn in order that it should form an adequate basis for the composition. He retained the two outer verses word for word as usual, and amplified the second verse with a troping* recitative text to form the third movement. The second movement takes up the themes of the second verse of the hymn in a freely versified form and carries them further: like Simeon, I will set eyes upon Jesus in death, and then He will see me too and allow no harm to befall me. The fourth and fifth movements are a free paraphrase of the third verse of the hymn. The trope*-text in the third movement combines a reference to the 'Light that lightens the Gentiles' from the canticle with an allusion to Mark 16.16: 'He who believes and is baptized shall be saved'. And the fifth movement establishes a link with Romans 3.25 ('Christ, for whom God has set forth a Throne of Grace') referring to God's act of grace. Still more clearly than Luther's hymn, then, the cantata text embodies the fundamental elements of the Reformation creed: justification by faith (no. 4) through the action of grace alone (no. 5).

Bach's composition makes us regret that today, due to the abolition of the Marian feasts which were still celebrated in his day, a more frequent opportunity does not arise for performing this remarkable work, which shows the Thomascantor at the height of his powers. The splendid, stirring opening chorus* contrasts strings with flute and oboe in its introductory sinfonia. Triplet chord sequences give rise to an extremely dense, highly expressive texture, thematically independent of the chorale, though derived from its initial leap of a fifth:

As in most opening movements of the chorale cantatas, the chorale melody is delivered by the soprano, line by line in long notes, against an orchestral texture with its own theme, as noted above, and supported by the three lower voice parts, which in lines 1, 2, and 5, reinforced by the strings, treat imitatively* the instrumental head-motive shown above. In line 3 the vocal substructure treats a related motive* in a similar fashion, but lines 4 and 6 ('Meek and quiet' and 'Death has become my sleep') are for illustrative reasons accompanied in a mainly chordal texture, sung 'piano' and characterized by chromaticism* and modulation to distant keys.

No less beautiful is the alto aria, no. 2, in which transverse flute* and oboe d'amore* play a concertante* duet in dotted rhythms and parallel thirds over a tranquil continuo part in legato repeated quavers. Rich suspension figures, appoggiaturas, and other ornaments reveal that an expressive interpretation of this movement lay particularly close to the composer's heart. The third movement, despite its constant alternation between recitative and chorale, is accompanied throughout by a joy motive on the strings in order to show that, now Jesus has come into the world, death is no longer felt as a source of terror but rather as a desirable and joyful end to life on earth. The chorale melody is delivered in a lightly varied form. Only the last line, 'In death and also in dying', is extended by two bars, richly decked out with chromaticism and profusely ornamented; and for this line the strings cease their motivically imprinted *accompagnato** in order to harmonize it in tranquil notes.

The fourth movement is a thematically unified quintet for first and second violins, continuo, and (in the vocal passages) the two low voices, tenor and bass. Its entire thematic material is stated in the opening six-bar ritornello, namely three motives *x*, *y*, and *z*, which are so disposed in imitative texture that *y* serves as counterpoint* both to the head-motive *x* in the antecedent phrase and to the continuation-motive *z* in the consequent phrase:

The principal section includes four vocal passages *a ab a ab*, in which *a* represents an expanded vocal version of the ritornello's antecedent (see bar 1 above), and *b*, vocal insertion* within the continuation of the ritornello (see bar 3 above). The exceptional inclusion of four vocal passages might perhaps have originated in the text, which tells of 'the entire circle of the earth', for according to an old tradition the number four stands for, among other things, the four corners of heaven. The middle section includes several text-engendered groups of motives: imitation and calling motives on 'Es schallet' ('There sounds') and held notes, followed by imitation and the closing cadence, on 'Wer glaubt . . .' ('Whoever believes . . .'). A *secco* recitative, no. 5, leads to the concluding chorale in a plain, four-part choral setting, accompanied by the entire instrumental ensemble.

Ich habe genung, BWV 82

NBA I/28.1, pp. 77, 111, 155 BC A169 Duration: *c.* 23 mins

1. ARIA B ob str bc/S fl str bc[1] c/e $\frac{3}{8}$

Ich habe genung.	I have enough.
Ich habe den Heiland, das Hoffen der Frommen,	I have taken the Saviour, the hope of the devout,
Auf meine begierigen Arme genommen;	Into my eager arms;
Ich habe genung!	I have enough!
Ich hab ihn erblickt,	I have seen Him,
Mein Glaube hat Jesum ans Herze gedrückt;	My faith has pressed Jesus to my heart;

[1] The first specified scoring and key refer to the C minor version (for the 1735 performance, read mezzo-soprano throughout in place of bass), the second to the E minor version.

Nun wünsch ich, noch heute mit Freuden
Von hinnen zu scheiden.
Ich habe genung!

Now I wish this very day with joy
To depart from here.
I have enough!

2. Recitativo B bc/S bc — A♭–B♭/C–D c

Ich habe genung!
Mein Trost ist nur allein,
Daß Jesus mein und ich sein eigen möchte sein.
Im Glauben halt ich ihn,
Da seh ich auch mit Simeon
Die Freude jenes Lebens schon.
Laßt uns mit diesem Manne ziehn!
Ach! möchte mich von meines Leibes Ketten
Der Herr erretten!
Ach! wäre doch mein Abschied hier,
Mit Freuden sagt ich, Welt, zu dir:
Ich habe genung!

I have enough!
My consolation is this alone,
That Jesus might be mine and I His own.
In faith I hold Him,
For I too see with Simeon
The joy of the other Life already.
Let us go with this Man!
Ah! would that from my body's chains
The Lord might deliver me!
Ah! were my departure indeed here,
With joy I would say to you, O world:
I have enough!

3. Aria B str + ob da c bc/S str + fl bc — E♭/G c

Schlummert ein, ihr matten Augen,
Fallet sanft und selig zu!
  Welt, ich bleibe nicht mehr hier,
  Hab ich doch kein Teil an dir,
  Das der Seele könnte taugen.
  Hier muß ich das Elend bauen,
  Aber dort, dort werd ich schauen
  Süßen Friede, stille Ruh.

Slumber, you tired eyes,
Close peacefully and blessedly!
  World, I remain here no longer,
  I have indeed no part in you
  That could be of use to the soul.
  Here I must put up with misery,
  But there, there I shall see
  Sweet peace, quiet repose.

4. Recitativo B bc/S bc — c/e c

Mein Gott! wenn kömmt das schöne: Nun!
Da ich im Friede fahren werde
Und in dem Sande kühler Erde
Und dort bei dir im Schoße ruhn?
Der Abschied ist gemacht,
Welt, gute Nacht!

My God! when will that lovely 'Now!' come
When I shall depart in peace
And rest in the sand of the cool earth
And there with You in Your bosom?
I have taken my leave:
World, good night!

5. Aria B ob str bc/S fl str bc — c/e 3/8

Ich freue mich auf meinen Tod,
Ach! hätt er sich schon eingefunden.
  Da entkomm ich aller Not,
  Die mich noch auf der Welt gebunden.

With joy I anticipate my death:
Ah! if only it had taken place already!
  Then I shall escape from all the misery
  That still binds me in the world.

As in all Bach's cantatas for the Feast of the Purification, only the account of Simeon is singled out from the Gospel* story of the presentation of Jesus in the temple and interpreted to the contemporary congregation. The anonymous librettist declares that now the Saviour has appeared the Christian can desire nothing with greater longing that to 'depart from here' and to be rescued from the chains of the body in order to be united with Jesus in 'sweet peace, quiet repose'. Of all the Purification texts, this is probably the most deeply penetrated by mystical yearning for the afterlife: the world serves only as a place of misery in which the Christian has no part.

Bach composed this cantata for performance on 2 February 1727 and later revived it on several occasions in semi-modified forms as follows:

1731 (or 1730?): as a solo cantata for soprano in E minor
1735: probably as a solo cantata for mezzo-soprano in C minor, or possibly E minor (two performances a short time apart?)
c. 1746–7: as a solo cantata for bass in C minor, a version that essentially corresponds with that of 1727

The great popularity of the work is also clear from the manuscript copy of extracts from it that appears in Anna Magdalena Bach's second *Clavierbüchlein*, which was begun in 1725. As shown in the Critical Report to NBA V/4, the movements concerned were copied from the cantata into the *Clavierbüchlein* rather than vice versa. The scoring is modest. A single voice is accompanied by strings and continuo together with an oboe, which in the E minor version, due to its high pitch, was replaced by transverse flute.* It is curious that this same scoring is required in all three arias almost without exception. Even the silence of the oboe in the third movement, as in former editions of the work, applies at most to one or two of the transmitted versions. An oboe da caccia* participated here in the C minor version before 1735—perhaps even in the first performance[2]—and again in *c.* 1747–8, and in the E minor version it was replaced by flute.

The opening movement begins with an eloquent oboe melody over a gently agitated string accompaniment. The oboe entry, with its upward leap of a sixth, recalls related themes in the aria 'Erbarme dich' from the *St Matthew Passion* and the duet 'Wenn kommst du, mein Heil' from the cantata *Wachet auf, ruft uns die Stimme*, BWV 140. This makes it clear that, bound up with the glad gratitude of 'I have enough', is the yearning desire 'to depart from here this very day with joy'. Bach here reveals himself as a master of motivic transformation. The oboe motive* is taken up by the bass soloist in its original form:

[2] The flute part of the E minor version (*c.* 1735) was based on a lost C minor part for oboe da caccia; see KB, NBA I/28.1 (1994).

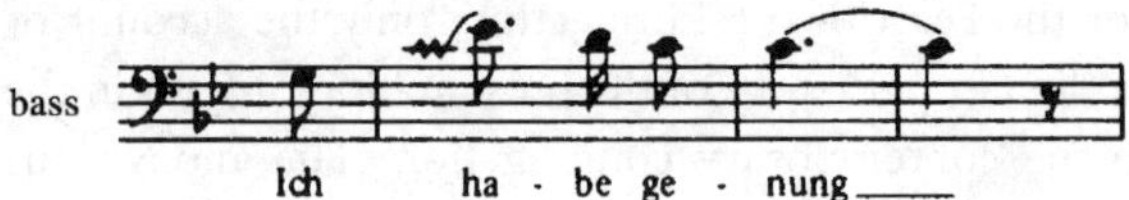

At the close of all three vocal passages (the overall form is A B B[1]), we hear a modified form, transposed to the keys of G minor, F minor, and C minor, but remaining similar in each case. In its G minor form it reads:

Section B opens with a further modification of the same motive to a different text:

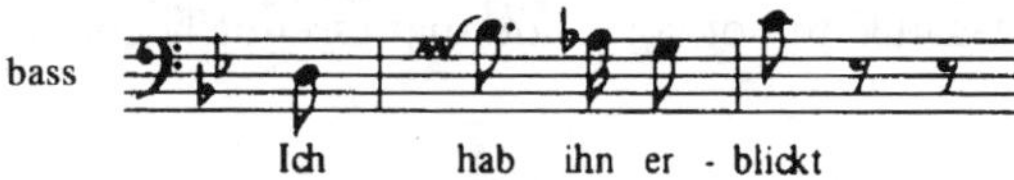

If more distantly related forms were included, we would arrive at a considerable number of additional transformations.

The second movement, a *secco* recitative, repeats the initial words of the cantata, this time in a new setting:

The call 'Let us go with this Man!', which draws the assembled congregation into the biblical narrative, is highlighted in a two-bar central arioso* passage, whose continuo-voice imitation* symbolizes the Christian's treading in the footsteps of Christ. The movement closes with yet another setting of the initial words of the cantata, whose cadential fall characterizes it as conclusive:

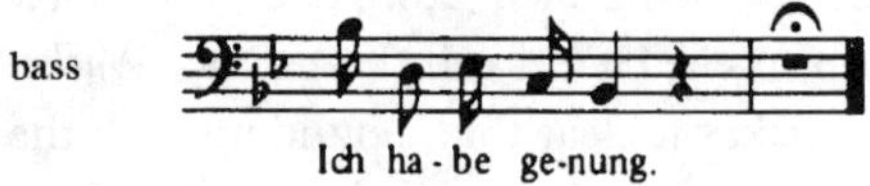

Next follows the so-called slumber aria, no. 3, which is rightly numbered among Bach's best-loved creations. Though representative of a widespread baroque type, it leaves all things typical far behind in its great richness of invention and fullness of expression. Its lullaby character is conveyed by the frequent pedal-point figures in the continuo; by a melodic tendency to the Mixolydian or minor seventh (d^2 flat at the beginning of bar 2 and often elsewhere) whose subdominant character evokes the impression of release; by the cradle rhythm, for which the syncopation is responsible; and by a repeated retardation of motion caused by fermatas (long pauses). The expanded da capo* form of the aria is exceptional. A reprise of the first vocal passage A is is heard in the centre of the middle section, with the result that a species of rondeau form emerges (*rit.* signifies instrumental ritornello):

rit.—A—*rit.*—B A C—*rit.*—A—*rit.*

A brief *secco* with arioso conclusion ('World, good night!') leads to the joyfully excited concluding aria, which is neither textually nor musically capable of sustaining the high level of the two preceding arias. It is one of those pieces close to dance—with clear, periodic phrase structure, enlivened by strong rhythmic impulses—that no doubt reveal Bach's great art, but in this case does not offer a balanced conclusion to what precedes it, with the result that the absence of a concluding chorale is doubly to be regretted.

Bekennen will ich seinen Namen, BWV 200

NBA I/28.1, p. 189 BC A192 Duration: *c.* 5 mins

ARIA A vln I,II bc E C

Bekennen will ich seinen Namen,	I will confess His Name:
Er ist der Herr, er ist der Christ,	He is the Lord, He is the Christ,
In welchem aller Völker Samen	In whom the seed of all peoples
Gesegnet und erlöset ist.	Is blessed and redeemed.
Kein Tod raubt mir die Zuversicht:	No death robs me of the assurance:
Der Herr ist meines Lebens Licht.	The Lord is my life's Light.

This aria, rediscovered in 1924 and first published in 1935, is in all probability the only surviving remnant of a larger work. According to documentary evidence, it originated around 1742. The text is a paraphrase of Simeon's canticle, the Nunc dimittis (Luke 2.29–32). Here, in contrast with the Purification cantatas that survive complete, it is not longing for death that forms the central focus, but rather the acknowledgement of Jesus as the Lord of all peoples. There is no documentary evidence for the assignment of the aria to the Feast of the Purification. It follows with some likelihood from the text, but nonetheless remains hypothetical as long as we remain ignorant of the context of the aria.

The composition itself, whose authenticity is established by the existence of an autograph draft, has a hymnic vigour reminiscent of Handel. The instrumental texture is part-homophonic* and part-imitative. The structure approximates to *Bar* form:* a text of the form *a b a b c c* is underpinned by the musical form A A^1 B C. This avoidance of the customary da capo* form, though found in earlier works too, accords well with the assumption of an origin within Bach's late period.

A number of cantatas written for other occasions in the church year were, from time to time, performed by Bach at the Feast of the Purification on account of their appropriate textual content, namely:

Komm, du süße Todesstunde, BWV 161
Ich lasse dich nicht, du segnest mich denn, BWV 157
Der Friede sei mit dir, BWV 158 (older version?)

3.2 The Feast of the Annunciation (25 March)

EPISTLE: Isaiah 7.10–16: The prophecy of the Messiah's birth.
GOSPEL: Luke 1.26–38: The angel Gabriel announces to Mary the birth of Jesus.

Siehe, eine Jungfrau ist schwanger, BWV Anh. I 199

1. [BASS SOLO? CHORUS?]: 'Siehe, eine Jungfrau ist schwanger'
2. ARIA: Ihr frohen Lippen, reget euch!
3. CHOR[ALE]: **Ei! meine Perle, du werte Kron**
4. RECIT[ATIVO]: Wir Menschen waren tot in Sünden
5. ARIA: Nur der Immanuel
6. CHOR[ALE]: **Das hat er alles uns getan**

According to textual discoveries made by Wolf Hobohm in St Petersburg,[3] this cantata, whose music is lost, was performed by Bach in Leipzig on 25 March 1724. That the work may have been composed by Bach himself is suggested by the formal correspondence of the text with those of other Bach compositions of 1724 and 1725.[4]

Wie schön leuchtet der Morgenstern, BWV 1

NBA I/28.2, p. 3 BC A173 Duration: *c.* 25 mins

1. [CHORALE] SATB hn I,II ob da c I,II vln conc I,II str bc F $\frac{12}{8}$

Wie schön leuchtet der Morgenstern	**How lovely shines the Morning Star,**
Voll Gnad und Wahrheit von dem Herrn,	**Full of grace and truth from the Lord,**
Die süße Wurzel Jesse!	**The sweet root of Jesse!**
Du Sohn David aus Jakobs Stamm,	**You Son of David from Jacob's stock,**
Mein König und mein Bräutigam,	**My King and my Bridegroom,**
Hast mir mein Herz besessen,	**You have taken possession of my heart;**
Lieblich, freundlich,	**Lovely, kindly,**
Schön und herrlich, groß und ehrlich, reich von Gaben,	**Fair and glorious, great and honourable, rich in gifts,**
Hoch und sehr prächtig erhaben.	**Highly and most splendidly exalted.**

[3] See W. Hobohm, 'Neue "Texte zur Leipziger Kirchen-Music" ', *BJ* 1973, 5–32.

[4] For details and a reproduction of the text, see Hobohm, 'Neue Texte'. A facsimile of the printed text of 1724 is given in BT, p. 427.

2. Recitativo T bc	d–g 𝄴
Du wahrer Gottes und Marien Sohn,	You true Son of God and Mary,
Du König derer Auserwählten,	You King of the elect,
Wie süß ist uns dies Lebenswort,	How sweet to us is this Word of Life,
Nach dem die ersten Väter schon	According to which the first fathers already
So Jahr' als Tage zählten,	Counted both years and days,
Das Gabriel mit Freuden dort	And which Gabriel promised with joy
In Bethlehem verheißen!	There in Bethlehem!
O Süßigkeit, o Himmelsbrot!	O sweetness, O heavenly Bread!
Das weder Grab, Gefahr, noch Tod	Which neither grave, danger, nor death
Aus unsern Herzen reißen.	Can tear out of our hearts.
3. Aria S ob da c bc	B♭ 𝄴
Erfüllet, ihr himmlischen, göttlichen Flammen,	Fill, you heavenly, divine flames,
Die nach euch verlangende gläubige Brust!	The faithful breast that longs for You!
Die Seelen empfinden die kräftigsten Triebe	Our souls feel the most powerful impulses
Der brünstigsten Liebe	Of the most ardent love
Und schmecken auf Erden die himmlische Lust.	And taste on earth heavenly delight.
4. Recitativo B bc	g–B♭ 𝄴
Ein irdscher Glanz, ein leiblich Licht	An earthly radiance, a corporeal light
Rührt meine Seele nicht;	Does not stir my soul;
Ein Freudenschein ist mir von Gott entstanden,	A joyful Light from God has arisen for me,
Denn ein vollkommnes Gut,	For a perfect Good,
Des Heilands Leib und Blut,	The Saviour's Body and Blood,
Ist zur Erquickung da.	Is there as refreshment.
So muß uns ja	Thus indeed
Der überreiche Segen,	The abundant blessing
Der uns von Ewigkeit bestimmt	Ordained for us from eternity,
Und unser Glaube zu sich nimmt,	Of which our faith partakes,
Zum Dank und Preis bewegen.	Must move us to thanks and praise.
5. Aria T vln conc I,II str bc	F 3/8
Unser Mund und Ton der Saiten	Our mouths and the sound of strings
Sollen dir	Shall to You
Für und für	For ever and ever
Dank und Opfer zubereiten.	Prepare thanksgiving and offerings.
Herz und Sinnen sind erhoben,	Heart and mind are raised
Lebenslang	As long as I live
Mit Gesang	In singing,
Großer König, dich zu loben.	Great King, to Your praise.

6. Choral SATB bc (+ instrs; hn II independent) F c

Wie bin ich doch so herzlich froh,	**How heartily glad I am indeed**
Daß mein Schatz ist das A und O,	**That my Treasure is the Alpha and Omega,**
Der Anfang und das Ende;	**The beginning and the end;**
Er wird mich doch zu seinem Preis	**He will indeed to His glory**
Aufnehmen in das Paradeis,	**Take me up into Paradise,**
Des klopf ich in die Hände.	**For which I clap my hands.**
Amen! amen!	**Amen! Amen!**
Komm, du schöne Freudenkrone, bleib nicht lange,	**Come, You fair Crown of Joy, do not delay for long,**
Deiner wart ich mit Verlangen.	**I await You with longing.**

This work, composed for performance on 25 March 1725, is the last chorale cantata* of the cycle of 1724–5. For although Bach's second church year in Leipzig did not come to an end till Trinity, from Easter 1725 onwards he returned to the setting of 'normal' cantata texts. According to an old tradition, Philipp Nicolai's hymn of 1599 was assigned to the Feast of the Epiphany, but it was also sung at the Annunciation. Bach's anonymous librettist preserved the wording of the outer verses, nos. 1 and 7, but paraphrased the remainder: verse 2 in the first recitative (no. 2), verse 3 in the first aria (no. 3), verse 4 and part of verse 5 in the second recitative (no. 4), and verse 6, as may be easily recognized, in the second aria (no. 5).

In many respects, Nicolai's hymn is easy to relate to the readings of the day, since it refers to the coming of the Saviour. Exceptionally apt in this regard are the last lines, 'Come, You fair Crown of Joy, do not delay for long, I await You with longing', which, strictly speaking, refer to the Second Coming but are nonetheless accorded an Advent significance in Cantatas 61 and 36 (first version). Further links between reading and hymn are established in the paraphrase of the middle verses, particularly in the second movement, which deals with the Messianic hope of the first fathers and with the promise of Gabriel. Altogether, the librettist must be credited with the empathy he shows for that fervour which characterizes Nicolai's poem and which has turned his hymns into an enduring possession of the Protestant Church. The librettist has, moreover, supplied Bach with verse which, if not inspired, is nonetheless thoughtful and appealing.

Bach's composition underlines still further the charm and depth of feeling of his textual model. The instrumentation derives its festive brilliance from the participation of two horns, two oboes da caccia,* and two concertante* violins alongside strings and continuo. On this basis a remarkable sound-picture emerges. The tutti of wind and strings creates a richly scored, full-sounding middle layer, over which the two solo violins play a lively figuration, easily recognizable as an image of the sparkling Morning Star—all the more so in view of the absence of the usual wind instruments of this pitch (flutes, oboes, and trumpets).

The design of the opening chorus* brings to our attention once more, at the very end of Bach's regular composition of chorale cantatas, the characteristic form of the great chorale-choruses. The chorale melody, divided into line sections, lies in the soprano in unison with first horn. The lower voices support the *cantus firmus** and at times prepare for its entry in an imitative* texture. In so doing they sometimes make use of thematic material expounded in the orchestra and elsewhere employ chorale-related or freely invented material. Characteristic examples of different kinds of treatment of the lower parts are found in line 2, 'Full of grace and truth from the Lord', and line 5, 'My King and my Bridegroom', where the chorale-line is richly prepared by a lengthy fore-structure, including a literal *cantus firmus* quotation in the tenor and alto. By contrast, in line 7, the setting of 'lovely' consists simply of two chords—here the contrast between the soprano *cantus firmus* and the lower-part complex, in counterpoint* with it, is abolished. The orchestra develops its own independent thematic material in a twelve-bar introductory sinfonia, which is related to the chorale melody only in the leap of a fifth that opens the theme and, more generally, in the insistently triadic nature of the figure-work. The semiquaver figuration of the solo violins, which, as mentioned above, lends the movement its distinctive hue, is maintained in the vocal passages too, whereas the other instruments are here only occasionally independent and frequently double the voices. A compositional problem arises from the inherent tendency of the chorale melody to maintain its tonic key throughout all ten lines. This, in an extended chorus of this kind, could easily have a monotonous effect. Bach avoids this danger, however, by seizing the opportunities for harmonic side-stepping within the vocal passages and by modulating to other keys in the episodes (at the beginning of the *Abgesang** and before the last line). All in all, what emerges is a movement of jubilant splendour, colourful profusion, and Advent joy.

The two recitatives, nos. 2 and 4, are set as plain *secco* accompanied by continuo. Special emphasis is given only to the words 'Freudenschein' ('joyful light') and 'Erquickung' ('refreshment') in the fourth movement by means of melismatic* decoration. On the other hand, it seems that Bach took special care over the composition of the two arias. The first, no. 3, presents the rare sound combination of soprano voice with an obbligato* instrument of tenor pitch, the oboe da caccia.[5] The melodic lines are solemn and song-like. The opening of the vocal section is achieved by adding text to the antecedent phrase of the ritornello, whose more instrumental-style, figurative continuation plays a notably

[5] The original performing material includes two copies of the oboe da caccia part for no. 3, but the second copy was evidently intended to replace rather than double the first.

small role in the vocal writing. In the second aria, no. 5, which is assigned to strings, the two concertante violins allow the composer the opportunity to introduce charming solo–tutti contrasts. Even within the tutti passages, Bach incorporates echo effects, and polyphonic* treatment is largely renounced. The impression thereby arises of a joyful, dance-like piece whose instrumentation and figure-work harks back to the opening chorus, despite the absence of direct thematic links. The thematic material is notably uniform, which strengthens the impression of joyful abandon. In musical terms, even the middle section turns out to be a variant of the principal section.

The concluding chorale again achieves a hymnic, festive character by virtue of its independent and markedly agile second horn part (the other instruments simply double the voices). In the previous aria, it was the figuration of the solo violins that harked back to the opening of the cantata, but here it is the full sound of the entire instrumental ensemble, enriched with wind and combined with the chorale singing of the choir, that formally rounds of the work by recalling the opening movement.

3.3 The Feast of the Visitation (2 July)

EPISTLE: Isaiah 11.1–5: The prophecy of the Messiah.
GOSPEL: Luke 1.39–56: Mary visits Elizabeth; Mary's song of praise (the Magnificat*).

Herz und Mund und Tat und Leben, BWV 147

NBA I/28.2, p. 65 BC A174 Duration: *c.* 34 mins

1.	CHORUS SATB tr str + ob I,II bsn bc	C $\frac{6}{4}$
	Herz und Mund und Tat und Leben Muß von Christo Zeugnis geben Ohne Furcht und Heuchelei, Daß er Gott und Heiland sei.	Heart and mouth and deed and life Must bear witness of Christ, Without fear and hypocrisy, That He is God and Saviour.
2.	RECITATIVO T str bc	F–a C
	Gebenedeiter Mund! Maria macht ihr Innerstes der Seelen Durch Dank und Rühmen kund; Sie fänget bei sich an, Des Heilands Wunder zu erzählen, Was er an ihr als seiner Magd getan. O menschliches Geschlecht, Des Satans und der Sünden Knecht, Du bist befreit Durch Christi tröstendes Erscheinen Von dieser Last und Dienstbarkeit!	Blessed mouth! Mary makes known the innermost part Of her soul through thanks and praise; She begins with herself, Recounting the wonders the Saviour Has done for her as His handmaid. O human race, Servant of Satan and of sin, You are freed Through Christ's comforting appearance From this burden and servitude!

Jedoch dein Mund und dein verstockt Gemüte
Verschweigt, verleugnet solche Güte;
Doch wisse, daß dich nach der Schrift
Ein allzuscharfes Urteil trifft!

However, your mouth and your hardened spirit
Are silent and deny this goodness;
Yet know that according to Scripture
A judgement all too sharp shall strike you!

3. Aria A ob d'am bc — a 3/4

Schäme dich, o Seele, nicht,
Deinen Heiland zu bekennen,
Soll er dich die seine nennen
Vor des Vaters Angesicht!
Doch wer ihn auf dieser Erden
Zu verleugnen sich nicht scheut,
Soll von ihm verleugnet werden,
Wenn er kommt zur Herrlichkeit.

Do not be ashamed, O soul,
To acknowledge your Saviour,
Should He call you His own
Before His Father's Countenance!
Yet whoever on this earth
Does not shrink from denying Him
Shall be denied by Him
When He comes in glory.

4. Recitativo B bc — d–a C

Verstockung kann Gewaltige verblenden,
Bis sie des Höchsten Arm vom Stuhle stößt;
Doch dieser Arm erhebt,
Obschon vor ihm der Erde Kreis erbebt,
Hingegen die Elenden,
So er erlöst.
O hochbeglückte Christen,
Auf, machet euch bereit,
Itzt ist die angenehme Zeit,
Itzt ist der Tag des Heils: Der Heiland heißt
Euch Leib und Geist
Mit Glaubensgaben rüsten,
Auf, ruft zu ihm in brünstigem Verlangen,
Um ihn im Glauben zu empfangen!

Stubbornness can blind the mighty until
The Highest's arm thrusts them from their seat;
Yet this arm,
Even though Earth's sphere trembles before it,
Exalts the wretched,
Whom He redeems.
O highly favoured Christians,
Rise up, make yourselves ready!
Now is the acceptable time,
Now is the day of Salvation: the Saviour calls you
To arm body and spirit
With the gifts of faith;
Rise up! call to Him in fervent longing
In order to receive Him in faith!

5. Aria S vln I solo bc — d C

Bereite dir, Jesu, noch itzo die Bahn,
Mein Heiland, erwähle
Die gläubende Seele,
Und siehe mit Augen der Gnaden mich an!

Prepare the way to You, O Jesus, even now;
My Saviour, choose
The believing soul,
And look upon me with eyes of Grace!

6. Choral S + tr ATB str + ob I,II bc — G 3/4 9/8

Wohl mir, daß ich Jesum habe,
O wie feste halt ich ihn,
Daß er mir mein Herze labe,

It is well for me that I have Jesus;
Oh, how firmly I hold Him,
That He may restore my heart

Wenn ich krank und traurig bin.
Jesum hab ich, der mich liebet
Und sich mir zu eigen gibet;
Ach drum laß ich Jesum nicht,
Wenn mir gleich mein Herze bricht.

When I am ill and sad.
I have Jesus, who loves me
And gives Himself to me for His own;
Ah, therefore I will not let go of Jesus,
Even though my heart should break.

Parte seconda. Nach der Predigt.

Second Part. After the sermon.

7. Aria T vc? bc — F $\frac{3}{4}$

Hilf, Jesu, hilf, daß ich auch dich bekenne
In Wohl und Weh, in Freud und Leid,
Daß ich dich meinen Heiland nenne
Im Glauben und Gelassenheit,
Daß stets mein Herz von deiner Liebe brenne.
Hilf, Jesu, hilf!

Help, Jesus, help, that I too may confess You
In weal and woe, in joy and sorrow,
That I may call You my Saviour
In faith and composure,
That my heart may ever burn with Your Love.
Help, Jesus, help!

8. Recitativo A ob da c I,II bc — C c

Der höchsten Allmacht Wunderhand
Würkt im Verborgenen der Erden.
Johannes muß mit Geist erfüllet werden,
Ihn zieht der Liebe Band
Bereits in seiner Mutter Leibe,
Daß er den Heiland kennt,
Ob er ihn gleich noch nicht
Mit seinem Munde nennt,
Er wird bewegt, er hüpft und springet,
Indem Elisabeth das Wunderwerk ausspricht,
Indem Mariae Mund der Lippen Opfer bringet.
Wenn ihr, o Gläubige, des Fleisches Schwachheit merkt,
Wenn euer Herz in Liebe brennet,
Und doch der Mund den Heiland nicht bekennet,
Gott ist es, der euch kräftig stärkt,
Er will in euch des Geistes Kraft erregen,
Ja Dank und Preis auf eure Zunge legen.

The almighty wonder-hand of the Highest
Works in the secret places of the earth.
John must be filled with the Spirit:
The bond of Love draws him
Even in his mother's womb,
So that he knows the Saviour,
Even though he does not yet
Name Him with his mouth;
He is stirred, he leaps and jumps,
While Elizabeth announces a miracle,
While Mary's mouth brings the offering of her lips.
If you, O believer, note the weakness of the flesh,
If your heart burns with love,
And yet your mouth does not confess the Saviour,
It is God who powerfully strengthens you:
He will stir up in you the power of the Spirit;
Indeed, He will lay thanks and praise on your tongue.

9. Aria B tr str + ob I,II bc — C c

Ich will von Jesu Wundern singen
Und ihm der Lippen Opfer bringen,

I will sing of the wonders of Jesus
And bring Him my lips' offering;

Er wird nach seiner Liebe Bund	He will, according to His Covenant of Love,
Das schwache Fleisch, den irdschen Mund	Subdue weak flesh, mortal mouth
Durch heilges Feuer kräftig zwingen.	Through His holy Fire.
10. CHORAL [Scoring as in no. 6]	G $\frac{3}{4}$ $\frac{9}{8}$
Jesus bleibet meine Freude,	**Jesus remains my joy,**
Meines Herzens Trost und Saft.	**My heart's comfort and sap.**
Jesus wehret allem Leide,	**Jesus obviates all misfortune,**
Er ist meines Lebens Kraft,	**He is my life's strength,**
Meiner Augen Lust und Sonne,	**My eye's delight and sun,**
Meiner Seele Schatz und Wonne;	**My soul's treasure and bliss;**
Darum laß ich Jesum nicht	**Therefore I will not let Jesus go**
Aus dem Herzen und Gesicht.	**From my heart and sight.**

This cantata is based on a Weimar text by Salomo Franck, which contained only the odd-numbered movements together with a different concluding chorale. Bach set this Franck text as BWV 147a for the Fourth Sunday in Advent, 1716. Since no cantata was performed in Leipzig on that occasion, the text was adapted to its new purpose by making various textual alterations, replacing the concluding chorale, adding the recitatives nos. 2, 4, and 8, and incorporating an additional chorale verse to conclude the first part of a work that was now expanded to two parts. Although Franck's Advent text was, in any case, not unsuitable for a Marian feast, references to the Visitation are made still clearer in the newly added portions of text. The principal theme—the acknowledgement of Jesus, originally by John the Baptist—is reinterpreted to refer to Mary, whose song of praise, the Magnificat* (Luke 1.46–55), is a grateful acknowledgement to God in which Christendom is called upon to join. In the manner of a preacher, the textual editor flies into a passion against the impenitence of the deluded (nos. 2 and 4), interweaving numerous references to the Gospel* reading—for example, when we are told in the fourth movement that the arm of the Most High thrusts the mighty from their seat and exalts the lowly (cf. Luke 1.52), or when the eighth movement mentions the leaping of John in his mother's womb. In the sixth and tenth movements—verses 6 and 16 respectively of the hymn *Jesu, meiner Seelen Wonne* by Martin Jahn (1661)—the assembled congregation, represented by the choir, acknowledges Jesus as a great treasure worthy of preservation.

Bach's autograph score offers us the rare opportunity of bearing witness to a spontaneous textual alteration on the part of the composer. In the fifth movement, Bach began to write Franck's text as we know it from his published verse:

Beziehe die Höhle	Occupy the cavern
Des Herzens, der Seele,	Of the heart, of the soul,

Und blicke mit Augen der Gnade mich an.	And look upon me with eyes of grace.

But he may have felt that the image of Jesus looking out of a cavern with merciful eyes was not entirely felicitous, for while still writing he altered the first two lines of the passage to the more tasteful version, 'Mein Heiland, erwähle die gläubende Seele' ('My Saviour, choose the believing soul').

Bach's composition was first performed in the version we know today in Leipzig on 2 July 1723. Its festive character is enhanced by the addition of a trumpet to the usual instrumental ensemble of two oboes, strings, and continuo (plus bassoon). The opening chorus* is a model of well-balanced symmetry. Owing to the grammatic unity of the text, it was hardly possible to divide it up in motet* style or just into principal and middle sections. Consequently, the entire text is delivered in all three sections of this free da capo*-form movement, which may well explain why Bach's setting to a striking extent assimilates the middle section to the outer sections: the form is A A^1 A, rather than A B A^1. Each section is dominated partly by the orchestra, with choral insertion,* and partly by the choir, in *a cappella** writing with continuo; and in the outer sections, choral fugue, with the instruments largely *colla parte,** is added as a third type of texture, which results in the following overall form (italics denote instrumental passages):

	Sinfonia a
Principal section:	Fugue b + *instruments*
	Sinfonia a^1 + choir
	A cappella passage x
Middle section:	*Sinfonia* a^1 + choir
	A cappella passage y
Free da capo:	Fugue b^1 + *instruments*
	Sinfonia a^1 + choir
	A cappella passage z
	Sinfonia a

The three recitatives are variously scored. The second movement is accompanied by plain string chords, with individual words emphasized by livelier motion; the fourth is in continuo texture, with an arioso* middle section; and the eighth, a motivically-imprinted *accompagnato,** is accompanied by two oboes da caccia,*[6] whose expressive motive* lends special emphasis to the wonders of God with which the text is concerned. Only at the point where the text tells of John's leaping inside his mother's womb is the fixed motive temporarily discontinued in favour of a descriptive figure.

[6] At a revival in the late 1730s the first oboe da caccia part was played on the oboe d'amore*; see KB, NBA I/28.2 (1995).

In Franck's text, the four arias follow one another without intermission, though in a different order. The first, no. 3, is notable for its suspended rhythm, in which normal 3/4 time and disguised 3/2 alternate in an irregular order and sometimes in different layers in the various parts. This rhythm, heard at the very outset on obbligato* oboe d'amore*—

—is taken up at the vocal entry to the words 'Schäme dich, o Seele, nicht' ('Do not be ashamed, O soul') and later to other lines of text. The second aria, no. 5 (like the first, a trio for obbligato instrument, voice, and continuo), is characterized by the virtuoso triplet figuration of a solo violin. The brilliance of this instrumental part is evidently designed to reflect a spirit of expectant joy over the coming of the Messiah. As in the first movement, the text is hardly subdivided at all, with the result that Bach adopts the unusual form of six vocal sections in succession, with the complete text delivered altogether five times. There is no vocal da capo. Instead, a rounding off is achieved by incorporating the last two sections as vocal insertion* within an almost complete statement of the extended ritornello before its final reprise in a purely instrumental form.

The tenor aria, no. 7, is a continuo movement whose instrumental bass line is elaborated in the triplet figuration of the cello. The head-motive of the ritornello, which also forms the opening of the voice part—

—recurs repeatedly in the course of the movement and at the end forms a concluding motto.* The few parts of the first three arias contrast with the full scoring of the last, no. 9, for which the entire instrumental ensemble is required, including trumpet, in order to praise the wonderful works of Jesus. Incidentally, in place of 'von Jesu Wundern' ('of Jesus's wonders') older editions give 'von Jesu Wunden' ('of Jesus's wounds'), which is based on a misreading. The movement is decidedly concerto-like in character. The prominent, signal-like head-motive is followed by a sequential continuation, and echo effects are derived from the presence or absence of the oboes. In the second section, 'Er wird nach seiner Liebe Bund', the instruments are at first much overshadowed by the voice, but at the end, as in no. 5, Bach creates the impression of a formal rounding-off by means of vocal insertion within an almost complete ritornello statement before its concluding instrumental reprise.

The chorales at the end of Parts I and II, nos. 6 and 10, are musically identical. A plain four-part vocal setting of the chorale is embedded line by line within an extended orchestral framework—including outer ritornellos and inner episodes—of a charming and overtly pastoral character. On this account the piece has achieved astonishing popularity (under the title *Jesu, Joy of Man's Desiring*), particularly in Anglo-Saxon countries. As the following comparison shows—

—the eight-bar ritornello is derived from the chorale melody, *Werde munter, mein Gemüte.*

Meine Seel erhebt den Herren, BWV 10

NBA I/28.2, p. 133 BC A175 Duration: *c.* 23 mins

1. [Chorale] SATB tr ob I,II str bc — g C

Meine Seel erhebt den Herren,	**My soul magnifies the Lord,**
Und mein Geist freuet sich Gottes, meines Heilandes;	**And my spirit rejoices in God, my Saviour;**
Denn er hat seine elende Magd angesehen.	**For He has regarded His lowly handmaiden.**
Siehe, von nun an werden mich selig preisen alle Kindeskind.	**Behold, from henceforth all generations shall call me blessed.**

2. Aria S ob I + II str bc — B♭ C

Herr, der du stark und mächtig bist,	Lord, You who are strong and mighty,
Gott, dessen Name heilig ist,	God, whose Name is holy,
Wie wunderbar sind deine Werke!	How marvellous are Your works!
Du siehest mich Elenden an,	You regard me in my lowliness,

Du hast an mir so viel getan,
Daß ich nicht alles zähl und merke.

You have done so much for me
That I cannot count or note it all.

3. Recitativo T bc — g–d C

Des Höchsten Güt und Treu
Wird alle Morgen neu
Und währet immer für und für
Bei denen, die allhier
Auf seine Hülfe schaun
Und ihm in wahrer Furcht vertraun.
Hingegen übt er auch Gewalt
Mit seinem Arm
An denen, welche weder kalt
Noch warm
Im Glauben und im Lieben sein;
Die nacket, bloß und blind,
Die voller Stolz und Hoffart sind,
Will seine Hand wie Spreu zerstreun.

The goodness and faithfulness of the Highest
Are new every morning
And last for ever and ever
For those who here
Look to His help
And, in true fear, place their trust in Him.
On the other hand, He wields power
With His arm
On those who are neither cold
Nor warm
In faith and in love;
Naked, bare, and blind:
Those who are full of pride and arrogance
His hand will scatter like chaff.

4. Aria B bc — F C

Gewaltige stößt Gott vom Stuhl
Hinunter in den Schwefelpfuhl;
Die Niedern pflegt Gott zu erhöhen,
Daß sie wie Stern am Himmel stehen.
Die Reichen läßt Gott bloß und leer,
Die Hungrigen füllt er mit Gaben,
Daß sie auf seinem Gnadenmeer
Stets Reichtum und die Fülle haben.

God thrusts the mighty from their seat
Down into the lake of brimstone;
God is wont to exalt the humble
So that they stand like stars in heaven.
God leaves the rich bare and empty,
The hungry He fills with gifts,
So that upon His sea of Grace
They always have riches and abundance.

5. Duetto e Choral AT tr or ob I + II bc — d 6/8

Er denket der Barmherzigkeit
Und hilft seinem Diener Israel auf.

He remembers His mercy
And helps up His servant Israel.

6. Recitativo T str bc — B♭–g C

Was Gott den Vätern alter Zeiten
Geredet und verheißen hat,
Erfüllt er auch im Werk und in der Tat.
Was Gott dem Abraham,
Als er zu ihm in seine Hütten kam,
Versprochen und geschworen,
Ist, da die Zeit erfüllet war, geschehen:
Sein Same mußte sich so sehr
Wie Sand am Meer
Und Stern am Firmament ausbreiten,
Der Heiland ward geboren,

What to the fathers in the days of old
God spoke and promised,
He also fulfils in work and deed.
What to Abraham,
When He came to him in his tents,
God promised and swore,
Did happen when the fullness of time came:
His seed had to spread as much
As sand at the sea
And stars in the firmament;
The Saviour was born,

Das ewge Wort ließ sich im Fleische sehen,	The eternal Word appeared in the flesh
Das menschliche Geschlecht von Tod und allem Bösen	To redeem the human race from death and all evil
Und von des Satans Sklaverei	And from Satan's slavery
Aus lauter Liebe zu erlösen;	Out of pure love;
Drum bleibts darbei,	Therefore it remains the case
Daß Gottes Wort voll Gnad und Wahrheit sei.	That God's Word is full of grace and truth.

7. Choral SATB bc (+ instrs) g C

Lob und Preis sei Gott dem Vater und dem Sohn	**Blessing and praise be to God the Father and to the Son**
Und dem Heiligen Geiste,	**And to the Holy Spirit,**
Wie es war im Anfang, itzt und immerdar,	**As it was in the beginning, is now and ever shall be**
Und von Ewigkeit zu Ewigkeit. Amen.	**From eternity to eternity. Amen.**

Among Bach's chorale cantatas* this work occupies a special place. It is not based on a Protestant hymn, and yet if ever a work deserved the description 'chorale cantata' it is this, for it is based on a genuine (Gregorian) chorale melody, that of the ninth psalm-tone (quoted here according to Schein's Cantional of 1627):

Since ancient times Mary's Magnificat* (Luke 1.46–55) had been a component of the liturgy for Vespers; and in Bach's day it was sung in German at the Leipzig afternoon service to the melody of the ninth psalm-tone in the four-part setting by Johann Hermann Schein (1627). At the Feast of the Visitation, the Magnificat also formed part of the Gospel* reading. It was thus a natural step to use it as the basis of a chorale cantata on that occasion in 1724.

The anonymous editor of the text retained the original wording of Luke 1.46–8 (no. 1), of verse 54 (no. 5), and of the doxology* with which psalm-singing customarily ends (no. 7). The remaining verses he paraphrased to form arias and recitatives: verse 49 in no. 2, verses 50–1 in no. 3, verses 52–3 in no. 4, and finally verse 55 in no. 6, whose text was expanded to include a reference to the birth of the Saviour. In addition, allusions to other biblical passages were repeatedly interwoven in accordance with baroque practice. Thus the third movement includes references to Lamentations 3.22–3 ('It is of the goodness of the Lord that we are not consumed; His mercy . . . is new every morning, and great is Your faithfulness') and Revelation 3.16 ('Since you are lukewarm, neither cold nor hot, I will spit you out'); and the sixth movement carries still further the appeal already made in Luke's Gospel to God's promises to Abraham (cf. in particular Genesis 18.1 ff.). However, the paraphrase lacks specific references to the Gospel reading apart from the Magnificat itself; there is no mention, for example, of Mary's visit to Elizabeth.

Bach's composition was written for performance on 2 July 1724 and thus forms the fifth work in his cycle of chorale cantatas. The first movement begins with a concertante* instrumental sinfonia, thematically unrelated to the psalm-tone—a trio texture made up of violins I and II (reinforced by oboes) and continuo, with the harmony filled in by viola. The choir enters after twelve bars, delivering the chorale half a verse at a time, with trumpet strengthening the *cantus firmus*.* In verse 1, the ninth psalm-tone lies in the soprano, while the lower voice parts, whose thematic material is derived from the orchestral music, accompany in free polyphony.* In verse 2, the *cantus firmus*, again reinforced by trumpet, migrates to the alto, yet this second section is essentially a reprise of the first with subdominant transposition and exchange of parts. A rounding-off, together with a return to the tonic key, is skilfully achieved by building a choral texture without *cantus firmus* into a concluding reprise of the introductory sinfonia.

The second movement, a soprano aria with string ensemble and oboes that enter or rest according to pitch, is also in concertante style. It is notable for its lively semiquaver motion which involves not only the upper parts but even the continuo. The middle section ('You regard me in my lowliness') is dynamically reduced, though it shares the same thematic material in its instrumental accompaniment, and closes with a passage accompanied by continuo only before the da capo* of the principal section. A *secco* recitative with arioso* conclusion, no. 3, acts as a transition to the next aria, no. 4, a movement in continuo texture whose introductory instrumental bars recur in the vocal passages in the form of a *basso quasi ostinato*.* In the first of the three vocal passages, it is only the antecedent phrase that recurs, but in the two others the continuation does also. The conclusion of the aria, like that of the opening chorus,* consists of a complete reprise of the ritornello with vocal insertion,* extended by a pedal-point.

In the following duet, no. 5, not only is the biblical text preserved in its original wording but the melody of the ninth psalm-tone is heard again. The alto and tenor have their own theme in an imitative* texture, accompanied by continuo, while the *cantus firmus* is played on trumpet or unison oboes (evidently as alternatives[7]), as in the setting of 'Suscepit Israel' from the *Magnificat*,

[7] The trumpet seems to have been replaced by unison oboes at a late revival, *c.* 1740–7; see KB, NBA I/28.2.

BWV 243/243a. Bach later transcribed this movement for organ as BWV 648, including it among the six chorales engraved by Schübler.

The sixth movement begins as *secco* recitative with continuo accompaniment. From the words 'Sein Same . . .' ('His seed had to spread as much as sand at the sea . . . the Saviour was born'), however, motivically shaped string figures are heard at an 'andante' tempo in order to underline words of particular significance for this feast and to emphasize the fulfilment of God's promise to Abraham and, later, to Mary. At the conclusion of the work, the two verses of the doxology are set in a plain four-part texture. The *cantus firmus* in the top part is, once again, the ninth psalm-tone.

4

The Feast of St John the Baptist (24 June)

Epistle: Isaiah 40.1–5: 'It is the voice of a preacher'.

Gospel: Luke 1.57–80: The birth of John the Baptist; the song of praise of Zacharias (the Benedictus*).

Ihr Menschen, rühmet Gottes Liebe, BWV 167

NBA I/29, p. 3 BC A176 Duration: *c.* 18 mins

1. Aria T str bc — G C $\frac{12}{8}$

Ihr Menschen, rühmet Gottes Liebe	You people, celebrate God's Love
Und preiset seine Gütigkeit!	And praise His goodness!
Lobt ihn aus reinem Herzenstriebe,	Bless Him from pure impulse of heart,
Daß er uns zu bestimmter Zeit	Since at the appointed time
Das Horn des Heils, den Weg zum Leben	The horn of salvation, the path of life
An Jesu, seinem Sohn, gegeben.	He has given us in Jesus, His Son.

2. Recitativo A bc — e C

Gelobet sei der Herr Gott Israel,	Blessed be the Lord God of Israel,
Der sich in Gnaden zu uns wendet	Who turns to us in Grace
Und seinen Sohn	And sends His Son
Vom hohen Himmelsthron	From the high throne of heaven
Zum Welterlöser sendet.	As Redeemer of the world.
Erst stellte sich Johannes ein	First John appeared
Und mußte Weg und Bahn	And had to prepare the path and highway
Dem Heiland zubereiten;	For the Saviour;
Hierauf kam Jesus selber an,	Thereupon Jesus Himself arrived
Die armen Menschenkinder	To gladden the poor children of men
Und die verlornen Sünder	And lost sinners
Mit Gnad und Liebe zu erfreun	With Grace and Love
Und sie zum Himmelreich in wahrer Buß zu leiten.	And to lead them in true repentance to the heavenly Kingdom.

3. Aria Duetto SA ob da c bc — a $\frac{3}{4}$ C $\frac{3}{4}$

Gottes Wort, das trüget nicht,	God's Word does not deceive:
Es geschieht, was er verspricht.	What He promises comes to be.
Was er in dem Paradies	What He pledged in Paradise
Und vor so viel hundert Jahren	So many hundred years ago

Denen Vätern schon verheißß,	To our forefathers
Haben wir gottlob erfahren.	We, God be blessed, have experienced.
4. Recitativo B bc	C–G C
Des Weibes Samen kam,	The woman's seed came
Nachdem die Zeit erfüllet;	After the fullness of time had arrived;
Der Segen, den Gott Abraham,	The blessing that God promised Abraham,
Dem Glaubensheld, versprochen,	That hero of faith,
Ist wie der Glanz der Sonne angebrochen,	Has broken forth like the radiance of the sun,
Und unser Kummer ist gestillet.	And our grief is stilled.
Ein stummer Zacharias preist	A mute Zacharias praises God
Mit lauter Stimme Gott	With loud voice
Vor seine Wundertat,	For the wondrous deed
Die er dem Volk erzeiget hat.	He has shown His people.
Bedenkt, ihr Christen, auch,	Consider, you Christians, also
Was Gott an euch getan,	What God has done for you,
Und stimmet ihm ein Loblied an!	And strike up for Him a song of praise!
5. Choral S + tr ATB str + ob bc	G $\frac{3}{4}$
Sei Lob und Preis mit Ehren	**Blessing and praise with honour be to**
Gott Vater, Sohn, Heiliger Geist!	**God the Father, Son, and Holy Spirit!**
Der woll in uns vermehren,	**May He increase in us**
Was er uns aus Genaden verheißt,	**What He promises us out of Grace,**
Daß wir ihm fest vertrauen,	**That we hold fast our confidence in Him,**
Gänzlich verlassen auf ihn,	**Fully rely on Him,**
Von Herzen auf ihn bauen,	**And build on Him from our hearts,**
Daß unsr Herz, Mut und Sinn	**That our heart, courage, and mind**
Ihm festiglich anhangen;	**May cleave firmly to Him;**
Darauf singn wir zur Stund:	**Whereupon we sing at this hour:**
Amen, wir werdens erlangen,	**Amen, we shall obtain it,**
Gläubn wir aus Herzens Grund.	**If we believe from the bottom of our heart.**

The text of this cantata, which is by an anonymous librettist, praises the love of God in accordance with Zacharias's song of praise, the Benedictus, which forms part of the Gospel* reading. Certain phrases, such as 'the horn of salvation' (no. 1) or 'Blessed be the Lord God of Israel' (no. 2), are adopted from it almost word for word (cf. Luke 1.68–9). In the second movement, the focus of attention shifts from Jesus back to John the Baptist, who paved the way for the Saviour. The librettist sees here the fulfilment of a promise already made by God in paradise (no. 3). This refers to God's words to the serpent after the Fall of Man: 'I shall put enmity between you and the woman and between your seed and her seed; it shall crush your head' (Genesis 3.15). According to traditional Christian teaching, this passage implies the promise that Jesus, the 'woman's seed' (no. 4), will one day stamp the serpent's head from out of paradise, thereby effacing Adam's sins.[1] The text ends by calling upon Christendom to consider God's good deeds and to follow Zacharias in singing Him a song of praise (no. 4). This is done in the concluding chorale, the fifth (supplementary) verse of Johann Gramann's hymn *Nun lob, mein Seel, den Herren* (Königsberg, Prussia, 1549).

Bach's composition was written for performance on 24 June 1723, soon after he took up the post of Thomascantor at Leipzig. It may be because he was new to the post that this cantata, which had to be produced on top of his regular Sunday music, makes use of a choir only in the concluding chorale and for its instrumental ensemble requires, in addition to strings and continuo, only one oboe (or oboe da caccia*) and trumpet[2] (merely to reinforce the chorale melody). In addition, it is notably brief in extent, containing only two arias.

The opening aria is of exceptional charm. It is a pastorale that reflects a mood of relaxed joyfulness rather than the injunction to praise God. The full-sounding string texture of the ritornello, with its dense sequences of sixth-chords, gives way to greater differentiation in the vocal passages: at times, a solo violin (with continuo) acts as the sole accompaniment of the voice; elsewhere, the singing is accompanied by the string tutti in a restrained *piano*. The compact sound is often broken up by brief, spirited passages of imitation,* and yet the texture is essentially homophonic* and disinclined to develop into strict part-writing. The second movement, a *secco* recitative, concludes with arioso:* the last two lines of text are sung against the background of a quasi-ostinato semiquaver motive* in the continuo as a means of highlighting the goal of the divine plan of salvation.

The quartet texture of the following duet with obbligato* oboe da caccia, no. 3, is, like the opening aria, not conceived in genuinely polyphonic* terms. The close proximity in pitch of the obbligato instrument and the voice parts again creates a dense, full sound. The concertante* element comes to the fore more prominently than in the first movement, of course, due to the presence of the obbligato 'hunting' oboe. After a six-bar introductory ritornello, the voice parts enter in homophony. Brief imitative motives ('Es geschieht, was er verspricht') then alternate with homophonic passages in a deft combination with ritornello excerpts played by the oboe da caccia. The middle section of this pure da capo*-form duet is unorthodox. The first half of it brings a change to common time and vocal canon,* whose head-motive—

[1] See H. Werthemann, *Die Bedeutung der alttestamentlichen Historien in J. S. Bachs Kirchenkantaten* (Tübingen, 1960), 71 ff.

[2] 'Clarino'—perhaps slide trumpet, or natural trumpet at the upper octave.

—is then incorporated in the texture as a repeated accompanying figure for oboe da caccia and continuo in alternation. The second half of the middle section returns to 3/4 time, but not to the thematic material of the principal section. Instead, the voices unite in jubilant parallel thirds and sixths with constant motivic repetitions, creating the impression of a joy that we wish would never end. Only then do we hear the da capo of the principal section. This movement illustrates how the duets of Bach and his time are, as we have often observed already, far more under the sway of a motet-like sectional form than are the solo arias.

The second recitative is again set as *secco* with arioso conclusion. This time, however, the closing arioso bars are not imprinted with an ostinato* motive but rather anticipate the melody of the concluding chorale, *Nun lob, mein Seel, den Herren*:

This concluding song of praise, no. 5, is the true high point of the work. Here all participants are united for the first time: strings, supported by oboe, choir (with trumpet doubling the chorale melody in the soprano), and continuo. The instruments surround and accompany the choral texture with their own thematic material, which in the chorale passages is skilfully combined with the prescribed melody, with the result that the work is crowned with an unexpected radiance.

Christ unser Herr zum Jordan kam, BWV 7

NBA I/29, p. 27 BC A177 Duration: *c.* 26 mins

1. [Chorale] SATB ob d'am I,II vln conc I,II str bc e C

Christ unser Herr zum Jordan kam	**Christ our Lord came to the Jordan**
Nach seines Vaters Willen,	**According to His Father's Will,**
Von Sankt Johanns die Taufe nahm,	**Was baptized by St John**
Sein Werk und Amt zu erfüllen;	**To fulfil His work and duty;**

Da wollt er stiften uns ein Bad,
Zu waschen uns von Sünden,
Ersäufen auch den bittern Tod
Durch sein selbst Blut und Wunden;
Es galt ein neues Leben.

There He would institute for us a bath
To wash us from sins
And to drown bitter death
Through His own Blood and Wounds;
It effected a new Life.

2. ARIA B bc — G c

Merkt und hört, ihr Menschenkinder,
Was Gott selbst die Taufe heißt!
  Es muß zwar hier Wasser sein,
  Doch schlecht Wasser nicht allein.
  Gottes Wort und Gottes Geist
  Tauft und reiniget die Sünder.

Hearken and hear, you children of men,
What God Himself calls baptism!
  There must indeed be water here,
  Yet not mere water alone.
  God's Word and God's Spirit
  Baptize and cleanse sinners.

3. RECITATIVO T bc — e–d c

Dies hat Gott klar
Mit Worten und mit Bildern dargetan,
Am Jordan ließ der Vater offenbar
Die Stimme bei der Taufe Christi hören;
Er sprach: Dies ist mein lieber Sohn,
An diesem hab ich Wohlgefallen,
Er ist vom hohen Himmelsthron
Der Welt zugut
In niedriger Gestalt gekommen
Und hat das Fleisch und Blut
Der Menschenkinder angenommen;
Den nehmet nun als euren Heiland an
Und höret seine teuren Lehren!

God has shown this clearly
In words and images;
At the Jordan, the Father let His Voice
Be heard clearly at the Baptism of Christ;
He said: This is my beloved Son,
In whom I am well pleased;
He has come from the high throne of heaven
For the world's benefit
In a humble form
And has adopted the flesh and blood
Of the children of men;
Adopt Him now as your Saviour
And hear His precious teaching!

4. ARIA T vln conc I,II bc — a 9/8 3/4

Des Vaters Stimme ließ sich hören,
Der Sohn, der uns mit Blut erkauft,
Ward als ein wahrer Mensch getauft.
Der Geist erschien im Bild der Tauben,
Damit wir ohne Zweifel glauben,
Es habe die Dreifaltigkeit
Uns selbst die Taufe zubereit'.

The Father's Voice made itself heard;
The Son, who purchased us with His Blood,
Was baptized as a true Man.
The Spirit appeared in the form of a dove,
So that we should believe without doubt
That it was the Trinity itself
Who prepared baptism for us.

5. RECITATIVO B str + vln conc I,II bc — e–b c

Als Jesus dort nach seinen Leiden
Und nach dem Auferstehn
Aus dieser Welt zum Vater wollte gehn,

When Jesus after His Passion
And after the Resurrection
Would go from this world to the Father,

Sprach er zu seinen Jüngern:
Geht hin in alle Welt und lehret alle Heiden,
Wer glaubet und getaufet wird auf Erden,
Der soll gerecht und selig werden.

He said to His disciples:
Go forth into all the world and teach all the Gentiles:
Whoever believes and is baptized on earth,
He shall be justified and saved.

6. Aria A str + ww + vln conc I + II bc e c

Menschen, glaubt doch dieser Gnade,
Daß ihr nicht in Sünden sterbt,
Noch im Höllenpfuhl verderbt!
Menschenwerk und -heiligkeit
Gilt vor Gott zu keiner Zeit.
Sünden sind uns angeboren,
Wir sind von Natur verloren;
Glaub und Taufe macht sie rein,
Daß sie nicht verdammlich sein.

Mankind, believe in this Grace
So that you do not die in sin,
Nor are destroyed in hell's slough!
Human deeds and sanctity
Count at no time before God.
Sins are inborn in us,
We are lost by nature;
Faith and baptism make them clean
So that they cannot be condemned.

7. Choral SATB bc (+ instrs) e–b c

Das Aug allein das Wasser sieht,
Wie Menschen Wasser gießen,
Der Glaub allein die Kraft versteht
Des Blutes Jesu Christi,
Und ist für ihm ein rote Flut
Von Christi Blut gefärbet,
Die allen Schaden heilet gut
Von Adam her geerbet,
Auch von uns selbst begangen.

The eye sees only water
As people pour it;
Faith alone comprehends the power
Of the Blood of Jesus Christ,
And for faith it is a red flood
Coloured by Christ's Blood,
Which fully heals all the wrongs
Inherited from Adam,
As well as those we ourselves have committed.

This work, the third in the cycle of chorale cantatas,* was composed for performance on 24 June 1724. It is based on Martin Luther's baptismal hymn of 1541, whose outer verses, nos. 1 and 7, were retained word for word, whereas the inner verses were each paraphrased by an anonymous author to form the like-numbered cantata movement. The cantata libretto adheres closely to Luther's hymn text, scarcely making any additions to it. In particular, it lacks any specific links with the Gospel* for the day, which is concerned with the birth of John the Baptist, not with the baptism of Jesus.

The most significant movement in the work is the opening chorus.* The presence of the *cantus firmus** in the tenor was determined in advance by the work's position as third in the cycle of chorale cantatas. The chorale melody, sung in long notes, is surrounded by the other voices in a freely polyphonic* texture with occasional imitation,* which is almost entirely unthematic in relation to the *cantus firmus*. Still more independent is the orchestral texture, whose thematic material, unrelated to the chorale, is expounded in a twelve-bar introductory sinfonia. The instrumental ensemble includes not only strings and continuo but two oboes d'amore* and two unison concertante* violins. And the movement's affinity with a violin concerto becomes clear if the chorale passages—invariably accompanied by figurative play on the two violins—are compared with the solo episodes of a concerto and the orchestral episodes with its tutti ritornellos. However, the instrumental passages themselves are also pervaded by the figure-work of the concertante violins; and perhaps it is right to see illustrated therein, as some interpreters have, the glittering play of the waves of the River Jordan. That Bach was in fact inspired by the image of the flowing Jordan is indicated by a figure which is unmistakably to be heard as a 'wave motive'. It enters at the outset in the continuo and thereafter in alternation with ripieno violins and viola, and it pervades the entire movement almost without interruption. At the beginning it reads:

Not so easy to interpret is the true tutti theme, to which the wave figure just quoted merely provides a background: it is a rugged, prominent, sharply rhythmic entity in which Arnold Schering saw the rocks 'through whose straits the river winds'.[3] Yet this interpretation is, in our view, in no way conclusive, and several other, no less conjectural interpretations might be put forward. More significant than such vague hermeneutics is the musical state of affairs. In contrast to the flowing, rhythmically neutral wave motive,* the tutti theme is clearly defined and rhythmically differentiated:

In the three arias, the scoring of the work undergoes a process of gradual enhancement. The second movement is a continuo aria, in which the choice of bass voice tells us clearly that Jesus Himself (or else John the Baptist) calls upon us to recognize the significance of baptism. The plunging demisemiquaver runs of the continuo have been interpreted, no doubt correctly, as the pouring of the baptismal water, which however, as the text instructs us, forms only the outward visible sign of the baptismal act. A *secco* recitative leads to the second aria, no. 4, which is gigue-like in character. Two solo violins in an imitative texture play

[3] '. . . durch deren Enge der Strom sich hindurchwindet' (preface to Eulenburg miniature score).

around the voice as it illustrates the individual phrases of the text: 'purchased us with His Blood' is represented by a falling chromatic* line, 'baptized' by a triadic figure tumbling into the depths; and at the words 'So that we should believe without doubt', that very doubt is, in true baroque fashion, represented by bold harmonic sequences and at one point by rhythmic complications. The formal design of the aria is also noteworthy. The three vocal passages (I II III in textual content) are strikingly alike in musical terms (A A^1 A^2), not least due to frequent ritornello quotations in the violins accompanied by vocal insertion.* Perhaps this stylistic resource, in conjunction with the triplet and triple-beat gigue rhythm and the threefold sectional structure, is designed to serve as a symbol of the Trinity, which forms the subject of the text.

The fifth movement opens as recitative accompanied by brief string chords. However, the baptismal command that forms the second half of the movement, 'Go forth into all the world . . .', is set as arioso* in order to underline its significance for the Christian doctrine of salvation. The last aria, no. 6, accompanied by strings with the support of oboes, is unorthodox in design. It belongs to the type known as *cavata*, in which the concertante* virtuosity of the Neapolitan da capo* aria is replaced by a song-like structure that approaches arioso. There is no introductory instrumental prelude. Instead, the first four vocal bars are followed by a four-bar instrumental ritornello that derives structural significance from its rondeau-like recurrence. The voice is largely accompanied by continuo only, but in the second section it is joined by unobtrusive string motives. The conclusion is exceptional. After the penultimate passage of text, the voice is no longer interrupted and replaced by the ritornello, but instead continues alongside it in the form of vocal insertion, after which the final vocal passage, accompanied by continuo, follows immediately. By way of compensation, as it were, an instrumental version of the opening vocal passage now prefaces the four-bar ritornello as an instrumental postlude. The overall form of the movement might be roughly sketched as follows:

alto + continuo	*strings + continuo*
lines 1–2: A	—
	ritornello in e
lines 1–3: A^1	accompanying figures
	ritornello in a
lines 4–5: B	—
	ritornello in b
lines 6–7: C	—
lines 8–9: D	ritornello in e
lines 8–9: E	—
	postlude A in e
	ritornello in e

The seventh verse of the chorale, in a plain choral setting with *colla parte** instruments, brings the work to an end.

Freue dich, erlöste Schar, BWV 30

NBA I/29, p. 61 BC A178 Duration: *c.* 40 mins

1. Chor SATB fl I,II ob I,II str bc — D 2/4

Freue dich, erlöste Schar,
Freue dich in Sions Hütten!
  Dein Gedeihen hat itzund
  Einen rechten festen Grund,
  Dich mit Wohl zu überschütten.

Rejoice, O redeemed host,
Rejoice in Zion's tabernacles!
  Your prosperity now has
  A truly sure foundation on which
  To shower you with blessing.

2. Recitativo B bc — b–G C

Wir haben Rast,
Und des Gesetzes Last
Ist abgetan.
Nichts soll uns diese Ruhe stören,
Die unsre liebe Väter oft
Gewünscht, verlanget und gehofft.
Wohlan,
Es freue sich, wer immer kann,
Und stimme seinem Gott zu Ehren
Ein Loblied an,
Und das im höhern Chor,
Ja, singt einander vor!

We are at rest
And the burden of the Law
Is abolished.
Nothing shall disturb this rest for us,
For which our dear forefathers often
Wished, longed, and hoped.
Well then,
Rejoice, whoever can,
And strike up in God's honour
A song of praise,
And in the higher choir
Indeed sing it to one another!

3. Aria B str bc — G 3/8

Gelobet sei Gott, gelobet sein Name,
Der treulich gehalten Versprechen und Eid!
  Sein treuer Diener ist geboren,
  Der längstens darzu auserkoren,
  Daß er den Weg dem Herrn bereit'.

Praised be God, praised be His Name,
Who has faithfully kept His promise and oath!
  His faithful servant is born,
  Who was long ago elected for this:
  That he should prepare the way for the Lord

4. Recitativo A bc — D–c♯ C

Der Herold kömmt und meldt den König an,
Er ruft; drum säumet nicht,
Und macht euch auf
Mit einem schnellen Lauf,
Eilt dieser Stimme nach!
Sie zeigt den Weg, sie zeigt das Licht,
Wodurch wir jene selge Auen
Dereinst gewißlich können schauen.

The herald comes and announces the King;
He calls, therefore do not delay,
But arise
With a swift pace
And hasten after this voice!
It shows the way, it shows the light
Whereby one day we shall certainly
Be able to see those blessed pastures.

5. ARIA A fl str bc — A C

Kommt, ihr angefochtnen Sünder,	Come, you besieged sinners,
Eilt und lauft, ihr Adamskinder,	Hasten, run, you children of Adam!
Euer Heiland ruft und schreit!	Your Saviour calls and cries!
Kommet, ihr verirrten Schafe,	Come, you straying sheep,
Stehet auf vom Sündenschlafe,	Awake out of sin's sleep,
Denn itzt ist die Gnadenzeit!	For now is the time of Grace!

6. CHORAL SATB bc (+ ww str) — A C

Eine Stimme läßt sich hören	**A voice may be heard**
In der Wüsten weit und breit,	**In the wilderness far and wide**
Alle Menschen zu bekehren:	**To convert all mankind:**
Macht dem Herrn den Weg bereit,	**Prepare the way of the Lord,**
Machet Gott ein ebne Bahn,	**Make a straight highway for God;**
Alle Welt soll heben an,	**All the world should begin**
Alle Täler zu erhöhen,	**To exalt all the valleys**
Daß die Berge niedrig stehen.	**So that the mountains may be made low.**

Secunda pars — *Second part*

7. RECITATIVO B ob I,II bc — e–f♯ C

So bist du denn, mein Heil, bedacht,	Then if You are intent, my Salvation,
Den Bund, den du gemacht	On keeping faithfully the Covenant
Mit unsern Vätern, treu zu halten	That You made with our forefathers
Und in Genaden über uns zu walten;	And on ruling over us with Grace,
Drum will ich mich mit allem Fleiß	Then with all diligence
Dahin bestreben,	I shall strive,
Dir, treuer Gott, auf dein Geheiß	Faithful God, at Your behest,
In Heiligkeit und Gottesfurcht zu leben.	To live for You in holiness and piety.

8. ARIA B ob d'am vln conc str bc — b 2/4

Ich will nun hassen	I will now hate
Und alles lassen,	And abandon all
Was dir, mein Gott, zuwider ist.	That is offensive to You, my God.
Ich will dich nicht betrüben,	I will not grieve You,
Hingegen herzlich lieben,	But rather heartily love You,
Weil du mir so genädig bist.	Since You are so gracious to me.

9. RECITATIVO S bc — f♯–G C

Und obwohl sonst der Unbestand	And although inconstancy is otherwise
Den schwachen Menschen ist verwandt,	Associated with weak man,
So sei hiermit doch zugesagt:	Let this nonetheless be promised herewith:
So oft die Morgenröte tagt,	As often as day dawns,
So lang ein Tag den andern folgen läßt,	As long as one day follows another,
So lange will ich steif und fest,	So long will I live rigidly and firmly,

Mein Gott, durch deinen Geist
Dir ganz und gar zu Ehren leben.
Dich soll sowohl mein Herz als
  Mund
Nach dem mit dir gemachten Bund

Mit wohlverdientem Lob erheben.

My God, through Your Spirit,
Wholly to Your honour.
My heart and mouth shall both exalt
  You,
According to the Covenant made with
  You,
With well-deserved praise.

10. Aria S vln I unis bc — e $\frac{9}{8}$

Eilt, ihr Stunden, kommt herbei,
Bringt mich bald in jene Auen!
  Ich will mit der heilgen Schar
  Meinem Gott ein' Dankaltar
  In den Hütten Kedar bauen,
  Bis ich ewig dankbar sei.

Hasten, you hours, come here,
Bring me soon to yonder pastures!
  With the sacred host I will
  Build my God an altar of thanks
  In the tents of Kedar
  Till I am eternally grateful.

11. Recitativo T bc — b–D C

Geduld, der angenehme Tag
Kann nicht mehr weit und lange sein,
Da du von aller Plag
Der Unvollkommenheit der Erden,
Die dich, mein Herz, gefangen hält,
Vollkommen wirst befreiet werden.
Der Wunsch trifft endlich ein,
Da du mit den erlösten Seelen
In der Vollkommenheit
Von diesem Tod des Leibes bist befreit,
Da wird dich keine Not mehr quälen.

Have patience: that acceptable day
Can no longer be far or long-delayed
When from all torment
Of the imperfection of the earth
Which holds you captive, my heart,
You shall be set completely free.
Your wish will finally come true
When with the redeemed souls
In that perfection
You are freed from this death of the body,
When no affliction torments you any
  longer.

12. Chor [Scoring as in no. 1] — D $\frac{2}{4}$

Freue dich, geheilgte Schar,
Freue dich in Sions Auen!
  Deiner Freude Herrlichkeit,
  Deiner Selbstzufriedenheit
  Wird die Zeit kein Ende schauen.

Rejoice, O hallowed host,
Rejoice in Zion's pastures!
  Of your joy's glory,
  Of your self-contentment
  Time shall see no end.

The occasion for the origin of this St John's Day cantata seems to have been of a more external nature. On 28 September 1737 Bach performed his cantata *Angenehmes Wiederau*, BWV 30a, in honour of the landlord at Wiederau, Johann Christian von Hennicke. Afterwards he no doubt decided that, rather than allowing the music composed (or in part reused) for that occasion to fall into oblivion, he would furnish it with a different text in order to render it reusable annually as a piece of church music. The secular text had been supplied by the experienced author Picander, and it is not impossible that it was he who wrote the sacred paraphrase too, for he had certainly demonstrated his skill at this procedure on numerous occasions in the past.

The paraphrase successfully achieves its double object of adhering to the range of affects* of the existing music and yet forging a link with the readings of the day. Movements of a general, laudatory character, such as the opening and closing chorus,* are certainly justified by the presence at the centre of the Gospel* reading of a song of praise, namely the Benedictus, the canticle of Zacharias. In addition, the third movement establishes a direct link with Luke 1.68 ('Praised be the Lord, the God of Israel') in its opening line, and then goes on to celebrate the birth of John the Baptist; and its closing line ('That he should prepare the way for the Lord') refers to the Epistle* reading. Moreover, the recitatives before and after this aria, nos. 2 and 4, celebrate the coming of the Baptist as the initial event in the process of Salvation. Part I of the cantata ends with an announcement of mercy for the sinner (no. 5) and with the third verse of the hymn *Tröstet, tröstet meine Lieben* by Johann Olearius (1671), which again refers to the Epistle reading. As often happens in the texts of the period, what follows is the application of what has been said to the individual Christian from among the assembled congregation. In response to the grace of God, the Christian resolves to desist from everything that runs contrary to God (nos. 8 and 9), hoping to be liberated soon from all earthly imperfection (nos. 10 and 11)[4] and to partake of eternal joy 'in Zion's pastures'—that is, in the heavenly Jerusalem (no. 12).

In its version as a St John's Day cantata, Bach's composition, which was probably first performed on 24 June 1738, or perhaps a year or two later, is one of his latest surviving church cantatas. The opening movement, whose original scoring (contrary to former assumptions) includes no trumpets and drums, is structurally related to dance forms. The choir enters immediately, but after only eight bars it gives way to a purely instrumental reprise of the same passage *a*, only slightly varied. The same happens to the next passage *b*, which is also eight bars long, with the result that, disregarding the participation or otherwise of the choir, the principal section exhibits the well-known structure of binary dance form with repeats:

Structure of section A:	‖: *a* :‖	‖: *b* :‖
Harmony (T: tonic; D: dominant):	T–D	D–T
No. of bars:	2×8	2×8

This A section of thirty-two bars is followed by a B section of the same length—likewise periodic in phrase structure but now performed by choir and instru-

[4] It is not altogether clear what the poet means by the 'Dankaltar in den Hütten Kedar' ('altar of thanks in the tents of Kedar'; no. 10), for in the passage from Psalm 120.5 to which he alludes the psalmist laments that, while endeavouring to keep the peace, he feels himself to be a stranger amidst the warlike tribe of Kedar. Evidently the poet wants to express his hope for a final time when peace shall prevail even among warlike tribes.

ments together throughout. Then comes a literal reprise of section A, a varied reprise of section B, and finally a da capo* of A. The rondeau form that thereby emerges, A B A B^1 A, is entirely articulated in four-bar phrases and their multiples. The total number of bars is $5 \times 32 = 160$.

An idiosyncrasy of this cantata is that even the texts of the recitatives, nos. 2, 4, 7, 9, and 11, are written as parodies, though Bach does not take the opportunity to reuse their music from Cantata 30a. Elsewhere Bach did not as a rule parody* the recitatives or replace them with new ones at a later stage (as he did in Cantata 134 and perhaps also Cantata 66). Why at such a late stage in his career he once again toyed with the idea of parodying the recitatives is beyond our knowledge. Perhaps it was because he feared that time would be short. In the event, however, the recitatives are new compositions. Nos. 2, 4, 9, and 11 are set as *secco*, but no. 7, which introduces the second part of the cantata, is a motivically-imprinted *accompagnato** for bass, two oboes, and continuo.

The underlying mood is joyful, relaxed, and unproblematic, not only in the opening chorus but in the four arias, where a dance-like style is often clearly evident. The third movement is in the style of a passepied, with a phrase structure no less clearly articulated than that of the opening chorus. The fifth movement is characterized by its fashionable syncopated rhythm. The instrumental ensemble is here made up of flute and strings, but the middle and lower parts merely serve as a *pizzicato** filling-in of the harmony; the melody is played by transverse flute* and muted first violin, partly in unison and partly in duet. It is not only the rhythm of the aria that is singular and dance-like but the binary form with repeats (analogous to the scheme of section A of the first movement, as described above) of the instrumental ritornello that forms its outer frame.

Similarly homophonic* in texture is the eighth movement, in which numerous echo effects strengthen the impression of a predominantly vertical orientation. Furthermore, the differentiation between solo violin and ripieno first violins serves to create additional tonal shading within an instrumental body made up of oboe d'amore,* strings, and continuo. Whereas in the fifth movement it was the syncopated rhythm that had a decisive effect on its character, here it is the Lombardic rhythm:

Again, all the features noted contribute to a decidedly modish style. Of all the arias, the tenth movement best fulfils the listener's expectations of an aria from one of Bach's church cantatas. Unison violins, soprano, and continuo here form a trio which, on account of its 9/8 rhythm, approximates to the style of a gigue. Partly as a consequence of its few parts, however, it is more polyphonic* in texture than any of the other arias. It is also more strikingly text-related, witness the call of 'Eilt, eilt, eilt!' ('Hasten . . .') at the first vocal entry and the later rising scale motives* on the same word.

Bach placed at the end of Part I a plain four-part chorale to the melody *Freu dich sehr, o meine Seele*. Part II, and thus the whole cantata, ends, however, like its secular model, with a reprise of the opening chorus with altered text. The work as a whole thereby acquires a conclusion which is not merely circumstantial in its mode of reference but rather general, ceremonial, and hymnic.

5

The Feast of the Archangel Michael (Michaelmas; 29 September)

Epistle: Revelation 12.7–12: Michael's fight with the dragon.
Gospel: Matthew 18.1–11: The Kingdom of Heaven belongs to the children; their angels look upon the countenance of God.

Herr Gott, dich loben alle wir, BWV 130

NBA I/30, p. 3 BC A179 Duration: *c.* 14 mins

1. [Chorale] SATB tr I–III timp ob I–III str bc — C c

Herr Gott, dich loben alle wir
Und sollen billig danken dir
Für dein Geschöpf der Engel schon,
Die um dich schwebn um deinen Thron.

Lord God, we all praise You
And shall rightly thank You,
Indeed, for Your creation of the angels,
Who hover around You, about Your Throne.

2. Recitativo A bc — F–G c

Ihr heller Glanz und hohe Weisheit zeigt,
Wie Gott sich zu uns Menschen neigt,
Der solche Helden, solche Waffen
Vor uns geschaffen.
Sie ruhen ihm zu Ehren nicht;
Ihr ganzer Fleiß ist nur dahin gericht',

Daß sie, Herr Christe, um dich sein
Und um dein armes Häufelein:
Wie nötig ist doch diese Wacht
Bei Satans Grimm und Macht?

Their bright lustre and excellency of wisdom shows
How God inclines to us men—
Such heroes, such weapons
Has He created for us.
They do not rest from honouring Him;
All their diligence is focused on this alone:
That they are around You, Lord Christ,
And around Your poor little company:
How necessary is this watch indeed
Amidst Satan's fury and might!

3. Aria B tr I–III timp (later str) bc — C ¢

Der alte Drache brennt vor Neid
Und dichtet stets auf neues Leid,
Daß er das kleine Häuflein trennet.
Er tilgte gern, was Gottes ist,
Bald braucht er List,
Weil er nicht Rast noch Ruhe kennet.

The old Dragon burns with envy
And constantly devises new harm,
So that he divides the little company.
He would gladly erase what is God's;
Soon he has need of cunning,
For he knows neither rest nor repose.

4. Recitativo [Duetto] ST str bc — e–G c

Wohl aber uns, daß Tag und Nacht

But happy are we that day and night

Die Schar der Engel wacht,	The host of angels watches,
Des Satans Anschlag zu zerstören!	Ready to destroy Satan's plot!
Ein Daniel, so unter Löwen sitzt,	A Daniel, who sits among lions,
Erfährt, wie ihn die Hand des Engels schützt.	Discovers how the angels' hand protects him.
Wenn dort die Glut	When the heat there
In Babels Ofen keinen Schaden tut,	In Babel's furnace does no harm,
So lassen Gläubige ein Danklied hören,	Believers let a song of thanks be heard;
So stellt sich in Gefahr	Thus, in danger,
Noch itzt der Engel Hülfe dar.	Even now the angels' help appears.

5. Aria T fl bc — G ¢

Laß, o Fürst der Cherubinen,	O Prince of cherubim,
Dieser Helden hohe Schar	Let this exalted host of heroes
Immerdar	Forever
Deine Gläubigen bedienen,	Minister to Your believers,
Daß sie auf Elias Wagen	That on Elijah's chariot they may
Sie zu dir gen Himmel tragen.	Carry them to You in heaven.

6. Choral SATB (+ str) tr I–III timp ww bc — C $\frac{3}{4}$

Darum wir billig loben dich	**Therefore we justly praise You**
Und danken dir, Gott, ewiglich,	**And thank You, God, for ever,**
Wie auch der lieben Engel Schar	**Just as the dear host of angels**
Dich preisen heut und immerdar.	**Praises You today and always.**
Und bitten dich, wollst allezeit	**And we pray that You would at all times**
Dieselben heißen sein bereit,	**Call them to be ready**
Zu schützen deine kleine Herd,	**To protect Your little flock**
So hält dein göttlichs Wort in Wert.	**That holds Your divine Word as worthy.**

This chorale cantata* was composed for performance on 29 September 1724. It is based on the hymn by Paul Eber (1554)—a paraphrase of the Latin *Dicimus grates tibi* by Philipp Melanchthon (1539)—whose first and last two verses, nos. 1, 11, and 12, are retained word for word, while the inner verses are paraphrased by the anonymous cantata librettist as follows: verses 2–3 form the recitative no. 2, verses 4–6 the aria no. 3, verses 7–9 the recitative no. 4, and verse 10 the aria no. 5.

In content, only general references are made to the readings of the day. Praise of God and gratitude for His creation of the angels (no. 1) is followed by a description of their character (no. 2) and then by a reference to the old dragon Satan, from whom the angels protect us (no. 3). At this point we find a connection with the Epistle* reading, which tells of the battle fought by Michael and his angels against the dragon. This reference was not added by the cantata librettist, for it was already present in the hymn. In the fourth movement, the protection afforded by the angels is supported by biblical examples. Daniel was saved by them from the lions (cf. Daniel 6.23), as were the men in the burning fiery furnace from being burnt to death (Daniel 3.1 ff.). Next follows a prayer that the angels will protect us until they carry off the believers into heaven, as they once did Elijah (cf. 2 Kings 2.11)—an image already found in earlier librettos (see, for example, the concluding chorale of Cantata 19). The cantata ends with praise and thanksgiving and with a prayer for our own future protection.

Bach's composition requires a festive orchestra of three trumpets and drums, three oboes, strings, and continuo. Accordingly, the opening chorus* is of great splendour. Significantly, the theology of Bach's day was still not accustomed to see in the angels any of the feminine weakness that later periods have imputed to them. Thus the opening movement is full of war-like aggression: here the angels appear as the conquerors of Satan and as the protectors of God's elect. The introductory sinfonia is characterized by triadic formations of various kinds, interchanged antiphonally between trumpets, oboes, strings, and continuo. As a result, a lively, excited concertante* texture emerges, thematically unrelated to the chorale melody. As in most of Bach's large-scale chorale-choruses, this melody is delivered in the soprano line by line in long note-values. The other voices support the chorale with counterpoints,* partly in imitation* and partly in free polyphony.* Like the instruments, the lower voices are motivically independent, being derived neither from the instrumental themes nor from the chorale melody, though they are themselves interrelated (see, in particular, lines 1, 3, and 4).

A brief *secco* recitative leads to the first aria, no. 3, which presents the rare scoring of three trumpets, drums, bass voice, and continuo in a graphic picture of the battle of the angels against the old dragon. The high demands made on the trumpet seem to have been Bach's motive for re-scoring the aria for strings at a subsequent revival, surely much to the detriment of this splendid battle scene. The contrast between this aria and the duet-recitative with strings that follows, no. 4, is as great as could be imagined. The calm and grace of this *accompagnato** reflects the security felt by believers 'even now' owing to the protection of the angels.

A mood of joyful abandon radiates from the second aria, no. 5, whose gavotte rhythm is probably to be understood in terms of gratitude for the service of God's angels to Christendom rather than as a reflection of the prayer of the text. The coloraturas* of the middle section ('Carry . . . in heaven') conjure up a graphic image of the soul being carried higher and higher by the angels. By contrast, the ceremonial trumpet sound of the concluding chorale establishes a link with the opening chorus. Voices, oboes, strings, and continuo here deliver the last two verses of the chorale in a plain four-part texture, while trumpets and drums crown the four line-ends of each verse with a radiant cadence.

Es erhub sich ein Streit, BWV 19

NBA I/30, p. 57 BC A180 Duration: *c.* 22 mins

1. [Chorus] SATB tr I–III timp str + ob I,II taille bc — C $\frac{6}{8}$

Es erhub sich ein Streit.
Die rasende Schlange, der höllische Drache
Stürmt wider den Himmel mit wütender Rache.
Aber Michael bezwingt,
Und die Schar, die ihn umringt,
Stürzt des Satans Grausamkeit.

There arose a great strife.
The raging serpent, the hellish dragon
Storms against heaven with furious vengeance.
But Michael conquers,
And the host that surrounds him
Overthrows Satan's cruelty.

2. Recitativo B bc — e C

Gottlob! der Drache liegt.
Der unerschaffne Michael
Und seiner Engel Heer
Hat ihn besiegt.
Dort liegt er in der Finsternis
Mit Ketten angebunden,
Und seine Stätte wird nicht mehr
Im Himmelreich gefunden.
Wir stehen sicher und gewiß,
Und wenn uns gleich sein Brüllen schrecket,
So wird doch unser Leib und Seel
Mit Engeln zugedecket.

Praise God! There lies the dragon.
The uncreaturely Michael
And his host of angels
Have prevailed over him.
There he lies in the darkness,
Bound with chains,
And his place is no longer
Found in the heavenly Kingdom.
We stand safe and secure,
And even though his roaring terrifies us,
Our body and soul shall be
Shielded by angels.

3. Aria S ob d'am I,II bc — G ¢

Gott schickt uns Mahanaim zu;
Wir stehen oder gehen,
So können wir in sichrer Ruh
Vor unsern Feinden stehen.
Es lagert sich, so nah als fern,
Um uns der Engel unsers Herrn
Mit Feuer, Roß und Wagen.

God sends Mahanaim to us;
Whether we stay or go,
We can stand in secure repose
Before our enemies.
Around us both near and far
Encamps the Angel of our Lord
With fire, horse, and chariot.

4. Recitativo T str bc — e–b C

Was ist der schnöde Mensch, das Erdenkind?
Ein Wurm, ein armer Sünder.
Schaut, wie ihn selbst der Herr so lieb gewinnt,
Daß er ihn nicht zu niedrig schätzet
Und ihm die Himmelskinder,
Der Seraphinen Heer,
Zu seiner Wacht und Gegenwehr,
Zu seinem Schutze setzet.

What is base man, that child of earth?
A worm, a wretched sinner.
See how even he is so loved by the Lord
That He does not regard him as too lowly
And disposes the heavenly children,
The host of seraphim,
For his guard and defence,
For his protection.

5. Aria T tr I str bc — e $\frac{6}{8}$

Bleibt, ihr Engel, bleibt bei mir!	Abide, O angels, abide with me!
Führet mich auf beiden Seiten,	Lead me on both sides,
Daß mein Fuß nicht möge gleiten!	That my foot may not slip!
Aber lernt mich auch allhier	But teach me also here
Euer großes Heilig singen	To sing Your great Sanctus
Und dem Höchsten Dank zu singen!	And to sing thanks to the Highest!

6. Recitativo S bc — C–F c

Laßt uns das Angesicht	Let us love the face
Der frommen Engel lieben	Of devout angels
Und sie mit unsern Sünden nicht	And with our sins not
Vertreiben oder auch betrüben.	Drive them away or grieve them.
So sein sie, wenn der Herr gebeut,	Then, when the Lord bids us
Der Welt Valet zu sagen,	To say farewell to the world,
Zu unsrer Seligkeit	For our Salvation
Auch unser Himmelswagen.	They shall also be our heavenly chariot.

7. Choral SATB tr I–III timp bc (+ ww str) — C $\frac{3}{4}$

Laß dein Engel mit mir fahren	**Let Your angel journey with me**
Auf Elias Wagen rot	**On Elijah's red chariot**
Und mein Seele wohl bewahren,	**And take good care of my soul,**
Wie Lazrum nach seinem Tod.	**Like Lazarus after his death.**
Laß sie ruhn in deinem Schoß,	**Let it rest in Your bosom,**
Erfüll sie mit Freud und Trost,	**Fill it with joy and comfort,**
Bis der Leib kommt aus der Erde	**Till my body comes out of the earth**
Und mit ihr vereinigt werde.	**And is united with it.**

Bach composed this cantata for performance on 29 September 1726. The text is derived from a strophic poem for St Michael's Day of 1724–5 by Picander, and it is not impossible that Bach himself undertook the task of converting it into a cantata libretto. This conjecture can neither be confirmed nor refuted, however, any more than the theory that Picander was responsible for editing his own text. The third movement was adopted literally from the original poem, the fourth is a somewhat freer madrigalian* rendering of the first strophe, and the sixth was more radically altered. The text of the first two movements was newly written, and the concluding chorale—the ninth verse of the hymn *Freu dich sehr, o meine Seele* (Freiberg, 1620)—was added afresh for the cantata version.

In the two new opening movements especially, the text closely follows the Epistle* reading, recounting Satan's defeat at the hands of Michael. In the third movement, the phrase 'God sends Mahanaim to us' is curious, for when used as a name, 'Mahanaim' (which means 'two hosts') signifies the place where Jacob once caught sight of God's hosts of angels (see Genesis 32.2). Here, however, it is applied to the hosts of angels themselves. In the same movement, the image of the angels encamped around us is drawn from Psalm 34.7, and 'fire, horse, and chariot' probably alludes to the rescue of Elisha by the heavenly hosts from the threat of capture (see 2 Kings 2.11 and 6.17). The opening of the fourth movement borrows a phrase from the psalms—Psalm 8.4 reads 'What is man, that You are mindful of him?' (Psalm 144.3 has something similar)—to illustrate the love of God, which manifests itself in the protection of mankind by the angels. Movements 5–7 pray for further protection and for safe conduct from the angels at the end of our life—the carrying away of the soul by the angels is here compared with the ascension of Elijah (2 Kings 2.11).

The first movement is one of the most monumental opening choruses* in all Bach's cantatas, a classic setting of that 'classic' text which had already been fashioned into an impressive chorus by Bach's highly gifted uncle Johann Christoph Bach, organist at Eisenach (Bach is known to have performed his uncle's twenty-two-part work in Leipzig, to general admiration). Bach's own chorus is based not on the biblical text itself (which is part of the Epistle reading) but on a madrigalian paraphrase of it. He therefore set the movement not according to the motet-style sectional principle favoured for choruses on biblical texts but rather in pure da capo* form. A fugue-like choral section with partly independent (and thematic) instrumental parts surrounds a middle section of a more homophonic* texture, though at times freely polyphonic,* again with largely independent instrumental parts. The festive scoring for trumpets and drums, with strings reinforced by oboes, enhances the overall impression of the movement. It is dominated by the choir, which enters immediately without any instrumental prelude and pauses only briefly. The absence of an introductory sinfonia removes the possibility of choral insertion,* and the movement is closely related to the motet* principle, not indeed in formal design (as we have seen) but in compositional technique.

The second movement, set as a plain, syllabically* declaimed *secco* recitative, is followed by a soprano aria, no. 3, with two obbligato* oboes d'amore,* which blend with the voices to form a homogeneous texture. Already in the opening theme, and later on too, text-engendered figures are in evidence, such as the held notes on 'stehen' ('stay') and 'Ruh' ('repose') or the semiquaver motion on 'gehen' ('go'). Yet, with all the text illustration of this bipartite aria, we are struck by the unity of its thematic material, which undergoes no far-reaching changes in the second half of the movement.

The second recitative no. 4, unlike the first, is accompanied by strings, though in its syllabic declamation and absence of melismas* it resembles its predecessor. The aria that follows, no. 5, is rightly regarded as one of the high points in all Bach's arias. The dotted rhythms of the siciliano—designated the 'angel rhythm' by Albert Schweitzer—pervade a movement whose melodiousness forms the greatest conceivable contrast with the turbulent opening chorus. It is at once an aria and a chorale arrangement, for during the vocal passages we hear the chorale melody *Herzlich lieb hab ich dich, o Herr* played line by line on the trumpet. When they heard this melody, the church-goers of Bach's day, familiar as they were with the text, could be in no doubt that the third verse of the hymn was intended: 'Ah Lord, at the end of my life let Your dear angel carry my soul into Abraham's bosom'. Another plain *secco* recitative, no. 6, forms a connecting link with the concluding chorale, a plain choral setting, reinforced by woodwind and strings, but with the addition of obbligato trumpets and drums, whose resplendence once again reminds us of the victory of Michael over Satan celebrated in the opening chorus.

Man singet mit Freuden vom Sieg, BWV 149

NBA I/30, p. 99 BC A181 Duration: *c.* 22 mins

1. Coro SATB tr I–III timp ob I–III bsn str bc — D $\frac{3}{8}$

'Man singet mit Freuden vom Sieg in den Hütten der Gerechten:	'They sing with joy of victory in the tabernacles of the righteous:
Die Rechte des Herrn behält den Sieg, die Rechte des Herrn ist erhöhet, die Rechte des Herrn behält den Sieg.'	The right hand of the Lord wins the victory, the right hand of the Lord is exalted, the right hand of the Lord wins the victory.'

2. Aria B vne bc — b C

Kraft und Stärke sei gesungen	Power and strength be sung
Gott, dem Lamme, das bezwungen	To God, to the Lamb who has conquered
Und den Satanas verjagt,	And driven away Satan
Der uns Tag und Nacht verklagt.	Who accused us day and night.
Ehr und Sieg ist auf die Frommen	Honour and victory have come upon the devout
Durch des Lammes Blut gekommen.	Through the Blood of the Lamb.

3. Recitativo A bc — e–D C

Ich fürchte mich	I am not afraid
Vor tausend Feinden nicht,	Before a thousand enemies,
Denn Gottes Engel lagern sich	For God's angels are encamped
Um meine Seiten her;	Around me on all sides;
Wenn alles fällt, wenn alles bricht,	Though all falls, though all breaks,
So bin ich doch in Ruhe.	I am still at peace.
Wie wär es möglich zu verzagen?	How would it be possible to despair?
Gott schickt mir ferner Roß und Wagen	God further sends me horse and chariot
Und ganze Herden Engel zu.	And whole hosts of angels.

4. Aria S str bc — A $\frac{3}{8}$

Gottes Engel weichen nie,	God's angels never retreat:
Sie sind bei mir allerenden.	They are with me everywhere.
Wenn ich schlafe, wachen sie,	When I sleep they watch,
Wenn ich gehe,	When I go,
Wenn ich stehe,	When I stay,
Tragen sie mich auf den Händen.	They shall bear me up in their hands.

5. Recitativo T bc	C–G c
Ich danke dir,	I thank You,
Mein lieber Gott, dafür.	My dear God, for this.
Dabei verleihe mir,	Grant me also
Daß ich mein sündlich Tun bereue,	That I may rue my sinful deeds,
Daß sich mein Engel drüber freue,	So that my guardian angel may rejoice
Damit er mich an meinem Sterbetage	And thus carry me on the day of my death
In deinen Schoß zum Himmel trage.	Into Your bosom in heaven.

6. Aria [Duetto] AT bsn bc	G c
Seid wachsam, ihr heiligen Wächter,	Be vigilant, you sacred watchmen,
Die Nacht ist schier dahin.	The night is nearly over.
Ich sehne mich und ruhe nicht,	I yearn and do not rest
Bis ich vor dem Angesicht	Till I am before the countenance
Meines lieben Vaters bin.	Of my dear Father.

7. Chorale SATB tr I–III timp bc (+ ww str)	C c
Ach Herr, laß dein lieb Engelein	**Ah Lord, let Your dear angel**
Am letzten End die Seele mein	**At my very end carry my soul**
Im Abrahams Schoß tragen,	**Into Abraham's bosom;**
Den Leib in seim Schlafkämmerlein	**Let my body rest in its bed-chamber**
Gar sanft ohn einge Qual und Pein	**Quite gently, without any anguish or pain,**
Ruhn bis am jüngsten Tage!	**Till the last day!**
Alsdenn vom Tod erwecke mich,	**Then awaken me from death,**
Daß meine Augen sehen dich	**That my eyes may see You**
In aller Freud o Gottes Sohn,	**In all joy, O God's Son,**
Mein Heiland und Genadenthron!	**My Saviour and Throne of Grace!**
Herr Jesu Christ, erhöre mich, erhöre mich,	**Lord Jesus Christ, hear me, hear me!**
Ich will dich preisen ewiglich!	**I will praise You for ever!**

The libretto of this cantata is drawn from Picander's cycle of 1728 and betrays numerous similarities with the text of Cantata 19, which is itself modelled on a poem by Picander. Both texts refer to the Michaelmas Epistle*—here with the support of another biblical quotation, Psalm 118.15 f. (no. 1)—and celebrate the defeat of Satan (no. 2). In both cases, the third movement tells us that God's angels are encamped around us (cf. Psalm 34.7) and that God sends 'horse and chariot' to help us (the phrase 'Gott schickt . . . zu' is common to both texts). In addition, the notion of the constant presence of the angels (formulated as a prayer in the fifth movement of Cantata 19) recurs here in the fourth movement. Finally, the wish that the angels might carry the soul up to God after death (sixth and seventh movements of Cantata 19) recurs here in the fifth and seventh movements. New in the present libretto is the notion of the vigilance of the watchmen ('the night is nearly over', sixth movement), which is based on Isaiah 21.11. However, the chorale 'Ach Herr, laß dein lieb Engelein'—the third verse of the hymn *Herzlich lieb hab ich dich, o Herr* by Martin Schalling (1569)—is again common to both works, assuming that the text-free quotation of the melody in the fifth movement of Cantata 19 is counted as part of the libretto; in the present cantata, this verse serves as the concluding chorale.

Bach's composition was probably written for performance on 29 September 1729, or possibly for Michaelmas 1728. The opening chorus* is a parody:* its music is drawn from the 'Hunt' Cantata, BWV 208, where it forms the finale. Three trumpets and drums here replace the two hunting horns of the original, and the movement is transposed from the key of F to D major. The rest of the instrumental ensemble (three oboes, bassoon, strings, and continuo) remains the same. Bach adapts the chorus to the new text with great skill—a task facilitated by the fundamentally joyful mood of both texts, which even share certain verbal roots: 'freudige Stunden / mit Freuden' ('joyful hours / with joy'); 'was Trauren besieget / behält den Sieg' ('what is victorious over sorrow / wins the victory'). If we did not possess the 'Hunt' Cantata, the parody character of the movement would probably not be obvious from the setting of the text (the choice of a biblical passage for the parody text in any case called for a freer revision procedure than usual), but rather from the texture, which is strikingly homophonic* for a biblical-text chorus, and from the pure da capo* form. These features are in keeping with the jubilant, indeed almost playful nonchalance of the movement, a mood that is no longer conscious of the 'battle in heaven' that took place beforehand.

Whether any of the other movements in this work are parodies we do not know—if they are, the original versions are lost, and the adaptations again exceptionally successful. The first aria, no. 2, is a continuo movement whose wide-ranging head-motive provides a convincing image of that visionary 'great voice' from Revelation 12.10 which announces the victory of the Lamb. A *secco* recitative, no. 3, leads to the second aria, no. 4, a string piece of enchanting beauty. Dance character is manifest in its song-like melody and its clear articulation into four-bar phrases and their multiples; and even the text-engendered melodic figures that depict going, staying, and being borne up in the hands of the angels do not alter this fundamental disposition.

The second recitative, no. 5, again a *secco* of brief dimensions, leads to the third aria, no. 6, a duet with obbligato* bassoon whose tone-colour, rare in a solo context, is possibly intended to reflect nocturnal darkness, or perhaps rather, in its lively figurations, the vigilance of the watchmen. This movement is again notable for its approachable melody, and even the frequent canonic writing for the two voices nowhere creates the impression of an elaborate contrapuntal texture, so unobtrusively is it adapted to the relaxed excitement of the piece. The plain concluding chorale ends with a surprise: at the final cadence the trumpets re-enter with a brief figure to crown the movement and thus the whole cantata.

Nun ist das Heil und die Kraft, BWV 50

NBA I/30, p. 143 BC A194 Duration: *c.* 5 mins

[Chorus] SATB I SATB II tr I–III timp ob I–III str bc D $\frac{3}{4}$

'Nun ist das Heil und die Kraft und das Reich und die Macht unsers Gottes seines Christus worden, weil der verworfen ist, der sie verklagete Tag und Nacht vor Gott.'	'Now the salvation and the power and the kingdom and the might of our God and His Christ have come, for he who accused them day and night before God is cast down.'

This movement poses many unresolved questions for scholarship with regard to its origin, use, and context (for instance, did it belong to a larger work that is now lost?). Its occasion may be inferred with some probability from the text on which it is based, Revelation 12.10, which belongs to the Epistle* for St Michael's Day. Being a single movement, however, the work is not a proper cantata but perhaps the opening (or closing?) chorus of a composition which is otherwise lost. The movement is preserved only in posthumous manuscript copies; and similar cases exist[1] in which later copyists showed interest only in the opening chorus of a cantata, so that if the original source material were lost we would know only the first movement of these compositions too.

The movement is constructed as a large-scale choral fugue,* in which the theme and its regular countersubjects are constantly interchanged in accordance with the permutation principle. This process unfolds within two similar sections, A A[1], each sixty-eight bars long and each made up of an extended fugal passage and a brief non-fugal epilogue. In the transmitted version, the individual counterpoints* are in many cases heard not just in linear fashion but in a chordally thickened form. The overall form may be sketched out schematically as follows:

A Fugue (8 permutations)
 Epilogue (antiphonal, imitative*)
A[1] Fugue (7 permutations)
 Epilogue (antiphonal, imitative)

The impressive effect made by the movement on the listener is due to the ingenious use of various techniques, among which the pseudo-inversion of the subject deserves special mention. The combination of this inversion with the original form of the subject within the same permutation creates the impression of enormous spatial breadth and splendour. As Werner Neumann

[1] Documented by Marianne Helms in KB, NBA I/30 (1974).

has observed, the movement 'represents the exhaustive realization of all the structural possibilities determined by the permutation principle and thus embodies the summit of its formal type'.

In the normal services at Leipzig, Bach did not have enough singers available to perform a double-choir work of this kind. It seems, therefore, that the exceptional display of splendour exhibited in this work might point to a special occasion. Some years ago, William H. Scheide[2] advanced the plausible theory that the movement might be traced back to an original form for single choir with five vocal parts (perhaps including divided altos) written for Michaelmas 1723 (Bach showed a preference for permutation fugue up to 1724), perhaps as an interpolation within a revived cantata of older origin, such as BWV Anh. I 5. The expansion to eight vocal parts might then be the work of an anonymous arranger. It has to be admitted that chordal thickening of the theme such as we encounter frequently in this piece is untypical of Bach. And the work loses none of its fascination if, in accordance with Scheide's proposal, it is reduced to five voice parts.[3]

Since Scheide's article was published in 1982 there has been much further scholarly discussion of this problematic work. Klaus Hofmann[4] accepts Scheide's hypothesis of a single-choir original version, but rejects the theory of outside intervention and casts doubt on the date Michaelmas 1723. Klaus Stein[5] argues that the special features of the work—the double choir, the two expositions* of the same material, and the simultaneous direct and inverted forms of the subject, one of which is treated chordally—might be explained as products of Bach's imaginative response to the text: the words of Revelation 12.10 are spoken by a 'great voice in heaven', which is perhaps conceived here as reflected from the earth and the clouds in a thunderous echo. Joshua Rifkin[6] raises the possibility that Bach was not the composer at all, citing the absence of his name in the oldest surviving source—a copy of the score in the hand of the Leipzig organist Carl Gotthelf Gerlach (1704–61)—as well as problems of voice-leading and the untypical overall A A[1] structure. Most recently, Scheide,[7] rejecting

[2] ' "Nun ist das Heil und die Kraft" BWV 50: Doppelchörigkeit, Datierung und Bestimmung', *BJ* 1982, 81–96.

[3] We must be cautious over the supposed connection with BWV Anh. I 5. Moreover, the assumption of 5-part vocal writing does not exclude the possibility that the movement originated before 1723: cf. BWV 31 (Weimar, 1715) and its problematic 1735 (?) Leipzig performance. The *Magnificat*, BWV 243a, Scheide's 'chief example' (*BJ* 1982, p. 91) of 5-part vocal writing in Bach's first year at Leipzig, is unsuitable for comparison with a Sunday or feast-day cantata, since it was performed at Vespers, not at the morning service.

[4] 'Bachs Doppelchor "Nun ist das Heil und die Kraft" (BWV 50): Neue Überlegungen zur Werkgeschichte', *BJ* 1994, 59–73.

[5] 'Stammt "Nun ist das Heil und die Kraft" (BWV 50) von J. S. Bach?', *BJ* 1999, 51–66.

[6] 'Siegesjubel und Satzfehler: zum Problem von "Nun ist das Heil und die Kraft" (BWV 50)', *BJ* 2000, 67–86.

[7] 'Nochmals BWV 50 "Nun ist das Heil und die Kraft" ', *BJ* 2001, 117–30.

the views of Hofmann, Stein, and Rifkin, returns to his theory that the work constitutes an anonymous arrangement of a lost Bach original, adducing a range of detailed arguments in support of this view. No doubt the controversy will continue. Meanwhile, one might well ask who other than Bach, in the vicinity of Leipzig in the early-to-mid eighteenth century, could have created a work of such breathtaking power.

6

The Reformation Festival (31 October)

Epistle: 2 Thessalonians 2.3–8: An injunction to steadfastness against the Adversary.
Gospel: Revelation 14.6–8: The everlasting Gospel: fear and honour God.

Ein feste Burg ist unser Gott, BWV 80

NBA I/31, pp. 67, 73 BC A183 Duration: *c.* 30 mins

1. [Chorale] SATB ob I–III in unis str bc (div) D ¢

Ein feste Burg ist unser Gott,	**A mighty fortress is our God,**
Ein gute Wehr und Waffen;	**A fine defence and weapon;**
Er hilft uns frei aus aller Not,	**He saves us freely out of all the trouble**
Die uns itzt hat betroffen.	**That has now befallen us.**
Der alte böse Feind,	**The old evil Enemy**
Mit Ernst ers itzt meint	**Now has serious intent;**
Groß Macht und viel List	**Great might and much cunning**
Sein grausam Rüstung ist,	**Are his cruel armament;**
Auf Erd ist nicht seinsgleichen.	**On earth there is not his equal.**

2. Aria [+ Chorale] SB unis str bc D ¢

Alles, was von Gott geboren,	Whatsoever is born of God
Ist zum Siegen auserkoren.	Is elected for victory.
Mit unser Macht ist nichts getan,	**With our might nothing is done,**
Wir sind gar bald verloren.	**We are very soon lost.**
Es streit' vor uns der rechte Mann,	**The right Man shall fight for us,**
Den Gott selbst hat erkoren.	**Whom God Himself has chosen.**
Wer bei Christi Blutpanier	Whoever to Christ's Blood-standard
In der Taufe Treu geschworen,	Has in baptism sworn fidelity
Siegt im Geiste für und für.	Is victorious in spirit for ever and ever.
Fragst du, wer er ist?	**Do you ask who He is?**
Er heißt Jesus Christ,	**He is called Jesus Christ,**
Der Herre Zebaoth,	**The Lord of Sabaoth,**
Und ist kein andrer Gott,	**And there is no other God;**
Das Feld muß er behalten.	**He must hold the field.**
Alles, was von Gott geboren,	Whatsoever is born of God
Ist zum Siegen auserkoren.	Is elected for victory.

3. Recitativo B bc — b–f♯ c

Erwäge doch,
Kind Gottes, die so große Liebe,
Da Jesus sich
Mit seinem Blute dir verschriebe,
Wormit er dich
Zum Kriege wider Satans Heer
Und wider Welt und Sünde
Geworben hat!
Gib nicht in deiner Seele
Dem Satan und den Lastern statt!
Laß nicht dein Herz,
Den Himmel Gottes auf der Erden,
Zur Wüste werden!
Bereue deine Schuld mit Schmerz,
Daß Christi Geist mit dir sich fest verbinde!

Consider well,
Child of God, what great Love
In that Jesus pledged Himself
To you with His Blood,
By which,
For the war against Satan's host
And against the world and sin,
He enlisted you!
Do not grant a place in your soul
For Satan and vices!
Do not let your heart,
God's heaven on earth,
Become desolate!
Bewail your guilt with anguish,
That the Spirit of Christ may be firmly united with you!

4. Aria S bc — b 12/8

Komm in mein Herzenshaus,
Herr Jesu, mein Verlangen!
Treib Welt und Satan aus
Und laß dein Bild in mir erneuert prangen!
Weg! schnöder Sündengraus!

Come into my heart's house,
Lord Jesus, my desire!
Cast the world and Satan out
And let Your Image shine forth from a renewed me!
Away, vile horror of sin!

5. Choral SATB in unis ob d'am I,II taille str bc — D 6/8

Und wenn die Welt voll Teufel wär
Und wollten uns verschlingen,
So fürchten wir uns nicht so sehr,
Es soll uns doch gelingen.
Der Fürst dieser Welt,
Wie saur er sich stellt,
Tut er uns doch nicht,
Das macht, er ist gericht',
Ein Wörtlein kann ihn fällen.

And though the world were full of devils
Who wished to devour us,
We will not fear so much:
We shall nonetheless prosper.
The prince of this world,
However grim he appears,
Yet does nothing to us:
This means he is judged;
A little Word can fell him.

6. Recitativo T bc — b–D c

So stehe dann
Bei Christi Blutgefärbten Fahne,
O Seele, fest!
Und glaube, daß dein Haupt dich nicht verläßt,
Ja, daß sein Sieg
Auch dir den Weg zu deiner Krone bahne!
Tritt freudig an den Krieg!

Stand fast, then,
By Christ's blood-stained banner,
O soul!
And believe that your Head does not forsake you,
Indeed, that His victory
Paves the way for your crown too!
Tread joyfully into battle!

Wirst du nur Gottes Wort	If only God's Word
So hören als bewahren,	Is both heard and kept by you,
So wird der Feind gezwungen auszufahren,	Then the Enemy will be forcibly cast out;
Dein Heiland bleibt dein Heil,	Your Saviour remains your Salvation,
Dein Heiland bleibt dein Hort!	Your Saviour remains your protector!
7. DUETTO AT ob da c vln bc	G $\frac{3}{4}$
Wie selig sind doch die, die Gott im Munde tragen,	How blessed indeed are those who carry God in their mouths,
Doch selger ist das Herz, das ihn im Glauben trägt!	Yet more blessed is the heart that bears Him in faith!
Es bleibet unbesiegt und kann die Feinde schlagen	It remains unvanquished and can strike its enemies
Und wird zuletzt gekrönt, wenn es den Tod erlegt.	And will at last be crowned when it defeats death.
8. CHORAL SATB bc (+ instrs)	D C
Das Wort sie sollen lassen stahn	**They shall let that Word abide**
Und kein' Dank dazu haben.	**And receive no thanks for it.**
Er ist bei uns wohl auf dem Plan	**He is indeed with us on the battlefield**
Mit seinem Geist und Gaben.	**With His Spirit and gifts.**
Nehmen sie uns den Leib,	**Let them take our body,**
Gut, Ehr, Kind und Weib,	**Goods, honour, child, and wife,**
Laß fahren dahin,	**Put them all away,**
Sie habens kein' Gewinn;	**They have no gain;**
Das Reich muß uns doch bleiben.	**The Kingdom must yet remain ours.**

This work is based on the Weimar cantata *Alles, was von Gott geboren*, BWV 80a, which was written for the Third Sunday in Lent 1715. Bach was unable to make use of that work in Leipzig, for no cantatas were performed there during the Lenten period. Since the original sources are almost all lost, the various stages in the origin of *Ein feste Burg* can only be imperfectly reconstructed. Between 1728 and 1731 it seems that Bach first designed a simpler version for the Reformation Festival, with a plain opening chorale but with the second movement presumably in the form in which we know it today. It is no longer possible to say anything more about this version. We do not know when the work acquired the splendid opening chorus* which is now familiar to us. Was it perhaps around the same time as Cantata 14 of 1735, whose opening chorus is designed according to a similar principle? In addition to all these problems, the scoring of the work is uncertainly transmitted and often falsified in modern editions: the trumpets and drums often found in the first and fifth movements were added by Wilhelm Friedemann Bach after the death of his father.

The adaptation of the original Lenten work to form a chorale cantata* was not difficult to accomplish, for two of the four verses of Martin Luther's hymn (1528/9) were already present in the early, Weimar version: verse 2 as the concluding chorale and an additional verse as the (presumably instrumental) quotation in the opening aria 'Alles, was von Gott geboren'. All Bach had to do, therefore, was to incorporate the newly composed movements, nos. 1 and 5, give the instrumental quotation in the bass aria, now no. 2, to the soprano, to be sung to the text of the second verse, and finally alter the text of the concluding chorale from verse 2 to verse 4. Thus revised, the cantata now contained all four verses of Luther's hymn. In addition, a line of text that referred too specifically to the Gospel* for the Third Sunday in Lent had to be altered to avoid misunderstanding: 'How blessed is the body that bore You, O Jesus!' (cf. Luke 11.27) became 'How blessed indeed are those who carry God in their mouths' (no. 7). This apart, the madrigalian* text, which refers to the expulsion of the devil recorded in the Lenten Gospel, could be retained without difficulty, especially in the light of Luther's third verse, 'And though the world were full of devils', and his second verse, which celebrates Christ as the victor who must hold the field. The first line of Franck's text, which now opens the second movement, is a paraphrase of 1 John 5.4, 'Whatsoever is born of God overcomes the world'.

The opening chorus probably represents the high point of Bach's chorale-based vocal music. The choir, reinforced by strings, sings a chorale motet;* in other words, each individual chorale line is stated fugally, with the melodic line slightly altered in some cases in order to render it better suited to the role of fugue* subject (note, in particular, the avoidance of note repetition at the beginning of lines 1 and 3). In addition, the fugal exposition* of line 2 (and 4) is combined with the repeat of line 1 (and 3). Towards the end of each chorale-line exposition, unison oboes (trumpets in W. F. Bach's version) and continuo bass deliver the unaltered chorale melody in canon.* Here, as in Cantata 77, the simultaneous statement of the *cantus firmus** at the highest and lowest pitch serves as a symbol of world-embracing validity: God's orbit of power embraces the entire cosmos. Amidst all his contrapuntal art, it is admirable how Bach still finds the opportunity for musical illustration of certain textual images, notably in the line 'Are his cruel armament' (a chromatic* line, first rising and then falling).

In the second movement, a chorale-aria, violins and violas are united in an obbligato* part whose tumult motives* in running semiquaver motion in the introductory ritornello sketch an effective battle scene. The entry of the bass aria part, rich in coloraturas,* is immediately followed by the entry of the soprano, whose lightly embellished delivery of the second verse of the chorale is doubled by the oboe, which itself adds further embellishments. In this fashion the principal section of the aria is combined with the two *Stollen** of the hymn, the middle section with the first four lines of the *Abgesang*,* and the pseudo-da capo* of lines 1 and 2 of the aria text (which is musically free, however, apart from isolated reminiscences) with the last line of the chorale.

The bass recitative with continuo accompaniment, no. 3, takes the form *secco*-arioso,* much used by Bach in Weimar. The arioso treatment of the last line, 'That the Spirit of Christ may be firmly united with you!', is expanded to almost the same length as the whole of the preceding recitative. The melodic charm of the soprano aria, no. 4, again accompanied only by continuo, forms a stark contrast with the two powerful introductory movements. As in most movements in continuo texture, the vocal melody unfolds freely and expressively over the continuo ritornello theme, which is repeated many times and in various modified forms.

The fifth movement, being a large-scale chorale arrangement, forms a counterpart to the first. Yet it is fundamentally different in character. By contrast with the motet-style contrapuntal texture of the first movement, the chorale melody is here sung in a lapidary choral unison and incorporated line by line within a concertante* orchestral texture. The antecedent phrase of the gigue-like theme is derived from the opening of the chorale, but its continuation is independent. The trumpet parts, which sometimes interject signal-like figures and elsewhere double the existing parts, are again an addition of W. F. Bach's.

The sixth movement is in structure similar to the third: a *secco* recitative with arioso conclusion for the last line of text, 'Your Saviour remains your protector'. In the seventh movement, an alto-tenor duet is united with the rare instrumental ensemble of oboe da caccia,* violin, and continuo to form a quintet texture whose depth of feeling forms a new high point in the work. With its heterogeneous, text-engendered motivic material, this partly homophonic* and partly imitative movement, which is divided into four sections according to the scheme A A[1] B C, resembles the series form of the motet. In particular, the lively, combative setting of line 3 (section B), 'It remains unvanquished and can strike its enemies', forms a tangible contrast with the graceful gestures of the other sections. As usual, the work concludes with a plain four-part chorale, a setting of the fourth verse of Luther's hymn.

Gott der Herr ist Sonn und Schild, BWV 79

NBA I/31, p. 3 BC A184 Duration: *c.* 17 mins

1. [Chorus] SATB hn I,II timp ob I,II (+ fl I,II) str bc — G ¢

'Gott der Herr ist Sonn und Schild. Der Herr gibt Gnade und Ehre, er wird kein Gutes mangeln lassen den Frommen.'	'God the Lord is sun and shield. The Lord gives grace and honour; he will not withhold any good thing from the devout.'

2. Aria A ob I (or fl I) bc — D $\frac{6}{8}$

Gott ist unsre Sonn und Schild! Darum rühmet dessen Güte Unser dankbares Gemüte, Die er für sein Häuflein hegt.	God is our sun and shield! Therefore our grateful spirit Praises the goodness He shows For His little body of men.

Denn er will uns ferner schützen,
Ob die Feinde Pfeile schnitzen
Und ein Lästerhund gleich billt.

For He will protect us further,
Though our enemies sharpen arrows
And the dog Blasphemy should bark.

3. CHORAL SATB hn I,II timp bc (+ ww str) G c

Nun danket alle Gott
Mit Herzen, Mund und Händen,
Der große Dinge tut
An uns und allen Enden,
Der uns von Mutterleib
Und Kindesbeinen an
Unzählig viel zugut
Und noch itzund getan.

Now thank the God of all
With hearts, mouth, and hands,
He who does great things
For us and in all quarters,
Who from our mother's womb
And from infancy onwards
Has done countless things for our benefit
And still does today.

4. RECITATIVO B bc e–b c

Gottlob, wir wissen
Den rechten Weg zur Seligkeit;
Denn, Jesu, du hast ihn uns durch dein Wort gewiesen,
Drum bleibt dein Name jederzeit gepriesen.
Weil aber viele noch
Zu dieser Zeit
An fremdem Joch
Aus Blindheit ziehen müssen,
Ach! so erbarme dich
Auch ihrer gnädiglich,
Daß sie den rechten Weg erkennen
Und dich bloß ihren Mittler nennen.

Praise God, we know
The right way to Salvation;
For, Jesus, You have shown it to us through Your Word,
So Your Name is still praised at all times.
But because many still
At this time
Must pull yoked to unbelievers
Out of blindness,
Ah! then have mercy
Graciously on them too,
That they may recognize the right path
And just name You as their Mediator.

5. ARIA [DUETTO] SB vln I + II bc b c

Gott, ach Gott, verlaß die Deinen
Nimmermehr!
Laß dein Wort uns helle scheinen;
Obgleich sehr
Wider uns die Feinde toben,
So soll unser Mund dich loben.

God, ah God, forsake Your own people
Nevermore!
Let Your Word shine brightly for us;
Even though greatly
Do our enemies rage against us,
Yet our mouths shall praise You.

6. CHORAL [Scoring as in no. 3] G 3/4

Erhalt uns in der Wahrheit,
Gib ewigliche Freiheit,
Zu preisen deinen Namen
Durch Jesum Christum. Amen.

Preserve us in the Truth;
Grant us eternal freedom
To praise Your Name
Through Jesus Christ. Amen.

The libretto of this cantata is not closely connected with any particular biblical reading. Instead, with reference to Psalm 84.11 (no. 1), it praises God for the protection He gives to His own people (no. 2), thanks Him for His good deeds (no. 3) in the words of the first verse of the well-known hymn by Martin

Rinckart (1636), and praises Jesus for showing us the 'right way to Salvation', asking Him to have mercy on those who have still not discovered this path but 'must pull yoked to unbelievers out of blindness' (no. 4). The cantata ends with a prayer for future protection, first in the form of madrigalian* verse (no. 5), then in the words of the last verse of Ludwig Helmbold's hymn *Nun laßt uns Gott dem Herren* (1575).

Bach probably wrote the work for performance on 31 October 1725. The instrumental ensemble for that performance was made up of two horns and drums, two oboes, strings, and continuo. For a subsequent revival, on 31 October 1730, Bach added two transverse flutes,* which double the oboes in the tutti movements (nos. 1, 3, and 6), while in the second movement the first flute took over the obbligato* part from the first oboe. The use of flutes is therefore not obligatory in present-day performances of the work. Around 1738 Bach adapted the opening chorus* and the two arias to Latin words in his Lutheran Masses. The first and fifth movements became the 'Gloria' and 'Domine Deus' of the Missa in G, BWV 236, and the second movement, the 'Quoniam' of the Missa in A, BWV 234.

The most imposing movement is the powerful opening chorus, whose introductory instrumental sinfonia is itself exceptionally grand in dimensions, amounting to forty-five bars. The extent of this sinfonia corresponds to its significance within the overall structure. Two themes are here stated which take on a decisive significance in later developments, namely the ceremonial opening horn theme (encountered again in the third movement)—

—and then, in bars 13 ff., a fugue* subject built on note repetitions:

The chorus proper is tripartite. It begins with four wide-ranging chordal or freely polyphonic* passages *a b a b* (against the fugue subject in the instruments), each followed by the horn theme as an articulating episode. In the second section ('He will not withhold any good thing from the devout'), a choral fugue is developed out of a vocally simplified version of the above subject, which is, however, doubled by the instruments in its original form. The third section is, like the first, a more homophonic* complex whose outer passages are moulded by choral insertion* into the beginning and end of the introductory sinfonia, and whose middle passage is a reprise of *b* from the first section.

After the alto aria with obbligato oboe or flute, mentioned above, it was a charming inspiration of Bach's to adopt the horn theme from the first movement in the chorale *Nun danket alle Gott*, no. 3. The chorale is thus expanded by independent horn music, continuing between the chorale lines to form episodes, which gives the first three movements the semblance of a united complex. Although there is no evidence that the cantata was divided into two parts, it would be quite conceivable for the sermon to follow at this point (after no. 3), so that the initial words of the fourth movement, 'Praise God, we know the right way to Salvation', would refer not so much to the preceding text, with which they have little in common, as to the exegesis of the preacher. This plain *secco* recitative is followed by a homophonic duet, no. 5, in a highly approachable, almost song-like melodic style. Curiously enough, the unison violins enter with the ritornello only after an introductory 'motto'* sung by the voices, and the concise eight-bar instrumental theme, frequently repeated, almost functions as an ostinato*—the movement as a whole is characterized by serial rather than cyclical form. The finale is a plain chorale setting, whose texture is expanded to six parts by the obbligato part-writing for the horns.

7

Church and Organ Consecration

Epistle: Revelation 21.2–8: The New Jerusalem.
Gospel: Luke 19.1–10: The conversion of Zacchaeus.

Höchsterwünschtes Freudenfest, BWV 194

NBA I/31, p. 147 BC B31/A91 Duration: *c.* 39 mins

1. [Chorus] SATB ob I–III bsn str bc — B♭ ¢ $\frac{3}{4}$ ¢

Höchsterwünschtes Freudenfest,	Most highly desired festival of joy,
Das der Herr zu seinem Ruhme	Which the Lord to His renown
Im erbauten Heiligtume	In the newly erected sanctuary
Uns vergnügt begehen läßt.	Lets us gladly celebrate.
Höchsterwünschtes Freudenfest!	Most highly desired festival of joy!

2. Recitativo B bc — B♭ c

Unendlich großer Gott,	Everlasting great God,
Ach wende dich	Ah, turn to us,
Zu uns, zu dem erwähleten Geschlechte,	The chosen generation,
Und zum Gebete deiner Knechte!	And to the prayer of Your servants!
Ach, laß vor dich	Ah, let our lips' offering
Durch ein inbrünstig Singen	Through fervent singing
Der Lippen Opfer bringen!	Be brought before You!
Wir weihen unsre Brust dir offenbar	We consecrate our breast to You publicly
Zum Dankaltar.	As an altar of thanksgiving.
Du, den kein Haus, kein Tempel faßt,	You, whom no house, no temple holds,
Da du kein Ziel noch Grenzen hast,	Since You have neither end nor boundaries,
Laß dir dies Haus gefällig sein,	Let this house be pleasing to You,
Es sei dein Angesicht	May it be to Your Countenance
Ein wahrer Gnadenstuhl, ein Freudenlicht.	A true throne of grace, a light of joy.

3. Aria B ob I str bc — B♭ $\frac{12}{8}$

Was des Höchsten Glanz erfüllt,	What the radiance of the Most High fills
Wird in keine Nacht verhüllt.	No night will black out.
Was des Höchsten heilges Wesen	What the holy essence of the Most High
Sich zur Wohnung auserlesen,	Has chosen for His dwelling

Wird in keine Nacht verhüllt,	No night will black out,
Was des Höchsten Glanz erfüllt.	What the radiance of the Most High fills.
4. Recitativo S bc	g–E♭ c
Wie könnte dir, du höchstes Angesicht,	How, You highest Countenance—
Da dein unendlich helles Licht	Since Your everlasting bright Light
Bis in verborgne Gründe siehet,	Sees as far as into secret motives—
Ein Haus gefällig sein?	Could any house be pleasing to You?
Es schleicht sich Eitelkeit allhie an allen Enden ein.	Vanity creeps in here on all sides.
Wo deine Herrlichkeit einziehet,	Where Your glory enters
Da muß die Wohnung rein	There the dwelling must be pure
Und dieses Gastes würdig sein.	And worthy of this Guest.
Hier wirkt nichts Menschenkraft,	Here human power works to naught,
Drum laß dein Auge offenstehen	Therefore let Your eye be open
Und gnädig auf uns gehen;	And graciously fall upon us;
So legen wir in heilger Freude dir	Then we will lay down in holy joy
Die Farren und die Opfer unsrer Lieder	Our bullocks and the offering of our songs
Vor deinem Throne nieder	Before Your Throne
Und tragen dir den Wunsch in Andacht für.	And bear our wish to You in devotion.
5. Aria S str bc	E♭ ¢
Hilf, Gott, daß es uns gelingt,	Save us, O God, that we will succeed
Und dein Feuer in uns dringt.	And that Your Fire will penetrate into us,
Daß es auch in dieser Stunde	So that at this time too,
Wie in Esaiae Munde	As in Isaiah's mouth,
Seiner Würkung Kraft erhält	It might receive its powerful effect
Und uns heilig vor dich stellt.	And bring us hallowed before You.
6. Chorale SATB bc (+ instrs)[1]	B♭ c
Heilger Geist ins Himmels Throne,	**Holy Spirit on the heavenly throne,**
Gleicher Gott von Ewigkeit	**Equal God from eternity**
Mit dem Vater und dem Sohne,	**With the Father and the Son,**
Der Betrübten Trost und Freud!	**Comfort and joy of the sorrowful!**
Allen Glauben, den ich find,	**All the faith that I find**
Hast du in mir angezündt,	**You have kindled within me;**
Über mir in Gnaden walte,	**Rule over me in Grace,**
Ferner deine Gab erhalte.	**Further preserve Your gift.**
Deine Hülfe zu mir sende,	**Send Your help to me,**
O du edler Herzensgast!	**O You noble Guest of the heart!**
Und das gute Werk vollende,	**And complete the good work**
Das du angefangen hast.	**That You have begun.**
Blas in mir das Fünklein auf,	**Blow up in me that little spark**
Bis daß nach vollbrachtem Lauf	**Until after my course is finished**

[1] Oboe III is largely independent on grounds of compass.

Ich den Auserwählten gleiche	**I become like the chosen ones**
Und des Glaubens Ziel erreiche.	**And attain faith's prize.**
Post concionem	*After the address*
7. Recitativo T bc	F–c C
Ihr Heiligen, erfreuet euch,	You saints, rejoice!
Eilt, eilet, euren Gott zu loben:	Hasten, hasten to praise your God:
Das Herze sei erhoben	Let your heart be raised
Zu Gottes Ehrenreich,	To God's Kingdom of Honour,
Von dannen er auf dich,	From which He looks upon you,
Du heilge Wohnung, siehet	You sacred dwelling,
Und ein gereinigt Herz zu sich	And draws a purified heart to Himself
Von dieser eitlen Erde ziehet.	From this vain earth.
Ein Stand, so billig selig heißt:	A situation so rightly called blessed:
Man schaut hier Vater, Sohn und Geist.	We see here Father, Son, and Spirit.
Wohlan, ihr gotterfüllte Seelen!	Well then, you God-filled souls!
Ihr werdet nun das beste Teil erwählen;	You will now choose the best part;
Die Welt kann euch kein Labsal geben,	The world can give you no refreshment:
Ihr könnt in Gott allein vergnügt und selig leben.	In God alone can you live contented and blessed.
8. Aria T bc	g C
Des Höchsten Gegenwart allein	The Presence of the Most High alone
Kann unsrer Freuden Ursprung sein.	Can be the source of our joy.
Vergehe, Welt, mit deiner Pracht,	Pass away, world, with your splendour:
In Gott ist, was uns glücklich macht!	In God is what makes us prosperous!
9. Recitativo Duetto SB bc	B♭–F C
Baß	*Bass*
Kann wohl ein Mensch zu Gott in Himmel steigen?	Can a man climb to God in heaven?
Sopran	*Soprano*
Der Glaube kann den Schöpfer zu ihm neigen.	Faith can incline the Creator to him.
Baß	*Bass*
Er ist oft ein zu schwaches Band.	It is often too weak a bond.
Sopran	*Soprano*
Gott führet selbst und stärkt des Glaubens Hand,	God Himself leads and strengthens faith's hand
Den Fürsatz zu erreichen.	To achieve its purpose.
Baß	*Bass*
Wie aber, wenn des Fleisches Schwachheit wollte weichen?	But what if the flesh's weakness would retreat?
Sopran	*Soprano*
Des Höchsten Kraft wird mächtig in den Schwachen.	The power of the Most High is made perfect in the weak.

Baß
Die Welt wird sie verlachen.
Sopran
Wer Gottes Huld besitzt, verachtet solchen Spott.
Baß
Was wird ihr außer diesen fehlen!
Sopran
Ihr einzger Wunsch, ihr alles ist in Gott.
Baß
Gott ist unsichtbar und entfernet:
Sopran
Wohl uns, daß unser Glaube lernet,
Im Geiste seinen Gott zu schauen.
Baß
Ihr Leib hält sie gefangen.
Sopran
Des Höchsten Huld befördert ihr Verlangen,
Denn er erbaut den Ort, da man ihn herrlich schaut.
beide
Da er den Glauben nun belohnt
Und bei uns wohnt,
Bei uns als seinen Kindern,
So kann die Welt und Sterblichkeit die Freude nicht vermindern.

Bass
The world will mock them.
Soprano
Whoever possesses God's favour despises such derision.
Bass
What will they lack beyond this?
Soprano
Their sole wish, their all is in God.
Bass
God is invisible and distant:
Soprano
Happy are we, that our faith teaches us
To see God in the spirit.
Bass
Their body keeps them captive.
Soprano
The favour of the Most High furthers their longing,
For He builds the place where one sees Him in His glory.
both
Since He now rewards faith
And dwells with us,
With us as His children,
The world and mortality cannot diminish our joy.

10. ARIA [DUETTO] SB ob I,II bc — F 3/4

O wie wohl ist uns geschehn,
Daß sich Gott ein Haus ersehn!

Schmeckt und sehet doch zugleich,
Gott sei freundlich gegen euch.
Schüttet eure Herzen aus
Hier vor Gottes Thron und Haus!

Oh, how fortunate are we
That God has chosen a house for Himself!

Indeed both taste and see
That God is friendly towards you.
Pour out your hearts
Here before God's throne and house!

11. RECITATIVO B bc — B♭ C

Wohlan demnach, du heilige Gemeine,
Bereite dich zur heilgen Lust!
Gott wohnt nicht nur in einer jeden Brust,
Er baut sich hier ein Haus.
Wohlan, so rüstet euch mit Geist und Gaben aus,

Well then, you holy congregation,
Prepare yourselves for holy delight!
God not only dwells in every single breast,
He here builds Himself a house.
Well then, arm yourselves with the Spirit and with gifts,

Daß ihm sowohl dein Herz als auch dies Haus gefalle!	So that both your hearts and this house may please Him!

12. Choral [Scoring as in no. 6] B♭ $\frac{3}{4}$

Sprich Ja zu meinen Taten,	**Say Yes to my deeds,**
Hilf selbst das Beste raten;	**Yourself help to counsel the best;**
Den Anfang, Mittl und Ende,	**Make beginning, middle, and end,**
Ach, Herr, zum besten wende!	**Ah Lord, turn out for the best!**
Mit Segen mich beschütte,	**Cover me with blessing,**
Mein Herz sei deine Hütte,	**My heart be Your tabernacle,**
Dein Wort sei meine Speise,	**Your Word be my nourishment**
Bis ich gen Himmel reise!	**Till I journey to heaven!**

In its transmitted form, this work first served as an organ consecration cantata at a public service on 2 November 1723 after the construction and testing of the organ at Störmthal near Leipzig.[2] The generalized content of the text, however, allowed the work to be revived subsequently in the context of the church year as a Trinity cantata. This took place during the following year, on 4 June 1724, and again (in an abridged version, with some reordering of movements and with obbligato* organ) probably on 16 June 1726, and finally for a third time on 20 May 1731. For this last performance a printed text is preserved that contains only Part I (nos. 1–6); the sources, however, testify to a performance of Part II also, no doubt after the sermon. Naturally, it is quite possible – indeed it may be assumed – that Bach revived his cantatas far more frequently than we are able to establish today.

The performance of 1723 was not the beginning of the work's history, however, for it is derived from a secular congratulatory cantata. That work differed from the surviving version in the absence of the chorales (nos. 6 and 12), in its recitatives, and in its dance-like finale, which was omitted when the work was adapted to form an organ consecration cantata. Unfortunately, only a few instrumental parts survive of this secular version, and since the vocal parts are lost, so too is the text. It may be considered certain, however, that we have here a fragment of a work from Bach's Cöthen period.

The text of the surviving version is geared more to church consecration than to that of an organ, for alongside the construction of the organ at Störmthal a renewal of the church's interior had been undertaken. Thus the text nowhere mentions the organ explicitly, but instead celebrates the 'newly erected sanctuary' (no. 1), thanks God, and prays, 'Let this house be pleasing to You' (no. 2). It announces further that the dwelling of the Most High is full of radiance and will not be dimmed by night (no. 3). The fourth movement warns against human

[2] Following the rediscovery of the original printed text, Peter Wollny (in 'Neue Bach-Funde', *BJ* 1997, 7–50) raised the question whether the first performance might have taken place on the previous Sunday, 31 October, which was both the 23rd Sunday after Trinity and the Reformation Festival.

vanity and, since human power achieves nothing, prays for the church in the words of Solomon from 1 Kings 8.29, 'that Your eyes may be open towards this house', and with reference to Hosea 14.2, 'so we will render the calves of our lips'. The fifth movement alludes to Isaiah 6.6f. in its prayer that we shall succeed in singing praises to the Lord. Part I concludes with the sixth and seventh verses of the hymn *Treuer Gott, ich muß dir klagen* by Johann Heermann (1630).

Part II brings no essentially new ideas, but it praises the divine Trinity (no. 7), whose presence alone brings blessing (no. 8). Textually, the most striking movement of all is the ninth, whose dialogue was perhaps suggested by a similar colloquy in the secular model, for its alternation between doubt (bass) and reassurance (soprano) is comparable with dialogues such as that of Fear and Hope in Cantata 66, which are likewise based on secular models. The other movements are concerned with the praise of God (in no. 10, after Psalm 34.8); and the work concludes with the ninth and tenth verses of Paul Gerhardt's hymn *Wach auf, mein Herz, und singe* (1647/53).

The distinctive feature of Bach's composition is that it represents the most consistent attempt within his works to adapt the form of the orchestral suite to the cantata. Inevitably, he renounces the unity of key in all movements which was essential to the suite, since it would have led to insurmountable monotony. Accordingly, the conjecture of several scholars that the cantata might have arisen by adding vocal parts to a real instrumental suite is not at all convincing. The first movement takes the form of a French Overture,* with the slow outer sections assigned to the orchestra alone (except for a brief choral conclusion) and the quick fugal middle section sung by the choir with partially independent instruments. In this case, it is indeed conceivable that the movement originated by choral insertion* within an existing instrumental piece.

Among the arias, the first (no. 3) has the character of a pastorale, the second (no. 5) is a gavotte, the third (no. 8) a gigue, and the fourth (no. 10) a minuet. This suite-like conception naturally originated in the secular model of the cantata, which, moreover, concluded with a movement in the style of a passepied. The extremely high pitch of the voice parts might also be derived from the secular model; it induced Bach to perform the work, upon its revival at Trinity 1724, in deep Chamber Pitch* and with bass recitatives at a lower pitch. We do not know to what extent the recitatives were newly composed or simply taken over from the secular original. They are throughout composed as *secco* with continuo accompaniment; only the duet-recitative no. 9 ends with an 'andante' arioso.* The two chorales are set in a plain four-part texture; the third oboe alone receives a largely independent part on grounds of compass—the instrument is pitched too high to double the tenor part.

8

Council Elections

Gott ist mein König, BWV 71

NBA I/32.1, pp. 3, 67 BC B1 Duration: *c.* 20 mins

1. Tutti SATB + SATB rip org, tr I–III timp, rec I,II vc, ob I,II bsn, str vne C/D[1] C

'Gott ist mein König von altersher, der alle Hülfe tut, so auf Erden geschicht.'

'God is my King from of old, who works all the salvation that comes to pass on earth.'

2. Air [+ Chorale] ST org e/f♯ C

'Ich bin nun achtzig Jahr', warüm soll dein Knecht sich mehr beschweren? Ich will 'ümkehren, daß ich sterbe in meiner Stadt, bei meines Vaters und meiner Mutter Grab'.

Soll ich auf dieser Welt mein Leben höher bringen,
Durch manchen sauren Tritt hindurch ins Alter dringen,
So gib Geduld, für Sünd und Schanden mich bewahr,
Auf daß ich tragen mag mit Ehren graues Haar.

'I am now eighty years old'; why should Your servant yet complain? I will 'return, that I may die in my own city, by the grave of my father and of my mother'.

Should I extend my life further in this world,
Taking many a bitter step as I press on into old age,
Then grant me patience, protect me from sin and disgrace,
So that I may wear my grey hair with honour.

3. Fuga SATB org a/b C

'Dein Alter sei wie deine Jugend. Und Gott ist mit dir in allem, das du tust.'

'May your old age be like your youth. And God is with you in all that you do.'

4. Arioso B org, rec I,II vc, ob I,II bsn F/G $\frac{3}{2}$ C $\frac{3}{2}$

'Tag und Nacht ist dein. Du machest, daß beide, Sonn und Gestirn, ihren gewissen Lauf haben. Du setzest einem jeglichen Lande seine Grenze.'

'Day and night are Yours. You cause both sun and stars to have their appointed course. To every land You set its borders.'

[1] The first specified key refers to *Chorton** or 'choir pitch', the second to *Kammerton* or 'chamber pitch'.

5. AIR A org, tr I–III timp C/D $\frac{3}{8}$ C $\frac{3}{8}$

Durch mächtige Kraft	Through mighty power
Erhältst du unsre Grenzen,	You maintain our borders;
Hier muß der Friede glänzen,	Here peace must radiate,
Wenn Mord und Kriegessturm sich allerort erhebt.	Though murder and the storm of war everywhere arise.
Wenn Kron und Zepter bebt,	Though crown and sceptre shake,
Hast du das Heil geschafft	You have created salvation
Durch mächtige Kraft!	Through mighty power!

6. [CHORUS] SATB + SATB rip org, rec I,II vc, ob I,II bsn, str vne c/d C

'Du wollest dem Feinde nicht geben Die Seele deiner Turteltauben.'	'We ask that You would not give the enemy the soul of Your turtle-doves.'

7. TUTTI [Scoring as in no. 1] C/D C $\frac{3}{2}$ C

Das neue Regiment	This new government
Auf jeglichen Wegen	In all ventures
Bekröne mit Segen!	Crown with blessings!
Friede, Ruh und Wohlergehen	Peace, calm, and prosperity
Müsse stets zur Seiten stehen	Must constantly attend
Dem neuen Regiment.	This new government.
Glück, Heil und großer Sieg	Good fortune, salvation, and great victory
Muß täglich von neuen	Must daily anew
Dich, Joseph, erfreuen,	Delight you, Joseph,
Daß an allen Ort und Landen	So that in all places and lands
Ganz beständig sei vorhanden	There remains quite constantly
Glück, Heil und großer Sieg!	Good fortune, salvation, and great victory!

As organist of the Blasiuskirche in the imperial free city of Mühlhausen from 1707 to 1708, Bach was responsible for providing a cantata for the annual service that took place on 4 February, the day after the council elections, to celebrate the change of council. As a rule, this composition was afterwards published, though in a small issue for display purposes only. Bach composed two such council election cantatas for Mühlhausen, the first in 1708 while organist of the Blasiuskirche, and the second in 1709 after his move to Weimar, and both were published. Only the earlier of the two works has survived, however; of the second (BC [B2]) we possess neither autograph nor original edition, and consequently it is impossible to ascertain whether the music might have been transferred to a work for a different occasion (the New Year's Day cantata BWV 143 comes to mind, for example) or whether it is entirely lost.

In keeping with the older style of church cantata, the text of the surviving work of 1708 is largely assembled from biblical words, to which a chorale verse is added in the second movement. The use of strophic verse in the finale also accords with the older cantata type, whereas a single strophe of freely versified text such as we find in the fifth movement occurs in both the older and the more modern type. It is not known who was responsible for the text. An obvious candidate is the Mühlhausen minister Georg Christian Eilmar, at whose request Cantata 131 was composed perhaps a few months before the present cantata. Or perhaps Bach himself assembled the text, a thesis espoused above all by Rudolf Wustmann, to which it might be objected that Bach could have had no motive for writing a bi-strophic poem for the finale and then disregarding its strophic structure when setting it to music.

The librettist's theme is derived from the occasion of the service: the handing over of office from the old to the new council. Consequently, he organizes the first half of his text around the age–youth antithesis. The opening movement already refers to it implicitly: 'of old' God has proved Himself to be our King and supported us, but now His servant, the old council, is too old and will return in order to die in its own city (no. 2). The theme reaches its culmination in the third movement, 'May your old age be like your youth', in which similar support is entreated for the new council. The movements that follow include praise (nos. 4 and 5), supplication (no. 6), and congratulations to the 'new government' (no. 7).

Bach's composition is entitled 'Motetto', but this may be taken merely as evidence of the intermixing of stylistic concepts in his time. The term 'Concerto',* which he used for the title of most of his later cantatas, would have been more appropriate here too. For the division of the orchestra into four choirs as follows derives from the practice of the polychoral concerto:

Choir I	three trumpets and drums
Choir II	two recorders and cello[2]
Choir III	two oboes and bassoon
Choir IV	two violins, viola, and violone

Added to this instrumental ensemble as a fifth participant is the vocal choir, itself graded in sound according to whether the ripienists* (which, as the heading in the autograph score informs us, are optional) rest or join in with the solo choir of concertists.* The sound world that emerges is highly variegated and dynamically differentiated in keeping with the formal articulation into small sections characteristic of Bach's youthful works. The movements for only a few vocal and instrumental parts are closely related to the seventeenth-century sacred concerto and should not be understood in terms of the genres aria and arioso* (let alone recitative).

[2] With its range of *G*–*e*[2] flat, the cello part lies exceptionally high. Evidently Bach had at his disposal an instrument whose lowest string was tuned to *G*.

The small-scale articulation of the first movement, which is based on Psalm 74.12, is held together by the recurring refrain-like figure, *a*:

This figure is a component of the framing tutti section A and, moreover, interrupts the two solo sections accompanied by strings only, B ('von altersher') and C ('der alle Hülfe tut, so auf Erden geschicht'), which results in the arch form A B a C A[1]. The vocal texture, part-chordal and part-freely polyphonic,* is accompanied in the tutti sections by alternating *concertato* choirs of instruments. The end of the movement dies away in a quasi-*pianissimo* on unaccompanied recorders.

The second movement is a sacred concerto in which 2 Samuel 19.35 and 37, sung by the tenor, is combined with the sixth verse of the hymn *O Gott, du frommer Gott* by Johann Heermann (1630), sung in an embellished form by the soprano. The movement is accompanied by the organ, partly in continuo fashion and partly as an obbligato* instrument with echo figures. The movement 'Dein Alter sei wie deine Jugend', no. 3, whose text is drawn from Deuteronomy 33.25 and Genesis 21.22, is one of the few purely vocal Bach cantata choruses* (the voice parts are assigned to the concertists only), being accompanied by continuo alone. Here we encounter one of the earliest instances in Bach's output of the technique of permutation fugue*—still of modest extent in this case, since the possibilities of enhancement through the gradual inclusion of instruments and ripieno singers are not explored, but all the more consistent in its avoidance of modulation (apart from the usual dominant transposition of the subject in *comes** form) or of an independent continuo part.

The bass solo 'Tag und Nacht ist dein', no. 4, based on Psalm 74.16–17, already exhibits the da capo* form of the modern aria, but its stylistic make-up is nonetheless still that of the sacred concerto. In the principal section, accompanied by choirs of recorders and oboes, the repeated traversing through an octave of the bass voice symbolizes the totality of divine power described in the text. The middle section provides a contrast of scoring (continuo only), metre, and intensity of rhythmic movement. The alto solo 'Durch mächtige Kraft', no. 5, a continuo movement with brief interjections from the trumpet choir and a somewhat longer trumpet ritornello at the close, is followed by no. 6, the most original and captivating movement in the whole cantata. The fervent prayer that

'You would not give the enemy the soul of Your turtle-doves' (Psalm 74.19) is heard in a homophonic* chorus (one might almost speak of a treble monody* harmonized in four parts) whose declamation is all the more effective for the narrow range of its melody. The strings double the voice parts, while choirs of oboes and recorders supply the brief prelude and episodes and mark the cadences of the choir. An inspired idea, greatly enhancing the effectiveness of the movement, is the heterogeneous continuo figuration. Violone and organ supply the 'staccato' supporting notes, the bassoon plays around them figuratively, and the cello, an octave higher, adds a figuration still further heightened in intervals and rhythmic motion:

The end of the movement is impressive. The choir delivers the text for the last time in unison on the *mediatio* (the first half-verse) of the first psalm tone;* the wind instruments accompany with complementary figures, at first in alternation; then for two bars the upper strings take up the cello's semiquaver figuration; and after choir and strings have come to rest, the music runs on for one more bar in the woodwind.

For the final chorus, no. 7, the complete instrumental ensemble is once more summoned. In form, motet-style sectional writing is predominant. Bach joins together brief homophonic passages in various metres and tempos, alternating solo and tutti scoring in the vocal choir. The one—admittedly very considerable—exception to this is the large choral fugue shortly after the beginning of the second strophe of text, a setting of the words 'muß täglich von neuen dich, Joseph, erfreuen' ('must daily anew delight you, Joseph'). The personage here addressed is Kaiser Joseph I, by whom the imperial free city of Mühlhausen was directly ruled. In this fugue, something new makes its appearance in Bach's works, namely his first attempt to succeed in a large form, to set the 'issue of unity' against the short-breathed formal multiplicity of the seventeenth century. The method he adopts is the permutation principle, which had already been employed in the third movement, though in a static manner, whereas here a constantly progressive enhancement is achieved by changing protagonists. The fugal exposition* is sung by the concertists accompanied by continuo only. Each voice then falls silent after it has sung through all four counterpoints,* and in each case an instrument enters in its place. The ripieno choir joins in, a full texture is achieved by adding the remaining participants, and finally the thematic entry of the first trumpet brings the fugue to a crowning conclusion. By contrast with this awe-inspiring stroke of genius, the remainder of Bach's setting of the second strophe of text seems like a mere coda. The last movement, like the first, ends with a quasi-*pianissimo* on two unison recorders.

Preise, Jerusalem, den Herrn, BWV 119

NBA I/32.1, p. 131 BC B3 Duration: *c.* 27 mins

1. [Chorus] SATB tr I–IV timp rec I,II ob I–III str bc — C C 12/8 ¢

'Preise, Jerusalem, den Herrn, lobe, Zion, deinen Gott! Denn er machet fest die Riegel deiner Tore und segnet deine Kinder drinnen, er schaffet deinen Grenzen Friede.'

'Praise the Lord, O Jerusalem, praise your God, O Zion! For He fortifies the bars of your gates and blesses your children therein; He makes peace within your borders.'

2. Recitativo T bc — G C

Gesegnet Land! glückselge Stadt!
Woselbst der Herr sein Herd und Feuer hat.
Wie kann Gott besser lohnen?
Als wo er Ehre läßt in einem Lande wohnen.
Wie kann er eine Stadt
Mit reicherm Nachdruck segnen?
Als wo er Güt und Treu einander läßt begegnen,
Wo er Gerechtigkeit und Friede
Zu küssen niemals müde.
Nicht müde, niemals satt
Zu werden teur verheißen, auch in der Tat erfüllet hat.
Da ist der Schluß gemacht:
Gesegnet Land! glückselge Stadt!

Blessed land! Happy city!
The very place where the Lord has His furnace and fire.
How better can God give reward other than
Where He lets honour dwell in a land?
How can He bless a city
With richer assurance
Than where He lets goodness and faithfulness meet together,
Where He never tires of letting righteousness
And peace kiss each other.
Not tired, never satisfied
With being preciously promised, it is also fulfilled by Him in deed.
Therefore we have to conclude:
Blessed land! Happy city!

3. Aria T ob da c I,II bc — G C

Wohl dir, du Volk der Linden,
Wohl dir, du hast es gut!
Wieviel an Gottes Segen
Und seiner Huld gelegen,
Die überschwenglich tut,
Kannst du an dir befinden.
Wohl dir, du Volk der Linden,
Wohl dir, du hast es gut!

Happy shall you be, you people of lindens!
Happy shall you be, it shall be well with you!
How much depended on God's Blessing
And His favour, which is able to do
Exceeding abundantly,
You can discover in yourself.
Happy shall you be, you people of lindens!
Happy shall you be, it shall be well with you!

4. Recitativo B tr I–IV timp rec I,II ob da c I,II bc — C c

So herrlich stehst du, liebe Stadt!	How gloriously you stand, dear city!
Du Volk! das Gott zum Erbteil sich erwählet hat.	You people, whom God has chosen for His inheritance!
Doch wohl! und aber wohl! wo mans zu Herzen fassen	It is good, it is very good, when one would take to heart
Und recht erkennen will,	And know aright
Durch wen der Herr den Segen wachsen lassen.	Through whom the Lord lets this Blessing grow.
Ja!	Yes!
Was bedarf es viel?	What more is needed?
Das Zeugnis ist schon da,	The witness is there already:
Herz und Gewissen wird uns überzeugen,	Heart and conscience will convince us
Daß, was wir Gutes bei uns sehn,	That what good we see among us
Nächst Gott durch kluge Obrigkeit	Happens, next to God, through prudent rulers
Und durch ihr weises Regiment geschehn.	And through their wise government.
Drum sei, geliebtes Volk, zu treuem Dank bereit,	Therefore, beloved people, be prepared for sincere thanksgiving,
Sonst würden auch davon nicht deine Mauern schweigen!	Otherwise not even your walls would hold their peace about it!

5. Aria A rec I + II bc — g $\frac{6}{8}$

Die Obrigkeit ist Gottes Gabe,	Authority is God's gift,
Ja selber Gottes Ebenbild.	Indeed God's very image.
Wer ihre Macht nicht will ermessen,	He who would not realize its might
Der muß auch Gottes gar vergessen:	Must also forever forget God's:
Wie würde sonst sein Wort erfüllt?	How else would His Word be fulfilled?

6. Recitativo S bc — F–C c

Nun! wir erkennen es und bringen dir,	Now! we acknowledge it and bring You,
O höchster Gott, ein Opfer unsers Danks dafür.	O highest God, an offering of our thanks for it.
Zumal, nachdem der heutge Tag,	Especially after today,
Der Tag, den uns der Herr gemacht,	The day that the Lord has made for us,
Euch, teure Väter, teils von eurer Last entbunden,	When you, dear fathers, are partly released from your burden
Teils auch auf euch	And partly have
Schlaflose Sorgenstunden	Sleepless hours of care
Bei einer neuen Wahl gebracht,	Brought upon you by a new election;
So seufzt ein treues Volk mit Herz und Mund zugleich:	Thus a loyal people sighs with heart and mouth alike:

7. [Chorus Scoring as in no. 1] — C c

Der Herr hat Guts an uns getan,	The Lord has done good things for us,

Des sind wir alle fröhlich.	Of this we are all glad.
Er seh die teuren Väter an	May He regard our dear fathers
Und halte auf unzählig	And keep them for countless
Und späte lange Jahre naus	And advanced long years
In ihrem Regimente Haus,	In their governmental house;
So wollen wir ihn preisen.	So we will praise Him.

8. Recitativo A bc — F–e c

Zuletzt!	At last!
Da du uns, Herr, zu deinem Volk gesetzt,	As You, O Lord, appoint us Your people,
So laß von deinen Frommen	Then from Your devout ones
Nur noch ein arm Gebet vor deine Ohren kommen	Let just one more poor prayer come before Your ears,
Und höre! ja erhöre!	And hear it! indeed, grant it!
Der Mund, das Herz und Seele seufzet sehre.	Mouth, heart, and soul sigh deeply.

9. Choral SATB bc (+ most instrs) — C c

Hilf deinem Volk, Herr Jesu Christ,	**Save Your people, Lord Jesus Christ,**
Und segne, was dein Erbteil ist.	**And bless what is Your inheritance.**
Wart und pfleg ihr' zu aller Zeit	**Look after and care for them at all times**
Und heb sie hoch in Ewigkeit!	**And raise them high in eternity!**
Amen.	**Amen.**

Among Bach's duties in Leipzig, as in Mühlhausen, was that of providing figural* music for the council election service, which took place annually in the Nicolaikirche on the Monday after St Bartholomew's Day (24 August), the day of the election. As the autograph date in the score testifies, the cantata *Preise, Jerusalem, den Herrn* originated during Bach's first year in Leipzig and was performed for the first time on 30 August 1723.

As usual on such occasions, the anonymous librettist refers to the council election in terms of praise and thanksgiving and finally beseeches God for future protection. The starting-point is Psalm 147. 12–14 (no. 1), and the following movements celebrate the welfare of the city where God 'lets honour dwell in the land' and 'lets goodness and faithfulness meet together' and where 'righteousness and peace kiss each other' (no. 2; cf. Psalm 85.10–11). In accordance with Romans 13, the poet praises the rulers as 'God's very image' (nos. 4 and 5)—rather too extravagantly for our way of thinking, alienated as we are from the doctrine of the Absolutist state. The other movements are devoted to thanksgiving and prayer. They give thanks to the city fathers and to the Lord, who 'has done good things for us' (cf. Psalm 126.3) and finally pray for future blessing in the words of Martin Luther's German version of the Te Deum (1529).

Bach's composition requires a splendid festive orchestra of no fewer than four trumpets and drums, two recorders, three oboes, strings, and continuo. No less splendid is the French Overture* design that he chose for the opening chorus.* Solemn, ceremonial dotted rhythms in the instrumental prelude and postlude frame the quick middle section, which, according to widespread tradition, should be designed as a fugue* but is here treated largely in homophony, with imitation* restricted to the outer parts, bass and soprano. In the plain *secco* recitative that follows, no. 2, the opening words 'Gesegnet Land! glückselge Stadt!' ('Blessed land! Happy city!') recur at the end. Bach lends this outer frame special charm by stating the reprise in reverse, as it were: the beginning of the first passage—

—corresponds with the end of the second—

The scoring of the aria 'Wohl dir, du Volk der Linden' ('Happy shall you be, you people of lindens!')[3], no. 3—for two oboes da caccia,* tenor voice, and continuo—with its pronounced emphasis on the middle register, gives the movement a mild, even warm sound, which is enhanced still more by the song-like, approachable melody. The second recitative no. 4, even more clearly than the first, is cast in a frame structure. The beginning and end are both marked by trumpet ritornellos, and the middle section—the true vocal section, allowing for the fact that the first two lines are still accompanied by trumpets—is filled out with woodwind chords. In the second aria, no. 5, the low woodwind instruments of the first aria are replaced by high woodwind (two recorders in unison). However, the two movements have in common their song-like—in this case, almost dance-like—melodic style. The *staccato* repeated quavers of the recorders are by many commentators interpreted as a mocking caricature of the text, 'Authority is God's gift, indeed God's very image', but this interpretation seems to us highly questionable. Surely modern conceptions of citizens who have come of age politically are here being anachronistically projected back onto the hierarchical thinking of the baroque period.

The following *secco* recitative, no. 6, leads directly into the chorus 'Der Herr hat Guts an uns getan' ('The Lord has done good things for us'), no. 7, which is cast in pure da capo* form. A predominantly chordal middle section,

[3] The name 'Leipzig' is derived from 'urbs Libzi', meaning place of lindens (lime trees).

occasionally broken up into imitation,* is surrounded by a choral fugue. Whether consciously or not, the fugue subject is similar to the opening of the chorale *Nun danket alle Gott*. The fugue, framed by a ritornello, gradually builds up from *a cappella** texture (with continuo), via the gradual addition of instruments (with partly independent and partly thematic woodwind), to a climactic threefold stretto* in which the trumpets participate. The ceremonial splendour of this chorus is followed by a brief *secco* recitative, no. 8, and then by a concluding movement in the style of a congregational hymn, a plain four-part setting of four lines from the German Te Deum with a lightly polyphonic* Amen at the close.

Ihr Tore zu Zion, BWV 193

NBA I/32.1, p. 203 BC B5 Survives incomplete[4]

1. Chorus Extant: SA ob I,II str	D c
Ihr Tore/Pforten zu Zion, ihr Wohnungen Jakobs, freuet euch!	You gates of Zion, you dwellings of Jacob, rejoice!
Gott ist unsers Herzens Freude,	God is the joy of our hearts,
Wir sind Völker seiner Weide,	We are the people of His pasture,
Ewig ist sein Königreich.	Everlasting is His Kingdom.
2. Recitativo Extant: S	b–e c
Der Hüter Israel entschläft noch schlummert nicht;	The Keeper of Israel shall neither sleep nor slumber;
Es ist annoch sein Angesicht	His Countenance has hitherto been
Der Schatten unsrer rechten Hand;	The shade upon our right hand;
Und das gesamte Land	And the entire land
Hat sein Gewächs im Überfluß gegeben.	Has yielded its increase in abundance.
Wer kann dich, Herr, genug davor erheben?	Who can exalt You enough for this, Lord?
3. Aria Extant: S ob I str	e 3/8
Gott, wir danken deiner Güte,	O God, we thank You for Your goodness,
Denn dein väterlich Gemüte	For Your fatherly disposition
Währet ewig für und für.	Endures for ever and ever.
Du vergibst das Übertreten,	You forgive our transgressions,
Du erhörest, wenn wir beten,	You listen when we pray,
Drum kömmt alles Fleisch zu dir.	Therefore all flesh shall come to You.
4. Recitativo Extant: A	b–G c
O Leipziger Jerusalem, vergnüge dich an deinem Feste!	O Leipzig, our Jerusalem, be content on your feast-day!
Der Fried ist noch in deinen Mauern,	Peace is still within your walls,

[4] A reconstruction by Reinhold Kubik has been published by Hänssler-Verlag (Neuhausen-Stuttgart).

Es stehn annoch die Stühle zum Gericht,	The thrones of judgement still stand,
Und die Gerechtigkeit bewohnet die Paläste.	And righteousness inhabits the palaces.
Ach bitte, daß dein Ruhm und Licht	Ah, pray that your renown and light
Also beständig möge dauern!	May thus endure constantly!

5. ARIA Extant: A ob I — G c

Sende, Herr, den Segen ein,	Send, O Lord, Your Blessing;
Laß die wachsen und erhalten,	Let them increase and sustain them,
Die vor dich das Recht verwalten	Those who administer justice before You
Und ein Schutz der Armen sein!	And act as a refuge for the oppressed!
Sende, Herr, den Segen ein!	Send, O Lord, Your Blessing!

6. RECITATIVO Not extant

7. CHORUS AB INITIO REPETATUR [repeat of opening chorus] — D c

This cantata was, in all probability, first performed on 25 August 1727 (see under BWV Anh. I 4, however), or else perhaps a year or two later. The text, by an anonymous librettist, refers to Psalm 87.2 in the first movement and to Psalm 121.4 in the second, praising God as defender of the 'Leipzig Jerusalem'. The music is, at least in part, a parody* of Cantata 193a. Perhaps both works share a common origin in a still older (Cöthen?) cantata. However, their incomplete transmission prevents us from forming any definite conclusions.

Wir danken dir, Gott, wir danken dir, BWV 29

NBA I/32.2, p. 3 BC B8 Duration: *c.* 28 mins

1. SINFONIA tr I–III timp str + ob I,II obbl org bc — D $\frac{3}{4}$

2. CHORUS SATB + SATB rip tr I–III timp bc (+ str + ob I,II) — D 2

'Wir danken dir, Gott, wir danken dir und verkündigen deine Wunder.'	'We thank You, O God, we thank You and declare Your wonders.'

3. ARIA T vln I solo bc — A ¢

Halleluja, Stärk und Macht	Alleluia, strength and might
Sei des Allerhöchsten Namen!	Be to the Name of the Most High!
Zion ist noch seine Stadt,	Zion is still His city,
Da er seine Wohnung hat,	Where He has His dwelling,
Da er noch bei unserm Samen	Where still among our seed
An der Väter Bund gedacht.	He remembers our forefathers' covenant.

4. RECITATIVO B bc — f♯–e c

Gottlob! es geht uns wohl!	Praise God! All is well with us!
Gott is noch unsre Zuversicht,	God is still our assurance;
Sein Schutz, sein Trost und Licht	His protection, His comfort and light
Beschirmt die Stadt und die Paläste,	Shield the city and the palaces,

Sein Flügel hält die Mauern feste.
Er läßt uns allerorten segnen,
Der Treue, die den Frieden küßt,
Muß für und für
Gerechtigkeit begegnen.
Wo ist ein solches Volk wie wir,
Dem Gott so nah und gnädig ist!

His pinions hold the walls firm.
He makes us blessed everywhere;
Faithfulness, which kisses peace,
Must for ever and ever
Meet righteousness.
Where else is such a people as we,
To whom God is so near and gracious?

5. Aria S ob I str bc — b $\frac{6}{8}$

Gedenk an uns mit deiner Liebe,
Schleuß uns in dein Erbarmen ein!
  Segne die, so uns regieren,
  Die uns leiten, schützen, führen,
  Segne, die gehorsam sein!

Remember us with Your Love,
Embrace us in Your mercy!
  Bless those who govern us,
  Those who guide, protect, and lead us,
  Bless those who are obedient!

6. Recitativo A + STB + SATB rip bc — D C

Vergiß es ferner nicht, mit deiner Hand
Uns Gutes zu erweisen;
So soll dich unsre Stadt und unser Land,
Das deiner Ehre voll,
Mit Opfern und mit Danken preisen,
'Und alles Volk soll sagen: Amen!'

Forget not henceforth with Your hand
To show us good things;
Then our city and our country,
Which are full of Your honour, shall
Praise You with sacrifices and thanksgiving,
'And all the people shall say: Amen!'

7. Aria A obbl org bc — D 2

Halleluja, Stärk und Macht
Sei des Allerhöchsten Namen!

Alleluia, strength and might
Be to the Name of the Most High!

8. Chorale SATB + SATB rip tr I–III timp bc (+ ww str) — D $\frac{3}{4}$

**Sei Lob und Preis mit Ehren
Gott Vater, Sohn, Heiligem Geist!
Der woll in uns vermehren,
Was er uns aus Gnaden verheißt,
Daß wir ihm fest vertrauen,
Gänzlich verlassn auf ihn,
Von Herzen auf ihn bauen,
Daß unsr Herz, Mut und Sinn
Ihm tröstlich solln anhangen;
Drauf singen wir zur Stund:
Amen, wir werdens erlangen,
Glaubn wir aus Herzens Grund.**

**Blessing and praise with honour be
To God the Father, Son, and Holy Spirit!
Who would increase in us
What He promises us out of Grace, that
We may hold fast our confidence in Him,
Abandon ourselves wholly to Him,
Build on Him from our hearts,
That our heart, courage, and mind
Should cleave comfortingly to Him;
Of this we sing at this hour:
Amen, we shall obtain it,
If we believe from the bottom of our heart.**

This cantata is dated 1731 in Bach's own hand, and therefore it must have received its first performance on 27 August that year. From the evidence of printed texts, we know that it was revived on 31 August 1739 and 25 August 1749. The anonymous librettist again adheres to the usual pattern for council-election cantatas, uniting thanksgiving for good deeds rendered by God with a prayer for future blessings. The opening biblical quotation is drawn from Psalm 75.1, and the madrigalian* verse that follows also includes several references to biblical texts. For the Christian congregation, Zion is no longer bound to a specific place, Jerusalem; it is rather the place where the Lord is worshipped. And when the words 'Zion is still His city, where He has His dwelling' are sung in the third movement, the churchgoer who knew his or her Bible might bring to mind 1 Chronicles 23.25 ('The Lord . . . will dwell in Jerusalem for ever'), interpreting Jerusalem as Leipzig. Biblical references are particularly numerous in the fourth movement. Alongside general formulations, such as 'God is still our assurance' (cf. Psalm 46.1, 62.8, and often elsewhere) or 'His protection . . . shields the city and the palaces, His pinions hold the walls firm' (cf. Psalms 122.7 and 36.7), we find an allusion to Psalm 85.10, which is also highlighted in other council-election cantatas (BWV 119/2, Anh. I 4/3 and 120/4): '. . . that goodness and faith are met together, righteousness and peace kiss each other'. Finally, the phrase 'And all the people shall say Amen!' from the sixth movement is drawn from Deuteronomy 27.26. The work concludes with the fifth verse (an addition, Königsberg, 1549) of the hymn *Nun lob, mein Seel, den Herren* by Johann Gramann (1530).

As in several other council-election cantatas, Bach resorts to an earlier composition for one of the movements: the splendid, ceremonial instrumental sinfonia is adapted with the highest mastery from the Preludio that opens the Partita in E for solo violin, BWV 1006. The violin part is taken over by obbligato* organ and the orchestral accompaniment newly composed. A more plainly scored version had already been employed in Cantata 120a. The original is still clearly recognizable in the restless figuration of the organ part, for there is no tutti ritornello theme in the orchestra as a counterweight to the solo part. The form of this sinfonia thus remains unique within Bach's works.

The following fugue-like chorus,* largely determined by canonic structures, is familiar from its later version as the 'Gratias agimus tibi' and 'Dona nobis pacem' of the B minor Mass.[5] Its principal theme is of a grand simplicity. In accordance with the dual text structure ('Wir danken dir . . . und verkündigen . . .') the musical setting is governed by two subjects, of which the first plays the greater part in determining the subsequent course of the movement:

[5] The mass and cantata versions probably stem from a common pre-1731 original; see Rifkin, notes to recording of B minor Mass, and Fröde, KB, NBA I/32.2, 41 f. and 51 ff.

Strings and woodwind double the voices, whose texture comprises a dense web of themes. The intensity is gradually enhanced, first by the addition of trumpet I, which doubles the subject in the soprano part; then by two entries of trumpets I and II with the subject in stretto,* augmenting the four-part choral texture to six parts; and finally by the unthematic entry of trumpet III and drums, which brings a further expansion to seven (or eight) parts.

The antiquated style of this chorus gives way to a modern concertante* style in the following tenor aria, no. 3. Solo violin and tenor voice act as equal partners and, together with the continuo, form a trio of sweeping vivacity. The movement is largely unified in character, for the vocal theme is derived from that of the introductory ritornello, and even the middle section of this da capo* structure maintains the ritornello theme in the violin part. A plain *secco* recitative, no. 4, leads to the soprano aria 'Gedenk an uns mit deiner Liebe' ('Remember us with Your Love'), no. 5, a charming siciliano with oboe and strings, whose melody, as in all Bach's movements of this type, emits an overwhelming warmth and intimacy. This impression is enhanced by the scoring: in the vocal passages, the continuo is silent, and the organ, playing *tasto solo* (that is, without filling in the harmony), joins the viola in the lowest part. Only the very last bars of the middle section form an exception to this (the aria is again in da capo form).

The next two movements are quite exceptional in design. In the *secco* recitative, no. 6, the words 'And all the people shall say:' introduce an 'Amen' sung in choral unison (or octaves), whereupon the principal section of the third movement immediately returns, without ritornello, transposed from A to D major and sung by the alto to the accompaniment of obbligato organ in place of violin. As a result, both thematically (no. 3 = no. 7) and in scoring (obbligato organ in nos. 1 and 7) the work is tightly held together to an exceptional degree. The concluding chorale once more allows us to hear the full ensemble. For the plain four-part choral texture, reinforced by oboes and strings, acquires a radiant crowning at the end of some of the lines from the obbligato trumpet choir.

Gott, man lobet dich in der Stille, BWV 120

NBA I/32.2, p. 55 BC B6 Duration: *c.* 26 mins

1.	[Alto Solo] A ob d'am I,II str bc	A 6/8
	'Gott, man lobet dich in der Stille zu Zion, und dir bezahlet man Gelübde.'	'O God, they praise You in the stillness of Zion, and they pay vows to You.'
2.	Chor SATB tr I–III timp str + ob d'am I,II bc	D C
	Jauchzet, ihr erfreuten Stimmen, Steiget bis zum Himmel nauf! Lobet Gott im Heiligtum Und erhebet seinen Ruhm Seine Güte, Sein erbarmendes Gemüte Hört zu keinen Zeiten auf.	Sing for joy, you glad voices, Climb up to heaven! Praise God in the sanctuary And exalt His renown. His goodness, His merciful disposition At no time comes to an end.
3.	Recitativo B bc	b C
	Auf, du geliebte Lindenstadt, Komm, falle vor dem Höchsten nieder, Erkenne, wie er dich In deinem Schmuck und Pracht So väterlich Erhält, beschützt, bewacht Und seine Liebeshand Noch über dir beständig hat. Wohlan, Bezahle die Gelübde, die du dem Höchsten hast getan, Und singe Dank- und Demutslieder! Komm, bitte, daß er Stadt und Land Unendlich wolle mehr erquicken Und diese werte Obrigkeit, So heute Sitz und Wahl verneut, Mit vielem Segen wolle schmücken!	Rise, you beloved city of lindens![6] Come, kneel down before the Most High; See how, In your ornament and splendour, In such a fatherly manner He preserves, protects, and watches over you And still holds His loving hand Over you constantly. Well then, Pay the vows that you have made to the Most High And sing songs of thanks and humility! Come, pray that city and country may be Further refreshed by Him without end, And that this worthy authority, Which today renews its seat and election, May be adorned with many blessings!
4.	Aria S vln conc str bc	G 6/8
	Heil und Segen Soll und muß zu aller Zeit Sich auf unsre Obrigkeit In erwünschter Fülle legen, Daß sich Recht und Treue müssen Miteinander freundlich küssen.	Salvation and Blessing Shall and must at all times Apply to our authorities In all desired abundance, So that justice and faithfulness must Kiss one another in friendship.

[6] See footnote 3 above, p. 729.

5. Recitativo T str bc D–f♯ c

Nun, Herr, so weihe selbst das Regiment mit deinem Segen ein,	Now, Lord, then consecrate this government with Your own Blessing,
Daß alle Bosheit von uns fliehe	That all wickedness may flee from us
Und die Gerechtigkeit in unsern Hütten blühe,	And righteousness flourish in our dwellings,
Daß deines Vaters reiner Same	That Your Father's pure seed
Und dein gebenedeiter Name	And Your blessed Name
Bei uns verherrlicht möge sein!	May be glorified among us!

6. Choral SATB bc (+ most instrs) b–D c

Nun hilf uns, Herr, den Dienern dein,	**Now save us, Lord, Your servants,**
Die mit deinm Blut erlöset sein!	**Who are redeemed by Your Blood!**
Laß uns im Himmel haben teil	**Let us have a share in heaven**
Mit den Heilgen im ewgen Heil!	**With the saints in everlasting Salvation!**
Hilf deinem Volk, Herr Jesu Christ,	**Save Your people, Lord Jesus Christ,**
Und segne, was dein Erbteil ist;	**And bless what is Your inheritance;**
Wart und pfleg ihr' zu aller Zeit	**Tend and nurse them at all times**
Und heb sie hoch in Ewigkeit!	**And raise them high in eternity!**

As in the council election cantatas discussed above, this specific occasion elicits praise and thanksgiving for the protection with which God has favoured the 'beloved city of lindens' and a prayer for blessing in future times. The introductory biblical passage, Psalm 65.1, supplies the theme for the next two movements, namely praise (no. 2) and making a vow out of gratitude (no. 3). The fourth and fifth movements beseech God for future blessing, and the sixth repeats this prayer in the words of Martin Luther's German Te Deum (1529).

Bach employed the chorus* and the two arias from this work, nos. 1, 2, and 4, in several different contexts. The arias possibly stem from his Cöthen years, and all three movements were used in the wedding cantata BWV 120a of 1729 and again in the cantata for the bicentenary of the Augsburg Confession, BWV 120b, of 1730. On the basis of the surviving source material, a watertight elucidation of all these relationships is hardly possible. It was formerly thought that the present cantata originated in some form before 1730 and was subsequently adapted to form BWV 120a and 120b. The autograph score, however, dates from around 1742, and more recently this date has been considered an accurate reflection of the cantata's status as the latest in this series of parody*-related works.[7]

In the opening movement, it is the text, and in particular the word 'Stille' ('stillness'), that must have induced Bach, contrary to his custom, to begin with a

[7] For the older view see in particular Dürr Chr 2, A. Glöckner, 'Neuerkenntnisse zu J. S. Bachs Aufführungskalender zwischen 1729 und 1735' (*BJ* 1981, 43–75), and K. Häfner, *Aspekte des Parodieverfahrens bei J. S. Bach* (Laaber, 1987). For the more recent view see J. Rifkin, notes to recording of the B minor Mass, *Nonesuch* 79036 (New York, 1982), Kobayashi Chr, and C. Fröde, KB, NBA I/32.2 (1994).

solo piece. The instrumental ensemble is made up of two oboes d'amore,* strings, and continuo. Friedrich Smend has advanced the plausible hypothesis that the aria was adapted from the slow middle movement of an instrumental concerto from the Cöthen period; and it has in fact a curious motivic affinity with the second movement of Cantata 35, of which the same conjecture has been made. The flowing coloraturas* of the alto part, which demand high skill and are incorporated in a frequently thematic instrumental texture, would then represent the remains of the original solo part (for violin?).

It is only in the second movement that full festive jubilation breaks out. Here the orchestra, now reinforced by trumpets and drums, plays a sinfonia-like introduction which includes the two principal themes of the following chorus: a triadic fanfare for 'Jauchzet' ('Sing for joy') and a sequence of stepwise rising semiquavers for 'steiget' ('climb'). Theses themes are partly adopted by the choir in a figurative and imitative* texture and partly used as the orchestral framework for passages of choral insertion.* The bipartite middle section of this da capo* form movement is taken up with largely homophonic* choral writing with accompanying instruments, leaving aside an articulating instrumental episode. The movement has become well known through the reuse of its principal section, albeit in a radically altered form, as the setting of the words 'Et expecto resurrectionem mortuorum' from the Credo of the B minor Mass.

A *secco* recitative leads to the soprano aria, no. 4, which is based on a presumably secular composition from the Cöthen period. The original itself does not survive, but we possess an early adaptation of it as a movement from the Sonata in G for violin and obbligato* harpsichord, BWV 1019a. The cantata version is an exceptionally lovely jewel among Bach's arias. With its intimate melody and the filigree-like figuration of the solo violin, accompanied by strings, it returns to the 'still' mood of the opening movement. A brief recitative follows (no. 5), whose prayerful character is furthered by its string accompaniment. The concluding chorale is a plain four-part setting of an extract from the German Te Deum.

Lobe den Herrn, meine Seele, BWV 69

NBA I/32.2, p. 113 BC B10 Duration: *c.* 27 mins

1. [CHORUS] SATB tr I–III timp ob I–III bsn str bc — D $\frac{3}{4}$

'Lobe den Herrn, meine Seele, und vergiß nicht, was er dir Gutes getan hat!'	'Praise the Lord, O my soul, and do not forget what good things He has done for you!'

2. RECITATIVO S bc — b–G C

Wie groß ist Gottes Güte doch!	How great indeed is God's goodness!
Er bracht uns an das Licht,	He brought us to the Light,
Und er erhält uns noch!	And He still sustains us!
Wo findet man nur eine Kreatur,	Where does one find a single creature

Der es an Unterhalt gebricht?	That lacks sustenance?
Betrachte doch, mein Geist,	Consider, my spirit,
Der Allmacht unverdeckte Spur,	The unhidden trace of the Almighty,
Die auch im kleinen sich recht groß erweist.	Which even in small things proves to be very great.
Ach! möcht es mir, o Höchster, doch gelingen,	Ah! if only I might succeed, O Most High,
Ein würdig Danklied dir zu bringen!	In bringing You a worthy song of thanks!
Doch, sollt es mir hierbei an Kräften fehlen,	Yet should I lack the powers for it,
So will ich doch, Herr, deinen Ruhm erzählen.	I would still, Lord, declare Your glory.

3. ARIA A ob I vln I bc — G 9/8

Meine Seele,	My soul,
Auf! erzähle,	Rise up! Declare
Was dir Gott erwiesen hat!	What God has shown you!
Rühme seine Wundertat,	Praise His marvellous deeds;
Laß, dem Höchsten zu gefallen,	To please the Most High, let
Ihm ein frohes Danklied schallen!	A joyful song of thanks to Him be heard!

4. RECITATIVO T str bc — e–f♯ c

Der Herr hat große Ding an uns getan.	The Lord has done great things to us.
Denn er versorget und erhält,	For He maintains and upholds,
Beschützet und regiert die Welt.	Protects and rules the world.
Er tut mehr, als man sagen kann.	He does more than one can say.
Jedoch, nur eines zu gedenken:	However, consider one thing only:
Was könnt uns Gott wohl Beßres schenken,	What better could God give us
Als daß er unsrer Obrigkeit	Than to grant our authorities
Den Geist der Weisheit gibet,	The spirit of wisdom,
Die denn zu jeder Zeit	Which then at all times
Das Böse straft, das Gute liebet?	Punishes evil and loves good?
Ja, die bei Tag und Nacht	Indeed, which by day and night
Vor unsre Wohlfahrt wacht?	Watches for our welfare?
Laßt uns dafür den Höchsten preisen;	Let us praise the Most High for it;
Auf! ruft ihn an,	Rise up! Call upon Him,
Daß er sich auch noch fernerhin	That He would henceforth
So gnädig woll erweisen.	Prove to be thus gracious.
Was unserm Lande schaden kann,	Whatever could harm our land
Wirst du, o Höchster, von uns wenden	Would You, O Most High, avert from us
Und uns erwünschte Hülfe senden.	And send us the salvation we desire.
Ja, ja, du wirst in Kreuz und Nöten	Yes, yes, in cross-bearing and necessities
Uns züchtigen, jedoch nicht töten.	You will chasten but not kill us.

5. ARIA B ob d'am str bc — b 3/4

Mein Erlöser und Erhalter,	My Redeemer and Preserver,

Nimm mich stets in Hut und Wacht!	Keep me ever in Your care and protection!
Steh mir bei in Kreuz und Leiden,	Stand by me in cross-bearing and suffering,
Alsdenn singt mein Mund mit Freuden:	Whereupon my mouth shall sing with joy:
Gott hat alles wohlgemacht.	God has made all well!

6. CHORAL SATB tr I–III timp bc (+ ww str) b–D c

Es danke, Gott, und lobe dich	**Let the people thank and praise You,**
Das Volk in guten Taten.	**O God, with good deeds.**
Das Land bringt Frucht und bessert sich,	**The land bears fruit and improves;**
Dein Wort ist wohl geraten.	**Your Word has succeeded well.**
Uns segne Vater und der Sohn,	**May the Father and the Son bless us,**
Und segne Gott, der Heilge Geist,	**May God the Holy Spirit bless us,**
Dem alle Welt die Ehre tut,	**To whom all the world pays honour,**
Für ihm sich fürchten allermeist,	**Fearing Him most of all,**
Und sprecht von Herzen: Amen!	**And says from the heart: Amen!**

This cantata was adapted from a work with the same opening lines, BWV 69a, written for the Twelfth Sunday after Trinity 1723. The joyful content of the Gospel* for that Sunday, which ends with the words 'He has made all well' (cf. no. 5 above), enabled the work to be reused as a council election cantata. This involved relatively minor alterations, which were undertaken by Bach during the very last years of his life: the revised version was performed on 26 August 1748. For the recitatives, both text and music were written afresh, and the former concluding chorale was replaced by the third verse of Luther's hymn *Es woll uns Gott genädig sein* (1524). The first and fifth movements, on the other hand, remained virtually unaltered, as did the third, which had already been revised for an earlier performance and was now subject to a few corrections only, clearly for textual reasons.

It is in the recitatives, then, that reference is made to the council elections. The first of them (no. 2), a *secco* with continuo accompaniment, praises God as our creator and preserver, to whom honour and thanksgiving are due. The second recitative (no. 4) enters more specifically into the given occasion. Again, it opens as a *secco*, but after the words 'However, consider one thing only', the strings enter to emphasize in musical terms the gratitude of the people for a wise government. At the point where God is addressed, the movement is enhanced still further, changing into a motivically accompanied arioso.* Altogether, then, it passes through three stages: *secco* (general deliberations), *accompagnato** (reflections on the town's government) and arioso (prayer for future assistance). The opening chorus* and the two arias, nos. 1, 3, and 5, are discussed above under Cantata 69a. The plain concluding chorale is augmented in texture by the independent parts assigned to the trumpet choir, which marks the ends of the lines and accompanies the whole of lines 5–6, the prayer for blessing in the *Abgesang*.*

The music of several other council election cantatas by Bach is lost. All that survives to prove that they once existed is their text or some other document. The works concerned are:

Council Election Cantata, Mühlhausen, 1709, BWV Anh. I 192

Although this cantata[8] (like its predecessor in 1708, BWV 71) was evidently published, it has so far eluded rediscovery. It is possible that its music is preserved in an adapted form in one of Bach's surviving works, but equally it may be altogether lost. See the above discussion of Cantata 71.

Wünschet Jerusalem Glück, BWV Anh. I 4

All that survives of this cantata is Picander's libretto, published in the second volume of his verse (Leipzig, 1729). It has so far proved impossible to find any evidence to support Spitta's precise statement that the cantata originated in 1727. The work is known to have been revived on 18 August 1741. See also the above discussion of Cantata 193.

Gott, gib dein Gerichte dem Könige, BWV Anh. I 3

Again, the printed text, which is dated 1730, is preserved among Picander's poems (Volume 3, Leipzig, 1732). The work was first identified by Arnold Schering in his article 'Kleine Bachstudien' (*BJ* 1933, pp. 50 ff.).

Herrscher des Himmels, König der Ehren, BWV Anh. I 193

Not only do we possess the printed text of 1740—*Nützliche Nachrichten von Denen Bemühungen derer Gelehrten und andern Begebenheiten in Leipzig* (Leipzig, 1740)—but it can be demonstrated that the seventh and last movement was a parody of the final chorus of the 'Hunt' Cantata, BWV 208/15. The remainder of the music is lost.[9]

There is no evidence to support Spitta's conjecture,[10] since adopted wholesale by Bach scholarship, that due to its suitable content Cantata 137, *Lobe den Herren, den mächtigen König der Ehren*, might have been performed not only on its proper occasion, the Twelfth Sunday after Trinity, but at a council election service (on

[8] Identified by Ernst Brinkmann, 'Neues über J. S. Bach in Mühlhausen', *Mühlhäuser Geschichtsblätter*, 31 (Mühlhausen, 1932), 294 ff.

[9] The work was identified by Werner Neumann, 'Eine verschollene Ratswechselkantate J. S. Bachs', *BJ* 1961, 52–7.

[10] Spitta II, 286 f.; Eng. version II, 455 f.

25 August 1732). Such a performance is, of course, conceivable, just as it is in the case of a number of other cantatas of similarly appropriate content, such as BWV 97, 100, 117, and 192. But we lack the evidence that might justify selecting one of these works and declaring it to be a council election cantata.

9

Weddings

Sein Segen fließt daher wie ein Strom, BWV Anh. I 14 (BC [B12])

It is apparent from the printed text, which is all that survives of this cantata, that Bach performed it at the wedding of Christoph Friedrich Lösner, 'Proviant- und Floß-Verwalter' (Provisions and Raft Manager), and Johanna Elisabetha Scherling in Leipzig on 12 February 1725. Both the opening lines and the text that follows them make frequent reference to the calling of the bridegroom, a widespread custom in wedding cantata librettos of the period which sometimes led to very curious results.

O ewiges Feuer, o Ursprung der Liebe, BWV 34a

NBA I/33, p. 29   BC B13   Survives incomplete

1. [Chorus] Extant: SATB vln I vla bc — D 3/4

O ewiges Feuer, o Ursprung der Liebe,	O eternal fire, O source of love,
Entzünde der Herzen geweihten Altar.	Enkindle the consecrated altar of their hearts.
Laß himmlische Flammen durchdringen und wallen,	Let heavenly flames penetrate and well up;
Ach laß doch auf dieses vereinigte Paar	Ah indeed on this united pair let
Die Funken der edelsten Regungen fallen.	The sparks of the most noble emotions fall.

2. Recitativo B bc — G–b c

Wie, daß der Liebe hohe Kraft	How is it that the lofty power of love
In derer Menschen Seelen	In those human souls
Ein Himmelreich auf Erden schafft?	Creates a heavenly kingdom on earth?
Was ziehet dich, o höchstes Wesen!	What draws You, O Highest Being,
Der Liebe Wirkung zu erwählen?	To choose the working of love,
Ein Herz zur Wohnung auszulesen?	To select a heart for Your dwelling?

3. Aria e Recitativo Extant: AT vln I vla bc — b–D c

'Siehe, also wird gesegnet der Mann, der den Herren fürchtet.'	'Behold, thus shall the man be blessed who fears the Lord.'
Wo dringt der Geist mit Glaubensaugen hin?	Where does the spirit enter with the eyes of faith?

Wo suchet er des Segens Quellen,
Die treuer Seelen Ehestand
Als ein gesegnetes, gelobtes Land
Vermögen darzustellen?
'Der Herr wird dich segnen aus Zion',
Was aber hat dein Gott dir zugedacht,
Dir, dessen Fleiß in Gottes Hause wacht?
Was wird der Dienst der heilgen Hütten
Auf dich vor Segen schütten?
'Daß du sehest das Glück Jerusalem dein Leben lang',
Weil Zion Wohl zuerst dein Herze rührt,
Wird sich auch irdisches Vergnügen
Nach deines Herzens Wunsche fügen,
Da Gott ein auserwähltes Kind dir zugeführt,
Daß du in ungezählten Jahren
Verneutes Wohlsein mögst erfahren.
'Und sehest deiner Kinder Kinder.'
So rufen wir zur Segensstunde
Von Herzen mit vereintem Munde:

Where does it seek the sources of blessing
By which the matrimony of faithful souls
May be represented
As a blessed, promised land?
'The Lord shall bless you out of Zion',
But what has your God destined for you,
Whose diligence watches in God's House?
What will service of the holy tabernacles
Pour on you by way of blessing?
'That you shall see the good fortune of Jerusalem all your life long',
Since Zion's good first stirs your heart,
Earthly contentment shall follow,
According to your heart's desire,
For God brings you a chosen child
So that for countless years
You may experience renewed welfare.
'And you shall see your children's children.'
So at this hour of blessing we call
From our hearts with united voices:

4. CHORUS Extant: SATB vln I vla bc — D c ¢

'Friede über Israel.'
Eilt zu denen heilgen Stufen.
Eilt, der Höchste neigt sein Ohr.
Unser Wünschen dringt hervor,
Friede über Israel,
Friede über euch zu rufen.

'Peace upon Israel.'
Hasten to those sacred steps.
Hasten, the Most High inclines His ear.
Our wishes arise to call:
Peace upon Israel,
Peace upon you.

Post copulationem — *After the wedding*

5. ARIA Extant: A vln I vla bc — A c

Wohl euch, ihr auserwählten Schafe,
Die ein getreuer Jakob liebt.
Sein Lohn wird dort am größten werden,
Den ihm der Herr bereits auf Erden
Durch seiner Rahel Anmut gibt.

Happy are you, you chosen sheep,
Whom a faithful Jacob loves.
His reward will there become greatest
To whom the Lord already on earth
Gives charm through his Rachel.

6. Recitativo S bc — f♯–D c

Das ist vor dich, o ehrenwürdger Mann,	That is for you, O honourable man,
Die edelste Belohnung,	The most noble reward
So dich vergnügen kann.	That you could desire.
Gott, der von Ewigkeit die Liebe selber hieß	May God, who from eternity was called Love itself
Und durch ein tugendhaftes Kind dein Herze rühren ließ,	And who lets your heart be stirred by a virtuous child,
Erfülle nun mit Segen deine Wohnung,	Now fill your dwelling with blessing,
Daß sie wie Obed Edoms sei,	That it may be like Edom's Obadiah
Und lege Kraft dem Segensworte bei.	And add strength to the word of blessing.

7. Chorus Extant: SB vln I vla bc — D c

Gib, höchster Gott, auch hier dem Worte Kraft,	Here too, Most High God, give power to the Word, which creates
Das so viel Heil bei deinem Volke schafft:	So much salvation among Your people:
'Der Herr segne dich und behüte dich.'	'The Lord bless you and keep you.'
Es müsse ja auf den zurücke fallen,	It must indeed redound upon those
Der solches läßt an heilger Stätte schallen:	Who let it be heard in holy places:
'Der Herr erleuchte sein Angesicht über dich und sei dir gnädig',	'May the Lord make His face shine upon you and be gracious to you',
Sein Dienst, so stets am Heiligtume baut,	His service, ever cultivated in the sanctuary,
Macht, daß der Herr mit Gnaden auf ihn schaut.	Makes the Lord look upon him with grace.
'Der Herr erhebe sein Angesicht über dich und gebe dir Friede.'	'May the Lord lift up His countenance upon you and grant you peace.'
Der Herr, von dem die keuschen Flammen kamen,	May the Lord, from whom the pure flames came,
Erhalte sie und spreche kräftig amen.	Preserve them and say heartily 'Amen'.

According to source studies, this cantata must have been performed during the first half of the year 1726.[1] Only a few performing parts survive, however. The text suggests that the bridegroom was a theologian. Bach later reused the first, fourth, and fifth movements in the Whit Cantata with the same opening lines, BWV 34; and the finale is related by parody* to that of Cantata 195 in its original version.

[1] It is possible that it had already been performed on 27 November 1725 at the wedding of Andreas Erlmann and Catherina Dorothea Hartranfft; see H.-J. Schulze, 'Neuerkenntnisse zu einigen Kantatentexten Bachs auf Grund neuer biographischer Daten', in M. Geck, ed., *Bach-Interpretationen* (Göttingen, 1969), 22–8, 208–10.

Der Herr ist freundlich dem, der auf ihn harret, BWV Anh. I 211

This cantata was written for the wedding of the doctor of theology Johann Friedrich Höckner and Jacobina Agnetha Bartholomaei on 18 January 1729. The libretto is by C. F. Henrici, alias Picander. The music is lost, but Bach is named as composer in the recently rediscovered printed text.[2]

Vergnügende Flammen, verdoppelt die Macht, BWV Anh. I 212

This cantata was written for the wedding of Christoph Georg Winckler and Caroline Wilhelmine Jöcher on 26 July 1729. The libretto is by C. F. Henrici, alias Picander. The music is lost, but Bach is named as composer in the recently rediscovered printed text.[3]

Herr Gott, Beherrscher aller Dinge, BWV 120a

NBA I/33, p. 77 BC B15 Preserved incomplete

1. [Chorus] Extant: SATB tr II vla bc — D C

Herr Gott, Beherrscher aller Dinge,	Lord God, Ruler of all things,
Der alles hat, regiert und trägt,	Who has, rules, and bears everything,
Durch den, was Odem hat, sich regt,	Through whom all that has breath stirs,
Wir alle sind viel zu geringe	We are all far too unworthy
Der Güte und Barmherzigkeit,	For the goodness and mercy
Womit du uns von Kindesbeinen	With which from childhood
Bis auf den Augenblick erfreut.	Up to the present time You delight us.

2. Recitativo [e Coro] Extant: SATB vla bc — b C 3/4 C

Baß	*Bass*
Wie wunderbar, o Gott, sind deine Werke,	How marvellous, O God, are Your works,
Wie groß ist deine Macht,	How great is Your might,
Wie unaussprechlich deine Treu!	How inexpressible Your faithfulness!
Du zeigest deiner Allmacht Stärke,	You showed Your almighty power
Eh du uns auf die Welt gebracht.	Before You brought us into the world.
Zur Zeit,	At a time
Wenn wir noch gar nichts sein	When we were still nothing
Und von uns selbst nichts wissen,	And knew nothing of ourselves,
Ist deine Liebe und Barmherzigkeit	Your Love and Mercy was
Vor unser Wohlgedeihn	For our welfare
Aufs eifrigste beflissen;	Most zealously solicitous;
Der Name und die Lebenszeit	Our name and lifetime
Sind bei dir angeschrieben,	Were prescribed by You

[2] See H. Tiggemann, 'Unbekannte Textdrucke zu drei Gelegenheitskantaten J. S. Bachs', *BJ* 1994, 7–22.

[3] See Tiggemann, 'Unbekannte Textdrucke'.

Wenn wir noch im Verborgnen blieben;
Ja, deine Güte ist bereit,
Wenn sie uns auf die Welt gebracht,
Uns bald mit Liebesarmen zu umfassen.
Und daß wir dich nicht aus dem Sinne lassen,
So wird uns deine Güt und Macht
An jedem Morgen neu.
Drum kommts, da wir dies wissen,
Daß wir von Herzensgrunde rühmen müssen:
Chor
'Nun danket alle Gott, der große Dinge tut an allen Enden!'
Tenor
Nun, Herr, es werde diese Lieb und Treu
Auch heute den Verlobten neu;
Und da jetzt die Verlobten beide
Vor dein hochheilig Angesichte treten
Und voller Andacht beten,
So höre sie vor deinem Throne
Und gib zu unsrer Freude,
Was ihnen gut und selig ist, zum Lohne.

When we still remained in secret;
Indeed, Your goodness was ready,
When it brought us into the world,
To embrace us soon with arms of Love.
And so that we do not let You out of our mind,
Your goodness and might
Are renewed for us every morning.
Thus it happens, since we know this,
That we must celebrate from the bottom of our hearts:
Choir
'Now thank the God of all, who does great things in all quarters!'
Tenor
Now, Lord, may this love and faithfulness
Also be renewed today for the betrothed;
And since the betrothed now both
Step before Your high and holy countenance
And pray, full of devotion,
Then hear them before Your throne
And grant, to our joy,
What is good and blessed for them as a reward.

3. ARIA Extant: S vla bc — G $\frac{6}{8}$

Leit, o Gott, durch deine Liebe
Dieses neu verlobte Paar.
Mach an ihnen kräftig wahr,
Was dein Wort uns vorgeschrieben,
Daß du denen, die dich lieben,
Wohltun wollest immerdar.

Guide, O God, through Your Love
This newly betrothed pair.
Make heartily true for them
What Your Word prescribed for us,
That to those who love You
You will do good for evermore.

Secunda parte post copulationem

Second part, after the wedding

4. SINFONIA str + ob I,II obbl org bc — D $\frac{3}{4}$

5. RECITATIVO [E CORO] SATB bc — b–c♯ C

Tenor
Herr Zebaoth,
Herr, unsrer Väter Gott,
Erhöre unser Flehn,

Tenor
Lord of Sabaoth,
Lord, God of our fathers,
Hear our supplication,

<table>
<tr><td>Gib deinen Segen und Gedeihn
Zu dieser neuen Ehe,
Daß all ihr Tun in, von und mit dir
gehe.
Laß alles, was durch dich geschehen,
In dir gesegnet sein,
Vertreibe alle Not,
Und führe die Vertrauten beide
So, wie du willt,
Nur stets zu dir.
So werden diese für und für

Mit wahrer Seelenfreude
Und deinem reichen Segen,
An welchem alles auf der Welt
gelegen,
Gesättigt und erfüllt.
Chor
Erhör uns, lieber Herre Gott.</td><td>Grant Your blessing and prosperity
Upon this new marriage, so that
All their deeds may go in, from and with
You.
Let all that happens through You
Be blessed in You;
Drive away all distress
And lead the betrothed pair
As You will,
Only always to You.
Then these shall be for ever and
ever—
With true joy of the soul
And Your rich Blessing,
On which everything in the world
rests—
Satisfied and fulfilled.
Choir
Hear us, dear Lord God.</td></tr>
<tr><td>6. ARIA [DUETTO] AT ob d'am I,II str bc</td><td>A $\frac{6}{8}$</td></tr>
<tr><td>Herr, fange an und sprich den Segen
Auf dieses deines Dieners Haus.
Laß sie in deiner Furcht bekleiben,
So werden sie in Segen bleiben;
Erheb auf sie dein Angesichte,
So gehts gewiß in Segen aus.</td><td>Lord, begin to pronounce Your Blessing
Upon this Your servants' house.
Let them be fixed in Your fear,
Then they shall remain in blessing;
Lift up Your countenance upon them,
Then they shall certainly go forth in
blessing.</td></tr>
<tr><td>7. RECITATIVO B bc</td><td>f♯–A c</td></tr>
<tr><td>Der Herr, Herr unser Gott, sei so mit
euch,
Als er mit eurer Väter Schar

Vor diesem und auch jetzo war.
Er pflanz euch Ephraim und dem
Manasse gleich.
Er laß euch nicht,
Er zieh nicht von euch seine Hand.

Er neige euer Herz und Sinn
Stets zu ihm hin,
Daß ihr in seinen Wegen wandelt,
In euern Taten weislich handelt.
Sein Geist sei euch stets zugewandt.</td><td>The Lord, the Lord our God, be with
you,
As He was with the host of your
fathers
Before this time and even now.
He plants you like Ephraim and
Manasseh.
He does not leave you,
He does not withdraw His hand from
you.
He inclines your heart and mind
Ever to Him,
So that you walk in His ways
And deal wisely in your deeds.
May His Spirit ever be turned towards
you.</td></tr>
</table>

Wenn dieses nun geschicht,
So werden alle eure Taten
Nach Wunsch geraten.
Und eurer frommen Eltern Segen
Wird sich gedoppelt auf euch legen.
Wir aber wollen Gott mit Lob und Singen
Ein Dank- und Freudenopfer bringen.

If this now happens,
All your deeds shall be advantageous
According to your wish.
And your devout parents' blessing
Shall lie doubly upon you.
But we will bring God with praise and singing
A thanks- and freewill-offering.

8. CHORAL SATB tr I–III timp bc (+ ww str) D $\frac{3}{4}$

Lobe den Herren, der deinen Stand sichtbar gesegnet,
Der aus dem Himmel mit Strömen der Liebe geregnet.
Denke daran,
Was der Allmächtige kann,
Der dir mit Liebe begegnet.

Praise the Lord, who has visibly blessed your caste,
Who has rained down from heaven with streams of Love.
Think upon
What the Almighty can do,
Who treats you with Love.

Lobe den Herren, was in mir ist, lobe den Namen.
Alles, was Odem hat, lobe mit Abrahams Samen.

Praise the Lord, all that is in me, praise His Name.
Let everything that has breath, together with Abraham's seed, praise Him.

Er ist dein Licht,
Seele, vergiß es ja nicht;
Lobende, schließe mit Amen.

He is your Light,
O soul, do not indeed forget it;
Those praising Him, conclude with Amen.

In all probability, this cantata dates from 1729, but nothing further is known about the wedding for which it was written. The recitatives (nos. 2, 5, and 7) are original compositions; the first, third, and sixth movements are related by parody* to nos. 2, 4, and 1 respectively of the council election cantata BWV 120; and the fourth movement is an adaptation of the Preludio from the solo violin Partita in E, BWV 1006. Here the solo part is assigned to obbligato* organ and an accompaniment for string orchestra (probably reinforced by oboes) was newly composed for the purpose. This version of the movement in turn supplied the model for the introductory sinfonia of Cantata 29, in which the instrumentation is enriched by trumpets and drums. Finally, the concluding chorale of the wedding cantata under discussion was adopted from Cantata 137.

The performing parts of this cantata survive only in a fragmentary form. In addition, we possess a fragmentary score which, in its existing form, begins towards the end of the fourth movement and continues to the end of the cantata. However, since the first, third, and fourth movements may be completed from other cantatas and the second seems to have survived in all essentials, no insuperable difficulties stand in the way of an attempted reconstruction.[4]

The content of the text is relatively generalized and offers no clues as to the personalities of the bridal couple. As mentioned above, the opening chorus* is related by parody to the second movement of Cantata 120, whose text-engendered motive* on 'climbs up to heaven' remains recognizable in this version. The kernel of the following *secco* recitative, no. 2, is a brief choral passage which, contrary to Frederick Hudson's view, is not a chorale variation on the hymn *Nun danket alle Gott* but a motet* on Ecclesiasticus 50.22. Even if certain reminiscences of the chorale melody may be heard at the outset, the text is not that of the hymn (but rather of the biblical passage just mentioned), nor is the musical form that of a variation.

The third movement is again familiar from Cantata 120 (no. 4), and the fourth has already been considered in connection with Cantata 29. The fifth, a newly composed *secco* recitative, flows into the words 'Hear us, dear Lord God' from the Litany, which Bach sets in liturgical style in a plain four-part texture. The sixth movement, which is related by parody to Cantata 120/1, nonetheless differs from it in including an additional part for tenor, which turns it into a duet, as well as a middle section of twenty-eight bars in F sharp minor. In the following *secco* recitative, no. 7, blessing is called down upon the bridal pair, and reference made to three relevant biblical passages, none of which is quoted literally, however: 1 Kings 8.57 f., Genesis 48.20–1 and 1 Chronicles 28.20. The work concludes with the fourth and fifth verses of the hymn *Lobe den Herren, den mächtigen König der Ehren* by Joachim Neander (1680) in a setting borrowed from Cantata 137, except that the trumpet choir is not added till the second verse.

Gott ist unsre Zuversicht, BWV 197

NBA I/33, p. 119 BC B16 Duration: *c.* 20 mins

1. [Chorus] SATB tr I–III timp ob I,II str bc — D ¢

Gott ist unsre Zuversicht,	God is our assurance,
Wir vertrauen seinen Händen.	We trust His hands.
Wie er unsre Wege führt,	While He leads us on our way,
Wie er unser Herz regiert,	While He rules our hearts,
Da ist Segen aller Enden.	There is blessing everywhere.

2. Recitativo B bc — A C

Gott ist und bleibt der beste Sorger,	God is and remains the best Provider,
Er hält am besten haus.	He keeps house best.

[4] A reconstruction by Frederick Hudson has been published by J. Curwen & Sons (London, 1955).

Er führet unser Tun zuweilen wunderlich,	He directs our activities at times strangely,
Jedennoch fröhlich aus,	Yet nonetheless joyfully,
Wohin der Vorsatz nicht gedacht.	To ends that our purpose had not considered.
Was die Vernunft unmöglich macht,	What reason regards as impossible
Das füget sich.	Comes about.
Er hat das Glück der Kinder, die ihn lieben,	The good fortune of children who love Him
Von Jugend an in seine Hand geschrieben.	He has written on His hand from their youth onwards.
3. ARIA A ob d'am str bc	A 3/4 c 3/4
Schläfert allen Sorgenkummer	Lull all sorrowful care
In den Schlummer	In the slumber
Kindlichen Vertrauens ein.	Of childlike trust.
Gottes Augen, welche wachen	God's eyes, which keep watch
Und die unser Leitstern sein,	And are our guiding star,
Werden alles selber machen.	Will themselves take care of everything.
4. RECITATIVO B str bc	f♯–A c
Drum folget Gott und seinem Triebe.	Therefore follow God and His impulse.
Das ist die rechte Bahn.	That is the right path.
Die führet durch Gefahr	It leads through danger
Auch endlich in das Kanaan	Finally into Canaan
Und durch von ihm geprüfte Liebe	And through love tested by Him
Auch an sein heiliges Altar	Even to His holy altar
Und bindet Herz und Herz zusammen,	And binds heart and heart together;
Herr! sei du selbst mit diesen Flammen!	Lord, be present Yourself with these flames!
5. CHORAL SATB bc (+ ww str)	A c
Du süße Lieb, schenk uns deine Gunst,	**You sweet Love, grant us Your favour,**
Laß uns empfinden der Liebe Brunst,	**Let us feel the fervency of love, so that**
Daß wir uns von Herzen einander lieben	**We may love one another from our hearts**
Und in Fried auf einem Sinne bleiben.	**And remain in peace and of the same mind.**
Kyrie eleis!	**Lord, have mercy upon us!**
Post copulationem	*After the wedding*
6. ARIA B ob obbl bsn vln I,II bc	G c
O du angenehmes Paar,	O you delightful pair,
Dir wird eitel Heil begegnen,	Sheer salvation shall befall you,
Gott wird dich aus Zion segnen	God shall bless you out of Zion
Und dich leiten immerdar,	And lead you for evermore,
O du angenehmes Paar!	O you delightful pair!

7. Recitativo S bc	C c
So wie es Gott mit dir	Just as God has had with you
Getreu und väterlich	Faithful and fatherly intent
Von Kindesbeinen an gemeint,	From your childhood onwards,
So will er für und für	So He will for ever and ever
Dein allerbester Freund	Remain your very best Friend
Bis an das Ende bleiben.	Until the end.
Und also kannst du sicher gläuben,	And thus you can firmly believe
Er wird dir nie	That He will never,
Bei deiner Hände Schweiß und Müh	Amidst the sweat and toil of your hands,
Kein Gutes lassen fehlen.	Let you lack any good thing.
Wohl dir, dein Glück ist nicht zu zählen.	Happy are you: your good fortune is beyond estimation.
8. Aria S vln solo ob d'am I,II bc	G 6/8
Vergnügen und Lust,	Pleasure and delight,
Gedeihen und Heil	Prosperity and salvation
Wird wachsen und stärken und laben.	Will grow and strengthen and refresh.
Das Auge, die Brust	The eye, the breast
Wird ewig sein Teil	Shall ever have its portion
An süßer Zufriedenheit haben.	Of sweet contentment.
9. Recitativo B ob I,II str bc	D–f♯ c
Und dieser frohe Lebenslauf	And this joyful course of life
Wird bis in späte Jahre währen.	Shall last until your latter years.
Denn Gottes Güte hat kein Ziel,	For God's goodness has no end:
Die schenkt dir viel,	It gives you many good things,
Ja mehr, als selbst das Herze kann begehren.	Indeed, more than the heart can even desire.
Verlasse dich gewiß darauf.	Of this you may be quite sure.
10. Choral SATB bc (+ ww str)	b c
[So wandelt froh auf Gottes Wegen,	**[Then journey gladly on God's ways,**
Und was ihr tut, das tut getreu!	**And whatever you do, do faithfully!**
Verdienet eures Gottes Segen,	**Earn your God's Blessing,**
Denn der ist alle Morgen neu:	**For it is new every morning:**
Denn welcher seine Zuversicht	**For whoever puts his trust**
Auf Gott setzt, den verläßt er nicht.]	**In God will not be forsaken by Him.]**

Bach composed this cantata for an unknown wedding in his late Leipzig period, around 1736/7. In the process, he made use of—or intended to make use of—several pieces composed at an earlier date. By contrast with Cantata 120, whose verse structure takes no account of the movements Bach earmarked for parody,* the anonymous librettist of the present cantata designed the arias so that the third movement should correspond with the aria 'Wieget euch, ihr satten Schafe' from the pastoral cantata BWV 249a and its parodies BWV 249b and 249, and the sixth and eighth with Cantata 197a, nos. 4 and 6 respectively. Only in the last two cases did Bach actually carry out the parody, however, either because he eventually found more time for composition than he had originally feared or because, for some reason, he considered it expedient to provide a new composition for the third movement.

As far as we can tell, the text, like that of Cantata 120a, makes no specific reference to the bridal couple. Proceeding from the opening line of Psalm 46, it urges trust in God (Part I), whose reward shall be God's unfailing kindness and His blessing (Part II). It is striking how often the text speaks of the path along which God will lead the bridal pair (no. 1: 'He leads us on our way'; no. 2: 'He directs our activities'; no. 3: 'our guiding star'; no. 4: 'that is the right path'; no. 6: '. . . and lead you for evermore'; no. 9: 'this joyful course of life'; and no. 10: 'on God's ways'). Should we see herein an allusion to the calling of the bridegroom? In the second movement, the remark that God has 'written on His hand' the good fortune of His children alludes to Isaiah 49.16. In the sixth movement, the words 'God shall bless you out of Zion and lead you for evermore' are based on Psalm 128.5, one of the psalms sung during the marriage service. And in the seventh movement, the words 'He will never . . . let you lack any good thing' may be understood as a reference to Psalm 84.11. Part I concludes with the third verse of Martin Luther's hymn *Nun bitten wir den Heiligen Geist* (1524). The chorale that ends Part II, no. 10, is transmitted without text in Bach's original score (the only surviving authentic source), yet there is no doubt that only the seventh and last verse of the hymn *Wer nur den lieben Gott läßt walten* by Georg Neumarck (1641) can be intended. It seems very doubtful whether the rewording 'So wandelt froh . . .' ('Then journey gladly . . .'), transmitted only in secondary sources from Zelter's circle and adopted in the standard modern editions, goes back to Bach. It should probably be regarded as a product of Zelter's editing and is consequently best replaced in performance by the original text, as used by Bach in, for example, Cantata 93, no. 7.

The principal section of the opening chorus,* which is cast in da capo* form and introduced by an instrumental sinfonia, is made up of a fugal exposition* for the choir, plus a chordal or freely polyphonic* continuation, which is largely dominated by the orchestra due to the technique of choral insertion.* The middle section, in a plain choral texture, takes up motives* from the introductory sinfonia in its independent instrumental parts and employs the fugue* subject in its instrumental episodes. The scoring (for trumpet choir, two oboes, strings, and continuo) is decidedly festive.

The four recitatives alternate between *secco* with arioso* conclusion and instrumentally accompanied settings. The second movement contains only a hint of an arioso conclusion, but in the seventh it takes up a full half of the movement. Within the instrumentally accompanied recitatives, there is a progressive increase in intensity: the fourth movement begins with short chordal strokes in the strings and continuo, and ends with long-held accompanying chords; the ninth is enriched by the addition of two oboes, and against their held chords, supported by continuo, we hear brief chordal strokes in the strings.

The three arias are again notably full in texture and instrumentation. The first, no. 3—essentially an alto aria with obbligato* oboe d'amore*—is filled out by accompanying strings in the form of a continuo realization, as it were, with the first violin reinforcing either the oboe or the alto part. Bach strikingly emphasizes the textual contrast between slumber and watchfulness by a change of time, livelier rhythmic movement, and freer treatment of the strings in the middle section. The two arias borrowed from Cantata 197a both had their scoring augmented. The sixth movement, which in its original form was probably scored with two transverse flutes* and obbligato cello or bassoon, is here given an additional oboe part, while its flutes are replaced by violins. The eighth movement, originally a bass aria with obbligato oboe d'amore, is rewritten for soprano and obbligato violin and enriched by two oboes d'amore, which fill out the harmony. The joyous affect* of this aria is so unspecific that the change of text proved unproblematic. In the sixth movement, on the other hand, its original character as a lullaby at the crib is clearly recognizable even in the parodied version. Both parts of the cantata end with plain four-part chorales.

Dem Gerechten muß das Licht, BWV 195

NBA I/33, p. 172 BC B14 Duration: *c.* 16 mins

1. [Chorus] SATB + SATB rip tr I–III timp fl I,II ob I,II str bc D C 6/8

'Dem Gerechten muß das Licht immer wieder aufgehen und Freude den frommen Herzen.	'For the just the Light must dawn time and again, and joy for devout hearts.
Ihr Gerechten, freuet euch des Herrn und danket ihm und preiset seine Heiligkeit.'	You just, rejoice in the Lord and thank Him and praise His Holiness.'

2. Recitativo B bc b–G C

Dem Freudenlicht gerechter Frommen	To the joyful Light of the righteous devout
Muß stets ein neuer Zuwachs kommen,	New growth must constantly come,
Der Wohl und Glück bei ihnen mehrt.	Which augments their prosperity and fortune.
Auch diesem neuen Paar,	For this new couple too,
An dem man so Gerechtigkeit	In whom we honour both justice
Als Tugend ehrt,	And virtue,
Ist heut ein Freudenlicht bereit,	A joyful Light is ready today,
Das stellet neues Wohlsein dar.	Which stands for new well-being.

O! ein erwünscht Verbinden!
So können zwei ihr Glück eins an
 dem andern finden.

Oh! what a desirable union!
Thus can two people find their happiness
 in each other.

3. Aria B ob I,II str + fl I,II bc G 2/4

Rühmet Gottes Güt und Treu,
Rühmet ihn mit reger Freude,
Preiset Gott, Verlobten beide!
 Denn eu'r heutiges Verbinden
 Läßt euch lauter Segen finden,
 Licht und Freude werden neu.

Extol God's goodness and faithfulness,
Extol Him with stirring joy,
Praise God, betrothed pair!
For your union of today
Let you find pure Blessing:
Light and Joy are renewed.

4. Recitativo S fl I,II ob d'am I,II bc e–D C

Wohlan, so knüpfet denn ein Band,
Das so viel Wohlsein prophezeihet.
Das Priesters Hand
Wird jetzt den Segen
Auf euren Ehestand,
Auf eure Scheitel legen.
Und wenn des Segens Kraft hinfort
 an euch gedeihet,
So rühmt des Höchsten Vaterhand.

Er knüpfte selbst eu'r Liebesband
Und ließ das, was er angefangen,
Auch ein erwünschtes End
 erlangen.

Well then, tie a bond
That prophesies so much well-being.
The priest's hand
Will now lay the blessing
Upon your matrimony,
Upon the crown of your head.
And when the blessing's power prospers
 in you henceforth,
Praise the fatherly hand of the Most
 High.
He Himself tied your bond of love
And lets that which He began
Also achieve its desired end.

5. Chorus [Scoring as in no. 1] D 3/4

Wir kommen, deine Heiligkeit,
Unendlich großer Gott, zu preisen.
 Der Anfang rührt von deinen
 Händen,
 Durch Allmacht kannst du es
 vollenden
 Und deinen Segen kräftig weisen.

We come to praise Your Holiness,
Everlastingly great God.
 This beginning arises from Your hands:
 Through omnipotence You can
 complete it
 And powerfully show Your blessing.

Post copulationem — *After the wedding*

6. Choral SATB + SATB rip hn II timp fl I,II bc (+ hn I ob I,II str) G C

Nun danket all und bringet Ehr,
Ihr Menschen in der Welt,
Dem, dessen Lob der Engel Heer
Im Himmel stets vermeldt.

Now all give thanks and pay honour,
You people of the world,
To Him whose praise the angelic host
Ever proclaims in heaven.

The history of this cantata is complicated and has proved difficult to unravel. Light has recently been shed on it, however, by the discovery of a printed text of 1736.[5] The lost earlier version, scored with recorders rather than transverse

[5] Reported by Peter Wollny in 'Neue Bach-Funde', *BJ* 1997, 7–50; he gives a facsimile of the text on pp. 29–32. The following reconstruction of the work's history follows Wollny.

flutes,* perhaps dates from the period 1727–32 (according to the likely date of the surviving wrapper for the performing parts). On 3 January 1736, it was performed at a wedding ceremony in Ohrdruf by the cantor and organist there, Bach's nephews Johann Christoph and Johann Bernhard Bach. The work they performed was in eight movements, divided into two parts as follows:

Vor der Copulation [before the wedding]

1. [TUTTI] Dem Gerechten muß das Licht
2. RECITATIVO Des Höchsten unerforschtes Führen
3. ARIA Habe deine Lust am Herrn
4. RECITATIVO So tretet nun, verbundne Zwei, zusammen
5. TUTTI Wir kommen, deine Heiligkeit, unendlich großer Gott, zu preisen

Nach der Copulation [after the wedding]

6. ARIA O heilige Stätte
7. RECITATIVO Wohlan! Es sei dies ausgesprochne Wort
8. TUTTI Gesegnet Paar! Dein Herrscher zeiget sich

Thus only the choruses* (nos. 1 and 5) correspond with their equivalents in the later, surviving version of Cantata 195. The music of all the other movements is lost, and all we know of it is that nos. 2–4 were for bass, tenor, and alto respectively and that the finale, no. 8, was related by parody* to the finale of another wedding cantata, BWV 34a of 1726.[6] Around 1742 Bach revived the work with the addition of four vocal (SATB) ripieno parts.

Finally, in the late 1740s Bach undertook a radical revision of the work. Nos. 2–4 were replaced by the movements whose texts are given in full above; the recitatives were newly composed; and the aria was parodied from elsewhere (perhaps from BWV Anh. I 13, no. 3, of 1738). According to a page of text, written around 1747/8 by Bach's son Johann Christoph Friedrich and enclosed in the surviving score, Bach originally intended to adopt a similar procedure in nos. 6–8. The recitative would have been composed afresh and the aria and chorus parodied from the homage cantata BWV 30a (nos. 5 and 1=13 respectively), so that Part II would have taken the form:

Post Copulationem [after the wedding]

6. ARIA Auf und rühmt des Höchsten Güte
7. RECITATIVO Hochedles Paar, du bist nunmehr verbunden
8. TUTTI Höchster schenke diesem Paar

It is uncertain, however, whether this intention was ever carried out. At any rate, in the score and parts of the final version, which dates from around 1748/9,

[6] See P. Wollny, 'Nachbemerkung zu "Neue Bach-Funde" (*BJ* 1997, S. 7–50)', *BJ* 1998, 167–9.

nos. 6–8 are replaced by a single plain four-part chorale (no. 6 of the version we know today).

Once we are familiar with the tendency of baroque poets to make allusions to the personal attributes of the bridal couple in their wedding carmina—a habit we have already observed in the text *Sein Segen fließt daher wie ein Strom*, BWV Anh. I 14—it requires no special acuteness to conclude that one version of this cantata was intended for the wedding of a lawyer. Not only the opening chorus, based on Psalm 97.11–12, but the statement in the following recitative that in this couple 'we honour both justice and virtue' are unmistakable pointers in this direction. The rest of the text is more generalized, praising God for the matrimonial knot here tied and imploring His future blessing upon it. It remains an open question whether the form of address 'Hochedles Paar' ('most noble pair') in the text of 1747/8—subsequently removed—points to a wedding among the nobility. According to our knowledge of the occasions on which Bach had to perform a wedding cantata (unfortunately, far from complete), it would be quite conceivable that the earlier version was performed at the wedding of Gottlob Heinrich Pipping, legal adviser and burgomaster at Naumburg, and Johanna Eleonora Schütz, daughter of a deceased pastor at the Thomaskirche, which took place on 11 September 1741. The calling of the bridegroom and the background of the bride (who was incidentally a great niece of Heinrich Schütz), would then by characterized by the allusions to 'justice' and 'virtue'.

The instrumentation of the cantata (three trumpets and drums, two flutes, two oboes, strings, and continuo) is exceptionally rich for a wedding cantata, and the choruses are 'scored' for four-part choirs of concertists* and ripienists.* The splendid opening chorus is bipartite, and each part has as its kernel a choral fugue* on one of the two psalm verses, 'Dem Gerechten muß das Licht . . .' and 'Ihr Gerechten, freuet euch . . .'. Both fugues are much interfused with non-fugal, concertante* elements—in the first, quotations of the instrumental introduction and choral insertion;* and in the second, sequential and canonic passages. Only seldom, therefore, do we form the impression of strictly linear writing.

The following recitative, no. 2, is close to arioso.* At the outset, we hear in the continuo a triplet figure, probably inspired by the word 'Freudenlicht' ('joyful Light'), which then pervades a large portion of the movement and demands recitative singing in strict time. The third movement, the only aria in the later version, shows an inclination to a popular, dance-like melodic style. The predominance of the Lombardic rhythm, or Scotch snap . is curious and not very common in Bach's works. Perhaps it should be taken to indicate a 'modernist' tendency in late Bach.

The second recitative, no. 4, 'Wohlan, so knüpfet denn ein Band', is set as *accompagnato*.* The rapid scale figures of the two flutes against the held notes of the two oboes d'amore,* which fill out the harmony, provide a background for the exhortation of the text. A largely chordal, homophonic* chorus in da capo* form, no. 5, concludes Part I, which was to be performed before the wedding. This movement again exhibits a dance-like quality and might be construed as a stylized polonaise.

In the later version, which is all that survives complete, only a plain chorale setting follows in Part II. The secondary origin of this piece is betrayed by its scoring with two horns (in place of three trumpets), of which the first reinforces the chorale melody while the second is independent. The opening verse of Paul Gerhardt's hymn *Nun danket all und bringet Ehr* (1647) is here sung to the melody *Lobt Gott, ihr Christen alle gleich*.

10

Funerals

Gottes Zeit ist die allerbeste Zeit (Actus Tragicus), BWV 106

NBA I/34, p. 3 BC B18 Duration: *c.* 23 mins

	German	English	Key	Time
1.	SONATINA rec I,II vla da g I,II bc		E♭/F[1]	C
2a.	[CHORUS] SATB rec I,II vla da g I,II bc		E♭–c/F–d	C $\frac{3}{4}$ C
	Gottes Zeit ist die allerbeste Zeit. 'In ihm leben, weben und sind wir,' solange er will. In ihm sterben wir zur rechten Zeit, wenn er will.	God's time is the very best time. 'In Him we live, move, and have our being,' as long as He wills. In Him we die at the right time, when He wills.		
2b.	T rec I,II vla da g I,II bc		c/d	C
	Ach Herr, 'lehre uns bedenken, daß wir sterben müssen, auf daß wir klug werden.'	Ah Lord, 'teach us to remember that we must die, so that we become wise.'		
2c.	B rec I + II bc		c–f/d–g	$\frac{3}{8}$
	'Bestelle dein Haus; denn du wirst sterben und nicht lebendig bleiben!'	'Put your house in order, for you shall die and not remain living!'		
2d.	SATB rec I,II vla da g I,II bc		f/g	C
	'Es ist der alte Bund:' Mensch, 'du mußt sterben!' *Sopran* 'Ja, komm, Herr Jesu!'	'It is the Old Covenant:' man, 'you must die!' *Soprano* 'Yes, come, Lord Jesus!'		
3a.	A vla da g I,II bc		b♭/c	C
	'In deine Hände befehl ich meinen Geist; du hast mich erlöset, Herr, du getreuer Gott.'	'Into Your hands I commit my spirit; you have redeemed me, Lord, You faithful God.'		
3b.	AB vla da g I,II bc		A♭–c/B♭–d	C
	Baß 'Heute wirst du mit mir im Paradies sein.' *Alt* **Mit Fried und Freud ich fahr dahin** **In Gottes Willen,**	*Bass* 'Today you shall be with Me in Paradise.' *Alto* **With peace and joy I go to that place,** **According to the Will of God;**		

[1] The first specified key refers to *Chorton** or 'choir pitch', the second to *Kammerton* or 'chamber pitch'.

Getrost ist mir mein Herz und Sinn,
Sanft und stille.
Wie Gott mir verheißen hat:
Der Tod ist mein Schlaf worden.

My heart and mind are established,
Meek and quiet.
As God has promised me:
Death has become my sleep.

4. [Chorale] SATB rec I,II vla da g I,II bc E♭/F c

Glorie, Lob, Ehr und Herrlichkeit
Sei dir, Gott Vater und Sohn bereit',
Dem Heilgen Geist mit Namen!
Die göttlich Kraft
Macht uns sieghaft
Durch Jesum Christum, amen.

Glory, praise, honour, and majesty
Be given to You, God the Father and Son
And to the Holy Spirit by name!
May the power of God
Make us victorious
Through Jesus Christ. Amen.

This cantata, known as the *Actus Tragicus*, may have originated during Bach's Mühlhausen period, shortly after Cantata 131 but probably still within the year 1707. We do not know what funeral service occasioned its composition. Perhaps it was intended as a memorial to Bach's uncle Tobias Lämmerhirt of Erfurt, who died on 10 August 1707, leaving fifty Gulden to the young Mühlhausen organist.[2] Despite its close temporal proximity to Cantata 131, which in form and stylistic attributes is everywhere in evidence, the *Actus Tragicus* is a work of genius such as even great masters seldom achieve. Here, in one stroke, the twenty-two-year-old composer left all his contemporaries far behind him. Of course, it could be argued that in later years Bach's art became a great deal more mature, but it hardly grew more profound. The *Actus Tragicus* belongs to the great musical literature of the world.

In form, the work belongs to the old type of church cantata. The text is made up largely of biblical words and hymns; only in no. 2a are a few free words inserted as connecting links. By contrast with Cantata 131, the text is assembled from a very diverse selection of biblical passages and hymns, as follows:

Second movement

a Acts 17.28
b Psalm 90.12
c Isaiah 38.1
d Ecclesiasticus 14.17 and Revelation 22.20
Instrumental quotation of the hymn *Ich hab mein Sach Gott heimgestellt* (Johann Leon, 1582/9)

[2] The occasion suggested by Hermann Schmalfuß ('J. S. Bachs "Actus tragicus" (BWV 106): Ein Beitrag zu seiner Entstehungsgeschichte', *BJ* 1970, 36–43)—the burial of Dorothea Susanna Tilesius (née Eilmar) on 3 June 1708—is in our view too late in the light of the cantata's stylistic attributes. J. Rifkin (recording notes, *L'Oiseau-Lyre* 417 323–2, New York, 1985) suggests the funeral of Johann Christian Hofferock, a prominent Mühlhausen citizen who died on 25 October 1707.

Third movement

a Psalm 31.5

b Luke 23.43 and verse 1 of the hymn *Mit Fried und Freud ich fahr dahin* (Martin Luther, 1524)

Fourth movement

a Verse 7 of the hymn *In dich hab ich gehoffet, Herr* (Adam Reusner, 1533)

The contents fall into two distinct parts: death under the Law and under the Gospel.* The first part touches on the theme of death, proceeding from general reflections on God and temporality. With increasing urgency it warns of the inevitability of death, culminating in the lapidary statement 'It is the Old Covenant: man, you must die'. Here the turning-point is reached: under the Gospel, death has lost its sting and brings the desired union with Jesus, which man can await with confidence. The work ends with praise of the Holy Trinity.

The instrumentation of this cantata is unique in Bach's works: a 'stille Musik' for two recorders, two violas da gamba, and continuo, particularly well suited to a funeral service. The musical structure of the work is related to the motet.* Brief passages that vary in scoring and thematic substance are grouped one after another in order to make the musical interpretation of the sung text as striking and intense as possible. Together, however, these individual sections form a symmetrical overall structure, and herein lies the forward-looking aspect of the work's conception:

1	2a	2b	2c	2d	3a	3b	4
Sonatina	Chorus	Solo	Solo	Chorus + solo + chorale	Solo	Solo + chorale	Chorale + fugue
E♭	E♭–c	c	c–f	f	b♭	A♭–c	E♭
F	F–d	d	d–g	g	c	B♭–d	F

The movement that brings the turning-point in content, no. 2d, a direct confrontation between the Law and the Gospel, is at once the centre and the musical high point of the work. Around it are grouped two pairs of solos, which are in turn framed by two choruses,* one introduced by an instrumental piece, the Sonatina, and the other prefacing a fugue on the last line of the chorale. Chorales in this cantata are assigned only to the second part, which deals with the Gospel. The sequence of keys is also ordered symmetrically around a central axis, but here the central point, B flat Minor / C Minor, is reached one movement later, in the alto solo 'In deine Hände', no. 3a.

The work is introduced by a preludial 'Sonatina', in which two obbligato* recorders play together, mostly in unison but with brief echo-dynamic and heterophonic* shadings, over a sonorous background of gambas and continuo. The entire piece is motivically imprinted and does not consolidate into themes. The chorus 'Gottes Zeit' is a tripartite motet as follows:

1. Homophonic* choral passage, partly with instrumental support
2. Fugato ('allegro') with part-doubling and part-independent instruments
3. Homophonic choral passage ('adagio assai') with the instruments largely *colla parte**

The sequence of sections is determined by the chief themes of the text: God's time–life–death. At the same time, individual words or phrases are strikingly illustrated by musical means: for example, 'solange [er will]' ('as long as He wills') by a held note. The first of the two solos that follow, for tenor, is a free chaconne, whereas the second, for bass accompanied only by two unison recorders and continuo, with its lively concertante* figuration and its extended vocal coloratura* on 'lebendig' ('living'), most approximates to the modern aria, except that it lacks a thematically functional ritornello.

In the central movement, several layers are piled up on top of each other. Here, new life is breathed into the old art of the polychoral motet on several texts, an art that had long ago sunk to the level of a humble craft, a patent formula by which worthy Thuringian village cantors attempted to unite dictum and chorale in their funeral motets. In the *Actus Tragicus*, however, it seems as if the genre reveals its true meaning and significance for the first time, since it arises of necessity from the succession of ideas in the text. First, the three lower voices sing a choral fugue to the words 'Es ist der alte Bund: Mensch, du mußt sterben' ('It is the Old Covenant: man, you must die'). This breaks off after two expositions,* and then the soprano, accompanied only by continuo, replies 'Ja, komm, Herr Jesu!' ('Yes, come, Lord Jesus!'). After five bars, the instruments enter with a three-part arrangement of the chorale melody *Ich hab mein Sach Gott heimgestellt*, of which at first only lines 1 and 2 are played. Thereafter, the sequence of choral fugue–soprano–chorale is repeated three times, so that the movement as a whole is made up of a fourfold sequence of its three component parts. In the process, however, a series of significant alterations are made. The individual stages become progressively shorter—twenty-five, twelve, six and twelve (including coda) bars—so that we seem to witness a gradual compression and a resulting increase in intensity. In the second stage, the soprano already enters during the choral fugue; and in the fourth, the order of entries of soprano and chorale is reversed, with the result that the chorale is combined with the choral fugue and the soprano ends the movement alone. In addition, the themes undergo a gradual but distinctive transformation. The fugue subject itself, which belongs to a type widespread in Bach's time—familiar from the *Musical Offering* and the *Art of Fugue* (a range of a fifth extended by a semitone above and below)—remains unaltered:

But its significance diminishes: the first stage contains six entries and the second stage two; the subject does not occur at all in the third stage, and in the fourth it enters only twice. At the same time, the countersubject gains increasing significance, though it is gradually modified in the process. In the first two stages, it is heard thus:

In the third, it takes the form:

And in the fourth, it turns into:

Finally, in the coda we hear the following version:

The contour of the countersubject is thus increasingly assimilated to the opening melody of the soprano:

It may be assumed that the bracketed portion of this melody was conceived as a quotation of the first line of the widely known chorale *Herzlich tut mich verlangen nach einem selgen End* ('Heartily do I long for a blessed end'), whose first verse ends with the words 'O Jesu, komm nur bald!' ('O Jesus, do come soon!'). Still another feature is worth pointing out: the eighteen verses of the chorale *Ich hab mein Sach Gott heimgestellt*, whose melody is quoted by the instruments, strikingly correspond with the succession of ideas in the text, as the following comparison of the most significant cases demonstrates:

Chorale verse	*Cantata text*
2. Mein Zeit und Stund ist, wann Gott will	In ihm sterben wir zur rechten Zeit, wenn er will
2. My time and hour is when God wills	In Him we die at the right time, when He wills
8. Ach Herr, lehr uns bedenken wohl, daß wir sind sterblich allzumal	Ach Herr, lehre uns bedenken, daß wir sterben müssen
8. Ah Lord, teach us to remember that we are altogether mortal	Ah Lord, teach us to remember that we must die
10. Wenn mein Gott will, so will ich mit hinfahrn in Fried	Mit Fried und Freud ich fahr dahin In Gottes Willen
10. When my God wills, then I shall go there in peace	With peace and joy I go to that place, according to the Will of God
16. Mein' lieben Gott von Angesicht werd ich anschaun, dran zweifl ich nicht,	Heute wirst du mit mir im Paradies sein
In ewger Freud und Seligkeit, Die mir bereit'; Ihm sei Lob, Preis in Ewigkeit.	Glorie, Lob, Ehr und Herrlichkeit Sei dir, Gott Vater und Sohn bereit'.
16. My dear God face to face shall I see, that I do not doubt,	Today you shall be with Me in Paradise
In the eternal joy and salvation	Glory, praise, honour and majesty be
Prepared for me; To Him be praise and glory in eternity.	Prepared for You, God the Father and Son.

The alto solo 'In deine Hände', no. 3a, is in its declamatory melodic style indebted to the seventeenth-century sacred concerto*, while its quasi-ostinato bass links it with the chaconne. It is followed immediately by the bass solo 'Heute wirst du mit mir im Paradies sein', no. 3b, also accompanied by the continuo, which now abandons its ostinato* figuration in favour of an imitative* relationship with the voice. Here, the bass voice is to be understood as the *vox Christi*, and the imitation between bass and continuo as a symbol of the imitation of Christ ('you shall be with Me'). While the bass is still singing, the alto enters again and, accompanied by the gambas, sings the chorale *Mit Fried und Freud ich fahr dahin* ('With peace and joy I go to that place') as the response of man to Jesus's promise. Here, Bach is careful that characterful turns of phrase such as 'sanft und stille' ('meek and quiet') or 'der Tod ist mein Schlaf worden' ('death has become my sleep') are marked *piano*.

The concluding chorale begins with the statement of each line in turn in a plain four-part choral setting, introduced by a brief instrumental prelude and divided by inter-line episodes, which mostly form an echo-like but embellished repeat of the line ending (on recorders). The last line, however, is expanded to form an 'allegro' fugue; and after a jubilant final climax, with the augmented subject in the soprano, the cantata—like BWV 71—dies away with an echo effect on the recorders.

If we attempt once more to become aware of the special qualities of this work, we are particularly struck by the overriding significance of the central fugue. An analogy might be drawn with the architecture of a baroque castle or church—such as the Frauenkirche in Dresden. Such a structure is not often found in Bach's later works; and where it does occur—perhaps in the early cantatas BWV 131 and 4, later in the *Magnificat* and the motet* *Jesu, meine Freude*—we never find anything like such a concentrated use of the means at Bach's disposal as in the *Actus Tragicus*. Here, the Law–Gospel* antithesis of the text is enhanced by simultaneous contrast and made prominent musically as follows:

	Law	*Gospel*
Texture:	in several parts (choral)	monodic (solo)
Style:	strict (fugue)	free (arioso*)
Pitch:	low (a symbol of God's relative distance)	high (a symbol of God's relative closeness)
Dynamics:	unmarked (= *forte*)	differentiated (echo effects, *pianissimo* ending)
Rhythm:	uniform motion, calm	differentiated, lively

To these resources the chorale is added as a symbol of the Church founded by Christ. It belongs on the side of the Gospel (see above), but against the relationship of the individual Christian to God it sets the supra-individual notion of the

Christian community. This further antithesis is clarified musically by means of the contrasting pairs monody*/polyphonic* texture, vocal/instrumental writing, and differentiated/uniform movement.

The *Actus Tragicus* is unique of its kind. A few years after its composition, Bach fundamentally altered the types of movement within his cantatas. Among the works created using the compositional means of his early period, however, this cantata far exceeds the others both in depth of expression and in spiritual penetration.

Ich lasse dich nicht, du segnest mich denn, BWV 157

NBA I/34, p. 43 BC B20 (= A170) Duration: *c.* 21 mins

1.	Duetto TB fl ob d'am vln I solo bc	b c
	'Ich lasse dich nicht, du segnest mich denn!'	'I will not let You go unless You bless me!'
2.	Aria T ob d'am solo bc	f♯ $\frac{3}{8}$
	Ich halte meinen Jesum feste,	I hold my Jesus firmly,
	Ich laß ihn nun und ewig nicht.	I do not let Him go now or ever.
	Er ist allein mein Aufenthalt,	He alone is my abode,
	Drum faßt mein Glaube mit Gewalt	Therefore my faith is fastened with might
	Sein segenreiches Angesicht;	Upon His Countenance, rich in blessing;
	Denn dieser Trost ist doch der beste.	For this consolation is indeed the best.
	Ich halte meinen Jesum feste.	I hold my Jesus firmly.
3.	Recitativo T str bc	A–D c
	Mein lieber Jesu du,	My dear Jesus,
	Wenn ich Verdruß und Kummer leide,	When I suffer vexation and affliction,
	So bist du meine Freude,	Then You are my joy,
	In Unruh meine Ruh	In unrest my rest
	Und in der Angst mein sanftes Bette;	And in fear my soft bed;
	Die falsche Welt ist nicht getreu:	The false world is not faithful:
	Der Himmel muß veralten,	Heaven must wax old,
	Die Lust der Welt vergeht wie Spreu;	The world's pleasure passes away like chaff;
	Wenn ich dich nicht, mein Jesu, hätte,	If I did not have You, my Jesus,
	An wen sollt ich mich sonsten halten?	To whom should I otherwise hold?
	Drum laß ich nimmermehr von dir,	Therefore I part from You nevermore
	Dein Segen bleibe denn bei mir.	Unless Your Blessing remains with me.
4.	Aria [+ Recitativo] B fl vln I solo bc	D c
	Ja, ja, ich halte Jesum feste,	Yes, yes, I hold Jesus firmly,
	So geh ich auch zum Himmel ein,	Then I also enter into heaven,
	Wo Gott und seines Lammes Gäste	Where God and His Lamb's guests
	In Kronen zu der Hochzeit sein.	Are in crowns at the Wedding.
	Da laß ich nicht, mein Heil, von dir,	There I shall not part from You, my Salvation,

Da bleibt dein Segen auch bei mir.	There too Your Blessing remains with me.
Ei, wie vergnügt Ist mir mein Sterbekasten, Weil Jesus mir in Armen liegt! So kann mein Geist recht freudig rasten! Ja, ja, ich halte Jesum feste, So geh ich auch zum Himmel ein.	Ah, how delightful To me is my coffin, For Jesus will lie in my arms! Then my spirit can rest most joyfully! Yes, yes, I hold Jesus firmly, Then I also enter into heaven.
O schöner Ort! Komm, sanfter Tod, und führ mich fort!	O lovely place! Come, gentle death, and lead me forth!
Wo Gott und seines Lammes Gäste In Kronen zu der Hochzeit sein.	Where God and His Lamb's guests Are in crowns at the Wedding.
Ich bin erfreut, Das Elend dieser Zeit Noch von mir heute abzulegen; Denn Jesus wartet mein im Himmel mit dem Segen.	I am delighted To put off the misery of this time This very day; For Jesus awaits me in heaven with His Blessing.
Da laß ich nicht, mein Heil, von dir, Da bleibt dein Segen auch bei mir.	There I shall not part from You, my Salvation, There too Your Blessing remains with me.

5. CHORAL SATB bc (+ instrs) D c

Meinen Jesum laß ich nicht, **Geh ihm ewig an der Seiten;** **Christus läßt mich für und für** **Zu dem Lebensbächlein leiten.** **Selig, wer mit mir so spricht:** **Meinen Jesum laß ich nicht.**	**I will not let go of my Jesus,** **I will go ever at His side;** **Christ lets me for ever and ever** **Be led to the Stream of Life.** **Blessed is he who says with me:** **I will not let go of my Jesus.**

On 31 October 1726, Johann Christoph von Ponickau, chamberlain, court counsellor and appeal judge, died at the age of seventy-five and a few days later was buried in the family vault at the church of Pomßen. He had been a personality of high repute and in many ways Saxony had been indebted to him. We do not know whether he had any direct links with Bach. In Picander's collection of verse, however, we find an extended funeral ode* on his death, followed immediately by the text of the cantata *Ich lasse dich nicht, du segnest mich denn*. This work was performed at a solemn memorial service at Pomßen Church on 6 February 1727. According to the commemoration print of the sermon (though not in Picander), this funeral music had a second part, performed 'after the sermon', namely the cantata *Liebster Gott, vergißt du mich*, BWV Anh. I 209. That work had been written for the Seventh Sunday after Trinity to a text from Georg Christian Lehms's collection *Gottgefälliges Kirchen-Opffer*, which required only

slight alterations for the funeral service.[3] Evidently, then, Bach reused an existing setting of this Lehms text, presumably one that he had composed himself.

Only the setting of Picander's text ('before the sermon') survives, however, and even then only in later manuscript copies which specify the Feast of the Purification as the occasion of the work. It seems that Bach revived it, at some time after it had fulfilled its original purpose, as an independent cantata for this Marian feast. The change of occasion was unproblematic, for the Purification Gospel* reading gives an account of the aged Simeon, whose words 'Lord, now let Your servant depart in peace . . . for my eyes have seen Your Salvation' (the Nunc dimittis*) have since come to be regarded as a paradigm of a Christian approach to death. A piece of funeral music whose subject was the death of one who had set his sights on Jesus could thus at any time be understood and performed as an interpretation of the Purification Gospel.

The freely versified text is prefaced (no. 1) by a dictum from Genesis 32.26—the words of Jacob to the angel who confronted him. In the text that follows, these words are understood and interpreted as being addressed to Jesus. The aria and recitative (nos. 2 and 3) commend firm attachment to Jesus as the best form of consolation in distress and temptation. The following aria, no. 4, then turns our attention to death: 'Then I also enter into heaven'. Here again, blessing is said to rest upon the person who will not part from Jesus. Integrated into this aria is a recitative, between whose lines the aria text is repeated one sentence at a time. The work concludes with the last verse of the hymn *Meinen Jesum laß ich nicht* by Christian Keymann (1658). Since the original sources are lost, it is no longer possible to establish whether the different wording of the opening line was intentional or merely a copying error (it should read 'Jesum laß ich nicht von mir').

Bach's setting may have taken account of local performance conditions, since the four voices come together only in the plain concluding chorale and the string orchestra is assigned an exclusively accompanying role, so that the main burden rests upon the three solo instruments and two solo singers. It appears to be no drawback, however, that on this occasion Bach was unable to make use of his full Sunday cantata orchestra. For instead he chose the select combination of transverse flute,* oboe d'amore* and solo violin,[4] a chamber-music type of ensemble rarely used outside his early cantatas (for example, BWV 152). The present cantata thus offers a happy combination of aural charm and compositional mastery.

[3] See H.-J. Schulze, 'Bemerkungen zu einigen Kantatentexten J. S. Bachs', *BJ* 1959, 168–70, and K. Hofmann, 'Bachs Kantate "Ich lasse dich nicht, du segnest mich denn" BWV 157: Überlegungen zu Entstehung, Bestimmung und originaler Werkgestalt', *BJ* 1982, 51–80.

[4] According to Klaus Hofmann, 'Bachs Kantate "Ich lasse dich nicht" ', the original version would have been scored with viola d'amore in place of solo violin and might have lacked a string ensemble, except perhaps in the concluding chorale. In no. 3 the first violin part would have been played by transverse flute and/or oboe d'amore and the second by viola d'amore. There was probably no viola part.

The introductory movement requires the three solo instruments just mentioned plus continuo. Since it is vocally a duet, the words 'I will not let You go unless You bless me!' are not conceived realistically. Moreover, the image of Jacob wrestling with the angel hardly seems to have served as the inspiration for Bach's setting, for what the music describes is no combat but rather the beseeching gesture of prayer. With typical baroque vividness, the following aria, no. 2, depicts firm attachment to Jesus in long-held notes and a spirited taking hold of faith in vigorous rising demisemiquaver figures. The relatively low pitch of the obbligato* oboe d'amore expands the cantata's range of sound after the generally higher pitch of the instrumental ensemble in the opening duet.

An accompanied recitative, no. 3, is followed by another aria, no. 4, whose obbligato instruments are now transverse flute and solo violin. A particularly elaborate form arises from the aforementioned incorporation of recitative passages. During the first half of the aria, the entire text is delivered one section at a time. The second half then brings a much abridged reprise of the opening section, three times interrupted by recitative insertions, which are accompanied by continuo only (first and third times) or by flute, violin, and continuo (second time). The vigorous intervallic leaps of the head-motive and the chosen voice type, bass, create the impression of joyfully secure confidence. The lively motion of the aria theme forms an effective contrast with the calm passages of recitative. It is worth noting how Bach holds together this multi-sectional aria by means of unifying motives:* each section begins in the bass voice with a melodic figure derived from the instrumental ritornello and preserved virtually unaltered. The same figure, moreover, prefaces the first section as a 'motto'* and recurs within each section. It is heard in the bass part altogether twelve times—an emblem of 'firm attachment' amidst the many-layered fabric of the movement:

A final chorale in a plain, four-part choral setting (no. 5), albeit more broken up into polyphony* than usual, ends the cantata.

Klagt, Kinder, klagt es aller Welt, BWV 244a

Funeral music for Prince Leopold of Anhalt-Cöthen
NBA I/34, Critical Report Music lost

Part I

1. Aria: Klagt, Kinder, klagt es aller Welt
2. [Recitative]: O Land! bestürztes Land

3. ARIA: Weh und Ach kränkt die Seelen tausendfach
4. [RECITATIVE]: Wie, wenn der Blitze Grausamkeit
5. ARIA: Zage nur, du treues Land
6. [RECITATIVE]: Ach ja! dein Scheiden geht uns nah
7. ARIA: Komm wieder, teurer Fürstengeist

Part II

8. [CHORUS]: 'Wir haben einen Gott, der da hilft'
9. [RECITATIVE]: Betrübter Anblick voll Erschrecken
10. ARIA: Erhalte mich, Gott, in der Hälfte meiner Tage
11. [RECITATIVE]: Jedoch der schwache Mensche zittert nur
12. ARIA: Mit Freuden sei die Welt verlassen
13. [RECITATIVE]: Wohl also dir, du aller Fürsten Zier
14. [CHORUS = reprise of no. 8]

Part III

15. ARIA: Laß, Leopold, dich nicht begraben
16. [RECITATIVE]: Wie konnt es möglich sein
17. ARIA: Wird auch gleich nach tausend Zähren
18. [RECITATIVE]: Und, Herr, das ist die Spezerei
19. ARIA à 2 CHÖREN: Geh, Leopold, zu deiner Ruh

Part IV

20. ARIA: Bleibet nun in eurer Ruh
21. [RECITATIVE]: Und du, betrübtes Fürstenhaus
22. ARIA: Hemme dein gequältes Kränken
23. [RECITATIVE]: Nun scheiden wir
24. ARIA TUTTI: Die Augen sehn nach deiner Leiche

Prince Leopold of Anhalt-Cöthen died on 19 November 1728. The funeral proper, together with the commemoration sermon, did not take place until March of the following year. For this occasion, Bach, who had spent perhaps the finest time of his life as Leopold's court Capellmeister in Cöthen between 1717 and 1723, and even after his departure remained Cöthen court Capellmeister 'von Haus aus', was entrusted with the composition and performance of the funeral music. It was performed during two separate events: at the funeral proper on the night of 23–4 March 1729, and alongside the commemoration sermon on the day of 24 March. The music for both events is lost, however.[5] All that survives is a text in four parts written by Bach's Leipzig poet Picander. According to Smend, Bach's setting of this text would have been heard complete

[5] According to Smend Kö, p. 90, the score of the night-time music was identifiable in the estate of the Göttingen music scholar Johann Nicolaus Forkel. As Klaus Hofmann has correctly observed, however ('Forkel und die Köthener Trauermusik J. S. Bachs', *BJ* 1983, 115–18), Forkel confounded Bach's funeral music with some by Johann Ludwig Bach of 1724.

on the morning of 24 March, and during the previous night another piece would have been performed, of which not even the text survives. This is quite possible, though it is questionable whether Bach really had at his disposal in Cöthen the means of performing more than four sections of such onerous and demanding music in swift succession. We simply do not know.

Although the music to Picander's text is lost, we find that, in setting the arias and choruses,* Bach made use of music familiar to us from other works—the correspondence in verse structure provides perfectly clear evidence. Admittedly, we know from similar cases elsewhere that Bach occasionally changed his mind during composition and wrote a new piece instead, but, judging by experience, at most only a small portion of the textual correspondences could be affected. Comparison shows that the majority of the arias and choruses were set to music borrowed from the *St Matthew Passion*,[6] and two further choruses are parodies of movements from the *Trauer-Ode*, BWV 198. The parody* movements are listed here; the following are drawn from the *St Matthew Passion*, BWV 244:

No.	*BWV 244*
3	Buß und Reu knirscht das Sündenherz entzwei
5	Blute nur, du liebes Herz
10	Erbarme dich, mein Gott, um meiner Zähren willen
12	Aus Liebe will mein Heiland sterben
15	Komm, süßes Kreuz, so will ich sagen
17	Gerne will ich mich bequemen
19	Ich will bei meinem Jesu wachen
20	Mache dich, mein Herze, rein
22	Ich will dir mein Herze schenken
24	Wir setzen uns mit Tränen nieder

The following movements are drawn from the *Trauer-Ode*, BWV 198:

No.	*BWV 198*
1	Laß, Fürstin, laß noch einen Strahl
7	Doch Königin, du stirbest nicht

Was ist, das wir Leben nennen (not in BWV)

This large two-part cantata was written as funeral music for Prince Johann Ernst of Saxe-Weimar and performed at a remembrance service on 2 April 1716. The music, which may well have been by Bach, is lost.[7]

[6] According to Smend Kö and others. I remain unconvinced by the converse hypothesis (D. Gojowy, *BJ* 1965, etc.) that the funeral music was the original and the *St Matthew Passion* the parody.*

[7] See A. Glöckner, 'Zur Chronologie der Weimarer Kantaten J. S. Bachs', *BJ* 1985, 159–64.

Schließt die Gruft! ihr Trauerglocken, BWV Anh. I 16
Mein Gott, nimm die gerechte Seele, BWV Anh. I 17

The music of neither of these two funeral cantatas is extant. In the first case, Bach's authorship is only conjectured, and in the second case too there is no definite proof of authenticity.

II

Various occasions

The various works listed under this collective heading will first be subdivided into separate groups.

Several cantatas owe their origin to specific occasions that do not belong under any of the previous headings:

Church cantata for the birthday of Prince Leopold of Anhalt-Cöthen:
Lobet den Herrn, alle seine Heerscharen, BWV Anh. I 5.
For 10 December 1718; text by Hunold.

Graduation cantata:
Siehe, der Hüter Israel, BWV Anh. I 15.
Date unknown. Reinmar Emans has conjectured that movements from this lost cantata might survive in the Sinfonia BWV 1045 and in the opening chorus* and bass aria (no. 5) of Cantata 104, *Du Hirte Israel, höre*.[1]

Three cantatas for the bicentenary of the Augsburg Confession:
Singet dem Herrn ein neues Lied, BWV 190a.
For 25 June 1730; text by Picander.
Gott, man lobet dich in der Stille, BWV 120b.
For 26 June 1730; text by Picander.
Wünschet Jerusalem Glück, BWV Anh. I 4a.
For 27 June 1730; text by Picander.

The music of all the cantatas listed above is lost, and only in the case of BWV 190a and 120b can it be reconstructed in part from extant works related by parody,* BWV 190 and 120.

In the following group of cantatas, the occasion for which they were written is not clear from the surviving source material. Consequently, we are unable to say with certainty whether Bach intended them for any suitable purpose or whether their occasion is simply unknown due to unfavourable transmission. The works concerned, all discussed below, are:

[1] See R. Emans, 'Überlegungen zur Genese der Kantate *Du Hirte Israel, höre* (BWV 104)', in K. Beißwenger et al., eds, *Acht kleine Präludien und Studien über Bach* (Wiesbaden, 1992), 44–50.

Nach dir, Herr, verlanget mich, BWV 150
Aus der Tiefen rufe ich, Herr, zu dir, BWV 131
Der Herr denket an uns, BWV 196
Nun danket alle Gott, BWV 192
Sei Lob und Ehr dem höchsten Gut, BWV 117
In allen meinen Taten, BWV 97
Was Gott tut, das ist wohlgetan, BWV 100
[Text unknown], BWV 1045 (only a fragment of the introductory sinfonia is extant)

Meine Seele soll Gott loben, BWV 223 (Mühlhausen, 1707–8?), mentioned by Spitta,[2] is lost and therefore was also for an unknown occasion.

Finally, in the case of two cantatas for a definite occasion, Bach stated that they could be used 'in ogni tempo'—that is, at any time during the church year. These works, discussed above under the Sunday on which they were performed, are:

Ich hatte viel Bekümmernis, BWV 21, for the Third Sunday after Trinity
Jauchzet Gott in allen Landen, BWV 51, for the Fifteenth Sunday after Trinity

Nach dir, Herr, verlanget mich, BWV 150

NBA I/41, p. 3 BC B24 Duration: *c.* 17 mins

1. Sinfonia vln I,II bsn bc b/d[3] c
2. Coro SATB vln I,II bsn bc b/d c

'Nach dir, Herr, verlanget mich. Mein Gott, ich hoffe auf dich. Laß mich nicht zuschanden werden, daß sich meine Feinde nicht freuen über mich.'	'For You, Lord, do I long. My God, I place my hopes in You. Let me not be ashamed, so that my enemies may not triumph over me.'

3. Aria S vln I + II bc b/d c

Doch bin und bleibe ich vergnügt,	Yet I am and remain cheerful,
Obgleich hier zeitlich toben	Although here for the moment
Kreuz, Sturm und andre Proben,	Cross, storm, and other trials rage,
Tod, Höll und was sich fügt.	Death, hell, and whatever else happens.
Ob Unfall schlägt den treuen Knecht,	Though disaster strikes the faithful servant,
Recht ist und bleibet ewig Recht.	Justice is and ever remains justice.

4. Tutti [Scoring as in no. 2] b/d c

'Leite mich in deiner Wahrheit und lehre mich; denn du bist der Gott, der mir hilft, täglich harre ich dein.'	'Lead me in Your Truth and teach me; for You are the God who saves me; daily I await You.'

[2] Spitta I, 339 f.; Eng. version I, 343 f.
[3] The first specified key refers to *Chorton** or 'choir pitch', the second to *Kammerton* or 'chamber pitch'.

5. Aria [Terzetto] ATB bsn bc — D/F $\frac{3}{4}$

Zedern müssen von den Winden	Cedars must from the winds
Oft viel Ungemach empfinden,	Often undergo much hardship;
Oftmals werden sie verkehrt.	They often become uprooted.
Rat und Tat auf Gott gestellet,	Counsel and work based on God
Achtet nicht, was widerbellet,	Disregard whatever howls against them,
Denn sein Wort ganz anders lehrt.	For His Word teaches something quite different.

6. Coro [Scoring as in no.2] — D–b/F–d $\frac{6}{8}$

'Meine Augen sehen stets zu dem Herrn; denn er wird meinen Fuß aus dem Netze ziehen.'	'My eyes always look to the Lord; for He shall pluck my foot out of the net.'

7. Tutti Ciacona [Scoring as in no. 2] — b/d $\frac{3}{2}$

Meine Tage in dem Leide	My days in suffering
Endet Gott dennoch zur Freude.	God nonetheless ends in joy.
Christen auf den Dornenwegen	Christians on their thorny paths
Führen Himmels Kraft und Segen.	Are escorted by heaven's power and blessing.
Bleibet Gott mein treuer Schutz,	If God remains my faithful defence,
Achte ich nicht Menschentrutz.	I may disregard human spite.
Christus, der uns steht zur Seiten,	Christ, who remains at our side,
Hilft mir täglich sieghaft streiten.	Daily helps me to fight victoriously.

This work, which is transmitted only in secondary sources, has had to endure much criticism and many doubts over its authenticity, though there are no convincing grounds for such doubts beyond a certain weakness of invention and occasional technical errors. The style is largely what might be expected of one of Bach's early cantatas,[4] and even the third-transposition of the bassoon part (the only woodwind instrument used) is familiar from Bach's Weimar works. We should therefore be cautious: why should Bach not have written a composition whose restrictions strike us today as uncharacteristically crude for a performance under conditions unknown to us? In recent years, it has been suggested that the work might be Bach's earliest surviving cantata of all, dating back to his Arnstadt period (1703–7).[5]

The instrumental ensemble consists only of two violins and continuo together with a bassoon, which partly reinforces the continuo and is partly independent. Of the four voices, only the soprano is employed as a soloist; the other three combine to form a terzetto in the fifth movement; it is likely that the artistic capabilities of the singers Bach had available for these parts were limited. The text is made up of biblical words and free verse (there are no chorales). The

[4] Details are given in Dürr St 2, 195–9.

[5] See A. Glöckner, 'Zur Echtheit und Datierung der Kantate BWV 150 "Nach dir, Herr, verlanget mich" ', *BJ* 1988, 195–203.

biblical words are throughout drawn from Psalm 25: the second movement is based on verses 1–2, the fourth on verse 5, and the sixth on verse 15. The other movements contain rhyming verse of varying metrical structure. The content shows man in peril but armed by trust in God, who will bring deliverance. The finale points to Christ, if only by allusion, as the ground of our hope for salvation.

The introductory instrumental prelude is a short, independent piece that nonetheless serves as an exposition* of the themes of the second movement. This chorus* displays the motet-like articulation in small units that we find elsewhere in Bach's early cantata choruses: imitative* passages alternate with homophonic* block chords. The chromatic* descent of the opening theme ('Nach dir, Herr . . .') is taken up once more in the fugally treated closing theme ('daß sich meine Feinde nicht freuen . . .'), which creates a form of rounding-off. The third movement is a brief, loosely constructed aria with obbligato* unison violins. The faint traces of concertante* treatment of the opening theme recede in favour of a simple succession of text-engendered melodic phrases. Only at the end is reference made once more to the opening theme.

The fourth movement introduces a succession of choral passages articulated in small units, of varying tempo and metre, as in the second movement but without its formal rounding-off. The opening words 'Leite mich . . .' ('Lead me . . .') suggested to the composer a form of pictorial representation: a scale, starting in the bass, climbs bar by bar through the four voices and then through the two violin parts, rising altogether from *B* to d^3. The fifth movement is a simple song-like terzetto with semiquaver figuration in the continuo, which at the end is briefly taken over by the bassoon, perhaps in order to create the effect of dying away.

A chorus follows (no. 6) whose opening in brief choral blocks recalls the articulation in small units of the preceding choruses, nos. 2 and 4. The lively figuration of the instruments clearly depicts the foot that has fallen into the net. The second half of the movement comprises a permutation fugue* in which the instruments take a thematic role, so that the overall structure is analogous to an instrumental prelude and fugue, a phenomenon that we also encounter several times in Cantata 131 (see below). The cantata concludes with another chorus, no. 7, now in the form of a *ciacona* (chaconne) and thus again analogous to a type that originally evolved within the field of instrumental music. The theme—

—is in the course of the movement transposed into various keys (b–D–f sharp–A–E–modulating–b) and, at one point, inverted. This theme, with a slight chromatic modification, was adopted by Johannes Brahms as the basis of the passacaglia that forms the finale of his Fourth Symphony.[6]

As a whole, this cantata seems in many ways immature, and it relates to Bach's early Weimar cantatas as a sketch does to a finished product. Yet we must not overlook the fact that it exhibits the characteristic features of Bach's early compositional technique, particularly *Stimmtausch** (exchange of parts), both in block-chordal writing and in contrapuntal textures, from brief imitative passages to permutation fugue. Moreover, the chaconne as a chorus recurs in Cantata 12 of 1714, albeit in a considerably more accomplished form. If Glöckner's proposed dating (pre-1707) is accepted, the work might be considered an authentic though very early cantata—perhaps the earliest of all.

Aus der Tiefen rufe ich, Herr, zu dir, BWV 131

NBA I/34, p. 69 BC B25 Duration: *c.* 24 mins

1. SINFONIA [+ CHORUS] SATB ob bsn vln vla I,II bc — g/a[7] 3/4 C

'Aus der Tiefen rufe ich, Herr, zu dir. Herr, höre meine Stimme, laß deine Ohren merken auf die Stimme meines Flehens!'	'Out of the depths, Lord, I call to You. Lord, hear my voice; let Your ears be attentive to the voice of my supplication!'

2. [BASS SOLO + CHORALE] SB ob bc — g/a [C]

'So du willst, Herr, Sünde zurechnen, Herr, wer wird bestehen? Denn bei dir ist die Vergebung, daß man dich fürchte.'	'If You should mark iniquity, Lord, who will stand? For with You is forgiveness, that You may be feared.'
Erbarm dich mein in solcher Last,	**Have mercy on me with such a burden,**
Nimm sie aus meinem Herzen,	**Take it from my heart,**
Dieweil du sie gebüßet hast	**For You have atoned for it**
Am Holz mit Todesschmerzen,	**On the Tree with the pains of death,**
Auf daß ich nicht mit großem Weh	**So that I do not from great woe**
In meinen Sünden untergeh,	**Perish in my sins,**
Noch ewiglich verzage.	**Nor forever despair.**

3. [CHORUS Scoring as in no. 1] — E♭–g/F–a C

'Ich harre des Herrn, meine Seele harret, und ich hoffe auf sein Wort.'	'I wait for the Lord, my soul waits, and I rest my hopes on His Word.'

4. [TENOR SOLO + CHORALE] AT bc — c/d 12/8

'Meine Seele wartet auf den Herrn von einer Morgenwache bis zu der andern.'	'My soul waits for the Lord from one morning watch to the next.'
Und weil ich denn in meinem Sinn,	**And since in my mind,**

[6] See S. Ochs, *Geschehenes, Gesehenes* (Leipzig & Zurich, 1922), 299 f., and A. Glöckner, 'Eine Abschrift der Kantate BWV 150 als Quelle für Brahms' e-Moll-Sinfonie Op. 98', *BJ* 1997, 181–3.

[7] The first specified key refers to *Chorton*,* the second to *Kammerton*.

Wie ich zuvor geklaget,	**As I have lamented before,**
Auch ein betrübter Sünder bin,	**I am also a troubled sinner,**
Den sein Gewissen naget,	**My conscience gnaws,**
Und wollte gern im Blute dein	**And in Your Blood I would gladly**
Von Sünden abgewaschen sein	**Be washed away of sins**
Wie David und Manasse.	**Like David and Manasseh.**

5. [Chorus Scoring as in no. 1] g/a C

'Israel hoffe auf den Herrn; denn bei dem Herrn ist die Gnade und viel Erlösung bei ihm.	'Israel, hope in the Lord; for with the Lord there is Grace, and with Him plentiful Redemption.
Und er wird Israel erlösen aus allen seinen Sünden.'	And He shall redeem Israel from all its iniquities.'

The above order of movements gives only a rough idea of the work. For, as one of Bach's earliest surviving cantatas, it consists not of independent, self-contained movements but of various kinds of sections that run straight into each other. It thus exhibits a form which, in the seventeenth-century cantata, had been derived from the series principle of the motet.* Motet, sacred concerto,* and chorale arrangement are the genres that lie behind this composition.

At the end of the autograph we find the words 'Auff Begehren Tit: Herrn D: Georg Christ: Eilmars in die Music gebracht von Joh. Seb. Bach Org. Molhusino' ('At the request of Dr Georg Christian Eilmar set to music by Johann Sebastian Bach, Organist at Mühlhausen'). It was thus composed during Bach's period as Mühlhausen organist, 1707–8, and the detail with which the commission is recorded points to the beginning of that period, as does the style of the work. Significantly, it was commissioned not by Bach's superior at the Blasiuskirche, Superintendent Frohne, but by the pastor of the Marienkirche, with whom at a later date Bach was to form still closer personal relations. If we were to draw the conclusion that Frohne showed less interest than Eilmar in Bach's cantata performances, this would imply that the tension between Orthodoxy and Pietism that overshadowed Bach's activity in Mühlhausen[8] was also reflected in the origin of this work.

The text consists exclusively of biblical words and hymns. The framework is the complete text of Psalm 130, within which the second and fifth verses of the hymn *Herr Jesu Christ, du höchstes Gut* (Bartholomäus Ringwaldt, 1588) are inserted. The cantata thus appears to have been written for a penitential service, perhaps in connection with the disastrous fire which, shortly after Bach took up his post, destroyed large parts of the town centre and rendered many families homeless.

The overall design of the composition is symmetrical and strikingly similar to

[8] Described fully in Spitta I, 354 ff.; Eng. version I, 358 ff.

that of the *Actus Tragicus*. In both cases, the beginning, middle, and end are marked by a chorus* and connecting links are provided by a solo combined with a chorale verse. An exceptionally early date is supported by the observation that neither permutation fugue* nor da capo* form, whether strict or free, is in evidence. Instead, the design of the choruses is largely analogous to the instrumental form of prelude and fugue—no doubt particularly pertinent to the young organist Bach. The first movement thus consists of an orchestral prelude (linked motivically with the opening of the chorus) immediately followed by the entry of the choir with loosely fugal calls of 'Aus der Tiefen' ('out of the depths') in alternation with the orchestra (psalm verse 1, 'adagio'). This flows into a quick ('vivace') choral fugue, again loosely constructed, as a setting of verse 2. Here, the fugue subject, 'laß deine Ohren merken . . .', is at each entry of the exposition* introduced by homophonic* choral blocks ('Herr, höre meine Stimme'). At the end of the movement, we hear a striking portrayal of supplication ('meines Flehens') in the repeated sigh figures performed in alternation by choir and instruments.

In the middle chorus, no. 3, a setting of verse 5 of the psalm, only a brief, five-bar, prelude-like introduction, marked 'adagio' ('Ich harre des Herrn'), precedes the choral fugue 'meine Seele harret'. This fugue, again broad in tempo ('largo'), is accompanied by a lively figuration on some of the instruments—at first, oboe and violin, later occasionally viola too—while the remainder merely provide a harmonic filling. The 'prelude' of the final chorus, no. 5, a setting of psalm-verse 7, most clearly reveals its origin in the series form of the motet. Here, the various portions of text are set with constant changes of tempo, texture, and motive* (one cannot speak of 'theme'):

'Israel': 'adagio', block chords

'hoffe auf den Herrn': 'un poc' allegro', chordal and freely polyphonic,* episodes with lively figuration in oboe and violin

'denn bei dem Herrn ist die Gnade': 'adagio', homophonic, with obbligato* oboe part

'und viel Erlösung bei ihm': 'allegro', freely polyphonic, lively figuration in oboe, violin, and bassoon

This is followed by the closing fugue, 'Und er wird Israel erlösen', a setting of psalm-verse 8 that is also transmitted as an organ fugue (BWV 131a), though Bach's authorship of the transcription is extremely doubtful. In the cantata, it begins with the voices accompanied only by continuo, and then the instruments, partly independent and occasionally thematic, are gradually added.

The two solo movements belong to the type of the sacred concerto* in few parts combined with a vocally delivered *cantus firmus*.* In the second movement, a motivic and figurative accompanying oboe is added; and in the fourth, ostinato* formations in the continuo ensure motivic cohesion.

Viewed as a whole, the cantata possesses all the merits and weaknesses of an early work. Forms here still put together in a fresh and nonchalant fashion would later be more purposefully and consistently united. Nevertheless, we already sense the power of genius here, particularly in the fugal movements, which provide confirmation of Carl Philipp Emanuel Bach's observation that his father's 'own reflection alone made him, even in his youth, a pure and strong fugue writer'.

Der Herr denket an uns, BWV 196

NBA I/33, p. 3 BC B11 Duration: *c.* 14 mins

1. SINFONIA str vc bc		C ¢
2. [CHORUS] SATB str vc bc		C ¢
'Der Herr denket an uns und segnet uns. Er segnet das Haus Israel, er segnet das Haus Aaron.'	'The Lord is mindful of us and blesses us. He blesses the House of Israel, He blesses the House of Aaron.'	
3. [ARIA] S vln I + II bc		a ¢
'Er segnet, die den Herrn fürchten, beide, Kleine und Große.'	'He blesses those who fear the Lord, both small and great.'	
4. [DUETTO] TB str vc bc		C $\frac{3}{2}$
'Der Herr segne euch je mehr und mehr, euch und eure Kinder.'	'May the Lord bless you ever more and more, you and your children.'	
5. CHORUS SATB str vc bc		F–C ¢
'Ihr seid die Gesegneten des Herrn, der Himmel und Erde gemacht hat. Amen.'	'You are the blessed of the Lord, who has made heaven and earth. Amen.'	

This cantata is an early work of Bach's. In the absence of the original sources, its early origin is testified not only by the text, which lacks freely versified movements and consists only of Psalm 115.12–15 plus a concluding 'Amen', but by its musical forms: recitative is altogether absent, and the forms represented—aria, duet, and chorus—are of extreme brevity. In every other aspect of style, too, the cantata may be dated without further ado between the Mühlhausen cantatas BWV 131, 106, and 71, which may have preceded it, and the first Weimar cantatas BWV 18, 182, etc., which no doubt followed it.

Wilhelm Rust, editor of the *Bach-Gesellschaft* edition (1864), and Philipp Spitta both concluded from the text that the cantata was written for a wedding. Spitta further argued that 'the House of Aaron' and 'the blessed of the Lord' point to a minister as bridegroom (using Aaron, the first High Priest, as an emblem for the priesthood generally), and 'you and your children' to the second marriage of a widower with children.[9] Seeking historical circumstances to match, he

[9] See Spitta I; Eng. version I, 370 ff.

advanced the thesis that the work was composed for the wedding of Johann Lorenz Stauber, who a few months earlier had officiated at Bach's own wedding, and Regina Wedemann, an aunt of Bach's first wife, on 5 June 1708. Since then, this connection has persisted. Yet where a text is drawn throughout from a single psalm, as it is here, it would be most unusual to make every detail coincide exactly with the situation of the performance. Moreover, Konrad Küster has recently cast doubt on the 'wedding-cantata' theory altogether, pointing out that the text is well-suited to almost any praise or thanksgiving celebration.[10]

This brief, readily intelligible composition hardly requires elucidation, but here a few typical stylistic traits might be pointed out. At this early period, Bach did not yet employ the technique of choral insertion.* Instead, he prefaces the opening chorus* with an independent, though thematically related instrumental sinfonia. The kernel of the chorus itself is a permutation fugue,* which is preceded by brief, imitative* choral passages, whose abridged da capo* concludes the movement. The most 'modern' of the five movements is the soprano aria, no. 3, which has an obbligato* part for unison violins, and is cast in pure da capo form. Here, for the first time within Bach's extant works, we find an instance of vocal insertion:* while the soprano is singing, the violins enter with an almost complete quotation of the introductory ritornello. The dimensions of this aria are, of course, still very modest.

By contrast, the small-scale articulation of the following duet, no. 4, makes an antiquated impression. Brief string ritornellos alternate with equally brief vocal passages. The concluding chorus, no. 5, is bipartite. A series of homophonic* choral blocks, accompanied by orchestral figuration, are followed by a very loosely constructed 'Amen' fugue, which intensifies as it proceeds, only to end (typically for early Bach) *piano*. Also characteristic of the young Bach, both here and occasionally in earlier movements, are the complementary figures—  —which create the impression of continuous motion.

Nun danket alle Gott, BWV 192

NBA I/34, p. 109 BC A188 Duration: *c.* 15 mins

1. CHORUS [VERSUS 1] SATB fl I,II ob I,II str bc G $\frac{3}{4}$

Nun danket alle Gott	**Now thank the God of all**
Mit Herzen, Mund und Händen,	**With heart, mouth, and hands,**
Der große Dinge tut	**Who does great things**
An uns und allen Enden,	**For us and in all quarters,**

[10] See K. Küster, ' "Der Herr denket an uns", BWV 196: Eine frühe Bach-Kantate und ihr Kontext', *Musik und Kirche* 66 (1996), 84–96.

Der uns von Mutterleib	**Who from the womb**
Und Kindesbeinen an	**And from childhood onwards**
Unzählig viel zugut	**Has done countless things for our benefit**
Und noch jetzund getan.	**And still does now.**

2. [Aria Duetto] Versus 2 SB str + fl I + ob I bc D $\frac{2}{4}$

Der ewig reiche Gott	**May the eternally bounteous God**
Woll uns bei unserm Leben	**Grant us in our life**
Ein immer fröhlich Herz	**An ever joyful heart**
Und edlen Frieden geben	**And noble peace,**
Und uns in seiner Gnad	**And in His grace**
Erhalten fort und fort	**Preserve us perpetually,**
Und uns aus aller Not	**And from all trouble**
Erlösen hier und dort.	**Redeem us both here and there.**

3. [Chorale] Versus 3 SATB str + fl I,II + ob I,II bc G $\frac{12}{8}$

Lob, Ehr und Preis sei Gott,	**Glory, honour, and praise be to God,**
Dem Vater und dem Sohne	**To the Father and to the Son**
Und dem, der beiden gleich	**And to Him who is equal to both,**
Im hohen Himmelsthrone,	**On the high heavenly throne,**
Dem dreieinigen Gott,	**To the triune God,**
Als der ursprünglich war	**As He was in the beginning**
Und ist und bleiben wird	**And is and will remain**
Jetzund und immerdar.	**Now and evermore.**

Although we do not know the specific occasion for which this cantata was written, it may nonetheless be approximately dated with some certainty. For virtually throughout the preparation of the performing parts the same scribes participated as in Cantata 51, *Jauchzet Gott in allen Landen*, which was in all probability performed in Leipzig during the period 1729–31. We may therefore assume that *Nun danket alle Gott* was performed, and probably composed too, around the same time, most likely as a wedding cantata.[11]

Unfortunately, both the original score and the tenor part are lost, with the result that the work survives in an incomplete state. It may be reconstructed, however, to the extent that no perceptible gaps remain and so that the presumed overall impression of the work is intact, regardless of a few questionable notes.[12] The cantata is one of the shortest that Bach ever wrote, for the three verses of the hymn by Martin Rinckart (1636) are preserved unaltered and without any addition. Yet not only is the number of performers required considerable,

[11] According to Günther Stiller, *J. S. Bach und das Leipziger gottesdienstliche Leben seiner Zeit* (Berlin and Kassel, 1970), 82; Eng. trans. as *J. S. Bach and Liturgical Life in Leipzig*, ed. R. A. Leaver (St Louis, 1984), 94.

[12] A completion of the tenor part is given by R. Higuchi in NBA I/34 (1986).

but all three movements are quite spaciously designed, and an extended chorale-chorus* replaces the usual plain concluding chorale.

The opening chorale-chorus essentially follows the form that Bach employed by preference. The chorale, sung by the choir with the melody in the soprano part, is incorporated line by line within an independent orchestral texture. The orchestral music is thematically unrelated to the chorale (provided that distant similarities are not counted as conscious references). The opening instrumental theme, which pervades the whole movement and undergoes manifold developments, is invented in double counterpoint:*

From it a lively concertante* texture develops in which the various instrumental groups become prominent in alternation. The choral texture is expanded and enriched beyond its usual extent, for the two *Stollen** and the *Abgesang** (chorale-lines 1, 3, and 5) are prefaced by a large-scale, imitative* fore-structure in the three lower voice parts, which are occasionally joined by the soprano in lines 1 and 3. The theme of this imitative texture is derived from the chorale-line that follows (line 5 is a dominant transposition of lines 1 and 3); in the case of lines 1 and 3, it reads as follows (entering in the tenor, which at this point may be reliably reconstructed):

Aural recognition of this theme is, however, impeded, since (as often in Bach) it only gradually detaches itself from homophonic block chords. In line 5, the bass, tenor, and alto enter in turn with imitation of the theme, which is here slighly modified. The accompanying texture of the other chorale lines is hardly plainer and often developed thematically out of the instrumental ritornello theme (see the unison violin II and viola theme quoted above). Finally, within the concluding reprise of the orchestral ritornello, Bach inserts a chordal shout of 'Nun danket alle Gott' to mark the final cadence.

The second movement also begins with an independent instrumental ritornello (for strings, reinforced by flute I and oboe I), whose clear, periodic articulation lends the movement the character of a ritual, stylized dance. The vocal theme, no less approachable and song-like, is derived not from the ritornello but from the opening of the chorale, which is extended by one bar on 'ewig' ('eternally') for illustrative reasons:

Also related to dance is the bipartite form that Bach employed (despite the *Bar* form* of the text) and the modulatory scheme: the first half closes in the dominant A, and the return to the tonic in the second half is achieved simply by reversing the order of entries (soprano–bass in place of bass–soprano). Otherwise, the two halves of the movement are, in musical terms, virtually identical:

Text:	I (*Stollen* 1 and 2)	II (*Abgesang*)
Music:	A	A
Key:	D-A	A-D

The finale is also dance-like in character—it is a gigue, like the finale of a suite. By contrast with the first two movements, its orchestral ritornello (for strings reinforced by all the woodwind) is derived from the chorale melody:

Once again, the chorale melody itself is given in long notes in the soprano part, interrupted by instrumental episodes between the lines. The lower voice parts accompany in free polyphony* and in lively triplet rhythms.

Sei Lob und Ehr dem höchsten Gut, BWV 117

NBA I/34, p. 153 BC A187 Duration: *c.* 26 mins

1. [Versus 1 Chorale] SATB fl I,II ob I,II str bc G $\frac{6}{8}$

Sei Lob und Ehr dem höchsten Gut,	**Praise and honour be to the highest Good,**
Dem Vater aller Güte,	**To the Father of all goodness,**
Dem Gott, der alle Wunder tut,	**To God who does all wonders,**
Dem Gott, der mein Gemüte	**To God who fills my spirit**
Mit seinem reichen Trost erfüllt,	**With His abundant comfort,**
Dem Gott, der allen Jammer stillt.	**To God who calms all woe.**
Gebt unserm Gott die Ehre!	**Give honour to our God!**

2. Versus 2 Recitativo B solo bc C–G c 3/8

Es danken dir die Himmelsheer,
O Herrscher aller Thronen,
Und die auf Erden, Luft und Meer
In deinem Schatten wohnen,
Die preisen deine Schöpfersmacht,
Die alles also wohl bedacht.
Gebt unserm Gott die Ehre!

The heavenly host thank You,
O Ruler of all thrones,
And those who in earth, air, and sea
Dwell in Your shadow
Praise Your creative might,
Which has well considered all things.
Give honour to our God!

3. Versus 3 [Aria] T ob d'am I,II bc e 6/8

Was unser Gott geschaffen hat,
Das will er auch erhalten;
Darüber will er früh und spat
Mit seiner Gnade walten.
In seinem ganzen Königreich
Ist alles recht und alles gleich.
Gebt unserm Gott die Ehre!

What our God has created
He will also maintain;
Over it early and late
He will rule with His Grace.
In His entire Kingdom
All is right and all equal.
Give honour to our God!

4. Versus 4 Choraliter SATB bc (+ instrs) G c

Ich rief dem Herrn in meiner Not:
Ach Gott, vernimm mein Schreien!
Da half mein Helfer mir vom Tod
Und ließ mir Trost gedeihen.
Drum dank, ach Gott, drum dank ich dir;
Ach danket, danket Gott mit mir!
Gebt unserm Gott die Ehre!

I called to the Lord in my distress:
Ah God, heed my crying!
Then my Helper helped me from death
And let my comfort prosper.
Therefore thanks, ah God, I thank You;
Ah, thank, thank God with me!
Give honour to our God!

5. Versus 5 Recitativo A str bc D c

Der Herr ist noch und nimmer nicht
Von seinem Volk geschieden,
Er bleibet ihre Zuversicht,
Ihr Segen, Heil und Frieden;
Mit Mutterhänden leitet er
Die Seinen stetig hin und her.
Gebt unserm Gott die Ehre!

The Lord has not yet and never will
Be parted from His people;
He remains their confidence,
Their Blessing, Salvation, and Peace;
With motherly hands he leads
His own continually here and there.
Give honour to our God!

6. Versus 6 [Aria] B vln solo bc b c

Wenn Trost und Hülf ermangeln muß,
Die alle Welt erzeiget,
So kommt, so hilft der Überfluß,
Der Schöpfer selbst, und neiget
Die Vateraugen denen zu,
Die sonsten nirgend finden Ruh.
Gebt unserm Gott die Ehre!

When the comfort and help must be lacking
That the whole world shows,
Then Abundance comes and helps,
The Creator Himself, and inclines
His fatherly eyes towards those
Who otherwise nowhere find rest.
Give honour to our God!

7. Versus 7 [Aria] A fl str bc D 3/4

Ich will dich all mein Leben lang,
O Gott, von nun an ehren;

I will all my life long,
O God, from now on honour You;

Man soll, o Gott, den Lobgesang
An allen Orten hören.
Mein ganzes Herz ermuntre sich,
Mein Geist und Leib erfreue sich.
Gebt unserm Gott die Ehre!

Your song of praise, O God,
Shall be heard in all places.
Let my whole heart be aroused,
Let my spirit and body rejoice.
Give honour to our God!

8. VERSUS 8 RECITATIVO T bc — b–G c

Ihr, die ihr Christi Namen nennt,
Gebt unserm Gott die Ehre!
Ihr, die ihr Gottes Macht bekennt,
Gebt unserm Gott die Ehre!
Die falschen Götzen macht zu Spott,
Der Herr ist Gott, der Herr ist Gott:
Gebt unserm Gott die Ehre!

You who profess the Name of Christ,
Give honour to our God!
You who confess God's might,
Give honour to our God!
Put false idols to scorn,
The Lord is God, the Lord is God:
Give honour to our God!

9. VERSUS 9 [CHORALE Reprise of no. 1 to new text] — G $\frac{6}{8}$

So kommet vor sein Angesicht
Mit jauchzenvollem Springen;
Bezahlet die gelobte Pflicht
Und laßt uns fröhlich singen:
Gott hat es alles wohl bedacht
Und alles, alles recht gemacht.
Gebt unserm Gott die Ehre!

Then come before His Presence
With jubilant leaping;
Pay your vowed duty
And let us sing joyfully:
God has considered all things well
And all, all He has done right.
Give honour to our God!

This cantata may be dated no more than roughly within the period 1728–31, nor can a specific occasion for its composition be ascertained. The hymn, by Johann Jakob Schütz (1673), was customary at weddings, and there is good reason to believe that, like BWV 97, 100, and 192, this cantata was written for a wedding service.[13] As in these other relatively late chorale cantatas,* Bach preserves the text of the hymn unaltered. Its associated chorale melody, however, is retained only in the first, fourth, and ninth movements, the remaining verses being set as recitatives and arias. Such a setting of a chorale text itself imposes certain restrictions on the composer, and in this hymn the regular recurrence of the last line, 'Gebt unserm Gott die Ehre!' ('Give honour to our God'), acts as an additional restraint. Bach responds by employing various means to lay special emphasis on this line.

The overall form of the cantata is determined by the literal reprise of the opening movement to the text of the concluding ninth verse. Accordingly, Bach created a splendid concertante* piece to act as a frame for the other movements. The fourth verse is also assigned to the choir: it is set as a plain four-part chorale such as normally concludes a cantata or the first part of a two-part cantata. Although there is no specific instruction to this effect, we may therefore assume that the cantata was performed in two parts, the first (verses 1–4) before the

[13] See Stiller, *J. S. Bach und das Leipziger gottesdienstliche Leben*, 82; Eng. trans., 94.

sermon and the second (verses 5–9) afterwards. Between the choruses,* verses 3, 6, and 7 are sung as arias and verses 2, 5, and 8 as recitatives. Curiously, despite the relatively large number of solo movements, not a single one is assigned to the soprano. This is surely to be attributed to a circumstantial dilemma rather than to artistic design. The chorale melody that forms the basis of Bach's setting is not the Crüger melody of 1653, often sung to this hymn today, but rather that of the chorale *Es ist das Heil uns kommen her*, the tune normally associated with the hymn in Bach's day.

The opening movement acquires its distinctive character from the contrast between a lively, concertante instrumental ensemble and a choir singing in solemn tranquillity and measured polyphony.* The participation of flutes and oboes as well as strings and the lively semiquaver motion of the continuo lend the instrumental texture a colourful hue. A ritornello theme derived from the first line of the chorale is tonally answered at once and then heard for a third time in the second half of the ritornello. The soprano states the unaltered chorale melody one line at a time. The three lower voices occasionally enter with brief passages of imitation* but essentially they have an accompanying function, developing greater independence only at the end of the last line. This not only allows Bach to emphasize that line, whose invariable wording in all verses has already been pointed out, but it also gives him the opportunity to let the final reprise of the ritornello enter quite imperceptibly before the voices have finished singing, giving rise to a brilliant interlocking of the last chorale line and the ritornello.

Verse 2 begins as a plain *secco* recitative, but the 'motto' last line is expanded into an arioso* in 3/8 time of such large dimensions that it divides the movement into two contrasting sections, recitative–arioso. Verse 3 derives its distinctive colouring from the combined effect of the minor mode and the two concertante oboes d'amore.* Its design, strikingly concise for an aria, is largely conditioned by the text, which precludes the standard da capo* reprise. Verse 4, a plain chorale setting, is followed by the second recitative, verse 5, whose bipartite design forms a counterpart to that of verse 2. In this case, the contrast between the recitative and the arioso setting of the 'motto' last line is further reinforced by the scoring: the recitative is accompanied by strings, the arioso by continuo only.

Verse 6, a bass aria with obbligato* violin, is related to verse 5 by the similar melodic setting of the 'motto' last line, there set as arioso but here as an aria passage with thematic interaction between violin and bass. Apart from this extended treatment of the last line, the movement is also noteworthy for its speech-like violin figures, which graphically illustrate various individual words such as 'nirgend' ('nowhere') or 'Ruh' ('rest'; note the low pitch). Verse 7 is set as a hymnic Largo for alto and strings, decorated by the coloraturas* of the flute, and is remarkable for its melodic inspiration. Owing to the repeat of the last three lines of text, a larger form is achieved than in the preceding arias. The melody of the 'motto' last line distantly recalls that of verses 5 and 6. Verse 8, the sole plain *secco* recitative and only a few bars long, avoids any special emphasis on the last line and, in a concise fashion, leads to the reprise of the first movement to the text of verse 9.

In allen meinen Taten, BWV 97

NBA I/34, p. 199 BC A189 Duration: *c.* 32 mins

1. [Versus 1 Chorus] SATB ob I,II bsn str bc — B♭ ¢

In allen meinen Taten	**In all my deeds**
Laß ich den Höchsten raten,	**I let the Most High counsel me,**
Der alles kann und hat;	**He who can do and has everything;**
Er muß zu allen Dingen,	**To all things,**
Solls anders wohl gelingen,	**If they should succeed well,**
Selbst geben Rat und Tat.	**He Himself must give counsel and deed.**

2. Versus 2 [Aria] B solo bc — g $\frac{6}{8}$

Nichts ist es spat und frühe	**Nothing comes, late or early,**
Um alle meine Mühe,	**Of all my trouble:**
Mein Sorgen ist umsonst.	**My care is in vain.**
Er mags mit meinen Sachen	**With my affairs He may**
Nach seinem Willen machen,	**Act according to His Will:**
Ich stells in seine Gunst.	**I place them in His favour.**

3. Versus 3 Recitativo T bc — E♭–d c

Es kann mir nichts geschehen,	**Nothing can happen to me**
Als was er hat versehen,	**Other than what He has prescribed**
Und was mir selig ist:	**And what is blessed to me:**
Ich nehm es, wie ers gibet;	**I take it as He gives it;**
Was ihm von mir beliebet,	**Whatever pleases Him from me,**
Das hab ich auch erkiest.	**That I have also chosen.**

4. Versus 4 Aria T vln solo bc — B♭ c

Ich traue seiner Gnaden,	**I trust in His grace,**
Die mich vor allem Schaden,	**Which protects me from all harm,**
Vor allem Übel schützt.	**From all evil.**
Leb ich nach seinen Gesetzen,	**If I live according to His commandments,**
So wird mich nichts verletzen,	**Then nothing will injure me,**
Nichts fehlen, was mir nützt.	**Nor will I lack anything beneficial to me.**

5. Versus 5 Recitativo A str bc — g–c c

Er wolle meiner Sünden	**May He free me from my sins**
In Gnaden mich entbinden,	**In His grace,**
Durchstreichen meine Schuld!	**Cancel my guilt!**
Er wird auf mein Verbrechen	**Upon my offences He will**

Nicht stracks das Urteil sprechen
Und haben noch Geduld.

Not immediately deliver judgement
And will yet have patience.

6. Versus 6 Aria A str bc — c C

Leg ich mich späte nieder,
Erwache frühe wieder,
Lieg oder ziehe fort,
In Schwachheit und in Banden,
Und was mir stößt zuhanden,
So tröstet mich sein Wort.

Whether I lie down late
Or wake up early,
Stay or go forth,
In weakness and in bonds,
And in whatever afflicts me close at hand,
I am comforted by His Word.

7. Versus 7 Duetto SB bc — E♭ $\frac{3}{4}$

Hat er es denn beschlossen,
So will ich unverdrossen
An mein Verhängnis gehn!
Kein Unfall unter allen
Wird mir zu harte fallen,
Ich will ihn überstehn.

If He has purposed it,
Then I will indefatigably
Go to my doom!
No accident among all
Will fall too heavily upon me:
I will endure it.

8. Versus 8 Aria S ob I,II bc — F $\frac{2}{4}$

Ihm hab ich mich ergeben
Zu sterben und zu leben,
Sobald er mir gebeut.
Es sei heut oder morgen,
Dafür laß ich ihn sorgen;
Er weiß die rechte Zeit.

To Him I have surrendered myself,
To die or to live
As soon as He commands me.
Whether it be today or tomorrow,
I let Him take care of it;
He knows the right time.

9. Versus Ultimus Choral S + ob I + II ATB str bc — B♭ C

So sei nun, Seele, deine
Und traue dem alleine,
Der dich erschaffen hat;
Es gehe, wie es gehe,
Dein Vater in der Höhe
Weiß allen Sachen Rat.

Then be true to yourself now, O soul,
And trust Him alone
Who has created you;
Whatever will be must be;
Your Father on high
Knows the right counsel for all things.

We know when this cantata originated from Bach's autograph date '1734', and while its specific occasion is unknown, it is most likely that it originated as a wedding cantata, like the other late chorale cantatas* BWV 100, 117, and 192.[14] Bach left the hymn by Paul Fleming (1642) unaltered; its associated chorale melody, however, *O Welt, ich muß dich lassen*, is employed only in the outer movements—all the inner ones are set without reference to it.

Fleming's hymn was originally written at the start of a long and dangerous journey (it included additional verses that specifically referred to this occasion), hence its character as 'making a start in God's name'. In his setting, Bach underlines this character by giving the opening movement the form of a French

[14] See Stiller, *J. S. Bach und das Leipziger gottesdienstliche Leben*, 82; Eng. trans., 94.

Overture* (though without the usual slow concluding section). The slow ceremonial section at the beginning, which strides along in taut dotted rhythms, serves as an instrumental introduction. The chorale is then embedded line by line within the 'vivace' fugal section. The chorale melody is sung in long notes by the soprano and supported by the three lower voices in an imitative* texture. Only after the end of the last chorale line, before the orchestral postlude, do all four voices unite in a chordal, homophonic* appendix. The instrumental texture has its own thematic material: allusions to the chorale worthy of mention are found neither in the slow introductory section nor in the quick main section. Even the theme of the imitative lower voice parts is, throughout all six chorale lines, invariably derived from the instrumental fugato theme, which reads:

Modifications arise only from the demands of textual underlay. The scoring is well-suited to the character of a French Overture. Two oboes and a bassoon at times detach themselves from the tutti texture of the main section to form a trio after the French model; and the instrumental ensemble is completed by strings and continuo.

The seven inner movements include only two recitatives but fully four arias and a duet. In musical substance, too, the recitatives are relatively unimportant. Both are brief, plainly declaimed movements, the first (verse 3) accompanied by continuo only, the second (verse 5) by strings also. The short hymn verses offer insufficient material for longer recitatives, and Bach forgoes the possibility of expanding them by arioso* insertions or—as the overall length of the hymn might have suggested—of uniting several verses to form a single recitative.

The importance that Bach attached to the arias is therefore all the greater. Verse 2 is set as a relatively undemanding continuo movement, with a song-like ritornello theme which is taken over by the vocal bass. Verse 4, however, includes a solo violin part so obviously designed for virtuoso effects that we might imagine some definite intention lay behind it. Perhaps Bach wanted to give a particular player the opportunity for virtuoso display, or perhaps the occasion of the performance for some reason suggested this mode of treatment. The text, which deals with the superabundance of divine grace, might well justify the procedure, but it seems doubtful whether it was the sole cause of it. Bach's setting of verse 6 enters more fully into the details of the text. As the vocal entry indicates, the opening string ritornello already includes the distinctive, text-engendered motives* for going to bed, waking up, lying down, and walking along.

In verse 7, a duet with continuo accompaniment, the brief introductory ritornello includes the subsequent vocal theme as its antecedent phrase, but the consequent is a typical instrumental figure whose energetic intervallic leaps were evidently inspired by the lines 'Then I will indefatigably go to my doom'. The continuo accompaniment temporarily becomes more flowing in the middle section, but the lines '. . . will fall too heavily upon me: I will endure it' once more call forth the energy-laden continuo figures before the free da capo* of the opening section (the movement is very unusual in not adopting the bipartite structure of the text in its compositional form).

Verse 8, with its two obbligato* oboes, is technically more demanding than the sixth movement but without achieving the level of virtuosity of the fourth. Indeed, a certain song-like simplicity adheres to the soprano part, even though it demands the same mastery that Bach requires of all the singers. Short melodic fragments interspersed with rests alternate with extended melismas.* The plain concluding chorale is augmented to seven parts by its obbligato string parts (the two oboes reinforce the chorale melody in the soprano). This hymnic crowning movement of the cantata may be regarded either as a formal counterbalance to the overtly ceremonial opening movement or else as a means of raising to prominence a verse that unites the content of all the preceding verses. Perhaps both these things were intended.

Was Gott tut, das ist wohlgetan, BWV 100

NBA I/34, p. 241 BC A191 Duration: *c.* 25 mins

1. Versus 1 [Chorale] SATB hn I,II timp fl ob d'am str bc G ¢

Was Gott tut, das ist wohlgetan,	**Whatever God deals is dealt bountifully:**
Es bleibt gerecht sein Wille;	**His Will remains just;**
Wie er fängt meine Sachen an,	**However He runs my affairs,**
Will ich ihm halten stille.	**I will hold still before Him.**
Er ist mein Gott,	**He is my God,**
Der in der Not	**Who in time of trouble**
Mich wohl weiß zu erhalten;	**Well knows how to uphold me;**
Drum laß ich ihn nur walten.	**Therefore I will just let Him rule.**

2. Versus 2 Duetto AT bc D c

Was Gott tut, das ist wohlgetan,	**Whatever God deals is dealt bountifully:**
Er wird mich nicht betrügen;	**He will not deceive me;**
Er führet mich auf rechter Bahn,	**He leads me on the upright path,**
So laß ich mich begnügen	**So I let myself be content**
An seiner Huld	**With His favour**
Und hab Geduld,	**And have patience;**
Er wird mein Unglück wenden,	**He will avert my misfortune,**
Es steht in seinen Händen.	**It lies in His hands.**

3. Versus 3 [Aria] S fl solo bc b $\frac{6}{8}$

Was Gott tut, das ist wohlgetan,	**Whatever God deals is dealt bountifully:**

Er wird mich wohl bedenken;
Er, als mein Arzt und Wundermann,
Wird mir nicht Gift einschenken
Vor Arzenei.
Gott ist getreu,
Drum will ich auf ihn bauen
Und seiner Gnade trauen.

He will consider me well;
He, as my physician and miracle-worker,
Will not pour out poison for me
As medicine.
God is faithful,
Therefore I will build upon Him
And trust His grace.

4. VERSUS 4 [ARIA] B str bc — G 2/4

Was Gott tut, das ist wohlgetan,
Er ist mein Licht, mein Leben,
Der mir nichts Böses gönnen kann,
Ich will mich ihm ergeben
In Freud und Leid!
Es kommt die Zeit,
Da öffentlich erscheinet,
Wie treulich er es meinet.

Whatever God deals is dealt bountifully:
He is my Light, my Life,
Who can grant me nothing evil;
I will surrender myself to Him
In joy and sorrow!
The time will come
When it shall openly appear
How faithful is His intent.

5. VERSUS 5 [ARIA] A ob d'am solo bc — e 12/8

Was Gott tut, das ist wohlgetan;
Muß ich den Kelch gleich schmecken,
Der bitter ist nach meinem Wahn,
Laß ich mich doch nicht schrecken,
Weil doch zuletzt
Ich werd ergötzt
Mit süßem Trost im Herzen;
Da weichen alle Schmerzen.

Whatever God deals is dealt bountifully:
Though I must taste the cup
That is bitter according to my delusion,
I do not let myself be afraid,
For nonetheless in the end
I shall be delighted
By sweet comfort at heart;
Then all sorrows shall retreat.

6. VERSUS ULTIMUS [CHORALE Scoring as in no. 1] — G C

Was Gott tut, das ist wohlgetan,
Darbei will ich verbleiben.
Es mag mich auf die rauhe Bahn
Not, Tod und Elend treiben,
So wird Gott mich
Ganz väterlich
In seinen Armen halten;
Drum laß ich ihn nur walten.

Whatever God deals is dealt bountifully:
I will abide by that.
Though I be driven on a rough road
By woe, death, and misery,
Even so God will
In a quite fatherly manner
Hold me in His arms;
Therefore I will just let Him rule.

This chorale cantata* is based on Samuel Rodigast's hymn of 1675 in its original wording. In 1724 Bach had composed an earlier chorale cantata, BWV 99, on the basis of the same hymn, though with madrigalian* paraphrase of the inner verses. The abundant original sources that survive for the present work tell us nothing about its intended occasion, but there is good reason to suppose that, like the roughly contemporary chorale cantatas BWV 97, 117, and 192, it was originally written for a wedding.[15] After the first performance in about 1734, Bach revived the work on several occasions (*c.* 1737 and *c.* 1742).

In its composition, Bach adopts the same overall scheme as in the cycle of chorale cantatas, setting the first and last verses of the hymn as chorale arrangements but remaining unfettered by the chorale melody in the four inner verses. It is nonetheless occasionally recalled: for example, in the upward leap of a fourth in the themes of the second, third, and fourth movements, but this makes no essential difference to the overall design. In setting these inner verses, Bach chose aria form exclusively (the first of them is a duet): recitatives are altogether excluded. The composer is thus confronted with the task of avoiding loss of concentration on the part of the listener by giving the maximum possible variety to his setting of four arias in succession.

In the first and last movements, Bach made use of music composed already (this in itself suggests that the work originated for a particular occasion rather than as a fresh attempt to interpret the chorale). The opening chorus* is drawn from the like-named chorale cantata BWV 99, but the instrumental ensemble is enriched by the addition of two horns and drums which give a decidedly festive colouring to the joyful elation of the movement. The concluding chorale originally ended each half of Cantata 75, *Die Elenden sollen essen*, Bach's Leipzig inaugural music. Evidently the plain concluding chorale of Cantata 99 was considered inadequate to the festive occasion of the new cantata, hence Bach's decision to borrow from elsewhere a movement with independent orchestral parts, and even to enrich its instrumentation. By this means he created a better balance with the opening movement, and only the scrupulously attentive listener is aware that the slight change to the chorale melody (its fifth note now rises to the sixth degree) indicates that the first and last movements are derived from different sources.

The relatively slim texture of Bach's setting of the inner verses forms a marked contrast with the richly scored outer movements. The duet, no. 2, is accompanied only by continuo. With its frequent imitation,* bordering on canon,* it represents the tradition-bound linear principle as opposed to the more 'modern', vertically articulated, concerted movement that precedes it. The soprano aria, no. 3, on the other hand, with its wide-ranging passage-work for the flute, brings the soloistic, virtuoso principle to the foreground. A minor-mode version of the chorale melody may be detected in the opening bars of the flute ritornello and of the soprano part. The text, which here runs directly from the second *Stollen** into the *Abgesang** ('Wird mir nicht Gift einschenken/ Vor Arzenei'), no doubt played an essential part in determining the extensive bipartite design, with its single episode between the vocal sections.

[15] See Stiller, *J. S. Bach und das Leipziger gottesdienstliche Leben*, 82; Eng. trans., 94.

Song and dance might have stimulated the composer in his setting of verse 4, for a clearly periodic phrase structure (ritornello: 4 + 4 + 8 = 16 bars), a cheerful major key, dance-like syncopations, and again chorale reminiscences in the opening bars characterize this particularly accessible aria. The clearly articulated formal structure A A B C (though with somewhat overlapping text) forges an especially close link with the *Bar* form* of the chorale, a form also common in folksong. After the full string texture of this aria, we again hear an obbligato* woodwind instrument, the oboe d'amore,* accompanied only by continuo, in the setting of verse 5. The words 'Though I must taste the cup that is bitter' were certainly a determining factor in the minor-mode character of this aria. The text may also have determined its bipartite form, in which the chromaticism* of the 'bitter cup' in the first part is contrasted with the 'sweet comfort' of the second.

Church cantata (text unknown), BWV 1045

NBA I/34, p. 307

Only the introductory sinfonia of this work survives, and even that is incomplete, breaking off after 149½ bars. In the Bach literature, this fragment is sometimes described as the opening of a violin concerto in D, but the heading of the autograph score (*c.* 1743/6) clearly reveals that the work as a whole required four voices:

> J J Concerto. a 4 Voci. 3 Trombe, Tamburi, 2 Hautb: Violino Conc: 2 Violini, Viola e Cont.

The title 'Concerto',* contrary to its modern associations, here excludes a secular occasion and indicates a church cantata (see 'concerto' in the Index of terms). The surviving fragment leaves a mixed impression and doubt has been cast on its authenticity:[16] possibly it is all that survives of Bach's arrangement of a concerto movement by another composer. It has also been conjectured[17] that the movement might have formed the sinfonia to the lost graduation cantata *Siehe, der Hüter Israel*, BWV Anh. I 15. The appearance of the score suggests that the wind parts are subsequent additions and that only the strings and continuo belonged to the sinfonia in its original form.[18]

[16] By Rudolf Stephan, 'Die Wandlung der Konzertform bei Bach', *Die Musikforschung* 6 (1953), 127–43 (see 143). The absence of the composer's name in the heading would provide insufficient grounds for doubts over the work's authenticity (the name might have been inscribed on the lost wrapper) if such doubts were not reinforced by stylistic considerations.

[17] By Reinmar Emans, 'Überlegungen zur Genese der Kantate *Du Hirte Israel, höre* (BWV 104)'.

[18] See R. Higuchi, KB, NBA I/34, 129–30.

PART 3

Secular cantatas

I

Festive music for the courts of Weimar, Weißenfels, and Cöthen

The popularity of the cantata genre in the seventeenth and eighteenth centuries resulted in numerous festive events of the time being marked by the performance of a work of cantata type. Before Bach's move to Leipzig, it was chiefly court entertainments that demanded the performance of a cantata. Apart from specific occasions such as the visits of non-resident princes, weddings, and so on, there were two annual occasions upon which it was customary to perform a cantata in central German courts: New Year's Day and the birthday of the reigning prince. Until 1717—as far as we can tell from the works that survive—Bach was only occasionally instructed to perform festive cantatas, but during his years at Cöthen (1717–23) one of his duties as Capellmeister was the preparation and performance of festive music every time it became due.

A considerable proportion of this festive music does not survive, for the mostly single opportunity for performance was less conducive to the conservation of the performing materials than in the case of church cantatas, which could be reused annually. A summary of the relevant occasions and of Bach's presumed performances of such festive works is given in the Critical Report to NBA I/35, pp. 7–10. The following works, written for the specified occasion, are today extant or identifiable:

a) For Weißenfels:

   Was mir behagt, ist nur die muntre Jagd ('Hunt' Cantata), BWV 208, probably first performed in February 1713 and revived subsequently at an unknown date. It is discussed below.

   Entfliehet, verschwindet, entweichet, ihr Sorgen ('Pastoral' Cantata), BWV 249a, composed for performance on 23 February 1725. It is lost but may be reconstructed and is consequently discussed below.

b) for Weimar:

   Was mir behagt, ist nur die muntre Jagd, BWV 208. Revival of the cantata composed for Weißenfels (see above), probably in 1716, with the name 'Christian' (Duke of Weißenfels) replaced by 'Ernst August', co-regent with Wilhelm Ernst of Saxe-Weimar.

c) For Cöthen:

Der Himmel dacht auf Anhalts Ruhm und Glück, BWV 66a, for 10 December 1718. All that is extant is the text, by Johann Christian Friedrich Hunold, and the sacred parody* BWV 66. For details of the presumed original form of the work see the Critical Report to NBA I/35, pp. 59–61.[1]

Die Zeit, die Tag und Jahre macht, BWV 134a, for 1 January 1719. This cantata is discussed below.

Dich loben die lieblichen Strahlen der Sonne, BWV Anh. I 6, for 1 January 1720. All that is extant is Hunold's libretto, which is reproduced in the Critical Report to NBA I/35, pp. 169–71 and elsewhere.

Heut ist gewiß ein guter Tag, BWV Anh. I 7, for 10 December 1720 (?). All that is extant is Hunold's libretto, which is reproduced in the Critical Report to NBA I/35, pp. 171–4, and elsewhere. In the same place, pp. 118 f., is a discussion of the date of the work.

(Text unknown), BWV Anh. I 8, for 1 January 1723. All that is extant is the title-page of the libretto, which is reproduced in the Critical Report to NBA I/35, pp. 175 f., and elsewhere.

Durchlauchtster Leopold, BWV 173a, for 10 December (year unknown). This cantata is discussed below.

(Text unknown), BWV 184a, date unknown. This work is almost completely lost and identifiable only by the reuse of some Cöthen performing parts in its sacred parody Cantata 184. For details of the presumed original form of the work, see the Critical Report to NBA I/35, pp. 138–42.

(Text unknown), BWV 194a, date unknown. This work is largely lost and identifiable only by the reuse of some Cöthen performing parts in its sacred parody Cantata 194. For details of the presumed original form of the work, see the Critical Report to NBA I/35, pp. 143–51.

Steigt freudig in die Luft, BWV 36a, for 30 November 1726 (?), the birthday of Prince Leopold's second consort. The music is lost, but we possess Picander's libretto, Cantata 36c, whose choruses* and arias were here parodied, and several other versions related by parody to Cantata 36c, namely Cantata 36b and two versions of Cantata 36. For details, together with references to further literature, see the Critical Report to NBA I/35, pp. 152 f.

[1] See also J. Rifkin, 'Verlorene Quellen, verlorene Werke: Miszellen zu Bachs Instrumentalkomposition', in M. Geck and W. Breig, eds, *Bachs Orchesterwerke* [conference report, Dortmund, 1996] (Witten, 1997), 65–7.

Was mir behagt, ist nur die muntre Jagd, BWV 208

NBA I/35, p. 3 BC G 1, 3 Duration: *c.* 39 mins

1. Recitativo S I bc — F–B♭ 𝄴

Diana

Was mir behagt,	What pleases me
Ist nur die muntre Jagd!	Is but the lively hunt!
Eh noch Aurora pranget,	Before Aurora dawns,
Eh sie sich an den Himmel wagt,	Before she ventures into the heavens,
Hat dieser Pfeil	This arrow has
Schon angenehme Beut erlanget!	Already found an agreeable target!

2. Aria S I hn I,II bc — F $\frac{6}{8}$

Diana

Jagen ist die Lust der Götter,	Hunting is the delight of the gods,
Jagen steht den Helden an!	Hunting is fit for heroes!
Weichet, meiner Nymphen Spötter,	Retreat, you mockers of my nymphs,
Weichet von Dianen Bahn!	Retreat from Diana's path!

3. Recitativo T bc — d 𝄴

Endymion

Wie? schönste Göttin! wie?	What, fairest goddess, what?
Kennst du nicht mehr dein vormals halbes Leben?	Do you no longer know your former other half?
Hast du nicht dem Endymion	Did you not give Endymion
In seiner sanften Ruh	In his gentle repose
So manchen Zuckerkuß gegeben?	So many sweet kisses?
Bist du denn, Schönste, nu	Are you now then, O fairest,
Von Liebesbanden frei?	Free from the bonds of love?
Und folgest nur der Jägerei?	And do you now pursue hunting only?

4. Aria T bc — d 𝄴

Endymion

Willst du dich nicht mehr ergötzen	Would you no longer delight
An den Netzen,	In the nets
Die Amor legt?	That Cupid lays?
Wo man auch, wenn man gefangen,	Where, when caught,
Nach Verlangen	To one's heart's desire
Lust und Lieb in Banden pflegt.	One cultivates pleasure and love in bondage

5. Recitativo S I T bc — B♭–C 𝄴

Diana

Ich liebe dich zwar noch!	Indeed I love you still!
Jedoch	However
Ist heut ein hohes Licht erschienen,	Today an exalted light has appeared,
Das ich vor allem muß	Which, above all,
Mit meinem Liebeskuß	With my loving kiss

Empfangen und bedienen! | I must welcome and serve!
Der teure Christian/Ernst August, | Dear Christian/Ernst August,
Der Wälder Pan/Lust, | The Pan/delight of the woods,
Kann in erwünschtem Wohlergehen | Can now in all desired prosperity
Sein hohes Ursprungsfest itzt sehen! | Celebrate his lofty birthday feast!

Endymion

So gönne mir, | Then allow me,
Diana, daß ich mich mit dir | Diana, with you
Itzund verbinde | To join now
Und an 'ein Freuden-Opfer' zünde. | And ignite a 'free-will offering'.

beide (both)

Ja! ja! | Yes, yes!
Wir tragen unsre Flammen | Let us carry our torches
Mit Wunsch und Freuden itzt zusammen! | Together now with joyful wishes!

6. Recitativo B bc — a–G c

Pan

Ich, der ich sonst ein Gott | I who am otherwise a god
In diesen Feldern bin, | In these fields,
Ich lege meinen Schäferstab | I lay down my shepherd's crook
Vor Christians/Ernst Augusts Regierungszepter hin! | Before Christian's/Ernst August's ruling sceptre!
Weil der durchlauchte Pan das Land so glücklich machet, | For the illustrious Pan makes the land so happy
Daß Wald und Feld und alles lebt und lachet! | That forest, field, and all live and laugh!

7. Aria B ob I,II taille bc — C c

Pan

Ein Fürst ist seines Landes Pan! | A prince is his country's Pan!
Gleichwie der Körper ohne Seele | Just as the body without the soul
Nicht leben, noch sich regen kann, | Can neither live nor move,
So ist das Land die Totenhöhle, | So a country is a den of death
Das sonder Haupt und Fürsten ist | That is without sovereign and prince
Und so das beste Teil vermißt. | And thus lacks its best part.

8. Recitativo S II bc — F–g c

Pales

Soll denn der Pales Opfer hier | Shall Pales' offering here
Das letzte sein? | Be last, then?
Nein! nein! | No! no!
Ich will die Pflicht auch niederlegen, | I too will do my duty,
Und da das ganze Land von Vivat schallt, | And when the whole land resounds with 'Vivat'
Auch dieses schöne Feld | Also urge this fair land,
Zu Ehren unserm Sachsenheld | For the honour of our Saxon hero,
Zur Freud und Lust bewegen. | To joy and delight.

9\. ARIA S II rec I,II bc — B♭ c

Pales

Schafe können sicher weiden,	Sheep may safely graze
Wo ein guter Hirte wacht!	Where a good shepherd keeps watch!
Wo Regenten wohl regieren,	Where rulers govern well
Kann man Ruh und Friede spüren	One can feel calm and peace
Und was Länder glücklich macht!	And whatever makes lands happy!

10\. RECITATIVO S I bc — F c

Diana

So stimmt mit ein	Then let us join with one accord,
Und laßt des Tages Lust vollkommen sein!	And let the day's delight be complete!

11\. CHORUS S I,II TB hn I,II str vc + ob I,II taille bsn bc — F c

Tutti à 4

Lebe, Sonne dieser Erden,	Live, sun of this earth,
Weil Diana bei der Nacht	As long as Diana by night
An der Burg des Himmels wacht,	Keeps watch on the citadel of heaven,
Weil die Wälder grünen werden!	As long as the woods turn green!
Lebe, Sonne dieser Erden.	Live, sun of this earth!

12\. ARIA DUETTO S I T vln solo bc — F 3/4

Diana, Endymion

Entzücket uns beide,	Enchant us both,
Ihr Strahlen der Freude,	You rays of joy,
Und zieret den Himmel mit Demantgeschmeide!	And grace the heavens with diamond jewels!
Fürst Christian/Ernst August weide	May Prince Christian/Ernst August graze
Auf lieblichsten Rosen, befreiet vom Leide!	Amidst the loveliest roses, freed from care!
Entzücket uns beide,	Enchant us both,
Ihr Strahlen der Freude!	You rays of joy!

13\. ARIA S II bc — F c

Pales

Weil die wollenreichen Herden	As long as the wool-rich flocks
Durch dies weitgepriesne Feld	Through this widely-praised land
Lustig ausgetrieben werden,	Are merrily herded,
Lebe dieser Sachsenheld!	May this Saxon hero live!

14\. ARIA B bc — F 3/8

Pan

Ihr Felder und Auen,	You fields and pastures,
Laßt grünend euch schauen,	Look verdant,
Ruft Vivat itzt zu!	Call out 'Vivat' now!
Es lebe der Herzog in Segen und Ruh!	May the Duke live in blessing and peace!

15. Chorus S I,II TB hn I,II ob I,II taille bsn str vc bc F $\frac{3}{8}$

Tutti

Ihr lieblichste Blicke! ihr freudige Stunden,	You loveliest sights! you joyous hours,
Euch bleibe das Glücke auf ewig verbunden!	May good fortune remain yours for ever!
Euch kröne der Himmel mit süßester Lust!	May heaven crown you with the sweetest delight!
Fürst Christian/Ernst August lebe! Ihm bleibe bewußt,	Long live Prince Christian/Ernst August! May he remain aware of
Was Herzen vergnüget,	What pleases the heart,
Was Trauren besieget!	What vanquishes sorrow!

[Additional strophe for no. 15, performed in 1713 or at a subsequent revival:]

Die Anmut umfange, das Glücke bediene	May charm encircle and good fortune attend
Den Herzog und seine Luise Christine!	The Duke and his Louisa Christina!
Sie weiden in Freuden auf Blumen und Klee,	They graze in joy amidst flowers and clover;
Es prange die Zierde der fürstlichen Eh,	May the ornament of the princely marriage shine,
Die andre Dione,	The other Diana,
Fürst Christians Krone!	Prince Christian's crown!

Like other German baroque princes, Duke Christian of Saxe-Weißenfels in his royal household sought to imitate the splendour of the 'Sun King', Louis XIV. The celebrations for his birthday, on 23 February, often lasted for several weeks; and since he was a passionate hunter, one or more hunts belonged to the annual programme of festivities. One of the more woeful aspects of this royal household was the prince's mismanagement of his land, which in later years induced the Kaiser to set up a royal commission to administer his finances. Among the more agreeable aspects was that in the year 1713[2] Bach helped to enhance the festivities, 'after the hunting contest held in the prince's hunting court',[3] with some *musique de table*.

Bach's 'Hunt' Cantata is his earliest surviving secular cantata, though it is not known whether there are still earlier congratulatory pieces whose loss we should lament. The libretto was supplied by the chief consistory secretary at Weimar, Salomo Franck. It contains a modest plot. One day Diana devotes herself exclusively to hunting, and her disappointed lover Endymion asks her whether she no longer loves him. Diana replies that she does indeed still love

[2] See A. Dürr, KB, NBA I/35 (1964) and H.-J. Schulze, 'Wann entstand J. S. Bachs "Jagdkantate"?', *BJ* 2000, 301–5.

[3] '. . . nach gehaltenen Kampff-Jagen im Fürstl. Jäger-Hofe.'

him but that today the priority must be to honour Prince Christian on his birthday. Now Endymion too no longer wants to hold back and with Diana he kindles a 'free-will offering' in honour of the prince. At this point Pan approaches and in his aria praises the good fortune represented by the prince of a country. Finally, Pales, goddess of shepherds and fields, rushes onto the scene to compare Christian's art of government with the watchfulness of a good shepherd. And then all four characters unite in a chorus* to offer their congratulations to the prince. This ends the plot, but thereafter the four gods—Diana and Endymion in a duet, Pales and Pan in an aria each—congratulate the prince once more, and a fully scored final chorus brings the work to an end amidst the general jubilation of all participants.

Bach's setting exudes all the youthful freshness of a first effort. Its constituent movements are still relatively brief, rather than broadly developed as in later works. But this very characteristic gives the cantata its spirited continuity and holds the listener captive. The recitative is far removed from the overly schematic form with which Bach's contemporaries were wont to handle it, including even such a celebrated figure as Telemann. In the opening movement, the free recitative rhythm changes after only four bars into an arioso,* which employs changes of tempo and varying figuration to depict the flight of Diana's arrow, her unconstrained joy over her quarry ('adagio'), and then, all of a sudden, the swiftness with which the hunting goddess chases after it ('presto'). Not all the arias employ the customary da capo* form. Diana's aria, which immediately follows the opening recitative, contains only a free, abridged da capo. Two horns are used here to highlight the hunting scene. Diana's part is full of trills and leaps—a truly virtuoso part, presumably first interpreted by a singer from the Weißenfels opera.

Endymion's recitative, no. 3, again changes to arioso at the end—a canon* at the fifth between voice and continuo, presumably inspired by the words 'And do you now pursue hunting only?'. His aria, no. 4, is an elaborate continuo piece over an ostinato* bass that recurs constantly in various transpositions, sometimes rather more freely treated. Diana and Endymion now unite in a dialogue-recitative, no. 5. This very soon develops into a polyphonic* duet in the style of the duets of Agostino Steffani, which were then widely admired. Its vitality results from the constant interchange of thematic material between the two singers. Pan enters in the following recitative, no. 6, now a pure *secco*. In his aria, no. 7, he is accompanied by three oboes (oboe I, II, and taille*), the characteristic shepherds' instruments. Technically, Bach is here confronted with the task of through-composing an aria text that contains hardly any caesuras and thus gives the singer no pauses of any length. Harmonically, the aria is exceptionally attractive due to its frequent side-stepping into remote keys.

Now, for the fourth time, the entry of a well-wisher, Pales, takes the musical form of recitative-aria (nos. 8–9). The aria 'Sheep may safely graze', no. 9, in which Pales praises Prince Christian's art of government—ostensibly so rich in blessings—has become widely known due to its scoring for recorders. It demonstrates not only the high standard of playing technique at the time but also Bach's ability to make two consecutive arias with woodwind scoring so different that nowhere does the impression of monotony arise. Diana now calls upon all four well-wishers to offer general congratulations in the chorus 'Lebe, Sonne dieser Erden', no. 11, whose vocal scoring—S I, II TB, rather than SATB—reveals that it was conceived as an ensemble of the four soloists.[4] It takes the form of a permutation fugue* and includes a charming exchange between voices and instruments. By contrast, the middle section of this da capo-form chorus is non-fugal, song-like, and homophonic.*

Since the plot is now over, the remaining movements follow without interpolated recitatives. In place of horns and woodwind, a solo violin now comes into its own as obbligato* instrument. The duet 'Entzücket uns beide', no. 12, is cast in homophony according to the French duet style, in contrast with the Italianate polyphony of Steffani. In accordance with baroque aesthetics, the cheerful character of the movement is darkened at the words 'freed from care': sorrow, even in its negation, is represented musically by minor-mode sounds and dissonances. Pales's aria 'Weil die wollenreichen Herden', no. 13, is less well-known than its sacred adaptation 'Mein gläubiges Herze' from the Whit Monday cantata BWV 68. This comes as no surprise, for in the simple melody of the secular model we hardly recognize the stirring excitement of the Whit cantata aria. Moreover, the 'Hunt' Cantata movement, virtually identical in its instrumental themes, is nonetheless substantially briefer in form: the short text is completely through-composed, lacking the contrast of a middle section. In the Whit cantata, the aria proper is immediately followed by an instrumental ritornello, whose original version is also found in the 'Hunt' Cantata, though not with Pales' aria but at the end of the score. We do not know for certain what function this instrumental piece had in the Weißenfels *musique de table*. By analogy with the Whit cantata, however, it seems reasonable to let it follow Pales's aria.

An aria for Pan, no. 14, accompanied only by continuo, with a song-like melody and in pure da capo form, concludes the individual singing of the well-wishers. It is followed by the concluding chorus, no. 15, which is again conceived as an ensemble of the four soloists, as we can tell from the vocal scoring (S I,II TB). Due to the participation of the entire instrumental ensemble, this largely homophonic-textured movement achieves antiphonal effects between

[4] This ensemble of four singers (two sopranos, tenor and bass) corresponds exactly with the regular membership of the ducal chapel at Weißenfels at the time of the cantata's first performance. See E.-M. Ranft, 'Zum Personalbestand der Weißenfelser Hofkapelle', *Beiträge zur Bach-Forschung* 6 (Leipzig, 1987), 5–36, and J. Rifkin, 'From Weimar to Leipzig: Concertists and Ripienists in Bach's *Ich hatte viel Bekümmernis* [BWV 21]', *Early Music* 24 (1996), 583–603 (see p. 593).

woodwind, strings, horns, and choir. A signal-like motive,* first heard on the horns, later often on bassoon and cello, and finally on unison woodwind or unison strings, reminds us yet once more of the occasion of the cantata's performance—the ducal hunt.

Entfliehet, verschwindet, entweichet, ihr Sorgen, BWV 249a

NBA I/35, Critical Report BC G2 Music lost[5]

1. SINFONIA
   a) [Allegro] tr I–III timp ob I,II str bsn bc — D 3/8
   b) Adagio ob I str bc — b 3/4
2. ARIA [DUETTO] TB (Da capo: SA) tr I–III timp ob I,II str bc — D 3/8

Menalcas, Damoetas	
Entfliehet, verschwindet, entweichet, ihr Sorgen,	Flee, vanish, fade, you cares,
Verwirret die lustigen Regungen nicht!	Do not unsettle our merry feelings!
Lachen und Scherzen	Laughter and mirth
Erfüllet die Herzen	Fill our hearts,
Die Freude malet das Gesicht.	Joy paints our countenance.
Doris, Sylvia	
Entfliehet, verschwindet, entweichet, ihr Sorgen,	Flee, vanish, fade, you cares,
Verwirret die lustigen Regungen nicht!	Do not unsettle our merry feelings!

3. RECITATIVO

Damoetas	
Was hör ich da?	What do I hear there?
Menalcas	
Wer unterbricht uns hier?	Who interrupts us here?
Damoetas	
Wie? Doris und die Sylvia?	What? Doris and Sylvia?
Sylvia	
So glaubet ihr,	Then do you believe
Daß eure Brust allein	That your breast alone
Voll Jauchzen und voll Freude?	Is full of jubilation and full of joy?
Doris	
Und daß wir beide	And that we two shall
Jetzt ohne Wonne sollen sein?	Now be without delight?

4. ARIA S fl bc — b 3/4

Doris	
Hunderttausend Schmeicheleien	A hundred-thousand compliments
Wallen jetzt in meiner Brust.	Well up now in my breast.
Und die Lust,	And of the delight

[5] Details of scoring and key, where present (that is, for the sinfonia and the arias), follow the reconstruction in NBA II/7, p. 99.

So die Zärtlichkeiten zeigen,	That tendernesses show
Kann die Zunge nicht verschweigen.	My tongue cannot keep silent.

5. Recitativo

Damoetas

Wie aber, schönste Schäferin,	But, fairest shepherdess,
Was habt ihr vor, wo wollt ihr hin?	What are you going to do? where are you going?
Doris	
Bei Buchen,	Among beeches,
Eichen oder Linden	Oaks or lindens
Die Blumengöttin aufzusuchen,	To seek out the flower goddess,
Um einen Kranz	To bind
Vor unsern teuren Christian	For our dear Christian
Zu winden.	A wreath.
Der ungemeine Glanz	The uncommon splendour
Von seiner hohen Feier,	Of his lofty celebration—
So meiner Seele wert und teuer,	So dear and precious to my soul—
Bricht jetzund an.	Breaks out now.
Menalcas	
Ihr geht mit uns auf gleichen Wegen.	You are going the same way as we.
Sylvia	
Wer aber wird die Schafe pflegen?	But who will look after the sheep?

6. Aria T vln I,II (+ rec I,II 8va) bc — G c

Menalcas

Wieget euch, ihr satten Schafe,	Rock yourselves, you satiated sheep,
In dem Schlafe	To sleep
Unterdessen selber ein!	In the meantime!
Dort in jenen tiefen Gründen,	There in those deep meadows,
Wo schon junge Rasen sein,	Where the young grass already grows,
Wollen wir euch wiederfinden.	We will find you again.

7. Recitativo

Damoetas

Wohlan!	Well, then!
Geliebte Schäferinnen,	Beloved shepherdesses,
Ihr sollt mit uns nach Hofe gehn	You shall go with us to the court,
Und unserm freudigen Beginnen	And at our joyful enterprise
Zur Seite stehn:	Stand at the side;
Allein,	However,
Wo werden Rosen und Narzissen,	Where shall we find roses and narcissi,
Jesminen, Lilien und Melissen	Jasmines, lilies, and balms
Zu unsern Kränzen sein?	For our garlands?
Sylvia	
Wahr ist es, ich kann nichts erblicken,	It is true, I can see nothing
Die Stirnen damit auszuschmücken;	With which to adorn our brows;

Doch wünsch ich mir, durch mein Bemühen
Die Blumen annoch vor der Zeit
Aus ihrer kalten Gruft zu ziehen.

Yet I wish, through my efforts
Before the time is ripe,
To draw the flowers from their cold tomb.

8. ARIA A ob I str bc — A C

Sylvia

Komm doch, Flora, komm geschwinde,
Hauche mit dem Westenwinde
Unsre Felder lieblich an,
Daß ein treuer Untertan
Seinem milden Christian
Pflicht und Schuld bezahlen kann.

Come then, Flora, come quickly,
Breathe with the west wind
Sweetly on our fields,
So that a loyal subject
To his gentle Christian
Can pay his duty and debt.

9. RECITATIVO

Damoetas

Was sorgt ihr viel,
Die Flora zu beschweren?
Was wird sich unser großer Fürst
Besonders an die Blumen kehren?
Ein Wunsch, den Treu und Liebe zeigt,
Und der als ein beständig Ziel
Durch Luft und Wolken steigt,
Wird seinen Ohren wohlgefallen.
Drum auf! Laßt euren Lobgesang
Mit untermischtem Paukenklang
Ertönen und erschallen!

Why do you take so much trouble
To burden Flora?
Why should our great prince
Especially heed flowers?
A wish that shows loyalty and love
And which, as a constant aim,
Climbs through air and clouds
Will be well pleasing to his ears.
Therefore arise! Let your song of praise,
Intermingled with the sound of drums,
Ring out and resound!

10. ARIA [QUARTET] SATB tr I–III timp ob I,II str bc — D C $\frac{3}{8}$

Glück und Heil
Bleibe dein beständig Teil!
Großer Herzog, dein Vergnügen
Müsse wie die Palmen stehn,
Die sich niemals niederbiegen,
Sondern bis zum Wolken gehn!
So werden sich künftig bei stetem Gedeihen
Die Deinen mit Lachen und Scherzen erfreuen.

May good fortune and well-being
Remain your constant lot!
Great Duke, your contentment
Must stand like palms,
Which never bow down
But rise up to the clouds!
Thus in future amidst constant prosperity
Your people shall rejoice with laughter and mirth.

The sources of Bach's 'Pastoral' Cantata—the original score and parts, together with manuscript copies of any kind—are lost. We possess only the printed libretto in the first volume of Picander's poems. However, we also possess the *Easter Oratorio* (in three different versions), and since Friedrich Smend has established that the music for all the arias of that work, including the duet and the quartet, was adopted from the 'Pastoral' Cantata, the movements concerned can be reconstructed without undue difficulty.[6] Only the recitatives are altogether lost, but if suitable music is invented for them the lost cantata can be restored in a performable version. This is all the more welcome in view of the failure of the *Easter Oratorio* to establish a permanent place in our musical culture on account of its clearly perceptible derivation from a secular congratulatory cantata. The *Christmas Oratorio*, on the other hand, though its choruses* and arias are again largely of secular origin, is better suited to its church purpose as a result of the inclusion of biblical words and chorale.

The composition of the 'Pastoral' Cantata was occasioned by the birthday of Duke Christian of Saxe-Weißenfels on 23 February 1725. Bach had long enjoyed good relations with the court of Weißenfels. Twelve years earlier, he had performed the 'Hunt' Cantata there (BWV 208), also for the duke's birthday; and from 1729 at the latest he boasted the title of 'Hochfürstlich Sächsisch-Weißenfelsischen würcklichen Capellmeister' (Actual Capellmeister to the Court of Saxe-Weißenfels).

With only slight modifications, Picander's text adheres to the tried and tested scheme invariably employed on such occasions. In view of the happy occasion about to be celebrated, the shepherds Damoetas and Menalcas drive away their cares. Their singing is interrupted by the shepherdesses Doris and Sylvia, who make it plain that all four have the same aim, namely to offer their congratulations to the prince. They leave in the hope that their sheep will rock themselves to sleep in the valleys where fresh grass is already growing. There are still no flowers on that February day, however, and Sylvia's entreaty that the flower goddess Flora will use the westerly winds to hasten their growth has little prospect of fulfilment in time. Yet even without flowers, Damoetas tells her, the prince will certainly accept with pleasure a song of congratulation 'intermingled with the sound of drums'.

Primitive as it is, the plot offers the composer ample scope for characterful shaping of the various movements. Among them the pastoral lullaby (no. 6) and, above all, the full-textured finale in praise of the prince belong to the regular repertoire of baroque opera and serenade music. Bach's setting, however, is of imperishable worth and towers above the general level of such congratulatory music. The opening Sinfonia comprises an Allegro and Adagio which were formerly thought to stem from a lost Cöthen concerto but are now believed to be original compositions.[7] It remains uncertain, however, whether this extensive instrumental introduction belonged to the Pastoral Cantata at all

[6] The 'Pastoral' Cantata (without recitatives), together with its sacred parody* the Easter cantata *Kommt, fliehet und eilet* of 1725, are published in a reconstruction by Paul Brainard in NBA II/7 (1977), Appendix B, p. 99. A performing edition by Friedrich Smend, with recitatives composed by Hermann Keller, appeared *c.* 1943/4 (Bärenreiter edn, No. 1785).

[7] See Rifkin, 'Verlorene Quellen, verlorene Werke', 74, note 57, and S. Rampe and D. Sackmann, *Bachs Orchestermusik: Entstehung-Klangwelt-Interpretation* (Kassel, 2000), 466, note 2.

or whether it was first added as part of its adaptation as an Easter cantata, in which case the Pastoral Cantata would have begun with the duet. In the Allegro, the various instrumental groups—trumpets and drums, woodwind (oboes and bassoon), and strings—consort together in antiphonal exchanges. Among them the first violin and bassoon at times come forward as soloists. In the Adagio, the first oboe is heard as soloist over a constantly repeated rhythmic figure in the strings (the trumpet choir is silent).

In the duet-aria 'Entfliehet, verschwindet', the voices—at first tenor and bass—enter after a substantial ritornello. Scale figures in the strings, repeated *pianissimo* in the oboes, depict the fleeing of cares. After a middle section, rich in coloraturas* ('Laughter and mirth . . .'), the reprise of the principal section is now sung by soprano and alto, for Doris and Sylvia interrupt the singing of Damoetas and Menalcas, as we are told in the following recitative. Doris's aria 'Hunderttausend Schmeicheleien', no. 4, is one of the movements that gain most from the reconstruction of their original version. The figure-work of the obbligato* flute is not only very idiomatic to the instrument, it also provides a graphic illustration of the 'welling up' of compliments (literally, 'flatteries') spoken of in the text.

The aural charm of the aria 'Wieget euch, ihr satten Schafe', no. 6, derives from its scoring with muted violins, doubled by recorders at the upper octave, over a calmly pulsating, pedal-like continuo bass. It directly conveys the impression of a cradle song and of shepherds' music. Despite its conventional type, the movement represents one of the most original inspirations among all Bach's secular-cantata arias. Sylvia's aria, no. 8, takes the form of a summons, 'Come then, Flora, come quickly!', which gives rise to vivacious accents. Oboe and strings open with a ritornello in pure concertante* style, whose theme is then taken up by the alto voice to the accompaniment of the oboe.

Finally, the concluding chorus, with its bipartite contrast, forms a curious counterpart to the Sanctus that originated around the same time and was later incorporated in the B minor Mass (BWV 232[III]). Both pieces open with a section in common time characterized by triplet rhythms. The voice parts constitute a largely chordal texture, only lightly broken up into polyphony.* The second section, a fugato in quick 3/8 time, provides the 'Pastoral' Cantata with a strikingly brief conclusion.

Die Zeit, die Tag und Jahre macht, BWV 134a

NBA I/35, p. 51 BC G5 Duration: *c.* 41 mins

1. Recitativo AT bc — B♭ **c**

Zeit

Die Zeit, die Tag und Jahre macht,	Time, which makes days and years,
Hat Anhalt manche Segensstunden	Has brought Anhalt many hours of blessing

Und itzo gleich ein neues Heil gebracht.	And now brings new welfare.
Göttliche Vorsehung	*Divine Providence*
O edle Zeit! mit Gottes Huld verbunden.	O noble Time! bound up with God's favour.

2. Aria T ob I,II str bc — B♭ 3/8

Zeit	
Auf, Sterbliche, lasset ein Jauchzen ertönen:	Arise, mortals, let jubilation ring out:
Euch strahlet von neuem ein göttliches Licht!	A divine light shines upon you anew!
Mit Gnaden bekröne der Himmel die Zeiten,	May heaven crown the times with grace;
Auf, Seelen, ihr müsset ein Opfer bereiten,	Arise, souls, you must prepare an offering;
Bezahlet dem Höchsten mit Danken die Pflicht!	Pay your duty to the Most High with thanksgiving!

3. Recitativo AT bc — g–E♭ c

Zeit	
So bald, als dir die Sternen hold,	As soon as the stars were propitious for you,
O höchst gepriesnes Fürstentum!	O most highly prized principality,
Bracht ich den teuren Leopold.	I brought you dear Leopold.
Zu deinem Heil, zu seinem Ruhm	For your welfare, for his renown
Hab ich ihn manches Jahr gepfleget	I have looked after him for many a year
Und ihm ein neues beigeleget.	And added a New Year for him.
Noch schmück ich dieses Götterhaus,	Still do I adorn this divine House,
Noch zier ich Anhalts Fürstenhimmel	Still do I grace Anhalt's princely heaven
Mit neuem Licht und Gnadenstrahlen aus;	With new light and rays of grace;
Noch weicht die Not von diesen Grenzen weit;	Still affliction retreats far from these borders;
Noch fliehet alles Mordgetümmel;	Still all murderous tumult flees;
Noch blüht allhier die güldne Zeit:	Still the Golden Age blooms here:
So preise dann des Höchsten Gütigkeit!	Then praise the benevolence of the Most High!
Göttliche Vorsehung	*Divine Providence*
Des Höchsten Lob ist den Magneten gleich,	The praise of the Most High is like a magnet
Von oben her mehr Heil an sich zu ziehen.	To draw more welfare to itself from above.
So müssen weise Fürsten blühen;	Thus wise princes must flourish;
So wird ein Land an Segen reich.	Thus a land grows rich in blessing.
Dich hat, O Zeit, zu mehrem Wohlergehn	You, O Time, for the increased prosperity

Für dieses Haus der Zeiten Herr ersehn.	Of this House, have been chosen by the Lord of Times.
Zeit	*Time*
Was mangelt mir an Gnadengaben?	What gifts of grace do I lack?
Göttliche Vorsehung	*Divine Providence*
Noch größre hab ich aufgehaben.	I have still greater ones in store.
Zeit	*Time*
Mein Ruhm ist itzt schon ungemein.	My renown is now already uncommon.
Göttliche Vorsehung	*Divine Providence*
Zu Gottes Preis wird solcher größer sein.	To God's glory it will be greater.
4. ARIA [DUETTO] AT str bc	E♭ ¢
Göttliche Vorsehung	*Divine Providence*
Zeit	*Time*
[Es streiten, es siegen die künftigen Zeiten	[Future times strive and conquer
Es streiten, es prangen die vorigen Zeiten]	Past times strive and shine]
beide	*both*
Im Segen für dieses durchlauchtigste Haus.	In blessing for this most illustrious House.
Dies liebliche Streiten beweget die Herzen,	This lovely strife moves our hearts
Zeit	*Time*
Die Saiten zu rühren,	To stir the strings,
Göttliche Vorsehung	*Divine Providence*
zu streiten,	to strive,
Zeit	*Time*
zu scherzen,	to jest;
beide	*both*
Es schläget zum Preise des Höchsten hinaus.	It redounds to the glory of the Most High.
5. RECITATIVO AT bc	C–g c
Göttliche Vorsehung	*Divine Providence*
Bedenke nur, beglücktes Land,	Consider, fortunate land,
Wieviel ich dir in dieser Zeit gegeben.	How much I have given you at this time.
An Leopold hast du ein Gnadenpfand.	In Leopold you have a pledge of grace.
Schau an der Fürstin Klugheit Licht,	Look at his consort's light of wisdom,
Schau an des Prinzen edlem Leben,	Look at the prince's noble life,
An der Prinzessin Tugendkranz,	At the princess's wreath of virtue,
Daß diesem Hause nichts an Glanz	So that to this House no brilliance
Und dir kein zeitlich Wohl gebricht.	And to you no temporal good is lacking.
Soll ich dein künftig Heil bereiten,	If I am to prepare your future welfare,
So hole von dem Sternenpol	Then fetch from the starry pole

Durch dein Gebet ihr hohes Fürstenwohl!
Komm, Anhalt, fleh um mehre Jahr und Zeiten!

Through your entreaty their lofty princely prosperity!
Come, Anhalt, plead for more years and times!

Zeit
Ach! fleh um dieses Glück.
Denn ohne Gott und sie
Würd ich nicht einen Augenblick
Für dich glückselig sein.
Ja, Anhalt, ja, du beugest deine Knie,
Dein sehnlichs Wünschen stimmt mit ein.

Time
Ah! plead for this good fortune.
For without God and it
I would not for one moment
Be blessed for you.
Yes, Anhalt, yes, you bend your knee:
Your most earnest wishes concur.

Göttliche Vorsehung
Allein, o gütigstes Geschick!
Gott schauet selbst auf die erlauchten Herzen,
Auf dieser Herrschaft Tugend-Kerzen,
Sie brennen ihm in heißer Andacht schön.
Um ihre Gott beliebte Glut
Kömmt selbst auf sie ein unschätzbares Gut
Und auf dies Land viel zeitlich Wohlergehn.

Divine Providence
However, O most kind fate!
God Himself looks upon these illustrious hearts,
Upon this sovereignty's candles of virtue:
They burn beautifully for Him in ardent devotion.
Around their blaze, beloved of God,
A priceless good comes upon them,
And upon this land, much temporal prosperity.

6. Aria A bc — g c

Göttliche Vorsehung
Der Zeiten Herr hat viel vergnügte Stunden,
Du Götterhaus, dir annoch beigelegt,
Weil bei der Harmonie der Seelen,
Die Gott zum Hort und Heil erwählen,
Des Himmels Glück mit einzustimmen pflegt.

Divine Providence
The Lord of Times has added many contented hours
To you already, you divine House.
For with the harmony of souls
That choose God as refuge and salvation
Heaven's fortune is wont to chime.

7. Recitativo AT bc — E♭–F c

Zeit
Hilf, Höchster, hilf, daß mich die Menschen preisen
Und für dies weltberühmte Haus
Nie böse, sondern gülden heißen.
Komm, schütt auf sie den Strom des Segens aus!
Ja, sei durch mich dem teursten Leopold

Time
Help, O Most High, help men to praise me
And for this world-renowned House
Never to call me bad but rather golden.
Come, pour out upon them the stream of blessing!
Indeed, may there be through me for dearest Leopold

Zu vieler Tausend Wohl und Lust,
Die unter seiner Gnade wohnen,
Bis in ein graues Alter hold!
Erquicke seine Götterbrust!
Laß den durchlauchtigsten Personen,
Die du zu deinem Ruhm ersehn,
Auf die bisher dein Gnadenlicht geschienen,
Nur im vollkommnen Wohlergehn
Die schönste Zeit noch viele Jahre dienen!
Erneure, Herr, bei jeder Jahreszeit
An ihnen deine Güt und Treu!

Too many thousand good things and delights
That dwell under His Grace,
Gracious until grey old age!
Refresh his divine breast!
Let these most illustrious persons,
Whom You have chosen for Your renown,
On whom Your Light of Grace has hitherto shone,
Be served only in complete prosperity
For many years yet by the fairest Time!
Renew, Lord, at every season
For them Your goodness and faithfulness!

Göttliche Vorsehung
Des Höchsten Huld wird alle Morgen neu.
Es will sein Schutz, sein Geist insonderheit
Auf solchen Fürsten schweben,
Die in dem Lebens-Fürsten leben.

Divine Providence
The favour of the Most High is new every morning.
His protection, His Spirit will in particular
Hover over such princes
As live in the Prince of Life.

8. Chorus SATB ob I,II str bc — B♭ $\frac{3}{8}$

Zeit
Ergetzet auf Erden,
Göttliche Vorsehung
erfreuet von oben,
Tutti
Glückselige Zeiten, vergnüget dies Haus!
Göttliche Vorsehung/Zeit
Es müsse bei diesen durchlauchtigsten Seelen
Die Gnade/Der Segen des Himmels die Wohnung erwählen;
Tutti
Sie blühen, sie leben, ruft jedermann aus.

Time
Delight on earth,
Divine Providence
gladden from above,
Tutti
Blissful times, give pleasure to this House!
Divine Providence/Time
With these most illustrious souls
The grace/The blessing of heaven must choose its dwelling;
Tutti
They flourish, they live, everyone calls out.

This work is the original model of the Easter cantata *Ein Herz, das seinen Jesum lebend weiß*, BWV 134. When preparing the parody* Bach made use of the performing material of the secular version, which was thereby rendered incomplete. As a result, in the *Bach-Gesellschaft* edition the work was published as a fragment, *Mit Gnaden bekröne der Himmel die Zeiten*. Only Philipp Spitta's discovery of the text, by Christian Friedrich Hunold, made it possible to retrieve the cantata in full.

According to Hunold's poetics, the text belongs to the 'serenata'* type and it takes the form of a dialogue. 'Zeit' ('Time', in the sense of time past) and 'Göttliche Vorsehung' ('Divine Providence', the future), two allegorical figures, whose appearance on New Year's Day seems significant, converse over the destiny of Anhalt and above all, as one might expect, that of its prince, Leopold. In accordance with the veneration of princes which was typical of the age, Leopold is assured that even now he signifies exceptional good fortune for his land and subjects and that the future will bring him and Anhalt still greater gifts of grace. The sequence of movements gradually turns our attention from the past to the future. The first aria, no. 2, is assigned to Time; the second, a duet (no. 4), brings Time and Divine Providence together in a dispute over the 'blessing of this most illustrious House'; and the third, no. 6, is assigned to Divine Providence, who promises future blessings. In the last recitative, no. 7, the words 'The favour of the Most High is new every morning' allude to Lamentations 3.23. In the finale, no. 8, the dialogue of the two allegorical characters is augmented to four voices ('Tutti' signifies SATB), representing the congratulations of Leopold's subjects.

Contrary to the normal type of *church* cantata, in which the opening movement—often a biblical dictum or chorale—states the theme as if on a placard, with all that follows having a merely interpretative character, the present text, like that of many other secular cantatas, is heightened towards the end and culminates in general jubilation. The opening words, set by Bach as a plain *secco* recitative, are followed by a lively aria involving the entire instrumental ensemble of two oboes, strings, and continuo. At times, the first oboe is predominant with its concertante* figuration, but in the middle section it is joined by the second oboe and first violin, which take on a concertante role in alternation. Another plainly declaimed *secco* recitative links this aria with the next, no. 4, a duet with string accompaniment. Lively tumult figures on the first violin (the second violin and viola merely accompany) here portray the contest between past and future times.

The fifth movement directs our attention towards the future, from which not only Prince Leopold but his family, and indeed the entire land, may anticipate good fortune. In the middle of the movement, the call 'Come, Anhalt, plead for more years and times!' is composed as arioso,* setting it off from the surrounding *secco* recitative. The aria for Divine Providence, no. 6, is accompanied only by continuo, a texture Bach often uses for particularly personal statements. The voice is here allowed the scope to unfold freely and eloquently over the ostinato* motives* of the continuo (which are derived from the ritornello).

In a *secco* recitative, no. 7, declaimed syllabically* almost throughout, the blessing of the Most High is implored upon Anhalt and its prince. Thereupon all participants unite in the finale. The vocal texture is here augmented to four parts, giving rise to a constant interchange between the duet of the two allegorical figures and the tutti of all the singers. The cheerfully animated 3/8 rhythm is related to that of the first aria, no. 2, so that a suggestion of formal rounding-off is given.

Durchlauchtster Leopold, BWV 173a

NBA I/35, p. 97 BC G9 Duration: *c.* 23 mins

1. [Recitativo] S str bc — D C

Durchlauchtster Leopold,
Es singet Anhalts Welt
Von neuem mit Vergnügen,
Dein Köthen sich dir stellt,
Um sich vor dir zu biegen,
Durchlauchtster Leopold!

Most illustrious Leopold,
We sing of Anhalt's world
Afresh with delight;
Your Cöthen presents itself to you
In order to bow down before you,
Most illustrious Leopold!

2. Aria S str + fl I,II bc — D C

Güldner Sonnen frohe Stunden,
Die der Himmel selbst gebunden,
Sich von neuem eingefunden,
Rühmet, singet, stimmt die Saiten,
Seinen Nachruhm auszubreiten!

Glad hours of golden suns,
Bound by heaven itself,
Have appeared anew;
Praise, sing, tune the strings
To spread his renown!

3. [Bass Solo] B str bc — b C

Leopolds Vortrefflichkeiten
Machen uns itzt viel zu tun.
  Mund und Herze, Ohr und Blicke
  Können nicht bei seinem Glücke,
  Das ihm billig folget, ruhn.

Leopold's splendours
Now give us much to do.
  Mouth and heart, ear and sight
  Cannot rest at the good fortune
  That rightly pursues him.

4. Aria [Duetto] SB fl I,II str bc — G–D–A 3/4

Baß
Unter seinem Purpursaum
Ist die Freude
Nach dem Leide,
Jeden schenkt er weiten Raum,
Gnadengaben zu genießen,
Die wie reiche Ströme fließen.
Sopran
Nach landesväterlicher Art
Er ernähret,
Unfall wehret;
Drum sich nun die Hoffnung paart,
Daß er werde Anhalts Lande
Setzen in beglückten Stande.
beide
Doch wir lassen unsre Pflicht
Froher Sinnen

Bass
Under his purple robe
Is joy
After sorrow;
He gives everyone ample scope
To enjoy the gifts of grace
That flow like rich streams.
Soprano
Like a father of the people
He nourishes us
And wards off mischance;
Therefore the hope now germinates
That he will place Anhalt's land
In a happy situation.
both
Yet we do not let our duty's
Gladder feelings

Itzt nicht rinnen,	Flow away now,
Heute, da des Himmels Licht	Today, when heaven's light
Seine Knechte fröhlich machet	Makes his servants joyful
Und auf seinem Zepter lachet.	And delights in his sceptre.
5. RECITATIVO SB bc	f♯–b **c**
Durchlauchtigster, den Anhalt Vater nennt,	Most illustrious one, called Anhalt's father,
Wir wollen dann das Herz zum Opfer bringen;	We would, then, bring our heart as an offering;
Aus unsrer Brust, die ganz vor Andacht brennt,	From our breast, which quite burns with devotion,
Soll sich der Seufzer Glut zum Himmel schwingen.	A blaze of sighs shall leap up to heaven.
6. ARIA S str + fl I + II bc	D ¢
So schau dies holden Tages Licht	Then see this lovely day's light
Noch viele, viele Zeiten.	Many, many more times.
Und wie es itzt begleiten	And as it is now accompanied by
Hohes Wohlsein und Gelücke,	High prosperity and good fortune,
So wisse es, wenn es anbricht	So when it dawns in the future
Ins Künftige, von Kummer nicht.	It shall know nothing of grief.
7. ARIA B bsn + vc bc	A ¢
Dein Name gleich der Sonnen geh,	May your name move like the sun,
Stets während bei den Sternen steh!	While it ever stays still with the stars!
Leopold in Anhalts Grenzen	Leopold in Anhalt's borders
Wird im Fürstenruhme glänzen.	Will blaze in princely renown.
8. CHORUS SB fl I,II str bc	D 3
Nimm auch, großer Fürst, uns auf	Accept us too, great prince,
Und die sich zu deinen Ehren	And let those who sing in your honour,
Untertänigst lassen hören!	Most obediently, be heard!
Glücklich sei dein Lebenslauf,	May the course of your life be happy,
Sei dem Volke solcher Segen,	May such blessing be to your people
Den auf deinem Haupt wir legen!	As we lay upon your head!

This cantata, for the birthday of Prince Leopold of Anhalt-Cöthen, is relatively unambitious. It has therefore been suggested that it might have been written in great haste in 1717. That year, after his release from a four-week detention imposed by the Weimar duke, who refused to grant his dismissal, Bach, newly appointed as Cöthen Capellmeister, had only a few days to prepare for the prince's birthday, which was celebrated on 10 December. The autograph score of the present cantata (perhaps a later fair copy) apparently originated a few years later, however, and it is possible that we ought to place the origin of the work itself within the period around 1722.

A curious feature of the libretto, whose author is unknown, is the absence of verse designed for recitative. The two recitatives in the eight-movement work are far too regular in verse structure (the first even includes a da capo* of its opening line) to have been written with recitative setting in mind. The tri-strophic structure of the fourth movement must also have seemed antiquated around 1717/22. Thus the librettist should no doubt be sought among the older generation of poets.

The instrumental ensemble includes not only strings and continuo but two transverse flutes* and bassoon. The only singers required are soprano and bass—we may assume that the finale too, though designated 'Chorus',* was sung by these two soloists alone. It is possible that the two singers were conceived as allegorical figures, for Bach often failed to enter such names in his score and the printed libretto has not survived. It might be thought that lines such as 'Leopold's splendours now give us much to do' (no. 3) had been put into the mouth of some tutelary godhead or personification of renown or poetry, but the text discloses no further details.

Despite the limitations imposed on him by the simple scoring and the rather antiquated form of the libretto, Bach shapes the succession of eight cantata movements with ease and abundant resource. The introductory recitative, scored with strings, flows into a virtuoso coloratura* at the reprise of the opening words. The following aria, no. 2, reminds us of a dance in the clear periodic articulation of its introductory ritornello. Its striking melody, interspersed with rests and pervaded by triplet rhythms, in conjunction with the tender scoring for flutes and strings, lends it an exceedingly amiable character. Its expressive power is heightened in the middle section by clearly speech-like gestures on the words 'rühmet, singet' ('praise, sing'), whose motive* is repeated in the strings for emphasis. The third movement, for which Bach no doubt deliberately avoids what would be a pretentious heading of 'aria' in this context, is strikingly brief. The lively 'vivace' tempo and the excited motion of the accompanying strings characterize the fervour with which Leopold's renown is spread. Despite its free da capo, the movement gives the impression of open rather than closed form, for the motivically imprinted melodic line in the violins, almost invariably in unison, nowhere consolidates into a theme.

The duet 'Unter seinem Purpursaum', no. 4, headed 'Al tempo di minuetto', is perhaps one of Bach's most original arias. The form is tripartite in accordance with the tri-strophic verse structure. The second and third sections are both variations of the first, subjecting it by various means to a process of progressive enhancement. The key sequence ascends through the circle of fifths from G (section 1), via D (section 2), to A (section 3). The opening ensemble of voice, strings, and continuo is augmented by two flutes from the second section onwards and by the addition of a second voice in the third section. Finally, as far as rhythmic movement is concerned, crotchets prevail at first, then quavers in the second section and semiquavers in the third.

The duet recitative, no. 5, consolidates after a few bars into an arioso,* in which scale and sigh figures graphically represent the rising of devoted sighs to heaven. The following aria, no. 6, like the two previous arias, has the character of a dance, in this case a bourrée. The transverse flutes,* which reinforce the first violin, provide dynamic shading in the middle section by alternately resting and playing. No. 7, another aria, provides the necessary contrast with its neighbours by employing an exclusively deep pitch in both vocal and instrumental parts. Combined with the singing of the bass voice, bassoon and cello play a unison concertante* part over a continuo bass made up of violone and harpsichord. The concluding chorus is again dance-like and should probably be construed as a polonaise. Formally, it falls into two sections. Within each section the instrumental music is first heard alone and then repeated with the vocal parts superimposed—an enhanced species of binary dance form.

2

Festive Music for the Electoral House of Saxony

The composition and performance of congratulatory cantatas for members of the Electoral House of Saxony was not one of Bach's regular duties. Yet after his move to Leipzig in 1723 Bach composed a series of such works, especially after 1729 when he took over the direction of the student Collegium musicum, which had been founded by Telemann. For a list of performances verified by the sources see the Critical Report to NBA I/36, pp. 8 f. The identifiable works are as follows:

Entfernet euch, ihr heitern Sterne, BWV Anh. I 9, for the birthday of Augustus II[1] on 12 May 1727. Only the libretto by Christian Friedrich Haupt survives. For details see the Critical Report to NBA I/36, pp. 11–15.

Ihr Häuser des Himmels, ihr scheinenden Lichter, BWV 193a, for the name-day of Augustus II on 3 August 1727. All that survives is Picander's text and the council-election cantata BWV 193, whose first, third, and fifth movements are believed to be related by parody* to BWV 193a/1, 7, and 9. For details see the Critical Report to NBA I/36, pp. 16–19.

Es lebe der König, der Vater im Lande, BWV Anh. I 11, for the name-day of Augustus II on 3 August 1732. All that survives is Picander's text, plus the movements believed to be related by parody to the first, seventh (?), and ninth movements of this work, namely BWV 215/1 (and 232^{IV}, 'Osanna'), 248/39, and 212/14. For details see the Critical Report to NBA I/36, pp. 20–3 (regarding BWV 212/14 see the Critical Report to NBA I/39, pp. 126–9).

Frohes Volk, vergnügte Sachsen, BWV Anh. I 12, for the name-day of Augustus III[2] on 3 August 1733. All that survives is Picander's libretto, which proves to be a parody of BWV Anh. I 18 in all but its recitatives. An indirect parody of the opening movement survives in that of the *Ascension Oratorio*, BWV 11. For details see the Critical Report to NBA I/36, pp. 24–7.

[1] So styled as King of Poland, but as Elector of Saxony he was Friedrich Augustus I ('Augustus the Strong').

[2] So styled as King of Poland, but as Elector of Saxony he was Friedrich Augustus II.

Laßt uns sorgen, laßt uns wachen, BWV 213, for the birthday of Prince Friedrich Christian on 5 September 1733. This cantata is discussed below.

Tönet, ihr Pauken! Erschallet, Trompeten, BWV 214, for the birthday of Maria Josepha, Queen of Poland and Electoress of Saxony, on 8 December 1733. This cantata is discussed below.

Blast Lärmen, ihr Feinde! verstärket die Macht, BWV 205a, for the coronation of Augustus III, performed on 19 February 1734. All that survives is the text, plus Cantata 205 which acted as the parody model for most of the movements. For details see the Critical Report to NBA I/37, pp. 7–14.

Preise dein Glücke, gesegnetes Sachsen, BWV 215, for the anniversary of Augustus III's election as King of Poland, on 5 October 1734. The cantata is discussed below.

Schleicht, spielende Wellen, und murmelt gelinde, BWV 206, for the birthday of Augustus III on 7 October 1734; the performance was, however, delayed till 1736. The cantata, which was revived for the name-day of Augustus III on 3 August 1740, is discussed below.

Auf, schmetternde Töne der muntern Trompeten, BWV 207a, for the name-day of Augustus III on 3 August, probably in 1735. The cantata is discussed below.

Willkommen! ihr herrschenden Götter der Erden, BWV Anh. I 13: a homage cantata on the occasion of the king's visit and to celebrate the wedding of Princess Maria Amalia, performed on 28 April 1738. All that survives is the text by Gottsched. For details see the Critical Report to NBA I/37, pp. 97–102.

Was mir behagt, ist nur die muntre Jagd, BWV 208a, for the name day of Augustus III on 3 August 1742. All that survives is the libretto, plus Cantata 208 which acted as parody model in most of the movements. For details see the Critical Report to NBA I/37, pp. 91–6.

Laßt uns sorgen, laßt uns wachen, BWV 213

Hercules auf dem Scheidewege	*Hercules at the Crossroads*

NBA I/36, p. 3 BC G18 Duration: *c.* 45 mins

1. CHORUS SATB hn I,II ob I,II str bc — F $\frac{3}{8}$

Ratschluß der Götter	*Decree of the gods*
Laßt uns sorgen, laßt uns wachen	Let us care for, let us watch
Über unsern Göttersohn!	Over our divine son!
Unser Thron	Our throne
Wird auf Erden	Will on earth
Herrlich und verkläret werden,	Become glorious and radiant,
Unser Thron	Our throne
Wird aus ihm ein Wunder machen.	Will make a wonder of him.

2. Recitativo A bc — C–g 𝄴

Herkules
Und wo? Wo ist die rechte Bahn,
Da ich den eingepflanzten Trieb,
Dem Tugend, Glanz und Ruhm und
Hoheit lieb,
Zu seinem Ziele bringen kann?
Vernunft, Verstand und Licht
Begehrt, dem allen nachzujagen.
Ihr schlanken Zweige, könnt ihr nicht
Rat oder Weise sagen?

Hercules
And where? Where is the right path
By which I can bring my inborn desire
To love virtue, brilliance, and glory, and
majesty
To fruition?
Reason, understanding, and light
Demand that I pursue all these things.
You slender boughs, could you not
Offer counsel or means?

3. Aria S str bc — B♭ 2/4

Wollust
Schlafe, mein Liebster, und pflege der
Ruh,
Folge der Lockung entbrannter
Gedanken.
Schmecke die Lust
Der lüsternen Brust,
Und erkenne keine Schranken.

Pleasure
Sleep, my dearest, and take your ease,
Follow the enticement of inflamed
thoughts.
Taste the pleasure
Of the wanton breast
And know no bounds.

4. Recitativo ST bc — F–f♯ 𝄴

Wollust
Auf! folge meiner Bahn,
Da ich dich ohne Last und Zwang
Mit sanften Tritten werde leiten.
Die Anmut gehet schon voran,
Dir Rosen vor dir auszubreiten.
Verziehe nicht, den so bequemen Gang
Mit Freuden zu erwählen.
Tugend
Wohin? mein Herkules, wohin?
Du wirst des rechten Weges fehlen.
Durch Tugend, Müh und Fleiß
Erhebet sich ein edler Sinn.
Wollust
Wer wählet sich den Schweiß,
Der in Gemächlichkeit
Und scherzender Zufriedenheit
Sich kann sein wahres Heil erwerben?
Tugend
Das heißt: sein wahres Heil verderben.

Pleasure
Rise! follow my path,
Where without burden or restraint
I shall lead you with gentle steps.
Charm goes ahead already
To spread roses before you.
Do not be reluctant to choose
With joy such a comfortable path.
Virtue
Whither, my Hercules, whither?
You shall miss the right path.
Through virtue, effort, and diligence
A noble mind arises.
Pleasure
Who would choose sweat
When in ease
And playful contentment
He could earn his true welfare?
Virtue
That is to say: destroy his true welfare.

5. Aria A (Echo: A) ob d'am bc — A 6/8

Herkules
Treues Echo dieser Orten,
Sollt ich bei den Schmeichelworten

Hercules
Faithful Echo of these parts,
Should I be led astray by honeyed words'

Süßer Leitung irrig sein?	Sweet guidance?
Gib mir deine Antwort: Nein!	Give me your answer: No!
(Echo:) Nein!	(Echo:) No!
Oder sollte das Ermahnen,	Or should the warning
Das so mancher Arbeit nah,	That so much work is at hand
Mir die Wege besser bahnen?	Better lead the way for me?
Ach! so sage lieber: Ja!	Ah! then say rather: Yes!
(Echo:) Ja!	(Echo:) Yes!
6. Recitativo T bc	D–a **c**
Tugend	*Virtue*
Mein hoffnungsvoller Held!	My hero, full of promise!
Dem ich ja selbst verwandt	To whom I myself am indeed related
Und angeboren bin,	And in whom I am inborn,
Komm und erfasse meine Hand	Come and grasp my hand
Und höre mein getreues Raten,	And hear my faithful counsel,
Das dir der Väter Ruhm und Taten	Which puts your forefathers' glory and deeds
Im Spiegel vor die Augen stellt.	In a mirror before your eyes.
Ich fasse dich und fühle schon	I embrace you and feel already
Die folgbare und mir geweihte Jugend.	Your obedient youth, dedicated to me.
Du bist mein echter Sohn,	You are my true son,
Ich deine Zeugerin, die Tugend.	I your witness, Virtue.
7. Aria T ob I vln solo bc	e **c**
Tugend	*Virtue*
Auf meinen Flügeln sollst du schweben,	On my wings you shall hover,
Auf meinem Fittich steigest du	On my pinion you climb
Den Sternen wie ein Adler zu.	To the stars like an eagle.
Und durch mich	And through me
Soll dein Glanz und Schimmer sich	Your lustre and gleam
Zur Vollkommenheit erheben.	Shall rise to perfection.
8. Recitativo T bc	b–d **c**
Tugend	*Virtue*
Die weiche Wollust locket zwar;	Pale Pleasure is indeed enticing;
Allein,	However,
Wer kennt nicht die Gefahr,	Who does not know the danger
Die Reich und Helden kränkt,	That afflicts empires and heroes?
Wer weiß nicht, o Verführerin,	Who does not know, O seductress,
Daß du vorlängst und künftighin,	That in past and future,
So lang es nur den Zeiten denkt,	As long as imaginable time,
Von unsrer Götter Schar	By our host of gods
Auf ewig mußt verstoßen sein?	You must ever be repudiated?
9. Aria A vln I bc	a $\frac{3}{8}$
Herkules	*Hercules*
Ich will dich nicht hören, ich will dich nicht wissen,	I will not listen to you, I will not acknowledge you,

Verworfene Wollust, ich kenne dich nicht.
Denn die Schlangen,
So mich wollten wiegend fangen,
Hab ich schon lange zermalmet, zerrissen.

Depraved Pleasure, I know you not.
For the serpents
That would seize me in my cradle
I have long since crushed and torn.

10. RECITATIVO AT bc — C–F c

Herkules
Geliebte Tugend, du allein
Sollst meine Leiterin
Beständig sein.
Wo du befiehlst, da geh ich hin.
Das will ich mir zur Richtschnur wählen.
Tugend
Und ich will mich mit dir
So fest und so genau vermählen,
Daß ohne dir und mir
Mein Wesen niemand soll erkennen.
beide
Wer will ein solches Bündnis trennen?

Hercules
Beloved Virtue, you alone
Shall be my guide
Constantly.
Where you command, there shall I go.
That I will choose as my rule of conduct.
Virtue
And I will be wedded to you
So firmly and so closely
That without you and me
No one shall discern my nature.
both
Who would break such an alliance?

11. ARIA DUETTO AT vla I,II bc — F $\frac{3}{8}$

Herkules
Ich bin deine,
Tugend
Du bist meine,
beide
Küsse mich,
Ich küsse dich.
Wie Verlobte sich verbinden,
Wie die Lust, die sie empfinden,
Treu und zart und eiferig,
So bin ich.

Hercules
I am yours,
Virtue
You are mine,
both
Kiss me,
I kiss you.
Just as the betrothed are united,
Just like the pleasure they feel,
Faithful and tender and ardent,
So am I.

12. RECITATIVO B str bc — B♭–F c

Merkur
Schaut, Götter, dieses ist ein Bild
Von Sachsens Kurprinz Friedrichs Jugend!
Der muntern Jahre Lauf
Weckt die Verwunderung schon jetzund auf.
So mancher Tritt, so manche Tugend.
Schaut, wie das treue Land mit Freuden angefüllt,
Da es den Flug des jungen Adlers sieht,

Mercury
See, you gods, this is an image
Of the Saxon Crown Prince Frederick's youth!
The lively passing years
Even now awaken our admiration.
So many steps, so much virtue!
See how the loyal land is filled with joy
When it sees the flight of the young eagle,

Da es den Schmuck der Raute sieht,	When it sees the adornment of rue,
Und da sein hoffnungsvoller Prinz	And when its Prince, full of promise,
Der allgemeinen Freude blüht.	Blossoms to general rejoicing.
Schaut aber auch der Musen frohe Reihen	But see also the glad ranks of muses
Und hört ihr singendes Erfreuen:	And hear their joyful singing:
13. CHORUS SATB hn I,II ob I,II str bc	F 2
Chor der Musen	*Chorus of the Muses*
Lust der Völker, Lust der Deinen,	Delight of the peoples, delight of your own,
Blühe, holder Friederich!	Flourish, gracious Frederick!
Merkur	*Mercury*
Deiner Tugend Würdigkeit	The radiance of your virtue's worth
Stehet schon der Glanz bereit,	Is already prepared,
Und die Zeit	And the time
Ist begierig zu erscheinen;	Is eager to appear;
Eile, mein Friedrich, sie wartet auf dich.	Make haste, my Frederick, it awaits you.

When Augustus the Strong died in 1733 and his son ascended the electoral Saxon throne as Friedrich Augustus II, Bach and his student Collegium musicum showed increased activity in the performance of congratulatory cantatas for the ruling House of Saxony. Perhaps Bach wanted to use this method of endorsing his petition for the title of court Capellmeister, which he had made through the dedication of the Kyrie and Gloria of the B minor Mass. Although the Elector was not normally present in person in Leipzig, Bach might have expected him to hear news of the performances, and this might convince him that his favour and title would not be bestowed upon an unworthy recipient.

Hercules at the Crossroads, as the libretto is entitled in Picander's edition, was performed by Bach and his student Collegium musicum in Zimmermann's coffee garden on the afternoon of 5 September 1733 to celebrate the birthday of Crown Prince Friedrich Christian of Saxony. Congratulatory cantatas often lacked plot, amounting to little more than a lyric poem in praise of the personage honoured, but here Picander created a genuine 'dramma per musica'.* Hercules, a favourite symbol of baroque ruling figures, was better suited than virtually any other mythical hero to glorify the grandson of Augustus the Strong, who was then just eleven years old. Son of Zeus and Alcmena, Hercules had already distinguished himself as a hero in his earliest youth. In his cradle he had, without hesitation, crushed the serpents sent by his enemy Hera, mother of the gods. For the plot of the present cantata, Picander selected the myth handed down by Prodicus, who relates that Hercules met two women at a point where two roads crossed. One promised him a comfortable, luxurious life if he followed her road, the other hardship, but also virtue and glory, if he decided in favour of hers. Hercules resolves to take the path of virtue. The true significance of the plot is then revealed by Mercury, god of tradesmen and thus a personification of Leipzig and its citizens: Hercules is an image of Crown Prince Friedrich, for in his earliest youth he too had resolved to take the path of virtue.

The present-day listener who is acquainted with Bach's *Christmas Oratorio* will discover much that he already knows in the music of this cantata, as the following list of reused movements illustrates:

Hercules Cantata (model)	*Christmas Oratorio (parody*)*	
1 Laßt uns sorgen, laßt uns wachen	IV/36	Fallt mit Danken, fallt mit Loben
3 Schlafe, mein Liebster	II/19	Schlafe, mein Liebster
5 Treues Echo dieser Orten	IV/39	Flößt, mein Heiland
7 Auf meinen Flügeln	IV/41	Ich will nur dir zu Ehren leben
9 Ich will dich nicht hören	I/4	Bereite dich, Zion
11 Ich bin deine, du bist meine	III/29	Herr, dein Mitleid, dein Erbarmen
13 Lust der Völker, Lust der Deinen	[V/43	Ehre sei dir, Gott, gesungen]

In the last case the parody was planned, as is clear from the strophic structure of the poem, but not carried out.

The initial motives* of the first chorus,* headed 'Decree of the gods', are designed to accord with the opening of the text. In the melodic fall of 'Laßt uns sorgen' ('Let us care for') we seem to hear the gesture of loving protection, and in the rise of 'laßt uns wachen' ('let us watch'), by contrast, a look-out for danger in readiness for defence. When exchanged between horns, oboes, and strings, these motives, in conjunction with a *staccato* counterpoint,* lend the movement a colourful vitality. As a result of its scoring for horns, in place of the more usual trumpets and drums, the cantata acquires a certain serene radiance, an almost contemplative character. Here Hercules is not the warlike hero of renown but a boy whose welfare the gods must watch over (Crown Prince Friedrich was, after all, just eleven years old!). Accordingly, the part of Hercules, who in the following *secco* recitative asks the slender boughs to guide him on the right path, is sung by an alto, and in Bach's day it was self-evident that this would not be a woman's voice but that of a boy or falsettist.

'Pleasure' replies in the celebrated cradle song, no. 3, familiar from the *Christmas Oratorio*. Here it is designed to lull the young hero to sleep and thus divert him from the right path. The scoring for strings only (the oboe colour was added for the Christmas version) heightens the bewitching character of the aria. On account of its higher pitch, however (here it is in B flat; in the oratorio*, in G) it lacks some of the tenderness that we admire in the oratorio version. Next 'Virtue' (tenor) appears, and the two allegorical characters unleash an argumentative discourse in recitative, no. 4. Hercules, still seemingly irresolute, asks Echo to tell him the right way (no. 5), a typical baroque device which here has the additional function of raising the tension by deferring Hercules' final decision—in outward appearance only, however, for a close look at the words of the youthful hero reveals that his resolution is already firm from the outset, as courtesy to the electoral House demanded!

Virtue now steps forward and, after an introductory recitative, announces to the young Hercules, 'On my wings you shall hover' (no. 7). For this movement Bach chose the form of fugue,* which is rare in solo arias. Oboe, violin, continuo, and tenor in turn enter with the subject (disregarding the initial supporting notes in the continuo) and are then united on equal terms in a contrapuntal texture. Soon afterwards we hear entries of the inverted head-motive (oboe), strettos* (violin, oboe, and tenor) and, at the end of both principal and middle sections, an entry of the complete inverted subject in the continuo. Again Virtue issues a warning in a brief *secco* recitative, no. 8; but Hercules has now made up his mind, as he reveals in the aria 'Ich will dich nicht hören', no. 9 ('I will not listen to you, I will not acknowledge you, depraved Pleasure'). Albert Schweitzer pointed out the entirely different affect* of this aria as compared with its adaptation in the *Christmas Oratorio* ('Bereite dich, Zion, mit zärtlichen Trieben'; 'Make ready, Zion, with tender desire'). The indication 'unisoni e staccato' in the obbligato* violin part (here again an oboe is included only in the oratorio version) underlines the energetic character of the aria, with its determined calls of 'I will not'. After a brief recitative, Hercules and Virtue now unite in a duet, no. 11, whose scoring with two violas (thus without high strings) lends warmth and tenderness to its enraptured love text.

Since all the previous recitatives were set only as *secco* with continuo accompaniment, Mercury's words of interpretation, no. 12, acquire all the greater emphasis from their string accompaniment. The four-part vocal ensemble, which in the opening chorus lent their voices to the gods, now form a 'Chorus of the Muses' to sing the finale in honour of the prince. The music—a gavotte in character—is adopted from the Cöthen congratulatory cantata BWV 184a, where the vocal ensemble consisted of two voices only. We are reminded of this by the extended bass passages which are inserted between rondeau-like reprises of the tutti ritornello. Though eminently well-suited to form a joyful conclusion to the Hercules Cantata, this chorus would hardly have served as a satisfactory introduction to Part V of the *Christmas Oratorio*, as Bach had originally intended. We may therefore welcome his decision to invent new music for the words 'Ehre sei dir, Gott, gesungen'.

Tönet, ihr Pauken! Erschallet, Trompeten, BWV 214

NBA I/36, p. 91 BC G19 Duration: *c.* 27 mins

1. Chorus SATB tr I–III timp fl I,II ob I,II str bc D 3/8

Tönet, ihr Pauken! Erschallet, Trompeten!	Sound, you drums! Ring out, you trumpets!
Klingende Saiten, erfüllet die Luft!	Resonant strings, fill the air!
Singet itzt Lieder, ihr muntren Poeten!	Sing songs now, you lively poets!
Königin lebe! wird fröhlich geruft.	'Long live the Queen' is joyfully cried.
Königin lebe! dies wünschet der Sachse,	'Long live the Queen' is the Saxon's wish,
Königin lebe und blühe und wachse!	May the Queen live, blossom, and thrive!

2. Recitativo T bc b–f♯ C

Irene

Heut ist der Tag,	Today is the day
Wo jeder sich erfreuen mag.	When everyone may rejoice.
Dies ist der frohe Glanz	This is the joyful radiance
Der Königin Geburtsfests-Stunden,	Of the Queen's birthday-celebration hours,
Die Polen, Sachsen und uns ganz	Which have found Poles, Saxons, and all of us
In größter Lust und Glück erfunden.	In the greatest pleasure and good fortune.
Mein Ölbaum	My olive tree
Kriegt so Saft als fetten Raum.	Finds both sap and fertile ground.
Er zeigt noch keine falbe Blätter.	It still shows no dark leaves.
Mich schreckt kein Sturm, Blitz, trübe Wolken, düstres Wetter.	No storm, lightning, dark clouds, or gloomy weather frighten me.

3. Aria S fl I,II bc A 3/4

Bellona

Blast die wohlgegriffnen Flöten,	Blow the well-bored flutes,
Daß Feind, Lilien, Mond erröten!	That foe, lilies, moon may blush!
Schallt mit jauchzendem Gesang!	Ring out with exultant singing!
Tönt mit eurem Waffenklang!	Make noise with the clash of your weapons!
Dieses Fest erfordert Freuden,	This celebration calls for joys
Die so Geist als Sinnen weiden.	That nourish both spirit and senses.

4. Recitativo S bc f♯–D C

Bellona

Mein knallendes Metall	My exploding metal
Der in der Luft erbebenden Kartaunen,	Of cannon shaking in the air,
Der frohe Schall,	The joyful sound,
Das angenehme Schauen,	The pleasant sight,
Die Lust, die Sachsen itzt empfindt,	The pleasure that Saxony now feels

Rührt vieler Menschen Sinnen.	Stirs many men's senses.
Mein schimmerndes Gewehr	My gleaming weapon
Nebst meiner Söhne gleichen Schritten	Alongside my sons' even steps
Und ihre heldenmäßge Sitten	And their heroic ways
Vermehren immer mehr und mehr	Increase more and more
Des heutgen Tages süße Freude.	The present day's sweet joy.
5. Aria A ob d'am bc	b 3/8
Pallas	
Fromme Musen! meine Glieder!	Devout Muses! My members!
Singt nicht längst bekannte Lieder!	Do not sing long-familiar songs!
Dieser Tag sei eure Lust!	May this day be your delight!
Füllt mit Freuden eure Brust!	Fill your breast with joy!
Werft so Kiel als Schriften nieder	Throw down both quill and script
Und erfreut euch dreimal wieder!	And rejoice three times over!
6. Recitativo A str bc	f♯–D c
Pallas	
Unsre Königin im Lande,	Our Queen in the land,
Die der Himmel zu uns sandte,	Whom heaven sent us,
Ist der Musen Trost und Schutz.	Is the Muses' comfort and protection.
Meine Pierinnen wissen,	My Pierians,
Die in Ehrfurcht ihren Saum noch küssen,	Who still kiss her hem in reverence,
Vor ihr stetes Wohlergehn	For her constant well-being know
Dank und Pflicht und Ton stets zu erhöhn.	How to raise constant thanks, duty, and sound.
Ja, sie wünschen, daß ihr Leben	Indeed, they wish that her life
Möge lange Lust uns geben.	May long give us delight.
7. Aria B tr I str bc	D 2/4
Fama	
Kron und Preis gekrönter Damen,	Crown and prize of crowned ladies,
Königin! mit deinem Namen	O Queen, with your name
Füll ich diesen Kreis der Welt.	I fill this circle of the world.
Was der Tugend stets gefällt	What is ever pleasing to virtue
Und was nur Heldinnen haben,	And what only heroines have,
Sein dir angeborne Gaben.	May they be to you innate gifts.
8. Recitativo B fl I + II ob I,II bc	G–D c
Fama	
So dringe in das weite Erdenrund	Then may the wide earth's orb be penetrated
Mein von der Königin erfüllter Mund!	By my voice, filled with the Queen!
Ihr Ruhm soll bis zum Axen	Her glory shall grow to the axis
Des schön gestirnten Himmels wachsen,	Of the fair starry heavens;
Die Königin der Sachsen und der Polen	May the Queen of Saxony and Poland
Sei stets des Himmels Schutz empfohlen.	Ever be commended to heaven's protection.

So stärkt durch sie der Pol	Thus the Pole strengthens through her
So vieler Untertanen längst erwünschtes Wohl.	The long-desired welfare of so many subjects.
So soll die Königin noch lange bei uns hier verweilen	Thus the Queen shall long dwell here with us yet
Und spät, ach! spät zum Sternen eilen.	And late, ah late, hasten to the stars.

9. Chorus [Scoring as in no. 1] D $\frac{3}{8}$

Irene	
Blühet, ihr Linden in Sachsen, wie Zedern!	Blossom, you lindens, in Saxony like cedars!
Bellona	
Schallet mit Waffen und Wagen und Rädern!	Resound with weapons, chariots, and wheels!
Pallas	
Singet, ihr Musen! mit völligem Klang!	Sing, you muses, with a full sound!
Fama et Tutti	
Fröhliche Stunden! ihr freudigen Zeiten!	Cheerful hours! you joyful times!
Gönnt uns noch öfters die güldenen Freuden:	Grant us still more often gilded joys:
Königin, lebe, ja lebe noch lang!	Queen, live, yes live long yet!

Among the considerable number of congratulatory cantatas from the years 1733 and 1734 is a work written for the birthday of Maria Josepha, Electoress of Saxony and Queen of Poland, and performed by the student Collegium musicum under Bach's direction on 8 December 1733. The music of such an occasional work fulfilled its function upon a single hearing. For this reason, as in Cantata 213, Bach later parodied several of the movements in the *Christmas Oratorio*, in which form they have become widely known. Here is a list of the movements concerned:

Queen's Cantata		*Christmas Oratorio*	
1	Tönet, ihr Pauken!	I/1	Jauchzet, frohlocket
5	Fromme Musen!	II/15	Frohe Hirten, eilt
7	Kron und Preis gekrönter Damen	I/8	Großer Herr, o starker König
9	Blühet, ihr Linden	III/24	Herrscher des Himmels

Bach reused, or intended to reuse, all the arias and choruses* from Cantatas 213 and 214 in the *Christmas Oratorio*, with the exception of the third movement of the present cantata. It is unlikely that there were aesthetic grounds for this decision. The most obvious explanation is that the aria was reused in some other work that no longer survives, though there is no evidence for this theory.

The librettist of the Queen's Cantata is unknown. Occasionally one hears the conjecture that Bach himself might have written the text, but this is contradicted by the observation that all three arias are designed according to the same verse scheme: it is most unlikely that Bach would have imposed this constraint upon himself without drawing the least consequences from it in his musical setting of the words. The work has the pretentious subtitle 'dramma per musica',* but there is no dramatic plot. The four voices represent four goddesses from ancient mythology: Bellona, goddess of war (soprano); Pallas, guardian of the muses and of knowledge (alto); Irene, goddess of peace (tenor); and Fama, goddess of fame (bass). Each goddess in turn praises the Queen within her own prescribed sphere. Nothing else happens.

Bach's music is all the more splendid by comparison with this uneventful plot. Indeed, it surpasses the modest secular libretto to such an extent that it could easily be heard as a '*Christmas Oratorio* with different text'. For, to our notions, Bach is here discovered in the role of one who pays a courtesy call not with a bunch of flowers but with real jewels. In order to grasp this state of affairs, we have to bear in mind the baroque world-view (often previously emphasized), which knew no general distinction between sacred and secular styles and saw in princely might not merely human arbitrariness but rather the realization of the divine will on earth. Thus it is no doubt a difference of degree rather than kind whether the trumpet aria exalts the Queen of Poland (cantata) or the powerful King, Jesus Christ (oratorio*).

Although most movements of the cantata are familiar to us from the *Christmas Oratorio*, salient features of Bach's musical invention often prove to be intelligible only with reference to the original text. Thus the order of instrumental entries in the opening chorus—drums, trumpets, strings—derives from the text of the Queen's Cantata, which calls upon 'drums', 'trumpets', and 'resonant strings' in turn to praise the Queen. Akin to aria in its da capo* form, this chorus, with its repeated alternation between the dominance of the orchestra (with choral insertion*) and of the choir (with doubling or accompanying instruments) and its grand dimensions, exhibits the rich multiplicity of form that Bach had at his disposal when at the height of his powers.

In the four recitatives, each of the four mythological figures offers her congratulations, Irene and Bellona in *secco* with continuo accompaniment (nos. 2 and 4), in places backed by dramatic figuration in the continuo, Pallas with string accompaniment (no. 6), and Fama with that of woodwinds (No. 8). Irene had to be content with recitative only, but those of the other three characters are each preceded by an aria. It goes without saying that the text 'Blow the well-bored flutes' (no. 3) is scored with flutes; today the war goddess summons folk not to battle but to a celebration. Equally self-evident is that the text 'Crown and prize of crowned ladies' (no. 7), Fama's promise to carry the Queen's renown throughout the whole world, is illustrated by trumpet scoring. The fifth movement, however, in which Pallas (Athene) calls upon the muses to celebrate the Queen's feast-day not with 'long-familiar songs' but with spontaneous enthusiasm, is accompanied by oboe d'amore.* Only in the later, Christmas version is the aria assigned to the flute, the shepherds' instrument.

The concluding chorus is a dance movement with clear, periodic phrase structure. Its 96 bars (6 × 16) are divided into two 48-bar halves, each of which takes the same course: an instrumental passage (a or b), followed by a freely polyphonic* vocal passage (x or y) in which the voices enter in turn, leading to choral insertion within a reprise of the instrumental passage. This results in the following formal scheme:

Overall form:	A			B		
Section:	a	x	a + choir	b	y	b + choir
Number of bars:	16	16	16	16	16	16

Preise dein Glücke, gesegnetes Sachsen, BWV 215

NBA I/37, p. 87 BC G21 Duration: *c.* 37 mins

1. Coro Choir I: SATB Choir II: SATB tr I–III timp fl I,II ob I,II str bc D $\frac{3}{8}$

Preise dein Glücke, gesegnetes Sachsen,	Prize your good fortune, blessed Saxony,
Weil Gott den Thron deines Königs erhält.	For God maintains the throne of your King.
Fröhliches Land,	Happy land,
Danke dem Himmel und küsse die Hand,	Thank heaven and kiss the hand
Die deine Wohlfahrt noch täglich läßt wachsen	That still daily makes your welfare increase
Und deine Bürger in Sicherheit stellt.	And keeps your citizens in security.

2. Recitativo T ob I,II bc b–D C

Wie können wir, großmächtigster August,	Most high and mighty Augustus,
Die unverfälschten Triebe	How could we lay our genuine feelings
Von unsrer Ehrfurcht, Treu und Liebe	Of reverence, faithfulness, and love
Dir anders als mit größter Lust	Other than with the greatest pleasure
Zu deinen Füßen legen?	At your feet?
Fließt nicht durch deine Vaterhand	Does there not flow by your fatherly hand
Auf unser Land	Upon our land
Des Himmels Gnadensegen	Heaven's gracious blessings
Mit reichen Strömen zu?	In rich streams?
Und trifft nicht unsre Hoffnung ein,	And does not our hope come true
Wir würden noch zu unsrer Ruh	That we would yet read, for our peace,
In deiner Huld, in deinem Wesen	In your favour, in your nature,
Des großen Vaters Bild und seine Taten lesen?	Your great father's image and his deeds?

3. Aria T str + ob d'am I,II bc G C

Freilich trotzt Augustus' Name,	Certainly Augustus's name,
Ein so edler Götter Same,	Such a noble, divine seed,

Alle Macht der Sterblichkeit.
Und die Bürger der Provinzen
Solcher tugendhaften Prinzen
Leben in der güldnen Zeit.

Defies all might of mortality.
And the citizens of the provinces
Of such virtuous princes
Live in the Golden Age.

4. Recitativo B bc e–A C

Was hat dich sonst, Sarmatien, bewogen,
Daß du vor deinen Königsthron
Den sächsischen Piast,
Des großen Augusts würdgen Sohn,
Hast allen andern fürgezogen?
Nicht nur der Glanz durchlauchter Ahnen,
Nicht seiner Länder Macht,
Nein! sondern seiner Tugend Pracht
Riß aller deiner Untertanen
Und so verschiedner Völker Sinn
Mehr ihn allein,
Als seines Stammes Glanz und angeerbten Schein,
Fußfällig anzubeten hin.
Zwar Neid und Eifersucht,
Die leider! oft das Gold der Kronen
Noch weniger als Blei und Eisen schonen,
Sind noch ergrimmt auf dich, o großer König!
Und haben deinem Wohl geflucht.
Jedoch ihr Fluch verwandelt sich in Segen,
Und ihre Wut
Ist wahrlich viel zu wenig,
Ein Glücke, das auf Felsen ruht,
Im mindsten zu bewegen.

What induced you formerly, Sarmatia,
To prefer for your royal throne
The Saxon Piast,
Great Augustus's worthy son,
Above all others?
Not only the brilliance of illustrious ancestors,
Nor his lands' might,
No! rather did his virtue's splendour
Inspire all your subjects'
And such diverse peoples' minds—
More him alone
Than his brilliant descent and inherited glamour—
To fall prostrate before him.
True, envy and jealousy,
Which, alas, often spare the gold of crowns
Still less than lead and iron,
Yet flare up against you, O great King,
And have cursed your welfare.
Yet their curse is transformed into a blessing,
And their rage
Is truly far too small
For a good fortune that rest on rock
To be in the least stirred.

5. Aria B ob I str bc A $\frac{3}{8}$

Rase nur, verwegner Schwarm,
In dein eignes Eingeweide!
Wasche nur den frechen Arm
Voller Wut
In unschuldger Brüder Blut,
Uns zum Abscheu, dir zum Leide!
Weil das Gift
Und der Grimm von deinem Neide
Dich mehr als Augustum trifft.

Rage, audacious swarm,
Within your own guts!
Wash your impudent arm,
Full of fury,
In your innocent brothers' blood
To our horror, to your misfortune!
For the poison
And the wrath of your envy
Affects you more than Augustus.

6.	Recitativo S fl I,II bc	f♯–b C
	Ja, ja! Gott ist uns noch mit seiner Hülfe nah Und schützt Augustens Thron. Er macht, daß der gesamte Norden Durch seine Königswahl befriedigt worden. Wird nicht der Ostsee schon Durch der besiegten Weichsel Mund Augustus' Reich Zugleich Mit seinen Waffen kund? Und lässet er nicht jene Stadt, Die sich so lang ihm widersetzet hat, Mehr seine Huld als seinen Zorn empfinden? Das macht, ihm ist es eine Lust, Der Untertanen Brust Durch Liebe mehr denn Zwang zu binden.	Yes, yes! God is yet near us with His help And He protects Augustus's throne. He causes the entire North To be content with its elected king. Does not the Baltic, Through the conquered Vistula's mouth, Already know Augustus's empire Together With his armaments? And does he not let that city Which has so long resisted him Feel more his clemency than his wrath? Thus it is a pleasure to him To bind his subjects' hearts More through love than constraint.
7.	Aria S fl I + II ob d'am vlns + violetta	b 2/4
	Durch die von Eifer entflammeten Waffen Feinde bestrafen, Bringt zwar manchem Ehr und Ruhm; Aber die Bosheit mit Wohltat vergelten, Ist nur der Helden, Ist Augustens Eigentum.	Through weapons enkindled with zeal To punish enemies Indeed brings much honour and glory; But to repay malice with kindness Is the property only of heroes, Of Augustus.
8.	Recitativo STB tr I–III timp fl I,II ob I,II str bc	A–G C
	Tenor Laß doch, o teurer Landesvater, zu, Daß unsre Musenschar Den Tag, der dir so glücklich ist gewesen, An dem im vorgen Jahr Sarmatien zum König dich erlesen, In ihrer unschuldvollen Ruh Verehren und besingen dürfe. *Baß* Zu einer Zeit, Da alles um uns blitzt und kracht, Ja, da der Franzen Macht (Die doch so vielmal schon gedämpfet worden) Von Süden und von Norden	*Tenor* Grant, O dear sovereign, That by our dear band of muses The day that was so happy for you, On which last year Sarmatia elected you king, In her guileless serenity, May be revered and celebrated. *Bass* At a time When all around us flashes and crashes, Indeed when the French might (Which, however, has already been subdued so many times) From south and from north

Auch unserm Vaterland mit Schwert und Feuer dräut,	Threatens even our fatherland with sword and fire,
Kann diese Stadt so glücklich sein,	This city can be so fortunate as to find
Dich, mächtgen Schutzgott unsrer Linden,	You, mighty tutelary god of our lindens—
Und zwar dich nicht allein,	And indeed not you alone
Auch dein Gemahl, des Landes Sonne,	But also your consort, the land's sun,
Der Untertanen Trost und Wonne,	Her subjects' comfort and delight—
In ihrem Schoß zu finden.	In its bosom.
Sopran	*Soprano*
Wie sollte sich bei so viel Wohlergehn	Amidst so much prosperity
Der Pindus nicht vergnügt und glücklich sehn!	How should Pindus not seem contented and happy?
zu dritt	*all three*
Himmel! laß dem Neid zu Trutz	Heaven! in defiance of envy,
Unter solchem Götterschutz	Under such divine protection,
Sich die Wohlfahrt unsrer Zeiten	Let the welfare of our times
In viel tausend Zweige breiten!	Spread into many thousand branches!

9. Coro SATB (Choir I + II) tr I–III timp fl I,II ob I,II str bc D $\frac{6}{8}$

Stifter der Reiche, Beherrscher der Kronen,	Founder of empires, Ruler of crowns,
Baue den Thron, den Augustus besitzt!	Fortify the throne that Augustus owns!
Ziere sein Haus	Adorn his house
Mit unvergänglichem Wohlergehn aus!	With imperishable prosperity!
Laß uns die Länder in Friede bewohnen,	Let the lands live in peace
Die er mit Recht und mit Gnade beschützt.	That he protects with justice and grace.

We are exceptionally well-informed about the external circumstances that led to the composition and performance of this cantata, and a graphic description of the surrounding events is given by Werner Neumann in the Critical Report to the *Neue Bach-Ausgabe*, Series I, Volume 37. Augustus III, Elector of Saxony and King of Poland, evidently took Saxony by surprise in announcing that he and his consort would visit Leipzig between 2 and 6 October 1734. Since 5 October was the anniversary of his election as King of Poland, the students of Leipzig University decided to present a serenade to him that evening, accompanied by a torchlight procession. The libretto was written by the Leipzig schoolmaster Johann Christoph Clauder and the music composed by Bach, a task that he may have had to accomplish within little more than three days. A graphic picture of the event is given by the Leipzig town chronicler Salomon Riemer:

At about 9 o'clock in the evening, the students here presented to their Majesties a most humble evening serenade with trumpets and drums, which had been composed by Mr. Capellmeister Johann Sebastian Bach, Cantor at St Thomas's, at which six hundred students carried wax torches and four counts acted as marshals in leading the musicians. The procession went from the notice-board along Ritter Street, Brühl, and Catherine Street to the King's lodgings. When the music had reached the weigh-house, trumpets and drums ascended it, as did then a similar chorus from the town hall. When the printed libretto was presented, the four counts were allowed to kiss the royal hand, and afterwards His Royal Majesty, together with his Royal Consort and the Royal Princes, did not leave the window as long as the music lasted but most graciously listened to it, and Their Majesties were heartily well pleased.[3]

Joy over the day's success was, however, marred by an unfortunate event. The Stadtpfeifer Gottfried Reiche, Bach's first trumpeter, died from a stroke, which is said to have been caused by the exertion of blowing, together with the smoke from the torches, during the 'Royal *Musique*'.

The text is on this occasion not put into the mouths of ancient gods or shepherds but directly refers to events of the previous months. After the death of Augustus the Strong, his successor as Elector of Saxony had again been elected King of Poland. An opposing king emerged, however, in the person of Stanislaus Leszczynski, who had to be vanquished before Augustus could take the throne. Stanislaus fled to Danzig, and the surrender of that city on 6 July 1734 determined the outcome of the struggle in favour of Augustus. Understandably, events that took place only a few months before the cantata performance find an echo in its libretto. The first three movements celebrate the good fortune that has befallen Saxony with regard to its king. Our attention is then directed towards the cause: Augustus is distinguished, we are told, not only by heredity but also by his own virtue. Dangers occur, however: such good fortune breeds envy, which is nonetheless powerless to achieve anything (no. 5). The third recitative-aria pair of movements, nos. 6–7, refers in still more detail to the incidents of the past few months. The 'entire North', the 'conquered Vistula', and Danzig, 'that city which has so long resisted him', know not just Augustus's military power but also his clemency. For, rather than punishing his opponents, the king 'repays malice with kindness'. Next, the ruler himself is addressed, gratitude to him is expressed, and finally heaven is called upon for future protection. Although the libretto does not surpass the norm in its use of flattery for the veneration of a baroque ruler, it nonetheless makes a refreshing change in its bearing on the historical facts of the day.

[3] 'Gegen 9. Uhr Abends brachten Ihro Majt. die allhiesigen Studirenden eine allerunterthänigste Abend Music mit Trompeten und Pauken, so Hr. Capell Meister Joh. Sebastian Bach Cant. zu St. Thom. componiret. Wobey 600. Studenten lauter Wachs Fäckeln trugen, und 4. Grafen als Marschälle die Music aufführeten. Der Zug geschahe aus dem schwartzen Bret durch die Ritter Strasse, Brühl und Catharinen Strasse herauf, bis ans Königs Logis, als die Music an der Wage angelanget, giengen auf derselben Trompeten und Pauken, wie den auch solches vom Rath Hause, durch ein Chor geschahe. Bey übergabe des Carmens wurden die 4. Grafen zum Hand Kuß gelaßen, nachegehnds sind Ihro Königl. Majestät, nebst Dero Königl. Frau Gemahlin u. Königl. Printzen, so lange die Music gedauret, nicht vom Fenster weg gegangen, sondern haben solche gnädigst angehöret, und Ihr. Majestät herzlich wohlgefallen.'

Due to the short time available to Bach for its composition, it is reasonable to suppose that a good deal of existing music found its way into the new cantata.[4] In no case, however, can this be demonstrated from surviving compositions; and the method of verifying parody* relationships with lost compositions whose texts survive on the basis of the verse scheme of the libretto, so successful elsewhere, also fails here. For it is evident that Bach did not find the opportunity to discuss details of parody procedure with Clauder, as he was often wont to do with Picander, before the preparation of the libretto. It was nonetheless possible for Werner Neumann to establish the original model of the principal section of the opening chorus,* namely the chorus 'Es lebe der König, der Vater im Lande' from the lost cantata of that name, BWV Anh. I 11, performed by Bach and his Collegium musicum on 3 August 1732 for the name-day of Augustus the Strong, though not then in the presence of the royal family and its entourage. When transferred to the later cantata, this chorus, with its eight-part double choir and its splendid scoring for trumpets and drums, flutes, oboes, strings, and continuo, met all the requirements of an open-air performance before the king. The irregular strophic structure of the new text, however, demanded all sorts of changes to the voice parts. At the very outset, for example, an upbeat had to be accommodated, so that the vocal entry (soprano and alto in unison, tenor and bass at the octave below), originally thus—

—now became:

Over a decade later, Bach returned to the original form of the initial motive* when he adapted the movement as the 'Osanna' of the B minor Mass, the form in which it is familiar to us today.

In the following movements, Bach dispenses with the double-choir disposition of voices, restricting himself to three vocal soloists (soprano, tenor, and bass) and uniting all the singers in a single choir of four parts in the concluding chorus. The instrumentation, however, is conceived richly, in accordance with

[4] Nevertheless, Stephen Crist concludes, on the basis of the character of Bach's script and the density of correction in the autograph score, that only nos. 1 (A section only), 3, and 5 (except bb. 133–61) are parodies. See his 'The Question of Parody in Bach's Cantata *Preise dein Glücke, gesegnetes Sachsen*, BWV 215', in R. Stinson, ed., *Bach Perspectives* I (Lincoln, Nebraska, 1995), 135–61.

the splendour of the occasion. Of the four recitatives, only one is *secco*; two are set as motivically imprinted *accompagnato** with oboes or flutes, and the last, which addresses the king, calls for all the instrumental groups in turn.

The arias are carefully coordinated one with another. The joyful, ceremonial melody of the third movement, 'Freilich trotzt Augustus' Name', is a fervent song of praise to the king (the long drawn-out opening syllable again hints at hidden parody relationships). By contrast, in the fifth movement (to the words 'Rage, audacious swarm!'), we hear a true satirical song addressed to the enemies of the king—Bach's intention is clear from the heading 'presto' and from the oboe indication 'staccato sempre'. The third and last aria, no. 7, which praises the clemency of the king, is altogether different. The unusual scoring for two unison obbligato* flutes, soprano doubled by oboe d'amore,* and a bassett* for unison violins and violetta (a type of viola) reveals the point that Bach wants to make here. The continuo bass, a symbol of 'having one's feet on the ground', is absent, for 'repaying malice with kindness' is a quite unearthly quality. Bach later reused the aria in the *Christmas Oratorio*, Part V, no. 47, to the text 'Erleucht auch meine finstre Sinnen' ('Illuminate also my dark thoughts'), this time with continuo, though in a lighter scoring than the other movements.

In the concluding homage to the king, tenor, bass, and soprano enter in turn in an *accompagnato* before uniting in an arioso* terzetto to implore the future protection of heaven. Finally, all participants join together in a hymnic concluding prayer—largely homophonic* and in rondeau form (A B A B[1] A)—addressed to the 'Founder of empires, Ruler of crowns'.

Auf, schmetternde Töne der muntern Trompeten, BWV 207a

NBA I/37, p. 3 BC G22 Duration: *c.* 31 mins

1. CHORUS SATB tr I–III timp fl I,II ob d'am I,II taille str bc D $\frac{6}{8}$

Auf, schmetternde Töne der muntern Trompeten,	Rise, blaring notes of lively trumpets;
Ihr donnernden Pauken, erhebet den Knall!	You thundering drums, raise your clap!
Reizende Saiten, ergötzet das Ohr,	Charming strings, delight the ear,
Suchet auf Flöten das Schönste zu finden,	Seek to find the greatest beauty on flutes,
Erfüllet mit lieblichem Schall	Fill with lovely sound
Unsre so süße als grünende Linden	Our lindens so sweet and verdant
Und unser frohes Musenchor!	And our cheerful chorus of muses!

2. RECITATIVO T bc b–f♯ C

Die stille Pleiße spielt	The calm Pleiße plays
Mit ihren kleinen Wellen.	With her little waves.
Das grüne Ufer fühlt	The green bank feels
Itzt gleichsam neue Kräfte	Now new powers, as it were,
Und doppelt innre rege Säfte.	And doubles its lively inner sap.

Es prangt mit weichem Moos und Klee;
Dort blühet manche schöne Blume,
Hier hebt zur Flora großem Ruhme
Sich eine Pflanze in die Höh
Und will den Wachstum zeigen.
Der Pallas holder Hain
Sucht sich in Schmuck und Schimmer zu erneun.
Die Castalinnen singen Lieder,
Die Nymphen gehen hin und wieder
Und wollen hier und dort bei unsern Linden,–
Und was? den angenehmen Ort
Ihres schönsten Gegenstandes finden.
Denn dieser Tag bringt allen Lust;
Doch in der Sachsen Brust
Geht diese Lust am allerstärksten fort.

It shines with soft moss and clover;
There many a lovely flower blossoms,
Here, to Flora's great glory,
A plant raises itself high
And would show its growth.
Pallas's lovely grove
Seeks to revive itself in finery and lustre.
The Castalians sing songs,
The nymphs go now and again
And want, here and there among our lindens—
Want what? to find a pleasant spot
For their most fair object.
For this day brings every delight;
Yet in the Saxon breast
This delight is by far the strongest.

3. Aria T ob d'am I str bc — b ¢

Augustus' Namenstages Schimmer
Verklärt der Sachsen Angesicht.
Gott schützt die frommen Sachsen immer,
Denn unsers Landesvaters Zimmer
Prangt heut in neuen Glückes Strahlen,
Die soll itzt unsre Ehrfurcht malen
Bei dem erwünschten Namenslicht.

Augustus's name-day's lustre
Transfigures the Saxon countenance.
God ever protects devout Saxons,
For our sovereign's chamber
Shines today in new fortune's rays,
Which our reverence shall now paint
By the long-desired daylight of his name.

4. Recitativo SB bc — G–A C

Sopran
Augustus' Wohl
Ist der treuen Sachsen Wohlergehn;
Baß
Augustus' Arm beschützt
Der Sachsen grüne Weiden,
Sopran
Die Elbe nützt
Dem Kaufmann mit so vielen Freuden;
Baß
Des Hofes Pracht und Flor
Stellt uns Augustus' Glücke vor;
Sopran
Die Untertanen sehn
An jedem Ort ihr Wohlergehn;

Soprano
The good of Augustus
Is the welfare of loyal Saxons;
Bass
Augustus's arm protects
The Saxons' green meadows,
Soprano
The Elbe provides
The merchant with so many joys;
Bass
The court's splendour and bloom
Show us Augustus's good fortune;
Soprano
His subjects see
Everywhere their prosperity;

Baß
Des Mavors heller Stahl muß alle Feinde schrecken,
Um uns vor allem Unglück zu bedecken.
Sopran
Drum freut sich heute der Merkur
Mit seinen weisen Söhnen
Und findt bei diesen Freudentönen
Der ersten güldnen Zeiten Spur.
Baß
Augustus mehrt das Reich.
Sopran
Irenens Lorbeer wird nie bleich;
beide
Die Linden wollen schöner grünen,
Um uns mit ihrem Flor
Bei diesem hohen Namenstag zu dienen.

Bass
Mars's bright steel must terrify all enemies
To protect us from all misfortune.
Soprano
Therefore Mercury rejoices today
With his wise sons
And finds in these joyful notes
A vestige of the first Golden Age.
Bass
Augustus augments the realm.
Soprano
Irene's laurel will never fade;
both
The lindens would turn a fairer green
To deck us with their blossom
On this lofty name-day.

5. Aria [Duetto] SB bc + Ritornello tr I,II ob d'am I + II + taille str bc D C

Baß
Mich kann die süße Ruhe laben,
Sopran
Ich kann hier mein Vergnügen haben,
beide
Wir beide stehn hier höchst beglückt.
Baß
Denn unsre fette Saaten lachen
Und können viel Vergnügen machen,
Weil sie kein Feind und Wetter drückt.

Sopran
Wo solche holde Stunden kommen,
Da hat das Glücke zugenommen,
Das uns der heitre Himmel schickt.

Bass
Sweet repose can refresh me,
Soprano
Here I can have my pleasure,
both
We both stay here most gladly.
Bass
For our rich seeds laugh
And can cause much pleasure,
For no enemy or storm oppresses them.
Soprano
Where such propitious hours come,
There that good fortune has increased
Which the fair heaven sends us.

6. Recitativo A bc A–G C

Augustus schützt die frohen Felder,
Augustus liebt die grünen Wälder,
Wenn sein erhabner Mut
Im Jagen niemals eher ruht,
Bis er ein schönes Tier gefället.
Der Landmann sieht mit Lust
Auf seinem Acker schöne Garben.
Ihm ist stets wohl bewußt,
Wie keiner darf in Sachsen darben,
Wer sich nur in sein Glücke findt
Und seine Kräfte recht ergründt.

Augustus protects the glad fields,
Augustus loves the verdant woods
When his exalted courage
In hunting never rests
Till he has felled a fine beast.
The countryman sees with pleasure
Fair sheaves in his field.
He is always well aware
How no one in Saxony need suffer want
Who but reconciles himself to his fortune
And judges his powers aright.

7. Aria A fl I,II vln I + II + vla bc — G 3/4

Preiset, späte Folgezeiten,	Praise, later generations,
Nebst dem gütigen Geschick	Alongside kind fate
Des Augustus großes Glück.	Augustus's great good fortune.
Denn in des Monarchen Taten	For in the Monarch's deeds
Könnt ihr Sachsens Wohl erraten;	You can divine Saxony's welfare;
Man kann aus dem Schimmer lesen,	One can gather from its lustre
Wer Augustus sei gewesen.	Who Augustus was.

8. Recitativo SATB str + ob d'am I,II, taille bc — D c

Tenor	*Tenor*
Ihr Fröhlichen, herbei!	You joyful ones, come!
Erblickt, ihr Sachsen und ihr große Staaten,	See, you Saxons and you great states,
Aus Augustus' holden Taten,	From Augustus's kind deeds
Was Weisheit und auch Stärke sei.	What wisdom and strength are.
Sein allzeit starker Arm stützt teils Sarmatien,	His ever-strong arm protects in part Sarmatia,
Teils auch der Sachsen Wohlergehn.	In part the Saxon welfare.
Wir sehen als getreue Untertanen	We see, as loyal subjects,
Durch Weisheit die vor uns erlangte Friedensfahne.	The banner of peace obtained for us through wisdom.
Wie sehr er uns geliebt,	How much he loves us,
Wie mächtig er die Sachsen stets geschützet,	How mightily he ever protects the Saxons
Zeigt dessen Säbels Stahl, der vor uns Sachsen blitzet.	Is shown by his sabre's steel, which flashes for us Saxons.
Wir können unsern Landesvater	We can now honour our sovereign
Als einen Held und Siegesrater	As a hero and counsellor of victory
In dem großmächtigsten August	In the high and mighty Augustus
Mit heißer Ehrfurcht itzt verehren	With ardent reverence,
Und unsre Wünsche mehren.	And further our wishes.
Baß	*Bass*
Ja, ja, ihr starken Helden, seht	Yes, yes, you strong heroes, see
Der Sachsen unerschöpfte Kräfte	The Saxons' inexhaustible powers
Und ihren hohen Schutzgott an	And their high tutelary god
Und Sachsens Rautensäfte!	And Saxony's rue sap!
Itzt soll der Saiten Ton	Now the sound of strings shall
Die frohe Lust ausdrücken,	Express joyful delight,
Denn des Augustus fester Thron	For Augustus's secure throne
Muß uns allzeit beglücken.	Must always make us happy.
Sopran	*Soprano*
Augustus gibt uns steten Schatten,	Augustus gives us constant shade,
Der aller Sachsen und Sarmaten Glück erhält,	He maintains the good fortune of all Saxons and Sarmatians:
Der stete Augenmerk der Welt,	The constant focus of the world,
Den alle Augen hatten.	On whom all eyes are fixed.

Alt	*Alto*
O heitres, hohes Namenslicht!	O serene, exalted light of his name!
O Name, der die Freude mehrt!	O name that augments our joy!
O allerwünschtes Angedenken,	O most desired commemoration,
Wie stärkst du unsre Pflicht!	How you strengthen our duty!
Ihr frohe Wünsche und ihr starke Freuden, steigt!	You joyful wishes and you great joys, climb!
Die Pleiße sucht durch ihr Bezeigen	The Pleiße, by displaying
Die Linden in so jungen Zweigen	The lindens with such young branches,
Der schönen Stunden Lust und Wohl zu krön'	Seeks, for the delight and benefit of these lovely hours,
Und zu erhöhn.	To be crowned and enhanced.

9. Chorus [Scoring as in no. 1] D **2**

August, lebe,	Long live Augustus!
Lebe, König!	Long live the King!
O Augustus, unser Schutz,	O Augustus, our protector,
Sei der starren Feinde Trutz,	Defy the inflexible enemy,
Lebe lange deinem Land,	Live long for your country,
Gott schütz deinen Geist und Hand,	God protect your spirit and hand;
So muß durch Augustus' Leben	Then through Augustus's life
Unsers Sachsens Wohl bestehn,	Our Saxony's welfare must endure,
So darf sich kein Feind erheben	Then no enemy may rise up
Wider unser Wohlergehn.	Against our welfare.

Appendix: Marche tr I–III timp str + ww bc D **C**

This cantata, whose occasion is clear from the third movement—the name-day of the Elector of Saxony and King of Poland—was performed on 3 August 1735 (or possibly on the same date in one of the surrounding years). For the most part, it is a parody* of Cantata 207 of 1726—only the recitatives (nos. 2, 4, and 6) were newly composed. The anonymous librettist was thus confronted with the task of adhering to the textual scheme of the existing work. This he accomplished quite skilfully, though without producing a text that rises above a plain, serviceable level to achieve intrinsic poetic worth.

Although it contains no real plot, the work belongs to the *dramma per musica** type. Framed by two full choruses,* the individual arias of the four soloists praise the outstanding qualities of the monarch and the consequent good fortune of his subjects. The soloists no doubt represent allegorical or mythological figures whose significance would have been disclosed in the printed text if an exemplar of it had survived. In its absence we can only conjecture that the soprano might have represented Peace (Irene? cf. no. 4), the bass War ('Mavors' = Mars? cf. no. 4), and the tenor perhaps Wisdom (Apollo? cf. no. 8) or possibly the city of Leipzig (cf. no. 2). The rivers Pleiße (nos. 2 and 8) and Elbe (no. 4) and the god Mercury (no. 4) are also mentioned, however, so that it is also conceivable that the singers represent altogether different figures. Least clear of all is the function of the alto soloist, whom at times one might suppose to be a godhead of the woods or of hunting (no. 6) and elsewhere a god of posthumous fame (no. 7).

The movements adopted from Cantata 207 (nos. 1, 3, 5, and 7–9) are, on the whole, altered only to the extent required by the new textual underlay. In the third movement an oboe is added to the strings, but it serves largely as tutti reinforcement for the first violin. The newly composed recitatives (nos. 2, 4, and 6) are accompanied by continuo only, but no. 2 is provided with characterful instrumental figures to represent the waves of the 'calm Pleiße', and no. 4 with motivic continuo episodes to mark the vocal caesuras. It was probably for this version of the cantata that Bach added the March, which was evidently performed by a considerable body of players. It does not really belong to the cantata, however, but was presumably used as processional music, as in the contemporary account of the performance of Cantata 215 (see above).

Schleicht, spielende Wellen, BWV 206

NBA I/36, p. 159 BC G 23, 26 Duration: *c.* 43 mins

1. Chorus SATB tr I–III timp fl I,II ob I,II str bc — D 3/8

Schleicht, spielende Wellen, und murmelt gelinde!	Glide, playful waves, and murmur gently!
Nein, rauschet geschwinde,	No, rush swiftly,
Daß Ufer und Klippe zum öftern erklingt!	So that shore and cliff often resound!
Die Freude, die unsere Fluten erreget,	The joy that stirs our floods,
Die jegliche Welle zum Rauschen beweget,	That moves every wave to rush,
Durchreißet die Dämme,	Breaks through the dams
Worein sie Verwundrung und Schüchternheit zwingt.	Wherein it is confined by astonishment and timidity.

2. Recitativo B bc — A C

Weichsel	*Vistula*
O glückliche Veränderung!	O happy change!
Mein Fluß, der neulich/immer dem Cocytus gliche,	My river, which recently/always resembled the Cocytus,
Weil er von toten Leichen	Since from dead bodies
Und ganz zerstückten Körpern langsam schliche,	And quite dismembered corpses it crept slowly along,
Wird nun nicht dem Alpheus weichen,	Will now not yield to the Alpheus
Der das gesegnete Arkadien benetzte.	That moistened blessed Arcadia.
Des Rostes mürber Zahn	Rust's worn-out tooth
Frißt die verworfnen Waffen an,	Corrodes the rejected weapons
Die jüngst des Himmels harter Schluß/	That heaven's harsh decision lately/
Die stets der Zwietracht tolle Wut	That discord's mad rage constantly

Auf meiner Völker/Bürger Nacken wetzte.
Wer bringt mir aber dieses Glücke?
August,
Der Untertanen Lust,
Der Schutzgott seiner Lande,
Vor dessen Zepter ich mich bücke,
Und dessen Huld für mich alleine wacht,
Bringt dieses Werk zum Stande.
Drum singt ein jeder, der mein Wasser trinkt:

Whetted on my people's/citizens' necks.
But who brings me this good fortune?
Augustus,
His subjects' delight,
The tutelary deity of his lands,
Before whose sceptre I bow,
And whose favour alone watches over me,
Brings this about.
Therefore may everyone who drinks my water sing:

3. Aria B str bc — A 2/4

Weichsel
Schleuß des Janustempels Türen,
Unsre Herzen öffnen wir.
  Nächst den dir getanen Schwüren
  Treibt allein, Herr, deine Güte
  Unser reuiges/kindliches Gemüte
  Zum Gehorsam gegen dir.

Vistula
Lock the doors of Janus's temple:
We open our hearts.
  Besides the oaths sworn to you,
  Your goodness alone, Lord, drives
  Our repentant/childlike spirit
  To be obedient to you.

4. Recitativo T bc — f♯–b C

Elbe
So recht! beglückter Weichselstrom!
Dein Schluß ist lobenswert,
Wenn deine Treue nur/stets mit meinen Wünschen stimmt,
An meine Liebe denkt
Und nicht etwann mir gar den König nimmt./
Da mir es itzt den König wieder nimmt.
Geborgt ist nicht geschenkt;
Du hast den gütigsten August von mir begehrt,
Des holde Mienen
Das Bild des großen Vaters weisen,
Den hab ich dir geliehn,
Verehren und bewundern sollt du ihn,
Nicht gar aus meinem Schoß und Armen reißen.
Dies schwöre ich,
O Herr! bei deines Vaters Asche,
Bei deinen Siegs- und Ehrenbühnen.
Eh sollen meine Wasser sich
Noch mit dem reichen Ganges mischen
Und ihren Ursprung nicht mehr wissen.

Elbe
Quite right, blessed River Vistula!
Your conclusion is praiseworthy,
If only/always your loyalty accords with my wishes,
Remembers my love,
And does not take the King from me./
Now that the King is taken from me.
To lend is not to give;
You have asked of me the most benevolent Augustus,
Whose kind countenance
Shows the image of his great father;
Him have I loaned to you;
You should venerate and admire him,
Not tear him from my bosom and my arms.
This I swear,
O Lord, by your father's ashes,
By your scenes of victory and honour:
Rather should my waters
Mix with the abundant Ganges
And no longer know their source,

Eh soll der Malabar
An meinen Ufern fischen,
Eh ich will ganz und gar
Dich, teuerster Augustus, missen.

Rather should the Malabar
Fish on my shores,
Than that I would altogether
Go without you, dearest Augustus.

5. Aria T vln I solo bc — b 6/8

Elbe
Jede Woge meiner Wellen
Ruft das göldne Wort August!
  Seht, Tritonen, muntre Söhne,
  Wie von nie gespürter Lust
  Meines Reiches Fluten schwellen,
  Wenn in dem Zurückeprallen
  Dieses Namens süße Töne
  Hundertfältig widerschallen.

Elbe
Every billow of my waves
Calls that golden word 'Augustus'!
  See, you Tritons, lively sons,
  How with delight never felt before
  My realm's floods swell
  When on the rebound
  This name's sweet notes
  Resound again an hundredfold!

6. Recitativo A bc — D–f♯ C

Donau
Ich nehm zugleich an deiner Freude teil,
Betagter Vater vieler Flüsse!
Denn wisse,
Daß ich ein großes Recht auch mit an deinem Helden habe.
Zwar blick ich nicht dein Heil,
So dir dein Salomo gebiert,
Mit scheelen Augen an,
Weil Karlens Hand,
Des Himmels seltne Gabe,
Bei uns den Reichsstab führt.
Wem aber ist wohl unbekannt,
Wie noch die Wurzel jener Lust,
Die deinem gütigsten Trajan
Von dem Genuß der holden Josephine
Allein bewußt,
An meinen Ufern grüne?

Danube
I too share in your joy,
Aged father of many rivers!
For know
That I also have a great right to your hero.
Indeed at the welfare
That your Solomon delivers to you
I do not look askance,
For Charles's hand—
Rare gift of heaven—
Bears among us the royal sceptre.
But to whom is it unknown
How still the root of that delight,
Which to your most benevolent Trajan
Only pleasure in the lovely Josephine
Makes known,
Prospers on my shores?

7. Aria A ob d'am I,II bc — f♯ C

Donau
Reis von Habsburgs hohem Stamme,
Deiner Tugend helle Flamme
Kennt, bewundert, rühmt mein Strand.
  Du stammst von den Lorbeerzweigen,
  Drum muß deiner Ehe Band
  Auch den fruchtbarn Lorbeern gleichen.

Danube
Scion of Habsburg's lofty line,
Your virtue's bright flame
Is known, admired, praised on my shore.
  You stem from the laurel branch,
  Therefore your marriage bond must
  Also be like the fruitful laurel.

8. Recitativo S bc — A–e C

Pleiße
Verzeiht,

Pleiße
Pardon,

Bemooste Häupter starker Ströme,
Wenn eine Nymphe euren Streit
Und euer Reden störet.
Der Streit ist ganz gerecht;
Die Sache groß und kostbar, die ihn nähret.
Mir ist ja wohl Lust
Annoch bewußt,
Und meiner Nymphen frohes Scherzen,
So wir bei unsers Siegeshelden Ankunft spürten,
Der da verdient,
Daß alle Untertanen ihre Herzen,
Denn Hekatomben sind zu schlecht,
Ihm her zu einem Opfer führten.
Doch hört, was sich mein Mund erkühnt,
Euch vorzusagen:
Du, dessen Flut der Inn und Lech vermehren,
Du sollt mit uns dies Königspaar verehren,
Doch uns dasselbe gänzlich überlassen.
Ihr beiden andern sollt euch brüderlich vertragen
Und, müßt ihr diese doppelte Regierungssonne
Auf eine Zeit, doch wechselsweis, entbehren,
Euch in Geduld und Hoffnung fassen.

Mossy heads of mighty rivers,
If a nymph disturbs your dispute
And your speeches.
That dispute is quite justified;
The matter that nourishes it, great and precious.
Only pleasure is
So far known to me,
And my nymphs' happy jests;
So we felt upon the arrival of our victorious hero,
He who deserves
That all his subjects should bring him—
Since hecatombs are too poor—
Their hearts as an offering.
Yet hear what my mouth is bold

To say to you:
You, whose flood is swelled by the Inn and the Lech,
With us you should honour this royal pair,
Yet cede them entirely to us.
You two others should co-exist fraternally,
And if you must go without this twofold reigning sun
For a time, yet in alternation,

Compose yourselves in patience and hope.

9. ARIA S fl I–III bc — G c

Pleiße
Hört doch! Der sanften Flöten Chor
Erfreut die Brust, ergötzt das Ohr.
  Der unzertrennten Eintracht Stärke
  Macht diese nette Harmonie
  Und tut noch größre Wunderwerke;
  Dies merkt und stimmt doch auch wie sie.

Pleiße
Do listen! The gentle choir of flutes
Gladdens the breast, delights the ear.
  The might of undivided concord
  Causes this pleasant harmony
  And does still greater wondrous deeds;
  Mark this and be in tune with it.

10. RECITATIVO SATB str bc — e–D c

Weichsel
Ich muß, ich will gehorsam sein.
Elbe
Mir geht die Trennung bitter ein,

Vistula
I must, I will be obedient.
Elbe
The separation is bitter to me,

Doch meines Königs Wink/deines Ufers Wohl gebietet meinen Willen.

Yet my King's nod/your shore's welfare commands my will.

Donau

Und ich bin fertig, euren Wunsch,
Soviel mir möglich, zu erfüllen.

Danube

And I am ready to fulfil your wish,
As far as I can.

Pleiße

So krönt die Eintracht euren Schluß. Doch schaut,
Wie kommt's, daß man an eueren Gestaden
So viel Altäre heute baut?
Was soll das Tanzen der Najaden?

Pleiße

Thus concord crowns your conclusion. But look,
How is it that on your banks they are
Building so many altars today?
Why should the Nayads be dancing?

Ach! irr ich nicht,
So sieht man heut das längst gewünschte Licht
In frohem Glanze glühen,
Das unsre Lust,
Den gütigsten August,
Der Welt und uns geliehen.

Ah! if I am not mistaken,
One sees today the long-awaited light
Glow in joyous radiance
That our delight,
The most benevolent Augustus,
Lends to the world and to us.

[or:]
Ach! irr ich nicht,
So seh ich, wie das längst gewünschte Licht
Durch einen Glanz mich rühret,
Von dem August,
Der Erden süße Lust,
Den teuren Namen führet.

Ah! if I am not mistaken,
I see how the long-awaited light
Stirs me with a radiance
From which Augustus,
The earth's sweet delight,
Derives his precious name.

Ei! nun wohlan!
Da uns Gelegenheit und Zeit
Die Hände beut,
So stimmt mit mir noch einmal an:

Ah! now then!
Since opportunity and time
Hold out their hands to us,
Then strike up with me once more:

11. CHORUS [Scoring as in no. 1] D $\frac{12}{8}$

Die himmlische Vorsicht der ewigen Güte
Beschirme dein Leben, durchlauchter August!
So viel sich nur Tropfen in heutigen Stunden
In unsern bemoosten Kanälen befunden,
Umfange beständig dein hohes Gemüte
Vergnügen und Lust!

May the divine providence of eternal goodness
Protect your life, Your Highness Augustus!
As many as the drops nowadays
Found in our mossy channels,
To that extent may your lofty spirit
Be constantly surrounded by pleasures and delight!

The origin of this cantata is quite complicated. Unless we are altogether mistaken, Bach originally intended to perform it on 7 October 1734 to celebrate the king's birthday. Upon hearing the news that the royal couple would be present in Leipzig a few days before the birthday, however, he postponed it and performed the hastily composed Cantata 215 in their honour instead. Not until two years later, for the king's birthday on 7 October 1736, did Bach complete and perform the postponed work. A few years later, on 3 August 1740, he revived it with insignificant textual alterations for the name-day of the king.

The work is designed as a 'dramma per musica'.* In its modest plot, four rivers enter as personified representatives of their countries or city: the Vistula (Poland), the Elbe (Saxony), the Danube (Austria; Augustus III's consort Maria Josepha was an Austrian princess), and the Pleiße (Leipzig). The Vistula, Elbe, and Danube put forward their arguments in favour of claiming the monarch for themselves. The dispute is finally settled by the Pleiße, who decides that the Danube should indeed honour the royal couple but should cede them entirely to the other rivers. She also concludes that the Vistula and the Elbe should in alternation share the presence of the sovereign. With heavy hearts the rivers accept her judgement and unite in a chorus* of homage to the ruler.

The anonymous librettist thus designed an original but, in effect, far from breathtaking plot. Bach's composition, on the other hand, is exceptionally rich in musical beauties. The festive scoring for trumpets and drums, flutes, oboes, strings, and continuo with four voice parts suggests an open-air performance, despite the advanced time of year of the Elector's birthday (7 October). Within a frame furnished by two large-scale choruses, each of the four rivers is assigned a recitative-aria pair in the ascending order bass, tenor, alto, soprano. A recitative for all four soloists, again in rising order of vocal entry, then brings the plot to its conclusion and also acts as a transition to the choral finale. The key sequence accords with the plot to the extent that, within the context of the overall tonic D (outer movements), the dominant and relative minors A, b, and f sharp are assigned to the disputing rivers, whereas the judgement of Pleiße, who sings an aria in the subdominant G, marks the turning-point both of the plot and of the modulatory scheme.

The opening chorus is an original tone-picture of roaring rivers. Its dynamic contrasts, already foreshadowed in the instrumental introduction, are suggested by the words 'murmur gently' and 'no, rush swiftly'. In the middle section, the 'dams of timidity' are finally broken through: here the four-part vocal ensemble, accompanied by woodwind and strings, flows along in a joyous Allegro. A *secco* recitative leads to Vistula's aria 'Schleuß des Janustempels Türen', no. 3, whose text refers to the upshot of the Polish troubles. Musically, it is a dance-like, ceremonial bass aria, accompanied by strings, out of which the first violin repeatedly comes to the fore in a concertante* role. The Elbe enters in the fourth movement, a *secco* recitative that flows into arioso.* Elbe's aria, no. 5, is decidedly virtuoso in character on account of its extensive passage-work for obbligato* solo violin. The tenor's calling out of the 'golden word Augustus' (and, before that, the word 'ruft'/'call') against the concertante violin has a bewitching effect. No less charming is the portrayal of the swelling and rebounding of the floods in the middle section by means of extended coloraturas.*

The Danube is introduced in the third *secco* recitative, no. 6. The aria that follows, which alludes to the lofty descent of the Electoress, strikes a more solemn note with its two obbligato oboes d'amore.* The melodic lines are notable for their syncopated rhythm, which at the time might have been considered fashionable. Finally, the Pleiße enters, first in a *secco* recitative and then in an aria, no. 9, in which the sound of three flutes is designed to induce concord, an effect the listener will happily concede to this captivating and original movement with its singular instrumentation.

The recitative that brings the plot to its conclusion, no. 10, begins in the form of a *secco* as the Vistula, Elbe, and Danube submit to the arbitration of the Pleiße. String chords are, however, added to her last words, which introduce the concluding chorus with reference to the royal birthday (for the name-day, the text was slightly altered). Like the finales of many of Bach's congratulatory cantatas, the gigue-like concluding chorus is in rondeau form. The rondeau theme is heard three times, in alternation with two episodes with reduced dynamics: in the first of these, the trumpets are silent; in the second, only soprano and alto sing against a bassett* of violins and viola, with the result that the final rondeau reprise concludes both movement and work with all the greater effect.

3

Festive music for Leipzig university celebrations

When Bach came to Leipzig in 1723, Johann Gottlieb Görner, organist of the Nikolaikirche, had already discovered how to claim for himself the post of university music director left vacant by the death of Johann Kuhnau. The pugnacious Bach did in fact succeed in bringing about a division of duties which assured him the supervision of music for the 'old service' (at Christmas, Easter, Whit, and the Reformation Festival, together with the so-called 'Quartalsorationen'). Yet perhaps due to the preferential personal position that Görner enjoyed within the university, Bach gradually lost interest in these duties after 1725. The festive music composed by Bach is thus largely peripheral to the official academic life of Leipzig, either because it was written for non-academic personages (BWV Anh. I 20, BWV 198) or because it was performed outside academic celebrations (BWV 205, 207, 36b). The last-named group also includes the cantata *Murmelt nur, ihr heitern Bäche*, BWV Anh. I 195, presented as a serenade in honour of the Leipzig lawyer Johann Florens Rivinus by his students on 9 June 1723. The music is lost, however, and, in the absence of evidence, Bach's authorship of it can only be conjectured.

Latin ode (text lost), BWV Anh. I 20

The music of this ode,* composed for the birthday of Duke Friedrich II of Saxe-Gotha, was performed at an academic ceremony within the University of Leipzig on 9 August 1723. Although the text for this occasion had been published, both libretto and music are lost. For further details see the Critical Report to NBA I/38, p. 10.

Zerreißet, zersprenget, zertrümmert die Gruft, BWV 205

Der zufriedengestellte Aeolus	*Aeolus Placated*

NBA I/38, p. 3 BC G 36 Duration: *c.* 41 mins

1.	CHOR DER WINDE	CHORUS OF THE WINDS	
	SATB tr I–III timp hn I,II fl I,II ob I,II str bc		D $\frac{3}{4}$
	Zerreißet, zersprenget, zertrümmert die Gruft,	Tear, break, smash the vault	
	Die unserm Wüten Grenze gibt!	That confines our raging!	

Durchbrechet die Luft,
Daß selber die Sonne zur Finsternis werde,
Durchschneidet die Fluten, durchwühlet die Erde,
Daß sich der Himmel selbst betrübt!

Break through the air,
So that even the sun will turn to darkness,
Cut through the floods, rake up the earth,
So that heaven itself will be distressed!

2. Recitativo B brass timp ww str bc G–f♯ C

Äolus
Ja! ja!
Die Stunden sind nunmehro nah,
Daß ich euch treuen Untertanen
Den Weg aus eurer Einsamkeit
Nach bald geschloßner Sommerszeit
Zur Freiheit werde bahnen.
Ich geb euch Macht,
Vom Abend bis zum Morgen,
Vom Mittag bis zur Mitternacht
Mit eurer Wut zu rasen,
Die Blumen, Blätter, Klee
Mit Kälte, Frost und Schnee
Entsetzlich anzublasen.
Ich geb euch Macht,
Die Zedern umzuschmeißen
Und Bergegipfel aufzureißen.
Ich geb euch Macht,
Die ungestümen Meeresfluten
Durch euren Nachdruck zu erhöhn,
Daß das Gestirne wird vermuten,
Ihr Feuer soll durch euch erlöschend untergehn.

Aeolus
Yes! yes!
The hour is now at hand
When for you loyal subjects
From your solitude I shall pave the way,
Soon after summertime is ended,
To freedom.
I give you power
From evening to morning,
From midday to midnight,
To storm with your rage;
Upon flowers, leaves, and clover
With cold, frost, and snow
To blow fearfully.
I give you power
To knock over the cedars
And rip open the mountain peaks.
I give you power
To raise the tumultuous waves of the sea
Through your energy,
So that the stars will suppose
That their fire, extinguished through you, shall perish.

3. Aria B str + ob I bc A C

Äolus
Wie will ich lustig lachen,
Wenn alles durcheinandergeht!
Wenn selbst der Fels nicht sicher steht
Und wenn die Dächer krachen,
So will ich lustig lachen!

Aeolus
How merrily I will laugh
When all is thrown into confusion!
When even rock does not stay secure
And when the roofs crack,
Then I will laugh merrily!

4. Recitativo T bc c♯–b C

Zephyrus
Gefürcht'ter Äolus,
Dem ich im Schoße sonsten liege
Und deine Ruh vergnüge,
Laß deinen harten Schluß
Mich doch nicht allzufrüh erschrecken;
Verziehe, laß in dir,

Zephyr
Feared Aeolus,
In whose bosom I normally lie
And delight your repose,
Do not let your harsh decision
Terrify me too soon;
Delay, and within you,

Aus Gunst zu mir,
Ein Mitleid noch erwecken!

As a favour to me,
Let pity be awakened!

5. ARIA T vla d'am vla da g bc — b $\frac{3}{8}$

Zephyrus
Frische Schatten, meine Freude,
Sehet, wie ich schmerzlich scheide,
Kommt, bedauret meine Schmach!
Windet euch, verwaisten Zweige,
Ach! ich schweige,
Sehet mir nur jammernd nach!

Zephyr
Cool shade, my joy,
See how sorrowfully I depart;
Come, lament my shame!
Twist, you orphaned branches,
Ah! I am silent,
Gaze after me in distress!

6. RECITATIVO B bc — D c

Äolus
Beinahe wirst du mich bewegen.
Wie? seh ich nicht Pomona hier
Und, wo mir recht, die Pallas auch bei ihr?
Sagt, Werte, sagt,
Was fordert ihr von mir?
Euch ist gewiß sehr viel daran gelegen.

Aeolus
You almost stir me.
What? do I not see Pomona here
And, if I am right, Pallas with her?
Tell me, worthy ones, tell me,
What do you ask of me?
You certainly set great store by it.

7. ARIA A ob d'am bc — f♯ c

Pomona
Können nicht die roten Wangen,
Womit meine Früchte prangen,
Dein ergrimmtes Herze fangen,
Ach, so sage, kannst du sehn,
Wie die Blätter von den Zweigen
Sich betrübt zur Erde beugen,
Um ihr Elend abzuneigen,
Das an ihnen soll geschehn?

Pomona
If the red cheeks
With which my fruits shine
Could not capture your angered heart,
Ah, then tell me, can you see
How the leaves of the branches
Bow down sadly to the earth
To avert the misery
That shall befall them?

8. RECITATIVO SA bc — c♯–E c

Pomona
So willst du, grimmger Äolus,
Gleich wie ein Fels und Stein
Bei meinen Bitten sein?
Pallas
Wohlan! ich will und muß
Auch meine Seufzer wagen,
Vielleicht wird mir,
Was er, Pomona, dir
Stillschweigend abgeschlagen,
Von ihm gewährt.
Pallas/Pomona
Wohl! wenn er gegen mich/dich sich gütiger erklärt.

Pomona
Then would you, enraged Aeolus,
Be like a rock and stone
To my entreaties?
Pallas
Well then! I will and must
Venture my sighs too;
Perhaps to me
What to you, Pomona,
He tacitly refused
Will be granted by him.
Pallas/Pomona
Well! if only he would express himself more kindly towards me/you.

9. Aria S vln I solo bc — E $\frac{12}{8}$

Pallas
Angenehmer Zephyrus,
Dein von Bisam reicher Kuß
Und dein lauschend Kühlen
Soll auf meinen Höhen spielen.
Großer König Äolus,
Sage doch dem Zephyrus,
Daß sein bisamreicher Kuß
Und sein lauschend Kühlen
Soll auf meinen Höhen spielen.

Pallas
Pleasant Zephyr,
Your kiss, rich in musk,
And your refreshing coolness
Shall play upon my heights.
Great King Aeolus,
Do tell Zephyr
That his musk-rich kiss
And his refreshing coolness
Shall play upon my heights.

10. Recitativo SB fl I,II bc — b–D C

Pallas
Mein Äolus,
Ach! störe nicht die Fröhlichkeiten,
Weil meiner Musen Helikon
Ein Fest, ein' angenehme Feier
Auf seinen Gipfeln angestellt.
Äolus
So sage mir:
Warum dann dir
Besonders dieser Tag so teuer,
So wert und heilig fällt?
O Nachteil und Verdruß!
Soll ich denn eines Weibes Willen
In meinem Regiment erfüllen?
Pallas
Mein Müller, mein August,
Der Pierinnen Freud und Lust
Äolus
Dein Müller, dein August!
Pallas
Und mein geliebter Sohn,
Äolus
Dein Müller, dein August!
Pallas
Erlebet die vergnügten Zeiten,
Da ihm die Ewigkeit
Sein weiser Name prophezeit.
Äolus
Dein Müller! dein August!
Der Pierinnen Freud und Lust
Und dein geliebter Sohn,
Erlebet die vergnügten Zeiten,

Pallas
My Aeolus,
Ah! do not disturb the merriments,
For my muses' Helicon
Has prepared a feast, a pleasant
celebration
On his summit.
Aeolus
Then tell me:
Why then do you hold
This particular day so dear,
So precious and sacred?
O bane and vexation!
Shall I then comply with a woman's will
Within my governance?
Pallas
My Müller, my Augustus,
The muses' joy and delight
Aeolus
Your Müller, your Augustus!
Pallas
And my beloved son,
Aeolus
Your Müller, your Augustus!
Pallas
Experiences glad times,
Since eternity
Prophesied his wise name.
Aeolus
Your Müller, your Augustus,
The muses' joy and delight
And your beloved son,
Experiences glad times,

Da ihm die Ewigkeit	Since eternity
Sein weiser Name prophezeit.	Prophesied his wise name.
Wohlan! ich lasse mich bezwingen,	Well, then! I admit defeat:
Euer Wunsch soll euch gelingen.	Your wish shall come true.
11. ARIA B tr I–III timp hn I,II bc	D $\frac{3}{8}$
Äolus	*Aeolus*
Zurücke, zurücke, geflügelten Winde,	Back, back, you winged winds,
Besänftiget euch;	Calm yourselves;
Doch wehet ihr gleich,	Yet though you blow,
So weht doch itzund nur gelinde!	Blow now but gently!
12. RECITATIVO SAT bc	G $\mathbf{c}$
Pallas	*Pallas*
Was Lust!	What delight!
Pomona	*Pomona*
Was Freude!	What joy!
Zephyrus	*Zephyr*
Welch Vergnügen!	What pleasure!
zu dritt	*all three*
Entstehet in der Brust,	Arises in our breast,
Daß sich nach unsrer Lust	That according to our desire
Die Wünsche müssen fügen.	Our wishes must be accommodated.
Zephyrus	*Zephyr*
So kann ich mich bei grünen Zweigen	Then among the green branches
Noch fernerhin vergnügt bezeigen.	I can henceforth express my pleasure.
Pomona	*Pomona*
So seh ich mein Ergötzen	Then I see my delight
An meinen reifen Schätzen.	In my ripe treasures.
Pallas	*Pallas*
So richt ich in vergnügter Ruh	Then in pleasant repose I prepare
Meines Augusts Lustmahl zu.	My Augustus's feast of delight.
Pomona, Zephyrus	*Pomona, Zephyr*
Wir sind zu deiner Fröhlichkeit	We are ready for your merriment
Mit gleicher Lust bereit.	With equal delight.
13. ARIA [DUETTO] AT fl I + II bc	G $\frac{3}{4}$
Pomona, Zephyrus	*Pomona, Zephyr*
Zweig und Äste	Branch and boughs
Zollen dir zu deinem Feste	Bestow upon your feast
Ihrer Gaben Überfluß.	Their gifts' abundance.
Zephyrus	*Zephyr*
Und mein Scherzen soll und muß,	And my jesting shall and must,
Deinen August zu verehren,	In honour of your Augustus,
Dieses Tages Lust vermehren.	Enhance this day's delight.
Pomona/Zephyrus	*Pomona/Zephyr*
Ich bringe die Früchte/mein Lispeln mit Freuden herbei,	I bring my fruits/whispers with joy,

Daß alles zum Scherzen vollkommener sei.	So that in the amusement all may be more complete.
14. Recitativo S bc	D C
Pallas	*Pallas*
Ja! ja! ich lad euch selbst zu dieser Feier ein;	Yes, yes! I myself invite you to this celebration;
Erhebet euch zu meinen Spitzen,	Ascend to my summit,
Wo schon die Musen freudig sein	Where the muses are already joyful
Und ganz entbrannt vor Eifer sitzen.	And sit quite inflamed with zeal.
Auf! lasset uns, indem wir eilen,	Rise! let us, as we hasten,
Die Luft mit frohen Wünschen teilen!	Part the air with joyful wishes!
15. Chorus [Scoring as in no. 1]	D 2
Vivat! August, August vivat!	Long live Augustus! Long live Augustus!
Sei beglückt, gelehrter Mann!	May you be happy, learned man!
Dein Vergnügen müsse blühen,	Your pleasure must blossom,
Daß dein Lehren, dein Bemühen	So that your teaching, your endeavours
Möge solche Pflanzen ziehen,	May raise such plants
Womit ein Land sich einstens schmücken kann.	As can one day adorn the land.

On 3 August 1725 the Leipzig students gave a reception to celebrate the name-day of the university teacher August Friedrich Müller, who enjoyed great popularity among his pupils. Born in 1684 (and thus about the same age as Bach), he became Master of Law in 1707, Doctor of Law in 1714, and attained the rank of professor in 1731; in addition, he held the post of 'Rector magnificus' in 1733 and 1743. Bach's cantata was probably performed as a student serenade outside Müller's house.

Designed as a 'dramma per musica',* the cantata is based on a libretto by Picander, who published it in the first volume of his verse. The plot is simplicity itself. Pallas Athene, together with the muses, celebrates a feast in honour of the learned man on Mount Helicon. She has cause, however, to fear that Aeolus, god of the winds, will already unleash the autumn storms. Aeolus does, in fact, inform his winds of their imminent liberation and himself rejoices in the approaching storms. Zephyr, god of mild summer breezes, and Pomona, goddess of fruit-growing, implore deferment. But it is Pallas who, by referring to the tribute being paid to the universally esteemed August Müller, obtains Aeolus's promise not to disturb the peace of the season for the time being. Thereupon Pallas invites all those present to take part in her celebration and to join in a 'Vivat' for the learned man.

Bach's composition is a model of sumptuously scored open-air music, requiring an instrumental ensemble of trumpets, drums, horns, flutes, oboes, strings, and continuo, together with four voice parts. It is introduced by a lively 'Chorus of Winds', whose poetic model was the well-known description of Aeolus and his winds in the first book of Virgil's *Aeneid*. In concertante* opposition and in upward and downward running scale figures, in which the continuo also participates, Bach paints a graphic tone-picture of the impatient winds. Aeolus's recitative, no. 2, pursues this image further: fully orchestrated scale figures surge against the declamation of the voice. Aeolus's aria, no. 3, continues in the same mood and, in frequent note repetitions, depicts the laughter of the god. At the words 'And when the roofs crack', the middle section is enhanced by lively demisemiquaver motion in the accompanying parts.

Next Zephyr enters and, after a brief recitative, sings a 'shade aria', a popular type whose contemplative description of nature places it among the permanent repertoire of Italian baroque opera (the most famous example perhaps being Handel's 'Ombra mai fu', from *Serse*). Bach's aria for Zephyr (no. 5) is, however, an exceptional gem that leaves its models far behind. After the blustering singing of Aeolus in previous movements, the obbligato* viola d'amore* and viola da gamba create an atmosphere of calm and repose. It is revealing how Bach was able to give a quite different character to the following arias for Pomona and Pallas, despite their similar underlying mood—like Zephyr's aria, they aim to placate Aeolus. The composer's purpose is served, in particular, by a change of obbligato instrument: viola d'amore and viola da gamba (Zephyr) give way to oboe d'amore (Pomona, no. 7), and then to a virtuoso violin part (Pallas, no. 9). Moreover, the key sequence, which leads upwards through the circle of fifths from b (no. 5) via f sharp (no. 7) and c sharp (no.8) to the latter's relative major, E (no. 9), helps to characterize the purposefulness of the plot, for it makes us aware that, after ever more insistent entreaties, the turning-point is reached with the entry of Pallas in a radiant major key.

The true turning-point takes place in the recitative 'My Aeolus, ah! do not disturb the merriments', no. 10, whose significance is marked by the addition of two flutes. At the same time, a change takes place in the key sequence, which suddenly returns to the tonic D (Aeolus's aria, no. 11) before turning towards the so-far unused region of the subdominant, G. Aeolus's aria forms a complete contrast to the three that precede it: along with the blustering Aeolus, trumpets, drums, and horns plus continuo enter as the exclusive accompanying instruments, a scoring unique in Bach's arias. It is charming to observe how Bach makes programmatic use of the contrast between the high pitch of the trumpets and the relatively low pitch of the horns: at the words 'blow now but gently!' in the middle section only the two horns remain from the *furioso* of the brass music.

A terzetto-recitative, no. 12, expresses the joy of the petitioners over the fulfilment of their wishes; and gentle sounds are heard once more in a duet for Pomona and Zephyr, no. 13, accompanied by unison flutes—as gifts Pomona brings her fruits and Zephyr the gentle wafting of the summer breeze. In conclusion, the entire cast are once more united in a congratulatory chorus,* whose boisterous, ever-renewed 'Vivat' pervades at first the instrumental introduction and then the vocal music. In the middle section, spirited calls of 'Vivat' from the instruments alone occur from time to time while the voices sing other words.

Vereinigte Zwietracht der wechselnden Saiten, BWV 207

NBA I/38, p. 99 BC G 37 Duration: *c.* 32 mins

1. Chorus SATB tr I–III timp fl I,II ob d'am I,II taille str bc — D $\frac{6}{8}$

Vereinigte Zwietracht der wechselnden Saiten,	United discord of changing strings,
Der rollenden Pauken durchdringender Knall!	The rolling drums' penetrating boom!
Locket den lüsteren Hörer herbei,	Entice the pleasure-seeking listener;
Saget mit euren frohlockenden Tönen	With your jubilant notes
Und doppelt vermehretem Schall	And doubly augmented sound
Denen mir emsig ergebenen Söhnen,	Tell those keenly devoted sons
Was hier der Lohn der Tugend sei.	What is here the reward of virtue.

2. Recitativo T bc — b C

Der Fleiß	*Diligence*
Wen treibt ein edler Trieb zu dem, was Ehre heißt,	He whom a noble impulse drives to what is called honour,
Und wessen lobbegierger Geist	And whose spirit, desirous of praise,
Sehnt sich, mit dem zu prangen,	Longs to shine with that
Was man durch Kunst, Verstand und Tugend kann erlangen,	Which can be achieved through art, understanding, and virtue,
Der trete meine Bahn	May he tread my path,
Beherzt mit stets verneuten Kräften an!	Heartened by ever-renewed powers!
Was jetzt die junge Hand, der muntre Fuß erwirbt,	What the young hand, the lively foot now acquires
Macht, daß das alte Haupt in keiner Schmach und banger Not verdirbt.	Ensures that the old head does not perish in shame and anxious distress.
Der Jugend angewandte Säfte	The applied humours of youth
Erhalten denn des Alters matte Kräfte,	Then sustain age's dull powers,
Und die in ihrer besten Zeit,	And those who in their best time—
Wie es den Faulen scheint,	When it seems laziness—
In nichts als lauter Müh und steter Arbeit schweben,	Hover in nothing but pure exertion and constant work,
Die können nach erlangtem Ziel, an Ehren satt,	They could, after achieving their goal, satisfied in honour,
In stolzer Ruhe leben;	Live in noble repose;

Denn sie erfahren in der Tat,
Daß der die Ruhe recht genießet,
Dem sie ein saurer Schweiß versüßet.

For they experience in action
That for him who rightly enjoys repose
It sweetens his sour sweat.

3. Aria T str bc — b ¢

Der Fleiß
Zieht euren Fuß nur nicht zurücke,
Ihr, die ihr meinen Weg erwählt!
Das Glücke merket eure Schritte,
Die Ehre zählt die sauren Tritte,
Damit, daß nach vollbrachter Straße
Euch werd in gleichem Übermaße
Der Lohn von ihnen zugezählt.

Diligence
Do not draw back your foot,
You who choose my path!
Good fortune marks your steps,
Honour counts your sour treads,
So that after the path has been trodden,
For you to the same extent shall
The reward of these things be enumerated.

4. Recitativo SB bc — G–D c

Die Ehre
Dem nur allein
Soll meine Wohnung offen sein,
Der sich zu deinen Söhnen zählet
Und statt der Rosenbahn, die ihm die Wollust zeigt,
Sich deinen Dornenweg erwählet.
Mein Lorbeer soll hinfort nur solche Scheitel zieren,
In denen sich ein immerregend Blut,
Ein unerschrocknes Herz und unverdroßner Mut
Zu aller Arbeit läßt verspüren.
Das Glück
Auch ich will mich mit meinen Schätzen
Bei dem, den du erwählst, stets lassen finden.
Den will ich mir zu einem angenehmen Ziel
Von meiner Liebe setzen,
Der stets vor sich genung, vor andre nie zu viel
Von denen sich durch Müh und Fleiß erworbnen Gaben
Vermeint zu haben.
Ziert denn die unermüd'te Hand
Nach meiner Freundin ihr Versprechen
Ein ihrer Taten würdger Stand,

Honour
To him alone
Shall my dwelling be open
Who numbers himself among your sons
And, instead of the bed of roses that pleasure shows him,
Chooses for himself your path of thorns.
My laurel shall henceforth adorn only crowns
In which an ever-stirring blood,
An unfrightened heart and an indefatigable courage
Is felt for all work.
Fortune
I, too, with my treasures will always be found
With him whom you choose.
I will set an agreeable goal,
Out of my love, for him
Who always has enough for himself, never too much for others,
Of those gifts acquired through exertion and diligence,
So he believes.
Then if the untired hand is graced,
According to my friend's promise,
By a situation worthy of its deeds,

So soll sie auch die Frucht des Überflusses brechen.	Then it shall also pick the fruit of abundance.
So kann man die, die sich befleißen,	Then those who endeavour
Des Lorbeers Würdige zu heißen,	To be called worthy of the laurel
Zugleich glückselig preisen.	Can also be rapturously praised.

5. Aria Duetto SB bc + Ritornello tr I,II ob d'am I + II + taille str bc D ¢

Die Ehre	*Honour*
Den soll mein Lorbeer schützend decken,	My laurel shall be his tutelary adornment,
Das Glück	*Fortune*
Der soll die Frucht des Segens schmecken,	He shall taste the fruit of my blessing,
beide	*both*
Der durch den Fleiß zum Sternen steigt.	Who ascends to the stars through Diligence.
Die Ehre	*Honour*
Benetzt des Schweißes Tau die Glieder,	If sweat's dew moistens his limbs,
So fällt er in die Muscheln nieder,	Then he falls down among the oysters,
Wo er der Ehre Perlen zeugt.	Where he begets Honour's pearls.
Das Glück	*Fortune*
Wo die erhitzten Tropfen fließen,	Where the heated drops flow,
Da wird ein Strom daraus entsprießen,	There a stream thereof will spring up
Der denen Segensbächen gleicht.	That resembles rills of blessing.

6. Recitativo A bc G c

Die Dankbarkeit	*Gratitude*
Es ist kein leeres Wort, kein ohne Grund erregtes Hoffen,	It is no empty word, no hope aroused without foundation,
Was euch der Fleiß als euren Lohn gezeigt;	What Diligence shows you as your reward;
Obgleich der harte Sinn der Unvergnügten schweigt,	Although the harsh minds of the dissatisfied are silent,
Wenn sie nach ihrem Tun ein gleiches Glück betroffen.	If, after their activity, a like fortune befalls them.
Ja,	Yes,
Zeiget nur in der Asträa	Show in Astraea,
Durch den Fleiß geöffneten und aufgeschloßnen Tempel,	Through the temple opened and closed by Diligence,
An einem so beliebt als teuren Lehrer,	In a teacher as dear as he is loved,
Ihr, ihm so sehr getreu als wie verpflicht'ten Hörer,	You listeners, as loyal as you are indebted to him,
Der Welt zufolge eim Exempel,	Show the world an example,
An dem der Neid	In which envy

Der Ehre, Glück und Fleiß vereinten Schluß
Verwundern muß.
Es müsse diese Zeit
Nicht so vorübergehn!
Laßt durch die Glut der angezündten Kerzen
Die Flammen eurer ihm ergebnen Herzen
Den Gönnern so als wie den Neidern sehn!

At the united conclusion of Honour, Fortune, and Diligence
Must marvel.
This age must
Not let it pass by!
Through the glow of ignited candles
Let the flames of your hearts, devoted to him,
See patrons as well as the envious!

7. Aria A fl I,II unis str bc — G $\frac{3}{4}$

Die Dankbarkeit
Ätzet dieses Angedenken
In den härtsten Marmor ein!
  Doch die Zeit verdirbt den Stein.
  Laßt vielmehr aus euren Taten
  Eures Lehrers Tun erraten!
  Kann man aus den Früchten lesen,
  Wie die Wurzel sei gewesen,
  Muß sie unvergänglich sein.

Gratitude
Etch this commemoration
In the hardest marble!
  Yet time decays stone.
  Let rather from your deeds
  Your teacher's work be divined!
  If one can tell by the fruits
  What the root was like,
  It must be imperishable.

8. Recitativo SATB ww + str bc — D C

Der Fleiß
Ihr Schläfrigen, herbei!
Erblickt an meinem mir beliebten Kortten,
Wie daß in meinen Worten
Kein eitler Wahn verborgen sei.
Sein annoch zarter Fuß fing kaum zu gehen an,
Sogleich betrat er meine Bahn,
Und, da er nun so zeitig angefangen,
Was Wunder, daß er kann sein Ziel so früh erlangen!
Wie sehr er mich geliebt,
Wie eifrig er in meinem Dienst gewesen,
Läßt die gelehrte Schrift auch andern Ländern lesen.
Allein, was such ich ihn zu loben?
Ist der nicht schon genung erhoben,
Den der großmächtige Monarch, der als August Gelehrte kennet,
Zu seinen Lehrer nennet.

Diligence
You indolent ones, come!
See in my beloved Kortte
How in my words
No vain delusion lies hidden.
His still tender foot scarcely began to move
When he trod on my path,
And since he began in such good time,
What wonder that he could achieve his goal so early!
How much he has loved me,
How zealous he has been in my service,
Can be gathered from his learned writings even in other lands.
But why do I seek to praise him?
Is he not exalted enough already,
He whom the high and mighty monarch, who knows him as Augustus the scholar,
Names as his teacher?

Die Ehre	*Honour*
Ja, ja, ihr edlen Freunde, seht! wie ich mit Kortten bin verbunden.	Yes, yes, you noble friends, see how I am linked with Kortte!
Es hat ihm die gewogne Hand	My well-disposed hand has
Schon manchen Kranz gewunden.	Already wound him many a wreath.
Jetzt soll sein höhrer Stand	Now his higher position shall
Ihm zu dem Lorbeer dienen,	Serve him as a laurel,
Der unter einem mächtgen Schutz wird immerwährend grünen.	Which, under a mighty protection, shall be perpetually verdant.
Das Glück	*Fortune*
So kann er sich an meinen Schätzen,	Then he can delight in my treasures—
Da er durch eure Gunst sich mir in Schoß gebracht,	Since through your favour he was brought to my bosom—
Wenn er in stolzer Ruhe lacht,	When he smiles in noble repose,
Nach eigner Lust ergötzen.	According to his own pleasure.
Die Dankbarkeit	*Gratitude*
So ist, was ich gehofft, erfüllt,	Thus what I hoped is accomplished,
Da ein so unverhofftes Glück,	Since a Fortune so unexpected,
Mein nie genung gepriesner Kortte,	My Kortte—never praised enough—
Der Freunde Wünschen stillt.	Satisfies you friends' wishes.
Drum denkt ein jeder auch an seine Pflicht zurück	Therefore may everyone recall his duty
Und sucht dir jetzt durch sein Bezeigen	And seek now by expressing it
Die Früchte seiner Gunst zu reichen.	To obtain the fruits of his favour.
Es stimmt, wer nur ein wahrer Freund will sein,	May whoever would be his true friend
Jetzt mit uns ein.	Now join with us.

9. Chorus [Scoring as in no. 1, but ob I,II in place of ob d'am I,II] D 2

Kortte lebe, Kortte blühe!	Long live Kortte! may Kortte flourish!
Die Ehre	*Honour*
Den mein Lorbeer unterstützt,	He whom my laurel favours,
Das Glück	*Fortune*
Der mir selbst im Schoße sitzt,	Who sits in my own bosom,
Der Fleiß	*Diligence*
Der durch mich stets höher steigt,	Who climbs ever higher through me,
Die Dankbarkeit	*Gratitude*
Der die Herzen zu sich neigt,	Who inclines our hearts to himself,
Tutti	*Tutti*
Muß in ungezählten Jahren	Must for countless years
Stets geehrt in Segen stehn	Ever remain honoured in blessing
Und zwar wohl der Neider Scharen,	And no doubt see envious crowds
Aber nicht der Feinde sehn.	But not enemies.

This cantata was composed in honour of Dr Gottlieb Kortte, a Leipzig university teacher who seems to have been no less popular among his students than August Müller, the dedicatee of Cantata 205 (see above). The initiator of this music of homage might have been one of Kortte's students, and the occasion was 'D. Korttens erhaltene Profession' ('the chair obtained by Dr Kortte'): on 11 December 1726 he gave his inaugural lecture as Professor of Jurisprudence (from memory, incidentally, since he had left his manuscript at home). The cantata would have been performed on the same day or shortly afterwards.

The author of the libretto is unknown. In the manner of the 'dramma per musica',* the four solo singers evidently represent allegorical figures whose names could no doubt have been gathered from the printed text if a copy of it had survived. Only in two places in the score does Bach himself shed light on the matter: the alto personifies 'Dankbarkeit' (Gratitude) and the bass 'Ehre' (Honour). In accordance with the substance of the text, the two other characters have been interpreted, so far without contradiction, as 'Glück' (Fortune, soprano) and 'Fleiß' (Diligence, tenor).

The opening chorus* is adapted from an earlier composition: it represents a choral version of the third movement of the Brandenburg Concerto No. 1, BWV 1046. The concertante* part for violino piccolo is taken by SATB voices, the two horns are replaced by three trumpets and drums, and two flutes are added to the three oboes. The movement is now in the key of D instead of F major, and its opening theme starts with an upbeat in accordance with the text (even in the instrumental parts the theme is prefaced by an upbeat quaver). Moreover, as a whole the movement is six bars longer than the Brandenburg version. Malcolm Boyd has argued persuasively that the vocal version is the original and the instrumental version a derivative, both having had a common source in an older vocal work, presumably a lost secular cantata from Bach's earlier years at Cöthen (1717–21).[1]

The inner movements comprise the usual alternation of recitatives and arias, organized in three recitative-aria pairs (the second pair, nos. 4–5, are set as duets, which enables all four singers to step forward as soloists). Afterwards, an additional recitative, no. 8, accompanied by strings and wind, gives all the soloists in turn a hearing once more. The three arias are richly diverse in form, scoring, and character. The first, no. 3, with full string accompaniment, captivates by virtue of its fashionably syncopated rhythms, clearly designed to illustrate the laborious strides ('die sauren Tritte') that ought to characterize the person who has

[1] See M. Boyd, *Bach: The Brandenburg Concertos* (Cambridge: Cambridge University Press, 1993), 61–70. Boyd's hypothesis has been fleshed out by Michael Talbot, who shows in detail how the lost cantata might have furnished material for BWV 207, 1046, and 1046a. See M. Talbot, 'Purpose and Peculiarities of the Brandenburg Concertos', in M. Geck and K. Hofmann, eds, *Bach und die Stile* [conference report, Dortmund, 1998] (Dortmund: Klangfarben Musikverlag, 1999), 255–89 (especially 271–6).

chosen the path of Diligence. In the second aria, no. 5 (a duet with continuo accompaniment), the two voices unite in the principal section in an imitative* texture. In the opening ritornello, the theme is stated by the continuo, which is restricted during the vocal passages, however, to an accompaniment in continuous quavers. In the middle section of this da capo* aria, the two voices, one after another, come forward as soloists. At the end there is a surprise: the reprise of the principal section is unexpectedly followed by the second Trio from the finale of the First Brandenburg Concerto, whose third movement we have already encountered in the opening chorus. This Trio is likewise in D major rather than F and scored with trumpets in place of horns. Moreover, its repeats are enriched by *staccato* chords in the strings and continuo. The inclusion of the trio is a clever device, in part no doubt intended to break up a series of three successive continuo movements (nos. 4, 5, and 6). In the third aria, no. 7, the alto voice is joined by two obbligato* flutes in an imitative texture. In addition, unison violins and violas keep restating a repeated-note motive in dotted rhythm, whose ostinato* persistence is no doubt intended to illustrate the words 'Etch this commemoration in the hardest marble'.

The sweeping finale (no. 9), simple and homophonic,* with its clearly defined sectional structure and its pithy rhythms, is manifestly dance-like in character. A twenty-eight bar, dynamically subdued middle section is framed by a principal section in two halves (4 × 16 bars) cast in binary dance form: each half is first stated with choral insertion* and then repeated by the instruments alone. A purely instrumental march included in the score of this cantata, and therefore often performed with it, is in all probability an independent piece of processional music belonging to the parody* Cantata 207a.

Laß, Fürstin, laß noch einen Strahl (Trauer-Ode), BWV 198

NBA I/38, p. 181 BC G 34 Duration: *c.* 35 mins

1. [Chorus] SATB fl I,II ob d'am I,II str vla da g I,II lute I + II bc — b c

Laß, Fürstin! laß noch einen Strahl	Let, Princess, let one more ray
Aus Salems Sterngewölben schießen.	Shoot out of Salem's starry vaults.
Und sieh, mit wieviel Tränengüssen	And see with how many showers of tears
Umringen wir dein Ehrenmal!	We surround your memorial!

2. Recitativo S str bc — f♯ c

Dein Sachsen, dein bestürztes Meißen	Your Saxony, your dismayed Meißen
Erstarrt bei deiner Königsgruft;	Grow numb at your royal tomb;
Das Auge tränt, die Zunge ruft:	The eye weeps, the tongue cries:
Mein Schmerz kann unbeschreiblich heißen!	My grief can be called indescribable!
Hier klagt August und Prinz und Land,	Here Augustus and prince and land lament,
Der Adel ächzt, der Bürger trauert,	The nobility moan, the citizens mourn;
Wie hat dich nicht das Volk bedauert,	How should the people not lament you

Sobald es deinen Fall empfand!	As soon as they received news of your fall?
3. Aria S str bc	b c
Verstummt! verstummt, ihr holden Saiten!	Silence! silence, you sweet strings!
Kein Ton vermag der Länder Not	No sound could convey the lands' distress
Bei ihrer teuren Mutter Tod,	Aright over their dear mother's death—
O Schmerzenswort! recht anzudeuten.	O sorrowful word!
4. Recitativo A ww str vla da g I,II lute I,II bc	G–f♯ c
Der Glocken bebendes Getön	The bells' vibrating sound
Soll unsrer trüben Seelen Schrecken	Shall awaken our troubled souls' alarm
Durch ihr geschwungnes Erze wecken	Through their swung bronze
Und uns durch Mark und Adern gehn.	And go through our marrow and veins.
O, könnte nur dies bange Klingen,	Oh, if only this disquieting sound,
Davon das Ohr uns täglich gellt,	That daily pierces our ears,
Der ganzen Europäerwelt	Could for the whole European world
Ein Zeugnis unsres Jammers bringen!	Bear witness to our sorrow!
5. Aria A vla da g I,II lute I + II[2]	D 12/8
Wie starb die Heldin so vergnügt!	How cheerfully the heroine died!
Wie mutig hat ihr Geist gerungen,	How courageously her spirit struggled
Da sie des Todes Arm bezwungen,	When death's arm subdued her
Noch eh er ihre Brust besiegt.	Before he conquered her breast.
6. Recitativo T ob d'am I,II bc	G–f♯ c
Ihr Leben ließ die Kunst zu sterben	Her life let the art of dying
In unverrückter Übung sehn;	Be seen in steadfast use;
Unmöglich konnt es denn geschehn,	It was impossible then for her
Sich vor dem Tode zu entfärben.	To go pale at the prospect of death.
Ach selig! wessen großer Geist	Ah! blessed is one whose great spirit
Sich über die Natur erhebet,	Rises above nature
Vor Gruft und Särgen nicht erbebet,	And does not tremble before tomb and coffin
Wenn ihn sein Schöpfer scheiden heißt.	When its Creator calls it to depart.
7. [Chorus Scoring as in no. 1]	b 2
An dir, du Fürbild großer Frauen,	In you, O model of great ladies,
An dir, erhabne Königin,	In you, O sublime Queen,
An dir, du Glaubenspflegerin,	In you, O protector of the faith,
War dieser Großmut Bild zu schauen.	This great-souled image was to be seen.

[2] Joshua Rifkin suggests that the lutes might have played the bass line only, and the continuo might have been realized by the harpsichord. See his 'Some Questions of Performance in J. S. Bach's *Trauerode*', in D. R. Melamed, ed., *Bach Studies 2* (Cambridge, 1995), 119–53.

Pars secunda. Nach gehaltener Trauerrede	*Second Part. After the mourning oration*
8. [ARIA] T fl I ob d'am I vln I,II vla da g I + II + lute I + II bc	e 3/4
Der Ewigkeit saphirnes Haus Zieht, Fürstin, deine heitern Blicke Von unsrer Niedrigkeit zurücke Und tilgt der Erden Denkbild[3] aus.	Eternity's sapphire house Draws, Princess, your serene glances Away from our lowliness And effaces the mental image of the earth.
Ein starker Glanz von hundert Sonnen,	A powerful radiance of an hundred suns
Der unsern Tag zur Mitternacht Und unsre Sonne finster macht, Hat dein verklärtes Haupt umsponnen.	That turns our day into midnight And makes our sun dark Has encompassed your transfigured head.
9. RECITATIVO B fl I,II ob I,II bc	G–b C 3/4 C
Was Wunder ists? Du bist es wert, Du Fürbild aller Königinnen! Du mußtest allen Schmuck gewinnen, Der deine Scheitel itzt verklärt.	What wonder is it? You are worthy of it, You model of all queens! You had to win all the adornment That now transfigures the crown of your head.
Nun trägst du vor des Lammes Throne Anstatt des Purpurs Eitelkeit Ein perlenreines Unschuldskleid Und spottest der verlaßnen Krone.	Now you wear before the Lamb's throne In place of purple's vanity A pure pearl robe of innocence And deride the crown you have left behind.
Soweit der volle Weichselstrand, Der Niester und die Warthe fließet, Soweit sich Elb' und Muld' ergießet,	As far as the full banks of the Vistula, Where the Niester and the Warthe flow, As far as the Elbe and the Mulde pour forth,
Erhebt dich beides, Stadt und Land. Dein Torgau geht im Trauerkleide, Dein Pretzsch wird kraftlos, starr und matt; Denn da es dich verloren hat, Verliert es seiner Augen Weide.	Your are exalted by both town and land. Your Torgau wears mourning-dress, Your Pretzsch grows weak, stiff, and dull; For since it has lost you It misses what its eyes feast on.
10. CHORUS ULTIMUS [Scoring as in no. 1]	b 12/8
Doch, Königin! du stirbest nicht, Man weiß, was man an dir besessen; Die Nachwelt wird dich nicht vergessen, Bis dieser Weltbau einst zerbricht. Ihr Dichter, schreibt! wir wollens lesen: Sie ist der Tugend Eigentum,	Yet, O Queen! you do not die; We know what we possessed in you: Posterity will not forget you Until this universe one day collapses. You poets, write! we would read it: She has been virtue's property,

[3] The reading 'Dreckbild' is an interpretative error on the part of the NBA editor.

Der Untertanen Lust und Ruhm,	Her subjects' delight and glory,
Der Königinnen Preis gewesen.	The prize of queens.

We are exceptionally well-informed about the origin of this work. Its composition was occasioned by the death of the consort of Augustus the Strong, the Electoress Christiane Eberhardine, on 5 September 1727. In Saxony she enjoyed universal veneration for not concurring with her husband's conversion to Catholicism (in order to acquire the Polish crown). Shortly after her death, the Leipzig student Carl von Kirchbach sought the permission of the university and the Elector to hold a mourning oration in her praise in the university church, the Paulinerkirche. A mourning ode* was to be performed with text by Gottsched and music by Bach. Within the university, attempts were made to have the music composed and performed by their favoured Görner, and only the perseverance of Kirchbach, who threatened to call off the whole event, enabled Bach to keep the commission. One consequence, both shameful and amusing, was that Bach was to be asked to sign a declaration stating that the commission would not serve as a precedent for the rights of Görner, the university music director, to be abused in future. On 11 and 12 October, however, the university registrar sought Bach's signature in vain.

According to the autograph date at the end of the score, Bach completed the work on 15 October 1727. Since the mourning event took place two days later, on 17 October, the time available for writing out the parts and for rehearsal must have been severely limited. Being an ode, a strophic poem, Gottsched's text differs from the orthodox form of a cantata libretto. Consequently, it is doubtful whether Gottsched would have approved of Bach's setting in arias and recitatives or his arbitrary division of a strophe among several movements. For Bach divides the nine strophes, each of eight lines, into the following movements:

Strophe	*Lines*	*Movement*
1	1–4	1. Chorus
	5–8	2. Recitative (soprano)
2	1–4	
	5–8	3. Aria (soprano)
3	1–8	4. Recitative (alto)
4	1–4	5. Aria (alto)
	5–8	6. Recitative (tenor)
5	1–4	
	5–8	7. Chorus
6	1–8	8. Aria (tenor)
7	1–8	9. Recitative (bass)
8	1–4	Arioso* (bass)
	5–8	Recitative (bass)
9	1–8	10. Chorus

In view of the shortage of time for the preparation of the work, it is hard to resist the conjecture that the bass was originally to have sung an aria as well as a recitative, like the soprano, alto, and tenor (in descending order). Judging by the distribution of the text elsewhere, the eighth strophe would have provided ample material for such an aria.

Bach's setting requires an exceptionally abundant instrumental ensemble: the woodwind is represented by two each of transverse flutes* and oboes d'amore,*[4] the strings are supplemented by two violas da gamba, and the continuo by two lutes. In addition, if we are to believe the chonicler Sicul, the continuo part was realized not just by the organ but also by the harpsichord, from which Bach himself directed the performance. The beginning, middle, and end of the work are each marked by a chorus* in which the entire instrumental ensemble participates. Each of these choruses represents a different musical principle. The opening chorus is governed by the principle of the concerto, or more specifically the group-concerto, for each instrumental group—flutes, oboes, upper strings, gambas—comes to the fore in alternation. The choral writing, broken up figuratively, is woven into this concertante* instrumental texture. The overall form is bipartite, A A[1], in which the four-line text is delivered complete within each half. The second chorus, no. 7, represents the principle of fugue.* Again, it is designed in two halves (divided by a thematic orchestral episode), each of which consists of a fugal exposition* plus a looser chordal postlude. Finally, the concluding chorus represents the principle of song and dance. It is a choral aria, whose partly obbligato* instruments at times approach an antiphonal concertante style, though without concealing the overall dance-song effect. The structure is easily recognized as binary dance form with repeats, framed by ritornellos, and with gigue-like melodic writing. It is worth pointing out the repeated choral unison in the B section. Introduced by the words 'You poets, write! we would read it', it lays special emphasis on the following quotation from the imaginary poets' writings: 'She has been virtue's property, her subjects' delight and glory, the prize of queens'.

In the three arias, interspersed among the three choruses, various instruments or instrumental combinations come to the fore as soloists: violins and viola (no. 3), two violas da gamba accompanied by continuo lutes (no. 5), and transverse flute and oboe d'amore, supported by gambas and lutes as a figurative decoration of the continuo and with accompanying chords in the violins (no. 8). Thus two full-textured arias surround a movement of quietly intimate character, dynamically subdued on account of its gamba and lute sonority.

[4] A contemporary account also mentions recorders, which are not specified in the autograph score (the original performing parts are lost). See Dok II, No. 232, p. 175, and NBR, No. 136, pp. 136–7. Rifkin ('Some Questions of Performance in J. S. Bachs *Trauerode*') suggests that the chronicler Sicul might have mistaken the oboes d'amore, which he does not mention, for recorders.

The remaining four movements (nos. 2, 4, 6, and 9) are set as recitatives. The poetic design of the work demands a more differentiated musical treatment of the recitatives than madrigalian* verse requires. Consequently, the first three recitatives are set throughout, and the last in part, as *accompagnato*,* often motivically imprinted in order to lend emphasis to a particular turn of phrase. In the second movement, the strings give a striking illustration of the words 'Your Saxony, your dismayed Meißen grow numb', first with brief chordal interjections and then, from 'The eye weeps', with a wave-like motion. In the fourth movement, flutes and plucked strings are used to give a still more graphic evocation of the sound of funeral bells of various sizes, from the miniature bells of the flutes to the deep, sonorous bells of the gambas and continuo. The sixth movement is another motivically imprinted *accompagnato*, but here the motives of the two oboes and the constantly recurring broken triads in the continuo seem to lack a clear illustrative connotation. In the ninth movement, the sixteen lines of text are divided between three sections: an introductory *secco* for bass and continuo, an arioso* for the same combination, and an *accompagnato* with woodwind, which on this occasion, however, lacks motivic imprint.

Bach later reused the two framing choruses (on several occasions) and the arias with different texts as follows. Movements 1 and 10 were first incorporated in the funeral music for Prince Leopold of Anhalt-Cöthen, BWV 244a, of 1729 (as nos. 1 and 7). Later, they found what was no doubt their definitive place in the lost *St Mark Passion*, BWV 247, of 1731 (as 'Geh, Jesu, geh zu deiner Pein' and 'Bei deinem Grab- und Leichenstein'). Movements 3, 5, and 8 were also reused in the *St Mark Passion* of 1731: for the movements 'Er kommt, er kommt, er ist vorhanden', 'Mein Heiland, dich vergeß ich nicht', and 'Mein Tröster ist nicht mehr bei mir'. No reuse of the central chorus (no. 7) is recorded. It is quite conceivable, however, that it found a new place in a work that no longer survives, possibly as one of the biblical-text choruses in the *St Mark Passion*.

Die Freude reget sich, BWV 36b

NBA I/38, p. 257 BC G 38 Duration: *c.* 30 mins

1. CHORUS SATB fl ob d'am str bc		D $\frac{3}{4}$
Die Freude reget sich, erhebt die muntern Töne,	Joy is astir, raise lively sounds,	
Denn dieser schöne Tag läßt keinen ruhig sein.	For this fine day lets no one be at rest.	
Verfolgt den Trieb, nur fort, ihr treuen Musensöhne,	Follow your impulse further, you loyal sons of the Muses,	
Und liefert itzt den Zoll in frommen Wünschen ein!	And deliver your tribute now in devout wishes!	
2. RECITATIVO T bc		D–f♯ C
Ihr seht, wie sich das Glücke	You see how the good fortune	

Des teuersten Rivins durch die gewohnten Blicke	Of our dearest Rivinus, through its habitual glances,
In dieser angenehmen Zeit	Is renewed at this agreeable time
Zu seines Hauses Wohl verneut.	For the welfare of his house.
Der Segen krönet sein Bemühen,	Blessing crowns his endeavour,
Das unsrer Philuris so manchen Vorteil schafft.	Which is so advantageous to our Philuris.
Und dieser Segen macht durch seine starke Kraft,	And this blessing through its great power
Daß Not und Ungemach von seiner Seite fliehen.	Causes affliction and adversity to flee from his side.
3. Aria T ob d'am (or vln?) bc	b $\frac{3}{8}$
Aus Gottes milden Vaterhänden	From God's gentle fatherly hands
Fließt seiner Kinder Wohlergehn.	Flows His children's welfare.
Er kann das Wahre, Gute schenken,	He can give us truth, goodness,
Er gibt uns mehr, als wir gedenken,	He gives us more than we imagine
Und besser, als wir es verstehn.	And better than we understand.
4. Recitativo A str bc	G–A C
Die Freunde sind vergnügt,	His friends are delighted
Den Fest- und Gnadentag zu schauen;	To see this festive day of goodwill;
Sie können ihren Wunsch auf sichre Gründe bauen,	They can build their wish on firm ground,
Auf dessen Huld, der alles weislich fügt,	On the favour of Him who disposes all things wisely,
Der manche Proben schon gewiesen,	Who has already shown many proofs
Daß dieser fromme Mann ihn tausendmal gepriesen.	That this devout man has praised Him a thousand times.
Allein!	However!
Wie? Dürfen wir auch froh bei seinem Glücke sein?	What? ought we also to be glad over his good fortune?
Verschmähe nicht, du gütiger Rivin,	Do not be scornful, O kind Rivinus,
Daß wir uns auch bemühn	That we too exert ourselves
Und lassen itzt, dich zu verehren,	And now in your honour
Auch unsre Lieder hören.	Let our songs be heard.
5. Aria A fl str bc	D C
Das Gute, das dein Gott beschert,	The good that your God bestows
Und was dir heute widerfährt,	And that befalls you today
Macht dein erwünschtes Wohlergehn	Makes your desired welfare
Vor uns auch schön.	Splendid for us too.
6. Recitativo S bc	f♯–c♯ C
Wenn sich die Welt mit deinem Ruhme trägt,	When the world is preoccupied with your renown,
Den dein gelehrter Fleiß stets zu vermehren pflegt,	Which your learned diligence is ever wont to increase,

Wenn deine Frömmigkeit ein wahres Muster gibet,
Wie man dem Nächsten dient und Gott dabei doch liebet,
Wenn sich dein edles Haus auf deine Vorsicht stützt,
Wodurch es auch den Armen nützt,
So sehn wir dies nur mit Bewundrung an,
Weil unsre Dürftigkeit nichts Höhers wagen kann.

When your devoutness provides a true model
Of how to serve one's neighbour and thereby love God,
When your noble house is supported by your prudence,
Whereby the poor also benefit,
We can only regard this with admiration,
For our inferiority can venture nothing more exalted.

7. ARIA S fl + vln I solo bc — A 12/8

Mit zarten und vergnügten Trieben
Verehrt man deine Gütigkeit.
  Erschallet aber einst ein Lied,
  Das dich der Sterblichkeit entzieht,
  So sind wir auch darzu bereit.

With tender and delighted impulses
We honour your goodness.
  But if a song is one day heard
  That withdraws you from mortality,
  Then we are ready for that too.

8. CHORUS / RECITATIVO SATB str + fl + ob d'am bc — D ¢/C

Was wir dir vor Glücke gönnen,
Wünscht man dir noch zehnmal mehr.
  Tenor
  Ja wohl! Du hasts verdient,
  Wer dich aus deinem Ruhme kennt,
  Des Unrechts Geißel nennt;
  Hingegen der Gerechten Schirm und Schutz,
  Der bietet Not und Unglück Trutz.
Dich soll kein Verhängnis quälen,
Nichts an deinem Wohlsein fehlen.
  Alt
  Dein ganzes Haus
  Seh als ein Tempel aus,
  Wo man mehr Lob als bange Seufzer hört,
  In dem kein Fall die süße Ruhe stört.
Diese Lust ergötzt zu sehr,
Mehr als wir entdecken können.
  Sopran
  Drum wirst du, großer Mann, verzeihen,
  Daß wir dabei, nach unsers Lehrers Treu,
  Uns auch mit ihm bei deinem Feste freuen;

What good fortune we wish you
May it be wished for you ten times over!
  Tenor
  Certainly! You have deserved it;
  Whoever knows you from your renown
  Names the scourge of injustice,
  But the shield and shelter of the just,
  Who defies affliction and misfortune.
Doom shall not torment you,
Your welfare shall lack nothing.
  Alto
  May your whole house
  Have the appearance of a temple
  Where one hears more praise than anxious sighs,
  In which no incident disturbs sweet repose.
This pleasure delights too much,
More than we can discover.
  Soprano
  Therefore you will pardon us, great man,
  That according to our teacher's faithfulness
  With him also do we rejoice at your feast,

Doch auch, daß unsre Pflicht	But also that our duty
Nichts mehr von neuen Wünschen spricht.	No longer speaks of new wishes.
Was wir dir vor Glücke gönnen,	What good fortune we wish you
Wünscht man dir noch zehnmal mehr.	May it be wished for you ten times over!

This cantata is chronologically the last of the group of cantatas numbered BWV 36, of which no fewer than five versions exist. The order of their origin is outlined above under Cantata 36 (First Sunday in Advent). This particular cantata (BWV 36b) originated around 1735 as a homage cantata for a lawyer (as we gather from the text), a member of the learned Leipzig Rivinus family. Although neither the dedicatee (several individuals come into consideration) nor the occasion can be established with certainty,[5] various chronological features of the sources suggest that the work might have been performed for the inauguration of Johann Florens Rivinus as Rector in October 1735.

Only the performing parts of the work survive, and even these are unfortunately incomplete. Due to the survival of the other versions, however, the reconstruction of what is missing presents no real problems, and Werner Neumann has undertaken the task for the *Neue Bach-Ausgabe* (Series I, Vol. 38). Modern performers will nonetheless tend to prefer one of the other versions, for the text of the present version is neither as fine poetically nor as well suited to the music as those of the other extant versions BWV 36 and 36c.

In *Die Freude reget sich* only the recitatives, nos. 2, 4, and 6, and the recitative insertions in no. 8 are newly composed; and of these only no. 4 requires string accompaniment, the others being set as *secco* accompanied by continuo (plus an arioso* conclusion in the third section of no. 8). The other movements, nos. 1, 3, 5, and 7, are parodies of the corresponding movements in Cantata 36c. Apart from changes to the voice parts to accommodate the new text, the alterations are insignificant. Two features worthy of note are the change of voice type in no. 5 from bass to alto and the addition of a transverse flute* in nos. 1, 5, 7, and 8.

[5] See W. Neumann, KB, NBA I/38 (1960), 163–6.

4

Festive music for Leipzig council and school celebrations

Apart from the church cantatas that Bach wrote for council election services, only a few known works were dedicated to the Leipzig council and school authorities, and none of them is preserved. The following works are identifiable:

Erwählte Pleißenstadt, BWV 216a, a homage cantata for the Leipzig town council which dates from after 1728. The precise occasion for its performance is unknown. All that survives is the text, plus the two vocal parts for Cantata 216, which served as parody* model in the non-recitative movements (nos. 1, 3, 5, and 7) of both works. For details see the Critical Report to NBA I/39, pp. 12 f.

Froher Tag, verlangte Stunden, BWV Anh. I 18, performed on 5 June 1732 for the consecration of the renovated Thomasschule. All that survives is the text by Johann Heinrich Winckler, a parody of the first movement as the opening chorus* of the *Ascension Oratorio*, BWV 11, and Picander's parody libretto for the cantata BWV Anh. I 12, whose music is likewise lost. Arnold Schering[1] conjectured that the music for the sixth movement, the aria 'Geist und Herze sind begierig', survives in the 'Domine Deus' of the Missa in F, BWV 233. For details see the Critical Report to NBA I/39, p. 16.

Wo sind meine Wunderwerke, BWV Anh. I 210, performed on 4 October 1734 to mark the departure of Johann Matthias Gesner, Rector of the Thomasschule. This cantata, whose music is lost, has recently been identified from its previously unknown printed text, by an anonymous author.[2] Bach is not named as composer of the music, but his authorship may be regarded as highly probable in view of his post as Thomascantor. The first movement possibly served as the original model for the aria 'Gott, wir danken deiner Güte' from Cantata 193 (no. 3 = BWV 193a no. 7).

Thomana saß annoch betrübt, BWV Anh. I 19, performed on 21 November 1734 to greet the new Rector of the Thomasschule, Johann August Ernesti. All that survives is the text, probably by Johann August Landvoigt. In addition, it has

[1] In 'Über Bachs Parodieverfahren', *BJ* 1921, 49–95 (see p. 93).

[2] See K. Hofmann, '*Wo sind meine Wunderwerke*: Eine verschollene Thomasschulkantate J. S. Bachs?', *BJ* 1988, 211–18.

been conjectured[3] that the concluding chorus*, 'Himmel, streue deinen Segen', was a parody of the equivalent movement in Cantata 201.

[3] By A. Schering, 'Über Bachs Parodieverfahren', p. 93.

5

Leipzig music of homage for nobles and burghers

Schwingt freudig euch empor, BWV 36c

NBA I/39, p. 3 BC G 35 Duration: *c.* 29 mins

1. [Chorus] SATB ob d'am str bc	D $\frac{3}{4}$
Schwingt freudig euch empor und dringt bis an die Sternen,	Soar up joyfully and break through to the stars,
Ihr Wünsche, bis euch Gott vor seinem Throne sieht!	You wishes, till God sees you before his throne!
Doch, haltet ein! ein Herz darf sich nicht weit entfernen,	Yet stop! a heart need not stray far
Das Dankbarkeit und Pflicht zu seinem Lehrer zieht.	That is drawn by gratitude and duty towards its teacher.
2. Recitativo T bc	b C
Ein Herz, in zärtlichem Empfinden,	A heart, in the tender feelings
So ihm viel tausend Lust erweckt,	That many thousand pleasures arouse in him,
Kann sich fast nicht in sein Vergnügen finden,	Can hardly rest content,
Da ihm die Hoffnung immer mehr entdeckt.	For hope reveals more and more to him.
Es steiget wie ein helles Licht	Like a bright light it climbs,
Der Andacht Glut in Gottes Heiligtum;	The blaze of his devotion in God's sanctuary;
Wiewohl, der teure Lehrerruhm	Though his dear teacher's renown
Ist sein Polar, dahin, als ein Magnet,	Is his pole—there, as to a magnet,
Sein Wünschen, sein Verlangen geht.	Go his wishes, his longing.
3. Aria T ob d'am (?) bc	b $\frac{3}{8}$
Die Liebe führt mit sanften Schritten	Love leads with gentle steps
Ein Herz, das seinen Lehrer liebt.	A heart that loves his teacher.
Wo andre auszuschweifen pflegen,	Where others are wont to digress,
Wird dies behutsam sich bewegen,	This one will move cautiously,
Weil ihm die Ehrfurcht Grenzen gibt.	For reverence gives him boundaries.
4. Recitativo B bc	e–D C
Du bist es ja, o hochverdienter Mann,	It is indeed you, O highly deserving man,
Der in unausgesetzten Lehren	Who in constant teaching

Mit höchsten Ehren
Den Silberschmuck des Alters tragen kann.
Dank, Ehrerbietung, Ruhm,
Kömmt alles hier zusammen;
Und weil du unsre Brust
Als Licht und Führer leiten mußt,
Wirst du dies freudige Bezeigen nicht verdammen.

With the highest honour
Can wear the silver trappings of age.
Thanks, duty, renown,
All here come together;
And because you must lead our breast
As light and guide,
You will not condemn these joyous protestations.

5. ARIA B str bc — D ¢

Der Tag, der dich vordem gebar,
Stellt sich vor uns so heilsam dar
Als jener, da der Schöpfer spricht:
Es werde Licht!

The day that once bore you
Presents itself to us as beneficial
As that on which the Creator said:
Let there be Light!

6. RECITATIVO S bc — b–f♯ C

Nur dieses Einzge sorgen wir:
Dies Opfer sei zu unvollkommen;
Doch, wird es nur von dir,
O teurer Lehrer, gütig angenommen,
So steigt der sonst so schlechte Wert
So hoch, als unser treuer Sinn begehrt.

Only this one thing concerns us:
That this offering is too imperfect;
Yet if only by you,
O dear teacher, it is kindly accepted,
Then its value, otherwise so poor, climbs
As high as our loyal spirit desires.

7. ARIA S vla d'am bc — A $\frac{12}{8}$

Auch mit gedämpften, schwachen Stimmen
Verkündigt man der Lehrer Preis.
  Es schallet kräftig in der Brust,
  Ob man gleich die empfundne Lust
  Nicht völlig auszudrücken weiß.

Even with subdued, weak voices
Our teacher's praise is proclaimed.
  It sounds forcibly in the breast,
  Even though the pleasure felt
  One does not fully know how to express.

8. RECITATIVO T bc — A–D C

Bei solchen freudenvollen Stunden
Wird unsers Wunsches Ziel gefunden,
Der sonst auf nichts
Als auf dein Leben geht.

In such hours, full of joy,
The goal of our wishes is found,
Which applies to nothing
Other than your life.

9. CHORUS [+ RECITATIVO Scoring as in no. 1] — D ¢/C

Wie die Jahre sich verneuen,
So verneue sich dein Ruhm!
  Tenor
  Jedoch, was wünschen wir,
  Da dieses von sich selbst geschieht,
  Und da man deinen Preis,
  Den unser Helikon am besten weiß,
  Auch außer dessen Grenzen sieht.
Dein Verdienst recht auszulegen,
Fordert mehr, als wir vermögen.

As the years are renewed,
Renewed be your renown!
  Tenor
  Yet what do we wish,
  Since this happens of its own accord
  And since your praise,
  Which our Helicon knows best,
  Is seen even beyond its borders?
Rightly to expound your merit
Demands more than we are capable of.

Baß	*Bass*
Drum schweigen wir	Therefore we are silent
Und zeigen dadurch dir,	And thereby show you
Daß unser Dank zwar mit dem Munde nicht,	That our thanks speak not with our mouths
Doch desto mehr mit unsern Herzen spricht.	But all the more with our hearts.
Deines Lebens Heiligtum	The sacred edifice of your life
Kann vollkommen uns erfreuen.	Can perfectly delight us.
Sopran	*Soprano*
So öffnet sich der Mund zum Danken,	Then let our mouths open in thanks,
Denn jedes Glied nimmt an der Freude teil;	For every member partakes of the joy;
Das Auge dringt aus den gewohnten Schranken	The eye breaks out of its usual limits
Und sieht dein künftig Glück und Heil.	And sees your future fortune and welfare.
Wie die Jahre sich verneuen,	As the years are renewed,
So verneue sich dein Ruhm!	Renewed be your renown!

It is not known exactly what occasioned the composition and performance of this cantata. The text reveals that it was conceived as a birthday cantata in honour of an elderly teacher; and diplomatic features of the autograph score, the sole surviving original source, suggest that it originated around April or May 1725, or possibly later in the same year. This date rules out the possibility that the person honoured might have been Johann Matthias Gesner, as has sometimes been conjectured, for he was resident in Leipzig as Rector of the Thomasschule at a later date, between 1730 and 1734. Moreover, since he was born on 9 April 1691 and was thus only 34 years old in 1725, he almost certainly would not yet have worn 'the silver trappings of age'.

Bach's music, often reused later, is today more familiar in its sacred parody* as the Advent cantata BWV 36 than in its original secular version. The reader is therefore referred to the above discussion of the movements reused in the church cantata, nos. 1, 3, 5, and 7. The overall form is symmetrical: three arias, linked by *secco* recitatives, are surrounded by two choruses.* At the centre is an aria with full string accompaniment, no. 5, whereas the outer arias nos. 3 and 7 are set as trios, each with its own distinctive obbligato* instrument: oboe d'amore* (?) in no. 3 and viola d'amore (replaced by muted violin in the church cantata) in no. 7. The subdued dynamic character of nos. 3 and 7 in relation to the central aria is justified by their text: the victorious 'Let there be Light!' of no. 5 contrasts with the 'gentle steps' and the cautious, reverential stirring of the heart in no. 3 and with the 'subdued, weak voices' of no. 7. Each of the outer, tutti movements embodies its own distinct musical principle: in no. 1 the concerto and in no. 9 the dance. This last movement, with good reason omitted from the church cantata, is a gavotte with three interspersed recitatives: for tenor with strings (*rec. 1* below), for bass with continuo (*rec. 2*), and for soprano with a motivic accompaniment for the entire instrumental ensemble (*rec. 3*). Since the gavotte is in itself symmetrically structured, the following overall form emerges:

A A + choir B B + choir *rec. 1* C + choir *rec. 2* D + choir *rec. 3* A A + choir B B + choir

Verjaget, zerstreuet, zerrüttet, ihr Sterne, BWV 249b

Die Feier des Genius — *The Celebration of Genius*

Bach performed this cantata on 25 August 1726 for the birthday of Count Joachim Friedrich von Flemming. All that survives is the text by Picander, which reveals that in all its non-recitative movements it was probably a parody of the lost 'Pastoral' Cantata BWV 249a. It is therefore possible to reconstruct it (without the recitatives) from the *Easter Oratorio*, BWV 249, another parody of the 'Pastoral' Cantata. It remains uncertain, however, to what extent the movements concerned were borrowed without alteration. For details see the Critical Report to NBA I/39, p. 41.

O! angenehme Melodei, BWV 210a

NBA I/39, p. 143 BC G 29 Duration: *c.* 36 mins

1. Recitativo S str bc[1] — A–D 𝄴

O! angenehme Melodei!	O pleasant melody!
Kein Anmut, kein Vergnügen	No charm, no pleasure
Kommt deiner süßen Zauberei	Approaches your sweet enchantment
Und deinen Zärtlichkeiten bei.	And your tendernesses.
Die Wissenschaften anderer Künste	The attainments of other arts
Sind irdnen Witzes kluge Dünste:	Are human wit's clever smokescreens;
Du aber bist allein	You alone, however,
Vom Himmel zu uns abgestiegen,	Came down to us from heaven,
So mußt du auch recht himmlisch sein.	So you must be truly heavenly.

2. Aria S ob d'am str bc — A 3/8

Spielet, ihr beseelten Lieder,	Play, you inspired songs,
Werfet die entzückte Brust	Cast the enraptured breast
In die Ohnmacht sanfte nieder;	Gently down into a swoon;
Aber durch der Saiten Lust	But through the strings' delight
Stärket und erholt sie wieder.	Strengthen and revive it again.

[1] Only the soprano part survives. The other scoring details are conjectural and based on BWV 210.

3. Recitativo S bc	f♯–E 𝄴
Ihr Sorgen, flieht,	You cares, flee,
Flieht, ihr betrübten Kümmernüsse!	Flee, you troubled woes!
Ein singend Lied	A song being sung
Macht herbes Grämen süße,	Makes bitter griefs sweet,
Ein kleiner Ton tut Wunderwerke	A little note works wonders
Und hat noch mehr als Simsons Stärke,	And has still more than Samson's strength,
Weil er,	Because
Wenn Schwermut oder Bangigkeit	When melancholy or anxiety,
Wie ein Philisterheer	Like a host of Philistines,
Sich wider unser Ruh erregt,	Chafes against our repose,
Die Qual zerstreut und aus dem Sinne schlägt.	It dispels the torment and thrusts it out of the mind.
4. Aria S ob d'am vln I bc	E 12/8
Ruhet hie, matte Sinnen,	Rest here, tired senses,
Matte Sinnen, ruhet hie!	Tired senses, rest here!
Eine zarte Harmonie	A tender harmony
Ist vor das verborgne Weh	Is for hidden woe
Die bewährte Panazee.	The proven panacea.
5. Recitativo S bc	c♯–b 𝄴
Wiewohl, beliebte Musica,	Although, beloved Musica,
So angenehm dein Spiel	Your playing is so agreeable
So vielen Ohren ist,	To so many ears,
So bist du doch betrübt und stehest in Gedanken da.	Yet you are distressed and stand there lost in thought.
Denn es sind ihr' viel,	For there are many
Denen du verächtlich bist;	To whom you are worthless;
Mich deucht, ich höre deine Klagen	I fancy I hear your complaints
Selbst also sagen:	Themselves speaking thus:
6. Aria S fl bc	b 𝄴
Schweigt, ihr Flöten, schweigt, ihr Töne,	Be silent, you flutes; be silent, you notes,
Klingt ihr mir doch selbst nicht schöne;	You do not sound fair even to me;
Geht, ihr armen Lieder, hin,	Go, you poor songs,
Weil ich so verlassen bin!	For I am thus forsaken!
7. Recitativo S str bc	D–A 𝄴
Doch fasse dich, dein Glanz	Yet compose yourself: your lustre
Ist noch nicht ganz	Is still not quite
Verschwunden und im Bann getan!	Faded and banned!
Ja, wenn es möglich wär,	Indeed, if it were possible
Daß dich die ganze Welt verließe	That the whole world forsook you
Und deine Lieblichkeit verstieße,	And rejected your loveliness,
So komm zu deinem teuren Herzog/ Flemming	Then come to your dear Duke/ Flemming,

In seinem Schirm und Schatten her.	Into his shelter and shade.
Er weiß allein,	Only he knows
Wie Wissenschaft und Kunst zu schätzen müsse sein.	How knowledge and art must be valued.
[Or:]	
So komm zu unsre werten Gönner	Then come to our honoured patrons,
In ihre Gunst und Neigung her.	Into their favour and inclination.
Sie wissen allein,	Only they know
Wie Wissenschaft und Kunst zu schätzen müsse sein.	How knowledge and art must be valued.

8. ARIA S ob d'am str bc — c♯ $\frac{3}{4}$

Großer Herzog,/Flemming, alles Wissen	Great Duke,/Flemming, all knowledge
Findet Schutz bei deinen Füßen,	Finds its protection at your feet:
Du stehest denen Künsten bei.	You stand by these arts.
Aber unter denen allen	But among them all
Liebt dein gnädiges Gefallen	Your gracious favour loves
Ein angenehme Melodei.	An agreeable melody.
[Or:]	
Werte Gönner, alles Wissen	Honoured patrons, all knowledge
Findet Grund bei euren Füßen,	Finds its foundation at your feet:
Ihr stehet denen Künsten bei.	You stand by these arts.
Aber unter denen allen	But among them all
Liebt eur gütiges Gefallen	Your kind favour loves
Ein angenehme Melodei.	An agreeable melody.

9. RECITATIVO S fl ob d'am str bc — f♯–A C

Durchlauchtigst/Erlauchtet Haupt, so bleibe fernerweit	Illustrious/Exalted head, then remain henceforth
Der edlen Harmonie mit deinem Schutz geneigt!	Inclined to noble harmony with your protection!
[Or:]	
Geehrten Gönner, so bleibet fernerweit	Honoured patrons, then remain henceforth
Der edlen Harmonie mit eurer Gunst geneigt!	Inclined to noble harmony with your favour!
Solange sie noch Kinder schöner Stimmen zeiget,	As long as it still exhibits lovely children's voices,
So wird sie alle Zeit	Then it will at all times
Dein/Eu'r Lob und deinen/euren Ruhm besingen,	Sing of your praise and your renown,
Und wenn es ihr erlaubt,	And if it be allowed,
Vor dein/eu'r beständig Blühn	For your constant flourishing
Sich itzt bemühn,	It now endeavours
Ein wünschend Opfer vorzubringen.	To make a desired offering.

10.	Aria S fl ob d'am str bc	A ¢
	Sei vergnügt, großer Herzog, / Flemming,	Be content, great Duke, / Flemming,
	Großer Herzog, / Flemming, sei vergnügt!	Great Duke, / Flemming, be content!
	Dein fürstliches / gräfliches Haus	May your princely / count's house
	Vermehre den Schimmer und breite sich aus,	Increase its lustre and spread it abroad
	Bis selber das Glänzen der Sonne verfliegt.	Till even the brilliance of the sun vanishes.
	[Or:]	
	Seid vergnügt, werte Gönner,	Be content, honoured patrons,
	Werte Gönner, seid vergnügt!	Honoured patrons, be content!
	Ein ewige Lust	May an eternal delight
	Bestelle die Wohnung in euerer Brust,	Make its dwelling in your breast
	Bis diese das Singen der Engel entzückt.	Till it is enraptured by the singing of angels.

This cantata was originally composed for performance on 12 January 1729 as a homage cantata for Duke Christian of Saxe-Weißenfels on the occasion of a visit to Leipzig.[2] Unfortunately, only the soprano part survives. For the most part, the cantata may nonetheless be reconstructed, since it belongs to a group of works linked by parody,* one of which survives complete, namely the wedding cantata BWV 210. Three of these works, which differ only slightly, are united under the BWV number 210a:

1. A homage cantata for Duke Christian of Saxe-Weißenfels.
2. A homage cantata for Count Joachim Friedrich von Flemming, the dedicatee of BWV 249b and Anh. I 10.
3. A homage cantata for unknown 'patrons', identifiable through textual alterations in versions 1 and 2.

Leaving aside alterations to the voice part, necessitated by the parody, the non-recitative movements (nos. 2, 4, 6, 8, and 10), as well as the opening recitative, accord musically with Cantata 210. The recitatives (nos. 3, 5, and 7), of which only the soprano part survives, were not adopted in Cantata 210. The recitative no. 9 begins like the equivalent movement in Cantata 210 but differs towards the end (the later version is longer).

So kämpfet nur, ihr muntern Töne, BWV Anh. I 10

Like BWV 249b and the second version of BWV 210a, this is a congratulatory cantata for Count Flemming, written for and performed on his birthday, 25

[2] This was recently established following the rediscovery of the original printed text. See H. Tiggemann, 'Unbekannte Textdrucke zu drei Gelegenheitskantaten J. S. Bachs', *BJ* 1994, 7–22.

August 1731. As in Cantata 249b, only Picander's text survives. The cantata's identification as a composition by Bach is based solely on Friedrich Smend's hypothesis[3] that a parody of the first movement survives in the opening movement (no. 54) of Part VI of the *Christmas Oratorio*—a second-hand parody, as it were, since Part VI is as a whole a parody of a lost church cantata. In addition, according to Smend the concluding chorus* of the Flemming cantata, 'Lebe und grüne, großer Flemming', no. 7, might have been parodied from Cantata 201/15. For details see the Critical Report to NBA I/39, p. 42.

Angenehmes Wiederau, BWV 30a

NBA I/39, p. 53   BC G 31   Duration: *c.* 47 mins

1. CHORUS tr I–III timp fl I,II ob I,II str bc	D $\frac{2}{4}$
Tutti	*Tutti*
Angenehmes Wiederau,	Pleasant Wiederau,
Freue dich in deinen Auen!	Rejoice in your meadows!
Das Gedeihen legt itzund	Prosperity now lays
Einen neuen, festen Grund,	A new, firm foundation
Wie ein Eden dich zu bauen.	On which to build you like an Eden.
2. RECITATIVO SATB bc	b–G C
Schicksal	*Destiny*
So ziehen wir	Then let us move
In diesem Hause hier	Into this house here
Mit Freuden ein;	With joy;
Nichts soll uns hier von dannen reißen.	Nothing shall here tear us away from it.
Du bleibst zwar, schönes Wiederau,	You indeed remain, fair Wiederau,
Der Anmut Sitz, des Segens Au;	The seat of charm, the mead of blessing;
Allein,	However,
à 4	*a 4*
Dein Name soll geändert sein,	Your name should be changed:
Du sollst nun Hennicks-Ruhe heißen!	You should now be called 'Hennicke's Rest'!
Schicksal	*Destiny*
Nimm dieses Haupt, dem du nun untertan,	Accept this head, to whom you are now subject,
Frohlockend also an:	Jubilantly thus:
3. ARIA B str bc	G $\frac{3}{8}$
Willkommen im Heil, willkommen in Freuden,	Welcome in cheers, welcome in joy,
Wir segnen die Ankunft, wir segnen das Haus.	We bless your arrival, we bless your house.
Sei stets wie unsre Auen munter,	Be ever lusty like our meadows,
Dir breiten sich die Herzen unter,	We submit our hearts to you,

[3] Put forward in 'Neue Bach-Funde' (1942).

Die Allmacht aber Flügel aus.

The Almighty spreads his wings over
you.

4. Recitativo A bc — A C

Glück
Da heute dir, gepriesner Hennicke,
Dein Wiedrau sich verpflicht',
So schwör auch ich,
Dir unveränderlich
Getreu und hold zu sein.
Ich wanke nicht, ich weiche nicht,
An deine Seite mich zu binden.
Du sollst mich allenthalben finden.

Fortune
Since today, O praised Hennicke,
Your Wiederau pledges itself to you,
So too do I swear
To be unalterably
Faithful and propitious to you.
I do not waver, I do not yield
From binding myself to your side.
You shall find me everywhere.

5. Aria A fl str bc — A ¢

Glück
Was die Seele kann ergötzen,
Was vergnügt und hoch zu schätzen,
Soll dir Lehn und erblich sein.
Meine Fülle soll nichts sparen
Und dir reichlich offenbaren,
Daß mein ganzer Vorrat dein.

Fortune
Whatever can delight the soul,
Whatever is cheerful and highly to be
prized
Shall be your fief and inheritance.
My abundance shall spare nothing
And be richly revealed to you,
So that my whole stock may be yours.

6. Recitativo B bc — f♯–D C

Schicksal
Und wie ich jederzeit bedacht
Mit aller Sorg und Macht,
Weil du es wert bist, dich zu schützen
Und wider alles dich zu unterstützen,
So hör ich auch nicht ferner auf,
Vor dich zu wachen
Und deines Ruhmes Ehrenlauf
Erweiterter und blühender zu machen.

Destiny
And as I am intent at all times,
With all care and might—
Since you are worthy of it—to protect
you
And to support you against all things,
So I do not cease from further
Watching over you
And making the honoured course
Of your renown more expansive and
more flourishing.

7. Aria B ob vln conc str bc — b 2/4

Schicksal
Ich will dich halten
Und mit dir walten,
Wie man ein Auge zärtlich hält.
Ich habe dein Erhöhen,
Dein Heil und Wohlergehen
Auf Marmorsäulen aufgestellt.

Destiny
I will keep you
And attend to you
As tenderly as one holds an eye.
I have placed your elevation,
Your benefit and well-being
On marble columns.

8. Recitativo S bc — f♯–G C

Zeit
Und obwohl sonst der Unbestand
Mit mir verschwistert und verwandt,

Time
And although otherwise inconstancy
Is closely linked and related to me,

So sei hiermit doch zugesagt:

So oft die Morgenröte tagt,
So lang ein Tag den andern folgen läßt,
So lange will ich steif und fest,
Mein Hennicke, dein Wohl
Auf meine Flügel ferner bauen.
Dies soll die Ewigkeit zuletzt,
Wenn sie mir selbst die Schranken setzt,
Nach mir noch übrig schauen.

May it nonetheless be promised herewith:
As often as the rosy dawn appears,
As long as one day follows another,
So long will I rigidly and firmly,
My Hennicke, build your welfare
Further on my wings.
Eternity shall in the end,
When it sets limits even to me,
See your welfare still remaining after me.

9. Aria S unis vlns bc — e $\frac{9}{8}$

Zeit
Eilt, ihr Stunden, wie ihr wollt,
Rottet aus und stoßt zurücke!
Aber merket dies allein,
Daß ihr diesen Schmuck und Schein,
Daß ihr Hennicks Ruhm und Glücke
Allezeit verschonen sollt!

Time
Hasten, you hours, as you wish,
Destroy and repel!
But note this only,
That this ornament and lustre,
Hennicke's renown and good fortune,
You must ever spare!

10. Recitativo T bc — G–f♯ C

Elster
So recht! ihr seid mir werte Gäste.
Ich räum euch Au und Ufer ein.
Hier bauet eure Hütten
Und eure Wohnung feste;
Hier wollt, hier sollet ihr beständig sein!
Vergesset keinen Fleiß,
All eure Gaben haufenweis
Auf diese Fluren auszuschütten!

Elster
Quite so! you are to me worthy guests.
I grant you meadow and shore.
Here build your huts
And your dwelling securely;
Here you would be, shall be steadfast!
Omit no diligence
In pouring all your gifts in a heap
On these fields!

11. Aria T fl I ob d'am I str bc — b $\frac{3}{4}$

Elster
So wie ich die Tropfen zolle,
Daß mein Wiedrau grünen solle,
So fügt auch euern Segen bei!
Pfleget sorgsam Frucht und Samen,
Zeiget, daß euch Hennicks Namen
Ein ganz besonders Kleinod sei!

Elster
Thus as I provide the drops
So that my Wiederau shall be verdant,
So you too add your blessings!
Carefully cultivate fruit and seeds,
Show that to you Hennicke's name
Is a quite special gem!

12. Recitativo SATB str bc — G–D C

Zeit
Drum, angenehmes Wiederau,
Soll dich kein Blitz, kein Feuerstrahl,
Kein ungesunder Tau,

Time
Therefore, pleasant Wiederau,
No lightning, no flash of fire,
No unhealthy moisture,

Kein Mißwachs, kein Verderben
schrecken!
Schicksal
Dein Haupt, den teuren Hennicke,
Will ich mit Ruhm und Wonne
decken.
Glück
Dem wertesten Gemahl
Will ich kein Heil und keinen Wunsch
versagen,
à 4
Und beider Lust,
Den einigen und liebsten Stamm,
August,
Will ich auf meinem Schoße tragen.

No poor harvest, no destruction shall
terrify you!
Destiny
Your head, dear Hennicke,
I will cover with fame and bliss.
Fortune
From his most esteemed consort
I will withhold no benefit and no good
wish,
a 4
And the pleasure of both,
Your own and that of the beloved House
of Augustus,
I will bear in my bosom.

13. Aria [Chorus: reprise of no. 1 with new text] D $\frac{2}{4}$

Tutti
Angenehmes Wiederau,
Prange nun in deinen Auen!
Deines Wachstums Herrlichkeit,
Deiner Selbstzufriedenheit
Soll die Zeit kein Ende schauen!

Tutti
Pleasant Wiederau,
Shine forth now in your meadows!
To your growth's splendour,
To your self-satisfaction
Time shall see no end!

On 38 September 1737, homage was paid to Johann Christian von Hennicke, a protégé of the all-powerful Count Brühl, on taking possession of his fief[4] at Wiederau near Leipzig. For this occasion, the text of a homage cantata was written by Picander and the music composed by Bach. In a slight and conventional plot, full of obsequious gestures, the libretto of this 'dramma per musica'* spreads the praise of Hennicke through the allegorical characters of Destiny (bass), Fortune (alto), Time (soprano), and the River Elster (tenor), which runs through the estate. Bach's music is as pleasing—indeed, at times positively fashionable—as it is original and captivating in invention. In some movements he perhaps resorted to earlier works. The eleventh movement, in particular, is related by parody* to the work-group BWV 210/210a (no. 8) and may be derived from the lost original model.

The majority of the non-recitative movements—the opening and closing choruses,* nos. 1 and 13 (musically identical, despite their different texts), and the arias, nos. 3, 5, 7, and 9—were not long afterwards, perhaps, reused by Bach in Cantata 30 for the Feast of St John the Baptist (see the above discussion of that work). Moreover, the first and fifth movements are related by parody to a lost intermediate version of Cantata 195. Only the recitatives, largely set as *secco* with

[4] His official status was 'Erb-, Lehn- und Gerichtsherr'.

continuo (only no. 12 is scored with strings) were not taken over into other compositions. Worthy of note are the four-part vocal passages in the framing recitatives, nos. 2 (middle) and 12 (end), in which significant passages of text are sung together by all four soloists.

Mer hahn en neue Oberkeet, BWV 212

Cantate burlesque *'Peasant' Cantata*

NBA I/39, p. 153 BC G 32 Duration: *c.* 30 mins

1. [Ouverture] vln vla bc — A $\frac{3}{4}/\frac{2}{4}/\frac{6}{8}$
2. Aria Duetto SB vln vla bc — A ¢

Mer hahn en neue Oberkeet	We have a new squire
An unsern Kammerherrn.	In the person of our chamberlain.
Ha gibt uns Bier, das steigt ins Heet,	He gives us beer that goes to our heads,
Das ist der klare Kern.	That's the plain truth of it.
Der Pfarr' mag immer büse tun;	The parson may well frown;
Ihr Speelleut, halt euch flink!	You players, look sharp!
Der Kittel wackelt Mieken schun,	Molly's frock is already swaying,
Das klene luse Ding.	The saucy little thing!

3. Recitativo SB vln vla bc — D–A c

Baß	*Bass*
Nu, Mieke, gib dein Guschel immer her;	Now, Molly, give me a kiss;
Sopran	*Soprano*
Wenns das alleine wär!	If only that were all!
Ich kenn dich schon, du Bärenhäuter,	I know you well, you old bearskin,
Du willst hernach nur immer weiter.	Then you just want more and more.
Der neue Herr hat ein sehr scharf Gesicht.	The new Master has a very harsh look.
Baß	*Bass*
Ach! unser Herr schilt nicht;	Ah! our Master won't scold us;
Er weiß so gut als wir, und auch wohl besser,	He knows as well as we, or even better,
Wie schön ein bißchen Dahlen schmeckt.	How lovely a little fondling tastes.

4. [Aria] S vln vla bc — A $\frac{3}{4}$

Ach, es schmeckt doch gar zu gut,	Ah, how good it tastes
Wenn ein Paar recht freundlich tut;	When a couple are really intimate;
Ei, da braust es in dem Ranzen,	Ah, it roars in your insides,
Als wenn eitel Flöh und Wanzen	As if nothing but fleas and bugs
Und ein tolles Wespenheer	And a mad swarm of wasps
Miteinander zänkisch wär.	Were quarrelling with one another.

5. Recitativo B bc — f♯–D c

Der Herr ist gut: Allein der Schösser,	The Master is good, but the tax-collector,
Das ist ein Schwefelsmann,	He's a real devil

Der wie ein Blitz ein neu Schock strafen kann,	Who can fine you like lightning
Wenn man den Finger kaum ins kalte Wasser steckt.	For barely sticking your finger in cold water.
6. ARIA B vln vla bc	D 3/4
Ach, Herr Schösser, geht nicht gar zu schlimm	Ah, Mr Tax-collector, don't be too hard
Mit uns armen Bauersleuten üm!	On us poor peasant folk!
Schont nur unsrer Haut;	Spare but our skins;
Freßt ihr gleich das Kraut	Though you devour the cabbage
Wie die Raupen bis zum kahlen Strunk,	Like a caterpillar to the bare stalk,
Habt nur genung!	Let that be enough!
7. RECITATIVO S bc	A–b c
Es bleibt dabei,	It is settled:
Daß unser Herr der beste sei.	Our Master is the best.
Er ist nicht besser abzumalen	You couldn't imagine a better,
Und auch mit keinem Hopfensack voll Batzen zu bezahlen.	Nor even pay for him with a hop-sack full of coins.
8. [ARIA] S vln vla bc	b 3/4
Unser trefflicher	Our excellent
Lieber Kammerherr	Beloved chamberlain
Ist ein kumpabler Mann,	Is an affable man;
Den niemand tadeln kann.	No one could find fault with him.
9. RECITATIVO SB bc	D–G c
Baß	*Bass*
Er hilft uns allen, alt und jung.	He helps us all, old and young.
Und dir ins Ohr gesprochen:	And let me whisper in your ear:
Ist unser Dorf nicht gut genung	Isn't our village good enough
Letzt bei der Werbung durchgekrochen?	To get by in the last recruitment?
Sopran	*Soprano*
Ich weiß wohl noch ein besser Spiel,	I know an even better game:
Der Herr gilt bei der Steuer viel.	The Master carries great weight with the taxes.
10. ARIA S vln vla bc	G 3/4
Das ist galant,	This is fine:
Es spricht niemand	No one speaks
Von den caducken Schocken.	Of the land taxes.
Niemand redt ein stummes Wort,	No one breathes a word of it,
Knauthain und Cospuden dort	But Knauthain and Cospuden
Hat selber Werg am Rocken.	Still have to pay.
11. RECITATIVO B bc	e–d c
Und unsre gnädge Frau	And our gracious Lady
Ist nicht ein prinkel stolz.	Is not a bit proud.

Und ist gleich unsereins ein arm und grobes Holz,	And even though folk like us are a poor and coarse wood,
So redt sie doch mit uns daher,	Yet she chats with us
Als wenn sie unsersgleichen wär.	As if she were one of us.
Sie ist recht fromm, recht wirtlich und genau	She is very pious, very hospitable, and careful,
Und machte unserm gnädgen Herrn	And for our gracious Master
Aus einer Fledermaus viel Taler gern.	She'd gladly make a lot of money out of a bat!

12. Aria B vln vla bc — B♭ $\frac{3}{4}$

Fünfzig Taler bares Geld	For fifty Thalers in ready money
Trockner Weise zu verschmausen,	To be used up just like that
Ist ein Ding, das harte fällt,	Is a thing that's hard to put up with
Wenn sie uns die Haare zausen,	When we get our hair pulled,
Doch was fort ist, bleibt wohl fort,	Yet what's gone is gone for good;
Kann man doch am andern Ort	If we could somewhere else
Alles doppelt wieder sparen;	Save it all twice over,
Laßt die fünfzig Taler fahren!	Let the fifty thalers go!

13. Recitativo S bc — C–D c

Im Ernst ein Wort!	Seriously, one word!
Noch eh ich dort	Before I turn my mind
An unsre Schenke	To our tavern
Und an den Tanz gedenke,	And to dancing,
So sollst du erst der Obrigkeit zu Ehren	You shall first hear from me, in honour
Ein neues Liedchen von mir hören.	Of the authorities, a new little song.

14. Aria S fl vln I,II vla bc — A $\frac{3}{8}$

Klein-Zschocher müsse	Let Klein-Zschocher be
So zart und süße	As gentle and sweet
Wie lauter Mandelkerne sein.	As pure almonds.
In unsere Gemeine	In our community
Zieh heute ganz alleine	Let only one thing enter today:
Der Überfluß des Segens ein.	An abundance of blessings.

15. Recitativo B bc — D–e c

Das ist zu klug vor dich	That's too clever for you
Und nach der Städter Weise;	And after the town manner;
Wir Bauern singen nicht so leise.	We peasants don't sing so delicately.
Das Stückchen, höre nur, das schicket sich vor mich!	Listen to the little piece that suits me!

16. Aria B hn vln vla bc — G $\frac{6}{8}$

Es nehme zehntausend Dukaten	Let him take ten thousand ducats
Der Kammerherr alle Tag ein!	Every day, the chamberlain!
Er trink ein gutes Gläschen Wein,	Let him drink a good glass of wine,
Und laß es ihm bekommen sein!	And may it do him good!

17. Recitativo S bc — D–A 6/8 C

Das klingt zu liederlich.
Es sind so hübsche Leute da,
Die würden ja
Von Herzen drüber lachen;
Nicht anders, als wenn ich
Die alte Weise wollte machen:

That sounds too uncouth.
There are such fine folks here,
Who would indeed
Laugh heartily over it,
Just as if I were to sing
The old tune:

18. [Aria] S hn vln vla bc — D 3/4

Gib, Schöne,
Viel Söhne
Von artger Gestalt,
Und zieh sie fein alt;
Das wünschet sich Zschocher und
  Knauthain fein bald!

Fair one, have
Many sons
With good looks
And bring them up well;
That's what Zschocher and Knauthain
  want, very soon!

19. Recitativo B bc — b–A C

Du hast wohl recht.
Das Stückchen klingt zu schlecht;
Ich muß mich also zwingen,
Was Städtisches zu singen.

You're probably right:
The little piece sounds too bad;
So I'll have to make myself
Sing something in the town style.

20. Aria B vln bc — A 3/8 ¢ 3/8

Dein Wachstum sei feste
Und lache vor Lust!
  Deines Herzens Trefflichkeit
  Hat dir selbst das Feld bereit',
  Auf dem du blühen mußt.

May your prosperity be secure
And laugh in pleasure!
  Your heart's excellence
  Has prepared the ground for you,
  On which you are bound to blossom.

21. Recitativo SB bc — A–b C

Sopran
Und damit sei es auch genung.
Baß
Nun müssen wir wohl einen Sprung
In unsrer Schenke wagen.
Sopran
Das heißt, du willst nur das noch
  sagen:

Soprano
And let that be enough.
Bass
Now we must venture a leap
Into our tavern.
Soprano
In other words, all you still want to say is:

22. [Aria] S vln vla bc — b ¢

Und daß ihrs alle wißt,
Es ist nunmehr die Frist
Zu trinken.
Wer durstig ist, mag winken.
Versagts die rechte Hand,
So dreht euch unverwandt
Zur Linken!

And as you all know,
It's now the time
For drinking.
Whoever is thirsty, just nod.
If your right hand lets you down,
Then turn right round
To the left!

23. [Recitativo] SB bc — D C

Baß
Mein Schatz! erraten!

Bass
My sweetheart! you guessed!

Sopran	*Soprano*
Und weil wir nun	And because we now
Dahier nichts mehr zu tun,	Have nothing more to do here,
So wollen wir auch Schritt vor Schritt	Let's amble along step by step
In unsre alte Schenke waten.	To our old tavern.
Baß	*Bass*
Ei! hol mich der und dieser,	Well, the devil take me!
Herr Ludwig und der Steur-Reviser	Mr Ludwig and the Tax Inspector
Muß heute mit.	Must come with us today.

24. CHOR SB vln vla bc F C

Wir gehn nun, wo der Tudelsack	We're going now where the bagpipe
In unsrer Schenke brummt.	Drones in our tavern.
Und rufen dabei fröhlich aus:	And merrily we cry:
Es lebe Dieskau und sein Haus,	Long live Dieskau and his house,
Ihm sei beschert,	May he be granted
Was er begehrt,	Whatever he desires
Und was er sich selbst wünschen mag!	And whatever he himself might wish!

Bach's Peasant Cantata, one of his most popular, original, and cheerful works, is the last of his cantatas that can be dated. The many corrections in the hastily written autograph score, evidently prepared within a very short period, indicate that only in a few cases did Bach make use of older music. Only no. 20 is unquestionably a parody* (it is based on the seventh movement of Cantata 201) and the music for no. 14 was probably borrowed from the lost cantata BWV Anh. I 11, no. 9. The other movements are probably all, or nearly all, new compositions.

We should not be misled by the title 'Peasant' Cantata or, as Picander's printed libretto styles it, 'Cantate en burlesque': this is no rustic piece, to be performed by or for peasants. It is rather a homage cantata like many others, performed on 30 August 1742 in honour of one Carl Heinrich von Dieskau. Upon the death of his mother in 1742, Dieskau, who was born of an old noble family, inherited a number of properties, and on 30 August he was paid the customary homage by his subordinates at the village of Klein-Zschocher near Leipzig. As superintendent of the collection of taxes in the Leipzig area, Dieskau was the immediate superior of Henrici, alias Picander, and it may have been Picander who, seeking Dieskau's favour through his poetic talent, requested Bach to set the text he had written and to perform the homage cantata.

The choice of a rustic setting for the typically modest plot is probably symptomatic of the gradual decline of the baroque gods-and-shepherds dramas towards the middle of the century. The libretto should not, however, be overestimated. While original, it serves the purpose of amusement and not at all that of social criticism. When the sixth movement, with its plea for indulgent treatment of the 'poor peasant folk', is cited in an attempt to label Bach a social revolutionary and champion of the exploited peasantry, the true purpose and occasion of this poem—of homage (which in any case is that of Picander, not Bach)—are forgotten. Nevertheless, the text illustrates many characteristic features of the peasant life of the times. The upper-Saxon dialect is employed in the opening duet but then largely dropped, lingering only in such isolated dialect forms as 'Mieke' (Molly), 'Guschel' (mouth), 'Dahlen' (fondling), and 'prinkel' (a little), etc. The dialogue of the two soloists alludes to circumstances of which we can have little inkling today. The tax-collector ('Schösser'; does Picander refer to himself or to a colleague?), for example, becomes the butt of the peasants for penalizing them 'for barely sticking their finger in cold water' (that is, presumably, for infringing the fishing rights) and for severely exploiting them in other ways. We also learn that, due to Dieskau's influence, Klein-Zschocher escaped lightly at the last recruitment and that the new master is very influential, particularly in taxation, with the result that the tax on fallow land ('caducken Schocken') had not been levied. Finally, the wish that the 'Fair one' should 'have many sons' (no. 18) was all too well-founded, for the Dieskau family had so far been blessed with five daughters but not a single son.[5]

The unpretentious plot, typical of such homage cantatas, introduces a young peasant girl Molly and her lover. The true purpose of paying homage to the new master is reached only after copious mutual bantering and a thorough settling of accounts with the unpopular tax-collector. The chamberlain, adept at using his influence in favour of the peasants, and his condescending wife are praised in a chain of recitatives and arias. In the contrast between the 'uncouth' rustic manner of singing and the 'town style' (which is really in place here, though regarded by Molly's lover as 'too clever' for her), the poet introduces a skilfully deployed stylistic discrepancy into a series of obeisant wishes that would otherwise be too uniform—a factor that proves beneficial to Bach's setting.

Bach's composition impresses by virtue of the unaffected naturalness with which popular and highly stylized forms grow together into a unity—something not dissimilar to what we later encounter, albeit on a different level, in Mozart's *Die Zauberflöte*. The ensemble as a whole is made up of soprano and bass voices, horn, flute, strings, and continuo, but Bach favours a rustic trio texture of violin, viola, and continuo, and the wind instruments are used only in isolated movements (the flute and horn might have been played by the same musician).

In the overture, which is made up of seven short movements in succession (a b c d e f a^1), Bach may have recalled the quodlibets* of Bach-family days during his youth. The opening and closing duets are bourrée-like in character, and the other arias also betray an affinity with dance: nos. 4 and 6 might be regarded as polonaises, no. 8 as a sarabande, no. 12 as a mazurka, no. 14 as a minuet, and no.

[5] In essentials, the present account of the text follows the commentary to the Peters edition (Leipzig, 1952), edited by Werner Neumann.

22 as a *paysanne* or peasant dance, while no. 20 resembles a passepied. Repeatedly, Bach seems to have interwoven well-known folk tunes into his composition. After the words 'I know you well, you old bearskin, then you just want more and more' in no. 3, and again at the end of the movement, a suggestive commentary is provided by an instrumental quotation of the song 'With you and me in a feather-bed, with you and me on straw; there no feather pricks us, there no flea bites us'[6] (with the lines reordered: 3–4, 1–2). In addition, no. 16 is a well-known hunting song from Bohemia, and since no. 18 is in the preceding recitative described as 'the old tune', it is presumably based on a familiar melody. It is worth pointing out a stylistic characteristic of folk music that recurs frequently in this cantata: strong beats are often split up and weak beats syncopated, as in the Adagio and second Allegro sections from the overture—

—and frequently in subsequent movements:

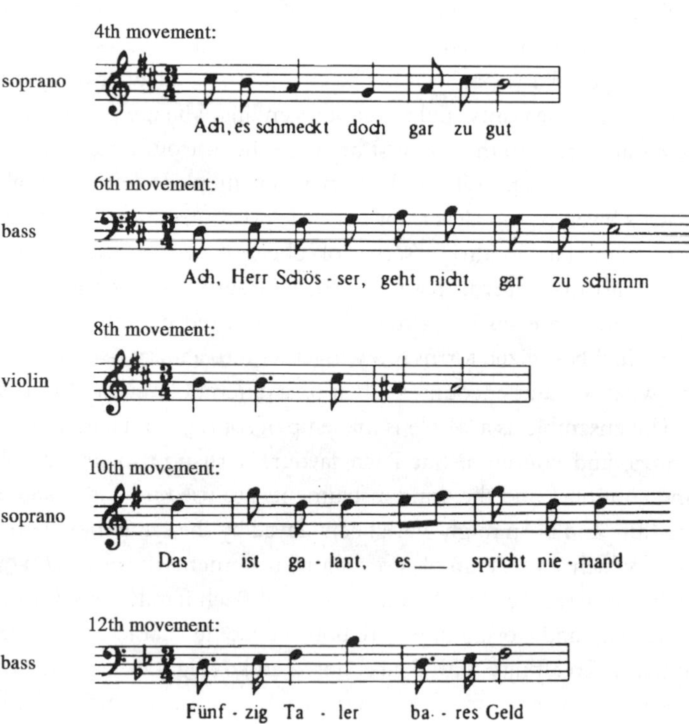

[6] 'Mit dir und mir ins Federbett, mit dir und mir aufs Stroh; da sticht uns keine Feder net, da beißt uns auch kein Floh.'

The musical sequence of events is such that each of the two soloists has to sing not only a series of movements in folksong or folkdance style but also a 'town-style' aria which forms the high point of the solo part concerned. The soprano aria 'Klein-Zschocher müsse so zart und süße', no. 14, is of quite exceptional charm; and listeners familiar with the Bach cantatas cannot fail to recognize in the shaking figures of the bass aria 'Dein Wachstum sei feste', no. 20, the 'shaking heart' from Pan's aria in Cantata 201, no. 7, though the parody text '. . . and laugh in pleasure' is not ill-suited to it.

In sum, it would be mistaken to go to the extreme of regarding the 'Peasant' Cantata as one of Bach's chief works. Nevertheless, we cannot help admiring the fact that Bach maintained his close link with dance and folk music, as well as hymn and chorale, throughout his life, and so successfully turned it to artistic account in his compositions.

6

Wedding cantatas

Weichet nur, betrübte Schatten, BWV 202

NBA I/40, p. 3 BC G 41 Duration: *c.* 23 mins

1. [Aria] S ob str bc		G c
Weichet nur, betrübte Schatten, Frost und Winde, geht zur Ruh! Florens Lust Will der Brust Nichts als frohes Glück verstatten, Denn sie träget Blumen zu.	Retreat, gloomy shadows; Frost and wind, go to rest! Flora's delight Will grant the breast Nothing but good fortune, For she brings flowers.	
2. [Recitativo] S bc		C c
Die Welt wird wieder neu, Auf Bergen und in Gründen Will sich die Anmut doppelt schön verbinden, Der Tag ist von der Kälte frei.	The world is renewed; On mountains and in valleys Charm would bind herself in doubled beauty; The day is free of cold.	
3. Aria S bc		C 12/8
Phoebus eilt mit schnellen Pferden Durch die neugeborne Welt. Ja, weil sie ihm wohlgefällt, Will er selbst ein Buhler werden.	Phoebus hastens with swift horses Through the newborn world. Indeed, because she pleases him well, He himself would become a lover.	
4. Recitativo S bc		a–e c
Drum sucht auch Amor sein Vergnügen, Wenn Purpur in den Wiesen lacht, Wenn Florens Pracht sich herrlich macht, Und wenn in seinem Reich, Den schönen Blumen gleich, Auch Herzen feurig siegen.	Therefore Cupid also seeks his pleasure When purple laughs in the meadows, When Flora's splendour looks glorious, And when in his kingdom, Like fair flowers, Ardent hearts conquer.	
5. Aria S vln solo bc		e c
Wenn die Frühlingslüfte streichen Und durch bunte Felder wehn, Pflegt auch Amor auszuschleichen, Um nach seinem Schmuck zu sehn,	When the spring breezes stroke And waft through motley fields, Cupid too is wont to creep out To look for his finery,	

Welcher, glaubt man, dieser ist,	Which is believed to be this:
Daß ein Herz das andre küßt.	That one heart kisses another.
6. Recitativo S bc	A–D 𝄴
Und dieses ist das Glücke,	And this is good fortune:
Daß durch ein hohes Gunstgeschicke	That through a lofty, favoured destiny
Zwei Seelen einen Schmuck erlanget,	Two souls attain one adornment,
An dem viel Heil and Segen pranget.	On which much welfare and blessing shine.
7. Aria S ob bc	D $\frac{3}{8}$
Sich üben im Lieben,	To cultivate love,
In Scherzen sich herzen	To embrace in jest
Ist besser als Florens vergängliche Lust.	Is better than Flora's transitory delight.
Hier quellen die Wellen,	Here the waves gush,
Hier lachen und wachen	Here laugh and watch
Die siegenden Palmen auf Lippen und Brust.	The victorious palms on lips and breast.
8. Recitativo S bc	G 𝄴
So sei das Band der keuschen Liebe,	So may the bond of chaste love,
Verlobte Zwei,	Betrothed pair,
Vom Unbestand des Wechsels frei!	Be free from the inconstancy of change!
Kein jäher Fall	May no sudden incident
Noch Donnerknall	Nor thunderclap
Erschrecke die verliebten Triebe!	Frighten your amorous desires!
9. Gavotte S ob str bc	G 2
Sehet in Zufriedenheit	May you see in contentment
Tausend helle Wohlfahrtstage,	A thousand bright days of well-being,
Daß bald bei der Folgezeit	So that in the near future
Eure Liebe Blumen trage!	Your love may bear flowers!

The origin of this wedding cantata is obscure. It survives only in a manuscript copy of 1730 whose notation is strikingly antiquated, a style of writing normally found in Bach only up to 1714. Moreover, it has been conjectured that the libretto might have been written by the Weimar poet Salomo Franck.[1] A Weimar origin, rather than the traditional dating in Bach's Cöthen years, is also suggested by certain stylistic features pointed out by Joshua Rifkin:[2] the brevity and arioso* endings of the recitatives; the sinuous oboe line and slow–fast–slow design of the opening aria, frequently paralleled in the arias of 1713–14 but seldom thereafter; and the specific mode of combining voice and obbligato* instrument in the aria no. 7, which finds no real counterpart in Bach's vocal works after 1715.

[1] See H. Streck, *Die Verskunst in den poetischen Texten zu den Kantaten J. S. Bachs* (Hamburg, 1971).

[2] In the notes that accompany his recording (L'Oiseau Lyre).

If the precise year of origin remains unknown, we nonetheless know the season in which the work was performed. In fanciful words, the libretto reveals that winter is drawing to a close: 'the day is free of cold' and flowers begin to shoot up (nos. 1–2), the sun climbs higher once more (no. 3), and so Cupid again keeps a look-out for prey (nos. 4–5). This gives the cue for mentioning the occasion of the work, namely to honour a bridal couple (no. 6), for love is 'better than Flora's transitory delight' (no. 7). The cantata ends with joyful good wishes.

In Bach's setting the plain garb of sound, which requires only solo soprano, oboe, strings, and continuo, suggests that the occasion of the work should be sought in a civil or possibly noble wedding rather than a royal one. Nor would the trifling, jesting tone have been well suited to a person of high rank. Arias alternate with recitatives, which invariably open as *secco* with continuo but solidify into arioso towards the close, a typical stylistic feature of Bach's Weimar and Cöthen periods which still occurs in the first Leipzig cantatas but not so often thereafter.

Among the arias, the opening movement in particular commands our admiration. Its unorthodox, prelude-like main section occupies the middle ground in form between quasi-improvisatory arioso and strictly-constructed aria. Above a repeated string motive, which depicts the vanishing of wintry shadows in rising chord sequences, the oboe extends a wide-ranging melody that turns into a soprano-oboe duet at the entry of the voice. This opening section, marked 'adagio', contrasts in tempo and thematic material with a livelier middle section ('andante'), just as the 'rest' to which the frost and wind return in the text gives way to the good fortune brought by 'Flora's delight'. A da capo* of the principal section closes this imposing movement.

In the second aria, no. 3, the trotting of Phoebus's 'swift horses' is unmistakably portrayed in the continuo figuration. Attention has often been drawn to the affinity between this aria and the finale of the Violin Sonata in G, BWV 1019. The third aria, no. 5, scored with obbligato violin, strikes a more elegiac note; and the fourth, no. 7, with obbligato oboe, is distinctly popular and folksong-like in character as a result of its dance-style triple time and its accessible melodic writing. The dance character of the finale is overtly proclaimed by its heading 'Gavotte'. A simple sixteen-bar melody, scored for the entire instrumental ensemble, is then repeated with voice in a lightly varied form, after which a da capo of the instrumental ritornello ends this exceptionally brief movement.

The overall form of the cantata might be described as a gradual transformation, achieved in a wave-like pattern, from a highly stylized, aperiodic, concerto-like movement to a popular-style, periodically articulated dance movement. The outer movements, nos. 1 and 9, represent the two extremes, no. 5 approaches the first type, and in nos. 3 and 7 the second type acquires an increasingly clearer profile.

Auf! süß entzückende Gewalt, BWV Anh. I 196

This lost cantata was written for the wedding of Christiana Sibylla Mencke and Peter Hohmann (who was in 1736 raised to the nobility under the name von Hohenthal) on 27 November 1725. All that survives is Johann Christoph Gottsched's libretto, which was published in 1730 (and several times thereafter) in his *Versuch einer critischen Dichtkunst*. Not long before the wedding, Gottsched had arrived in Leipzig and met with a warm welcome and encouragement from the highly reputed father of the bride; and he may have welcomed the opportunity to show both his gratitude and his skill as a poet. That Bach wrote the music was established by Friedrich Smend[3] on the basis of the similarity in metrical structure between two of the arias and two movements from the *Ascension Oratorio*, BWV 11, nos. 4 and 10. According to Smend, the first of the two arias, 'Entfernet euch, ihr kalten Herzen' (no. 3), cannot easily be reconstructed from its supposed parody,* the oratorio* aria 'Ach bleibe doch, mein liebstes Leben', but the second, 'Unschuld, Kleinod reiner Seelen' (no. 5), may be recovered in its presumed original form from the oratorio aria 'Jesu, deine Gnadenblicke'. Indeed, the autograph of the *Ascension Oratorio* here reveals traces of an older instrumental scoring for two transverse flutes* and two unison oboes da caccia,* which was probably valid for the wedding cantata but altered for the oratorio version. Thus at least one charming aria from the lost wedding music may be recovered.

Gottsched's libretto includes the allegorical figures Nature, Modesty, Virtue, and Foresight, and it closes with a 'Chorus of Nymphs on the River Pleiße'.[4] The aria 'Unschuld, Kleinod reiner Seelen' is sung by Modesty, who at first recoils from love out of fear of defilement until she is advised by Nature that a pure love exists that is pleasing to God. If we consider Bach's setting of the newly recovered aria, its 'bridal' character becomes truly apparent. Above all, the absence of continuo proves to be text-engendered. Here, as in the aria 'Aus Liebe will mein Heiland sterben' from the *St Matthew Passion* and elsewhere, Bach uses it as a symbol of innocence. The oboes da caccia consequently form a bassett* in place of continuo, which means that the aria includes parts at treble and alto pitch only. The special charm of this aria may perhaps act as some compensation for the loss of the other movements of the cantata.

Vergnügte Pleißenstadt, BWV 216

This cantata, composed to a text by Picander for the marriage of a merchant, Johann Heinrich Wolff, to Susanna Regina Hempel, was performed on 5 February 1728. Apart from the printed text, however, only two voice parts survive. The

[3] In 'Bachs Himmelfahrts-Oratorium', in K. Matthaei, ed., *Bach-Gedenkschrift 1950* (Zurich, 1950), 42–65.

[4] 'Natur', 'Schamhaftigkeit', 'Tugend', 'Verhängnis', and 'Chor der Nymphen an der Pleiße'.

aria 'Angenehme Hempelin', no. 3, and the duet 'Heil und Segen', no. 7, turn out to be parodies of Cantatas 204/8 and 205/13 respectively. The surviving fragment is published in NBA I/40, pp. 23–34, and details of its history and transmission may be found in the accompanying Critical Report, pp. 26–46. The cantata of the same title edited by Georg Schumann and Werner Wolffheim in 1924 cannot claim the validity of a reconstruction. It is rather a free re-creation of the work that paraphrases the original.

O holder Tag, erwünschte Zeit, BWV 210

NBA I/40, p. 37 BC G 44 Duration: *c.* 39 mins

1. RECITATIVO S str bc	A–D c
O holder Tag, erwünschte Zeit,	O propitious day, desired time,
Willkommen, frohe Stunden!	Welcome, joyful hours!
Ihr bringt ein Fest, das uns erfreut.	You bring a feast that delights us.
Weg, Schwermut, weg, weg, Traurigkeit!	Away, melancholy! away, away, sorrow!
Der Himmel, welcher vor uns wachet,	Heaven, which watches over us,
Hat euch zu unsrer Lust gemachet:	Has made you for our pleasure:
Drum laßt uns fröhlich sein!	Therefore let us be glad!
Wir sind von Gott darzu verbunden,	We are bound by God
Uns mit den Frohen zu erfreun.	To rejoice with the joyful.
2. ARIA S str ob d'am bc	A $\frac{3}{8}$
Spielet, ihr beseelten Lieder,	Play, you inspired songs,
Werfet die entzückte Brust	Cast the enraptured breast
In die Ohnmacht sanfte nieder!	Gently down into a swoon!
Aber durch der Saiten Lust	But through the strings' delight
Stärket und erholt sie wieder!	Strengthen and refresh it again!
3. RECITATIVO S bc	f♯–B c
Doch, haltet ein,	But cease,
Ihr muntern Saiten;	You lively strings;
Denn bei verliebten Eheleuten	For with enamoured couples
Soll's stille sein!	There should be calm!
Ihr harmoniert nicht mit der Liebe;	You do not harmonize with Love;
Denn eure angebornen Triebe	For your innate impulses
Verleiten uns zur Eitelkeit,	Lead us to vanity,
Und dieses schickt sich nicht zur Zeit.	And this is not suited to the present time.
Ein frommes Ehepaar	A devout couple
Will lieber zu dem Dankaltar	Would rather go to the altar of thanksgiving
Mit dem Gemüte treten	With their feelings
Und ein beseeltes Abba beten;	And offer up an inspired prayer to the Father;
Es ist vielmehr im Geist bemüht	They are, rather, diligent in spirit

Und dichtet in der Brust ein angenehmes Lied.	And compose in their breast an agreeable song.
4. ARIA S ob d'am vln I bc	E 12/8
Ruhet hie, matte Töne,	Rest here, subdued notes,
Matte Töne, ruhet hie!	Subdued notes, rest here!
Eure zarte Harmonie	Your tender harmony
Ist vor die beglückte Eh'	Is for a happy marriage
Nicht die wahre Panazee.	No true panacea.
5. RECITATIVO S bc	c♯–b C
So glaubt man denn, daß die Musik verführe	So is it believed that Music leads one astray
Und gar nicht mit der Liebe harmoniere?	And does not harmonize with Love at all?
O nein! Wer wollte denn nicht ihren Wert betrachten,	Oh no! Who, then, would not consider its worth,
Auf den so hohe Gönner achten?	Of which such exalted patrons are sensible?
Gewiß, die gütige Natur	Certainly, kind Nature
Zieht uns von ihr auf eine höhre Spur.	Draws us by it onto a higher track.
Sie ist der Liebe gleich, ein großes Himmelskind,	It is, like Love, a great heavenly child,
Nur, daß sie nicht, als wie die Liebe, blind.	Only it is not, like Love, blind.
Sie schleicht in alle Herzen ein	It steals into all hearts
Und kann bei Hoh' und Niedern sein.	And can be with the exalted or the lowly.
Sie lockt den Sinn	It entices the mind
Zum Himmel hin	To heaven
Und kann verliebten Seelen	And can tell enamoured souls
Des Höchsten Ruhm erzählen.	Of the glory of the Most High.
Ja, heißt die Liebe sonst weit stärker als der Tod,	Indeed, though Love is elsewhere called far stronger than death,
Wer leugnet? die Musik stärkt uns in Todes Not.	Who would deny that Music strengthens us in death's extremity?
O wundervolles Spiel!	O wonderful play!
Dich, dich verehrt man viel.	You, you are much revered.
Doch, was erklingt dort vor ein Klagelied,	Yet what lament is heard there
Das den geschwinden Ton beliebter Saiten flieht?	That eschews the nimble sound of beloved strings?
6. ARIA S fl bc	b C
Schweigt, ihr Flöten, schweigt, ihr Töne,	Be silent, you flutes; be silent, you notes,
Denn ihr klingt dem Neid nicht schöne,	For you do not sound good to envy;

Eilt durch die geschwärzte Luft,
Bis man euch zu Grabe ruft!

Hasten through the darkened air
Till you are called to the grave!

7. Recitativo S bc — f♯–E c

Was Luft? was Grab?
Soll die Musik verderben,
Die uns so großen Nutzen gab?
Soll so ein Himmelskind ersterben,
Und zwar für eine Höllenbrut?
O nein!
Das kann nicht sein.
Drum auf, erfrische deinen Mut!
Die Liebe kann vergnügte Saiten
Gar wohl vor ihrem Throne leiden.
Indessen laß dich nur den blassen Neid verlachen,
Was wird sich dein Gesang aus Satans Kindern machen?
Genug, daß dich der Himmel schützt,
Wenn sich ein Feind auf dich erhitzt.
Getrost, es leben noch Patronen,
Die gern bei deiner Anmut wohnen.
Und einen solchen Mäzenat
Sollst du auch itzo in der Tat
An seinem Hochzeitfest verehren.
Wohlan, laß deine Stimme hören!

What air? what grave?
Shall Music perish,
That gave us such great benefits?
Shall such a heavenly child die,
And indeed for an infernal crew?
Oh no!
That cannot be.
Therefore arise, revive your spirit!
Love can endure cheerful strings
Quite well before its throne.
Meanwhile, do but deride green envy;
What will your singing make of Satan's children?
It is enough that heaven protects you
When an enemy is aroused against you.
Be of good cheer, patrons still live
Who gladly dwell amidst your charm.
And one such patron
You shall now in fact
Revere at his wedding feast.
Well then, let your voice be heard!

8. Aria S ob d'am str bc — c♯ 3/4

Großer Gönner, dein Vergnügen
Muß auch unsern Klang besiegen,
Denn du verehrst uns deine Gunst.
Unter deinen Weisheitsschätzen
Kann dich nichts so sehr ergötzen
Als der süßen Töne Kunst.

Great patron, your pleasure
Must even vanquish our sound,
For you honour us with your favour.
Among the treasures of your wisdom
Nothing can delight you so much
As the art of sweet sounds.

9. Recitativo S fl ob d'am str bc — f♯–A c

Hochteurer Mann, so fahre ferner fort,
Der edlen Harmonie wie itzt geneigt zu bleiben;
So wird sie dir dereinst die Traurigkeit vertreiben.
So wird an manchem Ort
Dein wohlverdientes Lob erschallen.
Dein Ruhm wird wie ein Demantstein,
Ja wie ein fester Stahl beständig sein,
Bis daß er in der ganzen Welt erklinge.

Highly honoured man, continue to be
As well-disposed as you are now to noble harmony;
Then one day it shall drive away your sorrow.
Then in many a place
Your well-deserved praise shall resound.
Your renown shall be as constant as a diamond
—Indeed, as tempered steel—
Till it be heard throughout the entire world.

Indessen gönne mir, Daß ich bei deiner Hochzeit Freude Ein wünschend Opfer zubereite Und nach Gebühr Dein künftig Glück und Wohl besinge.	Meanwhile, permit me, Amidst your wedding joy, To prepare a welcoming offering And duly celebrate In song your future good fortune and welfare.
10. ARIA S fl ob d'am str bc	A ¢
Seid beglückt, edle beide, Edle beide, seid beglückt! Beständige Lust Erfülle die Wohnung, vergnüge die Brust, Bis daß euch die Hochzeit des Lammes erquickt.	Be happy, noble pair, Noble pair, be happy! May constant delight Fill your dwelling, please your breast, Till the Wedding of the Lamb refreshes you.

This cantata is the only work that survives complete from a related group of cantatas discussed above (see under Secular Cantatas 5, BWV 210a). It seems to have been used on at least two occasions, but only the later or latest version is transmitted. We do not know for what bridal couple it was intended. The diplomatic findings of the source material point to the period around 1738–41,[5] and a few hints may be gleaned from the text itself. The bridegroom must have been an influential man and it appears that he was particularly devoted to music. The lines 'Among the treasures of your wisdom nothing can delight you so much as the art of sweet sounds' (no. 8) do not necessarily point to a professional scholar, any more than a theologian should of necessity be inferred from the words 'A devout couple would . . . offer up an inspired prayer to the Father' (no. 3). In these allusions, however, the special interests of the patron concerned are evidently enshrined, among which we gather that music occupied first place.

In his text the anonymous librettist meditates over the interrelations between music and love. 'Inspired songs' put the breast into a state of rapture, but since they induce 'vanity' they do not harmonize with love. Nor are 'subdued notes' the right remedy for a happy marriage, and now more than ever the flute's lament must be silent, being ill-suited to this festive occasion. The poet then asks whether music should therefore die altogether, but he answers in the negative. 'Love can endure cheerful strings quite well before its throne', particularly as long as patrons of music still exist, and one such patron is to be honoured today. The text ends with praise of the bridegroom as a patron of music and with good wishes to the bridal pair.

Bach's setting not only shows the most mature artistry, it is also extremely demanding in vocal technique. Coloraturas,* trills, and rapid passage-work reaching as high as top c^3 are required of the soprano singer. In addition,

[5] According to Kobayashi Chr, 42 f.

considerable ability is expected of the instrumentalists, especially the flautist. Both librettist and composer were evidently convinced that the bridegroom was a connoisseur who would know how to appreciate such things. Bach may have given him and his bride a memento of the occasion: it has been suggested that the joint soprano and continuo part preserved among the original performing material[6]—perhaps the finest piece of calligraphy in Bach's hand that we possess—was intended as a presentation exemplar for the bridal couple.[7] The vocal restriction to soprano solo only (on the title-page Bach described the work as a 'Cantata a Voce sola') naturally demands a richly contrasting treatment of the various movements in order to counteract the risk of monotony. In this respect the librettist provides valuable assistance through his description of the diverse character of music.

The introductory accompanied recitative leads to a dance-like aria, no. 2, scored with strings (with first violin doubled by oboe d'amore*). Already in the opening ritornello, the changeable feelings of the 'enraptured breast' and the surging up and down of the spirits are vividly illustrated. A contrasting picture is painted in the second aria, no. 4. Here oboe d'amore and solo violin play a concertante* duet of inspired tenderness, characterized by a preference for the minor (Mixolydian) seventh, as in the setting of 'O holder Tag' from the opening recitative. The structure of the third aria, no. 6, whose solo instrument is this time transverse flute,* is conditioned by the text. After only a few notes, the flute melody is interrupted by the voice in the words 'Be silent, you flutes', and the opening ritornello is replaced by substantial instrumental episodes between the vocal phrases. This device not only diversifies the aria structure, it also leads to an animated exchange between the solo soprano and the elaborate and extensive flute figures.

The *decrescendo*, as it were, in the scoring of the first three arias reflects the rejection of such sounds as unsuitable for wedding music. When the bridegroom is addressed as a patron of music, however, a full texture is heard once more. The fourth aria, 'Great patron, your pleasure must even vanquish our sound' (no. 8), is scored for obbligato* oboe d'amore and continuo with the inner parts filled in by first and second violins. As in the second movement, the dance character of the music, reinforced by the echo effect in the instrumental ritornello, is unmistakable. The linking recitatives between the arias have thus far been set as *secco* with continuo accompaniment. In the ninth movement, however—a motivically imprinted *accompagnato** that forms a transition to the finale—Bach creates a counterpart to the opening recitative. Flute and oboe d'amore form a backcloth to the voice, playing continuous semiquaver figures

[6] See the facsimile, with preface by Werner Neumann, in *Faksimile-Reihe Bachscher Werke und Schriftstücke*, 8 (Leipzig, 1967).

[7] Though if that were the case, it would be hard to understand how the part remained in Bach's possession.

against the supporting chords of the strings. Finally, the concluding aria unites the entire ensemble in ceremonial congratulation of the bridal couple. This movement once again confirms that the work was written for a connoisseur, for Bach is not content, as he often is elsewhere, with a lively dance-finale in popular style, but instead invents a conclusion which, for all its melodic appeal, forms a well-nigh hymnic impression.

7

Secular cantatas for various occasions

O vergnügte Stunden, da mein Herzog funden seinen Lebenstag, BWV Anh. I 194

Birthday cantata for Prince Johann August of Anhalt-Zerbst, performed on 9 August 1722. The music is lost, but the printed text has recently been rediscovered.[1] The work belongs to the serenata* type and takes the form of a dialogue between two allegorical figures, 'Gloria' and 'Fama'.

Ich bin in mir vergnügt, BWV 204

Von der Vergnügsamkeit	*On Contentedness*

NBA I/40, p. 81 BC G 45 Duration: *c.* 31 mins

1. Recitativo S bc — B♭ **c**

Ich bin in mir vergnügt, Ein andrer mache Grillen, Er wird doch nicht damit Den Sack noch Magen füllen.	I am cheerful in myself, Let someone else mope, Yet he will thereby fill Neither purse nor stomach.
Bin ich nicht reich und groß, Nur klein von Herrlichkeit, Macht doch Zufriedensein In mir erwünschte Zeit.	Though I am not rich or great And have but little grandeur, Yet contentment is created within me By the time desired.
Ich rühme nichts von mir: Ein Narr rührt seine Schellen; Ich bleibe still vor mich: Verzagte Hunde bellen.	I do not speak proudly of myself: A fool rings his own bells; I keep quiet about myself: Faint-hearted dogs bark.
Ich warte meines Tuns Und laß auf Rosen gehn, Die müßig und darbei In großem Glücke stehn.	I attend to my affairs And on a bed of roses Let the idle lie and thereby Attain great happiness.
Was meine Wollust ist, Ist, meine Lust zu zwingen;	What my pleasure is Is to subdue my desire;

[1] See B. Reul, ' "O vergnügte Stunden da mein Hertzog funden seinen Lebenstag": Ein unbekannter Textdruck zu einer Geburtstags-Kantate J. S. Bachs für den Fürsten Johann August von Anhalt-Zerbst', *BJ* 1999, 7–17 (see pp. 12–17 for a complete facsimile reproduction of the text).

Ich fürchte keine Not,
Frag nichts nach eitlen Dingen.

Der gehet nach dem Fall
In Eden wieder ein
Und kann in allem Glück
Auch irdisch selig sein.

I fear no distress,
Ask nothing of vain things.

Such a person after the Fall
Enters Eden again
And can in all fortune
Even on earth be blessed.

2. ARIA S ob I,II bc g $\frac{3}{8}$

Ruhig und in sich zufrieden
Ist der größte Schatz der Welt.
  Nichts genießet, der genießet,
  Was der Erden Kreis umschließet,
  Der ein armes Herz behält.

To be tranquil and contented within
Is the greatest treasure in the world.
  He enjoys nothing who, enjoying
  What the earth's sphere encompasses,
  Maintains a poor heart.

3. [RECITATIVO] S str bc E♭–F C

Ihr Seelen, die ihr außer euch
Stets in der Irre lauft
Und vor ein Gut, das schattenreich,
Den Reichtum des Gemüts verkauft;
Die der Begierden Macht gefangen hält:
Durchsuchet nur die ganze Welt!
Ihr suchet, was ihr nicht könnt kriegen,
Und kriegt ihrs, kanns euch nicht vergnügen;
Vergnügt es, wird es euch betrügen
Und muß zuletzt wie Staub zerfliegen.
Wer seinen Schatz bei andern hat,
Ist einem Kaufmann gleich,
Aus andrer Glücke reich.
Bei dem hat Reichtum wenig statt:
Der, wenn er nicht oft Bankerott erlebt,
Doch solchen zu erleben in steten Sorgen schwebt.
Geld, Wollust, Ehr
Sind nicht sehr
In dem Besitztum zu betrachten,
Als tugendhaft sie zu verachten,
Ist unvergleichlich mehr.

You souls who, estranged from yourselves,
Constantly run into error,
And for a possession from the realm of shades
Sell the wealth of the spirit,
You whom the might of desires holds captive:
Search the whole world over!
You seek what you cannot obtain,
And if you obtain it you cannot enjoy it;
If you enjoy it, it will deceive you
And must in the end fly away like dust.
He whose treasure lies in others
Is like a merchant,
Rich from another's fortune.
Wealth has little value for him
Who, if he does not often suffer bankruptcy,
Nonetheless hovers in constant apprehension of it.
Riches, pleasure, glory
Are not much
To contemplate in their possession;
To regard it as virtuous to despise them
Is incomparably more.

4. ARIA S vln solo bc F C

Die Schätzbarkeit der weiten Erden
Lass' meine Seele ruhig sein.
  Bei dem kehrt stets der Himmel ein,
  Der in der Armut reich kann werden.

May the values of the wide world
Leave my soul in peace.
  Heaven is ever with him
  Who can become rich in poverty.

5. Recitativo S bc — d c

Schwer ist es zwar, viel Eitles zu besitzen	It is hard indeed to possess many worthless things
Und nicht aus Liebe drauf, die strafbar, zu erhitzen;	And not to be culpably inflamed for love of them;
Doch schwerer ist es noch,	Yet it is still harder
Daß nicht Verdruß und Sorgen Zentnern gleicht,	For a burden not to bring vexation and troubles,
Eh ein Vergnügen, welches leicht	Before a pleasure that is easy
Ist zu erlangen,	To attain
Und hört es auf,	And ceases,
So wie der Welt und ihrer Schönheit Lauf,	Like the course of the world and its beauty,
So folgen Zentner Grillen drauf.	Is followed by burdensome moping.
In sich gegangen,	To commune with oneself,
In sich gesucht,	To seek within,
Und sonder des Gewissens Brand	And without the fire of conscience
Gen Himmel sein Gesicht gewandt,	Turning its face towards heaven,
Da ist mein ganz Vergnügen,	That is my entire delight,
Der Himmel wird es fügen.	Which heaven will ordain.
Die Muscheln öffnen sich, wenn Strahlen darauf schießen,	Oysters open when the sun's rays flash on them
Und zeigen dann in sich die Perlenfrucht:	And then reveal the pearls' fruit within them:
So suche nur dein Herz dem Himmel aufzuschließen,	So seek but to open your heart to heaven,
So wirst du durch sein göttlich Licht	So that through its divine Light
Ein Kleinod auch empfangen,	You too will receive a jewel
Das aller Erden Schätze nicht	Which all the earth's treasures
Vermögen zu erlangen.	Are unable to attain.

6. [Aria] S fl bc — d 12/8

Meine Seele sei vergnügt,	May my soul be contented,
Wie es Gott auch immer fügt.	However God ordains things.
Dieses Weltmeer zu ergründen,	To fathom this ocean
Ist Gefahr und Eitelkeit,	Is peril and vanity;
In sich selber muß man finden	In oneself one must find
Perlen der Zufriedenheit.	The pearls of contentment.

7. Recitativo S bc — F–B♭ c

Ein edler Mensch ist Perlenmuscheln gleich,	A noble man is like pearl-oysters:
In sich am meisten reich,	In himself most rich,
Der nichts fragt nach hohem Stande	He asks nothing of high rank
Und der Welt Ehr mannigfalt;	Or the world's manifold glory;
Hab ich gleich kein Gut im Lande,	Though I have no property in land,
Ist doch Gott mein Aufenthalt.	Yet God is my abode.

Was hilfts doch, viel Güter suchen	What is the use of seeking many possessions
Und den teuren Kot, das Geld;	And that precious filth, money?
Was ists, auf sein' Reichtum pochen:	What good is it to boast of one's wealth
Bleibt doch alles in der Welt!	If it all remains in the world?
Wer will hoch in Lüfte fliehen?	Who would fly high in the air?
Mein Sinn strebet nicht dahin;	My soul does not strive for that;
Ich will nauf im Himmel ziehen,	I would rise up to heaven:
Das ist mein Teil und Gewinn.	That is my lot and prize.
Nichtes ist, auf Freunde bauen,	It is worthless to build on friends,
Ihrer viel gehn auf ein Lot.	Many of them amount to little.
Eh wollt ich den Winden trauen	In need I would rather entrust myself to winds
Als auf Freunde in der Not.	Than to friends.
Sollte ich in Wollust leben	If I were to live in pleasure
Nur zum Dienst der Eitelkeit,	Merely in the service of vanity,
Müßt ich stets in Ängsten schweben	I would have to hover in constant anxiety
Und mir machen selbsten Leid.	And cause harm to myself.
Alles Zeitliche verdirbet,	All things temporal perish,
Der Anfang das Ende zeigt;	The beginning points to the end;
Eines lebt, das andre stirbet,	One lives, another dies
Bald den Untergang erreicht.	And soon arrives at extinction.
8. ARIA S fl str + ob I,II bc	B♭ $\frac{2}{4}$
Himmlische Vergnügsamkeit,	Heavenly Contentment,
Welches Herz sich dir ergibet,	The heart that devotes itself to you
Lebet allzeit unbetrübet	Always lives untroubled
Und genießt der güldnen Zeit,	And enjoys the Golden Age,
Himmlische Vergnügsamkeit.	Heavenly Contentment.
Göttliche Vergnügsamkeit,	Divine Contentment,
Du, du machst die Armen reich	You, you make the poor rich
Und dieselben Fürsten gleich,	And like princes;
Meine Brust bleibt dir geweiht,	My breast remains consecrated to you,
Göttliche Vergnügsamkeit.	Divine Contentment.

This work, which is also transmitted under the title *Von der Vergnügsamkeit* ('Of Contentedness') or *Der vergnügte Mensch* ('The Contented Man'), is a genuine 'cantata', being written for a single (soprano) voice. It must have been composed in 1727 or 1728, but it is not known what occasioned its origin. Perhaps it was intended only for domestic performance within Bach's circle of family and friends. The text is based on Christian Friedrich Hunold's cantata libretto *Von der Zufriedenheit*, but with striking alterations. Leaving aside unimportant discrepancies, the differences between Hunold's text and Bach's cantata libretto may be outlined as follows:

No.	*Hunold*	*Bach*
1	= no. 7, lines 1–2 ('Ein edler Mensch')	Six-strophe poem *Der vergnügte Mensch*, also by Hunold
2–6	Virtually the same in both versions	
7	—	Hunold's first movement, followed by a six-strophe poem of unknown origin
8	—	Two-strophe poem of unknown origin

On closer scrutiny the obvious assumption that Hunold himself changed his printed text into the form set by Bach for a specific occasion proves to be implausible. Hunold died as early as 1721, and a poet as familiar with the rules of poetics as he would naturally have supplied texts in the usual madrigalian* form rather than strophic poems for the recitatives nos. 1 and 7. Werner Neumann, who gave the first complete account of the background of the work, therefore conjectures, surely correctly, that the text editor should be sought in the immediate proximity of Bach, and that well-known strophic songs such as were then in wide circulation were used to enrich Hunold's text. As we have seen in connection with the cantatas for Septuagesima Sunday, contentment with the fate that befalls us, or resigning ourselves to the destiny ordained by God, is one of the favourite, recurring themes of the time. In homespun moralizing terms, partly entertaining and partly edifying, the entire text praises contentment and self-sufficiency. Discontented striving after glory and wealth is feeble and meaningless, whereas a noble man carries his treasure within him and his 'heavenly contentment' will be rewarded in heaven by God.

Bach's setting consists of a fourfold sequence of recitative-aria pairs. Since the vocal music is throughout for solo soprano, changes of instrumental scoring are the principal means of diversification, alongside as much variety of musical character as the text permits. The instrumental ensemble is made up of flute, two oboes, strings, and continuo, from which various obbligato* instruments are selected for the arias: two oboes in the first, solo violin in the second, and solo flute in the third. Only the fourth and last aria demands the full instrumental resources: the string ensemble reinforced by two oboes and by a flute which is at times accorded an independent, concertante* role. Similarly, on account of their extensive text Bach found it expedient to diversify his setting of the recitatives. The first is set as pure *secco*, the second as an *accompagnato** with strings (including a brief 'presto' interpolation at the words 'fly away like dust'), the third as *secco* with occasional coloraturas* to illustrate the text, and the fourth as *secco* leading to arioso.*

Bach took no account of the strophic textual structure of the first movement, which results in a rather stereotyped succession of single-bar phrases for each line. In the seventh movement he divides the text into two halves, setting Hunold's two lines and the first three strophes as *secco* (again with stereotyped single-bar lines) and the other three strophes as a song-like arioso whose simple, natural vocal quality suddenly unveils the character of the text as a strophic song. It is almost as though the composer regrets having proceeded till then as if confronted with a madrigalian text.

It is not only this simple song-like style that lends itself to the musical representation of a calm, consolidated state of feeling, but also a certain uniformity of motion, such as we encounter in the violin figuration of the fourth movement, and, in particular, the stylistic resource of the pedal point. As a long-held accompanying note in recitatives this occurs frequently, of course (there is an example at the very beginning of the first movement), and would thus hardly be perceived as a special device. One cannot fail to notice, however, that the arias also make repeated use of pedal-point formations and held notes. In particular, they play an essential part in the third aria, no. 6, while the first and last arias, nos. 2 and 8, each open with a pedal point broken up into repeated notes, a combination of the stylistic resources of uniform motion and pedal point:

As a component of the theme in each case this also recurs frequently in the course of these movements.

For the rest, the shaping of the arias is richly diversified. The first, no. 2, is a siciliano in which the trio of two oboes and continuo is joined by the voice as a fourth part on an equal basis. In the second aria, no. 4, the simple song-like melody of the soprano is entwined with lively violin figurations made out of broken chords, together with echo effects, which creates a more flat-surfaced impression as a contrast to the linear interplay of the first aria. The third, no. 6, is pervaded by the scale figures of the solo flute which, like the soprano, launches into extended melodic arches—presumably an image of well-balanced inward equanimity. The last aria, no. 8, is more dance-like in character and compactly chordal in texture. In the ritornellos the instruments coalesce into a single body of sound, but in the vocal passages the flute disengages itself from the rest of the instrumental ensemble (which then functions as an accompaniment) and comes to the fore in an independent counterpoint* to the voice. The bi-strophic text is repeated, resulting in the textual form a b a b. Musically, all four sections are related, particularly the first and last (which differ in text), a form that can be represented only approximately by the scheme A B C A^1 or A A^1 A^2 A, and which creates the aural impression of a rondeau-like structure.

Geschwinde, ihr wirbelnden Winde, BWV 201

Der Streit zwischen Phoebus und Pan — *The Dispute between Phoebus and Pan*

NBA I/40, p. 119 BC G 46 Duration: *c.* 54 mins

1. Chorus SSAA T I,II B I,II tr I–III timp fl I,II ob I,II str bc — D 3/8

Tutti	*Tutti*
Geschwinde,	Quick,
Ihr wirbelnden Winde,	You whirling winds,
Auf einmal zusammen zur Höhle hinein!	Into your lair together all at once!
Daß das Hin- und Widerschallen	So that the to-and-fro sound
Selbst dem Echo mag gefallen	May be pleasing even to Echo
Und den Lüften lieblich sein.	And delightful to the breezes.

2. Recitativo S B I,II bc — b–G C

Phoebus	*Phoebus*
Und du bist doch so unverschämt und frei,	And are you, then, so impudent and frank
Mir in das Angesicht zu sagen,	As to say to my face
Daß dein Gesang	That your singing
Viel herrlicher als meiner sei?	Is far more splendid than mine?
Pan	*Pan*
Wie kannst du doch so lange fragen?	How can you indeed question it so long?
Der ganze Wald bewundert meinen Klang;	The entire forest marvels at my sound;
Das Nymphenchor,	The chorus of Nymphs,
Das mein von mir erfundnes Rohr	Which my reed, invented by me,
Von sieben wohlgesetzten Stufen	Of seven well-placed pipes,
Zu tanzen öfters aufgerufen,	Has often summoned to dance,
Wird dir von selbsten zugestehn:	Will of their own accord admit to you:
Pan singt vor allen andern schön.	Pan sings more beautifully than anyone else.
Phoebus	*Phoebus*
Vor Nymphen bist du recht;	For nymphs you are right;
Allein, die Götter zu vergnügen,	However, to please the gods
Ist deine Flöte viel zu schlecht.	Your flute is far too wretched.
Pan	*Pan*
Sobald mein Ton die Luft erfüllt,	As soon as my sound fills the air
So hüpfen die Berge, so tanzet das Wild,	The hills jump, the deer dances,
So müssen sich die Zweige biegen,	The branches have to bow,

Und unter denen Sternen
Geht ein entzücktes Springen für:
Die Vögel setzen sich zu mir
Und wollen von mir singen lernen.
Momus
Ei! hört mir doch den Pan,
Den großen Meistersänger, an!

And under those stars
An enchanted leaping takes place;
The birds perch by me
And would learn singing from me.
Momus
Ah! do listen to Pan,
That great master-singer!

3. Aria S bc — G 2/4

Momus
Patron, das macht der Wind!
  Daß man prahlt und hat kein Geld,
  Daß man das für Wahrheit hält,
  Was nur in die Augen fällt,
  Daß die Toren weise sind,
  Daß das Glücke selber blind,
  Patron, das macht der Wind!

Momus
Sir, it's all hot air!
  When one boasts but has no money,
  When one holds to be true
  Whatever but meets the eye,
  Taking fools for wise men
  Or Fortune itself as blind.
  Sir, it's all hot air!

4. Recitativo A B I,II bc — e–D C

Mercurius
Was braucht ihr euch zu zanken?
Ihr weichet doch einander nicht,
Nach meinen wenigen Gedanken,
So wähle sich ein jedes einen Mann,
Der zwischen euch das Urteil spricht;

Laßt sehn, wer fällt euch ein?
Phoebus
Der Tmolus soll mein Richter sein,
Pan
Und Midas sei auf meiner Seite.
Mercurius
So tretet her, ihr lieben Leute,
Hört alles fleißig an;
Und merket, wer das Beste kann!

Mercury
Why do you need to quarrel?
You certainly won't yield to one another
In my humble opinion,
So each choose a man
Who will pronounce judgement between you;
Let's see, who comes to mind?
Phoebus
Tmolus shall be my judge,
Pan
And let Midas be on my side.
Mercury
Then come here, you dear people,
Listen carefully to everything;
And note who can do best!

5. Aria B I fl solo ob d'am solo str bc — b 3/8

Phoebus
Mit Verlangen
Drück ich deine zarten Wangen,
Holder, schöner Hyazinth.
  Und dein' Augen küss' ich gerne,
  Weil sie meine Morgensterne
  Und der Seele Sonne sind.

Phoebus
With longing
I press your tender cheeks,
Charming fair Hyacinth.
  And I love kissing your eyes,
  For they are my morning stars
  And the sun of my soul.

6. Recitativo S B II bc — D–A C

Momus
Pan, rücke deine Kehle nun
In wohlgestimmte Falten!

Momus
Pan, jerk your throat now
In well-tuned folds!

Pan
Ich will mein Bestes tun
Und mich noch herrlicher als Phoebus halten.

Pan
I will do my best
And prove myself still more splendid than Phoebus.

7. Aria B II vln I + II (+ ob d'am I?) bc — A $\frac{3}{8}$ ¢ $\frac{3}{8}$

Pan
Zu Tanze, zu Sprunge,
So wackelt das Herz.
Wenn der Ton zu mühsam klingt
Und der Mund gebunden singt,
So erweckt es keinen Scherz.

Pan
For dancing, for leaping,
Thus shakes the heart.
If the note sounds too laboured
And the mouth sings with restraint,
It arouses no mirth.

8. Recitativo A T I bc — D–f♯ **c**

Mercurius
Nunmehro Richter her!
Tmolus
Das Urteil fällt mir gar nicht schwer;
Die Wahrheit wird es selber sagen,
Daß Phoebus hier den Preis davongetragen.
Pan singet vor dem Wald,
Die Nymphen kann er wohl ergötzen.
Jedoch so schön als Phoebus' Klang erschallt,
Ist seine Flöte nicht zu schätzen.

Mercury
Now judges, here!
Tmolus
The verdict is not at all hard for me;
The truth shall speak for itself
That Phoebus has here carried off the prize.
Pan sings for the forest,
The nymphs he might well delight.
Yet with such a lovely sound as Phoebus makes
His flute is not to be compared.

9. Aria T I ob d'am I solo bc — f♯ $\frac{12}{8}$

Tmolus
Phoebus, deine Melodei
Hat die Anmut selbst geboren.
Aber wer die Kunst versteht,
Wie dein Ton verwundernd geht,
Wird dabei aus sich verloren.

Tmolus
Phoebus, your melody
Was born of charm itself.
But whoever comprehends the art
By which your sound astonishes us
Is taken out of himself by it.

10. Recitativo T II B II bc — A–G **c**

Pan
Komm, Midas, sage du nun an,
Was ich getan!
Midas
Ach Pan! wie hast du mich gestärkt,
Dein Lied hat mir so wohl geklungen,
Daß ich es mir auf einmal gleich gemerkt.
Nun geh ich hier im Grünen auf und nieder
Und lern es denen Bäumen wieder.
Der Phoebus macht es gar zu bunt,

Pan
Come, Midas, declare now
What I have done!
Midas
Ah Pan, how you have invigorated me!
Your song sounded so well to me
That I have learnt it at once.
Now I shall go up and down here in the country
And teach it to the trees.
Phoebus makes it far too florid,

Allein, dein allerliebster Mund
Sang leicht und ungezwungen.

But your most lovely mouth
Sang easily and unforced.

11. ARIA T II vln I + II bc D ¢

Midas
Pan ist Meister, laßt ihn gehn!
Phoebus hat das Spiel verloren,
Denn nach meinen beiden Ohren
Singt er unvergleichlich schön.

Midas
Pan is master, let him go!
Phoebus has lost the game,
For to my two ears
Pan's singing is incomparably fine.

12. RECITATIVO SA T I,II B I,II bc b–e c

Momus
Wie, Midas, bist du toll?
Mercurius
Wer hat dir den Verstand verrückt?
Tmolus
Das dacht ich wohl, daß du so
ungeschickt!
Phoebus
Sprich, was ich mit dir machen soll?
Verkehr ich dich in Raben,
Soll ich dich schinden oder schaben?
Midas
Ach! plaget mich doch nicht so sehre,
Es fiel mir ja
Also in mein Gehöre.
Phoebus
Sieh da,
So sollst du Esels Ohren haben!
Mercurius
Das ist der Lohn
Der tollen Ehrbegierigkeit.
Pan
Ei! warum hast du diesen Streit
Auf leichte Schultern übernommen?
Midas
Wie ist mir die Kommission
So schlecht bekommen?

Momus
What, Midas, are you mad?
Mercury
Who has deranged your mind?
Tmolus
That I knew well, that you were so
inept!
Phoebus
Tell me, what should I do with you?
Do I turn you into a raven?
Should I flay you or scratch you?
Midas
Ah, do not torment me so harshly!
It struck me so indeed
To my hearing.
Phoebus
Well then,
You shall have ass's ears!
Mercury
That is the reward
For crazy ambition.
Pan
Ah! why have you made
Light of this contest?
Midas
How in this commission
Have I fared so badly?

13. ARIA A fl I,II bc e $\frac{3}{4}$

Mercurius
Aufgeblasne Hitze,
Aber wenig Grütze
Kriegt die Schellenmütze
Endlich aufgesetzt.
Wer das Schiffen nicht versteht
Und doch an das Ruder geht,

Mercury
Inflated passion
But few wits
Gets the fool's bell-cap
Put on in the end.
Whoever does not understand
navigation
But still takes the rudder

Ertrinket mit Schaden und Schanden zuletzt.	Drowns with harm and dishonour in the end.

14. Recitativo S str bc — G–D c

Momus	*Momus*
Du guter Midas, geh nun hin	Good Midas, go hither now
Und lege dich in deinem Walde nieder,	And lie down in your forest,
Doch tröste dich in deinem Sinn,	Yet console yourself in your mind:
Du hast noch mehr dergleichen Brüder.	You have yet more brothers like yourself.
Der Unverstand und Unvernunft	Folly and unreason
Will jetzt der Weisheit Nachbar sein,	Would now be the neighbours of wisdom,
Man urteilt in den Tag hinein,	People judge at random,
Und die so tun,	And those who do so
Gehören all in deine Zunft.	All belong to your fraternity.
Ergreife, Phoebus, nun	Now, Phoebus, take up
Die Leier wieder,	Your lyre again:
Es ist nichts lieblicher als deine Lieder.	There is nothing lovelier than your songs.

15. Chorus [Scoring as in no. 1] — D $\frac{2}{4}$

Tutti	*Tutti*
Labt das Herz, ihr holden Saiten,	Refresh the heart, you lovely strings,
Stimmet Kunst und Anmut an!	Let art and charm strike up!
Laßt euch meistern, laßt euch höhnen,	Let them outdo you, let them mock you,
Sind doch euren süßen Tönen	Yet to your sweet sounds
Selbst die Götter zugetan.	The gods themselves are devoted.

In this cantata Bach takes up his own cause, fighting for the high demands made by every true art, including his own music, and campaigning against the ignorant attitude that rests content with a light diet. For this subject, to him deadly serious, he chooses the form of the comic *dramma per musica*.* It may be assumed that the work was first performed in 1729 by the student Collegium musicum in Zimmermann's coffee garden, perhaps at Bach's début as director. It would be gratifying to be able to connect the origin of the cantata with specific events; and it is true to say that attacks of the kind ridiculed here were indeed made against Bach. In the *Criticus musicus* of 1737, for example, Johann Adolph Scheibe writes of him:

> This great man would be the admiration of whole nations if he had more amenity and if he did not deprive his pieces of naturalness through a bombastic and confused substance and obscure their beauty through too much art.

On a broader front, people were shaken by an attack on music and musicians in 1749. In a school prospectus the Freiberg Rector Johann Gottlieb Biedermann sought to prove that an intensive cultivation of music was harmful to youth. This caused widespread indignation among musicians, and Bach himself directly intervened in the controversy. Both incidents took place after 1729 when the cantata was first performed, however, and at most they may be linked with revivals: there is evidence of one in the late 1730s and another (with references to Biedermann) in 1749. Moreover, since the search for plain naturalness was a general attribute of the progressive aesthetics of the day, no specific occasion was necessary. From that viewpoint Bach's art must have seemed artificial, his strict part-writing confused and his ornamental style bombastic—an attitude that began to change only gradually with the growing historical understanding of the Romantic movement.

The libretto was supplied by the fluent writer Picander, who selected for it the old Greek myth that Phoebus Apollo had been challenged to a musical contest and, as victor, had severely punished the losers. Ovid gives a later and rather different version in the *Metamorphoses*, Book XI, and since this was Picander's source it may be summarized here briefly.

On Mount Tmolus (also called 'Timolus') in Lydia, Pan shows off in front of the nymphs with the flute named after him and challenges Phoebus Apollo, inventor of the cithara, to a musical contest. Tmolus, god of the mountain, is appointed judge. First Pan plays on the flute and then Phoebus on the cithara; and everyone has to agree with Tmolus, who awards the victory to Apollo—everyone, that is, except Midas, King of Lydia, who is also present (it is he whose foolish wish that everything he touched might turn to gold had brought him to the edge of death by starvation). He alone prefers the uncouth song of Pan and is rewarded with the ears of an ass. Ovid relates further that Midas sought to conceal his ass's ears under a Phrygian cap—presumably the 'bell-cap' mentioned in the cantata. But his servant, incapable of keeping the secret to himself, confides it to a fox-hole. The reed that later grows out of the hole makes the secret public in a whisper: 'Midas has asses' ears!'

Picander and Bach do not adhere very closely to Ovid's original. Tmolus and Midas become seconds to the two contestants, Phoebus sings to flute, oboe, and strings, and Pan is accompanied by unison violins rather than flute. Moreover, two additional characters are introduced: Momus, god of satire, and Mercury. The inclusion of Mercury is surely not without special intention: as god of merchants he represented the citizens of Leipzig (he has the same function in another Bach cantata, BWV 216a), and through his mouth they too take up Phoebus's cause.

Evidently Bach's prime concern was not to give as striking and dramatic a portrayal as possible of the ancient myth but rather to hammer out the topical antagonism between 'the elaborate, restrained, serious style and that which is light and merely pleasing' (Spitta). When Midas confesses that Pan's song 'sounded so well to me that I learnt it at once', one cannot help recalling the demand for the 'semblance of familiarity' made by the Berlin school of Lieder. The topical problems involved are illustrated in Momus's recitative, no. 14. In the 1749 revival, the last three lines of this recitative read:

Verdopple, Phoebus, nun	Redouble now, Phoebus,
Musik und Lieder,	Your music and songs,
Tobt gleich Birolius und ein Hortens darwider!	Though Birolius and Hortensius rage against them!

Here we find Bach's allusion to the aforementioned dispute over the school prospectus, hostile to music, by the Freiberg rector J. G. Biedermann, alias Birolius.

Bach's setting is quite exceptionally lavish. In addition to six principal vocal parts, plus duplicate soprano and alto parts in the outer movements, it requires trumpets and drums, two flutes, two oboes, strings, and continuo. The opening chorus* at once unleashes a turbulent sound that banishes the 'whirling winds' to their lairs so that the 'to-and-fro sound' of the musical contest may be heard undisturbed. The plot is then advanced in plain *secco* recitative, while the disposition of the interspersed arias is designed to achieve a carefully balanced contrast, with movements of bucolic and lyrical character alternating throughout. The effectiveness of the arias is also enhanced by their varying instrumentation: for example, when the satirical aria of Momus, 'Patron, das macht der Wind', no. 3, accompanied by continuo only, is followed by the richly scored aria of Phoebus, 'Mit Verlangen', no. 5. For this movement Bach evidently summoned up all his art, though without making it sound in the least 'learned' in consequence. Its clearly periodic phrase structure is recognizably dance-like in origin, despite the measured tempo expressly required ('Largo'). Pan's aria 'Zu Tanze, zu Sprunge', no. 7, on the other hand, is more than just a musical joke: it is cram-full of refinements (note, for example, the imitative* continuo entry at the beginning) and was therefore well-suited to its adoption in the Peasant Cantata thirteen years later to the text 'Dein Wachstum sei feste und lache vor Lust' ('May your prosperity be secure and laugh for pleasure'). To a greater extent than Phoebus's aria, of course, it aims to make an immediate effect, not only through its popular melodic style but in its graphic illustration of the 'shaking heart'.

The aria of Tmolus, 'Phoebus, deine Melodei', no. 9, with obbligato* oboe d'amore,* corresponds in style with the singing of Phoebus. The great pains taken by Bach to achieve compelling melodic expression are here illustrated by his careful marking of the parts with performance indications, which include a rare case of a specifically notated *crescendo* (surely the only possible interpretation of the following notation):

In Midas's aria 'Pan ist Meister', no. 11, the violins are united in a common obbligato part, as they are in the aria of Pan himself. The words 'For to my two ears Pan's singing is incomparably fine' are accompanied by a tell-tale musical commentary:

It is quite obvious that a donkey's braying is imitated here in order to show what kind of ears Midas has. The passage is thus an early forerunner of Mendelssohn's *Midsummer Night's Dream* Overture.

The entire drama is finally summed up by Mercury in a dance-like aria with two obbligato flutes, 'Aufgeblasne Hitze', no. 13. The final recitative, Momus's warning against the prevailing folly, acquires special emphasis through its string accompaniment. The concluding chorus is an enthusiastic hymn to music. In the principal section of its da capo* structure, the instruments are predominant and the voices incorporated within the reprise of each instrumental passage. The bipartite middle section, on the other hand, is dominated by the choir; the flutes are independent, the trumpets silent, and the other instruments often *colla parte*.* The overall form is thus as follows:

Principal section	*Middle section*	*Principal section*
a a+choir b b+choir	c c^1	a a+choir b b+choir

Schweigt stille, plaudert nicht, BWV 211

Kaffee-Kantate *Coffee Cantata*

NBA I/40, p. 195 BC G 48 Duration: *c.* 27 mins

1. Recitativo T bc — G–D c

Schweigt stille, plaudert nicht
Und höret, was itzund geschicht:
Da kömmt Herr Schlendrian
Mit seiner Tochter Liesgen her;
Er brummt ja! wie ein Zeidelbär;
Hört selber, was sie ihm getan!

Be silent, do not chatter
And listen to what happens now:
Here comes Mr Schlendrian
With his daughter Liesgen;
How he growls, like a bear!
Hear for yourselves what she has done to him!

2. Aria B str bc — D c

Schlendrian
Hat man nicht mit seinen Kindern
Hunderttausend Hudelei!
  Was ich immer alle Tage
  Meiner Tochter Liesgen sage,
  Gehet ohne Frucht vorbei.

Schlendrian
Don't we have with our children
A hundred-thousand vexations!
  What I always say every day
  To my daughter Liesgen
  Is quite fruitless.

3. Recitativo SB bc — e–f♯ c

Schlendrian
Du böses Kind, du loses Mädchen,
Ach! wenn erlang ich meinen Zweck:
Tu mir den Coffee weg!
Liesgen
Herr Vater, seid doch nicht so scharf!
Wenn ich des Tages nicht dreimal
Mein Schälchen Coffee trinken darf,
So werd ich ja zu meiner Qual
Wie ein verdorrtes Ziegenbrätchen.

Schlendrian
You bad child, you slack girl!
Ah! when will I achieve my purpose:
To do away with coffee?
Liesgen
Father, please don't be so harsh!
If three times a day I may not drink
My cup of coffee,
To my torment I'll become
Like a dried-up roast goat!

4. Aria S fl bc — b 3/8

Liesgen
Ei! wie schmeckt der Coffee süße,
Lieblicher als tausend Küsse,
Milder als Muskatenwein.
  Coffee, Coffee muß ich haben;
  Und wenn jemand mich will laben,
  Ach, so schenkt mir Coffee ein!

Liesgen
Ah! how sweet coffee tastes,
Lovelier than a thousand kisses,
Milder than muscatel.
  Coffee! I must have coffee;
  And if anyone would refresh me,
  Ah, then pour me some coffee!

5. Recitativo SB bc — A–e c

Schlendrian
Wenn du mir nicht den Coffee läßt,
So sollst du auf kein Hochzeitfest,
Auch nicht spazierengehn.
Liesgen
Ach ja!
Nur lasset mir den Coffee da!
Schlendrian
Da hab ich nun den kleinen Affen!
Ich will dir keinen Fischbeinrock

Schlendrian
If you don't give up coffee for me,
You shall have no wedding feast,
Nor go out walking.
Liesgen
Ah, indeed!
Just leave me my coffee!
Schlendrian
(Now I'll have the little monkey!)
I will not get you a whalebone skirt

Nach itzger Weite schaffen.
Liesgen
Ich kann mich leicht darzu verstehn.
Schlendrian
Du sollst nicht an das Fenster treten
Und keinen sehn vorübergehn!
Liesgen
Auch dieses; doch seid nur gebeten
Und lasset mir den Coffee stehn!
Schlendrian
Du sollst auch nicht von meiner Hand
Ein silbern oder goldnes Band
Auf deine Haube kriegen!
Liesgen
Ja, ja! nur laßt mir mein Vergnügen!
Schlendrian
Du loses Liesgen du,
So gibst du mir denn alles zu?

Of the current width.
Liesgen
I can easily agree to that!
Schlendrian
You shall not go to the window
And see anyone passing by!
Liesgen
That too; yet I beg of you,
Let me keep my coffee!
Schlendrian
You shall not have from my hand
A silver or golden band
Upon your bonnet!
Liesgen
Yes, yes! Just leave me my pleasure!
Schlendrian
You slack Liesgen, you!
Won't you have anything from me, then?

6. ARIA B bc e C

Schlendrian
Mädchen, die von harten Sinnen,
Sind nicht leichte zu gewinnen.
Doch trifft man den rechten Ort;
O! so kömmt man glücklich fort.

Schlendrian
Girls of stubborn dispositions
Are not easy to win over.
Yet if you hit the right spot,
Oh, then you'll be lucky!

7. RECITATIVO SB bc C–D C

Schlendrian
Nun folge, was dein Vater spricht!
Liesgen
In allem, nur den Coffee nicht.
Schlendrian
Wohlan! so mußt du dich bequemen,
Auch niemals einen Mann zu nehmen.
Liesgen
Ach ja! Herr Vater, einen Mann!
Schlendrian
Ich schwöre, daß es nicht geschicht.
Liesgen
Bis ich den Coffee lassen kann?
Nun! Coffee, bleib nur immer liegen!
Herr Vater, hört, ich trinke keinen nicht.
Schlendrian
So sollst du endlich einen kriegen!

Schlendrian
Now follow what your father says!
Liesgen
In everything, only not coffee.
Schlendrian
Well then, you must put up
With never taking a husband.
Liesgen
Ah yes, father, a husband!
Schlendrian
I swear that it will not happen.
Liesgen
Till I can give up coffee?
Now, coffee, stay put for ever!
Father, listen, I shall not drink any.
Schlendrian
Then you shall get a husband in the end!

8. Aria S str bc hpschd — G $\frac{6}{8}$

Liesgen	*Liesgen*
Heute noch,	This very day,
Lieber Vater, tut es doch!	Dear father, do it please!
Ach, ein Mann!	Ah, a husband!
Wahrlich, dieser steht mir an!	Truly, this suits me well!
Wenn es sich doch balde fügte,	If only it might happen soon
Daß ich endlich vor Coffee,	That at last instead of coffee,
Eh ich noch zu Bette geh,	Before I go to bed,
Einen wackern Liebsten kriegte!	I might get a gallant lover!

9. Recitativo T bc — e c

Nun geht und sucht der alte Schlendrian,	Now old Schlendrian goes and sees
Wie er vor seine Tochter Liesgen	How for his daughter Liesgen
Bald einen Mann verschaffen kann;	He can soon provide a husband;
Doch, Liesgen streuet heimlich aus:	Yet Liesgen secretly spreads it about:
Kein Freier komm mir in das Haus,	'No suitor may come to my home
Er hab es mir denn selbst versprochen	Unless he has promised me himself,
Und rück es auch der Ehestiftung ein,	And also included it in the marriage contract,
Daß mir erlaubet möge sein,	That I may be allowed
Den Coffee, wenn ich will, zu kochen.	To make coffee whenever I want'.

10. Chorus STB fl str bc — G [¢]

Die Katze läßt das Mausen nicht,	The cat won't leave the mouse,
Die Jungfern bleiben Coffeeschwestern.	Girls remain sisters in coffee.
Die Mutter liebt den Coffeebrauch,	Mother loves the coffee habit,
Die Großmama trank solchen auch,	Grandma drank it too,
Wer will nun auf die Töchter lästern!	Who would now blame the daughters?

This libretto by Picander, which in comic style takes aim at the contemporary vogue for coffee drinking, seems to have met with a very favourable response, for it was set by at least two other composers in addition to Bach. The story is simple. Liesgen, a young town girl, will not give up her daily coffee for anything in the world. No threat from her father, who goes under the splendid name of Schlendrian ('humdrum'), is of any use. Only when he promises to find a husband for her if she gives up coffee drinking does she change her mind: 'This very day, dear father, do it please! Ah, a husband! Truly, this suits me well!' At this point Picander's libretto and the other settings of it come to an end. Bach, however, adds an account of how Liesgen has secretly made it known that no suitor may come to her home who will not grant her permission, solemnly included in the marriage contract, to drink coffee at will. This not only adds a charming twist to the little plot, it also permits the re-entry of the narrator (tenor), otherwise used only in the opening recitative, and enables the work to end with an effective terzetto finale that sums up the moral of the tale: 'The cat won't leave the mouse; girls remain sisters in coffee'. It remains unclear whether Bach himself wrote the text for these two additional movements or whether he asked his friend Picander to do so.

Bach probably composed this entertaining little work in mid-1734, by which time Picander's libretto had already been published (in 1732, in Part III of his collected verse). The music was no doubt intended to amuse the frequenters of Zimmermann's coffee house at a performance given by the Collegium musicum. The oft-voiced opinion that the character of Liesgen alludes to Bach's daughter of the same name (Elisabeth Juliana Friederica) is easily disposed of, for Elisabeth, later wife of the Bach pupil and Naumburg organist Johann Christoph Altnickol, was not born till 1726, and it is quite certain that neither as a six-year-old for the poet Picander nor as an eight-year-old for her composer-father would she have formed a suitable model.

Bach's *Coffee Cantata* surely does not belong among the principal works of the Thomascantor, any more than the 'Peasant' Cantata. Yet for their time both works exhibit a relatively modern tendency. The subject is drawn neither from gods clad in the robes of baroque princes nor from the overworked shepherds and shepherdesses but, in the *Coffee Cantata*, from among local Leipzig citizens with all their little ruses and weaknesses. Bach's music makes these people, his fellow citizens, come truly alive in a manner that almost anticipates Mozart's art of characterization. We are almost tempted to regret that Bach did not compose operas!

The recitatives play an altogether subordinate part. Invariably set as syllabically* declaimed *secco*, their function is to further the plot and to cater for the dialogue. All the more pronounced is Bach's art of differentiation as revealed in the arias. Two tenor recitatives, nos. 1 and 9, and an ensemble, no. 10, provide a framework for the real plot, which takes place in four arias for Schlendrian and Liesgen in alternation, joined together by dialogue-recitatives (nos. 2–8).

The first pair of arias introduces the two characters in turn. Schlendrian appears as an irascible father exasperated by his ill-bred daughter. The opening ritornello, in full string texture with ostinato* head-motive, presents him as a stubborn blusterer who sticks to his opinion:

He almost tumbles over with rage as he moans about the 'hundred-thousand vexations' caused by his children:

However stubbornly her father stands by his prohibition, Liesgen, gently stirred, hankers after her coffee. Whereas her father's theme strides along confidently in a firm common time, she hovers among higher things with her feet well above the ground; for the head-motive of her aria ritornello, notated in 3/8 time, in reality wavers constantly between 3/8 and 3/4, and afterwards she takes up the same theme:

In addition, the fiorituras of the obbligato* flute stress her flighty character. In the middle section there is no end to her yearning for coffee, first in ardent fourths and fifths

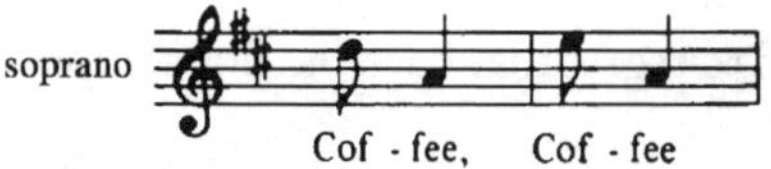

and finally in syncopated chains:

The second pair of arias brings the turning-point in the plot. Schlendrian proves to be the wiser of the two, at least at first—he knows how to make a girl change her mind. In his aria (no. 6), a continuo movement with ostinato formations, the theme, characterized by manifold chromaticism,* depicts the difficulty of the task, but also no doubt the cleverness with which Schlendrian sets about it. For her part, Liesgen is once more ardently aroused (aria, no. 8). Having been so recently in raptures about coffee, she now pines for a husband. Strings and harpsichord bass, broken up into figuration, provide a telling aural backcloth, and as in the fourth movement the thematic identity of the vocal and instrumental parts allows an effective interplay between the thematic leadership of soprano voice or instrumental ensemble, or else of both together in unison.

The terzetto-finale, accompanied by all the instruments (flute, strings, and continuo) is a bourrée whose principal section is designed in six-bar sentences, each followed by a varied repeat. The middle section, in which the voices are given the opportunity to sing at somewhat greater length, later recurs in varied form, giving rise to the overall structure A B A B[1] A.

Amore traditore, BWV 203

NBA I/41, p. 33 BC G 51 Duration: *c.* 14 mins

1. [Aria] B hpschd a $\frac{12}{8}$

Amore traditore,	Cupid, you traitor,
Tu non m'inganni più.	You deceive me no more.
Non voglio più catene,	I no longer want your chains,
Non voglio affanni, pene,	I do not want trouble, pains,
Cordoglio e servitù.	Sorrow and servitude.

2. Recitativo B hpschd C–G $\mathbf{c}$

Voglio provar,	I want to find out
Se posso sanar	If it is possible to heal
L'anima mia dalla piaga fatale,	My soul of its fatal wound
E viver si può senza il tuo strale;	And live if possible without your dart;
Non sia più la speranza	Let hope no longer be
Lusinga del dolore,	The allurement of sorrow,
E la gioja nel mio core,	And with joy in my heart
Più tuo scherzo sarà nella mia costanza.	Let my constancy no longer be your jest.

3. Aria B hpschd C $\frac{3}{4}$

Chi in amore ha nemica la sorte,	He who has adverse fortune in love
È follia, se non lascia d'amar,	Is mad if he does not stop loving;
Sprezzi l'alma le crude ritorte,	His soul should scorn its harsh ways
Se non trova mercede al penar.	If he finds no reward for his suffering.

Two cantatas with Italian texts are transmitted under Bach's name, BWV 203 and 209. Whether both works are really by Bach is doubted by many scholars, and since no autographs survive their authenticity cannot be established through source studies. On the other hand, so many Bachian characteristics are to be found within them that on stylistic grounds there is much to be said in favour of their authenticity. If those who remain doubtful ask why Bach should have set texts in Italian, of all languages, it might be rejoined that this was a fashion cultivated by other German composers (in many cases more often than by Bach) from which he would not have had the least reason to abstain. Finally, the secular solo cantata originated in Italy, and both works are 'cantatas' in this original sense of the word.

Andreas Glöckner has recently concluded from what we know of the lost principal source[2] that *Amore traditore* might have originated during Bach's period as Capellmeister at Cöthen (1717–23), where Italian chamber cantatas belonged to the regular repertoire of court entertainment music. In accordance with almost universal tradition, the text is a love poem. The unknown poet bewails the chains and painful wounds that accompany love and resolves to be ensnared by it no longer so that he may live henceforth in freedom. The scoring for solo voice and harpsichord is standard in Italian solo cantatas. The only unusual feature is the use of the harpsichord in the second aria not merely in a continuo role but as an obbligato* instrument, which admits a concertante* element into the work.

The formal structure is concise. Two arias are linked by a plain *secco* recitative of only eleven bars. The six-bar continuo ritornello that opens the first aria recurs frequently in the course of the movement, at times complete and elsewhere divided into segments. Such a consistent adherence to the stated thematic material, not only in the ritornellos but in the vocal passages too, is itself characteristic of Bach and might be taken as evidence of the work's authenticity. The second aria has a still more broadly conceived ritornello in concertante style, which is afterwards more freely treated but again recapitulated in segments on several occasions. This movement too, then, is notably unified and far from unBachian in character. Formally, both arias correspond to the standard Italian type, being cast in the conventional pure da capo* form.

Non sa che sia dolore, BWV 209

NBA I/41, p. 45 BC G 50 Duration: *c.* 24 mins

1. Sinfonia fl str bc — b 2/4
2. Recitativo S str bc — b–A C

Non sa che sia dolore	He does not know what sorrow is
Chi dall' amico suo parte e non more.	Who parts from his friend and does not die.
Il fanciullin' che plora e geme	To the little child who weeps and groans
Ed allor che più ei teme,	And then fears still more
Vien la madre a consolar.	Comes his mother to console him.
Va dunque a cenni del cielo,	Then go at the sign of heaven
Adempi or di Minerva il zelo.	And satisfy now the zeal of Minerva.

3. Aria S fl str bc — e C

Parti pur e con dolore,	Go then and, with sorrow,
Lasci' a noi dolente il core.	Leave us behind with aching hearts.
La patria goderai,	You will delight in serving your homeland,
A dover la servirai.	In doing your duty.

[2] See A. Glöckner, ' "Das kleine italienische Ding": Zu Überlieferung und Datierung der Kantate "Amore traditore" (BWV 203)', *BJ* 1996, 133–7.

Varchi or di sponda in sponda,
Propizi vedi il vento e l'onda.

Now you are crossing from shore to shore,
May you see propitious winds and waves.

4. Recitativo S bc — b–e C

Tuo saver al tempo e l'età contrasta,
Virtù e valor solo a vincer basta.
Ma chi gran ti farà più che non fusti?
Ansbaca, piena di tanti augusti.

Your knowledge contrasts with time and age;
Virtue and valour alone are enough to conquer.
But who will make you greater than you were?
Ansbach, full of so many great men.

5. Aria S fl str bc — G $\frac{3}{8}$

Rigetti[3] gramezza e pavento,
Qual nocchier, placato il vento,

Più non teme o si scolora,
Ma contento in su la prora
Va cantando in faccia al mar.

Reject anxiety and dread,
Like the steersman when the wind drops:

He no longer fears or turns pale,
But is content with his prow
And goes singing in the face of the sea.

The authenticity of this work, like that of the cantata just discussed, has often been questioned. Due to its more extended and ambitious structure, more substantial grounds for and against Bach's authorship can be adduced, though so far without being able to reach a definite conclusion. The unresolved questions begin with the text, which is written in Italian at times poor enough to be incomprehensible. Luigi Ansbacher[4] has conjectured that a text editor largely unfamiliar with Italian altered the original wording to render it suitable for the intended occasion. The very beginning points to this conclusion: 'He does not know what sorrow is who parts from his friend and does not die'. This seems greatly exaggerated, even for the pathos-laden baroque era, and our suspicion is aroused that in the original it was a much crueller fate that led the singer to the borders of death—perhaps (to name a favourite theme of the time) the irretrievable loss of the beloved. Ansbacher's conclusion has since been confirmed by the discovery of certain sources of the text. The first two lines of the recitative no. 2 are evidently drawn from the poem *Partita dolorosa* by Giovanni Battista Guarini (1538–1612; published in *Rime*, Venice, 1598); the last two lines of the aria no. 3 from the opera *Galatea* (Naples, 1722) by Pietro Metastasio (1698–1782); and all but the first line of the aria no. 5 from Metastasio's *Semiramide riconosciuta* of

[3] The source reads 'ricetti', but the emendation 'rigetti' was suggested by Luigi Ansbacher, 'Sulla cantata profana N. 209 "Non sa che sia dolore" di G. S. Bach: Bach librettista italiano?', *Rivista musicale italiana* 51 (1949), 98–116; reprinted in K. Matthaei, ed., *Bach-Gedenkschrift 1950* (Zurich, 1950), 163–77.

[4] 'Sulla cantata profana N. 209 "Non sa che sia dolore" '.

1728/9.[5] This last quotation, incidentally, provides a *terminus post quem* for the cantata libretto: it cannot have originated before Vinci's Roman and Porpora's Venetian settings of *Semiramide* for the carnival of 1729.

From the text we learn that the traveller is a scholar returning to his homeland in order to serve it. Wind and waves might be favourable for his journey (taken literally, this must apply to travel by sea). His knowledge is exceptional for his age (he is thus still young) and he seems to have active patrons in Ansbach. According to Ansbacher, this could point to Johann Matthias Gesner (1691–1761), who in 1729 left Weimar to return to his native Ansbach as Rector of the Gymnasium. We know that Gesner, as Rector of the Thomasschule in Leipzig (1730–4), later came to value Bach highly, and it is quite possible that they were already acquainted from as early as Bach's Weimar years (1708–17). But the libretto will not altogether correspond with the facts. Even if 'wind and waves' might count only as a metaphorical image for a journey by land, and even though we might try to account for the improbability of Gesner's friends organizing his farewell music in Leipzig by adducing an old friendship with Bach (of which there is no evidence), we are still left with the problem of his age. Does one still say of a thirty-eight-year-old that his knowledge is in advance of his years? In a recent study[6] Klaus Hofmann has proposed that the dedicatee of the cantata might be Lorenz Christoph Mizler (1711–78), who in many respects conforms better with the description in the text. Bach's cantata might then have originated in 1734. But it may well be impossible to reach final certainty in the matter.

The work begins with a concerto movement for solo flute, strings, and continuo, which casts no doubt at all on Bach's authorship, being altogether in the style of his B minor Suite for the same combination, BWV 1067. Characteristic both of this movement and of Bach in general is the dominating role of the opening motive (bars 1–2), which turns up again and again in the course of the movement, not only in tutti ritornellos but as an accompanying interjection for the strings against the solo figuration of the flute. A brief recitative accompanied by strings, no. 2, then tells of the wrench caused by the departure of Minerva's disciple.

Both of the arias make use of the entire instrumental ensemble, and in both cases the concertante* flute takes precedence over the string tutti. In the first aria, no. 3, the initial motive plays a dominant role, as in the sinfonia, but here it is more tender in accordance with the plaintive character of the text.

[5] The first quotation was pointed out by Klaus Hofmann, 'Alte und neue Überlegungen zu der Kantate "Non sa che sia dolore" BWV 209', *BJ* 1990, 7–25 (see p. 14), the second by Wolfgang Osthoff in W. Osthoff and R. Wiesend, eds, *Bach und die italienische Musik* (Venice, 1987), 17 f., and the third by Reinhard Strohm, 'Bemerkungen zu Vivaldi und der Oper seiner Zeit', *Vivaldi-Studien* [conference report] (Dresden, 1981), 81–99 (see p. 84, note 4).

[6] 'Alte und neue Überlegungen zu der Kantate "Non sa che sia dolore", BWV 209'.

Incidentally, this arouses the suspicion that, as in so many other Bach cantatas, the sinfonia might have been borrowed from an existing concerto, since it shows no direct correspondence with the affect* of the cantata. In the principal section of the aria, the soprano, accompanied by wide-ranging semiquaver passages on the flute, sings of the grief of those who are left behind. The middle section, on the other hand, strikes a more cheerful note, dealing with the joy of the scholar's homeland over his return.

A brief *secco* recitative, no. 4, this time accompanied by continuo only, forms a transition to the dance-like concluding aria, no. 5, which seeks to banish grief. It exhibits some decidedly 'modern', Italianate features and of all the movements gives most scope for doubts over authenticity. Polyphony* here yields to a more homophonic* texture, and the harmony is *galant* and full of sentiment. Nevertheless, the movement is a masterpiece of its kind and forms a worthy conclusion to a cantata which, though perhaps not very profound, is nonetheless exceedingly charming and rich in inspiration.

Appendix: doubtful and spurious cantatas

A New Year cantata, *Ihr wallenden Wolken*, BWV Anh. I 197, is entered under Bach's name in the estate catalogue of the Göttingen music scholar Johann Nikolaus Forkel (Göttingen, 1819). It is no longer extant, and its authenticity and specific purpose (church cantata? homage music?) cannot be established without knowledge of further details.

The following cantatas have been excluded from consideration here on the grounds that they are spurious (for a reference to the evidence that led to this conclusion, see the literature column; in the era of modern scholarship BWV 217–22 have never been seriously considered as works by Bach):

BWV	*Title*	*Composer*	*Literature*
15	Denn du wirst meine Seele	J. L. Bach	Scheide I
53	Schlage doch, gewünschte Stunde	G. M. Hoffmann?	Dürr St 2, p. 58[7]
141	Das ist je gewißlich wahr	G. P. Telemann	*BJ* 1951–2, pp. 31–5
142	Uns ist ein Kind geboren	?	Dürr St 2, pp. 57 f.
160	Ich weiß, daß mein Erlöser lebt	G. P. Telemann	*BJ* 1951–2, p. 35
189	Meine Seele rühmt und preist	G. M. Hoffmann?	*BJ* 1956, p. 155
217	Gedenke, Herr, wie es uns gehet	J. C. Altnickol	Preface, Carus-Verlag (Stuttgart, 1999)
218	Gott der Hoffnung erfülle euch	G. P. Telemann	*BJ* 1951–2, pp. 38 f.
219	Siehe, es hat überwunden der Löwe	G. P. Telemann	*BJ* 1951–2, pp. 39 f.
220	Lobt ihn mit Herz und Munde	?	KB, NBA I/41, p. 125
221	Wer sucht die Pracht, wer wünscht	?	KB, NBA I/41, p. 126
222	Mein Odem ist schwach	J. E. Bach	KB, NBA I/41, p. 127
224	Reißt euch los, bekränkte Sinnen	C. P. E. Bach?	*BJ* 1993, pp. 137–9

[7] See also *BJ* 1955, p. 15, note 9.

Bibliography

The essential resources for the study of Bach's cantatas are as follows (for full details, see the list of abbreviations, pp. xiv–xvi, where applicable, or else the alphabetical entries in this bibliography):

Neue Bach-Ausgabe (NBA): the modern collected edition of Bach's works; comprehensive information about their sources is given in the accompanying *Kritischer Berichte* (Critical Reports)

Bach-Werke-Verzeichnis (BWV): Wolfgang Schmieder's thematic catalogue of the works of Bach

Bach Compendium (BC): a more recent thematic catalogue by Hans-Joachim Schulze and Christoph Wolff

Bach-Jahrbuch (*BJ*): an annual periodical devoted to Bach studies

Bach-Dokumente (Dok I–III): the complete documents relating to Bach's life and work

The New Bach Reader (NBR): the chief documents relating to Bach's life and work in English translation

Sämtliche von J. S. Bach vertonte Texte (BT): Werner Neumann's complete edition of the vocal texts set by Bach, with facsimiles

Handbuch der Kantaten J. S. Bachs: Werner Neumann's standard reference book on the Bach cantatas

Studien über die frühen Kantaten J. S. Bachs (Dürr St 2): Alfred Dürr's chronological study of the pre-Weimar and Weimar cantatas

Zur Chronologie der Leipziger Vokalwerke J. S. Bachs (Dürr Chr 2): Alfred Dürr's chronological study of the Leipzig vocal works

The World of the Bach Cantatas, ed. C. Wolff: essays by various Bach scholars on all aspects of the cantatas and their background. Only Vol. 1 has so far appeared in English translation (*J. S. Bach's Early Sacred Cantatas*, New York, 1997); Vols 2 and 3, devoted to the secular cantatas and the Leipzig church cantatas respectively, are available in German (Stuttgart, 1997 and 1999)

www.bach-cantatas.com: website listing recordings with critical discussion, texts and translations, notes on the Lutheran church year, availability of scores, and much else.

Bach biography: the best modern biographies in English are W. Emery, C. Wolff et al., *The New Grove Bach Family* (London, 1983); M. Boyd, *The Master Musicians: Bach* (London, 1983; 2nd edn Oxford, 1995); and C. Wolff, *J. S. Bach: the Learned Musician* (Oxford and New York, 2000)

Bach bibliography: for literature up to 1980 inclusive, see C. Wolff, ed., *Bach-Bibliographie* (Kassel, 1985); for 1981–5, R. Nestle, 'Das Bachschrifttum', *BJ* 1989, 107–89; for 1986–90, R. Nestle, 'Das Bachschrifttum', *BJ* 1994, 75–162; and for 1991–5, K. Germerdonk, 'Das Bach-Schrifttum 1991 bis 1995', *BJ* 2000, 193–299

Bach dictionary: see M. Boyd, ed., *Oxford Composer Companions: J. S. Bach* (Oxford, 1999), a comprehensive A–Z covering every aspect of Bach's life and work

Introduction to Bach Studies by D. R. Melamed and M. Marissen (New York and Oxford, 1998)

Facsimiles of the autographs: for a full list, see Y. Kobayashi, *Die Notenschrift J. S. Bachs*, NBA IX/2, 217–20

Details of the original performing parts: for a full list, see L. Dreyfus, *Bach's Continuo Group* (Cambridge, MA, 1987), Appendix A

The following list of literature relating to the Bach cantatas is not exhaustive, but it aims to include most items of importance that have appeared up to 2000 (the 250th anniversary of the composer's death and celebrated worldwide in numerous festivals under the heading 'Bach Year 2000'). In the case of conference reports or collected essays in which most or all of the contents are relevant, only the overall title is given (e.g. W. Blankenburg and R. Steiger, eds, *Theologische Bach-Studien* I); for full details the reader should consult the contents page of the book concerned. Detailed information on the literature relating to each individual cantata may be found in BWV or BC.

In the case of publications before 1957 (and a few later publications, such as those of Paul Mies or W. Gillies Whittaker) it should be noted that their chronological information is out of date. Yet these writings are of lasting value, even though one has to ignore their chronological statements and heed only their descriptions of the cantatas. This applies not only to the writings about the cantatas and their background published by Arnold Schering, Friedrich Smend, or Woldemar Voigt, but also to the passages in which Philipp Spitta discusses the cantatas in his Bach biography.

Agricola, Johann Friedrich and Bach, Carl Philipp Emanuel: Bach obituary, pub. in L. C. Mizler, *Neu eröffnete musikalische Bibliothek* IV/1 (Leipzig, 1754), 158–76; reproduced in Dok III, No. 666; Eng. trans. in NBR, No. 306

Ambrose, Z. Philip: ' "Weinen, Klagen, Sorgen, Zagen" [BWV 12] und die antike Redekunst', *BJ* 1980, 35–45

——ed., *Texte zu den Kirchenkantaten von J. S. Bach, The Texts to J. S. Bach's Church Cantatas* (Neuhausen-Stuttgart, 1984) [the complete librettos in German–English parallel text]

Ansbacher, Luigi: 'Sulla cantata profana N. 209 "Non sa che sia dolore" di G. S. Bach: Bach librettista italiano?', *Rivista musicale italiana* 51 (1949), 98–116; reprinted in K. Matthaei, ed., *Bach-Gedenkschrift 1950* (Zurich, 1950), 163–77

Axmacher, Elke: 'Die Texte zu J. S. Bachs Choralkantaten', in W. Rehm, ed., *Bachiana et alia musicologica: Festschrift Alfred Dürr zum 65. Geburtstag* (Kassel, 1983), 3–16

——'Erdmann Neumeister: ein Kantatendichter J. S. Bachs', *Musik und Kirche* 60 (1990), 294–302

Bach, Carl Philipp Emanuel: see under Agricola

Beißwenger, Kirsten: *J. S. Bachs Notenbibliothek*, diss., Univ. of Göttingen, 1991 (Kassel, 1992)

——and Wolf, Uwe: 'Tromba, Tromba da tirarsi oder Corno? Zur Clarinostimme der Kantate "Ein ungefärbt Gemüte" BWV 24', *BJ* 1993, 91–101

Bertling, Rebekka: *Das Arioso und das ariose Accompagnato im Vokalwerk J. S. Bachs* (Frankfurt, 1992); also in *Musik und Kirche* 62 (1992), 327–34

Bischoff, Bodo and Siebert, Ulrich: 'Zum Rezitativ Nr. 2 aus der Kantate "Ihr Menschen, rühmet Gottes Liebe" BWV 167 von J. S. Bach: Versuch einer Analyse', *Bach-Studien* 10 (Leipzig, 1991), 137–54

Blankenburg, Walter: 'Bach geistlich und weltlich', *Musik und Kirche* 20 (1950), 36–46

—— 'Das Parodieverfahren im Weihnachtsoratorium J. S. Bachs', *Musik und Kirche* 32 (1962), 245–54

—— 'Die Bedeutung der solistischen Alt-Partien im Weihnachts-Oratorium J. S. Bachs, BWV 248', in R. L. Marshall, ed., *Studies in Renaissance and Baroque Music in Honour of Arthur Mendel* (Kassel and Hackensack, NJ, 1974), 139–48

—— 'Zur Geschichte des Kirchenkonzerts', *Musik und Kirche* 44 (1974), 165–75

—— 'Eine neue Textquelle zu sieben Kantaten J. S. Bachs und achtzehn Kantaten Johann Ludwig Bachs', *BJ* 1977, 7–25 [concerns BWV 17, 39, 43, 45, 88, 102, and 187]

—— 'Die Bachforschung seit etwa 1965: Ergebnisse, Probleme, Aufgaben', *Acta musicologica* 50 (1978), 93–154; 54 (1982), 162–207; 55 (1983), 1–58

—— *Kirche und Musik: gesammelte Aufsätze zur Geschichte der gottesdienstlichen Musik* (Göttingen, 1979)

—— 'Tendenzen der Bachforschung seit den 1960er Jahren, insbesondere im Bereich der geistlichen Vokalmusik', in R. Brinkmann, ed., *Bachforschung und Bachinterpretation heute* [conference report, Marburg, 1978] (Kassel, 1981), 86–93

—— *Das Weihnachts-Oratorium von J. S. Bach* (Munich and Kassel, 1982)

—— 'Theologische Bachforschung heute', *Augsburger Jahrbuch für Musikwissenschaft* 2 (1985), 91–106

—— and Steiger, Renate, eds, *Theologische Bach-Studien* I (Neuhausen-Stuttgart, 1987)

Blume, Friedrich: *Die evangelische Kirchenmusik* (Potsdam, 1931); 2nd rev. edn as *Geschichte der evangelischen Kirchenmusik* (Kassel, 1965); Eng. trans. as *Protestant Church Music: a History* (New York, 1974)

—— 'Umrisse eines neuen Bach-Bildes', *Musica* 16 (1962), 169–76; Eng. trans. as 'Outlines of a New Picture of Bach', *Music & Letters* 44 (1963), 214–27, reprinted in W. Hays, ed., *Twentieth-century Views of Music History* (New York, 1972), 225–38

Bolin, Norbert: *Sterben ist mein Gewinn: Ein Beitrag zur evangelischen Funeralkomposition der deutschen Sepulkralkultur des Barock 1550–1750* (Kassel, 1989)

Boyd, Malcolm: *The Master Musicians: Bach* (London, 1983; 2nd edn Oxford, 1995)

—— ed., *Oxford Composer Companions: J. S. Bach* (Oxford, 1999)

Brainard, Paul: 'Bach's Parody Procedure and the St Matthew Passion', *Journal of the American Musicological Society* 22 (1969), 241–60 [concerns BWV 244a]

—— 'Cantata 21 Revisited', in R. L. Marshall, ed., *Studies in Renaissance and Baroque Music in Honour of Arthur Mendel* (Kassel and Hackensack, NJ, 1974), 231–42

—— 'Über Fehler und Korrekturen der Textunterlage in den Vokalwerken J. S. Bachs', *BJ* 1978, 113–39

—— 'Textvertonungsrücksichten als bestimmendes Element des Bachschen Kompositionsverfahrens', in R. Brinkmann, ed., *Bachforschung und Bachinterpretation heute* [conference report, Marburg, 1978] (Kassel, 1981), 152

—— 'The Aria and its Ritornello: the Question of "Dominance" in Bach', in W. Rehm, ed., *Bachiana et alia musicologica: Festschrift Alfred Dürr zum 65. Geburtstag* (Kassel, 1983), 39–51

——'Aria and Ritornello: New Aspects of the Comparison Handel/Bach', in P. Williams, ed., *Bach, Handel, Scarlatti: Tercentenary Essays* (Cambridge, 1985), 21–33

——'The Regulative and Generative Roles of Verse in Bach's "Thematic" Invention', in D. O. Franklin, ed., *Bach Studies* (Cambridge, 1989), 54–74

——'The "Non-quoting" Ritornello in Bach's Arias', in P. Brainard and R. Robinson, eds, *A Bach Tribute: Essays in Honour of William H. Scheide* (Kassel and Chapel Hill, NC, 1993), 27–44

Brandt, Konrad: 'Fragen zur Fagottbesetzung in den kirchenmusikalischen Werken J. S. Bachs', *BJ* 1968, 65–79

Breig, Werner: 'Bemerkungen zur zyklischen Symmetrie in Bachs Leipziger Kirchenmusik', *Musik und Kirche* 53 (1983), 173–9

——'Das Finalproblem in Bachs frühen Leipziger Kirchenkantaten', in G. Allrogen and D. Altenburg, eds, *Festschrift Arno Forchert zum 60. Geburtstag* (Kassel, 1986), 96–107

——'Grundzüge einer Geschichte von Bachs vierstimmigen Choralsatz', *Archiv für Musikwissenschaft* 45 (1988), 165–85 and 300–19

——'Der Schlußchoral von Bachs Kantate "Ein feste Burg ist unser Gott" (BWV 80) und seine Vorgeschichte', in M. Just and R. Wiesend, eds, *Liedstudien: Wolfgang Osthoff zum 60. Geburtstag* (Tutzing, 1989), 171–84

Brusniak, F. and Steiger, R., eds: *Hof- und Kirchenmusik in der Barockzeit: Hymnologische, theologische und musikgeschichtliche Aspekte* (Sinzig, 1999)

Buelow, George J.: 'Expressivity in the Accompanied Recitatives of Bach's Cantatas', in D. O. Franklin, ed., *Bach Studies* (Cambridge, 1989), 18–35

Butler, Gregory G.: 'J. S. Bachs Gloria in excelsis Deo BWV 191: Musik für ein Leipziger Dankfest', *BJ* 1992, 65–71

Chafe, Eric: 'Luther's "Analogy of Faith" in Bach's Church Music', *Dialogue* 24 (1985), 96–101

——*Tonal Allegory in the Vocal Music of J. S. Bach* (Berkeley, 1991)

——'Bach's First Two Leipzig Cantatas: a Message for the Community', in P. Brainard and R. Robinson, eds, *A Bach Tribute: Essays in Honour of William H. Scheide* (Kassel and Chapel Hill, NC, 1993), 71–86 [concerns BWV 75 and 76]

——'*Anfang und Ende*: Recurrence in Bach's Cantata *Jesu, nun sei gepreiset*, BWV 41', in R. Stinson, ed., *Bach Perspectives* I (Lincoln, Nebraska, 1995), 103–34

——*Analyzing Bach Cantatas* (Oxford and New York, 2000)

Clement, A. A., ed.: *Das Blut Jesu und die Lehre von der Versöhnung im Werk J. S. Bachs* (Amsterdam, 1995)

Cowdery, William W.: 'The Early Vocal Works of J. S. Bach: Studies in Style, Scoring and Chronology', diss., Cornell Univ., 1989

Crist, Stephen A.: 'Bach's Debut at Leipzig: Observations on the Genesis of Cantatas 75 and 76', *Early Music* 13 (1985), 212–26

——'Aria Forms in the Vocal Works of J. S. Bach, 1714–24', diss., Brandeis Univ., 1988

——'Aria Forms in the Cantatas from Bach's first Leipzig *Jahrgang*', in D. O. Franklin, ed., *Bach Studies* (Cambridge, 1989), 36–53

——'The Question of Parody in Bach's Cantata *Preise dein Glücke, gesegnetes Sachsen*, BWV 215', in R. Stinson, ed., *Bach Perspectives* I (Lincoln, Nebraska, 1995), 135–61

——'J. S. Bach and the Conventions of the Da Capo Aria, or How Original was Bach?', in P. F. Devine and H. White, eds, *The Maynooth International Musicological Conference 1995: Selected Proceedings* I (Dublin, 1996), 71–85

——'Bach, Theology and Harmony: a New Look at the Arias', *Bach* 27 (1996), 1–30

Dadelsen, Georg von: *Beiträge zur Chronologie der Werke J. S. Bachs*, Tübinger Bach-Studien 4/5 (Trossingen, 1958)

——'Anmerkungen zu Bachs Parodieverfahren', in W. Rehm, ed., *Bachiana et alia musicologica: Festschrift Alfred Dürr zum 65. Geburtstag* (Kassel, 1983), 52–7

——'Bachs Kantate 77', in G. von Dadelsen, *Über Bach und anderes: Aufsätze und Vorträge 1957–82* (Laaber, 1983), 185–93

——'Herkules an der Elbe: Mythologie und Allegorie in Bachs weltlichen Kantaten', in G. von Dadelsen, *Über Bach und anderes: Aufsätze und Vorträge 1957–82* (Laaber, 1983), 212–21

Darmstadt, Gerhart: 'Kurz oder lang? Zur Rezitativbegleitung im 18. Jahrhundert', *Musik und Kirche* 50 (1980)

Daw, Stephen: *The Music of J. S. Bach: the Choral Works* (Rutherford, NJ, 1981)

Day, James: *The Literary Background to Bach's Cantatas* (London, 1961)

Dibelius, Martin: 'Individualismus und Gemeindebewußtsein in Joh. Seb. Bachs Passionen', *Archiv für Reformationsgeschichte* 41 (1948), 132–54; repr. in M. Dibelius, *Botschaft und Geschichte* I (Tübingen, 1953), 359–80

Donington, Robert: '*Amore traditore*: a Problem Cantata', in H. C. Robbins Landon and R. E. Chapman, eds, *Studies in Eighteenth-century Music: a Tribute to Karl Geiringer on his Seventieth Birthday* (London, 1970), 160–76

Dreger, Carl O.: 'Die Vokalthematik J. S. Bachs: dargestellt an den Arien der Kirchenkantaten', *BJ* 1934, 1–62

Dreyfus, Laurence: 'J. S. Bach's Experiment in Differentiated Accompaniment: Tacet Indications in Organ Parts to the Vocal Works', *Journal of the American Musicological Society* 32 (1979), 321–34

——'Zur Frage der Cembalo-Mitwirkung in den geistlichen Werken Bachs', in R. Brinkmann, ed., *Bachforschung und Bachinterpretation heute* [conference report, Marburg, 1978] (Kassel, 1981), 178–84

——'The Metaphorical Soloist: Concerted Organ Parts in Bach's Cantatas', *Early Music* 13 (1985), 237–47

——*Bach's Continuo Group: Players and Practices in his Vocal Works* (Cambridge, MA, 1987)

Drinker, Henry S.: *Texts of the Choral Works of J. S. Bach in English Translation*, 4 vols (New York, 1942–3)

Drüner, Ulrich: 'Violoncello piccolo und Viola pomposa bei J. S. Bach: zu Fragen von Identität und Spielweise dieser Instrumente', *BJ* 1987, 85–112

Dürr, Alfred: 'Zur Aufführungspraxis der Vor-Leipziger Kirchenkantaten J. S. Bachs', *Musik und Kirche* 20 (1950), 54–64

——'Über Kantatenformen in den geistlichen Dichtungen Salomon Francks', *Die*

Musikforschung 3 (1950), 18–26; repr. in A. Dürr, *Im Mittelpunkt Bach: Ausgewählte Aufsätze und Vorträge* (Kassel, 1988), 15–21

——*Studien über die frühen Kantaten J. S. Bachs* (Leipzig, 1951; 2nd rev. edn Wiesbaden, 1977)

——'Zur Echtheit einiger Bach zugeschriebener Kantaten', *BJ* 1951–2, 30–46; repr. in A. Dürr, *Im Mittelpunkt Bach: Ausgewählte Aufsätze und Vorträge* (Kassel, 1988), 22–34

——'Gedanken zu J. S. Bachs Umarbeitungen eigener Werke', *BJ* 1956, 93–104

——'Zur Echtheit der Kantate "Meine Seele rühmt und preist" (BWV 189)', *BJ* 1956, 155; repr. in A. Dürr, *Im Mittelpunkt Bach: Ausgewählte Aufsätze und Vorträge* (Kassel, 1988), 35

——'Zur Chronologie der Leipziger Vokalwerke J. S. Bachs', *BJ* 1957, 5–162; 2nd rev. edn Kassel, 1976

——'J. S. Bachs Kirchenmusik in seiner Zeit und heute', *Musik und Kirche* 27 (1957), 65–74; repr. in A. Dürr, *Im Mittelpunkt Bach: Ausgewählte Aufsätze und Vorträge* (Kassel, 1988), 62–9

——' "Ich bin ein Pilgrim auf der Welt" [BWV Anh. I 190]: eine verschollene Kantate J. S. Bachs', *Die Musikforschung* 11 (1958), 422–7; repr. in A. Dürr, *Im Mittelpunkt Bach: Ausgewählte Aufsätze und Vorträge* (Kassel, 1988), 70–5

——'Verstümmelt überlieferte Arien aus Kantaten J. S. Bachs', *BJ* 1960, 28–42; repr. in A. Dürr, *Im Mittelpunkt Bach: Ausgewählte Aufsätze und Vorträge* (Kassel, 1988), 76–86

——'Wieviele Kantatenjahrgänge hat Bach komponiert? Eine Entgegnung', *Die Musikforschung* 14 (1961), 192–5

——'Der Eingangssatz zu Bachs Himmelfahrts-Oratorium und seine Vorlage', in W. Brennecke and H. Haase, eds, *Hans Albrecht in Memoriam* (Kassel, 1962), 121–6; repr. in A. Dürr, *Im Mittelpunkt Bach: Ausgewählte Aufsätze und Vorträge* (Kassel, 1988), 109–14

——'Bachs Trauer Ode und Markus Passion', *Neue Zeitschrift für Musik* 74 (1963), 460–6; repr. in A. Dürr, *Im Mittelpunkt Bach: Ausgewählte Aufsätze und Vorträge* (Kassel, 1988), 115–25

——*J. S. Bach: Weihnachts-Oratorium BWV 248* (Munich, 1967)

——'Bach's Chorale Cantatas', in J. Riedel, ed., *Cantors at the Crossroads: Essays on Church Music in Honour of Walter E. Buszin* (St Louis, MO, 1967), 111–20; Ger. version as 'Gedanken zu Bachs Choralkantaten' in W. Blankenburg, ed., *Johann Sebastian Bach* (Darmstadt, 1970), 507–17; repr. in A. Dürr, *Im Mittelpunkt Bach: Ausgewählte Aufsätze und Vorträge* (Kassel, 1988), 126–32

——'Zur Entstehungsgeschichte des Bachschen Choralkantaten-Jahrgangs', in M. Geck, ed., *Bach-Interpretationen* (Göttingen, 1969), 7–11, 207–8

——'Zur Textvorlage der Choralkantaten J. S. Bachs', in W. Blankenburg et al., eds, *Kerygma und Melos: Christhard Mahrenholz 70 Jahre* (Kassel and Hamburg, 1970), 222–36; repr. in A. Dürr, *Im Mittelpunkt Bach: Ausgewählte Aufsätze und Vorträge* (Kassel, 1988), 133–45

——'Gibt es einen Spätstil im Kantatenschaffen J. S. Bachs?', lecture, 1973; often repr., most recently in A. Dürr, *Im Mittelpunkt Bach: Ausgewählte Aufsätze und Vorträge* (Kassel, 1988), 146–57

——'Bachs Kantatentexte: Probleme und Aufgaben der Forschung', *Bach-Studien* 5 (Leipzig, 1975), 49–61; repr. in A. Dürr, *Im Mittelpunkt Bach: Ausgewählte Aufsätze und Vorträge* (Kassel, 1988), 167–77

——'Bemerkungen zu Bachs Leipziger Kantatenaufführungen', in conference report, Leipzig, 1975 (Leipzig, 1977), 165–72; repr. in A. Dürr, *Im Mittelpunkt Bach: Ausgewählte Aufsätze und Vorträge* (Kassel, 1988), 192–7

——'Zur Problematik der Bach-Kantate BWV 143 "Lobe den Herrn, meine Seele" ', *Die Musikforschung* 30 (1977), 299–304

——'Zur Bach-Kantate "Hält im Gedächtnis Jesum Christ" BWV 67', *Musik und Kirche* 53 (1983), 74–7; repr. in A. Dürr, *Im Mittelpunkt Bach: Ausgewählte Aufsätze und Vorträge* (Kassel, 1988), 244–7

——'Neue Erkenntnisse zur Kantate BWV 31', *BJ* 1985, 155–9

——'Zum Eingangssatz der Kantate BWV 119', *BJ* 1986, 117–20

——' "Entfernet euch, ihr kalten Herzen": Möglichkeit und Grenzen der Rekonstruktion einer Bach-Arie', *Die Musikforschung* 39 (1986), 32–6 [concerns BWV 11/4 and Anh. I 196/3]

——'Noch einmal: wo blieb Bachs fünfter Kantatenjahrgang?', *BJ* 1986, 121–2

——'Die Bach-Kantate aus heutiger Sicht', *Studia musicologica norvegica* 12 (1986), 7–23; repr. in A. Dürr, *Im Mittelpunkt Bach: Ausgewählte Aufsätze und Vorträge* (Kassel, 1988), 248–59

——'Gedanken zum Partiturautograph von J. S. Bachs Kantate "O Ewigkeit, du Donnerwort" (BWV 20)', in F. Meyer et al., eds, *Komponisten des 20. Jahrhunderts in der Paul Sacher Stiftung* (Basle, 1986), 20–30

——'Merkwürdiges in den Quellen zu Weimarer Kantaten Bachs', *BJ* 1987, 151–7

——'Gedanken zu den späten Kantaten Bachs', in C. Wolff, ed., *J. S. Bachs Spätwerk und dessen Umfeld* [conference report, Duisburg, 1986] (Kassel, 1988), 58–63

——'Zum Choralchorsatz "Herr Jesu Christ, wahr' Mensch und Gott" BWV 127 (Satz 1) und seine Umarbeitung', *BJ* 1988, 205–9

——'Philologisches zum Problem Violoncello piccolo bei Bach', in D. Berke and H. Heckmann, eds, *Festschrift W. Rehm zum 60. Geburtstag* (Kassel, 1989), 45–50

——'Zur Textbeziehung der Arienritornelle bei Bach', *Beiträge zur Bach-Forschung* 9–10 (1991), 34–43

——'Zur Parodiefrage in Bachs h-moll-Messe: Eine Bestandsaufnahme, *Die Musikforschung* 45 (1992), 117–38

——'Zu J. S. Bachs Hallenser Probestück von 1713', *BJ* 1995, 183–4

Ehrmann, Sabine: 'J. S. Bachs Leipziger Textdichterin Christiane Mariane von Ziegler', *Beiträge zur Bach-Forschung* 9–10 (1991), 261–8

Eller, Rudolf: 'Gedanken über Bachs Leipziger Schaffensjahre', *Bach-Studien* 5 (Leipzig, 1975), 7–27; Eng. trans. as 'Thoughts on Bach's Leipzig Creative Years', *Bach* 21 (1990), 31–54

Emans, Reinmar: 'Gibt es eine Entwicklung im Wort-Ton-Verhältnis bei Bach?', *Beiträge zur Bach-Forschung* 9–10 (1991), 60–9

——'Überlegungen zur Genese der Kantate *Du Hirte Israel, höre* (BWV 104)', in K. Beißwenger et al., eds, *Acht kleine Präludien und Studien über Bach: Georg von Dadelsen zum 70. Geburtstag* (Wiesbaden, 1992), 44–50

——'Stylistic Analysis and Text Philology in the Service of "Inner Chronology", involving Stylistic Analyses of Selected Arias by J. S. Bach', *Bach* 26 (1995), 1–14

——'Überlegungen zum Bachschen Secco-Rezitativ', in M. Geck and K. Hofmann, eds, *Bach und die Stile* [conference report, Dortmund, 1998] (Dortmund, 1999), 37–49

Eppelsheim, Jürgen: 'Die Instrumente' in B. Schwendowius and W. Dömling, eds, *J. S. Bach: Zeit, Leben, Wirken* (Kassel etc., 1976), 127–42; Eng. trans. as 'The Instruments', *J. S. Bach: Life, Times, Influence* (Kassel etc., 1977), 127–42

Finke-Hecklinger, Doris: *Tanzcharaktere in J. S. Bachs Vokalmusik*, Tübinger Bach-Studien 6 (Trossingen, 1970)

Finlay, Ian F.: *J. S. Bachs weltliche Kantaten*, diss., Univ. of Göttingen, 1950 (London, 1950)

——'Bach's Secular Cantata Texts', *Music & Letters* 31 (1950), 189–95

Finscher, Ludwig: 'Zum Parodieproblem bei Bach', in M. Geck, ed., *Bach-Interpretationen* (Göttingen, 1969), 94–105, 217–18

Fischer, Albert and Tümpel, W.: *Das deutsche evangelische Kirchenlied des 17. Jahrhunderts*, 6 vols (Gütersloh, 1904–16; repr. Hildesheim, 1964)

Forchert, Arno: 'Bach und die Tradition der Rhetorik', in D. Berke and D. Hanemann, eds, *Alte Musik als ästhetische Gegenwart* [conference report, Stuttgart, 1985], 2 vols (Kassel, 1987), I, 169–78

Franke, Friedrich W.: *J. S. Bachs Kirchen-Kantaten* (Leipzig, 1925)

Fröde, Christine: 'Zur Entstehung der Kantate "Ihr Tore zu Zion" (BWV 193)', *BJ* 1991, 184–5

Geck, Martin: 'Bachs Probestück', in K. Dorfmüller, ed., *Quellenstudien zur Musik: Wolfgang Schmieder zum 70. Geburtstag* (Frankfurt, 1972), 55–68 [concerns BWV 22 and 23]

——'Spuren eines Einzelgängers: die "Bauernkantate" oder: vom unergründlichen Humor der Picander und Bach', *Neue Zeitschrift für Musik* 153 (1992), 24–9

——'Die *vox-Christi*-Sätze in Bachs Kantaten', in M. Geck and K. Hofmann, eds, *Bach und die Stile* [conference report, Dortmund, 1998] (Dortmund, 1999), 79–101

Gerlach, Reinhard: 'Besetzung und Instrumentation der Kirchenkantaten J. S. Bachs und ihre Bedingungen', *BJ* 1973, 53–71

Gerstmeier, August: 'Der "Actus tragicus": Bemerkungen zur Darstellung des Todes in der Musik J. S. Bachs', in H. Becker et al., eds, *Im Angesicht des Todes* (St Ottilien, 1987), 421–52

Glöckner, Andreas: 'Neuerkenntnisse zu J. S. Bachs Aufführungskalender zwischen 1729 und 1735', *BJ* 1981, 43–75

——'Zur Chronologie der Weimarer Kantaten J. S. Bachs', *BJ* 1985, 159–64

——'Anmerkungen zu J. S. Bachs Köthener Kantatenschaffen', *Cöthener Bach-Hefte* 4 (Köthen, 1986), 89–95

——'Überlegungen zu J. S. Bachs Kantatenschaffen nach 1730', *Beiträge zur Bach-Forschung* 6 (1987), 54–64; repr. in C. Wolff, ed., *J. S. Bachs Spätwerk und dessen Umfeld* (Kassel, 1988), 64–73

——'Zur Echtheit und Datierung der Kantate BWV 150 "Nach dir, Herr, verlanget mich" ', *BJ* 1988, 195–203

——'Die Musikpflege an der Leipziger Neukirche zur Zeit J. S. Bachs, *Beiträge zur Bach-Forschung* 8 (Leipzig, 1990)

——'Einige Beobachtungen zu J. S. Bachs Umgang mit den Vokalwerken seiner Zeitgenossen', *Beiträge zur Bach-Forschung* 9–10 (1991), 219–25

——'Bemerkungen zu den Leipziger Kantatenaufführungen vom 3. bis 6. Sonntag nach Trinitatis 1725', *BJ* 1992, 73–6

——'Bachs frühe Kantaten und die Markus-Passion von Reinhard Keiser', in K. Heller and H.-J. Schulze, eds, *Das Frühwerk J. S. Bachs* [conference report, Rostock, 1990] (Cologne, 1995), 257–66

——'Neue Spuren zu Bachs "Weimarer" Passion', *Leipziger Beiträge zur Bach-Forschung* 1 (1995), 33–46

——' "Das kleine italienische Ding": Zu Überlieferung und Datierung der Kantate "Amore traditore" (BWV 203)', *BJ* 1996, 133–7

——'Eine Abschrift der Kantate BWV 150 als Quelle für Brahms' e-Moll-Sinfonie Op. 98', *BJ* 1997, 181–3

——'Eine Michaeliskantate als Parodievorlage für den sechsten Teil des Bachschen Weihnachts-Oratoriums?', *BJ* 2000, 317–26

Gojowy, Detlef: 'Zur Frage der Köthener Trauermusik und der Matthäuspassion', *BJ* 1965, 86–134

——'Lied und Sonntag in Gesangbüchern der Bach-Zeit', *BJ* 1972, 24–60

——'Wort und Bild in Bachs Kantatentexten', *Die Musikforschung* 25 (1972), 27–39

——'Ein Zwölftonfeld bei J. S. Bach? Beobachtungen am Rezitativ BWV 167, Satz 2, Takte 13–19', *Bach-Studien* 5 (Leipzig, 1975), 43–8

——'Zur Vorgeschichte von J. S. Bachs Osteroratorium', *Die Musikforschung* 30 (1977), 309–28

——'Beobachtungen zur Arbeitsweise J. S. Bachs an Originalpartitur und -stimmen des Osteroratoriums BWV 249', in W. Hofmann and A. Schneiderheinze, eds, *Bach-Händel-Schutz Ehrung der DDR 1985* [conference report, Leipzig, 1985] (Leipzig, 1988), 181–92

Grüß, Hans: 'Analytische Beobachtungen an Kantatensätzen J. S. Bachs und ihre Konsequenzen für deren Aufführungspraxis', in R. Brinkmann, ed., *Bachforschung und Bachinterpretation heute* [conference report, Marburg, 1978] (Kassel, 1981), 161–4

——'Bemerkungen zur Aufführungspraxis des Actus tragicus BWV 106', in K. Heller and H.-J. Schulze, eds, *Das Frühwerk J. S. Bachs* [conference report, Rostock, 1990] (Cologne, 1995), 280–9

Gudewill, Kurt: 'Über Formen und Texte der Kirchenkantaten J. S. Bachs', in A. A. Abert and W. Pfannkuch, eds, *Festschrift Friedrich Blume* (Kassel, 1963), 162–75

Häfner, Klaus: 'Der Picander-Jahrgang', *BJ* 1975, 70–113

——'Zum Problem der Entstehungsgeschichte von BWV 248a', *Die Musikforschung* 30 (1977), 304–8

——'Picander, der Textdichter von Bachs viertem Kantatenjahrgang: Ein neuer Hinweis', *Die Musikforschung* 35 (1982), 156–62

——*Aspekte des Parodieverfahrens bei J. S. Bach: Beiträge zur Wiederentdeckung verschollener Vokalwerke* (Laaber, 1987)

Hamel, Fred: *J. S. Bach: Geistige Welt* (Göttingen, 1951)

Haselböck, Lucia: *Du hast mir mein Herz genommen: Sinnbilder und Mystik im Vokalwerk von J. S. Bach* (Vienna, 1989)

Herz, Gerhard: 'Bach's Religion', *Journal of Renaissance and Baroque Music* 1 (1946), 124–38

——ed., *J. S. Bach: Cantata No. 4 'Christ lag in Todesbanden': an Authoritative Score. Background, Analysis, Views and Comments* (New York, 1967)

——'BWV 131: Bach's First Cantata', in H. C. Robbins Landon and R. E. Chapman, eds, *Studies in Eighteenth-Century Music: A Tribute to Karl Geiringer* (London, 1970), 272–91; repr. in G. Herz, *Essays on J. S. Bach* (Ann Arbor, 1985), 127–45

——ed., *J. S. Bach: Cantata No. 140 'Wachet auf, ruft uns die Stimme': the Score of the New Bach Edition. Background, Analysis, Views and Comments* (New York, 1972)

——'Der lombardische Rhythmus in Bachs Vokalschaffen', *BJ* 1978, 148–80

——'Thoughts on the First Movement of J. S. Bach's Cantata No. 77 "Du sollt Gott, deinen Herren, lieben" ', in G. Herz, *Essays on J. S. Bach* (Ann Arbor, 1985), 206–17

Hindermann, Walter F.: *Bachs Himmelfahrts-Oratorium: Gestalt und Gehalt* (Kassel, 1985)

Hirsch, Arthur: *Die Zahl im Kantatenwerk J. S. Bachs* (Neuhausen-Stuttgart, 1986)

Hirschmann, Wolfgang: ' "Glückwünschendes Freuden-Gedicht": Die deutschsprachige Serenata im Kontext der barocken Casualpoesie', in F. Brusniak, ed., *Barockes Musiktheater im mitteldeutschen Raum im 17. und 18. Jahrhundert* (Cologne, 1994), 75–113

Hobohm, Wolf: 'Neue "Texte zur Leipziger Kirchen-Music" ', *BJ* 1973, 5–32

Hofmann, Klaus: 'Bachs Kantate "Ich lasse dich nicht, du segnest mich denn" BWV 157: Überlegungen zu Entstehung, Bestimmung und originaler Werkgestalt', *BJ* 1982, 51–80

——'Forkel und die Köthener Trauermusik J. S. Bachs', *BJ* 1983, 115–18

——'Alter Stil in Bachs Kirchenmusik: zu der Choralbearbeitung BWV 28/2', in D. Berke and D. Hanemann, eds, *Alte Musik als ästhetische Gegenwart* [conference report, Stuttgart, 1985], 2 vols (Kassel, 1987), I, 164–9

——'*Wo sind meine Wunderwerke*: Eine verschollene Thomasschulkantate J. S. Bachs?', *BJ* 1988, 211–18 [concerns BWV Anh. I 210]

——'J. S. Bachs Kantate "Jauchzet Gott in allen Landen" BWV 51: Überlegungen zu Entstehung und ursprünglicher Bestimmung', *BJ* 1989, 43–54

——'Alte und neue Überlegungen zu der Kantate "Non sa che sia dolore" BWV 209', *BJ* 1990, 7–25

——'Neue Überlegungen zu Bachs Weimarer Kantaten-Kalender', *BJ* 1993, 9–29

——'Bachs Doppelchor "Nun ist das Heil und die Kraft" (BWV 50): Neue Überlegungen zur Werkgeschichte', *BJ* 1994, 59–73

——'Perfidia und Fanfare: Zur Echtheit der Bach-Kantate "Lobe den Herrn, meine Seele" BWV 143. Ein Nachtrag zu meiner Ausgabe im Carus-Verlag', in B. Mohn and H. Ryschawy, eds, *Cari amici: Festschrift 25 Jahre Carus-Verlag* (Stuttgart, 1997), 34–43

——'Zum Schlußchoral der Kantate "Man singet mit Freuden vom Sieg" (BWV 149)', *BJ* 2000, 313–16

——'Über die Schlußchoräle zweier Bachscher Ratswahlkantaten', *BJ* 2001, 151–62

Husmann, Heinrich: 'Die Viola pomposa', *BJ* 1936, 90–100

Irwin, Joyce L.: *Neither Voice nor Heart alone: German Lutheran Theology of Music in the Age of the Baroque* (New York, 1993)

Jacobson, Lena: 'Musical Figures in BWV 131', *The Organ Yearbook* 11 (1980), 60–83

Jauernig, Reinhold: 'Zur Kantate "Ich hatte viel Bekümmernis" (BWV 21)', *BJ* 1954, 46–9

Kaiser, Rainer: 'Neue Erkenntnisse zur Chronologie der Kantate BWV 195', *Archiv für Musikwissenschaft* 44 (1987), 203–15

Kobayashi, Yoshitake: 'Zur Chronologie der Spätwerke J. S. Bachs: Kompositions- und Aufführungstätigkeit von 1736 bis 1750', *BJ* 1988, 7–72

—— *Die Notenschrift J. S. Bachs: Dokumentation ihrer Entwicklung*, NBA IX/2 (Kassel, 1989)

—— 'Quellenkundliche Überlegungen zur Chronologie der Weimarer Vokalwerke Bachs', in K. Heller and H.-J. Schulze, eds, *Das Frühwerk J. S. Bachs* [conference report, Rostock, 1990] (Cologne, 1995), 290–310

Koch, Ernst: 'Tröstendes Echo: Zur theologischen Deutung der Echo-Arie im IV. Teil des Weihnachts-Oratoriums von J. S. Bach', *BJ* 1989, 203–11

—— 'Die Stimme des Heiligen Geistes: Theologische Hintergründe der solistischen Altpartien in der Kirchenmusik J. S. Bachs', *BJ* 1995, 61–81

Kordes, Gesa: 'Self-parody and the "Hunting Cantata", BWV 208', *Bach* 22 (1991), 35–57

Krausse, Helmut K.: 'Eine neue Quelle zu drei Kantatentexten J. S. Bachs', *BJ* 1981, 7–22 [concerns BWV 64, 69a, and 77]

—— 'Erdmann Neumeister und die Kantatentexte J. S. Bachs', *BJ* 1986, 7–31

Krones, Hartmut: 'Kirchenstyl und Kammerstyl in den Rezitativen von J. S. Bachs Kantaten', in M. Geck and K. Hofmann, eds, *Bach und die Stile* [conference report, Dortmund, 1998] (Dortmund, 1999), 61–77

Krummacher, Friedhelm: 'Die Tradition in Bachs vokalen Choralbearbeitungen', in M. Geck, ed., *Bach-Interpretationen* (Göttingen, 1969), 29–56, 210–12

—— *Die Choralbearbeitung in der protestantischen Figuralmusik zwischen Praetorius und Bach* (Kassel, 1978)

—— 'Bachs Vokalmusik als Problem der Analyse', in R. Brinkmann, ed., *Bachforschung und Bachinterpretation heute* [conference report, Marburg, 1978] (Kassel, 1981), 97–126

—— 'Explikation als Struktur: zum Kopfsatz der Kantate BWV 77', in conference report, Leipzig, 1985 (Leipzig, 1988), 207–17

—— 'Gespräch und Struktur: Über Bachs geistliche Dialoge', *Beiträge zur Bach-Forschung* 9–10 (1991), 45–59

—— 'Bachs frühe Kantaten im Kontext der Tradition', *Die Musikforschung* 44 (1991), 9–32

—— 'Traditionen der Choraltropierung in Bachs frühem Vokalwerk', in K. Heller and H.-J. Schulze, eds, *Das Frühwerk J. S. Bachs* [conference report, Rostock, 1990] (Cologne, 1995), 217–43

—— *Bachs Zyklus der Choralkantaten: Aufgaben und Lösungen* (Göttingen, 1995)

—— 'Französische Ouvertüre und Choralbearbeitung: Stationen in Bachs kompositorischer Biographie', *Schweizer Jahrbuch für Musikwissenschaft, Neue Folge*, 15 (1995), 71–92

Kube, Michael: 'Bachs "tour de force": Analytischer Versuch über den Eingangschor der Kantate "Jesu, der du meine Seele", BWV 78', *Die Musikforschung* 45 (1992), 138–52

Küster, Konrad: 'Meininger Kantatentexte um Johann Ludwig Bach', *BJ* 1987, 159–64

——'Die Frankfurter und Leipziger Überlieferung der Kantaten Johann Ludwig Bachs', *BJ* 1989, 65–106

——' "Theatralisch vorgestellet": Zur Aufführungspraxis höfischer Vokalwerke in Thüringen um 1710/20', in F. Brusniak, ed., *Barockes Musiktheater im mitteldeutschen Raum im 17. und 18. Jahrhundert* (Cologne, 1994), 118–41

——' "Der Herr denket an uns" BWV 196: Eine frühe Bach-Kantate und ihr Kontext', *Musik und Kirche* 66 (1996), 84–96

Leaver, Robin A.: 'The Libretto of Bach's Cantata No. 79: a Conjecture', *Bach* 6 (1975), 3–11

——*J. S. Bach as Preacher: his Passions and Music in Worship* (St Louis, 1984)

——'The Liturgical Place and Homiletic Purpose of Bach's Cantatas', *Worship* 59 (1985), 9–29

——'Bach and the German Agnus Dei', in P. Brainard and R. Robinson, eds, *A Bach Tribute: Essays in Honour of William H. Scheide* (Kassel, 1993), 163–71

——'Music and Lutheranism', in J. Butt, ed., *The Cambridge Companion to Bach* (Cambridge, 1997), 35–45

——'The Mature Vocal Works and their Theological and Liturgical Context', in J. Butt, ed., *The Cambridge Companion to Bach* (Cambridge, 1997), 86–122

MacCracken, Thomas G.: 'Die Verwendung der Blechblasinstrumente bei J. S. Bach unter besonderer Berücksichtigung der Tromba da tirarsi', *BJ* 1984, 59–89

Mann, Alfred: 'Bach's Parody Technique and its Frontiers', in D. O. Franklin, ed., *Bach Studies* (Cambridge, 1989), 115–24

Marissen, Michael: 'On linking Bach's F-major Sinfonia and his Hunt Cantata, BWV 208', *Bach* 23 (1992), 31–46

Märker, Michael: 'Der stile antico und die frühen Kantaten J. S. Bachs', *Bach-Studien* 9 (Leipzig, 1986), 72–7

——'Strukturanalytische Befunde im Eingangschor der Kantate BWV 187 "Es wartet alles auf dich" ', *Bach Studien* 10 (Leipzig, 1991), 131–6

——'Die Tradition des Jesus-Seele-Dialoges und ihr Einfluß auf das Werk Bachs', *Beiträge zur Bach-Forschung* 9–10 (1991), 235–41

——*Die protestantische Dialogkomposition in Deutschland zwischen Heinrich Schütz und J. S. Bach* (Cologne, 1995)

——'J. S. Bach und der rezitativische Stil', in M. Geck and K. Hofmann, eds, *Bach und die Stile* [conference report, Dortmund, 1998] (Dortmund, 1999), 51–60

Marshall, Robert L.: *The Compositional Process of J. S. Bach: A Study of the Autograph Scores of the Vocal Works*, 2 vols (Princeton, 1972)

——'The Autograph Score of *Herr, gehe nicht ins Gericht*, BWV 105', commentary to the facsimile edition (Leipzig, 1983); repr. in R. L. Marshall, *The Music of J. S. Bach* [collected essays] (New York, 1989), 131–42

——'The Genesis of an Aria Ritornello: Observations on the Autograph Score of "Wie zittern und wanken", BWV 105/3', in R. L. Marshall, *The Music of J. S. Bach* (New York, 1989), 143–59

——'On Bach's Universality', in *The Universal Bach: Lectures Celebrating the Tercentenary of Bach's Birthday, Fall 1985* (Philadelphia, 1986), 50–66; repr. in R. L. Marshall, *The Music of J. S. Bach* (New York, 1989), 65–79 [pp. 76–9 concern BWV 78]

Marti, Andreas: '. . . *die Lehre des Lebens zu hören': Eine Analyse der drei Kantaten zum 17. Sonntag nach Trinitatis von J. S. Bach unter musikalisch-rhetorischen und theologischen Gesichtspunkten* (Berne, 1981) [concerns BWV 47, 114, and 148]

Martino, Donald, ed.: *178 Chorale Harmonizations of Joh. Seb. Bach: a Comparative Edition for Study*, rev. edn (Newton, MA, 1985)

Melamed, Daniel R.: 'Mehr zur Chronologie von Bachs Weimarer Kantaten', *BJ* 1993, 213–16

——*J. S. Bach and the German Motet* (Cambridge, 1995)

Melchert, Hermann: 'Das Rezitativ der Kirchenkantaten Joh. Seb. Bachs', diss., Univ. of Frankfurt, 1958; largely repr. in *BJ* 1958, 5–83

Mendel, Arthur: 'On the Keyboard Accompaniments to Bach's Leipzig Church Music', *The Musical Quarterly* 36 (1950), 339–62

Meyer, Ulrich: ' "Brich dem Hungrigen dein Brot": Das Evangelium zum ersten Sonntag nach Trinitatis', in W. Rehm, ed., *Bachiana et alia musicologica: Festschrift Alfred Dürr zum 65. Geburtstag* (Kassel, 1983), 192–200

——'Symbolik in J. S. Bachs Kantatenschaffen', in P. Gerlitz, ed., *Symbolon: Jahrbuch für Symbolforschung. Neue Folge, Bd. 12: Licht und Paradies* (Frankfurt am Main, 1995), 9–21

——*Biblical Quotation and Allusion in the Cantata Libretti of J. S. Bach* (Lanham, Maryland, 1997)

Mies, Paul: *Die geistlichen Kantaten J. S. Bachs und der Hörer von heute*, 3 vols (Wiesbaden, 1959–64)

——*Die weltlichen Kantaten J. S. Bachs und der Hörer von heute* (Wiesbaden, 1966–7)

Möller, Hans-Jürgen: 'Das Wort-Ton-Verhältnis im Weihnachtsoratorium J. S. Bachs', *Neue Zeitschrift für Musik* 133 (1972), 686–91

Moser, Hans-Joachim: 'Aus Joh. Seb. Bachs Kantatenwelt', *Die Musik* 17 (1924–5), 721–36

Neubacher, Jürgen: 'Raumgebundene Bildlichkeit in einer Kantate J. S. Bachs? Überlegungen zu "Himmelskönig, sei willkommen" [BWV 182]', in C.-H. Mahling, ed., *Florilegium Musicologicum: Hellmut Federhofer zum 75. Geburtstag* (Tutzing, 1988), 233–45

Neumann, Werner: *J. S. Bachs Chorfuge* (Leipzig, 1938; 3rd edn Leipzig, 1953)

——*Handbuch der Kantaten J. S. Bachs* (Leipzig, 1947; 5th edn Wiesbaden, 1984)

——'Zur Aufführungspraxis der Kantate 152', *BJ* 1949–50, 100–3

——'Das "Bachische Collegium musicum" ', *BJ* 1960, 5–27; repr. in W. Blankenburg, ed., *Johann Sebastian Bach* (Darmstadt, 1970), 384–415

——'Eine verschollene Ratswechselkantate J. S. Bachs', *BJ* 1961, 52–7 [concerns BWV Anh. I 193]

——'Über Ausmaß und Wesen des Bachschen Parodieverfahrens', *BJ* 1965, 63–85

——'Probleme der Aufführungspraxis im Spiegel der Geschichte der Neuen Bachgesellschaft', *BJ* 1967, 100–20

——'Eine Leipziger Bach-Gedenkstätte: Über die Beziehungen der Familien Bach und Bose', *BJ* 1970, 19–31

——'J. S. Bachs "Rittergutskantaten" BWV 30a und 212', *BJ* 1972, 76–90

——ed., *Sämtliche von J. S. Bach vertonte Texte* (Leipzig, 1974)

——'Das Problem "vokal-instrumental" in seiner Bedeutung für ein neues

Bach-Verständnis', in R. Brinkmann, ed., *Bachforschung und Bachinterpretation heute* [conference report, Marburg, 1978] (Kassel, 1981), 72–85

—— *Über das funktionale Wechselverhältnis von Vokalität und Instrumentalität als kompositionstechnisches Grundphänomen, dargestellt am Schaffen J. S. Bachs* (Berlin, 1982)

Niebergall, Alfred: 'Die Geschichte der christlichen Predigt', *Leiturgia: Handbuch des evangelischen Gottesdienstes* 2 (Kassel, 1955), 181–353

Nitsche, Peter: 'Konzertform und Ausdruck: Bemerkungen zu einigen Arien J. S. Bachs', in H. Danuser et al., eds, *Das musikalische Kunstwerk: Geschichte-Ästhetik-Theorie. Festschrift Carl Dahlhaus zum 60. Geburtstag* (Laaber, 1988), 385–94 [the cantata arias concerned are BWV 56/1, 82/5, 103/5, 132/5, 152/2, and 166/1]

Noack, Elisabeth: 'Georg Christian Lehms, ein Textdichter J. S. Bachs', *BJ* 1970, 7–18

Otterbach, Friedemann: *J. S. Bach: Leben und Werk* (Stuttgart, 1982)

Pankratz, Herbert R.: 'J. S. Bach and his Leipzig *Collegium musicum*', *Musical Quarterly* 69 (1983), 323–53

Parrott, Andrew: *The Essential Bach Choir* (Woodbridge, 2000)

Pelikan, Jaroslav: *Bach among the Theologians* (Philadelphia, 1986)

Petzoldt, Martin, ed.: *Bach als Ausleger der Bibel: Theologische und musikwissenschaftliche Studien zum Werk J. S. Bachs* (Göttingen, 1985)

—— *Ehre sei dir Gott gesungen: Bilder und Texte zu Bachs Leben als Christ und seinem Wirken für die Kirche* (Göttingen, 1988; 2nd edn Göttingen, 1990)

—— 'Schlußchoräle ohne Textmarken in der Überlieferung von Kantaten J. S. Bachs', *Musik und Kirche* 59 (1989), 235–40

—— 'Zur Frage der Textvorlagen von BWV 62 "Nun komm, der Heiden Heiland" ', *Musik und Kirche* 60 (1990), 302–10

—— 'Zur Differenz zwischen Vorlage und komponiertem Text in Kantaten J. S. Bachs am Beispiel von BWV 25', *Bach-Studien* 10 (Leipzig, 1991), 80–107

—— ' "Die kräftige Erquickung unter der schweren Angst-Last": Möglicherweise Neues zur Entstehung der Kantate BWV 21', *BJ* 1993, 31–46

—— 'Hat Gott Zeit, hat der Mensch Ewigkeit? Zur Kantate BWV 106 von J. S. Bach', *Musik und Kirche* 66 (1996), 212–20

Pirro, André: *L'Esthétique de Jean Sebastien Bach* (Paris, 1907)

Platen, Emil: *Untersuchungen zur Struktur der chorischen Choralbearbeitung J. S. Bachs*, diss., Univ, of Bonn, 1957 (Bonn, 1959)

—— 'Aufgehoben oder ausgehalten? Zur Ausführung der Rezitativ-Continuopartien in J. S. Bachs Kirchenmusik', in R. Brinkmann, ed., *Bachforschung und Bachinterpretation heute* [conference report, Marburg, 1978] (Kassel, 1981), 167–77

Prinz, Ulrich: *Studien zum Instrumentarium J. S. Bachs mit besonderer Berücksichtigung der Kantaten*, diss., Univ. of Tübingen, 1974 (Tübingen, 1979)

—— 'Zur Bezeichnung "Bassono" und "Fagotto" bei J. S. Bach', *BJ* 1981, 107–22

—— 'Anmerkungen zum Instrumentarium in den Werken J. S. Bachs', in *300 Jahre J. S. Bach* [catalogue of Stuttgart exhibition] (Tutzing, 1985), 89–97

Reimer, Erich: 'Bachs Jagdkantate als profanes Ritual: Zur politischen Funktion absolutistischer Hofmusik', *Musik und Bildung* 12 (1980), 674–83

—— *Die Hofmusik in Deutschland 1500–1800* (Wilhelmshaven, 1991)

Reul, Barbara: ' "O vergnügte Stunden da mein Hertzog funden seinen Lebenstag":

Ein unbekannter Textdruck zu einer Geburtstags-Kantate J. S. Bachs für den Fürsten Johann August von Anhalt-Zerbst', *BJ* 1999, 7–17 [concerns BWV Anh. I 194]

Richter, Bernhard F.: 'Über die Schicksale der der Thomasschule zu Leipzig angehörenden Kantaten J. S. Bachs', *BJ* 1906, 43–73

—— 'Über J. S. Bachs Kantaten mit obligater Orgel', *BJ* 1908, 49–63

Rienäcker, Gerd: 'Beobachtungen zum Eingangschor der Kantate BWV 127', *Beiträge zur Bach-Forschung* 2 (1983), 5–15

—— 'Beobachtungen zum Eingangschor BWV 25', *Bach-Studien* 10 (Leipzig, 1991), 108–30

—— 'Nachdenken über sinnvolles Musizieren? – Marginalien zu J. S. Bachs "Der Streit zwischen Phoebus und Pan" [BWV 201]', in M. Geck and K. Hofmann, eds, *Bach und die Stile* [conference report, Dortmund, 1998] (Dortmund, 1999), 161–8

Rifkin, Joshua: 'Ein langsamer Konzertsatz J. S. Bachs', *BJ* 1978, 140–7 [concerns BWV 156/1]

—— 'Bach's Chorus', paper read to the American Musicological Society, Boston, 1981; pub. in A. Parrott, *The Essential Bach Choir* (Woodbridge, 2000), 189–208

—— 'Bach's Chorus: a Preliminary Report', *The Musical Times* 123 (1982), 747–54; rev. Ger. version as 'Bachs Chor: Ein vorläufige Bericht', *Basler Jahrbuch für historische Musikpraxis* 9 (1985), 141–55

—— 'Some Questions of Performance in J. S. Bach's *Trauerode* [BWV 198]', in D. R. Melamed, ed., *Bach Studies* 2 (Cambridge, 1995), 119–53

—— 'From Weimar to Leipzig: Concertists and Ripienists in Bach's *Ich hatte viel Bekümmernis* [BWV 21]', *Early Music* 24 (1996), 583–603

—— 'Zur Bearbeitungsgeschichte der Kantate "Wachet! betet! betet! wachet!" (BWV 70)', *BJ* 1999, 127–32

—— 'Siegesjubel und Satzfehler: Zum Problem von "Nun ist das Heil und die Kraft" (BWV 50)', *BJ* 2000, 67–86

Robertson, Alec: *The Church Cantatas of J. S. Bach* (London and New York, 1972)

Rubin, Norman: ' "Fugue" as a Delimiting Concept in Bach's Choruses', in R. L. Marshall, ed., *Studies in Renaissance and Baroque Music in Honour of Arthur Mendel* (Kassel and Hackensack, NJ, 1974), 195–208

Ruhnke, Martin: 'Das italienische Rezitativ bei den deutschen Komponisten des Spätbarock', *Analecta musicologica* 17 (1976), 79–120

Scheide, William H.: *J. S. Bach as a Biblical Interpreter* (Princeton, 1952)

—— 'J. S. Bachs Sammlung von Kantaten seines Vetters Johann Ludwig Bach', *BJ* 1959, 52–94; *BJ* 1961, 5–24; *BJ* 1962, 5–32

—— 'Ist Mizlers Bericht über Bachs Kantaten korrekt?', *Die Musikforschung*, 14 (1961), 60–3

—— 'Nochmals Mizlers Kantatenbericht: Eine Erwiderung', *Die Musikforschung*, 14 (1961), 423–7

—— 'The "Concertato" Violin in BWV 139', *Bach-Studien* 5 (Leipzig, 1975), 123–37

—— 'Zum Verhältnis von Textdrucken und musikalischen Quellen der Kirchenkantaten J. S. Bachs', *BJ* 1976, 79–94

—— 'Bach und der Picander-Jahrgang: Eine Erwiderung', *BJ* 1980, 47–51

——' "Nun ist das Heil und die Kraft" BWV 50: Doppelchörigkeit, Datierung und Bestimmung', *BJ* 1982, 81–96

——'Eindeutigkeit und Mehrdeutigkeit in Picanders Kantatenjahrgangs-Vorbemerkung und im Werkverzeichnis des Nekrologs auf J. S. Bach', *BJ* 1983, 109–13

——'Nochmals BWV 50 "Nun ist das Heil und die Kraft" ', *BJ* 2001, 117–30

Schering, Arnold: 'Beiträge zur Bachkritik', *BJ* 1912, 124–33

——'Die Kantate Nr. 150 "Nach dir, Herr, verlanget mich" ', *BJ* 1913, 39–52

——'Über Bachs Parodieverfahren', *BJ* 1921, 49–95

——'Kleine Bachstudien', *BJ* 1933, 30–70

——*J. S. Bachs Leipziger Kirchenmusik* (Leipzig, 1936; 2nd edn Leipzig, 1954)

——'Bachs Musik für den Leipziger Universitätsgottesdienst 1723–1725', *BJ* 1938, 62–86

——*J. S. Bach und das Musikleben Leipzigs im 18. Jahrhundert. Musikgeschichte Leipzigs* 3 (Leipzig, 1941)

——*Über Kantaten J. S. Bachs* [prefaces to the Eulenburg miniature scores edited by Schering], ed. F. Blume (Leipzig, 1942; 3rd edn 1950)

Schmalfuß, Hermann: 'J. S. Bachs "Actus tragicus" (BWV 106): Ein Beitrag zu seiner Entstehungsgeschichte', *BJ* 1970, 36–43

Schmitz, Arnold: *Die Bildlichkeit der wortgebundenen Musik J. S. Bachs* (Mainz, 1950; repr. 1980)

——'Die oratorische Kunst J. S. Bachs', in conference report, Lüneburg, 1950 (Kassel, 1950), 33–49; repr. in W. Blankenburg, ed., *Johann Sebastian Bach* (Darmstadt, 1970), 61–84

Schmoll-Barthel, Jutta: 'Überlegungen zu Bachs Choralsatz', *Beiträge zur Bach-Forschung* 9–10 (1991), 285–92

Schneider, Max: 'Bach-Urkunden', *Veröffentlichungen der Neuen Bachgesellschaft* 17/3 (Leipzig, n.d.)

Schneiderheinze, Armin: 'Über Bachs Umgang mit Gottscheds Versen', in conference report, Leipzig, 1975 (Leipzig, 1977), 91–8

——'Zu den aufführungspraktischen Bedingungen in der Thomaskirche zur Amtszeit Bachs', *Beiträge zur Bach-Forschung* 6 (1988), 82–91

——'Zwischen Selbst- und Fremdbestimmung: Überlegungen um Kantate 174', *Beiträge zur Bach-Forschung* 9–10 (1991), 205–13

——' "Christ lag in Todes Banden": Überlegungen zur Datierung von BWV 4', in K. Heller and H.-J. Schulze, eds, *Das Frühwerk J. S. Bachs* [conference report, Rostock, 1990] (Cologne, 1995), 267–79

Schöne, Albrecht: *Emblematik und Drama im Zeitalter des Barock* (Munich, 1964; 2nd edn Munich, 1968)

Schrade, Leo: 'Bach: the Conflict between the Sacred and the Secular', *Journal of the History of Ideas* 7 (1946), 151–94

Schrammek, Winfried: 'Viola pomposa und Violoncello piccolo bei J. S. Bach', in conference report, Leipzig, 1975 (Leipzig, 1977), 345–54

Schulze, Hans-Joachim: 'Bemerkungen zu einigen Kantatentexten J. S. Bachs', *BJ* 1959, 168–70

——'Marginalien zu einigen Bach-Dokumenten', *BJ* 1961, 79–99

——'J. S. Bach und Christian Gottlob Meißner', *BJ* 1968, 80–8

——'Neuerkenntnisse zu einigen Kantatentexten Bachs auf Grund neuer biographischer Daten', in M. Geck, ed., *Bach-Interpretationen* (Göttingen, 1969), 22–8, 208–10

——'Melodiezitate und Mehrtextigkeit in der Bauernkantate und in den Goldbergvariationen', *BJ* 1976, 58–72

——' "150 Stück von den Bachischen Erben": Zur Überlieferung der vierstimmigen Choräle J. S. Bachs', *BJ* 1983, 81–100

——'Studenten als Bachs Helfer bei der Leipziger Kirchenmusik', *BJ* 1984, 45–52

——*Studien zur Bach-Überlieferung im 18. Jahrhundert* (Leipzig, 1984)

——*Ey! wie schmeckt der Coffee süße: J. S. Bachs Kaffee-Kantate in ihrer Zeit* (Leipzig, 1985)

——' "Entfernet euch, ihr heitern Sterne" BWV Anh. I 9: Notizen zum Textdruck und zum Textdichter', *BJ* 1985, 166–8

——'The Parody Process in Bach's Music: an Old Problem Reconsidered', *Bach* 20 (1989), 7–21

——'Wunschdenken und Wirklichkeit: Nochmals zur Frage des Doppelaccompagnements in Kirchenmusikaufführungen der Bach-Zeit', *BJ* 1989, 231–3

——'Bach's Secular Cantatas: a New Look at the Sources', *Bach* 21 (1990), 26–41

——'Florilegium-Pasticcio-Parodie-Vermächtnis: Beobachtungen an ausgewählten Vokalwerken J. S. Bachs', *Beiträge zur Bach-Forschung* 9–10 (1991), 199–204

——'Wann entstand J. S. Bachs "Jagdkantate" [BWV 208]?', *BJ* 2000, 301–5

——'Vom Landgut in die Stadtbibliothek: Zur Überlieferung der Bach-Kantate "Ach Herr, mich armen Sünder" [BWV 135]', *BJ* 2001, 179–83

Schureck, Ralph: 'The Restoration of a lost Bach Sinfonia for Organ and Orchestra', *Musicology* 5 (1979), 205–9 [concerns BWV 188/1]

Seidel, Elmar: *J. S. Bachs Choralbearbeitungen in ihren Beziehungen zum Kantionalsatz*, Parts I and II (Mainz, 1998)

Seiffert, Max: 'Praktische Bearbeitungen Bachscher Kompositionen', *BJ* 1904, 51–76

Siegele, Ulrich: *Kompositionsweise und Bearbeitungstechnik in der Instrumentalmusik J. S. Bachs*, diss., Univ. of Tübingen, 1957 (Neuhausen-Stuttgart, 1975)

——'Bachs Endzweck einer regulierten und Entwurf einer wohlbestallten Kirchenmusik', in T. Kohlhase and V. Scherliess, eds, *Festschrift Georg von Dadelsen zum 60. Geburtstag* (Neuhausen-Stuttgart, 1978), 315–51; repr. in *The Garland Library of the History of Western Music* 6 (New York and London, 1985), 195–233

Sirp, Hermann: 'Die Thematik der Kirchenkantaten J. S. Bachs in ihren Beziehungen zum protestantischen Kirchenlied', *BJ* 1931, 1–50; *BJ* 1932, 51–118

Smend, Friedrich: 'Bachs h-Moll-Messe: Entstehung, Überlieferung, Bedeutung', *BJ* 1937, 1–58

——'Bachs Markus-Passion', *BJ* 1940–1948, 1–35; repr. in *Bach-Studien* (see below), 110–36

——'Neue Bach-Funde', *Archiv für Musikforschung* 7 (1942), 1–16; repr. in *Bach-Studien* (see below), 137–52

——*Joh. Seb. Bach: Kirchen-Kantaten*, 6 vols (Berlin, 1947–9; 3rd edn Berlin, 1966)

——'Bachs Himmelfahrts-Oratorium', in K. Matthaei, ed., *Bach-Gedenkschrift 1950* (Zurich, 1950), 42–65; repr. in *Bach-Studien* (see below), 195–211

——*Bach in Köthen* (Berlin, 1951); Eng. trans. by J. Page, ed. and rev. by S. Daw (St Louis, 1985)

——'Bachs Trauungskantate "Dem Gerechten muß das Licht immer wieder aufgehen" [BWV 195]', *Die Musikforschung* 5 (1952), 144–52; repr. in W. Blankenburg, ed., *Johann Sebastian Bach* (Darmstadt, 1970), 150–61

——*Bach-Studien: Gesammelte Reden und Aufsätze*, ed. C. Wolff (Kassel etc., 1969)

Smith, Mark M.: 'J. S. Bachs Violoncello piccolo: Neue Aspekte, offene Fragen', *BJ* 1998, 63–81

Smither, Howard E.: *The Oratorio in the Baroque Era: Protestant Germany and England* (Chapel Hill, 1977), 154–71

Smithers, Don L.: 'The Original Circumstances in the Performance of Bach's Leipzig Church Cantatas', *Bach* 26 (1995), 28–47

Spitta, Philipp: *Johann Sebastian Bach*, 2 vols (Leipzig, 1873, 1880); Eng. trans. by C. Bell and J. A. Fuller-Maitland, 3 vols (London, 1884–5; repr. 1952)

——'Über die Beziehungen Sebastian Bachs zu Christian Friedrich Hunold und Mariane von Ziegler', in *Historische und Philologische Aufsätze, Festgabe an Ernst Curtius zum 2. September 1884*; repr. in 2 parts: in P. Spitta, *Zur Musik* (Berlin, 1892) [concerns M. von Ziegler], and in P. Spitta, *Musikgeschichtliche Aufsätze* (Berlin, 1894) [concerns C. F. Hunold]

Stalmann, Joachim, ed.: *Das deutsche Kirchenlied: Kritische Gesamtausgabe der Melodien* (Kassel, 1993–)

Steiger, Lothar and Renate: '. . . angelicos testes, sudarium et vestes: Bemerkungen zu J. S. Bachs Osteroratorium', *Musik und Kirche* 53 (1983), 193–202

——'Zeit ohne Zeit: J. S. Bachs Kantate BWV 20 "O Ewigkeit, du Donnerwort" I', in A. Dürr and W. Killy, eds, *Das protestantische Kirchenlied im 16. und 17. Jahrhundert: Text-, musik- und theologiegeschichtliche Probleme* (Wiesbaden, 1986), 165–233

——' "Es ist dir gesagt, Mensch, was gut ist": J. S. Bachs Kantate BWV 45: Ihre Theologie und Musik', in *Kerygma und Dogma* 32 (1986), No. 1, 3–34

——*Sehet, wir gehn hinauf gen Jerusalem: J. S. Bachs Kantaten auf den Sonntag Estomihi* (Göttingen, 1992) [concerns BWV 22, 23, 127, and 159]

Steiger, Renate: ' "Die Welt ist euch ein Himmelreich": Zu J. S. Bachs Deutung des Pastoralen', *Musik und Kirche* 41 (1971), 1–8, 69–79, 107

——'Methode und Ziel einer musikalischen Hermeneutik im Werke Bachs', *Musik und Kirche* 47 (1977), 209–24

——'Die Einheit des Weihnachtsoratoriums von J. S. Bach', *Musik und Kirche* 51 (1981), 273–80; 52 (1982), 9–15

——ed., *Sinnbildlichkeit in Text und Musik bei J. S. Bach* [conference report, Heidelberg, 1987] (Heidelberg, 1988)

——ed., *Parodie und Vorlage: Zum Bachschen Parodieverfahren und seiner Bedeutung für die Hermeneutik; die Messe BWV 234 und die Kantaten BWV 67, 179, 79 und 136* [conference report, Stuttgart, 1988] (Heidelberg, 1988)

——'*Actus tragicus* und *ars moriendi*: Bachs Textvorlage für die Kantate "Gottes Zeit ist die allerbeste Zeit" (BWV 106)', *Musik und Kirche* 59 (1989), 11–23

—— ' "Amen, amen! Komm, du schöne Freudenkrone": Zum Schlußsatz von BWV 61', *Musik und Kirche* 59 (1989), 246–51

—— 'Eine emblematische Predigt: Die Sinnbilder der Kantate "Ich will den Kreuzstab gerne tragen" (BWV 56) von J. S. Bach', *Musik und Kirche* 60 (1990)

—— ed., *J. S. Bachs Choralkantaten als Choral-Bearbeitungen* [conference report, Leipzig, 1990] (Heidelberg, 1991)

—— ed., *Die seelsorgliche Bedeutung J. S. Bachs: Kantaten zum Thema Tod und Sterben* [conference report, Schloß Beuggen, 1992] (Heidelberg, 1993)

—— ' "Fallt mit Danken, fallt mit Loben vor des Höchsten Gnaden-Thron": Zum IV. Teil des Weihnachts-Oratoriums von J. S. Bach', in F. Brouwer and R. A. Leaver, eds, *Ars et musica in liturgia: Celebratory Volume presented to Casper Honders on the Occasion of his 70th Birthday* (Utrecht, 1993), 198–211

—— ed., *'Wie freudig ist mein Herz, da Gott versöhnet ist': Die Lehre von der Versöhnung in Kantaten und Orgelchorälen von J. S. Bach* [conference report, Schlößchen Schönburg Hofgeismar, 1994] (Heidelberg, 1995)

—— ed., *Die Quellen J. S. Bachs: Bachs Musik im Gottesdienst* [conference report, Stuttgart, 1995] (Heidelberg, 1998)

—— ed., *Von Luther zu Bach* [conference report, Eisenach, 1996] (Sinzig, 1999)

—— ed., *J. S. Bachs Kantaten zum Thema Tod und Sterben und ihr literarisches Umfeld* (Wiesbaden, 2000)

Stein, Klaus: 'Stammt "Nun ist das Heil und die Kraft" (BWV 50) von J. S. Bach?', *BJ* 1999, 51–66

Stephan, Rudolf: 'Die Wandlung der Konzertform bei Bach', *Die Musikforschung* 6 (1953), 127–43

Stiehl, Herbert: *Das Innere der Thomaskirche zur Amtszeit J. S. Bachs*, Beiträge zur Bach-Forschung 3 (Leipzig, 1984)

Stiller, Günther: *J. S. Bach und das Leipziger gottesdienstliche Leben seiner Zeit* (Berlin and Kassel, 1970); Eng. trans. as *J. S. Bach and Liturgical Life in Leipzig*, ed. R. A. Leaver (St Louis, MO, 1984)

—— ' "Mir ekelt mehr zu leben": Zur Textdeutung der Kantate "Vergnügte Ruh, beliebte Seelenlust" (BWV 170) von J. S. Bach', in W. Rehm, ed., *Bachiana et alia musicologica: Festschrift Alfred Dürr zum 65. Geburtstag* (Kassel, 1983), 293–300

Stokes, Richard, ed.: *J. S. Bach: the Complete Church and Secular Cantatas* (Ebrington, Glos., 1999) [the cantata librettos in German–English parallel text]

Streck, Harald: *Die Verskunst in den poetischen Texten zu den Kantaten J. S. Bachs* (Hamburg, 1971)

Szeskus, Reinhard: 'Zu den Choralkantaten J. S. Bachs', in conference report, Leipzig, 1975 (Leipzig, 1977), 111–20

—— 'Zum Vokaleinfluß in Bachs Kantatenritornellen', in R. Brinkmann, ed., *Bachforschung und Bachinterpretation heute* [conference report, Marburg, 1978] (Kassel, 1981), 153–60

—— 'Zur motivisch-thematischen Arbeit in Kantaten J. S. Bachs', *Bach-Studien* 6 (Leipzig, 1981), 109–20

—— 'Zur Themenwandlung in Bachs Vokalschaffen', *Bach-Studien* 7 (Leipzig, 1982), 140–55

——'Bach und die Leipziger Universitätsmusik', in D. Berke and D. Hanemann, eds, *Alte Musik als ästhetische Gegenwart* [conference report, Stuttgart, 1985] (Kassel, 1987), 405–12; repr. in *Beiträge zur Musikwissenschaft* 32 (1990), 161–70

Tagliavini, Luigi F.: *Studi sui testi delle cantate sacre di J. S. Bach* (Padua and Kassel, 1956)

Terry, Charles S.: *Bach: the Cantatas and Oratorios* (London, 1925; repr. 1972)

——*Joh. Seb. Bach: Cantata Texts Sacred and Secular, with a Reconstruction of the Leipzig Liturgy of his Period* (London, 1926; repr. 1964)

Thalheimer, Peter: 'Der Flauto piccolo bei J. S. Bach', *BJ* 1966, 138–46

Thiele, Eugen: *Die Chorfugen J. S. Bachs* (Berne, 1936)

Tiggemann, Hildegard: 'Unbekannte Textdrucke zu drei Gelegenheitskantaten J. S. Bachs', *BJ* 1994, 7–22 [concerns BWV 210a, Anh. I 211, and Anh. I 212]

Treiber, Fritz: *Die thüringisch-sächsische Kirchenkantate zur Zeit des jungen Bach*, diss., Univ. of Heidelberg, 1937; pub. in *Archiv für Musikforschung, Jahrgang 2* (1937)

Unger, Hans-Heinrich: *Die Beziehungen zwischen Musik und Rhetorik im 16.–18. Jahrhundert* (Würzburg, 1941)

Unger, Melvin P.: *Handbook to Bach's Sacred Cantata Texts: an Interlinear Translation with Reference Guide to Biblical Quotations and Allusions* (Lanham, Maryland, 1996)

Voigt, Woldemar: 'Zu Bachs Weihnachtsoratorium, Teil 1 bis 3', *BJ* 1908, 1–48

——*Die Kirchenkantaten J. S. Bachs: Ein Führer bei ihrem Studium und ein Berater für ihre Aufführung* (Stuttgart, 1918; 2nd edn Leipzig, 1928)

Wachovsky, Gerd: 'Die vierstimmigen Choräle J. S. Bachs: Untersuchungen zu den Druckfassungen von 1765 bis 1932 und zur Frage der Authentizität', *BJ* 1983, 51–79

Wackernagel, Philipp: *Das deutsche Kirchenlied von der ältesten Zeit bis zu Anfang des XVII. Jahrhunderts*, 5 vols (Leipzig, 1864–77)

Walker, Paul: 'Die Entstehung der Permutationsfuge', *BJ* 1989, 21–41; Eng. version as 'The Origin of the Permutation Fugue' in *Studies in the History of Music* 3 (New York, 1993), 51–91

Walter, Meinrad: *Musik-Sprache des Glaubens: Zum geistlichen Vokalwerk J. S. Bachs* (Frankfurt am Main, 1994)

Werner-Jensen, Arnold: *Reclams Musikführer J. S. Bach 2: Vokalmusik* (Stuttgart, 1993)

Werthemann, Helene: *Die Bedeutung der alttestamentlichen Historien in J. S. Bachs Kirchenkantaten* (Tübingen, 1960)

——'Zum Text der Bach-Kantate 21 "Ich hatte viel Bekümmernis in meinem Herzen" ', *BJ* 1965, 135–43

Westrup, Jack A.: *Bach Cantatas*, BBC Music Guides (London, 1966)

Whaples, M. K.: 'Bach's Earliest Arias', *Bach* 20 (1989), 31–54

——'Bach's Recapitulation Forms', *Journal of Musicology* 14 (1996), 475–513

Whittaker, W. Gillies: *Fugitive Notes on Certain Cantatas and the Motets of J. S. Bach* (Oxford, 1925)

——*The Cantatas of J. S. Bach*, 2 vols (London, 1959; repr. 1964)

Wolf, Uwe: 'Eine "neue" Bach-Kantate zum 4. Advent: Zur Rekonstruktion der Weimarer Adventskantate "Herz und Mund und Tat und Leben" BWV 147a', *Musik und Kirche* 66 (1996), 351–5

——'J. S. Bach und der Weißenfelser Hof: Überlegungen anhand eines Quellenfundes', *BJ* 1997, 145–50

——see also under Beißwenger, Kirsten

Wolff, Christoph: *Der stile antico in der Musik J. S. Bachs: Studien zu Bachs Spätwerk* (Wiesbaden, 1968)

——'Die Traditionen des vokalpolyphonen Stils in der neueren Musikgeschichte, insbesondere bei J. S. Bach', *Musik und Kirche* 38 (1968), 62–80; Eng. trans. as 'Bach and the Tradition of the Palestrina Style' in C. Wolff, *Bach: Essays on his Life and Music* (Cambridge, MA, 1991), 84–104

——'The Organ in Bach's Cantatas', recording notes, 1975; repr. in C. Wolff, *Bach: Essays on his Life and Music* (Cambridge, MA, 1991), 317–23

——'Bachs Leipziger Kantoratsprobe und die Aufführungsgeschichte der Kantate "Du wahrer Gott und Davids Sohn" BWV 23', *BJ* 1978, 78–94; Eng. trans. in C. Wolff, *Bach: Essays on his Life and Music* (Cambridge, MA, 1991), 128–40

——'Wo blieb Bachs fünfter Kantatenjahrgang?', *BJ* 1982, 151–2

——'The Reformation Cantata "Ein feste Burg" [BWV 80]', *American Choral Review* 24 (1982), 27–38; repr. in C. Wolff, *Bach: Essays on his Life and Music* (Cambridge, MA, 1991), 152–61

——' "Intricate Kirchen-Stücke" und "Dresdener Liederchen": Bach und die Instrumentalisierung der Vokalmusik', in H.-J. Schulze and C. Wolff, eds, *J. S. Bach und der süddeutsche Raum: Aspekte der Wirkungsgeschichte Bachs* [conference report, Munich, 1990] (Regensburg, 1991), 19–23

——'Pachelbel, Buxtehude and die weitere Einflußsphäre des jungen Bach', in K. Heller and H.-J. Schulze, eds, *Das Frühwerk J. S. Bachs* [conference report, Rostock, 1990] (Cologne, 1995), 21–32

——' "Die betrübte und wieder getröstete Seele": Zum Dialog-Charakter der Kantate "Ich hatte viel Bekümmernis" BWV 21', *BJ* 1996, 139–45

——ed., *Die Welt der Bach-Kantaten*, 3 vols (Stuttgart, 1996–9); 1: *J. S. Bachs Kirchenkantaten: von Arnstadt bis in die Köthener Zeit* (Stuttgart, 1996); Eng. trans. as *The World of the Bach Cantatas: J. S. Bach's Early Sacred Cantatas* (New York, 1997); 2: *J. S. Bachs weltliche Kantaten* (Stuttgart, 1997); 3: *J. S. Bachs Leipziger Kirchenkantaten* (Stuttgart, 1999)

——*Johann Sebastian Bach: The Learned Musician* (Oxford and New York, 2000)

Wolff, Christoph and Emery, Walter et al.: *The New Grove Bach Family* (London, 1983), a rev. edn of the Bach articles in S. Sadie, ed., *The New Grove Dictionary of Music & Musicians* London, 1980)

Wolff, Leonhard: *J. S. Bachs Kirchenkantaten* (Leipzig, 1913; 2nd edn 1930)

Wollny, Peter: 'Bachs Bewerbung um die Organistenstelle an der Marienkirche zu Halle und ihr Kontext', *BJ* 1994, 25–39

——'Neue Bach-Funde', *BJ* 1997, 7–50 [concerns BWV 194 and 195]

——'Nachbemerkung zu "Neue Bach-Funde" (*BJ* 1997, S. 7–50)', *BJ* 1998, 167–9 [concerns BWV 34a]

Wustmann, Rudolf: 'Sebastian Bachs Kirchenkantatentexte', *BJ* 1910, 45–62

——*Joh. Seb. Bachs Kantatentexte* (Leipzig, 1913; 3rd edn Wiesbaden, 1982)

Zahn, Johannes: *Die Melodien der deutschen evangelischen Kirchenlieder*, 6 vols (Gütersloh, 1889–93; repr. Hildesheim, 1963)

Zander, Ferdinand: 'Die Dichter der Kantatentexte J. S. Bachs: Untersuchungen zu ihrer Bestimmung', diss., Univ. of Cologne, 1967; partially repr. under same title in *BJ* 1968, 9–64

Zehnder, Jean-Claude: 'Zu Bachs Stilentwicklung in der Mühlhäuser und Weimarer Zeit', in K. Heller and H.-J. Schulze, eds, *Das Frühwerk J. S. Bachs* [conference report, Rostock, 1990] (Cologne, 1995), 311–38

Ziebler, Karl: *Das Symbol in der Kirchenmusik Joh. Seb. Bachs* (Kassel, 1930)

Zieglschmid, Stefan: 'Theologische Metaphern in Bachs Kantaten, dargestellt am Beispiel der Kantaten zum ersten Pfingsttag sowie BWV 194', *Beiträge zur Bach-Forschung* 9–10 (1991), 226–34 [concerns BWV 34, 59, 74, 172, and 194]

Index of Names

Authors and editors listed in the bibliography are not included, even if their name occurs in the running text.

Index of terms and glossary

The purpose of the following list of words is twofold: a) it serves as an index of terms already explained in the course of the main text; and b) it explains terms used but so far left undefined, thereby rendering them comprehensible to readers who might be relatively unfamiliar with musical terminology. Accordingly, the alphabetically listed words are accompanied either by a brief definition or by a reference to the page or pages on which they are defined (though these are not necessarily all the pages on which the term occurs).

Abgesang (Ger.): see 'Bar'.

a cappella (It.): literally, in the style of music sung by the choir of a *cappella*, the musical establishment of a church or chapel. The term *a cappella* is often used in the sense of unaccompanied vocal music, especially in the style of sixteenth-century sacred polyphony. In Bach's day, however, instrumental doubling and an independent continuo (though not independent instrumental parts, other than those of the continuo group) were quite compatible with the *a cappella* principle.

accompagnato (It., 'accompanied'): see p. 17 f.

affect (It.: *affetto*): emotion or passion—such as love, joy, or anger—that might be evoked by music. According to many seventeenth- and eighteenth-century theorists, the chief aim of music was to arouse such feelings in the listener. 'Affective' music of that period differs from musical expression of the nineteenth or twentieth centuries in that the composer takes an objective stance in order to portray distinct, static states of feeling.

applicatio (Lat., 'attachment', 'application'): according to seventeenth- and eighteenth-century preaching doctrine, that part of the sermon in which the substance of the text, based on the lesson, is applied to the contemporary congregation.

aria (It., 'air'; see also 'strophic aria'): see p. 18 f.

arioso (It., 'air-like'): see p. 18 f.

a tempo (It., 'in time'): the resumption of a fixed tempo after a rhythmically free passage such as a recitative.

augmentation, diminution: techniques of polyphonic writing (used especially in canon, fugue, and *cantus firmus* arrangements) in which a distinctive melody—usually a theme or *cantus firmus* (q.v.)—is stated by one or more voices in note-values doubled or halved in relation to those of its previous statements.

Bar: the favoured song form of the *Meistersinger*, also employed in a large number of German folksongs and hymns. It consists of two similar *Stollen* followed by a different *Abgesang*, giving rise to the scheme A A B. Where the *Abgesang* flows into a reprise of the *Stollen* melody, the so-called *Reprisenbar* arises, A A B A, as for example in *Es ist ein Ros entsprungen*. Even larger formal complexes sometimes adopt *Bar* form or else turn it round to form the so-called *Gegenbar* (A B B).

bassett (Ger.: *Bassettchen, Bassettgen*; It.: *bassetto*): see p. 435.

basso (quasi) ostinato: *basso ostinato*, or ground bass, denotes a compositional technique in which a generally brief, striking, and constantly reiterated instrumental bass theme serves as the basis of a freely unfolding and constantly varied melody in the upper parts. In Bach's time the instrumental bass was, in general, no longer retained completely unaltered, but rather treated more freely as a 'basso quasi ostinato' (Hugo Riemann), e.g. transposed to other keys, divided into segments, and occasionally interrupted by free passages.

Benedictus: see 'psalm tone'.

canon (Gr., 'measure', 'rule'): denotes, among other things, the strictest style of imitation (q.v.), in which two or more melodically and rhythmically identical voices follow each other (either at the same pitch, or a certain interval apart). In musical composition there are numerous gradations between absolutely strict canon and voice-leading in canonic style.

cantata: for the use of the term to denote the secular solo cantata, see p. 9 f.

canticle: see 'psalm tone'.

cantus firmus (Lat., 'fixed song'): denotes an unchangeable, pre-existing melody upon which a composition is based. In Bach it is usually a Protestant chorale, less often a Gregorian chant. The immutability of the given melody—a requirement in principle—does not preclude its ornamentation or slight variation (e.g. to render it suitable for canonic treatment).

chamber pitch: see under 'Chorton'

choir pitch: see 'Chorton'

choral insertion (Ger.: *Choreinbau*): see p. 19 f.

chorale (= Protestant hymn): for the forms of Bach's chorale arrangements, see pp. 11 f. and 20.

chorale cantata: see pp. 29 ff. and 43.

Chorton ('choir pitch'): pitch standard a tone to a minor 3rd higher than the *Kammerton* ('chamber pitch') introduced from France. Up to the beginning of the eighteenth century the notation of church music was generally based on *Chorton*. The fact that organs, due to the length of their pipes, could not be retuned in the modern *Kammerton* induced Bach and his contemporaries to employ double notation in their church compositions: either the woodwind instruments (in *Kammerton*) received a part notated higher than the rest of the ensemble (Bach's practice before 1723) or the organ received a part notated lower (Bach's practice in Leipzig). The problems for present-day performance practice that arise from this state of affairs are at times hard to resolve. Evidence of surviving organs at *Chorton* suggests that they were pitched at an average of $a^1 = 465$ hertz (the modern pitch standard is $a^1 = 440$). By about 1700, the more common level of *Kammerton* was $a^1 = 415$, but $a^1 = 403$ and even $a^1 = 390$ (known as *tief-Kammerton*, or deep chamber pitch) were also of frequent occurrence.

chorus: for the forms of Bach's choral movements, see pp. 12, 19 f., 28, and 32.

chromaticism, chromatic: describes note sequences that employ not only the seven degrees of the diatonic scale but also the sharpened or flattened notes foreign to the scale (e.g. *c sharp* or *c flat* in relation to *c*). The chromatic scale, of twelve notes per octave, arises through upward or downward motion by semitonal steps (*c–c sharp–d–d sharp* etc.).

colla parte (It., 'with the part'): denotes particularly (in the present context, exclusively) the doubling of the vocal parts by instruments, e.g. in motet-style movements and in plain four-part concluding chorales.

coloratura (It., 'colouring'): exceptionally elaborate runs, trills, etc. in vocal music, especially in an aria or arioso (see also 'melisma').

comes (Lat., 'companion'): see 'fugue'.

concertante (It., present participle of 'concerto', q.v.): in a general sense, music that is in some way concerto-like; instrumental writing that is soloistic rather than accompanimental.

concertino (It., 'little concerto'): mostly used to denote a group of solo instruments as distinct from the 'tutti' (q.v.).

concertist: see pp. 24 and 49 f.

concerto (It.): in Bach's day, as now, an instrumental work in several movements. In the context of church music, however, it was often used specifically to denote settings of biblical words for an ensemble of voices and instruments; it was also synonymous with the present-day term 'church cantata'.

concerto, sacred: see p. 8.

continuo: abbreviated form of 'basso continuo' (It., 'uninterrupted bass'), i.e. in music of the thoroughbass era, the fundamental part over which chords filled in the harmony. The instruments that participated in the continuo in Bach's cantatas are, as a rule, cello and violone (today, double bass), organ (in church music) or harpsichord (in secular music), usually also bassoon, and occasionally, either as addition or replacement, lute or viola da gamba. The stringed instruments and bassoon would have been restricted to playing the notated bass line, while the keyboard instruments and/or lute would also have filled in chords (harmonized according to the system of figured bass) or provided some extra, improvised melodic figuration. See also 'bassett'.

counterpoint (from Lat. *punctus contra punctum*, 'note against note'): of the wide range of meanings of this word, the following may be selected: a) a set of rules in which the pupil progresses from note-against-note texture to ever more complex techniques of part-writing; b) the countersubject to a given part, e.g. to a theme or *cantus firmus* (q.v.); in permutation fugue (q.v.) it is applied to what is normally designated the subject in order to clarify the equality of all participating voices; c) compositional technique of exchanging independent parts, as in 'double' or 'invertible' counterpoint; d) in Bach's *Art of Fugue*, BWV 1080, the title 'Contrapunctus' is employed as synonymous with fugue.

cue: a short passage from another part included in a player's performing material just before the player's own entry, intended to help the performer know when to come in.

da capo (It., 'from the head', i.e. from the beginning): often abbreviated to 'D.C.', it occurs at the end of the middle (B) section of an aria or chorus to indicate that the opening (A) section should be repeated, creating an overall ABA form, as in the so-called 'da capo aria' (see p. 18).

de tempore (Lat., 'temporal'): derived from 'proprium de tempore', the liturgical songs that constantly change in the course of the church year. Also used in the substantive form 'detempore', it denotes characteristics related to the specific time in the church year, e.g. those of a cantata text based on the readings for the day.

diminution: see 'augmentation'.

doxology (Gr., 'word of glory'): in a general sense, any formula of praise, e.g. the close of the paternoster. In Christian psalm singing, it denotes the 'Gloria Patri', the formula in praise of the Trinity appended to the psalm text proper ('Glory be to the Father and to the Son and to the Holy Spirit. As it was in the beginning, is now, and ever shall be. Amen.').

dramma per musica: see p. 9.

dux (Lat., 'leader'): see 'fugue'.

Epistle: see 'lessons'.

exposition: the statement of a theme, as opposed to its development or to unthematic passages. In fugue the term applies to the opening section or to any section in which the complete subject is treated in imitation (q.v.).

false relation (also known as 'cross-relation'): a form of part-writing forbidden in strict composition, in which a semitonal step outside the scale (e.g. c–c sharp) or a tritone (e.g. f–b) is divided between two different voices (even if one of the notes is transposed to another octave), e.g. e^1–*c sharp*^{1}

$c^1 - a$

In setting words to music the false relation was, exceptionally, permitted in Bach's day for interpretative purposes in certain contexts, e.g. the setting of the word 'sin'.

flauto piccolo: see p. 34.

figural: characterized by the use of figuration, i.e. stereotyped ornamental figures.

fore-imitation (Ger.: *Vorimitation*; see also 'imitation'): preparation for the entry of a part—usually the *cantus firmus* (q.v.)—by imitative quotation of its melody in some or all of the other participating parts. The main entry thus prepared is often heard in augmentation (q.v.).

freely polyphonic: see 'polyphony'.

French Overture: denotes the typical overture form derived from French Baroque opera, in which the standard three-part scheme is: slow or moderate–quick–return to opening tempo (this last section was optional and often omitted). It was also used outside opera, especially as an introduction to the orchestral suite, and was at times transferred to other genres, e.g. to the cantata (cf. BWV 20, 61, 97, 110, 119, 194).

fugue (Lat.: *fuga* = 'flight'): a composition in strict part-writing, usually with a constant number of voices, imprinted with a distinctive theme or subject with which each voice enters in turn. This subject normally returns repeatedly in the course of the movement in so-called 'expositions'. Fugue differs from canon in its freer treatment of the parts, and from imitative texture (see 'imitation') in its formal unity. The beginning of a fugue, until full texture arrives, is designated an 'exposition' (q.v.). This is characterized by the answer at the 5th: i.e. the subject, normally stated in its basic ('dux') form at the first entry, is imitated or 'answered' by the second voice in a form transposed to the 5th above (or the 4th below)—the so-called 'comes' form.

This answer may be 'real' or 'tonal', depending on whether the 5th transposition is literal or slightly altered in accordance with its tonal context. See also 'stretto', 'permutation fugue', 'augmentation, diminution'.

Gospel: see 'lessons'.

hemiola (Gr., 'one and a half'): in the music of Bach's day, denotes the uniting of two triple-time bars to form a single bar with doubled beats, e.g. the change from

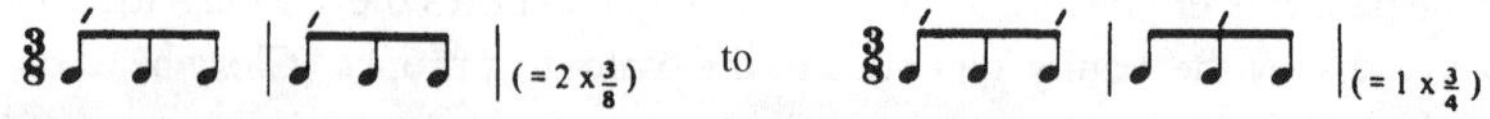

$\frac{3}{8}$ | | (= 2 x $\frac{3}{8}$) to $\frac{3}{8}$ | | (= 1 x $\frac{3}{4}$)

heterophony, heterophonic (Gr., 'different sound', 'different-sounding'): term derived from comparative musicology but transferred to similar phenomena in Western music, denoting a distinctive form of part-writing in which two or more voices are predominantly in unison but with occasional deviations from each other. These deviations are mostly conditioned by vocal or playing technique, e.g. when a melody delivered in plain form by the voice is doubled by an instrument, whose part is consequently furnished with instrumental-style embellishments.

homophony, homophonic (Gr., 'same sound', 'same-sounding'): see 'polyphony'.

hymn-sermons: see p. 29 f.

imitation, imitative: denotes a basic technique of part-writing in which a distinctive figure, theme or motive is stated in one part and then repeated ('imitated') in another while the first part continues. Such imitation is especially clear to the listener, and therefore particularly favoured by composers, where the parts enter thus one after another, e.g. in the exposition of a fugue (q.v.). In a narrower sense, the term 'imitative texture' is used above all where imitation occurs within a free texture, i.e. without reference to one of the strict forms such as canon, fugue, etc.

Kammerton: see *Chorton*.

lamento (It., 'lament'): a song of lamentation, particularly in seventeenth-century Italian opera. A typical form of *lamento*, developed at that time, was a vocal piece sung over an ostinato (q.v.) bass figure that descended chromatically through the interval of a fourth. Hence such figures (e.g. that of the Crucifixus of the B minor Mass) are designated '*lamento* basses'.

Leipzig: for Bach's cantatas and cantata performances during his Leipzig period, see pp. 22–53.

lessons (at mass or the principal morning service): Bible readings, two of which survived from a greater number in early Christian times: the Epistle, a reading from the Epistles or Acts of the New Testament; and the Gospel, a reading from one of the four Gospels. Chapter and verse were prescribed for each Sunday and feast-day during the church year. See also p. 4.

madrigal: see pp. 5 f. and 7.

madrigalian verse: a text devised according to the poetic rules of the madrigal. Also used as a collective term for all non-strophic, freely versified portions of text in the secular cantata or in the later form of church cantata (recitative, arioso, aria, chorus).

Magnificat: see 'psalm tone'.

melisma (Gr., 'song'): normally denotes the slurring of a single syllable of text over several notes. It also denotes coloraturas (q.v.) and embellishments. The converse is syllabic (q.v.) singing (one syllable per note).

monody: see p. 8.
motet: see p. 7.
motive, motif: a brief melodic and/or rhythmic figure out of which a whole movement, or a section of a movement, may be constructed.
motivically imprinted accompagnato: see p. 18.
motto: term coined by Hugo Riemann for a peculiarity of many arias of the seventeenth and eighteenth centuries, namely an advance statement of the vocal head-motive (invariably associated with a significant textual phrase) usually after an introductory instrumental ritornello. The motto is followed by an instrumental episode, then by an identical repeat of the vocal head-motive, this time followed by its continuation (see, for example, the aria 'Geduld, geduld' from Bach's *St Matthew Passion*). On occasion, the motto is placed at the end of an aria as a 'concluding motto', as in the aria 'Es ist vollbracht' from Bach's *St John Passion*.
Neapolitan sixth chord: chromatically altered sixth chord on the flattened second degree of the scale (e.g. in C major or minor, a D flat chord), though usually heard in its first inversion (so that in C major/minor its bass-note would be F); in cadences it therefore functions as a replacement for the subdominant. It is called a sixth chord in reference to the distinctive flattened sixth interval between the bass note (in this example, F) and the root (D flat). In C minor, a cadence with a Neapolitan sixth would be:

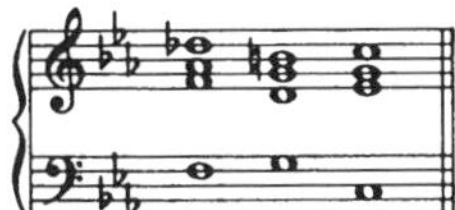

Nunc dimittis: see 'psalm tone'.
obbligato (It., 'obligatory'): an important accompanying part that should not be omitted, such as an elaborate instrumental part within a vocal aria.
oboe da caccia (It., 'hunting oboe'; see also 'taille'): type of oboe pitched a fifth lower than the normal oboe. Today it is usually replaced by the cor anglais.
oboe d'amore (It., 'oboe of love'): type of oboe with a distinctive tone colour, pitched a minor third lower than the normal oboe.
ode: in Bach's day, a strophic poem. The converse is madrigalian verse (q.v.).
oratorio: for Bach's use of the term, see p. 44 f.
ordinarium missae (Lat., 'ordinary of the mass'): those portions of the mass liturgy that remain largely constant throughout the church year. The converse is *proprium missae* ('proper of the mass'), the constantly changing portions specific to each week and festival.
organ: for its obbligato use by Bach, see p. 38 f.
ostinato (It., 'obstinate'): a brief musical pattern that recurs repeatedly in unaltered form. See also 'basso (quasi) ostinato'.
parody (Gr.): in musicological usage, the provision of a new text to an existing vocal composition, which is more or less radically altered in consequence. This form of adaptation was widely cultivated in Bach's day with the aim of rendering music written for particular occasions usable more generally, for different purposes.

permutation fugue (see also 'fugue'): see p. 12.

Phrygian cadence: cadential formula in the Phrygian mode (e f g a b c d e) but with the third of the final chord often raised, for instance:

Following the advent of major-minor tonality, the Phrygian cadence was conceived as a half-close with the bass descending a semitone to the dominant. As such it was often used by Bach—due to its effect as an incomplete ending—for the setting of a question.

pizzicato (It.): 'plucked'—direction to stringed-instrument players to pluck the strings with the fingers rather than using the bow.

polyphony, polyphonic (Gr., 'many sounds', 'many-sounding'): denotes, in particular, the type of texture in which each part preserves its melodic and rhythmic independence, as distinct from 'homophony', a rhythmically uniform, chordal texture in all parts, emphasizing harmony rather than melody. A polyphonically composed piece can either be bound to a particular theme, motive, or *cantus firmus* (q.v.), or else unbound in a free-ranging texture described as 'freely polyphonic'. The great bulk of Bach's music is essentially polyphonic in texture.

psalm tone: the Lutheran church adopted the nine 'psalm tones' from the old ecclesiastical tradition of psalm singing on the basis of fixed melodic patterns. By Bach's time these psalm tones were used only occasionally, chiefly for the singing of the three New Testament canticles, the Benedictus (Luke 1.68–79), the Magnificat (Luke 1.46–55) and the Nunc dimittis (Luke 2.29–32). See also pp. 657 and 678.

quodlibet (Lat., 'what pleases me'): a combination of several melodies, often well-known ones, performed either simultaneously (in counterpoint) or in succession, largely of playful intent. The singing of quodlibets is said to have been a popular activity on Bach family days.

recitative (from It. *stile recitativo* = 'reciting, narrating style'): see p. 17.

ripienist (from It. *ripieno* = 'full', 'filling'): see pp. 24 and 49 f.

secco (It., 'dry'): see p. 17.

serenata: see pp. 9 and 21 f.

solo (It., 'alone'): denotes the special prominence of a particular instrument or an individual singer. In scoring specifications it is used to indicate where a part is taken by a single performer as opposed to several performers. In concerto style it is used as a formal indication ('solo episode') as distinct from the 'tutti' (q.v.).

Stimmtausch (Ger., 'voice exchange'): see p. 12 f.

Stollen: see 'Bar'.

stretto: technique of polyphonic writing (especially used in fugue) in which a subject, stated by two or more voices, enters in the following voice before the end of its statement in the preceding voice.

strophic aria: see pp. 4 f. and 9.

syllabic (from Gr. *sullabe*): syllable by syllable; denotes a style of vocal delivery in which each syllable is sung to its own note. The converse is 'melismatic' (see 'melisma').

tacet (Lat., 'is silent'): a 'tacet' indication in a performing part denotes that the singer or player concerned does not participate in the portion of the work so marked.

taille (Fr.): in French music denotes middle pitch, particularly tenor pitch. In Bach 'taille' invariably indicates the part for tenor oboe (within a fully scored piece), nowadays normally played on the cor anglais.

theme: a musical idea with a clear rhythmic and melodic profile, often made out of several motives (q.v.). It has a formative effect upon the overall structure due to its recurrence and, in many cases, its development and transformation.

transverse flute: for its use in Bach's cantatas, see p. 34.

trope: see p. 3.

tutti (It., 'all'): the coming together of all the participants, or the great majority of them, in the performance of a piece. The converse is 'solo' (q.v.). In concerto style the alternation of 'tutti ritornellos' and 'solo episodes' is a crucial determinant of the form.

unison (It.: *unisono* = 'one sound'): denotes the simultaneous motion of several voices, which would otherwise usually be independent, at the same pitch (or perhaps in octaves).

violoncello piccolo: see p. 35.

vocal insertion (Ger.: *Vokaleinbau*): see p. 19 f.

Index of cantatas: alphabetical

The BWV number is given in brackets.

Index of cantatas: by BWV number

	DATE DUE		